Other Best-Selling Authors with Omnibus Collections from
Random House Value Publishing, Inc.

BARBARA TAYLOR BRADFORD
LaVYRLE SPENCER
ROSAMUNDE PILCHER
MARY HIGGINS CLARK
MAEVE BINCHY
DEAN KOONTZ
MICHAEL CRICHTON
JANELLE TAYLOR

THREE COMPLETE NOVELS

NELSON DEMILLE

THREE COMPLETE NOVELS

NELSON DeMILLE

WORD OF HONOR

CATHEDRAL

BY THE RIVERS OF BABYLON

WINGS BOOKS
NEW YORK

This 1999 edition is published by Wings Books®, an imprint of Random House Value Publishing, Inc., 201 East 50th Street, New York, NY 10022, by arrangement with Warner Books.

Wings Books® and colophon are registered trademarks of Random House Value Publishing, Inc.

Printed in the United States of America

Random House
New York • Toronto • London • Sydney • Auckland
http://www.randomhouse.com/

Library of Congress Cataloging-in-Publication Data

DeMille, Nelson.
    [Novels. Selections.]
    Three complete novels / Nelson DeMille.
        sp.   cm.
    Contents: Word of honor—Cathedral—By the rivers of Babylon.
    ISBN 0-517-08237-3
    I. Title
PS3554.E472A6   1992
813'.54—dc20   92-7596
                                                                                     CIP

8 7 6 5 4 3 2

CONTENTS

WORD OF HONOR

To Ginny, with love.

Acknowledgments

I would like to thank Tony Gleason for his insights
into military law, Reid Boates for his editorial suggestions
and Nick Ellison for his consistent support.
And many thanks to Kathleen Haley for her dedicated assistance.
Thanks also to Sergeant First Class Susan Rueger at Fort Hamilton,
and Dr. Russell Gilmore, Director of the Harbor Defense Museum.
Further thanks to Daniel Barbiero, still a Marine.
And to my men of Delta Company,
First Battalion of the Eighth Cavalry, warmest regards.

Part 1

It is easier to find false witnesses against the civilian than anyone willing to speak the truth against the interest and honor of the soldier.

—Juvenal

1

B en Tyson folded his *Wall Street Journal* and stared out the window of the speeding commuter train. The dreary borough of Queens rolled by, looking deceptively habitable in the bright May morning sunshine.

Tyson glanced at the man in the facing seat, John McCormick, a neighbor and social acquaintance. McCormick was reading a hardcover book, and Tyson focused on the title: *Hue: Death of a City.*

McCormick flipped back a page and reread something, then glanced over the book and made unexpected eye contact with Tyson. He dropped his eyes quickly back to the book.

Tyson felt a sudden sense of foreboding. He focused again on the book jacket. The cover showed a red-tinged photograph of the ancient imperial city of Hue, a low-angle aerial perspective. The city spread out on both sides of the red-running Perfume River, the bridges broken and collapsed into the water. Great black and scarlet billows of smoke hung over the blazing city, and the sun, a crimson half ball, rose over the distant South China Sea, silhouetting the dominant features of the town: the Imperial Palace, the high walls and towers of the Citadel, and the soaring spires of the Catholic cathedral. A remarkable picture, Tyson thought. He nodded to himself. *Hue.* Tyson said, "Good book?"

McCormick looked up with feigned nonchalance. "Oh, not bad."

"Did I get an honorable mention?"

McCormick hesitated a moment, then without a word, he handed Tyson the opened book.

Ben Tyson read:

On the sixteenth day of the battle of Hue, 15 February, an American rifle platoon found itself pinned down by enemy fire in the western suburbs of the city. The platoon was an element of Alpha Company, Fifth Battalion of the Seventh Cavalry Regiment, of the First Air Cavalry Division. As a point of historical interest, the Seventh Cavalry was the ill-fated regiment commanded by General Custer at the Little Big Horn.

The rifle platoon under fire was led by a twenty-five-year-old Auburn ROTC graduate, Lieutenant Benjamin J. Tyson, a New Yorker.

Tyson continued to stare at the open book without reading. He glanced at McCormick, who seemed, Tyson thought, embarrassed. Tyson continued reading:

The following account of what happened that day is drawn from interviews with two members of Tyson's platoon whom I will identify only as Pfc X and Specialist Four Y. The story, heretofore untold, was originally brought to my attention by a nun of mixed French and Vietnamese ancestry named Sister Teresa. Further details regarding the provenance of this story may be found at the conclusion of this chapter.

Tyson closed his eyes. Through the blackness an image took shape: a Eurasian girl, dressed in white, with a silver cross hanging between her breasts. Her body was fuller than that of a Vietnamese, and there was a slight wave in her long black hair. She had high cheekbones and almond eyes, but her eyes were soft brown, and there was just the suggestion of freckles on her nose. As he held the image in his mind's eye, the mouth turned up in a smile that seemed to transform her whole face, making the features more strongly Gallic. The Cupid's-bow mouth pursed, and she spoke softly, *"Tu es un homme intéressant."*

"Et tu, Térèse, es une femme intéressante."

Tyson opened his eyes. He looked back at the page:

The enemy fire directed at Tyson's men was coming from the vicinity of a small French hospital named Hôpital Miséricorde. The hospital, operated by a Catholic relief agency, was flying two flags: a Red Cross flag and a Viet Cong flag.

The firefight had erupted shortly before noon as the American platoon approached. The platoon quickly took cover, and there were no initial casualties. After about five minutes of intense firing, the enemy broke contact and withdrew toward the city.

Someone in the hospital then draped a white bed sheet from a second-story window, indicating surrender or "all clear." Seeing the white sheet, Lieutenant Tyson began moving his platoon up to take possession of the hospital and surrounding structures. The enemy, however, had left behind at least one sniper, positioned on the hospital's roof. As the Americans approached, shots rang out, killing one American, Pfc Larry Cane, and wounding two others, Sgt. Robert Moody and Pfc Arthur Peterson. There was a possible second sniper positioned at one of the windows.

Tyson paused again, and his mind returned to that day in 1968. It had been one of the worst days of the massive enemy offensive that had begun on the lunar New Year holiday called Tet, ushering in the Year of the Monkey.

He vividly recalled the sky, so blackened with smoke that he wouldn't have known it was an overcast day except for the cold rain falling through the ash.

He heard, in the steady rumbling of the train, the persistent pounding of impacting mortars and the ceaseless staccato chatter of automatic weapons.

The train whistle blew at a crossing, and Tyson recalled very clearly the blood-freezing shriek of incoming rockets, exploding with an earthshaking thunder so intense that it took a few seconds to realize you were still alive.

And the dead, Tyson remembered, the dead lay everywhere. Trails and fields surprised you with sprawled, slaughtered corpses; hamlets were littered with the unburied dead. The Graves Registration people wore gas masks and rubber gloves, recovering only the American dead, burning the rest in pyres stoked with diesel oil and ignited with flamethrowers. Bonfires, bone fires, crackling fat, and grinning skulls. He could still smell the burnt human hair.

Tyson recalled what his company commander, Captain Browder, had said: "The living are in the minority here." And Browder himself joined the majority not long after.

Death, he remembered, was so pervasive in that bleak dying city, in that bleak and rainy winter, that the living—civilian and soldier alike—had almost ceased to struggle against it. People would, out of instinct, duck or take cover, but you could see in their eyes that they had no prospects for the future. *Hue: Death of a City. Hue: City of Death.* No wonder, he thought, we all went mad there.

Tyson drew himself back to the book. He skipped a page and read at random:

> A French nurse, Marie Broi, attempted to stop the Americans from killing the wounded enemy soldiers, but she was struck with a rifle. An Australian physician named Evan Dougal began swearing abusively at the Americans. Clearly, everyone was overwrought; nearly hysterical might be a better term.
>
> Suddenly, with no forewarning, an American soldier fired a burst from his automatic rifle, and Dr. Dougal was hurled by the force of the rounds across the room. Spec/4 Y describes it as follows: "He [Dougal] was thrashing around on the tile floor holding his stomach. His white smock was getting redder and his face was getting whiter."
>
> The ward that had been in pandemonium a few seconds before was now very still except for the dying sounds made by Dr. Dougal. Pfc X remembers hearing whimpering and crying from the adjoining pediatric and maternity ward.
>
> What happened next is somewhat unclear, but apparently, having murdered the first Caucasian, several members of Tyson's platoon decided it would be best to leave no witnesses. The doctors, nurses, and nuns were ordered into a small whitewashed operating room and—

"Jamaica Station!" cried the conductor. "Change here for trains to New York! Stay on for Brooklyn!"

Tyson closed the book and stood.

McCormick remained seated and said hesitantly, "Do you want to borrow—?"

"No."

Tyson crossed the platform to make his connection, wondering why this had happened on such a sunny day.

2

Tyson looked down from his office window and focused on Park Avenue, twenty-eight stories below. One version of the American dream, he reflected, was an office aerie like this one—a commanding height from which the captains of industry and commerce directed the nine-to-five weekday battle against government, consumers, environmentalists, and one another. Having arrived here, Tyson discovered that he had no particular enthusiasm for the fight. But he had wisely not dwelt too long on this discovery. And besides, the world had changed for him somewhere between Hollis and Jamaica Station.

Miss Beale, his secretary, spoke. "Do you want to finish this letter?"

Tyson turned from the window and glanced at the seated woman. "You finish the letter."

Miss Beale stood, her steno pad held to her ample chest. "Are you feeling all right?"

Tyson looked Miss Beale in the eye. Miss Beale, like many secretaries, was alert to signs of weakness in her employer. A little weakness could be exploited. Too much weakness, however, foreshadowed visions of the unemployment line for both of them. Tyson replied, "Of course I'm not all right. Do I look all right?"

She was momentarily discomposed and muttered, "No . . . you . . . I mean . . ."

He said, "Cancel my lunch date and my afternoon appointments."

"Are you leaving for the day?"

"Most probably."

Miss Beale turned and left.

Tyson gazed around his office. He wondered what color offices were before the discovery of beige.

He opened his coat-closet door and looked at himself in the full-length mirror. He was just over six feet tall and he thought he carried it well. Tyson brushed his gray pinstripe suit, straightened his tie and vest, and finger-combed his sandy hair. There were few corporate images he did not fit, few armies in the world where he would not be described as every inch an officer and a gentleman.

Tall people were more successful, so said the studies done on the subject of success in business. Yet the president of his corporation was five feet, two inches. In fact, most of the principal executives in the company and the parent company were under five feet six. And with good reason, he thought: They were all Japanese.

Tyson closed the closet and walked to his desk. He sat and sipped absently on a cup of cold coffee, then his eyes drifted to a piece of company stationery: Peregrine-Osaka. When Peregrine Electronic Aviation had been acquired by

Osaka, Tyson had not been happy, and his spirits had not improved in the two
years since the takeover.

He was no racist, he told himself, and yet looking down on Mr. Kimura when
they conversed was awkward, and being addressed as Ty-sun was somehow
grating.

The Japanese were subtle, and their presence was delicate and gentle. Yet in
some indefinable way they ruled with an iron hand. Tyson, unasked, had removed his war mementos from his walls: his Army commission, citations, and
photographs—*objets de guerre* that had had some cachet with Defense Department customers, that had been looked on favorably by Peregrine's former
owner and founder, Charlie Stutzman, but which now did not fit the new re-
gime's psychological decor. Also making its way home in his briefcase was a
photograph of his father in his Navy flier's uniform. His father's Grumman
Hellcat could be seen in the background on the deck of the carrier *Lexington,*
three rising suns painted on the fuselage. Three dead Japs.

Mr. Kimura had studied the photo intently one day but had no comment.
Tyson waited one face-saving week before removing it.

Tyson stood, picked up his slim attaché case, and exited his office. He passed
Miss Beale's desk, aware of her keen gaze.

3

Ben Tyson walked east on 42nd Street and turned into a small bookshop
near Grand Central Station. On a table marked RECENT ARRIVALS
sat a tall stack of them, red, black, and white spines facing him. The top
of the stack was crowned with a standing display copy. Tyson took the copy and
leafed through it.

Interspersed with the text were photograph sections, and every few chapters
there were classical military map drawings of Hue and environs. The book fell
open to the title page, and Tyson saw that it was autographed by Andrew
Picard.

"The author was in here yesterday."

Tyson looked up into the eyes of a young woman dressed in jeans and a T-
shirt that said "New York Is Book Country."

She continued, "We just got those in last week. He bought a copy for me and
signed it. I read part of it last night. I try to at least scan the major books that
come in."

Tyson nodded.

She went on, "It's in the style of the big battle through the eyes of little
people." She appraised Tyson closely. "Were you there? Nam, I mean."

Tyson replied, "Quite possibly."

She smiled, "Well, I'd recommend it as a good read—if you were there. Not
really my taste."

Tyson said, "There's supposed to be a part in here about a massacre of a
French hospital."

She grimaced. "Right. Really gross." She thought a moment, then said,
"How could we do something like that?"

Tyson marveled at how the young used the first-person pronoun to include and indict themselves for the depredations of the government and the military. He said, "It was a long time ago. I'll take the book."

Tyson went to the corner of 42nd and Second and entered Ryan McFadden's, a sort of upscale Irish pub. His eyes adjusted to the dim light, and he moved to the long bar, taking an empty stool. The establishment's clientele was eclectic: foreigners from the nearby U.N., local media people from the WPIX-Daily News building across the avenue, and a smattering of literati whose presence seemed a mystery to the owners, who did not encourage that sort of trade. It was not the type of place frequented by businessmen, and he did not expect to run into any of his associates. One of the owners, Dan Ryan, greeted him warmly. "Ben, how's life been treating you?"

Tyson pondered several answers, then replied, "Not too bad."

Ryan ordered him a Dewar's and soda, with the traditional Irish publican's "Good luck."

Tyson raised his glass. *"Slainté."*

Ryan moved off to greet a group of newcomers. For the first time since he'd opened Picard's book that morning, Tyson's thoughts turned exclusively to his wife: Marcy was not the type of wife one saw on the news, standing staunchly beside a prominent husband accused of political corruption, embezzlement, or sexual wrongdoing. She was very much her own woman and gave her loyalty selectively, as it should be given. She was not, for instance, a good corporate wife, and in fact had a career of her own as well as a mind of her own. She had been and still was violently antiwar, antimilitary, and anti-anything that didn't fit neatly into her own left-of-center view of the world. Her reaction to the book would be revealing, Tyson thought.

Tyson opened his attaché case and took the book. He set it on the bar and scanned the pertinent chapter quickly, unwilling to actually read or comprehend any more of it, like someone who has gotten a Dear John letter or a telegram about a death. His name jumped out at him in various forms: Tyson's platoon; Lieutenant Tyson; Tyson's men; Tyson's medic; Tyson's radio operator. . . .

He shut the book, finished his drink, and ordered another. After some time he opened the book to a page he had dog-eared, and read a passage:

> As the platoon approached, they were presented with three conflicting signals: the Viet Cong flag, the Red Cross flag, and the white sheet. The latter may have lulled them into a false sense of security as they crossed the exposed courtyard in front of the building. Suddenly shots rang out, and Larry Cane was killed instantly. Moody and Peterson were hit. The platoon took cover and returned the fire.
>
> Of the two wounded, Moody's injury was slight, but Peterson's wound was critical. The morale of the platoon, not good to begin with, became worse. There was a feeling of helpless rage and impotence among the men, a feeling that they'd been duped and deceived.

Tyson nodded to himself. Yes, that was an accurate description. Rage and impotence. They'd been played for suckers. Not only by the enemy, but by their commanders in the field, their commanders at headquarters, their commanders in Washington. They were looking for something or someone to strike back at. In retrospect, Tyson realized those people in the hospital never had a chance.

Tyson skipped a page.

> On entering the hospital, Tyson demanded immediate medical attention for his two wounded.
>
> The hospital's chief of staff, a Frenchman named Dr. Jean Monteau, explained rather peremptorily to Tyson in passable English that the hospital was on the triage system: i.e., there were so many patients and so few staff and supplies that those who were clearly dying—like Peterson—could not be helped and those who were lightly wounded—like Moody—would have to wait. Whereupon, Dr. Monteau turned his back on Tyson and began attending a Viet Cong soldier whose arm was shredded by shrapnel and who apparently fell into the proper category to receive care.
>
> Dr. Monteau's medical judgment may have been sound, but his judgment of the situation could not have been worse.

Tyson looked up from the book. "You got that right, Picard." He tried to picture the face of Dr. Jean Monteau but he was able only to conjure up a sneering caricature of an arrogant little Frenchman. Surely, he thought, this was a defense mechanism of his mind, a justification for what happened. The real Dr. Monteau had addressed him with some dignity and politeness. What may have seemed at the time like peremptoriness was fatigue. He thought again, then concluded, *No, Monteau certainly was an arrogant little son of a bitch.* But he didn't deserve to die for it. Tyson stirred his drink, then read again at random:

> Tyson's platoon, as I've mentioned, had been operating independently of its company for over a week. They had already suffered high casualties in the preceding sixteen days of the offensive. Out of an original platoon of forty men, nineteen remained. Also, they had gone without rest or resupply for the seven days prior to this incident.
>
> These facts are not meant to suggest extenuating circumstances for what happened. They are provided only as background. Certainly soldiers have been more sorely tried, more lacking in comforts, more exposed to hostile action and the general horrors of war than this unfortunate platoon, without reverting to—

Tyson slammed the book. He lit a cigarette and watched the smoke rise, then abruptly turned the book over and looked closely at the picture of Andrew Picard. The photo seemed oddly blurred, but he saw the profile of a bearded man of about his own age, dressed in a light shirt with military-style shoulder tabs. There were lines running across the photograph, and Tyson saw that they were actually names. He suddenly realized that the photograph was of Picard's image reflected in a dark, glossy surface, and he comprehended that the surface was the black granite wall of the Vietnam memorial in Washington.

Tyson stared at the extraordinary photograph for some time, reading the etched names of the dead that ran across the black wall, across Picard's mirrored image, out to the edges of the dust jacket—that ran, he thought, across time and space; the army of the dead.

Tyson opened the book to the inside flap and read the short biography: *Andrew Picard is a graduate of Yale University. He served with the Marines as a Public Information Officer in Vietnam at Hue during the Tet offensive. He lives and works in Sag Harbor, Long Island.*

Tyson nodded. *Yale.* Probably went to Platoon Commander School the summer after graduation but had gotten himself a cushy public relations job and managed to avoid actually having to lead a combat infantry platoon.

Sag Harbor. A little town just north of the Hamptons. Tyson had rented a summer house out there some years before. He could vaguely recall a roadside mailbox that he passed often with the names Picard/Wells on it, but couldn't remember exactly where. It appeared that the lines of his life and Mr. Picard's had converged without touching: once in 1968 at Hue, then in the summer of '76, and most recently in a bookshop on 42nd Street. It appeared too that they were somehow fated to meet.

Over his third Scotch, Tyson recollected an incident nearly two years before; he had received a telephone call at his home from a man who said he was researching a book on Vietnam. Tyson recalled being as unhelpful as possible without being obviously evasive. Some weeks later the man had called again. Tyson had been abrupt and hung up. *Andrew Picard.* Tyson nodded in recognition.

Tyson thumbed through the book and regarded the photograph pages. There was the usual lineup of military commanders: Americans and their South Vietnamese allies on one side, Viet Cong and North Vietnamese on the other. Like a football program, he thought.

Then there were the shockers: the uncollected dead, the trucks and armored vehicles hauling the collected dead, the civilians on their knees weeping and wailing over inert bodies, the grotesquely wounded, and finally the mass graves. And it was all in black and white which he thought was wrong. World War II was in black and white. This war was in color.

Tyson stopped turning pages and looked down at a half-page photograph. Grouped around the ruined hull of an enemy armored amphibious vehicle were the men of the First Platoon, Alpha Company, Fifth Battalion, Seventh Cavalry. There were nearly forty of them, a team shot, taken before the Tet season began, before injuries cut the roster by more than half.

They were, he thought, a cocky-looking crew, arrogant and unfrightened. A good deal of that was posturing, of course. But he remembered that the picture had been taken in December 1967, around Christmas—before that first fateful day of Tet, January 30, 1968, when Alpha Company had lost a third of its people one morning in a village called Phu Lai.

December, though, had been a good month. The rain was light, the winds warm, and the sun not so cruel. Casualties were zero that month, and they'd tallied some kills on their side of the scoreboard. Christmas, if not a Currier and Ives one, had at least been bloodless. Ergo the smug faces of the men of the First Platoon of Alpha Company.

Tyson saw himself poised in the turret of the enemy vehicle, the warlord atop the scarred castle turret of the vanquished enemy, his victorious soldiers gathered about.

He scanned the faces more closely and was able to pick out the ones who were fated to die and those about to be wounded.

He studied the faces with the intensity of a man studying a high school yearbook before an upcoming reunion.

Tyson closed the book and slipped it into his attaché case. He picked up his drink and noticed the slightest tremor in his hand. He replaced the glass on the bar and drew a deep breath.

He headed for the door, stepped out into the bright sunlight, and began walking. By the time he reached Fifth Avenue, his mind had settled back into the present. He considered the consequences of this public exposure. He reflected for a while on his courses of action, his family, friends, and career.

The danger seemed unreal and remote at the moment, but that was the worst kind of danger: the kind you cannot or will not meet head-on. The kind that is amorphous at first, incorporeal, but which takes shape while you're busy denying it exists and then hardens into a physical entity.

It was very much, he thought, like when the jungle suddenly became quiet at night. *Nothing out there.* Then the bamboo would click in the wind, but there was no wind. Moon shadows would move across the outer perimeter, but there was no moon and no clouds to make shadows.

Then suddenly, between the beats of a speeding heart, the silent and shapeless shadows would appear, black-clad in the black night, dropping all pretense of not existing, moving toward your pathetic little perimeter of invented safety.

Tyson stopped walking and wiped a line of perspiration from his forehead. He looked around as though to assure himself he was on the sidewalks of New York. Then his mind went back once again to that rainy morning in Hue. It seemed that it had happened on another planet, in another life, and to another person. That Ben Tyson, he thought, was twenty-five years old, unmarried, had never held an infant in his arms or seen a corpse outside a funeral home. That Ben Tyson had only a vague conception of love, hate, tragedy, compassion, or even morality. Nothing in his sheltered American life had prepared him for Hue, 15 February 1968.

The question at hand, however, was this: *Had anything since then prepared him to face the consequences of that day?*

4

Ben Tyson boarded the 1:40 out of Penn Station and took a seat in the smoking car.

The train moved out through the dark tunnels of Manhattan, passed under the East River, then broke free into the sunlight of Queens.

At Jamaica Station there were the usual garbled PA announcements and the search for the right track before he boarded the correct train.

Twenty-two minutes out of Jamaica, the train came to a halt at Garden City station, and Tyson stepped out onto the sunny platform near the quaint station house.

He could smell the flowers, great colored protrusions of them, growing wild along the track beds. Out of instinct he turned right toward his house, then reversed his direction and walked along the raised platform toward the center of the village. He descended the short flight of steps and crossed Hilton Avenue.

Tyson realized that he hadn't been home on a weekday afternoon in some years. There were children walking and bicycling from school, housewives with

carriages, service vans, mail carriers, and all the other signs of activity that
made up the life of these commuter towns by day. He felt almost estranged
from these familiar streets where he'd spent his childhood.

Tyson stood before a picturesque brick building with arched windows. The
hundred-year-old structure had served as the village stable, public school, and
warehouse. Now it was a gentrified warren of law offices where Dickensian
scriveners spent the day bent over plea forms and wills. Tyson entered a ground
floor office and stood in the empty waiting room.

He shifted the attaché case to his left hand and was aware of the book, like a
tumor, he thought, nascent at the moment, newly discovered, awaiting diagno-
sis.

A woman appeared from the far door. "May I help you?"

"My name is Ben Tyson. I'm here to see Mr. Sloan."

She smiled in recognition, not of his face, but of his name. Like most of
Tyson's relationships, the one with Phillip Sloan's secretary was primarily tele-
phonic. "I'm Ann. Please have a seat."

She disappeared and a minute later returned with Phillip Sloan, a man in his
fifties. Sloan was dressed in an unfortunate checkered suit, tassled shoes, and
his club tie, whose colors never seemed to match anything. Sloan greeted Tyson
effusively, then said, "Ben, did we have an appointment?" Sloan made a silly
show of leafing through his secretary's appointment book.

Tyson moved toward the entrance to the inner offices. "This won't take long,
Phil."

Sloan shot his secretary a quizzical look, then followed. He directed Tyson
into the library. "I have a client in my office."

Tyson took a seat at a long reading table and regarded the book-lined walls.
Corpus Juris Secundum. The law of the land, codified and indexed, spelling out
in excruciating detail and obtuse prose the rights and obligations of a uniquely
lawless society.

Tyson placed an open book on the mahogany table and slid it toward Sloan.
Sloan glanced quickly at the front of the book, then began to read.

Tyson lit a cigarette and stared off at the far wall.

After some time, Sloan looked up from the book, a neutral expression on his
face.

Tyson saw that Sloan was not going to speak, so he said, "John McCormick
showed that to me on the train this morning."

Sloan gave a professional nod that conveyed nothing.

Tyson did not particularly like the man. But Sloan's father had been the
Tyson family attorney for years, and it seemed natural that Phillip Sloan should
continue to handle the Tyson's affairs. And Sloan was good, if not likable.
Tyson stood. "I just wanted to alert you to this before you heard it on the links
or wherever it is you disappear to on sunny days. If anything comes of it, I'll let
you know."

Sloan hesitated, then made a motion with his hand. "Sit down, Ben. I can
spare a few more minutes."

You're damned right you can, thought Tyson. *This is one of those walk-ins you
dream about.* Tyson remained standing.

Sloan began speaking with a tone of concern. "Well, this is distressing." He
thought a moment, then said, "I suppose you've given some thought to bringing
suit."

But Tyson was only half listening. He said abruptly, "Could this thing bring
about a criminal action?"

Sloan stayed silent for some time, staring at Tyson, then said, "That depends."

"On *what?*"

"Obviously on whether or not there is any substance to what is written in that book." He paused, then said, "Will you sit down, Ben? Let me see that book again."

Tyson sat and took the book from his attaché case.

Sloan examined it, reading the flap copy, scanning the index, then the front matter. He looked up at Tyson. "Major publisher. The author seems to have credentials. The book is annotated and has a bibliography. Seems like a respectable job."

Tyson shrugged.

Sloan said, "You understand, Ben, that whatever we say here is privileged conversation." Sloan drew a deep breath. "Well?"

Tyson hesitated, then said, "Look, what I want to know from you is whether or not I . . . or the men who served with me . . . can be called to account."

Sloan's voice had an edge of sharpness. "For what? You haven't answered my question."

"For murder!"

Sloan leaned back in his chair and thought a moment, then replied, "There is no statute of limitations on murder."

Tyson's face was impassive.

Sloan continued, "However, the Army would have to establish jurisdiction in this case."

"Meaning?"

"They'd have to get you back in."

Tyson nodded. "Can they do that?"

"That's the question." Sloan added, "If they can't, then no civilian court can try you. You see, you fall between the cracks. It would have to be an American military courtmartial or no trial at all. There are precedents for this."

"I'm sure there are." Tyson thought a moment. "Okay, worst scenario. They get me back in. Then what?"

"The key here is witnesses. Is there anyone in your former unit who would testify against you?"

"Apparently there is."

Sloan shook his head. "Talking to a writer is not the same as testifying in front of an Army grand jury."

Tyson stayed silent.

Sloan played with his pencil awhile, then said, "Look, what we have here is an alleged crime brought to light by a writer some seventeen—eighteen years . . . My God, is it that long ago? Anyway, many years after the alleged facts. The writer mentions three sources for his account: two unnamed GIs whom he claims were in your platoon and whose anonymity he is protecting and one Eurasian nun, identified only as Sister Teresa, who he says is the sole survivor of the massacre—" Sloan looked at Tyson. "Do you know this Sister Teresa?"

Tyson hesitated before replying, "I knew the nun in question."

Sloan did not pursue this but said, "Anyway, here is an alleged crime, committed in a foreign country with which we have no present relations—"

"I know all that."

"—during a military operation, during a time of war, and you are not specifically mentioned as one of the people who actively engaged in this . . . massacre."

Tyson stared at the book lying between them. "All right, now what's the bad news?"

Sloan leaned forward. "You know. As the commander—"

"Responsible for the actions of my men, I bear full responsibility, and so on. Yes, I know."

"Did you shoot anyone?"

"No."

"Were you at the scene of the alleged murders?"

Tyson began to reply, then said, "Picard says I was."

"Picard wasn't there. I'm asking you."

"No, I wasn't even there. Case closed."

"I'm afraid it isn't, Lieutenant." Sloan tapped his pencil on the table, then said, "Okay, let me play devil's advocate again. Or Army prosecutor, if you like. Based on what I read here, I, as a prosecutor, want to know if you actually *ordered* those murders or if you did anything to *prevent* them. I want to know if you *knew* of them and did not *report* them, or even if you *should* have known of them or should have *anticipated* them. Because if any of that is true, then the Army will charge you with the actual murders as though you committed them with your own hands."

After a period of silence, Tyson let out a breath and remarked, "Rank has its privileges."

Sloan stood and went to the far wall of the library. He pulled a large volume from a high shelf and literally dusted it off, then laid it on the table. He said, "Any case that the Army builds against you will probably be based in part on the precedents and principles established at the Nuremberg trials of Nazi war criminals and the Tokyo trials of Japanese war criminals."

"I'm in good company."

Sloan leafed through the book as he spoke. "The object of these trials was to get nooses around the necks of our enemies, of course. But some of those precedents have come back to haunt the American military." He stopped turning pages. "To wit: The landmark case of General Yamashita, commander of Japanese forces in the Philippines. Yamashita was accused by the Americans of having 'unlawfully disregarded and failed to discharge his duty as a commander,' by permitting men under his command to 'commit brutal atrocities and other high crimes.' " Sloan glanced at Tyson. "Nowhere was it alleged that Yamashita personally *committed* any of the atrocities or even that he *ordered* their commission or even that he had any *knowledge* of them. The charges merely stated that during the period of his command he failed to *anticipate* what his troops might do, *should* have known what they might do, and failed to provide effective control of his troops as was required by circumstances." Sloan closed the book. "General Yamashita was found guilty and hanged."

"Thanks for the pep talk, Phil."

Sloan looked at his watch. "I have to get back." He stood. "Look, the point about 'should have known' and all that is somewhat esoteric. The Army is not going to charge you with anything after all these years unless you were actually at the scene of the incident. Were you?"

"Quite possibly." Tyson stood.

"Did you actively participate in any way? I'm still not clear about what your role was in this alleged incident."

Tyson picked up his attaché case. "Well, it was a long time ago, Phil, and I'll have to think about what my role was."

Sloan seemed miffed at the evasive answer. He walked toward the door and turned back. "The best defense is an aggressive offense. That's true in football,

combat, and law. You ought to give serious consideration to suing this guy
Picard. If you don't sue, then this will be noted by the government and the
Army, and may well influence their decision on if and how to proceed." Sloan
waited for a reply, then added, "Also, you ought to consider how your friends,
community, family, and employers will look on this if you don't sue for libel."

Tyson had already considered all of that. He knew, too, that Sloan was baiting him, asking in an oblique manner, *Of the charge of murder, guilty or not
guilty, Tyson?*

"Of course I'll consider a lawsuit," Tyson said.

Sloan nodded slowly. "All right, Ben, keep me informed if anything further
develops. Meanwhile, leave me the book to read. Get another copy and do the
same." He walked through the door, and Tyson followed. They parted in the
corridor. Sloan said, "Don't make any statements, public or private."

Tyson looked over his shoulder. "I wasn't planning to."

"Best to Marcy."

Tyson left the office and walked up the tree-shaded avenue. The danger, he
thought, was more clear now and more palpable, which in a way made him feel
better. But the thing had grown another head, and the teeth were far bigger
than he'd thought from a distance.

Ben Tyson recrossed Hilton Avenue and entered the village library. He went
directly upstairs to the reference law library. After some searching he sat at a
small desk with four thick books. He pulled a yellow legal pad from his briefcase and headed the first page: *The Peers Commission Report on the My Lai
Massacre.* On the second page he wrote: *Byrne's Military Law.* Page three and
four he headed, respectively: *The Uniform Code of Military Justice* and *The
Manual for Courts-Martial.*

Tyson opened the Peers Commission report and began reading, making
notes as he went along. After half an hour, he pushed it aside and opened *The
Uniform Code of Military Justice.* He was familiar with this book and was fairly
certain it hadn't changed in the eighteen years since he'd last opened a copy of
it. Military law transformed itself at roughly the same rate as the evolution of a
new species.

As an officer he'd sat on court-martial boards and had even acted as defense
and trial counsel at Special Courts-Martial. Military law as written had seemed
fair, logical, and even compassionate. There was a certain element of common
sense to it that he knew instinctively was not present in civilian law. Yet some of
the courts-martial he'd observed, especially those overseas, had a surreal quality to them; grim, dreary, little Kafkaesque affairs whose sole function was to
process the accused into the convicted as quickly and quietly as possible.

Tyson skimmed the pertinent parts of the *UCMJ,* made some notes, then
picked up the *Manual for Courts-Martial.* The book was actually a three-ring
binder that held loose-leaf pages. He perused the book quickly, more out of
curiosity and a perverse sense of nostalgia than for legal strategy. The manual
was little more than a primer, a blueprint, and a script for a trial. Everyone's
part was neatly spelled out in black and white. As an officer he had gone to this
book only when all signs and omens pointed to court-martial. Tyson closed the
book, rubbed his eyes, and stood. The light was dying from the west-facing
window, and the library seemed unnaturally still, even for a library. Tyson
looked at his watch. Nearly 6 P.M. He collected his notes, slipped them into his
attaché case, and descended the stairs. He left the building and walked to a
bench in the small war memorial park, a stretch of lawn between the library
and railroad station. A late commuter train pulled in, and wives or husbands in

cars and station wagons were there to meet it. Across the street the large hotel sat serenely in its own treed park.

Several things that he'd read, especially in *Byrne's* and the *Peers Commission Report,* preyed on his mind. He had thought briefly that perhaps he was beyond the reach of the law; that time, distance, and the course of his own life had forever separated him from that fetid little white stucco hospital. But now he was not so sure.

Tyson stood, turned, and began walking. He pictured himself in his pressed officer greens, sitting again in a court-martial room, not on the government side but in the accused's chair. He held on to that image as he walked, trying to make it so vivid that he felt impelled to take any steps necessary to avoid its becoming reality.

He headed toward Franklin Avenue where there was a bookshop. And then, without further delay, he knew he must head home to his family.

5

B en Tyson walked up the flagstone path to his home, a prewar Dutch Colonial on a pleasant street lined with stately elms.

There was a good feeling to the house with its white cedar shingles, shutters, hipped roof, and Dutch dormers covered with reddish slates. Two carriage lanterns flanked the black-paneled door, and through the fanlight above the door he saw the foyer chandelier.

He opened the mailbox and extracted a thick sheaf of mail, mostly third-class junk, which reminded him that he lived in a prestigious zip code and was on every mail-order hit list in the nation. It also tipped him off that Marcy was not yet home.

He tried the door and found it was unlocked, meaning David was home. He entered and called out, "Dave!"

A stereophonic sound emanating from the second floor reverberated through the walls and floor, about a 4 on the Richter scale. Tyson threw the mail on the foyer table and went through the living room into the rear den, or as Marcy called it, "our office." The first time his father heard her say that he looked as if he was about to have another coronary.

Tyson threw his jacket over the desk chair and sat in an Eames recliner. He surveyed the room whose original masculine flavor had been altered, neutered by Marcy into a sort of eclectic potpourri of things that struck her fancy. Things that did not strike her fancy were conspicuously absent from the room, most notably his Army memorabilia, which couldn't seem to find a home.

The remainder of the traditional home had undergone the same transformation. Only David's room, which contained Tyson's boyhood maple colonial furniture, circa 1953, had escaped Marcy's imprint. David had shown a strong sense of territoriality that Marcy could not crack, though Tyson was fairly certain that the boy didn't care either way about the bedroom furniture.

Marcy was, he reflected, a coercive utopian. Their house was run as though it were a commune. Decisions were shared, housework was shared, things and thoughts were shared. Yet, Tyson felt that he was somehow not getting *his* share. If nothing else, he thought, he made twice her salary and worked longer hours. Although Marcy would not use Marx's words, her philosophical rebuttal was: *From each according to his ability, to each according to his needs.* Apparently his needs were less, though any suggestion that his ability was greater met with an icy silence. He often wanted to point out to her that he'd fought a war to keep a country from being run the way his house was run. But that was a lost cause, too.

Tyson put his head back and listened to the stereo. *Primitive. Jungle music.* He couldn't identify the song, if in fact it was a song. But he could not deny its appeal on some primal level.

Tyson drew from his attaché the two books that he'd purchased earlier, a paperback novel by Picard called *The Quest,* and *Hue: Death of a City,* which had set him back another $18.95, plus tax. At this rate, he thought, he'd drive the book onto the *Times* bestseller list and make Picard rich.

He set the novel aside and opened the Hue book, scanning some of the pages that did not relate to the incident at Hôpital Miséricorde. Picard, he judged, was not a terribly bad writer. The book was in the style and format favored by pop historians, stressing personal tragedy, anecdotes, and interviews with survivors—from peasants and privates to generals and provincial governors. And it was impressionistic—the big picture painted or suggested by a series of tiny points like a Seurat.

He read from an early chapter:

> Hue. The city had an almost ethereal nature to it. It was one of those small city-jewels of the world that transcended the meaning of city. It was the soul of Vietnam, North and South. It was a center of learning, culture, and religion; an historical and evocative place, the seat of the old Annamese Empire for twenty-one centuries. And like all great cities, it was a blend of the exotic and the sophisticated, the urbane and the bucolic. It was more Vietnamese than French, but the old cafés on the south side of the Perfume River still had a colonial air about them, and the great Phu Cam Cathedral was a tribute to the city's ecumenicalism.
>
> Hue was a mélange of sights, smells, sounds, and sensations. It was vitality and otherworldliness all in one. It was the heart and embodiment of the nation, and as long as it existed, the Vietnamese people, from the simple villager to the corrupt Saigon politician, had reason to hope. . . .

"Hi, Dad."

Tyson closed the book and looked up at his son. "Hello, David."

"Whatcha readin'?"

"Try that again."

"What are you reading?"

"A book. You didn't take the mail in."

"I took the garbage *out.*"

"You left the door unlocked."

"I took the milk and paper in. Where's Mom?"

"That was my question."

David smiled.

Tyson regarded his son. The boy dressed well, but then sartorial splendor was in vogue at the moment. His hair was of a length that would offend only a master sergeant, and the boy was good-looking, though in Tyson's opinion too lean, like his mother. But also like his mother, his coloring was dark and rich, and he had her striking green eyes.

David drew closer and glanced at the book in Tyson's lap. "Hew?"

"Pronounced 'way.' The French gave the Vietnamese the Latin alphabet, then misspelled every word for them."

"Oh. It's about Vietnam."

"Right. Jeet?"

David laughed. "No. What's for dinner? You cook tonight. I have K.P. Mom serves."

"Is that so?"

"Check the chart." He said it with barely concealed disdain. David picked up *The Quest.* "What's this?"

"Another book. I'll bet you've seen them in museums or on television. They make movies out of them."

David ignored the sarcasm and studied the cover art, then read the flap copy. "The Holy Grail. I read something about that. King Arthur. Is that a true story?"

"It is a legend, and a legend is like the truth, but a legend is also like a myth, and a myth is like a lie. Follow?"

"No." His eyes drifted back to the Hue book. "Is that a true story?"

Tyson did not reply.

David put the novel down on the end table, then said, "What's wrong, Dad?"

Tyson thought a moment, then replied, "I'd rather not discuss it at the moment."

"Are you and Mom getting divorced?"

"Not to my knowledge."

David smiled. "Okay. We can hold a family council later."

Tyson again detected a note of mockery in David's voice. "There are some things, David, that do not lend themselves to solutions by family councils. There are things in this world that children should not be privy to nor burdened with."

"Tell that to Mom."

"I will. But I will speak to you privately about what's troubling me without giving you all the details."

"Okay." The boy hesitated, then said, "You want me to call out for dinner?"

"Yes. Please. Make it a surprise. No pizza."

David nodded and moved toward the door. Tyson could see he wanted to say something more, but Tyson did not encourage him. David left, and Tyson stood, moving to the bar in the shelf unit. He poured himself a small Drambuie.

Tyson sometimes wondered if they should have had more children. He was one of four children, the other three, girls. Conversely, Marcy had three brothers, and he suspected that she had been somehow traumatized by the experience. He, on the other hand, had been treated affectionately by his sisters. David would know neither sibling affection nor rivalry. The decision not to have more children had been made eight years ago when Jenny was born, lived, suffered, and died, all within a week. Marcy said it was a result of the LSD she took in college. Tyson offered that it could have been Agent Orange. His minister, Reverend Symes, said it was God's will. The doctors had no opinion.

Yet, David was healthy in every way, and Tyson sometimes thought it was worth another try. But neither of them had the temperament to cope with a deformed child who lived.

Tyson put this out of his mind and picked up the Hue book. He looked at the index to see if his name appeared anywhere other than the pages dealing with the Hôpital Miséricorde incident. There was a page reference near the front of the book and one near the end. He turned to the earlier page and read while standing:

The soothsayers had foretold that the Year of the Monkey would bring bad luck, and never had the prophets of doom been proved so right so soon. The year was not three hours old when the enemy offensive began.

But notwithstanding this dire prediction, a festive mood filled Hue that day. It was a time of traditional family reunions, feasting, and street festivals. It was like Christmas, New Year's Eve, and Mardi Gras rolled into one. Ancestors were honored at family altars, and religious ceremonies were held at the city's many pagodas and temples. Paper dragons snake-danced through the streets, and, forebodingly, fireworks and skyrockets reverberated throughout the city.

There was a declared truce, but the military was uneasy. American troops were on normal alert, and the South Vietnamese had canceled holiday leaves for some, but not all of their troops. Nearly half the Vietnamese armed forces and a high percentage of key commanders were not on duty. And of those who were, it can be assumed that many were engaged in some sort of celebration.

On the evening of 30 January, seven thousand soldiers of North Vietnam's 4th, 5th, and 6th regiments marched boldly, in parade formation, across the bridges that spanned the canals in Hue's southern suburbs. And no one stopped them.

Within the city, thousands more Viet Cong had infiltrated and mingled with the holiday revelers. Other enemy formations were poised around the city, waiting to strike. Hue's time had come.

But the battle of Hue actually began earlier in the day, though at the time no one realized the significance of those opening shots. Alpha Company, Fifth Battalion of the Seventh Cavalry, First Air Cavalry Division, was patroling an area six kilometers west of the city in the late afternoon. The company, nearly two hundred strong, was commanded by Captain Roy Browder of Anniston, Alabama. Alpha Company began a standard sweep through the supposedly deserted village of Phu Lai when it encountered a unit of well-armed enemy troops, later identified as the Ninth North Vietnamese Regiment, whose strength was estimated at over a thousand men. The enemy regiment was hiding in the village in preparation for their midnight assault on Hue.

The first platoon of Alpha Company was led by Lieutenant Benjamin Tyson, of whom we will learn more later. Tyson's lead platoon was actually inside the village when, according to a survivor, whom I will call Pfc X for reasons that will become clear later, "All of a sudden the place started to move. I mean haystacks opened up, and gooks came out of the wells and holes in the ground. Gooks were standing in the windows and doors of the hootches around the village square, and we were in the middle. It was like a nightmare. I couldn't believe my eyes. No one fired for a really long time. But maybe it was a few seconds. Then it exploded."

Tyson found he was sitting in his chair again. He nodded to himself. It was curious to discover after all these years that his company was one of the first to make contact with the enemy before the Tet offensive actually began. But then the grunt in the field rarely saw the bigger picture. And though he never knew that he'd tangled with a thousand enemy troops, he could believe it. It was for people like Picard to supply the regiment designations and other details that seemed unimportant then, but which allowed others, veterans such as himself, to interpret what had happened. If they cared to.

He put his head back and yawned, feeling very drowsy. The book slipped from his hand onto the floor.

"What the hell are we going to do? *What? What?* What are we going to *do?*"

Tyson lay in the village square between the dead radio operator and the dead squad leader. He turned to the rifleman lying wounded beside him and replied, "We're going to die."

Machine-gun fire raked the square, and rocket-propelled grenades burst among the living and the dead. Tyson had never heard or seen such sustained and heavy enemy fire and had never been in so exposed a position to fully appreciate how quickly a cohesive military unit could wither and die. He knew of no tactics that would extricate them from this massacre in the muddy square. One just had to wait one's turn to die, or stand up and get it over with.

A rocket-propelled grenade landed in front of his face and splashed filthy water into his eyes. Tyson stared at it, half submerged in the brown puddle, realizing it was the last thing he'd ever see. But it did not explode, and he would learn later from other men who had stared that khaki egg-shaped death in the eye that many of those Russian-made grenades were faulty. Some unmotivated, vodka-soaked munitions worker in Volgograd had done something wrong, and Ben Tyson was alive for the time being.

A bullet nicked his right ear, and he yelled out, more in surprise than in pain. He saw men stand and run, only to be cut down, and he wondered where they were running to because the fire was coming from all sides of the square. They were cut off from the rest of the company, and they hadn't the men or resources to break out. He prayed earnestly for a quick death and drew his .45 automatic as insurance against being taken alive.

Then, as if God answered someone else's prayer, a bullet struck a smoke-signal canister hooked to the web belt of a dead man, ten meters to Tyson's front. Tyson watched as the red smoke billowed up slowly from the dead body as though the man were bleeding into a zero-gravity environment.

Tyson tore a smoke canister from his own belt, pulled the pin, and rolled it a few feet away. The canister popped, disgorging a stream of green smoke into the heavy, fetid air. Smoke canisters began popping all over the square as the survivors of his platoon comprehended that there might be a way out. Vivid plumes of red, blue, yellow, orange, and green smoke rose from the killing zone.

The enemy was temporarily blinded, and their fire lifted

higher, as was natural in obscured conditions; they began cross-firing into each other's positions across the market square.

Tyson reached out and pulled the radiophone from the stiffening fingers of the dead radioman. He steadied his voice and called Captain Browder. "Mustang Six, this is Mustang One-Six. We're backing out the same way we came in. Can you meet us halfway?"

The radio crackled, and Browder's voice came on with that practiced cool of a man who was used to talking and ducking bullets at the same time. "Roger. We're heavily engaged at the moment—still at the edge of the village. But we'll try a linkup. That's your smoke, I guess."

"Roger. Guide on that. We've got to leave the dead."

"Understand."

"How about air and artillery?"

"On the way. But don't wait for it. Get your asses moving. Papa's coming. Good luck, partner."

"Roger, over."

"Roger, out."

Tyson rose to one knee and called out through the smoke and noise, "Pull back! Take the wounded and leave the dead and know the difference!"

The first platoon of Alpha Company began their withdrawal across the mud-slick square. They crawled, ran, and stumbled back through the smoke-shrouded marketplace to the first line of huts that bordered the open area. They set the huts ablaze with incendiary grenades, threw the last of their smoke canisters, and tossed tear-gas grenades in their wake. They blasted away with M-16s, machine guns, shotguns, grenade launchers, and pistols, expending ammunition at a rate that testified to their desperateness. They fought for each meter through the cluster of bamboo huts, leaving a burning swath through Phu Lai in their efforts to break out of the trap that had severed them from their main body.

The linkup with their company came on a small village lane that ran between a duck pond and a pigsty. The wounded were handed over to the less fatigued troops of the second and third platoons and passed down the line to a concrete pagoda where the four company medics had gathered. The enemy was still firing, but the battle lines had become so obscured that Alpha Company was not drawing effective fire at the moment.

Browder approached, a stocky figure covered with grime, moving nonchalantly along the path. He spoke to Tyson gruffly. "Well, you're out of the neck-deep shit, sonny, but you got me wading in the knee-deep stuff."

"Thanks for coming."

"Yeah. Well, we can either form a perimeter here, dig in and fight it out until they break it off. Or we can make a break now and beat feet across that rice paddy dike we came in on. Any thoughts?"

Tyson rubbed his bleeding ear. "I don't like the smell of this. Too many gooks with too much ammunition, acting too ballsy. I think we hit something bigger than we are. Time to go."

Captain Browder said, "But we've got nonambulatory wounded to drag out, and I've got some KIAs."

Tyson shook his head. "I don't think Charlie's going to break contact and disappear this time. I think if we stay, they mean to finish us off."

Browder considered a moment, then nodded. "Let's pull out before they get a fix on us again. Let the artillery and gunships pound the shit out of this asshole of a village."

Browder spoke into his radio and gave the orders for a withdrawal. The Cobra gunships arrived and were surprised to meet heavy-caliber antiaircraft fire. One ship crashed in flames into the village. The artillery began landing in Phu Lai, round after round of incendiary white phosphorus as Browder had called for, and the village began to burn as Alpha Company reached the rice paddy dike that marked the western edge of the village.

They staggered across the sodden paddies, carrying the wounded and a few of the dead, leaving a trail of abandoned equipment. Tyson saw a boot stuck in the mud. The enemy fired after them, but Alpha Company paid little attention. Their sole objective was to distance themselves from the village of Phu Lai.

The gunships and artillery covered their withdrawal, which was in reality a rout. The enemy did not follow them across the exposed paddies but took to their underground bunkers and tunnels to wait out the rain of fire and steel.

Alpha Company regrouped on a high and dry piece of ground dotted with burial mounds: the village cemetery. They picked off the rice paddy leeches and began digging in. Bones were turned up, and they littered the reddish earth as the men dug deeper. Skulls were set on the edges of the foxholes, facing outward, a circle of grinning death's-heads stark white against the upturned earth. Someone dug into a fresh grave, and the stench caused the man to vomit. The grave was quickly closed again.

Casualty lists were prepared by the platoon sergeants. The officers read and tallied them: five known dead, present and accounted for. Thirty-eight wounded, ten critically. Fifteen were missing, and Browder reported by radio to battalion headquarters that the presumption of death was strong, but this did not save him from a fierce dressing-down for leaving Americans behind.

Under normal circumstances, Tyson thought, both he and Browder would have been relieved of their commands for the Phu Lai fiasco. It was, after all, a defeat, and a defeat equaled a blunder of some sort. But on that particular night of January 30, in the words of Roy Browder, the feces hit the rotary blades, and they were spared the humiliation of being fired. In the general confusion and panic that gripped the battered nation over the following weeks, trivialities such as the Phu Lai fuckup were forgiven and forgotten. After all, said Browder with a wink, everyone from the chiefs of staff to the chief of Army intelligence was a fuckup for not having noticed what was coming. Browder, when he had a free moment some days later, put himself in for a Silver Star and told Tyson to do the same, though Tyson did not.

Alpha Company spent a restless night among the bones and

pungent earth. A breeze from the South China Sea carried the sounds of explosions from the east, and they could see parachute flares and signal rockets in the vicinity of Hue. A sergeant on his second tour of duty commented, "That's just Hue celebrating. It's called Tet. The gook New Year. Happy New Year."

But it wasn't Hue celebrating. It was Hue dying.

At dawn the remainder of Alpha Company moved east toward the now besieged city, a journey of six kilometers that would take them nearly two weeks and, for many of them, a lifetime to complete.

"Ben!"

Tyson opened his eyes and focused on Marcy sitting in the club chair across from him, a drink in her hand. He cleared his throat. "Hello."

"Tough day?"

Tyson sat up. "I've had worse."

Marcy considered him for a moment. Then she said, "David ordered Chinese food."

"I smell it."

"Do you want to eat, or do you want to talk?"

"I want to drink." He held out his glass.

She hesitated, then stood and took it.

"Drambuie. Neat." He picked up the Hue book and slid it across the coffee table between them. She handed him his drink.

He said, "Have a seat, my love. I have good news and bad news. The good news is that your husband is famous. The bad news is the reason why. Page two-seventeen."

She took up the book and began reading. She dressed well, and for all her feminism, she favored frilly white blouses and cameo chokers. Her skirt was hot pink and fit tightly, with a slit up the side. She wore her dark brown hair in a short shag that framed a light olive complexion. She looked vaguely Semitic or Mediterranean, though her genetic pool lay in the north of Europe. Her eyes were what people noticed first; those large watery green eyes that were able to flash anger, sensuality, and iciness with equal intensity. Ben Tyson studied his wife as she read. Finally, she sensed his gaze and raised the book.

Tyson shifted his attention to the window. Bluebirds were feeding on the back lawn, and the sun was nearly gone, leaving long purple shadows over the terrace. The room was dark except for the circle of lamplight around Marcy.

"Is this true?"

He turned back toward her. She'd rested the open book in her lap and was staring at him, intently, expectantly.

Everything that came to mind sounded evasive. "As far as it goes, and in substance, yes, it is accurate."

She said nothing for a long time, then asked, "What more is there?"

"Much, much more."

"In your words, Ben. How is this book inaccurate?"

"It's a matter of perspective. It depends on where you were standing."

"Where were you standing?"

He ignored the question and said, "Also, after a long time it's hard to distinguish reality from fantasy from nightmare."

"It says here"—she tapped the open book—"it says you and your men massacred sick and wounded people. You shot men, women, children, and babies. Burned people alive. Did *that* happen?"

Tyson let a few seconds go by, then replied evenly, "It happened. It did happen. But not quite the way Picard says."

"Then tell me what you remember. What you know."

Tyson considered a moment, then answered, "No."

"Why not?"

"I made a promise never to speak of this."

"Whom did you promise?"

Tyson looked off at some indeterminate point and said distractedly, "We all promised. We swore to each other."

She showed a flash of anger. "That's absurd. I'm your wife."

Tyson stood and poured himself another liqueur. He turned and looked at her.

Marcy stood and tossed the book on the coffee table. "I think I have a right to know, and I don't really care about some vow you made . . . and obviously *someone* broke that vow. X and Y squealed, didn't they?"

"You weren't *there!* You were *here!* Don't ask me to explain to you what happened in that shithole eighteen years ago. Who the hell knows what happened? Who cares—?" Tyson got himself under control and sat back in his chair. "I don't remember what happened."

Marcy drew a deep breath and looked at him closely. "That's not true." She added, "I can remember what happened to me eighteen years ago—"

"You should. It was reported in a national magazine."

"Cheap shot, Ben." She moved to the door as if to leave, then walked to where Tyson was sitting and put her hand on his shoulder.

He took her hand and said, "Just give me some time to sort it out. I'll tell you. But I want to tell you the truth. And that's not possible now."

She didn't reply.

Tyson added, "Look, if this book triggers some sort of . . . investigation, then there will be different versions of the truth . . . and it's best if you wait—"

"What do you mean 'an investigation'? Can they . . . bring charges . . . ?"

"According to Phil Sloan they can."

She shook her head, then said, "You went to him? Before you spoke to me?"

"He has a law degree. You don't. He was available. You weren't. The subject was murder, not marital difficulties."

Marcy disengaged her hand from his. "Just tell me this: Did you . . . kill anyone? I mean, it doesn't say you killed anyone yourself. . . ."

He replied, "An officer is responsible for the actions of his men."

"Nonsense! That's so typically macho. Such egotistical military bullshit . . . Every sane person is responsible for his or her own actions."

He interrupted, "I'll tell you something else: Not only am I responsible for the actions of the men I commanded, but I'm liable for crimes they may have committed. That's the law."

"Idiotic."

"Be that as it may, you have to take into account *military* law, institutions, custom, and logic. Not your own personal philosophy."

"All right. I understand that, Ben. Just don't decide to be noble or stupid. If you didn't kill anyone, you're innocent of murder. And you'd better say that, if anything comes of this."

Tyson didn't reply but walked to the window and threw open the sash. A scented breeze came into the room, and the big sycamore tree rustled in the light wind. Children were playing in the next yard. It was an incredibly beautiful twilight, he thought. One of those evenings whose smells come back to you years later. "What is that? Honeysuckle?"

"I suppose."

"Why can't it always be May?"

"You said you liked the changing seasons."

"Right. But sometimes I like it to be always May."

Marcy stared at his back for some time, then spoke softly. "I'm frightened for you, Ben."

"I'm okay."

"No, you're not. That's the point. I know what's going through your mind: duty, honor, country, God. Or something like that. You've got a martyr streak in you—"

"Do I?"

"You may have survived combat, but you won't survive this. Not unless you—"

Tyson turned and faced her. "That's enough."

"All right. But I'll tell you this: As far as I'm concerned, everything that had to do with that war was criminal. But that's no reason to offer yourself up as the chief criminal, out of some misguided sense of responsibility, guilt or—"

"Enough! I don't need a lecture."

"What *do* you need from me?"

Tyson leaned back against the windowsill. He thought she would probably be more understanding if he'd come home and announced that he was an embezzler or a dope addict. Or better yet, that he'd machine-gunned a roomful of Republican fund-raisers. But this particular crime touched a raw nerve in her. He said, "I just wanted you to know."

"Thanks. I could have learned more at the supermarket."

He forced a smile, then spoke musingly. "Maybe I'm overreacting . . . maybe this will fade away. Probably I shouldn't have even gone to Phil's office."

She replied, "I hope you're right," then added, "But you know, Ben, even if it doesn't lead to anything in a legal sense . . . in other ways, here in this house, in this town, and on your job . . ."

"Yes, I know. Thank you."

She seemed to be lost in thought, and instinctively he knew her mind had returned to those pages of gory detail.

She looked up at him. "How did they kill the children? I mean *how* . . . ?"

There was a knock on the door, and it opened a crack. David peeked in. "The Chinese delicacies are congealing."

Tyson said, "Give it a shot of microwave. We'll be right there."

David closed the door.

Marcy and Ben Tyson looked at each other for some seconds, both wondering how much David had heard. They turned and walked silently toward the door.

She said, "Do you want wine?"

He held the door open for her. "Beer goes better with Chinese delicacies. How was your day?"

"Hectic. And I have a trip this week."

"Where?"

"Chicago. One night."

He didn't respond.

6

Tyson awakened. He threw the bedclothes back and turned his head toward Marcy. She slept in the nude, in all seasons, as he did. He regarded her naked body, dark against the plain, white cotton sheets. He watched her full, firm breasts rising and falling as she breathed, then his eyes traveled down to her pubic hair. The miracle of their marriage, he thought, was that after sixteen years the sexual attraction was as strong as the sexual drive.

Tyson knew that nearly everyone found them a classically mismatched couple. Tyson considered himself a traditional man, a result of growing up in a home that stressed traditional values and in a community that was locally famous as a conservative bastion. Unlike Marcy, he was never personally caught up in the turbulence of the sixties, partly because he went to college in the Deep South, partly because of his years in the Army, 1966 to 1969. He'd commented on occasion, "I missed the Age of Aquarius, but I saw it on TV."

Marcy Clure Tyson and Benjamin James Tyson had nearly opposite tastes in music, clothing, literature, and art. Politically, he was indifferent, and she was committed. Yet they married and stayed married while a good number of their friends were divorced, about to be divorced, or wished they were divorced. Tyson had often wished he'd never met her but rarely wished to see her gone.

Marcy rolled over on her side and faced him. She mumbled something, then let out a snore.

Tyson swung his legs out of the bed and stood. He walked across the carpet to the dormer windows as he did every morning to personally greet the day. The eastern sky was brightening, and he could see it was going to be another fine morning. Below in the dark street he saw two very early commuters, briefcases swinging in wide arcs, as they stepped out purposefully to catch the next train. Tyson heard the matin bells of a nearby church. *Each matin bell, the Baron saith, knells us back to a world of death.*

Tyson stepped onto the running trampoline and began to jog in place, his eyes still fixed on the east-facing window. There were lights in bedrooms across the road, and at the larger cross-street at the south end of the block, he saw cars making their way toward the parkways, expressways, and railroad stations. Suburbia was on the move, flowing westward to infuse the great city with its clean, oxygenated blood, to wow Wall Street and Madison Avenue with its tennis tans and tales of weekend bogies and eagles.

Tyson jumped off the trampoline and somersaulted to the middle of the gray carpet. He did a few minutes of calisthenics, then walked briskly into the master bathroom.

The bathroom had been modernized and sported a large Jacuzzi. Tyson turned it on. He shaved and brushed his teeth, then lowered himself into the hot, swirling eucalyptus-scented water. Through the rising steam he saw himself in a mirrored wall. He was, by any standards, powerfully built and somewhat on the hairy side. Some women liked that, others didn't. Marcy reveled in the forest on his chest. The Oriental girls, he recalled, found it beastly or amusing, but never sexy. However, they always commented favorably on his size; and it wasn't flaky, prostitute flattery. Westerners *were* bigger as he'd found out when he'd purchased a non-PX condom at a local *pharmacie*. He thought he should tell that amusing story to Mr. Kimura over lunch one day.

He put his head and shoulders back on the marble rim of the tub and floated in the turbulent waters. The dream had come again last night: He is back in the Army. There is a war on. It is a nameless war, with few of the elements of Vietnam. The landscape is the cold wintry woods of Fort Benning, Georgia, where he'd taken his infantry officer training. The combat fatigues he wears remind him of the foreign-looking uniforms worn by the aggressor army in the war games they played at Benning. In the dream these uniforms are filthy and torn. The weapons and equipment he carries are somewhat primitive. He does not interpret this to mean it is an earlier war, but rather a future war of long duration: an interminable, civilization-destroying conflict. Armies sweep back and forth across the scarred earth and the dying cities. That part at least is Vietnam.

In the dream he is no longer an officer, but an ordinary rifleman, and someone always says to him, "Tyson, you have five more years to serve," to which he always replies, "That's not fair. I was already in. This time I'll die."

Tyson pushed off the edge of the large tub, and let the waters swirl around his floating body. He had gone briefly to a psychiatrist who specialized in the war neuroses of upper middle-class and wealthy veterans, preferably ex-officers. That was about as specialized as you could get, Tyson thought, and only on Park Avenue would you find such a shrink. Tyson had rather liked the man, Dr. Stahl, and found his insights revealing and his knowledge of postwar-related stress nothing short of startling.

Stahl and he had talked about the dream, they talked about the guilt of having survived when others didn't and spoke of the special guilt of having killed. They discussed at length the unique problems of having commanded men in battle, of having given orders that led to the deaths of subordinates and the deaths of civilians. It was in this area that Stahl earned his two hundred dollars an hour, and they were both aware of that. Popular literature and conventional wisdom were confined to the depressingly ordinary problems of the grunt. Stahl recognized that analyzing the problems of the ex-officer was more interesting, more complex, and usually more remunerative.

Tyson had been on the verge of telling the man about Hôpital Miséricorde but knew intuitively that confession becomes a bad habit. After Stahl he would tell Marcy, and after Marcy the Reverend Symes. And thus having squared things away in privileged conversations with his shrink, his wife, and a representative of his God, he would eventually go to the Army Judge Advocate General. Therefore, he did not tell Stahl, and since further psychotherapy was of little value unless Stahl knew the Big Secret, Tyson had terminated the relationship, much to Dr. Stahl's surprise and regret. Stahl found Tyson interesting. Tyson found Stahl too perceptive.

The last thing Stahl had said to him, in a letter actually, written in Stahl's somewhat stilted middle-European style, was this: *There is something else on your mind which is a great and terrible secret, Mr. Tyson. I cannot see it, but I can see its shadow and feel its presence in everything you say.*

It would be idle to speculate on what it is, but please feel assured that in war everything is the norm. I have spoken to brave men who have had hysterics on the battlefield, who have run from the enemy, who have left their friends to die, and who have soiled their pants in the heat of battle. I have had revealed to me things of which you cannot even begin to dream. I tell you, my friend, war is hell, but take heart: When a soldier goes to war everything is pre-forgiven.

Tyson had never forgotten that cryptic last line: *Everything is pre-forgiven.* But by whom? How? When was it pre-forgiven? That line was meant to pique his curiosity; to entice him back onto the couch of Dr. Stahl. And it almost had. But in the end he did not answer the letter, because it was unanswerable.

Some time after that, Dr. Stahl, like a statistically significant percentage of his colleagues, had killed himself. The *Times* reported that the overdose of Quaaludes may have been accidental, but Tyson did not think so. Tyson thought that Vietnam killed by contact, association, and proxy.

Tyson floated to the edge of the tub and spread his arms out over the rim to steady himself. He stared up at the infrared lamp overhead and felt its waves warming his face. He recalled that he was not particularly surprised at Dr. Stahl's suicide. For all Stahl's assurances about not being judgmental, not being shocked, the man was after all human. He had listened to an army of sick men fill his ears with grief until it had filled his heart and soul, and like a slow-acting virus, had overcome his immunities. And one day he discovered he was dead and made it official.

Tyson had been unexpectedly saddened while reading the obituary. But on a practical level, he was concerned about what had happened to Stahl's case files, though he had never made any inquiries.

Stahl had ended most of his sessions with the words "You cannot run from the demons, so you must make friends with them." He had advised Tyson to recall the dream in detail, talk with the characters who peopled the dark landscapes of his mind, until one day they would become familiar, friendly, then perhaps banal and insipid. So, lying there in the Jacuzzi, Tyson went through it again. But this time—and there was no mistaking it—the characters in the dream had become more malevolent. The dream had taken on a special and prescient significance. In fact, the nightmare was becoming reality. *All is pre-forgiven, Dr. Stahl.*

Marcy walked naked into the bathroom and lowered herself into the tub. She drew a long breath, inhaling the eucalyptus, smiled, and closed her eyes.

Tyson watched her breasts bob in the water, then turned his attention to her face. Rivulets of sweat ran from her brow down her cheeks. He thought she looked fine without makeup. She extended her legs and floated atop the misty water. Tyson reached out and massaged her toes. She murmured, "Oh, that feels good."

Marcy spread her floating legs, and Tyson knelt, leaning forward, cupping her buttocks in his palms. As he moved his head between her legs, she said, "You'll drown if you try that."

"What a way to go."

"Ben!"

He buried his face deep in her groin, and she brought her thighs together, slipping down farther into the water, taking him down with her. He struggled for a moment, broke free, and surfaced, spluttering. "Bitch."

She laughed.

Tyson retreated moodily to his end of the bath.

Marcy lifted herself out of the sunken tub and stood on the tiled edge, her legs parted as she stretched and yawned.

Tyson watched her and was instantly reminded of the photograph. It had originally appeared in *Life* magazine and had been reproduced a number of times in books dealing with the 1960s. It was a black-and-white photograph showing a group of students in Los Angeles's Griffith Park during the winter recess of 1968. It must have been a mild day because they were all cavorting in the nude at Mulholland Fountain.

The occasion was a rock concert according to the *Life* caption, though when the picture had been used on a network TV documentary about the 1960s, the occasion had been described as a love-in. A photographic essay book described the event as an antiwar rally. Tyson had also seen the picture captioned as a happening and a be-in. Although the event may not have been clear, the picture of Marcy was. She was the most prominent of all the students, standing on the rim of the fountain much as she was now standing on the rim of the Jacuzzi, a full-frontal nude, one arm around the shoulders of a slender, shaggy-haired young man. The other arm was upraised, fist clenched, and her legs were parted. The expression on her face was a mixture of defiance and uninhibited joy. To the side could be seen two policemen approaching the fountain full of naked young men and women.

Tyson saw the picture again in his mind: Marcy's luxuriant pubic hair like a black bull's-eye, her breasts standing proud and erect. But for all the nakedness in that fountain, there was little that was erotic. The gathering was meant as a political statement, and it was.

Like other famous tableaux—the flag-raising over Iwo Jima or the girl weeping over the body at Kent State—the photograph transcended the particular event and captured the essence of an age. None of the subjects had been identified in print, their names as unimportant as the name of the photographer or the journal where the photograph first appeared. The picture had entered the public domain, the history books, and the public consciousness. No royalties were paid nor permissions asked nor rights protected. Yet for those who knew the subjects by name or who were the subjects, the famous photograph still remained personal and evoked a sense of grief, joy, or violated privacy.

Tyson looked up at his wife, still engaged in her stretching exercises. Her body and indeed her face had not changed that much in nearly two decades. In the picture, though, her hair hung in long, wet strands down to her breasts. When Tyson had first met her at a party in a friend's Manhattan apartment, her hair was still shoulder-length, and his mental image of her remained that of a young girl with long hair, barefoot, with little makeup, and wearing a peasant dress. He said, "I love you still."

She paused in her stretching exercises and smiled at him. "We are still in love. Remember that in the coming weeks and months."

"No matter how nasty we are to one another."

"Right."

Tyson shut the water off and lifted himself onto the tatami mat beside the tub. He rested his head on a cylindrical bamboo pillow and brought his knees up. He ran his fingers over the scar on his kneecap. It had turned reddish purple from the hot water. Most shrapnel wounds were jagged and ugly as they were supposed to be. This one was ludicrous: It looked like a large question mark.

Tyson said to his wife, "There was a picture of me and my platoon in the book."

"I didn't see it." Marcy reached into the large, tiled shower stall and turned on the six pulsating jets. She said, "Where did you leave the book, by the way? I don't want David to see it."

Tyson stood and stepped into the shower with her. He thought he'd remind her that the *Life* magazine of March 8, 1968, was stuck up on the bookshelf in plain view. He said, however, "I put it in my attaché case. But he'll have to read it eventually."

She let the water pound against her body and ran her soapy hands over her breasts and face. "Right. But you have to speak to him first."

"The book speaks for itself. I'll just ask him to read it from the beginning. So my . . . role will be seen in context."

She looked over her shoulder. "In or out of context it's gruesome, Ben, and it's going to upset him. Speak to him first." She added, "Perspective. Give him some perspective. Show him where to stand when he's reading it."

Tyson left the shower.

She called out, "Sorry."

Tyson tore a towel off the rack and quickly dried himself.

Marcy shut off the water and opened the stall door. "Tell me something. How did you live with this for all these years? Wait. Don't be angry. I don't mean that in a judgmental sense. I mean it in a practical sense. How did you keep it to yourself and not tell *anyone? Did* you tell anyone?"

"No."

She nodded and said, "You never even hinted at it. . . ." She thought a moment, then added, "You were blocking. You totally blocked it."

"Psychobabble." Tyson tossed the towel in the hamper. "I never *blocked* it. I just chose not to discuss it. Unlike many people, I don't have to pour my guts out and reveal my personal history to casual acquaintances or even to friends. Or even to you." He turned and walked into the adjoining dressing room, closing the door behind him.

He opened his closet and scanned his suits without really noticing them. It occurred to him that Marcy was going to be his toughest critic, but also his most honest one. He should listen to what she was saying so he could know what others were thinking. "Day two," he said aloud. "Each day brings forth something new."

7

B en Tyson pulled his yellow Volvo into the drive leading to the Garden City Hotel and joined a line of slow-moving cars waiting to be parked. He moved the car up a few feet. Directly in front of him was a Cadillac limousine. In his rearview mirror he saw the grillwork of a Rolls. He said, "Let's buy a new car. Something decidedly decadent."

She shook her head. "In your present situation, a new *tie* would look flagrant. Low profile, Ben. That's the word of the week." She added, "Also, your job may be a little shaky."

Tyson nodded. Nevertheless, he thought, the old battered Volvo needed replacing. But now, nearly two weeks after that Tuesday morning, even the most mundane and personal decisions had to be scrutinized with one eye on appearances.

Tyson moved the car up another few feet and looked out toward the hotel.

The nine-story building sat in the center of the suburban village, surrounded by ten acres of landscaped park. It was a new building, vaguely Georgian in style and topped by a reproduction of the cupola that had crowned the old Garden City Hotel. The setting sun blazed in red reflection from the windows, and Tyson squinted. He imagined the redbrick Georgian structure that had stood there when he was growing up. The May evening recalled to him his senior prom in the Regency Room. He remembered the annual cotillion, the weddings and celebrations, including his parents' twenty-fifth anniversary party in the Hunt Room. It was, he reflected, a privileged childhood and adolescence, a very good time. A time of hope, a time before the war and the turbulence had changed him; had changed everyone. Such had been the years of his growing up in the fifties and early sixties. He said, almost to himself, "Enjoy it while you can."

"What?"

"Life. Dance and be merry."

She glanced at him and said thoughtfully, "Philosophical musings don't become you."

"Perhaps. I was just trying to put my petty problems in perspective. *That* is still the word of this week, by the way."

"Glad to hear it."

"Also, the last refuge of a troubled spirit is religion. I'm going to pay a call on Reverend Symes."

She thought a moment, then said, "Why not? That's better than talking to your wife. And he can't testify against you either. Which reminds me, you never told me what Phil Sloan said."

"Why should I? I know by something you let slip that you spoke to him yourself. Privileged conversations, indeed. I'll give old Symes a shot at being discreet."

Marcy didn't reply.

Tyson expanded on his earlier subject. "But life is good. At least for us. There's no war, depression, famine, hunger, or civil strife."

"Not in Garden City, also known as the Garden of Eden. This place is zoned against reality."

Tyson exhaled a long breath. Subconsciously, he thought, he must have precipitated this conversation about Garden City—Marcy's favorite subject—in order to take his mind off other things. Marcy was a product of Manhattan's Upper West Side, whose population leaned as far to port as Garden City's citizens leaned starboard. And Marcy, he knew, wanted to move back to her old stomping grounds. As if she'd read his thoughts, she said, "You can't live here anymore, you know."

"I can live wherever the hell I please."

"But you can't." Marcy retreated into a moody silence. Just when Tyson thought he was on the verge of a marital dispute, she laughed unexpectedly. He glanced at her. She said, "Do you realize we always pick a fight when we don't want to go someplace?"

"Yes, I realize that. This car has made more U-turns than a boomerang." He stopped the car under the hotel marquee. "But this time we've arrived at our planned destination."

A green-liveried footman with top hat opened Marcy's door. An attendant held open Tyson's door, and Tyson exchanged the Volvo for a parking chit. A doorman saluted as they passed inside to the pink marbled lobby. A hand-painted sign announced:

THE NASSAU HOSPITAL AUXILIARY
ANNUAL CHARITY BALL
GRAND BALLROOM

The arrow pointed left.

Marcy said, "Let me buy you a drink first."

The tables in the dimly lit Hunt Room were full, but Tyson found an empty barstool and Marcy sat. Tyson stood beside her. He ordered a Scotch, and she ordered a glass of white wine. They both glanced around the room as their eyes adjusted to the low light, and nodded to a few people.

The drinks came, and Tyson stirred his Scotch. He said, "Am I crazy to come here? Or just brazen?"

Marcy picked up her wine. "At some point you'll know the answer to that. Up to now, no one knows how to deal with you."

Tyson leaned his back against the bar and again surveyed the room. English hunting prints on the paneled walls were a feeble reminder that the original Hunt Room had actually been a place where ladies and gentlemen of the Meadow Brook Hunt Club gathered after riding to hounds. Tyson mused, "I liked the old place better."

Marcy's eyes rolled. "Oh, Jesus, if I hear that one more time *from one of you original settlers,* I'll puke."

"Well, it was a hell of a place." He added maliciously, "The Nassau County Republican Club had its headquarters in the old hotel. I used to do volunteer work for them. We had a Goldwater fund-raiser here in sixty-four."

"I'm getting sick."

He smiled, then sipped his Scotch and drew on his cigarette. "History," he said aloud. "Teddy Roosevelt stayed here often. Charles Lindbergh spent the week before his solo flight at the old hotel. Once, when I was on leave, I took the Lindbergh suite. Did I ever tell you that? I slept in the bed Lindbergh slept in."

Marcy contrived a yawn and replied, "Based on what I've heard from people who don't romanticize the old fleabag, you probably slept in the same sheets, too."

Tyson stared into the dark recesses of the lounge. The clientele in the pre-World War I era included Astors, Morgans, Vanderbilts, Hewitts, Jays, Belmonts, Harrimans, even Lillian Russell. But history was a continuum. Someday, someone sitting where he was now sitting would say that Benjamin Tyson had frequented the new Hunt Room.

Benjamin who?

The guy who was court-martialed for murder. Remember? It was in all the papers. The hospital massacre in Vietnam.

Oh, right. He used to drink here? No kidding?

But that was future history. In the old Hunt Room, when he was drunk, he'd conjure up images of the past, especially the aviation greats who had drunk there between the world wars: Glenn Curtiss, Jimmy Doolittle, Billy Mitchell, Lawrence Sperry, Amelia Earhart, Leroy Grumman. . . . Tyson recalled his boyhood dream to be a fighter pilot, as his father had been; he thought of his plastic model of the Grumman Hellcat and wondered what had become of it. The world spun too fast now, and Tyson knew he would never fly a Grumman Hellcat, but what was worse, the desire to do so was dead.

Marcy broke into his thoughts. "Another?"

He turned his head toward her. "One more."

She ordered, and Tyson said to the young bartender whom he knew slightly, "Ed, you ever heard of the battle of Hue?"

"Midway? Yeah, it was on TV."

"Heard of the Tet Offensive?"

The bartender turned and ran Tyson's tab through the register. "Tet? Sure. Vietnam. The VC attacked Tet and the Americans got beat." He put the tab back on the bar in front of Tyson.

"Tet was a time, not a place."

"No kidding?"

"No kidding."

Ed shrugged and went off to serve someone else. Tyson said, "Smart kid." He sipped on his drink, then observed, "See . . . ultimately all battlefield deaths are in vain. No one really remembers any of it. So what's the big deal?"

"You tell me."

But Tyson could not. He sensed the alcohol working its magic and felt better. Marcy said, "Time to dance."

Tyson smiled and took her hand. They retraced their steps through the lobby, arm in arm, nodding to a few people as they made their way to the Grand Ballroom. As they entered the mauve-colored ballroom, Tyson scanned the pale-blue-clothed tables set around the large dance floor. The band wasn't playing, and there seemed to be a lull in the full room. Tyson said, "Let's split up and regroup at the bar."

"Okay . . . oh, Christ. . . ."

Mrs. Livander, the president of the Nassau Hospital Auxiliary, had spotted them and was sweeping across the room, arms prematurely spread for an embrace. Tyson stepped forward as though he were sacrificing himself so that Marcy might live. Mrs. Livander veered slightly and enveloped him in her plump arms. "Ben Tyson. Oh, you charming man. You're so devilishly handsome, if I were ten years younger I'd be after you."

Tyson thought twenty years was closer to the mark, but he hugged Lydia Livander and gave her a peck on the cheek.

Mrs. Livander turned to Marcy and effused, "You look *lovely*. What a stunning *dress!* How *do* you keep your figure?" She took Marcy by the shoulders as if to fix her in place and poured a steady stream of lavish praise on her. Tyson's eyes darted around until he spotted the bar.

Without warning, Lydia Livander took their arms in a firm grip and propelled them toward a photographer from the *Garden City News*. "Sam," she bubbled, "Sam, you *must* get a picture of this beautiful couple this *instant.*"

Tyson and Marcy smiled, the flash went off, and before Tyson could see clearly, Mrs. Livander had him on the move again. Tyson glanced at Marcy and shrugged. If he'd intended to slip in unobtrusively, he was making a bad start of it. As Mrs. Livander moved them around to meet people they already knew or didn't want to know, he had the distinct impression that heads were turning toward him.

Pleading an urgent call of nature, Tyson broke free of Mrs. Livander's ministrations and made directly for the bar. He ordered a Scotch and soda and carried it to a neutral corner. Shortly, Marcy came up to him and said, "You see, nothing has changed. Lydia did that for each of the two hundred couples who arrived tonight."

Tyson swallowed half his drink. "I felt like the only Negro at a Liberal party dance. There wasn't enough of me to go around."

Marcy smiled. "Hang in there, Benjamin. Balls."

"Right. Nevertheless, it's going to be a long evening."

"But a memorable one. And your last public appearance, I daresay."

"Perhaps." However, he suspected that his last public appearance would not be a black-tie affair but a dress-green appearance in a place less convivial than this one.

Ben Tyson sat at a round table and surveyed the full ashtrays, empty bar glasses, and discarded programs: the detritus of another tax-deductible bash. If the hospital got 10 percent of the take, they were doing well, he thought. The tables hadn't been assigned, and he'd found himself with different groupings of people throughout the evening. Now, finally, he found himself alone.

Tyson glanced at his watch. On balance, he thought, he was glad he'd come. If there was any truth to the old saying that public opinion was in advance of the law, then he felt somewhat relieved. No one had snubbed him, and no one had hustled him into the men's room to face a committee of peers with tar and feathers.

There had been some awkwardness and strained smiles, but this was not an age of absolutes, and there was no consensus on the correct behavior toward a suspected war criminal. Socially, he was still acceptable. Legally, he was innocent until proven guilty. Time to go home.

Tyson looked around the room. Half the crowd was gone, but he couldn't see Marcy. In fact, he hadn't seen much of her most of the evening, though he felt confident she'd danced with a good number of the men, annoyed an equal number of wives, gotten at least one serious proposition, and accepted one or two dates for lunch in the city.

Tyson began walking toward the door and saw he was on a collision course with Phillip Sloan. Sloan intercepted him near the exit. "Ben. Did you have a good time?"

"Hello, Phil."

"Where's your wife?"

"Where's yours?"

Sloan smiled tightly. "Do you have a moment?"

Tyson replied, "I'd rather not be seen speaking to my lawyer."

Sloan seemed miffed at being put into the same category as a bookie or loan shark. "Let's step out here." They went into the large anteroom, and Sloan indicated the men's room. Tyson said, "Branch office?" Sloan went inside and Tyson followed. Sloan said curtly, "Is this all right?"

"If you like pink marble."

"Listen, Ben, you haven't been the most cooperative client—"

"And you have not been the most discreet attorney, Phil."

Sloan began to respond, but said instead, "You know, our families have done business for years. I consider you more than a client, you're—"

Tyson turned and used the urinal.

"You're a friend. The wives are friends."

"We're all friends."

"Right. So don't give me this shit that you don't want us to be seen together in public."

Tyson turned from the urinal. "What did you want to see me about?"

Sloan glanced around to assure himself they were alone. An Hispanic attendant sat on a stool, reading the *New York Post.* Sloan said, "I've contacted an attorney in the city who specializes in publishing law."

Tyson washed his hands.

"He advised us to bring suit." Sloan waited, then went on. "His reasoning is that these alleged incidents are so old that a criminal action is extremely unlikely. That will leave Picard's allegations as basically hearsay. In lay language, Picard has his ass hanging out. Are you following me?"

The attendant gave Tyson a hand towel. "Sort of."

"Also, no one but you is mentioned in a pejorative way. Whenever he writes about someone shooting civilians, he doesn't give a name."

"I noticed that omission."

"But you are mentioned by name as a witness to the massacre. The point is made again and again that you did nothing to stop the killing." Sloan added, "There's even a line in there that suggests you masterminded the cover-up. There's also an ambiguous sentence about you ordering the enemy soldiers to be killed."

"That certainly was an ambiguous sentence. I did not order wounded and captured enemy soldiers murdered. I ordered my men to find and destroy any armed enemy soldiers still in the hospital who continued to resist."

Sloan seemed uninterested in the clarification. He said, "The point is, whoever spoke to Picard was out to get *you.* I think Picard believed a lot of crap and printed it as truth. This attorney and I agree that we have a very strong case for libel."

Tyson straightened his bow tie.

Sloan continued, "Ben, I'd like you to meet this attorney. His name is Beekman. He's a real crackerjack—"

"What does that make me? The prize? Are you a Milk Dud?"

"You're drunk." Sloan made a move to leave, then came back and took a deep breath. "Beekman has handled some famous literary libel cases. You may know the name."

Tyson looked at Sloan's reflection in the mirror. He said, "You and I have both heard of civil trials that took on the coloration of criminal cases. All sorts of muck is dragged up, the press reports it as though it were a murder trial instead of a lawsuit, and in the end, even if the plaintiff wins, he loses." Tyson took a bottle of Aramis and splashed some on his palm. "Let the damned thing *die.*" He slapped the cologne on his face.

"It won't die unless you *kill* it. If you don't sue and win, these allegations will hang over you for the rest of your life. Reviewers will quote from Picard's book, other authors will pick up bits and pieces, and this damned hospital incident will enter history as *truth.*"

Tyson didn't respond.

"Actually, it may be better to sit tight for a few weeks and see what kind of media exposure this gets."

Tyson tipped the attendant and looked at Sloan. "What does that have to do with it?"

"Well, according to Beekman, considering the book is recently published, the damages to you are small as of now. The book could be recalled by the publisher, further limiting damages. However, we could wait and . . . pretend we had no knowledge of the book. Then, in time, as a result of, let's say, author interviews and book reviews, plus the book's circulation, advertising, promotion, and so forth, your good name and reputation will be further damaged."

Tyson didn't reply.

"Let's say," continued Sloan carefully, "that you lose your job. That your son is harassed at school. That Marcy is . . . well, whatever. Then, wham! We sue. We go after not only Picard but the publisher, the distributor, maybe even the unnamed sources that Picard mentions. Assuming a jury finds for you, the award will be *huge.* You will be vindicated and rich."

Tyson observed, "The flip side of every problem is an opportunity."

"Exactly."

Tyson was intrigued by Sloan's offhand manner in engineering a conspiracy. He'd probably be more ethical in a criminal case where the money was paid up front, and the only thing he could lose was his client's liberty.

Sloan said, "Libel suits are very rare things. It's not often that a person gets libeled in print. Cases like this probably make up less than one percent of all civil suits. And the press covers them. So I understand you wanting to avoid further public exposure. But you're a fighter, Ben, and you won't let this blotch remain on your honor."

"Cut the crap, Phil."

Sloan pulled at his lip as though he were wrestling with a tough decision. He looked at Tyson and said, "You probably think no one is going to zero in on your small chapter in that big book. Well . . ." He reached into his pocket and pulled out a folded piece of paper. "Beekman got this for me. There's a trade magazine called *Publishers Weekly,* and they get galley copies of books months before publication. This is a book review in that magazine published seven weeks ago." He handed Tyson the photocopied page.

Tyson looked at it. There were six short book reviews on the page. His eyes went to the one captioned *Hue: Death of a City. Andrew Picard.* There was some publishing information, followed by a short review of about 150 words. He scanned it quickly and saw that the review was generally favorable. Halfway through he read:

> There is an account of a massacre by American troops at a French hospital filled with patients and European staff. Picard's writing vividly re-creates the massacre and leaves the reader wondering why no official inquiry ever grew out of this incident that ranks with My Lai in the annals of Vietnam atrocities.

Tyson refolded the page and handed it back to Sloan.

Sloan tapped the paper against his palm. "You see? Even in this little précis, you see what sticks out?"

"I see."

"Imagine longer reviews in newspapers and magazines."

Two men came into the rest room. Tyson walked out, and Sloan followed him into the anteroom. People were wandering out of the ballroom and standing around talking, or heading for the lobby. Tyson noticed a few people glancing their way. He said, "You know, Phil, when I got that Community Fund Service Award, no one seemed to hear about it. But as soon as I get myself mentioned in some obscure book as a war criminal, everyone has heard the good news in two weeks."

"That is life, my friend."

"So I've heard."

Sloan took Tyson's arm. "I have to tell you, Ben, a lot of people kept asking me tonight, 'Are you suing?' I don't know what to say anymore."

Tyson knew Sloan was maneuvering him toward a lawsuit the way a surgeon maneuvers a patient toward the operating room. He knew he needed a second opinion and not Beekman's. He said to Sloan, "If we sue and it went to trial, how many Army lawyers would be in the spectator seats? How many Justice Department lawyers?"

Sloan didn't reply.

Tyson continued, "You see, win or lose, in a civil suit, the government will hear enough to make them curious. Did that occur to you, counselor?"

Sloan shrugged. "That's a possibility, of course. But still, Ben, I'm assuming that in a strict legal sense you are not guilty of murder. That's what the government will conclude if they monitor a civil trial."

Tyson leaned closer to Sloan. "They will conclude no such thing, my friend." Tyson fluffed Sloan's red pocket handkerchief. "Good night." Tyson turned and walked toward the lobby where he found Marcy seated in an armchair. She stood as he approached, and without a word, he took her arm and they left the lobby of the hotel through the main doors. The night had turned cool and misty, with a soft wind blowing from the south. Tyson breathed deeply to clear his head. "I think I smell the ocean."

"You always say that after you eat canapés made with anchovy paste. You said that once in Switzerland."

Tyson gave the doorman his parking chit. About a dozen people waited under the marquee for their cars. Tyson looked at Marcy. "Did you have a good evening?"

Marcy considered a moment, then said, "No. For the first time, I felt I wasn't Marcy Clure Tyson but Ben Tyson's wife."

"Weak ego, Marcy."

Marcy did not reply.

Tyson lit a cigarette and leaned against a pillar. He looked out across the hotel grounds toward the road. To the left was the village's main street, a long block of little shops and banks. Everytown, USA; as Everytown had looked before the malls and commercial strips. To his left front was the library, and to the right of that, the small war memorial park. Directly opposite the hotel was the commuter station. In the distance, rising above the trees, he could see the tall Gothic spire of the Episcopal Cathedral of the Incarnation against the moonlit skyline, topped by an illuminated cross. This was familiar territory. Safe ground.

"Are you all right?"

He looked at his wife. "Yes."

"You were somewhere else."

"Sometimes I do that."

Marcy said, "Your mother called today. I forgot to tell you."

"What did she want?"

"She wants you to take care of yourself. Eat well. Relax. I think Florida made her Jewish."

Tyson smiled. He'd heard from a few old friends and some out-of-town family over the past two weeks. He was a little surprised at how fast news traveled. It reminded him of the Army, the rumor mill par excellence.

Marcy, as though she knew what he was thinking, said, "Anybody who didn't know about it when they got here knows now. Maybe you ought to issue an official statement in the village papers and the club newsletter."

Tyson smiled again. "Phil said no statements, public or private." But he himself had called a few people, close friends and relatives. And he'd been surprised by the variety of reactions: some people seemed insensitive; some were noncommittal; a good number seemed unimpressed by the seriousness of what had been written about him. A few people, as he'd noted tonight, sensed a developing celebrity status, albeit of a questionable nature, and he had the impression that these people were trying to get close to him to somehow share the limelight. Tyson said to Marcy, "The Grenvilles, who are important personages in the old guard, have asked us to cocktails. Next Friday, if you're interested."

Marcy replied, "I suppose they want you to autograph Picard's book. I'll bring the *Life* magazine to pass around."

Tyson smiled. Marcy, if nothing else, he thought, was well equipped to handle friends, neighbors, and family.

As Tyson saw his car coming down the drive, a voice behind him called out, "Ben. Marcy."

Tyson and Marcy turned. John McCormick and his wife, Phyllis, had come through the doors.

McCormick said, "I didn't get a chance to speak to you guys tonight." Greetings, handshakes, and perfunctory kisses were exchanged. McCormick said bluntly, "I have some more bad news for you, Ben. I hope you don't hold anything against the bearers of bad news."

Tyson rather liked McCormick, but two pieces of bad news from the same person in two weeks might, he supposed, prejudice him against the man. Tyson saw the thick newspaper under McCormick's arm and made a guess at what the news might be.

McCormick said, "Sunday *Times.* Just came in. The book got a major review. Your name is mentioned."

Tyson nodded. "Okay." He noticed that Phyllis McCormick looked at her husband in a way that suggested this was not her idea. Tyson saw McCormick hesitate, much as he had hesitated on the train before handing him the book. Tyson had a sense of déjà vu, coupled with a sinking stomach, as McCormick offered him the separated Book Review section. Tyson smiled gamely. "Do you want me to autograph it?"

McCormick's smile seemed more forced. "You can keep it."

The Volvo stopped at the curb, and the doorman held the passenger door open. The Tysons wished the McCormicks good night, and they parted. Tyson slipped behind the wheel of the Volvo and put it into gear as the attendant shut his door. He pulled up the curved drive toward the road. Marcy sat quietly with the Book Review section on her lap.

Tyson said, "Well."

"Well what?"

"Well, with a national circulation of about two million, things are going to begin happening."

Marcy nodded. "I'll arrange for an unlisted phone number Monday."

"Good idea."

"The school year is nearly over."

"Right."

"Should I list the house with the brokers?"

"Don't overreact."

She thought a moment, then inquired, "How are your employers going to take this?"

Tyson swung the car onto Stewart Avenue. "Who knows?" He headed west toward Eaton Road. "I can't get a handle on that bunch. They really are inscrutable."

"I'll let the racist remark pass, Ben, because I know you're under some strain."

Tyson didn't reply.

She asked, "Did Phil find you?"

"Yes." He turned left on Eaton Road. "Spoke to me in the men's room. Do you realize how much business is conducted in men's rooms?"

"What did he say?"

"Sue the bastards."

"He must be under the impression you're innocent."

"No, he's under the impression that the government is not clever enough or motivated enough to seek an indictment. Therefore, Picard is vulnerable to a civil suit. Poor Andrew Picard. He may find out that the truth doesn't pay as much as it costs."

She looked at him in the dim light. "Would you sue a man who told the truth?"

Tyson pulled into his long driveway and shut off the engine. He listened to the insects for a while.

"Would you?" she asked again.

8

Lieutenant General William Van Arken, the Army's Judge Advocate General, flipped through the personnel file in front of him. "I see he has two Purple Hearts. Score one point for Mr. Tyson."

Fraser Duncan, from the Secretary of the Army's office, looked at Tyson's medical file and commented, "Both wounds were superficial. Score only half a point."

Herbert Swenson, an aide to the Secretary of Defense, observed, "He has the Vietnamese Cross of Gallantry, awarded by the Vietnamese government for actions at Hue. That could get sticky."

Thomas Berg, a presidential aide, looked down the long, polished mahogany table. He said, "We were discussing the question of possible court-martial. Let's talk about relevant facts."

General Van Arken, sitting at the opposite end of the table, replied, "Mr. Berg, if you have ever witnessed a court-martial, you will know that is what we are doing."

Berg shrugged. He turned to Peter Truscott, a young attorney from the Justice Department. "I gather from what you've said that the Attorney General is not interested in pursuing this case."

Truscott stayed silent for longer than was considered polite, then replied carefully, "I didn't actually say that. I said it is a shaky case from a legal standpoint, Mr. Berg. Also, the Attorney General feels the matter is specifically military in nature."

Berg looked up and down the table at the four men present in the windowless room, located in the interior of the building. Green-shaded lamps illuminated the places where the men sat, leaving dark gaps at the long table.

The outer fringes of the large room were in darkness, and the only sound that penetrated the room was the susurrant rush of the air-conditioning ducts. *Dark things,* thought Berg, *belong in dark places.*

There was no stenographer present, and Berg had seen to it that there were no tape recorders in the room. No one was allowed to take notes. This was an unofficial, ad-hoc group whose agenda memos and daybooks showed they were meeting to discuss better methods of interdepartmental communication, which in fact they had discussed for about two minutes. And except for Van Arken, they were representatives of their respective government offices—special aides to their bosses. The feeling in the White House had been to keep it low-key. The subject of Benjamin Tyson, if anyone ever asked, had never come up.

Fraser Duncan spoke directly to Berg. "Could you give us some insight into the White House's thinking on this?"

Berg rubbed his lip thoughtfully, then replied, "The President knows nothing of this. His military aides asked me to prepare a background briefing in the event it becomes necessary to bring this to the President's attention. The President's only interest in this would derive from his position as Commander in Chief." Berg thought he ought to temper the lie and added, "His political aides are obviously concerned with the political ramifications of the case. No one has forgotten Nixon's part in the Calley case." He added quickly, "But politics are not the issue. The President's legal aides want to insure that the President acts in a legally correct manner each step of the way."

Berg looked at Van Arken, who as a young major had been on the prosecution staff in the My Lai case. Berg said to him, "We are here because so little precedent exists for this type of thing in this country—and thank God for that. In fact, with the exception of yourself, General, no one here has had any experience with war crimes, and no one is quite as sure of himself as you are." Berg saw a few smiles around the table.

Van Arken replied with forced civility, "I'm fairly certain that eventually this will land in my lap, and the Army will be obliged to proceed with a court-martial. If so, then I, too, want to be certain that we don't have a recurrence of the Calley-Medina fiasco."

Berg nodded. "So does the White House, General." Berg had taken the time to read Van Arken's file and to ask questions of people who knew the man. Van Arken was fifty-five, young for his position. He was military in his bearing, language, and attitude, an oddity in the Judge Advocate General's Corps, where the opposite qualities were held in some esteem.

Berg saw that no one was going to speak, another oddity in a government meeting, so Berg said, "Gentlemen, what we've established so far is that legally an officer can be tried for a murder, or murders, committed by his troops, depending on the circumstances. We've also noted that there is no statute of limitations on murder. Beyond these two elementary facts, we have not discovered anything. We can't even be certain a capital crime has been committed."

The General's voice carried loud and clear across the room. "Based on what we've all read in this Hue book, we have every reason to believe that some sort of capital crime has been committed."

Swenson said irritably, "Certainly you don't believe everything you read."

Van Arken replied with less assurance, "No, sir . . . but you can't come away from reading that without getting some sense of . . . of a criminal act." Van Arken sipped on a glass of water. "As in civilian law, where there is information or suspicion that a violation of law has occurred, then an official investigation must follow."

Berg had realized early in the meeting that Van Arken was disposed toward a full criminal investigation, rather than an unofficial fact-finding committee as the White House had hoped. Clearly, the man was out to make a reputation for himself; or to live down his previous reputation regarding the Calley-Medina trials. However, the Tyson case, more than the Calley case, had trouble written all over it. Not only domestic political trouble, but international problems as well. Berg said to the group, "As I understand it, there is a question of jurisdiction involved here. It is the opinion of the Justice Department that no state or federal court has jurisdiction in this case."

Truscott nodded. "That's correct. The alleged crime happened in a foreign country. The alleged perpetrator was at the time a member of the armed forces. However, he is not now a member of the armed forces. And that's where the problem lies."

Berg turned to Van Arken. "General?"

Van Arken stayed uncharacteristically silent for a few seconds, then said, "As Mr. Truscott indicated, the alleged crime was committed while the suspects—and I include Tyson's troops, of course—were subject to the provisions of the Uniform Code of Military Justice. There's no doubt about that. My opinion is that whether or not they are so subject at present is irrelevant—"

Truscott interrupted, "It is *not* irrelevant, General. It is crucial. Tyson, we know, is not in the Army now. The others may or may not be. We will find out. But the Army is not going to try civilians. Not ever."

Van Arken replied calmly, "Do you mean to tell me, Mr. Truscott, that if some of those men are still on active duty, only they will be unfortunate enough to be tried for murder? Will the civilians go free for the same crime?"

Truscott began to reply, but said instead, "The question is probably moot. Let's find out first if any of these men are still on active duty."

Van Arken continued, "All right, assume none of them are. Tyson we *know* is a civilian. So how must we change the jurisdictional status of these men?"

Truscott didn't reply, but Berg said, "You're suggesting, of course, that we call these men back to active duty."

Van Arken nodded. "Mr. Truscott is correct. The Army cannot and will not try civilians. Therefore, we cannot even begin an investigation of Mr. Tyson, but we can investigate Lieutenant Tyson."

There was silence in the room, then Berg said, "I've been advised that this question of a serviceman becoming a civilian before a crime has been discovered has never been fully resolved to anyone's satisfaction. It's apparently a glaring gap in our system of justice. Therefore, we must legally resolve this point before we proceed."

Van Arken added, "Every decade or so something like this comes up, and we are unprepared for this question of jurisdiction. Most of these past cases involved crimes of little importance. Here we have a crime of immense proportions, with implications beyond our borders."

Berg said, "Thank you, General. I think we realize that."

"The point," continued Van Arken, unperturbed, "is that, while the Uniform Code of Military Justice does not list war crimes as an offense, it does list first-degree murder, and that is the charge that must be investigated. Because—and this is the point, Mr. Berg—if it is not, I hold out to you the embarrassing possibility that, theoretically, the present government of Vietnam, or the governments whose nationals were alleged to have been murdered in that hospital, could file charges with the tribunal in The Hague. The charge would be crimes against humanity—war crimes."

No one commented and Van Arken continued, "Under U.S. law, we know neither Tyson nor his men would ever have to actually face such a tribunal. However, it is crucial that the charge of murder be promptly investigated to preempt anything of this sort."

Berg was unimpressed by Van Arken's foray into international law and diplomacy, but he knew Van Arken had a point. He said, however, "American citizens are not charged with murder to satisfy world opinion *or* domestic opinion."

Van Arken replied, "I wish that were so. But there have been cases where just that has happened to servicemen overseas. And, to some extent, that will happen with this case if you delay. This is a case where the law has to be in advance of public opinion so as not to give the appearance later that we were bending to any outside pressures. In other words, gentlemen, before a storm of media attention hits us, we ought to publicly announce an investigation."

Berg had the gut feeling that Van Arken, whatever his motives, was correct. But the President and his advisers hoped this mess would go away if left alone. Berg knew intellectually that it would not, but emotionally he hoped also. He felt he had enough bad news to carry back to the White House for the moment. He looked at Herbert Swenson.

Swenson understood the unasked question and replied, "From what I've heard, I don't believe this matter should be personally attended to by the Secretary of Defense. The Department of the Army ought to deal with it directly."

Fraser Duncan smiled thinly. "I'll recommend that the Secretary of the Army closely monitor the case, but I'm passing the buck down to the Judge Advocate General's Corps."

Peter Truscott spoke. "The resources of the Attorney General's office are, as always, available to the government in the interests of justice. But only in matters pertaining to questions of law. On questions of strategy, that's up to the Army, the JAG, and the Commander in Chief."

Berg nodded. There was, he thought, little legal precedent to fall back on. There appeared to be a violation of the Uniform Code of Military Justice; there appeared to be some machinery in existence to deal with this violation. But because of the unique and unusual nature of this case, there were many subjective decisions to be made along the way to the courtroom. Berg gathered his files and said, "I suggest we adjourn and do some homework and some . . . soul-searching." He stood. "We'll meet again to discuss interdepartmental communications. In the meantime, keep in mind that we are not dealing solely in abstract law problems or public relations problems, but with human beings. Specifically, with a man named Benjamin Tyson who may end up in front of a court-martial board, on trial for murder, for which the maximum penalty, if convicted, is death by firing squad. Good day."

9

David Tyson came into the kitchen where his father was sitting, drinking coffee and reading at the long breakfast counter. David said, "I'm going to bed."

Tyson looked up at the kitchen clock and saw it was nearly 11 P.M. Marcy would be back soon from her nocturnal grocery shopping. The night was warm, and Tyson was barefoot and shirtless, wearing only a pair of cutoff jeans.

David asked, "What are you reading?"

Tyson replied, "These are photostats of magazine pieces that I got from the library. Personal accounts of the battle of Hue."

"We're up to that now. I mean Vietnam. In school. In history."

Tyson smiled. "When I was a soph, we only had to get up to Eisenhower sending the Marines to Lebanon."

David pulled up a stool and sat opposite his father.

Tyson pushed the photostats aside. "How are you making out in school?"

"Okay."

"That's not what I hear."

"What do you mean?"

"You're catching some flak at school."

David looked at his father and replied, "I can handle it."

"Can you?"

"You always told me to handle my own problems. You bawled me out once when I was a kid and came home crying about something that somebody did to me. So I don't come home crying anymore."

Tyson regarded David for a few seconds. "But this is different. This is my fault. You can complain to me."

"I'm not complaining. Anyway it's not all bad. Some guys . . . and girls . . . are sort of friendlier than they used to be."

Tyson nodded. "I'm having the same experience. But watch out for that too."

"I know."

Tyson realized he was looking at his son in a new light. David was one of those boys who thought their own father was a better person than their favorite rock star or professional athlete. This was perhaps a rarity these days, but perhaps it was not so rare, just unspoken and never put to the test. Regardless, it was what it was and it must run in his family because Tyson had always hero-worshiped his own father. "Do you want a beer?"

David hesitated, then nodded. He went to the refrigerator and brought back two bottles. He opened them and slid one toward his father, then sat again.

Tyson and David drank. Tyson thought of Gene Conroy, who had come up to him in the Men's Club, a man Tyson barely knew, and apologized to Tyson for his son Derek's behavior toward David. That was the first Tyson had heard of any such problem. Yet he knew some of that must be going on and that there was great potential for cruelty among children. The children of Alpha Company had shown him the limits of cruelty. And Tyson wondered, without dwelling on it too long, if David could ever be a member of Alpha Company. In a way, he hoped his son had some of that cruelness in him, because if he did not, he would not survive in the world in which he lived. "Adults have deceived nearly every generation of youth into dying for them and their causes. Do you understand that?"

"I think so."

"I don't want you fighting for me. I'm talking about Derek Conroy, as one instance."

David studied the label on the beer bottle. "I don't have to take any crap from anybody."

"Okay, as long as you're defending yourself, responding to personal insults, or whatever. But don't defend *my* honor."

"Why not?"

"I just told you. Adults con the young into fighting their battles."

"You haven't conned me."

"Haven't I?" Part of the process of growing up, Tyson thought, of losing whatever innocence that was still part of childhood, was receiving a cruel blow from someone you cared about. It was time, Tyson decided, for David to be disabused of the notion that his father was innocent. In that way, David could grow, could fight for the real Ben Tyson if he chose to; not the idealized one. He said, "I'm going to tell you what no one outside of my platoon knows. I'm going to tell you, as best I can, what happened at Miséricorde Hospital. Okay?"

David nodded hesitantly. "Okay."

Tyson said, "First thing you should know is what Picard said in his book is mostly true. My platoon massacred over one hundred men, women, children, and infants. The youngest man in my platoon was not much older than you. His name was Simcox, and I saw him shoot a nurse about the same age as himself. Do you want me to go on or not?"

David bit at his lower lip. Finally he said, "No." He stood. "It doesn't matter. I knew it was all true. I don't care. I'm going upstairs."

"And pull the covers over your head?"

"I don't want to hear it, Dad."

Tyson nodded. "Okay. As long as you understand that what people are saying and writing about me is at least partly true. Understand too that this has nothing to do with you. You have nothing to be ashamed of. You are David Tyson, and you are your own person."

David walked toward the kitchen door, then turned back. "How about what people are saying about Mom?"

Tyson did not know quite how to deal with this. Somehow he was more willing to discuss mass murder with his son than the subject of Marcy's past. Tyson said, "A man or woman's past personal life is no one's business but their own. Your mother never hurt a soul, and no one has any right to hurt her or try to hurt me or you through her. Don't respond to any of that."

David replied, "I have to be honest with you, Dad. It wasn't you that asshole Conroy was talking about. It was Mom."

Tyson drew a deep breath. "Idiotic."

"I get these filthy notes shoved in my locker. Dad, if you want to talk to me about something, talk to me about all that crap about Mom."

"There's nothing to say. Most of it is lies."

"Is it?"

"Yes. Go to bed, then. It's late. We'll talk again."

David nodded. "Night." He left.

Tyson sipped on his beer. *My God,* he thought, *that kid's world fell apart. Yet, he showed no outward signs.* Tyson finished his beer. David, he decided, was tougher than he'd suspected. But it would be a race between the end of the school term and the end of David's ability to cope. *Poor David. Poor Marcy. Poor Ben.*

Marcy Tyson placed the grocery bag on the breakfast counter. Ben Tyson was still sitting on the stool reading, a cup of coffee in his hand. He said, "Hello. Back already?" He didn't look up.

"No, I'm still at the supermarket."

"Good." He turned a page and yawned.

Marcy said, "It was weird. Bizarre. I mean at the checkout. There I was on the *cover* of the *American Investigator.* Can you believe it? A housewife's dream come true."

Tyson looked up from the paper.

Marcy continued as she began unpacking the bag, "They covered my crotch with a black strip. But my tits are right there. Jesus. Who needs it? Right?"

Tyson watched her closely as she went about emptying the brown bag. She did not seem upset, but he suspected she was. She looked very young tonight, he thought, dressed in a cotton khaki skirt, sandals, and a navy blue knit shirt open at the collar.

He looked at the kitchen clock. It was nearly midnight, not the Tysons' normal hour to go marketing. He looked at the groceries piled on the counter. "Did you buy that rag—what's it called?"

"The *American Investigator*." She hesitated, then added, "It's in the car."

He nodded. Life in the Tyson household had become somewhat surreal, not to mention furtive and xenophobic. He had taken to varying his methods and times of commuting to New York, though Marcy continued to take her regular train. They generally avoided social contact, and he had dropped out of the tennis tournament at the club. They no longer dined at local restaurants, though he still went to the Men's Club, which was a world unto itself.

Tyson played with the sugar cubes, building a tower on the countertop. He spoke without looking up. "As a public relations person, can you explain to me the dynamics of this thing? I mean, how did we become hot news?"

Marcy put away some canned goods. "Lots of reasons. Andrew Picard is hot, for one thing. He's good on talk shows. Not bad-looking either. Maybe this is a slow news month. But remember, Ben, the central belief of the public relations business: 'There's no such thing as bad publicity.' "

"Well, this shit looks mighty like it." He added another course of cubes to his tower. *Picard.* After the *Times* book review, Picard had appeared on radio and television, hawking his wares. And Picard knew what interested his audience. And it wasn't the battle of Hue. That was an abstract subject, too boring for the electronic media. Picard spent his airtime wisely, focusing on the Miséricorde Hospital massacre, as it was now known.

Tyson had actually heard Picard on the car radio one morning, and if he hadn't read the book, Tyson would have believed that the entire thirty-nine chapters were devoted to Benjamin Tyson and his gang of psychotics shooting up a hospital with the rest of the massive month-long battle only a sideshow for that main event.

Marcy broke into his thoughts. "This is the sort of thing a publicist prays for. Moving from the fluff and entertainment pages to the news pages. Authors have wet dreams about being mentioned in somebody's column."

Tyson nodded as he concentrated on the tottering tower. *Hue: Death of a City.* The book had been given a piece in *Newsweek.* Could *Time* be far behind? The book had appeared on the Sunday *Times* bestseller list two weeks ago and was climbing. Picard must be pleased. Tyson added a flying buttress to steady the tower.

"These things achieve a critical mass of their own," explained Marcy. "You understand? It becomes news because it has become news. That's not to say it isn't a good story. I mean, let's be objective here, Tyson. And it doesn't hurt to be twenty-five miles from the news center of the world. We'd get off easier if we lived in Omaha. That's a fact."

Tyson blew gently on the hexagon-shaped tower and watched it sway.

"What the hell are you doing?"

"This is the gleaming white marble tower that stands on the desolate brown plains of Formica. It is the last bastion of civilization in a dying world. The last learned men and women have gathered here—" He blew again and a cube toppled to the brown countertop. "But savages have surrounded the tower, and—"

"Are you well? I mean, should I call a white van, or what?"

He looked up. "Just playing. Men never grow up. I think you said that once or twice."

"Anyway . . ." She turned and put some packages in the freezer. "Anyway, I spoke to the local fuzz this morning, and they were sympathetic. However, it seems that laws about harassment, blocking traffic, causing a public nuisance, and so on apply only to mortals and not to newspeople unless you get a court

order or something. . . . If those shits set up their cameras outside again—"
She slammed the freezer door.

Tyson recalled the local TV station that had thrown together a half-hour
news show on the unfolding drama. There was an interview with Picard, alternating with stock footage of the battle of Hue. The war had returned to the
American living room. And it was good footage, aerial stuff of the burning city,
then close-ups of the Marines trying to cross the Perfume River over the one
remaining railroad bridge, the university crammed with miserable refugees.
And not your typical peasants, but upper-middle-class Vietnamese, students,
doctors, priests, monks, and administrators. The cream of society, filthy and
forlorn, weeping for the cameras. Very good footage.

The show had ended with a reporter standing outside a house, and it had
taken Tyson a moment to realize it was his house. The reporter had done his
wrap-up as the camera panned the block of substantial houses, taking in a few
curious neighbors. Then the camera had zoomed in on Tyson's front door. The
reporter had closed with, "Behind this handsome door is the one man who can
answer Andrew Picard's questions. But that man is not talking. And it remains
to be seen whether or not he will ever talk about what happened at that hospital eighteen years ago."

Tyson tapped the countertop sharply and watched the tower bounce, then
settle back without collapsing. "Earthquake. Severe damage, but the tower
built by the world's last master builders stands." Tyson yawned again, then
turned back to his wife. "You know, Marcy, for all the interest people have
shown in me and my difficulties, I suspect that a good number of them haven't
actually gotten around to reading the relevant chapter in Picard's book. Yet
they all think they know what it's about."

Marcy yawned also. "They're waiting for it to be made into a TV movie,
Ben." Marcy put away the last of the groceries. "Thanks for helping."

"Sorry . . . I was thinking." He lowered his head, eye level to the sugar
cube tower. "I see the major damage—"

Marcy flicked her finger and the tower collapsed in a heap.

"Bitch." He swept the cubes to the side and blew away the sugar granules.
"Do you want me to re-create the battle of Hue with sugar cubes?"

"Maybe in the morning."

"After reading Picard's book I know what happened." He quickly laid out a
line of cubes. "This is the south wall of the Citadel. Okay? Each wall was two
miles long. All right, the south wall abutted the north bank of the Perfume
River—" He looked around, spotted the milk pitcher, and poured a stream of
milk over the countertop. "That's the Perfume River. Pretend. Okay, this is the
canal—" He trailed his finger through the milk and formed a small tributary.
"Okay, help me with the other three walls. Do you have any more sugar cubes?
We have to build the Imperial Palace here, and construct the walled enclave in
the northeast corner of the Citadel, where Picard had gotten himself trapped
with the South Vietnamese soldiers. That's over here. Three full battalions of
the First Cav were approaching from the north. Their mission was to relieve
the pressure on the Marines and ARVN—that's the South Viets—and to block
escape routes to the north and interdict enemy supply and reinforcement attempts. Got it? This sugar tong and these two spoons represent the three
cavalry battalions. Follow? Okay, the tong is my battalion, the Fifth Battalion
of the famed Seventh Cavalry. But my company was detached and we were
more to the west. Here. My platoon was further detached and I was operating
alone. Here. I was advancing along the north bank of the river. Hue was burn-

ing to my front. Now this little fucking sugar cube is Hôpital Miséricorde. Okay?" He looked at her. "Why aren't you building those walls?"

Marcy Tyson turned and went to the cabinet over the trash compactor. She retrieved a bottle of Grand Marnier and filled half a water tumbler. "Want one?"

"No thanks."

She noticed he had completed the four walls of the Citadel without her help. "Ben, cut it out. Seriously."

He looked up and his eyes found hers. He smiled and swept away the sugar cubes.

She let out a shallow breath. "Ready for bed?"

"Not yet. I was thinking . . . it must have been the neighbors. I mean the *Life* magazine picture. The media didn't stumble on that by accident. You weren't even identified by name in the original caption."

Marcy swirled the orange liqueur around the glass. "Actually, Ben, I tipped them off. I was tired of you getting all the press."

Tyson smiled. "I thought a good PR person is supposed to stay out of the spotlight."

Marcy raised the glass to her lips. "Well, I have an ego, too." She drank.

"It had to be someone in town. But why would anyone do that? I mean, what is gained by dragging you into this mess?"

Marcy leaned back against the sink. "People are petty, envious, and nuts. I thought everyone knew that."

"I thought you believed in the basic goodness of people. Brothers and sisters and all."

"I do believe in that. Sincerely and passionately. Nevertheless, an awful lot of people are flaming assholes." She finished her drink.

Tyson stared out the kitchen window. There was a light on in the sunroom of the Thompson house, and he could see their daughter Ginny, seventeen, parading around in her bra and panties. He saw a figure approach the sunroom. The French doors opened, and the figure entered. The lights went out.

Marcy glanced out the window. "Ginny?"

"Right."

"Did you rendezvous like that when you were a horny little guy?"

"Damn right. I knew every backyard and fence in this town."

Marcy laughed. "God, it was different in the city. We used to neck a little in the parks, and sometimes if it got serious we'd go to the roof of our building. The boiler room, in the winter."

"Peasant." Tyson walked to the refrigerator and opened it. "This is all pussy food. Yogurt, lettuce, strawberries." He closed the door.

Marcy spoke. "Two incidents. Hue and Griffith Park, occurring about the same time. What did the *New York Post* say? Something about the irony of Marcy making love while Ben made war. Christ, give me a break." She smiled. "You know you've arrived when the papers start calling you by your first name. And as a journalism major and a public relations lady, I can tell you, Mr. Tyson, you ain't seen nothin' yet." She finished her second Grand Marnier, and Tyson noticed her eyes had taken on a glazed duck à l'orange look.

Tyson sat on his stool at the breakfast counter. "Funny, I haven't had that nightmare since this began."

"Why should you? You're living it. 'Life is a dream in the night, a fear among fears, a naked runner lost in a storm of spears.' Arthur Symons." She filled his half-empty coffee cup with Grand Marnier.

"Thanks," Tyson said to his wife. "We have got to get David out of here as soon as the school term is finished. The kid must be going through hell, but he hasn't said a word."

Marcy nodded.

Tyson sipped on his coffee, laced with orange liqueur. David, he knew, had been aware of the infamous photograph long before this. In fact, about a year before, Tyson had found David sitting on the floor of the den with the original *Life* magazine spread out on his lap, staring at the picture of his mother.

Tyson had chosen not to let the incident pass without comment. Some days later, he'd sat David down and given him a brief sociological lecture on the Age of Aquarius. It was odd, he'd thought, that a middle-aged man had to defend his generation's looser morality to a teenager. But morality, like war and peace, was cyclical. Victorians did not approve of the morality, clothing, or literature of the Georgian age that preceded theirs. David's generation, while certainly not prigs, were nevertheless not quite as loose as their parents once were.

David had listened, nodded understanding, but something told Tyson that the boy did not approve, not only of the nude picture but of his parents' life-style.

Tyson realized that he himself affected a certain sophistication regarding the photograph, Marcy's past in general, and the marital relationship. Marcy had once observed to friends, "Ben has become more liberal and less inhibited, and I've become more conservative in my middle age. That's the story of the nine-teen eighties."

Tyson understood, too, that he was titillated by Marcy's past, as well as by her present job, which brought her into close contact with successful men. There were the business trips, the breakfasts, lunches, late dinners, late office nights, and the publicity events. There were ample grounds for jealousy, and in fact there had been some rather intense discussions on occasions when Marcy had staggered home in the small hours of the morning. The one thing this marriage did not suffer from was boredom. He said to her, "You're handling this well. And you're right. You don't need this."

She poured a third drink. Her voice was slightly slurred. "For better or for worse. That's what the hell it's all about." She thought a moment, then added, "You're handling it quite well, too. I . . . I always respected you . . . but there were times . . . you know, when I felt you were wishy-washy. I guess I promoted that . . . I never wanted to emasculate you . . . never. . . . And I'm glad to see you show real balls . . . I mean, adversity builds character, right? We all need a little stress to feel alive . . . it can strengthen us and our marriage . . . but too much stress and strain . . ." She tipped the glass back, drank, and suppressed a belch. "I don't know."

Tyson nodded. Marcy, he knew, was a self-assured woman. And she was alive, and where there was life there were problems.

He looked at her. "I just remembered that time I brought Kimura, Saito, and their wives here for dinner. And you served them take-out Chinese food from the containers."

Marcy said innocently, "Did I fuck up?"

Tyson smiled.

"You never said a word about it." She grinned. "I served the shit with chop-sticks, for Christ's sake." She added in an injured tone, "And I made up that neat drink out of sake and bourbon. The Hiroshima Bomber. Everybody liked it."

Tyson laughed.

"Don't laugh at me, you pompous, uptight twit."

Tyson stopped laughing and took a step toward her. "Who's uptight?"

"You, you stuffy, anal-compulsive—"

He seized her by the shoulders, lifted her in the air, and laid her out on the breakfast bar, amid the coffee cups, sugar cubes, and newspaper.

"What the hell are you doing, Tyson?"

"I'm going to fuck you, lady."

"Here?"

"Here." He unzipped her skirt and pulled it with her panties down around her ankles, over her sandals, and threw the bunched clothing on the floor. "Spread your legs."

She spread her legs, knocking cups and ashtrays off the counter. Tyson slipped his shorts off and lifted himself onto the counter between her thighs. Without any preliminaries, he mounted her, finding her wet and receptive.

Marcy extended her arms and clutched the edges of the counter.

Tyson's thrusts were short and rapid, but he found his knees had no traction on the smooth countertop. He rocked back on his haunches. "Turn over."

Marcy flipped herself onto her stomach, then rose to her hands and knees. Tyson clutched her shoulders and entered her from behind, ramming hard a dozen times in quick succession. Marcy slid forward, and her head rested against the splashboard. The counter shook, and the sugar bowl vibrated over the edge and crashed to the floor, followed by the milk pitcher.

Marcy spread her knees farther apart and lowered her head, looking back between her hanging breasts at Tyson's sliding penis and dangling testicles.

Tyson came suddenly, withdrew, and hopped back off the counter. He slapped her buttocks and strode out of the kitchen, calling back, "Clean up that mess."

Marcy remained motionless for a full minute, feeling the wetness running over her thighs, dripping onto the breakfast counter. Slowly, she lowered herself to the floor and surveyed the debris. Still naked from the waist down, she swept the milk and sugar together with the smashed ceramic, then knelt and pushed the mess into a dustpan with a sponge. She stood and began wiping the breakfast bar, wet with milk and splattered sperm.

Marcy stopped suddenly and stared down at the glistening streaks along the brown plastic counter. She felt humiliated and used. But tonight that was how she was supposed to feel. That was part of their sexual repertoire; Marcy taunts Ben, Ben treats Marcy like chattel. The acting out of a common sexual fantasy. And she enjoyed that submissive role about once a month. But this time there was something different . . . something was wrong. . . . Tears came to her eyes, and her hands shook as she continued wiping the counter.

10

Thomas Berg said, "Change of venue, gentlemen. I trust this suits you." Berg motioned around the small, tastefully decorated room in the Victorian-style Old Executive Office Building. Berg added, "We are getting closer to the White House, physically as well as metaphysically." He nodded toward the window at the Executive Mansion a few hundred yards to the east.

Berg lowered himself into a wingback chair. General Van Arken sat in a suede upholstered chair near the window. Peter Truscott, from the Attorney General's office, sat by himself on a leather couch. Absent were the representatives of the departments of Defense and of the Army. Berg explained, "We're limiting our options, so we're limiting our membership in this group to us three."

The air-conditioning in the hundred-year-old building was balky, and the east-facing room was warmed by the late morning sun. Truscott and Berg had slipped off their jackets and loosened their ties. Van Arken kept his green tunic on, and as per regulations, it was fully buttoned. Berg felt warm just looking at the man. He thought that the military had developed discomfort as a separate art form. A tray of carbonated mineral waters sat on the coffee table along with a bucket of ice and glasses.

Berg cleared his throat. "All right, at our first meeting, we discovered we had a potential problem. By our second meeting last week, General Van Arken's prophecy of media attention seemed to be coming true. General, any other prophecies?"

Van Arken sat forward. "I have no crystal ball, Mr. Berg. But I am in closer contact with the real world than the people over there are." He jerked his thumb over his shoulder at the White House.

Berg nodded. "Perhaps." He thought a moment, then said, "The President has a press conference scheduled in three weeks. This subject will come up unless it is ruled out beforehand. But the press doesn't like that. The President can, of course, take cover behind the fact that it would be improper to comment on a possible legal matter. But we'd like him to be able to say something more substantial than that." Berg looked at the two men. "We'll think about that."

The room fell silent, and Truscott helped himself to a glass of sparkling water. Outside on the White House South Lawn, a helicopter was landing, and the muted sound of the rotor blades penetrated the stillness of the small sunlit room.

Berg addressed Van Arken. "Another of your prophecies has come true, General. To wit: The State Department has, this week, received inquiries from the ambassadors of France, Holland, Belgium, Germany, and Australia, asking what is being done to investigate the alleged murders of their nationals by American forces in Vietnam, and so forth." Berg paused, then continued, "I am happy to report, however, that the Swiss ambassador, who as you know unofficially handles the affairs of Hanoi here, has not received any such note from the People's Republic intended for us. But that may be on the way. Also, no one in the U.N. has raised the issue as yet."

Van Arken interjected, "It would be hypocritical in the extreme for Hanoi to attempt any propaganda from this, considering what their own troops did at Hue."

Berg shrugged. "My theory is that Hanoi will let the countries involved and the Catholic Relief Agency make problems for us." Berg looked at Truscott. "Anyway, between our first and second meetings, General Van Arken contacted the Army Records Center at Fort Leonard Wood, and we believe now that no one who was in Tyson's platoon at the time of the alleged massacre is still in the military. So, based on that, we agreed that it would be best to offer the former enlisted men in that platoon immunity from prosecution in exchange for sworn testimony."

Peter Truscott responded, "As in the Calley trial, you have to let the small fish go, in order to land the big one." Truscott added, "Anyway, it's nearly impossible to recall enlisted men to duty. Tyson, as an ex-officer, is an easier catch. Correct?"

Van Arken said nothing, but Berg could see he was unhappy.

Truscott said, "Incidentally, I made some discreet inquiries at the Nassau County Clerk's office—that's the county where Tyson lives. It appears that Tyson has not initiated a libel suit against Picard or the book publisher."

Berg said, "What can we construe from that?"

Truscott shrugged. "Any one of a dozen things." He thought a moment, then said, "Sometimes I try to put myself in Tyson's place. . . . I wonder what I would do."

Berg smiled. "I'd think about it in Brazil."

Truscott smiled, too, then said seriously, "I believe that Tyson, like us, is playing a waiting-hoping game. And, like us, he doesn't know what he's waiting for or hoping for. And, like us, he's frightened."

Berg nodded slowly. After some time he said, "Well, that brings us to our next order of business—Mr. Tyson himself. How far can we delve into this case before it becomes necessary to recall Mr. Tyson to duty? Mr. Truscott?"

Truscott replied, "The Attorney General's office feels that you can proceed as you are now with informal meetings and research, until you feel there is substance to these allegations."

Berg looked toward Van Arken. The General shook his head and offered, "We are right now in a tenuous legal position."

Neither Truscott nor Berg replied.

Van Arken expanded on his opinion. "You must understand that a recall to duty would place Mr. Tyson not only under the *jurisdiction* of the Uniform Code of Military Justice but under its *protection* as well. As you noted in our first meeting, Mr. Truscott, the Army cannot court-martial a civilian. So, by extension, the Army cannot investigate a civilian. Such an investigation by my office or the Army Criminal Investigation Division would certainly be a violation of the man's civil rights."

Berg nodded to himself. Clearly, Van Arken had thought this out. Clearly, too, Van Arken was making a power play. Berg turned to Truscott.

Peter Truscott was rubbing his chin. "Well, this is difficult. . . . Perhaps the White House could order my office or the FBI to begin an investigation, then we could pass the findings on to the JAG—"

Van Arken interrupted, "I cannot accept the fruits of a civilian investigation in a case like this. Gentlemen, if you want this case killed or weakened because of procedural errors, then you are doing a fine job of it."

Berg glared at Van Arken for a few seconds but said nothing. Obviously, they'd reached an impasse.

Van Arken said suddenly, "I suspect that the White House doesn't want Mr. Tyson in uniform."

Berg stood and poured himself some mineral water. "Well, they see that as a point of no return."

"We've already reached and passed that point. Read the newspapers."

Berg ignored this and continued, "Also, from a legal point of view, wouldn't it be prejudicial to Mr. Tyson if he was recalled to duty before we even assembled the facts? It seems to me that would be premature and ominous. Truscott?"

Truscott answered, "Well . . . no more so than if a suspect were extradited from a foreign country. The government has to take certain steps in some cases to establish its jurisdiction. That shouldn't be construed as a presumption of guilt."

Berg remained standing and sipped on his mineral water. His eyes unconsciously went to the window, and he stared at the White House. He looked away and said, "Well, if we do that—recall Tyson to duty—it will make every newspaper in the country. I'd still like to retain the option of keeping a lid on this." He turned to Van Arken. "Let's address the human element. What if Tyson spends six months or a year in the Army and it turns out he's innocent? You can't fool around with a man's life like that because of unfounded suspicions. Why can't we let this man go about his daily life until we are more certain there is reason to put him back in uniform?"

Van Arken replied, "I told you why. And I don't think Mr. Tyson is going about his daily life. A recall might be merciful. I'm human, too."

Berg snapped, "An Army induction notice in the mail is about as welcome and merciful as a public health notice regarding your last sexual partner."

Truscott chuckled.

Van Arken's normally florid face turned redder. He moved to the center of the room, as though he were on the verge of walking out. He seemed to be trying to control his voice as he spoke. "We have sufficient information to suspect that a crime has been committed. We have a suspect. We either take steps to bring the suspect under our jurisdiction, or we drop the case. But keep in mind that if we turn our backs on two hundred alleged victims, as Tyson apparently did at the time, then we are as guilty as he is." Van Arken added ominously, "We can probably count on appearing before a congressional inquiry."

Berg exhaled a long breath and said, "I'll speak to the President personally about what we've discussed."

Van Arken, still standing, said, "Why don't you ask the President to sign an order as Commander in Chief recalling Tyson? It would be less subject to challenge than an Army-directed recall."

Berg's tone was sharp. "General, you know damned well the President does not want to do that. This is purely an Army affair, as we all agree. So let's leave the President out of it. This is a simple murder trial, not an international incident, all right? Now, how long do you think it will take the Army to get Tyson back in the saddle?"

Van Arken drew a short breath, then replied curtly, "I can't prophesy that. It depends on how hard Tyson fights the recall order."

Truscott added, "He can fight it all the way up to the Supreme Court."

Berg sat back in his chair. He wondered if a long legal battle over recall and jurisdiction would be such a bad thing. It would take the pressure off the executive branch and put it into the judiciary where it belonged.

Truscott seemed to sense what Berg was thinking. He said, "We can contact Tyson's attorneys or even Tyson directly."

Berg looked at him. "Why?"

"Sometimes," said Truscott, "the direct approach is best. If we informed him or his attorney that a recall was being considered in order for us to proceed with an investigation, we might get some indication of how he intends to . . . respond."

Berg glanced at Van Arken.

Truscott added, "If I were Tyson's attorney, I'd urge him to try to make a deal. In exchange for not challenging a recall order, I'd ask the Judge Advocate General's office for . . . well, something." He turned to Van Arken. "What would you offer?"

"Nothing."

Berg said, "Well, you'd offer him a fair court-martial, wouldn't you?" Berg wondered about Van Arken's actual motivations in pursuing this so aggressively. Berg had researched the General's psyche and philosophy, and on the surface the man appeared to be a staunch moralist and law-and-order advocate. Privately, he led a rather austere life, was unmarried, and lived in Army housing. It was rumored he owned two civilian suits: summer wool and winter wool. Both blue.

Berg stood. "All right, gentlemen, before we adjourn, I'd like to make a personal comment, and it is this: To some degree, society feels a shared sense of guilt and culpability with their armed forces that they don't feel with the common criminal. So, if we eventually court-martial, convict, and imprison Benjamin Tyson, we should not expect to be national heroes."

Van Arken's jaw hardened. "I'm not concerned with my popularity in the Army. And I'm not running for public office."

Truscott stood. "Well, let's not have a row over this." He turned to Berg. "Basically, the General is correct, and you ought to tell that to the President. Cover-ups don't work anymore. I'd rather do something unpopular than face a charge of conspiracy."

Berg nodded in agreement. "I'm not suggesting a cover-up. I'm suggesting we balance whatever good a court-martial would do against the harm it will cause the nation."

Van Arken replied, "If we don't—or can't—see this through, then the system will have failed. And I can't think of a greater harm to a nation founded on law than that its justice system should fail—except perhaps that its public officials should have failed to try. I think, too, that if Mr. Tyson were in this room and he were objective, he'd agree."

Berg smiled without humor. "Benjamin Tyson is fighting for his life, and he is not going to be objective. He is going to cause his government and his country great embarrassment. And I don't blame him." Berg picked up his attaché case. "This is going to open old wounds, and those wounds will run with fresh blood. That fucking war is going to come home again. God help us." Berg turned toward the door. "Meeting adjourned."

11

At 7:30 on a Tuesday morning, Benjamin Tyson walked into the clubhouse of the Garden City Golf Club, known unofficially as the Men's Club. The present building had been erected in 1899, the same year the women had been invited to leave, and the premises had developed, thought Tyson, that unique, ripe flavor peculiar to masculine establishments. Women, however, were invited to play the course once a year, though few availed themselves of this dubious honor.

Tyson surveyed the lounge area and saw a few men playing poker dice around a coffee table. He walked on, passed down the length of the bar, and entered the cathedral-ceilinged dining room. He walked through the room, nodded to a few people at the breakfast tables, and exited onto the rear terrace.

Phillip Sloan sat at a small round table under a blue-striped umbrella, read-

ing a newspaper. Tyson took the chair opposite. Sloan looked up. "Good morning." He poured Tyson a cup of coffee from a pewter pot.

"Thanks." Tyson drank the coffee black. He observed that Sloan's golfing
attire contained all three primary colors, plus orange. Tyson looked out across
the fairway. Men in bright plumage performed the repetitive rituals of ball and
club. A hundred years before, when these acres had been pristine glacial out-
wash, the Carteret Gun Club had set up pigeon shoots, massacring a thousand
birds at a shoot. And the Meadow Brook Hunt Club had also galloped through
from time to time, hounds barking, horns blaring: "the unspeakable in full
pursuit of the uneatable." Golf was tamer, but so were the times.

Golf was not Tyson's favorite sport, and neither was bird shooting or fox
hunting. But he felt somehow that these Elysian fields had been sanctified by a
century of hedonism; that regardless of what social changes enlightened the
world and defined American democracy, there ought to be a few acres set aside
for gentlemen to make asses of themselves. At least until the next glacier came
through.

Sloan looked up from his newspaper, apparently just noticing that his companion was wearing a suit. "I thought you were going to play a round with me?"

"No, I'm catching the eight-forty-two. So let's wrap it up by eight-thirty."

Sloan seemed disappointed, then regarded Tyson thoughtfully. He said,
"What is your status there?"

Tyson poured himself more coffee. "Where? On the eight-forty-two?"

"Your *job.*"

Tyson sipped on his coffee. Women, he noticed, alluded to the strains on his
marriage. Men usually inquired about his job. Nearly no one was solicitous of
his psyche. Tyson replied, "Hard to say, Phil. I mean, on the one hand you have
the famous Japanese paternalism. On the other hand you have Japanese efficiency. I'm not very efficient these days. Added to that is the Nipponese obsession with appearances, face, and that sort of thing. I embarrass them." He
smiled and added, "As a former samurai who has been disgraced, I should take
the honorable way out. But American managers haven't yet embraced Japanese necrophilia."

Sloan seemed uncomfortable with this line of conversation.

Tyson's tone was bitter. "You know, if old man Stutzman were still in charge,
he'd have offered me the corporation's law firm to fight this."

Sloan waved a dismissive hand.

A waiter came to the table, and Tyson ordered eggs and orange juice. Sloan
ordered sweet rolls and another pot of coffee. It struck Tyson that he had an
irrational dislike for men who ate sweet rolls for breakfast.

Sloan reached into his briefcase and pulled out a folded newspaper page,
handing it literally under the table to Tyson.

Tyson unfolded it and saw it was the front page of the *American Investigator;*
not the one featuring Marcy, but the most recent edition of the weekly tabloid.
One of the numerous headlines read: MR. PRESIDENT, WILL JUSTICE BE
DONE? That interrogatory headline, Tyson observed, was a sly way of suggesting to the *American Investigator*'s readership that the Chief of State received a copy of the rag on the White House doorstep. Tyson noticed another
front-page story titled MARCY'S FRIENDS AND LOVERS TELL ALL. Tyson refolded the page without reading the text and handed it back to Sloan.
"So?"

"Well, the story about Marcy goes beyond the bounds of common decency
and journalistic ethics. Even for this scandal sheet. The fellow Jones who's

been covering the story has interviewed some of Marcy's college friends and . . . people who claim to have been intimate with her.''

Tyson poured cream into his coffee.

Sloan continued, "The article is libelous. Filled with titillation, sarcasm, innuendos, and suggestions of radical activities of a violent nature. Marcy was radical, as we know, but to the best of my knowledge, never violent. There are also gratuitous remarks about drugs.'' Sloan hesitated, then added, "There is also a guarded mention of marital infidelity.''

Tyson didn't reply.

"Sleaze,'' Sloan continued. "Pure sleaze. And damned sure libelous. Look, this has gone on long enough. I think *she* ought to bring suit. I'm talking to you man-to-man, Ben. You don't have to get involved in the suit, but I thought I'd speak to you first. Now, we both know that Marcy is an independent woman, and she doesn't need her husband's permission to enter into a lawsuit. But tradition and common courtesy dictate that I speak to you first.''

"Don't let *her* hear you say that.''

Sloan affected a smile. "Well, we'll keep this conversation to ourselves. But she is my client, and I'm going to speak to her.''

"That's your prerogative.''

The breakfasts came, and Tyson buttered a slice of toast. Sloan bit into a sticky bun. Tyson asked, "Good?''

Sloan nodded as he chewed. "Want one?''

"No, thank you.'' Tyson took a forkful of eggs.

Sloan lifted a packet of sugar from a bowl and emptied the contents into his coffee. Tyson said, "They don't use sugar cubes anymore. Everyone uses those idiotic packets now. I'm going to speak to the manager.''

"These are more sanitary—''

"But you can't *build* things with packets. I was going to show you the battle of Hue. Here, I can do it with paper and pen.'' Tyson took a pen from his inside pocket. "Give me one of those yellow pads you people always carry.''

Sloan's eyes rolled slightly as he retrieved a legal pad from his briefcase.

Tyson began drawing as he ate.

Sloan glanced around the terrace and noticed a few people turn away. Both men ate in silence for a while as Tyson drew, then Sloan said, "Let's speak about your suit for a moment. All right, you have been libeled in print and slandered on TV and radio. All the damage that could be done is done. You have suffered acute personal embarrassment, irrevocable harm to your career and your character, causing you great psychological damage—''

Tyson glanced up from his drawing. "Are you sure? I feel okay.''

"Listen, Ben, if we delay any longer in initiating suit, we will be guilty of laches—that means sitting on our asses. The law specifically states that you may not unreasonably delay bringing suit for damages. The law recognizes that potential plaintiffs who do that are playing a game, trying to increase the harm—''

"*You* said to let my name get dragged through the slime so we could sue for bigger bucks, Phil.''

Sloan cleared his throat. "That's not exactly what I said. Anyway, the problem is, to avoid the appearance of laches we must begin now, today—''

"The problem was the layout of the city.'' Tyson swiveled the yellow pad around on the table. "See, within the Citadel, the old city was laid out in long, straight, narrow streets. There's no room for armor to maneuver. The ARVN tried, but the NVA easily knocked out their tanks with rockets. Okay, within the Citadel you also had the walls of the Forbidden City, which in turn held the

emperor's Palace of Heavenly Peace. See? Then there were these watchtowers
on the walls, which were seized early by the Viet Cong and North Viets. To
complicate the situation, the Perfume River cuts the city in two. Right here.
Farther south of the city you have the area of the emperor's tombs, which were
traditionally controlled by VC—tourists had to pay a VC tax. Crazy war. Anyway . . . you see . . . this is a difficult cityscape . . . too difficult. The
American commanders should not have chosen to fight the enemy on the
enemy's terms. That's what caused so much death and destruction. Hue became a sort of Verdun, with everyone converging on the center of the city to
slaughter each other. Bad tactics. The Americans and South Viets should have
withdrawn and established a *cordon sanitaire.* What do you think?"

"You know," said Sloan, trying to control his irritation, "because we're
friends, I let you get away with jerking me around. And I know you're under a
lot of stress. But it's time to cut out the nonsense and *act."*

Tyson contemplated the map he'd drawn and added another detail.

Sloan leaned across the table. "Here's the question—do we have a suit? Or is
Andrew Picard, through his witnesses, telling the truth? Did you, Benjamin
Tyson, or did you not, participate in any way in the murder of men, women,
children, nuns, medical staff, et al., at Miséricorde Hospital?"

Tyson pushed the legal pad aside and chewed thoughtfully on a piece of
toast, then met Sloan's eyes and said, "I suppose you ought to know. Yes, I am,
as suggested in Picard's book, guilty of murder."

To his credit, Tyson thought, Sloan did not feign surprise or any other emotion that he did not feel. Sloan simply nodded curtly.

Tyson continued, "So that's the end of the civil suit talk. Sorry to disappoint
you and sorry to have jerked you around so long. But you understand."

Sloan said a bit coolly, "I'm not disappointed. Well, in a way I'm disappointed that you didn't confide in me earlier and disappointed that you don't
think you're innocent—"

"I'm *not* innocent."

Sloan stayed silent a moment before replying, "That's up to the criminal
justice system to decide. Not you. Look, in the event charges are brought
against you and then dismissed, or otherwise disposed of, or if in fact you are
tried, then found not guilty, then you can most probably win a civil suit for libel.
Do you follow?"

Tyson nodded. The man *was* persistent and had obviously thought this
through.

Sloan went on. "But you must let me initiate the suit now. We can postpone
and delay any resolution of the suit for as long as it takes to dispose of any
potential criminal charges. That resolves your complaint about the possibility
of the government monitoring a civil trial. That puts them in a position of
having to try to outstall us. I can keep a civil suit alive for years without going to
trial. They can't do that with criminal charges without violating your rights."

Tyson thought legal strategies were more Machiavellian than even political
strategies. Military strategy, if nothing else, was based on simplicity, speed, and
commonly understood objectives. Tyson replied, "I'm getting dizzy. Anyway, as
I said, with a few minor corrections, Picard has related the truth—"

"Oh, who gives a shit about the truth?" Sloan leaned farther across the table
and spoke in a low voice. "Listen to me. I don't give a goddamn if you're guilty
or not, and you've wasted a lot of my time trying to obscure that irrelevant fact.
What I'm concerned with is what's happening *now.* You've been fucked around
by the press, jerked off by your employers, snubbed by your peers, and held up

to scorn on radio and TV by that schmuck Picard. Let's lay the groundwork for getting even."

Tyson looked out over the greens. Fred Riordon, a semi-retired pediatrician, was teeing off. He turned back to Sloan. "Picard is not a schmuck. I've read his book, and I've seen him on TV. I wish he were a schmuck, but he's not. He's an arrogant twit, but nobody's fool. Secondly, getting even through civil suit, while civilized, is also wimpy and a poor substitute for kicking people in the balls or cutting their throats. If I ever sue, it won't be for revenge. Third, your points about our criminal justice system are well taken, but I've been doing a lot of reading, and I'm not so sure a military tribunal would find me innocent."

"The rules of evidence still apply."

Tyson shrugged. "Go see a court-martial. Then we'll discuss it."

Sloan drummed his fingers on the table. "You know, it's time you made a public statement. Something . . . something like you were saying before . . . about the battle itself. Something to the effect that it was chaos . . . but more than that . . . that it was a military blunder . . . gross stupidity, leading to unnecessary deaths—"

"What the hell purpose would that serve?"

"Oh, you'd be surprised. Allegations are not charges."

Tyson watched as the shadow of an airplane passed over the links. Tyson turned his attention to Sloan. "No, but there are allegations and then there are allegations. I'm not a lawyer, Phil, but let me tell you what I know of human nature. Here we have wide public knowledge of an alleged crime of some magnitude. Just as you see dollar signs, there are Justice Department lawyers and JAG lawyers who see glory and challenge." Tyson lit a cigarette and added, "Here we have a public spectacle with all the right elements: murder, conspiracy, Vietnam, sordid revelations, and exposés—a three-ring circus, complete with acrobats, jugglers, magicians, clowns, and tightrope walkers. You're right: Innocence or guilt has little to do with this."

"That's cynical."

Tyson laughed. *"That,* from a lawyer?"

"Cut it out, Ben. I'm trying to help you. And I didn't like that remark about money."

"I know you're not in it just for the money, Phillip. You have an eye on press coverage, too. One man's misfortune is another man's fame and fortune. But that's okay. No sweat."

"You're becoming paranoid."

"Paranoia kept me alive once."

Sloan poured himself and Tyson more coffee. He said, "You certainly bring new perspectives to the legal system."

Tyson seemed not to hear. He said, "An important element, I think, in how I am ultimately going to be judged—either legally or in the eyes of my peers— lies in the ethnicity of the victims."

Sloan eyed him closely but did not respond.

Tyson nodded to himself and continued, "Some of them were Caucasian, Phil. White folk like us. The soldiers at My Lai had it easy. They had only to explain away two or three hundred slant-eyed gook bodies. I have to explain about a dozen dead Caucasians. In war, as in every facet of life, it's quality, not quantity, that counts."

Phillip Sloan seemed to miss the sarcasm of the observation and nodded agreement. He said softly, as if to himself, "Catholics . . . the Orientals were Catholic. . . ."

"Right, Phil. All the Vietnamese nuns were obviously Catholic. Probably many of the patients were, too. It was a predominantly Catholic suburb of Hue. Some of the Europeans may have been Protestant. Double trouble." Tyson lit another cigarette. "No priests, though."

"Thank God for that."

"A bunch of babies, however. Pregnant women, children, sick people, wounded people—"

"Jesus."

"That's what you find in a hospital, Phil. In war, you have to take what you get."

Sloan looked at him quickly. "Are you crazy?"

"Now, there's an interesting question, fraught with many possibilities." Tyson winked and stood. He handed Sloan the yellow pad. "Do you see the mistake the Marines made?"

Sloan seemed momentarily confused, then glanced at the legal pad. "Oh—"

"It's pretty obvious, isn't it? Look, instead of driving north across the river into the heart of the Citadel, they should have swept around to the west in an end run. *Then* north across the river to block the western gate in the Citadel wall." Tyson tapped his finger on the yellow, lined paper. "That was the key. The communists were pumping in supplies and reinforcements through the western gate. And no one was in a position to stop them. My company was moving toward the west wall, but we were understrength and spread thin. Picard glosses over this Marine blunder, which is interesting. You see, after all these years, there is a little part of him that is still a Marine. *Semper Fidelis.* Don't badmouth the corps. Even when you're supposed to be after the truth."

Sloan said, "He bad-mouthed you and your troops with no problem. That's what I was getting at before—command culpability at a level higher than yours. If you go before a court-martial board, you can subpoena every commander who was within twenty miles of Hue that day. Make it clear to the Army that you were a small cog in a malfunctioning wheel, that you're not taking the rap alone. Go for the brass."

Tyson stared at Sloan, then leaned down, close to Sloan's face. "But don't you see, my friend? That's not fair. Any fool, including an ROTC lieutenant like me, can be a military genius at the breakfast table twenty years later, after having read a comprehensive history of the battle. But real genius is the ability to grasp the essence of a situation as it is happening. To think—not on your feet but on your belly, with five radiotelephones screaming at you, men dying and crying in pain, your pants full of piss, and the thump, thump, thump of mortar rounds walking toward you." Tyson slapped the table three times. Thump, thump, thump!

Sloan glanced around quickly and saw that people were looking.

Tyson straightened up and threw his cigarette on the terrace stone. He said in a quieter voice, "Well, judge not, that ye be not judged. The Allied commanders at Hue killed more of their own troops through stupidity than the enemy killed through superior tactics. But I'd forgive those officers if they asked my forgiveness. Because, you know, buddy, in the heat of battle, there is no judgment to be made on anyone. When the battle ends and coffee is being served to the survivors, people ought to remember that. Thanks for breakfast, Phil."

12

Benjamin Tyson lay naked on the ceramic tile ledge and watched the steam rising to the ceiling.

The man on the tier above him waited until the steam stopped hissing, then said, "I hope you understand why I wanted to speak to you here."

Tyson felt the good sweat running over his body. He glanced up at the man sitting with his knees drawn up to his chest. Tyson replied, "I assume it has something to do with recording devices."

"Right." He added, "Everyone's paranoid these days. Well, what with mini-transmitters, directional microphones, and all, I don't blame people. But this place is good. I have a lot of meetings in steam rooms. We'll swim later."

Tyson sat up and propped his back against the wall. He had on past occasions discussed business here at the New York Athletic Club, but the place had been chosen to promote chumminess, not to put everyone at ease about tape recorders.

The man said, "What are your clubs?"

"Book-of-the-Month."

He laughed, then said, "Don't you belong to two suburban clubs? The Garden City Country Club and the Garden City Golf Club—that's men only, isn't it?"

Tyson said, "I'm afraid I'm not clear about who you represent, Mr. Brown."

"I represent the government."

"The whole government? All by yourself?"

The man smiled slowly. "Well, that's not important right now."

"It is to me. Look, you convinced me on the phone you had something important to say. That's why I'm here."

Brown looked down at Tyson, but said nothing.

Tyson stared back at him through the white steam. Brown was somewhat younger than Tyson, and Tyson, like most men who've recently discovered they are middle-aged, disliked authority figures who were younger than themselves. The man was well built and well tanned, Tyson noted, except for the outlines of a brief bathing suit and a watch on his left wrist. He had curly blue-black hair and manicured nails, and his general appearance was that of a man who took some care with himself. Tyson noticed he wore a wedding band and a religious medal. He didn't think Brown was military but felt he had once been. His accent hinted of private schools and an Ivy League college. Tyson said finally, "What can I do for you, Mr. Brown?"

"Call me Chet, okay?"

"Okay, Chet. What else can I do for you?"

The man smiled. "May I call you Ben?"

"Sure."

"Well," said Chet Brown, as he massaged his sweaty calves, "I want to speak to you about . . . things. This conversation will be unofficial but authorized. We can come to some binding decisions here."

Tyson remarked, "Sounds like the government is in trouble."

"Not at all. You are the one who is in trouble."

Tyson did not reply immediately, then said, "So why negotiate? What did old Ben Franklin say, Chet? 'Neither a fortress nor a virgin will hold out long after they begin to negotiate.' "

Brown laughed. "I like that. I think I'm going to like you, Ben. You don't look like a mass murderer."

Tyson resisted several responses, one of which was taking a swing at Chet Brown.

Brown continued, "You see, Ben, justice has to be balanced with compassion. More to the point, there are popular cases and unpopular cases. There is theory and there is reality."

Tyson tuned out as the man went through his warm-up. Tyson rubbed the sweat from his eyes, then looked at the glass door. An attendant had stuck up a sign, and Tyson assumed it said something like "keep out."

Tyson yawned and stretched. No, he reflected, he certainly didn't feel awkward sitting naked with this man. Nor did he feel at a psychological disadvantage. He felt somewhat relaxed and somnolent as he suspected he was supposed to feel. He also felt he should keep in mind that he was discussing his fate with his enemy.

Brown was still speaking, and Tyson tuned back in. "You see," said Brown, "this issue has obviously become too well known, nationally and internationally, to be ignored. We'd *like* to ignore it, but we can't."

"Try harder."

"You see, Ben, this has become a real emotional issue. We knew it would. All the old shit is being dredged up again."

Tyson closed his eyes.

Brown went on. "Public opinion is divided. Right? The national debate is following the old pattern—some columnists and commentators have pointed out that Picard's book discusses at length the infamous enemy atrocities at Hue. But, as usual, they say only America's alleged crimes are given media attention."

Tyson liked that argument.

"But," continued Brown, "other people have pointed out that America is expected to behave better than its enemies. Double standard. Right? And in any case, carping about enemy atrocities doesn't get you anywhere. The perpetrators of the Hôpital Miséricorde massacre"—Brown pronounced it in good French—"those perpetrators are within U.S. jurisdiction."

"But actually," replied Tyson, "they aren't any longer."

"Well," said Brown musingly, "that is the point, isn't it, Ben?"

"Yes, Chet, that is the point."

Neither man spoke for some time. Then Brown said, "People are beginning to talk publicly about court-martial. You may have read that in the newspapers. Or heard it on radio and TV."

"I think I did read that somewhere. I don't watch much TV. I listen to tapes on my car radio. Fifties sounds. Incredible stuff. Do you like fifties music?"

"I love it. I could listen to the Everly Brothers all day."

"How about the Shirelles?"

"They don't write them like that anymore. Listen, Ben, there are a lot of people on your side. Including me."

"What is *my* side, Chet?"

Brown leaned down so his face was just inches from Tyson's. "Please don't play games with me, okay?"

Tyson stared hard at the man until Brown returned to his sitting position on the tier above Tyson. The steam came on again, and Brown disappeared in the white vapor. Both men sat quietly listening to the loud hissing. Tyson closed his eyes. The steam stopped suddenly, and Tyson drew a breath through his nostrils.

Brown spoke in a soft voice. "This is how it stands—the people who are on your side are mostly the civilians: the White House, the secretaries of the Army and Defense, the Justice Department, and others. It is the Army itself that wants your ass."

"No gratitude."

"Whatever. I think the Army and the Judge Advocate General Corps in particular are very anxious to redeem themselves. I'm speaking of the My Lai screw-up, of course. They can't retry that one, but they've been given another one."

Tyson didn't reply.

Brown continued, "Regarding this hospital incident, the Army wants to clean its own house, and the JAG is anxious to provide the broom. Fellow by the name of Van Arken."

Tyson nodded. That name had been mentioned a few times in news stories.

Brown added, "You see, the Army's memory of My Lai is long and clear. There is a continuity in the Army ranks that you don't have in the White House, for instance, where a half dozen administrations have come and gone since My Lai. And the folks in the White House can't seem to call the JAG Corps off or even get them to pull a few punches."

Tyson nodded to himself. It made sense. The military would remain forever obsessed with honor lost and honor regained. Tyson suspected that somehow, in the collective psyches of the military, this case transcended Miséricorde Hospital and had to do with Vietnam as a whole.

Brown spoke slowly and deliberately. "The Army has initiated the procedure to recall you to active duty."

Tyson felt a tightness in his stomach, but his face revealed nothing.

"Do you understand you can't be tried except by court-martial?"

"I understand that."

"You have an attorney named Sloan."

"Right."

"Do you have any other lawyers?"

"Do I need more than one?"

"Just checking. Look, I want to be honest with you—"

"Good."

"The Army is going to have a hell of a time making that recall order stick in court. But you know what?"

"No, what?"

"They'll get you back. It may take two years, but they will. Do you have the *resources* to fight the government?"

"That's my secret."

"Do you have the will?"

"What are you getting at?"

Brown swung his legs down from the ledge and leaned forward. "I'd like to offer you some advice."

Tyson construed that to mean a deal. "Shoot."

"Don't fight the recall order."

Tyson slid off the tile ledge and stood. "Great advice, Chet." He bent down and touched his toes. "Okay, what's in it for me?"

"A speedy trial."

"You mean just like in the Constitution?" Tyson began a series of stretching exercises. "You're wasting my time."

Brown mused, "God bless America, Ben. How many countries in the world are there where a suspected mass murderer can jerk around a government man who's trying to offer him a deal?"

"One, at last count. And here we are."

"Right. But if this was someplace else, this white-tiled room would be used for another purpose. Like me beating the shit out of you."

Tyson straightened up. "Try it, sonny."

Brown seemed to be considering the offer, then shook his head. "Look, let me get my business out of the way. Then if you want, we can go a few rounds. We'll both feel better."

Tyson dropped into a push-up position.

Brown slipped down to the floor and came closer to Tyson. "I'm prepared to make you an offer in exchange for your cooperation."

Tyson jumped to his feet. He faced Brown, and the two men stood an arm's length apart. "Is this legal?"

Brown shrugged. "I'm not a lawyer. Neither are you. You said on the phone you'd meet me without a lawyer present."

Tyson walked toward the door. "Let's grab a shower." They exited and walked down a short passage to the showers.

Tyson felt his head clearing under the cool, pulsating water. Brown stood under a shower head a few feet away and said, "You see, Ben, Van Arken believes he has sufficient grounds to recall you. But if you challenge this recall, then the President may have to sign an executive order recalling you. He'd rather not be put in that position."

"Tell him I'd challenge his executive order."

"He's not only thinking of himself. He thinks that if he got personally involved in your case, it would prejudice the case against you."

Tyson shut off the shower and walked into the locker room. An attendant handed him a towel. Brown came up behind him and said, "I've reserved two masseurs. My treat." He led Tyson to a small massage room. Two tables sat side by side. Tyson jumped on the closer one and lay on his stomach. Brown sat on the table beside him. "They'll be along in a while."

Tyson closed his eyes and yawned. He felt relaxed despite the unpleasant subject of conversation. A dreamy lassitude came over him. He couldn't imagine what life would be like in jail, and in truth he was prepared to listen to anything that would keep him from finding out. He faced Brown on the nearby table. "If you really want to be honest with me, you'll tell me on what grounds this recall will be made. Then I'll tell you how I'm going to beat it."

"Once an officer, always an officer," Brown said.

"I don't feel like an officer. You'll have to do better than that, Chet."

Brown said, " 'To all who shall see these presents, greeting.' Sound familiar? That's what your presidential commission says. And mine too." He continued, " 'Know ye, that reposing special trust and confidence in the patriotism, valor, fidelity, and abilities of Benjamin James Tyson, I do appoint him a commissioned officer in the Army of the United States.' "

Tyson stared at Brown.

Brown went on. " 'This officer will therefore carefully and diligently discharge the duties of the office to which appointed by doing and performing all manner of things thereunto.' " Brown smiled. "The language is pretty archaic. But that's the kind of language that has some cachet in court. Sounds like it was handed down from George Washington's administration. Which it was. Anyway, here's the part that's of immediate interest to us—'This commission is to continue in force during the pleasure of the President of the United States of America.' "

Tyson snorted, "Nice performance, Chet."

Brown continued, "Your commission was signed by Lyndon Johnson, but any President could enforce it at his pleasure. And you accepted that commission. You raised your right hand and took a solemn oath."

Tyson didn't reply.

Tyson hung his toes over the edge of the diving board, bounced, and dove into the swimming pool. He did a few laps, then swam to the middle of the pool and treaded water.

Brown floated on his back close by. There were two other men in the pool, both elderly, some distance off. A disinterested lifeguard sat on a deck chair reading a paperback book. Brown said, "I'm glad there are a few places left where a man can swim *au naturel.* How much longer can these private clubs hold out? I'm going to write a book someday called *The Feminization of America.*" Brown yawned lazily. "Your wife, I understand, is an active feminist."

Tyson said nothing.

Brown rolled forward and treaded water beside Tyson. "The last point in this recall business. . . ." Brown's eyes moved toward Tyson. "Did you know you are still listed on the rolls of inactive reserve officers?"

"No, I didn't," Tyson lied.

"Well, it's a fact. You were asked once by letter to indicate if you wished to remain on the inactive rolls or be dropped from the rolls. You didn't check either box. Instead, you wrote a nasty little note on the letter and sent it back to the Department of the Army. You're not supposed to do that, Ben. You were supposed to check a box. A lot of modern life depends on what box you check."

Tyson swam to the edge of the pool and rested his head on the tile rim. He closed his eyes, extended his legs, and floated. He remembered that standard form letter from the Department of the Army. It had come in mid-April 1975. Cambodia had fallen to the Khmer Rouge, Laos was falling to the Pathet Lao, and the North Vietnamese Army and Viet Cong were about to enter Saigon. Tyson, like a number of men he knew who had served in Vietnam, was bitter and angry. He thought he'd gotten Vietnam out of his system years before, but the names in the news awakened old memories. City after city, camp after camp, fell to the enemy in rapid succession. Quang Tri, Hue, Da Nang, Pleiku, and one night, his former base camp, the First Cavalry headquarters at An Khe. And each name that he heard or read evoked images of blood, death, sacrifice, and bravery. He said aloud, "That letter came at a bad time."

Brown was standing beside him in the shallow water. He replied, "It must have. You scrawled across the letter these words: 'Fifty thousand Americans dead, one hundred fifty thousand wounded. For what?' "

Brown continued. "That little impetuous note has been seen by everyone in the JAG office. There was, I understand, some discussion regarding the type of man who would write something like that for the posterity of the Army Records Bureau."

Tyson opened his eyes. "I resent the fact that people are analyzing me and talking about me as though I were a specimen. I don't like people reading my Army records, though I know you have a right to do that. I'm getting pissed off, Chet."

"Of course you are. I don't blame you. But remember, please, that though we're not discussing mass murder at the moment, that's what this thing is ultimately all about."

Tyson glanced at the big wall clock across the natatorium.

Brown said, "I won't keep you much longer. You probably have work piling up on your desk. I just wanted to inform you of this recall. If you fight it, the Army will counterattack. Eventually, you know, they will break through. You'll have bought some time, but at great cost."

"That's better than going quietly to the slaughter."

"It's not a slaughter. It's a trial. And I'll tell you something else, Ben. Even if you reach the Supreme Court with this and they find for you, you'll be beaten. You will never have had the opportunity to have these allegations resolved. Your entire fight to escape jurisdiction will appear as an admission of guilt. If, on the other hand, you voluntarily come back to active duty, you will have gained an important psychological advantage, and you will have scored a tremendous public relations coup on your own behalf. The Army would look favorably on any such voluntary action on your part."

Tyson said, "What are you offering in exchange for my cooperation?"

Brown caught hold of the pool wall and rested his folded arms on the rim. "Well, I can't promise you anything concerning the legal proceedings themselves. I'm not in the business of thwarting an Army investigation, or if it goes to trial, I can't tamper in any way with a military court-martial. But I can make a few guarantees in exchange for some promises from you."

Tyson climbed the concrete steps of the pool and sat on the pool edge, his feet in the water. "Let's hear the guarantees."

Brown moved closer to him. "First, if you voluntarily place yourself under Army jurisdiction, you will be assigned to a post within twenty-five miles of the metropolitan area."

"Sounds like an enlistment pitch. How about a new uniform?"

"Sure. Also—and this is important—you will not be placed under restraint of any sort. You will be as free as you are now, within the parameters of your duties, if any. Okay so far?"

"No, but go on."

Brown's tone was impatient. "Look, Ben, if they get you back in after a court fight, it won't be so easy on you. They'll assign you to Fort Bumfuck in the Arizona desert, and you'll be confined to quarters."

"Don't threaten me, junior."

Brown stood in the shallow water on the concrete step and clenched his right fist, cracking his knuckles. He said, "You don't want to be confined to quarters, Ben. You won't like that. Neither will your family. Your wife. She'd probably have to stay in New York to work. It would get very lonely for her, buddy . . . or maybe it wouldn't—"

Tyson drove the heel of his foot into Brown's solar plexus. Brown's eyes and mouth opened wide as he doubled over and stumbled back down the pool steps.

The two old men at the far end of the pool didn't notice, and the lifeguard kept reading his book. A young man in a nearby deck chair stood suddenly and made eye contact with Tyson.

Brown straightened up and caught his breath. His head bobbed quickly several times, and he motioned with his hand toward the young man. Tyson stood and took a step back from the pool as he kept an eye on the man. The man sat back in his chair.

Brown drew several deep breaths and stared up at Tyson. "Okay . . . okay.

. . . I had that coming. . . ." Brown put his hands on the edge of the pool. "I'm getting out. Okay? Truce."

Tyson nodded.

Brown lifted himself out of the pool and turned from Tyson. He walked slowly to his deck chair and wrapped a towel around his waist. He sat on the edge of the chair and patted the chaise longue beside him.

Tyson walked to it, grabbed his towel, and put it around his waist.

Brown said, "Feel better? Sit down."

Tyson felt much better. He stretched out in the chaise longue.

Brown massaged his midsection. "Christ . . . you see, you *are* a violent man. You're normal." Brown affected a smile.

Tyson relaxed but kept his eye on Brown. It came to him that since Vietnam he hadn't felt much deep passion, anger, or challenge. In a way, he realized, he was reverting, regressing in time and temperament, to the type of person he had been before Marcy, suburbia, middle age, and the corporate structure began limiting his aggressiveness. He was taking more control over his life, which in other ways was coming apart. He said to Brown, "I'm sorry. But if you piss me off again, I'll hit you again."

Brown forced a weak smile. "Okay. Can I finish my business?" Brown leaned forward and rested his hands on his knees. "Where was I? Restraint. Right. If you are actually court-martialed I can also guarantee that you won't be placed under restraint even during the trial. Therefore, if things don't seem to be going well in the courtroom, you at least have the option of removing yourself in the ultimate sense from Army jurisdiction. In fact, you can go now if you wish. No one is watching you."

Tyson said nothing.

Brown added, "Your passport will not be revoked or confiscated as is the normal procedure. But if you decide to go, now or at anytime, please go someplace where you won't embarrass the government with an extradition problem. Brazil is the choice of most, but you might consider Sweden." He leaned closer to Tyson. "Listen, everything I'm offering is within the power of the executive branch to do—"

"Sweden! Are you trying to tell me that eighteen years after I served my country and came home, I should run to Sweden? *I* should run to Sweden where—"

"Please lower your voice."

Tyson sat up. "—where the deserters and draft-dodgers went? I should go to Sweden when all the draft-dodgers have been given a presidential pardon? Where's *my* presidential pardon?"

"It is rather ironic if you think about it—"

"Fuck you, Brown! Fuck you and whoever sent you."

"Not so loud, please."

"I'm not going anywhere, goddamn it! I'm an American citizen, and this is my country. Fuck Sweden and fuck the Army!"

Brown glanced around the pool area. "Calm down."

Tyson lifted himself out of the chair. "Listen, Chet, or whatever the fuck your name is, tell your bosses this: I may be a suspected mass murderer, but I am also a certified war hero. I have two fucking Purple Hearts—" Tyson pointed to the white scar tissue that disfigured his right ear, then to the thick purple line that curved around his kneecap and ran down his shin. "I have a fistful of medals and commendations. I am also a husband, a father, and a hardworking taxpayer. I am a respected member of my community, and I have never knowingly broken the law in my life. If something *did* happen in that shithole eighteen years ago, something that maybe lasted thirty minutes of my forty-year life, then . . . then. . . ." Tyson found his heart was beating heavily and his fists were clenched. He glowered at Brown, who was sitting very still.

Brown spoke in a soft voice. "This was the first war in our history that produced not one certifiable, media-anointed, publicly acclaimed war hero. Not one." Brown stood. He stared at Tyson for some time, then added, "Hey, you have to understand, my friend, there are no bad guys in this piece. Not me, not Van Arken, not the folks in the White House, not the media, and not even you. There is only the system. The law."

Brown touched Tyson's arm gently and cocked his head toward the locker room. As they walked, Brown said, "No one has anything against you personally. Everyone I spoke to wishes you well. But you have to understand, Ben, the military needs this one. You've read the Peers Commission report on My Lai, haven't you? Well, everything that General Peers said was wrong with that case, from beginning to end, will be right with this case. No cover-ups, no legal blunders, no undue command influence, no congressional whining, no journalistic Monday-morning quarterbacking, no fuckups. Just justice. Even if we have to script it and fake it. Okay?"

They reached the door that led to the locker room and stopped. Tyson said, "Tell them I'm a fighter, Chet."

"I will." Brown rubbed his stomach. "You are." Brown glanced around. "I'm going to do some laps. You have to get going." Brown hesitated, then said, "There's more. You see, Ben, you *can* hurt the Army, the government, and the country if you want. So if you're going to fight, fight fair. If you're going to run, run clean." Brown continued, "No swipes at the Army or the President or the system. No criticism of the Army justice system, no going on about the immorality of the war. No talking to reporters. No opening of old wounds."

"That's it? Or that's not it?"

"Almost. We want you to accept a JAG-appointed defense counsel." Brown glanced at Tyson, then continued. "We don't want you retaining an F. Lee Bailey. You couldn't control a hotshot.civilian lawyer. The deal wouldn't work with a civilian. You see, a civilian would drag it out, try to get all kinds of publicity for himself. We want the trial concluded before the reporters from the *Times* and the *Post* get their pens uncapped. We don't want the continuing saga of Ben Tyson on the nightly news. Neither do you." Brown continued, "Though you can't plead guilty, you *can* at least refrain from calling witnesses, cross-examining government witnesses, and that sort of thing. There's nothing irregular about not offering a defense. In fact, military court-martial boards look favorably on that. They'll probably hand you one to ten for being a gentleman. And you won't do a day of it anyway. As long as you accept this offer. Okay? Do you understand what is required of you? We'll remind you of what is required from time to time as certain situations arise." Brown added softly, "It's not a bad deal, Ben. It guarantees you won't be imprisoned. Will you think about it?"

"Sure."

Brown smiled, then gave Tyson a hard look. "If you turn this deal down, there will be no hard feelings. But do *not* mention this conversation to anyone. Not your wife, your lawyer, or anyone. If you do and we find out, then . . . then it becomes personal."

Tyson nodded.

Brown said, "I'll call you." He extended his hand. "No hard feelings."

Tyson took Brown's hand. "When I drove my heel into your solar plexus, it was not personal, Chet. I was acting out my rage against the system."

Brown laughed. He turned and walked toward the pool. Tyson watched him jump in, then passed through the door to the locker room. *Yes,* he thought, *justice will be done, even if it has to be scripted and faked.*

13

General William Van Arken stood behind a podium that bore the crossed sword and quill pen emblem of the Judge Advocate General's Corps. He addressed the four officers seated before him. "Although we have no authority at present to investigate the Tyson case, we may choose an investigating officer to contact Mr. Tyson on the day he receives his recall orders, to inform him that charges are being contemplated against him, and to inform him of his rights."

Van Arken looked at the three men and one woman seated in the row of writing desks in the small lecture room located in the third side of the Pentagon. Van Arken's adjutant, Colonel Sam Spencer, sat directly in front of him. To Spencer's right was Lieutenant Colonel Eugene Pellum, Van Arken's special legal counsel. To Spencer's left was Captain Lorraine Connelly from personnel. Next to her was Lieutenant Jack Gibbs, Van Arken's aide. Van Arken said, "As you know, the Uniform Code of Military Justice recommends that in felony cases, the investigating officer be a major or higher rank. Therefore I've asked Captain Connelly to assemble the microfilmed files of approximately twenty-five such officers who may be suitable to conduct this investigation." Van Arken motioned to the projection screen behind him.

"I'll remind you," he continued, "that in the interests of fairness, we should not discuss this case as such, but we can make references to certain facts that are relevant to the task of choosing an impartial investigator." He looked at his legal counsel. "Colonel Pellum?"

Pellum nodded. "Let me also remind everyone that just as we have the sworn duty to choose an investigator who will not be prejudicial toward the suspect, we should also choose someone who will not be sympathetic toward him."

Colonel Spencer added, "As we know, any JAG officer should be impartial and acceptable. However, in this case it would be appropriate to consider candidates."

Captain Lorraine Connelly said, "We should perhaps first come up with a profile. Credentials, requirements, character traits, and so forth. Then we can narrow the field."

Van Arken nodded in agreement. "Well, what *are* we looking for?"

Colonel Pellum replied, "Ideally, the investigating officer should be as free from negative or positive bias regarding the Vietnam War as possible." He smiled grimly. "That would either be someone who is young or someone who has spent the last two decades on the moon."

Lieutenant Gibbs spoke. "Maybe the investigating officer should be someone who has decided not to continue his military career." He hesitated before adding, "Someone who has nothing to lose and nothing to gain. An officer who won't feel . . . pressured to come to a conclusion that he feels will please the Army."

Van Arken didn't reply.

Colonel Spencer nodded. "That's a good point. No one can accuse us later of bringing in a gung-ho hatchet man who's trying to make rank."

Several heads nodded. The discussion continued for some minutes before Van Arken said, "In summation, then, everyone feels that this officer should not have served in Vietnam or even have been in the service during the Vietnam era. That would obviously be consistent with him not being a career officer. He should in fact be too young to have even been involved in college activities, pro- or antiwar during this period." Van Arken reflected a moment. "There can't be many men in that age group who are majors and who are not continuing their military careers."

Captain Connelly said, "I think someone who is fulfilling a four-year tuition assistance obligation will meet these requirements."

Van Arken mulled over these suggestions. This was not precisely what he had in mind. He said, "I want a man who will project a good image for the Army and for the Judge Advocate General's Corps."

No one responded.

Van Arken said, "Well, let's begin going through the files." He pressed a button on the podium to signal the man in the soundproof projection room.

"Excuse me, General." Captain Lorraine Connelly spoke. "May I make a suggestion?"

The lights dimmed, and the screen behind Van Arken brightened. The General looked at Lorraine Connelly in the reflected light of the screen. "Yes?"

She said, "I suppose it isn't proper for any of us to propose a candidate, but that's what I'm going to do."

"Whom do you have in mind?"

She replied, "Major Karen Harper."

There was a stillness in the darkened room. Captain Connelly added, "Some of you may know her. I met her when we worked together in Germany." Connelly paused, then said, "I included her file among the ones we're going to consider. Why don't we look at it first?"

No one responded.

Captain Connelly spoke into the silent darkness. "Major Harper fills the initial requirements that we've agreed on. In addition, she is very thorough. Good attention to detail. Fine judgment, shows outstanding initiative, and her personal appearance is always up to standards." Lorraine Connelly could see in the dim light that the General seemed to respond positively to these military buzz words. Taking heart, she continued, "Colonel Pellum made a humorous comment about finding someone who spent the last two decades on the moon. Well, more importantly, it would be favorably viewed if the investigating officer has spent the last month in a media vacuum. It so happens that Major Harper is recently returned from a thirty-day leave, which she spent in the Far East. I doubt if she bothered to pick up any American papers there."

Van Arken said curtly, "Choosing an Army investigator is not like jury selection. I don't think a JAG officer believes everything he—she—reads in the papers."

Colonel Spencer, Van Arken's adjutant, interjected, "Still, General, I like that idea. So will the media." He turned to Connelly. "Do you know of her personal history?"

Captain Connelly replied, "Yes, sir, I believe she comes from a large family. Rural people. Farmers, I think. Ohio." She was tempted to add "heartland," but resisted the overkill and went on. "Her undergraduate work was at Ohio State, as her file will show. I believe her education was touch and go because of finances. She entered American University Law when she was in her mid-twenties, and Defense picked up the tab."

Lieutenant Gibbs mumbled, "In exchange for four years' hard time, like me." He laughed to try to slough off the ill-considered remark.

Van Arken presided over the silence for a while, then abruptly pressed the intercom button on the podium and spoke to the projectionist. "Let's have Harper, Sergeant."

Within a minute the first page of the file was projected on the screen.

The five officers read the page on the screen. Colonel Spencer said, "She's presently assigned to the JAG School in Charlottesville. That's close to us here, but not too close. And she can hop on a shuttle to New York whenever necessary."

Colonel Pellum commented, "Her ETS is July sixteenth. That gives her enough time to complete the preliminary investigation and not have to stick around for the consequences."

Lorraine Connelly said, "The file will show she's successfully conducted Article 31 and 32 investigations. Also, she's a remarkable interrogator—"

"Meaning what?" asked Van Arken curtly.

"Meaning, sir, she gets at the truth. Suspects—men, I suppose you'd say—talk freely to her. She's not abrasive, officious, or intimidating—"

"I don't want anyone who's going to be soft on Tyson."

Lieutenant Colonel Pellum said, "General, Tyson is obviously a bright man. He knows he can cripple an Article 31 investigation in the two seconds it will take him to exercise his right to remain silent. I think, though, that if a woman called on him . . . Not to be sexist, but it may help. At this stage we're only empowered to conduct this informal inquiry. So we'd like to get the most out of it until such time as we can proceed further."

Van Arken saw the others nod in agreement. He said bluntly, "Tyson may not take kindly to being investigated by a woman." He hit a button, and the next page appeared. The five officers read the pages of Harper's file as they rolled across the screen. Van Arken commented, "She is unmarried." This elicited no response. Van Arken said into the intercom, "Sergeant, go on to the photograph."

The film advanced quickly, then stopped at a blurry file photograph. The projectionist adjusted the focus, and the screen filled with a black-and-white picture of a woman with light, tousled hair. She had a wide smile, big eyes, and freckles. No one spoke until Lieutenant Gibbs commented, "Looks like someone I'd let in the door."

There were a few chuckles. Van Arken heard Gibbs say something else and caught the word *wife*. There was some further laughter. Van Arken snapped, "At ease."

Captain Connelly regarded General Van Arken in the glare of the projector's beam. She could see that Van Arken was deep in thought. Lorraine Connelly had heard that Van Arken was not amused by the off-color jokes his junior officers were making about Tyson's wife. Lorraine Connelly strongly suspected, too, that General Van Arken was not favorably disposed toward a man with a wife like that.

Colonel Spencer's voice broke the stillness. "General, I know the choice of a woman could cause some problems; but if it's image you're after, then there's a good image for you." He pointed at Karen Harper's picture. "Looks like she stepped out of a Coke ad."

Van Arken rubbed his chin thoughtfully. Putting a woman in charge of the investigation, he understood, could very well enhance the image of the JAG

Corps. It would also defuse recent criticism regarding the postings and promotions of female personnel in his command. The Pentagon would be pleased.

Lieutenant Gibbs seemed to read Van Arken's thoughts. "This might give some credence to the recruiting slogan, 'Be all you can be.' "

Van Arken eyed Gibbs with some annoyance, then continued his ruminations. He realized that if Harper bungled the investigation, it might not reflect too unfavorably on the mostly male and mostly career officer corps. And if Major Karen Harper ran into trouble with the investigation, the White House could be pressured to quickly authorize the formal, grand jury type investigation, with subpoena powers, a working staff, and assistance from the Army CID and the FBI. There was, of course, the possibility that Major Harper would find no evidence to recommend that charges be forwarded to a grand jury. But Van Arken didn't think that was a strong possibility, given the nature of the allegations. Van Arken looked at the officers in front of him. He had the impression they favored assigning this Harper woman to the case. The General said, "Does anyone have any objections to this officer serving as the Article 31 investigating officer in the matter of Benjamin Tyson?"

No one objected.

Van Arken stared at Captain Lorraine Connelly in a way that suggested he thought she'd stuck her neck out and had better be prepared for the consequences. Van Arken said, "All right. Major Harper it is."

Van Arken turned and stared at the photograph of Karen Harper still projected on the screen. Beyond the fresh good looks and the warm smile, he thought he saw some strength of character, some keen intelligence; a result, he imagined, of the hard climb from rural poverty to an education, a law degree, a military tour of duty. He, too, had been born in rural poverty on a Pennsylvania farm not eighty miles from where he stood now. And like Karen Harper, he reflected, he had made the climb alone, without marrying. Dependents got heavy when you started so far down in the hole that it took half a lifetime just to reach ground level with everyone else.

General Van Arken turned back to the people in the small dark room. "Captain Connelly, you will not communicate this decision to Major Harper. On the day Tyson receives his recall orders, Major Harper will receive her orders assigning her to temporary duty as investigating officer. No one here will divulge anything that was said. No one here will have any contact with Major Harper until her investigation is completed. If there is nothing further"—he met everyone's eyes—"then thank you for coming. Dismissed."

14

T he old Volvo rolled east on Montauk Highway, through Southampton, then Water Mill. Tyson turned left at the Methodist Church and headed up Scuttle Hole Road. The late afternoon sun lay mellow and pleasant over the well-tended and prosperous potato farms. Scuttle Hole Road intersected with the Sag Harbor turnpike, and Tyson swung north.

He turned his head and spoke to David, who shared the rear seat with cartons and suitcases. "David, do you remember any of this?"

"Sort of. It's real nice."

Within ten minutes they entered the old whaling village of Sag Harbor. Stately homes with widow's walks lined lower Main Street, then at the Civil War monument the street widened into the business district.

Tyson joined the line of slow-moving traffic. The sidewalks were crowded with a happy-looking mixture of families, singles, gays, townsmen, fishermen, farmers, and yachtsmen from distant ports.

The Volvo continued slowly. Tyson scanned the storefronts, looking for the bookshop. In the front window was a hand-lettered sign announcing BOOKS BY LOCAL AUTHORS. Tyson was surprised to see there were nearly two dozen scribblers in local residence. There among the books he spotted the distinctive scarlet cover of *Hue: Death of a City*.

"Still a hot item."

"What?"

Tyson cocked his head to the side.

Marcy looked. "Oh. Sure. Five weeks on the *Times* bestseller list. Number twelve and climbing. Maybe you and Picard can do a little East End publicity together. Put a rocket up that book's ass, as we say in the business. I'll handle the PR."

"Not funny."

"No," agreed David, "not funny."

Marcy shrugged. "Just trying to kill time in traffic."

The Volvo approached the traffic circle at the end of Main Street. In the center of the circle rose a tall white flagpole. The stars and stripes snapped nicely in the wind that blew off the harbor, and the halyard slapped against the pole. Beyond the circle in a grassy patch was the windmill overlooking the harbor. To the right was the Long Wharf, thick with cars, people, and fishmongers. Sailing vessels swayed at their moorings, and Tyson could hear the creaking in the riggings.

David said, "I remember this. A red seaplane landed there."

Marcy said, "We used to have lunch at that restaurant on the wharf. See it?"

"Oh, yeah. I helped unload fish from a boat."

Tyson put in, "Catch of the day. Red snappers. I paid nine dollars a plate for them an hour later."

Marcy remarked, "You have a selective memory."

Tyson nodded. "You ain't seen nothing until you see my selective amnesia on a witness stand."

No one spoke. Tyson took the Volvo around the circle and headed to North Haven over the bridge crammed with joggers, bicyclists, and pedestrians. He turned left on Short Beach Road, then left again onto a small peninsula called Baypoint. "Which way?"

"Right over there on Cliff Road, left on Bayview. There it is. The gray-shingled Cape."

Tyson looked at the white-trimmed cottage as the car descended the curved road. The grass was brown and high; the mimosa hung in heavy pink bloom over the small portico. Wildflowers grew where they could, and untrimmed spruce and cedar darkened the left half of the property. Quite lovely, really. He said, "Does this place have electricity?"

"Don't get cute, Tyson."

He pulled the car into the gravel drive and shut off the engine. There was a silence as the Tysons surveyed the property from the car. Tyson said, *"This* was nine thousand dollars for the summer?"

Marcy snapped, "And we were lucky to get it. There's nothing left on the entire East End." She added, "It's quaint, and it's on the bay."

David opened the rear door. "I'm going to take a look." He shot out of the car and disappeared around the side of the garage.

Marcy and Ben sat in silence. The engine ticked, and a locust clicked somewhere. Tyson said, "You're right. This isn't far from the one we rented a couple of years ago."

"It was eight years ago."

"Was it? Time flies." He looked at the house and the trees, and he thought of that summer. Each Friday after work he'd take the Long Island Railroad from Penn Station to Bridgehampton, an unpleasant three-hour run made barely more tolerable by spending it in the bar car. Marcy and David would meet him at the station, and they'd usually have dinner in a Bridgehampton pub whose name escaped him at the moment. On Monday morning, at dawn, he'd board the Hampton jitney bus with other men and women who were making the commute back to the front lines. Marcy had been between jobs then, and she'd spent the entire summer in Sag Harbor with David.

Marcy broke into his thoughts. "Where are you?"

He looked at her. "That summer."

She nodded. "You took most of August off."

"Yes, I did. Things were slow at Peregrine. No one seemed to be building many fighter bombers or attack helicopters that year. That's all changed now."

"Unfortunately it has."

"How about you? No one needs any quick publicity fixes this summer?"

She replied, "I told you, I took an extended leave. The job is there when I want to go back. Tom was very good about it. Very understanding."

"Good old Tom."

They sat in silence for a while, then Tyson opened his door. "Well, let's see what sort of horror house you've rented this time."

They walked across the high weedy lawn, and Marcy found the key. They entered directly into an all-white living room furnished in what Tyson thought of as East End rental chic: chrome, glass, molded plastics, and beige cotton suede.

At the far end of the living room were sliding glass doors that led out onto a wooden deck. Marcy walked to the doors and slid one open. She took a deep breath. "Smell that sea."

Tyson slid the screen open and walked onto the redwood deck. Marcy followed. Tyson looked out over the property. The yard dropped off and ended in a tangle of bramble and a heap of bulkhead rocks. Beyond was the body of water called Sag Harbor Cove. David was picking his way over the rocks. Tyson said, "I hope there's some hot little number around here for him."

Marcy leaned on the deck rail and watched their son. "I hope he finds whatever he needs out here." She stared out at a sleek yellow-sailed catamaran gliding west toward the narrows. "A sailboat in the backyard. This is beautiful, Ben."

"Yes . . . but you'll miss the Big Apple. You may even miss Garden City."

"I'll miss New York, but I won't miss Garden City. It was insufferable these last few weeks."

"It's all in the mind." Tyson gave her a sidelong glance. The wind blew her hair, and the sun shone fully on her face. Her eyes were closed, and she looked about ten years younger than she'd looked yesterday.

Tyson walked along the deck and peered into a second set of glass doors.

"The kitchen looks decent. But . . . oh, God . . . I don't see a dishwasher. There's no trash compactor or microwave oven. Marcy, is this the right house?"

"Don't be a wiseass, Ben. Anyway, I have menus from fourteen take-out places."

"That's my girl. Resourceful in the face of privation. Well, hell, you may as well enjoy your vacation."

She replied coolly, "It is not a vacation, Ben. We're on the lam."

Tyson didn't reply.

Marcy looked across the hedgeline into the adjoining yard. Two men in their twenties were sunbathing on lawn lounges. They had on matching yellow bikini shorts.

Tyson followed her gaze. "They're probably gay."

Marcy turned her attention back to the water and didn't respond.

Tyson said, "Well, let's get the bags inside and unpacked."

Tyson sat in a cane rocker on the back deck, a Scotch in one hand, a thin cheroot in the other. He wore faded jeans, sandals, and a sleeveless sweatshirt with the ubiquitous Sag Harbor whale across the front. The remains of an improvised barbecue lay on the round picnic table. The sun was setting behind a line of cedars across the cove, and lighted boats made their way between channel markers.

Tyson listened to his neighbors' radio and was happy to discover they preferred soft over hard rock. Tyson reflected again on Andrew Picard. He was not quite as certain of Picard's exact location in Sag Harbor at this moment as he was of their relative positions at Hue in 1968—thanks to Picard's book with accompanying campaign maps. The night of Tet had found Picard in the South Vietnamese Army's First Division Headquarters, an enclave in the northeast corner of the Citadel. Tyson's platoon had been advancing eastward and, with a brief stop at Hôpital Miséricorde, had come a few kilometers from the Citadel walls. Their mission had been to link up with what was left of the ARVN First Division, which had broken out of their enclave and were driving west through the narrow streets of the Citadel itself. Tyson supposed that if he had accomplished his mission he might actually have met Picard, one of only a dozen or so Westerners who had taken refuge with the ARVN division. He supposed, too, that Picard would have been happy to see Americans and would have taken Tyson's picture and written a little piece about him. Perhaps they'd have shared a canteen cup of Japanese gin. And if Tyson could have seen into the future, he'd have put his .45 automatic to Picard's head and blown his brains out.

Tyson looked out across the cove at the bluff on the far shore. Backyards were strung with Japanese lanterns, and barbecue pits gave a distinctive charcoal smell and a chimerical glow. Someone who couldn't wait for July Fourth was sending skyrockets arching into the black eastern sky. The smell of the charcoal in the damp night air strongly reminded him of the pervasive smell in the Vietnamese villages at mealtime. He was reminded, too, of the colored paper lanterns hung before Tet and the night sky lit with fireworks that were not fireworks. He fancied that the cove at the narrows was the Perfume River, and the lighted boats were sampans gliding down to the South China Sea. At night it was easy to imagine things, to create moods, fantasies, or nightmares, to find peace or to refight wars. But one thing was certain about that distant lantern-lit shore: Andrew Picard lived there, and sometime before the summer was done, he would knock on Picard's door.

Tyson drew on his cigar. The glass kitchen door slid open, and Marcy stepped out to the deck. She went to the rail and surveyed the cove. "Do you remember the time we were swimming in the nude out there? It was a full moonlit night, and that cabin cruiser came up beside us, and the people insisted we come aboard for a drink?"

Tyson smiled and looked at her. She had on loose-fitting, blue cotton boating pants with a matching hooded jersey. He noticed she was barefoot and wore little makeup and no jewelry except for her wedding ring. The metamorphosis was nearly complete. Tomorrow she'd have color in her cheeks and sand between her toes. She'd smell of brine and charcoal, just like that summer. But it was not going to be a summer just like that summer. Tyson said, "How about the night we were screwing in the rubber raft and we floated through the narrows into the lower cove?"

"We fought that tide for two hours before we got back." Marcy sat on the edge of the round table, her bare feet on a chair. She poured a glass of red wine and said, "How did it go this morning?"

Tyson rattled the ice cubes in his drink. "Well, I'm afraid I lost my temper. Most unfortunate. Greatly embarrass Kimura-san and Shimamura-san."

"Cut the Mr. Moto talk, Ben. Were you canned?"

"No . . . oddly enough, I wasn't."

Marcy said, "So, did they offer you a raise?"

"Actually, they want me to request a transfer to Tokyo."

Marcy looked at him in the light of the flickering citronella candle. "Tokyo?" She thought for a moment, then said, "I have a career, and I don't see why I should give it up."

Tyson sat forward in the rocker, and his voice was sharp. "To save my ass, lady. And besides, *I* have the career. You have a *job*—from which you've absented yourself for three months with no problem. Anyway, who said you were invited?"

The crickets chirped, and the water lapped against the stone. A breeze rustled the crab apple tree. Tyson said, "I'm sorry."

Marcy didn't reply.

"I didn't mean that."

"Okay." She poured the last of the wine. "Are you going?"

Tyson had no intention of going to Japan but discovered to his surprise that he had no intention of telling her that. He said, "I'm weighing the decision." What, he thought, was the purpose of the lie? Lying had become habit. He lied to his attorney, his employers, to Brown, to his friends and family, and now to his wife. He supposed he was in training for the main event, trial by general court-martial. He settled back into his rocker. "Where's David?"

"He found some boys his age. They went night fishing down at the end of Whaler's Walk."

Tyson nodded. "Did you remind him his name is Anderson?"

"Yes."

Tyson blew cigar smoke into the misty air. "I feel like a criminal."

"Do you?"

Tyson looked at her in the flickering light but didn't reply.

She said, "Anyway, I think the real estate agent knew who I was even though I used my maiden name."

"Your maiden name and your picture, madam, are as prominent as my name and picture. You should have used a *nom de guerre.*"

"I don't think we'll be bothered out here." She watched him make his way across the dark lawn toward the rocks and bushes. She suddenly felt an unspecified fear grip her and jumped down from the table. "I'll go with you."

They walked together in silence and picked their way down the white rocks until they found a wide, flat piece of shale at the water's edge. They both sat. Marcy said, "It's cold here."

"Go back and get a sweater."

"Put your arm around me."

He did so, awkwardly.

She snuggled closer to him. At length she said, "What's bothering you?"

"Is that a joke?"

"No, it's a question. And I'll tell you what isn't bothering you. The massacre business isn't bothering you. Not today. You've coped quite well in recent weeks."

Tyson didn't respond.

She said, "It's me that's bothering you. Or rather what the schlock tabloids are saying about me, and the respectable media are intimating."

He shrugged. "It's not relevant. On a scale of one to ten, court-martial for murder is up there. Your past rates a one."

"I don't think so."

Tyson slipped his arm from her shoulders. "Well . . . I guess when they start interviewing a seemingly inexhaustible supply of ex . . . boyfriends. . . ." He threw his cigar in the water.

Marcy tucked her legs under her and wrapped her arms around her chest. "Are you embarrassed by me?"

He didn't reply.

"None of this would have come out if it weren't for *your* notoriety. But I don't blame *you.*"

"Right. Okay. Look, I'm not trying to blame you for my predicament. I was the one who—" Tyson drew a deep breath. "But can't you at least see that these steamy articles, the picture, and all this crap has kept the public interest alive in my case? It's had a sort of synergistic effect. You know? And David . . . I took the time to explain to him . . . I mean, my side of it. You never tried to explain to him that . . . I mean that there was a sexual revolution or some damned thing. All he's getting is what he's reading. And he *is* reading that crap." He looked at her.

Marcy threw a stone into the water.

Tyson listened to a frog croaking. Another skyrocket rose from the distant shore.

Marcy stood. "All right. I'll deal with David. But how do *you* feel about everything that's been written about me?"

He stood also. "You seem to believe everything they are writing about *me.*"

Neither spoke, then Marcy said in a calmer voice, "There are grains of truth in what has been written about each of us, I suppose . . . but . . . not infidelity, Ben. Not that."

Tyson nodded. "Okay."

She forced a smile and touched him lightly on the arm. "Hey, Tyson, one day we'll get roaring drunk and tell each other all our darkest, most intimate, most dangerous and embarrassing secrets. Then we'll file for divorce. Or fall in love again." She laughed softly.

Tyson smiled in return but didn't feel appreciably better. Intellectually he knew that what he did in 1968 was far worse than what she did in that same year. Yet he and society seemed harsher toward her, the traditional scapegoat: the whore. He drew a long breath and said, "Well . . . anyway, it sounds like you had more fun than I did. Maybe I'm jealous."

She took his arm in a firmer grip. "I'm sure, Ben, we both got what we really wanted out of that time." She hesitated. "You wanted to be there."

Tyson looked at her closely, then replied, "Yes, I've had that thought myself."

She ran her fingers down his arm and squeezed his hand.

He glanced out over the water. "I'd like to be alone here."

She hesitated, then said, "Don't jump in."

"No."

"Promise."

"See you later."

"Promise!"

He was momentarily startled, then nodded quickly. "Promise."

She turned and climbed back toward the lawn.

Tyson watched her as she picked her way barefoot over the rock, her dark clothing against the bleached stone, graceful in the moonlight; a sight to store away, then conjure up someday when they were no longer together.

There was a chill in the night air, and the central heat didn't seem to be working. Marcy lay sleeping on the couch. David was in his room. Tyson knelt before the fireplace and touched a match to the paper and cedar kindling beneath the oak logs. The fire caught, and the smoke drew nicely up the flue. He leaned back against the armchair and focused on the flaming wood. He pulled out another cigarette and struck a wooden stove match, watching the phosphorus ignite in a white flame.

Tyson slipped out the door and walked down the short corridor. Tony Scorello was standing at the entrance to the maternity ward. Tyson saw that a white phosphorus grenade had been thrown into the ward. If it had been thrown by Scorello, Tyson thought, he looked now as though he wished he could take it back.

But there was no taking it back and no putting it out. White phosphorus had peculiar properties when ignited, sticking like napalm and burning with a white-hot intensity, which needed no air to support its combustion. Neither water nor smothering would extinguish it. Willy Peter, it was called, because GIs have to call everything something else. Willy Peter was splattered on the whitewashed walls of the crowded ward and Tyson noticed that a large crucifix on the far wall was burning.

Tony Scorello turned to him, tears streaming down his dirty face, his mouth moving to form words, but only moans came forth. Scorello's rifle lay at his feet, and his arms were flapping like an excited child's.

Tyson pushed Scorello aside and stepped through the arched entrance to the ward. About half of the two dozen beds were burning and melted mosquito nets hung in black strands like giant cobwebs. Most of the bassinets had collapsed in fiery heaps. A naked woman staggered up the aisle between the beds, but there was no other movement. The bed closest to Tyson was burning, and through the flames and smoke he saw the shape of a woman lying very still, like a Hindu woman, he thought, performing suttee.

Tyson noticed that the louvered shutters were open, and he saw the rain falling outside. Somewhere in the dying hospital a generator still put out electricity because the three paddle fans spun and a light burned over the nurses' station.

Tony Scorello suddenly ran into the burning ward and Tyson went after him. The stench of the ward was overpowering: flesh, hair, bedding, the phosphorus itself, and the charred bones as the phosphorus ate deeper into the bodies.

Tyson found Scorello sitting on the floor, his face buried in his hands. He began sobbing, "Mother of God. Mother of God. I didn't do it. I didn't do it."

Tyson left him where he was and returned to the door he had first come through marked *Salle de Contagion.* Tyson opened it and went inside, pulling the door shut behind him.

Sister Teresa, dressed in a white linen habit, sat on the edge of the single bed, her hands resting in her lap. Tyson thought she looked very composed. He was annoyed that she hadn't gotten under the bed as he'd instructed her. He said, *"Le feu."* A Vietnamese phrase came to him. *"O day khong duoc yen*—It is not safe here."

She nodded in acceptance but remained sitting.

Tyson said, *"Est-ce qu'il y . . . une porte de toit?* A roof door?"

"Oui."

"Où?"

She said in English, "I do not wish to escape."

"Like hell." Tyson took her by the arm and raised her off the bed. They stood face-to-face for several seconds, and he could see tears welling up in her eyes.

She said, "Why are they doing this?"

Tyson had a dozen explanations but no answers.

Sister Teresa put her head on his shoulder and wept.

Tyson glanced up and saw the single paddle fan slowing to a stop. Through his boots, he felt the heat from the fires below. The sound of gunshots penetrated the thick-walled room, and the familiar acrid smell of burning humans permeated the air. Outside, the rain still fell, and a distant thunder from the direction of Hue rolled across the gray, sodden landscape. Benjamin Tyson felt a grayness in his soul such as he'd never felt before or since. He found he was squeezing Sister Teresa in his arms, and he heard her sobbing softly. "My God," he said, "My God, I thought I knew them." And a voice in the dim place in his mind answered, *You knew them. You always knew. You knew what they would do one day.*

"No!" Tyson dropped the match and looked at the black burn on his fingers.
"No, what?"

He stared at Marcy standing over him.

She said, "Would you like a drink?"

"Oh, no thanks."

She eyed him closely. "You look like you could use one."

"I always look like that." He turned his head back to the fire and stayed silent for some seconds before saying, "Afterward, that night in the bunker, he looked normal."

"Who?"

"Tony Scorello. Well, not really normal. None of us, I think, looked normal or acted normal for weeks . . . but Scorello was brewing a canteen cup of

coffee. His hands were wrapped in bandages. I suppose he'd gotten burned.
Later he played cards. I watched him by the light of the flickering candle."

Marcy looked puzzled.

Tyson stayed silent for a second, then added, "You know, I just realized
something. I might see him again. I might see them all again."

She knelt beside him and took his hand. "Ben . . . please . . ." she said
with concern, "please be all right."

The next morning, Ben Tyson sat at the round table on the back deck and
sipped a cup of steaming coffee. The table was damp, and he took care not to
get the sleeves of his suit wet.

The morning air had a chill to it, and he could see his breath. Tyson looked
out over the cove where a mist lay gently on the water. A red cloud-streaked
sun sat close over the North Haven Bridge, and sea gulls cut the still air with
that unexpected, early morning screeching.

Marcy came through the glass kitchen doors, wearing a short red robe.
"You're up early," she said in a husky voice. "I guess the living room floor
wasn't comfortable."

"You should have woken me."

"I did everything but kick you."

He stared off toward the water. A twenty-foot inboard open whaler was
maneuvering between the fog-covered channel markers. The tide was out, and
Tyson could see a man in the bow probing the bottom with a gaff.

Marcy said, "I didn't know you were leaving this early. I thought you'd stay
with David and me for a few days at least."

He shrugged.

Marcy walked barefoot across the wet deck and looked out over the lawn.
Tyson regarded her legs, the thin kimono drawn tight across her back and
buttocks.

Marcy turned and studied his face in silence. At length she said, "What's
bothering you this morning? Your notoriety or mine?"

"Yours," he answered before he had a chance to think.

"Oh, Christ, are you still on that?"

"What's changed?"

"Why can't you let it go?"

"I don't know why." He stared into his coffee cup, then said softly, "I
thought I was beyond jealousy and possessiveness. Yet . . . when my wife's
complete sexual history is national news, I feel a little foolish. But I guess I'm
not normal."

She snapped, "Men! My God, you're all so damned hung up on how
many—" She drew a deep breath. "Forget it. I'm not adding fuel to this."

Tyson nodded. "I'll try." But he thought that Marcy's attitude toward the
photograph and the stories had again become somewhat blasé. Tyson had discovered that the photograph had been reproduced in various pulp magazines
where it had been presented without blackout. In addition, several more articles about Marcy Clure had developed. These were less sensational than the
ones in the *American Investigator,* and purported to be serious examinations of
the life and times of a young radical turned suburbanite, wife, and career
woman. Still, Tyson thought, these pieces were little more than cleverly concealed titillation. Then, a week ago, Sloan had shown him a wall poster version
of the *Life* photograph which someone had picked up for him in one of those
funky card shops down in the Village. The poster was captioned, HAPPY
DAYS.

Sloan had remarked, "People of the eighties are often shocked by what people of the sixties did, and they are often the same people."

Marcy's past history, he understood, was irrelevant to his past history. Yet he knew instinctively that the photograph and the stories would hasten his downfall. He also understood that he was becoming obsessed with his wife's past, and he wanted very much to make amends, but couldn't.

Tyson stood and discovered his legs were shaky. He saw that tears had formed in Marcy's eyes.

She shouted, "I didn't do anything wrong! You knew, damn it! You knew all about *me* when we met. I never *hid* anything. I fucked. So what? You *killed*. You killed more people than I fucked."

"I wonder."

"Get the hell out of here!"

Tyson went back into the house, retrieved his attaché case, and exited through the front door. He began the two-mile walk to Main Street from where he would catch the jitney bus to Manhattan. As he came out of Baypoint onto the beach road, an old red Ford Mustang drew up beside him, and a young man called out, "Need a lift to town?"

Tyson nodded and hopped in. The driver, he saw, was no more than eighteen, dressed in jeans and a white T-shirt that had no message. Tyson thought he was a local. "Thanks. Can you drop me at the movie theater?"

"Sure. You going to catch the bus?"

"Right."

The young man drove off. "You out for the summer?"

"Yes."

"Where you staying?"

"Baypoint."

"Nice. You're on TV, aren't you?"

Tyson shook his head.

"Yeah, you are. A news show. Right?"

"A cooking show."

"No kidding?" He gave Tyson a sidelong glance, then observed, "Lot of famous people out here. I saw Norman Rockwell last week."

"He's dead."

"No, I saw him. I never read any of his books, but I saw him on TV a couple times."

"Norman Mailer?"

"Right. What did I say?"

"Rockwell."

"No, that's the Nazi."

"That's George Lincoln Rockwell. He's dead, too."

"Is he?" The young man seemed to be sorting this information. He said, "What's your name?"

"Jack Abbott."

"Right. You do a talk show."

"No, a cooking show."

"Right. My name's Chuck."

They drove across the North Haven Bridge and entered Main Street. Tyson said, "You can let me off here. I'll walk the rest."

Chuck pulled to the side. "You're early for the next bus. There's the Paradise Grill up the street. Good coffee."

"Thanks." Tyson opened the door.

"You going to do a show in New York?"

"Right." Tyson climbed out.

"What time? What channel?"

"Noon today. Channel Thirteen. Fried snapper with dill." Tyson patted his briefcase. "Got 'em right here. So long, Chuck." Tyson closed the door and headed toward the coffee shop.

He heard a horn honking behind him but didn't turn. The slow-moving car kept slightly behind him, and the honking became insistent. People on the sidewalk were looking. An old man motioned to him, then pointed to the car. Tyson kept walking. The last thing he wanted with his coffee was Chuck.

A voice called out, "Tyson, get your head out of your ass."

He turned. Marcy motioned him toward the car. He approached the open passenger-side window. She said, "Get in here."

He opened the door and slid in. She pulled away. They drove in silence through Main Street and out of the village, onto the Bridgehampton Road. She said, "I'll take you to the station."

"I felt like taking a bus."

"You'll take the fucking train and like it."

Tyson shrugged. The Volvo headed south through the outskirts of the village and into a forest of scrub pine and pin oak. There was little early morning traffic, and a ground fog crept through the stunted and misshapen trees onto the lonely road. To Tyson this landscape always seemed foreboding. He said, "I'm sorry."

"About what?"

"That remark."

"What remark? Which one are you sorry about?"

"The one about . . . forget it."

"No. Which one are you sorry about? The one where you suggested that I fucked more than a hundred people?"

"Right. That one."

"Well, what if I did? At least I left them smiling. How did you leave your hundred?"

"Let me out."

Marcy accelerated, and the speedometer showed sixty miles per hour.

"Hey, slow it down."

"Whores drive fast."

"Cut the crap and slow down!"

She pressed down on the accelerator and took a curve on the wrong side of the road. Tyson reached out, shut off the ignition, and pulled the key out. The car began to decelerate. He looked at her and saw she was fighting back tears.

The Volvo slowed to a near stop on an uphill grade, and Tyson turned the wheel, putting the car into the sandy shoulder. He threw the car into park, then got out and came around to the driver's seat. "Move over."

She slid into the passenger seat. Tyson got in and started the car. He threw it into low, and the wheels spun, then the Volvo lurched back onto the road, and he continued toward Bridgehampton.

Neither spoke until they reached the station parking lot. He said, "I need some time to think this out."

She seemed composed now and nodded. "Me too."

He said, "Call me with the unlisted number when you get the phone."

She kept staring out the windshield.

Tyson cleared his throat. "I won't be coming out this weekend."

"All right."

He said, "I've caused us a lot of pain."

She didn't respond.

He hesitated, then opened the door. "Will you be all right now?"

She nodded and handed him his briefcase.

He got out and closed the door, then put his head in the open window. "Careful driving. Tell David I'm sorry I didn't have a chance to say good-bye."

"Your train's coming."

Tyson glanced back and saw the big diesel's headlamp far down the misty tracks. He turned back to her. She looked at him, and they held each other's eyes for a long time, then the train whistle blew, and Tyson turned away.

Part 2

He who does not prevent a crime when he can, encourages it.
—Seneca: Troades

15

Miss Beale looked pale, Tyson thought. He'd noticed, too, that over the weeks she had become drawn and fidgety. He supposed she was having personal problems of some sort, but the astonishing notion came to him that Miss Beale was worried about him. Tyson said, "What is it?"

She handed him a large manila envelope. The first thing he noticed was that its shade of buff was darker than anything he'd seen in normal business correspondence. The second thing he noticed was the government franking mark. Lastly he noticed that the envelope was from the Department of the Army. But he knew where it was from when Miss Beale first came through the door.

Miss Beale said, "It came registered mail. I signed for it. . . ."

Tyson saw that the envelope was addressed to Lieutenant Benjamin J. Tyson. He placed it on his blotter. "Thank you. Have you typed the Taylor contract?"

"It's almost finished. . . ." Miss Beale seemed reluctant to leave.

Tyson said, "Anything else?"

"No . . ." She started toward the door, then said, "Will you be leaving us?"

Tyson replied, "It would appear so."

Miss Beale blurted, "Oh, we all think this is terrible, Mr. Tyson. Terrible. This isn't . . . isn't right. We're all upset. . . ."

Tyson assumed she was referring to the lunchroom clique who obviously discussed this at some length. The boardroom group was not so sympathetic. He recalled that in the infantry, after every battle, some promotions opened up, and people scrambling for them did not care if they had become available because of 81 millimeter mortar fire or 122 millimeter rocket fire. The corporate world was not so much different. Tyson said, "I appreciate your concern."

He saw that Miss Beale still seemed stuck to her spot and added, "Incidentally, you will continue here as long as you wish. I've spoken to Mr. Kimura about that."

She nodded. "Thank you." Miss Beale finally turned and left.

Tyson was as touched by this display of concern as he was mystified. He didn't think he was particularly popular with the rank and file, but apparently they decided he was being ill-treated by the world. This was something they could identify with. In fact, from what he could determine from the media, there was a ground swell of man-in-the-street support taking shape. He'd read that someone in Virginia had begun a Tyson Defense Fund, though no one had contacted him or Sloan about it. Odd, he thought, how Americans react to publicized stories of woe. He wanted to believe that there was a genuine altruism and sense of charity in the country, and perhaps there was, and perhaps he'd learn to believe there was.

He stared down at the manila envelope, then pushed it aside.

"It's your wife," said Miss Beale over the intercom.

"I'll take it." Tyson pressed the blinking phone button. "Hello."

"Hi." Marcy's voice sounded distant.

There was a short silence, then Tyson said, "Let me have the phone number."

She gave it to him and said, "We've had rain the last two days. How is it there?"

Tyson glanced back through the window. "Same."

"Sometimes the weather here is different."

"Sometimes it is. How's David?"

"Fine. He found some friends, and the rain doesn't seem to keep them from fishing. They found a hangout, too. A disco off Main Street."

"In Sag Harbor? What's it called? The Wailing Whaler's Top Deck? What's the world coming to?"

"Who knows? There's a steel band on the Long Wharf at night."

"Is there?"

"Yes, and that place where John Steinbeck used to hang out—the Black Buoy—well, it's got a new image."

Tyson wondered how she knew. He said, "Well, sometimes it's not a good idea to try to go back, is it? I mean, sometimes it's painful."

"Sometimes."

Tyson swiveled his chair around and stared at the rain-splattered window. He used to be ambivalent about rain, but after going through two monsoons, each of three months' duration, he had developed a deep dislike for wet weather.

Marcy said, "Are we still friends?"

"Sure."

"Good." Her voice still had a tentative tone. "Anything new at work?"

"No. The arms race is still making everyone here giddy with delight. Lots of work."

She hesitated before saying, "I was thinking . . . if . . . well, I'd consider going to Tokyo with you . . . I mean, I'd definitely go . . . if that's what you decided."

Tyson replied, "Tokyo is no longer an option."

"Why not?"

"Because I'm in the Army now."

"What . . . ?"

Tyson glanced at the papers on his desk. "The letter said, 'Greeting.' After that it was all downhill."

"Oh . . . oh, Ben . . ."

"Well, anyway, I had a meeting with Kimura, and I informed him of my new status." Tyson thought back to the meeting less than an hour before. There had been nothing inscrutable about Mr. Kimura's visage, and Tyson had read him well. Kimura, he was certain, knew about the recall order, though he feigned otherwise. Tyson said to Marcy, "Kimura offered me half pay during my time on active duty. I don't know if that includes jail time."

Marcy didn't reply.

Tyson continued, "Plus all my vacation pay, sick pay, and some year-end bonus money."

"That . . . that was very generous."

"Very." But Tyson didn't think generosity had anything to do with it. The government was subsidizing this, one way or another. They didn't want to leave him destitute. And that was not altruism, that was public relations strategy. But he didn't think he wanted to play their game. He said, "I don't know what first lieutenants make these days, and I really don't give a damn, but I figure with that pay and your salary we'll be broke within the year."

"What do you mean? Didn't you accept the offer?"

"No. In fact, I'm thinking of resigning as a matter of principle."

"Why? That's absurd, Ben. Take the half pay. You've put in years of hard work for that company—"

"But how about principle? You're a principled person, so I thought you'd understand. I thought you'd back me up on this. And you're an antimaterialist. So it can't be money you're worried about."

"Are you baiting me?"

"Quite possibly."

Marcy stayed silent for some time, then said, "What is the principle you're going to resign for?"

"The right to be financially ruined. The right to reject money you don't work for. The right to suffer the consequences of one's actions. The right to embarrass the government. How's that for antiestablishment rhetoric? Aren't you proud of me?"

"Look . . . I didn't call to fight . . . and I think I understand . . . but you have a family. . . ."

"We'll get by."

There was a silence, then Marcy said, "Yes, we'll get by. Do what you think is best."

Tyson nodded to himself. He had the feeling she meant it.

Marcy said, "What does this recall mean? Do you have to go somewhere?"

"Well, yes. I also received assignment orders." He glanced at the separate sheet of paper. "Could be a lot worse—"

"Where?"

"Fort Hamilton. Brooklyn. You know where that is? Near the Verrazano Bridge."

"Yes . . . well, that's good. Can you . . . are you confined or anything?"

"I don't know. I just have to report by fifteen July, as they say in the back-assward Army." He thought a moment. "Hey, when's my shark trip?" He looked at his daybook. "The fourteenth. Good. I can do that, then report in the next day. I'll bring the shark if I get one." He paused, then observed, "This sucks a mop."

She didn't reply, but he thought he heard her stifling a sob.

Tyson lit a cigarette and put his feet on the windowsill. If he were unmarried, he reflected, he'd have already quit his job and been in Hong Kong by now, a city he remembered fondly from his R and R. Everyone, including and especially the government, would be glad to see him go. But not, unfortunately, to Hong Kong, a British colony. He'd have to go, as old Chet indicated, someplace where the government could make a pretense of being unable to get him back. That is what he would do if he were not a husband and father. But he was. Still, it was enticing. He watched the rain running down the big windowpane, then said, "What do you think of the idea of me skipping out of the country? I mean, is that an alternative to this mess?"

"It is. But your ego and your overblown sense of responsibility will keep you here."

Tyson thought that her voice sounded stronger, more like Marcy. She always bounced back quickly. He said, "But I'd be saving you, David, and the government a lot of embarrassment and trouble. They're probably praying in Washington that I fly away and bother them no more."

"Well, if that's true, you should work out a deal of some sort. . . ."

Tyson thought Marcy and Chet Brown would get along well. "Right. Airfare and pension. Send for the family later. Brazil has no extradition, but I don't care for the tropics. Maybe Sweden. They have limited extradition. I'll get a job with Volvo. I'll talk them into putting electronic rocket-aiming devices in the four-door model. What do you think?"

Marcy forced a light tone in her voice. "Get yourself a big blonde Viking. You always liked blondes."

Tyson smiled. "Well . . . let's think about it. Fight or flight? I have a few weeks."

Neither spoke, then Marcy said, "How are we doing?"

Tyson was surprised to hear himself saying, "I love you."

She replied quickly, "I love you, too." She added, "But I think you've decided not to come home."

Tyson didn't reply.

She said, "I suppose you have enough on your mind without marital problems. Right?"

Tyson didn't offer an immediate reply, then said, "I found a place in the city. Paul Stein's. You know him. He's going to the Hamptons. I pay the utilities, keep the burglars away, forward the mail, and take phone messages."

Again, there was a long, awkward silence, then Marcy spoke. "Will they let you live . . . what is it called—?"

"Off-post. I hope so. Beats BOQ—bachelor officer's quarters. . . . My horoscope this morning said, 'You will exchange a well-paying executive position for a job as a house sitter. New careers in the armed forces will open up for you. You may go on a long trip at government expense, or you may go at your own expense to a place where the government can't find you. Your mate will be understanding if she gets a postcard from Rio de Janeiro signed Joao.' "

"Just keep me informed."

Tyson swung the chair around to his desk. "Okay. You have Stein's number. I'll be moving in this weekend."

"Well . . . watch out for those horny working girls."

"Best to David."

"I'll tell him."

"Okay. Take care."

"I will. You, too."

"Good-bye."

"Good-bye."

Neither hung up, and Tyson said, "'Bye."

"'Bye."

Tyson put the receiver in the cradle and saw that his hand was shaking. "Damn it." He slammed his hand on his desk, and the desk items bounced. "Damn it!" He stood and kicked the wastebasket across the room.

16

Ben Tyson stood in front of the round barbecue grill, a Scotch in one hand, a spatula in the other. He looked down at the single hamburger. There was something pathetic about it, he decided, and he scooped it up with the spatula, flipping it into the bushes. He finished his Scotch.

The stillness of the backyard was broken by a sudden, sharp report that quieted the birds. Somewhere out on the dark street there was a series of hollow popping sounds, and a dog began barking. A few backyards down, he could hear the sounds of recorded music and laughter. July Fourth was not his favorite holiday, but spending it alone was no treat either. Most years, if he was home, he, Marcy, and David would go to the country club. The club went to great pains to create a traditional Fourth with striped tents on the lawn, hot dogs, hamburgers, balloons, and cotton candy. People sat on the veranda and drank beer, children's games were organized, and a brass band played Sousa marches. The only thing missing, thankfully, was speeches.

He had considered joining the festivities, but decided he was not in the mood to meet the public, nor did he feel like spreading awkwardness among his neighbors. His objective for the evening was to get too drunk to consider taking the rented car out to Sag Harbor.

Tyson opened the French doors and went into the den. He poured himself another Scotch and took a few books from the shelf, dropping them into a carton. He intended to drive into Manhattan in the morning and move into Paul Stein's apartment.

The phone rang, but Tyson ignored it as he went through his desk drawers trying to find his pocket calculator. The phone kept ringing. Only about a dozen people had the unlisted number, and he couldn't think of one he wanted to speak to. He found his calculator and dropped it in his briefcase. The phone continued to ring. He suddenly realized it might be David, and he picked it up.

A female voice he didn't recognize said, "Mr. Benjamin Tyson?"

Tyson said, "Who is this?"

"This is Major Harper—"

He felt his stomach give a turn.

"I'm from the Judge Advocate General's office. I've been assigned to conduct an investigation under Article 31 of the Uniform Code of Military Justice to look into the facts surrounding certain allegations of wrongdoing at Miséricorde Hospital in the Republic—"

"Are you serious?"

"Yes, Lieutenant, I am."

Tyson sat in his desk chair. "How did you get my number?"

Major Harper replied, "It was given to me in my briefing papers—"

"This is an unlisted number."

"I don't see what relevance that has. I do apologize for calling on a holiday evening—"

"Where are you calling from?"

"Washington, which is also irrelevant, *Lieutenant.*"

"I don't wish to be called lieutenant."

"Did you receive your orders recalling you to active duty?"

Tyson leaned forward and doodled on his blotter. This call was not unexpected, yet he found he wasn't quite prepared for it. A few days ago he might have been able to leave the country legally. Today, he was an officer in the United States Army, and he did not have the freedoms that most American citizens enjoyed.

Major Harper said, "I have a registered mail receipt here—"

"Yes, I got the damned thing."

After a silence on the phone, Major Harper said, "I would appreciate it if you would address me with the respect that is due my rank."

Tyson rubbed his eyes and sat back in the chair. "Do you expect me to call you ma'am?"

"That is the correct form of address for a female officer of higher rank."

Tyson exhaled a long breath. His head was beginning to ache, and his stomach did another turn. He put a milder tone in his voice. "All right. I suppose I ought to be as polite as possible, ma'am."

Her tone was immediately conciliatory. "I'm sorry if I came on a little strong."

"No problem. What can I do for you?"

"Well, as I said, I'm conducting this informal investigation to determine if there is any substance to certain allegations put forth in a book called *Hue: Death of a City.* I assume you're familiar with the work."

"It certainly sounds familiar."

She said, "I was going to begin my investigation in other areas, then call you. But then the thought occurred to me that you may want to have the opportunity to give your side first."

"That's thoughtful."

Major Harper continued, "I'm supposed to advise you of your rights under Article 31 of the Uniform Code of Military Justice. You have the right to remain silent and the right to counsel. Also, I'm to advise you of any possible charge contemplated . . . which is . . . murder."

Tyson did not reply.

She continued, "You also have the right to question witnesses, but we have none at this time. As I said, I called you first. Look, as an officer you know your rights. What I want to know is if you'd like us to meet."

Tyson considered his reply. The woman was unusually open, admitting she hadn't done any preliminary work before calling. The usual procedure in an Army investigation, he recalled, was to suggest to the suspect that there were already battalions of witnesses against him, drawers full of signed depositions, and lockers overflowing with incriminating evidence.

He saw a faint possibility that this could be quashed at this stage. It depended to a large extent, he understood, on himself and this unknown woman. To be sure, there were other factors, but the recommendation of a preliminary investigating officer not to pursue the matter might kill it. Tyson said, "All right. Let's meet."

She replied, "Fine. Do you want to come to Washington?"

"Not particularly."

"Well, I'll fly to New York. How about tomorrow?"

Tyson thought a moment, then said, "Okay."

"What time would be convenient?"

"What *place* are we talking about, Major?"

"Well . . . several choices . . . the airport, Fort Hamilton—"

"No and no."

"Your office?"

"I don't think that would be appropriate unless you come in civilian clothes."

"Well, I could do that, but . . . can we meet at your home?"

He said, "Take the nine A.M. shuttle. Any Long Island limo should be able to find the address. You'll be here before eleven."

"All right, about eleven A.M., your house. And I assume that since we are meeting, you will waive your right to remain silent."

"I wouldn't ask you to come all the way to New York so I can plead the Fifth."

"Fine . . . because there is a possibility we can . . . I don't mean to hold out false hope, but perhaps if we just discussed this, we could get it into perspective. This matter may end after I interview you and the other members of your platoon whom we can locate."

"Good."

"May I ask if you're bringing civil suit against the author of that book? You don't have to answer."

"I'm considering it."

"Will you have an attorney present at our interview?"

"I'm considering it."

She didn't reply immediately, then said, "That's your right, of course. But as an officer and an educated man, you may not need one present." She continued, "You could have an attorney available by phone, but there's no use escalating this. If you have an attorney, then I may have to bring a stenographer, then—"

"Then I'll need a tape recorder, and before you know it we'll have TV cameras and a house full of people. Okay, no attorney."

"I don't mean to talk you out of anything. Under the UCMJ, you have a right —"

"I know the UCMJ. I took a refresher course at the library."

"Fine."

"May I ask you a question?"

"Certainly."

"If I'm a lieutenant and you're a major, why am I calling some of the shots? Now, you don't have to answer that. It's your right as a lawyer to dissemble."

There was a short silence before Major Harper replied, "Do you feel like an officer in the United States Army?"

"Not in the least."

"Then, rank aside, I'll be considerate of your feelings. This must be disorienting for you."

"It was disorienting the first time I was called to active duty. This time it just plain sucks."

Major Harper didn't reply.

Tyson said, "I hope this is a short tour of duty."

"So do I."

"Do you?" He asked abruptly, "Do you drink coffee? I hate to make a whole pot if you don't drink it."

"Coffee would be fine."

"I'll see you tomorrow. Have a happy Fourth." Tyson hung up.

He sat back and breathed deeply. He thought about the disembodied voice he had just heard and tried to picture a face. The voice was pleasant, soft, almost melodic, with a touch of the Midwest. She was, he thought again, very frank. Disarmingly so. And it wasn't because she was being particularly considerate. It was her interrogation style, and he'd be wise to remember that.

Also, the reason he had been able to call the shots wasn't because of any female deference or consideration for his feelings. It was because she had been ordered to take a soft approach. The JAG Corps, the Pentagon, and perhaps even the White House were handling him gingerly. "Good," he said aloud. "I like being handled gingerly by powerful people." He had been so engrossed in his own fears that he had forgotten they were afraid too.

Tyson stood and poured himself another Scotch. He surveyed the partially packed boxes around the den.

He threw open the French doors and stared out onto the dark patio with its glowing brazier. Fireworks echoed between the houses, and rockets from the county park lit up the eastern sky. He almost looked forward to the interview, to the prospect of having his fate hinge solely on his own resources. To hell with lawyers. Here was a challenge in a life that had become devoid of important challenges.

Tyson felt a long-forgotten flutter in his stomach: It is the night before the big Auburn-Navy game, it is the hour before the dawn attack. It is, he thought, the culmination of one life and the beginning of another. He said softly, "Not one game, not one battle ever turned out to be half as bad as the anticipation. Let's get on with it."

17

At ten minutes to eleven, Benjamin Tyson's doorbell rang. Tyson moved to the foyer and looked at himself in the full-length mirror. He regarded the navy blue blazer of summer wool, then fluffed the red silk pocket handkerchief. The crease in the beige trousers was, as they said in the Army, razor sharp. His black loafers were polished, and the white cotton shirt accented his tan. His intent was to look prosperous, self-assured, untouchable. This house was his castle, the clothing his armor.

The doorbell rang again. Tyson moved to the front door, reached out, and opened it quickly.

Subconsciously, he'd expected to see a woman in a light-colored uniform, but she wore what the Army called Class A greens: forest green skirt, matching tunic, light green blouse, and a crisscrossed black tie. On her head, at a jaunty angle, was a green garrison cap with officers' gold piping. A black handbag was slung over her shoulder, and she carried a black leather briefcase in her left hand. She smiled pleasantly. "Mr. Tyson?"

"No. I'm Lieutenant Tyson. I guess the mufti threw you." He extended his hand. "The gold oak leaf tells me you're a major, and your name tag says Harper. Hello, Major Harper."

As she took his hand she said, "There's no need for you to wear a uniform."

"Good." He looked her over quickly. Her hair was honey-colored, her eyes pale blue, and she looked well scrubbed. He pictured cornfields and church socials. Somewhere beneath the unflattering uniform dwelt a good body. He stepped aside. "Please come in."

She entered, removing her garrison cap. They exchanged some words about the cloudy weather, her flight, and his home.

Tyson took her cap and laid it on the foyer sideboard. He said, "Can I take your jacket?"

She hesitated, then said, "Yes, please." She set down her briefcase and handbag, then unbuttoned the four brass buttons of the tailored tunic and slipped it off. Tyson saw that her light green blouse was also well tailored and fit more snugly than the Army might have liked. He put her jacket in the foyer closet and turned back to her. They looked at each other for a few seconds before he said, "This way."

He led her through the living room into the rear den. Tyson indicated a suede armchair and she sat, remarking, "Nice room."

"Thank you." He'd removed the packing boxes and any other evidence to suggest he was removing himself from his primary residence. Tyson went to the wall unit that held a small bar, on which sat an electric coffeepot. He poured two cups and said, "Would you like some cream liqueur or cognac with this? Or don't officers drink on duty in the new Army?"

"They do. But I'll wait."

Tyson poured some Irish cream into his cup. "Hair of the dog." He assumed she'd noticed his bloodshot eyes, but having made the self-observation, he thought he should explain it. "Drinking with some friends. After you called. Actually, it was sort of a fund-raiser. My defense fund," he lied. "They have this annual July Fourth bash up at the club—my country club—and everyone was in a patriotic mood, so they passed the hat." Tyson realized he was not making a good job of it, but added anyway, "I've gotten a good deal of support in the community. I also understand that a national defense fund is forming . . . if I need one."

Karen Harper took a small printed card from her briefcase and said, "Let me get the formalities out of the way. Your rights and all that. I should do this again in person. Okay?"

"Cream?"

"Yes, please."

"Sugar?"

"Yes . . . I'd like to read you your rights now." She glanced at the card.

"I'm listening." He put cream and sugar into her cup.

"All right . . . you have the right to remain silent—"

"Excuse me. One lump or two?"

"Just one, please. You have the right to question any witnesses. You have the right to be represented by Army counsel." She continued reading from the card as Tyson placed a cup of coffee on the table in front of her.

Tyson considered sitting at his desk, then decided against it. He took the Eames recliner opposite her, across the coffee table, and put his cup down. He watched her as she read the short list of rights. He'd read that list to suspects at least fifty times, and each time he could feel the awkwardness, the tension, that hung in the air between him and the soldier standing before him.

Karen Harper looked up from the card. "Do you understand your rights under the Uniform Code of Military Justice?"

"Yes, ma'am."

"Do you wish to be represented by Army counsel?"

"No, ma'am."

"Do you wish to have your own attorney present at this time?"

"He's playing golf."

She looked at him and waited.

Tyson said, "As I indicated on the telephone, I do not."

She nodded perfunctorily, then continued, "I'm to advise you of the offenses charged against you. As yet, there are none. But obviously what we are contemplating is murder."

Tyson did not respond.

She went on. "As I said, there are no witnesses as yet, but you will have the right to cross-examine them if there is a formal investigation. You have the right, at this time, to suggest witnesses who may provide you with statements of defense, extenuation, or mitigation. Do you have any such witnesses?"

"No, ma'am."

"You have the right to make a statement. Do you wish to do so?"

"No, ma'am."

There was a long silence, then Tyson said, "I wish to answer questions. Shoot."

She glanced at her notes. "All right. . . . Have you read the book *Hue: Death of a City?*"

"Yes, ma'am."

"You can drop that. Are you the Lieutenant Benjamin Tyson mentioned in the book?"

"It would appear so."

"Were you in command of the platoon described in chapter six of said book?"

"Yes, I was."

"Were there any higher-ranking officers present?"

"No. I was operating independently of my company and battalion."

"Did you have radio contact with your chain of command?"

"Sporadically. The radio batteries were weak. Resupply was a problem at that time."

She nodded, then asked several more questions. Tyson knew she was just getting him into the habit of answering questions, avoiding anything too close to the central issue of mass murder. *She's good,* he thought. But he himself had done this before, and it was coming back to him.

Tyson decided to interrupt her stream of questions. He stood and poured more coffee for both of them. "Let's take a break."

She smiled, as though this was a good idea, but Tyson knew otherwise. He said, "Cigarette?"

"No, thank you."

"Do you mind if I do?"

"Not at all."

Tyson leaned back on the edge of his desk as he drew on his cigarette. He looked at Major Karen Harper. She must be, he thought, a bit anxious despite her calm exterior. She had a 180-pound fish on the line and he could break it anytime he wished.

She began to speak conversationally, as if this was not part of the interview, though Tyson knew it was. She said, "I found something interesting in your personnel file—that note you wrote on the Army questionnaire. Do you remember that?"

He let a few seconds pass, then replied, "Oh . . . that. . . . I must have been in a mood that day."

"I suppose. It was a rather strong note for an officer to have placed in his permanent file."

"I wasn't an officer."

"But you were. You are. You have always been, since the day you took the oath of office after college."

"Would it have made a difference if I had checked the damned box requesting that I be dropped from the rolls?"

"I don't know. That's not my department. I was only interested in what prompted you to write that."

"Do you have any recollection of the war? Of the fall of Saigon? I mean, you look very young."

"I was about fifteen during the 1968 Tet Offensive—"

"Fifteen? Christ, I wish I had been fifteen. By the way, Tet was a time, not a place. Do you know that?"

"Of course I do. Anyway, I was twenty-two when Saigon fell in 1975. I recall thinking at the time that the war had gone on since I could remember. I was relieved it was over."

"My wife was too. She proposed a toast to the National Liberation Front."

She said, "I think one of the reasons they picked me to conduct this investigation is my lack of involvement in the events in question."

"Perhaps." She exhibited, he thought, an ingenuousness beneath which was a certain cunning. Or maybe, he conceded, she really was simple and naive. He found himself studying her more closely. Neither the cut nor the color of the Army uniform did anything for her, but her face, her hair, her voice, and her movements more than compensated for that. Her mouth, he noticed, was expressive and capable, he guessed, of sensuousness in other situations. He said, "What are some of the other reasons they picked you? I mean, why *you?*"

She shrugged.

"Probably your experience in murder investigations."

"I've never investigated a murder before."

"I've never been suspected of a murder before. Small world."

She picked up the bottle of cream liqueur from the coffee table. "Do you mind?" She poured some in her coffee. "Anyway, in regard to the note and the questionnaire, I was wondering if you were planning to challenge your recall to active duty."

"Look, Major, once the government decides to start grinding you up, there's not much you can do unless you have unlimited resources."

She leaned toward him, across the coffee table. "You shouldn't feel as though you're being railroaded. If you think the recall was illegal, I suggest you find the resources, financial and otherwise, to fight it. That's your first line of defense, as the infantry would put it."

Tyson didn't reply.

They sat in silence for some time, then Tyson stood and walked to the bookcase, opened a drawer, and retrieved a cedar box. He spilled the contents out on the coffee table.

They both looked at the array of medals and ribbons, including the Purple Heart, the Combat Infantryman's Badge, the Air Assault Medal, and the Vietnamese Cross of Gallantry. Tyson picked up the brass cross by its yellow-and-orange ribbon and dangled it. "This is a Vietnamese decoration. It was given to me at an awards ceremony in the ruins of the Citadel at Hue, on a blistering hot afternoon after the city was retaken. I'll never forget the little Viet colonel who gave out the medals. He was badly burned, smelled of fish, synthetic Japanese Scotch, sweat, and putrid flesh. When he embraced and kissed me, I thought I was going to vomit." Tyson stared at the medal. "But he was a hell of a soldier. I'm sure he didn't survive the war. Neither did his government. So here I hold a useless medal from a defunct government." He let it fall on the table. "Does it count for anything?"

She nodded. "Of course. A court-martial—if there is one—will take that sort of thing into consideration. Do you have the paperwork for that?"

"I seem to have misplaced it. But I remember that the commendation cites me for bravery . . . for actions that took place on 15 February 1968, in and around the village of An Ninh Ha. The English is bad, and the language is general, but it may be that the Army will find it difficult to prosecute me for murders that allegedly took place at a battle for which I was decorated. What do *you* think?"

"Try to find the written orders."

"There was no copy in my file?"

"No, and I don't think the present government in Saigon—or Ho Chi Minh City—will be helpful."

"I was also supposed to receive a Silver Star for the same action. The Viets usually read the lists of proposed American awards and matched their version of the medal with the American one. That's how I got the Viet Cross. But I never got the Silver Star."

"Why not?"

He shrugged. "I saw the recommendation made by my company commander, Browder, now dead. But it was probably misplaced. That was fairly common at the time."

"Perhaps it was turned down."

"Perhaps, but I don't think so."

"Captain Browder, I assume, wrote up the recommendation based on verbal reports from your men. Browder, you indicated, was not at the hospital."

"That's correct. Standard practice."

"Which of your men made the recommendation?"

"Kelly, my radio operator, put me in for the star. Someone else would have had to corroborate Kelly's report of my valor. I don't remember who that was though. Not many of my platoon survived anyway. Did you locate any of them?"

"Yes."

"How many? Who?"

"I'll send you or your attorney a list of names and addresses . . . if necessary. You may not have to go to the time and trouble. And perhaps neither will I. We may just drop it." She pulled her pad toward her. "I'll make a note to check on the Silver Star."

"You're being very helpful, Major."

She said, "Again, let me make it clear that I'm not working for the prosecution. I'm here to gather facts."

"Yes. I remember how it's supposed to work."

She stared at the ribbons and medals lying on the coffee table. Tyson studied her face. She looked impressed, even a bit unhappy that it had come to this. *It's an act, of course,* he thought. *He's acting, she's acting. Souvenirs de guerre,* like mementos of the departed, called for a minute of respectful silence. Of course, he thought, both she and the Army would be highly skeptical of any medal proposed or awarded to him on 15 February 1968. But to suggest this aloud would be akin to sacrilege.

She said, "I read the citations for the two Purple Hearts. I can see—I hope this doesn't make you uncomfortable—I can see the wound on your right ear."

Tyson let the silence drag out, milking it for what it was worth, then replied, "Yes, a village called Phu Lai, on the first day of the Tet Offensive. I lost nearly half my platoon that day. That bullet had my name on it, but . . . an angel was sitting on my shoulder . . . and pushed my head an inch to the left."

She nodded.

He went on, "Then, as you probably read, I was wounded by shrapnel in the right knee. That was on February 29th—1968 was a leap year. The battle of Hue was declared officially over on February 26th, but somebody forgot to tell Chuck."

Again she nodded.

Tyson decided to break the gloomy pall. He grinned suddenly. "Do you want to see my knee wound?"

She smiled quickly in return. "Not right now." She added, "Great line, though."

"It used to work like a charm." Tyson held his smile, but his mind returned to that extra day in February. The hot shrapnel had sliced in from the left side, and he'd fallen to the ground. When he looked down, not knowing what to expect, he saw his fatigues covered with blood. He'd ripped open the light cotton material, and there was a large piece of meat—fat, flesh, ligaments— flapped over, exposing his patella. He recalled staring at the bare bone incredulously. He'd never seen such a thing. And if there had been any lingering doubts concerning his mortality, they were dispelled then as he gaped at the stuff he was made of.

Tyson sat back down in his chair. "Do you want to continue?"

Karen Harper leaned forward. She asked a few more warm-up questions, then, without any change in tone or expression, said, "Can you describe for me, in your own words, the events of that day, 15 February 1968?"

Tyson regarded her closely. "If I gave you a general account of what happened, I wouldn't want to be held to any of the details."

She put aside her pencil and paper. "I'm barely making notes, as you can see, and in any case this is not sworn testimony."

"And do I have your word as an officer that you have no recording devices with you?"

She sat back and crossed her legs. "Yes, you do."

Tyson took a few moments to collect his thoughts, then began. "We were dug into a defensive perimeter around a small clump of trees about five kilometers west of Hue. We had taken mortar and small-arms fire during the night and suffered two wounded. I had the wounded medevaced out at first light. It was rainy and chilly. It gets cold in February in the northern provinces. Anyway, we pulled out of the perimeter and began advancing on Hue, as per radio orders."

There was a rushing sound on the radio speaker, then a crackling, followed by Captain Browder's voice. "Mustang One-Six, this is Mustang Six. How do you hear me? Over."

Tyson took the handphone from Daniel Kelly, his radiotelephone operator, and squeezed the handle lever. "Six, this is One-Six. Weak but clear. How me?"

"Same. Orders from Big Six. Proceed in a Sierra-Echo direction toward Hotel Uniform Echo."

Tyson replied into the mouthpiece. "Solid copy. Anything specific?"

"Negative. Use your own judgment. Don't make the city today. We'll rendezvous tonight and advance on the west wall together."

"Roger. . . . Maybe we should link up now. I'm down to one-niner folks, and there're signs that Chuck is all over the damned place. In strength. Saw hoofprints last night before sundown. Estimate five hundred or more. Heading toward the city."

"Roger that, One-Six. Orders is orders. Everybody's spread thin, kiddo. Hey, are we having fun yet?"

Tyson glanced at Kelly, who had his hand around the radio aerial and was stroking it, which was Kelly's way of suggesting that the brass was jerking everyone off again. Tyson drew a deep breath and spoke into the radiophone. "Let me know how my two wounded make out."

"Roger." Browder hesitated, then said, "Keep to the open paddies. Avoid the bush and avoid the hamlets."

Tyson didn't think that was consistent with search and destroy, or harassment and interdiction. It sounded more like avoid and evade. He wondered if the Army Security Agency or any brass was monitoring. Tyson cautioned, "Big brother, big ears."

"Fuck them," snapped Browder, who was obviously on edge himself. "Anything further?"

"I need C's. And I don't have a map beyond An Ninh Ha."

"Ask at the next Chevron station. I'll get C's dropped in. I'll see about the map. Further?"

Tyson thought he should report that everyone had trench foot, fatigues were torn, boots and laces were falling apart, and the halogen-treated water they were drinking was making them all sick. But Browder knew that. Tyson said, "Negative further."

"Roger. Keep up the splendid work. Out."

Tyson handed the phone back to Kelly. "Let's move it. Order of march: one, B, three, A, then two."

Kelly's voice boomed out over the perimeter. "Saddle up! Movin'! Movin'! First squad on point."

Tyson walked out of the entrenched positions to a wide dike and moved down it, surveying the terrain around him. Kelly came up beside him, joined by Specialist Four Steven Brandt, the platoon medic, who set his medical bag down in the mud.

Tyson watched the men move at intervals out of the copse of willow trees and onto the dike toward him. First rifle squad consisted of five men out of the original ten, all Pfc's. Normally led by a staff sergeant, the squad was now led by Bob Moody, a nineteen-year-old black kid who had been chosen by Tyson because he'd been in country a month longer than the other four. He was also the only one who wanted the job.

Behind first squad was team B, one of the two M-60 machine-gun teams, consisting of a gunner, assistant gunner, and an ammo bearer.

Third rifle squad followed: three men, led by Pfc Larry Cane. Bringing up the rear was machine-gun team A and the squad leader of the two teams, Paul Sadowski, a twenty-year-old who had been a sergeant for five days.

Even as the platoon contracted, Tyson kept his machine-gun

squad up to strength by assigning riflemen to the two teams. Conventional wisdom had it that the life expectancy of machine gunners in battle was shorter than that of officers and radio operators. And Tyson believed it. At Phu Lai, every one of the original fourth squad was killed or wounded. Men were understandably reluctant to be assigned to the machine-gun squad but were perversely proud when they were; only the best, the brightest, and the strongest men could be trusted with this grueling and crucial job. The guns had to be manned and fed, and when a gunner was hit, someone else took his place, just as someone always picked up the fallen colors in the old cavalry regiments.

Personnel management, Tyson thought. *Just like they taught us in Personnel Management 401 at Auburn. Though it was a little more complex here.*

Tyson watched the last man come out of the copse of willows, Pfc Hernando Beltran, a hefty Cuban-American and the sole survivor of second squad. Beltran claimed he was now the second-squad leader and refused to be assigned to either of the remaining rifle squads or the machine-gun squad. Tyson could see his point and allowed Beltran to command his phantom squad, always in the rear guard.

Beltran carried a Browning automatic shotgun and slung an M-79 grenade launcher over his shoulder. He wore a Colt revolver, and judging from its ebony handles and chrome finish, Tyson doubted that it was standard Army issue. Probably West Miami standard, however. Also smuggled in from the States was Beltran's machete, made of gleaming surgical steel and with an ivory handle. Beltran said it had belonged to his late father, who had owned a sugar plantation in pre-Castro Cuba. Beltran also claimed that Nuestra Señora del Cobre had appeared to him one night in boot camp and instructed him to kill one hundred Communists to avenge his family's misfortunes. Tyson was somewhat skeptical of this but saw no good reason to disabuse Pfc Beltran of this useful notion.

Tyson's platoon command group, usually five men, consisted of himself, Brandt, and Kelly. His second radio operator, Johanson, had been killed at Phu Lai, and the platoon sergeant, Fairchild, was in Japan by now, contemplating the flat bed sheets where his legs should have been. Losing Fairchild, Tyson thought, had been particularly unfortunate. Fairchild had been the only regular Army man among them. At thirty-eight years of age, he had been a stabilizing influence, a father figure to the teenaged platoon. This war, Tyson thought, had become a children's war. And children, as any schoolteacher would tell you, were capable of astonishing acts of brutality if left unsupervised.

Tyson moved to the edge of the dike and watched the procession of men coming toward him. As each man passed by, Tyson laid a hand on him and said something. "How's the jungle rot today, Walker?" "Stand a little closer to the razor next time, Scorello." "How short, Peterson? Eighteen days? Hang in there. I'll get you out of the field in a day or two."

Brandt handed out malaria pills, and Tyson watched as each man dutifully placed his pill in his mouth. A few paces away, about half of them spit their pills out. In a choice between malaria and what had come to look like certain death or injury in combat, malaria seemed to be the preferred choice of half.

Tyson looked into each man's eyes as he passed and saw that too many of them had developed the Thousand-Yard Stare.

But perhaps today or tomorrow would be the day Alpha Company rotated to the rear; rest, recreation, refitting, and replacements. Not to mention a little debauchery, if the Quang Tri brothels had survived the enemy "cleansing" program. Tyson turned to his radio operator. "Well, Kelly?"

Kelly nodded in understanding. He said softly to Tyson, "I give them one or two more days, if things go right—no more mine fields, no snipers, no booby traps, and damn sure no more Phu Lais. A break in this shit weather would help."

Tyson lit a cigarette and blew the smoke into the gray, rain-sodden air. Kelly, like most radio operators, was a notch above the average grunt. Officers picked their RTOs for their ability to think fast and talk quickly on the radio. RTOs observed their officers at close quarters, and ostensibly some leadership ability rubbed off. In fact, Tyson thought Kelly to be officer material.

Inevitably, Kelly had become almost a friend, though the Army frowned on officers fraternizing with enlisted men. This quaint custom extended into combat, and due to the fact that Alpha Company had only two officers left of the six authorized—Browder and himself—Tyson's circle of potential friends was limited to Browder. It was, Tyson reflected, lonely at the top.

Kelly added, "I don't think anyone is real anxious to reach Hue."

Tyson considered a moment, then said, "There are a lot of Marines there waiting for the cavalry to arrive."

Kelly shrugged. "This bunch won't do them a lot of good." Kelly added, "Besides, the Marines got themselves into that shit, they can get themselves out."

Tyson threw down his soggy cigarette and glanced at Kelly, wondering how much more Kelly knew of the men's state of mind than he did. "Orders is orders."

Kelly snapped, "Come on, Lieutenant." Kelly hesitated, then said softly, "I don't trust them anymore."

"Who? The brass?"

Kelly snorted. "I haven't trusted those assholes since I set foot in this country. No, I mean *them.*" He cocked his head toward the straggling platoon.

Tyson nodded. He had stopped trusting them a week before, when Fairchild stepped on a land mine. The thought occurred to Tyson, as it had undoubtedly occurred to his men, that Lieutenant Tyson was the last vestige of military authority in the platoon; that if he were removed from the picture, things might, in some dimly perceived way, get better.

But there was, he hoped, a lot of emotional territory between wishing for the elimination of an officer and actually eliminating him. For the most part he was trusted and respected. Even the Phu Lai debacle hadn't hurt his standing with the platoon; he'd gotten them into the mess, but he'd also gotten them out.

Kelly, who seemed to be reading his mind, observed, "You're the only one in this platoon who knows how to read a map or call in artillery."

Tyson didn't reply.

"If you weren't here, the colonel would have to let us join up with the company. Or better yet, with Browder as the only officer left, he'd order us all to stand down."

"They'd send some rear echelon lieutenant out to take over."

"He wouldn't last long."

Tyson nodded to himself. *No, he would not last long.* Tyson watched the last man, Beltran, move past him. At ten-meter intervals, the line of troops stretched nearly a quarter kilometer along the muddy, rain-splashed dike. Tyson scratched at a leech bite on his forearm and contemplated the watery blood running over his pallid skin. "Damn it."

Brandt looked at the arm. "Still got teeth in there, Lieutenant. It's getting infected."

Tyson squeezed the raised red circle and felt the sharp microscopic teeth in his flesh. The leech had joined him sometime in the night, and by the time he'd awoken, it had engorged itself into a gray, pulsating tumescence the size of a fountain pen. Leeches injected an anticoagulant into the blood, and Tyson knew it would be hours before the holes clotted.

The leech, he thought, was probably the sole remaining object of disgust among the hardened veterans who had grown accustomed to the repulsive flora and fauna of Southeast Asia, who picked lice out of one another's hair, and who found poisonous snakes in their sleeping bags on cold nights. The blood-sucking leech was metaphor; it was Vietnam sucking them dry.

Brandt splashed iodine on the bite. "I'll give you a needle later so you can dig the teeth out. You shouldn't have squashed him. Heat their ass with a cigarette. They'll back off."

"I know that." But Tyson had smashed the obscene thing with his fist and had no regrets about it. He said, "Let's go." Tyson, Brandt, and Kelly moved quickly up the column to take their positions in the middle of the formation. Tyson turned to Brandt, who walked bent under the weight of his medical bag, the rain dripping from his camouflage net. Tyson asked, "Did anyone come to you this morning?"

Brandt raised his head, and Tyson was struck by the color of his flesh. Tyson had seen unhealthy skin that was chalky, mottled, yellow, grayish. But Brandt's face was actually deep gray, the color of clay. Tyson suspected that the man had been eating some sort of nitrate substance—probably the propellant envelopes from a mortar round—to feign illness but had overdone it. *Bastard.* "Any sick call, Brandt?"

Brandt replied tonelessly, "Only Scorello. Said his nerves were shot."

Tyson replied, "I told you to send those to me."

Brandt shrugged.

Tyson regarded his medic as they walked. Brandt, the only other college graduate in the platoon, had been a premed student at Bucknell. Having failed to get quickly accepted into a medical school, Brandt belatedly declared himself a conscientious objector and was drafted directly into the Medical Corps. Tyson said to him, "Next time you eat an explosive, Doc, do me a favor and swallow a lit match."

"What are you talking about?" Brandt turned his head away as he walked.

Tyson recalled that Brandt had been in country about seven months. Many COs began by refusing to carry a weapon, but within a month accepted a pistol for self-defense. Sometime later, depending on the depth of their belief and how frequently they brushed shoulders with death, they graduated to an M-16 automatic rifle. Some began requisitioning hand grenades and other nonpacifist ordnance. Brandt, on the other hand, had come to the field fully armed. Tyson made no moral judgment on that account. But, he had come to judge Brandt in other ways, and Spec/4 Steven Brandt was found wanting. Tyson asked, "No one had any physical complaints?"

Brandt shook his head.

Tyson reflected on this. There certainly wasn't a man in the platoon who was physically well. He didn't have to be a medic to hear the hacking coughs or see the effects of dysentery, fever, and vomiting. Blood and water blisters oozed into rotting boots, and there was barely a man who walked right. Yet no one had tried to go on sick call for at least a week. There was some message there, and Tyson thought it was this: The survivors of First Platoon, Alpha Company, were beyond pain, and that frightened him.

Tyson, Brandt, and Kelly reached a point in mid-column and fell into file. Kelly remarked to Brandt, "Someday, Doc, when you're sitting in your consulting office listening to some fat executive complain about his hemorrhoids, remember that you did something good here. Don't bug out on this platoon, Doc, or you'll never have that memory."

Brandt's eyes met Kelly's. Brandt said, "Fuck off."

Tyson opened a cellophane packet of stateside Nabisco cream-filled sugar wafers that his sister had sent him and passed it to Kelly, then to Brandt. Tyson took one himself and put it in his mouth, letting it dissolve slowly like a Communion wafer, his mouth salivating in response to the aromatic essence of vanilla and the richness of the cream and sugar. *Bless you, Laurie,* he thought. *Bless you for the sugar wafers. When I get home I'm going to buy you ten boxes of sugar wafers.*

They trekked on slowly through the dead and quiet countryside. After an hour, Tyson pulled his plastic-coated map from his pouch pocket and opened it. He studied the map as he walked, glancing at the terrain features around him. He reckoned he was about equidistant between Highway One to the northwest and the Perfume River to the south. Hue was about three kilometers to the east, off the map. In fact, whenever the rain lightened and the wind blew from the South China Sea, he could hear the far-off rumble of war.

Intellectually, Tyson was fascinated by the chaos. He understood that he was a direct participant in an historic event. The national life of twenty million people had almost ceased to exist. The country's social fabric and institutions were in shreds, and its army was near collapse. Hunger and disease stalked the cities and villages. From his small perspective, and from radio and written briefings, Tyson knew that the situation was serious. And if Alpha Company was a microcosm of the American fighting formations in the field, then the Green Machine was barely holding together.

Kelly's radio crackled, and the voice of the point squad leader, Moody, came over the speaker. "Hey, there's a bunch of gooks, about two o'clock, two hundred meters."

Kelly handed Tyson the radiophone. Tyson looked out across the rain-splattered rice fields. He spoke into the phone. "Roger. See them. Hold it up. I'll take a look. Cover me."

The platoon came to a gradual halt, and the men knelt in the mud of the wide dike, facing alternately left and right for security. The two machine guns were set up facing the group of unknown Vietnamese who stood on a small bare knoll.

Tyson motioned to two riflemen, Farley and Simcox. "Let's take a walk."

Tyson, Kelly, and the two men moved farther up the main dike, then turned right, onto a smaller dike, and headed out across the exposed paddies. Tyson drew a pair of field glasses from a plastic case and adjusted the focus. The people appeared to be civilians. "ICs or good actors."

Simcox remarked, "Yeah. I haven't seen a real innocent civilian since I left San Francisco."

They turned again onto a still smaller dike that was knee-deep in water, and sloshed forward, toward the Vietnamese. Tyson could see that the people were standing on a burial mound. In fact, they appeared to be burying bodies. He counted ten Vietnamese standing on the mound: five old men, one young boy, and four females, consisting of two women and two teenage girls. Typical of what was left in the villages. They appeared to be peasants, all dressed in black pajamas and conical straw hats. Normally, there would be some mixture of Western clothing, but since Tet, the peasantry had reverted to traditional garb, undoubtedly, Tyson thought, to curry favor with the ascendent power. If the communist offensive failed, the peasants would be back in jeans and Hawaiian shirts. Being a peasant was tough.

A few of the Vietnamese glanced at the approaching Americans, but otherwise they went about their unhappy business. Kelly remarked, "I can smell the stiffs from here."

Tyson came within twenty meters of the earth mound that rose from the gray water. He called out, *"Dung cu don!"* The Vietnamese stopped moving and faced him. They seemed to know the drill because they separated so he could see them all and kept their hands to their front. The boy and a young woman dropped their shovels.

Tyson, with Kelly beside him, walked out of the water onto the mound. Farley and Simcox covered. Tyson stood directly in front of the group; then looked down at the bodies. He counted eight of them, wrapped in good, white cotton bed sheets, which made him think the bodies had come from Hue. One of the shrouded corpses was a small child. Tyson surveyed the burial detail and met their eyes, one at a time. He said, "ID—*cho toi xem gian can cuoc.* ID."

The six males and four females produced plastic ID cards from their pajamas. Tyson inspected them perfunctorily, then following protocol, addressed the oldest male, a bald, age-spotted man with a wispy, gray beard. *"Ong lam gi o day?"*

The old man looked at the young boy, who replied in English, "We bury mama-san, papa-san. VC kill *beaucoup*—VC very bad, VC number fucking ten—"

"Okay, cut the bullshit." Tyson looked at the freshly opened holes and counted six finished graves and two more started. The Vietnamese had a strong prohibition against mass graves, and the holes must have taken hours to dig with the two shovels. Each body, he knew, had been wrapped first in black cloth, then in white. Grains of rice had been placed in the mouth. In the end, he thought, even a dying civilization tries to inter its dead properly.

Tyson could not imagine anything more depressing than this gray tableau of frightened villagers burying their families in the cold winter rain. He spoke again to the old man. *"Ong o dau den?"*

Again, the boy answered. "We from An Ninh Ha. Beaucoup VC come. Kill papa-san, mama-san, baby-san—"

"Okay, ace, cool it." Tyson looked at his map and located An Ninh Ha. "Which way is your village? *Con bao xa nua den lang?"*

The boy pointed to a mist-shrouded tree line in the far distance. Tyson estimated it at about a kilometer. He took a bearing with his compass, then looked at his map again and said to Kelly, "According to the map, there's a hospital there."

Kelly glanced at Tyson's map. "Don't count on it."

Tyson looked again at the white bed sheets and turned to the boy. *"Nha Thuong—hôpital?"*

The boy nodded vigorously. *"Beaucoup* VC in *Nha Thuong."*

Tyson's eyes met Kelly's, and Kelly observed, "Good place to avoid."

Tyson replied, "The mission, Kelly. The mission of the infantry is to—"

"Make contact with and destroy the enemy. Fuck it, Lieutenant." Kelly cocked his head toward the two riflemen at the edge of the mound and said quietly, "No one has to know about the *beaucoup* fucking VC. No one gives a shit."

Tyson spoke to the boy again. "VC in *Nha Thuong? Bac si* in *Nha Thuong?"*

The boy nodded again. *"Français. Français. Catholique. Catholique."*

Tyson looked again at Kelly.

Kelly's expression conveyed that he could not have cared less if the pope were in the hospital. He suddenly turned and knelt beside one of the bodies. Blood had seeped through the white sheet, and Kelly stared at the red, rain-soaked blotch. "Stinks." He grasped the shoulder of the corpse and shook the body. "Big sucker." Kelly drew his Marine K-bar knife, and made a slice through the white sheet from forehead to chest. The Vietnamese began wailing. Kelly ripped open the double shroud and exposed the blue-white features of a young man, the slice from Kelly's knife bisecting his bloodless face. Kelly ripped further and exposed the khaki tunic of a North Vietnamese soldier.

The wailing stopped, and a tense silence hung over the burial mound. Kelly stood slowly and looked grimly at the group of Vietnamese. He said to Tyson, "These bastards are burying enemy dead."

Tyson thought he didn't give a damn. He said, "Forget it."

"Like hell." Kelly leveled his rile, and the Vietnamese immediately huddled together, clutching at one another. Kelly shouted, "You die!"

One of the young women fell to her knees and began crying, "No! No kill me!"

Tyson snapped, "Knock it off, Kelly!"

Kelly lowered his rifle. "Fucking gooks."

Tyson turned and motioned to Farley and Simcox.

The two men climbed onto the mound. Tyson said, "Cut the wrappings open."

The men hesitated, then drew their knives.

Kelly was staring at the two shovels. He said to Tyson, "Look at this shit. A GI entrenching tool." He picked it up and swung it at the boy, who ducked. Kelly shouted, "Where did you get this, cocksucker? *O dau?*"

The boy was trembling, but like survivors everywhere, thought Tyson, not only could he speak the lingua franca of the occupying army and not only could he duck quickly, but he probably had a good answer for life-threatening questions. The boy cried out, "Buy from GI! Black market. Buy. Eight hundred piaster."

"You're full of shit," said Kelly.

Simcox called out, "Two more NVA."

Tyson said, "Throw them in the water." He looked at the Vietnamese. "No bury." He made a cutting motion across his neck. "Savvy? You *biet?*"

They all nodded in unison, affecting contrite expressions. *"Biet! Biet!"*

Tyson heard a splash and turned. The first enemy soldier floated face-down in the paddy. Farley and Simcox threw the second and third in after him. The floodwaters carried the corpses east, down toward the coastal plains, toward Hue, where they had begun their funeral journey. As he watched, a wake appeared at a right angle to one of the bodies, and Tyson saw a water rat scurry atop one of the corpses. The rat probed at the winding sheets with its long gray muzzle. Tyson turned away.

Farley said, "I hope those three fucks were at Phu Lai."

Simcox nodded and looked thoughtfully at the civilians. He said tonelessly, "Let's waste them."

"At ease, Simcox." Tyson was feeling petty. Even if they had been at Phu Lai, the three men had been soldiers and deserved a decent burial. But in the field, in the absence of a functioning judicial system, Tyson felt obliged to administer summary justice

to the living and the dead. He was wondering what to do with the
Vietnamese when Kelly called out, "We ought to search this
crew."

Tyson shrugged. "I suppose."

Kelly barked an order in Vietnamese, and the villagers, hesitantly at first, then more quickly, as Kelly leveled his M-16, began
to undress.

They stood there, naked in the cold rain, the five old men, the
boy, the two older women, and the two young women, their silk
pajamas and conical hats lying in the mud. Kelly, Farley, and
Simcox walked around them, kicking at their black pajamas,
trampling their laboriously woven straw hats into the mire.

Tyson turned away and lit a cigarette. The radio crackled, and
Larry Cane's voice came over the speaker. "One-Six, this is One-
Three. What are you guys up to over there?"

Tyson took the radiophone from Kelly and looked out across
the inundated checkerboard of rice fields, to the north where his
platoon was strung out along the high dike. "One-Six here. Saddle up and move out. Head toward that tree line at four-five
degrees. Try to stay on the dry dikes. We'll intersect with you.
Out." He handed the phone back to Kelly, then stared at the
miserable villagers standing over the open graves, naked and
shivering in the winter rain. He remarked softly, "My God, Kelly,
we're Nazis."

Kelly nodded in agreement. "We're shits, Lieutenant. I mean
to tell you, we are *shits.*"

Farley said, apropos of nothing, "Fucking gooks."

Simcox concurred, "Cocksuckers." He glowered at the pathetic wretches who had instinctively huddled closer to one another for warmth, despite their obvious embarrassment. Tyson
noticed that the women were shielded by the old men. The boy
was in the forefront, ready to do some fast negotiating if he
smelled a massacre, Tyson thought.

Farley shouted, "You're all fucking VC! VC!"

This standard accusation brought forth the standard exclamations of protest and shaking of heads. "No! No! No VC! No
VC!"

Tyson felt that if he turned his back, Farley, Simcox, and perhaps even Kelly would mow these people down with no more
regard than they had for slashing a machete through a trouble-
some vine. And the incredible thing, he thought, was that Farley
attended the company Bible study group, and Simcox was always
giving little GI luxuries like soap and ballpoint pens to village
schoolteachers. Kelly had a good rapport with village elders and
old mama-sans. But that was last month and the month before.
That was when the sun was shining, before the green-gray body
bags began filling with Alpha Company.

Today, Tyson understood, the war completely possessed their
minds, had insinuated itself deeply into their hearts, and had
sickened their souls. To say that war brutalized men was like
saying that famine made people hungry.

Tyson felt suddenly old, tired, and demoralized. Surely, he
thought, there was a spark of decency left in them. He said softly,

with no expression on his face, "Make them lie in the graves and shoot them."

Kelly looked at him quickly. Farley's eyes widened. Simcox lowered his rifle. No one spoke, no one moved. A full minute passed, then Tyson snapped, "Okay, heroes, confiscate the shovels. They can bury their dead with their hands."

Farley picked up the Army entrenching tool, and Simcox, the long-handled grave digger's shovel. Kelly motioned to the Vietnamese to get dressed, then said, *"Chao ong.* So long, suckers. Look me up when you get to the States."

Farley laughed.

Simcox kicked a clod of mud that splattered on the boy's groin.

The four soldiers moved down the opposite side of the burial mound, and Tyson took the lead along a narrow, bush-choked dike. He saw the main body of his platoon moving onto a submerged path in order to intersect with them.

Kelly walked directly behind Tyson. He said softly so the other two couldn't hear, "Are we going to that hospital?"

Tyson replied without turning, "Maybe."

"Don't push it, Lieutenant."

"Don't push *me,* Kelly. In fact, shut the fuck up."

They walked in silence awhile, then Kelly said, "Hey, I'm looking out for your ass."

"Look out for your own ass."

"I'm doing that too. What would I do if you got greased? I'd be a rifleman again." Kelly affected a laugh.

Tyson bent his head forward and lit a soggy cigarette with his Zippo lighter. He looked at the stainless-steel lighter, given to him at Christmas by his platoon. One side of it had the First Cavalry shoulder patch engraved on it. Etched on the other side was a ribald version of the Twenty-third Psalm: *Yea, though I walk through the valley of the shadow of death, I fear no evil, for I am the meanest motherfucker in the valley.*

Tyson dropped the lighter in his pocket and passed the cigarette to Kelly. Tyson said, "We'll give it a peek. I'm curious. If it looks dicey, we'll bypass it or call artillery on it. If it looks okay, maybe we can set up there awhile. They might have showers, hot chow, toilet bowls, and who the hell knows what else. Hot and cold running French nurses."

Kelly laughed. "Okay. We'll take a peek. I'm not real anxious to get to Hue anyhow."

"You said that."

"And I'll say it again tomorrow."

The four men intersected the other fifteen troops of the platoon at a place where two dikes crossed.

Moody said to Tyson, "What the hell was going on there, Lieutenant?"

"Burial detail. Local gooks planting some NVA. We took their shovels away. Mission accomplished." Tyson said to Kelly, "Report to Browder later; three confirmed NVA bodies. Okay, let's move."

The platoon began moving along the straight dike that pointed toward An Ninh Ha. Simcox called to Tyson as they walked, "Where are we heading now, Lieutenant?"

"Hue, sonny. Hue."

"Fuck Hue."

"Fuck Hue," agreed Tyson. He added, "There's a little Frenchy café on Tihn Tam Street with halfbreed honeys, Simcox. They serve Martel brandy and croissants."

"Not anymore, they don't. What's a . . . ? A what?"

"A croissant. That's French for a blow job under the table. It comes with the brandy."

"No shit?"

"No shit." After a minute he said to Brandt, Simcox, and a few others within earshot, "Intermediate objective: a hospital about two clicks from the Citadel's west wall. Pass that on."

The platoon trekked slowly east through the rain and mud. The distant tree line loomed larger, and the muted sounds of explosions grew more distinct. *Hue,* Tyson thought. Hue sounded like a meat grinder. What other species of living thing on God's earth would go willingly or unwillingly into a meat grinder? There was a lesson to be learned here, he reflected, but he was damned if he knew what it was.

The bloated, putrid carcass of a water buffalo lay on the dike, its belly full of rats and its hide covered with wiggling maggots. The platoon detoured around it, into the chest-deep, leech-infested rice paddies, holding their noses and swearing at this further outrage.

Tyson climbed back onto the slippery dike, Kelly pulling him up by his rifle muzzle. The platoon stopped for a leech check. Tyson glanced at his map and saw the little square with the cross nestled in the village of An Ninh Ha. *Nha Thuong.* Literally, house of love. He hoped so. They could all use some love.

Tyson looked at Major Harper. "Excuse me?"

"To recap, you said you moved out at first light. You received radio orders from Captain Browder to proceed to the village of An Ninh Ha, a sort of suburb of Hue that was reportedly controlled by the enemy. An Ninh Ha was along the main enemy supply route into Hue. A helicopter spotted a large concrete structure in the village. The structure flew an enemy flag. Your radio orders were to assess the situation in An Ninh Ha and determine if the concrete structure was in enemy hands, and if so, to occupy it and pull down the flag. Correct?"

Tyson nodded. "Correct."

She thought a moment, then said, "There's no way to verify that, of course." Tyson shrugged.

She continued, "Picard's book says you heard of this hospital from some local peasants who were burying their dead; that it was *you* who decided to go to the village and to the concrete structure which you knew was a hospital."

"Not true," he lied. "I was ordered to go there and make contact with the enemy. Intelligence reported that the . . . the structure—I didn't know it was a hospital then—that the concrete structure was in enemy hands. No one said anything about a hospital."

She nodded. "So you were psychologically prepared to meet the enemy?"

Tyson thought a moment, then replied, "Yes, that's a good way to put it."

"You advanced on this village. . . ." She glanced at her notes. "An Ninh Ha . . . am I saying it right?"

"Close enough for government work."

"Did you meet any resistance on the way?"

Tyson replied cautiously, "No . . . but we could see signs of them."

"Who?"

"Chuck, Charlie, Mr. Charles, VC, Viet Cong, Victor Charlie. Whom are we talking about?"

"What sort of signs?"

"Well, the usual stuff: strung-out commo wire, spider holes—those are gook-size foxholes—smothered cooking fires, hoofprints—what we called hoofprints: fresh VC sandal prints; they made their sandals out of old tires. And North Vietnamese Army boot prints—actually black sneakers. There was evidence of a large number of enemy troops moving in the same direction we were. Toward Hue." Tyson lit a cigarette. "We also saw unburied dead—VC and North Viets. I think Picard confirms all of this. We were not in friendly territory."

"Apparently not. And you knew the enemy was to your front?"

"Right. We suspected he was stalking us from behind as well. I think we all felt like lost lambs in a clearing, getting a little nervous about all those slanty yellow eyes staring out of the dark woods."

She cupped her chin in her hand and regarded him for some time, then smiled. "Did you? I saw a group photo of you and your platoon. To paraphrase the Duke of Wellington, I don't know what effect these men had on the enemy, but by God, they frightened *me.*"

Tyson suppressed a smile. "Well, they *looked* mean; but they were pussycats."

"Anyway, you approached this village?"

"Yes. Like most villages, it was heavily treed, and we moved carefully across the dike to the tree line that marked the edge of the village. According to my map, the village was nestled in a bend of a small river: a tributary of the Perfume River. The western wall of the Hue Citadel was about two kilometers farther—off my map. At this point I called for air recon, but the weather was awful and whatever was flying was committed elsewhere. So we did what soldiers have done since the beginning of warfare—we called out to the inhabitants to assemble where we could see them. But no one appeared. Intelligence had indicated that the village had been abandoned in the first days of the offensive. So we began probing fire—"

"You fired into the village?"

"Yes. That was standard procedure after a warning. But we drew no fire, so we moved cautiously along two parallel dikes, toward the tree line. This is always the worst part because when you come within, say, ten or twenty meters, if they're in there, then they chop you up."

"But no one fired?"

"No. But then another trick they had was to suck you into the village, then spring the door shut behind you. That's what happened to us at Phu Lai on the first day of Tet."

"So you were all . . . jittery?"

Tyson replied, "Cautious, but not trigger-happy."

"Please go on."

"The village was quite picturesque. It was, as you said, sort of a suburb of Hue, and it had some Western influence. There were some French-style villas, paved paths, well-kept gardens, and a few shops around a market square. Very different from the really rural villages that were all bamboo and buffalo shit. Anyway, on the concrete walls were painted VC and NVA slogans—"

"In Vietnamese?"

"Most of them."

"You could read them?"

"No . . ."

"Then how did you know they were VC and NVA slogans and not government slogans?"

"Well, they were painted in red. The enemy used red. Commies—Reds. Get it?"

"You said *most* of the signs were in Vietnamese?"

"Yes, there were a few in English. Routine crap—'Throw out the imperialist running dogs of American adventurism,' or something catchy like that." He added, "There were also these red silk banners strung between the trees with more slogans. It was obvious to me that the place had been under enemy control for some time."

Karen Harper nodded, then asked, "Were there any signs in English directed specifically toward American soldiers?"

Tyson replied, "Yes, I remember one in particular. It said, 'GI, who now sleeps with your wife?' " Tyson smiled. "I think Charlie hired Tokyo Rose as a media consultant."

Karen Harper nodded, then asked, "Any threatening sort of signs?"

"Sure. One said something like, 'GI, Death will come today.' "

"Did that sort of thing have any effect on your troops?"

Tyson considered a moment, then replied, "Sure, the signs and banners and brochures we found got to us a little. Why?"

"Just wondering. Anyway, notwithstanding the slogans and psy-warfare messages, the village was deserted? No civilians? No enemy?"

"No civilians to be seen. No sign of a government presence either. As for the enemy, he was usually unseen. Anyway, we saw this small concrete church and moved toward it. It was there that we discovered another open square, a *place* as they say in French. It was paved with concrete slabs and surrounded by stucco buildings with red tile roofs. On the far side of the square, at about fifty meters' distance, was a large concrete structure. It was two stories high and had two wings projecting from the front, forming a courtyard. There were a few smaller buildings to each side in the same style and painted the same cream color as the main building. I took it for a government complex of some sort. From the main building, on a flagstaff over the front doors, flew a Viet Cong flag, or perhaps a North Vietnamese flag. It was hard to tell the difference, and the difference didn't matter. Now, banners and slogans are one thing, but an enemy battle flag is another. They don't leave their flag behind any more than we do. An enemy flag equals enemy people."

"Was there a Red Cross flag on a pole in the courtyard, as the book indicates?"

"There was no such flag. No red cross, only a red star flag."

Karen Harper reached into her briefcase and took out Picard's book. Tyson looked at it but made no comment.

She said, "I read the entire book. In fact, I just finished it on the plane."

"Good for you."

She opened the book to a marked page and, without preamble, read:

> It was common at the time of the countryside offensive to run
> up the enemy flag as a sign of surrender, a gesture that the build-
> ing and the people should be spared. In Hue, however, a number
> of students and Buddhist groups were sympathetic to the com-

munist cause, and certain Europeans in the city had similar sympathies. Hue was cosmopolitan, sophisticated, liberal, and generally antiwar. When the enemy took possession of most of the city during the general offensive, these elements in the city's population sometimes hoisted the communist flag in a victory celebration. As the battle lines changed, however, so did the flags. To be fair and accurate, the North Vietnamese and Viet Cong often ran up their own flags over captured buildings. So in this case it was not known if that taunting red flag was raised over the hospital by the enemy or by the hospital staff. If by the staff, was it for reasons of protection, surrender, or in sympathy? Or was it perhaps some combination of the three?

Karen Harper looked up from the book and met Tyson's eyes. "Picard agrees that there was an enemy flag there, but he indicates that it might have been raised by the hospital staff for the reasons he indicates. Why did you assume, as you indicated, that enemy soldiers were there?"

Tyson stubbed out his cigarette and replied with a touch of annoyance in his voice, "I didn't have Picard's book with me. I had no idea, Major, of what the hell was going on in Hue or its environs. When I saw an enemy flag, I made the logical assumption that I was approaching a fortified enemy position."

"Yes, of course. Please go on."

Tyson leaned back in his chair and thought. *She is playing dumb, and she is imploring me to educate her. I am responding to this dumb woman by trying to teach her about war. Only she is not so dumb. She is using a very sophisticated method of interrogation. Careful, Tyson.*

"Mr. Tyson? You were saying something about the church and the square."

"Yes, we deployed on the near side of the square. There were, as I said, no villagers around to question. But it never occurred to me that I was looking at anything other than a large concrete building, a former French admin building or something, currently flying an enemy flag and in fact being used as a fort." Tyson leaned forward. "You have to understand, Major, that you can't be ethnocentric if you're trying to understand this. Picard says hospital, and you think of a big, sleek building with nice blue signs directing you to visitor parking and all that. You think that mistaking a hospital for an administration building is hard to swallow, like mistaking a water buffalo for an elephant. Well, try to imagine, if you will, a country without neon signs, McDonald's, or corner gas stations, a country where suburb doesn't mean PTAs and lawn mowers but means a shithole village close enough to a rinky-dink city to have a few buildings with glass windows and no pigs in the street."

Karen Harper did not reply immediately, then said somewhat coolly, "I just spent a month in Japan and the Philippines, a good deal of that time in the countryside. I've been all over the world in the last four years. I am not ethnocentric, but your point is well taken." She added, "Still, hospitals, especially in war zones, are somehow always well marked. But go on."

Tyson stared at her for some time, and their eyes met and held.

She said with a note of near sarcasm, "Do you need another break?"

Tyson stood and went to the side window. It was a soft gray day, damp and cool, an almost welcome relief from the bright sunshine and heat. He smelled rain in the air. Karen Harper, he decided, was ahead on points. He knew he should end the interview now, but his ego wouldn't buy that. Like his father, a gambler, he believed you couldn't win it back unless you kept playing. He turned from the window. "I don't need a break."

She nodded. "You were saying you were on the near side of the square."

Tyson moved back to his chair and sipped on his coffee. "Yes. We moved into positions of cover and concealment around the church. Kelly, my radio operator, who had a good voice, shouted across the square in Vietnamese for anyone inside the concrete building to come out. No one replied. We fired a few probing rounds. No return fire. We waited, called out again, then fired again. No return fire. But we knew they were in there. We could smell them." He looked at Karen Harper, but she did not challenge that statement.

Tyson continued. "We increased our rate of fire, trying to get them to give themselves away. I was beginning to wonder if anyone was in there when it happened. Someone, probably some scared kid, fired back. Now we *knew*. We stepped up our fire, blasting the windows. The enemy began firing back, very intense fire. Mostly small arms, but a few rockets and propelled grenades. Then a machine gun opened up from the roof. We exchanged fire for about five minutes, then I decided to assault the building. The square was not completely exposed. There were trees and ornamental gardens, a few low walls, and also a pool and fountain. We began moving out, firing and maneuvering. We took one killed and two wounded before we reached the front doors of the building. That's in the book—"

"Yes, but the book says the main enemy force had withdrawn sometime before you even got there. The three casualties were the result of a solitary sniper on the roof. Picard says through his two witnesses—two men in your platoon—that you never fired on the building, that civilians in the hospital signaled to you and hung out a white bed sheet. You believed the building held no enemy troops, and apparently so did the hospital staff. Seeing their signal to you, you advanced directly across the square, and the solitary sniper opened fire from the roof. So here we have a further divergence between your account and the account in the book."

"Well, I'm telling you what happened as I recall it. The enemy force had not withdrawn. We met with intense fire and we returned it."

"All right. By the way, did your field map indicate a hospital? What is the hospital symbol? A square within which is a cross with equal-length arms, like the Red Cross." Her eyes met his.

He said slowly, "Well, there was a hospital symbol on my map . . . as I'm sure you know . . . but old map symbols in a country at war for nearly thirty years are somewhat meaningless. Try checking into the hotel that you see on a Vietnam map, or crossing a bridge that's been down for twenty years."

"I understand that, but—"

"More to the point, I was temporarily disoriented, and I thought I was on the other side of the village. I thought the building designated as a hospital on the map was to the north."

"I see." She seemed to be mulling this over, then reached into her briefcase and drew out a plastic-coated map.

Tyson felt his mouth go dry.

Major Harper stood and came around the coffee table. Unexpectedly, she knelt beside Tyson's armchair and unfolded the map.

Tyson looked down at the colored Army ordnance map. The map was trilingual—French, Vietnamese, and English. It suddenly seemed very familiar: the rice paddies, the trails, the burial mounds, the rivers and streams, the woods and hills. After nearly two decades, he still knew the place. His eyes focused on An Ninh Ha.

Major Harper asked, "This was the standard issue map, was it not?"

"Looks like it."

She seemed to be studying it, her finger sliding across the Plasticine coating, stopping at An Ninh Ha. "Here it is."

"Yes. There it is."

"You see here . . . you said you saw a church on the near side, the west side of the square. Here's the church on the map, a box clearly marked with a Christian, or Latin, cross. The only church in the village. And across the square on the east side is the hospital, marked with the cross of equal-length arms. That seems clear. What I'm wondering is where you *thought* you were." She glanced over her shoulder at Tyson.

Tyson's eyes went from the map to her face, and they stared at each other in silence. Her proximity was somewhat unsettling. He could smell her scent, an unusual spicy fragrance. He saw that her hair had highlights he hadn't noticed. Between the buttons of her blouse, there was a gap, and out of the corner of his eye he saw the curve of her breasts and observed she was wearing a half-cut bra.

She said again, "Where did you think you were?"

Tyson drew a deep breath through his nostrils and leaned over the coffee table. He scanned the small village quickly. In the north end, near the bend in the river, was a pagoda whose symbol, a box with a projecting line, could conceivably be mistaken for that of a church. Some distance away, perhaps a hundred meters, was the symbol for a school: a black box with a pennant flag. Tyson said, "There. I thought I was there."

Major Harper nodded as though she accepted this. "So you thought the Catholic church you passed was a pagoda, and the hospital across the square was a school? You said you thought it was an administration building."

"Well . . . I meant a public building. . . ."

"I see." She looked at him with an expression meant to convey that she was a little confused. She said, "But the juxtaposition of these two sets of buildings is quite different. Also . . . here you have an open square, a *place*. Here, between the pagoda and the school, you have tiny black boxes which I presume are houses, and the distance is greater—"

"Look, Major, I don't need a course in map reading. You know, it's easy to sit here in a dry room with a nice new map and play devil's advocate. But *my* map was bent and folded so many times the plastic coating was cracked, and water had seeped into the paper. An Ninh Ha was nearly obliterated on *my* map." Tyson's voice was sharp. "Let's forget maps. Okay?"

Major Harper folded the map. Still kneeling, she handed it to Tyson. "These are hard to come by. I assume you don't have yours. My compliments."

Tyson took the map. "Thanks for the memories."

She stood. "Look it over when you get a chance. It may jog your memory."

Tyson did not reply.

She returned to her side of the coffee table. Still standing, she said, "All right. Where were we?"

"I was attacking the building. Do you want a blow-by-blow account of the assault? Or do you want to wait until they make it into a movie?"

"Actually, I'd like us to back up to when you're deployed around the church. You're looking at the building, fifty meters across the square. It's flying an enemy flag, and you're focusing on that. But did you see any written signs on the building, in English or in French? Do you know French?"

"As you know from my file, I have a working knowledge of it. There were no signs—written or otherwise."

She handed him a slip of paper. "What does that mean?"

Tyson looked at the Vietnamese words. *Nha Thuong.* He threw the paper on the coffee table. "I told you I didn't know the written language. I spoke a few words and phrases, most of which had to do with getting me laid." He smiled.

Major Harper smiled in return and sat. She said, "Well, that means hospital, of course."

"Does it?"

She pointed to the map on the coffee table and observed, "The maps were trilingual and were therefore like a Rosetta stone." She nodded to herself, as though arriving at a truth, then continued. "The legend on that map included the words '*Nha Thuong, hôpital,* hospital.' You saw this trilingual legend day in and day out as you consulted your map. So of course you know '*Nha Thuong*' when you see it written. The question is, Was it written on the concrete building?"

Tyson did not reply.

She seemed lost in thought for some time, stroking her chin with her finger. At length she said, "The question of whether or not you knew that building to be a hospital is pertinent but not crucial to the central issue. Let's assume you did not know it was a hospital."

"Right."

"You deployed, fired at a building with an enemy flag, drew fire in return, and began an assault. Believe it or not, I rather like a good war story. I saw *A Walk in the Sun* about ten times. Please continue."

Tyson leaned back in his armchair. He wanted a cigarette but decided this was not the time to display what could be construed as a nervous habit. He said, "We began by laying down heavy suppressing fire. You know—we blasted all the windows and doors with automatic fire to keep the enemy down. Then we began our final assault—"

"Excuse me again. The book said someone hung a white bed sheet from a window to indicate surrender or all clear. Apparently the two witnesses told Picard they saw this."

"Why the hell would the enemy hang out a surrender flag? They had an avenue of escape. Why the hell would I begin an assault if I or anyone in my platoon saw a white flag?"

"That goes back to the original point. The enemy had already withdrawn, according to the book. It was the hospital staff who hung the bed sheet from the window, also according to the book account. They waved to you from the windows. But you don't agree with any of that. So please continue."

"Right. So we began to fire and maneuver, working our way toward the building. We continued to draw heavy fire—"

"I'm sorry. It's just that I've done some basic infantry tactics research. I spoke to an infantry colonel who was there. A friend of mine. I sort of anticipated that, if I had the opportunity to hear your version, it would probably be that some sort of firefight took place. Excuse the comparison, but that's what was said about My Lai—"

"What's your point?"

"The point is that this colonel said a frontal assault on a concrete building was not something he would ever expose his men to."

"Maybe he's a wimp."

"Hardly. He did say he would fire some sort of incendiary devices into the place and burn the insides, which would be mostly wood, I guess. Then, he said, he might move in for an assault."

He regarded her for some time, then replied, "We didn't have any incendiary ordnance that could be fired from a launcher. We had only hand grenades—

fragmentation, white phosphorus, and concussion grenades. So we had to move in close."

"Why didn't you call in air strikes, aerial rockets, mortars, or artillery? Isn't that standard operating procedure in American infantry tactics? Send bombs instead of men?"

"Yes, that's standard procedure. But there was no fire support available. Nothing was functioning right at that time. So we moved in for an old-fashioned frontal assault. Fire and maneuver. We broke into the ground floor, just like in the war movies that you seem to like—"

"Where and when did the casualties occur? Was it before or after you got into the . . . the building?"

"I . . . we took two wounded on the initial assault. Peterson had a sucking chest wound . . . both lungs were involved . . . the bullet passed from side to side . . . he was drowning. The other man, Moody, was hit in the thigh . . . he was all right. . . . The third man, Larry Cane, was killed inside the building."

"Oh, I thought you indicated earlier that all the casualties occurred outside. That's what Picard's book said also, except he said they were caused by a single sniper. Anyway, there were remarkably few casualties for an assault on a fortified structure."

"Everyone's allowed to get lucky once in a while. I'm sorry I can't report more dead and wounded."

"I was just wondering. Please continue."

"There was no one on the first floor and still no indications that the place was a hospital. There were offices, a chapel, a lobby, some sleeping quarters, and a kitchen and dining room. We found two staircases. We reached the second floor and got into a room-by-room fight. It was then that a few phosphorus hand grenades were tossed around. The place started to burn—"

"How many enemy do you estimate?"

"Maybe thirty or forty—we were outnumbered."

"But you didn't know how many were in there when you attacked. There could have been two hundred."

"Well, I could tell by the amount of fire coming from the windows that there weren't two hundred."

"And you lost one killed in that room-to-room fighting? A man named Cane?"

"Yes."

"But a while ago you said all three casualties occurred outside, during the assault. Picard agreed, though his account of the severity of the fight is somewhat different from yours. Now you say Larry Cane was killed inside."

Tyson lit a cigarette. He drew on it, then replied, "Well, that's a result of having read Picard's book. You see, what's happening is that my memory is being jogged by all this, but Picard's book has put some false recollections in my mind. Cane *was* killed inside the hospital. I'm positive of that. I saw him get hit. Upstairs, in the main ward."

Karen Harper nodded. "I'm sure we can clear that up if it becomes necessary. And I understand what you mean about false recollections as a result of having recently read the book." She added, "Nonetheless, Mr. Tyson, I find it all a little hard to believe. I mean, nineteen very fatigued men making a frontal assault on a building held by a significant number of North Vietnamese regulars. And why didn't you surround the building so the enemy couldn't escape? That, I understand, would have been standard procedure. And what, may I ask, prompted you to such acts of heroism? If you couldn't get fire support to level the building, why not just bypass it? Pretend it didn't exist? Am I being cynical, or did American troops sometimes avoid a fight?" She leaned forward. "I don't expect you to answer any of thcsc questions because they presuppose that you are lying about the whole assault business."

Tyson looked at her.

Karen Harper continued, "In most murder investigations we look for motive. In cases of war-related massacres, investigators tend to overlook motive because motive, in the hands of the defense, becomes extenuation and mitigation. In other words, defense argues that the motive was a good one. For instance, you mentioned Phu Lai a few times, and I was wondering if perhaps your men were looking for revenge. . . ." She stared at him. "That would be understandable."

Tyson did not reply immediately, then said, "I would be lying if I told you that all of us were not looking for revenge. Killing breeds killing, as you may know. But combat deaths do not—should not—breed murder. We were looking for revenge on the battlefield, and we found it at Hôpital Miséricorde. In fact, there's your motive for my assault on the building, and there's the reason my men followed me. A payback for Phu Lai. But it had to be quid pro quo. Slaughtering civilians would not even the score. But taking that concrete building from the enemy would. Did."

She nodded. "You're a very bright man."

"Am I blushing?"

She said, "Still, your account is . . . not . . . not a good war story. In fact, it's unbelievable."

Tyson drew on his cigarette. He realized in retrospect just *how* unbelievable this story sounded from the standpoint of military tactics and logic. He saw that if even a JAG officer and a woman with presumably no knowledge of infantry tactics beyond an unlikely fondness for war movies and a friendship with an infantry colonel could punch holes in his story, then it would not stand up under closer scrutiny. Yet it seemed like a good story when it was first fabricated. It was standard Vietnam cover-up. Whenever a few ICs—innocent civilians—were killed by mistake—or in less blameless ways—you came up with a hair-raising story of a firefight. No one questioned you. No one said anything about your lack of casualties. And a good officer always made certain his men carried a few enemy weapons to turn in along with the bodies of old men, women, and children. It was that kind of war.

Tyson reflected: *The story sounded good at the time, because we'd told it to each other in a vacuum, without outside criticism, and because we wanted to believe it. . . . Damn her,* he thought. *Was the hospital marked? Why didn't you call in artillery? Why so few casualties in the assault?*

She broke into his thoughts. "So, anyway, the hospital was burning now. You had killed a number of the enemy. The rest, I assume, fled. How?"

"They jumped from the second-floor windows."

She nodded, then asked, "Did you see any patients, any hospital staff?"

Without hesitation he replied, "Yes, we saw patients and staff." *Stick to the damned story. Don't deviate. It's the only story we have. The only one we all know. It may sound improbable, but it's not impossible. Beyond a shadow of a doubt.* He said, "Most of them were dead. I don't know if they were killed in the assault or if they were executed by the enemy."

She said nothing.

Tyson continued his narrative. "It was total confusion at that point. I mean, you wouldn't believe what chaos it was—wounded VC and NVA soldiers in uniform—you couldn't tell if they were patients, if they were armed, if they

were surrendering, or if they were about to shoot you. There were a few
women, but one of them was a VC nurse, and she fired a pistol at us. Someone
killed her. It was incredibly confusing. I blame the goddamned VC and NVA
for using a hospital full of people. . . . By that time we could see that it was a
hospital. . . . Anyway, the place was burning by now, and we threw some of
the patients—the ones in the maternity and pediatric ward—out of the window
. . . to save them. . . . There were bushes below. . . ." Tyson stopped. He
realized he was rambling. He cleared his throat and continued. "Well, I suppose in a way you could call it a massacre . . . but certainly not an intentional
one on our part. I could see how that Eurasian nun could misinterpret what she
saw. . . . But most of the dead were a result of the assault or of the enemy
executions that took place before we assaulted the building. I think they massacred the staff and the patients, including their own wounded, when they saw
they were going to be overrun. . . ."

She said, "And Dr. Monteau?"

"I don't remember being introduced to anyone by name, Major."

"But one of Picard's sources—one of your men—related an incident—"

"Which man?"

"I don't know. I told you I came here first."

"By law you'd have to tell me who Picard's sources were, if you knew them.
That is the reason you came here first."

She didn't comment on Tyson's observation but said, "And the Australian
doctor—"

He said irritably, "Damn it, I told you there was a hospital full of patients
and staff. Yes, they were killed. Yes, some of them were probably killed by us.
But they were killed as an unfortunate consequence of military operations
against an armed enemy who made use of a place of sanctuary to conduct
operations against American forces. Write that down. End of statement."

She nodded and asked him to repeat it as she wrote. Then she said, "Why are
there such discrepancies between your story and the stories told to Picard by
two of your men?"

"Maybe Picard distorted what they said."

"Possibly." She seemed to be lost in thought, then said, "But Picard says in
his book that he learned of this incident as a result of a chance meeting in
France with this Sister Teresa. *She* apparently used the word *massacre*—"

"In what context? A massacre by whom? And how did she use the word? It is
spelled the same in French and English, and the meaning in French is close to
ours, but in French it has the added connotation of useless killing, the slaughter
of battle—not solely wanton or premeditated killing of unarmed people. I did
my homework, too—"

"So I see. Those are good questions. I'll call the Army language school and
get an opinion on that."

"Have you located this Sister Teresa?"

"No. Do you remember her?"

"I believe so. Will you interview Picard?"

"Of course." She said, "Your version is interesting because it is so subjective,
whereas Picard's account seems so objective."

"Meaning?"

"Meaning you've left room for interpretation of events, while he has been
unequivocal in saying he has heard the story of a massacre and reported it."

Tyson said nothing.

She added, "If Picard was embellishing, then I can see very clearly from your
version how he could do so. All the ingredients are there: a hospital, a large

number of deaths, the flags, the shooting in the wards. Anyway, Picard was a novelist once. Did you know that? He's used to making up stories. Don't forget to advise your attorney of that."

Tyson seemed not to hear her.

She continued. "Then again, it might have been that the two men from your platoon were embellishing or lying when they spoke to Picard. But why would they do that? It certainly brings no credit to them."

"It certainly does not."

"But it brings discredit on *you*. Did you have any enemies in your platoon?"

"I'll tell you that when you give me the names of those two men."

She nodded. "Also, Sister Teresa may make the worst kind of witness. She may not have understood what she saw or may not have communicated it very well to Picard."

"Probably."

She leaned forward and said, "I would imagine that at some point she made some sort of report to the Catholic authorities in Saigon or France who ran the hospital. Don't you think that's a possibility?"

Tyson had always thought that a distinct possibility. He replied, "Maybe."

She continued, "But I understand that the South Vietnamese government, and to some extent the Catholic church in Vietnam, had a tendency to bury any stories unfavorable to their allies and champions. They did not want to embarrass the Americans. Saigon tried to kill the My Lai investigation even as the JAG Corps was pursuing it. Foreigners don't understand why we insist on washing our dirty linen in public. So if this nun's report, if there was one, in any way reflected unfavorably on American soldiers, then it never would have gotten back to France. That's my theory."

"Which, as I see," said Tyson, "you've given some thought."

"I've given the whole incident some thought."

"Me too." Tyson stood and walked to the window. With his back to her, he said, "You know, a month or so ago I would have related this incident at a drunken stag party as a good shoot-'em-up war story. I had nothing to be ashamed of. We did a brave thing. A lot of officers *would* have bypassed that building—like your infantry colonel friend. I mean, it was unfortunate that so many innocent people got killed, but the bad guys were the ones in black pajamas." He turned toward her. "Now I'm getting very defensive. I'm having second thoughts about what happened. But I shouldn't have second thoughts. My perceptions at the time were the correct ones."

She nodded. "I know. You start to second-guess yourself. Every commander since the beginning of time refights his battles in his mind. Also, it's been a long time."

"A very long time."

Karen Harper said, "That's why we may need more statements. For instance, if Sister Teresa is found and her testimony turns out to be lucid. . . ." She looked at him. "Would you like her to be found?"

Tyson did not reply.

She observed, "It's odd that there were no other survivors."

He sat down again. "I told you we saved some people. But don't expect any long-distance calls from Nam."

"No. This is difficult. Too many years and too many miles." She commented, "You say you may remember Sister Teresa. What do you remember about her?"

"I remember she was scared. Maybe hysterical. Someone got her out a window. That's all I remember at the moment. I'll think about that."

"Fine. You know, I was thinking that if the investigation were broadened, we might try to contact Vietnamese refugees through their representative organizations. That might lead us to another survivor."

"It's a long shot that you'd find another survivor that way."

"True. Do you think the present government of Vietnam would cooperate? They have the advantage of access to the scene of the incident, which we do not."

Tyson began to feel that he had become her assistant, which was, he knew, another method of interrogation. He said, "If they did cooperate I don't think anyone that they present as a witness would have much credibility in front of a court-martial board of American officers. Do you?"

"I guess not. That was foolish."

Tyson nodded. Both suggestions were foolish. She was trying to shake him with the old unexpected-witness routine. What she didn't know—yet—was that there were absolutely no survivors. Except Sister Teresa.

Karen Harper poured coffee into their cups.

Tyson remembered a home-improvement salesman who felt that as long as he was drinking coffee, he wouldn't be tossed out. He was wrong. He said to Karen Harper, "I think that's about it."

She sipped on her coffee. "You've been very helpful. As I said, I'm trying to arrive at the truth, for your sake as well as in the interests of justice. You'd like this cleared up too, I suppose, so you can get back to your normal routine."

"Major, I never again want to go back to my normal routine. But I would like to get this done with and resign my commission. This time I'll check the correct damned box. Double-check it. How long will this last?"

"Oh . . . a few more weeks. I just need to contact Picard, then get the names of the two men who gave him his story. If necessary, we may contact other men from your platoon whose whereabouts we've tentatively determined."

"Who?"

"I told you—I'll send you or your lawyer a list as soon as we decide whether or not we even need their statements. I really hope I just find that Picard was, well, bullshitting a bit."

Tyson smiled in spite of himself.

She said, "Do you feel good about this interview? Do you think it was conducted fairly and properly?"

"Absolutely." He thought a moment, then added, "You're a remarkable woman. Why don't you get a civilian job?"

She smiled. "I'm getting out soon."

"Are you? You're not a career officer?"

"No. I'm paying back my tuition."

"I see. . . . Do you mind if I ask you whether or not you're married?"

"That's not relevant . . . but no, I'm not. Why?"

"Just curious." He saw she wasn't going to leave until asked to, and he wanted to end it before he said anything he'd regret. He stood. "I have a tennis date in half an hour."

She stood. "Yes, of course." She gathered her things and followed Tyson into the foyer. "I'm going to Manhattan. I understand there's a train."

"Yes." He looked at his watch. "The next one leaves in about twenty minutes. You can walk to the station."

"I'd like to freshen up first."

"Right. Up the stairs, to the left."

She climbed the long, sweeping staircase. He watched her and thought, *Tu-*

ition assistance program. That's like admitting you're dirt-poor. He tried to imagine what sort of background she came from. Her accent was definitely Midwestern. She was well spoken and carried herself well. She had made major within her four years of active duty, so she must be on the ball. He wondered what line of convoluted reasoning had led the JAG to send her to his door. What Machiavellian logic was behind this? He shrugged. Military logic, which was to say nonlogic. Yet there had to be some method to the madness. In this case, he admitted, there was definitely some method. . . .

She came down the stairs and walked toward the front door. "I have enough to do to keep me busy for some days, but I'd like us to meet again. Is that all right?"

Tyson thought a moment, then replied, "I'll have to think about that."

"Well, if you decide you'd like to, let's make a tentative date for a week from today. Why don't you come to Washington?"

Tyson knew he could not be ordered to speak about this case. But he could be ordered to go to Washington, to Fort Benning, Georgia, to Nome, Alaska, or to anywhere they decided he should go. He could exercise his right to remain silent from one end of the continent to the other. But he'd rather play ball in New York or Washington than Nome. He said, "I suppose I could meet you in Washington."

"Good. I'll call you with the details of the meeting." She handed him her card. "Please call me if anything else occurs to you in the meantime, or if you need assistance or just want to talk."

"That's what I used to say to suspects. It's trite, Major."

"I know. But I get lots of calls."

He took her jacket from the coat closet and helped her on with it, then he opened the door. Outside a light rain had begun to fall. He took an umbrella from the stand, and they walked together down to the street. She said, "Thank you for being so cooperative. I feel I'm getting closer to understanding this."

"Then you're a damned sight smarter than I am." He considered a moment, then said, "If charges are actually brought against me . . . what is the current Army policy on . . . restriction?"

She replied, "Of course that's on your mind. . . . I'm fairly sure . . . off the record . . . that as an officer, and taking into account all the sensitive aspects of this case, you would have almost complete freedom. . . . I'm sure you can live off-post, within the confines of your duties, if any. They may impose one restriction—"

"Don't leave the country."

"That's right."

"Am I restricted to this country as of now?"

"Not as far as I know. You are on administrative leave until you report to Fort Hamilton. Do you have any plans to leave the country?"

"No." He added, "And you can tell them that."

"Who?"

"Whoever is wondering, whoever is worried, or whoever is hoping. You've heard *that* sentiment expressed, I assume."

She nodded. "This thing has brought back so many bad memories of that time—Look, if you're innocent, I honestly feel that the Army, the nation, and others, including the media, will make full restitution to you. This is a country that knows how to say 'I'm sorry.' "

"Who's going to apologize to my wife?"

She looked into his eyes. "No one. That damage is done, and no one can ever make that right again. We're also a country that is obsessed with . . . with . . ."

"Fucking." He smiled. "On second thought, you're too honest to be a civilian lawyer." He paused, then said, "Well . . . it was good of you to come all the way here. I realize it could have been done differently. I think this informal format was best."

"I think so."

He looked around at the gently falling rain, then remarked, "I'd offer you the umbrella, but I remember that military people can't carry umbrellas."

"Silly custom . . . or is it a rule? It's sillier to get wet. I'll take the umbrella, unless you need it for your tennis game."

They exchanged smiles as he passed her the umbrella. She said, "I'll return it next week."

He looked at his watch. "You'd better hurry. Right at the end of this block, five more blocks, and you'll see the station. I'm not going to salute. The neighbors are watching."

She put out her hand and he took it. "Good-bye." She turned and walked away.

He stood under a tree and watched her moving down the street, carrying his umbrella.

His attention shifted back to the rain. It was a gentle rain, and when it rained in a certain way, he still thought of Vietnam: hot, steamy rain, vaporous ground clouds, and the steady, soft, susurrant sounds of water brushing the leaves. And the moldy smells of the wet earth, which he smelled now, brought back the jungle.

Vietnam, he thought suddenly, *is here, in this village.* He smelled it on the damp, rotting vegetation, heard it in the falling rain, and saw it in the vaporous air. Tyson walked slowly back toward his house in the rain.

18

Benjamin Tyson walked unhurriedly across the broad lawns of Constitution Gardens. It was twilight, breezeless and humid, and he could feel the sweat seeping through his white knit shirt and sticking to his poplin trousers.

There were a good number of people about, flying kites, lying on blankets, strolling, listening to radios. To Tyson's left lay the Doric Parthenon of the Lincoln Memorial, and to his right, the long Reflecting Pool running due east toward the massive obelisk of the Washington Monument. The setting sun cast a mellow aura over the park, the pool, and the surrounding buildings. On the north edge of the park, across Constitution Avenue, stood a phalanx of august and commanding buildings that Tyson thought looked familiar from photographs, though he couldn't identify them. He did not know Washington well, but even a stranger coming into this city by chance would know that he was in an imperial capital, a place of power, a new Rome.

It was no more than a black slash in the ground, a poignant contrast to the lofty white marble and limestone of this monumental city. It was cut into a

gently rising slope of grass, and critics had complained that it was antiheroic
and nearly invisible. Yet it was as easy to spot as the two presidential monuments that flanked it, because it was where all the people were.

Tyson approached slowly, and the nearer he drew, the quieter the park became, as if this were a protected zone, a place where it was understood that one
did not fly kites, throw Frisbees, or play radios.

The atmosphere around the black memorial was not unlike that of a funeral
home: silent, somber, subdued. An al fresco mortuary.

Though he had been to Washington on business, he had never come here.
Yet he felt he knew the place after years of media exposure. As he moved
closer, however, he realized that no photograph could capture the essence of
this vast headstone, no news film could convey the impact of its hushed presence. Unlike other shrines to the dead, this was a tactile and participatory
memorial. People were passing their fingers over the etched names, reading
them, pointing to them, making pencil rubbings of a name with any piece of
paper at hand.

Tyson stopped some ten feet from the black granite wall. On the rising lawn
behind and above the wall stood six men in jungle fatigues. They seemed to be
a permanent part of the site, soldiers frozen in time at the vertex of the black
wedges, standing precariously close to the precipice. Tyson had the impression
they were young men, but that was because he associated jungle fatigues with
young men. On closer scrutiny he saw they were men nearer to middle age, his
age.

Tyson moved closer to the wall and stood on the paved walkway that paral-
leled it. Other men of about his own age had on bits and pieces of uniforms. A
wasted man sat in a wheelchair; two men walked with canes. And there were
those in good clothing, with no visible signs of wounds, who in some subtle way
were nonetheless identifiable as veterans. Tyson saw in those faces something
he had not seen in nearly twenty years—the Thousand-Yard Stare. He felt he
was among a gathering of wraiths, and he swore they stank of the jungle and
were splattered with Asian mud. He had a sudden fear that he'd see a face he
knew. He wanted to turn and walk quickly away, before the black arms of the
outstretched walls engulfed him. He drew a breath, turned, and found himself
facing the bronze statues of the three soldiers clad in jungle fatigues. They each
seemed to be in a trancelike state, though it was not the Thousand-Yard Stare,
but an oddly lifeless look as though the sculptor had consciously tried to represent three ghosts.

He turned back and focused on the names in a tall black panel near the
vertex: *James B. Alexander, Robert J. Betz, Jack W. Klein, David J. W. Widder,
Lawrence W. Gordon.* There were no ranks, he noticed, no unit designations,
no clue as to whether they were Army, Marine, Navy, Air Force, or Coast
Guard, no hometown, age, or any vital statistic; just names arranged chronolog-
ically from the first deaths in 1959 to the last in 1975. And this, he thought, was
as it should be, just names. The mothers, fathers, wives, children, brothers, and
sisters knew all there was to know about the names.

Tyson saw flowers stuck between the stone panels, flowers strewn at the base
of the monument, photographs set against the wall. Here and there were more
impressive floral arrangements. To his right, lying on the black stone bordering
the base of the wall, was a first baseman's glove.

"Can I find a name for you?"

Tyson looked to his left. Beside him was a young girl of about sixteen, in
jeans and T-shirt. She had nice eyes and a good tan but was otherwise rather
homely. She carried a pad and pencil. Tyson said, "Excuse me?"

"I can find the location of a name."

"Oh . . . okay . . . Browder. Roy Browder."

The girl replied, "That might be a common name. Do you have a middle initial? A date of death?"

"Date of death, February 21, 1968."

"Okay. Be right back." She walked quickly to the east end of the memorial, and Tyson saw her approach a woman in the green uniform of the National Park Service. The woman had a thick registry book and was looking up names for people. The young girl, Tyson realized, was a sort of free-enterprise link between the overworked civil servant and the visitors.

Tyson looked back at the polished wall and stared beyond the white-etched names into the dark mirrored stone. The granite was reflective, he thought, in the sense that it reflected the living and that the living reflected on the dead. If that was its purpose, then the monument worked.

An attractive woman, a few years younger than Tyson, stepped onto the narrow grass border between the wall and the path. She touched her finger to a name, and Tyson looked at her reflection. He saw her lips pucker in a kiss, then turn up in a sort of wistful smile. She winked and turned. Tyson's eyes followed her, and he saw her join a man on the path. The man, Tyson thought, looked somewhat uncomfortable.

"Sir?"

Tyson turned to see the girl beside him.

"Panel 36 E. Line 95. That's over here." She pointed.

"Thanks. . . ."

She handed Tyson a green-and-black brochure. "This will help you locate other names if you know the approximate dates of death." She added, "If you'd like to make a donation to the memorial fund . . ."

"Sure." Tyson took out his wallet and gave the girl a five-dollar bill.

"Thank you." She hesitated, then said, "I like to know . . . I mean, who . . . a friend, relative . . . ?"

"A friend."

"Were you there?"

"Yes."

She nodded. "My father was killed in 1967. Before I was born. He was a career NCO. Army. Panel 22 E. Line 91. Patrick Duggan."

Tyson wondered if she was asking if he knew him. He said, "I'm sorry."

"Oh, it's not painful or anything. Just sad."

He nodded. She didn't seem anxious to leave, and it occurred to him that this rather plain-looking girl was lonely. He found that he was curious about the life of a soldier's posthumous child. Did her mother remarry? Did she live here in Washington? Did the Army really take care of its own? Or did they take her father and leave her and her family to struggle on less than a family on public assistance as he'd once read? But he knew he wasn't going to ask her any questions.

Tyson's eyes fell on the sunlit wall again. Long before there were military death benefits and widows' payments there were grand monuments to the fallen, conceived and built by the lobbies for the dead. And in the regimental mess halls, toasts were offered to the missing. But for the survivors, he thought, there was precious little in the way of glory or sustenance. If he could design a single monument to all wars, it would consist of a statue of a woman with the Thousand-Yard Stare.

The girl followed his gaze. She said, "Do you like it? The wall?"

He nodded again.

"Lots of people don't. Well, most people come here thinking they're not going to like it. But it gets to them somehow. You know?"

"Yes. I do."

"My mother said they should have put fifty-seven thousand gravestones on the west lawn of the Capitol."

"Yes, with my statue of the woman standing among them."

The girl didn't respond to this but pursued her own line of conversation. "They'd have to see them every day. The Congress. They should have done it while the war was going on. Each week they'd unload gravestones on the lawn. You know?"

"Sounds good."

The girl smiled.

Tyson and the girl stood in companionable silence for some time, then Tyson said, "Do you know who I am?"

The girl's eyes fell on his face, and she shook her head.

"Ben Tyson."

She shrugged.

Tyson shrugged in return and smiled.

The girl stuck out her hand awkwardly. "Pam Majerski."

Tyson took her hand.

She said, "My stepfather adopted me. Majerski."

Tyson squeezed her hand before he released it. "Thanks for your help. Panel 36?"

"Right. Line 95. Roy Browder. I think I had him before. Wife, I think."

Tyson turned and moved down the wall. He stepped in front of the panel. He saw the year 1968 etched in a nearby panel and saw, too, that 1968 took a lot of panels. A bad year. The worst year. It would have been a good year to spend somewhere else.

He found Browder's name and stared at it a moment, trying to remember the man and conjuring up the slightly pudgy face with the perpetual cigar jammed in the left corner of his mouth. Browder's death had moved him deeply at the time, though Tyson had not particularly liked his company commander. But Browder had been the Old Man, the embodiment of gruff, fatherly discipline, the essence of authority, the place where the buck stopped in Alpha Company.

And, on Captain Browder's death, six days after Miséricorde Hospital, Lieutenant Benjamin Tyson, twenty-six years old and with an ROTC Commission, had become commanding officer of Alpha Company. Had Browder lived, Tyson thought, he would have ultimately confessed to him. And in some way what was happening now would not be happening. The Old Man would have made it right.

Tyson moved to the next panel, then the next. He spotted the names of men he knew, men he'd seen die, men he'd seen evacuated with grisly wounds, and men he'd said goodbye to when he'd left Vietnam. He couldn't say for certain how many people from Alpha Company had contributed their names to this wall, but he thought there were at least fifty.

Tyson consulted the brochure, moved on to other panels, and saw the names of men he knew from other times and places: a childhood friend, two college classmates, men he'd trained with and served with in the States. He thought he knew an inordinate number of the 57,939 Americans listed here.

He walked slowly along the length of the wall until he realized the sun was nearly gone. He moved back to the panels that represented the year 1968. He saw the names Frederick Brontman and Irwin Selig, who had been alive when he left Vietnam, and it was the first he knew of their deaths. He found the names of Peter Santos and John Manelli, who had been killed at Hue on the same day Browder had died. He found the name of Arthur Peterson, who had been wounded in the chest and died at Miséricorde Hospital. He discovered the name of Michael DeTonq, the only man in Alpha Company to be reported missing in action. Following DeTonq's name was a cross, denoting that he was still missing, but Tyson strongly believed he was not MIA. DeTonq was MOP—missing on purpose. DeTonq, a Cajun from Louisiana, spoke passable French and had undoubtedly chosen to terminate his short military career before it terminated him. Tyson often pictured DeTonq in the arms of a sympathetic French woman. Good for him. Tyson hoped he'd survived the fall of Vietnam and somehow made it back to the States.

Tyson took out a handkerchief and wiped the sweat from his brow. He turned away from the stone and looked out over the park. Long purple shadows lay in the groves of trees. About a hundred yards away stood a solitary man in full camouflage fatigues and bush hat. Tyson thought for one uncomfortable moment that this was a true ghost, that no one but he saw the man. Then the man raised a bugle to his lips, and the last sunlight glinted off the polished brass. The air was suddenly split with the doleful, haunting sound of taps.

The dwindling crowd turned, watched, and listened. The final note hung in the hot, humid air. The man returned to a position of attention, turned smartly, and walked away.

The people around the memorial began moving off as well. Tyson stepped away from the wall, hesitated, then turned back. He ran his hand over the smooth black granite, feeling its radiant warmth, the grit-blasted names, the seams between the panels. His hand slid upward to a height of nearly eight feet, and his fingers rested on the name of Lawrence F. Cane. Killed in action at Miséricorde Hospital. Tyson had written the official letter of condolence to Cane's mother: *Dear Mrs. Cane, You may take some comfort in the knowledge that your son Larry died in the service of his country.* Which was true, Tyson thought. People did take some comfort in that. Better than losing a son in a gang war. *I knew Larry well, and he was as fine a soldier and human being as I've ever had the honor to serve with.* Well . . . but after all, speak only good of the dead. He wasn't a bad sort really. *Larry was a valuable and respected member of my platoon, and he will be missed by everyone who knew him.* All riflemen are valuable, and they're all missed. Nothing personal, just practical. *I was with him at the time of his death, and I assure you he died quickly and without pain.*

Which was, Tyson thought, the only absolutely true line in the letter. Tyson *had* been with him and *could* verify that Larry Cane died quickly and without pain because Tyson had shot him through the heart.

Sincerely yours,
Benjamin J. Tyson,
First Lieutenant,
United States Army, Infantry

19

B enjamin Tyson sat in the Garden Terrace Lounge of the elegant Four
  Seasons Hotel located at the edge of Georgetown. The Four Seasons was
  where he stayed when he traveled for Peregrine-Osaka, so this, he reasoned, was where he should stay when he traveled for the Army. He doubted,
however, that the Army was going to reimburse him. But really this was for Ben
Tyson, he thought; this was for each of the three hundred twenty-two nights
he'd stayed awake in the jungles and swamps, in fear and discomfort. They
owed him.

He hadn't changed his clothes and still wore the sweat-stained shirt and
slacks he'd worn to the monument. The air-conditioning made his skin feel
clammy, and he recalled those occasions when he'd come directly from the field
into a frigid officers' club, the Vietnamese waitresses with blue noses and toes,
coughing and sniffling, the Americans drinking cold beer and moving animatedly as though they'd just been revived with a bucket of ice water over the head.

He sprawled deeper in his armchair, put his feet on the cocktail table, and
kicked off his loafers. He regarded his toes awhile, then drank the last of his
Scotch.

A waitress approached, and Tyson ordered his third drink. He was vaguely
aware that he should be better dressed for this lounge and for this meeting. But
his socioeconomic status being vague at the moment, he thought he could dress
as he pleased.

Tyson glanced at his watch. She was late.

He reflected that he had not experienced survivor guilt to any great degree.
But sitting here in comfort in the nation's capital, surrounded by memorials
and mausoleums of one sort or another, he began to feel a certain unease, or
perhaps it was a maudlinism brought on by a combination of the black wall and
the alcohol. Tyson decided he ought not to meet her in his present state of
mind. His drink came, and he paid the bill, then rose to leave.

He spotted her coming in from the lobby and felt an unexpected disappointment in seeing that she wasn't wearing civilian clothing. Her garrison cap was
tucked in a side pouch of her black handbag, and she still carried the black
briefcase.

Karen Harper looked around the dimly lit lounge, her eyes adjusting to the
light. Tyson sat as she approached. She said, "Good evening." She extended her
hand. "I was afraid you'd left."

"Would an officer and a gentleman do that?"

She smiled as he motioned her to an upholstered chair diagonal to his. Tyson
signaled to a waitress, and Karen Harper ordered a white wine. She said to
Tyson, "This is a very nice hotel."

"Nothing but the best for our boys in uniform."

"You were authorized to stay at the Presidential. Did you get your travel
vouchers in the mail?"

Tyson swirled his glass and stared at the ice cubes. At length he replied, "My attorney advised me not to accept any government funds. In any case, I stay at the Four Seasons when I'm in Washington."

"If you got a haircut and dressed up a bit you could use one of the officers' clubs in the area. Cheap drinks." She asked, "Do you intend to report to Fort Hamilton as ordered, in uniform?"

"I'm not sure."

"I'd strongly advise you to do so."

"My status is not settled."

"Your status is clear. You are on active duty."

He shrugged.

She asked in a conversational tone, "Did you get your business taken care of today?"

Tyson nodded. "I met with a fellow who has done the legal groundwork to establish a nonprofit national defense fund for me. Then I met with a lawyer from the Reserve Officers Association, over on Constitution Avenue. Then I had lunch with some people from the Disabled American Veterans. I have a ten percent disability as you know. Actually I think it's seven and a half percent, but what the hell. Anyway, they asked me to join, and I did. After lunch I met with a delegation from the Veterans of Foreign Wars, and then I called on my congressman."

"You've had a peripatetic day."

"Right. And I moved around a lot too."

She smiled, then said, "It's good to keep busy."

"Well, Major, you have to hustle when you're trying to beat a firing squad."

"Don't be melodramatic."

Tyson picked up his drink. "I had the feeling today that I have a lot of support. That the government and the Army are following an unpopular course of action."

Karen Harper replied, "Well, that's the strength of a pluralistic society, Mr. Tyson. Free people rally around a cause or issue and fight the government. I think that's very healthy."

"Do you understand what I'm telling you?"

"Yes. The government is aware of all this. But to use a military expression, the Rubicon has been crossed."

"Are they looking for a way to retreat with honor?"

"I don't think so. They can't."

Tyson commented, "Then the hell with them. They'll get a fight."

She said, "I've always thought that ninety percent of wars, trials, and fistfights were started because no one knew how to back off while saving face. Perhaps if people didn't feel the *need* to save face, we could avoid conflict."

Tyson snorted. "That's a very feminine attitude. Face *is* important, and conflict is not necessarily bad."

The waitress brought Karen Harper's wine.

Tyson raised his glass. "To a short relationship."

She touched her glass to his. "Don't be sulky."

They both drank.

She said, "I forgot your umbrella."

"So I see."

"I think I left it on the plane."

"It was a gift from my grandmother, right before she died."

"Then she won't know I lost it."

They stared at each other awhile, then smiled simultaneously. Tyson noticed she was in a somewhat lighter mood than last time. He wondered if this was because she had some good news for him. But based on the conversation so far, that wasn't likely. More likely she'd just gotten some good news for herself or had sex or bought a new shade of lip gloss.

She said, "I'm to advise you again of your right to remain silent and to have an attorney present and of your other rights in regard to this investigation."

"I'll waive that."

"Okay." She surprised him by signaling to a waitress. The waitress approached, and Karen Harper motioned toward the nearly full glass of wine. "Please take this and bring me a glass of Principessa Gavia. Do you have that?"

"Yes, ma'am. Only by the bottle."

"Fine."

The waitress took the glass and moved off.

Tyson said, "When in Rome . . ."

She replied, "It's actually a Piedmont wine from the Banfi estate at Gavia."

"Really."

"I visited the winery once."

"Are you going to drink the whole bottle?"

"I only want a glass."

"You wouldn't have ordered that at the Presidential."

"Probably not." She continued, "I've done some further work on this investigation. Mostly telephone calls plus some records research. I contacted Andrew Picard by phone. He was very reluctant to tell me the names of your two platoon members who gave him his story. But I persuaded him it would be in the best interests of justice."

Tyson recalled that Picard was an ex-officer and might also be vulnerable. He replied, "I'm sure you were convincing." He lit a cigarette.

She stared at him awhile, then said, "Well, aren't you going to ask me who they were?"

"No, I'm playing it cool."

She replied, "Well, I'll pretend you asked because then I have to tell you. One of the men who related the Miséricorde Hospital story to Picard was your former platoon medic, Steven Brandt." She glanced at him. Tyson showed no reaction.

She continued, "He's now a physician in Boston. An orthopedist. I spoke to him by phone."

"Did you?"

"Yes. And he reiterated and confirmed the story he gave to Picard about the massacre."

"Did he?"

"And he elaborated on it somewhat. That is, he'd read Picard's book, of course, and he added some details."

Tyson knew it was Brandt, hoped it was Brandt, and not one of the others. But there *was* another man, and Tyson had no idea who it could be.

Karen Harper continued, "I'm obligated to tell you about Brandt; that is, the name of a possible witness against you. But because his testimony was unsworn, there was no transcript and no recording made. Therefore I'm not obligated to tell you precisely what he said. However, if we proceed to a formal investigation, you or your attorney will have the opportunity to cross-examine any sworn testimony Dr. Brandt might give. Do you understand this point of law?"

"I remember."

"Good." She seemed thoughtful, then said, "Was there any bad blood between you and Dr. Brandt?"

"He wasn't a doctor then, only a scared punk kid like the rest of us. The title 'doctor' has some cachet, and I don't want it used in these proceedings. How's that for a point of law?"

"I'll make a note of it. How about the bad blood?"

"No."

"Are you certain? Mr. Brandt—Spec/4 Brandt—was a conscientious objector. There were often bad feelings between—"

"That's not true. The medics who were COs were as fine a group of soldiers as you could find. I respected their beliefs, their bravery, retrieving wounded under fire, carrying that huge medical bag that made them a better target than my lieutenant bar made me."

She nodded, then said, "But you're speaking in general terms. Did you feel that way about Brandt?"

"I'll think about that." Tyson stubbed his cigarette into an ashtray. "Okay, who was the other man who spoke to Picard?"

"Richard Farley."

"Farley?"

"Yes. Do you remember him?"

"Vaguely."

"What do you remember about him?"

"Nothing of any consequence."

"Was he a good soldier?"

"Check his record."

"I'm asking you."

Tyson thought a moment. *Farley. Why Farley? Why not?*

"Mr. Tyson?"

"He was . . . not particularly bright, not particularly brave—somewhat below average in all areas."

"Any bad blood between you? I ask that because if there was an incident it might be possible to show that Farley is not unbiased toward you."

"I understand. But there was no bad blood between us. Neither was there any love lost between officers and enlisted men. Actually, it was a classical love-hate relationship."

"You and Farley?"

"Me and them."

A busboy brought a wine bucket and stand, setting it beside Tyson. A sommelier approached followed by the waitress. Tyson observed to Karen Harper, "This is getting serious."

The waitress set down two glasses and the sommelier displayed the label to Tyson. Tyson said, "I only read Scotch labels. The lady ordered the wine."

The wine steward bowed his head. "Very good, sir." He pivoted smoothly and held the bottle toward Karen Harper. "Major?"

She nodded.

He drew the cork and set it on the cocktail table in front of her, then poured a few ounces into her glass. She sipped the wine. "Fine."

"Very good, Major." He filled her glass and turned to Tyson. "Sir?" he said, with the expertise of one who recognizes an oenophobe when he sees one.

Tyson shrugged. "Good chaser for the Scotch."

The sommelier filled Tyson's glass, submerged the bottle in the bucket, bowed, and left.

The waitress lingered a moment, looking at Tyson, then glanced at Harper, and recognition dawned on her face. She said, "Can I get you anything else?"

"The bill," said Tyson.

She turned and left.

Karen Harper sipped her wine in silence.

Tyson tasted his. "Not bad. How would you describe it?"

She replied, "It has a fresh, perfumy bouquet. It is clean, well balanced, with a light frizzante and a haunting aftertaste."

"That's just what I was thinking." He set his glass down and said, "By the way, the waitress recognized me. Maybe you too."

She nodded. "I thought she might have."

He said, "In New York, there are waitresses and such who get paid by gossip columnists to report on newsworthy people having a tête-à-tête in a dark lounge."

Karen Harper seemed a bit surprised by that. "Well, I don't think—"

"I don't want to be here when a photographer from the *American Investigator* arrives." He stood.

"We could go to a pub I know in Georgetown. About five minutes' walk—"

"I'm tired of bars. Room 618, if you want to come up. Five-minute intervals, sound and light security, three knocks, password is 'lollipop'—the enemy can't say that. They say 'rorripop.' Did you know that?" He nodded toward the wine bucket. "That's on the Army." He turned and left.

20

B en Tyson stood at his room bar and poured a miniature bottle of Scotch into a glass of ice and soda. He looked around the room. A hanging lamp cast a soft glow over the sitting area. The triple-sized bed was lit by a table lamp, and Tyson switched it off, leaving the bed in darkness.

There were three solid raps on the door, and he moved toward the foyer. "Password."

After a moment of silence, he heard her say, "Rorripop."

He smiled, then opened the door.

She stood at the threshold a moment, then entered wordlessly.

He motioned her toward the couch on the far side of the room. She went to it but did not sit.

Tyson took a split of white wine from the bar refrigerator and filled a stem glass. He set the glass on the coffee table in front of her. "Domestic. Okay?"

She didn't reply.

Tyson took his drink to an upholstered chair opposite the couch and sat.

After a full minute of mutual silence, she said, "I really shouldn't be here."

"Neither should I."

"I have to put this in my report. I mean, where we are conducting this interview."

"You're free to leave."

She said, "I'm thinking of your interests too. You're a married man. . . ."

"That is the least of my problems. Listen, Major Karen Harper, I didn't ask for a female investigator. And I'm cooperating in this investigation. If I choose to conduct this interview in the privacy and comfort of my room, and if you're uncomfortable, we can reschedule this for another time and place. I can't promise I'll be as talkative then, and I may have a lawyer present."

She seemed indecisive for a moment, then sat on the couch. "Where were we?"

"Downstairs in the lounge. Farley and I." Tyson settled back in his chair.

"Yes. Farley is a paraplegic. He was badly wounded by shrapnel in the spine about two months after you left Vietnam. Did you know that?"

"I seem to remember someone writing to me about that." He'd maintained some contact with the platoon for a few months. Then, through normal attrition—death, wounds, sickness, rotation back to the States, and transfers—there was no one left. The first platoon of Alpha Company had, like a college fraternity, metamorphosed into a different platoon, only the name remained the same—new blood in; old, tired, and dead blood out. A succession of new officers and new riflemen, who became old men if they lived longer than ninety days. Stories and myths were handed down: tales of cowardice and bravery, and the tales changed with each telling as the oral history of the platoon was transmitted like a compressed epic poem in the vernacular of the GI. He often wondered what legacy he'd left.

Karen Harper broke into his thoughts. "Farley lives in Jersey City now. He spends a good deal of time in VA hospitals. He is drug-dependent and suffers from emotional disturbances."

"Good witness for the prosecution." Tyson added, "Sorry to hear about that though."

"I spoke to him briefly by telephone. His story seems to corroborate that of Brandt."

Tyson kicked off his loafers and rubbed his feet against the thick rug. "You can make yourself comfortable."

"I'm comfortable." She glanced around the softly lit room. "Very nice. Your company does quite well with government contracts."

"Those are not unrelated thoughts."

"No."

"I worked hard to get where I am—was."

She nodded. "I didn't mean to be offensive."

"No, I don't think you did. We're from different worlds, Major." He thought a moment, then said, "To use a lover's expression, this is not working."

She stared at him before replying, "Let's try to make it work."

He shrugged.

She said, "Richard Farley is a potential witness for the prosecution. You will have the right to cross-examine him if—"

"How did Picard find him? How did Picard find Brandt?"

"Interesting. It seems that Picard, after his chance conversation with Sister Teresa in France, placed an ad in the locator section of the First Cavalry Division newspaper." She opened her briefcase and handed Tyson a photocopy of the locator section dated some two years before.

Tyson looked at the circled ad and read: *Historian looking for veterans of Alpha Co., First Battalion, Seventh Cav. who served during the first three months of 1968. Specifically would want to hear from anyone from the second platoon who was at the battle of Miséricorde Hospital at Hue. Researching same for private client. All replies kept strictly confidential, anonymity assured.*

Which, thought Tyson, was bullshit. He noticed a post office box address in Sag Harbor. He laid the ad on the coffee table.

She said, "The First Cavalry Division informs me that they send *you* that newspaper."

Tyson nodded. About the only thing he ever glanced at in that newspaper was the sometimes interesting locator section: men looking for lost buddies, women looking for wayward men, historians doing research—that sort of thing. But he'd obviously missed this one. Brandt had not. *Fate*. He said, "Brandt and Farley answered this?"

"Actually only Brandt did. Sometime later, at Picard's urging, Brandt supplied a corroborating witness in the person of Richard Farley."

Tyson nodded. "How did Brandt know the whereabouts of Farley? Why did Brandt come forward in the first place?"

She shrugged. "When I spoke to Brandt he confined his answers to what he saw at Miséricorde Hospital. If he's subpoenaed, we'll discover the answers to your other questions."

"Was Brandt perhaps the medic who treated Farley after he was hit?"

"Funny, but I asked that too. According to Farley, he was."

"That's interesting. What else did Farley say?"

"Not much that was comprehensible. He seemed very distraught. He cried actually."

Tyson's eyes met hers, and she turned away. Tyson stood. "Want another?"

"I haven't touched this one."

He walked to the refrigerator and opened it. "Hey, here's a bottle of champs." He popped the cork on a split of Moët and poured two glasses of the champagne, then carried the glasses back to the sitting area. "Here. Join me in a toast."

She took the glass. "To what?"

Tyson raised his glass. "To Richard Farley and the other two million seven hundred thousand who returned to pollute our society with wasted limbs, damaged chromosomes, and sick minds."

She lowered her glass. "I won't drink to that."

"Well, I will." He raised his glass, then suddenly flung it across the room where it shattered against the bar cabinet. He strode quickly out of the room into the bathroom and slammed the door.

Karen Harper sat motionless and listened to the water running. She noticed her hands were shaking. She reached for her briefcase, then released it, then reached for it again and stood.

Tyson came back into the room, motioned her into her seat, and sat down without a word.

She noticed he'd splashed water on his face and combed his hair. She detected the faint scent of a good cologne.

Tyson said, "Go on."

Karen Harper cleared her throat. She said, "May I have a cigarette?"

"You don't smoke."

"Sometimes I do."

He held his pack of cigarettes toward her, and she took one. He lit it, noticing that she held it awkwardly and drew on it as though she were sucking through a straw. She exhaled and continued, "As I indicated in our first meeting, I've located some members of your platoon. Two, to be exact. Since I last spoke to you I've spoken to them by telephone."

Tyson did not reply.

She continued, "One is a former squad leader named Paul Sadowski, who lives in Chicago, and the other is Anthony Scorello, who now lives in a suburb of San Francisco. Do you remember them?"

"Vaguely."

"I thought men remembered who they served with in combat."

"Macho myth."

Karen Harper regarded him for some time, then asked, "Do you want to know what Sadowski and Scorello said?"

"Sure." Tyson felt his heart thumping, and his mouth went dry. "Sure. What did they say?"

She leaned toward him and watched him, making no pretense of not noticing his unease. Tyson stared back at her, angry that she would play it out like this. He snapped, "Well, what did they say, Major?"

"They said," she replied evenly, "exactly what you said."

Their eyes met, and neither looked away. Tyson settled back in his chair. "So. There you have it."

"Have what?"

"*My* corroboration. Two against two. And if I offer sworn testimony in my own behalf—"

"Neither a grand jury nor a court-martial takes a vote of witnesses, Lieutenant. They would be interested, however, in who is perjuring himself."

Tyson felt his confidence returning and said curtly, "I would be interested in *why* Brandt and Farley would perjure *themselves.*"

She nodded appreciatively, drew on her cigarette, then stubbed it out. She said, "Whether it is perjury or truth, Mr. Tyson, I think that ultimately only you can tell me why they told Picard this story. Only you can tell me why Sadowski and Scorello told me a different story." She stared at him, but he did not reply.

She leaned across the cocktail table and lowered her voice. "Lies are destructive and spread like malignancy to the innocent and guilty alike. I want the lies to stop. I want *you* to put an end to them, if not for your own sake, then for the sake of the innocent and for the sake of your country. End the nightmare for everyone. Tell me what happened on 15 February 1968. What *happened?*"

Tyson spoke with no inflection in his voice. "If I know the truth, and I haven't told you, it's because I'm not convinced that you, the country, the Army, or anyone deserves to know the truth."

"What can I do to convince you?"

"Probably nothing. Maybe just get closer to it by stages. Truth should be hard-won. The truth is only recognized as the truth after all the lies are told and discounted. You won't appreciate the truth or even begin to fathom it unless you take a tortuous road to find it."

She nodded. "But you *will* tell me? I mean, sometime after this is all over? You will tell me, personally and privately, if not publicly?"

"I may. I may very well."

"But now I have to work hard."

"Yes. I had to work hard."

"Fair enough." She sat back in her chair.

Tyson looked at her in the dim light of the lamp. He had the sudden impression that she was more obsessed with this thing than she ought to be. It occurred to him that if he could understand the source of her obsession he could outflank her and the Army.

Like every good interrogator, she had made a sudden switch from inquisitor to confessor. That often worked with the smug patriot or religious fanatic, happy in their martyrdom, or with the mentally deficient who didn't understand the consequences of confession. But since he didn't fit any of these types, he saw no reason to offer a confession. And it wasn't the truth they wanted anyway. The truth reflected more unfavorably on them, on the system, than it did on him. What they wanted was a final offering to Mars, a last scrap of flesh, because 57,939 sacrifices weren't enough, and the soothsayers had somehow divined that 57,940 was what was required to put the war to rest for all time.

But, Tyson thought, since he didn't recall having started the war, he saw no good reason for sacrificing himself to end it. Marcy, he realized, would be pleased with that reasoning.

He said aloud but not to Karen Harper, "I made it home. I'm standing on home base. You can't tag me out now. What is the statute of limitations on being tagged out?"

Karen Harper stood and moved to the large picture window. She looked up Pennsylvania Avenue toward the lighted White House. She said, "There in that mansion lives a man who knows your name, who has memos on his desk with your name on them."

Tyson looked at her dark profile against the window.

She continued, "That man deals with issues of global importance and national survival every day. From time to time, because of the structure of our laws, he must personally deal with the cases of individual citizens. He is Commander in Chief of the armed forces, your boss and mine. He can grant clemency, immunity, and pardons. He can commission you into the armed forces, and he can rescind your commission. Somewhere along the line, he will have to make a decision regarding you—before, during, or after a court-martial." She turned her head toward Tyson. "Soon, in the next few days, he is scheduled to hold a press conference. Your name will come up. He, or his aides, have prepared a brief statement regarding your case." She added, "I strongly suspect that he wishes he'd never heard your name and hopes he never hears it again after that press conference."

"That would make two of us."

"The nation, Mr. Tyson, wishes they'd never heard your name."

"Then that makes all of us." He asked, "How about you?"

"I'm glad I met you. You are a remarkable man. . . ." She added self-consciously, "A man by whom I will probably judge other men."

He stared at her for a moment, then remarked, "Having said that, you probably want to leave."

"Should I?"

He rubbed his lip contemplatively, then replied, "No. I don't think we will speak again like this, alone and without witnesses or counsel. We may as well both get the most out of it."

"Yes, there are certain dynamics that take place when only two people are present. . . . It gets complicated and phony when there is even one more person. We couldn't speak like this."

Tyson put his right leg on the cocktail table and abruptly pulled his trouser leg up, revealing his shin and knee. "Come here. Look at this."

There was something of the infantry officer in his voice that compelled her to respond quickly and automatically.

"Look. This is something I wouldn't do at a formal hearing. Closer."

She stepped closer and looked down at the thick, curving purple scar.

"Not much as far as wounds go, Major. But when it happens to you, your stomach heaves and your skin goes all clammy."

She kept staring at the old wound as if studying it for some meaning.

Tyson said, "A shrink once spent two hours telling me about the synergistic effect of a physical scar on a mental scar. The great truth he revealed was this: The disfigurement and pain is a daily reminder of the traumatic episode." Tyson pulled the trouser leg down. "Well, no kidding."

She looked up and said, "A shrink?"

Tyson realized he should not have revealed that information. He replied, "A friend. Cocktail party chatter."

She nodded, but he saw she didn't believe that. She asked, "Did Brandt treat you?"

Tyson glanced up at her but didn't reply.

"Did Brandt treat you?"

"No." Tyson stood. He paced to the center of the room, turned, and faced her.

"Why not? He was your platoon medic."

Tyson did not reply.

"Was he there at the time you were wounded?"

"Ask him."

"I'm asking you."

"Ask *him!*"

She was momentarily startled, then said, "All right. I will." At length she said, "In addition to the chapter in Picard's book that deals with the Miséricorde Hospital incident, Picard mentions you in two other chapters."

She stooped down and retrieved Picard's book from her briefcase, placing it under the light of the hanging lamp over the cocktail table. She said, "You are mentioned in an early chapter—the firefight at Phu Lai on the first day of the Tet Offensive. Then you are mentioned at the end of the book, the aftermath of the battle of Hue."

She opened the book to a marked place and, still kneeling, read:

> The battle was officially declared over on 26 February, and military communiqués spoke of "mopping-up operations." But the battle was not over just because the American military declared it to be. For the Marines and Army personnel still engaged in shooting matches with communist troops in and around the city, there was precious little difference between battle and "mopping up."
>
> Ironically, one of the last American casualties at Hue was the man whose platoon had made one of the first contacts of the Tet Offensive, Lieutenant Benjamin Tyson.
>
> Tyson's platoon, badly mauled in the market square at Phu Lai on 30 January, had gone on to Miséricorde Hospital on 15 February, then was helicoptered to a secure beach area for a few days of rest and refitting. But the battle of Hue raged on, and the barely fit platoon was helicoptered with the rest of Alpha Company, Fifth Battalion, Seventh Cavalry, to an area two kilometers north of Hue. The company, still under the command of Captain Roy Browder, patrolled south toward the city.
>
> On 21 February, Alpha Company found themselves on the north bank of the Perfume River. Across the river was the Gia Hoi quarter of Hue, a triangle-shaped point of land nestled in a sharp bend of the river. Most of the Gia Hoi suburb was still under communist control.
>
> Captain Browder, apparently on his own initiative, commandeered a number of flimsy watercraft from the local villagers and crossed the river at dusk. After they reached the opposite bank, the company came into contact with an enemy unit dug into the high ground above the riverbank. The two groups exchanged fire in the growing darkness. Several men of Alpha Company were wounded, and two men of Tyson's first platoon, Peter Santos and John Manelli, were killed. Also killed was Captain Browder.

At daybreak, Tyson, the last officer in the company, received radio orders making him Alpha Company's commander. The enemy had disappeared during the night, and Tyson moved Alpha Company away from the river into an area known as the Strawberry Patch. This was a semirural section of the Gia Hoi suburb of Hue, a place we would describe today as a gentrified exurb. There, in the Strawberry Patch, Alpha Company encountered thousands of wretched refugees. And there they also discovered the first of the mass graves that held the approximately three thousand citizens of Hue massacred by the Viet Cong and North Vietnamese.

Meanwhile, a South Vietnamese ranger battalion had also crossed the river and was making its way south. On 26 February, this unit, with supporting fire from Alpha Company, stormed the last stronghold in Gia Hoi, the Cambodian Pagoda across the street from the high school. It was then that Gia Hoi was considered clear, and the battle of Hue was declared over. But this was premature. Whether by design or circumstances, hundreds of enemy troops remained in Hue's main suburb of Gia Hoi.

On 29 February, Alpha Company was engaged in aiding refugees and searching for Viet Cong hiding among the masses of displaced civilians. Tyson had set up checkpoints on a road that led to the east gate of the Citadel wall. His men examined civilian ID cards, handed out C rations, and set up a medical aid station. Suddenly rockets streaked out of a nearby grove of fruit trees. Several soldiers and civilians were hit by flying shrapnel, and Lieutenant Tyson suffered a wound to the knee. As the refugees scattered, the enemy began firing automatic weapons at the Americans who had taken cover in a drainage ditch and were firing back. After ten or fifteen minutes, the enemy broke contact.

The wounded of Alpha Company, including its last officer, Benjamin Tyson, were medevaced to a hospital ship in the South China Sea.

Another irony of this tale is that Lieutenant Tyson, whose platoon had acted so inhumanely at Miséricorde Hospital, was wounded while on a mission of mercy. Alpha Company itself, now without a single officer and with over half its men killed or wounded, was finally ordered to stand down. They were helicoptered to Camp Evans, the First Air Cavalry Forward Base Camp, and given two weeks of relatively safe perimeter guard duty. Replacements of officers, sergeants, and enlisted men filled the ranks of the decimated company, as the original men found increasingly ingenious ways of removing themselves from that illfated unit.

Hue, that smoking, burning cauldron where so many had died, was peaceful on the morning of March the first. The birds had returned, and no gunfire could be heard for the first time in over a month. But the proud city, often described as the most precious piece of Vietnam, lay devastated, its inhabitants totally demoralized, their once legendary spirit crushed for all time.

And yet the killing was not quite over. There was still the matter of revenge. This writer personally observed the National

Police "Black Squads" rounding up hundreds of men, women, and students accused by their neighbors of having aided the occupying communist invaders. These unfortunate people were taken to various places in and around the city and presumably executed since they were never heard from again.

As a young Marine officer, standing on a tower of the Citadel, I watched the endless funeral processions winding through the rubble-strewn streets. Hue, which had thumbed its nose at the war, would never be the same again, and neither would the American soldiers who fought there.

Vietnam's most celebrated songwriter at the time, a young man named Trihn Cong Son, was living in Hue during the battle. In March, with the Vietnamese spring in full bloom, he wrote a ballad, a stanza of which is translated here:

> When I went to the Strawberry Patch
> I sang on top of corpses
> I saw, I saw, I saw on the road
> An old father hugging the corpse of his
> Frost-cold child.
> When I went to the Strawberry Patch
>   of an afternoon
> I saw, I saw, I saw pits and trenches
>   filled with
> The corpses of my brothers and
>   my sisters.

Karen Harper closed the book and looked up at Tyson. The room was still, and neither spoke.

Finally Tyson said, "I just realized that it must have been as unsettling for Picard to write that book as it was for me to read it. He smelled the same evil smell that I did."

Karen Harper nodded. She said, "I'd like to know what happened to you during that ten or fifteen minutes of the firefight."

"I bled."

"Yes, of course you did. And you were in pain. And a medic should have gotten to you. But . . ." She stood. "Well, you said there was no bad blood between you and Brandt, but I strongly suspect there was."

Tyson sat on the edge of the bed. He said, "If you suspect that Brandt did not tell Picard everything that happened at the Strawberry Patch, why would you believe Brandt's selective perceptions of the events at Miséricorde Hospital?"

"I never said I did. What did Brandt do or fail to do at the Strawberry Patch?"

"You find out. Then you tell me. Then I'll tell you if you're right."

"All right." She paused, then said, "Picard lives in Sag Harbor on Long Island. Did you know that?"

"That was on the book jacket."

"Yes . . . and it's an odd coincidence that you and your family are summering there."

Tyson rose from the bed and crossed to the cocktail table. He picked up his drink. "Partly coincidence, partly fate. Partly . . . reading that on the jacket reminded me of the place. We used to go out there . . . long ago."

She said, "You may run into him out there."

"Right." He reflected a moment, then said, "People out there have these neat mailboxes by the side of the road with their last names on them." He glanced at her. "I guess you know about rural mailboxes. Anyway, you read all sorts of famous names. But there is an unwritten rule of privacy. Well, I used to see the name Picard, but I never associated it with Andrew Picard the novelist, probably because I never heard of him. Anyway, down the road from a house I rented some years ago was a mailbox with the name Algren. I found out it was Nelson Algren, the guy who wrote *The Man with the Golden Arm.* I loved that book, and I had a copy of it. I wanted to knock on his door and ask him to autograph it. But I didn't want to violate that rule of privacy. Then some months later I read that he died. So my book is unsigned. But I have this other book, by Andrew Picard, and I think I'd like his autograph, before something happens to *him.*"

She raised her eyebrows. "Don't do anything . . . that will get you into trouble."

Tyson sat on the arm of the upholstered chair and stared out the window.

She said abruptly, "Are you separated?"

He was taken aback by the question, but answered, "Yes."

"Is there any chance of a reconciliation?"

"I suppose . . . I don't think it's . . . I mean I think we're just separated for the duration. Not legally. Why?"

"Just curious."

"Are you?" Tyson lit a cigarette.

Karen Harper said, "I'm sorry. I mean about your marriage. And your job."

"Well, that's life though. You can't be suspected of mass murder without there being a few inconveniences attached."

"It's easy to be bitter—"

Tyson suddenly jumped to his feet. He felt tired, angry, sick of the subject of murder. "Oh, Christ, Major, I don't need any more damned sympathy. I've had enough of that today."

"Sorry—"

"If I'm a mass murderer, then I don't deserve the sympathy. If I'm not, I'll sue the pants off everyone and retire to Switzerland." Tyson continued, "Do you know where else I was today? I went to the memorial. . . . I could stand here all fucking night and tell you what passed through my mind in ten minutes there. But it's all been said. I mean it's all there in that great big black fucking wall. Do me a favor. Go there. Look at yourself in the wall. Take your god-damned list of Alpha Company and find them in the wall. Listen, I don't care about myself. But how in the name of God can the government bring further discredit on those poor bastards? Go there, Major, and talk to the dead and explain your course of action to them."

She nodded slowly. "I *will* go there."

Tyson suddenly felt fatigued and slumped back into his chair. He closed his eyes.

Karen Harper walked to the window and stared out of it. Finally she turned from the window and said, "Can I make you a drink?"

He looked at her in the dim light and nodded.

She crossed to the bar and made him a Scotch and soda, then carried it back and handed it to him. She said, "I'm not feeling very well. Can we continue this another time?"

"No. Finish it up."

"Are you sure . . . ?"

"Finish it. Tonight."

She nodded and sat on the couch across from him. "I'm not feeling sorry for you. I'm feeling sorry for myself."

"Good. Press on, Major."

Karen Harper looked across the cocktail table at Benjamin Tyson, then drew a typed sheet of paper from her briefcase and glanced at it. She said, "Based on Picard's book and on Army records and on the statements of Brandt, Farley, Sadowski, and Scorello, I've compiled this list of five additional men who were present at the hospital and who we believe are alive today." Harper read, "Dan Kelly, Hernando Beltran, Lee Walker, Harold Simcox, and Louis Kalane." She handed the list to Tyson and said, "Could you add any names to this list?"

Tyson took the list and scanned the names. "No . . . well, yes. Holzman and Moody."

She replied, "Kurt Holzman was killed in a motorcycle accident fifteen years ago. Robert Moody died of cancer two years ago. That's why they're not on the list."

"I see. . . ." He put the paper on the cocktail table. Picard had mentioned the names of most of the platoon members in his book but had not included the usual appendix of "Where They Are Now." Picard obviously did not know where they were, or he'd have contacted them as he'd contacted Brandt and Farley and had tried to interview Tyson himself. Picard, though, when he'd had his photograph done at the wall, could have taken the trouble to look at the names behind him. Tyson said, "I just learned today that Brontman and Selig were killed in action after I left Vietnam."

"Yes, they were. How did you learn that?"

"I saw their names."

She nodded. "Yes, of course." She inquired, "By the way, did you find your personal journal, or platoon log, or whatever you kept?"

"I didn't keep a log."

Her eyebrows rose to indicate incredulity. "I was told all officers kept some sort of logbook or journal. How could you remember radio frequencies, platoon rosters, promotions, guard duty, grid coordinates, and all that, without written entries in some sort of book?"

Tyson sat back and stared thoughtfully at a point above Karen Harper's head. In a steamer trunk in his basement, that held much of his war memorabilia, he'd found his tattered, water-stained log, bound in furry gray hide, which according to the itinerant Chinese stationer who'd sold it to him was elephant hide, though Tyson suspected the deceased animal to be a rat. The daily entries were written in GI-issue blue ballpoint pen, now turned light violet. The paper was yellowed and water-stained, and the writing was barely legible. It was, however, legible enough to spark his memory, and as he'd flipped the pages, names, places, and incidents returned to him in a way that Picard's book was not able to conjure up for him.

The entry for 15 February had begun in much the same way as other days: *BMNT* [Beginning of Morning Nautical Twilight] *0632 hrs. 68 F, rainy, cold, windy.* Then followed the platoon roster, people on sick call, notes regarding resupply, a change in a radio frequency, grid coordinate objectives, and other small details of infantry life in the field. He'd made one personal note that morning that read: *Morale awful.*

The next entry for that date was written in almost total darkness sometime after sundown, the words scrawled across two pages. It read: *Platoon on verge of mutiny. Overheard death threats. Filed false radio report re: hospital battle this* A.M. *Investigate. God—*

And there it ended. *God what?* he thought. *God forgive? God help us?* He'd forgotten what he was going to write.

He had slid the book into his waistband as someone drew close in the dark and spoke to him; they might not think to search his body for his logbook.

Investigate. And they were. But not, unfortunately, posthumously. The entry in itself was not revealing, but in light of recent developments it was incriminating enough; incriminating enough to put him behind bars. Yet he could not bring himself to destroy the book and had mailed it to his sister Laurie in Atlanta for safekeeping.

"Lieutenant Tyson? *Did* you keep a log?"

He looked at her. "Actually I did. But I recall that after I was evacuated to a hospital ship it was lost."

"Lost."

"Yes, along with most of my personal effects. They helicoptered you onto the ship, pretty nurses stripped you and scrubbed you, and injected you, and what personal effects you had were put into a small plastic bag. Government property was put into another bag. Give back to Caesar that which is Caesar's. You were damaged meat that needed processing and mending. And if you couldn't be mended, then *you* were put into a plastic bag. Give back to God that which is God's. Get it?"

She seemed to have some trouble following him, then said, "So . . . the logbook was . . ."

"Probably put into the government bag and recycled or burned or whatever they did with bloody clothes and equipment. When my bag of personal effects was returned—watch, wallet, letters, and cigarette lighter—I noticed my diary was missing."

She nodded, and Tyson had the impression she appreciated a well-constructed lie. She said, "That would have been a nice keepsake, the basis for your memoirs."

"I don't think anyone is interested in my memoirs."

"But they are."

Tyson lit a cigarette. "So, these five—Kelly, Beltran, Walker, Simcox, and Kalane—are unaccounted for?"

Karen Harper nodded. "But we're looking for them." She drew another piece of paper from her briefcase. "I'll give you a rundown." She glanced at the typed sheet. "There were, we believe, nineteen of you who approached that hospital on the afternoon of 15 February 1968. Does that sound right?"

"I suppose. Except we didn't know it was a hospital."

She looked annoyed. "The building. Structure. Edifice."

"Right."

"Of the nineteen, we are in contact with five—Brandt, Farley, Sadowski, Scorello, and you." She continued, "Arthur Peterson was wounded by a bullet to the chest during the . . . assault or approach to the hospital and died there. Correct?"

"Correct."

"Moody was lightly wounded but was returned to duty the following week."

"Correct."

"According to what you told me, Larry Cane was killed in the room-to-room fighting. The Army death certificate lists a bullet through the heart. Correct?"

Tyson said nothing.

She looked at him a few seconds, then said again, "A bullet through the heart."

Tyson nodded.

She continued, "Two men, Peter Santos and John Manelli, were killed at Hue in the incident described in Picard's book. Correct?"

"Correct."

"That was the day Captain Browder was killed and you became company commander."

"Right."

"And Michael DeTonq disappeared in the city of Hue on 29 February, the same day you were wounded. He has never been accounted for."

Tyson did not respond.

She added, "And you were evacuated that day, leaving your platoon with thirteen men who had been at the scene of that incident. Later, after you'd gone back to the States, Brontman and Selig were killed, as we know. Holzman and Moody died, as I said, in civilian life, leaving five possible witnesses: you, Brandt, Farley, Sadowski, and Scorello, whose whereabouts we know; and five witnesses who we believe to be alive but whose whereabouts are unknown at present: Kelly, Beltran, Walker, Simcox, and Kalane. Also one possible witness, Michael DeTonq, who is officially listed as missing in action and presumed dead. Is that correct?"

Tyson glanced at his copy of the typed sheet. "Sounds right."

"Have you ever heard from any of these men who are unaccounted for?"

Tyson shook his head. Men sometimes kept in touch after having shared the common experience of war. In fact, there were reunions sponsored by the First Cavalry Division Association. *But,* he thought, *we shared something that would make it unlikely we would attend such reunions or that we'd send Christmas cards to one another.*

"What do you think happened to Michael DeTonq?"

"How would I know?"

"Do you think he deserted?"

"He's listed as missing. Why dishonor his memory?"

"If he deserted, there is no honor attached to his memory."

Tyson replied curtly, "Why cause pain to his family?"

"What sort of pain? If he deserted, he may be alive. That would give them some hope."

"Hope is nothing more than deferred despair. Leave it alone."

She said, "This is important. He is a potential witness, perhaps a witness for you. The Army commission on MIAs will investigate his status, if even a shred of evidence can be found to suggest he may be alive . . . perhaps a statement from you indicating why you believe he deserted, as opposed to the official conclusion of missing, presumed dead."

"Even if he did desert I doubt he survived the fall of Vietnam."

"He may have made it back to the States before then. If so, he could be back with his people in rural Louisiana. And the statute of limitations on desertion has run out."

"Has it? Who writes these laws? And who gives a damn anyway? Not Michael DeTonq. Not me."

She seemed deep in thought, then said, "Under the category of silver linings, then. Okay? If nothing else comes of this, help the Army account for another one of its lost men. Tell me something I can transmit to the Army commission on MIAs."

Tyson rested his chin in his hand contemplatively, then replied in a faraway tone, "When I was wounded, as the helicopter was landing to take me away, Michael DeTonq knelt beside me, lit a cigarette for me, and said, 'The war is over for you today. For me too. We'll meet again, back in the world. *Adieu, mon ami.'* "

Karen Harper leaned forward. "May I write that down?"

"Yes."

She took a notebook and pen from her purse and wrote, then read it back to him. "Is that correct?"

"Yes."

"And from what he said and perhaps how he said it and under the circumstances, you had the impression he was going to desert?"

"Yes."

"Thank you." She added, "Back in the world—that was GI jargon for back in the States—he meant to make it back."

"So did everyone."

"Would you consider making a public appeal for these men—DeTonq, Dan Kelly, Hernando Beltran, Lee Walker, Harold Simcox, and Louis Kalane—to come forward?"

"No."

"Why not? Won't they corroborate your story? If you line up enough witnesses for the defense, there may be no court-martial." She added, "I told you I would help locate witnesses for the defense. That's my job."

"Then do it. Work hard."

"I will. Why won't you help?"

Tyson contemplated his glass of Scotch and soda, pressing an ice cube down with his fingertip. At length he said, "I thought about what you're suggesting. I've decided that it would be unfair of me to make such an appeal. Each man has to be found by you or has to decide in his own way to come forward." He looked at her. "Do you understand?"

She nodded. "But you will at least give me some clues? Some background?"

"Within limits."

"All right, then let's continue. Have you ever heard from Dan Kelly?"

Tyson observed, "This is beginning to sound like a class reunion attended by only us two. Except you weren't in my class."

"How long was Kelly your radio operator?"

"Want another cigarette?"

"I understand he was your radio operator for about seven months. I understand, too, that you had a close relationship. So I wonder if you heard from him recently."

"No."

"A long time ago, then?"

Tyson realized that as the scope of the investigation widened, as she spoke to more people, she would learn things or pretend to have learned things, and his chances of getting caught in a lie grew exponentially. For all he knew, Kelly had already spilled his guts into a tape recorder, and Karen Harper would pluck the recorder and tape out of her black bag of tricks and replay it for him. He said, "Have you spoken to Kelly?"

"No. I'd have to tell you if I did."

"But I have to ask."

She shrugged. "You make me ask the right questions."

"I have more rights than you. I'm the suspect."

"I have to work harder."

"Right."

"Have *you* heard from Kelly?"

"Actually I did. In about August of '68, then again about seven or eight years ago."

She waited.

Tyson lit another cigarette. "Kelly enjoyed soldiering. He enjoyed war. There are always a few like that. . . . Anyway, he wrote to me in August 1968, saying he was taking his discharge at an American installation in Ethiopia instead of back in the States. You probably know from his personnel file that he was discharged overseas."

"Yes. I know that a soldier can take his discharge almost anywhere there is an American military installation. But I found it odd that he should pick Ethiopia instead of Rome, for instance."

"Well, there was no war in Rome at the time. But there *was* one in Biafra. Remember that one? Anyway, he wrote me saying he was going to join the mercenaries in Biafra. I figured he was killed there. Then . . . yes, it was 1976 . . . Bicentennial time, remember? . . . he wrote to me again, from Portugal—"

"Excuse me. How did he have your address after so many years?"

"Well, he alluded to the fact that he was working for a civilian concern. In Nam this used to mean the CIA. And they have everyone's address, don't they?"

She asked, "What did he write to you about?"

"About joining him in Portugal. Then taking a little trip down to Angola to look into the civil war there. A thousand a week, banked in Switzerland, and all expenses paid."

"Were you enticed?"

Tyson thought a moment, then replied, "I was married . . . had a son by then. I remember thinking that the Army paid me eighty dollars a week as an infantry officer in Nam and that the CIA paid twelve hundred percent more for the same shit work." He smiled grimly, then added, "And I'll bet the CIA never asked their people questions like the Army is asking me. If you want to investigate suspicious deaths, ask the CIA about their Operation Phoenix in Nam. They murdered, or caused to be murdered, about five thousand civilians who may or may not have been VC sympathizers. Go down to Langley tonight and ask them, Major. They're open all night. I'll go with you."

"Did you respond to Kelly's letter?"

"No."

"Did you hear from him again?"

"No. I remember seeing the published names of American mercenaries who were captured and executed by the leftist faction in Angola after they'd won the war. But Kelly's name wasn't among them."

"I may be able to check on that."

"Right. Go ask the spooks if they know of him or of his whereabouts. If you think I'm good at stonewalling, wait until you talk to those jokers. Maybe you'll learn something else about the law at Langley."

"If you hear from any of these men as a result of the national publicity surrounding the case, will you let me know?"

"Perhaps." Tyson stubbed out his cigarette.

"I'll let you know immediately if I locate any of them."

"A little more immediately than you let me know about Sadowski or Scorello, please."

"I have the right to question possible witnesses first."

"So do I, if I find them first." He looked at his watch.

"Just one or two more things." Karen Harper regarded Tyson and said softly,

"Of course there is one more possible witness, someone whose testimony would be, I think, beyond reproach."

"And who might that be, Major?"

"You know. The French government is cooperating in trying to find her. So is the Vatican." Major Harper took a sip of her wine and continued, "It should not have been difficult to locate a French-Vietnamese nun, but it is proving so. We believe she really exists, beyond what Picard has said and you have said. Actually the records of the Catholic Relief Agency list a Sister Teresa at that time and place, with other pertinent details of age and ancestry. What do you remember about her? Her age, for instance."

Tyson said, "The Eurasian nun I knew was then in her mid-twenties. She was strikingly beautiful, though the Catholic Relief Agency might not have that fact in their records. She worked at the dispensary attached to the Joan of Arc School. She lived at a convent nearby."

"How did you know she was a nun?"

"Little clues. Like the nun's habit. A cross around her neck. Living in a convent. Didn't date much."

"You're being sarcastic. I asked because the Vatican has no record of her having taken her final vows."

Tyson remembered something Sister Teresa had said to him. *If we sin, it is not so great a sin as you think.* He said to Karen Harper, "You know, over there, credentials were not carefully checked. If this woman had been educated by the Catholics, especially in a convent, and if she'd somehow acquired passable medical knowledge, then she could present herself as a nursing nun whether or not she was a nurse or a nun."

Karen Harper nodded. "So . . . if she were an impostor then and continued to be when Picard met her in a French hospital, she might be lying low as a result of all this."

Tyson shrugged. "Possibly. But you should not use a pejorative word like *impostor.* Understand that Eurasians were outcasts in Vietnamese society. A woman like that would find protection, comfort, and a means of survival within the Catholic Church. I'm sure she earned her keep."

Karen Harper replied, "I'm sure she did. It's hard to comprehend that, isn't it? I mean being born into a society where the moment you are born you are an outcast with limited prospects. And you have to do something like impersonate a nun . . . and lead a life of . . . confined social opportunities. . . ."

"Celibacy."

"Yes."

"Well, most Eurasian women—those born of French soldiers and Vietnamese women—had the choice of the convent or the whorehouse. The whorehouse provided a similar sort of comfort and protection, without the celibacy requirement obviously."

"Obviously." She asked, "Did you know Sister Teresa before this incident?"

Tyson did not want to lie about peripheral matters, but neither did he want to fashion a hangman's rope for the Army out of small threads of truth. The less said about Sister Teresa, the better. On the other hand, she, like the others, might appear at any moment. He said, "Yes, I knew her prior to that day."

"How did you know her?"

"I met her briefly, in happier times, before Tet."

"How?"

"By chance. At mass in the Phu Cam Cathedral."

"What were you doing there?"

"Looking for my dog."

"I meant, you are not Catholic."

"I went with a Catholic officer. To see the cathedral mostly."

"When was the next time you saw her?"

"A week before Christmas. I was delivering some . . . aid packages to the convent. She happened to be there. Then a day or so later there was a children's Christmas party at the Joan of Arc School in Hue. The MAC-V civic action officer was looking for someone to play the piano."

"You play the piano?"

"As well as I speak French. But I can do Christmas carols. I'll play for you someday."

"We'll wait until Christmas. So you met her then—at the Christmas party—and spoke to her?"

"Yes. A short conversation."

"In what language?"

"French, Vietnamese, and English."

"What was discussed?"

"Nothing that has any bearing on this case. We spoke of war, children, God's grace . . . that sort of thing."

"Are you a Christian?"

"Yes, it's fashionable now. Except at Peregrine-Osaka. There I'm a Buddhist from nine to five."

"Were you a Christian then, in 1968, when it wasn't quite so fashionable?"

"I tried to be. Why?"

She shrugged, then asked, "Did you see Sister Teresa again, after that Christmas party?"

"Yes."

"How often?"

"Perhaps four times."

"In what context?"

"What do you mean?"

"Did you see her officially? By chance? By design? Socially? How did you see her?"

"All of the above. What difference does it make?"

"I'm trying to preestablish her bona fides. Now that I see that you knew her, she may not be an unprejudiced witness as I was first led to believe. So I'd like to determine the extent of your involvement."

Tyson didn't respond.

She asked, "After the Christmas party, when and how did you see her?"

"I saw her twice more around Christmas. There was a truce, a cease-fire. I apparently made such a hit at the Christmas party that MAC-V requested that I do temporary civic action work in Hue."

"Could Sister Teresa have had anything to do with MAC-V's request?"

"Ah, the plot thickens, does it not?"

"Well?"

Tyson shrugged. "Possibly."

"So you saw her twice more during the period of the Christmas cease-fire. How about after that?"

"Yes. In mid-January. I was asked to come to Hue to discuss job opportunities with MAC-V."

"They offered you a job?"

"Yes."

"Did you accept?"

"Yes. Frankly, I'd seen enough combat."

"So how was it that you wound up still leading an infantry platoon?"

"Timing. I was to report to the MAC-V compound on or about January 30 to begin my new duties of winning hearts and minds. A staff officer said something about my arriving for the Vietnamese New Year party. He used the word *Tet,* but I didn't know what that meant. Anyway, when January 30 rolled around, Alpha Company was in the field, as usual. I decided not to take the morning resupply helicopter back to base camp, but to take the evening helicopter instead. I guess I was feeling a little guilty about leaving my platoon and company. Browder was razzing me about becoming a rear echelon flunky. So that morning I went out on what was to be my last patrol."

She nodded. "And the morning of January 30 found you in the market square at Phu Lai?"

"Yes. As I was lying there waiting to die, I thought it might have been better if I'd taken that morning resupply chopper. But as fate would have it, I lived, and by January 31, the MAC-V compound at Hue was surrounded by thousands of communist troops. They never broke through, but a lot of Americans died defending the compound, and a lot more were caught outside the compound walls, at Tet parties, and were found later with their hands tied behind their backs and bullets through their heads." He lit a cigarette. "So . . . it's all written somewhere in God's daybook. Isn't it? 'January 30—A.M.—Tyson misses appointment with helicopter. Meets VC at Phu Lai instead. Bullet nicks ear. P.M.—Dinner with Alpha Company. C rations in the cemetery. Begin Tet offensive.' " He looked at the smoke rising from his cigarette. "But I wasn't fated to die at Phu Lai or at the MAC-V compound or Miséricorde Hospital or the Strawberry Patch. Instead, it was my fate to sit here with you tonight."

She lowered her head in thought, and Tyson could see she was processing something. She finally looked up and continued her question in a neutral tone. "So during the time you were in Hue in mid-January interviewing for a staff job, you had the opportunity to see Sister Teresa again. How many times?"

"I don't recall exactly. Once or twice. I was there only about two days."

"And you didn't see her at any time after that, until 15 February at Miséricorde Hospital?"

"That's correct."

"That must have been a surprise."

"To put it mildly."

"You didn't know she worked there?"

"I didn't know the place existed, Major."

"Of course. But she never mentioned that she worked at another hospital?"

"No. I only knew she worked at the Catholic dispensary near the Joan of Arc School and Church."

"Where did you meet her on those occasions after that Christmas party? What is there to do in Hue? I mean where does an American officer take a nun?"

"Are you being sarcastic or just nosy?"

"I'm intrigued."

"Perhaps I *should* write my memoirs."

"The locale is exotic, the unsuspecting city is on the eve of a great cataclysm, you are a young soldier about to return to the front. You meet a strikingly beautiful woman, a nun—"

"When you put it like that, it sounds like melodrama. A woman's story."

"Don't be sexist. Where did you take her?"

"That's my business."

"All right. How do you suppose she wound up at Miséricorde Hospital, outside the city walls?"

"Beats the hell out of me."

"Fate?"

"Yes, fate."

Major Harper nodded. "And that was the last time you saw her?"

"Yes."

"Did you ever wonder what became of her?"

"Often."

"Picard's book, then, brought you some good news."

"Yes, that was the good news."

"Would you like to see her again?"

"No."

"Why not?"

"For the same reason I don't attend class reunions."

"Why is that?"

"I have nothing to say."

"Reminisce."

"The young have aspirations that never come to pass, the old have reminiscences of what never happened."

"Who said that?"

"I did."

"Originally?"

"I don't remember."

"Did you speak to her then? At the hospital?"

"Just a few words."

"Such as?"

"I don't remember. You can imagine what sort of words—hurried words, words of comfort. Then . . . someone took her away. The building was burning."

"That was the last time you saw her?"

"I said it was."

"But where did she go? Certainly she would have stayed close by until the shooting was over. She would have put herself under your protection, or your platoon's protection. They were offering protection, weren't they?"

Tyson spoke softly. "They were not . . ."

She waited, then said, "They were not?"

"I mean, they were not in a . . . position to. . . ."

Her eyes met his and held contact. Finally she said, "Did you look for her when the shooting stopped?"

"Well, yes, of course. But we had to move on. To pursue the enemy. I thought she'd died. . . ."

"Pursuing the enemy was more important than offering protection to the survivors of that hospital?"

"Unfortunately it was. They have a name for it. War."

"But there were Europeans there, Vietnamese Catholics, wounded—"

"We didn't distinguish between types of refugees."

"Didn't you? How often did you come across Europeans? Catholic nuns? Excuse me, but that would have been a great feather in your cap to have rescued these people and gotten them to an American base camp. Where did they go, these survivors of the battle?"

Tyson saw she was tired and noted that her tone had become argumentative. He had the impression she was becoming frustrated and obsessed.

She snapped, "Where did they *go*, Lieutenant?"

"They fled."

"Why did they flee from you?"

"They did not flee *from* us. They just fled."

"The wounded fled?"

"The wounded . . . were carried away by the survivors."

Karen Harper's voice rose. "There *were* no survivors, Lieutenant! They all died there. That's what Sister Teresa told Picard. Your platoon murdered everyone. That's what she said. That's why the Catholic Relief Agency lists all those doctors and nurses as missing. They died at Miséricorde Hospital."

Tyson stood and nearly shouted. "They were killed by the goddamned communists, before, during, and after the battle. They panicked and fled and were killed by enemy troops in and around this village."

"No! They died in the hospital." Karen Harper stood also. "The question is did Sister Teresa, in her hysteria, witness an ill-advised and perhaps blundered assault that led to the deaths of innocent people and the burning of the hospital? Or did she witness a cold-blooded massacre, followed by the deliberate burning of the hospital to cover the evidence?" She looked him in the eyes. "If you just made a stupid blunder, for God's sake say so, and we can forget about murder. Forget your ego and your pride, and tell me if you made a dreadful mistake that led to the deaths of those people. There *is* a statute of limitations on that sort of thing—on manslaughter—and it has expired. Tell me."

"If I tell you that, will you return a report saying I admitted to manslaughter but not to murder and that this is your finding as well?"

"Yes, I will."

"Will that be the end of it? For me? For my men?"

She hesitated, then said, "I'll do everything I can to see that it is the end of it."

"Will you? Why?"

She shook her head. "I'm sick of it."

"You're sick of it? Everyone is sick of it. But how about truth and justice?"

"The hell with that." She rubbed her eyes with the back of her hand, the way a child would do, then composed herself. "I'm sorry. I'm tired." She looked at him and cleared her throat. "Of course we'll pursue this with the intent of either clearing your name completely or forwarding charges to the proper court-martial convening authority, if necessary."

He saw the moment had passed and had some regrets about it. "I think you'd better go."

"Yes." She gathered her things and turned toward the door. Tyson watched her as she crossed the long room. She opened the door, turned, looked at him a moment, then left.

Ben Tyson surveyed the cluttered cocktail table—the ashtray, the glasses, the papers. His eyes wandered to the bar area where his champagne glass lay shattered on the floor. He looked around the room, like a detective wondering what had happened here.

Tyson stepped to the window and stared out into the city lights. He looked down at the sidewalk six stories below and saw her walking up Pennsylvania Avenue. He watched her closely, noticing even from this distance that her gait was not jaunty or purposeful. Rather she walked like he felt: deflated and unsure. He was glad he wasn't alone anymore.

21

Benjamin Tyson turned off the lights of his hotel room, made himself a fresh drink, and sat in the armchair, his feet on the cocktail table. He felt drained and weary. He stared out the window at the summer sky and watched a succession of aircraft make the approach to National Airport.

The imperial city, a city of monuments. *Hue. Washington.* They were becoming confused in his mind. He closed his eyes.

Lieutenant Benjamin Tyson consulted the city map spread out on the passenger seat of his open jeep, held down by a .45-caliber Colt automatic.

Hue was divided into three parts: the old city within the Citadel walls, built on the north bank of the Perfume River; the Gia Hoi district, a new suburb outside the city walls; and the South Side, the European Quarter on the left bank of the river.

He turned cautiously into an unmarked street in the South Side and scanned the block. When he'd borrowed the jeep from MAC-V—Military Advisory Command-Vietnam—a motor pool NCO in the compound had instructed him on urban driving. "Don't drive down no deserted streets," drawled the big bony sergeant from South Carolina.

"Right."

"Pick streets with lots of kids. Even Charlie don't shoot up a street with kids."

"Can I bring my own kids?"

"Don't pick up no hitchhikers, includin' pussy, and watch for them motorbikes. Charles likes to flip you a little something from them bikes."

"Maybe I need a tank."

"Naw, Hue's pretty safe really. A whole lot safer than the streets of New York, Lieutenant."

Well, perhaps. But Tyson thought he'd rather be on Third Avenue at the moment.

"Bring my jeep back in one piece. Okay?"

Tyson had pointed out that if the jeep were in several pieces, the chances were good that he would be, too.

Tyson now scrutinized the white stucco houses and courtyards. Looked okay. He headed up the long straight road.

As he'd left the MAC-V compound, he'd spotted the old French Cercle Sportif, with its verandas overlooking the Perfume River, its tennis courts and gleaming white concrete driveway, and he was reminded of an incident that took place on his first trip to Hue, a month earlier in November. He had gone alone to a French café on Tihn Tam Street and practiced his French on an elderly half-breed bartender. A middle-aged Frenchman of slight build had moved down the bar and introduced himself as Monsieur Bournard, the proprietor of the establishment. Monsieur Bournard had unexpectedly invited Lieutenant Tyson to Le Cercle Sportif, *"pour jouer au tennis."*

After a set of lawn tennis, they had sat on the veranda, furnished with Art Nouveau pieces, and drank cold beer. Monsieur Bournard had remarked, "Hue has changed little since I was a boy. In the Buddhist myth, Hue is the lotus flower growing from the mud. It is serenity and beauty amidst a sea of carnage. Hue is eternal because she is sacred to communist, Buddhist, and Christian alike. Hue will survive the war, Lieutenant. You may not."

"And you?" Tyson had inquired.

The Frenchman shrugged. "The communist cadres enjoy my little café."

"You entertain communists in your café?"

"Certainement. They have been good customers long before you arrived. You are shocked? Annoyed?" he'd asked in a tone that suggested he'd made this little confession before in similar circumstances. "One must be *très pratique.* They will be good customers long after you and your countrymen are gone. Don't be naïve."

Tyson had replied, "I grew up in a place where naïveté is a virtue. However, Monsieur Bournard, I am not shocked, nor annoyed. But I may report you to the National Police."

"As you wish. But most of them use my little place to do business with the communists. The National Police are also *très pratique,* you see." Monsieur Bournard had leaned across the marble table. "This was a nice manageable little war until you arrived." The Frenchman made it sound personal. As Tyson considered pointing out that he hadn't come here by choice, the Frenchman made a sudden sound of exasperation and muttered, *"Les Américains,"* as though this said it all.

Tyson had risen from his chair. "Thank you for the tennis and the beer."

The Frenchman looked up, but did not stand. *"Pardon.* You are my guest. But I saw too many of my countrymen die here. In the end the Asians will have their way."

"With you too."

"Non. Me, I am like a little cork bobbing on a raging yellow sea. You and your Army are . . . well, like the *Titanic."* Monsieur Bournard turned his attention back to his beer.

As Tyson walked away he heard the Frenchman call out, "Take care of yourself, my friend. I can't think of a worse cause to die for."

Tyson had then gone into the changing room, showered, and returned his borrowed white tennis clothes. He received in exchange his combat fatigues, freshly laundered, and his boots, polished. The Vietnamese attendant had presented him with his holstered .45 automatic in the way a porter in an English club might give a gentleman his walking stick. To say that Le Cercle Sportif was an anachronism was to understate the extent of the establishment's improbable existence. Yet it existed the way his own club back home existed: as a bastion of cultivated lunacy surrounded by a justifiably hostile and suspicious world.

Riding now in another borrowed jeep from the MAC-V compound, Tyson recalled that incident of a month earlier and reflected on what Monsieur Bournard had said. He concluded that it was Monsieur Bournard who was naïve in the extreme. Neither Monsieur Bournard nor his café nor his club would survive this war. The communists represented something new under the sun, and those like Monsieur Bournard and his sporting friends who thought they could accommodate those grim puritans had obviously not learned anything from life, history, or the daily news.

But in one respect, the Frenchman had been correct: The Asians would have their way. Tyson saw no possible victory in this war, and like the other half million Americans in the country, he was beginning to concentrate on the only victory that made sense: victory over death.

Tyson drove slowly through the busy tree-lined streets of the South Side, crowded with three-wheeled Lambrettas, Peugeots, cyclo-cabs, and motorbikes of every make and color. Military traffic was light. The late afternoon air was suffused with pungent and exotic smells. A line of pretty high school girls crossed the street, dressed in their flowing silk *ao dai.* They stole glances at him, giggled, and chattered. Their teacher, a stern-looking old nun, reprimanded them. The procession passed, and Tyson drove on.

It was Christmas week, and so long as he saw no signs of Christmas in this tropical city, he was neither nostalgic nor homesick. But here in the mostly European and Vietnamese Catholic quarter, he saw little reminders: a Christmas tree in a window, a boy carrying a wrapped present, and from the shuttered loggia of a villa, he heard a piano playing "O Holy Night."

Tyson drove through the square in front of the Phu Cam Cathedral. On the north side of the square was a sandbagged machine-gun emplacement. A few ARVN soldiers were strolling, holding hands as was the custom of Vietnamese men. But otherwise, there was no sign that Hue was at war. Quang Tri to the north and Phu Bai to the south were desecrated by barbed wire, gun emplacements, and green vinyl sandbags. Hue remained unspoiled, a hauntingly attractive illusion, as Monsieur Bournard had suggested, its energy and charm heightened by the realities of the terror beyond its useless walls.

Tyson turned down a narrow lane and stopped in front of a fenced courtyard. He jumped down from the jeep, slung his rifle, then reached in the rear and lifted out a heavy box wrapped in PX Christmas paper.

He looked up and down the lane, then opened a rotting wooden gate and walked through the courtyard garden choked with hibiscus and poinsettia.

Tyson pulled at a bell rope, and a minute later the mahogany door was opened by an old servant woman. Tyson said, *"Allo. Toi trung-uy Tyson. Soeur Térèse, s'il vous plaît."*

The old woman smiled, flashing an uneven set of teeth dyed

reddish brown with betel nut. She motioned him into the dark foyer, then led him to a sitting room.

Tyson stood his rifle against a credenza and sat in a musty armchair, its threadbare fabric home to a few darting silverfish. The chair, indeed all the furniture, looked to be European, pre-World War II vintage. A lizard climbed up a dingy white stucco wall and disappeared behind a cheap print of the Blessed Virgin. The mortar between the red terra-cotta floor tile was green-black with mildew, though the floor seemed to be freshly scrubbed. The tropics, he thought, were not hospitable to man's creations. That, added to forty years of war, made it a wonder anything still stood or functioned in this wretched country.

Tyson didn't hear her come into the room but saw her shadow pass along the wall. He stood and turned. She wore a white cotton *ao dai* with a high mandarin collar. The floor-length dress had slits up to the thighs, but she also wore the traditional silk pantaloons beneath the dress. She seemed, he thought, somewhat embarrassed that he'd called at the convent. Thinking about it, Tyson was embarrassed also. War was justification for much that was uncivilized, but a man calling on a woman ought to have a good reason for doing so. He said, *"Je suis en train de venir . . . à MAC-V. . . ."* He thought that "just passing through" sounded as trite in French as in English. *"Comment allez-vous?"*

She inclined her head. *"Bien. Et vous?"*

"Bien." He hesitated, then lifted the box from the floor and set it on the credenza. *"Pour vous . . . et pour les autres soeurs. Bon Noël."*

She looked at the box but said nothing.

Tyson vacillated between leaving and pressing on with his unexpected visit. He knew that if his heart were pure, suffused with Christian charity and the spirit of Christmas, he would not be acting so awkwardly. But the fact was he had other things on his mind.

Sister Teresa took a step forward and laid her long fingers on the box.

Tyson drew his K-bar knife from its scabbard and sliced open the gift-wrapped box, then pulled the corrugated lid open, revealing a potpourri of PX treasures: soap, stationery, tinned fruit, medicated talc, a bottle of California wine, and other consumer products whose nature and usefulness would probably have to be explained.

Sister Teresa hesitated, then reached into the box and withdrew a bar of Dial soap wrapped in gold foil. She studied the foil and the clock on the wrapper, then sniffed it, and an involuntary smile passed across her lips.

Tyson said, *"Pour tout le monde,"* attempting to further depersonalize the gift. *"Pour les enfants, pour le dispensaire. Une donation."*

She nodded. *"Merci beaucoup."* She placed the soap back in the box. *"Bon Noël."*

They stood in silence awhile, then Tyson said, *"Je vais maintenant."*

She said, "Could you . . . take me . . . a ride?"

He smiled at the unexpected English. "Where?"

"Le dispensaire."

"Certainly."

Tyson slung his rifle, and she led him to the door.

He followed her out through the garden and helped her into the jeep. He did a walk-around to see if any parts had been appropriated, or worse, if anything lethal had been added. Satisfied but not positive, he climbed in, unlocked the ignition, and pushed the starter button. The jeep didn't explode, and the gas gauge still read half full. The ubiquitous VC and local slicky boys were sleeping on the job. He decided it wasn't such a bad country after all.

They drove in silence along the Phu Cam Canal, crossed the An Cuu Bridge, and headed north on Duy Tan Street, a section of Highway One. The buildings here were mostly two-story wooden clusters, with narrow fronts, wooden sidewalks, and alleyways between them. Tyson was reminded of an Old West town.

Here on the South Side of the river were the university, the Central Hospital, and the sports stadium, as well as the treasury, the post office building, and the French-style provincial capitol. None of these institutions or services had existed in the imperial walled city, but the French had grafted them neatly onto the South Bank while the emperors reigned in splendid isolation within the Citadel. But neither the emperor nor the French ruled here any longer. In fact, no one ruled here any longer. Instead the city was a collection of fiefdoms: the military, the civil government, the Catholic and Buddhist hierarchies, the students, and the Europeans. The Americans had found the place too perplexing, and Hue was the only city in Vietnam where no American combat forces were committed. The small MAC-V compound was like the Emperor's Forbidden Palace, secluded and forlorn. And everywhere, in every quarter of the city, in every government building, every school and pagoda, on every block, was the invisible presence of the communist cadres, Hue-born and educated, mingling easily in the cafés, lunching with Monsieur Bournard one day, the National Police commander another, and all the while waiting. Waiting.

Tyson picked up speed, checking the side and rearview mirrors, staying to the center of the road, and keeping a close watch on the motorbikes that passed him. He found Hue more unnerving than the jungle. He glanced at Sister Teresa, sitting placidly with her hands in her lap. He said, "Do the VC bother you? At the school?"

She remained staring straight ahead. "They leave us alone."

"Why?"

She shrugged. "In Hue everyone leaves everyone alone."

"They say there are many VC and sympathizers in Hue."

"There are many intellectuals in Hue."

"They also say Hue is very anti-American."

"The Europeans in Hue are sometimes anti-American."

Tyson smiled. "Hue is very antiwar."

"All the world is antiwar."

"Hue reminds me of Greenwich Village. Even the people dress the same."

She looked at him. "Where is that?"

"In America."

She nodded. "There are riots in America."

"So they tell me." Tyson sometimes felt adrift between a once-familiar world that had become increasingly alien the last time he'd seen it and a true alien world that was becoming uncomfortably understandable. They said that if a day came when you completely understood the Orient, you should seek professional help.

The jeep approached the Joan of Arc Church, a yellowish stucco building with a colonnaded front and an impressive steeple. There was a school close by, and a small dispensary building marked with a red cross. Sister Teresa said, "I will walk from here."

Tyson pulled to the side of the busy street. Sister Teresa remained sitting in the seat beside him, then said, "When do you leave?"

Tyson glanced at her. "Vietnam? I'm leaving on 17 April. If not sooner. No later."

She nodded slowly.

"Why do you ask?"

She shrugged, a very Gallic shrug, he thought. He wondered which parent was French. He said, "Do you have family in Hue?"

"*Oui.* The family of my mother. My father, he is *un para.*"

"A French soldier. A paratrooper?"

"*Oui. Un para.*"

"In France?"

She shrugged again. "I never knew him."

"Have you ever been to France?"

"No. I have been only to Da Nang. To the convent school."

"You speak French well. You are educated, a nun, you are half French. Why don't you leave here? Go to France."

She looked at him. "Why?"

Tyson thought he should tell her there was a war going on, that eventually, as Monsieur Bournard said, the communists would win, that she was a beautiful woman, and that she would do well anywhere. Instead he changed the subject. "Why did you become a nun?"

"My mother wished it. My father was Catholic."

"How old are you?"

She seemed somewhat surprised at the question but replied, "Twenty and three."

He nodded. She would have been born in 1945, the year the Second World War ended, the year the Japanese surrendered Vietnam and the French and the communists began their war to determine who was going to be in charge here. He looked at her, hesitated, then asked, "Don't you find it difficult? Not being able to . . . marry?"

She looked away from him.

He said quickly, "That was not a proper question."

She replied, "I am content. There are many of us of mixed

blood in Hue, and we are . . . how do you say? . . . *Les paria. . . ."*

"Outcasts."

"Oui. Outcasts to our people. The Europeans treat us well, but we are not as good as them. We find peace in the Church."

Tyson realized her view of the world was rather limited. He had a dislike for men who played Svengali or Professor Higgins with women of other cultures or lesser stations in life, so he dropped the subject for a more immediate one. "When can I see you again?"

She turned toward him and looked him fully in the face for the first time. He met her eyes and held them. Seconds ticked by. Finally, she said, "Tomorrow if you wish. There is a—*une soirée pour les enfants. A l' école. Pour Le Noël.* . . . Do you . . . ?" She made a fluttering motion with her fingers. *"Le piano."*

"Oh . . . sure. *Un peu."*

"Bien. Les chansons de Noël?"

"That's about all I can play. Except for 'Moon River.' "

"Bien. A onze heures. A l' école." She pointed.

"I'll try to be there."

She smiled. "Good." She put her legs over the side of the jeep and looked back. *"Merci,* Lieutenant."

"A demain, Térèse."

She seemed surprised at being addressed that way, then said, *"A demain* . . . Benjamin." She slid down from the jeep and walked toward the dispensary in the church compound.

Tyson watched her. She looked back, smiled shyly, then hurried on.

He thought of the first time he had seen Teresa, a month earlier on his first trip to Hue. He had gone to the Phu Cam Cathedral with a Catholic officer and attended mass. Two dozen nuns were taking communion together, and among them was this singularly beautiful Eurasian, hands pressed together, returning from the communion rail to her pew. The officer he was with noticed her, too, and so did most of the Europeans around him, or so he believed.

After mass he saw her again in the square speaking with a Vietnamese Catholic family. At Tyson's urging he and the American officer he was with approached. Tyson introduced himself and the officer in French.

Even then, he reflected, he couldn't imagine not seeing her again. And today he had. And now they both understood that any subsequent meetings were at their own peril.

Tyson sat in the jeep a while longer, then noticed it was nearly dark. Hue had a late curfew, midnight to 5 A.M., but MAC-V wanted their charges safely tucked into the compound by dark. Unless you'd made other sleeping arrangements and informed them of the lady's address.

Tyson threw the jeep into gear and traveled the few hundred meters to the MAC-V compound. The sentry waved him through the barbed-wire gate between the high concrete walls.

Tyson opened his eyes and saw by the illuminated clock on the nightstand that it was three-fifteen. The city was darker now, and he could see stars high above the horizon.

Several images vied for attention in his mind: Teresa, Karen Harper, Marcy, the wall, the hospital, and Hue. It was as if the past were overtaking the present and about to become the future.

22

Benjamin Tyson entered Sag Harbor from Brick Kiln Road. He drove slowly through the narrow streets, past early eighteenth-century houses of white clapboard and gray shingle.

The drive in the rented TR6 had taken nearly three hours from his apartment in Manhattan, and it was already twilight here on the eastern end of Long Island. There was no streetlighting, and the treelined roads lay in darkness.

Tyson realized he was in a part of the town that he did not know. He pulled the Triumph to the curb and got out. The air was damp and briny, with misty auras shimmering around the post lamps near the entrance to the tightly spaced houses.

Tyson reached back into the car and retrieved a book. He zippered his windbreaker and began walking west, toward the setting sun. At length he recognized a street and turned into it, and within a few minutes he came to Main Street. There were a good number of people promenading to the Long Wharf and back, entering and leaving several taverns and restaurants. People sat on the veranda of the old American Hotel, rocking in their bentwood rockers, throwing back drinks on the aft roll and returning the glass to a rest position on the forward roll.

Tyson crossed Main Street and turned into a small lane, following it downhill toward the water. He had remembered where he'd seen the mailbox so long ago and found the house, a very old cedar-shingled saltbox sitting on a small bluff above the body of water called the Lower Cove. A tilted picket fence surrounded the house and the unkept grounds. The mailbox still said Picard/ Wells. The lights were on.

Tyson opened the gate and approached by way of a footpath paved with broken shells. With no hesitation—because he had not come this far to have second thoughts—he raised the brass knocker and brought it down hard on the black-painted door. He heard footsteps, and the door opened. "Yes."

Tyson did not reply.

Andrew Picard peered at his visitor in the dim light of the porch lamp. Finally Picard's eyebrows rose. "Oh. . . ."

Tyson stared at him, and neither spoke for some time. Picard showed what Tyson thought was a good deal of cool, or perhaps it was the alcohol that Tyson smelled on his breath.

Tyson regarded the tall, lanky man standing a few feet from him. He was wearing blue jeans and a button-down oxford shirt with the sleeves rolled up. He was very tan, and his longish hair appeared to be bleached by the sun and salt. Tyson knew him to be a preppie and a Yalie, and had heard his voice on radio and TV, so the words *tweedy* and *madras-covered marshmallow* entered his mind. But the reality belied this unkind prejudice, and Tyson reminded himself he was looking at an ex-Marine officer who by all accounts had done his duty.

Picard said simply, "Come in."

Tyson followed him into the foyerless room. A stereo was playing Paul McCartney's "Hey Jude." Tyson's eyes adjusted to the darkness of the room. It was, he saw, a large open space, created by the removal of all the interior walls where hand-hewn posts still stood. The simple painted furnishings all looked as if they had been bought at a Quaker garage sale. Three hooked rugs sat on the rough floorboards, and a fireplace of round river stone dominated the left-hand wall. A small coal fire in the grate warmed and dried the sea air.

At the rear of the open room was a long countertop separating an enclosed porch that held what had once been called a summer kitchen. The rear windows of the kitchen looked out onto the cove, and Tyson saw the lights of Baypoint across the water and picked out the deck lights of his house. Shadows moved in front of the sliding glass doors, and he felt his heart give a sudden thump.

Picard said, "Are you here to kill me?"

Tyson turned from the window. "The thought never crossed my mind."

"Fine, then how about a drink?"

"I don't need one, but if you do, go ahead."

Picard did not reply. His eyes dropped to the book in Tyson's hand.

"I came for your autograph." He held out the book.

Picard took it and smiled. *"The Quest.* One of my early ones. Did you like it?"

"Not bad."

"Fiction is fun. Nonfiction sometimes gets people upset." Picard placed the book on the oval dining table and opened it. "This is a library book. Garden City. And it's overdue." Picard shrugged. "Pen?"

Tyson handed him a pen.

Picard thought a moment, then wrote: *For Ben Tyson, Where have all the soldiers gone? Long time passing. Best, Andrew Picard.*

He handed the open book to Tyson, and Tyson read it, then closed the book. "Indeed." He laid the book back on the table.

Picard went to the stereo and turned it off. Both men stood in silence, though it did not seem to Tyson an embarrassing silence, but a time to reflect on a shared experience and to go through the mental leaps necessary to get to the here and now. Finally Picard said, "If you wanted a drink, what would it be?"

"Scotch."

Picard went into the open kitchen and put ice in two glasses. "Neat?"

"Soda."

He rummaged through the refrigerator, then held up a bottle of Perrier. "Wimp water of the Hamptons. Okay?"

"Fine."

Picard split a bottle of Perrier between the glasses. "How'd you find me? I'm not listed."

"Mailbox."

"Right. Mailbox. Have to paint that out. Getting too much attention these days."

Picard poured from a bottle of Cutty Sark, then came around the counter

and handed Tyson his drink. Picard held out his glass. "To those who met their
fate at Hue, including us." He touched his glass to Tyson's, and they drank.

Tyson's eyes wandered around the room. Under a side window was a writing
desk cluttered with papers and pencils. "What are you doing for an encore?"

Picard shrugged. "Hard act to follow."

"Well, you can do the court-martial of Benjamin Tyson."

Picard for the first time seemed ill at ease. "I don't think so."

Tyson put his glass on an end table. He glanced at a steep open staircase that
ran along the right-hand wall, up to the loft. He said, "Are you alone?"

Picard replied, "Yes, but I'm expecting company any moment." He added
with a smile, "Five duck-hunting friends with shotguns."

Tyson did not acknowledge the quick wit.

Picard swallowed more of his drink, and Tyson suspected he was a bit under
the influence. Picard said, "I almost called you a few times."

"Did you? Actually you called me twice some years ago. I probably should
have met with you then."

Picard nodded. "I found it easier to write about you because I hadn't met
you. Had I met you, had we gotten drunk together, I might have chucked the
whole chapter into the fire."

"Then you'd still be an unknown author."

"But a happier one. I'm not gloating, you know."

"No, I don't think you are."

Picard sipped on his drink thoughtfully, then observed, "I assume you read
the entire book, so you'll know I lost friends there, too. And most of my friends
didn't even have the chance to die fighting. They were staff officers with MAC-
V, like myself, and they were caught by the communists outside the compound,
marched to a ditch, and were shot in the head. Or worse, some were buried
alive." Picard stared down at the floor for a few seconds, then added, "Some
men talk to their shrinks. Writers write."

Tyson nodded. "And how are you feeling now, Picard? Are the nightmares
gone? How are your ghosts doing?"

Picard rubbed his chin contemplatively. "Well . . . I think about it more
now. I opened the wrong door. . . . It started when I began researching the
book, talking to survivors. That brought it back. . . ."

Tyson commented, "You didn't do the survivors any favors either."

Picard seemed not to hear. He went on, "I didn't really see much action
there . . . until Tet. Then I saw things I was ill prepared to see. Things I could
barely comprehend. I'd lived in Hue for nearly a year and became enchanted
with the place. It was a city of light in a country where night had descended. I
fully believed the myth that Hue was special. Then after the battle I walked
through the gray ash and the black corpses, and I remember thinking, 'Nothing
is sacred,' and I began feeling sorry for the whole fucked-up human race."

Picard ran his fingers through his long hair, then continued, "And sometimes
now—you asked about ghosts—I have this dream. You remember the Army
medical expression 'the walking wounded'? An innocuous expression only
meaning ambulatory cases. But in this dream I see these bandaged . . . things
. . . part zombie, part mummy . . . and they're walking through gray ash,
their hands held out as though they were pleading, and they drop in their
tracks, but more keep coming out of the white smoke. . . ." He looked at
Tyson. "I can tell you this."

Tyson nodded.

Picard stared off into space awhile, then said, "I saw a little boy about six years old wandering down the street naked. He had his genitals blown off . . . but he seemed more concerned with the glass shards in his arms . . . and . . . I can't forget that face . . . he was alone, with no one to help him, tears running down his cheeks. . . ." Picard looked at Tyson. "But you must have seen worse . . . I mean in the infantry."

Tyson didn't respond for a while, then said, "In the infantry, one is not just a spectator, but often the cause of the suffering, as you pointed out so well."

Picard stared at the floor.

Tyson drew a long breath and said, "You know, sometimes after you've shot first and asked questions afterward, and the old mama-san or little baby-san is not answering, then you feel like the worst monster God has ever created. So the next time you react more cautiously to a perceived threat, and you take a bullet for your trouble. And your buddies vow to shoot first the next time, in memory of you. And the march of death goes on until everyone is in step, shooting first—blowing away anything that moves, cutting a grim swath, death's premature harvest, through the rice fields and fruit orchards. . . ." Tyson's eyes drifted to the coal burning on the fire grate. He watched the blue flames for a minute, then turned back to Picard. "Did you help that little boy?"

Picard replied haltingly, "I . . . he . . . he saw me . . . he raised his arms . . . like he was surrendering . . . but he was showing me that he was badly cut . . . There were still pieces of glass in his hands and arms. He said, '*Bac-si. Bac-si.*' " Picard closed his eyes for a moment, then said, "I wanted to scream at him, 'Not your arms, you idiot! Your balls! Your balls!' . . . but he was a little boy. I took a step back as he came closer, then . . . I leveled my rifle and shouted, 'Go away! *Di-di.*' Then I turned and ran." Picard drew a breath. "I couldn't let him get near me. I simply could not handle it." His eyes met Tyson's.

Tyson nodded. "It happens."

Picard finished his Scotch. "Yes . . . but other men around me did better than I did."

"That day."

Picard walked slowly back to the kitchen and made himself another drink. "Right." He seemed to come out of his dark mood and added, "Some days were better than others. You had a bad day on February 15. On February 29 you were attending the sick and wounded. Later that day you were one of the wounded. *C'est la guerre,* as our little friends used to proclaim ten times a day."

Tyson finished his drink and put the glass on the coffee table. It occurred to him that Picard was the first man he'd spoken to about this who had actually been there. Beyond their differences in experiences and perceptions there lay the same residual malaise, the little time bombs waiting to go off.

"Another?"

"No."

"Have a seat."

"I'll stand."

Picard came around the breakfast bar and sat on a Boston rocker off to the side of the fireplace. At length he replied, "I told your friend Harper I would only offer impartial testimony—regarding my sources. Especially Sister Teresa. You can tell your attorneys that also."

Tyson nodded. He also wondered why Picard had referred to Harper as his friend.

Picard added, "I'm not looking to crucify you."

"That's what I like about artists and writers, Picard. They're always doing this little dance around the shit pile, but they never step in it, never have to eat any of it, and by God they don't even smell it."

Picard leaned forward in his rocker. "*I* stepped in it up to my ears."

"You fell in it by accident. And when the stink was gone two decades later, you decided to describe your brief combat experience to the world."

Picard rocked slowly for some time, and the floorboards creaked in the silent house. He said, "I reported what I saw and what I heard from witnesses. . . . But sometimes I think that I never should have written that chapter."

"Why do you think that?"

"Well . . . it wasn't . . . well documented, and . . . it leaves me open to a libel suit—"

"That's not why. Why shouldn't *you* have written that chapter?"

Picard replied without hesitation, "Because I didn't help the little boy with his genitals blown off and because I didn't put that in the book. Because one night when the communists were storming the walls of the ARVN compound, I went to pieces in front of the ARVN soldiers, and a Vietnamese colonel punched me. And I didn't put that in the fucking book either. And I realize now that you can't put it behind you until you hold it up and show it to everybody." He looked at Tyson. "I may have done you a favor I couldn't do for myself."

"Thanks, buddy. I'll return that favor first chance I get."

Picard smiled grimly.

Tyson thought a moment, then said, "You reported your own heroics, however. The day the ARVN broke out of their compound and began their counterattack into the Citadel. You were a hero that day, carrying wounded ARVN to safety through machine-gun fire. Is that true?"

"Oh, yes. Two little guys at a time. Bullets and rockets splattering all over the fucking street. Who can figure it? They weren't even Americans." Picard crossed his legs and swirled his drink. He said, "I suppose if you're an honest writer, you write about the times you pissed in your pants. I suppose your platoon did things that would make the Army proud. I suppose I should have dwelt on those things a bit more."

"Well, Picard, maybe if you meet my men in some closed hearing, you'll recall the things you discovered tonight."

"I'm sure I will. But I don't know what good it will do anymore."

Tyson watched the smoke rising from his cigarette. He said, "I didn't come here to coach the witness, Picard. I came here to see if we fought in the same war. I think we did." Tyson tossed his cigarette into the fire. He continued, "We all have secrets, and sometimes we tell them to each other, because we understand one another. But we usually don't tell these things to other people. We are embarrassed by some of the things we did and appalled by most of the rest. But among ourselves, we can speak without explanations or apologies." He moved closer to Picard. "I'm not saying the story of Miséricorde Hospital should not have come out, but I don't think *you* were the person it should have come from."

Picard stood. "But *you* were."

Tyson nodded. "Yes. And now that you broke the understood rule of keeping your mouth shut, I may very well tell my story."

"But according to Dr. Brandt, you all swore to lie. That was not an unspoken rule but a blood oath. What are you going to say to your men about telling the truth?"

"I will tell them that the truth shall make ye free."

"Is the truth . . . I mean is it close to what I wrote . . . ?"

Tyson smiled. "You will find out in court."

"Are you going to sue me?"

"Quite possibly." Tyson looked around the room with a proprietary interest. "Nice place. Do you rent or own?"

Picard laughed. After some reflection he said, "You are not the sort of man to engage in blackmail. I am not the sort of man who will be blackmailed."

Tyson looked at him appraisingly, then changed the subject abruptly. "Who is Wells?"

"Wells. . . . Oh, on the mailbox. Lady who used to live here. I should paint over the name."

"You live alone?"

"Sometimes. They come and go."

"Do they? You never married?"

"Once. I have a twelve-year-old daughter. Lives with her mother and stepfather in California. I miss her. Life . . . I mean, life in the good old USA ain't what it was when I was a kid. If there was someplace less fucked up I'd go there. Know anyplace?"

"I'm afraid I don't. Do you hang out with the local literati?"

"Christ, no. They're bigger assholes than I am." Picard went back to the kitchen. "One more, Tyson. Then you can go if you want."

Tyson noticed Picard had trouble navigating. He said, "Short one."

Tyson lit another cigarette and tossed the match in the fireplace. He looked at Picard moving about the kitchen. He did not particularly like the man, but neither could he bring himself to dislike him. Picard was like a fraternity brother, and allowances had to be made. Picard had revealed two acts of pure cowardice. That may have been a way of making amends or a way of making Picard feel better about himself. In either case it had the effect of making Tyson feel like the recipient of an unwanted gift, the keeper of yet another appalling secret. Had they been friends, Picard would have hated him the next morning. Tyson said, "You spent nearly a year in Hue before the Tet attack?"

"Right."

"You knew the place."

"Pretty well." Picard came around the counter with the two drinks.

Tyson took his glass from Picard. "Did you ever go to a café on Tihn Tam Street? *Le Crocodile?*"

Picard sipped his Scotch. *"Certainement.* That little shit who owned the place had a foot in every camp."

"Bournard?"

"I think that was his name. Why?"

"I sometimes wonder what became of him."

"Friend of yours?"

"No. I met him only once. He advised me to go home."

"He should have taken his own advice."

"Why?"

"Well, I can tell you what I heard, though it might not be true. You know what the VC did to Vietnamese who had any commerce with Americans, like barbers, prostitutes, cleaning women, and all."

"I heard."

Picard nodded. "Well, Monsieur Bournard and the staff of his café, according to what I heard, showed up at the Central Hospital minus their hands."

Neither man spoke for some time, then Tyson said, "My father once said to me, about his war, 'That was a war I would go to again.' " He looked at Picard. "I don't think we can say that about our war."

Picard replied, "No, we don't have that. And that, I think, is at the heart of this post-stress syndrome. Not what happened there—because all war is the same shit—but what happened here."

Tyson finished his drink and set the glass down. "Could be."

Picard cleared his throat. "By the way, a word of advice: Dr. Brandt would like to see you in front of a firing squad. Don't ask me how I know, because he seemed cool, logical, and objective. But, Christ, Tyson, he indicted you for murder in no uncertain terms."

"I'm sure he did."

Picard seemed on the verge of asking why but apparently thought better of it.

A silence enveloped the room, broken only by the ticking of the mantel clock. Tyson glanced at it and said, "I should go." He zipped his windbreaker.

Picard hesitated, then said, "Are you going home? I mean, the place you're renting here."

Tyson gave him a quick look. "Perhaps. Why?"

"I met her."

"Who?"

"Marcy. Your wife. She was here."

Tyson nodded. Of course Marcy would have called on Picard.

"She's very nice."

"Was she?"

"She was to me. No rancor, no hysterics. A remarkable woman. All she wanted to know was whether or not I told the truth in my book."

Tyson didn't respond.

"So how do you answer a wife who asks you to reveal a truth about her husband? I told her I was not an eyewitness to the event. I was only a reporter. Typical writer—right, Tyson? Dancing around the shit pile again. Well, she let me off easy. Told me I probably did what I thought was right."

"Very gracious. Now you can sleep better—despite your ghosts."

Picard didn't respond directly but said, "Why did she ask *me?* Why doesn't she ask *you?* Well, of course, she's asked you. But you're not talking. Not even to the woman who shares your bed."

Tyson walked toward the door, then turned back to Picard. "How did she look?"

"Marcy? Fine. Nice-looking woman."

"No, I meant Sister Teresa. How did she look, Picard?"

Picard glanced at him quickly, then replied, "Fine. Serene—"

"Physically. Good-looking?"

Picard considered a moment, then replied, "She went through a very difficult time after the communist victory."

Tyson nodded. She would be about forty now and not an American forty. A real world forty. "What happened to her over there?"

"Bad things. Prison camps, forced labor, that sort of thing." Picard regarded Tyson for some time, then said, "She never mentioned you by name. Only referred to you as the lieutenant. But lately, after speaking to Karen Harper and thinking about all that Sister Teresa said and now after your questions about her . . . I think I missed something. . . ."

Tyson opened the door. "Thanks for the drinks."

"You forgot your book."

"I don't really want it. Good evening."

"Go home, Tyson. She might actually miss you."

Tyson closed the door and walked down the path of broken shells.

The door opened behind him, and a shaft of yellow light fell over the front yard. Picard's voice called out into the damp night air. "What would you have done? If the situation were reversed, Tyson, what would you have done in my place?"

Tyson called back, "I would have helped the little boy."

"No, I mean about putting that chapter in the book."

Tyson knew what he meant and did not reply as he opened the gate and passed through it. He stood on the sidewalk and looked up the path at Picard's silhouette in the lighted doorway. He said finally, "I would have done what you did, Picard. And if you had been in command at Miséricorde Hospital instead of me, nothing would have been any different there either."

"I know. I know that. Fuck Nam, Lieutenant."

"Yes, indeed, Lieutenant."

23

Ben Tyson left the dark road and made his way through the bulrushes down to the water's edge. The cove was misty, and the moon was obscured by haze. Yet he could see the lights of the far shore about a fifth of a mile across the gently swelling seawater. Red-blinking channel markers swayed about halfway across the cove, and a sailboat passed silently into the narrows. The tide was out, and the low-tide terrace was strewn with pebbles, shells, and marine life.

The lights of Baypoint seemed to beckon him, to draw him closer to the edge of the lapping water. He recalled clearly a night before the Tet Offensive, standing on the north bank of the Perfume River, staring at the mesmerizing lights of the European Quarter across the water. He felt soothed now, as he'd felt then at the water's edge, at peace with himself and enchanted by the colors on the water, beguiled by the rhythmic rippling of the swells. Impulsively he stripped down to his shorts and threw his clothing into a tangle of bayberry. He waded into the water. He began swimming, only in circles at first, the water cooling and cleansing his warm, sweaty skin. Then, without realizing it, he struck out across the cove for Baypoint.

The tide was running strong, pulling him east toward the outer harbor, and he compensated by angling in a northwesterly direction. The swells were higher than they looked from the shore, and he found he was becoming fatigued.

Reluctantly he made for a channel marker and held on to its bell cage.

He could see his house clearly now, less than three hundred yards farther to the north. Tyson drew a deep breath and headed out. About halfway to the shoreline he felt his right knee begin to throb, then suddenly the knee gave out, and his leg hung useless in the water. Tyson swore silently and turned over on his back. He floated east with the tide toward the North Haven Bridge inlet.

The water seemed warm, and the swells were undulating with a soothing rhythm. A hazy moon with its beautiful corona looked down on him, and Tyson felt strangely in tune with his world.

He was vaguely aware of floating beneath the North Haven Bridge, through the inlet, and past the lighted Long Wharf a few hundred yards to his left. He floated through the ship opening in the stone jetty and out into the great harbor. He tried to move his left leg but found that the knee had seized up. "Damn it." This had happened before, and it would pass if he let it rest.

After what seemed like a long time, he felt the tidal pull slackening. A while later he was conscious of a change in direction caused by the land breeze coming from Shelter Island to the north. He tried to picture a map of the coastal region around Sag Harbor and concluded that if the wind prevailed from the north and the tide began its flood, he should wind up at the disco on the Long Wharf. In his underwear. He laughed and swore at the same time. He tried to flex his knee, but it seemed tighter.

After a time Tyson noticed that the wind was picking up, and small but ominous whitecaps broke over his body. What was worse, the wind had come around and was blowing from the south and west now, taking him away from Sag Harbor, out to sea. The water that had seemed so warm was cooling him rapidly, and the wind, too, had a chill in it. He found he was having difficulty catching his breath now, diminishing his ability to stay afloat. "No good."

He righted himself and treaded water with his arms and good leg. He scanned the horizons for boats, but his visibility was limited by the rising sea as the swells gave way to the first random breaking waves, and for the first time he was frightened.

Tyson was lifted onto the crown of a large swell and looked around quickly. There were boat lights on all horizons, but none of the craft seemed close enough to hail. The lights of Sag Harbor twinkled enticingly about a quarter mile to his southwest, but they may as well have been on the hazy blue moon. The changing tide was too slack to pull him back, and his drift was determined by the rising wind from the southwest. To the northeast Tyson saw the Cedar Point Lighthouse, beyond which was Gardiners Bay where he was headed, and beyond that the Atlantic, next stop France.

The swell flattened, and Tyson dropped into a trough. He tried to distance himself from the problem and think about it objectively as he'd done in combat. As for passing boats, they'd have to be passing damned close to see him at night with these waves. And if he was reading the wind and tide right, it didn't seem likely he'd be washed ashore anywhere. But if he was, it might not be on a sandy beach because too much of these coastlines were bulkheaded with rock and timber. That was all the bad news except for sharks, which he wouldn't think about. The good news was that he was able to think at all.

As he expected, the waves began to build, and floating on his back became impossible. He tried to ride the back of the waves, slipping down into the trough before the wave ascended and crested, then timing the next wave to break before it reached him so that he was lifted again on the back of that curling wave and dropped into the following trough. The wavelengths and periods of crest were still far enough apart to do that, and the heights were running only three to four feet. But this seemed to be changing for the worse.

Tyson thought he saw a boat's lights nearby as he was lifted onto a wave. But the sea had become too loud to waste his breath calling. And his field of vision and his own visibility were narrowly confined within the walls of the black and white water around him. The moon and stars had disappeared, and the night was darker. The smell and taste of brine began to churn his stomach, and he heaved up a mouthful of seawater.

He was fighting for his life now. He suddenly realized that if he didn't make it they'd think it was suicide. "No. *No!*"

He pictured his house in Baypoint, its deck lighted in the distance, and he saw himself moving closer to it. David and Marcy were having a quiet dinner at the round redwood table. A candle lamp burned between them, and he saw their faces in the flickering light and heard the soft sussurant sound of the radio playing, Willie Nelson drawling out "All of Me."

As he'd feared, the wavelengths and the intervals of crest shortened as the heights rose. The troughs were shorter, less than ten feet from the back of one wave to the wall of the oncoming one. The curl of an eight-foot wave blocked the sky above him like an unrolling canopy, then crashed down around him, blinding and deafening him.

As he struggled to the surface, fighting for air, he knew there was no riding this out any longer. One or two more like that and he'd be gone.

Tyson concentrated on his numbed knee, trying to will it to respond, to move, to get his leg kicking. In his youth, before Vietnam, before the Purple Heart, he'd swum in worse seas than this, far out into the treacherous Atlantic, out of sight of land. *This is a goddamned harbor. Benjamin Tyson will not drown in a harbor, in moderately high seas, in the middle of summer. No.* He shouted, "FUCK NAM! FUCK NAM! FUCK NAM!" He shouted until the words were indistinct, even to his own ears. "Fucknam, fucknam, fucknam, fucknam—!"

He marveled at lights that could be so bright and hands that could be so clean. The white sheets felt cool against his naked body, and the hovering nurses were solicitous. The USS *Repose,* he thought, was a halfway station between death and life, a salvage ship that collected the flotsam and jetsam from the ravaged shore.

You're going home, soldier.

You'll have complete recovery of that knee.

Oh, the nurses at Letterman are going to love this one.

Here are your personal effects, Lieutenant.

There will be no disability.

Seen some shit, did you, ace?

There's a movie in the lecture hall tonight, Ben. Would you like me to take you?

This war is obscene. Obscene.

Captain Wills and Lieutenant Mercado have been transferred to another ward. They're fine. No, you can't see them.

No psychological counseling recommended. This one has all his marbles.

Your brigade commander is coming aboard to pin medals on pajamas. Some men fake sleep, then he pins it on their sheets. Your choice.

You're flying to Da Nang tomorrow. They want you at a special awards ceremony in Hue next week.

I don't know where they keep the corpses, Lieutenant. What difference does it make?

You'll be able to run, jump, swim, play tennis, even climb mountains.

No combat duty.

Good luck, Tyson.

Good-bye, Ben.

That knee will be good as new in a month. Swimming will be good for it.

The white life ring lay about ten feet to his left, then it moved far away in a backswell and disappeared. It surfaced again and shot across the churning waters directly at him as though it were homing in by remote control.

Tyson grabbed it firmly with both hands, ducked under it, and slipped up into the hole. The lifeline tautened and broke water. Tyson followed the dripping line with his eyes and for the first time saw the lighted boat not fifty feet from him. It was a cabin cruiser, about a forty-footer, with a flying bridge. Tyson bobbed in the wake of the craft, then as he drew closer felt the churning turbulence of the propellers. As he was pulled closer he saw across the white transom the boat's name: *Tranquillity II*. Then everything went black.

Tyson opened his eyes. He was aware that he was wrapped in a robe. He tried to stand but couldn't.

A man knelt beside him. "Dick Keppler." He pulled aside the flap of the robe exposing Tyson's right knee. "War wound?"

Tyson looked at him.

Dick Keppler said, "They have a sort of signature—pockmarks where minute particles of debris were blown in by an explosive force. Don't get that from a football injury. Seen it before. Is this what's bothering you?"

Tyson realized the man must be an M.D. He replied, "Just fatigued. Cramped."

"Could be. You'll be back on the courts in a week."

"No combat duty."

The doctor laughed. "No. Here, let me help you up."

Tyson took his arm and stood. A woman who introduced herself as Alice handed him an eight-foot gaffing hook, and Tyson supported himself with it. He asked if they could take him to Baypoint, and within fifteen minutes they approached the Baypoint Peninsula. Tyson scanned the near shore and pointed. "There."

Keppler cut the throttle and swung to starboard, heading for the long dock. Tyson felt the keel scrape bottom once or twice before the boat eased alongside the dock.

Alice looped a line around a piling, and everyone shook hands. Tyson said, "If you'll wait, I'll return the robe and gaff."

Dr. Keppler replied, "Keep them as a souvenir. Do you need a hand getting up those rocks?"

"No, just get me started."

Keppler jumped onto the dock, took Tyson's hand, and helped him ashore. "Thanks again." They exchanged farewells.

Tyson stood on the rickety dock and watched the *Tranquillity* ease back into the channel. They waved and he waved in return.

Tyson rested his weight on the gaff pole and turned toward the shore.

He climbed the rocks backward, in a sitting position, and reached the lawn. He stood and looked at the house set back a hundred feet. The deck was lit, and he could see someone reclining in a lounge chair. He moved across the lawn using the gaff as a walking staff. As he drew near he saw through the deck rail that there were in fact two people in the lounge chair, lying face-to-face groping at each other. The woman had her back to him, and he could see that her T-shirt was hiked up to her armpits. Tyson coughed and took a few more steps.

The man on the lounge chair jumped up and adjusted his trousers, then came quickly to the rail. "Who's that?"

"Hello, David."

"Dad! Dad!"

David vaulted over the rail onto the lawn and stopped short. "What happened?"

"Where?"

David seemed confused. "What . . . why . . . ?"

Tyson could see the girl had gotten herself together and was standing at the railing. Tyson imagined he presented an odd appearance dressed in a white robe, barefoot, with his hair tangled, and leaning on a gaff pole. Tyson said, "I was boating with friends. Went swimming, got a cramp, and they dropped me off. Introduce your friend."

"Oh . . . right." David looked over his shoulder, then back to his father, then again to the girl. "Right. This is my dad—Melinda. Dad, Melinda."

Tyson said, "Hello, Dad."

Melinda laughed. "Nice meeting you."

Tyson started toward the steps, and David took his arm. "Are you sure you're okay?"

"Just a bad cramp." He walked up to the terrace and sat in a folding chair. "Where's your mother?"

"Oh, out. Be back by ten."

Tyson nodded.

David said, "Are you staying . . . ?" He glanced quickly at Melinda.

Tyson yawned. "I guess. I live here, don't I? How about getting me some kind of cordial? Straight up."

"Right." David darted into the house.

Tyson and Melinda regarded each other for some time. Tyson judged her to be older than David by a few years. She was a nice golden brown, a little pudgy but cute. "Live here?"

"Just for the summer. We live in Manhattan."

"Where are you staying?"

"Down the road. The gray-shingled house."

"That narrows it down to twenty."

She laughed. "Green shutters." She added, "Last name is Jordan. My father comes out on weekends. My mother is having dinner with Mrs. Tyson."

Tyson nodded. That answered the question he would not ask David and also told him that the Anderson cover was blown. He supposed it didn't matter. "And you and David are baby-sitting each other?"

She smiled with only enough embarrassment to show she knew she should be but wasn't. Tyson recalled the summer his father had discovered him in a beached skiff with a tarp over it. The skiff rocking on the sand must have looked suspicious if not ghostly. Tyson smiled.

David returned with a half-filled tumbler. "Crème de cacao. Okay?"

It wasn't, but Tyson assured him it was. "Sorry to butt in on your time together."

David and Melinda made sounds of protest though Tyson knew they must be frustrated. Tyson sipped on the liqueur. He felt an odd burning in his throat and stomach and thought he might get sick. He put the drink down on the armrest and took a deep breath.

David said, "You don't look good."

"I'm just tired. I'm not sick or anything." Tyson added, "I'm going upstairs to shower the salt off. Then I'm going to catch some z's." He raised himself on the arms of the chair and grasped the gaff pole with his right hand. "No, I don't need help. Just slide the door open."

Melinda slid the screen back, and Tyson passed into the living room. He called back, "David, I have a shark boat chartered for tomorrow. Be downstairs by five A.M."

"Aye, aye, sir."

Tyson climbed the stairs the way he'd climbed the rocks, buttocks first, then crawled into the large bedroom. He laid the gaff against the footboard, climbed into the low platform bed, and stretched out. He yawned. "Shower." He yawned again. The evening had taken on an unreal quality: the old town, the mist, Picard, the bay, the *Tranquillity* and her crew, the climb to his house, and finally David into some heavy petting. Little David. Time flies. He closed his eyes, and his last thought was that he should not be here. He should be, he knew, at the bottom of the sea.

24

"You smell like a fish."

"I feel like a fish. A cod, I think."

"What happened?"

Tyson yawned and rubbed his eyes. Marcy's face came into clearer focus above him. She was sitting on the edge of the bed close to him. He noticed that the gaffing hook was still at the foot of the bed. The window was open, and the breeze rustled the blinds. The night-table lamps were on, and the room was softly lit.

"Whose robe is that?" she asked.

"Dick's."

"I think it's a woman's robe."

"Then it must be Alice's."

"Who is Alice?"

"She's married to Dick." Tyson raised himself and sat up against the headboard. "The people on the boat. Didn't David tell you?"

"Yes. Why were you swimming in the cove with these people, bare-assed?" She parted his robe, exposing his groin.

He pulled the robe back. "I didn't start off bare-assed. Don't I get a hello?"

"Hello." She asked, "How do you know these people?"

"Met them while I was swimming. They took me aboard."

"I see." She glanced at his bare knee. "How does it feel?"

"Fine. I've been soaking it in salt water."

"Very funny. Can you move it?"

He tried to flex his knee. "Not yet." Tyson looked at his wife. Her normal olive complexion was nearly black, and the white of her teeth and eyes contrasted starkly against her skin. She wore a white jumpsuit, cut low in the front, revealing the curve of her tanned breasts. When she leaned over, Tyson could see she was braless and saw the white flesh an inch above her nipples. She looked at him. "Are you staying or visiting?"

He replied, "My shark trip is booked for tomorrow. I thought I'd stay here tonight."

She smiled without humor. "I think you've had enough of the sea."

"We'll see how the knee feels."

She asked, "How did you get here? To Sag Harbor?"

"Rented a car."

"Where's the car?"

"On the other side of the cove."

"Where are your clothes?"

"In my pocket. Cut the inquisition. I'll need to borrow the Volvo in the morning and some money. I'll bring you a mako to clean and fillet."

She seemed pensive, then asked softly, "You didn't try to . . . you know?"

Tyson began to reply in the negative, then said, "I don't know. . . . I think I just wanted to swim. I was swimming here actually."

She nodded dubiously.

He said, "I came about as close as you can get and still get back. Now that I've caught a glimpse of the far shore my curiosity is satisfied. I don't want to go there. Not for some time."

"I hope not." Marcy stood and went to the French doors leading to the balcony. She looked out into the cove as she spoke. "How are you making out in the big city?"

"Okay. Paul Stein has a nice apartment. You were there once before he got divorced." He added, "It's a little lonely. How about you?"

"I'm doing fine. Lots of people we know are here. Coincidentally, Paul stopped by, and we had dinner. He wanted to let me know he wasn't promoting our separation by loaning you his apartment."

"That was thoughtful."

She turned from the window and faced him. "Also, Jim, my boss, came by. We went swimming. And Phil Sloan was out last weekend."

"Sounds like a public rest house. I thought we were hiding out."

"I'm not hiding." She took a step toward him. "It's idiotic and sneaky. And it doesn't work. Those two guys who are renting next door knew who I was right away."

Tyson didn't reply.

Marcy inquired in a neutral tone, "What are you doing with yourself?"

Tyson shrugged. "Not much. Reading, exercising, walking a lot. I've never been unemployed. What am I supposed to do?"

"Are you keeping out of trouble?"

He smiled.

She frowned in return, a mock-annoyed frown. "I don't like you out of my sight, Tyson."

He didn't respond, but he felt a little happier. Against his better judgment he asked, "Are you keeping out of trouble?"

She shrugged.

Tyson waited.

Marcy moved to the side of the bed. She said, "Jim came with his wife. So did Phil. Paul Stein had his girlfriend with him, and the two guys next door are married—to each other." She laughed. "God, it's true that all the men are taken, gay, mental basket cases, too young, too old, or sexual deviates."

"Don't rule out the sexual deviates."

She looked at him sternly. "Anyway, I'm not available. Yet."

Tyson sat up straighter. He said, "It's best if you get used to not having me around . . . I mean, beyond the question of our recent problems is the possibility that I'll be in some sort of . . . custody for some time . . . so it's best if you get used to—"

"I want you here for just that reason. I want you to be with your family until this is resolved."

Tyson didn't respond.

Marcy drew a deep breath, then said, "Look, Ben, I understand why you left. Your wife became an embarrassment, the locker-room talk got smutty, people were laughing behind your back. So you did what all self-centered males do. You said, 'Look, guys, I left the slut.' Is that about it?"

Tyson said unconvincingly, "I told you your past is your business. My past is not. I left to save *you* embarrassment."

"Bullshit." Still standing beside the bed, she leaned closer to him. "How do you feel about me? In your heart?"

"I love you."

"Then fuck the world, and especially fuck the past. Let's go away from here."

Tyson shook his head. "I have orders to report to Fort Hamilton day after tomorrow."

"Don't. Do you still have your passport?"

"Yes—"

"Then go, for God's sake. Go while you can. I'll tie up all the financial ends here. Give Phil power of attorney. We can clear a nice sum on our house. David and I will join you in a few months."

"Where do you propose I go?"

"Who cares? Anyplace where they'll leave us alone."

"I'm an American. This is my country."

She snorted. "The last refuge of a patriot is somewhere without extradition."

Tyson smiled grimly. He stared at Marcy awhile, and their eyes met. He said, "Fight or flight? That is the question. I think I'd rather fight."

She sat again on the edge of the bed. "Let me ask you something. If I was the one who was facing a jail term, would you consider leaving the country with me?"

"Yes."

"Well, I'm willing to go with you. You're not dragging me. I'm suggesting it. I won't ever hold it against you."

"Easy to say now."

"Ben, why are you staying?"

"I'm optimistic. I think I can win."

"You once said to me, on the day this began, that this will be the Army's game, with their rules. That was good insight. Don't forget you said that."

"I've come to respect military justice now that I see it and remember it."

"You know what I think? I think the Army has already sent a memo to the commander of Leavenworth instructing him on the sort of accommodations they want for you."

Tyson cleared his throat. He replied, "Well, if that happens, when I get out I'll have paid my debt to society. And I can live a normal life."

"*What* society? This society doesn't give a rat's ass about what you did or didn't do in some benighted non-country over two decades ago. Half the nation doesn't care if you're guilty or not, and the other half is ecstatic that you bagged a hundred gooks in one day."

"No, that's not my country you're talking about."

She looked at him curiously, then replied, "I'm afraid it is. It's poor Picard's blood the country wants, not yours."

"Nonsense."

"Is it? You're out of touch."

"You sound like me when I was a member of the silent majority twenty years ago."

"I've woken up a bit. In fact, a curious incident happened to me about a week ago. I was in the American Hotel bar with Gloria Jordan, Melinda's mother. Now, this is not one of your blue-collar reactionary pubs. Not at four bucks a pop. There are city people and local gentry in there. And what do you think the subject of conversation was at the bar?"

"The resurgence or decline of the Broadway stage."

"No, sir. The subject was you."

"No kidding?"

"And the consensus was 'guilty, but who cares?' Also 'guilty with loads of extenuation and mitigation.' A few people suggested that you might be innocent as a result of temporary insanity."

"There's nothing temporary about it. I'm still married to you."

"One gentleman suggested you be given a medal, though he didn't specify which one he thought appropriate."

"I already got the Vietnamese Cross of Gallantry for that action. Let's not overdo it."

"One lady seriously doubted that such a good-looking man could do anything like that."

"Did you get her name and phone number?"

"Point is, Tyson, the public, if that was an accurate sampling—and I think you'd find even more support at the Sandpiper—the public thinks you're getting a raw deal whether or not you and your soldiers murdered a hundred men, women, and children. They think Picard is a shit."

"Poor Picard. What were you doing in a bar?"

"Getting drunk."

"You're supposed to say, 'Looking for my dog.' How did you vote?"

"I was very tempted to deliver my standard lecture on the immorality of the Vietnam War, but I remembered I couldn't testify against my husband. So I took Gloria's arm, and we slipped out."

"Before they recognized you and carried you down Main Street on their shoulders."

"It was very embarrassing. With Gloria there, I mean." She rubbed her chin contemplatively, then said, "But public opinion will not get you acquitted any more than it will get Picard indicted. It's not *that* kind of democracy."

"I guess not."

She glanced at her husband, then said, "Someone told me that federal agents are watching Picard's house—to protect him. Did you know that?"

"No. How would I know that?" But he should have known, he realized. He should have suspected that Picard's coolness in inviting him in was a result of having some heavy artillery on call. Interesting. He had to keep reminding himself that this was not a personal problem but a national one; that there were unseen players in the wings and people like Chet Brown who entered the stage for a moment, then faded back into the shadows, and their numbers were legion. He said, "Is anyone watching us?"

She shrugged. "If they are, it is not to protect us from an angry lynch mob. We have not been harassed by anyone except the media, and we've been threatened by no one. What does that tell you about your country?"

"It tells me I am innocent until proven guilty."

"Yet Picard is guilty. Guilty of smearing the name of a war hero. You, my friend, like your former boss, Westmoreland, are a sacred cow. You fought for your country, you were wounded in battle, and you are being persecuted by an ungrateful Army and a biased press. Well, that is the perception. The truth, as we both know, is that the government is actually doing its job in spite of the unpopularity of its course of action. The press, for all its faults, is seeing that the government doesn't lose its nerve."

Tyson said, "Whose side are you on?"

"Yours, damn it." She thought a moment, then said softly, "The test of how we feel about our convictions is whether or not we stand up for them when we are personally involved. If your case was one that I was reading about, I'd be inclined toward wanting to see you tried and convicted. But you are my husband, and I love you. So I say you ought to run, to become a fugitive from justice, because . . . . because I'm afraid you may be guilty. . . ." She turned away from him, and Tyson could see she was near tears.

He waited, then said, "Somehow I don't see Marcy Clure Tyson aiding and abetting a suspected war criminal. But you're right: If the suspected criminal is the man you love, then you have to make a choice. Well, lady, I'm damned flattered. But I'm not running. I've run and run for nearly two decades, pursued by a hundred bloody ghosts. And they would have let me run until the day I died. That was my punishment on earth. I don't know what they have in store for me when I finally join them, but I hope to God they are merciful when we meet."

"Stop it. Stop that."

"Well, anyway, the least I can do now is face this imperfect system of justice we've created. As I said, I've already had my punishment, and anything the Army does to me now is inconsequential."

"To you. Not to me." She put a cool tone in her voice and informed him, "I will not wait for you."

Tyson felt a tightening in his stomach but replied lightly, "That's my girl."

She added, "I will not wait for a fool."

He said nothing.

Marcy lowered her head in thought, then spoke. "You said fight or flight. But there are people who do neither. People who wait for the state apparatus to knock on their door in the middle of the night—"

"Oh, spare me your Kafka nightmares. I have enough nightmares of my own. This is America. The only people who knock on your door here in the middle of the night are drunks. And I'm not waiting like a paralyzed rabbit. I'm fighting."

"In your mind perhaps. But no one else sees any sign of it. Phil Sloan—"

"Fuck him."

She drew away from him and said, "Why are you optimistic? Has Major Harper said anything?"

Harper's name caught him by surprise, though it shouldn't have. He said, "Well, no. But I have a feel for the Army's case against me. It isn't strong. I think she may recommend that no charges be forwarded."

"Do you?" Marcy stood, went to the dresser, and opened the top drawer. She moved some underclothes aside and took out a newspaper. "I didn't want this lying around for David to see." She held up a copy of the *American Investigator*. "Have you seen this one?"

"Actually the supermarket was out of them. I bought toilet paper instead."

She laid the newspaper across his knees. "I know it's a rag, but this stuff seems to find its way into more respectable publications. Worse, other publications dig deeper for any grains of truth."

Tyson looked at the inside page to which she had opened. The story was headlined: *Splitsville for Tysons?* A subline announced: *Major Karen Harper Not the Cause, Say Friends.* Very sly, thought Tyson.

Tyson looked at the head-and-shoulders photo of himself and Marcy together. They were wearing evening clothes, and both had rather silly smiles. Tyson recognized it as the photo taken at the hospital charity ball. There was also a photograph of Karen in uniform, probably an Army PR handout.

Marcy said, "Can I get you something?"

Tyson looked up. "How about a glass of ice water?"

Marcy left.

Tyson scanned the article. He read a few lines at random: *Marcy has taken up residence on the chic East End of Long Island, while Ben is living in a bachelor pad on Manhattan's fashionable East Side. Friends say they are not legally separated but "just living apart."* He read another line farther down the column: *He was seen having drinks with her in the cocktail lounge of Washington's exclusive Four Seasons Hotel. A hotel spokesperson would not confirm that Tyson was registered there, but employees of the hotel said he was. We don't know who picked up the bill for Tyson's room or for the cocktails with Major Karen Harper, but we hope it wasn't the taxpayer.*

"Me neither," said Tyson aloud. "The nerve of those people flaunting their looks and money in exclusive cocktail lounges." He read a few more lines, getting the subliminal message that the *American Investigator* was trying to get across, and it had less to do with the American taxpayer getting screwed than with the possibility that Tyson and Harper were getting it on. He threw the paper aside, then opened the night-table drawer and found the pack of cigarettes he'd left there. He lit one with a paper match.

Marcy came into the room with a tray on which was a glass of ice water and a glass of white wine. She passed him the water and said, "I'm taking you to Southampton Hospital."

"Why? To get me neutered?"

"That's not a bad idea either." She picked up the newspaper and dropped it back in the drawer. She sipped on her wine, then said, "Interesting piece."

Tyson shrugged.

Marcy said, "I didn't know that investigations for capital crimes were conducted in cocktail lounges."

Tyson replied, "Better than a holding cell."

Marcy said, "I suppose you're trying to smooth-talk her. Turning on the charm."

Tyson knew there was no sarcasm or rebuke in that statement; only an appreciation of a possible explanation for his interest in Karen Harper. He said, "I'll tell you something you'll never read in that rag or anyplace else, and it is this: If by compromising that woman I could weaken or kill the government's case, I still would not do it. Not to her, not to you, and not to myself."

Marcy nodded. "Still, the story, for what it's worth, hints at some impropriety. You'll see that suggestion again in the *Washington Post* in a more genteel form." She added, "Anyway, if you wanted to try that route, I give you my conditional permission." She smiled.

"Conditional on what?"

"Conditional on results."

Tyson drank most of the water.

Marcy said in a carefully neutral tone, "Is she nice?"

Tyson had heard that loaded question enough times to know the correct response. "From the standpoint of looks, you can see for yourself, though she's certainly not my type. Her personality is abrasive, bitchy, and entirely too officious. Typical . . . of some people with newfound power." He glanced at Marcy surreptitiously over the rim of his glass.

Marcy seemed to be mulling this over, and if it had a ring of familiarity she didn't say so. She said, "Well . . . anyway, as long as it's only business, do what you have to do. I do in my business." She smiled mischievously.

Tyson put down his glass and finished his cigarette, throwing the butt in the glass. He said, "What prompted you to pay a visit to Andrew Picard?"

Marcy shrugged. "Curiosity." She added, "I could see his house across the cove, and one day while I was out alone in the skiff, I just came ashore in his backyard. He was cutting the grass. I introduced myself. We talked, then I left."

"I suppose if he lived inland that meeting never would have happened."

She looked across the bedroom at him. "Is that where you were tonight?"

"Yes. And I felt damned silly finding out you'd been there. He probably thinks all the Tysons are going to drop by to check him out. Maybe I can get my mother to fly in from Florida. She'd rap him over the head with her cane."

"I'm allowed to call on whomever I please. This concerns me too, you know."

"I trust you didn't ask him to do me any favors regarding testimony."

She shook her head. "I didn't."

"Good." He adjusted the pillow behind his head. He didn't like this feeling of physical disability. He could see why permanently disabled people were sometimes cantankerous. He said to her, "Picard's testimony is not that important. So you don't have to be nice to him if you see him downtown. You can snub him if you want."

"All right. But I doubt if I'll run into him."

Tyson glanced at her. Her response was somewhat out of character, he thought. But perhaps his perceptions were getting cloudy with fatigue.

Marcy sat in the dresser chair and kicked off her sandals. She regarded her toes awhile, her wineglass held in her lap.

Tyson decided he wanted to be alone. He managed a convincing yawn. "I'm going to get some sleep. Could you shut off these lights for me?"

Marcy remained seated. She said, "I want to speak to you about David. He's involved with that girl."

"Good. She seemed nice. Great tits."

"I think he's having sex with her."

"Terrific."

"That's not . . . I mean, how are we to react to that?"

"Well, if we had a daughter, we're supposed to get upset, angry, and frantic. With a son you say, 'terrific.' "

"You're baiting me. And this is serious. The boy is just sixteen. Aside from any moral issues, there are practical issues here. Psychological issues."

"Right." Tyson was aware that sometimes a call to perform some sort of parental duty was a spouse's way of trying to get an errant partner back into the fold. He said, "Have you spoken to him?"

"Well . . . no. It's more a father-son thing."

Tyson said straight-faced, "What does that mean?"

"You know. That's something a father should discuss with his son. It would be awkward for him and me if I spoke to him about it."

"It might be awkward for me too if I had to ask him if he's fucking the socks off his girlfriend. Why, by the way, do you think he is?"

"Well . . . sometimes you can sense these things," she said.

"Really? How?"

"Oh, stop being an ass, Ben. You can tell when people are doing it."

"Now you're getting me nervous."

"Will you speak to him?"

"Yes. Tomorrow. On the boat."

"We'll see about the shark trip."

"I'm going."

"Why is this important to you?"

"My grandmother was eaten by a shark. And on the subject of sex, close the door."

Marcy hesitated, then stood and moved to the door. "I thought you were tired."

"I was, but you were talking dirty."

She smiled. "Get Melinda Jordan off your mind, Tyson." She closed the door and moved toward the bed. "Do you want to see *really* great tits?"

Tyson pulled off the robe and threw it on the floor. "Do you want to see my war wound?"

Marcy smiled slowly as she unzipped the jumpsuit and pulled it down to her waist. Her white breasts stood erect from her dark bronze torso.

Tyson felt his penis move as it hardened.

She said, "Want to see more?"

"All of you."

She slid the jumpsuit and panties down to her ankles and kicked the bunched clothing to the side. Tyson stared at her black pubic hairs, which seemed to cover more area than the bathing suit she'd worn when she'd gotten her tan. She came beside the bed. "How do you want to do this?"

"Female superior, as they call it in our manual. I don't think I can get my leg moving even for this."

"Are you sure you want to do this?"

"Sure. Thought about it while I was drowning."

She came into the bed and straddled him with her knees.

"Too heavy?"

"I'm fine." He reached out and massaged her breasts, then let one hand slip down to her crotch and ran his fingers between her labia. "Long time, Marcy."

She nodded. "Feels good." She cupped his testicles with one hand and stroked his stiffening penis with the other. "If we can get this as stiff as your knee, we'll be in business."

He smiled as he felt her getting moist on his fingers.

She leaned forward and kissed his lips. "Salty."

He put his moist finger to his mouth. "Very salty."

"Pig."

Tyson felt her hand guiding him, and he slipped into her easily. She wiggled her groin until she fully enveloped him, then still in the kneeling position began a slow rhythmic movement. "Ben . . . oh, my. . . ."

He stroked her back and buttocks, then massaged her feet.

Marcy stretched out, covering him with her body, and they embraced. She picked up the tempo, and Tyson heard her deepening breath in his ear. She murmured, "Oh, God, Ben. I missed your cock."

"My cock missed you." He felt her coming—not all at once, but in small rippling tremors with rests between each series of undulating waves; like the sea, he thought, the primeval seas from which we came, the salty moon tides that still surge within us. She took in a short, deep breath of air, then her body stiffened a moment and went limp. He thrust upward hard and felt a sharp pain in his knee shooting up and down his leg, but he thrust again, the pain fighting for attention with the pleasure. He came and almost passed out.

Tyson breathed slowly and steadily. His fingers ran through the cleavage of her buttocks, and he felt the sweat that always formed when her orgasm was intense.

She whispered in his ear. "Are you all right?"

He nodded. "Yes."

"Hurt?"

"A little."

She rolled off carefully and lay on her side. "You're pale."

"All the blood went south. Just give me a second."

Marcy slid out of the bed and walked to the bathroom. She returned with aspirin and a tube of liniment.

Tyson took the aspirin, and Marcy rubbed the liniment into his knee. He felt drowsy but was aware of her leaving again and returning with a basin and sponge. She washed his groin, then sponged the salt from his body. She lay down beside him and covered them both with the sheets. "Shock and exposure. You need rest and body warmth."

"Wake me at four."

"Okay." She snuggled up to him, and he fell asleep with her arms around him.

Marcy waited, then got out of bed. She put the clock radio on the floor, turned off the table lamps, put her robe on, and walked to the door. She turned back and looked at her husband in the shaft of light coming from the hallway. He never slept in a supine position, and that he was doing so now was vaguely disturbing. She watched the rise and fall of his chest thinking how much she felt for him and wondering why the best man she had ever known had to suffer for the past sins of an army and a nation. She left the room and closed the door softly.

Tyson opened his eyes and saw that the ceiling had lightened almost imperceptibly. He could hear gulls and jays screeching, and a boat's horn echoed over the cove. A faint touch of dawn lightened the window, and he could see the tree outside.

"I'm alive," he said. "I'm home."

25

Ben Tyson drove west on the Shore Parkway. The Triumph's top was down, and the afternoon sun shone brightly in the southwest sky. To his left he saw the parachute towers of Coney Island, and beyond, the deep blue Atlantic. It was a fine afternoon for a drive.

Tyson had chosen a nice tan suit of summer-weight wool in which to report for duty, though the Army had requested something green: a uniform actually. "Well," he said aloud, "maybe they won't notice."

The radio was turned to WNBC-FM, golden oldies, and Bobby Darin was belting out "Somewhere, Beyond the Sea," and Tyson hummed along.

Tyson thought about the first time he'd reported for active duty, September 15, 1966. The draft was sweeping up young men by the thousands, and the procedure in his draft board was to report to a parking field on the campus of Adelphi University. From there, chartered buses took the draftees to the induction center on Whitehall Street in lower Manhattan. Reporting time at the parking field, recalled Tyson, had been 6 A.M. And Tyson never knew if that was simply because the Army liked to begin the day at dawn or because the Army thought it wise to take away these suburban boys under the cover of morning darkness.

He looked down now at the dashboard clock. He would arrive at Fort Hamilton before 5 P.M., early enough to report directly to the post adjutant, but late enough not to have to begin the processing procedure of getting a physical, ID card, payroll records, and all the other details of in-processing that he vaguely remembered as clearly distasteful.

He looked at his hands on the steering wheel, then he looked at the speedometer. He was doing sixty-five, but since he was in no hurry, he slowed down and slipped the Triumph into the right-hand lane. The song on the radio was "Mr. Tambourine Man," Bob Dylan's version.

A half mile ahead, the massive Verrazano Bridge spanned the Narrows from Fort Hamilton to Fort Wadsworth. Traffic sped by in the outside lane, and gulls circled overhead. The Fort Hamilton exit approached. Tyson downshifted the Triumph, cut the wheel sharply, and exited into the ramp. He came off the ramp, made a series of right turns, and approached the main gate that sat under the bridge's elevated approach road. He stopped in the middle of the road, took a deep breath, and pulled up to the MP booth.

The MP, a woman of about twenty with short red hair and a pug nose, stepped from the booth. Tyson handed her his orders. She glanced at them, then handed them back. "You have to report to post headquarters. Do you know where that is?"

Tyson thought he detected a note of snippiness in her voice, and had he been a civilian, he would certainly have let it pass. He looked at her name tag, then said, "The next time I pass through this gate, Pfc Neeley, I will have an officer bumper sticker on this car, and you will salute as the car passes. If I should stop to address you, you will address me as sir."

The young woman came to a position of attention. "Yes, sir."

Tyson didn't feel the least bit petty. It's like riding a bicycle, he thought. Once you learn, you never forget. He snapped, "Carry on."

She saluted. He returned the salute, his first salute in nearly two decades, and drove through the gate onto Lee Avenue. To his right was a row of vintage artillery pieces on display. To his left stood an old white wood frame building with a sign on the lawn informing him that the house had once been home to Robert E. Lee. As he drove he realized he didn't know where the headquarters building was but knew he'd eventually find it. He remarked to himself on the extraordinary neatness of the place, the lack of even a scrap of paper on the grounds, and he remembered those prebreakfast police calls, the entire garrison turned out to scour the post for offending litter.

He noticed, too, that the uniforms had changed; male and female soldiers wore camouflaged battle fatigues somewhat similar to the ones that in his day had been authorized only for Southeast Asia. He tried to picture himself dressed like that now but could not.

Tyson came to a building marked with a sign that said, HEADQUARTERS NYAC COMMAND GROUP. He pulled into a visitor parking slot and shut off the engine. The building was a two-story rectangular redbrick affair, nearly indistinguishable from a 1950s elementary school.

Tyson straightened his tie, took his attaché case, and got out of the car. His knee was stiff, and he was aware that he was dragging his leg. He entered through glass doors into a hallway of painted cement block, further reinforcing

his impression of an institution of lower education. The asphalt tile floor, however, was polished to a luster found only in military establishments.

Tyson approached a sort of ticket window on the right-hand wall. A duty
sergeant, another young woman, looked up from her desk and came to the
window. "Yes, sir?"

Tyson passed his orders through the opening. The young sergeant looked at
the name. "Oh. . . ."

"Am I expected?"

"Yes, sir, we've been expecting you." She hesitated and noted his civilian
attire but said nothing. Tyson thought that reporting without uniform was the
least of his problems today. The woman slid a sign-in book across the counter
along with a black government ballpoint pen. Tyson hesitated, then took the
pen and signed in. The pen clotted and skipped.

The duty sergeant said, "Welcome to Fort Hamilton, Lieutenant." She
handed him back his orders. "Please proceed to the adjutant's office, up the
stairs to the right."

"Thank you."

"Yes, sir."

At least, he thought as he walked, no one here said, "Have a good day." That
alone might be recompense for this whole mess. He climbed the stairs and
came to an open door above which was a sign that said ADJUTANT. He entered a
small outer office staffed by four young soldiers: two male, two female. He
found the sight of all these female personnel more than slightly disorienting.
Still, the presence of women lent a little reality to what he remembered as an
unnatural environment.

One of the young men, a specialist four, stood at his desk. "Can I help you?"

"Lieutenant Benjamin Tyson to see the adjutant."

He looked over Tyson's shoulder as though trying to spot the officer, then
looked at Tyson. "Oh! Yes."

"Right." Tyson was aware that the other people in the room were stealing
glances at him. Tyson handed the young man his orders. The man said, "Please
follow me, Lieutenant."

Tyson followed him into a small office that was marked CAPTAIN S. HODGES,
ASSISTANT ADJUTANT. The office was sparsely furnished and sparsely populated.
In fact, there was nobody there.

The soldier said, "I'll let the adjutant know you're here. You can wait here in
the captain's office." The man went through a communicating door into another office.

Tyson went to the window behind the desk. He could see the great bridge, its
massive gray steel piers rising up from the north end of the post and completely
dominating the skyline. Across the Narrows, a mile away where the bridge was
anchored on the far shore of Staten Island, was Fort Wadsworth, which, like
Hamilton, held an old coastal artillery battery, built to protect the sea approaches to New York Harbor. National defense, reflected Tyson, had been
simpler in the last century; an enemy warship sailed toward the Narrows, and
just in case there was any doubt if it was friend or foe, the ship considerately
flew the enemy flag. The coastal guns fired. The ship fired back. The stone forts
were picturesque, and so were the ships. Defending New York Harbor, he
thought, must have been a piece of cake.

The communicating door to the next office opened, and an officer strode
into the room. "Tyson?"

Tyson turned from the window. His eyes took in the pertinent information to
be gleaned from the uniform: The name tag said Hodges, rank of captain;

branch, Adjutant General Corps; awards and decorations, none. Tyson noticed the West Point ring. The man was in his middle twenties, his bearing was too stiff, and he wore a rather unpleasant, almost nasty expression. Tyson did not like the way the man had addressed him and had the urge to bury his fist in the captain's supercilious face. Tyson hesitated, then with great and obvious reluctance, came to a position of attention and saluted.

"Sir, Lieutenant Tyson reports."

Hodges returned the salute perfunctorily, then ruffled the papers in his hand. "It says here you are to report in uniform."

"I don't own a uniform."

"Do you know a barber?"

"Yes . . . yes, sir."

"How dare you report like *that?*" He jabbed a finger in Tyson's direction.

Tyson did not reply.

"Well?"

"No excuse, sir."

"I should think not." Captain Hodges seemed to realize that Tyson was actually standing behind Hodges's desk while Hodges was standing in front of it. He said, "Stand over here." He switched places with Tyson, then sat in his swivel chair. He said, "Before you report to the adjutant, I want you in proper uniform and your hair cut to regulation length."

"I'd like to see the adjutant now."

Hodges's face reddened. *"What?"*

"Captain, I have until midnight to report for active duty. This is an unofficial call. I would like a word with the adjutant."

Hodges seemed to be processing the protocol of such a request. He stared at Tyson.

Tyson stared back.

Hodges nodded to himself as though coming to the conclusion that it might not be a bad idea for Tyson to make a negative impression on the adjutant. He stood. "Wait here." Hodges disappeared into the adjoining office.

Tyson let out a long breath. He had sudden and vivid fantasies of perpetrating ingenious acts of violence on the person of Captain S. Hodges. But in a way he had provoked the man by his appearance. Tyson may as well have shown up barefoot in dirty jeans and wearing shoulder-length hair and a T-shirt that said FUCK THE ARMY. Still Hodges had not displayed even a modicum of the military courtesy that was due an officer of lower rank.

Tyson looked around the sparse office. Hanging on the walls were Hodges's West Point diploma, his commission, and a few certificates of completed courses. Tyson also noticed a framed paper with typing on it and came closer to it. It was headed, "An Excerpt from General MacArthur's Farewell Speech at West Point." Tyson read:

> The shadows are lengthening for me. The twilight is here. My days of old have vanished tone and tint; they have gone glimmering through the dreams of things that were. Their memory is one of wondrous beauty, watered by tears, and coaxed and caressed by the smiles of yesterday. I listen vainly for the witching melody of faint bugles blowing reveille, of far drums beating the long roll. In my dreams I hear again the crash of guns, the rattle of musketry, the strange, mournful mutter of the battlefield.
>
> But in the evening of my memory, always I come back to West

Point. Always there echoes and re-echoes Duty—Honor—Country.

Today marks my final roll call with you, but I want you to know
that when I cross the river my last conscious thoughts will be of
The Corps, and The Corps, and The Corps.

I bid you farewell.

Tyson turned away from the wall and stared through the window. "Yes, all
right. I see." Captain Hodges, young West Pointer, about ten years old at the
time of the Tet Offensive, considered Benjamin J. Tyson a disgrace to the
Corps, to the nation, and to humanity.

Tyson thought about that, putting himself in Captain Hodges's place, and
found himself disliking Benjamin Tyson. *I understand,* he thought. *And I'm
relieved to have finally found some overt moral outrage.* He suspected he would
run into more professional soldiers like Captain Hodges before this was ended.
The Army was much tougher on its own than civilians could ever be.

The door opened and Hodges snapped, "The colonel will see you now."
Tyson replied, "Thank you, Captain."

Hodges stood at the door as Tyson entered the adjutant's office. Tyson strode
in and stopped, as was customary, in the center of the room facing the desk. He
saluted. "Sir, Lieutenant Tyson reports."

The colonel returned the salute from a sitting position but said nothing.

Tyson heard Hodges's footsteps retreating behind him and heard the door
close. Tyson, while keeping head and eyes straight ahead, managed to see the
person to whom he was reporting. The adjutant was a rather stocky man, about
fifty years of age, and what was left of his hair was gray. His face was doughy,
and his jowls hung like pancake batter. Tyson realized he didn't even know the
man's name, and what was more, he didn't care to.

At length the colonel said, "Sit down, Lieutenant."

Tyson sat in a chair opposite the desk. "Thank you, sir."

Tyson did not overtly look around at the office, nor would he do that in
civilian life. He did note, however, that the room was spartan: a steel-gray desk,
a number of vinyl chairs, blinds on the windows, and gray asphalt tile on the
floor. The walls were the same cream-painted cement block as the rest of the
building. Tyson recalled his office at Peregrine-Osaka with more fondness than
he'd felt for it while he was there. This office, however, did have something his
did not: The wall behind the desk was covered with military memorabilia,
photos, certificates, and other symbols of recognition and accomplishment.
Tyson realized that he could finally hang his framed military certificates in his
new office. He also realized he wasn't going to.

The adjutant inquired, "Have you been to Hamilton before?"

The man's voice was gravelly, and the stink of cigar smoke that permeated
the room was a clue why. Tyson replied, "No, sir."

"Had no trouble finding us, did you?"

"No, sir." Tyson looked at him. He saw that the man wore the silver oak
leaves of a lieutenant colonel, not the eagles of a full colonel. Tyson's eyes went
to the black name tag over the right pocket: *Levin.* Tyson looked at the desk
nameplate. *LTC Mortimer Levin.*

Colonel Levin said bluntly, "Are you surprised to find a Jew sitting here?"

Tyson thought of several possible replies but none that would do him any
good, so he said, "Sir?" which was the military way of responding to a superior
officer without responding.

Colonel Levin grunted and stuck an unlit cigar in his mouth. "This, I take it, is a social call."

"Yes, sir. I meant to report in. But I had second thoughts after meeting Captain Hodges."

"I'm sure he had second thoughts after meeting you."

Tyson cleared his throat. "Colonel, I'm considering registering an official complaint, under . . . I believe it's Article 138 of the Uniform Code of Military Justice, with respect to my treatment by Captain Hodges."

"Are you?" The colonel nodded appreciatively. "A good defense is an aggressive offense. Well, don't try to confuse the issues, Tyson. Why don't you just invite Captain Hodges to meet you in the basement of the gym? That's where I like to see officers talk over their differences. Five rounds, sixteen-ounce gloves, referee must be present."

Tyson looked the colonel in the eyes and saw the man was not being glib or facetious. Tyson replied, "I may do that."

"Good. Listen, Tyson, it is my duty as adjutant to say welcome to Fort Hamilton and to arrange for you to meet Colonel Hill, the post commander. But in candor, Lieutenant Tyson, Colonel Hill does not want you here and would rather not meet you. So don't embarrass everyone by asking to meet him. And don't show up at social events that by custom you will be invited to. Please arrange to mess separately. Do I make myself clear?"

"Yes, sir."

Levin tugged at his jowl and seemed to be thinking. He looked at Tyson. "Let's say you are reporting in now so you don't have to come back later in uniform. Okay?"

"Yes, sir."

Levin shuffled some papers on his desk and found what he was looking for. "Your special instructions said you were to bring your passport. Did you do that?"

Tyson hesitated, then replied, "Yes, sir."

Colonel Levin extended his hand across the desk. "May I see it?"

Tyson reached into his breast pocket and drew out his passport. He put it in Colonel Levin's open hand.

Levin laid it on the desk and flipped through it. "You've been around."

"Yes, sir."

Levin dropped the passport into his top drawer and shut it. He folded his hands on the desk and regarded Tyson.

Tyson said, "By what authority are you taking my passport?"

Levin shrugged. "Beats me. Those are my orders. Take it up with the State Department or the Justice Department. You can have it back for authorized travel." He added, "I have instructions from the Pentagon assigning you temporarily to my office. So for the time being I am your commanding officer. However, I don't think you will want to share space with Captain Hodges, so I will try to find something for you to do away from this building."

"Yes, sir."

Levin took a deep asthmatic breath and said, "Is there anything you might be interested in doing on this post?"

Tyson found himself replying in an irritated voice. "Not a thing."

Levin's doughy face seemed to harden, then soften again. He finally lit his cigar and blew a puff of smoke into the air. "The Army," said Levin, "gave me a few special instructions. I am to assign you a duty commensurate with your abilities and experience." Levin tapped the thick personnel file. "You were an infantry officer."

"For less than two years—a long time ago. Most recently I was a vice-president of a large aerospace corporation."

"Is that a fact?" Levin tapped his cigar into a coffee mug. "We'll find something for you. By the way, do you know how much you make? Now, I mean."

"No, sir."

"You make $1,796 a month. Does this recall to duty impose an undue financial hardship on you?"

"One might say that. In fact, sir, if this tour of duty lasts very long I may have to sell my house."

Levin rubbed his jowls, then said, "I don't think this tour of duty will last very long. But please keep me informed regarding your financial situation."

"For what purpose, sir?"

"Well, the Army will help in any way it can. There's a credit union for one thing. All right?"

"Thank you." Tyson knew that Levin's concern was not personal; it was the government that was concerned about his economic welfare, which is why Levin had brought it up, to see what Tyson would say. In America, he'd learned, the worst thing that could befall a citizen, short of going to jail, was the ruination of his credit rating. Ruined reputations and ruined marriages and crises of the soul and psyche were small tales compared to a bad TRW rating. Tyson was happy to see that the government was concerned, that it was worried.

Levin said, "I'm confident you will figure out a way not to have to sell your house. Which reminds me, I have been instructed to offer you post family housing, though we're a bit tight here."

"Thank you, Colonel, but I don't think my family will be joining me here, and I wouldn't want to put another officer and his family out on the street. In fact, if the Army has no objections, I'd like to continue living off-post, and I will not require bachelor officer's quarters or any other Army accommodations."

Levin leaned across his desk. "Let me be a little more precise, Lieutenant. The Army orders you to take a family housing unit. Frankly the Army does not want to give the media or the public the impression that you are being put into a hardship situation. There is a nice two-bedroom brick row unit assigned to you, and it will have your name on it by morning. It is partly furnished, and you are authorized to move your household goods into it at government expense. You are also authorized to move your wife and son into it, though of course you do not have to do that. Clear?"

"No, sir, it's not. Do I have to live on post or not?"

Levin said, "I'm afraid you do."

"That," said Tyson strongly, "is most irregular. That would constitute an undue hardship, and there is no justification for that type of restriction."

Levin cleared his throat. "Unfortunately there is. A preliminary investigation into your case is being conducted under Article 31 of the Uniform Code of Military Justice, and it is the right of the Army to restrict its personnel to insure your continued availability for this investigation. Restriction, as you know, is a moral rather than a physical restraint, and it is enforced only by your moral and legal obligation to obey this order."

Tyson nodded. "I know all that, Colonel. What are the limitations of this restriction?"

Levin looked at a sheet of paper on his desk. "You are to be in your post quarters between twenty-four hundred hours and six hundred hours—that's midnight to six in the morning. You may, though, stay away overnight on the evening preceding your off-duty days. Your off-duty travel, however, is restricted to fifty miles from this post."

Tyson said nothing for a long time, then remarked, "My family is on the East End of Long Island. That, as you know, is about a hundred miles from here."

"Then obviously you cannot visit them."

"That would present an undue hardship."

"I hardly think, Lieutenant, that the Army's refusal to allow you to summer in the Hamptons is a hardship. You will have some duties here, and it is not reasonable that you should attempt to travel a great distance every day after work and be back here by midnight. Fifty miles, and you may not travel by boat or airplane unless it is first cleared by me or the post commander." Levin hesitated, then added, "I was under the impression you were not living with your wife."

"I was not, but I intended to do so again."

"Well, then. . . ." Levin looked at Tyson's orders. "You have a principal residence in Garden City. That's well within fifty miles of here, isn't it?"

"Yes, sir. That's the house I may have to sell."

"Well, Lieutenant, until that time comes, your wife can move back to that house in Garden City. As a practical matter, you can spend weekends at home there. Also your wife and son may want to spend some weeknights with you here in your family housing unit."

"Colonel, I do not think my wife will set foot on an Army installation."

Levin said irritably, "You'll have to work out your conjugal visits yourself, Lieutenant. It is not my duty to become involved in that."

"No, sir."

Levin tapped his fingers on his desk. After a time he said, "I realize this is very difficult for you, but if it will make you feel any better, this will all be over soon."

"Will it?"

"Yes. Actually the imposition of restrictions on you makes it necessary for the government to dispose of your case one way or the other without delay. In fact, your right to a speedy trial or the Army's decision not to pursue the case must come within ninety days of any sort of restriction. The civilian courts may not know what a speedy trial is, but a trial by court-martial is, if nothing else, speedy. So this restriction is a blessing in disguise. The clock is running for the Army as of now. Before mid-October this will be finished one way or the other."

Tyson nodded. "I see."

Levin said in a kinder tone, "Also, the restrictions are not very onerous. And no one is watching you. But be careful, for your own sake."

"Yes, sir."

Levin asked, "By the way, are there any other addresses I should know about?"

"Yes, sir. As you may have read in the papers, I'm currently living on the fashionable East Side."

"You've got more addresses than I've got bathrooms."

"Yes, sir."

"I want that East Side address and the Sag Harbor address. Give them to Hodges."

"Yes, sir."

Levin turned another page of Tyson's file. "Two Hearts. Where and where?"

"Right knee and right ear."

Levin nodded, and his eyes focused on Tyson's scarred right ear. He said, "I noticed you were limping. Is that a result of your wound?"

"Yes, sir."

"Are you fit for active duty?"

"No, sir."

"Well, you're fit enough for what they have in mind."

Tyson did not reply.

Levin said, "I half didn't expect you, Tyson."

"I was ninety percent sure I wasn't coming."

Levin smiled.

Tyson added, "My attorney has filed a motion in federal district court to have this recall to duty rescinded."

"That's none of my concern. You're here now, and you were right to report as ordered, uniform or not."

"Yes, sir. That's what my lawyer said."

"One last thing. Your oath of office. They require you to do this again, and they asked me to administer it upon your arrival."

Tyson nodded. Levin was being open with him, revealing to him the fact that the Army and the government had thought this out. Pull the passport, assign family housing, administer the oath. Slam bang, we got you coming and going. Only you're not going anywhere.

Levin picked up a piece of paper and handed it to Tyson. "No need to do it aloud. Just read it to yourself and sign it." He drew on his cigar.

Tyson read: *I, Benjamin J. Tyson, having been appointed an officer in the Army of the United States, in the grade of First Lieutenant, do solemnly swear (or affirm) that I will support and defend the Constitution of the United States against all enemies, foreign and domestic, that I will bear true faith and allegiance to the same; that I take this obligation freely, without any mental reservation or purpose of evasion; and that I will well and faithfully discharge the duties of the office upon which I am about to enter: SO HELP ME GOD.*

Tyson looked up from the paper and saw that Levin was extending a pen across the desk. Tyson hesitated, then took the pen and noticed irrelevantly that it was a good Waterman fountain pen. Tyson said, "I have some mental reservations."

"Is that so?"

"So . . . can I make a note of that on here? Cross that out and initial it?"

"You'd better not. Look, Lieutenant, this is the Army, and that is your oath of office, not a home improvement contract. You will sign it as is, or you may refuse to sign it."

"Then I refuse to sign it."

"Fine. Give it back."

Tyson handed the paper back with the pen.

There was a silence in the room, then unexpectedly, Levin said, "You been fishing, or loafing in the sun?"

"Both."

"There's good fishing at Sheepshead Bay, not too far from here." He glanced at his watch. "I take it you were not warmly received by Captain Hodges. That is not a presumption of guilt."

"Then what was it, Colonel?"

"It was an anticipation of problems: media nosing around here, maybe demonstrations, curiosity seekers. This is a nice quiet little post. Less than five hundred military. People like it here. Actually I was born and raised a few miles from here. Brighton Beach."

"I didn't ask to come here, Colonel."

"No. But the Army assigned you here as a courtesy to you; however, it is no big treat for us. I personally believe you should have been stationed at one of the larger bases, perhaps down South. A place like Bragg, which dominates the community around it, instead of vice versa as it is here."

Levin continued, "We are ill equipped to provide the necessary logistics and security in the event a . . . a judicial proceeding takes place here. It would be a media circus. And you see, Tyson, the careers of several officers like myself and Hodges who are responsible for you and for maintaining good order and discipline here could be jeopardized."

"I appreciate your problems. I won't add to them."

Levin nodded and stubbed out his cigar, then looked down at the papers spread across his desk. When he spoke again, he spoke as the post adjutant delivering the required advice to the newcomer. "I don't know how you've been treated by your civilian peers these last few months, but here you are an officer, and if you act like one, eventually you will be treated like one—even by people like Captain Hodges." He added, "Do the best you can in the time you are here. Whether you leave here a free man or under guard, you should be able to look on this time with a sense that you acted correctly and with honor."

"Yes, sir. I understand that."

"Good." Levin said more lightly, "I'd like us to have dinner. Maybe talk about things. Meet me at the O Club at eighteen hundred hours."

Tyson had a dinner engagement with his accountant in Manhattan and began to decline automatically, then recalled that he was in the Army, and in the Army the colonel's wish was a direct command. He said, "Yes, sir, Officers' Club at six o'clock."

"You say it your way, Lieutenant, I say it my way. Be there then."

"Yes, sir."

"See Captain Hodges on your way out, and he will give you some orientation literature. Give him those addresses. That will be all."

Tyson stood. "Yes, sir." He saluted, turned, and left the adjutant's office, closing the door behind him.

Tyson stood near Hodges's desk, but the captain was bent over paperwork and did not look up at him. Tyson drew his notebook from his breast pocket and scribbled the addresses Levin had asked for. He laid the paper on Hodges's desk. "Colonel Levin asked me to give you these—"

"Fine." Hodges added without looking up from his desk, "Take that packet. Familiarize yourself with the post and its facilities."

Tyson picked up a large brown envelope stuffed with papers and put it in his attaché case.

Hodges said, "Begin your in-processing tomorrow."

"Yes, sir." Tyson headed toward the door.

"Tyson?"

"Yes, sir?"

Hodges looked up at him. "We didn't need this."

Tyson wasn't certain if the *we* referred to Hodges and Levin or Fort Hamilton or the Army or the officer corps or the nation. Probably all of the above. Tyson replied, "No, sir."

"If you should ever have reason to come into this office again, and I hope you don't, I expect you to look like a soldier."

Tyson took a step toward Hodges's desk. He wanted to ask this young staff officer what the hell he knew about being a soldier. Tyson took a deep breath.

Hodges glared at him.

Tyson said, "Good afternoon, sir." He turned quickly and left.

He was vaguely aware of passing between the desks in the outer office, striding quickly through the corridor, down the stairs, past the reception window, and out the glass doors into the sunlit parking area. He walked to his car and flung his attaché case into the front seat. He kicked the car door and put a dent in the panel, then shouted, "Damn it! Damn—" He suddenly looked back at the headquarters building. In an open second-story window he saw the stocky figure of Lieutenant Colonel Mortimer Levin, his hands behind his back, a cigar stuck in his mouth, watching him.

Tyson composed himself, got into his car, and pulled away from the headquarters building. As he drove through the narrow streets of the small post, he came to the belated realization that he was in the Army. He said it aloud. "I'm in the Army. I am *in* the Army."

His first tour of duty and subsequent release from active duty had always had a feeling of tentativeness, of unfinished business, an unfulfilled obligation to the Army, to his country, and to himself.

But this time, he understood, was the final muster, the last call to arms. In reality, this recall to duty was but a continuation of his service after a long furlough. He did not know how this would end, but for the first time, here at Fort Hamilton, he saw the end in sight.

26

Benjamin Tyson climbed the steps to the Officers' Club, housed in the gray granite artillery fort.

The foyer and the hallways that ran to the left and right were arched and vaulted, constructed of stone and brick, and covered in places with stucco. The floor was made of flagstone, and the lighting fixtures were black wrought iron. Because it had been a fort, there were few openings to the outside world: only small gun ports, and these were bricked over.

A man in his twenties, dressed in a gray suit, was sitting at the reception desk. "Your name, sir?"

"Tyson. Where is the bar, please?"

The man ignored the question. "May I see some identification, Lieutenant?"

Tyson replied, "What for?"

"Club regulations."

Tyson showed the man his driver's license, and the man checked the name against a list, then asked Tyson to sign in, which he did. The man said, "Thank you, sir. Bar is to the right."

Tyson walked down an arched corridor. Shorter arched cul-de-sacs extended at right angles in the direction of the Narrows. These were, he knew, the casemates, the places where the big guns had sat overlooking the Narrows. The gun ports here were bricked up also.

He entered a long windowless chamber that might have been the magazine where powder and shot had been stored but which now was the lounge. A long mahogany bar ran along the left side of the room, and tables sat along the right wall. A hand-painted sign said PATRIOTS' BAR.

The barroom was filled, and Tyson was surprised to see more civilian-attired people than uniformed officers. He supposed the clientele consisted of retired military personnel, government workers, civilian guests, and spouses.

The decor could have been East Side pub, but the patrons were not. For one thing, he noticed, despite the crowd, there was not that raucous noise that you hear in an after-work place. Rather, there was a subdued tone to the room, punctuated by an occasional laugh of the type a lieutenant gives when his captain has said something witty.

Tyson spotted Colonel Levin sitting by himself at the far end of the bar. Tyson walked down the length of the room and joined him. "Good evening, Colonel."

"Good evening, Lieutenant. Have a seat."

Tyson sat on the barstool beside Levin.

Levin said, "Did you get a chance to explore the club?"

"No, sir. I just got here."

"It's an interesting place. They don't make them like this anymore. It's a national historic landmark."

"Is it?"

"Yes, that's in the post information book. I suggest you read it."

"Yes, sir."

"Do you want to become a member here?"

Tyson lit a cigarette. "I'm not certain."

"Every officer is urged to join."

"Yes, sir, I know."

"In fact, I took the liberty of signing you up."

Tyson drew on his cigarette. "Thank you, Colonel."

Levin regarded him. "What's your drink, Tyson?"

Tyson thought that Levin put the question the way someone might ask, "What's your religious affiliation?" as though each man were born with or chose a drink for life. He looked at Colonel Levin. The man was an odd amalgam of U.S. Army and New York Jewish. Tyson would rather have had to deal with either of those two types but not both in the same personality.

"Tyson? Something to improve your hearing?"

"Sorry, Colonel. Dewar's and soda."

Colonel Levin said to the barmaid, "Sally, meet Lieutenant Tyson, a new member."

The middle-aged woman gave a friendly smile. "Welcome to Fort Hamilton . . . Lieutenant."

"Thank you, ma'am."

She looked at him curiously, taking in his longish hair and probably, he thought, wondering about a lieutenant in his forties. Sally suddenly brightened. "Oh, police."

This, thought Tyson, was a logical deduction. A police lieutenant would be in his forties, and that was how Sally fit Tyson's age to his rank.

Tyson waited for Levin to say something tactful. Levin said, "No, this is Lieutenant Benjamin Tyson, United States Army, who is the subject of a murder investigation."

Sally's mouth dropped open. "Oh . . . yes."

Tyson thought that was probably the best way to do it. He decided he liked Levin.

Colonel Levin informed Sally that Lieutenant Tyson's drink was Dewar's and soda, and Tyson knew he'd be unwise to order anything different next time he came in.

Levin ordered another Manhattan for himself, then said to Tyson, "Did you get over to finance? You're entitled to some pay."

"No, sir. My attorney advised me not to accept any money."

"Did he? Well, try not paying *him* and see if he gives you the same advice."

"Yes, sir. You see, that's also why I don't know about joining the club. I've signed in as ordered, but there are certain things I can't or won't do on advice of counsel. On the other hand, as you suggested, I would be well advised to act like an officer, to become part of this post and its community. So I'm in somewhat of a quandary, and I hope you understand if I don't appear as gung-ho as most newly assigned lieutenants."

Levin replied curtly, "I'm sure it isn't only the advice of counsel that's making you less than eager to fit in here."

"That's correct, Colonel. No offense, but I was doing okay as a civilian."

Levin lit a new cigar and didn't reply.

Tyson continued, "As you just witnessed, I'm a little old to be wearing a first lieutenant's bar, Colonel."

The barmaid set down the drinks and added them to the colonel's chit. Levin raised his glass. "Welcome."

Tyson raised his glass also but did not touch it to Levin's. "Thank you, Colonel Levin."

Both men drank, then Levin said, "Tomorrow you will get your ID card, your physical, your uniform, and all that. Start early. I expect you firmly established in the Army and ready for duty by eight hundred hours, day after tomorrow."

"Yes, sir. What sort of duty?"

"The Department of the Army has instructed the post commander to instruct me to assign you casual duties so that you have ample time to attend to any personal problems that may have arisen as a result of your unexpected recall to duty. Also to allow you time to attend to any legal necessities that may arise as a result of this ongoing investigation." Levin ate the cherry from his Manhattan. "In other words, you are attached to my office as I said, and I'm supposed to find something for you to do that won't take up any of your time."

"Why can't I just report to you every morning, then knock off for the day?"

"I thought about that, Tyson. But that's not consistent with the Army work ethic and, I suspect, not consistent with your own work ethic. Casual duties are often boring, demeaning, and demoralizing."

"Yes, sir." Tyson remembered being on casual duty once and concluding the same thing: It was stressful to be pretending to be doing something when you weren't. But that was then. Now he'd just as soon spend the time before the final disposition of his case with his family and lawyer.

Levin said, "Did you notice that granite triangular-shaped building as you came into the club?"

"Yes, sir."

"That was the old fort's caponier."

"I thought so."

"Don't be sarcastic, Lieutenant. A caponier is a fortification to protect the landward side of the coastal battery. Anyway, that's where the Harbor Defense Museum is housed. Did you know we have a museum here?"

"Yes, sir. There was a booklet in the orientation literature."

"Right. The curator is a fellow named Dr. Russell. Nice eccentric sort of chap. He's civil service. In fact, there he is over there." Levin cocked his head toward a table in the corner. "The guy with the glasses."

Tyson looked toward the cocktail table and saw a tall lanky man not more than thirty years old sitting with three other civilians.

Levin said, "I spoke to him earlier about taking you on as an assistant."

"Assistant *what?*"

"Museum curator."

Tyson said nothing.

Levin asked, "What's wrong with that?"

"Well . . . I don't . . ."

"Look, Tyson, I'm doing you a favor. First of all, it's a job that won't take up much of your time or mental energies. Secondly, it has dignity, as opposed to some other jobs I could cook up for you. Finally, it's outside the normal activities here, and it will keep you segregated from your brother officers, which is desirable for all parties. And your immediate supervisor will be Dr. Russell, who's a civilian and an okay guy. And four, it's across the lane from the O Club so you can hang out here if you get bored. Also it's a nice little museum and sort of interesting. So what do you say?"

"I . . . don't know. . . . Do I have to wear my uniform?"

"Only on certain occasions. Like when dignitaries come to visit or school groups come."

"School groups?"

"Yes, you'll give tours to school kids. And senior citizen groups."

"Tours . . . ?"

"Do you need another drink to improve your hearing?" He called to the barmaid. "Another round, Sally." He looked back at Tyson. "Look, Lieutenant, I'm under orders to walk on eggs with you. That's between us. And I'm becoming media-conscious. The museum job is good. It *looks* good. Take it."

"I'll take it."

"Fine." Levin held up his glass, and Tyson took his fresh drink and touched the glass to Levin's.

Levin said, "I'll introduce you to Dr. Russell later."

"Yes, sir."

Levin finished half of his drink, and Tyson could see he was feeling the effects. His unhealthy pallor had turned a nice ruddy color, and his wheezing seemed less stertorous. Tyson suspected that Colonel Levin looked good every night around this time.

Levin said, "The public affairs office has been handling newspeople all day."

Tyson looked up from his drink. "Sir?"

"This is an open post. We really can't stop the press from coming through the gates unless we have special orders from higher up to keep them out."

"I see."

"We can, however, keep them out of *here* because this is a private club."

Tyson nodded. "I had trouble getting in."

"So did a lot of other people tonight, thanks to you. Point is, you can get waylaid by the press anyplace else on post that isn't a restricted area or isn't your place of work, like the museum. That's the instructions the Department of the Army is giving to the media. So you're safe in the museum and the club. You have about ten yards to run between the two places and twenty yards to the parking lot. So it's up to you to use your good judgment in dealing with these people. From what I read, you've displayed good judgment in the past."

Tyson said, "Is that your personal opinion, Colonel, or is that a compliment you've been asked to relay to me?"

"Both. Subject closed." Levin said, "Take your drink." He rose and made his way a bit unsteadily toward the table at which Dr. Russell was sitting. Levin said, "Dr. Russell, may I present Lieutenant Tyson?"

Dr. Russell stood and took Tyson's hand warmly. "Has Colonel Levin told you I'm in need of an assistant?"

Tyson replied, "Yes, he has." Tyson noted that Dr. Russell had a pleasant professorial accent. The man was taller than Tyson, very thin, and wore the sort of rumpled suit one might expect of a museum curator, not to mention a civil servant.

Dr. Russell introduced Tyson to the three men he was drinking with, and they seemed genuinely happy to make his acquaintance, as though they'd been introduced to a celebrity. Tyson had come to expect a wide range of reactions from people who knew who he was, and there was always that interesting few seconds as people processed the name and face and decided if they were happy to meet him or not.

Levin, Russell, and the three other men were making small talk, and Tyson tuned back in as Dr. Russell addressed him, "I've always thought it desirable to have a uniformed officer conduct some of these tours. I'm glad this opportunity came up."

Tyson replied, "So am I."

Dr. Russell's brow knitted as though he were thinking about what he had just said. He added, "Of course I realize this won't be a lengthy arrangement. You won't be here long, will you?"

"I think not."

Colonel Levin took Tyson's arm and announced, "We have a table waiting."

Tyson and Levin left the bar and went into the main corridor. Levin observed, "Dr. Russell seemed happy to have you aboard."

Tyson responded, "He'll be sad to see me leave."

They entered a medium-sized dining room that looked to be fairly new. Large windows let in the red light of a beautiful dusk. Levin explained, "This is a recent addition. The exterior is built of granite to blend in with the old fort, but Dr. Russell is nonetheless appalled. Everyone else is happy about the room."

Tyson saw that about half the tables were empty, and Levin asked the hostess to seat them away from other diners. They were shown to a table near one of the large windows looking out toward the Narrows.

Tyson said, "You could do a nice court-martial here."

Levin didn't reply immediately, then said, "I thought of it, but it would inconvenience people who normally have lunch here."

Tyson put his blue napkin on his lap. "Still, it's a great view." He asked, "Where do you hold trials now?"

"Oh, we have a small room in the JAG building. But that wouldn't do."

"I've sometimes wondered why there are no courthouses in the Army."

Levin shrugged. "Maybe because there is no permanently convened court. Military justice is ad-hoc, Tyson, unlike civilian justice. Therefore, anyplace will do."

A young waitress came to the table and greeted Levin. She said, "Manhattan, sir?"

"Right. Ann, this is the Lieutenant Tyson who's been in the news recently. Dewar's and soda, and I'd appreciate it if you told the staff not to talk to reporters."

The waitress took a second to digest all of that, then quickly looked at Tyson. "Oh. Hello . . . hello."

"Hello."

"Soda and water?"

"Dewar's and soda."

"Yes, sir." She dropped two menus on the table and hurried off to get the drinks. Levin lit a new cigar.

Tyson perused the menu. "How is the food, Colonel?"

"Compared to what? The Four Seasons or the mess hall?"

"The Four Seasons, sir."

"Never been there. Hey, I guess I should stop baiting you. It's not your fault you were a successful civilian. I recommend the steak. Good meat, and they have a charcoal grill."

Tyson put his menu down. "Fine." He lit a cigarette. Neither spoke. A new waitress came with the drinks and left with their dinner order. Levin observed, "We'll have the whole staff come and check you out by dessert." Levin raised his glass, and Tyson realized the colonel was one of those men who felt that alcohol was a sacred nectar that needed to be offered to some worthy sentiment before it was imbibed. He also realized Levin was getting a little rocky. Levin said, "I wish you a happy stay here."

They drank, and they spoke in general terms for a while, discussing the post and how the Army had changed in the last two decades and how it had remained the same.

Levin had another drink, and Tyson admired his capacity. Levin said apropos of nothing, "I told you I was raised in Brighton Beach. My father used to work here at Hamilton. He was a maintenance supervisor, a government employee. My brother and I used to tell everyone he was a G-man." Levin laughed.

Tyson stirred his drink. He didn't know where this was heading, but he was fairly sure he didn't want to get there.

Levin continued, "Anyway, I used to come to work with him sometimes on weekends—when I was in high school—this was during the Korean conflict."

"War."

"Whatever. Anyway, I guess I was very impressed by the officers strutting around. They had nicer uniforms then, and some of them carried swagger sticks. I was very impressionable."

Tyson said, "My father claims he saw Lindbergh take off for Paris, and that inspired him to be a flier. He was a Navy pilot. When was this addition to the club built?"

Levin seemed intent on his own narrative. "And I would sweep the floors and change the light bulbs. Right here . . . well, I mean in the original section. This was the O Club then, too. Anyway, I would see these gentlemen at their mess on Sundays, and I guess it stuck with me, being from a hard-up family. So in college I joined the ROTC program, and here I am." Levin drank some water and cleared his throat. "You can put a Jew in the Army, Tyson, but you can't put the Army in the Jew. I don't know why I stayed. I guess there must be something about it I like."

Tyson commented, "A military career can be very rewarding."

"I guess the officer corps is a quick way to achieve genteel respectability. It's always been for southerners. Why not a Jew from Brighton Beach, Brooklyn? Right, Tyson?"

"Why not?"

"Look, I'm not that drunk, and there is a point to this. We are all equal in social standing, we are all gentlemen by act of congress."

"Yes, sir."

Levin leaned across the table. "But I want to reveal to you an inequity in the system. Even though the Army does not care about your background, breeding,

or social standing for purposes of promotions, assignments, or career advance-
ment, they do care about that when they court-martial you. Follow?"

"Sort of."

"Let me make an unfortunate but necessary comparison. Lieutenant Calley,
the platoon leader of My Lai fame, was an underprivileged kid, as I recall,
lower-middle-class background. You were quite the opposite type of officer and
gentleman." Levin drew on his cigar and lowered his voice. "Now, I don't know
what the *fuck* happened at that hospital, Lieutenant, but let's assume *something*
happened that was not entirely kosher, not precisely in keeping with 'The Rules
of Engagement' or 'The Rules of Land Warfare.' Okay? Then you, Benjamin
Tyson, were supposed to be able to make finer distinctions of morality than a
man like Calley. Follow?"

Tyson did not respond.

Levin continued, "You are more accountable and more liable than the poor
schnooks around you who are firing their rifles into helpless people. No one
will be sympathetic or understanding or offer the defense that you were just an
underprivileged, teenage draftee who was as much a victim as a victimizer. You
were an educated, mature man, a volunteer, and an officer." Levin pointed his
cigar at Tyson. "You may not have pulled a trigger, but if you did nothing to
stop it—*even at the risk of your own life*—then God help you." He jabbed his
cigar toward Tyson. The two men stared at each other, then Levin said, "That's
the point."

Tyson replied, "Social rank, too, has its problems."

"Right." Levin settled back in his chair. "I've been following this in the news.
And I'm trying to put myself on the court-martial board. I'm sitting there
listening to testimony and looking at you. Maybe I'm envious of your good
looks, your advantages in life. Also maybe I'm a little awed. I'm thinking to
myself as I sit on that board—that jury—that you are supposed to represent the
culmination of our civilization, the final product of the great American experi-
ment. And I look at you in the defendant's chair, and it's hard for me to
comprehend how you could have been a party to what they are saying happened there. And that would frighten me, Lieutenant Tyson, because if you
were capable of that, then what hope is there for the rest of us?"

Tyson said, "To be honest with you, Colonel, after Vietnam I never again
thought there was any hope for any of us."

Levin looked sad.

Tyson finished his drink and lit another cigarette. At length he said softly,
"And regarding your estimation of me as a product of our country you are
partly right. My concept of right and wrong and of duty in that year of 1968 was
influenced less by what I learned in the Army than by what I saw happening in
America. I found it difficult to do my duty to a country that wasn't doing its
duty to me. The essence of loyalty, Colonel, is reciprocity. A citizen or a soldier
owes allegiance to the state in exchange for protection, for the state's allegiance to and duty toward the individual. That is an implicit social contract. I
may not have put it so well in 1968, but in my guts I felt my country had
abandoned me and my men and in fact the entire Army in Southeast Asia."

Levin nodded in understanding. "Heavy stuff before a beef dinner. Here's
our food. Bon appétit."

The two men ate in silence, then Colonel Levin began speaking in a pleasant
tone as though the previous conversation had been entirely amiable. "Do you
want to sign your oath now?"

"Do you have it with you?"

"Right here." Levin tapped his side pocket. "Want to sign it?"

"No, I just wondered if you had it."

"Be careful, Lieutenant."

"Sorry, Colonel."

Levin shrugged. "Doesn't matter. I called the JAG school in Virginia for a legal opinion. They said the one you signed in 1967 is still good. Be advised that you're still bound by that oath of office."

"I understand."

Levin chewed thoughtfully on a piece of bread, swallowed it, and said, "Do you want some advice?"

Tyson thought he had gotten enough advice over the past weeks to last him twenty years. He replied, "I don't think it would be appropriate for you—"

"Let me worry about that. You've been assigned to me, so I can give you advice as your commander."

"Yes, sir."

Levin sipped on his water, then said, "In case you don't know it, the Army is very nervous about this. They're afraid of you."

Tyson nodded. "So there's some advantage after all to being a respected member of society?"

"Right. And I'll tell you what scares the Army—they're like organized religion in this respect—the Army is scared of scandal."

"Scandal."

"Right. Listen to what I'm saying, Tyson. It might save your neck." Levin looked around the dining hall, then leaned forward and spoke in a confidential tone. "As far as the Army is concerned, any officer who fucks up is ipso facto a renegade, atypical of the officer corps, no matter how fine a background he comes from. The officer corps is like the priesthood. It is a calling, and when you answer the calling, you leave your world behind and enter a new one. It's not like being vice-president in charge of whatever you were in charge of at whatever that company was you worked for. When you are an officer in the United States Army your conduct reflects on the Army and the officer corps. Like a priest and his church. So it is not only you who are being judged but all of us: you, me, Captain Hodges, and the Joint Chiefs of Staff. Follow?"

"Yes, sir. But Captain Hodges was about ten years old at the time of the incident, and the Joint Chiefs of Staff have turned over a few times."

"But there is a continuity in the military, an institutional memory. If they can claim honors from the past, then they must accept the guilt as well. Your old unit, the Seventh Cavalry, is still trying to live down the Little Big Horn. Conversely, when you finally get your uniform on you'll wear a presidential unit citation given to the Seventh Cav long before you were even born. Point is, you have to somehow convince the Army that you are a *typical* product of the fucked-up state of the whole military system—not now, perhaps, but certainly at that time. And that you, who used to be a sensitive boy, a boy who got upset when his little pet canary croaked, became really psychotic during all that infantry training. You were a victim of a system that issued little plastic cards called 'The Rules of Engagement' telling you whom you were allowed to kill in less than a hundred words, then turned you loose with an undertrained, undisciplined, and demoralized platoon of seventeen-year-old armed savages from the Ozarks and the slums and made *you* liable for *their* actions. Ha, ha, what a laugh! Right? You had as much control over them as I have over the weather. Right?"

Tyson didn't reply.

Levin continued, "If you can threaten to bring the whole temple down around their heads, if you can hint that not only did American boys kill indiscriminately, but got killed in great numbers because of bad training, bad leadership, bad tactics—are you following me, Tyson? This isn't easy for me to say. But I *know* what it was like then. I was there, Tyson. Not in the infantry, but close enough to the front to see and hear all I wanted to see and hear." Levin looked at Tyson closely and said, "Tell them that if they stand you in front of a court-martial, you will testify for a week, indicting the Army, and that you'll give lots of interviews to the media. Tell them you'll take them with you."

Tyson pushed his plate away and lit a cigarette. He thought about Chet Brown telling him not to do exactly what Colonel Levin was suggesting he do. Apparently everyone thought he had great secrets to reveal. But Tyson did not recall thinking at the time that the Army was the cause of Miséricorde Hospital. He did not at that time blame them for his actions or the actions of his men. He had not protested the bad training, the immaturity of the troops, the vague guidelines of conduct, or his own unpreparedness as a combat infantry leader. If he had one scrap of evidence that he'd had such thoughts then—a letter home or a memo to his superiors—then, yes, he might reverse the blame for Miséricorde Hospital and indict the Army. But he'd accepted the blame then, and it was not justifiable to rewrite history in order to escape the blame now. He said to Colonel Levin, "I think I have to take this walk alone, Colonel."

Levin sighed. "Yeah. You and Jesus Christ, Tyson. Wise up." Levin hunched over the club chit with a pencil and tallied it. "How many drinks did you have?"

"Four."

"You drink too much. But at these prices you might as well." He looked at Tyson. "Listen, I'm not saying you should indict the Army. I'd never say that. But you should mention the fact that if they indict you, you'll return the favor. They'll back off."

"I'm not much of a bluffer. But thank you for the advice."

"We talked baseball." Levin stood. "One parting piece of advice, Lieutenant. Get the best goddamned certified military lawyer money can buy. Don't take one of those assigned yo-yos from the JAG office. They cost nothing, and that's exactly what you get."

Tyson stood also. "I've heard of certified military lawyers, but I'm not certain of what they are."

"Civilian lawyers certified by the military to serve as defense counsel at general courts-martial. There are only a few of them. Check the bar association."

"Could you recommend one?"

"No way." Levin picked up the chit and flipped it to Tyson. "You sign for it, Lieutenant. Your club number is T-38. I wrote it in. Thanks for dinner." He left.

Tyson picked up the chit and saw, written in pencil in the signature space, the name *Vincent Corva, Esq. N.Y.C.* He erased the name and signed his own.

27

Benjamin Tyson stood in front of the tunnel-like opening of a large artillery casemate and faced a group of about twenty senior citizens crowded around waiting expectantly for his next piece of useless information. There was no one else in the museum except this group, and he suspected that very few people came on their own.

The museum itself was interesting, as Levin had said. The caponier was a nearly perfectly preserved specimen of mid-nineteenth-century military architecture. The redbrick pillars rising into the arched ceilings were an appropriate setting for the martial displays. The displays themselves—cannon, muskets, sabers, uniforms, and such—were not unique or particularly good examples of their type, but set in the old fort, *in situ,* so to speak, they took on a more immediate significance. Still, Tyson thought, as someone once said, museums were the graveyards of the arts—in this case the martial arts, which were themselves inextricably tied to graveyards.

Tyson laid his hand on a four-foot-high section of black wrought-iron fence that ran the six-foot width of the casemate opening. He smiled at the group. "This fence has a personal significance for me."

He saw several sets of perfect white dentures smile back. For the life of him he could not understand why people that age would want to hear any of this. Yet they were attentive and polite. Conversely, the Boy Scout group of the day before, who were supposed to show the curiosity of youth, not to mention some hormonal interest in the subject of war, were bored and restless. Tyson thought perhaps he didn't have the hang of it yet. He said, "This fence dates back to about the 1840s. You can see here among the finely scrolled ironwork, the federal shield and American eagle, which was a common motif in those days."

Tyson badly wanted a cigarette and/or a breath of fresh air. The massive walls of the caponier held out some of the afternoon heat, but by the same token, the air was stagnant and redolent with cloying floral perfume and dusting powder. Also, the modern track lighting was hot. He supposed it was difficult to vent or air-condition such a structure. No, they didn't build them like that anymore.

A man said, "What personal significance does that fence have for you, Lieutenant?"

"What? Oh, yes. I did say that, didn't I? Well, this fence section is not from Fort Hamilton. It was salvaged from the old Federal Building on Whitehall Street before it was torn down. Now, to most men in the New York metropolitan area the words Whitehall Street are synonymous with induction into the armed forces." He smiled and saw a few of the old men nod and smile back.

"Anyway," he continued, "I remember this old fence from when *I* reported in for active duty, and I was surprised to see it *here."* He smiled again. In truth he didn't remember the fence at all. He'd had other things on his mind that morning than the architecture of that gloomy old processing facility that had sent a million men to the battlefields. He looked to his right to see the next station of the cross and caught a glimpse of himself in a glass display case. He was honest enough to admit he rather liked the way he looked in uniform. Most men did. He straightened his tie.

A woman's voice asked, "Did you see combat in Vietnam?"

He turned toward the voice. She was standing at the back of the group, somewhat taller than the generation born at the beginning of the century. Tyson wondered how long she'd been there. Most of the white heads were turned toward her.

Karen Harper added, "What are all those medals for?"

He cleared his throat and replied, "Mostly good conduct. I got one every time I was good. I have seven medals."

A few people laughed.

Tyson said to his tour group, "Why don't you look around on your own awhile? I'll be right back." He moved through the group, took Karen Harper's arm, and led her toward the front door. Outside, on the lane between the museum and the Officers' Club, she disengaged her arm from his hand. She said, "Lieutenants do not take the arm of female majors like that."

"Do you want a drink?"

"No. The last time I had a drink with you it got in the papers."

He smiled. "That caused me some trouble . . . at home."

"Did it?" She stood silently a moment, then said, "Me too. I mean . . . I have that friend I told you about. The infantry colonel, in Washington. But I shouldn't be telling you this."

Tyson felt just a twinge of jealousy. He'd somehow assumed she had a boyfriend, but he didn't particularly want it confirmed. He forced a smile. "I'll write him a letter explaining. You write one for me."

"Sure. Listen to me, Lieutenant, I think you're becoming a little too familiar."

"Sorry. I missed you."

"Stop that. Secondly, you're a lousy tour guide."

"I know."

"Third, I have some important things to tell you."

Tyson drew a deep but discreet breath. He said in a light tone, "So you've finally reached a conclusion in your investigation?"

"I've reached many conclusions." She turned toward the Officers' Club. "Follow me."

Tyson followed her into the club, through the foyer area to a steep and narrow stone staircase that wound up to the second floor of the club. As they walked Tyson said, "Observe that this level is built of brick, not granite, indicating it was built afterward. The big guns originally sat here when this was an open parapet and—"

"I know all of that. I've had this tour. What is going to become of your tour group?"

"They'll get back on the bus and talk about us all the way back to the home." She suppressed a smile. "You're being mean. I thought they were cute."

"It's mean to call them cute too. I don't want to get that old."

"You may not." They came to a long, roofed terrace whose seaward side was walled-in glass. Bright sunlight flooded through the glass, casting prismatic colors over the floor. Tyson said, "I found two reception rooms up here, either one of which would be perfect for a court-martial. Want to see them?"

"The Washington room and the Jackson room. I know them."

"Good. What do you think? The Washington has a really neat cathedral ceiling, but the Stonewall Jackson room is rather more *intime,* if you know what I mean."

"You're in a flippant mood this afternoon."

Tyson looked through the glass. Below he could see the new dining wing to his right, the Shore Parkway beyond that, then the Narrows, spanned by the Verrazano Bridge. A mile away was the Staten Island shoreline. Tyson could make out the gray artillery fort called Battery Weed, which was the sister fort to the one he was standing in. "Nice view." He lit a cigarette and asked, "Do I look as good in uniform as you imagined?"

"I assure you I never gave any thought to how you would look in uniform. But, yes, you look fine. You didn't get much hair taken off."

"I did. It grows back very quickly. By the way, did you ever find my umbrella?"

"No. I told you I left it on the plane. Do you want me to pay you for it?"

"It was a gift. Why don't you just buy me a similar one? Black."

"All right. Black." Karen Harper said, "I've been instructed to submit the report of my findings within five days."

"Good. Then we'll all know where we stand."

"Yes, the waiting is the tough part. I didn't mean to drag this out, but my resources have been limited by the provisions of Article 31 of the UCMJ, which, as you know, stipulates only a preliminary inquiry. Anyway, I'm to recommend one of two things: that the matter be dropped or that there is probable cause to believe that there was a violation of the Uniform Code of Military Justice and that charges be drawn up and forwarded to an Article 32 investigating body for consideration." She continued, "My recommendation would not be binding, as you know."

"But still it carries some force, and you're wondering what the Army wants you to recommend."

She replied strongly, "I don't care what they want—"

Tyson went on, "You're trying to figure out if they want you to be the heavy. If Harper says go with it, then the machinery is set in motion to take the investigation to a grand jury, and it will be you who prodded them into it. But if Harper says 'No go,' then they shrug and reluctantly drop the case even though your recommendation is not binding. Then the media flak is diverted toward you. I don't envy you."

Karen Harper let out a short breath. "Can I speak to you in confidence?"

"Of course."

She hesitated, then began, "Well, I always thought this thing was partly staged, partly a put-up job. I mean, why would the Army place so much responsibility on one individual? Why me?"

"Now you're thinking."

"This investigation should have been handled from the beginning by a trained staff—CID, FBI, Justice Department, and so forth. It should have lasted only long enough to determine if the facts warranted a grand jury investigation."

"True. But they've done nothing illegal so far."

"Well . . . perhaps not illegal. Just . . . unusual." She looked directly at him. "Let me ask you something. Has anyone . . . anyone from the government approached you . . . with an offer?" Karen Harper waited. "Well? Has anyone other than me been speaking to you?"

"No."

"You see, Lieutenant, I don't like being played for a fool any more than you like being a scapegoat."

"I certainly know how you feel."

"And I don't think either of us likes being pawns in a game that we know nothing about."

"No, we do not. Listen, Major, if you thought this was a straight case of seeing that justice was done, then you were naïve in the extreme. This case has gone beyond anything we said to one another and any evidence you may have gathered. Don't be surprised if someone approaches *you* and recommends to you what you should recommend to the Army."

She turned toward the glass wall and stared off into the distance. Tyson, too, looked out the windows. An ocean liner, the *Rotterdam,* cut through the Narrows and slid beneath the central span of the bridge, rocking the small pleasure craft in its wake. A jetliner approached from the south, making its descent into Kennedy Airport. Tyson recalled the vacations he'd taken with Marcy, the places where they'd been happy together. And it struck him with full force that that life was gone, that the life to come was shrouded with images of jail, divorce, financial troubles, and the stigma of criminality, proven or unproven.

Karen Harper broke into his thoughts. "I must tell you, Lieutenant, and you already know, that I've found sufficient facts to recommend that a grand jury consider the charge of murder."

"Then do it."

"But I've also begun to . . . suspect that the government is tampering with this case. And if that is true, then your rights may have been violated somewhere in this process—"

"Oh, look, Major, my rights were violated from the day the obstetrician slapped my ass without provocation. But sometimes the authorities have to do certain things for the general good of society and even for the good of the individual they are slapping around. Where did you get your legal training? In a convent?"

"You sound as though you're defending the government."

"I'm certainly not doing that. But I do understand that they're engaged in damage control."

"Did you make some sort of deal with the Army or the Justice Department?"

"No."

"Would you consider any sort of deal?"

"Depends on the deal. You never take the first one."

"So someone did approach you? That's illegal during an Article 31 investigation. Only I may approach you and only with your permission."

"You may stand on ceremony. I'm trying to stay out of Leavenworth."

"How were you approached? What were the circumstances?"

"Is this still off the record?"

She replied, "No. I can't hear anything like that off the record. I would have to report that."

"Then drop it."

She nodded reluctantly, then said, "Can I give you some basic advice?"

"You'll have to take a number."

She ignored this and said, "Get a qualified lawyer. Not Sloan. I've spoken to him, and he's out of his league on this. Get a good JAG lawyer or a certified military lawyer."

"That's excellent advice, Major. A little odd coming from my investigator but excellent nonetheless. I assume that means you're through with me."

"Yes. I'm going back to Washington tomorrow to finalize my report. That's one of the reasons I wanted to speak to you. To see if you want to include a written or oral statement in the report."

Tyson thought she could have asked that over the telephone. "I'll think about it." He inquired, "Aren't you due to be released from active duty?"

"I was. But I'm not being released. After I submit my report I am officially through with this case. However, if they need any clarifications they'd rather not have to subpoena me from civilian life. So I'm being held until the final disposition of this case."

"Tough break. I suspect, also, that the Army doesn't want you making any clarifications to the press, which is the real reason they're holding on to you. In other words, you've seen and heard too much to be allowed to go free. That should have occurred to you when you accepted this case. Well, they'll let you out eventually."

"I'm not upset about being held on duty . . . it changes my civilian plans a bit though. I was supposed to join a law firm . . . here in New York."

"I'll look you up if I need a new will."

"But my problems are insignificant compared to yours."

"Your problems will be a lot more significant if you pursue your theory or suspicions that the government is tampering with this case. They'll eat you alive, Major. So take some advice from an older man who's survived many corporate jungles as well as the Asian jungle. Don't try to be a hero. Let me worry about what the government is up to."

"I'm not concerned about you personally, you understand. I'm only concerned that justice—"

"Please. That word stimulates my gag reflex these days. Look, just play the game, keep your back to a solid object, and watch out for anyone heading for the door or the light switch."

She snorted. "That's nonsense."

"There are times, Karen, I wish you were a man and others times I'm glad you're not."

"That's sexist and entirely too personal. You may not use my first name."

They both stayed silent, then Tyson asked, "Other than the trouble you had with your friend, was there any official trouble?"

She rubbed her lower lip, then replied, "Well, yes. That's why they wanted me to wrap it up."

He laughed.

"It's not funny."

"Men and women are funny." He added, "Who's giving you a hard time? That stuffed shirt, Van Arken? I've heard and read a few things about that character."

She didn't respond but said, "I think they may have you under some sort of surveillance."

"That's all right. I'm not skipping the country, meeting with foreign agents, or sleeping around."

"Good. May I have a cigarette?"

"Another one? You had one last week." He took out his pack and shook one loose. She took it, and he lit it. She drew on it and exhaled, then coughed. She caught her breath and said, "You should quit."

"You're the one who coughed."

"Listen, Lieutenant . . . to deny . . . well, to pretend that . . . there has not been some . . ." She drew on her cigarette again, then looked at her watch. "I have to go."

"Finish the sentence."

She nodded. "Well . . . some words and feelings, I guess you would say

. . . that have passed between us . . . that were other than professional or germane to the inquiry . . ."

"I'm losing the subject and object of the sentence. Do you mean that you think we've developed a personal rapport?"

"Yes, that's what I meant."

"An attraction of sorts."

"I suppose."

"Well, me too." He looked at her and reminded her, "You said on our first interview that wouldn't happen."

"Did I?"

"Yes. Well, anyway, I like you very much, and now the air is clear."

"Yes."

He could see her hand with the cigarette shaking, and he realized his mouth had gone dry. "Well . . . so . . . what should we do about that?"

"Nothing." She cleared her throat and threw the cigarette down. "If you want to include a statement in my report, notify me before noon tomorrow."

"Where are you staying?"

"The guest house. Here."

"Can we have dinner tonight?"

"Certainly not. Not unless you want to get me into more trouble than I'm already in."

"Sorry about that. It wasn't intentional."

"If it were anyone but you, I'd say it was an intentional ploy to gain some advantage. Anyway, it was as much my fault as yours." She extended her hand. "Good-bye, Lieutenant."

He took her hand. "I'll be in my quarters tonight."

"And I'll be in mine." She turned and walked away.

Tyson watched her moving briskly down the bright sunny terrace. He said to himself, *Well, there is flesh and blood there after all.* He knew that he would see her again, and he knew, too, that nothing would come of it—not in a carnal sense anyway. But he understood, just as she must, that if the circumstances were different, then the outcome would be different. And when the time came that they parted for the last time, they would both be content in the knowledge that they had changed each other's life for the better.

28

Ben Tyson lay stretched out on the couch of his darkened living room. The small room was stifling hot, and he wore only a pair of running shorts. A cold bottle of beer dripped onto the coffee table. He sat up and took a deep breath. His two-mile run around the post had left him exhausted. "You smoke too much, you drink too much, and you're old." He recalled the grueling infantry training he'd once accomplished with relative ease: thirty-mile forced marches with full combat gear, a hundred push-ups at a time, rock climbing a five-hundred-foot waterfall during jungle training in Panama. "My God, you were tough then."

He stood slowly and walked to the small window fan. He didn't know what the policy was on air conditioners, and he didn't care because he'd decided to rough it out though his resolve was weakening. "Pussy, Tyson. You're a pussy." He did fifty quick jumping jacks, then began a series of bends. As he did he looked around the room. It was freshly painted and judging by the size of it, a half gallon would have done the job. The rest of the ground floor consisted of a small dining area and a kitchen. Upstairs were two bedrooms and a small bathroom. All the units in the row of redbrick attached houses were similar. Families with one and even two children were his neighbors. "Tyson," he said aloud, "you've been out of touch."

Cheap maple furniture, government property, was placed here and there, but he could bring his own, he was told. He tried to picture his furniture in this place and decided he'd have to stand it on end to make it fit. He'd have much preferred bachelor officers' quarters, which were more motel-like and efficient than this pretense of a home. But somewhere in the bowels of the Pentagon some bright half-wit had decided that Ben and Marcy should be given the opportunity to cohabitate. Presumably this decision was made in the spirit of the zookeepers who decide when and where the prize pandas should be allowed to mate.

There were no rugs or carpets on the wood floors, but in Army tradition the floors were highly polished. There were blinds on the windows but no drapes. His bedroom furniture consisted of a box spring and double mattress on a steel frame, one nightstand, and a mismatched chest of drawers. The second bedroom had a single bed, presumably for David. He'd had to sign for linens and towels but was expected to eventually get his own.

The kitchen held a stove and refrigerator and little else. There was no dishwasher, but he had no dishes so it worked out well. He wondered if he should get a coffeepot and invite the colonel and his lady for coffee. Medals will be worn. Bring your own cups and spoons.

Tyson straightened up and took several deep breaths. The sun was fully set now, and the only illumination in the room came from the street lamps casting stripes of light and dark through the blinds. He hadn't been given a television and hadn't bothered to buy a radio. American primitive. He understood how fragile and statistically beyond the norm had been his existence in the magic suburb.

This wasn't exactly house arrest, he reminded himself. He only had to be here between midnight and 6 A.M. He could conceivably take the subway into Manhattan and have dinner with someone. He could even drive into Garden City and go to his club or to his house and turn on the air conditioner, watch television, or jump into the Jacuzzi. But that wasn't what he wanted to do. He wanted to stay here, sweat, be bored, be alone, think, suffer, and get tough. "Tough," he said aloud.

Tyson ended his exercises and stood in front of the window fan again. A movement outside caught his eye, and he peered between the blinds. On the small lane that cut between the facing row houses he saw a figure approaching: a woman dressed in light slacks and dark top. She was carrying something in each hand, looking at the nameplates on the houses. She stopped in front of his unit, hesitated, then strode up the path. In the light of the porch lamp, Tyson saw it was Karen Harper, carrying a furled umbrella.

He saw her lean the umbrella against his door, then the mail slot opened and a folded Army-tan envelope began to appear. Tyson stepped quickly to the front door, knelt, and pushed the envelope back outside. The envelope reappeared, and Tyson pushed it back but this time met with some resistance. Karen Harper called out softly, "What are you doing? Get away from there."

He spoke through the mail slot. "Is this a bill?"

"Don't be an idiot. Take this."

He yanked on the envelope and pulled it in through the slot. He stood and opened the door, and the umbrella fell at his feet. He looked up the path and saw Karen Harper halfway to the lane. He picked up the umbrella, noticing it had a PX tag on it, and threw it back into the living room. He pulled the door shut and followed her, the envelope still in his hand. He caught up with her as she turned onto the lane. They walked side by side in silence. She finally said, "Get some clothes on if you intend to walk next to me."

"It's hot. What's in this envelope?"

"You'll see when you open it. When are you going to get a telephone?"

"When I think of someone I want to call."

"You were asked to put in a telephone to facilitate this investigation."

"I have telephones in Garden City, Sag Harbor, and my borrowed apartment in Manhattan. I don't think I can afford another one on my salary."

"Well, no one can order you to install a telephone in your quarters, but it would be more convenient for everyone, yourself and your family included, if you did."

"I'll give it some consideration. Come on back. I'll give you a beer."

"I've got work to do."

"I want to discuss your request for a statement."

She slowed her pace. "All right. But we can't talk in your quarters."

"I'll get some clothes on, and we'll walk. Come and take a look at my accommodations."

She hesitated, then followed him back. He showed her in and turned on the table lamp beside the couch. He looked at her in the light, noticing the simple blue short-sleeve blouse and the light cotton slacks. She wore white tennis shoes.

Karen Harper glanced at him a few times, keeping her eyes focused on his, taking care not to drop them to his mostly bare body.

Tyson thought she looked rather good in civilian clothes. He noticed, too, that she was actually thinner than she appeared in uniform—smaller breasts and hips, more lithe, and longer limbed. He waved his arm around the room. "Not bad for an officer and a gentleman." He added, "I think it needs a mirror to make it look larger."

She didn't reply but looked at him oddly. He said, "Oh, yes. Bugs. Not cockroaches, to be sure." He smiled. "Ben Tyson is wising up. I had a private security firm here this morning, and they pronounced the premises bug-free. Cost me a bundle. I'd have liked for them to have found something. Then you could have seen the stuff hit the fan."

"You're a thorough man."

"I'm becoming so. Also, if I had a phone, I wouldn't discuss anything sensitive on it." He added, "As for *me* having a bug here to record you or anyone, you have my word again, as an officer and a gentleman, that there is no recording or transmitting device here."

She replied, "You didn't have to say that."

"No, we're beyond that. But just to be sure, can I check you for recording devices?"

She smiled. "Certainly not."

Tyson shrugged. "Can't hurt to ask. Anyway, this game is getting damned serious, isn't it? I mean, they've lifted my passport, I'm fairly certain I'm being watched, and I've been placed on restriction."

"The restriction is not very onerous."

"This house is onerous. Do you want to see the rest of the palace?"

"No." She added in a less than cordial tone, "If you think you are a martyr, you need to get some perspective." She looked around the room. "Most people have never had the kind of house or life you had. I don't know why anyone is supposed to feel sympathetic when we hear about someone who has lost his manor and now lives in the gatehouse. Half the world would give their left arm for the gatehouse."

Tyson did not respond.

She stayed silent a moment, then said, "You know, your real problem is that you may be charged with murder. Your problem of reduced life-style is minor. I'd advise you to give more thought to the murder charge and less to your creature comforts." She paused. "I'm sorry, I shouldn't be lecturing you."

"But you're right. And I've come to the same conclusion. I mean to spend as much time here as possible until this is resolved. If I wind up in Leavenworth the transition will not be so shocking. If I wind up home I will kiss my garbage compactor." He smiled.

She smiled in return. "I admit it *is* hot as hell in here."

"Want a beer?"

"All right."

Tyson went into the kitchen and came back with two opened bottles of beer. He handed her one and said, "I got these glasses at Bloomingdale's. They look just like Budweiser bottles. *Très chic.*" He added quickly, "I'm not whining. I like beer out of a bottle."

"I doubt it."

Tyson hoisted his bottle and gulped down half the beer. She drank from her bottle. Tyson said, "What's in the envelope?"

"Just some forms for you to sign."

"I don't sign Army forms."

"I heard."

"Did you? Word travels fast."

"You're the subject of many people's attention these days. Don't let it go to your head. Anyway, these are just forms stating the times and locations of our meetings and confirming that you were read your rights. You can discuss them with your attorney before you sign them, but I'd like to have them before I leave tomorrow."

"And if I can't reach my attorney?"

"Well . . . then mail them to me in Washington."

"You need them to include in your report."

"Yes."

"The one that's due five days from today?"

"Well . . . I thought I'd get this taken care of while you were here. Also there was the umbrella—"

"It was good of you to walk across post to deliver these forms and the umbrella. Especially considering you could have had everything delivered to the museum tomorrow morning. But I like the personal touch."

"Yes, it was good of me." She changed the subject. "Will your family be joining you here?"

Tyson replied, "I think that given a choice between a beach resort and here, they'll opt for the beach."

She didn't respond, but he knew what she was thinking. He added, "It's not a matter of loyalty or being a fair-weather family or being supportive. It's simply a practical matter. I don't want them here, and I've told them so. I'll see them on weekends."

She nodded.

He added, "Tight quarters can lead to unnecessary stress. My son wouldn't have any friends. Marcy might be subject to some harassment—by the media. That sort of thing."

Karen Harper nodded again.

Tyson cleared his throat. "Of course I realize they could go back to Garden City, and we'd be much closer. But I think everyone is better off staying where they are for the summer at least."

"I think so." She put her beer on the coffee table and looked at her watch. "We've been here about ten minutes. That's about as long as we should be here."

"In case someone is watching."

"Yes, in case someone is watching. As it turns out, they knew I went back to your room that night. So I'm glad I put it in my report. But I don't want to have to do any more explaining." She moved toward the door.

Tyson set down his beer bottle and slipped on his sandals and a T-shirt. He opened the door, and they left together.

They walked down to Sterling Drive, which overlooked the Shore Parkway. Tyson gazed out over the water. There was something undeniably magical about harbor lights and boats on a summer evening.

She said, "I suppose you think I came to your quarters because I wanted to see you. Well, I'm not sure if that's true or not. When I got there and saw the lights were out, I thought you weren't in. And I felt . . . I felt . . ."

"A combination of relief and disappointment."

"Yes. I thought about taking a walk and coming back with that envelope and the umbrella, but then . . . then I decided to just drop them off. . . ."

"And the thought crossed your mind that I might be at the guest house looking for you and that we'd miss one another."

She nodded. "Why don't I feel foolish?"

"Because you know I don't find it foolish." He stopped walking but did not face her. Instead he looked out at the indistinct horizon where the black ocean met the black sky. He said, "The circumstances under which we met were intense and emotional, and so we could have expected one of two intense and emotional reactions: hate or . . . well, repulsion or attraction might be better words."

"I know that. I'm wondering if I'd met you under normal circumstances if I'd have given you a second look."

Tyson smiled. "If I'd met you under other circumstances, I'd have taken notice."

She began walking again, and he followed. She said, "Let's talk about something else. I wanted to give you some pointers regarding any statement you might choose to include in my report."

He replied, "I gave you a statement you could use when we first met. What would be the purpose of another one?"

"Well, in that statement you said you were conducting military operations against an armed enemy. It was fine as far as it went. But what you have to do is to categorically deny the allegations of the witnesses against you. Brandt and Farley. You see, those witnesses are all that the government has against you. Picard's interview with Sister Teresa is hearsay and not admissible. Also, there is no documentary evidence against you and no physical evidence. So the Army's case, if there is one, revolves around Brandt and to a lesser extent Farley."

Tyson nodded. He'd figured that out by himself. "So I should directly contradict what they said?"

"Yes. Or show why they would lie or why they would not be impartial witnesses for the prosecution. In other words, weaken their credibility by revealing whether or not there was any bad blood between you. As we say in law, impeach the witnesses."

"That's good of you to tell me that."

"Any lawyer would tell you the same thing. But when it comes from me, it is a hint that if you discredit Brandt—and Brandt is the key—then the Army may very well drop the investigation."

Tyson nodded.

"Can you discredit Brandt?"

"Perhaps in a sense I could. But that would mean saying something about what he did over *there,* of course. Not how he's led his life since then, because I don't know anything about him except what I read and that seems to indicate he's a fine doctor, married for sixteen years, with a son my son's age and a daughter. Why would I want to tell a tale that happened nearly two decades ago? Is saving my own skin that important?"

"I hope so."

"But that would be contrary to what I believe, which is that the past ought to be forgiven. If I want to be judged by how I've lived my life since Vietnam, how could I justify dragging up the past and throwing it in Brandt's face?"

"He threw it in your face."

"That's his problem. I won't make it mine."

She shook her head. "Colonel Levin was right."

Tyson gave her a sidelong glance. He said, "It's not that I have no sense of self-preservation. It's that I do. Every piece of advice I've gotten so far has been somehow repugnant to me. I'm the one who has to live with Ben Tyson after this is over. I'm going to try to beat this thing, but not by deception, compromise, or name-calling. I want a clean verdict on this, even if the verdict is guilty."

She nodded. "You're entitled to do it your way." She added, "But given the facts I've assembled and given the fact that you won't make a statement impeaching Brandt's statement, then I hope you understand that if I recommend that charges be served on you, I have no choice."

"I won't take it personally."

She walked off the drive onto the sloping grass and stared at the traffic passing on the Shore Parkway, her hands in the pockets of her tan slacks. She said, as if to herself, "What else can I do?"

Tyson stood off to the side and looked at her. A land breeze was coming up, and her hair began to blow. Tyson thought she looked very at home out-of-doors, very at ease in the elements. He said, "Why don't you believe Sadowski and Scorello? Are you calling them blatant liars? And me a liar?"

She turned her head toward him. "No. But as a practical matter, allegations of wrongdoing are given more weight than denials of wrongdoing."

"Why?"

"It's obvious. It's common sense. Steven Brandt is a respected physician and—"

"Never mind. I understand that too." He looked to his left. About ninety miles east along this same shore was Sag Harbor, and he felt some anger and bitterness that he wasn't there with his wife and son on the back terrace of his summer home. But he felt, too, that if he were with them at Thanksgiving, he would be with them in a better way. He said, "Ninety days?"

"Yes, that's the law."

"Can the Army wrap this up in ninety days?"

"They can wrap it up next week if they choose to drop it. But if they choose to press on, then all that remains to be done in a case like this is to contact the remaining witnesses and determine whose witnesses they will be."

"Did you find any of the remaining witnesses?"

"I put a memo in the envelope."

"What did the memo in the envelope *say?*"

She looked at him. "You'd have heard it on the news tonight. It will be in tomorrow's papers. Harold Simcox was killed in an automobile accident. Near his home in Madison, Wisconsin. His car hit a bridge abutment at a very high speed. There was a high alcohol level in his blood."

Tyson contemplated the shimmering water for a while and tried to conjure up Simcox's face but was surprised to discover he could not. Even his recent perusal of his Army photo album did not help. Simcox was always somewhere else, or his face was turned from the camera or covered with grotesque camouflage makeup or in deep shadow under the Australian bush hat he liked to wear. Harold Simcox. Tyson felt bad about that, but he also felt a sense of foreboding: spooky actually. He said to Karen Harper, "Accident?"

"I don't know." She added, "He was divorced, out of work, alcoholic, and sort of a loner from what I've been told. He left no note."

"Well, sometimes there's nothing to say." *And,* he thought, *sometimes there is too much to say that is better left unsaid. Harold Simcox,* he reflected, *a possible suicide. Moody dead of cancer.* He recalled the patrols through the defoliated areas. That was a war that would not stop killing and maiming. Richard Farley would be next. He said slowly, "I'm not superstitious . . . but the Army has bad-luck outfits like the Navy has bad-luck ships. I always somehow felt that the Seventh Cavalry was an ill-fated unit. The Little Big Horn was not the only bad day that outfit had." He drew a deep breath. "Well, perhaps it's not luck or fate but a matter of the collective psyches of military units, an institutional memory, as Colonel Levin suggested."

She didn't respond, and they both stood in silence. The wind was picking up, and heat lightning flashed over Staten Island. After some time she turned and began walking back the way they'd come. Tyson followed. She came to a park bench and sat. Tyson sat on the opposite end. He said, "Did you go to the monument?"

She nodded.

He waited, then said, "It's the sort of monument you put off seeing. I did."

"Yes, so did I. Because it's a gravestone." She added, "But seeing that wall with all those names gave me some perspective. I kept thinking that each man there did not die alone but died in combat among his friends, and those friends had the means to avenge those deaths, which is so unlike civilian death. And I thought that the chevron shape of that wall, which could stand for Vietnam, could also stand for vengeance. I thought that war, which is conceived in terms of global strategy, is ultimately fought by men who take it personally. And I tried to use that perspective to help me understand what may have happened at Miséricorde Hospital."

Tyson did not respond.

At length she said, "Well, anyway, regarding the witnesses. Precluding any more deaths, there will be at least four witnesses present at any judicial proceeding. There will be the two witnesses for the prosecution, Brandt and Farley, and the two for the defense, Sadowski and Scorello. Louis Kalane, Hernando Beltran, and Lee Walker will eventually be found. Dan Kelly and Michael DeTonq may never be accounted for. And then there's Sister Teresa."

He looked down the length of the bench at her.

She said, "No luck there. I'm beginning to wonder why she hasn't turned up."

Tyson replied, "I'm beginning to wonder if she ever existed. I mean, this whole thing has a strong sense of unreality about it. I can't believe it is happening, so I can't take any of it too seriously. This is very much like my first combat experience. It was so unreal—people firing rifles with live ammunition at *me*. Do you know what I did? I laughed. It was too ludicrous. It was a war movie. So, now, nearly two decades later, people are asking me to relive an experience that I didn't believe was happening *while* it was happening. Am I making sense?"

"Yes. I've heard that before, including the part about laughing in combat." She looked away from him and said, "That reminds me. The Army will want you to see a panel of psychiatrists before too long. That's standard these days for capital crimes investigations."

"Is it? What does that say about us as a nation? Why, I wonder, don't they order me before a board of chaplains to test if I am morally healthy? If my moral health is unsound, then I need religious and ethical therapy, not a court-martial."

She smiled. "Somehow that's not as absurd as it sounds. Nevertheless, you will be extensively tested—psychologically." She added, "I suppose you resent all of this. I mean, being ordered here and there to do this and that."

"That is an understatement. I resented having to take a physical, having my picture taken for an ID card, being assigned to post housing, being told to get a haircut, being told what the uniform of the day is, and so on, and so on."

Karen Harper said, "You're a real civilian. But if you recall, you get used to it."

"That's what I'm afraid of. I'd like not to get used to it. I'd like to retain my personality and my sense of myself."

"You have to bend a bit in the service. Don't be angry or bitter. Or if you are, don't show it. It's not productive."

He nodded. "You're right. I don't want to hate the Army or my country or anyone associated with this investigation. There are no evil geniuses out there looking to crucify me. There are only paper-shufflers who are doing their jobs according to the law as it is written. The fact that many may be guilty, but only one is indictable, should not make me question the wisdom of the law."

"You *are* angry."

"Anyway, the way to beat the legal system is with lawyers. So with your advice in mind to get a better lawyer, I called one whose name was given to me. He called me back after I returned to the museum this afternoon."

She inquired, "Have you retained him?"

"I think I may. He sounded fairly bright. I have a meeting scheduled with him tomorrow morning. But I have a group of summer-school kids coming in for the tour. What do you advise?"

She smiled. "Go see the lawyer. By the way, did your group of senior citizens wait for you?"

"Oh, yes. They have nothing but time. They asked me embarrassing questions about you. Wanted to know what my intentions were actually."

She smiled again but did not respond. She said, "If you retain this lawyer, let me know so I can enter his name and address in my report."

"I'll tell you his name now. It's Vincent Corva."

She nodded slowly. "Yes, I know him. He's certified by the JAG office."

"So he said. But is he good?"

"Well, that's not my place to say. But I saw him in court once at Fort Jackson."

"Who won?"

"The Army. Well . . . it was a tough case. The accused—a captain—was charged with manslaughter." She added, "He'd found his wife in bed with her lover."

"Ah! This sounds good. Continue."

She shrugged. "Well . . . this captain was officer-of-the-guard one night, and while he was driving his jeep checking the sentry posts, he detoured back to his house. I guess he had a suspicion. Anyway, he found them . . . his wife and a young lieutenant . . . together . . . *in flagrante delicto* . . . drew his forty-five, fired, and killed the lover."

Tyson leaned toward her, feigning more interest than he had in the case. "How close was he when he fired? How many shots? Who was he trying to hit?"

She smiled again, and he could see she thought him amusing. She replied, "It's funny you should ask that. Corva, in his summation, said something like, 'Any soldier who can hit a . . . moving target with an Army forty-five, with one shot, at twenty-three feet, without injuring the person . . . directly beneath the intended target, should be commended for his marksmanship, regardless of his inability to exercise the same sort of control over his emotions' . . . or something like that." She added, "It was an absurd statement and rather idiotic . . . but you know, it worked."

"Did the court find it amusing?"

"Yes. There was laughter. That statement appealed to all that was . . . macho . . . on that board of officers."

"So how did the defendant do?"

"He received one to ten . . . for the manslaughter. But they slapped him with two years for leaving his post and dereliction of duty."

"Typical Army," commented Tyson. "He would have been in more trouble if his pistol had misfired because it was dirty."

Karen Harper stretched her legs out and settled back on the bench. "That's a bit of an exaggeration. But your point, I assume, is that the military gives different priorities to some offenses than do civilian courts. That's something you and Mr. Corva ought to keep in mind. I'm sure you both will. Anyway, I understand he's rather good though his record is not so good. He takes mostly hopeless cases." She looked out toward the ocean. "There's a storm coming. See it?"

Tyson turned from her and gazed out over the water. He could see whitecaps forming on the dark blue expanse of open sea, and the stars on the horizon were obscured by a blurriness that he knew was rain.

She stood. "I'd better get back. I have work to do."

He stood also, and they began walking. A few drops of rain began falling, and the hot blacktop steamed. He said, "I'll lend you my umbrella again if you promise not to lose it."

She picked up her pace. "Well. . . ." The rain became heavier. Ahead were the lights of the officer family housing. The guest house was a quarter mile away. She said, "All right," and began moving quickly toward his housing unit. The rain became heavier. They both broke into a run.

They reached the front door soaking wet. Tyson hadn't locked the door, and he threw it open. They ducked quickly inside, out of breath. Tyson wiped the rain from his eyes and cheeks. He said, "Let me get you a towel to dry off."

"If you don't mind."

"No, I have three Army towels. Do you want to stay until this passes over?"

"No. I'll just take the umbrella."

"I can drive you to the guest house."

"I'll walk."

"Beer?"

"No thanks. A towel."

He looked at her, rainwater running down her face, and he reached up and wiped her brow and cheeks with his fingers. Their eyes met and held. He put his hands on her shoulders. She stood perfectly still, then put her left hand on his side, then hesitantly her right hand rested on his forearm. Tyson could hear his own heart beating and saw that a vein was fluttering in her throat. He felt his hands and her hands shaking. He drew her closer.

A footstep on the stairs broke the silence, and they stood apart. Around the corner of the landing appeared Marcy. She said, "Hello. I thought I heard voices."

Tyson said, "Marcy, may I present Major Karen Harper?"

29

General William Van Arken sat in the rear of the lecture hall and listened to the instructor, Colonel Ambrose Horton, deliver the final words of his talk to the two dozen military students sitting in the front row. Horton's deep, Virginia-accented voice, unaided by a microphone, echoed through the nearly empty amphitheater of the United States Army's Judge Advocate General School. The school, located within the Charlottesville campus of the University of Virginia, was a three-hour car ride from the Pentagon.

Colonel Horton's eyes drifted up into the rear rows and rested on General Van Arken, who was wearing a civilian suit of dark blue. It would have been correct to introduce the Army's Judge Advocate General, the boss, to the JAG School students, and indeed they would have been honored. But Colonel Horton's instincts told him that the General wanted to remain anonymous. Horton directed his attention back to the first row and spoke. "It has been said by combat commanders that the battlefield is the most honest place in the world. It has also been said by legal types such as us that, regarding war crimes, there are unique complexities in discovering the truth about a combat soldier doing his duty in the field."

General Van Arken listened to the echoes of Colonel Horton's words die away in the open spaces around him. The chimes of the clock tower struck eight, but the students did not move. The sun was fading from the large vertical windows, and the interior lighting seemed to grow harsher.

Colonel Horton concluded, "The next time we meet, we will examine those two statements and attempt to reconcile them. Specifically we will discuss atrocities, how they happen, and how we, as Army lawyers, must ultimately deal with them. Thank you."

The students stood in unison as Colonel Horton moved from the lectern up the center aisle. General Van Arken met him halfway. Horton said, "Good evening, General. An unexpected pleasure."

They shook hands. "This is not official," General Van Arken said. "Let's walk."

The two men left the lecture hall and went out into the hot night, walking through the nearly deserted campus. Van Arken said, "I'd like your opinion on the Tyson case."

Colonel Horton nodded. "Unofficially?"

"Of course." Van Arken gave Horton a sidelong glance. The man was well into his seventies and had the distinction of being the only man still in the Army who had been involved in the Nuremberg trials. He was considered by many to be the dean of Army jurisprudence and taught the philosophy of law and ethics to civilian as well as military students. Notwithstanding Horton's stature, he had been passed over for promotion to brigadier general twice, and in almost any other branch of the Army he'd have been asked or forced to resign. Van Arken said, "Would you like to sit awhile?" He indicated a wooden bench.

Horton nodded and lowered himself heavily onto the bench. He commented, "I've had a busy schedule today."

Van Arken sat on a facing bench and replied diplomatically, "This heat has drained me too." He looked into the old man's eyes. "Can I speak to you in confidence?"

Colonel Horton unbuttoned his green tunic and loosened his tie. He replied in a slow drawl, "As long as we don't stray into prohibited areas, General."

Van Arken regarded Colonel Horton for a moment. Horton caused him some measure of unease. The man was a maverick and a nuisance. He lectured widely on the Nuremberg trials, the Calley-Medina case, and on other controversial areas of military law. The Army did not always appreciate his views. Neither did Van Arken, which was one reason Horton would remain a colonel. But Van Arken needed straight answers, and Horton gave them. Van Arken said, "There is some talk that Major Karen Harper has inadvertently damaged the Army's case against Tyson."

"Well," said Colonel Horton, "what happened between Tyson and Harper as far as I can determine was magic. There is the doctrine in law which says we cannot enjoy the fruits of the poison tree. But we know they taste as good. Better. So, consider the Article 31 investigation a success, General. And end it. Soon."

Van Arken said, "I have."

"Good. Do you have any guesses as to what Harper will recommend?"

Van Arken shook his head. "It is really up to Tyson to impeach Dr. Brandt's testimony. If he does and if there is some substance to whatever he says about Brandt, then it doesn't much matter what Brandt has said about Tyson. I would not want to go into a courtroom with no evidence beyond two shaky witnesses. And neither would an Army prosecutor."

"But as it stands now," asked Colonel Horton, "Dr. Brandt is unimpeachable?"

"To the best of my knowledge. I have no contact with Major Harper, of course." Van Arken looked at Horton. "Do you want to walk?"

"Yes." He stood and buttoned his tunic. They walked on a path that cut diagonally across the Green Lawn. The multipaned windows of the buildings cast light patterns on the dark grass. Van Arken said, "During the Calley business, there was little sympathy for the accused within the JAG. We have a different situation here. Certain people at the top—in the White House and the Justice Department—are beginning to waver. I believe we owe it to the Army and to the nation to press on. And I was wondering if you felt the same way."

Colonel Horton looked around at the lighted buildings. He loved this old university founded nearly two centuries before by Thomas Jefferson. It was a magnificent showplace of neoclassical architecture: colonnades, cupolas, rotundas, and balustrades. But more than that, it was a place of mellow moods, an institution that still placed some value on chivalry, honor, and tradition. Horton mused, "What would Jefferson advise us, General?"

Van Arken took the question to be rhetorical and did not reply. Colonel Horton answered his own question. "Jefferson did not see the law as a narrow vocation but as a means of understanding the history, culture, morals, and institutions of a society. I think if we ran into him on this path now, he'd ask us how it came to pass that the American government is not certain it has the right to judge its citizens."

General Van Arken responded, "The question I put to you is, do we owe it to the nation to press on despite our . . . well, our shared culpability in the events of 15 February 1968?"

Colonel Horton smiled wryly, then said, "Are you looking for me to put something in writing, General? A memo to the White House or the Justice Department?"

"Well, yes. A sort of white paper from you as a respected jurist. Legally, we are on the right track. But people have raised these moral and ethical questions on both sides of this issue. We'd like to address those, to put this legal framework on a firm philosophical foundation."

Colonel Horton rubbed the side of his nose with his bony index finger and spoke contemplatively. "You know, General, when I was a young lieutenant working the prosecution side of the bench at Nuremberg, virtually the entire world was on our side. The press corps covered every minute of the trial, but there was no real scrutiny as we know it today. Consequently, we got away with a great deal. Errors in procedure, that sort of thing. But more importantly, we got away with making up the law as we went along. We hanged who we wanted to hang and were amazed at ourselves when we actually handed out prison terms instead of the death penalty. And there was no appeals process. Death meant death."

Horton reflected a moment before continuing. "There were only a handful of voices raised against the Allied tribunals. I was not among those who had the wisdom or foresight to see that what we were meting out was not justice but revenge. And even if I had understood that, I would not have had the moral courage to raise my voice." He looked at Van Arken. "I mean, my God, Hollywood blessed us with Spencer Tracy and *Judgment at Nuremberg*. There was not even the slightest doubt that we were not wholly on the side of the angels."

They continued on in silence awhile, then Colonel Horton said, "General, when you were a young captain working on the prosecution side in the My Lai cases, you were operating in a different world, a different moral climate. The media did their own investigations and in fact forced the Army investigation. The President did not see it as something to be proud of, and national opinion polls showed a majority in favor of letting the accused go free."

"Yes, I recall that clearly."

"Yes, so here we are today, both of us veterans of two of the most important military trials of this century, and I hope we'll keep in mind the lessons we both learned. We have no excuses for errors in judgment."

Van Arken replied with a touch of impatience, "What I learned from the My Lai trials, Colonel, was that the nation and the world will not tolerate barbarism in the armed forces of the United States no matter how that barbarism tries to disguise itself as battle." Van Arken drew a breath, then continued, "And Nuremberg, for all the faults, showed the world that civilization will not tolerate barbarism even when it becomes the national policy of a sovereign state. It is my considered opinion that if we are ever again to judge our enemies, legally or morally, we must first judge ourselves no matter how painful it may be to do so." Van Arken continued, "Any contemplated trial of Benjamin Tyson must serve as a warning to every combat officer in future wars that he will be held accountable for his actions until the day he dies."

Colonel Horton wondered how much of what Van Arken said was in the interests of justice, humanity, the Army, or the nation and how much was in the interests of General Van Arken and his career. But he did not want to be uncharitable toward the man. He might well be sincere. Horton spoke in a conciliatory tone. "Certainly, General, what you say is correct. But on a less theoretical level, I want to point out to you those unique complexities in discovering the truth about a combat soldier who was doing his duty in the field. Tyson was sent to Vietnam to kill. Any court-martial that is convened will not have to determine whether or not he killed but if he killed the right people in the right way."

Van Arken replied tersely, "My concern is that the entire question of the morality of the war will be raised as a defense. At Nuremberg you operated from a position of moral certainty."

"So did the Nazis. If you raise philosophical questions and try to drag me into it as an apologist for the government, you will give the case more stature. And that will play into the hands of the defense. That is my advice to you, though I give it grudgingly because I quite frankly don't believe that justice is being done."

"Why not?"

"Because the climate that existed in 1968 allowed not only the crime but the cover-up to flourish. Something had gone fundamentally wrong with the ethics and standards of the officer corps, the Army, and the nation. We've corrected much of that. But we can't go back and start court-martialing lieutenants until we call the generals to account. *And* the civilians in those past administrations. That's another thing I learned at Nuremberg."

Van Arken nodded. *"That* is what I'm afraid the defense is going to say. I'm afraid they're going to offer what has come to be called the Nuremberg defense."

"Good for them," snapped Horton. "I often have fantasies of convening a national inquisition and subpoenaing every son of a bitch who got us involved in Vietnam."

They continued in silence, then came ᴜ ᴀ crosswalk. Van Arken stopped. "Can I buy you dinner, Ambrose?"

Colonel Horton shook his head. "Thank you, ᴜ ᴀeral, but I have to work on tomorrow's lecture." He stared at Van Arken awhile, then said, "You know, Bill, you've been a force in getting this case under way, and I'm not certain that is your function. I'm not being critical. You've filled a vacuum left by the Justice Department, who should be pursuing this, and I congratulate you on your devotion. However . . . you see, I feel our civilian bosses are setting us up. They learned something from My Lai, too. As our enlisted men would say, we've pulled some shit duty."

Van Arken nodded. "I've figured that out. But that doesn't alter our obligation. My obligation."

Colonel Horton said impatiently, "You're rather sure of yourself, aren't you? I mean, you're sure you're on the side of truth and morality. Well, I'm not so sure."

"Just what does that mean?"

"I mean, Bill, you've spoken of accountability. And I'm thinking that if Lieutenant Benjamin J. Tyson did in fact command a platoon that massacred approximately one hundred men, women, and children, then where is the moral justification, sir, in offering the platoon survivors—the actual triggermen—immunity?"

Van Arken didn't reply.

"So you see, General, don't tell me you want to pursue this because of some moral absolute, because there is none. *That* is the main lesson I learned at Nuremberg."

Van Arken began to reply, but Horton interrupted. "At Nuremberg, I often wondered why the SS guards and the hangmen and the torturers were not called to account in greater numbers. Then I came to realize that had they been called, they would have simply said, 'I was only following orders.'" Horton added, "As you well know, General, the military constructs a unique subculture whose teachings supersede everything a man has learned in church or Sunday school, everything he has been taught by parents, teachers, and the community —indeed everything he knows in his own heart. So when a soldier says, 'I was only following orders,' he has offered a formidable defense and an embarrassing one for his superiors. He has offered the Nuremberg defense.

"And so, the buck is passed onward and upward, and at every echelon of command we hear the same thing—'I was only following orders'—direct orders, inferred orders, implied orders, standing orders, and so on. Until we finally come to the top where the sewerage begins flowing downhill again, as I saw at Nuremberg. The top Nazis would say, 'I could not possibly know how my orders were being misconstrued.' Or the line I heard over and over again, 'I had no idea this was happening among my subordinates.'"

Van Arken drew a short breath and said slowly and deliberately, "You've taught the philosophy of the law too long, Ambrose. You ought to get down to cases, as we say. But as I indicated, it wouldn't be altogether proper for us to discuss this case."

Colonel Horton smiled, then replied in a thoughtful tone, "Then let me discuss the fictional case of Lieutenant X who is court-martialed for murder. Everyone assumes that even if he is found guilty, he will not suffer the ultimate penalty—will not stand in front of a firing squad. And that's a safe assumption since a firing squad has not been constituted to shoot an American in the armed forces for over two decades. But *my* philosophy of law is this—if you try a man for a capital crime, be it murder or sleeping on guard duty in time of war, then you should fully acknowledge that you may in fact send him to his death. Do not assume that judicial reviews of the sentence will reduce the penalty or that an executive pardon will stay the execution. That's a game, and the law is not a game. So if you cannot justify in your own conscience a firing squad putting ten bullets into a man—if you have no stomach for that, then you must reduce the charge."

"There is no lesser charge for which the statute of limitations has not run out."

Colonel Horton's eyes narrowed. "Ah, I see. We are down to cases. So whereas Mr. Tyson at some previous point in time might be more correctly charged with, let's say, conspiracy to conceal a crime, at *this* point in time, it must be first-degree murder or nothing."

Van Arken nodded slightly.

Colonel Horton nodded too, as if he were just discovering an interesting fact. He said, "Well, I must be going. I think I have an idea for my lecture tomorrow. Thank you, General." Colonel Horton saluted, turned on his heel, and walked off.

General Van Arken watched him for a few seconds, then turned and walked in the opposite direction. For the first time he began to feel less confident about the justice of his own position. Privately he thought Tyson was guilty; but as Horton had pointed out, he would not want to see the man shot down by a firing squad. He only wanted to hold him up as a bad example for the rest of the officer corps. However, in his zeal to promote the ethical revolution that was sweeping the armed forces since Vietnam, he had reopened issues and debates best left in the past.

Nevertheless, the thing was started, and there was almost no way to stop it. Like a shout that begins an avalanche, this was growing and gathering force and momentum and thundering with deadly energy toward Benjamin Tyson.

30

Ben Tyson regarded his wife standing on the bottom landing. She wore shower clogs, cut-off jeans, and a white T-shirt. In blue letters across the front of the T-shirt was the Army reenlistment slogan: *Keep a Good Soldier In.* He wondered where the hell she had gotten that. He noticed her hands were red, and he smelled ammonia. She'd been cleaning.

Marcy Tyson crossed the small living room and extended her hand to Karen Harper. Marcy said, "I'm so glad we finally met."

Karen Harper took Marcy's hand. "So am I."

Both women regarded each other for a few seconds longer than Tyson considered necessary. He said, "Well, I'm glad too." He addressed Marcy. "Major Harper and I were walking and talking."

Marcy looked from one to the other, then remarked, "Perhaps you'd like to go upstairs and dry off."

Karen Harper replied, "I'll just borrow an umbrella, if I may. It's a short distance to the guest house."

"Stay awhile," said Marcy.

"No, thank you."

"I've brought a bottle of champagne. Help us drink it." She took Karen Harper's arm and led her to the staircase.

Karen Harper seemed to sense that to insist on leaving would be more awkward than staying. She said, "Thank you." She went up the stairs.

Marcy looked at her husband, smiled sweetly, then went into the kitchen without a word.

Tyson mumbled to himself, "Typical Tyson luck these days." He headed up the stairs, passed the closed door to the bathroom, and heard the hair dryer running. He entered the master bedroom and was surprised to see the bed covered with garment bags and the floor crowded with suitcases. He slipped off his running shorts and wet T-shirt, dried himself with his terry-cloth robe, and put on a pair of jeans, a tennis shirt, and sandals. He combed his damp hair and went out into the tiny hallway where he bumped into Karen Harper, whose hair and blouse were now dry. She had touched up her makeup and looked, Tyson thought, rather good.

She said, "I'm finished in the bathroom if you want to use the dryer."

"That's all right."

They looked at each other, and Tyson said, "Please stay for a drink."

"I'd rather not."

"I sense that my wife is upset about something, and if you had a drink with us, she might feel better."

"I doubt that, but if you mean you'd like ten minutes of calm before the storm, I'll stay."

Tyson smiled. "I guess that's what I meant." He motioned toward the stairs. "After you."

They descended the stairs in tandem, and Marcy greeted them in the living room. "There, you both look much better." She popped the cork on a bottle of champagne and filled three plastic champagne glasses that sat on the coffee table. She said to Tyson, "When you told me there was no dishwasher, I brought lots of plastic and paper with me."

"Good thinking. Where's David?"

"The Jordans are looking after him. Melinda is only too happy to have him as a houseguest."

Tyson explained to Karen Harper, "She's my son's girlfriend. The Jordans are summering in Sag Harbor. The Tysons are apparently now summering in Brooklyn."

Karen Harper addressed Marcy, "Will you be staying here then?"

Marcy handed her a glass as she replied, "Yes. I thought Ben was probably lonely here." She smiled and turned to Tyson. "Are you surprised? You looked very surprised."

"Did I?" Tyson picked up his glass. "I suppose that surprise is as good a word as any to describe my joy."

Marcy added, "David will join us shortly."

Tyson replied, "I don't think that's a good idea."

"Nevertheless," said Marcy, "we're cutting our vacation short to be with you." She looked at Karen Harper. "When will this be resolved?"

"By mid-October. The law—"

Tyson interrupted, "Why don't you and David just return to Garden City? We'll be close, and—"

"No, darling, we want to be *with* you. Here." She motioned around the room with her glass. "It's . . . cute. Like our first apartment."

Tyson didn't see any comparison with their first apartment. He said, "Major Harper thinks it will do me some good to experience a reduction in my life-style."

"I'm happy to see Major Harper is interested in the development of your character." She added, "I sublet the Sag Harbor house for August and got a nice price. So there's no turning back there. As for Garden City, I don't think the climate is quite right for David or me to return." She looked directly at Karen Harper. "David has suffered far more peer persecution than he's let on. Children are such savages. Do you have children?"

"No, I've never been married, as you may have read."

Marcy held up her glass. "Well, before it goes flat—here's to our new house."

They drank. Tyson put his glass down on the coffee table. "Anyway, I'm glad the two women in my life had this opportunity to meet. So—"

Karen Harper addressed Marcy, "I want you to know, Mrs. Tyson—I told your husband this—that I personally feel very badly about the way the press has carried on regarding your . . . your counterculture activities and other forms of protest during the Vietnam War. I myself was not old enough at that time to comprehend much of it, though I think I can understand your commitment to the peace movement as well as the forms of protest you chose to exhibit . . . to demonstrate that commitment. And I want to assure you that the negative publicity you are receiving is in no way influencing the Army's handling of this case."

Marcy Tyson regarded Karen Harper for some time. The sound of the rain outside filled the small room. At length Marcy responded, "I would have guessed you to be old enough to recall the war. But I'll take your word for it."

Tyson thought he ought to change the subject, but some perversity in his character made him want to hear more.

Marcy moved closer, then said, "I want you to know that I never gave any credence to those asinine innuendos in the tabloids regarding you and my husband."

Karen Harper replied coolly, "It's good of you to say that. I wish others could be as mature." She put her glass down and with her hand out approached Marcy. "Thank you for the wine."

Marcy took her hand and held it. She looked into Karen Harper's eyes and said, "But I'm also not so foolish or naïve as to believe that you and Ben have not established a close rapport. I'm sure you've discovered that my husband is a remarkable and decent man and if the law is at all compassionate, he is deserving of that compassion."

Karen Harper held Marcy's gaze and replied, "That is precisely what I've discovered, Mrs. Tyson, and unfortunately not much else. Good evening."

Marcy released her hand.

Karen Harper retrieved her handbag and briefcase. Tyson picked up the umbrella that was propped beside the front door. Karen Harper walked to the door, then she turned back to Marcy. "I had an image of you that was quite different and probably influenced by the media. In fact, I thought you were a liability to your husband's cause, but I see you are an asset. He needs all the assets he can get now." She turned to Tyson. "The best of luck to you."

Tyson smiled. "Alas, the Tyson luck has run out. But the Tyson wit, charm, and intelligence will suffice. Good night, Karen."

"Good night, Ben."

Tyson handed her the umbrella and opened the door. He watched her raise the umbrella and walk off in the gusty rain. He was reminded of the first day they'd taken leave of each other in front of his house, another house, long ago in the May rain, with his borrowed umbrella above her head. He closed the door and turned to his wife. Marcy's eyes were fixed on him, and he knew from long experience that she would not speak unless he did. He said, "Women are very stiff and formal with each other when they first meet, but they can still get some good zingers in. All in all, I'm happy to see you finally learned something from the ladies in Garden City."

Marcy peered at him through narrow eyes.

He cleared his throat and added, "There are times when savoir faire is preferable to salty language and emotional outbursts. You are, after all, an officer's wife. I'm quite proud of you."

"Go fuck yourself."

"Now, now—"

"You were both here *before* you took a walk, weren't you? That's when she said something about this place being good for you or something. How long were you here?"

"Not long enough for a man my age to consummate the sexual act." He poured himself more champagne and added, "Look, I'm flattered that you're jealous. But I'm being extremely faithful to you and chivalrous to her."

Marcy seemed to have calmed down somewhat. "All right . . . but things sometimes happen even when we don't want them to."

He drank the champagne. "What the hell is this stuff?"

"Cordón Negro."

"What? African champagne?"

"No, idiot. It's Spanish. It's not bad, and it's cheap."

"Spain is off the boycott list?"

"Yes, since Franco died. Didn't I tell you?"

"No. Can I buy sherry now?"

"Absolutely. And real Spanish olives for your martinis. And I think you fucked her. Psychologically, I mean. She's old enough to understand a man like you but still young enough to be spiritually seduced."

"How much a bottle?"

"Less than seven dollars. Incredible. The dollar is strong against the peso. She wished you luck with some finality. Does that mean your official relationship is over?"

"Yes. I don't think champagne is the place to cut corners, though."

"You have domestic beer in the refrigerator."

"Don't tell anyone. By the way, I didn't see the Volvo outside."

"I guess not, or you two wouldn't have charged in here hot as three-dollar pistols."

"That's hardly the way I would characterize our taking shelter from the rain. Where's the Volvo?"

"It died, and I gave it a Viking funeral. That new Toyota outside is ours."

"What? You bought a Nipponese automobile? Are you crazy? I won't drive it. How could you do that knowing how I feel about Japanese products flooding the country, and—"

"Don't try to change the subject. Will you have any occasion to go to Washington to see her again?"

"None. The preliminary investigation is concluded. And I'm not speaking to anyone again without counsel present."

"All right." Marcy drank her champagne. "You do have taste. She's quite good-looking. A natural wholesome beauty. She even looked good wet. I wonder why she never married. Did you ask her?"

Tyson didn't think this was a subject he wanted to discuss any longer. He said, "She's engaged to a colonel. The papers never tell you that."

"I didn't see an engagement ring."

"Well . . . engaged to be engaged. Anyway, are you really moving in?"

"Yes. David is coming as soon as we're set up."

"Why?"

"Because we had a family council and decided you couldn't be trusted alone. Also, your mother called *again.* This time to inform me that a wife's place is with her husband. I didn't know that. Did you know she lived in a converted chicken coop near Fort Stewart, Georgia, while your father was training in the Army Air Corps?"

"I believe she mentioned it a few hundred times when I was growing up. In fact, I was conceived in that chicken coop. Born in a private hospital on Park Avenue, to be sure, but conceived in a chicken coop."

"That explains a lot. Anyway, if she can do it, I can damned well do it."

"Don't put yourself out on my account."

Marcy looked at him. "Actually David was coming with or without me. He decided he loves you and is willing to give up his first lay in order to be here with you. Knowing men as I do, I would say that is a supreme sacrifice." She added, "Sometimes adolescents act like adults. Sometimes it's vice versa."

Tyson said, "I do miss you both, but it's . . . embarrassing . . . I mean, for you to see me like this. . . ."

She replied, "You're not on the Bowery. You are an officer in the United States Army. And that's nothing to be embarrassed about."

Tyson tugged on his ear. "I must be hearing things."

"I'm not as subversive as you like to think," she said. "Anyway, the point is the minister said for better or worse, and I said yeah, okay, and we've had it mostly better for our whole married life, and what the hell, it could be even worse. And I love you and missed you like hell."

Tyson put his arms around his wife, and they embraced.

Marcy said, "You are a proud man, Benjamin Tyson. Entirely too proud and too macho to survive in this sort of world. You have to show your weaknesses, let your friends and family share your pain."

He squeezed her tighter. "You know, Marcy, I've been a careless husband, indifferent father, shallow friend, and undedicated employee. I haven't shown any commitment to you, David, my job, or anything. And it started sometime before this mess."

"I know. Other people noticed. But don't be too hard on yourself."

"Why not? I'm glad I got this kick in the ass to wake me up. I'm not going to romanticize how things were before this started, but life *was* good. It was my perceptions of home, family, job, and friends that had gone wrong. I don't know why it did, but it did."

"It was partly my fault. I needed this, too, Ben. Our marriage, our life together, had become unnecessarily pointless. We're going to be one hell of a happy couple when this is behind us."

Tyson stayed silent for some time, then said, "I may be away awhile."

She dug her fingers into his back. "No! No, you won't be!"

He kissed her, and they clung tighter to each other. She put her head on his shoulder, and he could tell she was crying. He said in a light tone, "Where'd you get that idiotic T-shirt?"

She spoke without looking up. "Oh . . . I had it made at that shop in South-ampton. It struck me as a double entendre. Keep a good soldier in." She laughed. "Get it?"

"No. And I don't find it very funny."

She drew away from him, and he saw that her eyes were moist. She said, "Then I'll remove the offending article." She pulled the shirt off and threw it on the floor. "Better?"

Tyson found he was staring at her bare breasts. "Yes. Oh, yes." He smiled.

She cleared her throat and wiped her eyes with her hand. "Well, what am I supposed to do as an Army wife? I mean, besides cleaning the upstairs la-trine?"

He poured the last of the sparkling wine into their glasses. "Well, get a dependent's ID card first, a bumper sticker for the car, join the officers' wives' club, volunteer for something worthy, get the downstairs squared away, and invite some of the officers' ladies for tea, familiarize yourself—"

"Whoa, Tyson. Let's just start with the bumper sticker so I can park."

"That reminds me—"

"Oh, I didn't buy a Toyota. Just pulling your chain a little. I bought a Jeep."

"A what?"

"Jeep. Very practical. Good for your image. It's out front. Take a look."

Tyson looked out the window and saw a light-colored vehicle glistening in the rain.

"Jeep Cherokee. Four-wheel drive. It's got a CB radio and a gun rack."

"Are you serious?"

"It's only a year old. Bought it from a local out east. It's also got a winch so you can pull in fishnets or small boats or pull yourself out of mud or snow. That's neat. Go look at it."

Tyson turned from the window. "Maybe later."

"Can I see you give a tour of the museum tomorrow?"

"If you wish."

"Great. Hey, put on your uniform."

"No."

"Yes. I want to see how you look." She held his arm and pulled him toward the stairs.

"No, really—"

She rubbed her breasts against him. "Come on. I've never done it with a soldier." She winked.

"Well, if you put it like that. . . ."

They climbed the stairs and went into the master bedroom.

Marcy sat on the edge of the bed and crossed her bare legs. "Okay, soldier, strip off those civilian duds and get into uniform."

Tyson found he was self-conscious as he began undressing.

Marcy whistled.

"Cut it out." He stood before her, naked, and drew a deep breath. "Warm up here."

"Turn around. Let me see your body."

Tyson turned around, then faced her again. She said, "Good officer material. Come here."

He approached the bed. She reached out and cupped his testicles in her right hand. "Turn your head and cough."

He did as she said.

She pronounced, "Okay, you're in." She reached around and slapped him on the buttocks. "Get dressed."

He went to the closet and began putting on his greens without underwear. "This is silly—"

"Speak when you're spoken to."

He mumbled something, knotted his tie, and slipped on his tunic, buttoning it as he turned to her.

She nodded. "Not bad. Good fit. Brass all shiny. Ribbons straight. Okay, take a shower. Then report to me here."

"Yes, ma'am."

He undressed again and walked naked to the bathroom. He showered the sweat off, dried himself, and came back into the bedroom. The bed was clear of luggage, and Marcy lay on the rough white sheets, her legs spread and a pillow under her rear. She was wearing his fatigue shirt, which was hiked up to her waist, and his forage cap sat on her head. She said, "Let's clip those horns, Lieutenant, before you get into trouble."

He got into the bed, on top of her, and slipped in easily, finding her wet.

They made love in the small, hot, airless room, and they both knew this was a sort of parody of what could have happened with Major Karen Harper. Marcy whispered in his ear as she neared orgasm. "I don't usually do this with married men."

"My wife's a bitch."

"I know. I know."

"Keep a good soldier in," he said.

She wrapped her legs around his back and locked her ankles together. "I am. I am."

31

Marcy and Ben Tyson sat across from each other at the small table. Tyson was dressed in a maize-colored linen suit. Marcy wore a yellow cotton-knit sweater and matching skirt.

Marcy said, "This was a fort?"

"Not this part. This is the new dining room. Most forts don't have picture windows."

"Don't get smart."

Tyson picked up the menu. "The steak here is good."

"I don't see any quiche on the menu."

"Nor will you ever."

"You say that with relish."

"With steak sauce."

"I'll bet you stay in if you're acquitted."

"The military has a certain masculine appeal."

"Don't get carried away." She looked at him. "Would you . . . would you ever go back in—I mean, under other circumstances—if they called you in a national emergency? Another war?"

Tyson replied, "Yes, I would serve my country again."

"Even after what the Army has done to you?"

"They've done nothing to me. They think I've done something to them."

"Would you go back in for an unpopular, Vietnam-type, undeclared war?"

"Mine is not to reason why. I didn't even fight this recall as hard as I could have."

"Boy, once they've got you, they've got you forever, don't they?"

"I'm afraid so. Military service exerts a lasting influence on a man far beyond the short number of years he was on duty. Just like jail time. Ask anyone who was in—jail or the Army."

"I believe you. I just don't understand. I never understood how millions of men could clash on the battlefield, leaving piles of corpses, then do it again and again."

"Men love war. They love fucking the enemy, and when they withdraw, there is a postcoital depression that lingers for the rest of their lives."

"Scary, Ben. Scary."

"Don't I know it?"

They sat in silence for a few minutes. Marcy looked out over the nearly empty dining room and saw a couple turn their faces away. She said, "Why do you suppose people are staring at us?"

"They are absolutely dazzled by the dashing new officer and his lady."

She smiled grimly. "As long as they're not saying, 'There's that war criminal and his whore.'"

"My dear, in the officer corps all the brothers are courageous and all the sisters virtuous."

"I didn't know that." She sipped on her gin and tonic as she looked out the window. The night sky had cleared as suddenly as it had darkened earlier, and a stiff wind from the south fluttered the illuminated Stars and Stripes on the lawn. On the patio a barbecue was in progress, and she heard the sound of a steel band and saw the flames of the charcoal pit and the Tonga torches. She said, "There's something vaguely anachronistic about this place."

"That's what you say about Garden City. In truth, *you* are the anachronism, a time-traveler from the sixties."

"Perhaps you're right. Still, this is a very closed society, isn't it?"

"It's supposed to be. It has its own internal reality, which is based in part on its own history, exclusive of the society outside the gates."

"Now that I'm here in this environment, I'm beginning to understand you better."

"I'm beginning to understand me better too."

She asked, "Were you invited to that party out there?"

He glanced out the window. "All members are invited to all club functions. But I'm supposed to send my regrets."

"I see."

The waitress came, and they ordered their food and a bottle of Mouton Cadet. They chatted pleasantly, just like old times, they agreed. They held hands across the table, and the waitress smiled at them as she brought the food. Marcy and Ben ate in companionable silence.

Tyson finished his steak and poured himself and Marcy more wine. He looked across the dining room and said, "We're about to have company."

Marcy turned and saw a large ruddy-faced man with sandy hair, about fifty years old, making his way toward them from the direction of the patio. The man wore casual slacks and a rather silly flowered shirt. She said, "Who is that?"

"That is the Reverend Major Kennard Oakes, a Baptist chaplain. He has befriended me."

"Well, you need all the friends you can get."

The Reverend Oakes drew up to their table and smiled widely. He drawled in a deep southern accent, "Ben, are you drinking the devil's brew again?"

Tyson shook hands with the minister. "I'm Episcopalian. Drunkenness is a sacrament."

"Blasphemy. Is this Mrs. Tyson?"

Tyson made the introductions. Reverend Oakes sat without an invitation and took Marcy's hand across the table, patting it. "You are a very beautiful woman."

"Thank you."

Tyson said, "I'd offer you a glass of wine, but I don't want to tempt you."

The minister smiled. "Why aren't you two outside?"

Tyson replied, "Marcy and I just made wild passionate love, and we wanted to be alone."

Marcy's eyebrows rose, and there was a silence at the table. Finally the Reverend Oakes smiled and said lightly, "So, Ben, how was your day?"

"Fine."

"Are you free tomorrow morning? I have to drive down to Fort Dix, and I'd like the company."

Tyson lit a cigarette. "I have a group tomorrow morning."

"Then perhaps tomorrow afternoon. I can reschedule my appointment at Dix."

Tyson exhaled a stream of smoke. He said to Marcy, "Major Oakes is on temporary duty here like I am. But unlike me, he's not awaiting court-martial." He addressed the minister. "What did you say you were doing here?"

He turned to Marcy. "I'm here on special orders from the Army Chaplain School to evaluate the Bible classes given to young people at the various posts and installations in the New York metropolitan area."

Marcy said, "How interesting."

Tyson said, "You won't be conducting any services at the post chapel then?"

"No, I'm afraid not. The Reverend Perry is an excellent preacher if you want to see a good Baptist service."

Tyson nodded. "I'm glad you're here." He put his hand firmly on the minister's arm. "I had an argument with a fellow in the lounge last night, padre. He insisted it was John who said, 'The Pharisees also came unto him, tempting him, and saying unto him, "Is it lawful for a man to put away his wife for every cause?" ' I say it was Luke. So who was it?" He stared at Reverend Oakes.

"John."

"No, it was Mark."

"That's right."

"No, that's wrong," said Tyson. "It was Matthew. You fail Bible class."

The Reverend Oakes smiled and replied, "Who gives a shit, Tyson?"

Marcy's eyes widened.

The man pulled his arm away from Tyson, and they both stood. Tyson said, "Beat it, bozo."

The man glared at Tyson for a second, then nodded. "Chaplains are hard to do. I told them that. You're good though." He turned and left.

Tyson sat.

Marcy said, "What in the name of God . . . ?"

"In the name of God indeed. What swine!"

"Who?"

"That is the question," said Tyson.

"That man was spying on you?"

"I suppose you'd call it that." Tyson finished his glass of wine. "Well, there's a lesson for you. Be careful who you speak to."

Marcy drew a deep breath. "This is bizarre."

"Amen." Tyson looked at his watch. "I have to make a phone call. This new lawyer, Corva." He stood. "Be about ten minutes. Order coffee and dessert."

She said, "I want a telephone installed."

"Call about it tomorrow."

"I can't. I don't have a telephone."

He smiled and walked out of the dining room. Tyson passed the pay phones and headed toward the exit. He'd made his phone call earlier in the day, and it wasn't his lawyer he'd called but the *American Investigator.*

Tyson walked across the cobbled drive, still wet with the earlier rain, and opened the heavy oak door of the museum with his key. He entered, leaving the door partly ajar. Dim security lights illuminated uniformed mannequins with sabers and rifles, giving the impression of an evil place. Tyson glanced at his watch again. He heard a sound at the door, then a weak rap, and the door swung in. Tyson said, "Come in."

A figure stood on the cobble drive, then stepped up into the lobby area. "Mr. Tyson?"

"Right. Mr. Jones?"

"Yeah." Wally Jones stayed near the door and peered into the shadowy room.

Tyson looked at him in the doorway, silhouetted against the lights of the Officers' Club on the far side of the drive. He was heavyset and wore an ill-fitting bush jacket with matching light trousers. He had a leather bag slung over his shoulder. Tyson couldn't see his face clearly, but he appeared to be a man in his early fifties. Tyson said, "Come on in and shut the door."

Jones took another step into the museum's lobby but did not close the door. "Is this where you want to talk?"

"Yes. I have an office in the rear."

"You want to give me your side of the story?"

"That's what I told your editor."

"Okay. That's good. That's what we always wanted. Your side of the story. We never want to be unfair. Nobody wanted to do a hatchet job on you. Least of all me. I was in Korea. Most of our readers are the patriotic type. You know? So this is good."

"I want to tell you how the Army shafted me. But if your readers are the patriotic type, maybe you won't print that."

"Oh, we'll print it! We'll print anything you say."

"Okay. Follow me." Tyson turned and took a few steps. He looked back over his shoulder. "This way."

Jones chuckled nervously and said, "Hey, are you alone?"

"Yes. Are you?"

"Yeah. Look, why don't we step outside? Someplace sort of public but private. Like take a walk down to the water."

Tyson replied, "I can't be seen talking to you. But . . . okay. Let me get my notes." Tyson walked off into the dark recesses of the museum, slipped off his loafers, and, carrying them, circled back and stood at the doorway behind Wally Jones. "Ready?"

Jones gave a start and spun around. "Oh . . . Christ, you scared—"

Tyson delivered a powerful blow to Jones's solar plexus. Jones doubled over, and Tyson brought his knee up into Jones's face, hearing and feeling the man's nose break. Jones stumbled around, bent over, one hand on his midsection and the other over his face. Tyson slipped his shoes on and planted a savage kick to his rear, and Jones sprawled across the stone floor, moaning in pain.

Tyson heard a sound behind him and turned. A flash blinded him, followed by another. He charged out of the museum toward the photographer, who got off another shot before he turned and ran. Tyson followed.

Suddenly two men in jogging suits appeared from around the side of the museum. One grabbed the photographer around the arms, and the other pulled the camera from his hands, smashed it on the pavement, then came at Tyson. Tyson crouched in a defensive stance and waited.

The man drew abreast of the open museum door and shined a flashlight on Wally Jones lying inside on the floor. The light revealed a small puddle of blood forming around Jones's face. The man swung the flashlight toward Tyson and shined it in his eyes. He said, "Just stay where you are and keep your hands where I can see them."

"Who the hell are you?"

"The man with the forty-five automatic pointed at you."

Tyson heard the metallic double click of the hammer being cocked.

The headlights of an approaching vehicle rounded the side of the museum, and the vehicle drew up beside Tyson. A man poked his head out of the rear window. "You *are* a violent man."

Tyson clearly recognized the voice of Chet Brown. Brown said, "Get in the car, killer."

The car sped over the Verrazano Bridge. Tyson lit a cigarette. The driver, a young man with a hard look, called back, "Would you mind not smoking?"

Tyson exhaled a stream of smoke toward the front. Brown laughed softly. Tyson looked at Brown at the far end of the rear seat. He was wearing a white tennis outfit. Brown said, "How's your new job?"

Tyson drew on his cigarette and looked out the side window at the Statue of Liberty standing tall in its eerie green splendor.

Chet Brown said, "By the way, someone will escort your lady back to your quarters with an explanation."

Tyson inquired, "Was Oakes yours?"

"Maybe. Chaplains are hard to do."

"I know."

"We'll have to set up a special class for that now."

"Who? Who are you?"

Brown replied, "You wouldn't recognize the name. We're so shadowy, even the CIA doesn't quite believe we exist."

"Sounds like bullshit to me."

Brown changed the subject. "As for Wally Jones, I don't blame you, Ben. That bastard had it coming. If he'd written things about my wife like that, I'd have done the same thing. Anyway, that one was free—on us. But if you do anything like that again, you can deal with the police yourself. I can't obstruct justice more than once a month or so."

"Don't do me any favors."

"Well, that's my job, Ben. I'm your assigned guardian angel. That's why I'm wearing white."

Tyson retreated into a moody silence.

The car went through the far right lane of the toll plaza without paying, swung around to the right, and approached the main gate of Fort Wadsworth. The MP waved them on, and the car wound its way through the dark, deserted streets of the mostly unused fort. They drove down an incline toward the Narrows, passed a dock, and pulled up to the foreboding granite walls of Battery Weed.

Brown got out of the car and motioned for Tyson to follow. They walked to a set of huge double doors on the landward side of the three-tiered artillery battery. Brown pulled a door open and entered a cavernous chamber partially lit by small hanging light bulbs. Iron staircases ran off in different directions, and Tyson followed Brown to one of them, their footsteps echoing in the damp, still air. Brown led the way through a wide arched corridor that was lined on one side with wooden doorways. He said, "Pick any door."

Tyson indicated one, and Brown opened it. Tyson followed him into a room illuminated only by the light coming from two open gun ports.

Brown stood at one of the openings and looked out across the Narrows. "Some view. Hamilton, the Shore Parkway, Coney Island, Kennedy Airport, the bridge, and the harbor. Smell that salt air."

Tyson's eyes adjusted to the weak light, and he noticed that the stone walls were covered with grotesque depictions of animallike creatures painted in fluorescent colors.

Brown followed his gaze. "Cult stuff. The CID says they're Satanists. They find slaughtered dogs, cats, and chickens in these rooms."

Tyson didn't respond but moved to the far right gun port and stared out across the Narrows. Brown, he admitted, had a flair for choosing interesting places to chat. "How long have you been snooping on me?"

"Long enough to deduce that you and Harper are on the verge of something wonderful."

Tyson leaned out over the three-foot-thick sill of the gun port. It was about thirty feet to the embankment below.

"You came close tonight, lover. But you didn't count on your wife showing up. I literally held my breath when you and Karen ran into your digs. You must have done some fancy footwork because an hour later there you were holding hands with the missus over dinner. What a man!"

Tyson lifted himself onto the sill and sat lengthways in the big gun port, his back to the stone wall and his knees drawn up. He lit a cigarette and looked out over the far horizon. He noticed that Brown's manner was somewhat less cultured than it had been at the Athletic Club. Brown seemed more the tough guy here, and Tyson suspected the man had the chameleonlike ability to blend into his surroundings. He wondered which one was the real Chet Brown. Probably neither.

"You've had a hell of a day." Brown moved closer to Tyson. "Hey, are you practicing? I mean, sitting in a stone room and staring forlornly out the window."

Tyson flipped his cigarette toward Brown. "Keep your distance."

Brown retreated a step. "I'm just so thrilled to see you again. Anyway, as a guardian angel I can do certain things or not to them to alter the fate of mortals. But you control your own destiny on my days off. So watch the fucking and the fighting and don't call journalists unless you intend to beat them up. Okay?"

Tyson yawned. "Are you finished?"

"No. Does the name Colonel Eric Willets mean anything to you?"

"No."

"Well, your name means something to him. He's Karen's lover, and he'd like a piece of your ass."

"Tell him not to believe everything he reads in the papers. That's what I tell my wife."

Brown laughed. "I'll pass that on." He said, "You know, Ben, I like you. But you are the cause of much unhappiness. There is a black cloud following you, and everyone near you gets rained on. And on a national level, you have caused unhappiness in Washington. Did you read this morning's *Times?*"

"No."

"Well, you're the subject of a congressional inquiry. Also the U.N. Commission on Genocide has expressed interest in the case. They're talking about sending a fact-finding mission to Hue, and Hanoi says they're quite welcome to do that. I mean, who needs this shit, Ben?"

"Not me."

"Not your country either."

Tyson stared at Brown in the pale light. Things were becoming more clear. He felt his mouth going dry. He swung his legs around and slid down from the gun opening.

"Now you keep *your* distance." Brown continued, "We could get mad at

Brandt too, I guess. He had the big mouth. If he weren't around, the case would collapse."

Tyson slipped his hand in his jacket pocket and found his Swiss Army knife.

Brown went on ruminatively, "I voted for Brandt to go, but . . ." He shrugged. "There are those who think justice would be better served if it were you."

His hand still in his pocket, Tyson worked the clasp blade out of the handle, slicing his fingers as he levered it open.

"We offered you a deal."

"Offer it to me again."

"Okay. Will you take it?"

"Shove it up your ass."

Brown smiled tightly. "You are a cool one. I'll give you that." Brown glanced around the room, then his eyes focused again on Tyson. He drew a small automatic from an elastic band on his waist, and Tyson saw the black dull silencer in sharp contrast to the silvery nickel plating of the pistol. Brown said, "Climb out on the sill."

Tyson remained still. The distance between him and Brown was about ten feet, or about five feet too many according to his old hand-to-hand combat manual.

Brown snapped, "Get up there."

"Go fuck yourself."

Brown said coolly, "I want to help you do what you tried to in the bay. This is easier and faster than drowning, Ben. Just get up there, close your eyes, and roll back."

"What the hell are you talking about?"

"What the hell do you think I'm talking about?"

Tyson stared at Brown. "I didn't try to commit suicide, you asshole."

Brown seemed confused. He snapped, "Well, too bad. They really hoped you'd be honorable about it."

"Don't talk to me about honor. If you want me dead, do it yourself."

Brown shook his head and lowered the pistol. "At this point in time, I am authorized only to encourage you to terminate yourself. But please believe me when I tell you termination has been discussed. And if you do meet an untimely death, it will be a suicide or an accident, as happened to Mr. Harold Simcox. If you want to reach me, post a lost-and-found notice on the O Club bulletin board. 'Found—Copy of Camus's *The Stranger*—pick up at club office.' I'll contact you. In the meantime, keep alert, Lieutenant. You're on patrol."

Tyson said, "I don't need you to tell me that."

Brown stuck the automatic back into the elastic band and opened the door. He looked back at Tyson. "You can call for a taxi at the main gate. Enjoy the day."

Tyson watched the door close, then went to it and listened to Brown's footsteps echoing away in the damp corridor. He drew his hand from his pocket and saw it was covered with blood, and there were deep gashes in his fingers. He wrapped his handkerchief around his fingers and opened the door. The corridor was empty. He thought, *With a guardian angel like that, who needs the grim reaper?*

As he walked slowly through the dark corridor, Tyson suppressed the feeling of gratitude that he was still alive, which was the feeling Brown had wanted to leave him with. He also fought back the feelings of anger and outrage; Chet

Brown and company would have no effect on his emotions or decisions. Chet Brown did not exist.

"Enjoy the day." *Oh, Christ,* he thought, *is that going to be the new variation of 'Have a nice day'?* He hoped not. Things were bad enough.

32

B enjamin Tyson sat across the desk from Vincent Corva.
Corva said, "Coffee?"
"Fine."
Corva spoke to his secretary over the intercom.

Tyson regarded the small man in the morning light of the east-facing window. Corva was perhaps a few years younger than Tyson, very thin, with pale sunken cheeks and bulging eyes, giving an appearance of malnutrition. His black hair was swept back from his forehead, and his Adam's apple bobbed, moving the knot on his tie. The suit was very much Brooks Brothers, though Tyson suspected it had needed much alteration to fit so slight a frame.

Tyson lit a cigarette and held it clumsily with his bandaged fingers. Corva looked at the wrapped bandages but said nothing. He leaned forward, his arms on the desk, then inquired, "Who did you say referred you to me?"

Corva's voice, Tyson noticed, seemed much stronger and deeper than he'd expected from a man who couldn't have weighed a hundred and forty pounds. Tyson replied, "I didn't."

"Well, who did?"

"I called the bar association, and they gave me a list."

"So you picked Vincent Corva because the name sounded good."

"Something like that." Tyson looked around the office. It was an off-white room with acoustical ceiling tiles, gray carpet, and furniture that looked like it had been carried out of Conran's that morning. The wall decorations were a series of sepia prints that might have been named "Great Moments in Law," and Tyson was surprised there were more than two of them. On the windowsill sat a single plant that looked suspiciously like marijuana.

"Basil."

Tyson looked at Corva. "Excuse me?"

"Sweet basil. Smell it? Can't get fresh basil, even in New York. Do you like *pasta al pesto?*"

"Love it."

"You have to pick it fresh and make the sauce within fifteen minutes. Captures the essence of the basil. Makes all the difference."

"I'm sure of it." Tyson was briefly nostalgic for Phillip Sloan and his woody, leathery office.

"My father used to put a sprig behind his ear—some kind of superstition. Never got it clear though." Corva straightened up and drew a yellow legal pad toward him. He made a notation, and Tyson wondered if it had to do with sweet basil or murder. Corva said, "The press has reported that you are on restriction. Is that correct?"

"Yes." Tyson gave him the terms of his restriction.

Corva nodded thoughtfully. "That's odd, because that began the ticking clock. The Army may not have time to perfect a murder case in ninety days. But someone—higher up—has ordered restriction as a means to move the Army along. I suspect the government theorizes that the longer this is unresolved, the more harm it will cause."

"That's my theory too. Can you perfect a defense within the time remaining?"

"Well, they've had a few months' jump on me, but I'll see what I can do."

Tyson drew on his cigarette and looked over Corva's head at the framed diplomas and various professional accreditations on the wall behind the desk. He noticed a framed color photograph of soldiers in jungle fatigues standing on a desolate plain with black smoke rising in the distance. Tyson said, "You were in Nam?"

"Yes. Here's my background, Mr. Tyson: I was admitted to the New York State bar in 1967 and was shortly thereafter drafted directly into the Judge Advocate General's Corps and went to the branch school at Charlottesville. I was with the Staff Judge Advocate at Fort Benning. I used to watch the infantry OCS guys training sometimes. I never saw men pushed so hard. Then one day as I was walking past one of those full-length mirrors in the lobby of the JAG building, I saw this pale, skinny nerd with a briefcase that was pulling him over like a listing ship. So in a moment of pure lunacy, I decided I wanted to be an infantry officer." He looked at Tyson.

Tyson smiled and said, "Perhaps it was a moment of crystalline sanity."

"No one else thought so. Anyway, after months of red tape and bureaucracy, I got out of the JAG Corps and got assigned to the infantry school at Benning. I died six times during the first month of training. But I never let them know. I graduated, and shortly thereafter I shipped out for Nam and was assigned to the Twenty-fifth Infantry Division, down near Cu Chi."

Tyson nodded.

"I was a platoon leader like you and saw action, and went through the Tet Offensive like you. Unlike you, I wasn't wounded. Any questions?"

"Not at the moment."

"All right, on my return I was assigned to the Pentagon and performed various legal duties. Actually I was sort of a JAG mascot, and they liked to show me off—a JAG lawyer with a Combat Infantry Badge, living proof that even lawyers have balls."

Tyson smiled.

Vincent Corva added, "When you're five-six and scrawny, the infantry has a certain appeal that a man like yourself might not appreciate. I would not have been much of a warrior before gunpowder, but God gave us little squirts M-16 rifles and lightweight field gear and made us all equally deadly. But up here"—he tapped his forehead—"there are still vast differences among men. And up here is where this fight is going to take place." He rose. "I'm going to take a piss, Mr. Tyson."

"Okay."

"If you're not here when I come back, that's okay, too." Vincent Corva left his office.

Tyson stubbed his cigarette into an ashtray. He stood and went to the framed photograph behind Corva's desk. It was a posed shot, like a sports team, front row kneeling, back row standing. There were about forty men, armed with the basic ordnance of the rifle platoon. The background appeared to be a flat, endless expanse of black ash or soot, running out to the horizon of black smoke. It was a color photograph, but there was little color in it.

Standing in the middle of the back row was Lieutenant Vincent Corva. He looked almost comical sandwiched between two huge black men. But Tyson looked closer and saw something in Corva's features, in his eyes, that he understood. It was not the Thousand-Yard Stare, but the look of a hungry predator, a man who knows he is dangerous.

Tyson went to the window and plucked a dark green leaf from the basil plant. He crushed the leaf between his thumb and forefinger and sniffed its unique fragrance.

The door opened behind him, and he heard Corva say, "Smells jog the memory in a surprising way. Sweet basil always brings back my parents' house in early fall, canning tomatoes on the sun porch." He handed Tyson a mug of coffee. "They make coffee, but they won't bring it anymore."

Tyson said, "Well, why should they?"

"She's my wife."

"More reason not to."

Corva sat in his chair. Tyson remained standing. Corva said, "After I was released from active duty, I forgot about military law. But then came the Calley case, and I followed it closely. There is something uniquely fascinating about a court-martial. Don't you think so?"

"Absolutely."

"You were involved with special courts-martial I assume."

"About a dozen."

"Well, I missed that—I do mostly real estate law—so I boned up on military law and got certified. I've done about fifteen general courts-martial in the last fifteen years."

"I heard of one at Fort Jackson. Army captain. Shot his wife's lover."

Corva smiled.

Tyson looked at him, wondering what sort of impression he made on a court-martial board of officers. At least, Tyson thought, Corva didn't have shifty eyes like Phillip Sloan.

Corva leaned forward. "Look, Mr. Tyson, we could waltz around all morning, me pretending I'm sort of interested in taking your case and you pretending you might take your business elsewhere. I don't have time for that, and neither do you. I know every detail of this case that's been reported and some things that haven't been reported. Also I've read Picard's book. Twice. And I want the case. And there are only two certified military lawyers as good as me on the East Coast, and I don't remember their names. So you're fortunate you picked me from the list the bar association gave you."

Tyson said, "Okay, you're hired."

"Fine. I get two hundred dollars an hour. Double for courtroom time. This will cost you a small fortune."

"I'm broke."

"Who isn't these days? Do you have a rich aunt?"

"Lots of them. But I also have some defense fund groups here and there."

"I know," replied Corva. "I'll contact them. Or more likely they'll contact me. Don't worry about money. If there's not enough of it, I'll make up the difference. *Pro bono publico.* That's Latin, not Italian. Means for the public good." Corva stood. "Deal?"

"Deal." They shook hands.

Corva said, "I don't have time to go into any details, but the first piece of advice I'm giving you is not to speak to Major Karen Harper again. Not under *any* circumstances. Understood?"

Tyson nodded.

"I'd like to contact your personal attorney. Sloan. Garden City."

"Right."

Corva seemed deep in thought, then said, "I knew Van Arken, by the way. At the Pentagon. Not personally, but I knew of him. After My Lai hit the fan, I saw his name mentioned a few times. He's an uncompromising son of a bitch."

"The whole Army, Mr. Corva, is made up of uncompromising sons of bitches. I wouldn't want any other type of Army."

"Me neither. And the JAG is not much different than the infantry in that respect. There is no plea bargaining as we know it in civilian law."

"I'm not interested in plea bargaining."

"Nor am I, Mr. Tyson. But sometimes the government jumps over the Army's head and approaches you with a deal. Has that happened to you?"

"No, it hasn't."

"Let me know."

"Of course."

Corva opened the door. "Well, go meet my wife, Linda. She's the brunette with the pink dress in the outer office. She thinks you are handsome. She'll work hard for you, too. Sometime down the line, you and your wife will come over for dinner. In the early fall, when the sweet basil is at its best."

"If I'm available I'll be there."

"You'll be available, Mr. Tyson."

Tyson stopped at the door and turned back to Vincent Corva. "You understand, don't you, that a violation of the Uniform Code of Military Justice did take place on 15 February 1968? A violation for which there is no statute of limitations."

"Is that so?"

"You understand that most of what Andrew Picard wrote in his book is true."

"Is *what?*"

"True."

"How do you know?"

"I was *there.*"

"Were you?" He stepped closer to Tyson and lowered his voice. "Let me tell *you* something—let me reveal to you the one great truth about war, Mr. Tyson, and it is this: Ultimately all war stories are bullshit. From a general's memoirs to an ex-Pfc's boasting in a saloon, it is all *bullshit.* From the *Iliad* to the Grenada invasion, it is all *bullshit.* I have never heard a true war story, and I never told one, and neither have you. And if we do enter a courtroom, we will shovel the bullshit faster and higher than the Army, and by the time we are ready to walk out of there, we will all be up to our eyebrows in spent shell casings and bullshit. Don't burden me with the truth, Mr. Tyson, I am not interested."

Tyson looked into Corva's eyes. "You mean you don't want to know what—"

"No. What the hell do I care what happened there? When you have heard one war story, you have heard them all. Keep the details to yourself. And if I should have to ask you for a detail or two in order to form a strategy for the defense, do me a favor and bullshit me." Corva pointed his finger at Tyson. "The only story I want from you is the cover story, my friend. The one Mr. Anthony Scorello and Mr. Paul Sadowski are putting out. You see, Mr. Tyson, I am not much of a courtroom actor, and when Brandt and Farley get on the stand and start their version of the bullshit, I want to look appropriately incredulous. You know the Japanese play *Rashomon?* Read it. See you tomorrow.

Fort Hamilton. Buy me dinner, seven P.M. Coffee at your place. I want to meet your wife."

Tyson remained standing in the doorway. At length he said, "I once heard a true war story. A Confederate officer's account of Gettysburg. He wrote, 'We all went up to Gettysburg, the summer of sixty-three, and some of us came back from there; and that's all except for the details.' "

Corva smiled appreciatively. "Yes, except for the details. Good-bye, Mr. Tyson."

"Good-bye, Mr. Corva."

33

Benjamin Tyson said, "Pass the cucumbers, please."
David passed the cucumbers.
Marcy said to Vincent Corva, "More iced tea, Vincent?"
"No, thank you."

Tyson sat in his rolled-up shirt sleeves and loosened his black uniform tie. "Hot."

Marcy rose and closed the blinds, blocking out the noon sun from the small dining room.

Tyson surveyed the room, a ten-foot-square area, opening onto the living room. Marcy had purchased a dinette table from the post thrift shop and carried it home in the Jeep along with some framed pictures, including a scene of Mount Fuji painted in iridescent colors on black velvet. Tyson regarded the picture as he picked at his cucumbers. On the opposite wall of the dining room hung his commission.

Marcy said to Vincent Corva, "More chicken salad?"

"No, thank you, Marcy. That was a good lunch."

Tyson snorted, "Bullshit."

"No, really—"

"Protestant food, Vincent. You are what you eat. Today you're cool cucumbers and chicken salad made with Miracle Whip on white bread. By tonight you'll be speaking in aphorisms and lose your sex drive."

Corva smiled embarrassedly.

Marcy gave Tyson a look of mock scorn. "Ethnic slurs are not welcome at my table." She turned to Corva. "Wasn't that a good lunch for a hot day?"

"Yes."

David said, "Dad, I'm taking the bus and subway to Sheepshead Bay this afternoon. I'm going to hang around the boats and help out. Okay?"

Tyson said, "Why not?"

Marcy said, "Because I don't think I want him taking a bus and subway."

"How are we ever going to live on West Seventy-something Street if he can't take buses and subways?"

"Well . . . he has no experience with public transportation, and—"

"I had no experience with combat until a machine gun opened up on me one day. You talk about suburban turkeys—" He turned to Corva. "What do you think, Vincent?"

"Well . . . how old is—"

Tyson interrupted, "What's the kid going to do around here all day?"

Marcy snapped, "What do *I* do around here all day?"

Tyson snapped back, "What do *I* do all day? I have a two-minute commute to work, I give guided tours to geriatrics and stare at the damned cannon the rest of the day. Don't I take you to the club for dinner and lunch?"

"I know the damned menu by heart, including the printer's name and address."

David cleared his throat. "Well, can I go or not?"

"Yes."

"No."

Tyson slammed his hand on the table. "Yes!" He turned to Corva. "Italian wives aren't like this."

"Well—"

Marcy addressed Corva. "Would you let your fifteen-year-old son—"

"Sixteen," said Tyson and David simultaneously.

"Sixteen-year-old son take a subway?"

"Subways are safe," declared Tyson. "Don't believe everything you read in the papers. That's the trouble around here. Everybody believes what they read in the papers."

David said, "Maybe I'll just go down to the baseball field."

"Okay," said Tyson. "Why don't you go now?"

"Right." He stood, grabbed some plates, and disappeared into the kitchen, calling out good-byes. The kitchen screen door opened and shut.

Marcy looked at Corva. "Why do you and Ben have to see Colonel Levin today?"

Corva replied, "Some administrative matter, I suppose."

Marcy stared at him for some time. "Bullshit."

Tyson said, "Let's stop browbeating our guest." He turned to Corva. "The food may be dull, but the company isn't."

"I really like chicken salad."

Marcy laughed without humor. "Oh, God, sometimes I think we're going stir-crazy in this place." She addressed Corva. "It has been three weeks since you've been on this case. What have you done or discovered or whatever?"

"Well, I've spoken to Phillip Sloan, filed various motions in the Federal District Court, sent telegrams to the Department of the Army, Justice Department, the JAG, and the White House. I've held a press conference, and I've got my picture in *Newsweek, Time, U.S. News,* and the *American Investigator.*"

Marcy smiled, then turned to Tyson. "I haven't seen Wally Jones's byline for the last three weeks."

"Really? Probably on vacation."

Marcy turned back to Corva. "And you've contacted the witnesses?"

"Well, the government's witnesses' attorneys. And Karen Harper. She wasn't obligated to give me the fruits of a preliminary investigation, but she was most helpful."

"Yes, she was helpful to Ben, also. But what do you think she recommended?"

Corva glanced at Tyson, then said to Marcy, "Based on the expected testimony of the two government witnesses she probably recommended pursuing the case."

"Further investigation? A formal hearing? More months of this?"

"I'm afraid so."

Tyson said, "Anyone want a drink? Gin and tonic, out on the patio?"

Marcy stood. "There is no patio, Ben. And I have no tonic or limes."

"Well, call Gristedes and have them deliver tonic and limes and a patio. On the double."

"How about wine spritzers on the front stoop instead?" suggested Marcy.

"Fine." Tyson stood. He came around the table and kissed his wife. "Good lunch."

Marcy patted his cheek. "Bullshit."

Corva stood also. "I'll be out front." He took his suit jacket from the back of the chair and walked through the living room, leaving by the front door.

Marcy said, "Do you have faith in him?"

"Do you?"

"I'm not the one facing murder charges. Answer the question."

Tyson considered a moment before replying. "He has an unusual philosophy of the law. Sometimes I think truth and legality are Protestant obsessions. Mr. Corva takes a more subjective view of life. He's not interested in the crime but in the law's perception of it, the witnesses against me, and why they are against me. Sloan was always quoting the law, asking what happened at that hospital. Corva wants to know all there is to know about Brandt and Farley and is trying to determine what they *think* happened at the hospital. Different approach."

She nodded. "But it makes sense, especially after all these years have gone by."

Tyson said, "On my first meeting with him he asked me to read the Japanese play *Rashomon*. So I did. Do you know it?"

She shook her head.

"Well, it was about a rape and a killing. And it was four perspectives of the crime, told by four people at a trial. No two people reported the same thing. The bandit said he killed the husband, the wife said she killed the husband, the ghost of the husband said he killed himself, and a woodcutter said the husband fell on his own sword by accident. Obviously at least three people were lying, perhaps all four. The point is that truth is in the eye of the beholder, and no single objective explanation for a human event can ever be found." He smiled grimly. "Of course everyone on the receiving end of what happened at that hospital had the same ultimate experience. But if they were around to testify I think they would relate different perceptions."

Marcy nodded. "So Vincent Corva's defense is based on a Japanese play?"

Tyson shrugged. "Why not? Better than an Aesop's fable where everyone gets his just desserts."

Marcy looked doubtful. She looked into his eyes and said, "Ben, what is happening today?"

"Don't know, love. But I don't think it's an award ceremony." Tyson said, "Why don't you and David go back home?"

"We are home."

He let out a breath. "Well, why don't you go back to the big air-conditioned house we own with the patio out back?"

"You mean the house in Garden City where our country club is and all our friends are and where we have membership to the swimming pool and where all the nice stores and shops are, and the MPs don't ticket me every day for not having a parking sticker? That house?"

"Right. That's the place."

"Why would I want to go there if it meant leaving you?"

"Be still, my heart. Look, have you thought about David starting school?"

"Yes. I don't think he can go back to public school. Not here or in Garden City or anywhere. They would make his life miserable."

Tyson nodded.

Marcy said, "Your mother has a room for him, and he could stay with her in Florida and go to school under another name, or have a tutor—"

"No. He's staying here. With me. And if there's a court-martial he will attend."

"No, he will not."

"Yes, he will. Find a private school or a tutor in the area."

They stared at each other. Tyson looked at his watch. "Forget the spritzers. I have to go. Get this table cleaned up, then go down to the Laundromat and—"

"Buzz off."

Tyson grabbed her and kissed her hard on the lips. "I love you."

"Me too. Good luck."

Tyson walked into the living room and took his tunic from the sofa. He left the house and found Corva sitting on the front stoop looking through his briefcase. Tyson said, "Sorry to keep you waiting. I couldn't find the wine."

"That's all right."

"How about a drink at the club? It's on the way, sort of."

"Thanks, anyway. We should get moving. We should be there by now." He closed his briefcase and stood.

Tyson ignored him and asked, "Did you ever play stoop-ball when you were a kid in the slums?"

"Actually I grew up in a nice section of Staten Island." He motioned across the Narrows. "Right over there. Big house and garden."

"Your father grew sweet basil and tomatoes and all that?"

"Right. Zucchini and eggplant. We had fig trees. Had to wrap and insulate them every winter. You ever taste a fresh fig?"

"No. But I saw them once at Gristedes for fifty cents apiece. My father grew roses and boxwoods. My mother couldn't cook."

"Why would anyone want to cook roses and boxwoods?"

"I don't know. Protestants eat funny things."

Corva smiled. "Listen, I'll take you and Marcy and David to the Feast of San Gennaro next month. Down on Mulberry Street. You can get fresh figs for a quarter."

"Good. Looking forward to it." Neither man spoke. Finally Corva glanced at his watch. "Well, I think it's time."

Tyson nodded. "Right."

Corva said, "Remember, it's only words. It's not incoming rounds."

Tyson smiled. "Right."

"And if we don't like the words they're saying, we can just beat the shit out of them."

"Can we do that?"

"Sure. Article 141. Let's go."

They began to walk to post headquarters.

Benjamin Tyson and Vincent Corva sat in the office of the assistant adjutant, Captain Hodges. Tyson glanced at the communicating door that led into Colonel Levin's office. He said to Corva, "Levin was the person who recommended you."

Corva nodded.

"Do you know him?"

"No, but I had a manslaughter case at Fort Dix about a year ago, and Levin was on the court-martial board. He asked me a lot of questions."

"Good questions?"

"Too good."

"You lost?"

"Well . . . the accused was found guilty."

"Is that the same as you losing?"

"I guess so." Corva yawned.

Tyson inquired, "Do you win any?"

Corva was leafing through his notebook. "What's that?"

"Do you *win* any?"

"Oh. . . ." He seemed to be searching his memory. "A few." He leaned toward Tyson. "How many did *you* win? I mean, when you were defense counsel at special courts-martial."

Tyson said impatiently, "That's not relevant. I wasn't a lawyer. And nearly everyone I defended was patently guilty."

"Right. Or they wouldn't have been there."

"That's right," said Tyson.

Corva added, "The Army rarely convenes a court-martial unless they know the accused is guilty. If there's any doubt, they usually dismiss the charge, or they offer the accused nonjudicial punishment and see if he bites. Occasionally they'll order further investigation. But they don't enter a court-martial room with their fingers crossed the way a civilian DA does." He looked at Tyson and smiled. "So how many did you win when you were the *prosecution? All?"*

"Most of them pleaded guilty. The rest were pretty much open and shut. I mean like AWOLs. Either you are there when you're supposed to be or you are not. But this is not a special court-martial. This is a general court-martial, involving a capital crime, a very complex case. So I don't see any analogy."

"But there is a similarity. Most of the people I defend are as patently guilty as an AWOL soldier. By the time they call me they've fired their free Army attorney, and they are desperate. In this rather limited field I am known as Saint Jude, patron saint of hopeless causes."

"Now you tell me."

Corva smiled. "Be of good cheer, Benjamin. I'm due for a miracle."

"Me too." Tyson stood and went to the window. He stared out over the small post, watching the activity of military life below. "Sometimes I remember the faces of the accused men who were marched into a court-martial room. I don't like to see that look on men's faces. It's demoralizing to me to see men who are so frightened. It's embarrassing to everyone in the courtroom. I don't want to have that look on my face, Vince."

Corva said, "You're allowed to *be* frightened. But you will not *look* frightened. Not in front of a court-martial board. You know that."

"I know it. I won't even flinch when they hand me twenty to life."

"Twenty to life? Christ, *I'll* flinch."

Tyson turned from the window and stared at Corva.

Corva said, "By the way, when we get in there, feel free to speak your mind. You say you have a good relationship with Levin, so you don't have to let me do all the talking. Also he doesn't represent the prosecution. He's just your immediate commander, and he's only doing his job."

"What's his job today, Vincent?"

"Being a prick."

The door opened, and Captain Hodges stuck his head in.

Tyson said to Corva, "Speaking of which . . ."

Corva laughed.

Hodges looked both annoyed and confused. He cleared his throat. "The colonel will see you now."

Corva stood and led the way into Levin's office. Corva stepped aside to the right, Hodges to the left. Tyson went straight to the desk, saluted, and said, "Lieutenant Tyson reports, sir."

Levin returned the salute, then stood to shake hands with Vincent Corva and introduced Corva to Captain Hodges, who also shook hands with Corva. Colonel Levin sat, Corva sat in the chair indicated by Hodges, and Hodges sat. Tyson remained standing at attention. He was sure every facet of protocol was satisfied, but somehow he felt left out. He thought he should remind them that he was the reason they were all there.

Colonel Levin said, "Have a seat, Lieutenant."

Tyson sat in the only empty chair, between Corva and Hodges.

Levin let a moment go by before saying, "I have here a copy of Major Harper's preliminary investigation report, conducted under Article 31 of the Uniform Code of Military Justice." He opened a legal-sized file folder on his desk and addressed Tyson. "I've asked Captain Hodges to be present as a witness, owing to the fact that you have legal counsel present."

Tyson nodded.

Hodges said, "Please respond verbally, Lieutenant."

Tyson said, "Yes, sir."

Levin looked down at the folder. "I have been instructed, as your commanding officer, to make you aware of certain aspects of the investigation."

Corva said, "May I have a copy of the preliminary investigator's report, Colonel?"

"No, you may not. You and I know, Mr. Corva, that unlike an Article 32 investigation report, this is an internal communication. This report is between Major Harper and General George Peters, post commander of Fort Dix, who has general court-martial convening authority in this case. However, I have been instructed by General Peters, on advice of his Staff Judge Advocate, to read to the accused pertinent sections of this report."

Corva said, "May I request, Colonel, that you begin with the end? What is her conclusion?"

Captain Hodges stirred in his chair and made a sound that clearly indicated he did not like to have his colonel interrupted or otherwise annoyed. Under other circumstances Tyson might have enjoyed Hodges's frustration in dealing with a civilian.

Colonel Levin seemed to take Corva's suggestion well. He nodded. "Of course. I don't mean to drag this out and cause Lieutenant Tyson any unnecessary anxiety." He looked directly at Tyson and said, "Major Harper did not recommend that the case be dismissed."

Tyson nodded. He never expected that she would. Yet somewhere in the back of his mind he thought she might.

Corva said, "Then we are to have an Article 32 investigation?"

Colonel Levin seemed not to hear. He drew a typed sheet of paper toward him. "I'll read you certain parts of this as I've been instructed." He cleared his throat. "She states: 'My preliminary investigation did not uncover any documentary evidence or physical evidence of a crime, nor was it likely to, considering the locale of the alleged crime and the length of time that has elapsed since the crime allegedly took place. Further investigation for this type of evidence is not likely to be fruitful. Therefore, I have considered only the statements of the witnesses in reaching my conclusion. The statements of Dr. Steven Brandt and Mr. Richard Farley, if taken at face value, clearly indicate that a violation of the Uniform Code of Military Justice took place at the time and location in question. Further, their statements indicate that this violation would come under

Article 118, murder, for which there is no statute of limitations. Further, the government has established its jurisdiction over the suspect but has not established such jurisdiction over other possible suspects. Therefore, though there appears to be testimonial evidence that would incriminate other former members of the United States Army, this report is confined to the subject of Lieutenant Benjamin Tyson.' "

Colonel Levin looked at Tyson briefly, then at Corva. He said to Corva, "Any questions so far?"

"No, sir."

Levin nodded and continued reading. " 'The statements of Paul Sadowski and Anthony Scorello, on the other hand, are in almost direct contradiction to those of Brandt and Farley and refute the most damning points of those two statements. During extensive interviews with Lieutenant Tyson, as noted in some detail earlier, he made statements which were strikingly similar to those of Sadowski and Scorello. It should be further noted, however, that Lieutenant Tyson did not impeach the statements or character of either of the potential witnesses against him; he merely told a different version of the events in question. There is, though, some evidence based on various statements made by Paul Sadowski that Dr. Brandt may harbor some hostility or bias toward the accused. This hostility or bias would have had its genesis during the time Lieutenant Tyson and Dr. Brandt served together, as there is no evidence to suggest they saw or communicated with each other since the day Lieutenant Tyson was medically evacuated from the Republic of Vietnam.' " Colonel Levin looked at Tyson, then at Corva. "Okay so far?"

Corva turned to Tyson. "Okay?"

Tyson shrugged. "I guess. Am I supposed to add anything or question anything?"

"No," said Corva. "Just listen closely because we're not entitled to see this, only to hear it, and that only as a courtesy."

"And," interjected Hodges, "in the interests of justice."

Corva turned to Hodges and smiled. "Thank you, Captain. We know that."

Hodges's face reddened.

Levin cleared his throat. "Okay. Major Harper further states: 'This preliminary investigation has noted the existence of five additional witnesses to this incident: Daniel Kelly, Hernando Beltran, Lee Walker, Louis Kalane, and Michael DeTonq. The status of these witnesses is covered in a separate section of this report.' " Levin looked at Corva. "They have not been located."

Corva nodded.

Levin continued reading: " 'There is, in addition to these eyewitnesses, the author Andrew Picard, whose role in this matter is well known. Mr. Picard's statements to me on the telephone confirm that any testimony he would offer would be no more than hearsay. Mr. Picard, however, is the link to the last known and possible eyewitness, Sister Teresa. This matter is also covered in a separate section.' " Levin flipped a page and read, " 'In conclusion I believe that the evidence I have uncovered to date indicates that there is probable cause to believe that a violation of the Uniform Code of Military Justice occurred. Therefore, I recommend that this matter be referred to further investigation under Article 32 of the Code.' " Levin looked up from the report.

No one spoke. Finally Corva said, "And has General Peters acted on that recommendation?"

Levin took a cigar from his drawer and peeled off the cedar wrapper. Tyson noted irrelevantly that Levin had switched to a better brand. Levin said, "General Peters, on receipt of this report, forwarded it to his Staff Judge Advocate who in turn made his recommendation to General Peters regarding the disposition of this case. The Staff Judge Advocate concurred with Major Harper that an Article 32 investigation be initiated. General Peters in turn concurred with his SJA."

Corva observed, "That's a lot of concurrence. I hope there is no command influence present in those concurrences."

Levin replied, "Command influence would be illegal, Mr. Corva. This matter is being judged wholly on its legal merits."

"Really? I wonder if the decision not to dismiss this rather weak case is not a result of some sort of subtle command influence or the perception of same. In other words, to name titles, if not names: the Judge Advocate General, the Attorney General, the secretaries of the Army and of Defense, and the President of the United States. If I were General Peters, I'd hear those drums beating cadence, and I'd damned sure march to that beat."

Levin finally lit his cigar and drew on it until the tip glowed red. He said, "That is a serious allegation. And I'm not the one to hear it."

"No," said Corva, "but until I put it in writing and send it off to everyone I can think of, would you be kind enough to pass on my thoughts to General Peters?"

"If you wish." Levin handed Tyson a sheet of paper. "These are the orders convening the Article 32 hearing. The date, as you can see, is 9 September, which gives you sufficient time to locate any additional witnesses for the defense as may exist. The place is here, at Fort Hamilton. Specifically the Stonewall Jackson room on the second level of the Officers' Club. The hearing will be closed to the media and the public. Any questions?"

Tyson glanced at the orders. He replied, "No, sir." He handed the paper to Corva.

Corva examined the convening orders with some care before putting them in his briefcase. He addressed Colonel Levin. "I'd like you to pass on another comment to General Peters and his Staff Judge Advocate. I wish to remind them that the accused has a specific right under the UCMJ to request of the Army their assistance on his behalf. Therefore, if we are to have a formal investigation and hearing, I want the Army, at the Army's expense, to continue their efforts to locate missing witnesses and to advise the accused of the steps taken to accomplish that."

Colonel Levin nodded. "I will pass on your reminder to the convening authorities." Levin glanced at Captain Hodges, then made eye contact with Corva and said, "But my advice to Lieutenant Tyson and to you is that you should expend some effort yourselves in locating these witnesses if you believe they are going to be witnesses for the defense."

Corva replied, "There is no doubt in my mind that they are, Colonel. And in the interests of justice I'm certain the government will use its considerable resources to assist me in finding them and that the government will do so with the same zeal they've shown thus far in pursuing this case. And if they don't, I am going to take appropriate steps to have this case dismissed. I'll put that in writing, and you can forward it to General Peters."

Levin drew on his cigar. "Anything further, Mr. Corva?"

"No, Colonel."

The intercom buzzed, and Levin picked it up. He listened, then said to Captain Hodges, "Sergeant Wolton needs some orders signed. We'll take a five-minute break here."

Hodges stood and left the office.

Colonel Levin leaned across his desk and looked at Tyson. "Real crock of shit, eh, Tyson?"

Tyson was momentarily taken aback by the sudden shift in tone and manner. He replied, "Yes, sir. Real crock."

Levin glared at Corva. He said gruffly, "Save the legal razzle-dazzle for the hearing. You're giving me a headache."

Corva smiled. "You gave me a headache at Fort Dix."

Levin looked again at Tyson. "Smoke if you like."

Tyson shook his head. The thought occurred to him that Levin had contrived to send Hodges out of the room.

Levin said to Tyson, "You understand that, as your commanding officer, this is my job."

Tyson replied, "Of course. That's what I used to say to the men I was screwing."

Corva laughed.

Levin glowered at Tyson, then he smiled wryly. He said, "Just keep remembering that for the rest of this session."

"Yes, sir."

Corva said, "Colonel, as Lieutenant Tyson's commanding officer, I would like you to offer testimony as to his character if this ever gets to the sentencing stage."

Levin chewed ruminatively on his cigar. He finally replied, "I hope this doesn't get that far. But if it does I don't know if my brief association with Lieutenant Tyson would count for much."

"I think it would help for a court-martial board to hear that Lieutenant Tyson performed his duty here satisfactorily. Yes or no, Colonel?"

Colonel Levin put his cigar in the ashtray. He looked at Corva. "You may have noticed that I'm a little old to be a lieutenant colonel. You may also have noticed that Fort Hamilton is not the Pentagon or NATO headquarters. The long and the short of it is that I've been passed over once for promotion to full colonel, and I've gotten shit duty to boot. Be that as it may, *I* like Hamilton, even if the Army considers it the waiting room to oblivion. I'm up for full bird again, and there's talk I will be post commander when Colonel Hill leaves in October."

Levin looked at Corva closely. "Maybe you can understand, Mr. Corva. My father was a maintenance man here. And this will be my last duty station, being I've got nearly thirty years in. From here I'll go home, back to Brighton Beach, down the Shore Parkway a bit. And I'll have come full circle. And once in a while I'll return here and bring my wife to dinner at the club and appear at a few functions as the former post commander and do whatever old soldiers do who retire around Army installations. And it will have been a good life." He looked at Tyson.

Corva said, "Does that mean the answer is no?"

Levin turned back to him. "No. It doesn't. The answer is actually yes. I'd be happy to testify as to Lieutenant Tyson's good character. I just wanted you to appreciate it."

Corva smiled.

Tyson said, "Thank you, Colonel."

Levin grunted. No one spoke for the next few minutes. The door opened, and Captain Hodges took his seat without a word.

Levin shuffled some papers on his desk. "All right . . ." He drew a long wheezy breath. "All right. . . ." He turned to Tyson and cleared his throat. "Lieutenant Benjamin Tyson, I have been instructed to read to you the charges that have been preferred against you." Levin drew a long form from the folder, held it up so it hid his face, and read: "Lieutenant Benjamin J. Tyson, you are charged as follows: Violation of the Uniform Code of Military Justice, Article 118, murder. Specification One: In that Benjamin J. Tyson, First Lieutenant, United States Army, presently assigned to the adjutant at Fort Hamilton, Brooklyn, New York, then a member of Alpha Company, Fifth Battalion, Seventh Cavalry, of the First Air Cavalry Division, did, in or about the city of Hue, in the province of Thua Thien, in the former Republic of Vietnam, in or about the vicinity of Hôpital Miséricorde, on or about 15 February 1968, engage in acts which were inherently dangerous to others and evinced a wanton disregard of human life, causing the murder of an unknown number, not less than ninety, Oriental human beings, males and females, of various ages, whose names are unknown, patients and staff of said hospital, by means of shooting them or causing them to be shot, or ordering them to be shot, with rifle and/or pistol fire, or causing their deaths with incendiary hand grenades, and/or by other lethal means and devices not yet known."

Levin looked over the charge sheet, and his eyes passed briefly over Tyson's face. Tyson sat with his chin in his hand, his eyes focused on the wall behind Levin, his mind on some distant time and place. The room was absolutely still.

Levin cleared his throat again and continued, "Specification Two: In that Benjamin J. Tyson did, in or about the city of Hue, in the province of Thua Thien, in the former Republic of Vietnam, in or about the vicinity of Hôpital Miséricorde, on or about 15 February 1968, engage in acts which were inherently dangerous to others and evinced a wanton disregard of human life, causing the murder of approximately fourteen Caucasian human beings, male and female, in the manner stated in Specification One, whose names are as follows: Jean Monteau, male, physician, French national, age forty-six; Evan Dougal, male, physician, Australian national, age thirty-four; Bernhard Rueger, male, physician, German national, age twenty-nine; Marie Broi, female, nurse, French national, age twenty-five; Sister Monique (Yvette Dulane), female, nurse/nun, French national, age twenty-one; Sister Aimee (Henriette La Blanc), female, nurse/nun, French national, age twenty-one; Sister Noelle (Reine Mauroy), female, nurse/nun, Belgian national, age twenty-three; Pierre Galante, male, nurse, French national, age thirty; Henri Taine, male, nurse, French national, age thirty-one; Maarten Lubbers, male, laboratory technician, Dutch national, age twenty-three; Brother Donatus (full name unknown), male, staff assistant, nationality unknown, age forty-one; Sister Juliette (full name unknown), female, nurse/nun, nationality unknown, age fifty-three; Susanne Dougal, female (wife of Evan Dougal), Australian national, age thirty-five; Linda Dougal, female (daughter of Evan and Susanne Dougal), Australian national, age fifteen."

Colonel Levin stared at the charge sheet for a few more seconds, then put it down. He relit his cigar and puffed on it.

Tyson could hear the typewriters in the outer office. Through the open window came the sound of the Twenty-sixth U.S. Army Band practicing on the drill field. They were playing "Sweet Georgia Brown."

Levin drew a copy of the charge sheet from his folder and handed it directly to Tyson. Tyson, without looking at it, gave it to Corva, who dropped it into his open briefcase without a glance.

Levin handed Corva several stapled sheets of paper. "These are the names and brief biographies of the alleged Caucasian victims specified in the charge sheet. They were supplied to Major Harper by the Catholic Relief Agency in Paris and represent that agency's missing personnel—plus two dependent family members—who were assigned to duty at Miséricorde Hospital at the time of the alleged incident." Levin said to Corva, who was flipping through the pages, "Questions, Mr. Corva?"

"Dozens of them, Colonel, but unfortunately you could not answer any of them."

"No, I probably couldn't." Levin ground out his cigar.

Corva said, "Will that be all, Colonel?"

Hodges answered, "The colonel will let you know when that is all."

Corva smiled and leaned toward Hodges. He said in an amiable tone of voice, "How would you like to spend the rest of the day in the hospital?"

Hodges jumped to his feet. "How dare you threaten—"

Corva stood. "That was no threat. That—"

Levin bellowed, "At ease! Sit down, Captain!" He turned to Corva. "Please take your seat, Mr. Corva."

Hodges and Corva sat. Tyson stared out the window in pointed disinterest. The Army band had struck up George M. Cohan's "Over There," and Tyson tapped his foot to the lively tune.

Levin said to Hodges, "Captain, you will address Mr. Corva with the courtesy which an officer in the United States Army extends to all civilians. This is not Prussia, and you are not in the Prussian Army. Loosen up, man."

Hodges's face had gone from red to livid. He snapped, "Yes, sir!"

Tyson smiled absently as his foot beat faster to the quickening cadence of the song.

Levin said to Corva, "I'll let your remark pass, being it was provoked." He said to Tyson, "Lieutenant, if you're going to break into a tap dance, could you wait until you're clear of this building?"

Tyson stopped tapping. "Yes, sir."

Levin picked up a piece of paper and read it to himself with some concentration, as though he were trying to make sense of it. Finally he put down the paper and turned to Tyson. "Lieutenant Tyson, I have been instructed by Colonel Hill, the post commander, to place you in arrest."

Tyson made brief eye contact with Corva, then stared at Levin.

Levin looked away. He continued, "You may know from your prior service that military arrest is a moral and legal restraint, not a physical restraint. However, it is a greater restraint of freedom of movement than the restriction which you are now under. Please don't interrupt, Mr. Corva. Just listen. Lieutenant Tyson, the conditions of your arrest are as follows: You are not required to perform your full military duties, and in fact, your duties at the museum are herewith terminated, and your name has been removed from all post duty rosters. You will not leave this post without permission from me or an officer designated by me to grant such permission. You will report in to this office at nine hundred hours each day, to me or to Captain Hodges or to the weekend duty officer. You will sign in, in a book provided for that purpose, every three hours until twenty-one hundred hours. You will be in your quarters after that time and remain there until you report in the following day at nine hundred hours. You will not bear arms. You will confine your post activities to the PX, the commissary, the Officers' Club, your quarters, and the gymnasium if you wish to use it. The provost marshal has been instructed to monitor the period when you are restricted to quarters." Levin handed Tyson a sheet of paper. "This is the arrest order. Do you have any questions?"

Tyson shook his head, which normally would have provoked Hodges into telling him to answer the colonel verbally. But Hodges seemed permanently rebuked, albeit content with the ultimate outcome of this session.

Corva said, "I intend to protest this arrest to Colonel Hill. It is onerous, unnecessary, and it is most irregular to treat an officer in this manner. Also, it sucks."

Levin nodded as though in agreement. He said, however, "You have no legal remedies concerning an arrest order. But if you want a meeting with the post commander, I can arrange that."

Corva stood. "Is *that* all?" He glared at Hodges.

Levin nodded. "That's all *I've* got to say. How about you or your client?"

Corva said, "My client requests permission to leave the post at eighteen hundred hours for the purpose of getting drunk with me."

Levin replied, "Permission granted." He said to Tyson, "You will report here to me at nine hundred hours tomorrow."

"Yes, sir."

Levin stood, followed by Tyson and Captain Hodges. Levin looked at Tyson, then with a barely perceptible shrug said, "That will be all, Lieutenant."

Tyson saluted, did an about-face, and walked smartly out of the office.

34

Ben Tyson passed through the corridor and down the stairs, vaguely aware of where he was going, and less aware of the footsteps following him. Corva caught up with him. Tyson lit a cigarette as he left the headquarters building. He said to Corva, "Did you know that was going to happen?"

"Sort of."

"Why didn't you tell me?"

"You knew, Ben. Let's stop pretending this is some sort of silly bureaucratic screwup. These people are serious. They are charging you with *murder.* You knew that from the first day your friend handed you Picard's book."

Tyson drew on his cigarette. He replied, "I knew long before then." Tyson said, "Well, Vince, why didn't we beat the shit out of them?"

Corva smiled. "You're sounding like a hotheaded dago now."

They walked along Lee Avenue, past the antique cannon display, and approached the main gate.

Corva said, "Where are you going? You can't leave post until eighteen hundred hours."

"Fuck 'em. I don't even know what time that is." He passed through the pedestrian walk of the gates, absently returned the MP's salute, and turned left, under the elevated bridge ramp toward the Shore Parkway.

Corva said, "That's six o'clock. Come on. Let's go back. I am responsible for you."

"No one is responsible for me but me. They can take their arrest order, roll it up, put a light coat of oil on it, and shove it up their ass. And if you don't want to be responsible, leave."

Corva drew a deep breath but said nothing. They made their way through a small park down to the shore. Tyson walked east along the water's edge.

Corva followed a few feet behind. He said, "People who are accused of a heinous crime often delude themselves into thinking they didn't do it. So when the law starts to inconvenience them, they get outraged. Listen to me, Ben. I haven't asked you for many details of what happened, but *you* know, *I* know, and the *Army* knows that a terrible slaughter of innocents took place at that hospital. You heard the roll call of the dead, as the prosecutor will undoubtedly say. Not to mention 'not less than ninety Oriental human beings.' "

"I liked that. The way they neatly divided the white folk from the Oriental folk."

"They had the Caucasians' names, that's why they did that, not because of any racial bias, or—"

"Oh, bullshit. Would I be here now, twenty years later, if it was just a village of a couple hundred gooks? Slopes? Dinks? Zipperheads? Slants? What else did we call them, Vince? What did *you* call them? Anything but Oriental human beings. But I fucked up good. I zapped fourteen real people."

"Okay, you don't have to tell me all that. I know what we did and how we behaved. Christ, if I could go back . . ."

"Yeah."

Corva kept up with Tyson's brisk pace. Corva said, "The point is that you, I, and the Army also know that this slaughter was perpetrated by men directly under your command. Furthermore, there is probable cause to suspect that you were present and witnessed all or part of that slaughter. And they're going so far as to suggest you may have even pulled the trigger yourself a few times."

"I didn't." Tyson stopped and stared out over the water. Small ripples ran up to the pebbly beach. He drew in a deep breath of salt air. "I did not," he repeated.

Corva came up beside him. "Who cares? Not me. You know and I know that the Army does not care if you shot anyone or not. They do not care why it happened or if you tried to stop it or if your troops mutinied and held you at gunpoint or if you just stepped out a minute to take a piss and missed the whole thing. They only care that you did not report that massacre, which was your legal duty, not to mention, if you will, your Christian duty. For reasons known only to yourself you did not wish to see those murderers brought to justice. The irony here is that the men under your command most probably committed a crime of passion. Perhaps they were suffering from battle fatigue, which the Army recognizes under Article 118 as extenuating circumstances for murder. And undoubtedly your men were suffering from a fatal sickness of the soul. Fatal, that is, to others. But you, on the other hand, committed a crime of dispassion each and every day you did not report what you witnessed. You've had nearly two decades to set things right, Ben, and you did not. So now the Army is going to set things right, not only for them but also for you. As for the murderers, they have many defenses, but they don't even need them in a court of law. The peculiarities of this imperfect system pretty much assures they won't be called to account. Their crime was of the moment, a moment of madness. Your crime is an ongoing one. Army justice may not be perfect, but it is instinctive, unclouded by civilian hocus-pocus, and often uncannily just. You know that. And you also know and I know and the Army knows you are guilty. The charge sheet may not precisely reflect your role in that massacre. But I assure you that after all the witnesses testify and lie, that court-martial board, made up of men like Colonel Levin, men who as officers and leaders see and evaluate the human condition daily, will arrive at the truth. The verdict is a foregone conclusion. You might as well accept that. The only thing I can guarantee you is that when you walk out of that courtroom, even if you are in handcuffs and under armed guard, you will be free. You understand what I mean by free?"

"Yes."

"Good. So am I fired?"

"No. But I'd like to beat the shit out of you."

"Later. Do you want to get drunk tonight?"

Tyson nodded distractedly. He said, "Why don't we plead guilty?"

"Another quirk of military law. You are not allowed to enter a plea of guilty to a murder charge."

"Right. I remember that. Good rule."

"So to recapitulate, I'm not fired, and you want to get drunk with me tonight?"

"Right. Anything to get off this post. Even drinking with you."

"Fine. Let's walk back before the post Gestapo realizes you're missing."

They turned back toward the bridge and began walking slowly. Corva said, "When we are both very drunk we are going to swap peace stories. R and R stories. I have to tell you about this whorehouse located in an old French villa outside of Tay Nihn, run by a very crazy half-breed madam."

Tyson smiled. "Sounds like the same one we had outside of Quang Tri. Must have been a chain."

They passed under the bridge. The traffic overhead made a constant low humming noise, and sea gulls circled beneath the huge superstructure. Tyson said, "I was a damned good combat leader. But by the time I reached the hospital, I was a burnout case. I stopped doing my job. I really didn't give a shit anymore. I didn't even care if I lived or died."

Corva said, "Then eventually you would have died. But you got lucky and got wounded first. In the Strawberry Patch. And Brandt tended your wound. War is full of ironies."

"So I've heard."

They were back on 101st Street now, a commercial street of two- and three-story brick buildings. Tyson looked at the fort's gates beneath the bridge. "It's like jail."

"No. Jail is like jail."

"I always thought," said Tyson, "that if lawyers take a third of what they win for you in a civil case, they should do a third of the time their clients get in a criminal case."

"They would be permanently in jail," Corva pointed out.

Tyson stopped on the sidewalk outside the gate. "You took the subway here?"

"Right. Didn't want to run up your bill with a taxi. I'll walk to the station from here."

Tyson nodded.

Corva said, "I'm ready to talk to the witnesses for the defense. Sadowski and Scorello. I'm going to go at Army expense. You are authorized to come along. Sadowski lives in Chicago. Scorello lives in a suburb of San Francisco. Get you off post for a few days. Nice reunion."

Tyson shook his head. "I don't want to see them."

"Why not?"

"They don't want to see me. We don't want to see one another."

"Okay. I understand. It's not important. Do you want to see Brandt and Farley? You have the right to be present at a cross-examination. To confront them before a hearing or court-martial."

"Can we beat the shit out of them?"

"You bet."

Tyson smiled. "You're all talk, Corva." He lit a cigarette. "I considered killing Brandt."

"Did you? That would put a quick end to this business. That's the Nam solution to an annoyance. Blow it away."

"But now I'm under tight scrutiny. Couldn't get away with it."

Corva smiled slowly. "WASPs don't know anything about these things. You put out a contract. I'll take care of it if you want."

"Are you serious?"

"Are you?"

Tyson shook his head. "No."

"Well, don't talk about it if you're not. Do you want to see him? And Farley?"

"Just Brandt. Sometime before the court-martial."

"Good. Did you ever fuck what's-her-name? Harper?"

Tyson looked at him quickly. "No."

"Too bad." Corva looked at his watch.

Tyson threw down his cigarette. "By the way, I read *Rashomon.*"

"Did you learn anything?"

"Is this a test? Well, the answer is that an act—killing—can be legal or illegal, can be interpreted as battle, self-defense, murder, and so forth. And the odd thing is that not even the *victim* is always sure of his absolute innocence in the act. Such was the case of the samurai in *Rashomon.* Similarly, as Dr. Jean Monteau lay dying on the floor of Miséricorde Hospital, the thought must have crossed his mind that he contributed to his own death." Tyson stared at Corva.

Corva said, "And the perpetrators?"

"Yes, that's odder still. A man engaged in intercourse or killing is not always certain even in his own mind if he is making love or committing rape, waging war or committing murder."

Corva nodded again. "That's what juries are for." He added, "Your case is a bit simpler than *Rashomon,* however, because there are no surviving witnesses to give their impression of what they thought happened to them. And unlike *Rashomon,* I doubt if the ghosts of any of the victims will be called to testify at the trial." Corva added, "However, there is that one surviving witness. Did she see much?"

"Enough."

Corva thought a moment before speaking. "I said before that the verdict was a foregone conclusion."

"Right. That's what a defendant likes to hear from his attorney."

"Well, I was trying to set you up for the worst scenario. That's an old lawyer's trick. The real situation is more in the balance. What you have here is a bunch of tainted soldiers giving self-serving testimony. It's quite possible a court-martial board will be so confused and frustrated that they will decide the government hasn't proven its case beyond a reasonable doubt. Therefore, they'll have no choice but to return a verdict of not guilty though they know you are. But let me tell you something. It's the nun that concerns me. If she appears out of the blue and takes the stand, they will accept her testimony as gospel. And I'm assuming that testimony will be very damning for you."

"Do you want to know what she'll say?"

"Not particularly. If they find her, you can give me a few details. If they don't find her, it doesn't matter. Point is, nuns don't lie. At least that is the conventional wisdom in trial law. And defense counsels don't try to browbeat or attack the testimony of nuns, priests, rabbis, or ministers, except at their own peril."

Tyson said, "I wonder why she hasn't been found or hasn't come forward?"

Corva rubbed his chin reflectively. "If I were paranoid, I'd say the government already knows the whereabouts of not only Sister Teresa, but also of Hernando Beltran, Lee Walker, and Louis Kalane. Kelly and DeTonq are another matter. Your former heros are lying low on advice of counsel. They may never have to be called. But if they are, they will probably be your witnesses. Correct?"

"Probably."

"Because you all made a blood oath to lie. You all gave your word of honor that you would stand by one another. Correct?"

"Very astute, Vince."

"Oh, astute, my ass. Even a JAG lawyer could figure that out. What did Harper say in her report? Lieutenant Tyson made statements which were strikingly similar to those of Sadowski and Scorello. What do you think she was saying? You concocted a story nearly twenty years ago, rehearsed it, until finally you almost believed it. Christ, even if the government presented me with three or five more witnesses for the defense, I doubt if I'd march them all up to the stand to say the exact same thing. But no one can accuse *me* of coaching them. *You* coached them, Ben. Twenty years ago. You were their leader, you had the imagination to turn a massacre into an heroic epic. That's how you saved your life afterward."

Tyson's eyes met Corva's. Tyson said, "Don't be humble, Vince. You *are* astute."

"You're right," agreed Corva. "Point is, all war stories are bullshit. Did I tell you that?"

"You know you did."

"Don't forget it. See you tonight. Meet me at my office."

Tyson turned toward the fort. Every time he came away from a meeting with Corva, he felt just a bit more frightened yet paradoxically more at peace with himself. Freedom was just down the road, though it looked suspiciously like the walls of Leavenworth from here. He reentered the post without returning the MP's salute.

35

B enjamin Tyson stepped off the train at Garden City Station. It was one of those hot, dry August afternoons when everything seemed to move in slow motion, and there was an odd quietness in the still air. Tyson loosened his tie and slung his sport coat over his shoulder. He walked down from the platform and headed toward the taxi stand.

Three black Cadillacs sat empty in their spaces. Three black drivers sat under the shade of the station house overhang, reading newspapers and drinking canned soda. Tyson approached, and one of the men stood and smiled widely. "Mr. Tyson. You get off that train?"

"Hello, Mason. Just in for a few hours. Can you drive me around?"

"Sure can."

Tyson fell in step beside Mason, a heavyset man in late middle age, dressed in black chauffeur livery. "Hot today," observed Tyson.

"Sure is. Least it's dry." Mason opened the rear door of his Cadillac, and Tyson entered. Mason got in and started the engine. "Get that AC workin'."

"How have you been?" inquired Tyson.

"Fine, sir. Fine. How you been keepin' yourself?"

"Not bad."

"You lookin' good. Gettin' your exercise?"

Tyson smiled. "Doing five miles a day now."

"That's real good. When you gonna stop smokin'?"

"New Year's Day."

Mason laughed. "Where we headin'?"

"My house first."

Mason put on his billed cap and pulled out of the small parking field. He drove slowly through the tree-shaded residential streets lined with imposing homes. The town seemed deserted. Tyson inquired, "Had a neutron bomb attack while I was gone?"

Mason laughed again. "August. Folks pulled out. I get a few runs a day. Airports. Couple out east. Slow."

"Why don't you take the month off?"

"The bills don't stop in August."

"That's true." Tyson said, "How is Mrs. Williams?"

"Gettin' old. Just like me. Can't get up those stairs no more. I been lookin' at a place with an elevator. Air-conditionin' too."

Tyson considered inviting the Williamses to house-sit at his place for the next few months. But his experiences in social engineering were limited, and he didn't know if it was a good idea. He suspected that Mason and his wife would rather be home, wherever that was. Tyson looked around the immaculate car interior. He said, "You remember that Lincoln you had?"

"Sure do. Sixty-four. Block and a half long, wide as my mama-in-law's butt. They gettin' smaller. Can't find nothin' big enough no more. What those turkeys in Detroit thinkin' about?"

"The world's getting smaller and tighter, Mason. Just do me a favor and don't buy a Japanese car."

"Hell no! You seen them things? I got a 'frigerator bigger than them."

They talked cars for the next few minutes. Mason pulled up to the curb in front of Tyson's house.

Tyson said, "Come on in." He opened his own door and stood on the sidewalk, staring at his house. The gardener had kept up with it, and no doubt the maid had too. The pest control men did their scheduled spraying, and the seven-zone sprinkler system was on timer, as were all the outside lights. The burglar and fire alarms were hooked up to central station monitoring. The house, in effect, was on automatic pilot. It didn't need the Tysons. Tyson often envisioned a perfect upper-middle-class suburb, devoid of redundant residents, tended to by machines and service people.

He walked up the brick path, deactivated the alarm with a key, and stepped inside, followed by Mason.

The house smelled unfamiliar, not like his house. There was an odd mixture of odors, dominated by the smells of various cleaning products. The maid, Piedad, probably thought it was amusing to clean an empty house every week. Anglos were *loco*.

Tyson hung his sport coat on the clothes tree and went to the parsons table in the foyer where the mail was stacked. He leafed through it. Phil Sloan had a key and took care of small details such as sorting the mail and sending the important items to Tyson at Fort Hamilton. There was a stack of junk mail, a bundle of letters that looked like fan mail, and some bills that Sloan hadn't gotten around to forwarding. There were also a few parcels on the floor that Sloan had probably picked up from the post office. Tyson lifted one of them, a shoebox-sized package marked "Fragile." He opened it with his pocket knife, fished around in the Styrofoam packing, and drew out a particularly hideous Hummel of a boy and girl that looked as though it had been designed by Norman Rockwell for Hermann Goering. He placed it on the table and read the enclosed card: *Dearest Baby Brother, I've treasured this since Aunt Millie gave it to me five years ago, but remembering how much you always admired it, I'm thrilled to send it to you in your hour of need. Keep your nose up. Love to Marcy and David. Love, Laurie.*

Tyson smiled as he placed the card on the table. He dug deeper into the packing foam and extracted his platoon logbook, which he slipped into his hip pocket.

Tyson turned to Mason. "Can you give me a hand with something in the basement?"

"Sure can."

Tyson went down the basement stairs to the storage room and knelt in front of an old black steamer trunk. The padlock was still shut, but it was obvious by the disturbed dust in the area that someone had been there. *Bastards.* They'd gotten through the burglar alarm and the supposedly unpickable door locks. And they'd undoubtedly been through the entire house, every drawer, every closet, his desk, photo albums, diaries, checkbooks, address books, investment portfolios—every nook and cranny. They had penetrated into the very core of his privacy and had probably cataloged, photographed, and photocopied every-thing. "Bastards!"

"Sir?"

"Nothing." He was fairly certain they were opening his mail, too. But the heavily taped parcel from his sister had shown no sign of tampering. He felt somewhat good about beating them at their own asinine cloak-and-dagger game. Tyson said to Mason, "Let's get this trunk upstairs."

They each took a handle and carried the trunk into the living room and set it before the fireplace. He took a box of firestarter candles from the log bin and threw it onto the grate, lighting the entire box with a match.

Mason looked around the living room. "Some castle you got here, Mr. Ty-son."

"Yes, it is." He stood and went into the kitchen, coming back with two frosted mugs filled with beer. He passed one to Mason. Tyson raised his mug. "To liberty and justice for me."

"Amen." They touched glasses.

Tyson finished half the beer in one swallow. He took a key from his wallet, knelt, and opened the trunk.

On the left-hand side of the divided trunk were neatly folded jungle fatigues and khakis, plus a pair of canvas jungle boots, a bush hat, and a powder blue infantry fourragère. On the right was a photo album, maps, R and R brochures, and bundled letters from Hope Lowell, the girl he'd been seeing before he shipped out. There was also a metal ammunition box that held an Army com-pass, Army watch, Army flashlight, and other purloined government issues.

It didn't appear that anything had been disturbed, but when he looked through the photo album, he saw a few photos missing. Also missing were his orders for the Vietnamese Cross of Gallantry awarded for actions on 15 Febru-ary 1968. Missing, too, was his logbook, but he'd lifted that himself.

Tyson turned to Mason and saw he was eyeing the contents of the trunk. Tyson said, "I don't know why men keep junk like this."

Mason said, "I had a brother in Korea. Durin' that war they was havin' there. Only thing he came home with was underwear. Stole three duffel bags of underwear."

"Sounds like a practical man," observed Tyson. He took a tied bundle of letters. "Well. . . ." He hesitated, then threw it on the blazing mass of wax and watched as the flames licked around the edges. Item by item, beginning with the most combustible, he fed the fire until all that remained were the metal items, the boots, and the photo album. He picked up the boots and crumbled the dried mud in his fingers. "Southeast Asia. Instant Nam; just add water." What a peculiar slime it was, he thought. Three thousand years of intense recycling: rice, dung, blood, rice, ash, blood, rice, dung. And so on. He dropped the boots back into the trunk, then leafed through the photo album. He extracted a single picture, a snapshot of him and Teresa standing in front of the Hue cathedral. There had been two more, but they were gone. He slipped the picture into his breast pocket and threw the entire album into the fire.

Sweat ran down his face, and the smell of mustiness and ash clung to his nostrils. He closed the trunk, locked it, and gave Mason the key. "You can have the trunk if you want. The flashlight and the other odds and ends too. I'd like you to throw the boots and the rest in the garbage."

"Yes, sir." Mason put his beer carefully on the coffee table. He stared at Tyson. "You feelin' better, or you feelin' worse?"

"I'm not feeling."

Mason nodded.

"Can you take the trunk by yourself? I have a few more things to do."

"Yes, sir." Mason hefted the nearly empty trunk onto his shoulder.

Tyson said, "I'll meet you outside." He reached into his hip pocket and drew out the small hide-bound logbook. He sat cross-legged on the floor and opened it, leafing through the pages with his sweaty fingers. A drop of perspiration rolled from his chin and fell upon a page already stained by sweat and water twenty years before. He came finally to the entry for 15 February and read the last lines: *Platoon on verge of mutiny. Overheard death threats. Filed false radio report re: hospital battle this* A.M. *Investigate. God—*

He tried to recall how he felt after the massacre but could only remember the fear for his own life. He tried to imagine that he gave serious thought regarding the best way to report his platoon to Captain Browder or to the battalion commander. But his mind wouldn't play the game. In reality he knew he had never once seriously considered swearing to murder charges against the men of his platoon.

Tyson continued to turn the pages, noticing that the days after 15 February were represented by only a line or two of insignificant details, mostly grid coordinates and radio frequencies. He came to 29 February, the day he was wounded, and noted the only entry for the day read: *Refugee assistance. Battle for Hue officially closed, as per radio message.*

The next entry was for 3 March. He read: *USS Repose; South China Sea. Logbook returned today by orderly. Did anyone read entry for 15 Feb? Who cares? Nice to be alive. My hands look very clean. Knee giving me pain. Darvon only. No morphine. Doctor said, "You don't take morphine well." He wouldn't take it well either if he'd been given a triple dose.*

Tyson lowered the logbook and let his mind go back to the Strawberry Patch.

Ben Tyson lay on his back in a drainage ditch, actually the local honey pit, the place where offal was collected for sale to vegetable farmers. Green tracer rounds streaked over the ditch, lustrous against the dull gray sky. He could hear the muted chatter of automatic weapons and the occasional explosion of small rounds: 50-mm rifle grenades, 60-mm mortars, an occasional rocket. It was a desultory firefight between two spent armies, like two exhausted boxers, moving leaden limbs, taking a few obligatory swings at one another. A month before, he'd have taken this very seriously. But today, 29 February, he would describe the incident as light contact. The only remarkable thing about the day's contact from his point of view was that he'd finally been hit.

As the shock wore off, the pain became more severe, until finally it dominated his entire consciousness. The stench around him didn't matter, neither did the bone-chilling water or the occasional thump of the enemy mortar trying to put a round into the ditch where dozens of civilians were leaping for cover.

Within a few minutes the ditch had become crowded with Vietnamese: old men, a few young men who were ex-ARVN amputees, women, and children who did not cry. Only the babies cried.

A pig had gotten into the ditch, and it sniffed around him, then licked the blood from his knee. Tyson kicked the pig in the snout with his other foot. About ten of his men had withdrawn toward the ditch, and they slid in, cursing the muck and the Vietnamese refugees. One of his men, Harold Simcox, spotted him and called, "Medic! Lieutenant's hit!"

Of the two remaining company medics, it was Brandt who answered the call. Brandt worked quickly and professionally, first examining Tyson for wounds more serious than the obvious knee injury. He checked Tyson's pulse, felt his forehead, and looked at his eyes. It was only then that Brandt cut away the trouser leg and squeezed a tube of antibiotic ointment onto the open wound. He folded the flaps of flesh and stringy pink ligaments over the exposed patella. Tyson picked up his head to watch, but Brandt reached out and casually pushed his head back into the muck. "No peeking," said Brandt as he always said when dressing a wound. "Don't want you getting sick on me."

Tyson said irritably, "I've seen worse than this."

"Not on yourself. Just relax." Brandt applied a pressure bandage, tying the strings loosely. "Pain?"

"Some."

"Do you want morphine?"

Tyson wanted something for the pain, but he didn't want to become drowsy while there was still enemy contact. "Maybe just some APCs."

"Right." Brandt put two of the aspirin compound tablets in Tyson's mouth and placed the remainder of the bottle in Tyson's breast pocket. He pulled out a red grease pencil and wrote on Tyson's forehead, *NM*. No morphine given. He said, "They'll give it to you on the chopper."

"Right."

The gunfire had slackened, and Tyson noticed more of his men rolling into the ditch as they made their way across the exposed area where they'd been pinned down. Brandt found a helmet in the water and put it under Tyson's head.

"Thanks."

Brandt stared at him, then lit a cigarette and put it in Tyson's mouth. Brandt lit one for himself as there didn't seem to be any more customers for him at the moment. Brandt said, "It's a good wound. A good-bye wound."

"Million dollar?"

"Eight hundred thousand. You're going to limp. But you'll be limping in New York."

"Right." Tyson propped himself up on one arm and looked along the wide, shallow trench. About a dozen soldiers were kneeling, firing short bursts at the far-off line of fruit trees from where the rockets and gunfire had originated. But Tyson didn't think they were drawing return fire any longer. The rest of Alpha Company had decided not to participate in this particular firefight and were hunched down, smoking cigarettes, eating C rations, bantering and bartering with the civilians. Farley had a chicken perched on his head, and the Vietnamese thought that was comical. Michael DeTonq was talking very seriously to a young girl, and Tyson guessed the subject without hearing a word. Lee Walker had the pig in a neck lock and was writing or drawing something in grease pencil on its face. The men around him thought it was pretty funny whatever it was. Tyson was glad everyone was relaxed.

Tyson lay back on the helmet. The thought occurred to him, not for the first time, that he would miss this, miss the ability to indulge in eccentric if not actually atavistic behavior. Now that it was nearly over for him, he admitted to the excitement of combat, of living on the edge, of being free to release without constraint all of his aggressive energy. And he would miss too the sense of community offered by combat, the sense of bonding between men that was as profound as any between lovers, if not more so. It was a bond, unlike marriage, that could never be broken by divorce or separation or by anything other than death.

As he lay there in the slime, he thought again about that hospital and what they had done there. And again he felt no sense of failed duty, though by all legal, rational, and moral standards, he had failed miserably.

Tyson turned his head toward Brandt. "Who else was hit?"

Brandt replied, "Two guys from third platoon. Not bad."

"Did anyone call medevac?"

"I guess Kelly did."

"Where is Kelly?"

"Out there somewhere. But he's okay. I heard his voice over the squawk box down the line. How'd you get separated?"

Tyson had never been more than an arm's length from his radio operator, and he felt strangely powerless without Kelly and without the reassurance that personal radio contact with the outside world gave him. Tyson said, "When the firing broke out, a mob of panicky Viets got between us. You're sure he's okay?"

"Yes, sir. No bullshit. You're not hit bad enough for me to lie to you." Brandt drew on his cigarette and threw it, still lit, to a Vietnamese boy a few yards away. The boy fielded it with expertise and had it in his mouth before Brandt exhaled his smoke.

Tyson said, "You know . . . I feel a little better. Maybe I should take charge of this herd."

"No. You lay there. Your pulse is a little off, and if you could see the color of your face you wouldn't be thinking about taking charge of anything."

Tyson tried to remember who the ranking man was, but his head felt strangely light. He said, "Do me a favor, Doc. Find out who's the senior sergeant. Tell him to report here to me."

Brandt replied disinterestedly, "Okay. But I don't think anyone wants the honor of leading Alpha Company."

Tyson said, "Also find Kelly. And if I don't get a chance, tell everyone I said *adiós.* Okay?"

"Okay." But Brandt made no move to follow orders. Instead, he said, "We're finished. Not an officer or senior NCO left. They'll pull us in. Right?"

"I guess so. Hey, good luck, Brandt."

"Thanks."

Tyson said, "I'm feeling kind of funny."

"Shock."

"No . . . very funny . . . woozy. . . ."

"Really?"

"Did you . . . you give me something . . . ?"

His mind was becoming clouded, and things seemed to free-float around him. Michael DeTonq appeared from somewhere and was telling him something about deserting. Tyson thought he was hallucinating at first, but he realized DeTonq was real. Then Bob Moody, recently returned to duty from his wound at the hospital, was looking down on him. Moody said, "You'll be back in a week, Lieutenant, just like me."

Tyson thought he answered him, "No, not me," but he couldn't be sure he spoke.

Kelly was suddenly at his side, but he didn't say much. Kelly called the battalion commander, Colonel Womrath, on the radio. The colonel spoke to Tyson, telling him what a fine job he had done and how good it had been to have him as Alpha's acting company commander. Tyson replied in similar stock phrases, though somewhat disjointed, telling the colonel that it had been an honor to serve under him and to be part of the Seventh Cavalry and that he'd do it again if he was able. DeTonq said, "Bullshit." Kelly said, "Amen."

Then a line of men came at him in a low crouch, each one taking his hand and shaking it, then, against field regulations, saluting him; Richard Farley was first, the chicken still on his helmet, then came Simcox and Tony Scorello. Scorello said, "Thanks for saving my life," though Tyson didn't recall saving the man's life. Hernando Beltran came up to him and said, *"Adiós, amigo.* Watch out for those hippies in Frisco." Selig said his goodbye, then Louis Kalane, then Paul Sadowski gave him a religious medal, and Kurt Holzman accidentally bumped his knee. Finally Lee Walker, a black man, came up to Tyson, still holding the pig.

He turned the pig's face toward Tyson, and Tyson saw that Walker had drawn slanty eyebrows and a mandarin mustache on the animal's face. Walker said, "Charlie says good-bye too." The pig squealed and tried to get away, but Walker held it tightly. Tyson's eyes became clouded, and all he could see was the pig's malevolent red eyes squinting at him, then everything went black.

Tyson looked down at the book in his lap, then shut it. Sitting cross-legged on the floor had caused his knee to stiffen, and he stretched out his right leg. He vaguely recalled being carried to the medevac helicopter and the ride, like a floating dream, out to sea.

After, when he woke on the hospital ship, he was told by the ward physician that he'd gone into shock, possibly morphine shock, and nearly died. The doctor questioned him about whether or not he'd received morphine in the field. Tyson had replied that he didn't think so. But blood and urine tests showed high levels of morphine. He overheard a doctor using the words *therapeutic accident*. The consensus was that Tyson, who as an officer sometimes carried a Syrette of morphine, had injected himself to relieve the pain. Then one or both of the company medics, not aware of any previous dose being given, injected him again, and finally the helicopter medic had inadvertently given him the near fatal overdose. But that didn't fully explain the *NM* on his forehead, they agreed. Tyson had the impression that they wanted to let the unfortunate incident pass without official inquiry since it had not happened before. Tyson had considered giving the doctors his own conclusion, which was that medic Brandt had tried to murder him. But why rock the *Repose?* Brandt had nearly committed a perfect crime, and it was no less perfect for Tyson having survived.

Tyson stared down at the small logbook in his hands, then without further thought he threw it in the fire. He picked up a bellows and pumped air onto the fire until it blazed furiously, consuming the last scraps of his wartime reminders.

Tyson stood and began walking through the house. There were memories here too; ghosts in every chair, friends and family around the dining room table, people around the piano, bridge games in the den, making love to Marcy in front of the fireplace. There was the living room chair where his father had always sat, the place near the front windows where the Christmas tree always went, the corner in the kitchen where David's high chair had been, and the place in the foyer where David took his first step.

He went upstairs and wandered into David's room and stood there awhile, then looked into the two guest rooms and the spare room used as a second-floor sitting room. On the third floor was the garret with another whole suite for the maid's quarters, which were standard when this house was built. But these days, as Tyson was fond of saying, the live-in help slept in the master bedroom, so the third floor was totally unused. "What did we need all this space for? Were we trying to avoid each other?"

He recalled the house where he grew up, ten blocks away. It was about the same size as this one, but it was filled with people: his parents, his three sisters, his mother's mother and occasionally a spinster aunt, and a succession of mongrel dogs. "We are too selfish to have children anymore. We farm out the elderly, and indigent relatives know better than to ask for a place to stay. No wonder we're all alone at the end."

He went into the master bedroom and picked up the telephone. He dialed. Marcy answered, "Hello."

"It's me."

"Hello, you."

"I want a baby."

Marcy replied, "Okay."

"Maybe two. And a dog."

"Whoa. How's the house?"

"Empty. Lots of nurseries."

"Are you all right?"

"I'm fine. Mason is with me. I like Mason."

"He's probably a Democrat."

"He'd be a fool not to be." He said, "I don't think either of us is a nominee for the spouse of the year award this year. But I want you to know I love you."

Marcy said, "I love *you*. Very much. Hurry home. You're to be back at nine o'clock. I think I like the Army keeping you on a short leash."

He hung up, bounded down the staircase, and took his sport jacket from the foyer, activated the alarm, and left the house.

Mason opened the door of the running car, and Tyson got in. Mason slid behind the wheel. Tyson said, "We have a lot of stops. Got the time?"

"If you got the stops, I got the go."

Tyson laughed. "Okay. First stop, the country club."

Mason drove to the club, Tyson got out, went inside to the club secretary's office, and resigned his membership. They stopped next at the Men's Club, and he did the same. He got to his bank before closing and withdrew most of his savings in cash. He glanced in the side-view mirror a few times and said, "Mason, we're being followed."

"Know that."

"No sweat. Just my guardian angels."

"Okay."

The limousine went up Franklin Avenue and stopped at the suburban branches of Bloomingdale's, Saks, Lord & Taylor, Abraham & Straus, and smaller chain shops in between. At each place, Tyson paid his charges off in real money, which caused some consternation, and he canceled all his accounts, which gave him a sense of acting out a long-held fantasy.

He directed Mason to some of the local merchants where he settled up all house accounts and canceled them. He took care of the last merchant, a florist, and got back in the limousine with a box of long-stemmed roses. He passed the box over to the front seat. "These are for Mrs. Williams from Mrs. Tyson and me. Tell her we hope she's feeling better."

Mason lifted the lid of the long box. "Why, thank you, Mr. Tyson. Thank you."

Tyson sat back in his seat. "Let's just drive around town for a while. Fifty-cent tour."

"Yes, sir."

Tyson lit a cigarette and watched the familiar landscape from his window: the cathedral, the hotel, the churches, the clubs, the parks, the wide tree-lined streets, the shops, the schools, and the little railroad stations. He said, "Do you know what this is called, Mason?"

"No, sir."

"In the military they call it burning your bridges behind you so you can't retreat but are forced to advance. Civilians might say it's just a last farewell."

Mason said, "You not ever coming back?"

"I have to act as though I'm not. If I do come back, well, that's the way it was meant to be. If I never see this place again I want to remember it as it was when I was happy here, long ago, and happy here again on a late August afternoon."

Mason glanced at his passenger in the rearview mirror. He said, "In your head you never leave the place where you was born and raised. I ain't been back to Dillon, South Carolina, since I was seventeen. But I still has the place in my head. Strange, 'cause I wasn't none too happy there. Oh, some of it was happy. I remember we used to go to this little church, and . . . aw, hell, ain't nothin' left there. 'Cept an old aunt."

"Go see her. See the place where Mason Williams walked the streets and went to school and church."

"Might do that."

Tyson lit another cigarette. He said, "Mason, are you following all this in the news? Of course you are."

"Yes, sir."

"And? What are your thoughts?"

"Well . . . hard for me to say, Mr. Tyson."

"How long have we known each other? I remember you driving me places when I was in grade school. My father used to put me in your car and say, 'Take this fathead to school. He missed the bus again.' "

Mason laughed.

"Or, 'Take him and his juvenile delinquent friends to the movies.' And a few times you took me into the city to meet my parents for dinner."

"Yes, sir. Them was good days. I liked your father."

"Me too. So give it to me straight. What do you think about all this?"

"Well . . . I think, Mr. Tyson . . . you could have found some friends . . . could have stuck closer to your friends . . . and they would've stuck closer to you. You got a lot of friends in this town."

"Do I?"

"Yes, sir. There was people who was on your side. There was talk of honorin' you at the Fourth of July party at the club. . . . I hear things when people sit back there, 'cause they don't think I hear nothin'." He chuckled. "The other drivers talk too. Anyways, I never heard of nobody sayin' nothin' bad about you. Mostly they was unhappy for you."

Tyson nodded. "Maybe I got real paranoid."

"Maybe. Maybe you was unhappy in a lot of ways so you took it out on everybody."

"Could be. I'm happy now though."

"I know that."

"Do you?"

"Yes, sir, I seen it in your face and in your walk. I hear it in your voice. Ain't seen you like that in lots of years now."

"A few other people have told me that. Why do you suppose I'm happy? I'm about to go on trial for murder."

Mason drove for a while before answering, "You're startin' over. Lots of folks don't get that chance. You goin' to get that thing squared away, then you goin' on, and this time you goin' to get things right. You got a fine missus, and she'll stand beside you."

Tyson smiled. "I hope to God you're right. Listen, drive past my father's house."

Mason nodded and swung into Whitehall Street. He stopped in front of the house where Tyson grew up, a brick and stucco Tudor. Tyson couldn't recall the name of the people who lived there now and didn't care. He stared at the second-floor window that had been his room. He said, "When my father died, the cortege detoured past this house on the way to the cemetery. All the neighbors were out front. I didn't know that was going to happen. Took me by surprise. I cried."

"I know. You was in my car." Mason pulled away from the house. "Now you done thinkin' about the past, Mr. Tyson. Where you want to go now?"

"I don't know. I don't have to be back until nine. They don't let me out that often." He glanced at his watch. It was a few minutes to seven, and the shadows outside the car were lengthening. Commuters were home by now, and he could visit any one of a number of people. But on what pretext? Did he need a pretext? "Drive over to Tulamore."

Mason headed west, and Tyson directed him to a white clapboard colonial, the home of Phillip and Janet Sloan. He couldn't tell if anyone was at home and realized he didn't really want to see Phil Sloan. "Go on to Brixton."

They drove past the McCormicks' house without stopping, then the houses of a few more friends, some of whom were in, some apparently not. Mason said, "You wantin' to stop anywhere?"

"I don't think so. I just feel like an outsider who wants to look in. Do you think I should stop?"

Mason tipped his hat forward and scratched the back of his head. He said, "I guess you know what's best."

"Well, I'm a little shy these days." Tyson looked at his watch. "I guess I can catch the eight-ten to Brooklyn."

"Yes, sir."

The black limousine pulled up to the station. Tyson said, "Mason, if you were a betting man what odds would you give me?"

Mason opened Tyson's door. Tyson got out, and both men looked at each other. Mason replied, "I said you looked happy. No man who done what they sayin' you done looks happy about it. You just tell them the truth. Let them see your eyes."

"Okay, I'll do that." Tyson held out a fifty-dollar bill.

Mason shook his head. "You been overtippin' me since you was a boy. This one's on me. You take care now." They shook hands. "Hurry on. I hear the train."

Tyson walked up to the platform and saw the train approaching from the east. A soft breeze was blowing, and it was from the north in contrast to the usual southerly ocean breeze. A harbinger of autumn. The sun was below the horizon, and the large houses on the south side of the station plaza sat in deep shadow. A few cars remained in the parking field, a few wives waited for the city train. Farther down the tracks were tennis courts, and he saw a couple he knew, the Muellers, playing doubles with another couple. The station plaza, the new hotel, the library, and the parks formed a sort of old-fashioned village commons. This was the kind of place people pictured for themselves if they ever got nostalgic for the type of town that used to typify American life. Like many of the other commuter enclaves strung out along the great commuter rail lines radiating from New York, this was the best of worlds and the worst of worlds. It was both insular and part of the main. Marcy was right, and Marcy was wrong. It depended, he realized, on what was on your mind and what was in your heart.

He liked Robert Frost's definition of home: the place where, when you have to go there, they have to take you in.

But home was also the place where, when you strayed from it, they came looking for you.

That was not this place anymore.

The train stopped, and he boarded. He thought, There *is* something evocative about trains and railroad stations. The tracks and trains *do* run both ways. But there is a time in your life—and you don't always know which time—when you are going only one way.

He took a seat in the empty coach and drew from his breast pocket the picture of him and Teresa in front of the Hue Cathedral. He stared at it a moment, trying to reconcile the all-American boy in the photo with the man who had turned into a monster less than four weeks later. He stared at Teresa and marveled that even after a lifetime of warfare and death she looked very naïve, very shy and innocent. But perhaps that was the answer. She'd been inoculated at birth against the sickness of the soul that follows on the heels of war. His mind and soul had no immunities whatsoever, and he'd become sick the day he went out on his first patrol through the countryside and seen the massive destruction of lives, property, and family.

He put the picture back in his pocket and closed his eyes. He realized that Fort Hamilton might be the last place he saw before an armed escort took him to a federal prison. He opened his eyes and looked out the window. Everything was looking better than he'd ever seen it. If he passed this way again, he'd have to remember that.

36

The early morning sun slanted in through the venetian blinds of Tyson's living room. The rented television was balanced unsteadily on a folding snack table pushed against the staircase wall. Dressed in a warm-up suit, Tyson sat at the edge of the couch with a mug of coffee, watching a PBS news show. Marcy was in the armchair with coffee and a buttered corn muffin. David, sitting cross-legged on the floor with a glass of orange juice, said, "Can we rent a VCR?"

Tyson replied, "Not on my salary."

"Well, then, can we get one of the ones from home?"

"No."

David grumbled something.

Tyson glanced at his son. The boy was becoming surly. Perhaps he was just bored or maybe nervous about starting school.

The news commentator said, "The House Judiciary Committee is meeting to discuss the Tyson case. Lieutenant Tyson's attorney, Vincent Corva, stated that any such inquiry would only serve to further prejudice his client's legal and civil rights since the case has not yet been tried. But the House appears to be responding to outside pressure. The agenda for the House Committee includes studying legislation that would clarify jurisdiction in such cases. The Justice Department in past cases has taken the position that an honorably discharged serviceman cannot be tried for a war crime committed prior to his discharge, either by court-martial or in a federal court. Tyson's status as an ex-officer, however, made it possible to return him to active duty for the purpose of investigating charges against him stemming from this incident."

Tyson glanced again at David. The boy was reading a car magazine and seemed to have little interest in this. Bizarre, he thought. Adults give children too much credit. That, too, was a story of the sixties: adults seeking the wisdom of shallow adolescents.

The PBS commentator continued, "In another development, Colonel Ambrose Horton, an instructor at the Judge Advocate General School at the University of Virginia and a respected jurist, has directed a memo to General William Van Arken, the Army's Judge Advocate General. The contents of that memo have been revealed through an unidentified source. The memo reads in part: 'As you know, General, under the Geneva Convention of which the United States is a signatory member, the United States is obligated to enact any legislation necessary to provide effective penal sanctions for persons committing grave breaches of the laws of war.'" The commentator continued, "Colonel Horton further points out that in the nearly four decades since the U.S. signed the Geneva Convention treaty, Congress has failed to enact such legislation though most other signatories have. His conclusion to General Van Arken is that the Army should not take it upon itself to selectively prosecute Lieutenant Tyson while not prosecuting other suspects over whom Congress has failed to establish federal or military jurisdiction. It would appear then that no one in Lieutenant Tyson's platoon will be or can be charged with a crime. And so it is that at the Army hearing, one week from today, at Fort Hamilton, Brooklyn, only one man will face indictment for that crime: Benjamin J. Tyson."

Tyson leaned forward and turned off the television. He didn't know who Colonel Ambrose Horton was, but he knew that the man ought to put his retirement papers in if he hadn't already done so.

Tyson sipped on his coffee. He avoided news stories about himself. But when he did watch or listen, he tried to be objective to determine how he felt about this fellow Tyson. Generally the stories seemed to be slanted in his favor. The stuff about Marcy popped up once in a while, but even that seemed to be handled with more sympathy than sleaze recently.

Marcy said, "Is that going to affect anything?"

Tyson shrugged. "I don't think it will for me."

Marcy nodded. "Sometimes it takes a landmark case to restructure justice in this country. Even the Civil Liberties Union is behind you on this. That's comforting."

"To *you* perhaps."

David looked up from his magazine. "Dad, why is it if everybody's on your side . . . I mean, all those people who are contributing money and coming out on your side and all—why is the Army going to court-martial you?"

Tyson thought about that a moment. He replied, "Because I violated a trust, I broke my oath of office. So they want to . . . to set an example for other Army leaders, now and in the future."

"But it happened so *long* ago. Why can't they just forget something that happened thirty years ago?"

"Twenty." Tyson had read a front-page story once in the *Wall Street Journal* about how unaware college and high school students were of the war. A professor reported that a senior asked him what napalm was. Another instructor claimed three-fourths of his students never heard of the Tet Offensive. Tyson said, "The Army has the memory of an elephant, and for the first time in our history, the Army failed in its mission, and they will discuss this defeat forever." He drew a long breath. "Deep down inside, the Army wants a rematch. They would like to be sent again to Vietnam, to regain their lost honor—"

Marcy interjected, "Oh, God, Ben, don't even think that."

"It's true, Marcy. I know it's true." He looked at David. "But until then, anytime something about Vietnam comes up, they are going to overreact to it."

David stayed silent, digesting this. He said, "But you didn't kill anyone. You said you didn't kill anyone. The other guys did it, didn't they?" He looked at his father. "Didn't they?"

Tyson met his son's eyes. He said, "If you were hanging around with a bunch of guys and they got really wild one day and beat up a bunch of younger kids—really beat them badly—and you saw all this but did nothing to stop it, and afterward didn't tell your mother or the police—would you be as guilty as the rest of the guys? Less guilty? More guilty?"

"More guilty," David said softly. "If I couldn't stop them, then I should have told on them."

"Would it make any difference if the guys were very sorry for what they did? I mean, if they didn't brag about it but were ashamed of it?"

"I . . . I don't think so. They hurt people." David stood. "I'm going out." Marcy asked, "Where are you going?"

"Out. I'm bored. This place is driving me nuts."

Tyson inquired, "Have you made any friends here?"

"No."

"Do you want to go to Sag Harbor this weekend?"

David hesitated a moment. "No. . . ."

"Don't you miss Melinda?"

"Yes. But . . . if you guys can stick it out here . . . Dad, as long as you're under arrest I'm staying here."

"*You're* not under arrest." He turned to Marcy. "Look, why don't you and David drive out east today? You can find a place to stay. I have a lot of work to do with Vince."

Marcy shook her head. "We made this decision already, Ben. I'm staying here until this is finished. Anyway, the damned media comments on every move we make. If I go out to the beach, the *American Investigator* will say something like . . . Marcy enjoys the sun while Ben stews under house arrest."

Tyson replied, "Okay. That's your decision. I was looking forward to not having to wait to use the bathroom." He smiled. "But you'll notice the *Investigator* has not been too hard on us recently."

"I noticed that. And Wally Jones's byline is completely gone. Why is that?"

Tyson looked at David, who was hovering impatiently by the door. Tyson said, "David, you have stuff in my gym locker, right? I'll meet you there in about an hour."

"Okay." David left.

Tyson turned to Marcy. "I've gotten into incredible shape. It's my mind that's shot now."

"Sound mind, sound body—take your pick. So why do you think the *Investigator* dropped us?"

Tyson poured himself more coffee from a carafe. "Well . . . perhaps having reached new lows of journalistic depravity, they couldn't follow their own act. Especially with Major Harper out of the picture." Tyson added, "Also, I beat the shit out of Wally Jones." He stirred his coffee.

She laughed. "I bet you'd like to. By the way, I didn't think you handled David's questions very well."

"Why not?"

"I don't know . . . it's just that you press him too hard."

Tyson lit a cigarette. He could see this was going to be a bad day. The strain of this confinement and inactivity, coupled with uncertainty, was beginning to tell on Marcy and David. He rifled through some envelopes on the coffee table.

Marcy said, "The mortgage payment is late and there's a notice there from the village saying they're going to list the house for a tax sale unless we pay up."

"Is that so?"

"You see? The Tysons have paid taxes in that fucking village since year one, but miss one goddamned payment—you see what I mean?"

"No."

"I mean, damn it, that it doesn't matter how you've lived your life, brought up your kids, paid your stinking bills for twenty years. You miss a few payments, and you go to the top of the shit list. You're a nobody. A deadbeat."

"Yes, that's what I keep saying about my situation. Just one lousy massacre, and everybody gets on your case."

"Poor analogy."

"Anyway, take heart. I heard from Phil Sloan yesterday that our bank is suspending our mortgage payments and paying all property taxes for us. It's a loan of sorts which we will eventually have to repay."

Marcy looked doubtful. "Are you sure?"

"Yes. Now, isn't that a nice bank? Doesn't it restore your faith in humanity?"

"I guess it does."

"Well, don't be too reassured. Near as I can figure it, someone went to the bank and twisted their nuts."

"Who?"

"Who cares? A guardian angel, I think. A G-man. Someone from this shady cabal that has been reading our mail and dogging our every movement. The point is, even if we wanted to commit economic suicide, declare bankruptcy, and all that, we couldn't. The Army doesn't want that in the news before the trial. What if, God forbid, I'm innocent, and they've ruined me? Well, this is an enviable position in which most Americans will never find themselves."

She stayed silent for some time, then announced, "I don't like this." She raised her voice. "I do not *like* being watched, being—"

"Sh-h-h! You'll damage the microphones."

She stood, took a heavy glass ashtray from the coffee table, and flung it at the front window. It went through the blinds, smashed a windowpane, and ripped the screen. "Fuck the Army!"

"Calm down." He stood and surveyed the damage, then looked at her and said seriously, "We *are* being watched, you know. I do *not* want them to see us cracking up. Okay? Steady on, soldier."

She put her arms around him and laid her cheek on his shoulder. "Okay."

Tyson's eyes moved around the small room as he held her. It cost him a good deal of money each week to satisfy himself that the place didn't have electronic plumbing, but still he wondered. He said, "Did you get David enrolled at the local stiletto high?"

"It's actually supposed to be a good school according to the mothers I spoke to on post. The bus will pick him up on Lee Avenue. I spoke to the principal, and she's aware of the special problems involved."

"All right. How is David reacting?"

"Ask him."

"He always gives me the macho line. Takes after his old man. What did he say to you?"

"He's nervous."

"Understandable."

"Also he misses his friends."

"So do we all. But they're probably not his friends anymore."

"He says the school looks junky. Actually it is old but well kept."

"Well, he shouldn't compare a city high school with that suburban country club he got used to."

"It's good for his character. That's what you said."

Ben Tyson smiled. "Right." He held her tighter. "You know, without sounding too macho, a man likes to give his family the best. And when he can't he doesn't always feel like a man. Is that too patriarchal?"

"Yes, but I know how you feel."

"The private schools were just too expensive, Marcy—"

"Don't worry about it. We'll all make do."

"This might hurt his chances for a good college."

She shook him gently by the shoulders. "Stop that. You went to a lousy college, why shouldn't he?"

"Hey, there's nothing wrong with Auburn. Columbia was a pigpen."

She laughed, and they held on to each other.

Tyson cleared his throat. "Have you considered what you will do if I go up the river for a few years?"

"Sing Sing is up the river. Leavenworth is in Kansas. Across the river."

"Answer the question."

"I don't think about it. I *won't* think about it. So I can't answer your question."

"Okay . . . no use worrying about that now."

"Are you worried about the hearing?"

"No. Corva said not to waste energy worrying. I'll be indicted for sure."

"Oh. . . . Are you worried about *Corva?*"

"A little. Yes, a little. He's erratic. Sometimes I think he's a genius. Other times I think he's a dolt. He's fatalistic too. Well, maybe *realistic* is a better word."

She moved away from him and poured coffee for both of them. "He seems to really care about you, Ben. That's a good thing."

Tyson took his mug of coffee. "Corva and I were both infantry commanders, and our tours of duty coincided. I don't even have to say to him, 'Look, Vince, Nam sucked, the leeches sucked, the homecoming sucked, so don't let them make the peace suck, too.' He knows that, and I think if I went to jail, he knows that a little bit of him and all the rest of us would go to jail, too."

She stared into the blackness of her coffee, then looked up. "I think I understand that. I can see it when you're both together. Just promise me one thing."

"What's that?"

"When this is over, don't invite him and his wife over so you can bore us with war stories." She smiled.

He smiled in return. "Mercifully, he doesn't tell or listen to war stories."

Tyson thought a moment, hesitated, then asked, "So what's happening Tuesday? Are you going back to work?" He glanced at her, and she turned away.

Marcy sat on the arm of the upholstered chair. "Well . . . if I don't, I think I'm fired."

"I thought you were irreplaceable there. I thought Jim liked you."

"Don't let's get into an ugly scene, Ben. Jim has to fill the job."

"He could hold it another week until we see if I'm indicted or not."

"He's been very patient. A lot more patient than *your* employers were. And *you* were supposed to be irreplaceable."

"No salary slave is irreplaceable. That's what I learned. I wouldn't work for anyone again if my life depended on it. I'd rather be a self-employed handyman. *I* learned how the bosses treat you even if *you* didn't. I *was* a boss, and I let people go who had personal problems. There's no room in corporate America for personal problems. If this guy can't give you a little more time, the hell with him."

"We need the money, Ben. Get off your high horse. You are so damned hubristic about *everything.* You have to kiss some ass once in a while."

"No, I do not. But I do need you . . . I need your companionship. And your support. And David needs you more than ever."

"I realize all of that," she said in measured tones. "But quite frankly, Ben, I am going out of my fucking mind here. You may have noticed."

"No. I see no change."

"And I'll be a better companion to you and David at night and on weekends if I can get out of here for a few hours a day."

Tyson slammed the coffee mug on the end table. "Oh, bullshit. It was never a few hours. It was, and will be, long hours and paperwork at home and business trips and your mind on the job at dinner and phone calls in the evening—do you realize, lady, that I'm facing murder charges? How much more time do you think we might have together?"

She stared down at the floor and said softly, "I told him I'd be there Tuesday." She added, "We have new clients in Atlanta, and I have to fly down with him Thursday. I'll be back Friday night."

"Good. You can read in the paper whether or not I was indicted Friday afternoon."

"I'm sorry, Ben."

Tyson went to the door. "I'll be at the gym." He hesitated a moment, then said, "Look, I understand. Try to understand what it's like for me to be confined here by law. Maybe I'm just envious of free people." He waited for a reply to his conciliatory statement, but there was none, so he left.

37

At 7:30 P.M. there was a knock on the door, and Tyson opened it. Vincent Corva said, "Traffic was awful."

Tyson showed him in. "Thanks for coming on a holiday night."

Corva walked into the living room carrying a briefcase. He wore jeans and a polo shirt and looked, Tyson thought, more diminutive than he did in a suit. He wondered how Corva had carried the basic seventy pounds of field gear, food, water, and ammunition in hundred-degree heat.

Corva said, "I dropped my wife and kids off in Montclair."

"Oh, is that where you live? That's Jersey, isn't it?"

"Yes. And we spent the weekend at our summer place in Ocean City."

"Where is that?"

"The Jersey shore."

"Oh . . . I didn't know people went there."

Corva smiled. "Maybe not your people." He placed his briefcase on the floor near the sofa.

Marcy came into the living room. "Hello, Vince." She gave him a peck on the cheek. Tyson watched her. She had an easy way with men and put men at ease. He could see Corva was taken with her. Apparently Picard had been, too.

Corva said, "I'm sorry I couldn't get Ben released for this weekend. They are being real hardnoses. Usually an officer can give his word as his bond that he won't skip out."

Marcy observed, "This officer-and-gentleman routine is only for when it suits them. When it doesn't suit them, an officer's word is not enough."

Corva said, "Well, I think this has to do with keeping Ben clear of the media."

Tyson had the impression he was some sort of invalid whom relatives talked about as though he weren't there.

Corva continued, "Which reminds me. I've got a six-figure offer from a publisher. Christ, I've had to hire extra staff to keep up with these phone calls. Anyway, this is a respectable publisher. You want to tell your story for about a quarter million?"

Tyson looked at Marcy, and she looked back at him. Marcy spoke to Corva. "No, he does not. We both decided long ago that we will not make one penny from this mess. All we want at the end is to cover your legal expenses."

Corva nodded. "Okay. I'll never mention these offers again." He smiled. "Even saints can be tempted."

Marcy said, "Sit down. I bought a bottle of that awful stuff you said you drink. *Strelger?*"

"*Strega. Significato* witch."

She shrugged and disappeared into the kitchen.

Corva sat at the far end of the sofa. He said softly to Tyson, "I want to speak to you alone."

Tyson nodded. "She and David are going to the post movie."

Marcy came back with a tray on which were three fluted glasses and a long, slender bottle filled with a yellow liquid. She set the tray down and poured. They each took a glass, and Corva said, "Careful. They don't call this 'witch' for nothing." He poured the drink down his throat, as did Tyson and Marcy. They all gasped, looked at one another, and wiped their eyes. Tyson cleared his throat. *"Mamma mia.* This is paint remover."

Corva explained, "It takes getting used to." He lifted a mason jar from his briefcase and put it on the coffee table. "I promised you pesto sauce." He spoke to Marcy. "Don't open the jar until you're ready to use it. Don't heat it, or you'll lose the bouquet. Spoon it at room temperature on hot pasta. Okay?"

She examined the jar suspiciously. "Looks like the paint the strega took off." She stared at Corva. "Is all this Italian stuff an affectation? I mean, you don't do this as a shtick, do you?"

"Certainly not. It's my heritage." He winked at her.

She smiled in return. "You could use a good PR lady when this is all over. I'll make you into an Italian F. Lee Bailey. What's your middle name?"

"Marcantonio."

"Oh, I love it! V. Marcantonio Corva. Or Vincent Mark Anthony Corva. Or—"

Tyson said, "Won't you be late for the movie?"

Marcy looked at her watch. "Oh!" She stood and said to Corva, "They're showing *Creator,* with Peter O'Toole." She went to the stairs and called up, "David! Show time!" She turned back to Corva. "Image is important, but unlike a lot of PR people, I believe in substance too. That comes across with you."

Tyson said to Corva, "Lift your feet; the stuff is getting deeper."

Marcy looked at him icily.

Tyson added, "She's getting into practice. She's going back to work tomorrow."

Corva sipped on his drink. He'd noticed that the Tysons weren't speaking directly to each other, and there was something in Tyson's voice that sounded strained.

David came downstairs. "Hello, Mr. Corva."

"Hi, David. All ready for school tomorrow?"

"I guess."

"Just remember, kids are the same all over, even if they have Brooklyn accents."

David forced a laugh.

Marcy and David went to the door. Corva said, "Enjoy the movie. If I don't see you later, good luck to both of you tomorrow."

Marcy and David left, and Corva noted that no one offered any good-byes. Corva looked at Tyson awhile before speaking. "This is not a personal question, it is a professional concern. Are you having domestic difficulties?"

Tyson nodded as he lit a cigarette. "I've had them for seventeen years of marriage. So don't let it concern *you*. It doesn't concern *me*."

"What is the nature of these domestic difficulties?"

"Are you a divorce lawyer?" He poured himself another strega. "Well, since you won't drop it—it's Marcy's decision to return to work."

"You don't like that?"

"I guess not."

"You'll be home all day with the housework and trying to defend yourself against a murder charge, and she'll be having lunch with interesting people."

"You got it, Vinny. Boy, you *are* quick."

"Now, don't take it out on me."

"And I doubt if her clients are interesting. And I don't intend to do any housework. Fuck it, I'm getting a maid."

Corva stroked the bridge of his thin nose with his index finger. He said, "You may be right. I mean, to feel hurt and angry and abandoned. However, that is not going to help your defense of the murder charge." Corva leaned across the coffee table toward Tyson. "Let me tell you something that I think you will agree with: This murder case against you is more important than your marriage. Get some perspective, my friend, and stop being so fucking self-indulgent."

"Don't swear at me."

"I'd like to beat the shit out of you."

"You're all talk."

Corva stood and pointed at Tyson. "Look, you don't have the luxury to brood over your marriage or your lifestyle. If you don't keep your mind on this case, I'm walking out on it."

Tyson stood too. His voice became loud. "I'm not a goddamned robot. I'm angry. I feel betrayed."

"So *what?* You can't do a thing about it. Before this is over, *everyone* will betray you in some way. Your duty is to yourself now. And that duty is to keep out of jail. And when you are free of all this, then you can settle up the scores. *Capice?*" He stared at Tyson.

Tyson nodded slowly. "Yeah, I *capice*."

Corva stuck his hand out. "Friends?"

Tyson took his hand. "You're one of the scores I'm going to settle, you little wop."

Corva laughed.

They sat and drank in silence awhile. Tyson commented, "This stuff grows on you."

Corva poured another round. "The old men where I grew up made a home-brewed version of this. The government bought the recipe, and that's what Agent Orange is." He let loose a slightly alcoholic laugh, followed by a belch.

Tyson asked, "Did you hear or read that thing that Colonel Horton said?"

Corva nodded. "I know of Horton. Everyone respects him. Like they respect God. He has about that much actual influence on Army justice too. But he did pull the philosophical rug out from under Van Arken. What this all means to you as a practical matter is minimal. But at least there are people out there—not just your VFW fans but intellectuals—who are saying you are being shafted. None of this will stop the Army juggernaut, but you can take some comfort in knowing your case has raised some important constitutional issues."

"That's what martyrs are for, Vince. To suffer so mankind can progress into a more perfect society."

Corva said, "You may think you are being sarcastic. But I'll tell you, there will be millions of words written about the *United States* versus *Benjamin Tyson*. You will become case history. Did you know that the present French code of military justice was instituted as a direct result of the French Army's gross mishandling of the Dreyfus court-martial?"

Tyson lit another cigarette and sank back onto the sofa. "Ask me if I care."

"Someday," continued Corva, warming to his subject, "when you pass on to that great courtroom in the sky, your obit is a sure thing for the *Times*. Mine too."

"Really?" Tyson blew smoke rings. "What will they say about you? Never won a case?"

Corva was looking at the window. "What happened there?"

Tyson explained, "She went screwy a few days ago. You see, she's opposed to violence and is not completely understanding of how those poor bastards in my platoon cracked up and went on a rampage. But, out of ennui, she blasts an ashtray through the window. But I'm not being judgmental. I'm only pointing out that people who live in small houses shouldn't throw glass ashtrays."

Corva nodded. "Speaking of screwy, the Army intends to give you a battery of psychological tests. Any objections?"

"Yes. We can't offer an insanity defense two decades after the fact, and we're not going to claim that I'm incompetent to stand trial at this time. So, I'm not going to be a guinea pig for a bunch of crackpot shrinks."

"All right. I'll do what's necessary to block the testing." Corva inquired, "Have you ever seen a psychoanalyst?"

Tyson stubbed out his cigarette. "Briefly."

"Would his notes help us?"

"I don't know. How?"

"Will his notes indicate that you felt remorse and guilt for covering up the hospital incident?"

"I don't think so. I never told him."

"How can you go to a shrink and not tell him what is bothering you?"

Tyson smiled. "That's what *he* wanted to know."

"Would you have any objections if I contacted him?"

"Not at all, but you'll need a Ouija board."

"Oh. . . ."

"Suicide. If you contact him, tell him I didn't forget the last bill."

"You're drinking too much." Corva considered a moment. "What happened to his files?"

"Don't know. They're privileged information, aren't they?"

"While the therapist is alive. Afterward . . . well, I'll look into it." He took out a pen and yellow pad, and Tyson gave him Dr. Stahl's name and last address.

Corva extracted a folded page of the *New York Times* and held it up. "Did you see this?"

"I don't read the papers anymore. I'm reading Agatha Christie."

"Well, this is a story dealing with the international implications of this case." Corva scanned the page. "There is some talk of Vietnam taking the United States to the world court in The Hague. The moves toward normalization of relations between us and them have suffered a setback. That's another reason some people in Washington don't like you. Of course there are others who like you just fine for screwing it up."

"That's no concern of mine. Fuck Hanoi and Washington."

"Right. Also, it seems that the governments whose nationals were alleged to have been among the victims—France, Belgium, Germany, Holland, and Australia—have taken a formal interest in the case. They are our allies, as you may know."

Tyson shrugged. "Last month there was talk of the U.N. Commission on Genocide investigating. *Genocide?* Christ, that hospital was a virtual U.N. itself. We didn't discriminate. Why is everyone trying to crucify us?"

"They don't like us, Ben. Anyway, the Vietnamese ambassador to the U.N., according to this article, has stated that the People's Republic would be favorably disposed toward allowing an international fact-finding team, including an American, to visit the site of the alleged incident—Miséricorde Hospital and environs. The Vietnamese ambassador also suggested there may be witnesses available. Also, Hanoi has sent out a photograph of the former hospital which the *Times* has reproduced." He handed the full-page story to Tyson.

Tyson looked at the photograph. It showed a two-story white stucco building without a roof. Its walls were remarkably whiter than when he'd last seen fire licking out of the windows. But it couldn't have been repainted because it was obviously just a shell. Perhaps the monsoon had washed it, and the sun had bleached it like a bone. There were vines climbing up the sides, and he could see through the windows to the sky beyond.

> The hospital blazed in the dirty winter rain. The men of the first platoon of Alpha Company stood close, within ten meters, warming their sodden fatigues by the fire. Tyson noticed the steam rising from their uniforms and saw the red flames reflected in their wet, shiny faces.
>
> In the distance, artillery shells exploded, and a war plane streaked overhead, only its jet flame visible through the overcast. Tyson became aware of the crackling sound coming from the hospital as its teak timbers ignited and began splitting. There were noxious odors drifting out of the fiery windows—medical supplies, bedding, flesh.
>
> Without orders the men had formed a cordon around the walls of the rectangular building. They had shown good initiative, Tyson thought, an instinctive deployment without verbal orders, an understanding that the horror inside that hospital had to be kept inside.

A figure appeared at the front doors, a young woman in a white dressing gown carrying an infant. The baby was heavily wrapped in what looked like a GI-issue olive-drab towel. The woman gently pitched the infant into a tangle of ground vines to the side of the entrance just as a burst of gunfire slammed her back through the doors.

Tyson looked at where the shooting had come from and saw Richard Farley loading another magazine into his M-16.

Another figure appeared from a set of French doors at a second-story balcony on the east side of the building. Tyson saw it was a naked boy about twelve years old with an amputated leg. The boy hesitated, looked quickly back through the French doors, then closed his eyes and vaulted over the balcony railing. He dropped into a kitchen garden, landing on his knee and amputated stump. As he struggled to right himself, Tyson saw he had a white handkerchief that he was waving. Tyson heard the dull pop of Lee Walker's grenade launcher and saw the boy's chest explode in a mass of flying blood.

Suddenly a man with his head swathed in bandages burst out of the front doors of the hospital and raced across the courtyard at full speed, barefoot and wearing only pajama bottoms. He passed within twenty meters of Tyson, and Tyson realized he'd actually made it through the cordon.

Hernando Beltran swung his machine gun around and began firing furiously as the man approached a thick hedgerow at the edge of the plaza. The man was obviously a soldier because he moved like a broken-field runner, avoiding the bursts of gunfire. Beltran was swearing in Spanish. The man reached the hedgerow and jumped, but his body suddenly contorted as a burst of bullets hit him, and he landed, tangled in the hedges. The probing red fingers of the tracer rounds found him and tore into him, mowing the hedges down until the man lay lifeless in a tangled clump of twigs and leaves.

Tyson turned away, back toward the hospital. He noticed a movement on the pitched roof. About six people had come up through the louvered dormer that acted as an air vent to the attic and were clinging to the red terra-cotta tile. One of them, a man wearing the white pants and shirt of the hospital staff, moved cautiously toward the branches of the huge overhanging banyan tree. He chinned himself on a branch and began making his way toward the tree trunk, disappearing into the dense foliage. A Vietnamese nurse followed him. Tyson watched with mixed feelings, wanting them to escape, but knowing if they did, they would eventually make contact with the Vietnamese or American authorities.

Tyson's mind raced ahead. The platoon would be called back to base camp. As soon as they got off the helicopters, they would be surrounded by MPs, disarmed, and marched en masse to the stockade. He'd seen that happen once at Camp Evans, though he never learned what it was about. But the image of that once-proud fighting unit, hands on their heads, being ordered around by a platoon of spit-polished, sneering MPs, had affected him deeply.

Tyson kept staring at the spreading banyan tree. He saw that it was possible to escape that way. And that was comforting because that was the way Teresa had gone earlier, before his men had left the burning hospital and surrounded it.

Paul Sadowski said, "What do you see, Lieutenant?"

Tyson turned away from the tree and didn't answer.

Sadowski's eyes widened. "Oh, shit! Oh, Christ!" He called out to Beltran. "Put some fire in that tree."

Beltran picked up the M-60 machine gun and, firing from the hip, began spraying the banyan tree with long bursts of rounds, while Brontman fed the ammunition belts from a metal box. The second machine gun, manned by Michael DeTonq and Peter Santos, began raking the sloping roof. The red tile cracked and splattered into flying fragments. Tyson saw what they were shooting at on the roof: Partly hidden by branches of the tree were two female patients in hospital gowns, an old man, and a little girl with bright red legs, burned legs, the color of the tile. DeTonq's machine gun got the range quickly, and the four bodies, one after the other, tumbled down the roof, hit the rain gutter, bounced, and dropped along the wall to the ground. The machine gun followed them even in death and spewed burst after burst into the bushes where they'd fallen. Infantrymen, Tyson reflected, had seen too many kills suddenly get up and run away or shoot at them as they approached. As the expression went, "They're not dead until they're dead."

Beltran's machine gun, which was still firing into the tree, was now joined by DeTonq's and by a few M-16s and shotguns. The banyan tree was losing branches, dropping leaves, and shedding bark rapidly. The nurse fell out of the tree first and dropped to the ground by the far side of the hospital where Tyson could not see her. Harold Simcox ran toward the base of the tree, and Tyson saw him raise his rifle and empty an entire magazine at the ground.

Tyson looked back at the top of the tree. He could make out the white clothing of the man trying to hide in the foliage. The man seemed to be hit, and Tyson thought he saw red stains on the white clothing, but the man hung tenaciously to the trunk. Lee Walker fired a grenade, which burst on a branch over the man's head. Tyson heard a long mournful cry as the man released his grip and fell, bouncing through the branches. Again Simcox, still under the tree, finished the job.

There was no sound for some time except for the rain and crackling fire, and no one else appeared at any of the hospital doors or windows. Tyson saw several men glancing at him and figured it was his turn next. They had taken his rifle and .45 automatic pistol in the hospital, and he felt oddly naked without the weapons he'd carried and slept with for nearly a year.

Kelly was beside him now, his PRC-25 radio on his back, the radiophone in his hand. He was speaking to someone. Kelly gave the phone to Tyson. "Captain Browder."

Tyson took the radiophone. He was aware that several men had moved closer to him. He squeezed the transmit button and spoke. "Mustang One-Six here. Over."

Browder's voice came across weak. "Roger, One-Six. Need a sit rep and hawkeye," he said, using the radio code word for grid coordinates.

"Roger. Situation . . . sniper fire. Village of An Ninh Ha—Hawkeye of Yankee Delta, seven-two, five; two-one, six. How copy?"

Browder read the coordinates back and asked, "Need help? Artillery or gunships?"

"Negative. Light, ineffective fire. Vicinity of stucco buildings. We'll take a look-see."

"Roger. I haven't monitored any radio traffic from you in a while. I thought you'd all gone to sleep or died."

Tyson licked his lips and replied, "Nothing to report."

"Sniper fire is something to report. You still drawing fire?"

"Roger. We're going to move closer."

"Okay, be careful. Keep me informed. Hey, are you all right?"

Tyson was momentarily thrown off-guard by the question. He replied, "We're all okay. Tired."

The radio was quiet a few seconds, then Browder said, "Roger that. Take care of the snipers and proceed toward Hue."

"Roger."

"Out."

Tyson gave the radiophone back to Kelly. He looked at the men around him but showed no fear. He looked back at the hospital and saw it was fully ablaze now, and every window had bright orange flames curling out of it.

The remainder of the platoon had assembled in the open plaza in front of the hospital, knowing there was no one left alive inside. Nobody spoke, and the only sound was the rain in the palm fronds, the rain on the plaza, the rain in the puddles, and the rain on their helmets, heavier now, washing away the sound of the burning hospital and the movement of boots and rifles.

A sudden loud report caused everyone to turn, and a few men dropped into firing positions, aiming toward the hospital. The heated roof tiles were exploding, scattering hot shards of clay over the plaza. The men moved back. They waited. Finally the roof sagged and caved in, dropping onto the second floor which in turn collapsed onto the ground floor, leaving the hollow concrete shell of the building standing like a giant glowing oven. As if that were the signal they had been waiting for, the men began picking up their field gear and ammunition.

They divided up into their decimated squads, ready to move out. A few men looked at Tyson, waiting out of habit for an order, a signal, though Lieutenant Tyson was clearly not in charge any longer. Kelly pulled a .45 pistol from his web belt—Tyson's .45—and handed it to Tyson. Tyson slipped it into his holster, noting that no one came forward with his rifle. Kelly said quietly, "Get them moving."

Tyson didn't respond.

Kelly said more urgently, "Let's get the hell out of here."

Tyson looked around the plaza, beyond his assembled platoon, and scanned the picturesque houses and neat gardens bordering the open area. He wondered where she had gone, if she was watching them from some hiding place. He realized now that she would tell what happened, and he realized also that there might be other witnesses in this apparently dead and abandoned village.

Kelly seemed to understand at least part of what he was thinking. Kelly said, "Don't worry about the villagers. They can't say for sure what happened. The people in there"—he nodded toward the hospital—"they won't say a thing. Let's put some distance between us and this place. Before a command chopper comes by and asks what's going on." Kelly looked at Tyson awhile, then raised his arm and called out. "Saddle up! Movin' out!" He brought his arm down and pointed east toward a wide village lane that opened onto the plaza. Kelly gave Tyson a nudge, and the platoon began moving. Kelly said to him loudly, "Hell of a firefight. Right?"

Tyson looked down the line of men and saw Bob Moody being carried by Brontman and Simcox on a stretcher that they must have gotten from the hospital. Moody was smoking a cigarette and talking animatedly, the way the lightly wounded always did when they realized what could have happened to them and didn't.

Farther down the line, Holzman and Walker were carrying a bamboo pole on their shoulders. Slung from the pole was a green-gray rubber poncho, and in the poncho was the fetal-curled body of Arthur Peterson, who had died sometime during the time his platoon had been killing the doctors and nurses who might have saved him.

Behind him, Richard Farley was trudging under a heavy weight: Strapped to his A-frame, in place of his pack, like a deer, was the body of Larry Cane. Cane's head bobbed above Farley's left shoulder, his face covered with a big olive-drab handkerchief as was the procedure. But the tied handkerchief had slipped, and Tyson saw Cane's face, one eyelid still open. Someone had wiped the blood that had gushed from his nose and mouth, but there was still a smear of it on his chin, and his parted lips revealed red teeth.

Tyson stared at the white face as Farley drew nearer. Then Tyson looked at Farley's face in bizarre juxtaposition to the dead face behind him. Tyson's and Farley's eyes met and held. Farley's lips formed words, but Tyson heard nothing. Tyson reached out and retied the handkerchief firmly around Cane's face, feeling the cool clammy skin.

Tyson turned and began walking with his platoon. At least, he thought, they had two KIAs to back up a story of a battle. He hoped no one back at graves registration could tell that Cane had been shot at point-blank range with an Army .45-caliber pistol.

Kelly said, "Where we heading?"

Tyson looked at him. "Hell."

Kelly nodded. "Well, get out your map, Lieutenant, and show us the way."

"Ben? Are you listening to me?"

Tyson's eyes focused on the photograph of the hospital. The banyan tree was still there, bigger now, its branches dropping into the roofless hulk. He handed the newspaper page back to Corva. "Don't recognize the place."

"Nevertheless, the Hanoi government states this is Hôpital Miséricorde. Or was."

"Commies lie. Everyone knows that."

Corva continued, "I wonder if a team of experts could tell by the bullet pocks on the concrete what sort of shooting took place there. I mean, I assume the shot groups or shot patterns of a massacre might look different from those of a firefight."

Tyson didn't respond.

"Also the Hanoi government is excavating the ground-floor rubble, though I imagine the bodies must have been removed sometime after the Tet Offensive ended."

Tyson lit a cigarette.

Corva said, "Whatever was left there would have been used as ash fertilizer by the villagers. The vultures, beetles, and worms got the rest. Still, the concrete shell may reveal something, and this is the first possible physical evidence we've had to deal with."

"Should I be concerned?"

Corva thought a moment. "The *Times* story doesn't indicate that anyone in our government has accepted this invitation."

Tyson observed, "This invitation comes from the same people who massacred two thousand men, women, and children of Hue on the other side of the city. Where the hell do they get their nerve? I'd like to take an international commission to the Strawberry Patch and show them where I found the mass graves."

Corva said ironically, "That's not the way it works, Ben. American atrocities are more atrocious than communist atrocities. You know that." Corva added, "Anyway, this mess is making our government unhappy." He sighed deeply. "Damn it. I always knew this thing would make us look bad. Why do we always do this to ourselves?"

"Because," replied Tyson, "we do it better than anyone else could do it to us."

Corva shook his head absently. "Anyway, in answer to your question, it is my guess that the White House will tell the North Viets to take their kind invitation and shove it up their asses. Diplomatically."

"But the other countries *will* send people to Hue."

Corva rubbed his lower lip. "Yes, and they may discover something. But I've already informed the Justice Department that if they think they are going to introduce at an American court-martial any evidence gathered in a communist country by foreigners, they'd better be prepared for a ten-year legal battle, not to mention public outrage. I think they understood. We'll see."

Tyson commented, "You place a lot of faith in American public opinion."

"You should too. There is not much we can do about negative world opinion. But did you see that poll that indicated that an incredible seventy-eight percent of the American public thinks you are being made a scapegoat?"

"I missed that one."

"I have a clipping service that sends me anything with your name in it."

"Good."

"You've become a focal point, Ben, for a lot of pent-up feelings here and abroad."

Tyson shrugged. "Not my fault. I'd as soon drop the whole thing."

Corva added, "Like the Dreyfus court-martial, this is perceived as a case that transcends Benjamin Tyson and the first platoon of Alpha Company."

"Is that so?"

Corva pulled a sheet of paper from his briefcase. "Enough of international diplomacy and the state of the Union. Let's move on to more important business. I had a pleasant chat with Major Harper last week. In my office."

Tyson said casually, "Did you?"

"Nice piece of goods, Ben."

"I hadn't noticed."

"Well, I did. Anyway, she's too tall for me."

"Actually you are too short for her. What did she want?"

"Oh, just wanted to brief me on a few items. The most significant of which is that the FBI has located Hernando Beltran, Lee Walker, and Louis Kalane."

Tyson said nothing.

Corva went on, "That was quick work. Of course they knew all along where these men were. But the Justice Department wanted to see if you were going to be charged before they told you that."

Tyson said, "I never really understood why they weren't found sooner."

"And the government never released the names of the men in your platoon because if they had, people who knew these men would have blown the whistle to the media."

Tyson nodded thoughtfully. "But you know, Karen Harper wanted me to make a public appeal for them to come forward."

"Karen Harper was operating in a vacuum. For every hour she put in on the investigation, there were bureaucrats, JAG people, Justice Department lawyers, and FBI agents who were putting in hundreds of hours. She was the visible tip of an iceberg she didn't even know was attached to her. I think she knows that now. Doesn't matter though. Point is, she was asked to contact Beltran, Walker, and Kalane by telephone. And she did."

Tyson stood and walked to the window. He stared out at the headlights of the traffic crossing the bridge.

Corva said, "Harper reports that she spoke to each of the three men briefly by phone. Beltran and Kalane put her in touch with their respective attorneys. Walker did not have a lawyer. He is a mechanic, someplace outside of Macon, Georgia. Anyway, the attorneys for Beltran and Kalane indicated that their clients would not make any statements unless they were subpoenaed. Beltran is a successful Miami businessman. Kalane is involved somehow in the tourist business in Honolulu. Harper asked these two attorneys if their clients' prospective testimony would characterize them as witnesses for the defense or the prosecution."

Tyson lit a cigarette and continued to stare out the window.

Corva said, "Harper informs me that they are your witnesses."

Tyson exhaled a stream of smoke.

"So," observed Corva, "it seems you engender some sort of loyalty in your troops, Lieutenant Tyson."

Tyson said, "They kept the faith, Vince."

"So they did. I'll tell you something though. If I had been the attorney for either of them, I would have advised them to jump on the government side."

Tyson turned from the window. "Why?"

"Well, they will never be charged with murder even if they get on a witness stand and give a blow-by-blow account of a massacre. On the other hand, if they tell the altered version of the hospital incident but you are convicted anyway, they may then be liable for charges of perjury."

Tyson said, "I'm sure their attorneys advised them of that."

"I'm certain they did. Yet they want to stand up for you, Ben. I'm deeply touched. But not too deeply."

"Meaning?"

"Well, meaning that if this case had come to trial in 1968 or anytime before these men had been honorably discharged, then *they* would have been charged with the actual murder. Also, whether or not they are immune from prosecution, they are still not going to stand up in a public trial and admit to mass murder. I'd like to think they are going to stand up for you totally out of loyalty, but they have other motives as well."

"Perhaps, Vince. Perhaps. But it's not up to us to judge their motives."

Corva stood. "Do you have any loyalty to them?"

"Meaning?"

"Would you protect their reputations on a witness stand?"

"I suppose I would. But I do feel ambivalent toward them. They did something for which I'm now left holding the charge sheet, as you pointed out."

"That's your fault, Ben. I can see why you didn't prefer charges immediately. But afterward . . . when you were safely on that hospital ship and had time to think—what was that if not loyalty?"

"I suppose I felt loyal. The Army ingrains in you the concept of loyalty between an officer and his men. But when something like this happens, that loyalty can cause a miscarriage of justice."

"I know that."

Tyson went on, "When I was wounded, they all said good-bye. And they were truly sorry to see me go. A small thing, but it loomed large while I was lying on the hospital ship, a writing pad in my hand, wondering if I should write a love letter to my girlfriend or a memo to the battalion commander."

"I understand." Corva poured two more glasses of strega and handed one to Tyson. Corva said, "What I meant by my question about loyalty is this: If you are convicted, it is *essential* that you take the stand and offer true testimony in extenuation and mitigation before the board votes on a sentence. True testimony—as much as any war story can be true—would obviously be very damning toward Messrs. Sadowski, Scorello, Beltran, Walker, and Kalane. And it might leave them all open to perjury charges, which the Justice Department might well pursue in a federal court. And perjury is a very bad rap." He looked at Tyson.

"Why don't we cross that bridge when we come to it?" He put down his drink. "Tell me about Lee Walker."

"Oh, yes." Corva took a sheet of paper from the coffee table and perused it. He said, "Karen—Major Harper reports that Mr. Walker's initial statements to her led her to believe he was a witness for the defense."

Tyson nodded. Somehow he'd had no anxieties about Walker's testimony.

Corva continued, "Unlike when she questioned you, Sadowski, and Scorello, she was obligated to end the interview with Walker as soon as she determined that he was a witness for the defense, because you have now had charges preferred against you, and you have an attorney. So, Major Harper turned Mr. Walker over to me. I spoke to him by telephone. What do you remember about him?"

Tyson finished his drink and noticed the bottle was nearly empty. He put his glass down and lit another cigarette. "I don't know . . . a simple man. Honest. Kept out of trouble. Rural southern black. You know the type."

Corva said, "He was a little jumpy. Kept saying you didn't do anything wrong."

"Put him on the stand."

Corva smiled. "Well, that is the question. Who of the five do we put on the stand?"

"All of them."

"No, I told you why we can't do that. It would sound like they were all reading from the same teleprompter. What I have to decide is not only who will do the best acting, but who will stand up under cross-examination. That is very important."

Tyson observed, "You haven't gone to see Sadowski or Scorello yet."

"No, I have not."

Tyson said with a touch of sarcasm, "I've heard of armchair detectives. Now I've met an armchair lawyer."

Corva looked at him awhile. "There is such a thing as overpreparing for a case. I've seen that."

Tyson laughed despite himself. "Okay, you're the lawyer."

"That's right," agreed Corva. "Anyway, in conclusion, Major Harper also advised me that neither Daniel Kelly nor Michael DeTonq has been located. Nor has Sister Teresa."

Tyson nodded. The blinds rattled as a breeze blew in off the water. Tyson spoke musingly. "It's cooling off. It was a hot summer. Summers are sort of memory markers of the mind. I'll remember this summer for quite some time. I recall the summer of 1966, before I reported for duty. I was out of college, and I took the entire summer off. It was one of those perfect times in one's life: no obligations, no pressures, a sense of accomplishment at having graduated, and the prospect of a new adventure in front of me." He looked at Corva. "At times like these, it's normal to return to the past. But not particularly healthy, is it?"

"It's all right. If there is a refuge in the mind, Ben, hide out there awhile."

Tyson sat again and poured the remainder of the liqueur into his glass.

Corva shuffled through his papers. He said, "I was impressed with her." He looked at Tyson. "You were too. And she was impressed with you."

"Maybe if she gets out of the Army before my court-martial, I'll fire you and hire her."

Corva finished his drink. "Well, she won't get out of the Army while this is going on. They want her where they can keep an eye on her."

Tyson went into the kitchen and came back with a bottle of port. "Real Portuguese stuff. Thirty-five bucks a bottle. Float a little of this on top of the strega." He filled Corva's glass to the brim, then filled his own. They both drank the port, then drank another. Corva mumbled something about having to drive. He suppressed a belch, then said, "Also, Harper would not take the job of defending you, Lieutenant—"

"Cut the Lieutenant shit."

"Because she believes you are guilty."

Tyson slumped into the armchair and poured himself another. "How about you?"

"I would not have taken this case if I did not totally believe you should not pay for what happened there. I was there, buddy, and *I* would not want to pay again."

"You didn't say *you* thought I was innocent."

Corva shook his head several times. "Of course I didn't say that. I think you are guilty. I only said you should not have to pay."

Tyson leaned forward and stared at Corva. "You said you would not want to pay *again*. Are *you* indictable? What did *you* do over there?"

Corva stood but did not move from his spot. He swayed slightly, and his eyes seemed to be focused on something a long way off. At length he said, "Pretty much what you did, Ben. Looked the other way. Oh, it wasn't as grand as a massacre . . . but it was more than one incident."

"Tell me," prompted Tyson out of a perverse curiosity. "Picard told me. You tell me."

"Fuck Picard." Corva seemed to forget what it was he was going to say, then blurted, "My machine gunner mowed down three enemy soldiers who approached us under a white flag. I was sick for a week over that. Three kids who'd had enough and wanted to surrender. He cut them down like they were nothing . . . nothing." He glanced at Tyson. "I had a sharpshooter, Ben, with one of those fancy hunting rifles and high-powered scopes . . . he used to like to check the rifle's aim by shooting peasants running through the fields to get to their villages before curfew. He said his watch was fast. Get it? His watch was fast. He did it three times before I put a stop to it. Another time, we approached a village bomb shelter where a few villagers had taken cover, and—"

"All right!" Tyson stood. "All right, Vince. Enough. For God's sake, enough."

Both men stood in silence for some time. Then Corva walked over to Tyson and, to Tyson's utter amazement, embraced him.

Tyson stiffened, not knowing what to do. He hadn't been embraced by a man or embraced a man since . . . Vietnam. He moved his arms awkwardly and patted Corva on the back.

Corva stepped away. "Sorry . . . you know how Italians are."

Tyson cleared his throat. "Oh, it's all right. I was getting . . . emotional too."

Corva took a deep breath. "And those were only the offenses that are indictable today—the murders. There were other things—the beatings, the sexual . . . well, you know." He looked at Tyson. "Why did I let him do it *three* times before I put a stop to it, Ben? Why?"

Tyson replied, "Because you didn't believe what you were seeing the first two times."

Corva nodded quickly. "Yes. Yes, that was it. I guess. . . ."

Tyson rubbed his face and said wearily, "Is that about it? I mean, are we finished here?"

Corva began packing his briefcase. He said, "This is Monday night . . . the Article 32 hearing convenes Friday morning. I guess we ought to talk about that next time. See what we can do about not getting you indicted."

Tyson said, "I might be a free man by Friday afternoon."

Corva nodded. "Might be."

"And they will probably release me from duty the following week."

"Probably."

"Except none of that is going to happen, is it?"

"Probably not."

Tyson could see that Corva was both upset and drunk and had become taciturn.

Corva picked up his briefcase and walked to the door. He said, "I tried to get you a pass to meet me in the city tomorrow. But I think Colonel Hill thinks if you skip out, his career will be over. And he's right."

"I'm not running."

"I know that. But they don't know you. So I'll be here tomorrow, sometime before noon. Will you be here?"

Tyson forced a smile. "Call my secretary, and she'll give you my schedule for the morning."

"Right." Corva opened the door and drew in a long breath. He looked back at Tyson. "I broke my rule. About war stories. Sorry."

"It's okay."

"Won't happen again." He stepped onto the stoop. "Kiss your wife good-bye when she leaves for work tomorrow. Kiss your son too."

"Can you drive?"

"No. I'll take a cab." Corva walked unsteadily down the path.

Tyson watched him turn toward the main gate. He said softly to himself, "God, do we *all* have blood on our hands? Did anyone return from that place with his honor intact?"

Corva, he thought, like so many of them, had seemed to come through it without a scratch until you looked inside his head.

38

T he rain beat heavily against the windows. Tyson threw the morning newspaper aside and turned on the television, then shut it off. He poured himself another coffee but did not drink it, then lit another cigarette and stubbed it out. "Damn it!"

He stared at the broken windowpane and smelled the damp cool air that blew in. He paced the length of the living room: five paces, turned around, five paces. He dropped to the floor and did thirty push-ups. He stood and wiped his face with the sleeve of his gray sweat suit. The sweat suit was grimy, and he wondered if he was allowed to go to the post Laundromat, or if he had to send his son after school or his wife after work.

His eyes focused on a bud vase atop the TV in which was a single yellow tea rose. Somehow the idea of that flower in this dismal place offended him. Marcy's efforts to make the place a home angered him. He picked up the vase and went to the front door as the door bell rang. He stood motionless, resisting the urge to answer it quickly. It was probably Corva, and he could stand in the rain awhile. Good for his character. The door bell rang again. Tyson waited a full minute, then opened the door.

Vincent Corva hurried in and closed his umbrella. He looked at the vase and tea rose in Tyson's hands. "For me?"

Tyson opened the door again and threw the bud vase out on the lawn.

Corva said, "Hell of a day for the first day of school. I had to march my kids to the bus at gunpoint." He took off his black raincoat. "Reminds me of a monsoon I once walked in for two months. Did you have the monsoon up north?"

"I don't remember." Tyson took Corva's raincoat and hung it in the minuscule coat closet.

Corva observed, "Everything is small here. This place is so small you have to go outside to change your mind." Corva moved into the living room.

Tyson looked at his watch. "It's noon. What kept you?"

Corva put his briefcase on the coffee table. "Traffic. I said before noon."

"It's after noon. Five after."

"Your secretary said for lunch." He looked at Tyson. "Are you stir crazy?"

Tyson didn't reply.

Corva opened his briefcase and took out a brown paper bag. "My wife made sandwiches. Italian cold cuts, provolone, and caponata. I want you to taste this."

"I'm not hungry. I'm bored. I can't even take a walk in this fucking weather."

"Well, you have to walk to post headquarters to sign in. That's a nice break in the day." Corva began unwrapping the sandwiches.

"Fuck post headquarters. I haven't signed in for three days."

Corva looked at him. "Hey, don't break the rules of your arrest, Ben, or they will put you in confinement. That means the slammer. All they need is an excuse."

"At least there are people to talk to in jail."

Corva shrugged. He spotted the coffee carafe and a clean mug on the end table. He poured himself some coffee. "I want you to sign in after we are done here."

"Fuck them. They're not going to throw me in the slammer, and you know it."

"Why not?"

"Because they're worried about their image, that's why."

Corva put cream in his coffee. "I wouldn't count on that." He added, "And if you wind up at the Fort Dix stockade, I damn sure don't want to drive down there to see you. And that place is grim, buddy. Also, it's in New Jersey, and you wouldn't be caught dead in New Jersey." He smiled.

Tyson didn't acknowledge the humor.

Corva sat in the armchair and opened his briefcase. "Did you kiss Marcy and David this morning?"

"No." He lit a cigarette. "No one was in a kissing mood. David was sulky. Marcy was trying to contain her exaltation at going back to the office. She almost floated out of here. Also, I slept on the couch. It sucks, Vince."

"Oh, I know."

"What am I supposed to do when she goes on a business trip? It will only be David and I here. And I can't even take the kid anyplace." He picked up his metal ashtray, filled with cigarette butts, and heaved it at the opposite wall.

Corva pretended not to notice as he rifled through his papers.

Tyson sat down on the far end of the couch. He said, "I told them to stay in Sag Harbor, then go home to Garden City. But, no, they wanted to share my martyrdom and mortification. Now they're as screwed up as I am."

Corva picked up a piece of paper and said absently, "Sorry about last night."

"Oh . . . tell you the truth, I was so drunk, I don't remember much."

Corva nodded. "My wife was pissed off because she wanted the car today. I had to promise to stay sober and drive it home."

"Don't let her push you around. You fought a war."

"I don't think anybody gives a shit, Ben."

"Right."

Corva slid a wrapped sandwich across the coffee table and unwrapped his own.

Tyson opened his wrapper and lifted the long piece of Italian bread. "What the hell is this?"

"It's eggplant, capers, olives, tomatoes, and some other good stuff. Beneath that is provolone. Then Genoa salami, prosciutto, capocollo, mortadella—"

"This will put a hole in my stomach. I could taste that fucking strega when I woke up."

Corva bit into his sandwich. He spoke between mouthfuls. "Anyway, the hearing convenes at nine A.M. in the Jackson room. It has some of the features of a grand jury except there is no jury—only the Article 32 investigating officer, this fellow who took over from Harper, Colonel Farnley Gilmer." He peered at Tyson. "Where do WASPs *get* these names?"

"Family names. Had a friend at school named Manville Griffith Kenly."

"Christ. What did you call him?"

"Shithead." Tyson picked up his sandwich and bit into it. He chewed cautiously, then nodded. "Not bad. . . ."

Corva glanced at his notes. "Anyway, Colonel Gilmer is supposed to be impartial, like Harper. He is not supposed to be perfecting a case for the government. But he knows who pays him every month. Also, he is conducting a different sort of investigation than Harper did. Mostly he's reading her report, coordinating the efforts of the Army CID and the FBI in locating witnesses, using government resources to try to turn up any documentary evidence in the Army records bureau, and writing letters abroad regarding Sister Teresa. In addition, he's speaking to the newly appointed Army prosecution team and calling me when the mood strikes him. On the phone he sounds like an all-right guy, but you can tell he's nervous about fucking up. He's so cautious that when I say, 'How are you?' he says, 'Allegedly fine.'"

Tyson smiled for the first time that day.

Corva continued, "In the hearing itself, Gilmer is sort of a judge, jury, and moderator. However, there are instances when he performs some of the functions that are performed by a district attorney in a civilian grand jury. He does not have to literally change hats for this, but I always thought it would be good comic relief if that were required."

"Christ, Vince, no wonder they won't let the press in." Tyson sprawled out on the couch. "I'm practicing my military bearing for the hearing. Continue."

"Right. There will also be a court reporter present. We will be present, and most importantly, the prosecuting team will be present. We will have an opportunity to see the face of the enemy. There are three of them."

"There is one of you."

"I could ask for one or two Army-appointed lawyers, if you'd like."

"Do you want them?" asked Tyson.

"I prefer to work alone."

Tyson considered a moment. He said, "Wouldn't it be better from the standpoint of appearances and psychology if we had JAG lawyers in uniform present?"

Corva picked a piece of cheese out of his sandwich and chewed on it. "Well, it would look good to Colonel Gilmer and to any court-martial board that is convened to hear your case. However, the presence of Army defense lawyers in uniform will give the subtle appearance that we concur with this whole travesty of justice. *You* have to be in uniform, of course, but I want you to somehow look and act like a civilian, with a civilian lawyer, who is being tried by a military tribunal. That is very un-American looking, and that's the way I want it."

Tyson rubbed his jaw in thought. "Okay, just you and me, Vince. Do you know anything about the prosecution team?"

"Yes, I know they are a very tough bunch. Their names are Colonel Graham Pierce, Major Judith Weinroth, and Captain Salvatore Longo."

Tyson put his head back on the couch's armrest and stared up at the ceiling. He observed, "The Army is an equal opportunity employer."

"So it seems," Corva said. "The real problem is Colonel Pierce."

Tyson lit a cigarette and blew smoke rings into the air. He flipped his ash on the floor. "What do you know about him?"

Corva thought a moment. "You want it straight?"

"Sure."

"Okay. . . . First, he does mostly murder cases. He, like Van Arken, was on the prosecution staff in the Calley case. Before that he was an Army prosecutor at Long Binh. He tried capital cases there too. Sent a good many GIs home early. To Leavenworth. He is a protégé of Van Arken and, therefore, a prick. He may one day be the next Judge Advocate General."

Tyson sat up on the couch. He looked closely at Corva. "Tell me more."

"All right . . . he is an accomplished trial performer but no buffoon, and the jury will never sense what a performer or a prick he really is. Only another lawyer can spot those sterling qualities. Also, he is a genius in the true sense of the word. I've seen him introduce pages of documentary evidence, then without looking at it, quote long sections verbatim. He could be a stage actor."

Tyson leaned forward, his eyes on Corva.

Corva went on, "When he approaches the bench over some point of law, he can quote from the Manual for Courts-Martial, the UCMJ, and case law, chapter and verse, the way a Holy Roller can quote from the Bible. But he's not pedantic. He's quick-witted and has an analytical mind. He can switch tactics when he senses something isn't working, like a good battlefield tactician. Thinks on his feet."

Corva went on in a quickening voice. "He smells the weak points in the defense and attacks those weak points until he breaks through. Then when he's behind your lines, he blows up your ammo dump, pisses in your water wells, and eats your food. Then if you try to retreat, he blocks you, turns you around, and pushes you into the arms of an ambush. If you attack, he makes a strategic withdrawal, then outflanks you and surrounds you. And he doesn't let up until you raise the white flag. Then he's magnanimous, like it was all just a jousting tournament, and he comes over to you wanting to shake hands and buy you a drink."

Tyson said, "Sounds like he might be a bit of a problem."

Corva drew a deep breath. "Well, I didn't mean to scare you."

"Not at all."

"I mean," continued Corva, "he is not invincible. He can be beaten."

"Has he been?"

"No. He's never lost one."

"Then you both have perfect records."

"Right. But I'm due for a miracle."

"That's right." Tyson stood, went into the kitchen, and came back with a bottle of Sambuca. He poured a few ounces into his and Corva's coffee mugs. "This is the first and last drink you're getting here."

Corva lifted his mug. *"Salute."*

"Cheers." Tyson drank and put down his mug. "That's not bad. Like drinking a licorice stick."

"This is good for digestion."

"I think two fingers down my throat is what I need." He sat on the arm of the couch. "So, have you ever faced Colonel Pierce?"

Corva nodded. "Once. At Fort Bragg. Eighty-second Airborne major. Violation of Article 114. Dueling."

"Doing what?"

"Dueling. You know—ten paces, turn, and fire. That's been outlawed in the Army for over a hundred years. Takes a lot of fun out of garrison life. Anyway, I tried to show the jury that my client was defending his honor as an officer and a gentleman. It was a very unusual case."

"But with the usual outcome."

"Be fair, Ben. They had this major dead to rights. He slapped a young captain who he suspected was diddling his fiancée, then invited the captain to a clearing in the woods for a duel—forty-five automatics, no seconds to be present."

Tyson waited. "Well?"

Corva was picking up stray pieces of the sandwich from the wrapper and putting them in his mouth. "Oh . . . well, the captain showed up with six seconds—all MPs—and they dragged this major off. The captain was no fool. Anyway, Colonel Pierce decided he wanted to prosecute this one even though dueling is not a capital offense. Even if someone gets killed. That's quaint. Anyway, you don't get many Article 114s."

"What's the Army coming to? I was thinking of committing an Article 114 with Captain Hodges."

"You are not allowed to bear arms. That's quaint, too. Lots of quaint customs in military life."

"Right. So, what did this chivalrous major get?"

"Well, the rounds in the forty-five were short-loaded. Not enough powder to kill anyone according to my expert witness. The major was no fool either. Anyway, the jury loved this guy. I got him off with one year suspended and not even a separation from the service. Colonel Pierce was very upset. That was the one and only time he failed to get jail time awarded."

"He's after you, Vince."

"No, Ben, he is after *you.*"

Tyson smiled grimly.

Corva said, "But I'm ready for the son of a bitch." Corva seemed lost in thought for some time. He said, "So that is how the hearing will stack up Friday. Colonel Gilmer officiates, Colonel Pierce and his two cohorts listen and watch." Corva leaned forward. "Your demeanor should be one of cool detachment."

"Like the bloodless upper-middle-class WASP that I am?"

"Yes, that's right. Stay in character." Corva reached for the Sambuca bottle, but Tyson moved it away. Tyson said, "I need this to unplug the sink."

Corva continued, "Well, anyway, there are two theories regarding how the defense ought to proceed at a hearing. One: We can go into that hearing room prepared to fight every inch of the way to get the case dropped. Or two: We can assume that they mean to indict you even if we bring in six Carmelite nuns and the Archbishop of Hue, who swear you were taking communion with them in Da Nang that day."

"Where are the six nuns and the archbishop?"

"Doesn't matter. Point is, I believe they are going to indict you based on Brandt's statement, which, by the way, Colonel Gilmer had Brandt swear to in writing. Farley's statement is also a sworn statement now. I have a copy of both. Do you want to see them?"

"No. But what makes you certain they are going to indict me?"

"I guess you're not following this case much."

Tyson shrugged. "If they're going to indict me anyway, do I have to show up?"

"Only in body," replied Corva. "You see, Ben, I could drag in Sadowski, Scorello, Beltran, Walker, and Kalane. And they might just make one hell of a case for you. But this guy Colonel Gilmer will say to himself, 'Why are these guys saying one thing, and Brandt and Farley are saying another?' And he'll answer himself, 'Let's have a court-martial to find out. Let's have a seven-person jury decide.' Or words to that effect. You see, Ben, unlike a civilian grand jury where a lot of people vote in secret, Gilmer has the only vote. And if that vote is cast to not indict, everyone will guess that was his vote because he's the only one voting. *Capice?*"

Tyson nodded.

"And," continued Corva, "this obscure colonel will be suddenly well known to his superiors. So let's suppose Gilmer reads all the testimony, examines the facts, and we let him talk to our witnesses, and he *does* recommend that no indictment be forwarded. His decision, unlike a civilian grand jury's decision, is not binding."

"Then why bother with this farce?"

"Because some years ago the Army was forced to institute a grand jury system in order to protect the rights of the accused who were subject to too many discretionary command decisions. So the Army came up with this watered-down Article 32 hearing that still lets higher commanders reverse any decision of the make-believe grand jury type of hearing. The President at that time bought the goods and signed it into law. And so far the Supreme Court has been reluctant to hear any challenges to it. You see, the federal courts try to avoid this land mine of military justice. The premier of France, after the Dreyfus case, commented, 'Military law is to law as military music is to music.' If the federal courts had legal jurisdiction over you, you would still be a civilian. I would have raised three hundred legal questions by now, and eventually I would have plea-bargained this down to a fifty-dollar fine. But that's not the case. You are going to sit in a room with some scared colonel who wants you out of that room as quickly as possible. If Colonel Gilmer goes home that night and prays for guidance from above, he will not be praying to God, but to General Van Arken. And even if Colonel Gilmer for some reason does not vote to indict you, then General Peters, post commander at Dix, will. And if Peters doesn't vote to indict you, it can go right up to the Secretary of the Army, then Defense, then the Commander in Chief of the Armed Forces, who happens to be a politician. But the government does not want those people to have to stick their necks out and make an unpopular decision. And I strongly suspect poor Colonel Gilmer senses that and would not want to cause anyone above him such anguish. So he will forward the indictment to General Peters, who, on the advice of his Staff Judge Advocate, will concur. General Peters will then issue orders convening a general court-martial."

Tyson stood and walked to the window. He watched the rain awhile. "The script is already written."

"No, never written. Just understood by everyone who plays."

"I used to respect military justice."

"I still do. I told you I'd beat this in a federal court. But I'm having a hell of a time beating military justice. Point is, you are guilty. So you had better still respect it."

Tyson continued to stare out the window. "I don't like not putting up a fight, even if it's a losing fight."

"If we put the defense witnesses on the stand, they will be subject to cross-examination. We will have prematurely revealed to Colonel Pierce our positions, our strengths and weaknesses." Corva added, "But the decision is yours."

Tyson regarded the gloomy, rain-sodden landscape. "Okay, we'll hold the witnesses for a court-martial. Will Brandt and Farley testify for the prosecution?"

"Colonel Pierce will not call them for the same reasons I won't call our troops. Colonel Gilmer will consider their sworn statements. I do have a lot of questions for Brandt and Farley, but I'll have to ask them in front of a court-martial board."

"What sort of questions?"

"Well, I'm glad you asked. Maybe you can answer a few of them ahead of time."

Tyson turned from the window.

"You see, Ben, there *is* one way of convincing Colonel Gilmer that he doesn't have to forward an indictment. And if his reasons are sound, the chain of command will concur, and you will be free."

Tyson said nothing.

Corva fixed his eyes on Tyson's and asked, "Is there something you can prove, either through Army records or through witnesses, that would show Colonel Gilmer and everyone that you and Brandt were enemies?"

Tyson stayed silent a moment, then replied, "No."

Corva continued staring at him. "Why does Brandt hate you?"

"I didn't say he did."

"Do you hate him? I don't mean because of this. I mean because of something that happened over there?"

Tyson considered the question. He replied, "No, I don't hate him. I personally despise him. He was morally corrupt."

"Will the accused expand on that?"

"Not at this time."

"Can I tell you what Sadowski said to me? What he hinted to Harper and what she mentioned in her report?"

"What did Sadowski say?"

"He said you once beat the shit out of Brandt in front of the whole platoon. You kicked him and punched him repeatedly in the face. Then you threw him into a flooded rice paddy and wouldn't let him out until he was covered with leeches." Corva stared at Tyson. "He was half hysterical from the leeches, crying and begging you to let him come onto the dike."

Tyson lit a cigarette and exhaled a long stream of smoke. "I seem to remember something like that."

"What in the name of God would prompt an American Army officer to beat and humiliate one of his own men? A medic, of all people."

"I guess I was having a bad day."

"Don't be facetious, Ben."

"Oh, look, Vince, you don't want to hear it. It's a war story."

"I'll listen to this war story."

"Some other time. It's not pertinent."

"Not *pertinent?* It's very pertinent to why Brandt has come forward and told this story."

"It doesn't change the *story.* Or the facts."

"I'm not interested in *facts!* I'm only interested in showing that Brandt, in his hate for you and his desire for revenge, is not a credible witness."

Tyson replied evenly, "Brandt is a respected doctor. And he has a corroborating witness."

"What does Farley have against you?"

"I'm not sure."

"Why did Brandt know to tell Andrew Picard that Farley was the one who would back up his story? He didn't give Picard any other names. Only Farley."

Tyson shook his head. "Maybe Farley was the only one whose whereabouts he knew. Maybe they kept up their wartime acquaintance."

"A medical doctor and a strung-out paraplegic junkie? I doubt that. Were they good friends over there?"

"Not that I recall."

Corva sat. "This is like pulling teeth. You are not going to tell me what motivates Brandt and Farley, though I think you know."

"Maybe later, Vince, if it gets down to that."

Corva snapped his briefcase shut. "Okay. So Friday it will be you and I and Colonel Gilmer and the prosecution team, a court reporter, and no witnesses for the defense or prosecution. Also, there will be two other people present."

"Who?"

"Karen Harper, for one. She is in an advisory capacity to Colonel Gilmer." Tyson didn't respond.

"Also, Colonel Gilmer has subpoenaed Andrew Picard."

"Picard?"

"Yes. Not for the defense or prosecution, but as Gilmer's own witness."

"What does Gilmer want Picard to testify about?"

"Well, apparently Mr. Picard told Karen Harper a few things that didn't appear in his book or in subsequent interviews, and Gilmer feels that oral testimony is the best way to discover more about those things." Corva added, "You had a chat with Picard yourself."

"Yes."

"Was it pleasant?"

"It was revealing."

"Will he help us or hurt us on the stand?"

Tyson replied, "We actually hit it off all right. But you know how writers are. They think they have a special relationship to the truth. I'm sure even Wally Jones believes that, or he'd have gone to court to have himself legally declared a cockroach."

Corva said, "Things are so rigged against us, Picard's testimony can't hurt. I don't want an eyewitness up there who can be cross-examined. But I'll take a chance with Picard and not raise any objections to his testifying. It should be interesting if not enlightening."

"Could be."

Corva went to the closet and got his raincoat. "I'll speak to you tomorrow. If you recall why Brandt would like to see you in Leavenworth, please let me know."

"I'll think about it. What amazes me is why you and Harper don't just accept the most logical explanation for Brandt's actions. He was tired of living with the damned thing."

"Did he participate in the incident?"

"No. No, he didn't. But like me, he was a little ahead of the rest of the boys in education and maturity. And he was not infantry like the rest of us. He was trained as a healer. So he was particularly sensitive and upset. And now he wants to do the honorable thing. He wants justice."

Corva nodded thoughtfully. "That is what he will say, won't he?"

"Yes, that is what he will say. He will also say he respected me and I respected his work and having to testify against me is the toughest thing he has ever done in his life and he feels very badly for me and wishes it didn't have to be this way. But it's best for everyone if the truth is finally told. And so forth."

Corva buttoned his raincoat. "But deep down he hates your guts so bad that when he thinks about you he can taste the bile in his mouth. He has wished you dead a thousand times, and at the Strawberry Patch, he did something . . .

something . . . and in the last twenty years, he has fantasized about smashing your face with a rifle butt or throwing you in a tank full of leeches. Right?"

"Most probably."

"And one day . . . he sees this inquiry in the locator section of the First Cav newspaper and takes it as a sign. He throws caution to the wind, doesn't consider the ultimate consequences to himself if this comes to light, because his judgment is completely obscured by hate. And he spills his guts to Andrew Picard. And I'll bet by now he feels very ambivalent about what he did. It got a little bigger than he thought. He's ecstatic, of course, to see you being crucified, but he realizes there is some danger to himself as well. Right, Ben? He was an accomplice to this cover-up too. Meanwhile, Ben Tyson has figured out a way to finally settle the score. Right, Ben?"

"What do you mean, Vince?"

Corva pointed his finger at Tyson. "You know fucking well what I mean. I mean that you intend for the trial of Benjamin Tyson to also be the trial of Steven Brandt. Right?"

"You're very bright, Vince, even if you are Italian."

"And you're very, very vindictive for a coolheaded WASP, Ben. Christ, a Sicilian would wait twenty years to carry out a vendetta, but . . ." He shook his head. "I think you're nuts. But if this is what you want . . . you must want it bad. Bad enough that you did damned little to fight your recall to duty, damned little to show Harper you were a victim of a man who hates you, and damned little to try to make a deal with the government. Now I see *your* motive."

Tyson handed Corva his umbrella. "You may be partly right, of course. But it's all rather complex. I need this court-martial for me too. *Capice?*"

"Sure." Corva opened the door. "Well, it's still two hundred dollars an hour and double for court time even if you are nuts and even if you are enjoying yourself."

"Hardly that, Vince, and I'm still counting on you to save me in the end."

Corva laughed without humor, turned, and left, calling back, "Sign in at post headquarters. Now!"

"Thanks for lunch." Tyson closed the door, turned, and stared at the empty room. "Yes, Brandt and I will take each other down together; but only one of us will rise again."

39

Ben Tyson put his coffee cup on the white tablecloth and looked out the picture window of the Officers' Club dining room. White sea gulls soared against the gray sky, dived, and skimmed the whitecaps of the choppy Narrows. "Birds are free."

"Very profound," observed Corva as he helped himself to Tyson's toast. He looked up from his omelet and commented, "That uniform is hanging a little loose on you, Lieutenant."

"I'll see my tailor."

Corva pointed at Tyson's ribbons with his fork. "What is that there? Is that the gook cross?"

"Yes, the Vietnamese Cross of Gallantry. We don't say gook anymore, Vince."

"I know that." Corva swallowed a forkful of eggs. "Odd, isn't it? Wearing an award given by a country that no longer exists. Does that mean the award no longer exists? Makes you think."

"About what?"

"About the transient nature of things we think are forever. About Babylon and Rome, Carthage and Saigon."

"Ho Chi Minh City."

"Precisely." Corva went back to his breakfast.

Tyson poured more coffee. He asked, "Did you get a medal for valor?"

Corva nodded slowly. "Bronze Star."

"Tell me a war story."

Corva said, "There are two versions of that story. One version got me the Bronze Star."

"And the other version?"

"Would have got me . . . well, anyway, it had to do with tunnels. Tunnel complex near Dak To. Gooks would narrow the tunnels at some points so only gooks could get through. Well, I'm gook-sized. So I belly into this tight fucking hole, slithering like a worm, a silenced forty-five in one hand. Dark as hell, right? So I snap on my miner's lamp to take a quick look, and I'm face-to-face with Charles." Corva put sugar in his coffee.

Tyson said, "You're not going to tell me the rest, are you?"

Corva smiled mischievously. "No. No war stories." He leaned toward Tyson. "Do you know why the Italian Army lost in World War II?"

"No, Vince, why did the Italian Army lose in World War II?"

"They ordered ziti instead of shells."

Tyson lit a cigarette. "I don't get it."

Corva shrugged. He looked around the dining room. "Do you know who's behind you? Don't look."

"How many guesses do I get?"

"Having breakfast on the far side along the wall are Colonel Pierce, Major Weinroth, and Captain Longo."

"What are they eating? Babies?"

Corva observed, "We're going to have to share this dining room with them for some time if they hold the court-martial here at Hamilton. If you run into them in the club, be aggressively sociable—'Good morning, Colonel. Captain, do you have a light? Major Weinroth, may I suggest you visit the post beauty parlor?' " Corva laughed. "Well, don't say that. But you know what I mean. The Patriots' Bar is a little tight, and so are the urinals in the men's room, and you're going to be rubbing elbows with these people."

"Maybe they'll take a liking to me. Do you think Major Weinroth will use the men's room urinal?"

"Quite possibly. And I think Pierce and Longo squat to piss. Point is, Army facilities for courts-martial are such that I've seen a lot of awkward encounters. I mean, here's this guy Pierce trying to put you away for life, and you find yourself squeezed into a corner of the bar with him. Same goes for the prosecution witnesses and our witnesses. You and the dirty half dozen might run across Brandt or Farley."

Tyson nodded.

"Farley is in a wheelchair so you can't touch him."

"Can I beat the shit out of Brandt?"

Corva rubbed his nose thoughtfully. He said, "Do what you feel you have to do to Brandt if your paths cross. I can't tell you what to do."

Tyson looked toward the dining room entrance. Corva followed his gaze. Standing at the door waiting to be seated was Karen Harper. With her was a handsome older man in uniform.

Corva said, "That's the Article 32 investigating officer, Colonel Gilmer. And the broad looks familiar too."

"We don't call them broads anymore."

"Right. What's wrong with me this morning?"

The hostess was escorting them to a table near Tyson and Corva's, but Colonel Gilmer said something to the hostess. She pointed to another table near Pierce. Gilmer shook his head, and after some discussion he and Harper found a neutral corner.

Corva said, "Christ, somebody ought to brief the staff here."

Tyson watched Karen Harper sit in the chair pulled out for her by Gilmer. As Gilmer came around to his chair, she looked at Tyson, and their eyes met across the room. She smiled first: the sort of brief but intimate smile old lovers pass to each other in restaurants when they are with their new lovers.

Tyson put on a smile he hoped was passable, though he didn't know how he felt toward her.

Corva nodded to Karen Harper and Colonel Gilmer. Corva said, "He looks as uptight as he sounds on the phone. I'm going to have fun with this guy." He added, "She *is* a beautiful woman. I wonder why she never married. Probably fucks her brains out."

Tyson said coolly, "You really are a Neanderthal this morning."

"I know. I'm psyching myself."

Tyson glanced at his watch. "It's a few minutes after eight. What are we supposed to do for the next hour?"

"I've arranged to have a conference room at our disposal. Here in the club. We'll sit and chat. And at precisely five to nine we will enter the fittingly named Stonewall Jackson room. By noon we will be back here for lunch."

"Why don't you get fat? You eat like a horse."

"I weigh two hundred pounds. But it's all muscle." Corva stared across the room at Colonel Pierce for a while.

Tyson said, "I want to see what they look like." He turned in his chair at the same time Pierce looked toward him. Tyson didn't turn away, but Pierce did. Tyson looked back to Corva and commented, "They look grim."

"That's how prosecutors are supposed to look; like they are doing society's dirty work." Corva asked, "Did you hear from Marcy this morning?"

Tyson shook his head. "She never calls when she's traveling on business. I don't call her when I'm traveling either. It's a rule."

"What kind of rule is that?"

"The kind of rule some couples who travel eventually discover."

Corva bobbed his head slowly. "I don't know if I would want my wife traveling. Is that insecure?"

"Yes."

"I'm an old-fashioned dago."

"That's your problem."

"Is your mind on this hearing?"

"Absolutely."

Corva finished his coffee. "Let's go." He motioned for the waitress, and for some reason got all five of them, plus three busboys and the hostess.

There was a stillness in the dining room as the hostess stepped forward and spoke. "Lieutenant Tyson, we all would like to wish you the best of luck and to let you know it has been a pleasure serving you, your wife, and son these last few months. We want you to know that we all think you are an officer and a gentleman." She led the small group in a brief round of applause.

Tyson stood and to his surprise felt a lump form in his throat. He reached out to the woman and gave her a spontaneous hug and a peck on the cheek. She blushed and said, "Oh . . . my. . . ."

Tyson said hoarsely, "Thank you all so much."

Corva started another round of applause, and this time a few of the diners joined in. The staff bowed in unison, turned, and left.

Tyson remained standing. His eyes fell on the table where Pierce, Weinroth, and Longo sat. They were eating their breakfast with exaggerated obliviousness. On the opposite side of the room, Colonel Gilmer studied the breakfast menu with intensity. Karen Harper gave him a quick wink.

Corva stood. "How does such a snob like you inspire such loyalty in the masses?"

"I'm handsome."

"Yes, like Billy Budd. They hanged him, though." Corva picked up his briefcase. "Well, I don't see a chit, so I guess there is such a thing as a free breakfast." He led the way out of the dining room.

They made their way to the northeast corner of what had been the old fort and approached a heavy oak door. Corva said, "I have to go upstairs and pick up some paperwork. Go on in. There is supposed to be coffee and pastry laid on. I'll be back in a few minutes." He turned and walked quickly away.

Tyson stepped up to the door. He didn't know who or what was behind the door, but it wasn't just coffee and pastry. He glanced back and saw Corva disappear around the corner. He opened the door and recognized the room.

It was an old powder magazine with walls of reinforced concrete, painted a nice beige now, with a royal blue carpet on the floor.

The room was dimly lit by a floor lamp, but an odd glow emanated from the ceiling which Tyson knew was a result of the ceiling being constructed of glass rods embedded in thick concrete; a means to let the daylight in so oil lamps did not have to be used in the powder room.

They were all sitting at a round table, drinking coffee, eating, and talking in low voices. A miasma of cigarette smoke hung in the air, enhancing the feeling that he'd stepped into a dream.

Tyson shut the door behind him. The talking had stopped, and the men sat self-consciously in silence, fidgeting with cigarettes and coffee cups.

Paul Sadowski smiled and stood. He bellowed, "Ten-hut!" The other four rose hesitantly and stood, not at attention, but not at ease either.

Tyson took a few steps into the room. Sadowski, he saw, had gotten huge. His hair was thinning, and he sported a mustache that looked like two arched caterpillars. He was wearing what had to be the last leisure suit in the country.

Tony Scorello was thin as ever, but had sprouted a thick black beard to replace the hair that was missing from his nearly bald pate. Tyson wouldn't have recognized him except for the big brown doe eyes. He was well dressed in gray slacks and navy blazer but wore, in place of a tie, a heavy gold chain.

Louis Kalane looked remarkably the same, his Polynesian features having become, if anything, more handsome. He had a full shock of jet-black hair and wore a taupe-colored suit of worsted wool in a style that Tyson had never seen in New York.

Lee Walker hadn't changed much either, though the seventeen-year-old that

Tyson had known was now a little taller and a little more muscular. Walker wore a maroon polyester suit with a spread-collar shirt.

Hernando Beltran looked very old, and it took Tyson by surprise. His face was puffy, and beneath the finely tailored pearl-gray suit lurked a fat man. Beltran sported gold rings and a Rolex oyster. He was smiling from ear to ear, showing a gold-capped tooth.

My God, thought Tyson, *how do I look to them?*

Sadowski stepped forward as if this had been rehearsed. He came to an exaggerated position of attention, sucked in his stomach, puffed his chest out, and saluted. "Sergeant Sadowski reports, sir!"

Out of old habit, Tyson wanted to remind him that the "sir" came first in the American Army, and last only in old British war movies. Instead Tyson returned the salute without comment. He said, "At ease."

Sadowski reached out and took Tyson's hand, grasping it firmly and pumping his arm.

Tyson wished Corva was in the room—not so Corva could share this moment with him, but so Tyson could beat the shit out of him. Tyson gave Sadowski a warm look. "How you doing, Ski?"

"Fine, Lieutenant."

"Ben."

"Ben." He laughed. "Sounds funny."

Tyson walked to the table, and Beltran grasped him by the shoulders. "You borrowed twenty dollars from me, *amigo.* With compounded interest that is now two million dollars." He laughed deeply.

Tyson took his hand. *"Cómo está, amigo?"*

"Oh, you speak Spanish now?"

"No, Puerto Rican." He patted Beltran's stomach. "How are you going to carry an M-60 with that?"

Beltran laughed as he patted his own stomach. "Good living. I own half of West Miami. You come down, and I show you a hell of a time." He winked.

Tyson turned to Lee Walker. "How you been, Ghost?"

"Not too bad, Lieutenant—Ben. I don't own half of nothing, but if you come down to Macon, I'll take you bird shooting. You still good with a shotgun?"

"We can find out. I'd like that." Tyson moved around the table to Louis Kalane and took his hand. Tyson pulled at the lapel of his elegant suit. "You dealing dope again, Pineapple?"

Everyone laughed.

Kalane smiled abashedly. "Just got lucky with them turkey mainlanders. I run tours. Come check it out." He added, "You look pretty nifty yourself, Lieutenant." He grinned. "Where'd you get all those medals?"

"You don't remember that war?" Tyson moved to Scorello. They shook hands, and Scorello mumbled, "Nice seeing you again."

Tyson replied, "Same here, Tony. You're living in Frisco, right? Great town."

"Right. I work for the city."

"How long have you had that pussy tickler?"

Scorello forced a smile. "Long time."

They all stood in silence awhile, then Tyson said, "Thanks for coming," though of course they had little choice. He said, "I didn't know any of you would be here." He thought that Corva must have switched tactics. He asked, "Are you testifying today?"

Beltran spoke. "No, no. Mr. Corva just asked us to come and say hello to you. A little reunion." He added, "But we will be back for the court-martial to testify."

Again, no one spoke. Tyson said, "There may be no court-martial."

"Good," said Beltran.

Sadowski said, "Sit down. Have some coffee. Hey, this fort is something else. Looks like those old Frenchie forts around Quang Tri."

Tyson sat at an empty place, and everyone sat. He drew coffee from a silver urn.

Beltran looked around the table as though he were at a board meeting. He said, "So this is it. Out of forty-five men, this is what is left of the first platoon of Alpha Company, Fifth Battalion of the Seventh Cavalry. *Mi Dios,* Custer had more survivors."

A few men laughed halfheartedly.

Sadowski said, "Don't forget Kelly and DeTonq. They're out there someplace."

Scorello snorted. "DeTonq is dead, Ski. He never made it back. Kelly is probably dead, too."

No one spoke until Walker said quietly, "There's Doc and Red, too."

The room was silent again until Beltran smashed his fist on the table. "Those *maricones!* Doc I could understand. He was not one of us. But Red—that I cannot understand."

Tyson watched them through the haze of blue smoke caused by Beltran's cigar. He searched their faces for something, though he didn't know what. Perhaps there was a little guilt there, but mostly there was defiance, self-justification. If you couldn't justify the cold-blooded murder of babies, children, and women, then you died inside, or you died like Harold Simcox—inside and outside. Tyson said, "Smallpox was almost here." He looked at Scorello. "He was a buddy of yours, wasn't he, Tony?"

Scorello played with his beard. "Didn't hear from him much the last few years. He got fucked up."

Tyson took out a cigarette, and Kalane lit it with a gold Dunhill. Tyson said, "I guess you know how Moody died."

No one replied. Tyson had the impression that everyone was ambivalent about this reunion. Tyson asked, "How did Brontman and Selig die?" He looked around the table.

Sadowski answered, "Freddie died at Khe Sanh. Got hit by one of those little sixty-millimeter mortars the gooks liked so much. Selig was killed in the A Shau Valley. What a fucking mess that was, Lieutenant! Fucking gooks had armor, quad fifties, all kinds of bad shit. Selig stepped on a land mine. They sent him home in an envelope."

Tyson drew on his cigarette.

Kalane added, "You thought Hue was bad. Let me tell you, the A Shau sucked major cock. Khe Sahn was no picnic either. You missed the good stuff."

Tyson nodded. "I've always been lucky."

Sadowski continued the oral history of Alpha Company. "After you left, we got sent to Evans for rest and refitting. Some dork named Neely became CO. Then they sent four new second lieutenants out; bunch of fucking cherries right out of OCS; looked about sixteen years old. Then they sent us a hundred replacements, all pfc's, not a sergeant among them, and they're still pissing water from infantry school. Well, fuck it, by that time I got transferred to the rear, and Hideaway rotated home. Ghost . . . where'd you go?"

Walker replied, "Unloading ships at Wonder Beach."

"Right. And Tony . . ."

Scorello said to Tyson curtly, "I shot myself in the fucking foot. Got court-martialed and did a month in Long Binh."

Tyson didn't respond.

They settled into a more relaxed atmosphere, telling a few war stories, talking about family and jobs.

Beltran took a cigar out of his breast pocket and handed it to Tyson. "Real *Habana.* Got contacts there." He winked in a conspiratorial way. Beltran liked to wink, Tyson remembered. Beltran expanded on the wink. "I still fight communists. I finance anti-Castro groups. I know how to fight those godless pigs even if the *maricones* in Washington don't."

Tyson put the cigar in his inside pocket.

Beltran said, "We killed a lot of communists at Hue, so what the hell are they complaining about now?"

No one seemed to have an answer.

Finally Walker spoke. "Lieutenant, we want you to know we . . . we were talking, and like we decided, it's nobody's business what happened. We'll stand up for you, like you did for us."

Kalane said, "When you got evacuated . . . I told the guys you were going to squeal. But the MPs never came, and we're not going to forget that."

Beltran looked around the table and declared, "If they tortured me, roasted me on hot coals, I would not betray this man."

Sadowski said, "When that Major Harper called me on the phone, I nearly shit." He laughed and looked at Tyson. "My lawyer explained why they're nailing your ass to the wall and not ours. My fucking lawyer said to cooperate with the government."

A few heads nodded.

Sadowski continued, "But I told him where to put that idea."

Tyson had the impression everyone wanted him to know they were doing him a favor. Or repaying the favor he did for them. But if they hadn't obliterated a hospital full of people in the first place, there would be no favors to repay. Tyson looked at Scorello, who hadn't offered any favors so far.

Scorello looked away and said, "Let's stop the bullshit here. We're not going to talk because . . . because we have jobs and families and all. I work for a liberal city government. And things have been a little tough for me since this thing broke and my name got mentioned. Yeah, we'll help the lieutenant. But we're here to cover our own asses again, too." He looked at Tyson. "I had a kid when I was sent to Nam. I'm divorced now, but that kid—a son—is twenty-one. He's heard all the wild whore stories and all the times I shot it out with Charlie. Now he wants to know what the fuck I did there on February fifteenth."

Sadowski said, "I have a kind of sensitive wife. She cries a lot when she sees this shit on TV. When they say we killed the kids . . ." Sadowski cleared his throat. "This sucks."

Beltran rubbed his double chin. He said, "It does no good to speak of this. We all know what we have to do. Maybe you are doing it to save your reputations. In Miami I get no flak. So I am doing it only for Ben Tyson." He nodded with finality.

Tyson marveled that this was the same man who wanted to machine-gun him in the hospital. Well, he thought, people grow up.

Sadowski suddenly blurted, "I'd like to kill that fucking Doc. And that shithead Red."

Everyone looked at Tyson as if they wanted a second to the motion. Tyson said nothing.

Sadowski continued, "I know guys in Chicago who would break their fucking legs and arms . . . but I want them . . . wasted." Sadowski turned to Beltran. "You got any guys who can do something about those two fucks?"

Beltran sat back with his hands on his paunch. He nodded slowly and winked.

Tyson looked at them, each in turn. Any five men who had not been to war would have been shocked at the turn the conversation had taken. But these were not any five men.

Walker said, "Only Doc. Not Red."

Scorello cleared his throat. "It should happen before the court-martial."

Kalane looked at Beltran. "I'll pay for it. You arrange it."

Tyson thought he ought to say something sane. "I don't think that will make us feel any better."

Kalane leaned across the table. "We gave our word, Ben, on pain of death. We weren't fucking around then. We're not fucking around now. That fuck Brandt gave his word. What the *fuck* makes him think he can break it without something happening to him?"

Tyson didn't think this was the time to mention that Corva wanted him to tell the whole story if he were convicted.

Kalane added, "Listen, Ben, I wanted you dead that night after the hospital thing. Not because I didn't like you. I liked you a lot. But I liked me more. If *I* had shot my mouth off like Brandt, I would deserve to get wasted, too."

Tyson looked around the table. He spoke in a voice that he hoped still had some of the old command authority in it. "I covered for you *once.* I failed to do my duty *once.* But not again. If anything happens to Brandt or Farley, you might as well put me on your list, too, because by God I'll see to it that you all go to jail this time."

No one met his eyes and no one spoke. Finally, Scorello said, "Enough of this, for Christ's sake. Enough of this kind of talk. We're not killers."

No one seemed to know how to reply to that remarkable statement. Tyson stared at the blue smoke hanging above the table, and his eyes drifted upward to the concrete ceiling with the small circles of thick glass, like blue-green bottle bottoms.

Tyson looked up at the pinpoint of light on the domed ceiling of the bunker and was reminded of a bright star in the night sky of the Hayden Planetarium. He guessed that an armor-piercing shell had once made a direct hit on the foot-thick rounded concrete top of the pillbox, probably during some long-forgotten engagement between the French and Viet Minh.

Someone struck a match, and the sudden phosphorus flare gave several of the men a start. A candle was lit, and its wax was puddled on the floor, then the candle was stuck in it. The small flame seemed inordinately bright and cast shadows of the men along the round wall.

Tyson lit a cigarette with the lighter his platoon had given him. *Yea, though I walk through the valley of the shadow of death, I fear no evil for . . . for I am the meanest . . . for Thou art with me.*

Tyson leaned back against the clammy concrete and drew his knees up to his chest. He smelled, as much as saw, the wet canvas field gear strewn around the bunker. In the half light he picked out each of his men: Kelly to his right, Brandt to his left, both sitting with their backs to the wall. Spaced along the wall, also sitting, were Beltran, Scorello, Sadowski, Holzman, Brontman, Selig, Walker, Simcox, Kalane, Santos, Manelli, and DeTonq. Opposite him, about fifteen feet across the floor, was Richard

Farley sitting between the poncho-wrapped bodies of Cane and
Peterson. Moody lay on the floor in front of him and Brandt,
moaning softly. Tyson leaned over to Brandt and said softly, "Is
he going to be all right until morning?"

Brandt replied in a whisper, "I'm just afraid of blood poisoning. Otherwise he's okay."

Tyson leaned forward and spoke to Moody, "How you doing,
kid?"

Moody took a few seconds to answer, then spoke through a
morphine-induced haze. "Oh . . . Lieutenant . . . feeling bad
and good . . . send me home . . . checking out. . . ."

"Okay," replied Tyson. "Home."

"Sign the orders."

"Okay. Doc and I will both sign the orders."

"Browder too."

"Browder too," said Tyson.

"No fuckups."

"No fuckups." Tyson whispered to Brandt, "Home?"

"No," replied Brandt. "Fit for duty in a few weeks. Superficial.
Just worried about the blood poisoning."

Tyson leaned back against the wall again and drew on his cigarette. There were four long narrow gun slits at eye level, and
DeTonq was now peering out of the one facing Hue, Sadowski
out of the opposite one facing An Ninh Ha. Tyson could see the
flames and flares of night battle flickering at the gun slits, and he
heard the rumble of impacting artillery and air strikes. He
thought it was a bad sign that the only two sergeants in the platoon were doing what they should have ordered their men to do.

Scorello spoke softly, "Doc?"

"Yeah."

"Are they going to stink?"

Brandt replied, "Yeah. They're dead."

"Can't we put them outside?"

Farley's voice cut through the damp air. "No! The animals'll
get them."

Brandt said, "Double-bag them. Two ponchos each, twist-tie
them at both ends. No guarantee though."

A few of the men moved toward the two bodies and did as
Brandt instructed.

Tyson stubbed out his cigarette on the floor and felt for the
handle of his .45 automatic in his holster. He wondered if they
knew Kelly had given it to him. He wondered, too, if he'd use it
or if he'd even have a chance to use it. He heard whispering
around him and had the feeling that the whispering could end in
the crack of a rifle shot. He worked his logbook out of his back
pocket, drew his legs up farther, and made an entry, then slipped
the book under his shirt into his waistband.

The night passed slowly. Boots came off, feet were dried, socks
changed, and boots were put back on. A few heat tablets were lit,
and canteen cups of water were boiled over them. The smell of
tea, coffee, and cocoa competed with the noxious fumes of the
tablets, the moldy concrete, and the stink of fear given off by
seventeen bodies.

A card game started but broke up quickly. A few other men took turns at the gun slits. A few men went out into the rain to urinate or vomit. The radio speaker, its volume turned to the lowest setting, still filled the bunker with a continuous electronic crackling. Every half hour, Browder's radio operator would call the platoons for a situation report.

Tyson noticed the acrid smell of the local marijuana, but he didn't think he was in a position to make any arrests. In fact, he thought ironically, the more they smoked, the better he liked it. He pulled his fifth of Scotch from his rucksack, took a short pull, and passed it to Kelly. Kelly drank some and passed it to his right. By the time it went around the wall and reached Brandt beside him, it was empty. Someone said, "Hope Charlie don't hit us," then laughed. A few other men laughed, but Tyson thought the laughs sounded shallow.

The radio came alive again. "Mustang One-Six-India, this is Six-India," the voice said, identifying itself as Browder's radio operator. "Put your Six on for my Six, please." Kelly hesitated, then handed the radiophone to Tyson. The bunker fell silent as Browder's voice came on in those low, distinct tones used at night in the field. "One-Six, this is Six. I need some details of your contact for Big Six."

Tyson licked his lips and spoke into the phone, "Roger. Can't it wait until morning? We're trying to be quiet here."

"Roger, that. I'll advise Battalion. You people okay?"

"Roger. But I've got listening posts out there. Hear lots of movement. If we make further contact, you'll hear from us loud and clear. Meanwhile, negative sit rep," said Tyson in what he hoped sounded like an impatient tone.

"Roger. Keep cool. Dawn's coming."

"Right, over."

"Roger, out."

Tyson handed the phone back to Kelly. Kelly said, "As we approached the hospital, we took heavy fire. Peterson and Moody were hit. We took cover and returned the fire. There was a sizable enemy force in the building. We didn't know it was a hospital. Lieutenant?"

Tyson spoke in the quiet bunker. "There was a sizable enemy force in the building. I decided on an assault. We fired and maneuvered toward the structure. We got inside and engaged the enemy in room-to-room fighting. Sadowski?"

"We got inside and engaged the enemy in room-to-room fighting. DeIonq?"

"We got inside and engaged the enemy in room-to-room fighting. Beltran?"

"We got inside and engaged the enemy in room-to-room fighting. Kalane?"

The litany continued as Tyson listened. When it came around to him again he added another line and again the congregation responded.

The hours passed, partly in silent thought, partly in restructuring the details of what had happened inside the hospital. Tyson noticed that the ponchos that shrouded the two bodies were bloating like balloons. He noticed, too, that the men had become lethargic—a natural result of fatigue, marijuana, and post-stress behavior. They also seemed receptive to anything he said. Hour by hour he was regaining control.

A false dawn, peculiar to the tropics, broke through the east-facing gun slit, then it became very dark, the darkest hour. Tyson said, "The structure was completely burned, and there are no weapons or bodies to turn in. But I estimate an enemy body count of twelve."

Kelly said, "That sounds about right. Ski?"

Sadowski actually seemed to think about it before replying, "Are you counting the two that Kalane killed with the frag?"

Kalane said, "I reported those two, didn't I, Lieutenant?"

"Yes," replied Tyson, "I have those two." Tyson lit his cigarette and drank some tepid canteen water. He said, "We pursued the fleeing enemy toward Hue but lost their trail."

"Right," said DeTonq. "I spotted this old bunker half covered with growth, and we decided to check it out."

"We moved toward it carefully," said Beltran. "Walker, he throws a concussion grenade inside, then we rush it."

"It was empty," said Walker. "So we decided to hole up here 'cause we were pretty beat."

Tyson watched the gun slits. The fires of the night faded as the sky lightened with the new dawn. The rain had stopped, and there was an odd stillness outside as the enemy made their usual dawn withdrawals.

Tyson stared at the sputtering candle awhile, then moved in a crouch to the center of the bunker near the candle. Kelly, then Sadowski, drew toward him, followed by DeTonq, then the remainder of the men. Tyson put his hand out, and Kelly put his on top of his lieutenant's. Tyson watched as each man put his hand into the circle, and Tyson looked at each face in the light of the wavering candle. He did not know precisely what he felt for these men, but the overpowering emotion seemed to be pity. Tyson spoke in measured tones. "We give our word as soldiers, as brothers, as comrades in arms, as men, as friends, as fellow sufferers, and maybe as Christians. And we know what we are giving our word about. And it is forever. Kelly?"

"I give my word. Doc?"

"I give my word. Sadowski?"

"I give my word. DeTonq?"

"I give my word. Beltran?"

Hernando Beltran said, "Any one of us could have gone running to the colonel and told on the others. But we gave our word that night. And our lips were to be sealed to our death. I told no one, not even a priest. So I have this mortal sin on my soul . . . this killing of nuns. . . . And I must pray each day that God will forgive me when I meet Him. If He does not, then I am damned for eternity. This I did for us."

Tyson listened for a while as they spoke, then said abruptly, "Enough. We'll discuss Brandt at another time." He switched to a mundane subject. "Where are you all staying?"

Sadowski answered, "The Army put us up at the guest house here. We got in last night. But your lawyer told us to make it a surprise."

Beltran added, "I want to take you all to a Cuban restaurant in the city, called Victor's. Then we go to another place for something else." He turned to Tyson, but Tyson winked at him first and Beltran laughed. "Yeah! You coming, okay?"

Tyson said, "I'm under house arrest. But I can take you to dinner here at the club tonight."

Kalane smiled. "They don't let pfc's in here, Lieutenant."

Tyson said, "They do if pfc means private fucking civilian."

Everyone laughed. They made small talk for a while. The door opened and Corva entered. He looked around the table, and his eyes rested on Tyson's.

Sadowski called out, "Another fucking officer. Right, Vince?"

Corva smiled. "Right, Ski. First Lieutenant, infantry. The Twenty-fifth Division—Jungle Lightning. Best outfit in the fucking Nam."

There were groans and jeers from the five men. Beltran said, "The Cav was the number-one ass kickers, and you know that if you were really in the Nam."

Kalane added, "Charlie shit when he saw the Cav coming."

Corva pointed at Tyson's First Cavalry shoulder patch, a shield-shaped emblem with a black horse's head above a diagonal black stripe against a color known as cavalry yellow. "See this?" He tapped the horse's head. "This is the horse that you never rode . . ." He ran his finger along the diagonal stripe. ". . . this is the line you couldn't hold. And the yellow speaks for itself."

"Oh, bullshit!" snapped Sadowski.

"Fuck you!" said Kalane.

"Eat shit," suggested Walker.

Corva held up his hand. "Just joking, men. Old Army joke. Everybody was jealous of the Cav."

"Fucking-ay-right," said Kalane.

Corva glanced at his watch. "Well, time to go." He said to the five men, "I'd appreciate it if you'd hang out here, though I don't think I'll be calling on you."

Tyson stood, and the other men rose also. Beltran produced a fifth of rum from his attaché case and emptied it into seven fresh coffee cups. "A little toast, gentlemen." He raised the delicate cup in his beefy hand with the style of a man who is used to presenting toasts. He said, "A toast to the dead—God forgive me, but I can't remember all their names, but He knows who they are."

They all drank. Walker said, "And good luck to you, Lieutenant."

Corva put down his cup and picked up his briefcase. "Well, into the valley of death rode the First Cavalry."

Tyson shook hands with each man and left with Corva.

Out in the corridor Corva said, "Good to see unit pride."

"It's remarkable after nearly two decades."

"Yes, isn't it?" He added, "It can't hurt us at the court-martial either." Corva asked, "Were you happily surprised?"

"I wanted to beat the shit out of you."

"But you looked like you were having a good time."

"Well . . . I *was* glad to see them again after the initial awkwardness."

"They seem like a fine bunch of men."

Tyson walked in silence awhile, then said, "They are all murderers."

"Yes, but they are our murderers."

They climbed the stairs and stopped at the door of the reception room marked "Stonewall Jackson."

Corva said, "Look everyone in the eye when you enter. It's not necessary to salute Colonel Gilmer. Our table is on the right as you walk in. Any questions?"

"How did I get here?"

"You took the long way." Corva opened the door, and they entered.

40

It was a large handsome room with a highly polished wood floor, used for informal receptions and stag smokers. The front wall was brick with a fieldstone fireplace. The other walls were paneled in dark wood. Flanking the fireplace toward the ends of the brick wall were French windows with fanlights. Above the fireplace, appropriately enough, was an oil portrait of Thomas "Stonewall" Jackson, who once served at Fort Hamilton before heading south.

In front of the fireplace was a podium, and behind the podium stood Colonel Farnley Gilmer. To Gilmer's right was a bridge table at which sat Major Karen Harper.

Tyson and Corva took their places at a long banquet table along the right-hand wall. Directly across from them along the left wall was another banquet table at which sat Colonel Pierce, Major Weinroth, and Captain Longo. To the prosecution's left front, Tyson noticed, was a court reporter, a pretty young pfc with blond hair, freckles, and a sexy overbite, sitting at a portable olive-drab field desk of the type Tyson remembered from Vietnam. Other than the uniforms, that desk, and perhaps the oil painting of Jackson, there was nothing in the room to suggest a martial event was taking place.

The banquet tables were covered with floor-length white linen tablecloths. Tyson detected the faint odor of beer and stale smoke in the air.

In the far rear of the room were stacked about a hundred folding chairs. One of them had been opened and placed between the defense and prosecution tables, facing the podium. This, Tyson assumed, was the witness chair. An American flag on a stand had been positioned behind Karen Harper's table.

Between the flag and the door, standing at a modified position of parade rest, was a young black sergeant in dress greens. Tyson assumed he was the sergeant at arms, though he was not armed and wore no helmet as he'd seen at courts-martial he'd witnessed.

Tyson noticed that the defense, prosecution, and investigating team were spaced far enough apart so that private talk carried on in a low voice could not be heard by the other parties.

Colonel Gilmer looked at his watch.

Tyson looked at Karen Harper, but she was reading something in her lap.

Pierce, Weinroth, and Longo had their heads together and were conferring.

The court reporter hit a few keys on her stenotype.

Vincent Corva was making notes on some typed papers. He put his pencil down, leaned toward Tyson, and whispered, "Ziti instead of shells. Why don't you get that?"

Colonel Gilmer said, "Good morning. We are here to conduct a formal investigation into certain charges against Lieutenant Benjamin J. Tyson, ordered pursuant to Article 32b of the Uniform Code of Military Justice."

Colonel Gilmer looked at Tyson. "Lieutenant, you were informed of your right to be represented by civilian counsel at no expense to the United States or by military counsel of your own selection if reasonably available or by military counsel detailed by the Staff Judge Advocate at Fort Dix. You stated that you desire to be represented by Mr. Vincent Corva of New York City."

Tyson regarded Gilmer a moment. He was about sixty, with short gray hair, a pleasant square face but a vacuous expression.

Gilmer continued, "Let the record show that Mr. Corva is present here with you." Gilmer looked toward Corva. "Mr. Corva, I will ask you to step forward and enter your appearance by filling out item three on the official Investigating Officer's Report."

Corva stood and walked to Harper's table. They exchanged a few words that Tyson couldn't hear, and Harper slid a form toward Corva.

Tyson looked across the room and saw that Colonel Pierce was looking at him pensively. Tyson continued to stare at Pierce. He was not more than fifty years old, a young colonel. He had dark red hair and wore it longer than the Army would have liked. He affected a pair of reading glasses, but Tyson had seen him reading with and without them at the same distance. His complexion was strikingly red, and Tyson couldn't tell if he'd been out in the sun too long or had dangerously high blood pressure.

Corva returned to the table and took his seat.

Colonel Gilmer referred to a procedural guide and began reading, glancing at Tyson from time to time. "Lieutenant, I want to remind you that my sole function as the Article 32 investigating officer in this case is to determine thoroughly and impartially all of the relevant facts of this case, to weigh and evaluate those facts, and determine the truth of the matters stated in the charges. I shall also consider the form of the charges and make a recommendation concerning the disposition of the charges which have been preferred against you. I will now read to you the charges which I have been directed to investigate. They are as follows: Violation of the Uniform Code of Military Justice, Article 118, murder. Specification One." Gilmer began reading the long, convoluted sentence of the first specification. Tyson tuned out and focused instead on Major Judith Weinroth.

She was about forty, he guessed, and he saw no wedding ring, though that meant nothing anymore. The uniform looked awful on her, and Corva was right about recommending her to the post beauty parlor. Her expression was serious, all businesslike, the expression of the professional woman. But as he looked at her, Pierce whispered something in her ear, and she smiled one of the brightest, prettiest little-girl smiles Tyson had ever seen, and her whole face radiated beauty. But then the smile faded, and the face looked forbidding again.

Gilmer finished reading the second specification and said, "Lieutenant Tyson, I will now show you the charge and specifications."

Karen Harper stood and walked across the polished floor. She stopped in front of Tyson and presented him with the charge sheet. Tyson took it with his outstretched hand as he turned to Corva and said loud enough for everyone to hear, "Don't we have one of these?"

Corva said, "You can always use an extra one."

The court reporter giggled, and Gilmer looked annoyed. Harper, too, seemed annoyed and gave Tyson a look to show it before she turned and went back to her chair.

Gilmer let a full minute pass, during which time Tyson was supposed to read the charge sheet to himself. Instead, he looked at Captain Salvatore Longo. He was young, perhaps in his late twenties, and probably not too long out of law school. His uniform seemed perfectly tailored, and his curly blue-black hair was perfectly styled. His skin was deeply tanned in the way that Tyson had seen only on people who did a lot of boating. Tyson didn't think he was handsome, but he had no doubt Captain Longo had no trouble with women.

Colonel Gilmer again referred to something hidden behind the podium and said, "Lieutenant Tyson, I advise you that you do not have to make any statement regarding the offense of which you are accused and that any statement you do make may be used as evidence against you in a trial by court-martial. You have the right to remain silent concerning the offenses with which you are charged. You may, however, make a statement either sworn or unsworn and present anything you may desire, either in defense, extenuation, or mitigation. If you do make a statement, whatever you say will be considered and weighed as evidence by me just as is the testimony of other witnesses." Colonel Gilmer poured himself a glass of water.

Corva said into Tyson's ear, "What are the first five words a black guy hears after he puts on a three-piece suit?"

"What?"

"Will the defendant please rise?"

Tyson put his hand over his mouth. "Cut it out."

Gilmer was looking at the defense table with impatience. He said, "Lieutenant Tyson, do I have your attention?"

"Yes, sir."

"Good. Your defense attorney, Mr. Corva, and the government attorneys, Colonel Pierce, Major Weinroth, and Captain Longo, have previously been given a copy of the investigation file which has thus far been compiled in your case. It contains the sworn statements of Dr. Steven Brandt—"

Corva stood. "Objection, sir."

Colonel Gilmer's eyebrows rose quizzically. *"What* is your objection, Mr. Corva?"

"My objection is to the use of the title 'Doctor' in regard to Steven Brandt."

"Isn't . . . Steven Brandt a medical doctor?"

"He may well be, Colonel. That has no bearing on this case. At the time of the alleged incident, nearly twenty years ago, Steven Brandt was a specialist four. If we have frozen my client's rank as lieutenant, then we can freeze Brandt's rank as well. Or we may call him 'Mister' in these and any subsequent proceedings. I think you see my point."

Colonel Gilmer seemed to be trying to see the point.

Colonel Pierce rose. "Mr. Corva . . . is that all right? *Mister* Corva? Or would you prefer *Signore?"*

Weinroth and Longo laughed.

Corva replied, "You can call me Vince, Graham."

The court stenographer giggled again.

Gilmer looked as though he wanted to bang a gavel, but he had no gavel. He said, "There is a certain informality at an Article 32 hearing, but let's not overdo it, gentlemen. Colonel Pierce? Your point?"

"My point, Colonel, is that Mr. Corva's point is pointless and petty. If he's suggesting that the use of Steven Brandt's title is somehow prejudicial to his client, then I suggest he's too infatuated with medical doctors. I, for instance, might think medical doctors are arrogant, insensitive, and avaricious."

Gilmer turned to Corva.

Corva said, "I wonder if Colonel Pierce would repeat that in the presence of his star witness?"

This time Gilmer smiled. Karen Harper stood and came up beside him. They conferred in low tones. Colonel Gilmer said, "Major Harper informs me that Lieutenant Tyson made this point to her before he was represented by Mr. Corva. So we'll assume the accused has a real objection to the use of Steven Brandt's title in these proceedings, and I can appreciate his point. Therefore, from here on we will all use the term 'Mister' in referring to Steven Brandt. The issue is closed."

Colonel Gilmer began again. "The investigation file contains the sworn statements of Mr. Steven Brandt, Mr. Richard Farley, Mr. Paul Sadowski, Mr. Anthony Scorello, Mr. Hernando Beltran, Mr. Lee Walker, and Mr. Louis Kalane. The file also contains the unsworn statement of Mr. Andrew Picard. There is also in the file relevant documents, letters, and other incidental materials too numerous to identify individually." Gilmer looked at Corva. "Do you agree?"

"Yes, sir."

Gilmer continued, "I do not intend to call as witnesses Mr. Brandt or Mr. Farley, but intend rather to consider their sworn statements as contained in the file, in reaching my recommendation." Gilmer addressed Tyson and Corva. "Even though I do not intend to call Mr. Brandt or Mr. Farley, whose sworn statements I intend to consider in arriving at my recommendation, it is your right to have an opportunity to cross-examine the witnesses on matters limited to their written statements, if those witnesses are available. If you wish, I will arrange an appearance of those witnesses for that purpose. Do you want me to call Mr. Brandt and/or Mr. Farley as witnesses?"

Corva conferred with Tyson. "We could ask for them to be present, but that might take a week."

Tyson said, "I thought the prosecution was supposed to call prosecution witnesses."

"No, Gilmer slipped on his DA hat. Didn't you see that? He calls prosecution witnesses or doesn't call them. Of course he confers privately with the prosecution first."

Tyson said, "I keep looking at that American flag there just to be sure."

Corva smiled. "I thought I'd let you see a little of this so you can reconsider our strategy if you want. A few minutes ago Gilmer told you that you could present evidence in extenuation or mitigation. Did you catch that?"

"Yes. That's like assuming I'm already guilty, and would I like to make excuses for what I did."

"That's about the size of it. I'm glad you're paying attention. Also, if I call Brandt or Farley I can only cross-examine them based on what is contained in their written statements. At a court-martial I can get into the real issues."

Tyson nodded. "I don't want to delay this a week. Let's get on with it."

Corva stood. "Sir, for the record we do not accept the sworn statements of Mr. Brandt or Mr. Farley in lieu of their presence. However, we will waive our right to cross-examine them for the purposes of this hearing."

Colonel Gilmer addressed Karen Harper. "Mark Mr. Corva's statement as an exhibit under item 6A." He turned to Corva. "I may consider your statement in arriving at my recommendation."

"I hope, Colonel, you will also consider that the nature and seriousness of these charges is such that one would have expected you to call the government witnesses or have them present for cross-examination. It is most unusual to consider written statements alone in a case such as this."

Gilmer's face reddened slightly. "Well, then, do you want to call them for cross-examination or not?"

"No, sir. I think you should have called them so you could have examined them here in the presence of the accused. But if the written statements are cogent enough for you to consider how to proceed with an indictment for murder, then so be it. I only wish to register my utter amazement for the record."

Gilmer glared at Corva.

Pierce stood. "If it please the Colonel, I would like to register my own amazement that the counsel for the defense is questioning you on matters that are no concern of his."

Corva smiled at Pierce. "And no concern of yours. The colonel can take care of himself."

Tyson sat back in his chair. He was actually enjoying himself even if no one else was. He glanced at the court reporter and saw she was having fun too. She looked up from her machine and caught his eye. She smiled.

Colonel Gilmer tapped his fingers on the podium. "Will you both please take your seats?" He looked at Corva and said bluntly, "Do you want Brandt and Farley here? Yes or no?"

"No, sir."

Tyson leaned toward Corva. "Why are you busting everyone's balls?"

Corva was staring across the room at Pierce, and he replied without taking his eyes off Pierce, "I want to let Pierce know Vinnie Corva is back in town. As for busting Gilmer's balls, I want him to know we are not sitting still for any of this; that if there is to be a general court-martial, the counsel for the defense is going to attack the very form and substance of Army justice. That may give the people upstairs some second thoughts about a public trial."

Tyson said, "Can I smoke?"

"Why not? Gilmer and Pierce are blowing smoke."

Tyson produced the long fat cigar Beltran gave him and lit it. Great billows of blue-gray smoke rose in the air.

Gilmer regarded Tyson a moment, apparently trying to decide if he should tell Tyson to put it out. Gilmer let it go with a look of annoyance. He continued with the procedural manual. "Lieutenant Tyson, you also have the right to call available witnesses for my examination and to produce other evidence in your behalf. I have arranged for the appearance of those witnesses previously requested by you. If you desire additional witnesses, I will help to arrange for their appearance or for the production of any available evidence relating to your case."

Tyson noticed that Major Weinroth had a folder in her hand and was fanning the smoke away from her face. She stood. "Colonel Gilmer, may I request that there be no smoking allowed in here?"

Gilmer looked at Tyson. "Do you need that cigar, Lieutenant?"

Tyson stood. "I'm afraid so, sir."

"Well, let's take a ten-minute break then. Smoking in the corridor."

Tyson and Corva walked into the corridor, followed closely by Major Weinroth, who hurried off toward the rest rooms. Corva said, "That was insensitive of you."

"You said I could smoke."

"I thought you smoked little cigarettes."

"Beltran gave this to me. So how are we doing, Vince?"

"Not too bad. Gilmer is pissed off, and I even got to Pierce a little."

"That's swell, Vince. Do you want to see now if you can get me free?"

"First things first."

The door of the hearing room opened, and Karen Harper came out. She hesitated, then walked up to them. "Hello, Mr. Corva, Lieutenant Tyson."

Tyson said, "Aren't you sick of this case?"

She didn't reply but said, "Are you both quite pleased with yourselves?"

Corva answered, "Oh, really, Major, farcical proceedings call for farcical behavior."

"This is a very serious matter and . . . I think you are doing your client a disservice."

"Let me worry about my client. Your relationship with him is terminated." Tyson's eyebrows rose.

She turned to him, and they looked at each other awhile. She said finally, "I insisted that Andrew Picard testify today. I hope my insistence helps clear up this matter."

Tyson dropped his cigar to the floor and ground it out with his heel. "Sometimes I think that you're the only one who wants the whole truth and nothing but the truth."

"I'm not sure *that's* true either. But if it is, then everyone else is wrong. Also, if you decide to take the stand yourself today, you might want to clear up the matter of how Larry Cane died."

Tyson drew a deep but discreet breath. "I told you how Larry Cane died."

"Well, think about it." She turned and walked toward the rest rooms.

Pierce came into the corridor, turned down the hall, stopped, and walked back. He stood in front of Corva, and Tyson saw he had at least a head on Corva and about sixty pounds. Pierce smiled unpleasantly. "You see, what I forgot to establish is at how many *paces* the major intended to conduct the duel. After the trial I learned that within ten paces those bullets *would* have killed, and therefore, the weapons to be used *were* deadly weapons. Your analogy about dueling with ripe tomatoes impressed the board, but it was faulty."

"I suppose it was, Colonel, now that you bring up the question of distance. How forgetful of me."

"No, Mr. Corva, it was forgetful of *me*. But I'll be more attentive to omissions on your part this time."

"I'm sure you've learned something useful from that case."

Colonel Pierce gave Corva a look that was not friendly. He fixed his eyes on Tyson a moment, smiled at some secret delight, turned, and walked down the corridor.

Corva watched him go. "Very obsessed man. He ought to watch his blood pressure."

"What is he obsessed with, Vince?"

"Unlike Van Arken, who may be an idealist, Colonel Pierce is an egotist. He has the temperament of a star tennis player. If he ever lost a case, he'd be impotent for months."

"Well, that would be tough on Mrs. Pierce."

"Probably not. Point is, prosecuting is an individual sport, and if he lost he'd have no one to blame but himself. But he picks and chooses his cases carefully. None of them are cakewalks, but he doesn't pick cases that he thinks are too weak to win either."

"Not like you, Vince."

"No."

"But he picked my case and picked it probably at a time after he knew you were the defense counsel. I thought you scared him off last time."

Corva smiled and looked at his watch. "Let's go back in. And stop ogling that little court reporter. Harper is annoyed at you."

They entered the hearing room and took their seats. Within a minute, Karen Harper, Major Weinroth, and Colonel Pierce returned and took their places.

Colonel Gilmer said, "Let's resume." He looked around the room and said,

"In addition to the sworn statements for the defense and the prosecution, we have an unsworn statement from Mr. Andrew Picard, whose role in this case is well known to all parties. It is within my power as investigating officer to call Mr. Picard to testify under the category of an additional witness. This is done in the interests of justice, fairness, and a complete investigation." He looked at Corva. "Do you understand that Mr. Picard is my witness and not the government's witness?"

Corva stood. "I fail to see the distinction between you and the government, Colonel, but I'll play ball."

Colonel Gilmer seemed to want to explain the difference but had second thoughts and went on to the next required point. He looked at Tyson. "Would you please rise, Lieutenant?"

Tyson stood.

Colonel Gilmer read from his guide. "Lieutenant Tyson, before proceeding further, I now ask you whether you have any questions regarding your right to remain silent concerning the offenses of which you are accused; your right to make a statement, either sworn or unsworn, if you choose to; the use that can be made of any statement you do make; your right to cross-examine witnesses against you; or your right to present anything you may desire in your own behalf; and to have me examine available witnesses requested by you either in defense, mitigation, or extenuation."

Tyson wondered who made up these endless sentences.

Corva replied, "My client has asked me to explain to him why he is being offered the right to present statements or evidence in mitigation or extenuation. He says this is like being asked to give an excuse for something you never said you did. I admit to you, Colonel, I'm stumped by my client's question, and I thought that maybe somebody in this room could answer him."

Colonel Gilmer cleared his throat and referred again to his procedural guide. At length he said, "I may not proceed further until I am convinced that the accused understands what I have just read. It is general practice in these cases, Mr. Corva, that if the accused is represented by counsel—and he apparently is—"

The prosecution desk chuckled.

"Defense counsel generally indicates that he has explained these matters to the accused beforehand, and they are understood." He added, "I have never had any other experience after reading that statement to the accused."

"Nevertheless," said Corva, "my client, who is as innocent of the law as he is of the charge, has asked a commonsense question that I, as a lawyer, am not qualified to answer."

Colonel Pierce rose and said, "If it please the colonel . . . I am not in the habit of assisting the defense or the accused in comprehending what their rights are. But in the interests of fairness and justice, I would like to explain the meaning of extenuation and mitigation as it relates to this hearing." He looked directly at Tyson. "In commonsense language, Lieutenant, suppose you were called in to the school principal and accused of hitting Tommy Smith. And you say, 'I never hit him, and he deserved it anyway.' That is a statement in defense, extenuation, and mitigation, all in one."

Tyson replied, "It sounds a lot like an admission of guilt to me, Colonel."

Colonel Pierce smiled.

Tyson leaned toward Corva. "Is this guy serious?"

"We are on the wrong side of the looking glass. Everyone here is nuts, and if we stay much longer we will start believing them. Tell the asshole you understand."

"Which asshole?"

"Oh . . . Gilmer."

Tyson looked at Colonel Gilmer. "Colonel, I fully understand and accept Colonel Pierce's explanation and example of how I may offer excuses for something I don't admit I did."

Gilmer nodded, pleased that the matter was resolved.

Tyson took his seat, and Corva sat also. Corva said to Tyson, "We made our point."

"We're making lots of points, Vince. But when I got here, the scoreboard showed they'd started without us and won."

"No sweat."

Colonel Gilmer said to Corva, "You have indicated that you wish to call as witnesses the following individuals whose sworn statements are in the files: Mr. Paul Sadowski, Mr. Anthony Scorello, Mr. Hernando Beltran, Mr. Lee Walker, Mr. Louis Kalane. I have arranged for the appearance of those witnesses at government expense, and they are present. Mr. Corva, you may call the first witnesses by instructing Sergeant Lester"—Gilmer nodded toward the sergeant at arms—"as to their whereabouts and which of them you want called first."

Corva stood. "I do not wish to call any witnesses." He sat.

Colonel Gilmer leaned forward across the podium. "Is it not your intention, Mr. Corva, to call the witnesses for the defense?"

"No, sir, that is not my intention." Corva doodled on a sheet of yellow paper.

Colonel Gilmer said, "Mr. Corva, these five men were brought here at your request. They were transported, lodged, and fed at government expense. If you did not intend to call them to testify in your client's behalf, why did the government, at taxpayers' expense, go through the trouble of bringing them here?"

Corva looked up from his doodling. "Colonel, the government sent these five men to Vietnam for a year at the taxpayers' expense. They can send them to New York for a reunion at taxpayers' expense too. Small recompense."

Colonel Gilmer's voice rose. "Mr. Corva, I've been quite patient with you. If you had no intention of calling those witnesses, there was no reason to bring them here."

Corva replied, "Colonel, the decision to call or not call defense witnesses is solely mine and the accused's and can be made at any time. I choose not to call these witnesses."

Colonel Gilmer nodded tersely. "That is certainly your right."

Tyson looked at Sergeant Lester, who seemed disappointed, then at Colonel Pierce, Major Weinroth, and Captain Longo. They were concealing their disappointment much better. He looked at Karen Harper and caught her eye, but she looked away, so he turned to the court reporter, who smiled at him again. They held eye contact for a while until Colonel Gilmer said, "Lieutenant Tyson, do I have your attention?"

"Yes, sir."

"In lieu of defense testimony, I will consider the sworn statements of the five named defense witnesses, if that is your wish."

Corva answered, "That is our wish, Colonel."

"Fine. Do you want me to call any witnesses whose names have not been entered as witnesses? If so, give me their names and organizations or addresses."

Corva replied, "We would like to call the following witnesses as either defense witnesses or impartial witnesses: Daniel Kelly, Michael DeTonq, and the French-Vietnamese nun known only as Sister Teresa."

Colonel Gilmer seemed prepared for this. He said, "Do you have their organizations or addresses, Mr. Corva?"

"I have last-known addresses, Colonel. I believe you have those too."

"Yes, I do. And I've made every effort to contact these people but have been unsuccessful."

"Then we must consider the investigation incomplete."

Colonel Gilmer shook his head. "Mr. Corva, since there is no way you can convince me or anybody that the appearance of these witnesses would aid your client's defense, it would not prejudice your client's rights if they were not present. The prosecution could just as easily claim they are government witnesses. The witnesses being absent and having shown no sign of life for approximately ten, eighteen, and two years, respectively, we might assume they are dead."

Corva replied, "I know government workers who have shown no sign of life for decades but are promoted nevertheless—"

Sergeant Lester stifled a laugh and wound up coughing.

Corva continued, "But for purposes of this investigation and hearing I will table this request if you will assure me that the government will continue looking for these witnesses until these charges are finally disposed of in one way or the other."

Colonel Gilmer thought a moment, and Tyson wondered if he was thinking about the taxpayers again. Gilmer said, "That is a reasonable request, and you have my assurances on that."

"Thank you, Colonel."

Tyson said to Corva, "I never said I wanted them found."

"Don't worry about it. Adds to the drama."

"What if they *do* turn out to be witnesses for the prosecution?"

"Sh-h-h—Colonel Gilmer wants to speak."

"Vince!"

Colonel Gilmer cleared his throat. "Lieutenant Tyson, if you are aware of any military records which you want me to consider and which you have been unable to obtain, give me a list of those documents at this time."

Corva said, "We have been trying for some time, through Major Harper, to obtain the orders authorizing Lieutenant Tyson to wear the Silver Star for valorous acts performed in the line of duty in connection with military operations against an armed enemy, on 15 February 1968, in the vicinity of Hue City."

Colonel Pierce said to his assistants, loudly enough for everyone to hear, "What the hell does he think this is—an awards ceremony?"

Colonel Gilmer looked briefly at Pierce and then turned to Karen Harper. "Major."

Karen Harper stood. "Mr. Corva, I have with me Lieutenant Tyson's orders authorizing the Silver Star."

Tyson glanced at Corva, then turned back to Harper.

She continued, "The orders were apparently never forwarded, or they were believed to be forwarded. In any case they are in my possession."

Corva stood. "May I put them in my possession?"

She replied, "Certainly." She came around her table and carried a large manila envelope to Tyson. She said, "In addition to the orders, the envelope contains the actual medal and a ribbon."

Tyson replied, "Thank you, Major. That was thoughtful of you to procure the medal itself."

"Not at all." Her back to the room, she smiled at him, turned, and returned to her chair.

Corva said, "She's got it for you, lover."

"Fuck off."

Corva said to Gilmer, "May I take a moment to look at this?" He opened the envelope and slid out the contents. He read the citation proposed by Daniel Kelly and endorsed by Captain Roy Browder. It was a description of the action and the heroism that led to the award. It was general, describing the usual valor, self-sacrifice, and actions above and beyond the call of duty. But there were few specifics, and there was no mention of a hospital. Most importantly, the citation stated the date of 15 February and mentioned daylight action to distinguish it from something that might have happened before dawn or after sundown that day.

Corva drew a small blue box toward him and opened it. Inside, on a piece of white satin, lay the Silver Star. Beneath it was the small red, white, and blue rectangular ribbon. Corva took the ribbon from the box. "Turn this way."

"I can't wear that, Vince."

Colonel Pierce stood. "This is *not* an awards ceremony, Mr. Corva."

Corva paid no attention and pinned the ribbon over Tyson's two rows of existing ribbons. "There, it's the first one you wear, so we don't have to move any." Corva patted the rows of service ribbons. "Good. Real hero." He stood and turned to Pierce. "Colonel, Lieutenant Tyson has waited eighteen years for the Army to find this. You can damned sure wait thirty seconds while I pin it on him."

Pierce seemed about to say something, thought better of it, and sat down.

Corva turned to the front of the room. "Thank you, Colonel, and thank you, Major Harper."

Gilmer said to Tyson, "Congratulations. Now if we may—"

Corva interrupted. "Excuse me, Colonel, but I would like to point out to you that this award should be considered by you as evidence as you weigh and evaluate the facts in determining the truth of the matters stated in the charge sheet."

Colonel Gilmer didn't reply.

Corva continued, "I don't have to point out that the citation for this award and the charge sheet are two completely different documents which address themselves to the same event."

"No," said Gilmer, "you don't have to point that out. I figured that out for myself."

"Good," said Corva. "One can't be too careful when defending a man charged with murder."

Colonel Gilmer let out a long breath. He turned a page in the book before him and said, "Lieutenant Tyson, if you have any physical or real evidence which you have not introduced, you may introduce it at this time."

Corva replied, "We have no such evidence."

"Are you aware of any other evidence that you want me to consider and which you have been unable to obtain? If so, let me know now."

Corva stood. "We have no such evidence. And, I should point out, neither does the prosecution. I would like you to consider, Colonel, that the government has not even established that any deaths, legal or illegal, took place as specified in the charge sheet. Specifically, there are no corpses nor any photos of corpses nor any death certificates nor anyone who personally knew any of the alleged victims who can testify as to that alleged victim's present condition. I realize that it is not mandatory for the government to produce a corpse to substantiate a charge of murder, but a corpse or two is not too much to ask, if they are alleging over a hundred deaths."

Colonel Pierce stood and said sharply, "Mr. Corva, the government has no corpses to provide in order to satisfy your ghoulish sense of curiosity or your inane suggestion that there were no deaths at that hospital. If you—"

Corva's voice cut him off. "I am not saying there were no deaths! I have here a citation for a Silver Star that speaks of deaths. And if the government has no corpses, the defense does: Larry Cane and Arthur Peterson. Killed in action against an armed enemy, Colonel Pierce. And I have death certificates giving time, place, and cause of death. And until recently, I would have said I even knew *why* they died. Now that the government is trying to strip these men— living and dead—of their honor and their dignity, I can no longer say why." Corva sat.

The room was very still. Pierce sat slowly. Tyson was impressed by Corva's expression of outrage. And Corva, as he'd said himself, was no courtroom actor. Corva *was* outraged, because Corva had kept himself purposely ignorant of the actual events of February 15. Corva believed every word of the Silver Star citation.

Colonel Gilmer looked around the room. He said, "Does the defense have anything further to present?"

Corva shook his head. "No, sir."

"All right," said Gilmer, "I would like to call the additional witness, Andrew Picard." He turned to Sergeant Lester. "Please show Mr. Picard in."

Sergeant Lester snapped to attention, turned smartly, and strode out the door.

Tyson lit a cigarette. Corva drank water. Corva leaned close to him and asked, "How *did* Larry Cane die?"

Tyson replied, "I shot him through the heart."

Corva didn't seem particularly surprised.

The door opened, and Andrew Picard entered. Picard was dressed in brown tweeds, and Tyson thought he was rushing the season a bit and playing author a lot. Sergeant Lester showed him to the front podium, facing Gilmer.

Colonel Gilmer said, "Mr. Picard, will you raise your right hand, please?"

Picard raised his hand.

Gilmer said, "You swear that the evidence you shall give in the case now being investigated shall be the truth, the whole truth, and nothing but the truth. So help you God."

"I do."

"Please take your seat in the witness chair."

Picard walked toward the back of the room and sat in the chair facing Gilmer.

Colonel Gilmer said, "Please state your full name, occupation, and residence address."

"Andrew Picard, writer, Bluff Point, Sag Harbor, New York."

"Do you know the accused?"

Picard looked at Tyson. "We've met once."

Gilmer said, "I have an unsworn statement made by you in the presence of Major Karen Harper. My purpose in asking you here is to have you expand on this statement and to answer other questions I might have regarding your part in this case. And also to answer such questions as may be asked of you by the counsel for the defense or the prosecution."

Picard crossed his legs.

Colonel Gilmer said, "I am going to ask Major Harper to conduct this examination."

Harper stood and walked toward the witness chair. "Mr. Picard, we can dispense with a good deal of the background and so-called establishing questions because I don't think there's a person in this room who doesn't know the background on this case and your part in it."

"Fine with me, Major."

"Mr. Picard, did you make any efforts to substantiate what Mr. Brandt and Mr. Farley told you?"

"I did look for more witnesses but couldn't find any. They corroborated one another's story. For my purposes that was fine."

"Did you set out to expose alleged American atrocities during the battle of Hue?"

"Not at all. I wanted to—and did—expose communist atrocities. Lots of them. I was an eyewitness to some of them."

"But not to the Miséricorde Hospital incident?"

"No. I was trapped in the Citadel during that time."

"Did you *hear* anything about that hospital while you were there?"

Corva stood. "We really can't allow hearsay evidence, Major."

Colonel Gilmer said, "Mr. Corva, there is no jury present, and the strictest rules of evidence and examination do not apply. This is an informal format. If it weren't, I would have thrown you out long ago."

Picard laughed, joined by a few other people.

Corva made a mock bow toward Harper. "Please continue."

"Thank you." She addressed Picard. "*Did* you hear anything about the hospital while you were in Hue?"

"Yes, but only that it had been destroyed in the fighting and that Caucasian civilians and Vietnamese Catholics had been killed. That was the kind of news that made the rounds. The gooks—Viets—Buddhist-type Viets—were about as important as the local leech population. Not nice but true."

"Do you recall any sort of investigation at the time?"

"No. You have to understand the conditions in Hue. The destruction of one hospital was not remarkable in any way. Plus, we had our own casualties." He thought a moment, then said, "Also . . . the type of Westerner who was in Hue was . . . how shall I put this . . . ?"

"Any way you like, Mr. Picard."

"They were considered by the military to be mostly pinkos, wimps, and bleeding hearts."

"So this story of a possible massacre did not make the rounds among the troops the way, for instance, My Lai did?"

Picard shook his head. "This was not an open secret. Not to my knowledge anyway. Notwithstanding what I said about the type of Caucasians that were in Hue, I think the men in Tyson's platoon knew they screwed up pretty bad. I think—"

Corva stood. "Mr. Picard was not *at* that hospital. I really must object."

Harper answered, "I'm trying to establish the provenance of what Mr. Picard wrote."

"Then ask him where he got the story, and let's not give the witness free reign to engage in hearsay testimony."

Harper turned back to Picard. "From whom did you hear this story, and when did you hear it?"

"I heard it from Sister Teresa. In a hospital in Orléans, France. Nearly two years ago. I had pneumonia. There is a record of that."

"What hospital?"

"Mercy Hospital. Known in French—can you believe it?—as Hôpital Miséri-corde."

"How did the subject of the alleged massacre come up?"

"I had my manuscript with me. She saw the word *Hue.* That was all it took to start her talking about the war. I told her I was there. One thing led to another, and pretty soon I had an inkling that something very dark happened at Miséri-corde Hospital."

"You followed up on it?"

"Yes. When I got back to the States, I told my publisher I was on to some-thing and the manuscript would be delayed. I knew about locator ads, so I got the address of the First Cav newspaper and placed an ad. A month passed. I placed it again. Then I received a letter from this Dr. Brandt in Boston. I went to interview him.

"Brandt at first refused to give me the names of anyone who could corrobo-rate this story. He did give me the name of the platoon leader, Ben Tyson, who he said lived in a Long Island suburb of New York. I went through the subur-ban phone books and called a Benjamin Tyson. He said he wasn't the man in question. At this point I wasn't going to include this incident in the final draft, and I wrote a note to Brandt to that effect. Then Brandt came back with the name of Richard Farley, who he said could be contacted through the VA hospi-tal in Newark. Brandt also said that the Benjamin Tyson I located in Garden City on Long Island was the man I was looking for. He said he was certain of that, but he wouldn't say how he was so certain. I phoned Tyson again, but again he said I was mistaken. Anyway I interviewed Farley. He was a little strung-out. But he corroborated Brandt's story in substance and also the nun's story. I figured if it was all bullshit I'd know soon enough after it was published. I half expected about a dozen lawsuits from the platoon's survivors. But, as you see, no one is suing. . . . Though I suppose if Tyson beats the rap, they may all sue me then."

Harper asked, "Are you covered by insurance?"

"No . . . but that isn't making me try to get Tyson convicted, if that's what you're getting at."

Major Harper asked, "What do you think Mr. Brandt's motive was in con-tacting you and telling you this story?"

Picard smiled. "He had the idea from the locator ad I was on to it anyway. I suppose I led him to believe I already knew all there was to know. Doctors are kind of naïve. Also, I think he wanted to get it off his chest. Hell of a secret, right?"

"You never suspected him of ulterior motives?"

"Such as wanting to screw up Tyson? Yes, I did. But I don't know what would have prompted these motives, and I don't care."

"Why did Brandt give you Farley's name and no one else's?"

"Farley was the only man whose location he knew—except for Tyson's. I suppose he was able to clear it with Farley. He couldn't do that with the others because he didn't know where they were. He never gave me another name."

"How did Brandt know Farley's location and Tyson's location?"

Picard shrugged.

The reporter looked up and said, "Colonel, should I show that the witness shrugged?"

Picard laughed. "No, you can show that I said, 'How the hell should I know? Ask Brandt.' "

Major Harper inquired, "Have you found your notes yet, Mr. Picard?"

"I told you, all my written notes and taped interviews were transferred to a word processor disc and were accidentally erased. They are in that great data bank in the sky along with everyone else's erased tapes and discs. Christ, I'd like to tap into that."

"You didn't keep the printouts?"

"No one with a word processor stores reams of paper. Why is the military always ten years behind everyone else?"

Major Harper said, "One or two more questions. I was never clear on how Sister Teresa was able to identify the unit involved in the alleged incident."

Picard replied, "She identified the division . . . by their shoulder patches—*Ky binh*—cavalry. Everyone knew the First Cav patch. That's why I put the locator ad in the Cav paper, of course. Marines don't wear unit patches. We had the crazy idea that we didn't want to give the enemy any free field intelligence about the locations of units."

"What I'm getting at is this: Did Sister Teresa know any of the men . . . by sight?"

Picard nodded slowly. "As I said on the phone, she recognized the officer—Tyson—but only referred to him as *dai-uy*—lieutenant. I couldn't get her to remember his name."

"What did she say about him?"

Picard let a long time go by, then replied cautiously, "She said—now this is in a combination of Vietnamese, English, and French—she said he came into a room where she was hiding. He saw her and he spared her life."

"Spared?" asked Karen Harper. "Not *saved* her life? According to Lieutenant Tyson's account and the other five witnesses, the platoon saved some lives by throwing people from the burning hospital."

"Is that so? Well, the hospital *was* burning, according to the nun." He paused. "I'm not trying to crucify Tyson . . . I can't think of the word she used. It was French, though. *Sauver?* To rescue or to save? Or was it *épargner*—to spare or to save? It's a matter of translation, I guess."

"It's an important point, I should think. But not important enough to include in your book."

Picard glanced for the first time at Tyson. "An error of omission. It didn't fit Brandt's description of what happened, or Farley's. Sorry."

Harper let some time go by, then said, "You also told me that Sister Teresa mentioned the *bac si.*"

Picard nodded. "Another point I overlooked in the book. But for good reason. However, I do want to tell you about that . . . I've been a bit remiss. I wish I had my damned notes. My memory has been jogged by all this. . . ."

"What about the *bac si*—the medic? Steven Brandt?"

Picard leaned forward. "She said that she also recognized the *bac si* . . . from what we would call the Medcap program. Medics went around to the schools, churches, villages, and all that. Anyway she described Brandt as . . . '*un homme qui viole les jeunes filles.*' You don't need a lot of French to translate that."

Harper said, "Nevertheless, I will translate. A man who violates or abuses young girls."

Picard nodded again. "Of course there are many, many interpretations of that. What medical person hasn't been accused . . . I couldn't possibly include that in my book. Talk about a lawsuit. Christ!"

Karen Harper looked at Andrew Picard a moment, then said, "Did Sister Teresa say anything else to you about her relationship with Lieutenant Tyson?"

Picard glanced again at Tyson before replying, "Sister Teresa told me she had met the *dai-uý* earlier, at some function at Hue Cathedral. She knew that the *bac si* was in the *dai-uý*'s unit, and she took the opportunity to speak to him about this medic's predilection for underage virgins." He looked around the room. "I don't think any of this detracts from the central issue. I'll tell you what the nun and Brandt and Farley *did* agree on. They agreed that American soldiers willfully and with malice murdered a hospital full of unarmed and defenseless people."

Major Harper said, "We may be able to establish that, beyond a reasonable doubt. But there is only one man accused of that as it turns out—the officer in charge, Lieutenant Tyson. Now we have some reason to believe that his role in the alleged crime may not have been as great as we were led to believe—or as you suggested in your book—"

Picard said, "You know, Major, I was a Marine officer, and I know what Tyson's responsibility was. If he failed to discharge that responsibility he ought to be called to account for it. But not this way. This is a goddamned travesty—"

Colonel Pierce stood, but Corva stood as well and said loudly across the intervening space, "If the witness can give hearsay evidence, he can damned sure give his opinion."

Gilmer said curtly, "Please be seated. Both of you. Go on, Mr. Picard."

Picard continued, "I just want to add that I think Dr. Brandt lied to me about one important thing. I don't think Tyson ever gave a direct order to shoot anyone in that hospital. I think Tyson's troops mutinied. I think he was as much a victim as anyone else in that hospital. In fact, I think his platoon were victims too. Victims of war, combat fatigue, and shock. I think if you find Sister Teresa, she will tell you more about Lieutenant Tyson's actions that day than anyone else can."

Harper waited a moment, then asked, "Why didn't you include some of these things in your book, Mr. Picard?"

Picard replied, "I've asked myself that question. I have no answer."

"All right." She asked, "Did Sister Teresa tell you *how* Lieutenant Tyson saved or spared her?"

"No. You must understand that we had not only a language problem, but also I was rather ill and not in the best of form. I often wish I had another chance to conduct that interview."

Karen Harper observed, "So do we all." She drew a breath and said, "I have no further questions."

Colonel Gilmer addressed Colonel Pierce. "Does the government wish to cross-examine the witness?"

Colonel Pierce seemed unprepared for the question. He conferred with his assistants, then stood and said, "We have no questions."

Colonel Gilmer turned to Corva. "Does the defense wish to cross-examine the witness?"

Corva stood. "I have one question for Mr. Picard." He looked at Picard. "You were not an eyewitness to the events in question, and therefore neither the defense nor the prosecution has seen fit to claim you as their own witness. But you are the only link to Sister Teresa. I ask you this: Did the story you heard from Sister Teresa coincide with the story you heard from Steven Brandt in respect to the role of the accused in the hospital incident?"

"No, it did not."

"Thank you." He looked at Karen Harper. "I have no further questions."

Karen Harper said to Colonel Gilmer, "I have no further questions."

Gilmer said to Pierce, "Do you wish a recross?"

"No, I don't."

Colonel Gilmer said to Andrew Picard, "The witness is excused."

Picard stood and walked to the defense table. He said to Tyson in a soft voice, "You're a little old to be dressed like that, aren't you?"

"Tell it to the Army."

Picard smiled, "Luck." He walked toward the door held open by Sergeant Lester and left.

Colonel Gilmer drank from a glass of water. Karen Harper returned to her table. The room was still.

Corva said into Tyson's ear, "Why did the monkey fall out of the tree?"

"Why?"

"He was dead."

Tyson drew a deep breath. "I don't need any more jollying."

Colonel Gilmer addressed Tyson. "Lieutenant, will you please rise?"

Tyson stood.

"Lieutenant Tyson, earlier in this investigation, I advised you of your rights to make a statement or to remain silent. Do you want me to repeat this advice?"

Tyson said, "It is my understanding that if I make an unsworn statement, I may only be cross-examined on what I've said and not about other matters pertaining to this case."

"That's substantially correct. Do you desire to make a statement in any form?"

Corva stood. "No, sir."

Tyson said, "Yes, sir. I intend it to be unsworn, so I'll just make it from here, and I'll keep it short. Now that I understand all about making statements in extenuation and mitigation without incriminating myself, I'd like to make one. I want to say to you, Colonel Gilmer, that I am quite prepared to face a court-martial board in order to clear myself if you believe these charges can be disposed of in no other way. But if you choose not to forward these charges to a general court-martial, then I think you must recommend a way for the Army to publicly restore my reputation and my honor. The dropping of charges will not be sufficient to undo what has been done." Tyson sat.

Corva whispered to him, "I don't think that asking for a public apology will endear you to the Army or to General Van Arken. I think they would rather court-martial you, which is what you seem to want."

Tyson replied, "This court-martial is eighteen years overdue."

Colonel Gilmer turned toward the prosecution table. "Do you wish to cross-examine Lieutenant Tyson on anything he said?"

Colonel Pierce replied, "No, I do not, but I can't let that statement pass without comment." He looked at Tyson. "Contrary to what you said, the dropping of charges is all that the Army has to do to restore your honor and reputation in the eyes of the Army. If you have problems in civilian life that is no concern of the Army."

Tyson stood again, but Corva pulled him into his seat.

Colonel Gilmer looked at Corva. "Does the defense have anything further to offer?"

"No, sir, it does not."

Colonel Gilmer glanced at his watch, cleared his throat, and said, "The purpose of this investigation was to determine if there was any substance to the charge and specifications initiated against the accused and to determine if that charge and those specifications were in proper form. The recommendation of this investigation is advisory only and is in no way binding upon the authorities who ordered it."

Gilmer referred to a sheet of paper. "In arriving at my conclusions, I will consider not only the nature of the offense and the evidence in this case, but likewise the military service record of the accused and the established policy that trial by general court-martial should be resorted to only when the charges can be disposed of in no other manner consistent with military discipline."

Colonel Farnley Gilmer looked around the quiet room. "My report and my recommendation will be forwarded to the authorities who ordered this investigation. A copy will be forwarded to the accused. These proceedings are closed."

41

Benjamin Tyson began the last leg of his run, across the large open athletic field that lay behind the post headquarters.

The field was shrouded in a late September evening ground fog that obscured all but the lights of the surrounding buildings. Tyson moved at a slow pace through the clinging fog, realizing he'd lost his way in the disorienting white haziness.

He saw the tall white flagpole rising like a ship's mast above the vapor and altered his course, passing to the left of the pole. He crossed a concrete sidewalk and found himself on Lee Avenue. He slowed his pace and turned toward post headquarters.

An MP Jeep drew up beside him, and the man in the passenger seat called out, "You still at it, Lieutenant?"

Tyson recognized the voice. He turned his head toward the Jeep, which was keeping pace with him. "This wouldn't do you any harm either, Captain."

Captain Gallagher grunted. He called out, "As long as you're heading that way, why don't you sign in at HQ? It's nearly twenty-one hundred."

Tyson didn't answer. He changed his speed a few times, making the driver brake and accelerate to keep abreast.

Captain Gallagher added, "Then it's back to your room, sonny. No kidding. You've been making us look bad, and we're cracking down on your all-night runs."

Again Tyson didn't answer.

Gallagher inquired in a sarcastic tone, "Doesn't your wife miss you?"

"Go fuck yourself."

"Watch it, Lieutenant. I'll haul your ass in." He added in a conciliatory tone, "I'm trying to be helpful."

Tyson said to the MP captain, "There must be a felony in progress somewhere, Captain. Why don't you go find it like a good flatfoot?"

Captain Gallagher said something to the driver, and the Jeep sped away.

Tyson slowed to a walk and turned up the path of the headquarters building. He wiped the sweat from his eyes and shouldered the glass door open.

The duty sergeant behind the ticket window was Sergeant Lester of recent Article 32 fame.

The young buck sergeant looked up from his desk in the small duty room. "Hey, Lieutenant, how you doing?"

"Not bad, for a pack-a-day man."

Lester laughed and stood. "You here to sign in?"

"No, Sergeant, I'm looking for my dog."

"No dogs allowed on base."

"That's what I told him. Where's the book?"

"Oh . . . yeah . . . yes, sir. Colonel Levin has it. He's upstairs, and wants you to report to him."

"Is that like him wanting to see me?"

"Same shit. Only you got to do the hand jive." Lester whipped off a snappy salute and laughed.

Tyson took the steps three at a time, shadowboxed down the corridor to the amusement of two female clerks, and entered the adjutant's outer office. He walked to Colonel Levin's door and knocked sharply.

"Come in," called Levin.

Tyson opened the door, stepped to his desk, and saluted. "Sir, Lieutenant Tyson reports."

Levin returned the salute. "Sit down. You look bushed."

"Yes, sir." Tyson sat in a chair facing the desk. The room was in almost complete darkness, lit only by a gooseneck desk lamp that illuminated the papers in front of Levin but left his face in shadow.

Levin spoke from the shadows. "You've missed a good number of sign-ins."

"Yes, sir."

Levin observed, "You were running again."

"Yes, sir. Practicing for my escape."

Levin laughed. He stood and went to a file cabinet, returning with a bottle of premixed Manhattans and two water tumblers. He poured two drinks and handed one to Tyson.

Tyson put his drink on the edge of the colonel's desk. He regarded Levin's hands in the pool of light. The fingers of his left hand were nicotine-stained. Tyson waited, then broke the silence himself. "Working late?"

"Yes, tomorrow is a holiday. Yom Kippur. The day of atonement. I want to finish up by noon tomorrow."

"Right. My son has the day off from school."

"How are things going at home?"

"As well as can be expected. Child care and child amusement are a bit of a problem."

"I know. I have three sons. But they're grown now."

"Career Army?" Tyson smiled.

"No, no. They saw too much of it. It's very tough on family life. I had three hardship tours. One was for a year and a half in Korea. It takes a special woman to be an Army wife. It takes a lot of trust, too, when people are separated for that length of time."

Tyson wondered if there was supposed to be a message there for him. He drank some of the warm Manhattan.

Levin observed, "Autumn is here. I used to like the season, but as I get older, it's the spring and summer that I look forward to. 'Now it is autumn and the falling fruit and the long journey toward oblivion . . . have you built your ship of death, oh have you?' "

Tyson finished his drink. "Is that a direct question?"

"No, that was D. H. Lawrence." Levin picked a half cigar from the ashtray and lit it, his match briefly illuminating his face. Billows of smoke disappeared into the dark. Levin said, "What angers me is that the Army doesn't really *want* a trial. They feel obligated in some way to the press, the White House, the

Congress who approves their budgets, the Army and Defense secretaries, and even their own legal branch."

Tyson unwrapped a piece of foil in which he kept a cigarette and a pack of matches. He lit the cigarette without permission. "There's something obscene about carrying a cigarette in your jogging suit."

Levin seemed not to hear, intent on his own thoughts. "If this case had come to light eighteen years ago, while you were still on active duty, the Army would have a dozen options open to them and to you. But ironically the passage of time has worked against you." He added, "The options are limited to indicting or not indicting for murder."

Tyson stubbed out his unsmoked cigarette in Levin's ashtray. "I gave them the option of a public apology."

Levin smiled weakly. "The Army does not accept apologies from its officers and men, so I don't think you can expect to receive one."

"Quaint custom."

Levin said, "I have some business to conduct with you." He lifted a manila envelope from the right-hand drawer and laid it on the desk, then drew a sheaf of legal-size paper from the envelope and said, "The courier from Fort Dix arrived awhile ago. This"—he handed Tyson a printed form with typed papers attached—"is your copy of the Investigating Officer's Report. If you go to the bottom of page three, item seventeen, you will see that Colonel Gilmer recommended trial by general court-martial."

Tyson put the papers on Levin's desk without looking at them.

Levin continued, "General Peters, on the advice of his Staff Judge Advocate, agreed with the recommendation. Here"—he handed Tyson a single sheet of typed paper—"is your copy of the orders convening a general court-martial."

Tyson held the paper near the lamp and read the short document:

> *From: Major General George Peters, Post Commander, Fort Dix, New Jersey.*
>
> *A general court-martial is hereby convened. It may proceed at Fort Hamilton, Brooklyn, New York, on 15 October, to try such persons as may be properly brought before it. The Court will be constituted as follows:*
>
> *Military Judge: Colonel Walter Sproule.*
>
> *Members of the board: Colonel Amos Moore, Lieutenant Colonel Stanley Laski, Lieutenant Colonel Eugene McGregor, Major Donald Bauer, Major Virginia Sindel, Captain Herbert Morelli, Lieutenant James Davis.*
>
> *Trial counsel: Colonel Graham Pierce, Major Judith Weinroth, Captain Salvatore Longo.*
>
> *Defense counsel: Vincent Corva.*
>
> *[Signed] George Peters, Major General, United States Army.*

Tyson placed the sheet of paper atop the others. He looked at Levin awhile, then inquired, "Who do you think is the person who may be properly brought before this court-martial?"

Levin replied, "You may ask for a postponement. Speak to your lawyer."

Tyson shook his head. "October 15th sounds fine."

Colonel Levin handed Tyson a printed legal form. "The charge sheet."

"I have several of these. Do I need another?"

Levin explained, "As you can see, at each stage of the process, more boxes are checked, more lines filled in. This is signed by Colonel Pierce now, and he will formally serve you with a copy of this tomorrow at a time and place to be arranged. You may have your lawyer present, but it's not necessary."

Tyson placed the charge sheet on Levin's desk. "So that's it? Indicted, charged, and ready to be tried. All tidied up. I know that justice delayed is justice denied, but as Corva said, the JAG Corps ought to wear his old Jungle Lightning patch."

Levin did not respond.

Tyson stood and rubbed his neck. "My God, I was a commuter in May." He laughed. "I'm glad it's happening fast. Not much time to brood over it."

Levin said, "There is one item on that charge sheet that disturbs me."

"What is that, Colonel?"

"The endorsement."

"What endorsement?"

"On page two," said Levin, "where it says 'subject to the following instructions.' It is here that the convening authority usually gives special instructions to the court."

"What sort of special instructions?"

"Usually a limit to the punishment that the court can impose. It is within the power of General Peters or the chain of command right up to the Commander in Chief to state a maximum punishment that can be awarded. For instance, in a capital crime, this space"—he pointed to a line on the charge sheet—"will often state something like . . . the death penalty may not be imposed. . . ."

Tyson picked up the charge sheet. There was nothing written in the place provided for special instructions. He looked at Levin. "Are you telling me I could be shot?"

"Well . . . that's highly unlikely. An impossibility actually. . . . But I'm disturbed that General Peters didn't exclude the death penalty as a possible—"

"You're *disturbed?* Colonel, I'm outraged."

"Well, of course you are. It's a threat. I'm really surprised . . . usually the government, the Justice Department, or someone will offer the accused some sort of guarantee in a capital crime—in exchange, of course, for something else. But I'm not qualified to talk about that. I do know, however, that no court-martial board is going to impose the death penalty."

"How do you *know* that, Colonel? If the chain of command didn't instruct General Peters to exclude it, this court-martial board which has been constituted"—Tyson tapped the convening orders—"may take that as a sign that the death penalty is precisely what the chain of command wants."

"That's an interesting observation," admitted Levin. After a moment, he added, "But any sort of command influence, even subtle influence, is illegal."

"That's reassuring. I'm sure Colonel Gilmer's recommendation to indict was based solely on the facts." Tyson gathered the paperwork and stuffed it into the envelope. "If there's nothing further, I'll leave you to your work."

Levin cleared his throat. "There is one thing further. You are, as of now, confined to your quarters. Confined means confined. You may not leave unless there is a medical emergency. If you feel you have a need to leave your quarters for any other reason, you must put a request in writing directed to General Peters at Fort Dix."

"He's the guy who wants to shoot me. And I don't even know him."

Levin poured Tyson another drink. "It's not personal. There is nothing personal in any of this."

"That's the horror of it, Colonel."

Levin swallowed half his drink. "Yes. I'm sorry about the confinement. I put in a good word for you, but when the honchos came here from Dix and looked at all the blanks in the sign-in book, the shit hit the fan." Levin finished his drink. "Could have been worse. Could have been jail."

Tyson took some of his Manhattan. He said quietly, "May I walk in my backyard?"

Levin looked down at his desk a long time. "I'm sure no one will mind that." He added, "The confinement to quarters won't be too long—only until the conclusion of the trial."

Tyson nodded. "Then I go home. Wherever that may be."

"Yes, then you go home." Levin went to the window and contemplated the white clinging mist that carpeted everything below the second floor of the building. He said, "I've seen so many wonderful places in my life. I found peace once in a Swiss village. A peace that I never felt before or since." He sipped his drink, then drew on his cigar. "At the end of the Book of Numbers, chapter thirty-five, there is a mention of creating six cities of refuge, places where a suspected killer may go to live in peace until passions cool and justice may be done. 'Then the congregation shall judge between the slayer and the revenger of blood.' Between the murderer and the man who killed for justifiable revenge or in the heat of the moment."

Tyson didn't reply.

Levin turned, put his glass on the desk, and put his cigar in the ashtray. "Your passport is in the middle drawer of my desk. I'll be back in five minutes. You'll be gone by then so I'll say good night now. No need to salute." He extended his hand, and Tyson took it.

Levin turned and left the room. Tyson came around the desk and opened the middle drawer. His blue-and-gold passport lay on top of a cigar box. He looked at it awhile, then closed the drawer.

Tyson left Levin's office with the envelope of legal documents. He walked out into the vaporous night and headed back to his quarters. A pair of headlights appeared out of the fog behind him and lit the way. The vehicle stayed with him as he walked slowly down to the officer housing units.

He reached his front door, and the vehicle stopped at the curb. Captain Gallagher's voice called out in the damp air. "Good night, Lieutenant Tyson."

"Go fuck yourself, Captain Gallagher."

Tyson entered the house and pulled the door shut behind him, realizing he would not open it again until the morning of his court-martial.

Part 3

I shall tell you a great secret, my friend. Do not wait for the last judgment. It takes place every day.

—Camus

42

Ben Tyson opened the front door of his housing unit and walked down the path. The MP driver saluted, and opened the rear door. Tyson took off his billed officer's cap and slid in beside Vincent Corva.

Captain Gallagher, in the front passenger seat, turned his head, smiled, and said, "Where to?"

Tyson didn't reply, but Corva said, "Take us to church."

The driver pulled away from the curb. He drove slowly toward the U.S. Army Chapel on the corner of Roosevelt Lane and Grimes Avenue.

Within two minutes they approached the large redbrick chapel, with a long adjoining office wing. The extensive chapel complex had been built during the brief period when Fort Hamilton was the Army Chaplain School. As the staff car approached the chapel from the south, Tyson regarded the wide lawns and maple trees now a rich golden yellow. Beyond the chapel's single spire rose the gray suspension tower on the Brooklyn side of the Verrazano Bridge. Tyson noticed that there were nearly a hundred people milling around the chapel steps.

The staff car jumped the curb and drove across the lawn, stopping directly in front of a small doorway in the north office wing of the chapel. Captain Gallagher turned to Corva and Tyson. "They want you to use this door."

Corva replied, "Is that why you drove across the lawn and stopped right in front of it?"

Gallagher bit his lip. "Yes, sir."

Corva opened his door and slid out. Tyson followed. They stood in the crisp

October morning sunlight, between the parked car and the door. Tyson looked over the roof of the car. "Why are all those people standing there?"

"Because they can't get in. It's by invitation only. But they'd like to say they were part of it. So they stand there."

Tyson didn't reply.

Corva added, "In fact, they must be military or military dependents, because this base has been off limits to all civilians as of last night. Except those who work here, of course, and those with trial passes."

"We should have charged for the trial passes, Vince."

"Right. Would pay my fee."

Tyson realized the people on the chapel paths were looking at him. Some waved, some took pictures. They would have gotten closer, but there were about a dozen MPs cordoning this section of the lawn.

Corva said, "Enough photo opportunities. Let's get inside." Corva reached for the door, but it was pulled inward by an MP wearing a polished white helmet and a white pistol belt from which hung a holster and .45 automatic pistol. Corva waved Tyson through the door.

Tyson removed his hat as he entered the long white corridor. There were doors on either side, and above each door was a wall bracket from which hung red signs: CHAPEL ACTIVITY SPECIALIST; CAPTAIN SMYTHE; BLESSED SACRAMENT; and finally a sign that was marked RABBI ELI WEITZ, MAJOR, CHAPLAIN CORPS.

Corva stopped at the door. He said to Tyson, "When I drove in, there were literally thousands of people around the main gate with signs proclaiming everything from 'Free Tyson' to 'Shoot the Bastard.'" He paused. "There are a lot of emotions running loose out there, Ben. Lots of old questions, but I don't see anyone with any answers."

"That's because the questions are wrong."

Corva knocked on the rabbi's door, then opened it.

Rabbi Weitz, a heavyset man with gray curly hair, rose from his desk. He was wearing civilian clothing, a brown flannel suit. "Good morning, gentlemen." He shook hands with Tyson and Corva.

Corva said, "It was good of you to offer us your office, Rabbi."

"Offer? I didn't offer anything. They said, 'The court needs offices.' We drew lots, and mine said 'defense.' So I'm saying good-bye. But I wanted to say hello first." Rabbi Weitz picked up his attaché case. "How long will this last?"

Corva shrugged. "Can't say. Today is Monday. . . . It may be wrapped up by Friday."

"I need the office Friday night before services. That's the Sabbath."

"Yes, sir. I know that."

Tyson asked, "Will you be in the spectator seats?"

Major Weitz walked to the door and turned. "They offered me passes as compensation for commandeering my office. But there is nothing here that I want to see. But good luck, and may the Lord bless you." Rabbi Weitz left his office.

Corva put his briefcase on the rabbi's desk, and Tyson threw his hat beside it. Corva said, "The physical layout here lends itself to a court-martial."

"I still think it's bizarre."

"Where else on post could they do this? We didn't want it at Dix."

Tyson said, "What the hell difference does it make?" He went to the window and peered between the slats of the blinds. There were vehicles, including television vans, parked end-to-end along Roosevelt Lane. MPs were directing traffic.

Corva said, "They had to call in two MP platoons from Dix, and the city put on a hundred cops outside the gates."

Tyson turned from the window. "I've never been the center of a public spectacle before."

"Oh, you get used to it."

Tyson asked, "Wasn't there any way to do this in private?"

"I'm afraid not, Ben. I would have liked just enough press and civilian spectators to keep everyone honest. But once the Army bowed to pressure and announced an open trial, then the list of people who absolutely *must* be there seems to get bigger. The post commander's wife, Mrs. Hill, asked for thirty passes." Corva added, "The chapel holds about two hundred people, but out of common decency the Army is trying to limit the number of actual spectators to about one hundred."

Tyson smiled grimly. "I never saw a hundred people at Sunday services."

Corva commented, "The room they used for the Calley trial held fifty-nine people, and every seat was filled every day of the trial."

Tyson saw that Major Weitz had brewed a fresh pot of coffee and helped himself to a cup. He said to Corva, "Want some?"

"No. You have to consider your bladder. Lawyers get windy."

Tyson put the cup of coffee down untouched and lit a cigarette. He looked at his watch, then picked up a book and flipped through it for a few seconds until he realized it was in Hebrew.

Corva said, "Everyone has stage fright. Within ten minutes after you're in there, you'll be all right."

"I'm all right now."

"Good."

Tyson said, "I keep waiting for someone to call this off."

Corva didn't respond.

Tyson looked at his watch again. He searched for an ashtray, couldn't find one, and dropped his cigarette in the coffee cup.

Corva was flipping through a yellow pad of notes.

Heavy-booted footsteps sounded in the corridor. They stopped, and there were three knocks on the door. The door opened, and a tall young MP sergeant addressed Tyson. "Sir, will you accompany me, please?"

Tyson picked up his hat, and Corva picked up his briefcase.

The MP, whose name tag read Larson, said, "You can leave your cover here, sir."

"What? Oh. . . ." Tyson put his hat back on the desk, straightened his tunic and tie, and walked into the corridor, followed by Corva. The MP, Sergeant Larson, overtook them with long strides and led the way.

They came to a cross corridor and turned left. Sergeant Larson opened the door at the end of the corridor, and Corva went through it, followed by Tyson.

Tyson walked behind Corva, across the red carpet of the altar platform. He was aware of the murmur of a large number of people in the pews to his left. Corva indicated a long oak table on the far side of the raised altar floor, and Tyson went around the table and sat in a hard wooden chair. Corva sat to his left.

The first thing Tyson noticed was that the altar table had been removed. Across the red carpet from the direction he'd entered sat the long table that would hold the members of the court-martial board—the jury. Seven empty chairs faced him. Tyson looked to his left. The rear wall of the chapel, paneled in light pecan wood, rose two stories to the arched cathedral ceiling. In the center of the wall hung gold drapes stretching from ceiling to floor. Behind the drapes, Tyson knew, was a large recessed area, the presbytery, where the high altar sat beneath a large cross. The drapes were closed for Jewish services and for nonreligious events such as this one. In fact, he noticed, there was no longer anything visible to make this altar area look sanctified; it could have been an auditorium stage, and was no doubt designed to be transformed from religious to secular by the switching of a few stage props.

The wooden pulpit had been moved from its usual place and was now standing on a higher platform in front of the closed drapes, to be used, he assumed, as the military judge's bench. To the left of the pulpit was an American flag on a stand. And, hung on the paneled wall above the flag, where a religious tapestry usually hung, was the prescribed photograph of the President, flanked by photographs of the Secretary of the Army and the Secretary of Defense. But why anyone present cared in the least what the chain of command was, was anyone's guess. Tyson supposed that every institution needed its symbols, and the symbols of Army justice were less intrusive than those of the institution that normally used the premises.

To the right of the military judge, as he faced the pulpit, was a witness chair as in a civilian courtroom. To the left front of the pulpit was the court reporter's desk, also as in a civilian court.

Tyson turned to his right. Toward the edge of the raised platform, near the communion rail, was the prosecution desk, its chairs arranged with their backs to the pews, facing the judge's bench, or pulpit. Sitting at the desk were Colonel Pierce, Major Weinroth, and Captain Longo. Their table was covered with paperwork, whereas Corva had not yet opened his briefcase.

Corva checked the desk microphone to be certain it was off, then said to Tyson, "Looks like more than a hundred to me."

"I haven't looked yet." He turned his head to the right and looked into the nave. The pews, which he'd never seen more than half full for services, were completely occupied now, and there were people standing in the aisles. "Somebody must be counterfeiting tickets."

Tyson heard a subdued, almost somber murmur from the assembled court spectators. They'd come to see a play, but they behaved as though they were in church.

Tyson looked over the pews, above the front doors where the choir loft hung, running the width of the nave. At the rear of the loft were three slender lancet windows of stained glass that let diffused light into the dark loft. Corva had told him that the loft was reserved for General William Van Arken and his staff, other Army and government VIPs, including the Fort Dix post commander General Peters and a few local politicians and security people. By the light of the windows, Tyson saw figures moving around the loft. No doubt his old pal Chet Brown was up there too. He said aloud, "The night gallery."

Corva followed his gaze. "No one is supposed to know they are there. That might be construed as command influence."

"I saw the secret staff cars outside with flags and stars."

"Right."

Tyson looked along the walls of the nave. There were four tall stained-glass windows in each of the walls, and the morning sun poured through the south windows, casting a multi-hued luminescence over the pews. The depictions on the windows were somewhat abstract, designed like the rest of the chapel to satisfy all Christians and Jews, but ultimately satisfying no one. Most of the windows had patriotic or military themes, in red, white, and blue. Two windows had Old Testament motifs.

Tyson finally looked into the pews themselves. About three-fourths of the spectators were uniformed men and women. A whole block of pews had been reserved for a group of JAG students from Charlottesville. The civilian-attired people seemed to be middle-aged and well dressed. The type of people one saw at Wednesday matinees.

Marcy had made the arrangements for the Tysons' friends and family to be present, and she had handled the challenge in a way that only a public relations person could. Most of the people he knew seemed to be seated in the left front rows, including John and Phyllis McCormick sitting with a few other people from Garden City.

Conspicuous by their height were Messrs. Kimura, Nakagawa, and Saito. Tyson had to look twice to be sure it was them. He knew he should be amazed, but nothing amazed him anymore. With the gentlemen from Japan was his former secretary, Miss Beale, looking like she'd lost some weight and found a decent dress shop.

He spotted Andrew Picard, who had somehow made the acquaintance of Phil and Janet Sloan and was chatting with them.

He saw Paul Stein, in whose apartment he had sojourned too briefly. He spotted Colonel Levin and a woman he took to be Mrs. Levin. They were sitting with Tyson's boss of short duration, Dr. Russell. He saw Captain Hodges, who was looking at his watch. Tyson wondered who was running the post.

He kept scanning the pews looking for Karen Harper and finally saw her sitting in the last row. Beside her was a good-looking man in officer's uniform, speaking to her in a way that led Tyson to believe they were more than professional acquaintances. In fact, he thought, that was probably the man that Brown had mentioned—Colonel Eric Willets. Tyson somehow suspected that Colonel Willets would like to see him draw a life term, and he was there to witness it, if it happened.

Tyson had received a letter a few days before, a letter of support and sympathy from Emily Browder, Captain Roy Browder's widow. And she was out there in the pews somewhere, though there was no way for him to know who she was.

In the front left pew he saw his mother talking with the Reverend Syms, his minister and her former minister. It looked as if they were gossiping about the congregation, which was the only reason his mother used to speak to the man.

To his mother's right were his sisters, Laurie, June, and Carol, without their husbands. And to his sisters' right were Marcy and David. Marcy caught his eye, smiled, and blew a kiss. Tyson contrived a smile in return. He turned to Corva. "Is your wife here?"

"No. I get nervous when she's in the spectator benches."

"Really? Should I be nervous that everyone I know, including my sixth-grade teacher, is out there?"

"Not at all," Corva assured him. "You don't have much to say. Just watch me make a fool of myself."

Tyson looked at the right front pews, which had been reserved for the media. You could always tell the members of the press, he thought; they looked like reluctant refugees from the sixties.

Corva poured water from a glass pitcher into two paper cups.

Tyson noticed a metal ashtray and lit a cigarette.

Corva said, "You ought to quit, you know."

"Let's see first if I'm going to be shot."

"Makes sense." Corva took some papers from his briefcase and began laying them out on the table.

Tyson looked down at a copy of the charge sheet and read: *Jean Monteau,*

Evan Dougal, Bernhard Rueger, Marie Broi, Sister Monique, Sister Aimee, Sister Noelle, Pierre Galante, Henri Taine, Maarten Lubbers, Brother Donatus, Sister Juliette, Susanne Dougal, Linda Dougal.

Tyson did not think he was a man with any mystical leanings, yet somehow he felt the presence of the dead in this quasi-chapel, the presence of Captain Browder, the dead of Alpha Company, and the dead of Miséricorde Hospital.

Tyson looked at Corva. He thought his lawyer seemed a little anxious, which was understandable. But the bottom line was that if Corva lost the case, Corva was not going to jail. Tyson said, "I think I got the joke about the ziti and the shells."

Corva smiled. He laid a row of pencils beside a yellow pad. He said, "An oddity of the court-martial procedure, as you'll see, is that the prosecution performs some procedural functions that would be done by the judge at a civilian trial." Corva glanced at Pierce. "That bastard tried to confuse me on procedural matters in that dueling case. Most military lawyers will give the civilian defense lawyers a little slack on military procedures. But Pierce plays it tough."

Tyson said, "He's playing to a lot of civilians this time, and to the press. That might throw him off-balance."

Corva nodded. "I think it might. See how his hands are shaking?"

Tyson looked at Pierce closely, but all he could see was a picture of composure. "No." Tyson drew a deep breath and stubbed out his cigarette. The spectators seemed to be getting restless. The door in the wing of the altar area opened, and a man in uniform strode across the red carpet. An expectant hush fell over the pews. Then the man, a middle-aged sergeant, took his seat at the court reporter's desk. After everyone was satisfied that his appearance did not augur anything important, the talking began again.

Tyson commented, "Typical military. Hurry up and wait. Right, Vince?"

"Right."

The side door to the corridor opened again, and an MP stood at attention beside it. The MP, Tyson noticed, was unarmed, no doubt so as not to give the civilians or the press the impression that Tyson was dangerous. Through the door filed the seven-member board, led by Colonel Amos Moore, who was the president of the board, a sort of jury foreman but with far more power.

Colonel Moore walked directly to the long table and stood at the middle chair, facing Tyson. The other six members of the board followed in descending order of rank and peeled off to take their places. To Colonel Moore's right stood Lieutenant Colonel Stanley Laski, Major Donald Bauer, and Captain Morelli at the end. To Moore's left stood Lieutenant Colonel Eugene McGregor, Major Virginia Sindel, and the junior member, Lieutenant James Davis, who walked to the far left chair.

Tyson watched with some curiosity. He studied the faces of the seven members, but they had probably practiced impassivity in front of a mirror all morning. Corva knew something about each of them, but all Tyson knew for certain was that they were career Army officers. Some of them wore the branch insignia of the infantry and the combat infantryman's badge. All of them, except Virginia Sindel and Lieutenant Davis, were heavily beribboned.

The unarmed MP walked to the center of the floor where the missing altar table had crushed the nap of the red carpet. The MP faced the spectator pews and announced in a loud voice, "All rise!"

Tyson and Corva stood as did the prosecution and the court reporter. The spectators rose noisily, and Tyson could now see the silhouettes in the choir loft against the lancet windows. Several people from the press section came forward and Tyson could see they were sketch artists. They came right up to the communion rail, but no one was passing out wafers.

Through the open door behind the board table strode Colonel Walter Sproule, the military judge. He wasn't wearing robes, but wore the Army green dress uniform with colonel's eagles, and the branch insignia of the Judge Advocate General's Corps.

Colonel Sproule walked to the pulpit and took his place behind it. Tyson thought that the juxtaposition of Sproule, the high pulpit, and the gold drapes looked either magisterial or theatrical.

Colonel Sproule, a man nearing seventy, Tyson guessed, looked around briefly, noting that everyone was in place. There was no gavel, Tyson knew; and none was needed at a court-martial. Colonel Sproule didn't bother to adjust the pulpit microphone, but his strong voice carried over the silent pews. "The court will come to order."

43

Colonel Pierce remained standing after everyone sat. Pierce adjusted his microphone and spoke. "This court is convened by court-martial convening order one-thirty-nine, Headquarters, Fort Dix, New Jersey, a copy of which has been furnished to the military judge, each member of the court, counsel, and the accused."

Tyson looked into the spectator section. He wasn't imagining it; he had never seen so many enraptured expressions.

Pierce continued, "The following persons named in the convening orders are present." Pierce read the seven names of the court-martial board, the military judge, the three trial counsels including himself, and the defense counsel. Pierce addressed Colonel Sproule. "The prosecution is ready to proceed with the trial of the case of the United States against Benjamin James Tyson, First Lieutenant, United States Army, Fort Hamilton, New York, who is present in court." Pierce took his seat.

Colonel Sproule surveyed the court, his hands on the sides of the pulpit, and said, "It is my duty at this time to give the court preliminary instructions regarding your duties concerning the proper conduct of this trial."

Tyson looked closely at Sproule. He was a crochety-looking old man with a powder-pale face, a few strands of gray hair combed neatly over his bald pate, and eyes that seemed unfocused. Tyson suspected he was nearsighted, but he wore no glasses. Tyson did see a hearing aid behind his right ear. Here was a man, Tyson suspected, who had seen about forty years of courts-martial and had little patience left for posturing lawyers, inarticulate witnesses, and guilty men. Tyson didn't think that even this trial impressed Colonel Sproule much.

Sproule glanced briefly toward Corva and said, "It is the duty of the defense counsel to represent the accused in a manner consistent with the special requirements of military justice. It is the defense counsel's right and obligation to insure that the rights of the accused are maintained throughout these proceedings. It is not the duty or right or obligation of the defense counsel to willfully obfuscate the facts of this case or to engage in any courtroom tactics which may compromise the dignity of this court or to delay or obstruct justice."

Colonel Sproule surveyed the prosecution team opposite him and said, "It is the duty of the trial counsel to prove to the members of the board, beyond a reasonable doubt, the truth of the charge and the specifications that you have forwarded to this court as stated in the charge sheet. The government has had ample time to investigate this charge and to put it into proper form. I will assume that the case you are presenting here has close relevance to the charges you have sworn to. I want to remind you that in trial by court-martial, the trial counsel's primary duty is *not* to convict; it is to see that justice is done. I have no wish to quell the natural desire of counsel to win a case. However, this zeal must be tempered with the realization of your responsibility for insuring a fair and impartial trial, conducted in accordance with not only proper legal procedures, but also in accordance with the needs, customs, and traditions of the United States Army."

Colonel Sproule turned toward the seven-member board. "It is your duty to hear the evidence that is presented." He paused. "To hear only the evidence that is presented in this courtroom. You must remove from your minds, as much as is humanly possible, anything you have read or heard about the case now before you. Your ultimate purpose here is to decide whether the accused has violated the Code as charged and, if so, to adjudge an appropriate punishment, if any, for the offense." Sproule looked at Colonel Moore. "Colonel, you have served as president of the court on previous occasions, and I trust you will offer guidance and knowledge to those members who may not have had experience in sitting on the board."

Colonel Sproule faced the front and said, "It is the wish of this court that the spectators to this trial will conduct themselves in the quiet and dignified manner which is consistent with the seriousness of the matters being decided here."

Tyson thought about Sproule's preliminary statements to Corva and Pierce. What Sproule had done in effect was to tell the rabbits not to run.

Colonel Sproule turned to Colonel Moore. "President and members of the board, I will now introduce to you the other participants to this trial." Sproule formally introduced Sergeant Reynolds, the court reporter, then Corva, then the prosecution: Pierce, Weinroth, and Longo.

Colonel Sproule addressed Colonel Pierce. "The members of the court will now be sworn."

Colonel Pierce stood and announced, "The members will now be sworn. All persons please rise."

Everyone stood, including the spectators, though Tyson noticed many of the press corps did not stand, but continued to sit, taking notes. Apparently Colonel Sproule noticed as well. He said, "When the instruction is given by any member of the court to all rise, that instruction should be interpreted to include everyone who is not crippled."

There were a few chuckles in the pews as the press rose.

Colonel Pierce, still standing behind his desk, turned and faced the board. "As I state your name, please raise your right hand." Without referring to notes, Pierce began, "Do you, Colonel Amos Moore . . . Lieutenant Colonel Stanley Laski . . . Lieutenant Colonel Eugene McGregor . . . Major Donald Bauer . . . Major Virginia Sindel . . . Captain Herbert Morelli . . . Lieutenant James Davis . . . swear that you will faithfully perform all the duties incumbent upon you as a member of this court; that you will faithfully and impartially try, according to the evidence, your conscience, and the laws applicable to trial by court-martial, the case of the accused, Benjamin James

Tyson, Lieutenant, United States Army; and that you will not disclose or discover the vote or opinion of any particular member of the court unless required to do so in due course of law, so help you God?"

The seven members of the board replied in unison, "I do." They lowered their hands but remained standing as Pierce turned to Colonel Sproule, who raised his right hand. Pierce said, "You, Colonel Walter Sproule, do swear that you will faithfully and impartially perform, according to your conscience and the laws applicable to trial by court-martial, all the duties incumbent upon you as military judge of this court, so help you God?"

Sproule replied, "I do," and lowered his hand. Sproule then addressed the prosecution bench, who now raised their hands. Sproule said, "You, Colonel Graham Pierce, Major Judith Weinroth, Captain Salvatore Longo, do swear that you will faithfully perform the duties of trial counsel in the case now in hearing, so help you God?"

The prosecution team replied in the affirmative and lowered their hands.

Sproule next turned to Corva, who raised his right hand, and Sproule swore him in.

Colonel Pierce said into his microphone, "All be seated."

Colonel Sproule announced, "The Court is assembled."

Tyson said to Corva, "I see what you mean about the trial counsel. I've never heard of a DA swearing in a judge."

Corva nodded. "It's a subtle way for the Army to put the judge in his place. The Army instinctively mistrusts an independent judiciary, especially since no one in the chain of command can write efficiency reports on them."

Colonel Sproule looked out over the pews and announced, "Unless they are required to be present for other reasons, all persons expecting to be called as witnesses in the case of Benjamin Tyson will withdraw from the courtroom."

Tyson noticed that the spectators were looking around to see if there was a witness among them. Tyson spotted an MP walking up the aisle. The MP stopped and pointed to Andrew Picard. Picard pointed to himself in that idiotic way people do. *Who, me?* Picard rose reluctantly, said something to Phillip Sloan, and made his way clumsily out of the pew, all eyes on him.

Tyson leaned toward Corva. "Is Pierce going to call him?"

Corva covered his microphone. "No. I subpoenaed him. I may or may not call him. Let Pierce think about it." Corva added, "I have a subpoena waiting for Picard when he's brought to the head chaplain's office. He can cool his fucking heels there for a few days. Why should he see the trial?" Corva smiled.

After Picard was led out the main doors by the MP, Colonel Sproule said to Pierce, "Will the trial counsel distribute copies of the charge sheets to the members of the board, and will the members please take time to read these now?"

Captain Longo stood and approached the jury table, carrying a stack of papers. Beginning with Colonel Moore, and moving left to right like a shuttlecock, in descending order of rank, Longo set down before each member, not only the charge sheet, but a yellow pad and several pencils. Pierce remained standing as the board read the charge sheets.

Corva said to Tyson, "In a few minutes we'll be asked if we have any challenges against any of the board. Do you recognize any of them?"

"I recognize the type."

Corva smiled. "Not sufficient grounds for a challenge. We also have one peremptory challenge, and if we use it, I'd like to use it wisely."

"Wisely meaning what?"

"Meaning whose face don't you like?"

Tyson looked at the board reading the charge sheet. "I don't like any of their faces. Can we challenge the president of the court—Colonel Moore?"

"Yes. But the judge has already indicated to me and Pierce that he would not look favorably on that." Corva explained, "Before, in his preliminary statement, that reference to Moore's experience was for me and Pierce."

"Oh. I'm glad you understand the language spoken here."

Corva pulled a piece of paper toward him and said rapid-fire, "Colonel Moore commanded a company of the Fourth Infantry Division. You can see he was highly decorated. Next, Lieutenant Colonel Laski was an infantry platoon leader, like us, Ben. He served with the Americal Division, Calley's former unit. His tour of duty coincided with the Tet Offensive and with My Lai. Next is Lieutenant Colonel McGregor, also a former infantry platoon leader. He was with the Cav, and if you look, you'll see why he wears the Purple Heart."

Tyson looked at McGregor and noticed now that a good piece of the man's left ear was missing, and there was a scar that ran down the side of his neck and disappeared under his collar. "I see it."

"Okay, then we have Major Bauer, who is old enough to have caught the tail end of the war. He was a MAC-V adviser and saw action with a Vietnamese Ranger Battalion. So those are the four who have tasted blood. Next, Major Sindel is a public information officer at Fort Dix. She was a newspaper reporter before joining the Army. She will probably listen closely and ask too many questions for clarification. Captain Morelli is in the Adjutant General's Corps, and is stationed at Dix also. He is about thirty years old, so he was about twelve at the time of the incident we're here to discuss. Who knows how he'll react when the witnesses start getting into blood and gore."

Tyson said, "I'm not sure how anyone is going to react. This has got to be painful for those old troopers."

Corva glanced at Tyson, then concluded, "Lieutenant Davis is a West Pointer, who is awaiting orders for Germany. He is a product of the new Army, and has had more courses in ethics and morality than he's had in calling in artillery fire. He has no idea where you're coming from. He was about three or four years old at the time of the incident, and the date on the charge sheet looks to him like D-Day, June 6, 1944, looks to us."

Tyson nodded. The composition of the board was supposedly random. But with four Vietnam infantry veterans it was obvious to Tyson that the majority of the board had some expertise in evaluating the sort of testimony to be presented.

Colonel Moore looked at the board members to either side and saw they were finished reading. He announced, "The board has read the charges and specifications."

Colonel Pierce nodded and addressed the open court. "The general nature of the charge before this court is violation of the Uniform Code of Military Justice, Article 118, clause three, murder, in which the accused is alleged to have engaged in an act which was inherently dangerous to others and evinced a wanton disregard of human life." Pierce paused shortly for effect before adding the mandatory statement, "The charges were prepared by General George Peters, post commander, Fort Dix; forwarded with recommendations as to disposition by Colonel Farnley Gilmer and investigated by Colonel Gilmer under Article 32; and investigated by Major Karen Harper under Article 31 of the Code." Pierce added, "Neither the military judge nor any member of the court will be a witness for the prosecution."

Tyson said to Corva, "I hope not."

Corva smiled. "There was a time when that was possible. But everything is fair now."

"Right."

Pierce gave the defense table a look of impatience. He waited a moment longer as if to see if Corva and Tyson were quite through talking, then said, "The records of this case disclose no grounds for challenge to the military judge or to any member of the board."

Sproule and Pierce began a series of procedural questions and statements, and Tyson thought they harmonized well. Tyson looked at Colonel Sproule. "Do you know him?"

"I know of him. He's a bit stuffy but not above a little sarcasm, like most judges. He doesn't put up with courtroom antics as you heard him suggest. Basically he's fair. If he jumps on Pierce, he'll look for an opportunity to jump on me and vice versa. Someone told me he keeps a little score sheet in front of him for that purpose. But none of that really concerns you. He does not have the power of a civilian judge. The real power, as it has always been in courts-martial, lies there." He nodded toward the board of officers.

Tyson said, "I remember a bit of this. I told you I sat on a general court-martial board once. Right where Lieutenant Davis is sitting. I had to sharpen pencils, count ballots, and arrange for coffee."

Corva continued, "You know that unlike a civilian trial they don't have to be unanimous for a verdict. They only need two-thirds for a conviction. With seven members, they need four-point-six members to convict you. Call it five. If we exercise our one peremptory challenge, then they need four. Or, the other way to look at it, with seven members, we need three to vote not guilty. So, from the standpoint of a numbers game, our number is three. And we don't want to bump anyone who might be one of those three." Corva looked at Tyson. "So now that you've seen their faces, do we want to bump one of them? And if so, which one?"

"What do *you* think?"

Corva studied his yellow pad of handwritten notes. He said, "Morelli is a *paesano,* Sindel is a woman, Moore is the designated president. They're already accustomed to Davis running their errands. So that leaves the lieutenant colonels, Laski and McGregor, and Major Bauer. The Veterans of Foreign Wars. My vote would be for one of them to go. They know too much. They feel qualified to judge you."

Tyson nodded.

Corva said, "Let's see if Pierce exercises a peremptory challenge first."

Colonel Sproule said to Colonel Pierce, who was now sitting, "Does the prosecution have a peremptory challenge?"

Pierce answered from his chair, "The prosecution has no peremptory challenge."

Sproule looked at Corva. "Does the defense have a peremptory challenge?"

Corva stared across the twenty feet of open space that separated the defense table from the facing jury table. He looked at each member in the eye, and each met his stare and held it. He wrote something on a scrap of paper, folded it, and said to Tyson, "Write a name."

Tyson, too, looked at each member of the board. He wrote a name and slid the paper toward Corva. Corva opened his folded paper, and they both looked at the names they had written, which were the same name: Laski.

Corva stood and addressed Colonel Sproule. "The defense challenges Colonel Laski peremptorily."

Colonel Pierce stood. "If it pleases the court, let the record show that Mr.

Corva responded as required that it was the accused, not defense counsel, who exercised the peremptory challenge."

Colonel Sproule looked at Pierce for some time, then said, "That will be noted by the reporter." Sproule turned and addressed Lieutenant Colonel Laski. "The challenged member may be excused."

Lieutenant Colonel Laski stood, almost reluctantly, thought Tyson. He turned and left through the side door.

Captain Longo approached the board table and assisted in reseating everyone according to rank.

Corva stood and addressed Colonel Sproule. "If it please the court, I would like to suggest that any errors I may make in the future be brought to the court's attention by your honor. I only suggest this in the interest of freeing Colonel Pierce's mind so he may concentrate on presenting the government's case."

A few spectators tittered, and Colonel Sproule looked out over the pews, which fell silent. He said to Corva, "It is the proper function of Colonel Pierce to raise procedural points." He looked at Pierce. "However, I would appreciate being given the opportunity to make these points myself."

Pierce bowed his head but said nothing.

Colonel Sproule added, "One of these points being that the prosecution should now remove the empty chair from the board table."

Captain Longo sprang to his feet, went back to the board table, and moved the chair into the wing, out of view.

Colonel Sproule now turned to Tyson. "Will the accused please rise?"

Tyson stood.

Colonel Sproule said in a voice louder than he'd used previously, "Lieutenant Benjamin Tyson, you are charged with violations of Article 118 of the Uniform Code of Military Justice. How do you plead to the charge and to the two specifications?"

Benjamin Tyson replied in a clear voice free of any emotion, "To the charge, and to both specifications, I plead not guilty, sir."

There was the expected murmur from the spectator pews. Sproule ignored it and turned to the board. "President and members, your task then is to hear evidence and return findings." Sproule looked at Pierce and said, "Does the prosecution have an opening statement?"

Pierce replied, "Yes, your honor, I do."

Sproule said, "I remind the prosecution that in trial by court-martial, opening statements are not required and not customary. But when they are made, they are brief, and they should serve to clarify how you propose to present this case."

Pierce did not acknowledge the admonition. He stood, and Tyson noticed that Pierce's bright red hair was now military length, perhaps to make points with the board.

Pierce moved around the table and stood in the center of the floor where the altar had been. He faced the board, so that his profile was to Sproule and to the spectator section. He began, "President and members, the accused is charged with two specifications of murder under clause three of Article 118 of the Code. We are not charging premeditated murder, but we are charging that the accused, by his actions, engaged in, or allowed others to engage in, acts which showed a wanton disregard for human life leading to and causing mass murder."

Pierce spoke in even, measured tones. "These murders took place nearly eighteen years ago. The victims in Specification One are unnamed, and I cannot give you their names. I cannot give you their ages, nor can I tell you how many there were of either sex. I can produce for you no bodies, no death certificates, no pictures, no graves. I can, however, produce two witnesses who can attest to these deaths." Pierce paused in thought.

Tyson looked out at the pews. He realized that without a microphone, Pierce's voice was not carrying well, but the effect was to make everyone strain to hear every word, and there was not even the sound of breathing from the hundreds of men and women out there.

Pierce continued, "In Specification Two we have names and ages and sexes. We have this information from the Catholic Relief Agency for whom these people worked at Miséricorde Hospital. These people, fourteen of them, according to that agency, simply disappeared one day during the Tet Offensive in the month of February, in the year 1968. They were never heard from again. Now we think we know what happened to them."

Pierce paused again and turned his head toward Colonel Sproule, then glanced briefly over his shoulder and looked at Tyson. Pierce faced the board again. "In order for the government to prove a charge of murder against the accused, we must establish several connecting points: We must first establish that Lieutenant Tyson was in command of the platoon involved in this incident. We must establish that Lieutenant Tyson's platoon was at Miséricorde Hospital on 15 February 1968. We do not have to establish that Lieutenant Tyson was physically present at the scene of the alleged murders, but we will do so. We will also establish that willful and wanton murder took place there. And we will establish that Lieutenant Tyson ordered those murders, *or* did nothing to prevent those murders, *or* conspired to conceal the facts of those murders from his superiors. It is not necessary to establish that Tyson himself committed any of those murders with his own hands; and in fact, the government will not try to establish that."

Pierce looked at each member of the board. "As officers, you understand and appreciate the fact that Lieutenant Tyson, as the officer in charge of the body of men at Miséricorde Hospital, had the lawful responsibility to either anticipate, prevent, stop, or report the unlawful actions of his men. If the government can prove that he failed to carry out any one of his lawful responsibilities, then the law and Army traditions and customs clearly indicate that Lieutenant Tyson is guilty of willful and wanton murder."

Colonel Pierce drew a thoughtful breath and went on, "I would like to draw to the attention of this court the Department of the Army's own Law of Land Warfare. Specifically, Article 501, a copy of which will be submitted to the court. The article is headed 'Responsibility for Acts of Subordinates' and reads as follows." Pierce quoted without reference notes, " 'In some cases, military commanders may be responsible for war crimes committed by subordinate members of the Armed Forces, or other persons subject to their control. Thus, for instance, when troops commit massacres and atrocities against the civilian population of occupied territory or against prisoners of war, the responsibility may rest not only with the actual perpetrators but also with the commander.' "

Pierce, still facing the board, half turned and pointed behind him to Tyson. "Lieutenant Tyson, as an officer, had direct knowledge of the Law of Land Warfare and in fact was required to instruct his troops in the provisions of this law. He carried with him at all times, as per MAC-V orders, a plastic card on which was printed a condensation of the Law of Land Warfare." His voice rising, Pierce said, "This should have been a constant reminder to him, if indeed one was needed, that the massacre of unarmed, unresisting, and, in this case, sick and wounded nonbelligerents was a violation of the Law of Land

Warfare, not to mention a violation of the Uniform Code of Military Justice and of the Geneva Convention. And it was also in direct contradiction to his training and to what he learned and was required to teach his men on the subject of the rules of engagement in Vietnam. In point of fact, as an officer and a troop commander, who had served ten months in Vietnam, the accused knew full well what his lawful responsibilities were in regard to command and control of his troops."

Pierce moved a step closer to the board and said, "You members of the board, as officers, are fully aware that an officer with command responsibilities may commit a violation of the Code through the actions of his men, that an Army officer may commit murder without having personally murdered. That indeed, many of the most infamous and brutal acts of murder perpetrated by soldiers against civilians have been committed in the manner set forth in the charge and specifications."

Pierce added, "The testimony you will hear should leave no doubt that the accused did in fact commit acts of murder as defined by the total body of military law, rules, regulations, customs, and the traditions of the officer corps. Thank you." Pierce walked back to the prosecution table, glancing briefly at the spectators for the first time.

Colonel Sproule turned to Corva. "Does the defense have a preliminary statement?"

Corva stood behind his table. "Yes, your honor. And the defense will keep in mind the court's instructions regarding such statements."

"Proceed," said Sproule.

Vincent Corva surveyed the court, then said, "The defense, in the interests of justice and keeping in mind that a trial by court-martial ought not to be a vehicle for obfuscating self-evident truths, has made several pretrial stipulations. The first stipulation was that Lieutenant Tyson was in fact the platoon leader of the first platoon of Alpha Company, Fifth Battalion of the Seventh Cavalry. The second stipulation we made was that his platoon was in fact engaged in operations in or about the area in question. We further stipulated that these operations led to an engagement in the vicinity of a building that was discovered to be a hospital or infirmary. We even went so far as to stipulate that, though no one at the time knew the name of this facility, we would be willing to assign it the name of Miséricorde Hospital for the purposes of this case. The fourth stipulation was that Lieutenant Tyson was present when the alleged events occurred. Therefore, the prosecution's contention that it must establish those connecting points is in error. The defense has stipulated to those points, and any questioning of the witnesses that makes it appear to the court that the prosecution is uncovering new and incriminating truths would be . . . misleading to the court."

Corva looked at Pierce for a moment, then continued, addressing the board directly, "At some length, the prosecution has appealed to you as officers to understand what you undoubtedly already knew: that an officer is responsible for his men." Corva paused as though reluctant to pursue the point, then said, "I do not mean this in a pejorative way, but it is the sort of thing that an officer of the Judge Advocate General's Corps might think it necessary for you to be reminded of, though you, as career officers in the mainstream of Army life, live that fact every day."

Tyson glanced at the prosecution table and saw that Pierce's face was quite red, though it wasn't embarrassment that caused the interesting color, but anger. Tyson looked at the board, but again he saw nothing beyond the impassive expressions that are peculiar to juries.

Corva cleared his throat and said, "I had the honor of serving my country as a combat infantry officer in Vietnam. And during that time, I had no difficulty remembering my duties or responsibilities or the rules of engagement or the Law of Land Warfare or that I was ultimately responsible for the actions of my men. I assure you that Benjamin Tyson as a combat leader knew his duties and responsibilities as well. Yet, the prosecution has asked you to keep all these things in mind as though they were the central issues for you to consider as you hear this case. However, the issue is not whether or not Benjamin Tyson was responsible for the actions of his men. He was. The issue is what did his men *do*." Corva stroked the bridge of his nose in thought. "And," he added, "what did Lieutenant Tyson do."

Tyson suddenly realized that Corva had prepared no preliminary remarks; that Corva was extemporaneously rebutting what Pierce had said and was doing a fine job of it.

Corva again met the eyes of each member of the board. He said, "The prosecution has appealed to you as officers to understand the unique circumstances of command culpability and command responsibility. I appeal to you as *soldiers*—soldiers who have seen combat or have heard of combat from your fellow officers and from your men. I appeal to you to keep in mind that whatever you hear in this case, including the testimony of the defense's own witnesses, is the testimony of an event that took place eighteen years ago. But more importantly, it is the testimony of an event that was seen through the eyes of men who had already seen too much of war. Through the eyes of men who were themselves confused and frightened. Through the eyes of men who were, at the time of the alleged crime, caught up in the heat of battle. It is the intention of the defense to show that whatever deaths took place at Miséricorde Hospital, including the deaths of two American soldiers, took place as a result of hostile action and hostile action only. But if the accounts of that action seem to differ, I ask you to remember your own war stories or those you have heard. I ask you to consider that when the soldier comes home, what he remembers is a fraction of what he forgets, and what he forgets is what he chooses not to remember. Ultimately, all war stories, all the war stories you will hear in sworn testimony, are as true as they are false. The details are as clearly remembered as they are fabricated. And the motive for all testimony is as noble as it is self-serving. Thank you." Corva lowered himself slowly into his chair.

Colonel Sproule stared fixedly over the heads of the silent spectators. There was no movement in the chapel for some time, then Sproule looked at Pierce. "The prosecution may call its first witness."

Pierce stood and turned to the sergeant at arms standing at the side altar door. "The prosecution calls its first witness, Mr. Richard Farley."

44

Richard Farley came through the door in a battery-powered wheelchair, guided by Sergeant Larson. Pierce himself moved aside the witness chair and indicated to Larson where to position Farley's chair. The MP turned Farley toward the pews. Pierce said solicitously, "Is that all right, Mr. Farley?"

"Yes, sir," replied Farley in a weak voice.

Corva grumbled, "Next comes 'Are you comfortable?' "

Pierce asked Farley, "Are you comfortable?"

"Yes, sir."

Tyson stared at Richard Farley, dressed in an ill-fitting blue suit, his hair long, and his complexion unhealthy. His trousers hung loosely over his wasted legs.

Colonel Pierce seemed to be trying to think of another solicitous question when Colonel Sproule said, "The witness will be sworn in."

Pierce adjusted the floor microphone so it was closer to Farley, then said, "Please raise your right hand."

Farley raised his right hand, and Pierce recited, "You swear that the evidence you shall give in the case now in hearing shall be the truth, the whole truth, and nothing but the truth, so help you God."

"I do."

Pierce said, "Please state your full name, occupation, and residence."

Farley's thin voice barely carried, even with the aid of the microphone. "Richard Farley . . . unemployed, and I live on Bergen Street in Newark, New Jersey."

"Could you also please state your former grade and organization?"

"Yes . . . I was a pfc with Alpha, Fifth of the Seventh, First Air Cav."

"What were your duties in this unit?"

Farley thought awhile, then replied, "I was a soldier."

"A rifleman?" prompted Pierce.

"Yes."

Tyson looked at Farley and said to Corva, "This is pathetic."

Corva nodded.

Pierce asked, "Do you know the accused?"

"You mean Lieutenant Tyson?"

Pierce hid his annoyance and said patiently, "Yes, do you know him?"

"I did."

"Will you, Mr. Farley, point to the accused and state his name?"

Farley looked at Tyson, pointed, and said, "Lieutenant Tyson."

Tyson and Farley looked at each other for a moment, then Farley dropped his hand and turned away.

Corva stood. "Your honor, now that the dramatics are over, I wish to object. Pointing and naming are not necessary unless the question of identification is an issue."

Colonel Sproule said, "Objection sustained. Colonel Pierce, you can omit that if you call additional witnesses."

Tyson thought that Pierce had the chagrined look of a man who had tried to pull a fast one and got caught.

Pierce asked Farley a series of preliminary questions, and Farley seemed to be responding better as he got used to the format. Pierce said to Farley, "On the morning of the incident in question, before you reached the village of An Ninh Ha, did you see any Vietnamese civilians?"

Farley nodded before the question was finished, and Tyson knew they were into the rehearsed part of the testimony, though he didn't know why Pierce would ask that question.

Farley said, "There was 'bout ten civilians on a burial mound."

"What were they doing?" asked Pierce.

"Burying gooks."

Pierce looked at Farley sharply, and nearly everyone guessed that Pierce had instructed Farley not to use this pejorative term. But, thought Tyson, a gook was a gook was a gook. He began to feel sorry for Farley.

Pierce said to Farley, "Did you approach these Vietnamese civilians?"

"Yes, sir."

"Who approached them?"

"Me, the lieutenant, the lieutenant's RTO, Kelly, and Simcox."

"You, Lieutenant Tyson, Daniel Kelly, and Harold Simcox."

"Right."

"Can you tell us in your own words, Mr. Farley, what happened as you made contact with these ten Vietnamese civilians?"

"We never made contact with them. They were civilians."

Pierce looked confused and tried to rephrase the question, then realized the problem was one of semantics and not the witness's memory. "I meant contact in the sense of . . . you met them."

"Yes, sir."

"In your own words, Mr. Farley, tell us what happened."

Tyson wondered whose words Farley would use if not his own. As Farley related the story of the burial mound, Corva whispered to Tyson, "What's this all about?"

Tyson shrugged. "Beats me."

Corva said, "Neither Farley nor Pierce mentioned this in our pretrial conference."

"I barely recall the incident. I'm surprised Farley can."

Farley continued his story, and Tyson leaned toward Corva. "I think I know what he's getting at."

Pierce said to Farley, "And it was Lieutenant Tyson who ordered these people to remove their clothes?"

"Yes, sir."

"Was this common practice?"

"Well . . . sometimes. Not like this though. Usually it would happen in a hootch. The medic, maybe an officer. Maybe an older guy. A sergeant. One at a time. In a hootch."

"But Lieutenant Tyson ordered them to strip there?"

"Yes, sir."

"People of different sexes?"

"Yes, sir."

"What happened next?"

"He told us to make them lay in the graves, then shoot them."

Pierce straightened up, as though shocked and surprised. He looked briefly around the silent court, then turned back to Farley. "And did you?"

"No, sir. They hadn't done nothing wrong except burying the . . . the NVA bodies."

"No one complied . . . no one followed this order?"

"No, sir."

"But you clearly heard Lieutenant Tyson give the order?"

"Yes, sir. He said something like 'Make them lay in the graves and shoot them.' The peasants got the idea of what was going on, and they got real frightened and started begging."

Pierce delved further into this, then said, "So, after no one responded to the order, what happened?"

"Lieutenant Tyson told us to get going, and we went back toward the platoon."

"Where were you heading?"

"I'm not real sure. But somewhere around Hue."

"What was your mission?"

Farley shrugged. "Just get on to Hue. Marines were in heavy contact there."

Pierce said, "Did you have as an intermediary objective the village of An Ninh Ha and/or the hospital there?"

"Yes, sir. The gooks at the grave told us about a hospital. Lieutenant Tyson passed the word that this was an intermediate objective. He told one of the men . . . I think Simcox, that there'd be broads there."

"Women. At the hospital."

"Right. And showers and hot chow. Everyone got real anxious to get there."

"Did you have the impression that Lieutenant Tyson meant to commandeer this hospital?"

"Well, I guess so. We usually took what we wanted."

"And you're quite sure that Lieutenant Tyson and everyone knew they were headed toward a hospital?"

"Yes, sir. Like I said, we couldn't wait to get there. But once we got there we wished we never went."

Pierce let that sink in a few moments, then said, "Mr. Farley, in your own words, please tell what happened as you reached the village of An Ninh Ha. Spare no details, no matter how unimportant they may seem to you."

"Okay." Farley began a long disjointed narrative. He seemed confused and unsure, but Pierce never once interrupted, though he prodded often with "Go on" and "What happened next?" Tyson thought Pierce was quite clever to let an inarticulate witness tell it his own way.

As Farley began relating his story of the massacre, Tyson glanced around the court and looked into the pews. People were actually bent forward, listening with the sort of rapt attention that no minister, rabbi, or priest was ever able to elicit in this place.

Farley stumbled through it, groped for words, forgot names, contradicted himself a dozen times, showed no remorse, and even inadvertently made points for the defense. But the overall effect of this, the first testimony, was damaging. More than that, Tyson thought, when Farley finished, there probably wasn't a person in the chapel who didn't conclude that the first platoon of Alpha Company massacred an entire hospital full of people.

An hour and fifteen minutes after he began, Farley said, "By dawn, we all got it straight. Then one of the guys—I think it was Louis Kalane—made everyone put their hands in a circle . . . you know . . . we put our hands in the middle and swore we would all stick up for each other. They were good guys like that. We always stuck up for each other." Farley wiped the sweat from his forehead with his hand.

Pierce looked at his witness, torn between inquiring about his present mental and physical state and inquiring about more important matters at hand. Finally Pierce said, "And did the accused join hands with you and the others and swear to cover up the facts of the massacre?"

"Yes, sir. He's the one who straightened our story out. He had a lot on the ball."

"Really?" Pierce allowed himself a smile. Feeling good, he asked, "Do you want a drink of water?"

Farley's mind was not yet in the present, and his brows knit in concentration at the question.

Pierce said, "Do you want to take a rest?"

Farley nodded.

Pierce said to Sproule, "Your honor, we don't need a formal recess. Perhaps five minutes right in place."

Sproule replied, "Take what you need."

Pierce motioned to Captain Longo, who brought Farley a glass of water.

Corva leaned toward Tyson. "Do you have an explanation for the incident at the burial mound?"

Tyson thought Corva's tone was a bit sharp. He replied, "Yes. Vietnam."

"That won't do. Did you order those peasants to be shot?"

"Yes."

Corva unconsciously drew away from him.

Tyson said, "Look, Vince, I'll tell you what happened, then you can decide if you're defending a monster or not. Okay?"

Corva nodded. "Tell me before I cross-examine him." He added, "I'm . . . I'm sure there's an explanation. You see what Pierce is doing?"

"Yes. Suggesting that I was prone to ordering massacres that day." Tyson thought a moment, then said, "Farley is believable, isn't he?"

Corva replied, "Inarticulate witnesses frighten me. But on the cross, they always fall apart. I'll take Mr. Farley apart piece by piece."

Tyson looked at Farley. "I'm not enjoying that man's discomfort."

"Don't worry about him. He might put you in jail." Corva asked, "If I had to assign a motive to him, I'd say that Brandt has some sort of hold on the wretch. Maybe drugs. But I don't think we'll ever know."

Tyson replied, "I remembered something after you asked me about motive. I never knew too much about the interpersonal relationships of my platoon—an officer doesn't. But I do recall now that Farley and Cane were best buddies. Funny thing was that after the incident, I never put two and two together. But now it's making sense. Yet Farley never said a word to me afterward. Probably brooded about it, then forgot it. Then perhaps Brandt put the bug in his ear again. Farley looks and sounds like a guy who hasn't had a close friend since the day the shrapnel severed his spine. He may romanticize the past, though God knows there's not a thing to romanticize."

"There is if you were able to walk on your own two legs in the past." Corva thought awhile then said, "We'll keep this motive in mind. Meanwhile, I want enough information from you during the lunch recess to completely demolish him. I want him so demolished that Pierce will not call him back on a redirect exam to try to, as they say, rehabilitate the witness. *Capice?*"

"Right."

Pierce said to Colonel Sproule, "I think we're ready, your honor." Pierce turned to Farley. "Mr. Farley, you stated that you were in the operating room of this hospital when Lieutenant Tyson got into an argument with a French-speaking Caucasian whom you took to be a doctor. The argument concerned the doctor's apparent refusal to treat one of your wounded, Arthur Peterson. Is that correct?"

"Yes, sir."

"And you personally observed Lieutenant Tyson strike this doctor in the face?"

"Yes, sir."

"And you stated that you then struck the doctor with your rifle."

Farley hesitated, then said, "Yes, sir."

"Why did you strike the doctor with your rifle?"

"I . . . thought maybe he was going to swing at Lieutenant Tyson. The lieutenant didn't put him out, only pissed him off. So I hit the guy with my rifle."

"Where did you hit him?"

"In the stomach."

"With your M-16 rifle? You were carrying an M-16?"

"Yes, sir. It's real light. It has a plastic stock. I only gave the guy a tap really. Doubled him up a little."

"Did you knock him down?"

"No, sir. He was on his feet and chattering again a few minutes later."

"You thought Lieutenant Tyson might be assaulted by this man."

"Yes, sir. The guy was really hot. So I cooled him down a little." Farley seemed to be remembering a time when he could do such a thing.

Pierce asked, "Did you think it was wrong to hit this man with your rifle?"

"You should never have to hit anybody without a reason. But I figured there was a good reason, because the lieutenant belted him first."

Pierce nodded, then said to Farley slowly and distinctly, "After this incident, you say that Lieutenant Tyson ordered Hernando Beltran to pull a patient off one of the operating tables—there were six or so in this large operating theater —and put Arthur Peterson on it."

"Yes, sir. The lieutenant was looking out for his man, but this led to a big argument with the other doctors there. Then this one doctor who spoke English goes after one of our guys, and the guy just reacted and pulled the trigger, and this doctor goes down."

"Did Lieutenant Tyson say or do anything at that point?"

"No, sir."

"He didn't say anything to the man who shot the English-speaking doctor?"

"No, sir."

"Then, you say someone shot the French-speaking doctor."

"Yes, sir."

"And you don't remember who shot these doctors, except that you think it was the same man?"

Farley licked his lips. "Well . . . I hate to say a guy shot someone if he didn't, but I think it was Simcox."

"Harold Simcox."

Corva stood. "If it please the court, I would like the record to show that Harold Simcox is deceased and can obviously not defend himself against this allegation."

Colonel Sproule said, "Let the record reflect this. Continue, Colonel Pierce."

"Why do you think the man who shot the first doctor then shot the second?"

"Don't know. The first one sort of had it coming. The second one was the French guy who wouldn't help Peterson."

"The doctor whom Lieutenant Tyson struck."

"Yes, sir."

"What did Lieutenant Tyson do or say upon the shooting of the second doctor?"

"Nothing."

Pierce asked, "Did he approve? Did he say 'Stop that'? Did he make any statement?"

"No, sir. He didn't seem to care. You see, Brandt had yelled out that Peterson was dead. And I don't think Lieutenant Tyson cared about the doctors anymore. I think he was very angry."

"You stated that Lieutenant Tyson at some point gave an order—a direct order—to locate the wounded and sick enemy soldiers in the hospital and shoot them. He said, 'Waste them.' "

Farley's lips curled up in a smile that looked almost wistful. "Yes, sir. That's what we used to say. Waste them."

"Meaning what?"

"Kill them."

"Lieutenant Tyson said to waste enemy soldiers who were in the hospital for wounds and sickness."

"Yes, sir. So a bunch of guys went out and did it."

"Did you see this?"

"No, sir. I was still in the operating room. Well, I saw two of them get wasted. Somebody drew a forty-five and found two NVA on the tables there—one was really on the floor where Beltran put him—and this guy shot the two NVA in the head."

"Did Lieutenant Tyson observe this?"

"Sure. He was right there."

"Did he say anything? Do anything?"

"No, sir. He just stood there most of the time."

"You stated earlier that there was no resistance, armed or otherwise, inside the hospital."

"Yes, sir."

"What, then, in your opinion, led to the shooting of other patients who were *not* enemy sick or wounded? And to the shooting of other staff members after the initial two doctors were shot? In other words, Mr. Farley, how did the general massacre that you described begin?"

Farley replied, "Everybody just got carried away. They found seven or eight NVA in the beds and shot them. Then some people—nurses and doctors—started to run, and the guys started shooting at them. Then one thing led to another. I don't know. I never moved from the operating room. All I saw was what happened there."

"Did you yourself fire at anyone in the hospital?"

Farley licked his lips. Then he said, "A couple shots . . . but only the people who were trying to get away."

"After the men began shooting other patients and staff, after they'd gone beyond Lieutenant Tyson's orders to shoot wounded and sick enemy soldiers, did Lieutenant Tyson do anything to stop them at this point?"

"No, sir."

"Were you near him most of this time?"

"Yes, sir. We mostly stayed in the operating room. I did leave there once for a few minutes. After all the shooting stopped, and when I came back, he was gone. I didn't see him again until outside. The guys had surrounded the building now. I told you some of the guys had thrown white phosphorus grenades and the place was burning. So we all went outside. Some people inside tried to get out, but the guys shot them. Lieutenant Tyson waited until the roof caved in, then ordered us to move out. Then we got to a bunker near Hue, and we put up for the night. Lieutenant Tyson called Captain Browder a few times and told Browder we'd gotten into a fight. Well, there was the sniper who killed Peterson and wounded Moody, so that was a fight. Lieutenant Tyson came up with a body count of ten or twelve, I think."

"And Cane had been killed by the sniper, too," Pierce reminded him.

"Right. I think that's what caused the whole thing. This sniper firing at us from the hospital. Everybody was hot. So when we got in there, we went a little crazy. I mean, here's these NVA soldiers and all, laying in beds, and these doctors—white guys—saying they can't help us, sorry about that. So, sure, we got hot. And I want to say I don't really blame the lieutenant for saying 'Waste the gooks.' But I think a lot of guys didn't understand the order."

"The order to shoot North Vietnamese Army personnel who were patients in the hospital."

"Yes, sir."

"Did Lieutenant Tyson do anything to clarify his order?"

"No, sir. But I don't think he wanted all them other people killed. But once it started, he sort of got scared and just let it unroll. It was sort of payback time anyway."

"Payback time?"

"Yes, sir. What we used to call payback. Like getting even. Everything had to have a payback. Like once—before Lieutenant Tyson took over the platoon— we lost some guys in a mine field outside of Quang Tri. So we rounded up the gooks from the closest village and made them walk through the mine field ahead of us. That's payback. But that's another story."

Pierce turned away and raised his eyebrows, affecting a look to show everyone that Farley might be his witness, but he wasn't his good friend. Pierce cleared his throat and said, "So this was payback for the sniper?"

"Yeah, the sniper. And for the mortar fire the night before. And for Phu Lai. And for everything. And because we were going to Hue. And because the people in that hospital treated us like shit. Excuse me."

"And that's why Lieutenant Tyson ordered the NVA soldiers killed and didn't stop anyone who went beyond his orders," said Pierce, trying to bring the subject around again.

"Yes, sir. That's why."

"And that's why Lieutenant Tyson fabricated a cover-up story."

"Yes, sir."

"Payback."

"Yes, sir."

"Thank you. Your honor, I have no further questions, but I reserve the right to recall the witness."

Colonel Sproule looked at Corva. "Does the defense wish to cross-examine the witness?"

Corva stood. "Yes, your honor, but as it is approaching the lunch hour, may I recommend we recess at this time?"

Sproule replied, "I would not want to keep you from your lunch, Mr. Corva. May I take a minute to instruct the witness?"

A few people laughed, including Pierce, Weinroth, and Longo. The board, caught unawares by the sudden humor, smiled.

Corva smiled good-naturedly, but replied somewhat tersely, "Your honor, I'm quite prepared to forgo my lunch in the interests of justice. If the witness, who appears somewhat befuddled, is able to continue, I will begin my cross-examination this very moment."

Colonel Sproule regarded Corva closely for a few seconds, then said, "We will recess for lunch, Mr. Corva." Sproule looked down at Farley and said, "Mr. Farley, thank you for testifying. You are excused temporarily. As long as this trial continues, do not discuss your testimony or knowledge of this case with anyone except the counsel who are now present or the accused. You will not allow any witness in this case to talk to you about the testimony he or she has given or intends to give. If anyone other than counsel or the accused attempts to talk to you about your testimony in this case, inform Colonel Pierce, Major Weinroth, or Captain Longo. Do you understand the instructions, Mr. Farley?"

Clearly Farley didn't but he was already reaching for the power switch on his wheelchair. "Yes, sir."

Sproule said, "The witness is excused, subject to recall."

Farley's chair made an electrical whirring sound as it moved forward. Pierce had to step aside as Farley swung around and made his way past the board table toward the side exit.

Sproule waited until he was through the door, then said, "The court will recess until fourteen hundred hours."

Tyson and Corva stood, and Corva collected his papers. Tyson said, "This is depressing."

"No one said it would be uplifting. Where do you want lunch?"

"Paris."

The MP car dropped them off at the bachelor officers' quarters located in the north section of the post. Tyson recognized the modern three-story redbrick structure. "Does this place swing?"

"Actually, it does. I worked late here one night, and all I heard were stereos and giggling women."

They entered a plain vestibule and climbed the stairs to the third floor. Corva opened a door marked "3F" and showed Tyson into a good-sized living room/ dining room area, furnished in passable Swedish Modern. The reddish carpeting looked like basement rec room quality, and there was nothing on the walls but notes, Corva's notes, taped all around the dining area. Tyson said, "I'll take it."

Corva showed him to a round blond-wood table on which were heaped books, yellow pads, and reams of typed material. On the floor were stacks of newspapers, more books, and cartons of files. Tyson said, "I thought you worked out of your hat."

"They gave me this as an accommodation. This is where we will conduct our sessions from now on. I told the post commander we could not prepare a proper defense if we had to work in your quarters with your wife and son there. So, you are authorized to come directly here anytime I call you. Okay?"

"Okay."

"And if things get a little tense at home, call me at my office or home and I'll come here, and we'll meet and cool out awhile."

"Thanks."

Corva went to a small bar refrigerator and came back with two beers and two wrapped sandwiches. Corva sat on the far side of the table. Tyson popped the top on his beer and unwrapped his sandwich.

Corva bit into his sandwich and said as he chewed, "Payback."

Tyson nodded. "Did you call it that?"

"I guess. I don't think we institutionalized it, but I remember the philosophy."

Tyson sipped on his beer. "I guess it *was* payback. What did the Nazis call it? Reprisals."

"Right. Reprisals are outlawed under the same Rules of Land Warfare that Pierce was going on about. I'm glad war has rules. Can you imagine how dangerous it would be without them?"

Tyson lit a cigarette and said, "The one thing Farley seemed to grasp in his befuddled mind was the fact that the people in that hospital didn't like us. And in fact did not treat us as well as they undoubtedly treated the enemy who'd been there before us. I don't know if they were enemy sympathizers or if they just feared the enemy more than us. But they didn't fear us. Which I guess was

good. Our reputation was not that bad. But this show of contempt on their part
. . . they didn't understand we were itching to pay back for what we got in the
past few weeks." He looked at Corva. "Sounds like self-justification, doesn't
it?"

Corva shrugged. "I'll reserve my moral judgments." Corva drank some beer.
"Tell me about the burial mound incident."

Tyson related the incident as he remembered it and concluded, "Farley was
an uncomplicated man, as you may have noticed. He took things literally. One
time when he was complaining about something, I told him if he didn't like
being a rifleman, I'd ask the battalion commander to take him on as an intelligence analyst. The next day he actually asked me about it. It was very frustrat-
ing having to deal with people who didn't understand my wit."

Corva smiled.

Tyson added, "But thinking back on that incident, I think he *did* understand
that I was telling them to put up or shut up. I got tired of these idiotic threats
they'd make toward the Vietnamese. I wouldn't have let them do it, of course."

"You don't have to say that. Sorry if I got a little worried back there. Point is,
this was not a good story. It shows you in a bad light. Let's discuss the cross-
examination."

"There won't be any cross-examination," said Tyson.

"What?"

"I don't want you to take him apart."

"Why not?"

"Because if you pull apart his testimony, by the time you face Brandt, Pierce
will have rearranged the parts of Brandt's story that he sees won't hold up.
Farley is the gook in the mine field, Vince. Pierce wants him to show him where
the mines are, the hard way, so he can make a map for Brandt. *Capice?*"

Corva chewed awhile on his sandwich. *"Capisco."* Corva bit and chewed
again thoughtfully. He said, "For instance, if I try to get Farley to admit that
you shot Larry Cane in order to try to stop the massacre, then Brandt is fore-
warned that we are going to reveal that, and he can be prepared."

"Right."

"And the more I take Farley apart, the more Brandt will be able to come up
with versions that hew closer to the truth, even if it contradicts some of Farley's
testimony, and you don't really want that, because you want to expose Brandt
as a total liar. Right?"

Tyson didn't reply.

Corva said, "Well, your reasoning may be screwed up, but the tactics are
sound. I don't want to tip off Pierce, who will tip off Brandt. And you want
payback. So, okay, we will skip the cross on Farley, subject to recalling him if we
have to. As for the burial mound incident, I could cross-examine him for a
month, and I could not get across to the board what you just told me and what I
believe. I'll let that rest until or if we decide to put him on the stand again. They
can have that round. The only thing I am wondering is this: Where, when, and
how are we going to expose Steven Brandt as a liar?"

"Sometime after he gets on the stand and lies."

"I can do it through my cross-examination of Brandt, or I can do it through
one of our sterling witnesses. Or I can try to do it through your testimony."

"We'll see. Stay fluid."

Corva snorted. "Yeah, fluid." He leaned across the table, his hands on a pile
of books, and said to Tyson, "I just want to remind you that it is *you* who are on
trial, not Steven Brandt. You are what we call the accused. I often defer to the
wishes of my clients, which is why so many of them are in jail. But your wishes

are not all coinciding with my needs. You're the one who has to live with the outcome, Ben. If you perceive this trial as a rite of exorcism and you'll feel better about yourself while you're making scratches on the wall of your cell in Leavenworth, then we'll try to do it your way."

"Good. I'm glad we see eye-to-eye."

"Right. You want that sandwich?"

"No."

"Neither do I."

The court reconvened at 2 P.M., and Colonel Sproule said to Corva, "Your witness, Mr. Corva."

Corva stood and said, "The defense has no questions for the witness, your honor."

There was a stir in the court, and Colonel Sproule glared out at the spectators. He turned back to Corva and said, "You do not wish to cross-examine?"

"No, your honor. But we reserve the right to recall the witness at a later time."

Colonel Sproule seemed to resist shrugging, then turned to Colonel Moore. "Are there any questions by the board?"

Colonel Moore replied, "The board has questions, your honor."

Corva leaned toward Tyson. "There are times when I like the idea of a jury who may ask questions. There are other times when I don't. Let's see if I like this bunch or not."

Colonel Sproule was instructing the court. "The format that I have decided is proper for these questions has already been explained to you in pretrial instructions. You may ask your questions individually or through the president of the board, Colonel Moore. I remind you, however, that your questions to the witnesses must not be misleading, must not show bias, must relate to the testimony, must serve to clarify a point in your mind, and should be short and succinct. If you have any doubts as to the admissibility of your questions, you may reduce them to writing and show them to me. If you ask a question that I think is improper, I will not allow the witness to respond. Colonel Moore?"

Moore referred to his notes and said, "Major Sindel would like to put the first question to the witness."

Pierce stood and said to Farley, "Mr. Farley, you are reminded that you are still under oath."

Farley answered from his wheelchair, "Yes, sir."

Tyson had the distinct impression that Farley, after nearly two decades, was still intimidated by the trappings of military authority. Tyson had the urge to shake him and remind him that he was a civilian.

Major Virginia Sindel leaned in Farley's direction and asked, "Mr. Farley, you indicated you fired a couple of shots at people who were trying to get away. Did you hit anyone?"

Farley chewed on his lower lip a moment, then replied, "No, ma'am."

"Thank you. I have one further question. You stated several times that Lieutenant Tyson did nothing and said nothing in response to a variety of events that occurred. You also stated that he was frightened. What was he frightened of?"

Farley thought for some time, then replied, "He was frightened of us."

"Thank you."

Tyson looked at Major Sindel. She was about forty years old, with dark blond hair and blue eyes. The eyes were intelligent, and her voice had a touch of the South. She had beautiful hands that played with a pencil in an almost sensual way. She wasn't attractive, but Tyson thought she had enough going for her to be desirable.

Lieutenant Colonel McGregor asked, "Mr. Farley, you stated that Lieutenant Tyson gave an order to shoot any enemy sick and wounded that were in the hospital. I realize a great deal of time has elapsed, but could you recall the words he used?"

Farley tapped the fingers of both hands on the armrests of the wheelchair. Finally he replied, "Something like . . . 'go find the gooks' . . . no, he said, 'NVA' and maybe 'VC' . . . 'Go find them and waste them.'"

"He meant the NVA and VC in the beds?"

"Yes, sir."

"Did he say that?"

"I think so."

"How do you know he meant the NVA and the VC in the beds?"

"There was no other NVA and VC around."

"There were no armed enemy troops in or around the hospital?"

"No, sir. They ran off."

"Thank you."

Captain Morelli, the Adjutant General's Corps officer, asked, "Mr. Farley, just a point to clarify language. The word 'gooks.' Does this mean the enemy? Or civilians? Or both?"

Farley seemed glad someone posed an easy question. "Gooks could be both. Slants and slopes were civilians. Dinks could be both. It depended a lot on where you were and what you was doing. Charlie was always the enemy."

"Charlie was always a gook? But a gook wasn't always Charlie?"

Farley smiled for the first time. "You never knew when a gook was Charlie."

"I see. Thank you."

Colonel Moore asked, "In the hospital, did Lieutenant Tyson ever give you a direct order of any sort?"

Farley shook his head. "No, sir. He only gave the one order. To kill the sick and wounded. He shouted it to everybody."

"He did not personally supervise the carrying out of this order?"

"No, sir. He stayed in the operating room."

"Did you personally see his order carried out?"

"No, sir. I was in the operating room."

"But there were two wounded enemy soldiers in the operating room whom you did see get shot."

"Right. I saw that."

"What came first, Mr. Farley, the shooting of the two doctors in the operating room or Lieutenant Tyson's order to kill sick and wounded enemy soldiers?"

Farley replied, "I think the shooting of the two doctors. I can't remember. It was too long ago."

"How could you or the men of the platoon identify who of the patients were enemy soldiers?"

Farley thought about that for some time, then replied, "I don't know."

"Did Lieutenant Tyson instruct the men on methods of identification?"

"No, sir." Farley seemed to sense an opportunity. He said, "That's why the order was crazy. Once he gave it, you could shoot anybody. Women were VC, too. Old men were VC."

"But the women and babies in the maternity ward were not VC."

"I guess not."

"And the hospital staff were not VC or North Vietnamese Army."

"No, sir. But they were taking care of them."

"Did you ever observe anyone in your platoon trying to stop the shooting?"

"No, sir. But some guys didn't shoot. At least I never saw them shoot."

"Can you name anyone who didn't shoot?"

"Only one I know for sure was Doc Brandt. He never fired his rifle."

"Thank you." Colonel Moore said to Colonel Sproule, "The board has no further questions."

Colonel Sproule looked down at Richard Farley. "The witness is excused, subject to recall." Sproule looked at his watch and said to Pierce, "Do you wish to call your next witness?"

Pierce stood. "No, your honor. The next witness's testimony may be lengthy. I would prefer to begin tomorrow morning."

Sproule said, "The court will adjourn until ten hundred hours tomorrow."

Everyone stood as Colonel Sproule left the pulpit and exited the court.

Corva said to Tyson, "Bunch of amateurs."

"I thought they asked pretty good questions. Could you tell anything by their questions?"

"Yes. They've bought the story of a massacre. Nobody as stupid as Farley could make up over an hour of testimony about something that never happened. Tomorrow, Brandt will fine-tune the story. All the board wants to discover is your precise role, if any, in the massacre. They do not want to hear about firefights and room-to-room fighting." Corva picked up his briefcase. "I had a feeling this would happen. And as soon as Farley got into it, I felt that everyone in this place knew that what he had read in Picard's book was basically true."

"Well," said Tyson, "it was."

Corva watched the pews emptying and noticed that Marcy hadn't stayed behind. He turned back to Tyson. "Where do you want to go now?"

"Paris."

"My BOQ or your quarters?"

"Your place." Tyson looked around the chapel, empty now except for a few MPs waiting for him, and Colonel Pierce obsessively putting his papers in order. Tyson walked over to him, and Pierce looked up from his chair.

Pierce said, "Yes?"

Tyson said, "Yes, indeed."

"Can I help you?"

"Yes. You can. You can tell Richard Farley for me that I bear him no ill will. Will you do that?"

"Yes."

"And tell Dr. Brandt that it's payback time. Will you do that?"

Pierce, still in his chair, replied, "I think Dr. Brandt knows that."

Corva put his arm on Tyson's shoulder and moved him away. Corva said to Pierce, "You've improved quite a lot, Graham. I'm very impressed."

Pierce smiled tightly. "The best is yet to come."

"I think you should spend the night holding Dr. Brandt's hand," Corva said. "Two aspirins, see him in the morning. Good day." Corva turned and walked with Tyson out the side door into the corridor.

45

I f one were walking from Building 209, also known as Gresham Hall or the bachelor officers' quarters, and one were going to the officer family housing quarters, one might choose Pence Street, a quiet lane with few buildings, cutting through more of the flat treeless terrain of Fort Hamilton. And if one were coming from the Officers' Club and walking to the guest house, one might also use Pence Street, heading the other way. So, it was not completely fate, Tyson thought, that put him on the same street with Steven Brandt.

Tyson spotted him long before Brandt spotted Tyson, though they were the only two people walking on the grass that edged the narrow street. And, oddly, he knew it was Brandt long before he could clearly discern his features in the widely spaced street lighting.

It was a few minutes after 10 P.M., and he'd just left Corva's accommodations at the BOQ where the main topic of conversation had been the man who was less than fifty feet from him now. Tyson was still in his uniform, not having gone home to change. He saw that Brandt was wearing a bulky overcoat against the chill night air and had his hands thrust deeply in his pockets, his chin resting on the front of his coat, which was probably why he didn't see Tyson approaching him.

Tyson looked around but didn't see his usual MP escort. Tyson was within fifteen feet of Brandt now, and Brandt, sensing someone approaching, veered a few more feet onto the grass to allow room for the man coming toward him.

Tyson saw that not only was the overcoat bulky, but so too was the body it covered. Brandt had puffed out like a biscuit, and his face seemed to have the same appearance and complexion of flour and buttermilk. And he was quite bald except for a fringe of ludicrously long hair that fell on the collar of the dark blue overcoat. Tyson wondered how he'd recognized him from that distance; he barely recognized him now.

"Hello, Doc."

Brandt stopped, though *froze* might be a better word, Tyson thought. They were less than five feet apart, hand-shaking distance if anyone had the inclination.

Brandt didn't seem surprised, nor did he seem uncomfortable. If anything, he looked as if he'd just run into a dimly remembered patient, and he regarded Tyson with a cool clinical detachment, actually looking him up and down. Tyson had the urge to break the man's neck right then and there. Literally grab him as they'd taught him in hand-to-hand class and snap the neck at the third and fourth cervical vertebrae. "Out for a walk?" inquired Tyson.

Brandt nodded. "Yup."

"Coming from the club?"

"Yeah."

"Small post," observed Tyson.

Brandt remained in the position in which he'd frozen, one foot in front of the other, body slightly turned toward Tyson. "I'm not allowed to talk to you."

"On the contrary, Doctor, a witness may talk to the accused. If you don't *want* to talk to me, that's another matter."

"I have nothing to say."

"Save your voice for tomorrow."

Brandt neither moved nor responded. He seemed to sense that this chance meeting had to have a resolution.

"Hey, when's the last time we saw each other, Doc?" said Tyson as though the response should be, "The party after the Princeton game." In case Brandt thought the question was rhetorical, Tyson said, "When?"

"The ditch at the Strawberry Patch."

"Right. Right. What a day that was. What happened later?"

Brandt shrugged. "Don't remember."

"You did a nice job on me in the ditch."

"Thanks," said Brandt.

"The surgeons on the hospital ship said it was a professional wrap job."

"There's not much I could have done right or wrong with a wound like that. I'm glad to see you're walking well."

"Gives me a little pain in this damp weather."

"It'll always do that."

"Really? I thought I'd grow out of it."

Brandt straightened up and looked around.

Tyson said, "You're married now."

Brandt nodded.

"Children?"

"Two. Boy and a girl. Sixteen and twelve."

"Perfect family."

"Yes."

Tyson said, "Hey, I saw some of the old crew about a month ago. Beltran, Scorello, Sadowski, Walker, and Kalane. They asked about you."

For the first time Brandt smiled, but it was more of a grimace. "Did they?"

"Yes. They inquired about your future health."

Brandt didn't respond.

"See much of Farley?"

"Now and then." Brandt yanked his hand from his pocket and looked at his watch. "I have to go."

Tyson didn't acknowledge the statement. "What happened to the pictures?"

"What pictures?"

"The pictures, Doc. Your field study in female anatomy."

Brandt took a step, and Tyson took a step to intercept him. They were closer now, about three feet, swinging distance if anyone wanted to. Tyson said, "It's not even safe to hide them. You could die or something, and they'll turn up in your possessions. Maybe one of your children will get Daddy's war souvenir trunk and open it ten years from now. Bad for your posthumous reputation. Better to burn them, no matter how painful it may be to do so."

Brandt replied, "I don't know what you're talking about."

Tyson continued, "The ones I saw you take are classics, though. Hard to part with. You remember the one with the net hammock? That was clever of the National Police tying her in the hammock like a sausage. Every time they gave her a jolt of juice to the vagina, that hammock jumped, didn't it? Hard to capture that with snapshots."

Brandt looked around, but the long flat road was deserted.

Tyson said, "Look, Doc, everybody is a little kinky, but those people in the villages that we cordoned were in *pain*. Do you remember that woman who aborted after the National Police nearly drowned her in the well? And what was really *disgusting* was that you showed your corruption in front of the Vietnamese. It was one thing for us all to be crazy, but you compromised us and yourself with those people."

All Brandt could manage was, "Racist."

Tyson smiled. "I guess. And on the subject of morphine, I don't mind that you gave me more than my share, but I'd like to know what happened to the stuff that was missing."

Brandt said almost indistinctly, "Let me go."

"Yet, you were a good medic. You were no hero, but you were no coward, either. You knew your business. Lousy bedside manner, though. Those men who got hit were just meat to you. Just like the woman in the hammock with the electrode up her vagina. You are one of the *least* human beings I've ever come across. What do you do now? Orthopedic surgeon? Can I make any inferences from that? I guess not. That would be too psychoanalytical for me."

Brandt looked directly at Tyson for the first time. He said, "You never liked me from the beginning."

"I guess not."

"And I'll tell you why. Because you didn't like the competition. You liked being the honcho, the big college grad, with all your little adoring peons around you. I was an outsider, another college grad, and I had my own job separate from you and your lunatics. You all made such a thing about being infantrymen —First Cav troopers. What a laugh. If that was an elite unit, I shudder to think about the rest of the divisions."

Tyson looked into Brandt's eyes. "You may be on to something there, Doc."

"You see, I thought about that while I was there. I had a functioning brain, unlike the rest of them. You fancied yourself a knight, a tall handsome chivalrous knight with forty armed warriors at your side. I was the wizard, you see, the healer, whose presence you had to suffer and who reminded you—and your men—of death. And I watched for eleven months as men got chewed up and never said a word. But back in the aid stations and the hospitals, where *my* people were, they could at least cry together over the carnage. While I was with you, I shut my mouth. You hated me because the men looked up to me. But I wouldn't have competed for the approval of that bunch if they were the last human beings—or whatever they were—on the face of the earth."

Tyson nodded. "Doc, I'd be a liar if I said you were all wrong. But that doesn't change what *you* did or what you were. Or what I did or what I was, for that matter. But I did my duty up until that day. There's no stigma attached to me before February 15."

"You did your duty after you defined it for yourself. There were not many officers who would have reacted like you did to the . . . the cordon incident. That was your white knight complex. You liked being morally superior to everyone. I saw you once, by the way, coming out of a whorehouse in An Khe."

"How did you know it was a whorehouse?"

"Well," said Steven Brandt, "the past is the past, and we shouldn't stand here in the cold and talk about things that happened nearly two decades ago."

"No, and we shouldn't talk about them tomorrow either."

Brandt said nothing.

Tyson said, "We are all flawed, Dr. Brandt."

Brandt said, "I'd like to go."

"In a minute, Doc. I'm still the warrior, and you're not in the best of physical shape, as far as I can see. I want to ask you one question while I have this opportunity. Why didn't *you* report what happened at Miséricorde Hospital?"

Brandt said, "Don't you know?"

"No. I thought about it. But I never understood why you, who had nothing to do with it, didn't report it."

"Well, then, I'll tell you. When I first realized you were actually going to cover up that massacre, I felt my fingers closing around your balls. And every morning I woke up with a smile, wondering if I should make that the day I gave them a yank. And every day that passed, without you making a report, I knew you were in deeper trouble. The first few days were a little edgy for me, because I thought you would finally come to your senses and beat me to it. I thought perhaps you'd made a secret report, and that we'd be taken into base camp one day for R and R and find ourselves under arrest. But I gambled and waited, and by the end of February, I was going to yank you by your nuts off your high horse. I was going to see you in jail and me back in Saigon spending the rest of my tour of duty with the JAG people at MAC-V headquarters. But then fate stepped in again at the Strawberry Patch." Brandt shrugged and smiled. "So here we are."

Tyson stayed silent a long time, then said, "You could have still reported it and reported me. Men have been served charges in hospital beds before."

"Yes, but after the . . . the morphine . . . I was a little jumpy. I waited a week to see if we got a communication about your death. Then we got word that you were being sent to Japan and wouldn't be back. I thought about it. I decided that you were bright enough to figure out what I'd done to you and bright enough to know you didn't have a shred of evidence. So I considered us even. Or even enough for the time being." He stared at Tyson a very long time, then said, "I came from a good family, like you did, and I was always told I was special, like you were. I developed a big ego, like yours. So, to have you throw me in a leech-infested rice paddy and humiliate me in front of all those people, then have to face them and you every day. . . . and you wonder why I answered that locator ad? You find it hard to believe anyone can hate so charming a man as Ben Tyson. I assure you, I hate you." Brandt's eyes met Tyson's. "I still have nightmares about those leeches. I wake up sometimes feeling them pulsating against my skin."

"Do you? I'd recommend my shrink, but he killed himself."

Brandt said, "Can I go now?"

Tyson nodded. "Sure, Doc. But you have to remember one thing. Payback. Tomorrow won't end this."

"Well, it might for ten to twenty years. Good night." He took a tentative step, saw Tyson wasn't going to stop him, and hurried off.

Tyson continued on his way without looking back.

46

"Steven Brandt," said Colonel Pierce, "you swear that the evidence you shall give in the case now in hearing shall be the truth, the whole truth, and nothing but the truth, so help you God."

"I do."

"Could you state your residence and occupation?"

"I live in Boston, Massachusetts, and I am a medical doctor."

"Could you state your former grade, organization, and duties while you were a member of the armed forces serving in Vietnam?"

"Yes, I was a specialist four, with the Fifteenth Medical Battalion, and I served as a combat medic with Alpha Company, Fifth Battalion of the Seventh Cavalry, First Air Cavalry Division."

Tyson looked at Brandt as the preliminary questions continued. Brandt was dressed in the expensive bad taste that seemed to be common in the medical profession. He wondered if they all bought their clothes from an AMA catalog.

Tyson looked into the first pew and made eye contact with Marcy, who smiled somewhat enigmatically, he thought. They had been strange to each other for some weeks now, but there had been no open arguments. He had taken Corva's advice and put the marriage on hold while the trial was on fast forward.

As he scanned the pews, he observed that everyone who had come for act one had returned for act two. The weather was still nice, too, and that always brought people out, he thought.

Brandt's testimony began to move to more specific, though still peripheral, matters. Tyson turned his attention to the board. The combat veterans—Colonel Moore, Lieutenant Colonel McGregor, and Major Bauer—looked more relaxed with Brandt's testimony than with Farley's going on about gooks and human minesweepers and soldiers who took what they wanted. Of course, Brandt was saying similar things, but his choice of words was better.

Tyson looked again at Pierce and Brandt and listened. Pierce was proceeding very slowly, very logically, and very cautiously, unlike he'd proceeded with Farley. Brandt was articulate and answered the questions well, as though he were used to this sort of thing, and Tyson suspected he'd probably been involved in some way in civil cases of compensation claims or medical malpractice. Tyson glanced at Corva, who was scribbling notes as he listened to Brandt and Pierce sing their duet. Corva hadn't objected to anything so far, and there was little to object to, except that Pierce was referring to Brandt as "Doctor" in violation of a pretrial agreement. But Tyson thought Corva was smart not to draw attention to the point.

Pierce said, "How far were you from the burial mound, Doctor?"

"About two hundred meters."

"And you saw these people taking off their clothes?"

"Yes."

"Did you observe any actions on the part of Lieutenant Tyson, Farley, Simcox, or Kelly that you would construe as threatening gestures toward these approximately ten civilians?"

"Yes, though I couldn't say with certainty who made the gestures. But there was some pushing of the civilians, rifles were pointed at them. And I saw one of the soldiers kick mud at them."

Tyson glanced out over the pews again. The spectators were attentive, but it was not the rapt attention that Farley's testimony had engendered. Farley had laid the rough groundwork, now Pierce and Brandt were building on it, block by block, mortar and brick, until an unshakable structure would stand for Corva to try to take apart.

Pierce asked, "Were you often called on to assist in these strip searches of civilians?"

"Always. It was general policy. This type of search could only be done under the direction of an officer or senior NCO. They were to be conducted with as much tact as the situation allowed. It was my duty to perform the intrusion aspect of the search."

"What is the intrusion aspect?"

"The intrusion into the anus and vagina. Enemy documents were sometimes rolled into an aluminum tube and transported in that manner."

"Based on past experience, do you believe that what you observed was a necessary or legitimate search?"

"I don't think so. It seemed to me to be nothing more than . . . how shall I put this . . . ? A quasi-sexual event."

Corva and Tyson simultaneously looked at each other. Corva said, "This guy has more balls than a bull."

Pierce glanced sharply at the defense table, then said, "I'd like to ask you now your opinion of the desecration of the dead bodies of the enemy soldiers who were wrapped for burial."

Corva stood. "Your honor, the defense objects."

Colonel Sproule turned toward Corva with the look of a man who was rudely interrupted while listening to something interesting. "What is the nature of your objection?"

"Your honor, the defense fully understands that the prosecution is attempting to show a link between the alleged events at the burial mound and the alleged events later in the day. We have not objected to some of this testimony, but I think it has gone on long enough. It is, in fact, taking on a prurient aspect which might hold some interest to some people, but has little relevance to the case at hand."

Sproule thought about this a moment, then said to Pierce, "Colonel, we've spent nearly an hour at that burial mound listening to the testimony of a witness who was two hundred meters from the scene. Now, I will allow you to go on, but I expect, as I told you in an earlier session, that what you present has some relevance to the charges you have sworn to. Objection overruled."

Pierce nodded as though Colonel Sproule had made an interesting point, then turned around and continued the questioning of Brandt on the desecration of the bodies of the enemy soldiers.

In excruciating detail, the first platoon of Alpha Company continued its patrol toward the village of An Ninh Ha and Miséricorde Hospital. Tyson's own recollections of that rainy day coincided with Brandt's, and he was surprised at how good a memory Brandt had. And when Brandt didn't remember, he said so.

Pierce said to Brandt, "Doctor, the events that I am about to question you on concern your platoon's approach to this hospital. These events are discussed at some length in a book titled *Hue: Death of a City,* by the author Andrew Picard. Did you, in fact, supply any information for that book?"

"Yes, I did."

"Have you read the book?"

"Yes, I did."

"Generally speaking, how much of Mr. Picard's reporting was based on information that you gave him?"

"A good portion of his written account was based on my oral account to him, though I saw details and facts that I could not have given him."

"Such as?"

"The names of some of the hospital staff. He told me that he had interviewed a survivor of the incident—a nun named Sister Teresa, whom he later credited in the book."

Pierce pursued the provenance of the story for a while, then asked, "As the platoon medic, what was your usual physical location in the platoon formation?"

"Normally, on patrol, I traveled with what we called the platoon command group. This would consist of the platoon leader, one or two radio operators, and the medic. When the platoon halted for the night, the platoon sergeant would join us in the center of the defensive perimeter and form the command post."

"So you were usually close to the platoon leader, Lieutenant Tyson, day and night?"

"Yes."

"You knew him well?"

"As well as you can know a man you spend ten months with, night and day. There was, of course, a barrier to any real intimacy due to the fact that he was an officer and I an enlisted man. But we did at times confide in each other."

"How would you describe your relationship with him?"

Brandt turned and looked at Tyson. He gave Tyson a smile that Tyson and anyone who saw it would think idiotic.

Brandt turned back to Pierce and said, "There were differences between us, but we generally respected each other. He often praised my work."

"Did you often praise his?"

Brandt smiled again. "I was sometimes impressed with his ability to lead. He seemed a natural leader. I may have praised him on occasion."

Tyson listened to Pierce eliciting Brandt's opinion of him, and Tyson was surprised at what a high opinion Specialist Four Brandt had of Lieutenant Tyson.

Pierce went on in this vein for some time, and Tyson thought it was smart of Pierce to sandwich this personal element in between the burial mound incident and what was to come.

Pierce said, "Doctor, one final question before our expected recess. As the platoon's medic, did you feel that Lieutenant Tyson was adequately concerned with the mental and physical condition of his men?"

Corva stood. "Objection, your honor. The witness has no psychiatric training, to the best of my knowledge, and I should point out that, at the time we are discussing, he was a twenty-three-year-old medical corpsman, not a middle-aged doctor."

"Objection sustained. Colonel Pierce, do you wish a recess at this time?"

Pierce had no intention of breaking for lunch on that note. He replied, "I would like to rephrase the question, your honor."

"Please do."

Pierce turned to Brandt. "Doctor—"

Again Corva was on his feet. "Objection, your honor."

"To *what?*"

"Your honor, I didn't mind when Colonel Pierce addressed the witness as 'Doctor' the first thirty or forty times. But now that he's trying to elicit some sort of retrospective medical opinion, I think he's trying to give that opinion more worth than it has by referring to the witness as 'Doctor.' "

Sproule thought a moment and said, "Objection sustained. Colonel Pierce, perhaps you'd like some time to rephrase your question. This court will recess until thirteen-thirty hours."

In the BOQ, Tyson and Corva sat across from each other in the Swedish Modern armchairs, a light-wood coffee table between them. Corva had the

Officers' Club send over box lunches and explained to Tyson, "It's on your bill. I gave them your number."

"Thanks." Tyson added, "Short recess."

"Yes. Sproule could see that Brandt and Pierce will be at it for some time. I've seen testimony at courts-martial go until ten at night. No one has to worry about the jurors getting annoyed. Or overtime for the court reporter or guards." Corva dug into a plate of cold pasta salad. He said, "Tell me all about the good doctor's moral corruption. Was that the reason for the incident of the leeches in the rice paddy?"

Tyson nodded. "Did you ever participate in any of those cordon operations with the Vietnamese National Police?"

Corva nodded. "Just one. That was one too many."

"Right you are. My company did about four or five of them. Well, after we cordoned off the village before dawn, the National Police—the fucking Gestapo—would arrive in American choppers. Then they would go strutting in with their crisp uniforms to conduct search and interrogation operations. Is that the way they did it where you were?"

"Pretty much."

"No Americans were allowed in the village. What went on between the police and the villagers was not for American eyes. But American officers could sometimes enter to discuss coordination with the Gestapo commander. I entered a few times. Brandt, as a medic, could get in, too."

Corva nodded. "He enjoyed himself, did he?"

"Did he? He was in heaven. Talk about tactless strip searches. These police goons did some strip searches and intrusions that weren't in any field manual I've ever seen. And, of course, there was the torture—the whippings, the water treatments. I myself was disgusted by what these sadists were doing in the guise of a counterinsurgency operation. Brandt, on the other hand, was ecstatic. It was strictly forbidden to take pictures, of course, but Brandt had a cozy relationship with these National Police pigs. On the particular operation that led to his leech bath, I saw him snapping away with his camera. He didn't see me. Kelly was with me, and we followed him into a hootch. I caught him with two National Policemen, raping three young girls."

Corva shook his head. "Hearts and minds."

"You want to hear all the details, or do you want to finish your lunch first?"

"What do you think?"

"Have your lunch first."

The court reconvened at one-thirty, and Colonel Pierce said to Brandt, "You are reminded that you are still under oath."

Brandt nodded an acknowledgment.

Colonel Pierce apparently had not thought of a way to rephrase his last question because he asked instead, "Dr. Brandt, you have testified that your platoon had knowledge that they were approaching a hospital in the village of An Ninh Ha, a western suburb of Hue."

"That is correct."

"What was the platoon's reaction to this?"

Corva stood. "Objection, your honor. How is the witness supposed to gauge the reaction of nineteen men strung out over a distance of perhaps a quarter kilometer?"

"Objection sustained." He looked at Pierce. "Could you rephrase the question?"

"Yes, your honor." He looked at Brandt. "Did you hear any reaction to the information that you were on your way to a hospital?"

Brandt crossed his legs, and Tyson saw he wore light gray loafers with little tassels on them. His socks were almost sheer, and Tyson could see his white skin underneath.

Brandt replied, "During the rest breaks, I would often walk up and down the file to check on the physical condition of the platoon. During this time I heard reactions from several men about Lieutenant Tyson's decision to make this hospital an intermediate objective on our march to Hue."

"How would you characterize these reactions that you heard?"

"Mostly positive. The men seemed excited by the prospect of encountering some civilization."

"So they had no preconceived negative feelings about this?"

"On the contrary. I heard Lieutenant Tyson give a few of the men incentives. He spoke about hot chow, showers, and women."

"Could you be more specific?"

"I heard him speak to a man named Simcox and tell him that he might get a blow job at the hospital."

A few people in the spectator pews gasped. A man laughed, then became abruptly quiet.

Pierce waited a moment, then said, "Did you take this to mean that Lieutenant Tyson was suggesting to Simcox that he . . . Simcox . . . how do I phrase this . . . ?" Pierce smiled self-consciously.

Dr. Brandt volunteered a clarification. "A blow job, of course, is slang for fellatio. Lieutenant Tyson was telling Simcox that there was a chance of having this performed on him—Simcox—at the hospital. I assume Lieutenant Tyson meant by a woman."

"Thank you. Did you have the impression that Lieutenant Tyson meant to commandeer this hospital?"

"I don't know if he did or not. But by his statements about women and other comforts at the hospital, the men became quite aroused, and as the patrol moved toward the hospital, the expectations of the men became somewhat unrealistic."

Pierce continued mining this vein, and Tyson thought it was rather smart of Pierce to show that the men had positive feelings before reaching the hospital and that these feelings were a result of their platoon leader promising them rape, pillage, and plunder. Neither Pierce nor Brandt was going to be satisfied with proving only that he was a murderer. They wanted, also, to show that he was without integrity, venal, and debased. And there were two hundred people listening to this, including the press, people he knew, his wife, son, and mother. He wondered why he hadn't broken Brandt's neck.

The examination of Steven Brandt went on. Six or seven times Pierce drew the platoon to the hospital, then pulled them back with tangential or background questions posed to Brandt. Brandt seemed in no hurry either. He answered each of Pierce's questions fully and apparently objectively.

When Pierce finally took the court to the open square in front of the hospital, everyone was ready not only to hear but also to believe what Dr. Steven Brandt was going to say.

Pierce asked, "How many shots rang out from the vicinity of the hospital?"

"About five or six in quick succession."

"Could you tell approximately where they were coming from?"

"No. And neither could anyone around me."

"So you can't say for sure if they actually came from the hospital?"

"No."

"But in Picard's book and in previous testimony, it was stated that the hospital was the source of the sniper fire."

"I never told Picard it was. I don't know where Picard heard that. I thought the hospital was the least likely place an enemy sniper would choose."

"Did anyone around you at the time believe the firing was coming from the hospital?"

"Yes. Lieutenant Tyson did. He directed some fire back toward the hospital. I almost never got involved in tactical questions, but this time I asked him to stop the firing at the hospital."

"What did he reply?"

"He told me to mind my own business. Which I did. We had two wounded and one killed."

"Could you name them?"

"Yes. Robert Moody was wounded in the leg. A light flesh wound. Arthur Peterson was hit here—" Brandt pointed to a spot on his right side, just below the armpit. "The bullet passed through the . . . Can I use medical terms?"

Pierce smiled in sympathy. "Best not."

"Well, then, through the body and exited a bit lower on the other side. Both lungs were involved. Peterson was drowning in his own blood."

"And the third man?"

"Yes . . . Larry Cane . . . he was shot in the heart and died instantly."

"And you treated these men under fire?"

"No. The firing had stopped almost as soon as it had begun, and I was in no danger," said Brandt modestly.

"What happened after the firing stopped?"

"The platoon directed a few more rounds of fire at the hospital. There were no glass windows. Only screens and louver shutters, and I recall these being shot up. As I said, I still didn't think the five or six rounds that hit the three men came from there. Finally, Lieutenant Tyson gave a cease-fire."

"Then what happened?"

"Then Lieutenant Tyson ordered four or five men to maneuver toward the hospital. They did and got right to the front door without anyone firing at them. I should point out that, as we approached the hospital, there were white sheets hanging from three or four of the windows, which I took to be a sign of peace or a signal that the hospital was neutral. Also, as I said, there was the Red Cross flag flying on a staff from the front of the building."

"And there was no resistance from anyone inside the hospital?"

"None at all."

Tyson listened as Pierce backed up a bit, then took everyone to the threshold of the hospital again, then back again to the square in front of the hospital, then forward over the threshold into the front lobby. Pierce was pushing buttons on his tape recorder, forward, back, forward, and Brandt was responding like an audio tape. Corva objected now and then, but even Tyson could tell he didn't object to all he could have. He was giving Pierce a lot of leeway, and Pierce was growing a little cockier, letting Brandt make statements that Brandt would have a rough time explaining on the cross-examination.

Finally Pierce got the platoon up the stairs of the hospital to the second floor where the main drama would unfold.

Pierce asked Brandt, "How would you describe your reception inside the hospital?"

"Well, it was rather cool. We had just fired a few hundred rounds at the place, and if my guess is correct about the sniper not even being in or on the building, I can certainly see why they were less than enthusiastic to see us."

"Was anyone openly hostile?"

"I wouldn't go so far as to say that. The men of the platoon were not very friendly visitors, either. I don't entirely blame them, though. It was this solitary sniper who caused what one might characterize as a misunderstanding, a feeling of distrust and hostility. It was not the happy arrival that the platoon had been expecting."

Pierce looked pointedly at his watch.

Colonel Sproule did likewise, and Tyson thought they looked like they were doing a pre-attack watch synchronization. Colonel Sproule said, "Colonel Pierce, if you have no objections, I'd like to adjourn this court until eighteen hundred hours."

"I have no objections to a night session, your honor."

Sproule looked at Corva. "Does the defense have any objections to a night session?"

"No, your honor."

"Then the court is adjourned until eighteen hundred hours."

Tyson and Corva again went to the BOQ. Some of Brandt's morning testimony had been transcribed and was waiting for Corva, who took it from an MP at the door.

Corva and Tyson entered the apartment, and Corva took a bottle of premixed martinis from the bar refrigerator. He sat at the dining room table and began looking through the transcripts.

Tyson had a martini and a cigarette. He said, "Where's dinner?"

"I'm not hungry," said Corva.

"What if I am?"

"Eat your olive."

"There is no olive."

Corva shrugged as he read and drank.

Tyson said, "How is the prosecution doing?"

"Not bad."

"How is the defense doing?"

"Too early to say."

Tyson paced around the living room. "You're not objecting to some of Pierce's leading questions."

"Why should I object to them? They're interesting. Look, Brandt is Pierce's witness. A prosecutor leading his own witness is just a shortcut to getting to what Brandt is going to say anyway. Let them dance."

Tyson shrugged.

Corva said, "I'm going to ask you about some of these statements that Brandt made, and you'll give me short and succinct answers that I can use on the cross-examination, which will probably be tomorrow."

"Okay."

Corva said, "I hope *our* witnesses are as articulate and orderly in their answers."

"I hope you are as articulate and orderly in your questions."

Corva looked at Tyson. "I wish all our witnesses weren't going to tell about a room-to-room battle in the same location and at the same time as Brandt and Farley told about a wanton massacre. It might confuse the jury."

* * *

The court reconvened at 6 P.M., and Pierce pronounced, "All the parties to the trial who were present when the court adjourned are again present in the court."

Which, Tyson thought, was true. And if anyone took attendance in the pews, he could probably announce the same thing. The Army had an obsession with "all present or accounted for."

Pierce reminded Brandt that he was still under oath, but Tyson didn't think that was going to do any more good this time than it did last time.

Pierce began with warm-up questions, then questions of recapitulation, then moved again to the front doors of Miséricorde Hospital. Pierce and Brandt by this time had developed that sense of timing and mutual understanding of speech patterns that characterized long question-and-answer periods. But Brandt did not once anticipate a question, and though the examination was smooth, it did not appear rehearsed.

Pierce had finally gotten to the second floor of the hospital, and there was a palpable sense of expectation in the court, as Pierce asked, "What did you see when you entered this room?"

"I saw immediately that it was an operating room. From what I could see, I didn't think the hospital was ever meant to fulfill the function of a general hospital. It seemed more a sanitorium than a hospital. My guess was that it was built by the French as a country rest home or convalescent hospital."

Pierce seemed infinitely patient as Steven Brandt gave his professional opinion of the architecture, layout, and setting of the place. Tyson thought that if Steven Brandt had been a crippled, unemployed veteran instead of a medical doctor, neither Pierce nor anyone else would have had much patience for this. Brandt got down to specifics. "The operating room consisted of seven operating tables in an open space about thirty by forty feet. The walls were whitewashed stucco, as was the beamed ceiling. The windows were screened but not glazed as I said, and the floor was red terra-cotta tile. It was stark. There was electricity in the hospital, probably provided by a generator, and the operating room was lit by hanging incandescent fixtures. It was under these fixtures that the operating tables had been placed. Ceiling fans moved the air around, but the room stank of putrefying flesh and open body cavities. There were flies everywhere. I saw in an adjoining room a sink and toilet, and I assumed the water source was a collecting cistern on the roof. Hot water was boiled on a charcoal stove, also located in this adjoining room. The conditions were primitive, to say the least, and not very sanitary. My feelings for the men and women who were going about their jobs there was one of admiration."

Pierce nodded in complete accord, though Tyson suspected he hadn't listened to a word of it.

Pierce asked, "Who entered the operating room with you?"

"I can't recall everyone who was there, but I know I entered with Lieutenant Tyson, his radio operator, Kelly, Richard Farley, and I believe two more men. Farley was assisting Moody, who'd been hit in the leg. The other two men were carrying Peterson, who was semiconscious and crying out."

"How many other people were in the room, and who were they?"

"There were about twenty hospital staff there. It was quite a mixture. All the doctors seemed to be Caucasian males. There were Oriental orderlies of both sexes. There were female nurses of both races—that is, Caucasian and Oriental. Most of the nurses wore white cotton dresses that I thought resembled nuns' habits. They wore crosses around their necks. There were religious adornments throughout the hospital, and I made the assumption it was a Catholic facility."

Corva leaned toward Tyson. "I've seen courts-martial run until midnight."
Tyson said, "Brandt seems fresh. He's enjoying himself."

Corva observed, "Pierce is in fine form, too. I think he'd like to finish up with Brandt tonight, while they're both on a roll. Sometimes you get a witness back the next day and the magic is gone."

Pierce asked Brandt, "Did any of the staff in the operating room formally greet you?"

"No. But Lieutenant Tyson said something to the doctor who was closest to the door. The doctor was working on a patient with a badly mangled leg. Lieutenant Tyson walked over to the operating table—it was the closest one— and began talking to this doctor."

"In what language?"

"English, at first. But the doctor was intent on his patient. He said a few words to the nurse in what sounded like French, then Lieutenant Tyson switched to French."

"Do you speak French, Doctor?"

"No. But I'd heard enough of it over there by this time to recognize it."

"Were Lieutenant Tyson and the doctor speaking amicably?"

"Not at all. I could tell from the beginning that they were having strong words."

"About what?"

"I suppose about Lieutenant Tyson's insistence that someone do something for Peterson. Actually, Lieutenant Tyson did make several asides to me and Kelly in English, so I knew what was going on."

Pierce continued his questions, and the responses provided more detail than Picard had done in his book and Farley had given in his testimony. After fifteen minutes of examination concerning a segment of the incident that probably lasted one minute, Pierce asked, "What was your opinion—your opinion at the time—not in retrospect, but at the time—of Peterson's condition?"

"I told Lieutenant Tyson my opinion several times. Peterson's wound was mortal. Only a thoracic surgeon in a well-equipped hospital room could have saved him. I saw a similar wound at a place called Phu Lai. I told Lieutenant Tyson that if Peterson had any chance at all, it was to get him on a medevac chopper. But he hadn't called one."

"Did he give you any reason for not calling one?"

"No, except that he was obsessed with the idea that if he were in a hospital, he should be able to get aid for his man. I explained that the hospital didn't look like it was equipped for what would have been open chest surgery. I think that was what this doctor was trying to tell him, too." Brandt paused and said, "Actually, I told him to forget Peterson. The man's blood pressure was dropping, and his breathing was very shallow. It was a difficult thing to say, but the man was as good as dead."

"How did Lieutenant Tyson react to what you were telling him?"

"Not very well. He was very agitated, and I had the impression he was more interested in imposing his will on that doctor and the staff of that hospital than he was in helping Arthur Peterson."

Tyson stood suddenly, sensing his chair falling backward. All noise including the court reporter's stenotype stopped. No one said anything for a second or two as Tyson stared at Brandt, his hands visibly shaking.

Corva looked at him but made no movement to get him in his seat.

Colonel Sproule said to Tyson, "Will the accused please be seated?" Before Tyson could comply or not comply Sproule said hastily, "The court will recess for fifteen minutes."

* * *

Tyson and Corva walked in silence to Rabbi Weitz's office. Corva closed the office door and said, "You scared the shit out of old Sproule."

Tyson didn't reply.

Corva added, "Brandt went a little white, too." Corva went on, "And the board will have no trouble believing that you belted the French doctor."

Tyson walked to the window and lit a cigarette.

Corva added, "Of course, there was a positive side to that little scene. Colonel Amos Moore smiled for the first time in two days. I saw it. A tight little smile of approval."

Tyson shrugged.

Corva said, "They don't like the little shit, Ben."

Tyson nodded slowly. "But they believe him." Tyson drew on his cigarette. "Do you think Pierce himself believes that I ordered enemy soldiers to be shot?"

"Oh, yes. And it gives him the moral resolve he needs to prosecute this case. The fact of you not reporting the massacre may be legal or technical murder, but neither he nor the government would have had much heart for this case if that's all they had against you. No, they *have* to believe that your illegal order to commit selective murder led to the mass murder of everyone else in that hospital."

There was a knock on the door, and an MP called out, "Time."

Colonel Pierce looked at his witness for some time, then asked, "What was the result of this altercation between Lieutenant Tyson and the French-speaking doctor?"

"Lieutenant Tyson slapped the man across the face."

Pierce nodded thoughtfully as if he'd heard this someplace before. Recalling that both Picard and Farley had described what followed as confusion, he said to Brandt, "Would you tell us now, in your own words, what happened after Lieutenant Tyson struck this doctor. Take your time, Doctor, and relate the incident as you recall it from your perspective."

Brandt crossed his legs and leaned back in his chair. He put the tips of his fingers together and cocked his head slightly to the side so that he was looking obliquely at Pierce. Tyson thought Brandt was about to tell Pierce that he was a very sick man. Instead, Brandt said, "The very next thing that happened was that Richard Farley swung his rifle and delivered a butt stroke to the doctor's groin. The doctor doubled over in pain. Then Lieutenant Tyson turned to one of his men, Hernando Beltran, and told him to pull the doctor's patient off the operating table. Beltran did this, literally throwing this man with the mangled leg on the floor. Two men lifted Peterson to the table. A white Caucasian female then placed a suction tube in Peterson's throat and with a foot-pedal device began aspirating Peterson's blood. But Peterson would have needed transfusions of whole blood in order to stabilize his pressure, and he would have needed immediate exploratory surgery to see if blood was collecting in the abdomen. I think the hospital staff or some of them were ready to make a show of saving his life in order to avoid an ugly scene."

Brandt looked at his surroundings, and his eyes went to the stained-glass windows where the light had long since faded. He seemed suddenly aware of the fact that he'd been testifying since morning, and he slumped a little in the chair. He cleared his throat and went on. "Now that Peterson was on the table, Lieutenant Tyson began giving orders regarding other matters. His first concern, and properly so, was that the hospital should be searched thoroughly for hidden enemy soldiers. He ordered a room-to-room search."

Pierce interrupted. "Excuse me. Who did he give this order to? Who was present in the operating room? Could you describe the general command structure and deployment of this platoon?"

Brandt replied, "There were a total of nineteen men who approached the hospital. As I said, it was a much reduced platoon. It was difficult to keep track of the comings and goings of everyone. Men were coming in and out, making hasty reports to Lieutenant Tyson. There were no sergeants in the platoon to give orders or supervise the men except Paul Sadowski, who had just been promoted to sergeant but who was not very experienced. There was virtually no command structure or organized deployment of the platoon. But eventually, about twelve men wound up in the operating room. It was then that Lieutenant Tyson began to attempt some organization. But the men were not at home, so to speak, in this sort of situation. They were running about, gawking at patients and staff. Some of them had not been in contact with . . . with other people for close to a year. That's the general impression I had. One of undisciplined behavior. Inappropriate behavior for the surroundings."

Pierce seemed to find this interesting. "Did this cause friction between the men of the platoon and the hospital personnel?"

"Oh, yes. There were several incidents."

"Did Lieutenant Tyson correct the behavior of his men?"

"Not that I saw or heard. He'd promised them a little treat, and he let them run loose. But as I said, most of them had gravitated toward the operating room where he was. Someone reported to him that the adjoining ward held six or seven wounded North Vietnamese soldiers. Their bloody khakis had been found lying around, and somehow the men matched the khakis to the soldiers, or perhaps there were other signs to indicate who was an enemy soldier."

"And there were about twelve men in the operating room now."

"Yes. And one of them was now having a verbal altercation with an English-speaking doctor. Then Beltran called out that Peterson had died. Then Lieutenant Tyson gave an order to shoot any enemy soldiers who were found in the hospital." Brandt knew to stop there.

Pierce said, "You heard him give this order?"

"Yes. He was five feet from me."

"Can you recall in what form the order was given?"

"Not precisely. It was more of a response to these reports he was getting from a few men concerning the discovery of enemy soldiers in the beds. Lieutenant Tyson simply said something like, 'Shoot them.' "

"Meaning the enemy soldiers."

"That was the subject at hand, yes."

"Did anyone appear to follow this order?"

"Yes. A few men hurried off, and we heard five or six shots. Almost immediately afterward, I heard a loud burst of gunfire right in the room. I turned, and this English-speaking doctor lay on the floor bleeding. I couldn't tell who shot him or why. I dropped to one knee, behind the operating table. There were more bursts of automatic fire. I saw the French-speaking doctor drop to the floor. Then I heard two loud single shots, and I discovered later that someone had executed the two North Vietnamese patients in the operating room. I saw them sometime later with bullet wounds in their heads. I should point out that I couldn't see much from where I was on the floor. I had no idea at first where the gunfire was coming from except that it was close. I even thought it might be enemy fire. But within a minute I realized it wasn't, because no one was reacting as though it was. No one was saying 'take cover' or returning any fire. Everyone was on their feet within a minute. Then someone began ordering the hospital staff into the adjoining room, making them leave their patients on the tables."

"What was Lieutenant Tyson doing during this time?"

"He seemed to be doing nothing. He had his rifle cradled in his arm, he was smoking a cigarette and speaking to his radio operator, Kelly. I should say that a state of chaos existed now. There was random shooting throughout the hospital. I could hear voices screaming in Vietnamese. Most of the platoon had gone off into the rest of the hospital. There was a time when only Lieutenant Tyson, Kelly, and I were in the operating room. Tyson seemed unable or unwilling to move from the spot and see what was happening."

"Did you speak to him during this time?"

"Yes. I said to him, 'They're shooting everyone.' "

"And what did he reply?"

"He said he'd go see about it. He seemed almost unconcerned . . . detached. He and Kelly left, and I never saw them again until we'd all assembled outside the hospital."

Pierce said, "Let's go back to the time when the men were reporting to him about finding suspected wounded enemy soldiers. How many men reported this to him?"

"Two or three."

"Did any of them make a suggestion as to what should be done with them? Or did they ask for instructions?"

"One of them, actually it was Sergeant Sadowski, told Lieutenant Tyson that the enemy soldiers were under guard. He asked what to do with them. That's when Lieutenant Tyson said, 'Shoot them.' "

"Those were his exact words."

"Yes. 'Shoot them.' "

Pierce began a series of questions meant to replay the entire episode of the operating room. He tried to establish elapsed time, sequences, distances, positions of men, and names. But Brandt wouldn't commit himself to details or specifics, which, Tyson thought, was the right way to handle an incident that was chaotic when it happened eighteen years before. He noted, too, that Brandt's testimony did not perfectly coincide with Farley's, nor should it. It would have been suspicious if it had. He thought about his own five witnesses and their stories, and the sudden realization came to him that these men could not testify. Brandt and Farley diverted from the truth only on occasions when they sought to incriminate Tyson. But Beltran, Sadowski, Kalane, Walker, and Scorello would have to relate an entire battle episode that never happened. As Brandt went through his account again, Tyson leaned to Corva and said, "We have no defense witnesses."

Corva replied, "We never did. I'll talk to you about that tonight."

Pierce took Brandt finally out of the hospital, into the rain-splashed courtyard, and it was as though everyone in the chapel breathed easier as they moved from the blazing fire, screams, and gunfire into the quiet rain.

Pierce said, "So now you were all together again."

"Yes. Then Kelly, Lieutenant Tyson's radio operator, saw someone leap from a window of the hospital. He fired at the figure, a female, and she fell over before she could run. Then Lieutenant Tyson ordered one squad of men to deploy on each of the other sides of the hospital."

"Why?"

"He said to shoot anyone who tried to escape. I stayed with him and Kelly and a machine-gun team on the courtyard side of the hospital."

Tyson looked at his watch. It was 8:15 P.M. Corva must be hungry, he thought. The pews were still full, though there was some coming and going as MPs let people outside come in whenever others left. There seemed to be an inexhaustible supply of spectators, and Tyson found that interesting.

Pierce said to Brandt, "Do you want a recess?"

"No. I'm fine."

Pierce said to Sproule, "If the court has no objections, we'd like to continue."

Sproule replied, "You may continue until twenty-two hundred hours, then we ought to adjourn."

Pierce turned to Brandt again and picked up the questioning. "You said Lieutenant Tyson was making false radio reports to his company commander, Captain Browder."

"Yes. He was reporting enemy contact and giving progress reports regarding the approach to the structure which he described to Captain Browder as a large government building. He was, in effect, going back in time and creating incidents that did not happen. Meanwhile, we were putting distance between ourselves and the burning hospital."

Pierce, to everyone's surprise, moved quickly ahead to the French bunker. He asked Brandt, "What was the mood in the bunker?"

"Somewhat subdued. We had the two bodies with us—Peterson and Cane. Some of the men smoked marijuana. Lieutenant Tyson passed around a bottle of Scotch. A few men played cards. Lieutenant Tyson seemed intent on making them understand that they had to agree to a cover story for the incident. He coached everyone on what he should say if questioned. He congratulated them on a fine job. Then he even congratulated a man—Scorello—on using a phosphorus grenade to burn the hospital. He said something to the effect that there was no evidence to incriminate any of them. He even made up a body count."

"Did Lieutenant Tyson indicate why he was going through this trouble of fabricating a story—why he simply didn't report to Captain Browder on the sniper and leave it at that?"

"Yes. He indicated that too much time had elapsed. He had to account for several missed radio reports. Also, we were supposed to join up with Captain Browder and the main body of the company before dark. But Lieutenant Tyson did not want his men mingling with the rest of the company in the state they were in. So he reported we were still in the village of An Ninh Ha and would spend the night there. He also stated to Kelly, and I overheard this, that he wasn't going to have two dead and one wounded without being able to show an enemy body count. He was a man who did not like to look bad in front of his superiors. So, he fabricated a battle that would bring credit on him. His radio operator, Kelly, wrote up a proposal for a Silver Star for Lieutenant Tyson."

Colonel Pierce concentrated on Brandt's recollections of the night in the bunker. Brandt, whose testimony had been almost dry, now described the atmosphere in the bunker in lyrical terms. He spoke about the flickering candlelight, the men speaking long into the night, the sound of nearby artillery fire, and the burning city of Hue, whose west wall was less than a kilometer away. Brandt described Tyson spinning his tale of a battle, and Brandt's story became a tale within a tale. Brandt described Moody crying out from the pain, administering morphine to him, and offering tranquilizers to the men, who declined, preferring marijuana and the lieutenant's Scotch instead.

Brandt ended his story by describing the dawn breaking and the men climbing atop the concrete bunker watching the smoke rise from Hue, silhouetted against the rising sun.

Pierce let an appropriate amount of time pass, then asked, "Did anyone in the bunker show any remorse?"

"A few men were quite shaken. But by and large, there was a feeling that the people in the hospital got what was coming to them. This was stated several times and in several ways by different people."

Pierce, through Brandt, examined the psyches of the men of the first platoon. At five minutes to ten, Pierce said to Brandt, "Did you ever consider reporting the incident as it actually occurred?"

"Yes. Nearly every day. At first, it wasn't physically possible for me to make contact with anyone who I could report to. But then we were given a brief two-day rest in a rear area. But on the way to camp, a delegation of six or seven men from the platoon took me aside and told me that if the story got out, they would assume it was me who let it out. They further stated that it would do no good to report the incident, anyway, since no one would believe me if everyone else swore that there had been no massacre. They were right about that, of course. Considering the time, place, and general conditions that prevailed, I saw no benefit in reporting what I'd seen. Of course, I should have, and that has been haunting me for nearly twenty years now. So when the opportunity arose to assist the author, Picard, by supplying the details of this incident, I immediately took it. I thought that a book would be an excellent format to tell the story of Miséricorde Hospital. I thought that if the Army and the government wished to pursue it, they would, and I would make myself available for any investigatory or legal proceedings that came out of the book's revelations. And I did, and that is why I am here."

Pierce said, "Thank you, Doctor." Pierce looked at Colonel Sproule.

Sproule looked at his watch and nodded in satisfaction. Sproule announced, "The court will adjourn until ten hundred hours tomorrow."

Twelve hours after he'd taken the stand, Steven Brandt rose and walked off toward the side door.

47

At 10 A.M. on Wednesday, Colonel Sproule surveyed the chapel and announced, "The court will come to order."

Colonel Pierce said, "All parties to the trial who were present when the court adjourned are again present in the court."

Everyone sat except Pierce, who turned to Corva and asked, "Does the defense wish to cross-examine the last witness?"

Corva replied from his seat, "It does."

Pierce instructed the sergeant at arms, and within two minutes, Steven Brandt appeared.

Brandt took the witness chair, and Pierce said to him, "You are reminded that you are still under oath."

Brandt gave a slight wave of the hand in acknowledgment, which seemed an inappropriate gesture.

Tyson lit a cigarette and leaned across the table. He studied Brandt's face, but there was no sign of any apprehension at having to face a cross-examination.

The spectator section was again full, and Tyson noticed that some people seemed to be in the same seats as the day before, though perhaps he was imagining it. The press corps all seemed to have made friends with one another and with some of the MPs.

Corva was reviewing the previous day's testimony and made no move to rise and walk toward Steven Brandt, who seemed somewhat confused. Several minutes went by, then Pierce stood and addressed Colonel Sproule, "Your honor, did the defense answer in the affirmative?"

Sproule said to Pierce, "I believe so." Sproule turned to Corva. "Does the defense wish to cross-examine this witness or not?"

Corva stood, "Yes, your honor." He came around the table, strode directly to Brandt, and stopped a few feet from him. Corva said to Brandt, "Shoot them."

Brandt seemed to move farther back in his chair.

"Shoot them," repeated Corva. "Is that what he said?"

"Yes."

"To whom did he say it?"

"To . . . Sadowski."

"And Sadowski replied what?"

" 'Yes, sir.' "

"And what did Sadowski say to elicit the order of 'Shoot them'?"

"He said, 'We found wounded and sick NVA.' "

"And Lieutenant Tyson replied what?"

Pierce was on his feet. "Objection. Your honor, counsel is badgering the witness."

"Objection sustained."

Corva said to Brandt, "And Sergeant Sadowski left and shot them."

"Yes."

"Did you see him shoot them?"

"No."

"How do you know he shot them?"

"I heard the shots."

"That is how you know that Sergeant Sadowski shot them."

"No . . . I heard afterward that he shot them."

"Who told you this?"

"I don't recall."

"Not Kalane?"

"Maybe it was. . . ."

"Not Walker?"

"No, it was . . ."

"Objection." Pierce was on his feet again. "Counsel is badgering the witness."

"Sustained. Mr. Corva, if you don't mind."

"Yes, your honor." He looked directly at Brandt again. "What did you say to Lieutenant Tyson when Lieutenant Tyson said to Sadowski, 'Shoot them'?"

"Nothing."

"Did you think Lieutenant Tyson's order was an illegal order?"

"Yes."

"Yet you said nothing."

"I was only the medic."

"Only the medic."

"Yes."

"Did you tell Lieutenant Tyson that Peterson's wound was mortal?"

"Yes."

"Then why did he not listen to you?"

"I don't know."

"Did you tell him that only a medevac helicopter could save Peterson's life?"

"Yes."

"Then why didn't you use one of the two platoon radios to call one?"

"It . . . it really wasn't my job to use the radio."

"Did you know how to use it?"

"No."

"You didn't learn how to use a radio at Fort Sam Houston?"

"No."

"Wasn't radio use a three-hour class at Fort Sam Houston?"

"No. Yes."

"Why didn't you call for medevac?"

"It wasn't . . . I didn't have the frequency."

"The platoon medic didn't have medevac's frequency."

"No."

"Would anyone have given it to you if you'd asked?"

"I don't know."

"Did you ask either of the radio operators to call medevac?"

"Yes. Yes, I did."

"Who shot the Australian doctor?"

Brandt seemed momentarily thrown off by the switch in subject. "I don't know."

"Was it an American?"

"Yes."

"You said you didn't know."

"I didn't see who shot him."

"Who shot the French doctor?"

"I don't know."

"The burial mound was in the center of a rice paddy."

Brandt changed positions as though the change in subject necessitated it. "Yes."

"Where could a search be done to insure privacy?"

"I don't know."

"Were there trees or bushes around the burial mound?"

"I think so."

"There are no trees or any vegetation on Vietnamese burial mounds. How would *you* have conducted the search?"

"I don't know. I wouldn't have."

"Why?"

"It wasn't necessary."

"You were two hundred meters away."

"Yes."

"Did Larry Cane die instantly?"

Brandt licked his lips. "Yes. Bullet through the heart."

"You said he was in the operating room."

"Yes."

"Dead."

"Yes."

"Did you have him carried there?"

"Someone carried him there."

"Why?"

"I . . . I don't know."

"Why did someone carry a dead body up a flight of stairs?"

"I don't know."

"Who killed Larry Cane?"

"A sniper."

"He didn't die in the hospital?"

"No. Outside."

"What was he doing upstairs?"

"I don't know."

"Was he shot upstairs?"

"No."

"Did Lieutenant Tyson ever strike you?"

"No."

"On an occasion previous to this, did he not strike you in front of the entire platoon?"

"No . . . we had words . . . some pushing. . . ."

"Did you like Lieutenant Tyson?"

"Yes."

"Did he like you?"

Brandt took a breath. "No."

"Why not?"

"I don't know."

"Why did you like him?"

"He was a good leader."

"Was he a good leader on 15 February 1968?"

"No."

"The day before?"

Pierce stood again. "Your honor, this is really too much. These questions are designed to intimidate and confuse the witness."

Sproule said simply, "Objection overruled. Continue."

Corva continued, jumping from one incident to another. Brandt did not seem to enjoy the format. He began contradicting earlier answers, then he withdrew more and more into "I don't know" and "I don't recall" answers. Finally Corva said, "Shoot them."

Brandt ran his tongue inside his cheek.

"That was a direct order to Sergeant Paul Sadowski."

"Yes."

"You knew it was an illegal order?"

"Yes."

"You watched Sergeant Sadowski leave to carry it out?"

"Yes."

"Did Sergeant Sadowski leave by himself?"

"No."

"Who was with him?"

"I don't remember their names."

"How many?"

"Two or three."

"You heard six or seven shots?"

"Yes."

"Did Sergeant Sadowski or anyone report back that the order had been carried out?"

"No. Well, yes . . . someone yelled into the operating room, 'They're wasted.' "

"Who was the someone referring to as wasted?"

"The six or seven wounded enemy soldiers."

"You're quite sure."

"Yes."

"Who opened fire in the operating room?"

"I don't know."

"How long were you with the platoon after 15 February?"

"Another month or so."

"And you never found out who fired bursts of rounds into a crowded operating room full of patients, staff, and Americans?"

"No."

"Previous testimony indicated it was Simcox."

"It may have been. He was there."

"And Lieutenant Tyson did not reprimand him?"

"No."

"Do you expect anyone to believe any of this?"

"Objection!" Pierce was quite flushed by now. "Your honor—"

"Objection sustained. Mr. Corva, this is the last warning you are getting."

"Yes, your honor. Mr. Brandt, you stated that Lieutenant Tyson concocted a cover-up story for this alleged massacre."

"Yes."

"You stated that you went along with it."

"No. I did not go along with it."

"Then you reported a massacre."

"No."

"Why not?"

"They would have killed me."

"Who?"

"The men in the platoon."

"Do you think your superiors would have returned you to the platoon after you charged all the men in your platoon with mass murder?"

"I . . . didn't know if they would—"

"Really? You thought you might have been ordered to go back to the platoon after you alleged that they were all mass murderers."

"I thought the higher-ups wouldn't believe me. Or they'd try to cover it up."

"Really?" Corva glanced toward the board, then back at Brandt. "After you rotated back to the States in May of 1968, did you report the incident?"

"No."

"Why not?"

"I . . . wanted to forget it."

"You said it haunted you."

"It did. It does."

"Based on what you observed, who did you actually see commit murder in that hospital?"

"I'm not sure."

"Can you name any names?"

"No. Except perhaps Beltran. I saw him shoot the wounded man he pulled off the operating table."

"Did Lieutenant Tyson see this?"

"Yes."

"Did he take any action against Beltran?"

"No."

"Mr. Brandt, I listened to your testimony for a number of hours yesterday, and if there is *any* similarity to previous testimony, it has mostly to do with Lieutenant Tyson. The other participants in this incident have variously been described as doing a variety of things that they could not have done unless they were in two places at the same time. I realize that many years have elapsed since the event, and I wouldn't expect you or anyone to recall exactly the movements, or even the names, of nineteen men. Yet your testimony and previous testimony place Lieutenant Tyson in the same spot. Near the first operating table. And it pretty much leaves him there the whole time. Is that a correct assessment of Lieutenant Tyson's activities?"

"Yes. He was in the operating room."

"And he never said much."

"No. Except for a few orders."

"Such as?"

"Such as, 'Shoot them.' "

"He didn't attempt to stop this alleged massacre?"

"No."

"Did he aid or abet it?"

"Yes. By remaining silent."

"Did he ever fire his rifle?"

"Not that I saw."

"He mostly stood there, according to your testimony and previous testimony."

"Yes. He never tried to stop it."

"He stood there with his radio operator, Daniel Kelly, and had a cigarette."

"Yes."

"And you stood there in the same room with him."

"Yes."

"Were you afraid for your life?"

Brandt hesitated.

"Is that why you did nothing?"

"Yes."

"Did Lieutenant Tyson appear to be afraid for his life?"

"I don't know."

"Would you say that his troops went beyond the alleged order to shoot the enemy wounded?"

"Yes. They shot everyone."

"Did Lieutenant Tyson order them to shoot everyone?"

"I never heard him give that order. Only the first order."

"Were you surprised at that first order?"

"No."

"Why not?"

"He was angry."

"At what?"

"At the hospital staff."

"So he gave the order to shoot enemy wounded."

"Yes."

"But no one else?"

"Not that I heard."

"Did anyone threaten Lieutenant Tyson?"

"No."

"Did anyone point a gun at him?"

"No."

"Did anyone strike him?"

"No."

"What happened to the hospital personnel who were ordered into the scrub room?"

"I already stated that someone threw a hand grenade in there."

"Beltran."

"Yes."

"In earlier testimony you said you didn't remember."

"Did I? I remember now."

"Do you?"

"Yes. Beltran."

"Beltran was a machine gunner. He fired his machine gun from the window."

"Yes."

"Did machine gunners carry hand grenades?"

"How should I know?"

"Did Lieutenant Tyson leave the operating room during the alleged massacre?"

"Yes. Toward the end. I didn't see him again until we were outside."

"Where were you?"

"In the operating room. The whole time."

"Why?"

"I didn't know where to go."

"Why not go outside?"

"I suppose I should have."

"Lieutenant Tyson tried to impose his will on the staff of the hospital."

Brandt hesitated a moment, then replied, "I don't know."

"Did he care about Arthur Peterson?"

"I don't know."

"Did you?"

"Of course. I was the medic."

"Did you do everything you could for Peterson?"

"There was nothing to be done."

"Except call medevac."

Pierce stood again. "Your honor, Steven Brandt is not on trial."

Corva looked at Pierce, then at the board, then at Colonel Sproule.

Sproule said, "Objection sustained. Mr. Corva . . . your line of questioning is becoming abusive."

"Your honor, the line of questioning concerning Arthur Peterson stems from a totally uncalled-for remark made by the witness in earlier testimony."

"That may be. But I think you made your point."

"I think so, too, your honor."

"Objection sustained. Proceed, Mr. Corva."

Tyson listened as Corva continued the questioning. Brandt, Tyson thought, was not at ease with Corva's style of questioning. Corva returned to the same points several times, but each time rephrased the question and received a slightly different response. Corva would then recapitulate the various answers to the same question. Brandt was in trouble, thrown off-balance, and unable to recover his composure. His face and mannerisms betrayed that he was a man on the run.

After nearly two hours of questioning, Corva asked Brandt, "Did you shoot anyone?"

"No."

"Did you see Richard Farley shoot anyone?"

"No."

"Did you see Larry Cane shoot anyone?"

"No."

"Larry Cane was dead, Mr. Brandt."

Pierce got to his feet as Corva said, "I have no further questions, your honor."

Colonel Sproule almost breathed a sigh of relief and announced, "The court will recess until thirteen hundred hours."

Ben Tyson stared out the third-floor window of the BOQ. He said to Corva, "What do you think?"

Corva lay sprawled on the couch and yawned. "I think the board has reasonable doubt that you gave an order to shoot enemy soldiers."

Tyson was able to see the Officers' Club a few hundred yards away. He saw a group of uniformed people whom he took to be the board. Then he saw Brandt, then Pierce, Weinroth, and Longo. He envied them their freedom of movement. There were people dressed in civilian clothing outside on the cobblestones who he realized were media people. There were TV vans parked near the museum, and he saw two men holding cameras. "What is the fascination with this?"

"What?"

"Media coverage. People outside the gates. I can see the main gate from here. Newspaper headlines. *Headlines*. There are important things happening in the nation beyond those gates."

Corva yawned again. "Don't be modest."

Tyson turned from the window. "How about the second assertion that I aided and abetted the massacre by doing nothing to stop it?"

"Also reasonable doubt. I think the board understands the troops mutinied and that you were no longer in command." Corva sat up on the couch. "But I couldn't get Brandt to help me on that. If I were on the jury, I'd have lots of questions. Which is what will happen after lunch."

"Right. So we're down to the cover-up."

"Yes. That's about it. I wish I could think of a way to address that."

"We could say that it haunted me, like Brandt said it haunted him; I kept meaning to report it, but with one thing and another I kept putting it off."

Corva stood. "We could say that. Hey, open the refrigerator."

Tyson opened the bar refrigerator and took out a brown bag and two cans of beer. "What is it today?"

"Chinese food." Corva took the bag and began laying out containers on the dinette table.

"It's cold, Vince."

"So what?" Corva found plastic forks in the bottom of the bag. "Do you save these tea bags?"

Tyson said, "Do you think the board would return a verdict of guilty based only on the cover-up?"

Corva nodded. "Afraid so." He heaped food from the containers onto a paper plate. "Help yourself."

Tyson helped himself to a beer. He said, "Chinese food is what I had the night I saw Picard's book."

"Really?"

"That was a long time ago."

"It's almost over, Ben." Corva cut into a piece of egg foo yung.

"For years after I returned from Vietnam, I wouldn't eat rice."

"Me neither."

Tyson remained standing near the window as Corva ate. Tyson said, "You did fine with Brandt."

"Thanks. That's how you handle articulate witnesses. You don't let them articulate. Everyone was tired of his windy bullshit anyway. The court reporter last night wanted to shoot him."

Tyson smiled. "I didn't expect him to start coming apart like that."

Corva sipped on his beer. "I couldn't have or wouldn't have done that with a pfc or with Farley. But Sproule gave me a lot of latitude with Dr. Wonderful."

"I think you planted some questions in the board's mind."

"I think so. We'll see when they get a crack at him later."

"You don't want to delve too deeply into the matter of Larry Cane."

"No. He would have denied it." Corva lifted a forkful of rice. "You want to try any of this?"

"It's cold."

"Right. So, what do you think? About our five witnesses?"

Tyson sat opposite Corva. "They can't get up there and tell the story of the firefight, can they?"

"I really don't think so."

"That was an okay story eighteen years ago when we were bullshitting Browder and the battalion commander. I don't think it's going to fly anymore."

"No," agreed Corva, "and we shouldn't even let it on the runway." He looked at Tyson. "We have a problem, you know."

"Yes, I know." Tyson lit another cigarette. "Will Sadowski, Scorello, Walker, Kalane, or Beltran take the stand and tell the *truth* about the massacre? And testify that I did not order anyone killed? That I shot Cane in an attempt to stop it? That my life was in danger? That the troops mutinied? And that the cover-up was not my idea?"

Corva wiped his mouth with a paper napkin and swallowed. "That's what I'm trying to find out now. I've spoken to each of their attorneys, and they're not being very cooperative. Now that the trial has begun, everyone is having second thoughts about 'all for one and one for all.' "

"Are they?"

"I told you, Ben, that before this is over, everyone will betray you in one way or another."

Tyson drank his beer silently for a while. "You're saying they won't testify on my behalf?"

"We're still talking about it. You see, there are questions of immunity, of perjury, and Fifth Amendment rights. But the bottom line, Ben, is that those men do not want to get up on the stand and have Pierce ask them if they killed babies and pregnant women. Or did they only shoot doctors and nursing nuns? Who killed the babies, by the way?"

"Scorello. With a phosphorus hand grenade."

Corva shook his head.

Tyson tapped his fingers on the table.

Corva said, "What did Brandt actually do?"

"Pretty much what he said. Nothing. He was petrified. He thought they were going to kill him, too."

Corva picked at some fried rice. "Medics are always suspect, aren't they? They are never fully initiated into the psychotic circle. Medics, Army scout dog handlers, chaplains and chaplains' assistants, artillery forward observers . . . all those people who joined up with us from time to time . . . they looked at us funny, didn't they? Like they were visiting a traveling psycho ward where all the patients were armed to the teeth. They couldn't wait to get the hell back to camp. And when they left, we'd all laugh at them. But you know what? We *were* crazy."

Tyson finished his beer. "The platoon's instincts were correct about Brandt, as it turns out. They should have made a clean sweep of it."

Corva said, "They made a clean sweep of the hospital. They knew that they couldn't shoot a few people there like they did in the villages and get away with it."

"No. That was civilization. So they destroyed it."

Neither Corva nor Tyson spoke for some time. The phone rang, and Corva got up to answer it. He listened for a minute, then said, "All right. Keep me informed." He hung up and turned to Tyson. "That was my office. They're still negotiating with our reluctant witnesses' attorneys."

"And?"

"I don't know. They have very valid reasons for not exposing their clients to sworn testimony and cross-examination. If you were in their position and I was your attorney, I would not let you testify."

"How about comrades in arms and blood oaths by the light of a flickering candle and all that?"

"I'd say my client doesn't recall any of that. I'd say that in the latter part of the twentieth century in a country run by lawyers, you can forget all of that. I'd also say, to save face, that my client's oaths, if any were in fact made, had to do with relating the story of a fierce firefight. Not a massacre." Corva added, "But we're still negotiating with them."

Tyson said nothing.

Corva drew a deep breath. "Sometimes, Ben, I think the less said, the better. Sometimes it is the defense and not the prosecution who winds up removing the reasonable doubt from the minds of the jury who had reasonable doubt until the defense witnesses start getting cross-examined. *Capice?*"

"I guess. But we're not offering much of a defense."

"The prosecution didn't offer much of a case either. I'd like to throw it to the jury as soon as possible."

"Do you want me to take the stand?"

"I'll let you know. And if you think of a good reason why you chose to ignore a mass murder, let me know."

The phone rang again, and Corva picked it up. He listened. "Okay, Sergeant. Tell them to start without us." He hung up and said to Tyson, "They're not going to start without us."

"The court will come to order," said Colonel Sproule.

Pierce made his announcement regarding all the parties being present.

Colonel Sproule addressed Colonel Moore. "You informed me during the recess that the board has questions for the witness, Steven Brandt."

Moore replied, "Yes, your honor."

Sproule said to Colonel Pierce, "Recall the witness."

Pierce motioned to the sergeant at arms. Brandt did not immediately appear, and after some minutes two MPs were sent to look for the sergeant at arms and for Brandt. Finally, after five full minutes, Brandt appeared and walked across the floor to the witness stand. Colonel Pierce said to him, "The witness is reminded that he is still under oath."

Brandt sat.

Colonel Sproule addressed the court. "I have had an opportunity to see and hear the questions the board intends to pose to the witness and have ruled on their admissibility." Sproule looked at Pierce, then at Corva, then back to Colonel Moore. "You may begin."

Lieutenant Davis, the junior member of the board, began. "Dr. Brandt, did you discuss the hospital incident with your own commanding officer? That is, the commander of the Fifteenth Medical Battalion?"

"No."

"Could you tell us why not?"

Brandt shifted in his chair and crossed his legs. "As I stated, I was frightened."

"Would your commanding officer, a medical doctor, have been unsympathetic to your story?"

Brandt replied, "I don't know."

Corva leaned toward Tyson. "Dr. Steve is going to like this format even less."

The questioning from the six-member board went on for nearly an hour. Tyson could tell by the questioning that the board did not find Steven Brandt to their liking. Their questions focused on Brandt's reasons for not reporting the crime and his reasons for coming forward after all these years. They questioned him on his relationship with Tyson and with the other men of the platoon. Tyson didn't doubt that they believed Brandt's story of a massacre in broad outline. But, just as with Farley, they couldn't seem to focus on the details. Finally, Colonel Moore asked the last questions. "You stated earlier that you and Lieutenant Tyson had an altercation sometime previous to this incident."

"Yes."

"You mentioned pushing."

"Yes."

"Who pushed whom?"

"Lieutenant Tyson pushed me."

"Did you fall to the ground?"

"Yes."

"Did you make a formal complaint against him?"

"No."

"Could you tell us what the altercation was about?"

"I don't recall."

"Did you bear him any ill will?"

"None."

"Did you discuss the hospital incident with Lieutenant Tyson afterward?"

"No."

"Why not?"

"He was part of the cover-up."

"Did you discuss this incident with *anyone?* Anyone in the military or in civilian life?"

"No. Not until I discussed it with Andrew Picard."

"Did you, after you discussed it with Andrew Picard, attempt any communication with any government agency regarding this matter?"

"No."

"Did the Army, then, contact you regarding this matter?"

"Yes."

Colonel Moore looked to either side, and each member of the board shook his head to indicate that there were no further questions. But from where Tyson was sitting, the five heads turned toward the center, all shaking in unison, gave the appearance of five disgusted people.

Colonel Sproule said to Steven Brandt, "Thank you for testifying. You are excused, subject to recall." Sproule repeated the warning against discussing his testimony.

Tyson looked at Pierce, Weinroth, and Longo. They didn't look quite as smug as they had after Pierce's direct examination of Brandt. But neither did they look worried. In fact, they looked to Tyson like people who realize that the worst is over. That the end is near and that they are ahead and running downhill, while the opposition is only beginning the uphill portion.

Colonel Sproule finished with Brandt and said, "The witness is excused, subject to recall."

Brandt stood and walked, not too fast, toward the side door.

Colonel Sproule addressed Colonel Pierce. "Does the prosecution wish to call a witness?"

Pierce replied, "No, it does not, your honor."

"Does the prosecution have anything further to offer at this time?"

"No, it does not, your honor."

Colonel Sproule pronounced, "The court is adjourned until ten hundred hours tomorrow."

Tyson and Corva walked on the path leading to the BOQ. Tyson said, "When will we know if we have any defense witnesses?"

"Tonight, I hope. I may have to ask for a continuance."

"That's legal mumbo jumbo for a postponement."

"Right."

"I don't want a postponement."

"Well, Ben, neither do I. But we need some time."

"No. I want to be in court tomorrow."

"We'll discuss it later."

They came to a cross path on the lawn. The sun was behind the redbrick housing structures, and long shadows lay over the lawns. Corva said, "It gets cold here at night." He looked at Tyson. "Going home?"

"Yes. To see David awhile. Marcy is still trying to accomplish some work, and she has dinner with a client tonight. You know how it is. Trying to juggle being a homemaker, mother, career lady, and still put in six to twelve hours in court."

"Now, now." Corva glanced at his watch. "I'll be in the BOQ very late. Come over around ten, and we'll have a drink."

Tyson asked, "Where have all the soldiers gone, Vince?"

Corva replied, "They all have lawyers now."

48

Ben Tyson and Vincent Corva sat at the defense table. Tyson looked at his watch and noted that it was ten minutes to ten. The spectators were in place, and the prosecution was in place. The board began filing in.

Corva said to Tyson, "I know how you must feel."

Tyson lit a cigarette and replied, "I don't feel betrayed. I don't feel bad. I don't know what those five men would have said that would make a difference."

"They did all offer to make unsworn statements in extenuation and mitigation if a guilty verdict is returned. I think the presentencing presentation of extenuating circumstances is ultimately more important than the verdict in a case like this."

"From the standpoint of how long I would have to spend in jail, I agree."

Corva nodded. He added, "It's possible that they will return a verdict of not guilty."

Tyson said nothing.

Corva said, "Seeing as we don't seem to have any defense witnesses in the witness room at the moment, would you like a postponement?"

Tyson replied, "No. You have a defense witness sitting next to you."

Corva stayed silent a few seconds. He looked at the board, who were sitting at their table, talking quietly to one another. Corva said, "It is very rare for the accused in a case like this to take the stand in his own defense."

"You said last night I could make a statement."

"Did I say that?"

"Yes."

Corva put his hand on Tyson's arm. "Listen, Ben. If you go on that stand and make even a two-minute statement, you open a deep can of worms."

Tyson didn't reply.

Corva went on. "I thought about it. Last night, after you left. I stayed awake and thought about it. You have to understand that if you are sworn in, and make a statement, Pierce will cross-examine you on that for a week. I mean that literally, Ben. And when he's through with you, Sproule has the right to question you. And when Sproule is through, the six members of that board will go at it. You are the celebrity. And if you decide to step out in public, they will own you for as long as they can get away with it. I'll try to limit the questions as superfluous and such, but it would be several days before I could make a case for that. Understand?"

Tyson nodded.

"The choice is yours. You may remain silent. That is your right, and if you do so, no inference will be drawn from it, and it will not count against you in any way. Nor can it be commented on in any way."

Tyson said nothing for several minutes. The sergeant at arms strode toward the middle of the floor. Tyson said to Corva, "But I *will* make a statement, later, in extenuation and mitigation."

"Yes. If you are found guilty, you will have that opportunity. I hope you don't have to take advantage of that opportunity. I know this goes against your grain. But trust me."

"Sure."

"All rise!"

Colonel Sproule walked to the pulpit and stood behind it. "The court will come to order."

Pierce confirmed that all the parties were present.

Colonel Sproule addressed Colonel Pierce. "Does the prosecution have any further evidence to present?"

Pierce, still standing, said, "The prosecution rests."

Sproule turned to Corva. "Has the defense any evidence to present?"

Corva stood. "The defense has no evidence to present."

There was a stir in the court, and Sproule did not wait patiently for it to die down. He looked toward the pews and the spectators fell silent. Sproule turned back to Corva. "Does the defense, then, rest?"

"The defense rests."

Colonel Sproule nodded perfunctorily and turned to Colonel Pierce. "Does the prosecution have anything further to offer?"

Pierce answered, "It does not." Pierce said to Sproule, "Does the court wish to have any witnesses called or recalled?"

"It does not," replied Colonel Sproule. He, in turn, readdressed Pierce. "Does the prosecution wish to present a final argument?"

"It does," answered Pierce.

Colonel Sproule responded, "Colonel Pierce"—he turned to Corva—"and Mr. Corva. I wish to remind both of you that in trial by court-martial final arguments are not required. If they are made they can be written or oral. In either case, they are customarily short. They are made generally in order to call to the attention of the court reasonably pertinent facts of the case and how they relate to the law. They may include elements of a summation, but they are not to be lengthy recapitulations of the trial." He looked at Pierce. "You may begin."

Colonel Pierce came from behind the table and stood in the center of the floor as he had done when he made his opening statement.

Tyson watched him, then focused on the board. The six members sat ramrod straight, very military, Tyson thought. Pierce carried himself reasonably well for a JAG lawyer. Tyson looked at the spectators. On this Thursday morning, in the fourth day of the trial, the pews were again full. Marcy had come in late. David had gotten excused from school again. Tyson's mother, staying with friends in Garden City and taking a limousine in every morning, looked weary. As Tyson scanned the sea of mostly white faces, he saw a big moon-shaped black face smiling, trying to catch his eye. Mason nodded at him from the fifth or sixth row. Tyson smiled and nodded back.

Colonel Pierce began with the traditional "May it please the military judge, members of the court. You have heard the case of the United States against Lieutenant Benjamin Tyson. You have heard the testimony of two witnesses, Richard Farley and Steven Brandt, who related to the court the story of a cold-blooded massacre of civilians and enemy soldiers, of patients and staff, of infants and children. No, their testimony did not always agree in detail, their testimony was often contradictory, and their recall of names, events, and other specifics, which we have come to expect in trial testimony, was at times vague. But we did hear, did we not, the story of a massacre. And if the details were vague after some eighteen years, the broad outlines were still clear."

Pierce rubbed his upper lip and hung his head a moment, then continued. "Steven Brandt and Richard Farley were eyewitnesses to the events they described. These are events which are indelibly burned into their memories for all time—and not solely on account of their being eyewitnesses to the events, but on account of their having been participants in those events. But their participation is not the issue here. What is the issue is the involvement of the accused in those events. If you remove from your mind the extraneous details of the testimony and the cross-examination and consider only the facts which relate to the accused and to the charges brought against him, then what remains is this: The first platoon of Alpha Company entered a building which two eyewitnesses describe as a hospital. By their testimony, we learned that there were upwards of one hundred—possibly two hundred—living human beings in that hospital. Their platoon leader, Lieutenant Benjamin Tyson, gave a verbal order to shoot sick and wounded enemy soldiers. Members of the board, if we stop right there, and if we are to believe the sworn testimony of two independent and unbiased witnesses, then the government can rest its case. But if we are to right a terrible wrong, if we are to redeem the honor and integrity of the American Army, then we cannot rest there. No, we must consider the remainder of the corpses that the witnesses saw with their own eyes, piled in the wards, strewn in the hallways, lying in the operating room, and sprawled about the grounds of the hospital. We must consider that these unarmed and defenseless people were shot and killed by troops under the command of the accused. We must consider that the testimony of two eyewitnesses agrees that the accused did not do or say anything to halt the actions of his rampaging troops. That, in fact, the accused, by his inaction, aided and abetted the massacre you have heard described. That, indeed, the accused, by his inflammatory order to shoot unarmed and convalescent soldiers, precipitated the general massacre which followed."

Pierce turned and looked at Tyson, then looked out over the spectator pews for the first time, then again addressed the board. "You could, I could, anyone with an ounce of human compassion and understanding could make or find reasons and excuses for everything the accused did or failed to do in that twenty or forty minutes. But who can excuse what happened afterward? Who can excuse or understand an officer of the United States Army willfully entering into a conspiracy with men under his command to obstruct justice, to fabricate a series of events that were intended not only to obscure the facts of a heinous crime but also to turn that crime into an honorable engagement with enemy forces? Who can excuse or understand *that?* Who can excuse an ongoing cover-up of a capital and infamous crime that has continued up until this moment? Who can excuse an officer who, by his dereliction of duty, has perhaps and most probably insured that no one else will be brought to justice for this mass crime? Who can excuse a commissioned officer of the United States Army, in whom was placed special trust and confidence, from the obligations that he freely undertook when he took his oath of office?"

Pierce walked a few steps back toward the defense table, then turned and concluded, "The government has presented the facts which prove, beyond a reasonable doubt, that a violation of the Uniform Code of Military Justice occurred and that the violation was murder and that the specifications, as written, accurately reflect the nature of the violation; that the accused engaged in acts which were inherently dangerous to others and which evinced a wanton disregard of human life."

Colonel Pierce took his chair.

Colonel Sproule turned to Corva. "Does the defense wish to make a final argument?"

Corva stood. "It does, your honor."

"Proceed."

Corva came out to the center of the court and began, "May it please the military judge, members of the board. You have heard the case of the United States against Benjamin Tyson. You have heard two witnesses, Richard Farley and Steven Brandt, who constituted the whole of the prosecution's case against the accused—whose testimony constituted the whole of the evidence which is necessary to prove the serious charge of murder. If we are to believe that the witnesses are unbiased and unprejudiced toward the accused, then we have failed to understand the true nature and underlying meaning of the testimony. Even if we are to believe that Messrs. Brandt and Farley witnessed a massacre —and the defense does not contend anything to the contrary—then we must focus on two words: 'Shoot them,' the words that Brandt contends were used by the accused in giving an unlawful order. Farley's testimony as to that direct order was somewhat different. So, we are to ignore the fact that two prosecution witnesses cannot recall, after eighteen years, names, places, or words of their comrades. But we are to believe Steven Brandt when he says he can recall

Lieutenant Tyson saying, 'Shoot them.' And we are to believe Steven Brandt
when he states that Lieutenant Tyson did nothing to stop the troops under his
command from committing murder. Yet Steven Brandt cannot even remember
who committed the acts of murder which he says he saw or which he says he
thinks he saw. Steven Brandt has a very selective memory."

Corva paused and glanced at the empty witness chair, then at Pierce. He
turned again to the board and continued, "The prosecution has called to your
attention the fact that the testimonies of the two prosecution witnesses do not
agree in all respects. But when the witnesses made reference to Lieutenant
Tyson, there seemed to be little inconsistency in their statements. If we are to
believe that the variations in the testimony were due to the fact of the witnesses
perceiving the event from different perspectives or that their different perceptions were a result of different personalities or sensibilities, then why are they
in such agreement on the facts which tend to incriminate the accused?"

Corva paused, pulled at his lip awhile, then said, "Brandt. Brandt has told
you that he feared for his life. That he was approached by members of the
platoon after the incident and threatened. If we believe that, why not believe
that Lieutenant Tyson, too, feared for his life? The prosecution has stated that
the accused engaged in a conspiracy to cover the facts of this alleged crime. If
we believe Brandt that a conspiracy was hatched in that bunker and that Brandt
went along with it only to save his own life, then why not believe that of the
accused? For surely, if there were two outsiders among the men of that platoon, they were Benjamin Tyson and Steven Brandt. The testimony of the
witnesses has in fact painted a picture of not only a massacre but a mutiny. And
though the defense has stipulated to certain facts, the defense does not accept
as fact that Lieutenant Tyson made no oral or written report regarding the
incident in question. The prosecution asks you to infer from the lack of physical
evidence that no report was made. But no such inference can or should be
drawn. In deciding on whether or not Lieutenant Tyson properly reported to
his superiors the events in question, the board should consider that no reasonable man would attempt to make such a report while his life was in imminent
danger. If Lieutenant Tyson radioed false reports to his company commander
while in the physical presence of at least a dozen men who had just committed
mass murder, I think you can conclude that he acted reasonably. And in the
days that followed, while still in the field, at a time of intense enemy activity,
you can conclude why he made no report to his superiors. But sometime between 15 February and 29 February, the day Lieutenant Tyson was wounded
and evacuated, can the prosecution, can the two witnesses, can anyone say that
no oral or written report was made? Would it be beyond the realm of possibility
for you to believe that an oral report was made to Alpha Company's commander, Captain Browder, and that Captain Browder had no time to alert his
superiors before he was killed on 21 February? Would any amount of searching
in the Army archives come up with a scrap of documentary evidence to show
that the accused fulfilled his obligation to report a violation of law? Probably
not. But that does *not* constitute proof that the accused made no such written
report. And if the accused made such a report, oral, written, or both, and he
observed that no action was taken on that report, what is he to do? Make a
second report? Yes. And what if he did? And what if still no word comes to him
acknowledging his report? What is he to conclude? That it was lost? That it was
purposely lost? Would that be the first time such a thing happened? And when
Lieutenant Tyson was wounded and medically evacuated and eventually left the
Southeast Asian theater of operations, what was his responsibility regarding
this incident? Should he have pursued it? Undoubtedly. Did he? Perhaps. Did

the prosecution prove anything to the contrary? It did not. Is it the responsibility of the prosecution to prove the charges it has alleged, or is it the responsibility of the defense to disprove the charges?"

Corva came closer to the board table so that he was within a foot of it and looked up and down the table at the six members. "The prosecution has proved to me beyond a reasonable doubt that a massacre of innocent and defenseless people occurred at the time and place stated in the charge sheet. I am convinced. But the enormity of this crime ought not to cloud anyone's judgment regarding the culpability of the accused in those events. The fact of a crime does not constitute the presumption of guilt of everyone at the scene of that crime. If it did, then the defense table ought to have at least two more people sitting at it: Brandt and Farley."

Corva nodded, turned, and walked back to the table.

Colonel Sproule stood behind the pulpit, nearly motionless for close to a full minute.

Corva began straightening and stacking the papers on his desk.

Colonel Sproule said finally to Colonel Pierce, "Does the prosecution have a rebuttal argument?"

"Yes, your honor." Pierce stood and snapped at Corva, "The suggestion that the government witnesses are indictable is obscene. If the accused had done his duty as an officer none of us would now be sitting here."

Corva got to his feet and glared at Pierce. "If the witnesses engaged in lies and cover-ups eighteen years ago, there is no reason to believe they are telling the whole truth now."

Colonel Sproule said tersely, "That will be all, gentlemen." He asked Pierce, "Does the prosecution have anything further to offer?"

"It has not."

Sproule addressed Corva. "Does the defense have anything further to offer?"

Corva stood. "It does not."

Sproule said to the board, "The prosecution and the defense have rested. It only remains for you members to consider the evidence. This court will adjourn for the purpose of completing administrative matters and securing transcribed testimony that you may require in your deliberations. You are advised not to deliberate this case or discuss it in any way among yourselves until I have instructed you in your duties. The court will adjourn until ten hundred hours tomorrow."

Tyson stood.

Corva put his papers into his briefcase.

Tyson lit a cigarette.

Corva snapped his briefcase shut.

Tyson watched the pews emptying and saw Marcy and David walking down the aisle, their way being cleared by MPs.

Corva said, "Well."

Tyson said, "The defense rests."

"Yes."

"But the defense never played the game."

"Nevertheless, the defense rests."

Tyson shrugged. He looked at his watch. "Lunch?"

"Why not?"

Tyson followed Corva toward the side door.

The last MP in the place, Sergeant Larson, stood at parade rest near the door. He said, "Very nice, Mr. Corva."

"Thank you."

"See you both tomorrow."

Tyson nodded as he entered the corridor. It occurred to him that tomorrow there would be armed MPs as was customary on the day of the verdict. And that Sergeant Larson would be in charge of the escort that took him away in cuffs.

He suddenly remembered his dream and the man in the dream telling him he had five more years to serve. And the dream seemed now to be a presentiment of his sentence.

49

At 10 A.M. Colonel Walter Sproule called the court to order.

Sproule looked tired, Tyson thought, and he was sitting more on the high stool than he was standing. His face seemed whiter, and his eyes had a sunken appearance. Sproule waited until the court was assembled and the spectators had settled down. Then, as if someone had pumped air into him from behind the pulpit, he straightened up, rested his hands on the side of the pulpit, leaning slightly forward like a preacher about to deliver a message of hellfire and brimstone. Sproule's voice even sounded stronger as he spoke into the microphone. "President and members of the board, you have heard the testimony in the case of the United States against Lieutenant Benjamin J. Tyson."

Sproule began his charge to the jury, reading from typed sheets, behind the pulpit wall. He spoke in a steady voice with no inflections that would give color or weight to any point he was making.

Within ten minutes of Sproule's opening sentence, Tyson knew that Sproule, who had been almost taciturn up to now, was going to give a detailed and lengthy charge to the six members who had, Tyson suspected, already made up their minds.

Sproule went on. He made the point that Pierce had made in his preliminary remarks, the point about technical murder.

"In assessing the witnesses," Colonel Sproule said, "you may consider the witnesses' relationship to the accused, their apparent intelligence, and general appearance of candor. In considering the extent of culpability of the officer charged, you may consider his rank, background, education, Army schooling, and his experience in the field during prior operations involving contact with hostile and with friendly Vietnamese. You may consider his age at the time of the alleged incident and any other evidence which might help you in determining if the accused willfully aided, abetted, ordered, or concealed a mass murder. But first you must be certain beyond a reasonable doubt that the testimony of mass murder which you have heard was truthful."

Sproule went on in a somewhat convoluted manner, explaining the merits of the government's case, then the merits of the defense. He pointed out weaknesses in both cases and said, "You must be satisfied from the evidence, which consists solely of testimony, that the accused acted unlawfully, and further that any unlawful acts that the accused may have committed constitute murder. You must have an abiding belief, amounting to a moral certainty, that Lieutenant Benjamin Tyson is guilty as charged. I must remind you that because of the statute of limitations, there is no lesser included offense of which you may find him guilty. You may not return a verdict of manslaughter. You may not return a verdict of dereliction of duty, conspiracy, or any other lesser offense. You may only return a verdict of guilty or not guilty to the charge and to one or both of the specifications."

Colonel Sproule explained the procedures under which the board had to operate, and it was apparent that he was explaining it not only to the board, who most probably knew the procedures, but to the civilian spectators and the press. He said, "There is no possibility in a trial by court-martial of a hung jury. The first vote on the charge will be decisive. To convict, four or more of you must have voted guilty. To acquit, three of you or more must have voted not guilty. So I urge you to deliberate for as long as you feel necessary before you cast your first and only ballot. If you vote to convict on the charge of murder, then you must vote on the specifications. You may vote to approve one or both of the specifications. If you cannot in good conscience vote for either specification as written, but you have voted to convict on the overall charge, then it is within your power and your duty to change the wording of one or both specifications so that it comports with your reasoning behind your guilty verdict. I warn you, however, that a rewording of the specifications may change their meaning to the extent that they define manslaughter. In such a case, the accused would be not guilty of any chargeable offense under the Code."

Colonel Sproule said, "If you have reached a verdict by sixteen-thirty hours, you will return to this court to announce that verdict. If you have not reached a verdict by that time, you will be housed in the post bachelor officers' quarters and will not deliberate there. If you wish to deliberate this evening, you must arrange to be taken back to the deliberation room that has been set aside for you in the adjoining office wing."

Colonel Sproule continued, "I must remind you that you have sworn not to disclose or discover the vote or opinion of any particular member of the board. That is to say your vote and your reasoning for it are to remain secret after this court is adjourned and for all time."

Colonel Sproule leaned farther to the side of the pulpit toward the board and concluded, "The final determination as to the weight of the evidence and the credibility of the witnesses in this case rests solely upon you members of the court. You must disregard any comment or statement made by me during the course of the trial which may seem to indicate an opinion as to the guilt or innocence of the accused, for you alone have the independent responsibility of deciding this issue. Each of you must impartially resolve the ultimate issue as to the guilt or innocence of the accused in accordance with the law, the evidence admitted in court, and your own conscience." Colonel Sproule straightened up and announced, "The court will be closed."

Tyson looked at his watch. The charge to the jury had taken a full forty-five minutes, and now all the words that could possibly influence them had been spoken.

Benjamin Tyson stared silently out the window of Rabbi Weitz's office. It appeared that all the spectators had left the chapel and were now milling about over the lawns in the cool autumn sunshine. There were, in addition, several hundred people across the road behind MP barricades.

Corva poured himself a cup of coffee. "Do you want to go outside?"

"No."

"Don't you want to see your family?"

Tyson continued to stare out the window. "No."

Corva came up beside him and glanced out the window. "They look properly subdued. Respectful. It wasn't such a circus."

"Yes." The scene actually reminded him of a cigarette break outside a funeral home; people are introduced, there is the occasional brief smile. Everyone has their back to the place, not wanting to be reminded of why they are there. The final sermon is about to begin, so no one strays too far.

Corva turned from the window and stood beside the desk. He put cream in his coffee. "Are you satisfied with how the trial went?"

Tyson said with a touch of sarcasm, "I suppose if one has to be tried for murder, that was as good a trial as one can expect."

"I mean," said Corva, a bit impatiently, "are you satisfied with how I represented you?"

"I'll let you know after the verdict." Tyson noted that Corva's manner was somewhat cool. He supposed that was a defensive response. He felt badly for Corva having to wait here with him. Tyson said, "Why don't you take a walk?"

"You mean I'm fired?"

"No. A *walk*. In the fresh air."

"I wouldn't get fifteen steps before the media surrounded and annihilated me. I'll stay here until we're called. Or until four-thirty." Corva added, "But if you're going to smoke, open the window."

Tyson opened the window and felt the rush of cool, crisp autumn air. "How long do you think this will take?" He turned from the window.

Corva shrugged. "The trial was relatively short. There isn't much to consider except testimony. They may ask for transcripts of that."

Tyson waited, then asked again, "How long? Days? Hours? Minutes? Do I have time to finish a cigarette?"

"Court-martial deliberations are usually short. There is only one vote, and it is binding." He paused. "I suspect that everyone's mind was made up as they rose from their seats."

Tyson nodded distractedly.

Corva said, "There is no reason for them to pretend they agonized for days. In fact, there is subtle pressure on them to make up their minds. They are officers. They have heard the case. They have duties awaiting them. They would rather be back with their units than here. So, to give you a precise answer, I expect a verdict before four-thirty."

Tyson looked at the wall clock. "Six hours."

"Yes. More than ample time."

Tyson contrived a smile. "Nervous?"

"Anxious."

"You going to break your streak?"

Corva smiled wanly but didn't reply.

Tyson and Corva conversed on various irrelevant topics. No subject seemed appropriate, and each short foray into idle chatter inevitably led to something they didn't care to pursue. After an hour and a half, Corva opened the door and asked the MP to bring them newspapers and magazines. He said to Tyson, "I'll ask you one more time—you're authorized to go back to your quarters— do you want to go?"

"No."

"Do you want to go to the club for lunch?"

"No. I'm not particularly hungry. You can have something brought in."

"Are you feeling sorry for yourself?"

"No. I'm feeling sorry for you. And for my family."

"Can I send an MP to bring your wife here?"

"No."

"Your son?"

"No. And not my mother or my sisters or my minister or anyone." Tyson's voice rose. "Why can't you understand that I cannot face anyone now? Why can't you understand that if I see anyone . . . I don't want anyone to see me in my present condition. . . . Can't a man suffer alone, in dignity, anymore?" He pointed to Corva. "Would *you* want your family around you?"

Corva replied in a soothing tone, "I might, Ben. I might want their support—"

"Oh, fuck support. That's an idiotic word."

Corva drew a deep, patient breath. "I just wanted to make sure you understand that this may be the last time . . . for some time . . . that you can speak to them without . . . guards present. . . ."

Tyson paced across the small office. At length he said in a calmer tone, "I don't mean to take this out on you. You just happen to be here. So leave."

"No, sir. My personal policy is to stay with the accused."

Tyson stopped pacing and turned to Corva. "Well? Take a guess. As long as you're here, entertain me. Take a guess."

Corva said evenly, "Within the narrow confines of the charges and from a legal point of view, the government proved its case."

Tyson said, "So what is taking them so long? They're officers. Why can't they make up their minds?"

"Because the defense proved other things. Things that went beyond what they'd expected to hear." He looked at Tyson. "I'm not upset with you for holding some of this back. I asked you to. I wanted it revealed spontaneously, in its own time. And the board listened, and their impassive faces betrayed their emotions. They are human; therefore, they are now questioning *themselves.*"

Tyson didn't respond.

Corva said, "Right now, one or two of them are making arguments to try to influence a second or third member to say, 'The hell with the law.' That can be the only reason for any delay."

"Will it happen? Will three of them say, 'The hell with the law'?"

Corva glanced at Tyson, then looked off at the rabbi's bulletin board. He said, "If they say the hell with the law, then they are saying the hell with the Army. They are part of the system, the embodiment of the Code. They are sworn officers. They have more of a vested interest in this system than any civilian juror has in the civilian judicial system. What would you do in their place? How do you vote?"

Tyson thought a moment, then replied, "I vote guilty."

"Me too."

"So what is taking so long?"

"I honestly don't know. I told you . . . they are having some problems getting to the vote. Colonel Moore is not calling for the vote because one or two of them is sticking his or her neck out and making a pitch for you. Maybe Moore is making the pitch himself. Maybe Davis is on your side, too. Maybe Sindel is the one pushing for a quick guilty vote. Maybe Laski would have been the third person we needed on your side. I don't know. Nobody knows . . . juries never fail to surprise me."

"Even military juries?"

"Even them sometimes."

"You'd be damned surprised if you won this case."

Corva began to smile, but the sound of footsteps in the corridor brought him to his feet. There was a knock on the door, and an MP opened it, carrying a stack of newspapers and magazines. He said, "Got next month's *Playboy,* too. Get you anything else, Mr. Corva?"

"No, thanks."

The MP left. Tyson and Corva read desultorily. At half past noon, there were again footsteps outside the door. They stopped. There was a knock, and the door opened. Sergeant Larson said, "Can I take your lunch order? Or are you going out?"

Corva replied, "Have sandwiches and coffee sent, Sergeant. Surprise us. But no white bread and no mayo."

They waited a half hour, and Tyson commented, "It usually takes fifteen minutes to get sandwiches from the mess hall. Maybe they've reached a verdict."

"We'd still get the lunch before we were called. Try to relax."

"I'm relaxed. I'm bored."

Again there were footsteps, a knock, and the door opened. Sergeant Larson entered with a cardboard box which he set down on the desk. Tyson saw it was crammed with sandwiches, salads, and desserts. Larson said, "My wife. She's been insisting," he added with some embarrassment. "Hope it's okay."

Corva said, "Tell her we appreciate it."

Tyson took a wrapped sandwich, though he didn't want one. "That was thoughtful of her, Sergeant."

Larson smiled and left.

Corva found a chicken cutlet sandwich on rye bread and bit into it. He said, "As I told you once, and as you see and hear every day, you are not guilty in the public mind."

"I never thought much of American public opinion and judgment before. I'm a snob and an elitist. I don't deserve to take comfort in what they think now."

Corva found a can of cola and popped it open. "You have a good grasp of who you are and the world you live in. Unfortunately, who you are and the world you live in don't get along."

Tyson discovered two beers in the cardboard box and drank both of them without offering one to Corva.

Corva ate with no apparent loss of appetite.

Tyson went to the men's room under escort. Corva went on his own. The afternoon played itself out in boredom and anxiety. The sunlight was beginning to fail, and a wind came up off the water, scattering the red and gold leaves over the lawns and sidewalks, and rustling them against the side of the building. Tyson went to the window and noticed that the crowd had thinned and those who had not gone back in the chapel were huddled against the chill wind. Tyson said, more to himself than Corva, "Last autumn I raked the leaves and threw around the football with my son. I split logs and built fires in my fireplace. We went to a farm out east and bought pumpkins and gourds and apple cider. We came home, and I made hot rum toddies. I like the smell of autumn."

Corva replied in an equally distant voice. "Me too. I missed it in Cu Chi. I had my brother send me a shoebox full of leaves." He smiled to himself. "I gave them to people who said they missed the fall."

Tyson said, "Sounds like you were fishing for a psychiatric discharge."

Corva picked up the *Daily News.* The headlines read simply: *VERDICT TO-DAY?*

Tyson looked at it. "Good question." He looked at the wall clock. It was four-sixteen.

At four-twenty, Corva stood and went to the window. "No one seems to be leaving. The press vans are still there."

At four twenty-five, Tyson stood. "I didn't want to have to sleep on this. Have me put up in the BOQ. I'm not going home tonight."

Corva replied, "All right. I won't argue with you." He added, "It may be nerve-racking to have to wait, but it is not a bad sign. Something happened in that deliberation room."

"But what?"

At four-thirty, Corva snapped his briefcase shut and took his trench coat from the coat tree.

Neither Tyson nor Corva heard the footsteps this time, but they heard the gentle knock on the door, as gentle, Tyson thought, as the footsteps must have been, and he knew they hadn't come to excuse him for the day.

The door opened, and Sergeant Larson stood a moment without speaking; a moment too long for Corva, who snapped, "Well? Are we excused?"

"No, sir. The board has reached a verdict."

Corva nodded stiffly. "Thank you." He rehung his coat and said to Tyson in a strained voice, "Let's hear what they have to say."

Tyson walked toward the door being held open by Sergeant Larson. Larson said to Tyson, "Sir, you should take your cover."

"What . . . ?" Tyson stood motionless for a moment, then said, "Yes, of course. I won't be coming back here either way, will I?"

"No, sir."

"Thank the rabbi for us, if you should see him."

"Yes, sir."

Corva led the way into the corridor. Again, Larson caught up and walked ahead. He seemed to sense that his charges were in no hurry, and his pace was not fast. They entered the courtroom, and Tyson heard a hush fall over the crowd in the pews. He looked and saw that the chapel was completely full, like Easter Sunday, with people in the aisles and in the vestibule.

He strode purposefully past the table where the board was already assembled, past the prosecution table without looking at Pierce, Weinroth, or Longo, and took his place beside Corva at the defense table. Corva had remained standing, so Tyson did the same. He noticed, too, that the prosecution was now standing, though this was not required.

Tyson brought himself to look at the right front pew. Marcy was dressed conservatively in a tweed business suit. She crossed her legs, smiling at him encouragingly. David, seated next to her, looked sad, he thought, though perhaps *scared* was a better word. He wondered what was going on inside the mind of a sixteen-year-old. Tyson's three sisters, all pretty, lively women, were maintaining a show of optimism. His mother, who rarely showed any emotion other than haughtiness, impatience, or annoyance, now looked bewildered and old. Tyson contrived a look of unconcern and faced the board. He tried to read their expressions, but there was less there to read than there had ever been. The only flicker of emotion came from Major Virginia Sindel, who inadvertently made eye contact with him, then dropped her eyes.

Tyson realized Corva was speaking to him. Corva whispered, "There is a quirk in the wording of the Manual for Courts-Martial. Verdicts of not guilty are announced with the words, 'It is my duty to advise you . . .' Guilty verdicts with the words 'inform you.' I wanted you to know that so you could prepare yourself before you hear the actual verdict."

Tyson kept his head and eyes straight ahead and said, "Thank you."

Not more than a moment later, Colonel Sproule turned on his microphone and announced, "The court will come to order." Sproule looked out at the pews, then regarded the press section a moment, then looked at the prosecution and finally the board. He said, "All parties to the trial who were present when the court closed are now present."

Colonel Sproule addressed Colonel Moore, asking, "Has the court reached the findings in this case?"

Moore stood and replied, "It has."

Sproule then asked, "Are the findings reflected on the finding worksheets you were given?"

"They are," replied Moore.

Sproule looked at the prosecution table. "Will the trial counsel, without examining it, bring me the findings?"

Major Judith Weinroth stood and went directly to Colonel Moore, who handed her the findings. She made a show of not looking at the long sheets of paper and walked the five paces to the pulpit, handing the two pages up to Colonel Sproule. She waited in front of the pulpit facing it.

Colonel Sproule adjusted the pulpit light and examined the sheets of paper closely, turning them both over several times. Tyson, Corva, and everyone in the chapel, including the court reporter, had their eyes on Sproule's face to see any trace of emotion. But Colonel Sproule's face revealed nothing but concentration on the forms before him, and Tyson thought he had the look of a man grading a school essay on a dull subject.

Colonel Sproule looked up abruptly and said to Moore, "I find no defects of form." He handed the two pages down to Major Weinroth and said, "Will you return this to the president of the court?"

She took the papers, but they somehow got loose from her grasp, and they fell to the red-carpeted floor. She knelt hastily to retrieve them and lingered perhaps a half second too long in gathering them before she rose. Her face was flushed as she strode across the floor and handed the papers back to Colonel Moore, who gave her a sympathetic look. Major Weinroth turned and walked back to the prosecution table, carrying herself the way someone does who knows there is a room full of people looking at them. As she approached the table, her face still toward the spectators, she made eye contact with Pierce, and her head bobbed slightly, but no one could say for sure if it was in apology for the dropped forms or in triumph.

Colonel Sproule turned and looked at Tyson. He said, "Lieutenant Benjamin Tyson, please report to the president of the court."

Tyson replied in a strong voice, "Yes, sir."

Corva reached out and, in full view of the court and the spectators, squeezed Tyson's hand.

Tyson came around the table and walked across the red carpet, centering himself directly in front of Colonel Moore. Tyson saluted but maintained the protocol that this was one of the few occasions when no verbal report was made.

Colonel Moore and Benjamin Tyson faced one another. The remainder of the board stayed seated. Corva had remained standing, though it wasn't required that he do so. The prosecution was standing also, and they blocked the view of some of the spectators sitting on the left side of the nave. The media stood, perhaps to get a better view, and the people behind them began standing, perhaps because the press was blocking them. Then others began standing, even those whose view was not obstructed, and within a few seconds the entire chapel full of people was on its feet, standing and waiting.

Colonel Sproule began to say something into his microphone, then hesitated and turned to Colonel Moore. "Proceed with the verdict."

Out of the corners of his eyes, Tyson saw that the board was staring straight ahead, resisting their natural desire to look at him. Moore, without referring to the findings sheet and looking Tyson directly in the eye, spoke to him as though they were the only two people in the room. "Lieutenant Benjamin Tyson, it is my duty as president of this court to inform you—"

There were audible reactions from a few of the people in the pews who understood what the wording signified.

"—that the court, in closed session and upon secret ballot, two-thirds of the members present at the time the vote was taken concurring in each finding, finds you, of the charge of murder, guilty."

Tyson stood perfectly still, showing Colonel Moore and the board no more emotion than they'd shown him all week.

Someone in the pews shouted something, and a woman sobbed, though he didn't think it was Marcy or his mother, neither of whom was prone to sobbing.

Colonel Moore continued, "Of Specification One, guilty, and of Specification Two, guilty; excepting that in both specifications the words 'shooting them,' and the words 'ordering them to be shot,' will be deleted, leaving the words 'causing them to be shot.' " Colonel Moore looked at Tyson and gave a brief nod to indicate he was finished.

Tyson saluted, turned, and walked to the defense table, not meeting Corva's or anyone's eyes, not once looking at his wife and son.

Colonel Sproule surveyed the chapel and the altar area where no one was sitting but the five members of the board. He had the quizzical appearance of a man who had never seen such a thing. He announced into the pulpit microphone, "This court will reconvene Monday at ten hundred hours for the purpose of arriving at an appropriate sentence. This court is adjourned."

But no one moved toward the doors. Instead, everyone stood silently as Sergeant Larson, now armed and wearing a helmet, approached Tyson with another armed MP. The MPs stood self-consciously before the defense table. No one said anything until finally Larson asked politely, "Sir, will you come with me?"

Tyson shook hands with Corva, took his hat from the table, and came around to join the MPs, still not trusting himself to look at his family. The MPs moved to either side, flanking him, and walked across the altar floor through the side door and down the long white corridor. Tyson noticed that the corridor was deserted and quiet except for the sound of their footsteps.

They came to a door that exited to the back of the chapel grounds, and an MP standing there opened it.

Tyson put on his hat and walked out into the cool twilight. He noticed first the western sky to his front, a deep blue, then toward the horizon a nice orange and yellow beyond the lights of the bridge.

Burly MPs formed a wedge around him and escorted him toward a dark-colored staff car. The chapel and corridor had been deathly still, but now a raucous noise assailed him: the shouts of dozens of people, then dozens more as people converged on the rear of the chapel. He saw a television camera. Then there were flashbulbs lighting up the pleasant, comforting dusk. Microphones were pushed toward him, but the MPs pushed back hard. Above the general bedlam he heard a man shouting, "Let him go! Let him go!" A woman had somehow slipped past the phalanx of MPs and reached out to him sobbing,

"God bless you, God bless you." As she reached him, an MP caught her arm and pulled her away.

Tyson found himself at the car, then in it. Sergeant Larson slid in the rear beside him, then the other door opened and another MP slid in to Tyson's left, jamming him in between them. Both doors slammed shut, and Sergeant Larson said, "Please put your hands on the back of the seat in front of you."

Tyson did as he was told, and Sergeant Larson snapped a pair of handcuffs over his wrists. Tyson was surprised at how heavy they were.

The car began moving slowly over the back lawn, through the milling crowd, the headlights flashing from low beam to high, and the horn honking in a rhythmic cadence. The driver swore.

The MP to Tyson's left said, "I don't have to worry about your all-night runs anymore. Do I?"

Tyson turned his head and found himself looking straight into the beady eyes of Captain Gallagher. Tyson began to say something unpleasant, then realized he was no longer free to say to Captain Gallagher the things that needed saying.

Gallagher seemed to sense this, and realizing, too, that the sport was gone, his face softened. He said, "We were parked there for an hour waiting, but to tell you the truth, Tyson, I didn't want to see you in this car."

"Yes, sir."

The dark staff car was clear of the crowd and had picked up a two-Jeep escort. They were rolling fast now up Lee Avenue.

Tyson noticed for the first time that the man in the front passenger seat was a civilian. The man turned in his seat and said, "We have some talking to do before they sentence you, ace."

Tyson looked at Chet Brown. Tyson replied, "I don't think so."

Brown shrugged and turned back toward the front. He said, "We'll see."

Gallagher produced a hip flask and unscrewed the cap. "Let me buy you one."

Tyson said, "Don't need one."

Gallagher, too, shrugged and put the cap back on. He hesitated, then shoved the flask in the side flap pocket of Tyson's tunic. "Keep it."

Tyson realized they were not heading off-post and knew they were not going to Fort Dix.

Gallagher watched him a moment and said, "Just the post lockup. Over the weekend. Until the sentencing Monday. Then . . . then . . ."

"Then," said Brown from the front seat, "it depends on the stubborn son of a bitch where he goes next."

Tyson ventured a soft "Fuck you," and no one seemed to mind.

The car stopped at the provost marshal's office, and Tyson found himself in a small cell whose walls were made of glazed beige block. Sergeant Larson removed the handcuffs and left, slamming the barred cell door. Brown stood on the other side of the bars as the MPs went into the office to do the paperwork on the prisoner. Brown said, "All we want is an assurance from you—in writing —that you will never speak of any of this ever again for the rest of your natural life."

"Go fuck yourself."

"Except, of course, for a few well-chosen words now and then regarding the positive side of your experience with the government and with military justice."

"Take a walk."

"In effect, you've lived up to your end of the deal so far without even agreeing to it. You haven't said one word to the media about anything. We appreciate that. And your lawyer has been decent, too." Brown pulled a folded sheaf of papers from his breast pocket. "You read this and you sign it."

"Shove it, Chet."

"One of the things this says is that you won't bring up questions about your recall to duty or about the fact that the actual perpetrators of the crime are beyond the reach of the law. The government is very sensitive about that."

"I'm a little sensitive too."

Brown leaned closer, his hands on the bars, and his face between them. He kept a close eye on Tyson standing about eight feet away, as though acknowledging that Tyson, though caged, was dangerous. Brown said musingly, "Did you know, Ben, that of the twenty-five men originally implicated in My Lai, about eighteen never had charges brought against them because they had been discharged by that time? Well, the government has had ample time to plug that loophole but hasn't. And of the men implicated who were still in the service, most were never charged because the local commander didn't bring charges, such as General Peters brought in your case. Of course, Peters needed a little prodding. But the Army likes their system. And of the other men who were charged for My Lai, all were acquitted except Calley. That's what we call the My Lai mess now. And after all these years, the system hasn't changed. The government, the Justice Department, would like to change that system so that the United States is never again embarrassed by an inability to prosecute its servicemen for war crimes. That's a noble goal."

"It's so noble that no one has thought about it for twenty years."

"Well, it takes something like this, doesn't it? The point is the Army doesn't want its system changed. So there's a fight on now. What we don't need is you confusing the issues."

"Who are *we?* If I knew who you worked for, I might listen to you. You may be an Army man for all I know. You may be a JAG man."

"I may be. I may be a civilian. Doesn't matter."

"Sure does."

Brown ruffled the papers in his hand. "If you sign this, then no matter what sentence you are given, the President will give you a full pardon within thirty days. While you're still at the Dix stockade. You'll never see Kansas."

"Where were you before the verdict, bozo? When I needed you?"

Brown smiled. "Oh, I couldn't do anything about the verdict or even the sentence they hand you. I can't get to a military jury. But I can get to the chain of command and see that you are released by . . . let's say, Thanksgiving. Turkey in your dining room in Garden City. Tastes better than the turkey in Leavenworth."

"You searched my house."

"K and K Cleaning Service cleaned your house."

"You're a shit."

Brown threw the folded papers through the cell bars, and they landed in the center of the concrete floor. "Among other things, you agree not to talk to the press, you agree the government has treated you fairly, you agree not to write, lecture, or utter any public statements, and so on. And I agree to make you whole again. Including your overpaid job."

Tyson looked at the papers on the floor. "Okay, Chet. I'll read it if you'll beat it."

"Right. *Adiós, amigo.* Get a good night's rest. And, hey, you handled yourself well. I would have been shaking in my boots. And Monday, if you play ball, and they hand you ten to twenty, you can smile at them."

"Right."

"You'll have no visitors tonight, so don't think about giving that to your lawyer to smuggle out of here. I want it back at six A.M. tomorrow. Signed or unsigned."

"How about my copy?"

Brown laughed as he turned and left.

Tyson looked around the cell, then sat on his bunk. He glanced again at the papers lying on the floor, then took off his hat and shoes and lay back on the narrow Army cot. "The quarters keep getting smaller."

Sergeant Larson came to the cell door. He said, "You want dinner?"

"No thanks."

"Okay. Your lawyer called. He said he'll see you at seven A.M."

"Okay."

"He said to think about a statement you'd like to make in extenuation and mitigation before the sentencing."

"I'll think about it."

"Anything I can get you?"

"The keys."

Larson smiled. "The evening papers will be full of this. You want the papers?"

"You read about one court-martial, you read about them all, Larson."

"Right. Was everything okay?"

"What . . . ?"

"The lunch. I have to tell my wife."

"Oh. Yes. Great veal cutlets."

"It was chicken."

"That's right."

"Hey, what was it like over there?"

"Where?"

"Nam. What was it like in combat?"

Tyson thought a moment, then replied, "I couldn't tell you."

"Weren't you in combat?"

"I guess. But I'm home now. The war is over."

50

At five-thirty on Saturday morning Tyson was awakened by an MP and taken, in his underwear, to the latrine and shower room. The MP provided him with a standard-issue box of toiletries. The MP also gave him the rules and added, "You have twenty minutes."

Tyson shared the small facility with two other prisoners, who didn't have much to say, though one of them offered, "You got the biggest royal fuck I ever heard of."

The other one only commented that he'd never shared a latrine with an officer. Tyson didn't know if the man meant it was an honor or an inconvenience and thought it best not to ask.

Tyson shaved and showered and folded his towel into a square as he'd been told, placing it on the sink. He helped the other two prisoners clean the latrine and was wiping the shower dry when the MP returned. "Back to the cells, men."

Tyson was escorted back to his cell in his underwear. He dressed in his uniform but left the tunic in the metal wall locker. He combed his hair in a small polished metal mirror, an Army field mirror, that was hung too low on the wall and didn't reflect his image well, which might be more of a blessing than a nuisance, he thought.

At 6 A.M. sharp, Chet Brown arrived with a container of coffee.

Brown looked at the papers still on the floor where he'd thrown them. He said, "This offer is not good after the sentencing. So don't try to play it that way." He offered the container through the bars.

"Keep it."

Brown shrugged, peeled off the lid, and drank the coffee himself.

Tyson sat on the edge of his cot and lit a cigarette.

Brown continued, "Don't think if you get off with a year or two you can do that standing on your head, Ben. Jail sucks. And people like you don't do well in jail."

"Who are people like me?"

"They could hand you ten to twenty. And I won't be back with this offer. Because if they give you ten to twenty, then nobody has to worry about you becoming a public nuisance."

Tyson flipped his ash into a tin can filled with water.

Brown added, "They could order you hanged, you know."

Tyson yawned.

Brown said, "What's the big deal about agreeing to do something that you're already doing?"

Tyson looked at his cigarette as he replied, "Because, shithead, if I want to do something, then that's all right. If I don't, then that's all right, too. But if you try to put a gun to my head to make me do something, then all I can do is say fuck you. *Capice?*"

Chet Brown looked annoyed. He said in a sarcastic tone, "You didn't have all these scruples when you watched your men mow down nuns and babies."

Tyson drew a deep breath. "No. No, I didn't. That's why I'm here. But that doesn't mean I have to deal with you. Leave."

Brown began to say something, then changed his mind. He looked at the papers on the floor. "I'll take those."

Tyson stood and kicked the folded papers near the bars.

Brown said, "Step back, killer."

Tyson stepped back.

Brown squatted quickly and snatched the papers, spilling coffee on his trousers. "Damn it!"

"You're a little jumpy this morning, Chet."

Brown blotted the coffee with a handkerchief. He said to Tyson, "Look, if everything goes all right for you, maybe we can talk about government job opportunities. Look me up."

"How do I look you up, Chet?"

"Just make a public statement I don't like. You'll hear from me."

"Don't threaten, Chet. It makes me mad."

"Just trying to be helpful. I like you."

Tyson said, "You wouldn't know anything about the whereabouts of Dan Kelly and Sister Teresa, would you?"

"I might."

Tyson and Brown looked at each other, then Brown said, "You may hear from them shortly. Then again, you may not." He turned and walked through the door into the provost marshal's office.

A quarter of an hour later, an MP appeared with a breakfast tray from the mess hall and a newspaper. The MP opened the cell door and set the tray on the cot and handed the newspaper to Tyson. "Last night's final."

Tyson looked at the copy of the *New York Post*. The headline in red shouted, GUILTY! Tyson said, "Get it out of here."

The MP shrugged and left with the newspaper.

Tyson found he was hungry and finished the breakfast of scrambled eggs, bacon, and coffee. There were also grits, which the Army apparently still blithely served to soldiers, who stuck their cigarettes in them. "Typical." He wanted another cup of coffee but didn't ask. A radio in the provost marshal's office was playing a sort of music, a hard screaming rock that he thought shouldn't be allowed over the public airwaves until after 6 P.M. He decided he didn't like prison life.

The cell was cold, and Tyson put on his tunic and tightened his tie. There was no window, and he didn't know what the weather was like outside, but since he wasn't going outside, it didn't matter.

At 7 A.M., the door of the provost marshal's office opened again, and Corva came into the small passageway between the three cells. The MP opened the cell door, Corva entered, and the MP closed and locked the door.

Corva took the plastic molded chair and pulled it up facing Tyson, who was sitting on the cot. He opened his attaché case and laid it on his lap. Tyson noted that the attaché case made a better prison lap desk than the briefcase Corva usually carried. Tyson observed, "You seem at home here. I guess you've visited a lot of your clients in jail. Like all of them."

Corva ignored this and said without preamble, "Our goal now is to keep you out of jail."

"I'm *in* jail, Vince."

Corva produced a pint of Dewar's from his briefcase and threw it on the cot. "Put that out of sight. They don't mind if you drink, but they don't want to see it."

Tyson put the bottle under his pillow from which he took Captain Gallagher's hip flask, which was empty. "Give this back to Gallagher." He threw it to Corva, who put it in his attaché case. Corva said, "Is there anything else you need? Stamps—"

Tyson laughed derisively. "Writing paper, candy? Christ, Vince, I used to say that to the guys in my company who got locked up."

Corva said coolly, "Well, you won't be here long."

"Will you come to Kansas to see me? We can have a reunion. Corva's clients."

Corva smiled unexpectedly, then laughed. "Corva's clients. I like that. Corva's cases. No, clients."

Tyson regarded him icily for a moment, then leaned forward on his cot and said slowly and distinctly, "Get me the hell out of here."

"Working on it." He looked at Tyson and said pointedly, "Just for the record —you wanted a trial."

Tyson didn't speak for some time, then said, "No one *wants* to be tried. I may have thought I needed it. I'm not sure *how* I felt before Sproule said, 'The court will come to order.' " Tyson added, "Also for the record, someone with brains would have convinced his client that a court-martial was not a good idea. Someone with brains would have gotten this thing dismissed before it got this far."

Corva seemed to be counting to ten, then said, "There was a time, not so many years ago, when these charges might have been dismissed. But I don't think that was so good a thing either. Point is, this is the new Army."

"I'm old Army."

"Good point. I'll bring it up. Anyway. . . ." His eyes fell on the place above Tyson's top left pocket where the service ribbons were worn. "I see you've undecorated yourself."

Tyson nodded. "I couldn't very well wear the Silver Star or the Vietnamese Cross of Gallantry for heroism on 15 February 1968. Could I?"

"I suppose not." Corva said, "Let's do some work. Okay, if you were paying attention during the verdict reading, you might have heard Colonel Moore say, 'Two-thirds concurring.' The actual number tally of votes guilty or not guilty is secret, but they will announce an approximate fraction. With a six-member board, if the vote was five to one for conviction, Moore would have said, 'Three-fourths concurring.' But now we know what I suspected. Two people on that board voted for acquittal, which means there are two people on that board who will argue very strenuously for a light sentence. Follow?"

Tyson nodded.

Corva continued, "So, Pierce is pissed and a little worried. So he's prepared to go into the sentencing session with a strong argument when they ask him for his recommendation for an appropriate sentence. But now that we've got him on the run a little, he's come to me with a proposition. To wit: If we don't sit there for a week—offering extensive extenuation and mitigation—like everything from bringing in Levin and your wife to testify to your character and the reading of award citations and on and on—then he will recommend an appropriate sentence of five years. Now, understand, this session is very important in a court-martial. I've seen serious crimes extenuated and mitigated to the point where a board will hand out less than a year jail time. The Army is different from civilian life, as you may have noticed. A soldier can be reduced in rank, forfeit pay, confined to barracks, and all of that. So actual jail time tends to be less than you'd expect for some crimes. And the board will base the sentence not so much on what you did, but who you are, the sum total of everything you've accomplished as a man and as an officer. And even how you've behaved at the court-martial."

"How about how you've behaved?"

Corva nodded. "Yes, that too. And that's no joke, Ben. I couldn't get away with my civilian theatrics with that bunch. There is a very famous case of a captain who hired a civilian lawyer who was not only obnoxious but insulting to the board, threatening them with civil suit over something or other. The captain got the max in Kansas. So if I didn't seem like the lawyers you see on TV, that's why. Okay?"

"Okay."

"So what should I tell Pierce?"

"How about 'Pierce, go fuck yourself'?"

Corva smiled. "Okay. But I'll put it a little differently. Next point. The board, as you noticed, changed the wording of the specifications. In other words, they didn't believe Brandt or Farley that you, yourself, ordered your men to waste everyone or that you, yourself, engaged in any acts which were inherently dangerous to others or evinced any wanton disregard of human life. That was a slap in the face to Pierce, not to mention the fact that they called Brandt half a liar, and Farley, too. One of the commentators on a late-night news show last night said Brandt stands convicted as a liar. So you've got your Pyrrhic victory, and Brandt has a public relations problem. But you're the one in the slammer. Worth it?"

Tyson shrugged. "We'll see when the sentence is announced. And I'm not through with Dr. Brandt yet. When I take the stand in extenuation and mitigation, I have a few things to say—"

"Like hell you will. When you get up there, you'll talk about *you,* not Brandt. We had our chance to impeach Brandt's testimony." Corva studied Tyson's face. "When you take the stand, Ben, you tell the truth. You'll tell the court who murdered the people and who did not. You'll tell them you killed Larry Cane. You'll tell them your troops mutinied, went on a rampage, and you were almost shot trying to stop it—who pointed the rifle at you by the way?"

"Farley, Simcox, and Beltran."

Corva shook his head. "Anyway, you'll tell the court you were scared shitless and that's why you failed to make a report and swear to criminal charges. And you'll tell them you felt some loyalty toward your troops, misguided though it was. You will not tell them about Brandt fucking the little girl. *Capice?*"

Tyson nodded. "Do I . . . I mean, about Cane . . . is that necessary?"

"Absolutely." Corva looked at him closely. "The board understands that what they heard from Brandt and Farley was the story of a mutiny. They don't like to hear about troops mutinying. It scares officers. But they like it even less when they hear that the officer in charge stood there with his finger up his ass, whistling 'The Stars and Stripes Forever.' "

Tyson nodded. "I understand."

Corva went on, "The annals of military history are filled with stories of officers quelling mutinies though they were outnumbered by their troops a zillion to one and full of stories of officers dying in an attempt to prevent mutinies, massacres, rapes, pillaging, and what have you. A good part of the officer's code is based on this mental image of chivalry and is a direct product of the knight's code. They teach you that?"

"I missed that class."

"Anyway, you will get up there and tell them that indeed you did put your life on the line, shot an American soldier as was your duty, and were assaulted and knocked unconscious and so forth. You will tell them you did your duty. Right up to the point when you reached the safety of a base camp and did not initiate charges of mutiny, mass murder, arson, striking an officer, and so on. *That* is where you fucked up. That is what you will tell them."

"Will they believe any of it?"

Corva leaned across his attaché case. "If you tell it to them, Ben, they will believe it. It is the story that fills in the missing pieces for them. It also happens to be the truth. And just as that board knew Brandt and Farley were lying, so they will know you are not."

Tyson sat quietly for a long time, then said, "I feel bad for the rest of them. The ones who signed sworn statements and for the dead, whose families thought they were heroes. For Larry Cane's family, who thought he died in action. . . ." Tyson looked at Corva. "But it's time to set the record straight, isn't it?"

"Yes, it's time. Especially if there are men who didn't shoot anyone. Are there?"

Tyson nodded. "Some of them are dead now. Only Kelly, me, and Brandt never pulled a trigger."

"How do you know that Kelly and Brandt didn't? You weren't there the whole time."

"It came out afterward. But I assumed from the beginning they didn't. Brandt was a lot of things, but he wasn't a . . ."

"A what? A killer?"

"Right." Tyson said, "If we're setting the record straight, why can't we set it straight regarding Brandt?"

"That is one story I don't think they will believe, if *you* tell it." Corva added, "That's why I'm going to have Kelly tell it."

Tyson stood.

Corva remained seated.

He explained. "I heard from Colonel Farnley Gilmer, who was good enough to keep the Article 32 investigation open as is sometimes done even during trial. He informed me that Daniel Kelly has shown some signs of life. Specifically, a law firm claiming to represent Kelly has contacted Gilmer. The firm, incidentally, is Conners, Newhouse, and Irving, who coincidentally are secretly famous for representing CIA people. So, apparently somebody somewhere decided it was okay to surface Kelly for a one-shot public appearance."

"Kelly decided. He would have insisted."

Corva observed, "But not to testify at the early part of the trial. That would have put him in a position of having to lie if he were our witness or having to tell the truth as a prosecution witness. If indeed Pierce called him at all. Now that the smoke has settled, he's coming in as your witness in extenuation and mitigation only. He can be cross-examined on anything he says, but I think Pierce will have the sense not to do that."

Tyson said, as if to himself, "Daniel Kelly . . . God, he could have blown this case wide open. His story would not have agreed with ours or the prosecution's. He would have told the truth."

Corva nodded. "The old infantry vets on that board will understand that Kelly, as your radio operator, was rarely more than an arm's length from you every minute you were in the field. He was your shadow, your aide, your *consigliere.*"

Tyson said, "I don't know about that last thing. But I do know that he even followed me when I went off in the bush to take a crap. The only two times I can recall when we were separated for any length of time was when he knocked me out in the hospital and then later at the Strawberry Patch when we got separated by refugees."

Corva said, "I could reopen the whole case because of his appearance. But I don't think it would lead to an acquittal. The point remains that your cover-up amounted to condoning mass murder, and the words 'caused to be shot' and 'inherently dangerous acts' and so forth would be interpreted as your striking of Dr. Monteau which ignited the massacre." He looked at Tyson. "It did, you know."

"I know."

"But, anyway, if we reopen the case, Pierce may just switch around some wording on the charge sheet now that he has more of the facts."

"I don't want a retrial, Vince. Everyone's had enough. I just want to keep out of jail. I can live with the guilty verdict."

"I understand. And you can live quite well with Kelly testifying that he saw Brandt raping a young girl."

Tyson drew a long breath. "Yes."

"What, by the way, happened at the Strawberry Patch? Harper thinks Brandt failed to go out after you under fire. Failed to treat you."

Tyson shook his head. "He treated me. He treated me to an overdose of morphine."

Corva's eyes widened. "Jesus Christ. . . ."

Tyson said, "But, obviously, neither Kelly nor anyone was witness to that. I'm not one hundred percent sure of it myself. The nearly perfect crime."

Corva nodded. "And you can't tell that in court, Ben. He'll sue the pants off you. The board may believe it, but . . . without corroboration . . . and coming only from you . . . forget it. That's done with. You'll never settle that score." He glanced at Tyson and said, "That was a hell of a crew you had there, Lieutenant . . . rape, murder, conspiracy, revenge, mutiny . . . what else? Steal chickens, too?"

Tyson snapped, "As a matter of fact, they were not bad. Not in the beginning. But you can only log so many miles on a man and imprint so many obscenities on his brain before he begins to malfunction. You know that. Don't *you* judge them!"

"Sorry."

"*I* don't judge them too harshly. I don't even judge Brandt harshly. I mean, about trying to kill me."

"Because you'd thought about killing *him.*"

"Yes, that's why." Tyson smiled. "I related to that. I could see his point. The Nam solution—someone bothering you? Annoyed? Upset? Administer five to ten rounds of 5.56-millimeter M-16 ammunition. Or, if you're a medic, a good-bye dose of pure morphine."

Corva snapped his attaché case closed and stood. "I'll be back tomorrow. I'm going to mass at the chapel at ten A.M. Then I'll be here. And we'll go over the E and M."

"Do you want to do it this afternoon? I'm free."

Corva smiled. "Today I'm going to spend the day with Daniel Kelly at his lawyers' midtown office."

"Good. You'll like him."

"I might have, eighteen years ago. Men change."

"Do they? I don't think so."

Corva walked toward the cell door. He hesitated, then said, "One more thing. . . . This is not certain, but Colonel Gilmer tells me he has heard from Interpol. . . ."

Tyson moved toward Corva. "They've found her."

"Maybe. And not in France where everyone was looking. But in Italy. They think it's the same woman. I'll know today."

"I don't think I want her called."

"Well . . . we may not be able to."

"What do you mean?"

"I'll talk to you about it after I speak to Gilmer."

"There's no reason to call her. The case is done. We have Kelly for E and M. And I'll testify on my own behalf."

Corva rubbed his nose and said, "She can tell the court that you saved her life at the hospital."

Tyson didn't respond.

Corva added, "Ben, if this woman in Italy is *the* Sister Teresa, I'd like to talk to her. And I think if she is your friend, she'd want the opportunity to help you. You helped her." Corva looked at Tyson awhile, then said, "If it was more than a friendship . . . and it went bad . . . then maybe it would be best to leave her be. . . ."

Tyson looked at the floor awhile, then stated, "The woman was a nun, Vince."

"Of course."

Tyson rubbed his lip for some time. "None of your surprise reunions. Okay?"

"Okay." He drew an envelope from his side pocket. "A letter from your wife."

Tyson took it.

Corva said, "She loves you deeply, madly, passionately."

"Are you reading my mail?"

"No, no. My wife told me. My wife is staying with your wife this weekend."

"Who are you staying with this weekend?"

"Kelly and his rather unorthodox lawyers. And this Sister Teresa is a hard call. I have an interpreter lined up just in case."

"Really? You're not as incompetent as you look. What language? Greek?"

"No, French."

"Why not Vietnamese?"

"For one thing, they're harder to find. For another, the last thing I want in that courtroom is a Vietnamese. You know?"

Tyson nodded. *"Compris."*

"Anyway, if I can't get the whole show on the road by ten hundred hours Monday, I'll ask for another day or two." Corva glanced at his watch. "I need my breakfast. You screwed up my whole weekend."

"Mine is a little screwed up too. I have theater tickets for tonight. I want out of here, Vince. Monday night I want to be watching football at home. In Garden City."

"I'll do everything I can. You know there's no bail in the Army. But I may be able to secure what they call deferment. That's like back to house arrest until the case is finally settled with reviews and appeals and all that."

"Do it."

Tyson thought of Chet Brown. He said, "Is there any way we can negotiate the sentence? I mean, is that legal?"

Corva looked at him. "In military law, there is virtually no plea bargaining or sentence negotiations. And by law it must originate with the accused and his lawyer. Why do you ask? Has someone been talking to you?"

"No. I just wondered."

"By the way," said Corva, "you can have visitors in addition to your attorney."

"I don't want visitors."

"Okay. I had to ask." Corva turned and pushed a call button on the wall near the cell door.

Tyson commented, "You know your way around these places."

"I've been in jail before. A piece of advice about that: Follow all their idiotic rules. Military prisons are no place to try to exercise your rights."

An MP came with the keys and opened the cell door.

Tyson said to Corva, "I want you to tell me how you got the Bronze Star in the tunnel."

Corva smiled. "One of these days." He walked from the cell, and the MP shut the door. Corva said through the bars, "The first platoon of Alpha Company has nearly completed its exorcism." Corva left with the MP.

Tyson stood in the center of the small cell for a full minute, then stared down at the envelope in his hand. He opened it and read the note inside:

> *Dear Ben,*
> *I understand why you didn't want to see me while you were awaiting the verdict, and I'll understand if you don't want me to visit you*

*now. But I will not understand if you don't send me a letter today to
tell me you still love me.*
   David sends you his love, as I do.

Marcy

   *P.S. You looked quite brave up there. Your mother says you
should punch Colonel Pierce in the eye.*

Tyson read the short note again, then rang the bell. When the MP came,
Tyson asked him for writing paper and pen.

51

The cell door opened at nine-thirty on Monday morning, and Tyson and
Corva walked into the provost marshal's office. Corva said to Captain
Gallagher, "No cuffs. Right?"
Gallagher nodded. "But if he gets away, you will be held accountable."
Corva said, "Don't be an ass, Captain."
"Yes, sir. I try not to be."
Corva and Tyson left the office and got into the backseat of an olive-drab
staff car. Two MPs whom Tyson had never seen sat in the front. The car headed
toward the post chapel.
Tyson said, "That was not one of my better weekends."
The car delivered them to the rear door of the chapel's office wing. They
were met by two more armed MPs and taken directly to the courtroom.
It was a brilliantly clear day, and the four south-facing windows were alight
with the morning sun. Tyson took his place at the defense table and remarked
to Corva, "I feel at home here."
Corva nodded as if he'd heard this before.
No one else had arrived yet except the spectators, and Tyson looked out at
the pews. The press was in full attendance, but the pews were only about three-
fourths full, and most of the spectators were military. His sisters had gone
home to husbands and jobs, and only Marcy, David, and his mother remained
in the first pew, the remainder of the seats being left vacant. Marcy wasn't
looking at him, but David waved and Tyson waved back.
He didn't see anyone else he knew except Colonel Levin, who, he'd been
told, had taken leave time to attend each session.
Tyson began to turn his attention back to the court, but some movement
caught his eye, and he saw, walking down the middle aisle, Steven Brandt.
Brandt took an empty place in the pew almost directly behind Marcy. Tyson
nudged Corva. "Look."
Corva looked, and his eyes widened.
"What," asked Tyson, "is *he* doing here?"
Corva replied, "A witness may be present after the verdict. I guess he's here
to see you sentenced."
Tyson stared at Brandt until finally Brandt looked up. Brandt leaned back
and folded his arms. He smiled at Tyson.

Tyson, still staring at Brandt, said to Corva, "I'm going to kill the son of a bitch."

"Cool down, people are watching you."

Tyson saw that was true. People were looking from Brandt to Tyson and back again. Tyson sat back in his chair. He lit a cigarette. "Bastard."

After a few minutes he became aware again of his surroundings. He sensed a somewhat less tense atmosphere in the court, though he didn't know why there should be. He didn't consider his sentencing an anticlimax; it was the most important thing in the world for him at the moment. And today or tomorrow, he knew, depending on testimony, he'd take the stand himself. He looked at Marcy again, but she was still not looking at him. She was staring straight ahead. His note to her had been simple: *"I love you. But if I am sent to prison, I don't want or expect you to wait."*

He thought that was all right, but apparently, according to Linda Corva, it was not. *Women,* he thought. When he was younger, he'd never liked female intermediaries involved in his *affaires d'amour.* But they could be useful as a source of information, if not comprehension. He'd have to write another note.

The prosecution walked in, and Tyson thought they looked like three pigs heading back to the slop buckets for seconds.

The board entered very solemnly, together and in order of rank as usual. Tyson suspected that Colonel Moore ran his whole life by the manual for drill and ceremonies. Tyson said to Corva, "In a three-seat crapper, would he take the middle seat or the far right?"

Corva looked up from his papers and followed Tyson's gaze. "Oh . . . the place of honor is usually the far right. But at a dais or court-martial, he takes the middle. I'd say it was the same for a three-seat crapper. I'll check, though."

The sergeant at arms strode to the center of the floor and the spectators began to rise before he announced, "All rise!"

Colonel Sproule entered, and Tyson noticed for the first time that Sproule's pants were too long.

Sproule stepped up behind the pulpit, turned on the light, adjusted the microphone, and surveyed the court with his myopic eyes, as though, Tyson thought, he wanted to be sure he was in the right place. Sproule said, "The court will come to order."

Pierce stood and said, "All parties to the trial who were present when the court closed are now present."

Colonel Sproule glanced at something on the pulpit and said, "The purpose of this session is to hear testimony and to present to the board other evidence and documented facts which may be considered by them as extenuating or mitigating facts or circumstances which may be considered by the board in determining an appropriate sentence. The court will now hear the personal data concerning the accused shown on the charge sheet and any other information from his personal records relevant to sentencing. The court will also receive evidence of previous convictions, if any."

It was Captain Longo who stood and said, "The first page of the charge sheet shows the following data concerning the accused." Longo began reading the personal data sheet.

Tyson leaned toward Corva. "We're playing the B team today."

Corva said, "They are all the B team every day."

Longo continued to read the standard data from the charge sheet, but when he came to "term of current service," he paused and said in a snide tone, "Indefinite."

Corva was on his feet. "Objection, your honor."

Sproule didn't bother to ask what the objection was. He said to Captain Longo sharply, "Captain, this is not an audition. Just *read.*"

Longo seemed crushed and bowed his head. "Yes, sir."

Tyson noticed that Pierce and Weinroth exchanged looks as if to say, "I knew we shouldn't have let that schmuck open his mouth."

Longo completed the reading in a monotone, then sank low into his chair, as Major Weinroth stood. She began reading data from Tyson's old personnel file, though little of it seemed relevant any longer. Tyson realized he'd never heard her speak more than a word or two before, and he was surprised to find she had a deep, husky voice, which he found sexy. Then he discovered that he was thinking about sex, then his mind drew him to Kansas and a place where there was no sex of the type he favored. He had a sudden urge to bolt, to dash into the pews, into the arms of his supporters, who would carry him to safety. He whispered to Corva, "I'm making a break for it."

"Pay your bill first. Calm down."

"I'm getting restless."

"I see that. You want a recess?"

"No. I'll be all right."

Corva poured them both some water. Tyson lit a cigarette and blew the smoke toward Weinroth, who glanced up at him as she read. She finished reading the data and said to Corva, "Does the accused have any objection to the data as read?"

Corva replied, "Not the way you read it."

A few people laughed, and Corva said, "Give me a moment." He leaned toward Tyson. "All right?"

Tyson shrugged. "I wasn't paying attention."

Corva whispered, "The medals and citations and letters of commendation from your first term of service sound good to the board. And Levin's letter was a bit of a surprise. The board knows you did your job the first time around, and they know you've been a good soldier under Levin's command, too." He added half jokingly, "That's an automatic ten years off the sentence."

"That brings us down to sixty years. What if I can recite the Infantryman's Prayer by heart?"

Colonel Sproule cleared his throat pointedly.

Corva remained in his seat and said, "The accused has no objection to the data as read."

Tyson said to Corva, "Why am I still the accused?"

"I don't know. Never thought about that."

Colonel Sproule announced, "These documents will be marked as exhibits and made a part of the court record. Copies of all documents and records that are relevant to the imposition of an appropriate sentence will be presented to the members of the board preceding deliberations on sentence."

As the exhibits were marked, Tyson studied the board closely. Two people there had voted for acquittal, but for the life of him, he couldn't guess which two.

Corva saw where he was looking and said, "Major Sindel. That was who my wife said."

"Possible. Who else?"

"Beats me. The rest of them look like they spent the weekend building a scaffold."

Tyson said, "Maybe McGregor . . . no, Morelli . . . he liked your style . . . you remind him of his Uncle Vito's mouthpiece."

"Are you all right today?"

"I didn't sleep well."

"I'm not surprised." Corva looked at his client with some concern.

Colonel Sproule addressed Colonel Pierce. "Does the prosecution have evidence in aggravation?"

Pierce replied, "It does not."

Sproule turned to Corva. "Does the defense have evidence in extenuation and mitigation?"

"It does, your honor."

"Does the defense have evidence to be submitted and marked as exhibits?"

"It does not, your honor."

"Does the defense, then, intend to call witnesses in extenuation or mitigation?"

"It does, your honor."

"Then call your first witness, Mr. Corva."

Corva turned to the sergeant at arms and said, "The defense calls as a witness Mr. Daniel Kelly."

The door opened, and Daniel Kelly strode into the court. Tyson saw at once that the slight twenty-one-year-old he remembered was now a powerfully built forty-year-old man who walked with the movements of an athlete. Kelly's fair skin was bronze, and his long straw-colored hair fell across his forehead. Tyson noticed that his eyes darted everywhere at once, taking in the whole scene, noticing possible ambush sites, registering places of cover and concealment, heeding signs of booby traps, and discerning good fields of fire. Kelly wore black flannel slacks, a white turtleneck sweater, and a beige-colored suede sport jacket. Kelly stopped at the witness chair, looked at Tyson, and gave a thumbs-up. Tyson returned the greeting.

Corva said to Sproule, "Your honor, we intend that this be sworn testimony."

Sproule nodded to Pierce, who approached the witness chair with the impatient movements of a man who thinks he should be somewhere else by now. "Raise your right hand."

Kelly, still standing, raised his hand.

Pierce recited quickly, the words running together, "Do you swear that the evidence you shall give on the case now in hearing shall be the truth, the whole truth, and nothing but the truth, so help you God?"

"I do." Kelly sat without Pierce inviting him to do so.

Pierce said, "Please state your name, residence, and occupation."

"Daniel Kelly, Edgerton, Ohio, importing and exporting."

Pierce, who had been given some general information by Corva regarding expected testimony, had apparently learned a few other things about Daniel Kelly and didn't intend to let his first statement go unquestioned. "You are a *current* resident of Edgerton, Ohio?"

"Yes."

Pierce seemed skeptical. "Could you be more specific concerning your occupation?"

"Yes. I import and export things."

Someone laughed.

"From Edgerton, Ohio?" asked Pierce dubiously.

"Yes."

Corva said, "Your honor—"

Sproule put out his hand toward Corva and said to Pierce, "Perhaps you'd like to hold the cross-examination until after the defense has examined its witness, Colonel Pierce."

Again, a few people snickered.

Colonel Sproule said, "Mr. Corva, you may begin."

Pierce returned to the prosecution table, as Corva stood under the pulpit facing Kelly. Corva began, "Mr. Kelly, could you state your former grade, organization, and duties while serving in the Republic of Vietnam."

Kelly replied in a well-modulated voice, "I was a Specialist Four, serving with the first platoon of Alpha Company, Fifth Battalion of the Seventh Cavalry, First Air Cavalry Division. I was the platoon leader's radiotelephone operator, known as an RTO."

Tyson noticed, too, that Kelly's diction and choice of words had improved since Vietnam.

Corva said, "You were Lieutenant Tyson's personal radio operator, were you not?"

"For most of the time I was there, yes."

"And as an RTO, you had close and frequent contact with your platoon leader."

"Every day. We slept in the same foxhole. I had to provide him with radio contact at a second's notice, so we stayed fairly close."

Corva asked a series of questions to establish Kelly's past and present relationship to Tyson, then asked, "Are you generally aware of the circumstances of this trial?"

"Yes, I am."

"You are aware that Lieutenant Tyson has been convicted of murder."

"Yes, I am."

"And you have offered to appear in his behalf to offer testimony that may establish extenuating circumstances for the crime of which he stands convicted."

"Yes, I have."

"Mr. Kelly, could you tell the court what happened on the morning of 15 February 1968? The incident of the burial mound. Begin, please, at first light."

Kelly replied, "At first light, nineteen of us moved out of our night defensive positions." Kelly continued his narrative in the short concise sentences favored by the military, using military terminology of the period and using it accurately. Tyson had the impression that Kelly was relating last week's events, and he thought others shared that impression.

Tyson watched the board. He could see that Moore, McGregor, and Bauer were favorably impressed with Daniel Kelly. But he didn't know if that was going to do Benjamin Tyson any good. He glanced at Brandt, who seemed to be getting a little uneasy.

Kelly concluded, "We resumed the patrol, in a southeast direction, toward Hue."

Corva asked, "So, the only men who were with you on that burial mound were Lieutenant Tyson, Richard Farley, and Harold Simcox."

"Yes."

Colonel Pierce stood. "Your honor, if it please the court. I have been exceedingly patient, listening intently for anything that sounds like it might be extenuation or mitigation for the offense of which Lieutenant Tyson has been convicted."

Sproule looked down at Corva. "Mr. Corva?"

Corva replied, "Your honor, the nature of testimony offered in extenuation or mitigation is often such that it does no more than to establish the accused's state of mind or his intentions or the general conditions that prevailed at the time. I intend, your honor, for Mr. Kelly to be up here for some time. Now, the prosecution can object to this and that, but I assure the court that I will get this story told one way or the other, even if it means Mr. Kelly sitting here for the next week while I reply to objections. Your honor, do not take offense. Lieutenant Tyson stands here convicted of murder. And I am standing here to do everything in my power to see that the board has every pertinent detail that surrounds this incident, so that they may arrive at an appropriate sentence. I want the members of the board to discover as much as I know and Mr. Kelly knows about Lieutenant Tyson and about Miséricorde Hospital before they vote on a sentence. Though it may not all appear to be pertinent as it unfolds, I assure the court that this evidence is pertinent and that the court will recognize it as such by the time the witness steps down. That is my intention, your honor."

Sproule thought about that for a moment, then said, "Colonel Pierce, Mr. Corva, would you approach the bench?"

Pierce and Corva stepped up to the higher level of the pulpit on the side away from the witness chair. Colonel Sproule faced them and addressed Pierce in a low voice. "Colonel, if I am to believe Mr. Corva, he is attempting to establish what he believes are extenuating and mitigating circumstances for the crime which you have proven. I suggest you let him do that. Unless you have good and substantive objections to the testimony, I will overrule you. If this testimony takes you somewhat by surprise because of the sudden appearance of this witness, I will give you ample time to prepare a cross-examination during which you may address these objections within that format. I remind you that the defense has the benefit of the doubt in these matters. The charges having been proven, I intend to give the defense even more leeway in presenting facts which might lessen the sentence. I believe the board is looking for those facts."

Pierce stayed silent for a moment, then responded, "Yes, your honor."

Sproule turned to Corva. "I'll let the man talk, Mr. Corva, but I strongly suggest you do not attempt to retry this case in this session." Sproule looked from one to the other and said tersely, "Understood?"

They both answered in the affirmative.

Sproule faced forward on the pulpit and said, "Proceed with the examination."

Pierce went back to the prosecution table, and Corva to the witness chair. Corva addressed Kelly. "During the burial mound incident, did you hear Lieutenant Tyson give an order to shoot the peasants who were burying the dead?"

"Yes."

"Now . . . I'm going to ask for an opinion, Mr. Kelly. . . ." He glanced sharply at Pierce. ". . . And the court knows it is only your opinion. But as a man who had served with Lieutenant Tyson in the field for approximately eight months before that incident, what was your opinion of that order?"

Kelly replied, "On the face of it, it was an illegal order. But it is my opinion that it was not given in earnest. It was meant to shame."

"To shame whom?"

"Me, for one. Farley, Simcox, and I were making threatening gestures toward the peasants, generally being abusive. The strip search, for instance, could have been handled with more tact. I could see that Lieutenant Tyson was becoming annoyed with us. So, in a manner of speaking, he called our bluff. And we *were* bluffing. We had no intention—at least I didn't—of shooting those people. It was a bluff that we used too freely with the Vietnamese. After Lieutenant Tyson gave the order, no one moved for some time. He did not repeat the order or attempt to enforce it in any way. He then said, 'Okay, heroes, let's get moving.' Or words to that effect. He said it with sarcasm."

Corva asked, "Did you discuss this with him afterward?"

"No. There was nothing to discuss. If I had thought he was serious about the order, I would certainly have discussed it with him. But the order was too out of character to take it as anything but what I said it was."

"Did you discuss it with Farley?"

"No."

"Do you think Farley understood that the order was a bluff? Meant to shame?"

Pierce got to his feet, thought better of it, and sat.

Tyson could see that the board and Sproule were intent on hearing the story. And Pierce, as Corva had suggested some time ago, knew when to withdraw. Pierce had to weigh the effects of letting Kelly tell the story against the effects of not letting him tell it.

Corva repeated the question to Kelly.

Kelly replied, "Farley was not a man who understood subtleties. Yet, on this occasion, I believe he understood that Lieutenant Tyson did not mean for us to shoot those people. Simcox understood it. He commented to me as we left the burial mound that Lieutenant Tyson was too soft on the gooks. I don't think he would have said that if he believed that Lieutenant Tyson's order to shoot them was meant in earnest. Farley was in earshot and responded, 'Yeah.' "

Corva nodded, then said, "Thank you. We can move on or rather, move back, to an incident of some months previous to this incident which occurred in either late November or early December. I'm referring to an operation that was known as a cordon. Alpha Company was working with the Vietnamese National Police at a village south of Quang Tri. Do you recall this operation?"

"Yes. We'd done four or five of them before. Regarding this particular one, everything went as planned. The village was surrounded two hours before dawn. At dawn, we sent a few squads in to be sure the village was not infested with armed enemy soldiers. Then the squads withdrew. Sometime later, within the hour, a large Chinook helicopter landed, and about forty or fifty National Policemen got out. Their officers exchanged some words with our officers, who assured them the village did not harbor any large enemy force. The National Police then entered the village with the objective of finding VC who might be hiding in holes or tunnels, VC sympathizers, VC political cadres, arms caches, documents, and that sort of thing."

"What was your personal opinion of this sort of operation? I ask that, because I was an infantry officer and know my opinion of it."

Kelly replied, "These operations were distasteful to me personally and to many other men in the company. The National Police usually—no, always— behaved very badly toward the local population. After we'd swept through the village, we were normally not allowed to go back to see what they were doing, but you could hear the screams."

"Screams."

"Yes. They would vigorously interrogate the villagers."

"How vigorously?"

"Usually with the aid of electric shock treatments to the genitals. They brought their own hand-cranked generators. They would also suspend people by rope or wire upside down into the wells until they nearly drowned. They used other means of interrogation which were peculiar to the Orient and which probably should not be discussed here."

"Of course. Now, you said Americans were not allowed in the village during this period of interrogation."

"Correct. However, the officers in the American unit involved sometimes entered the village for purposes of discussing tactical matters with the National

Police commanders. As Lieutenant Tyson's RTO, I, of course, would go with him. On those occasions, I personally observed what I stated earlier."

"How did Lieutenant Tyson feel about these operations?"

"He had negative feelings toward using American troops as accomplices to this sort of thing. He wrote a memo once to the battalion commander protesting what he said amounted to condoning these brutalities. He made the point that it was demoralizing for his troops to see the results of it, as we always went through the village after the police had gone. After his letter to the battalion commander, Alpha Company never again participated in these joint operations with the National Police."

Corva asked, "What happened on that particular operation? The one that led to the altercation."

"Lieutenant Tyson's platoon was stretched out along a dike, forming a side of the cordon. From here we could see into a part of the village. The National Police had a dozen people, all naked, of all ages and sexes, lined up at a well. We could see them lower the first person down the well."

"What was the purpose of this sort of thing?"

"It was supposed to encourage the villagers to point out the VC spider holes, tunnels, arms caches, and to turn in any VC among them. But, to my mind it was—or became—nothing more than a thinly disguised sado-sexual orgy. They often got a VC or two and a weapon or two, but the price was too high."

Tyson looked at the board, then at Colonel Sproule, then at Pierce. And finally at the spectators. Kelly's narrative had created an atmosphere of intense interest, except at the prosecution table where the atmosphere was more one of uneasiness.

Corva said to Kelly, "Go on, please."

"Yes. Lieutenant Tyson suggested we go into the village to talk to the local Viet commander. He always did that."

"Why?"

"To try to get them to take it a little easy. The presence of Americans usually accomplished that, until you turned your back. Lieutenant Tyson's objections to this sort of operation were partly humanitarian but partly practical. He doubted if any hearts or minds could be won by subjecting an entire village to mass torture and humiliation. He observed that after the National Police went back to their barracks, we would still have to deal with the locals in our area of operations."

"So you went into the village."

"Yes. We went into the village. And while walking, we spotted Steven Brandt."

Pierce was on his feet. "Objection. Your honor, this has gone on long enough. This is totally irrelevant."

Sproule looked down at Corva, then at Pierce, then back to Corva. He said to Corva, "Explain to the court, Mr. Corva, how the line of questioning you are pursuing will extenuate or mitigate the circumstances surrounding the incident for which Lieutenant Tyson stands convicted."

Corva replied, "Your honor, it is my intention to demonstrate to the court that there was bad blood between Lieutenant Tyson and the prosecution's witness, Steven Brandt, and that the hostility that existed between Lieutenant Tyson and his former medic was of such intensity that it has prevailed up until the time that Mr. Brandt took the stand in this court. I intend to show that Mr. Brandt's statement, that there was no such hostility and animosity, was a lie."

Sproule said, "It's a little too late for that, isn't it, Mr. Corva?"

"Your honor, if I can demonstrate through this witness's story that Mr.

Brandt's feelings for the accused were biased and hostile, then I can demonstrate that Mr. Brandt's testimony was likewise biased and hostile, which in turn will let the board put the proper coloration on Mr. Brandt's testimony and may influence their deliberations on an appropriate sentence, which is the purpose of this session."

Sproule's eyebrows arched slightly. "That is stretching it a bit, Mr. Corva. I don't know what your true purpose is in pursuing this story. However, you may continue, with caution. Objection overruled."

Pierce sat and slapped his hand against the table in a rare show of ill temper.

Corva said to Kelly, "You saw Mr. Brandt in the village. Did he belong there?"

"To some extent. Medics, as well as officers, could and did enter these villages while the police were conducting their searches and interrogations. The medics were often needed."

"What happened next?"

"Lieutenant Tyson said to me, 'Keep back. I want to follow him,' meaning Brandt."

"Why? What did he mean by that?"

"It was Lieutenant Tyson's observation that Brandt was acting improperly."

"How so, Mr. Kelly?"

"Brandt was taking pictures. This was strictly forbidden by the National Police. They did not want pictures."

"What was Mr. Brandt taking pictures of?"

"Mostly of naked women being tortured and humiliated."

Corva waited for Pierce, but Pierce did not object. Corva said, "Go on."

"Lieutenant Tyson noticed that the National Police were not stopping Brandt from taking pictures. In fact, they seemed quite friendly toward Brandt."

"Did you notice this also?"

"Yes. And I once saw Brandt on a previous cordon operation give a National Police captain what looked like medical supplies from his bag."

"Continue."

"After Brandt finished with his pictures, he entered a hootch—a Vietnamese house—with two National Policemen. Lieutenant Tyson and I discussed this for some time, then went into the house. A policeman put his hand on Lieutenant Tyson's arm to detain him. Lieutenant Tyson pushed the man away, and we entered the house in which Brandt had gone."

"And what did you—*you* see, Mr. Kelly?"

Tyson turned from Kelly and stared at Steven Brandt, whose expression was fixed and rigid. Tyson kept his eyes on Brandt as Kelly replied, "I saw three naked females. One of them was curled up in a corner weeping, and a policeman was pulling her by the arm. Another female was performing fellatio on a second policeman, and the third female was being raped by Mr. Brandt."

Pierce jumped to his feet and shouted something that was drowned out by other sounds in the chapel, which ranged from gasps to a few shouts. Tyson caught Brandt's eye for a moment before Brandt turned away.

Colonel Sproule signaled to the sergeant at arms, who went to the communion rail and held up his hand for silence. The well-disciplined crowd fell silent.

Colonel Sproule announced, "If there are any more outbursts, I will clear the court." He looked at Pierce, who was about to state his objection again, and Sproule said, "Objection overruled." He said to Corva, "I wish to put some questions to the witness."

"Yes, your honor."

Sproule looked down the side of the pulpit. "Mr. Kelly, the court would like to know how you determined that what you saw was rape and not . . . not the normal activities of men and women."

Kelly glanced up at Sproule, then turned back to his front and replied, "I don't see anything normal in group sex, your honor, but that might be my personal prejudice. To answer your honor's question, I assumed from the circumstances that the men did not know the females very long. About five minutes, I think. Also, the females were weeping. All of them. Also, they were very young, your honor. The one who was with Mr. Brandt was not more than twelve or thirteen. Even making allowances for cultural differences and the earlier onset of puberty in tropical climates and such, this was quite young. Also, when Mr. Brandt stood, I could see blood on his genitals and his thighs, and I remember making the assumption that the girl had been a virgin, though, of course, she may have been having her period. Also, your honor, the girl looked to me as though she had been struck in the face. It was for these reasons, your honor, that I concluded that what I was witnessing was a mass rape and not a party."

Sproule nodded and swallowed. "I see."

"And also, your honor, Mr. Brandt had a look of fear on his face when he saw Lieutenant Tyson and me. He jumped immediately to his feet—he was on a sleeping mat on the floor—and exclaimed, 'Don't!' "

Sproule asked, "Don't what?"

"Lieutenant Tyson and I had both leveled our rifles at our hips. This was a precaution against any attempt by the two policemen to go for their guns. They could sometimes be hostile. But Brandt thought Lieutenant Tyson or I was aiming at him. So he shouted, 'Don't!' Then he shouted, 'Please!' as he grabbed his fatigue pants. He was still wearing his bush jacket and boots. Then he bolted through a window, leaving behind his medical bag and rifle."

Colonel Sproule asked, "Did you follow him?"

"Yes, your honor. But first we gathered up Brandt's equipment and escorted the two policemen out of the hootch. Several policemen were converging on the hootch now, and an ugly scene seemed about to take place. There was some shouting back and forth between Lieutenant Tyson and myself on one side and about a dozen police on the other."

"Did you feel you were in danger?" asked Sproule.

"There was an element of danger. But in the end, we simply turned and walked away. We got back to the dike, and Brandt was there, fully clothed by now. Lieutenant Tyson approached him. I should have pointed out before, your honor, that Lieutenant Tyson had mentioned to me on a few previous occasions that he thought Brandt was taking advantage of his status as a medic to further his private interests in the local women. Lieutenant Tyson was concerned about this."

Sproule said, "So this was the incident that caused this alleged animosity between Lieutenant Tyson and Mr. Brandt?"

"Yes, your honor, but the animosity deepened after Lieutenant Tyson confronted Mr. Brandt on the dike."

"What did Lieutenant Tyson say to Mr. Brandt when he confronted him on the dike?"

"Not too much, your honor. Lieutenant Tyson kicked Mr. Brandt in the groin. Then he slapped him around but only hit him once or twice with a closed fist. Then Lieutenant Tyson threw Mr. Brandt into the flooded rice paddy, drew his forty-five, and instructed Mr. Brandt to sit in the water or have his brains blown out. Mr. Brandt sat in the water. Then Mr. Brandt began to complain that the leeches were finding him. He became quite agitated and began to weep, then he became hysterical."

Colonel Sproule said nothing for some time. He touched his fingers to his lips in thought, then asked, "Were there any other witnesses to this incident on the dike?"

"Yes, your honor, the entire platoon could see this from their positions on this long straight dike. But no one thought it wise to interfere with what appeared to be a personal matter. In fact, I passed the word down the line for the men to remain in position and continue with their mission of watching the village for anyone trying to escape from it."

"But no one else knew the cause of this incident on the dike?"

"No, your honor. And never did know. But I think there were some good guesses."

"Do you know if Lieutenant Tyson took any legal action against Mr. Brandt or if Mr. Brandt took any such action against Lieutenant Tyson?"

"There was no such action taken by either party, your honor. Not that I know of."

Sproule asked Kelly, "How did the incident end?"

"After about thirty minutes, Lieutenant Tyson had calmed down somewhat and told Mr. Brandt that he could come out of the water. Mr. Brandt did so. Mr. Brandt then undressed on the dike, and I observed perhaps thirty leeches on his body. He was very agitated. He was weeping actually, pleading for someone to help him take the leeches off. Several men went to his assistance with insecticides and lit cigarettes. Mr. Brandt had lost some blood to the leeches, and as a result of his physical and mental state, we called in a helicopter to take him away."

Sproule asked, "Would a man have rejoined his unit after such an incident?"

"Not normally, your honor, but Lieutenant Tyson and I went back to the rear area that night on a resupply helicopter and paid a sick call on Mr. Brandt, who was in the battalion aid station. Lieutenant Tyson informed Mr. Brandt that he expected him back in the field within twenty-four hours, or he would have him court-martialed on a variety of charges. Mr. Brandt indicated that he didn't want a public record of this incident as he planned to go to medical school. Lieutenant Tyson felt that he had solved Mr. Brandt's problem and thought that Mr. Brandt's continued presence in a combat infantry company would be useful to Mr. Brandt and to the company. Mr. Brandt was a good medic. So the matter rested there, which answers your honor's question of Mr. Brandt's return to his unit."

Colonel Sproule nodded. "And that was the end of the incident?"

"No, your honor, this is the end of the incident."

"Quite so, Mr. Kelly." Colonel Sproule looked at Corva for some time, then nodded to indicate he should proceed.

Corva said to Kelly, "And from that time on, how would you characterize the relationship between Lieutenant Tyson and Mr. Brandt?"

Kelly replied, "I don't think Mr. Brandt liked being humiliated in front of the entire platoon, nor did he like the leeches. I think I would characterize the relationship between the two men as cool."

"Do you think Mr. Brandt held a grudge against Lieutenant Tyson?"

"I believe so. Neither of them was what you would call the forgiving type."

"Do you think Mr. Brandt held this grudge up until the time of the hospital incident, some two or three months later?"

"Yes. In fact, that morning of the burial mound incident, he and Lieutenant Tyson had words."

"About what?"

"About Mr. Brandt feigning illness to get out of the field."

Corva asked a few further questions, then said to Colonel Sproule, "I have no further questions regarding this incident, your honor. I would like to go on to the hospital incident if you have no further questions."

"I have none. And if the board has any, we will ask them at the end of your examination of Mr. Kelly. We will take a recess at this time and reconvene at fourteen hundred hours. I would like to see Colonel Pierce and Mr. Corva in my chambers. The court is closed."

Tyson looked out to the pews and saw Brandt hurrying, head down, toward the doors.

Corva said to Tyson. "Feel better now?"

"No."

"Good. You should not. But I can."

52

The court reconvened and Daniel Kelly retook the stand.

Colonel Pierce stood and said, "Mr. Kelly, you are reminded that you are still under oath."

Corva stood under the pulpit and faced Kelly. After a few preliminary questions, he said to Kelly, "Could you relate to the court the events that led up to the hospital incident?"

Kelly replied, "Yes, I can," and began a clear detailed account of the approach to Miséricorde Hospital. The account, Tyson noticed, was much more lucid than Brandt's or Farley's, but did not differ from those accounts in any major details, nor did it differ from the account in Picard's book, which Tyson knew everyone in the court had read.

Tyson glanced into the choir loft and saw a few silhouettes. The pews, which had been one-fourth empty at the morning session, were now full again, no doubt as a result of word getting out about the testimony. He did not see Brandt, and suspected the good doctor was on his way back to Boston.

Tyson looked at the press section and saw that those pews were full as well. There had been no sketch artists at the morning session, but there were five at the communion rail just now, kneeling, their sketch pads on the rail, their eyes on Kelly.

Tyson looked into the right front pew and saw that David was not there, though Marcy was, and the expression on her face was taut.

Tyson had picked at his lunch in his cell, waiting for Corva to join him, but Corva never came. And they had barely five minutes together before Sproule called the court to order. During that five minutes Corva had told him that the session in Sproule's chambers—the head chaplain's office—had been heated. And Tyson did not know how much more Corva could get away with. He saw, though, that Corva was being a bit more cautious in the wording of his questions, and so far Pierce had no reason to object. Corva's questions emphasized the physical and mental condition of the platoon since he was no longer trying to prove that nothing illegal had occurred, but was now showing why it had occurred. Tyson felt more at ease with this approach.

Corva said to Kelly, "So you entered the hospital after you were certain the enemy sniper had fled. You had two wounded: Robert Moody, who was lightly wounded in the leg, and Arthur Peterson, whose wound was serious. You have stated that you knew it was a hospital before you ever reached it and that no firefight of any significance occurred as you approached the hospital. There was a single sniper. Correct?"

"Correct."

"Now, Mr. Kelly, you are in the hospital, and here is where previous testimony diverged even further. What happened in the hospital to cause the incident for which Lieutenant Tyson has been convicted?"

Kelly paused for the first time in his testimony, then spoke. "We carried Moody and Peterson inside. The staff was preoccupied with their duties and I remember thinking that they showed no signs of having been affected by the recent shooting. Lieutenant Tyson detained a nurse who informed us that all the doctors were upstairs. We carried Moody and Peterson upstairs—"

Colonel Sproule interrupted. "Mr. Kelly, I think the court is wondering about a missing detail. There seem to be two versions of the death of Cane. One is that he was killed outright by the sniper outside the hospital. The other version is that he died in room-to-room fighting. Since it appears there was no room-to-room fighting, I assume he died outside the hospital. Yet, you don't mention his death in your account."

"That is because Larry Cane was still alive when we entered the hospital, your honor."

Sproule thought a moment, then said to Corva, "Proceed."

Corva addressed Kelly. "What did you find upstairs?"

"There were three wards. One was a sort of general ward filled to overflowing with wounded. Mostly civilian refugees from Hue, I believe. The second ward was marked in French, CONTAGION. We only glanced into that ward, a small room with ten beds, all filled. The third ward was pediatric and obstetrics. This had perhaps thirty beds and was full, also. In addition, there were wounded and sick all over the corridors. There were people who appeared to be neither wounded nor sick, but just refugees. There were perhaps a hundred people in the hospital, but there could have been two hundred, for all I know. We discovered also an operating room. It was there that we carried Arthur Peterson. I should point out that we were not completely certain the hospital was secure and that the platoon was making room-to-room searches. We found a pile of bloody khakis which we took to be enemy uniforms and in fact found about a half dozen young men in the beds whom we took to be enemy sick and wounded."

"What was the platoon's reaction to this?"

"Pretty much the same reaction they had to the peasants burying the enemy dead. It was not rational, but then neither were we. It is only in retrospect that it seems we overreacted to the fact that the hospital held enemy sick and wounded."

"Did anyone threaten these sick and wounded enemy soldiers?"

"Not that I could see. But Sergeant Sadowski put a few men in the ward to keep an eye on them."

"What happened in the operating room?"

"I was in the operating room with Lieutenant Tyson and several other men. It was a large room that actually held six or seven operating tables. It was very primitive, as I recall. There were people on each of the tables, and there were nurses and doctors in attendance. Lieutenant Tyson spoke to a man who identified himself as the chief of staff."

"In what language did they speak?"

"Mostly French, but some English. The gist of the conversation, most of which I learned of afterward, was that Lieutenant Tyson, of course, was asking —actually insisting—that Peterson and Moody be treated. Peterson was at this point lying on the floor of the operating room. Moody was sitting against a wall. This doctor knelt down and examined Peterson perfunctorily and announced that the man was beyond saving. Lieutenant Tyson told him to try. The doctor explained—and again this is what Lieutenant Tyson told me afterward—that the hospital was on the triage system. That is, anyone whose wounds were very severe would not be helped because that would tie up too much of the hospital's resources for little or no gain. The lightly wounded, such as Moody, would not be helped because they could live with their wounds. It was only those people in the middle group who would be tended to. Apparently neither Peterson nor Moody qualified for this group. Moody was actually being tended to by Brandt right there on the floor of the operating room anyway."

"But Peterson was dying?"

"Yes. He'd been shot in the side, and the bullet exited on the other side. He was gagging and spitting up frothy white blood. Apparently he was drowning. He was semiconscious, and kept calling out for help. In fact, while he was lying on the floor, he pulled at Lieutenant Tyson's pant leg. Lieutenant Tyson knelt a few times while he was arguing with this doctor. I was kneeling on the floor, holding Peterson's hand."

"Do you recall who else was in the room?"

"People kept coming in and out. But Farley and Cane were there almost the entire time. There were several Oriental staff in the room, again coming and going. There were also perhaps five or six Caucasians, which was one of the reasons the men of the platoon kept coming in and out."

"Why?"

"To see the Caucasians. Other than GIs, none of us had seen Caucasians in some time. It was a novelty. There was one Caucasian woman, too, a rather good-looking woman, and that caused a little stir. As I suggested, it wasn't an operating room of the type we picture, but only a large whitewashed room with a red tile floor and six or seven tables."

"How long did this altercation between the doctor and Lieutenant Tyson last?"

"Hard to say. Maybe five minutes before Lieutenant Tyson finally leveled his rifle at the man and ordered him to do something for Peterson."

"And what did the doctor say?"

"I'm not sure, but I could tell by his motions and his tone of voice that he wasn't intimidated. He seemed to want to return to his patient, who was an Oriental male lying naked on the closest table. The man's leg had been shredded pretty badly by some sort of explosive device. The man's clothing, a khaki North Vietnamese Army uniform, was on the floor. So, the doctor turned away. Lieutenant Tyson spun him around and slapped him across the face." Kelly paused.

Corva let the silence continue for some seconds, then said, "What happened next?"

"Several things were happening concurrently now. First, Farley delivered a horizontal butt stroke to the doctor's abdomen, which caused him to double over. Hernando Beltran had entered the room and gone to the operating table where the wounded enemy soldier was. Beltran pulled the man off the operating table and onto the floor. The man was screaming. Peterson was crying. The doctor was moaning in pain. The nurses were becoming frightened. Then from the rear of the operating room comes this tall Caucasian, running at us. He was shouting in English and had an accent that I believe was Australian. We'd worked with Australian troops for a week once, and that was how I could identify the accent."

"What was the man shouting, Mr. Kelly?"

"He was being very abusive. Everyone was stunned to hear this English-speaking man. He hadn't said anything up until that point."

"What was he saying now?"

"He began by telling Lieutenant Tyson to get out and take his men with him. Then he began to swear, calling us all fucking murderers. Then he moved on to larger issues, such as the fact that all we knew how to do was kill and hurt people. That we had no right to be there—in Vietnam. That the war was this and that. The sort of stuff you saw in the stateside newspapers."

"Did Lieutenant Tyson respond?"

"No. The man was obviously overwrought. But while this was going on, Beltran and someone else had laid Peterson on the now vacant operating table. Another doctor approached, but he spoke no English or French. I believe he was German or Dutch. He was indicating by his motions that he would operate on Peterson. In fact, someone had put a tube down Peterson's throat, I suppose to suck the blood out. But no one was paying much attention to this doctor by now. The French doctor was somewhat recovered now from the butt stroke, and extremely angry, but I had the distinct impression that the medical staff there had properly evaluated the situation and were about to cooperate. But there was still this Australian doctor who wouldn't calm down. And then there was Beltran, who had found another NVA soldier and had thrown him off the operating table, too. Lieutenant Tyson shouted to Beltran to get out. I'm telling you what I remember, but it was somewhat confusing, because everyone was very hyper. I would imagine that these people had had about as little rest as we had, and tempers were very short. But as I said, the Australian was exhibiting the most provocative behavior."

"What do you mean by provocative?"

"He began pointing."

"Pointing."

"Yes. At each of us. He would point and shout things such as, 'You! Get out!' or, 'You are a bloody fucking murderer. You. You. How dare you.' That sort of thing."

"How did the men react to this?"

"Not too well. As I said, we were wet, tired, frightened. We knew we were headed toward Hue. I don't think anyone expected to come back from there. And then here was this doctor, one of our own, so to speak, calling us names. Someone shouted to him that he wouldn't speak to the VC or NVA that way, which was probably true. Also, I think the general feeling was that the enemy had caused all this misery, not us. As I said, the rest of the staff were willing to cooperate regarding Peterson, but I had the impression they were not pro-American types. They didn't greet us very warmly. That, I think, set up the psychological atmosphere for what eventually happened to them."

"And the Australian doctor was still being abusive?"

"Yes. He couldn't get himself under control. Something inside him had obviously snapped. Two Caucasian males tried to pull him away, but he pushed them aside. Most of us were ignoring him, but somehow Larry Cane got into a screaming match with him. They traded insults for some seconds. Then the

Australian poked Cane with his finger and said, 'You're a stupid son of a bitch.' Cane pulled the trigger on his rifle and fired a burst into the Australian's abdomen."

Corva said, "This was the first shot that was fired?"

"Yes. But that's all it took. Beltran went over to the two North Viets on the floor, pulled his pistol, and shot them both in the head. Then Cane, for a reason I'll never comprehend, fired his M-16 into the far wall, splattering stucco all over. People were screaming, dropping to the floor. The Australian doctor was lying against a wall where he'd been thrown by the impact of the bullets, bleeding badly from the abdomen. Then Brandt, apropos of nothing really, yelled out, 'Peterson's dead.' Cane then turned and shot this French doctor in the back."

"What was Lieutenant Tyson doing during this time?"

"Same thing as I was doing. Diving for the floor. Cane had obviously gone around the bend. It happened really very quickly. At least I think it did. Then Lieutenant Tyson got to one knee and drew his pistol. He aimed it at Cane and ordered him to drop his rifle. Cane was reloading another magazine. Lieutenant Tyson again told him to drop the rifle. It was all very tense."

"And did Cane drop the rifle?"

"He did after Lieutenant Tyson shot him in the chest."

Ben Tyson sat with his elbows on the table, his chin resting in his hands, staring intently at Daniel Kelly, as was everyone. Tyson listened hard for a sound, but there wasn't any. Corva seemed to have nothing to say and neither did Kelly.

Finally, Colonel Sproule asked Kelly, "Are you saying that Lieutenant Tyson shot Cane?"

"Yes, your honor. Shot and killed him."

Sproule nodded, almost wearily, thought Tyson. Tyson looked at the board and saw Colonel Moore staring at him, as though seeing him for the first time. Tyson also saw Major Bauer's head nodding slowly and rhythmically.

Corva came back to the defense table and poured himself some water and drank it. He never looked at Tyson but turned and went back to Kelly.

Tyson sat back in his chair and turned his head toward the prosecution table. Pierce seemed not upset and not uncomfortable. He seemed, if anything, relaxed, as if it were all beyond his control now. Tyson looked at Colonel Sproule, who seemed thoughtful. Probably, thought Tyson, this case, whose facts had eluded him, was now becoming clear and tidy in his mind.

Corva said to Kelly, "What happened next?"

"The operating room was in pandemonium, as I recall. Beltran was at the door and wouldn't let anyone leave. Richard Farley ran over to Cane and knelt beside him. Cane and Farley were from the same town somewhere in South Jersey and had enlisted together under the buddy system, which guaranteed that the men would stay together during their enlistment. Farley was very distraught and was screaming at Tyson that he had killed his friend to save a bunch of gooks. Of course, Cane had in fact killed two Caucasians, but as I said, Farley was distraught. No one and nothing was making much sense. Even now I can't make much sense of it."

"Did Lieutenant Tyson at any time give an order to kill wounded enemy soldiers? Or to kill anyone?"

"No, he did not."

"You were with him the entire time?"

"Yes. Except for a period later, after the shooting began."

"How much time had elapsed since you entered the hospital?"

"About fifteen or twenty minutes."

"You described the operating room scene as pandemonium. Could you give any details?"

"I recall that Beltran began giving orders. Nearly the entire platoon was in the operating room by now and Beltran ordered them to find all the gooks and shoot them."

"Was Beltran in a leadership position?"

"No. He was a pfc. He was a machine gunner. But he was prone to giving orders. Lieutenant Tyson told him to shut up. But Farley was now standing to Lieutenant Tyson's side, aiming his rifle at him. Lieutenant Tyson was still on one knee with his pistol in his hand and his M-16 on the floor. Farley told him to drop his pistol."

"Did he?"

"No, Lieutenant Tyson stood and told Farley to drop his rifle. But now Beltran had his machine gun trained on Lieutenant Tyson. A few of the men meanwhile had gone back to the ward where the enemy soldiers were lying in bed. We heard six or seven shots, and I assumed they'd killed the wounded NVA."

"What were you doing during this time?"

"Not too much. It was a very chaotic situation. I tried to calm people down, but it was beyond that at this point. Another man, Harold Simcox, was pointing his rifle at Lieutenant Tyson now. Lieutenant Tyson told them—Beltran, Farley, and Simcox—to drop their weapons, but they didn't. Simcox was one of those men who had a bad attitude toward any authority. There was no bad blood between Lieutenant Tyson and Simcox, but Simcox was a rabble-rouser, and as soon as he smelled a mutiny, he joined the mutineers. There are always a few like that."

"So now three men were pointing their weapons at Lieutenant Tyson. What was his response?"

"His response was to tell the three men they were under arrest. He told me to call battalion headquarters and make a report."

"Did you?"

"No. Lieutenant Tyson's estimation of the situation was faulty. Had I attempted to make a radio call, I'd have been shot. And so would Lieutenant Tyson. He was letting his ego get in the way of his judgment."

"What was the response of Beltran, Farley, and Simcox to being told that they were under arrest?"

"They had a negative response to that. Farley again told Lieutenant Tyson to drop his pistol, and this time he threatened to shoot him if he didn't. At this point, it seemed to be a standoff. Then we were momentarily diverted when one of the staff, a young Caucasian male, leapt from the window. It was two stories, but there was shrubbery outside. Beltran ran to the window, rested his machine gun on the ledge, and fired."

"Did he hit the man?"

"He said he did. Then Beltran turned from the window and ordered all the remainder of the staff into a side room that looked like a scrub-up room. It had sinks and a toilet. Then he sent a few men out to round up any other staff members, Caucasian and Orientals."

"Would you say that Beltran, then, was *the* leader or *a* leader of this mutiny?"

"Sort of. He was giving orders, and people were taking them. He was on a power trip. He was also shouting that this was a communist hospital. It was actually Catholic, and there were crosses and such all over the place, but he didn't seem to perceive this."

"And Farley and Simcox still had their weapons trained on Lieutenant Tyson?"

"Yes. And the Australian doctor was taking his time about dying. He was still on the floor crying out in pain. But Farley wouldn't let the hospital people go near him. His reasoning as best I could determine was that if they couldn't find the time or space for Peterson, then they shouldn't worry about the Australian. There was a certain degree of symmetry and logic to that. During these few minutes, other people in the hospital were trying to run away, but they were shot by the men of the platoon whose natural reaction was to shoot anyone running away. At this point there was no full-scale massacre in progress, but the deaths were mounting up, and I believe that some of the men were thinking along the lines of eliminating evidence and witnesses."

"Including eliminating Lieutenant Tyson?"

"Yes. I think so. Farley and Simcox looked as if they were trying to get up the nerve to shoot him. Beltran was inciting everyone who would listen to him. Lieutenant Tyson was ordering me to give him the radiophone. At this point, I decided that Lieutenant Tyson was part of the problem and not part of the solution. So I struck him and knocked him to the floor."

"What was your intention in doing that?" asked Corva.

"Partly to get him out of there since he wasn't going to leave on his own. Partly to save his life. After he was on the floor, Farley and Simcox, I believed, wouldn't think it necessary to shoot him. Apparently this was an accurate assessment, because they then turned away from him and joined Beltran and a few others who were shoving people into this washroom. I asked a man named Walker to give me a hand, and together we carried Lieutenant Tyson out of the operating room, down a short corridor, to the first door we came to, which turned out to be a small room that appeared to be a laboratory. We put him on the floor, and I told Walker to stay there with me. We sat there awhile, listening to the shooting and the screaming. I never actually saw the indiscriminate shooting. Up until that point, the deaths had been caused by some specific factor, no matter how unjustified or illogical."

"How long did you stay there?"

"Walker and I stayed there about ten minutes. Then the shooting stopped, and we left to see what was going on. In retrospect, I should have stayed with Lieutenant Tyson, but I didn't think he was in any real danger any longer. I saw all I wanted to see in the hospital and came back to the laboratory about ten minutes later, but Lieutenant Tyson was gone. I guessed that he'd left the hospital, because I hadn't seen him while I was looking around the hospital, so I went outside and looked around."

"Did you see him there?"

"No. And I didn't want to go back inside that hospital. I had some fear for my own safety. I was also angry at Lieutenant Tyson for leaving the laboratory."

"Would you describe what you saw in the hospital after you left the laboratory?"

"I'd rather not."

"All right . . . what did you do outside the hospital?"

"I was trying to sort all of this out in my mind. I sat on a stone bench in the courtyard and had a cigarette. I saw the hospital begin to burn. The platoon began to assemble outside. One of the last people out was Lieutenant Tyson. The platoon surrounded the hospital and watched it burn. Several people who had not been shot tried to escape through the windows and doors, but they were shot. We stood around in the rain and waited until the hospital roof collapsed. Then we formed up and began moving toward Hue."

"Did anyone threaten Lieutenant Tyson at that point?"

"During the rest breaks in the patrol there was some discussion about killing him, but no one did anything about it. Lieutenant Tyson was sort of a prisoner, and he never said a word to me or anyone as we walked. We carried Moody in a stretcher and Peterson's body in a poncho. Farley carried Cane's body for a while, then we took turns carrying it. We walked in single file, and no one could see anyone else's face. It was very surreal. The more we walked, the more the adrenaline boiled out. The rain was coming down hard, and the villages seemed dead. To our front we could see Hue burning in the rain. We could actually see the flames now and hear the small-arms fire. It was early, but we decided it was time to pull in for the day. Everyone was very tired. We found an old French pillbox—a round concrete bunker—and set up there. Lieutenant Tyson kept making radio reports to Captain Browder of this sniper fire, and as long as he did that, he was safe. But everyone was wondering what he'd say when he got a chance to go back to base camp."

Corva asked, "What happened in the bunker?"

"We sat around. A few candles were lit. Everyone was soaked. We changed into dry socks and we heated C rations. We had to keep the two bodies in the bunker so the animals wouldn't get them. Normally, we would have called for a chopper to get rid of the dead and wounded, but we were supposed to still be in An Ninh Ha exchanging fire with snipers, so we couldn't give our grid coordinates. Browder kept calling asking if we needed artillery support and all that. Lieutenant Tyson said no, there were civilians in the area. Finally Browder said to do something about the snipers. So Lieutenant Tyson reported that we were going to move on this building where the sniper fire was coming from. Actually, it had been two hours since we left the village of An Ninh Ha. Finally, Lieutenant Tyson reported that we were now in heavy contact with an NVA force in a large building. Then he reported an assault on the building, then reported a room-to-room fight, then victory. It was bizarre. Browder said fine job. Browder reported that he was near Hue already. So were we, but he didn't know that. He gave us his grid coordinates. He wasn't more than a kilometer from us. But we said we couldn't reach him before nightfall and we'd stay in An Ninh Ha and link up in the morning. We were making this all up, of course, and feeding it to Lieutenant Tyson as he was talking with Browder on the radio. After Lieutenant Tyson reported that we were going to stay in An Ninh Ha, we started to talk about the battle as though it had really happened. I think the men reasoned that everything about the war was so unreal anyway that this battle and the body count we came up with was as real as the stuff MAC-V put out. So we smoked some grass, and Lieutenant Tyson passed around a bottle of Scotch. We played some cards. We slept. We woke up in the middle of the night. A few guys threw up outside. Brandt gave Moody another shot of morphine. The radio crackled all night, and every hour or so I made scheduled night reports. By dawn, we had our story down pretty well. In fact, by dawn, it was not a story, it was the truth. What really happened became that night's collective nightmare. We had done a neat switch with reality. I even wrote up a Silver Star for Lieutenant Tyson that night. The next morning we linked up with the rest of the company, got Moody medevaced, and got rid of the corpses. We swapped war stories with the other two platoons. Captain Browder said he was very proud of us. We reported, I think, twelve enemy KIA. We didn't want to overdo it. Actually Browder didn't believe a word of it. The time sequences and all the little details were wrong. We'd never asked for artillery to support us, for instance. Browder was a pro, and Lieutenant Tyson wasn't exactly convincing on the radio or in person. But we had two killed and one wounded, though we had no captured weapons. One of the other platoon sergeants asked us sarcastically if the twelve NVA we killed were unarmed. But the after-action reports were written, and no one higher up asked any questions or even did an after-action survey of the battle scene to the best of my knowledge. But it was a very tumultuous time. We moved on to other problems. Within a week, nobody cared what happened in An Ninh Ha in the hospital that now has a name. But I told you what happened, though I swore in the bunker I never would. So even though I swore to you here that I would tell you the truth, you understand that my story could be as phony as the rest of them."

After a full minute, Corva said, "The defense has nothing further."

Sproule asked, "Does the prosecution wish to cross-examine?"

Pierce replied in an almost weary tone, "The prosecution does not."

Colonel Sproule looked at Colonel Moore. "Are there any questions by the court?"

Colonel Moore replied, "The court has no questions."

Colonel Sproule said to Kelly, "The witness is excused."

Kelly stood, but instead of turning to his left and leaving, he turned right and walked toward Tyson with the self-assurance of a man who knows no one is going to challenge his movements.

Tyson stood, and they grasped each other's hands. Tyson said in a quiet voice, "Hello, Kelly."

"Hello, Lieutenant."

"Thanks for coming."

"No problem. You should have come to Angola with me. You wouldn't be here now."

"No, I'd be dead now."

Colonel Sproule looked at Kelly and Tyson, then looked at his watch and said, "The court is adjourned until ten hundred hours tomorrow."

The board, the prosecution, and the spectators stood and began drifting off.

Tyson saw the MPs approaching and said to Kelly, "See you later maybe."

"Don't think so," said Kelly. "Flying out in about two hours."

"Where to?"

"Here and there. Doing a gig in Central America now."

"Your number is going to come up one of these days, Kelly."

"Maybe. But it's been fun playing."

"You missed a good reunion. Sadowski, Scorello, Kalane, Beltran, and Walker. Only DeTonq is not present or accounted for."

"DeTonq's still there, Lieutenant."

"Maybe. Maybe he made it back."

"No, he's there. In place."

"In what place?"

"Hue. Agent in place. Posing as a Frenchman. We need intelligence there."

"You're making that up."

"Maybe. But we'll be back there someday."

"Without me."

"With or without you."

Tyson said, "Thanks again."

"Anytime, *amigo*. I'll look you up next time around."

"Try Leavenworth."

"I'll try Garden City first." Kelly winked, turned, and walked away as the MPs flanked Tyson.

53

The MP car pulled up to Tyson's housing unit at 7:30 A.M., and Sergeant Larson unlocked Tyson's handcuffs. He said to Tyson, "One half hour, sir. We'll honk at eight hundred hours."

"Right."

Larson added, "There will be an MP stationed at the rear door of your unit, sir."

"Swell." Tyson opened the car door and walked quickly up the path of his attached unit. David opened the door before he reached it and stood smiling in the doorway.

"Hello, Dad."

"Hello, kid." They shook hands, then embraced. Tyson went into the house, and David closed the door. Marcy came quickly down the stairs, dressed in a gray suit and high heels, suitable for trials or business meetings.

Tyson embraced her, and they kissed, but they both sensed an estrangement between them. She said to him, "Would you like breakfast?"

"No thanks. They serve breakfast early there. I had eggs and grits."

Marcy, David, and Ben Tyson went into the dining area and sat around the table, half of which was piled with Marcy's paperwork. They talked about David's school for most of the next twenty minutes. Tyson had coffee, David had two bowls of cereal, and Marcy sipped on a weak herb tea. "My stomach," she explained. "Tension. Not really sleeping well."

Tyson looked at his watch. "I'd better start saying goodbye now." He stood and said to his wife, "I'll see you in court, as they say."

"Do you want David there?"

Tyson looked at his son eating his cereal. Tyson said to him, "Do you want to go to a court-martial, or do you want to go to school?"

David smiled weakly. "Court-martial."

"Good. Maybe you'll be a JAG lawyer when you grow up."

Marcy said to Tyson, "Say hello to Vince for me."

"Okay." He found his hat on the couch.

She added, "What is happening today, Ben?"

He replied, "I'm not certain. Except that we're still presenting extenuation and mitigation. Corva may ask Levin to testify today."

She asked, "What time do you think it will end?"

"I'm not sure. Depends on how many people Corva has lined up." He paused and asked, "Do you want to testify?"

"Me?"

"Yes. The wife often testifies to her husband's character during E and M."

"Really? How bizarre."

Tyson shrugged. "The Army is all one big family."

She thought a moment, then smiled. "Do I have to tell the truth?"

"No, no. They expect wives to lie."

"Well, I will of course. But I don't think you really want me to testify."

"No, I don't. It's not my style. But Corva thinks it's a good idea. You know how these Italians are with family. In Italian courts they herd in the whole family—old grandmas and little bambinos, all screeching and crying."

Marcy frowned. "I hate it when you make ethnic generalizations."

"Corva seems to enjoy it. He does it to me. Why should it bother you?"

She started to say something, then just shrugged.

Tyson nodded toward the paperwork and her attaché case on a chair. "Do you have an appointment this afternoon?"

She nodded. "But I've arranged it for five, in midtown. If the court adjourns at four-thirty, I can make it easily."

"I'll pass a note to Judge Sproule."

Marcy drew a deep breath and said nothing.

As Tyson checked his watch, the car horn blew twice. He said, "There's my limo."

David stood and again they embraced. Marcy took his arm and walked with him to the front door. She said softly, "I never know when I'm going to see you again."

"Well, if you come to court at ten, you'll see me."

"You know what I mean."

"Tomorrow," said Tyson. "I'll work out something for tomorrow."

She squeezed his arm. "Can you get forty-five minutes?" She winked suggestively.

He smiled. "I'll try."

"I know you would like to be a little nicer to me, but you're trying to make this easier on me by being . . . cool. It's not making it easier." She said, "Ben . . . Kelly's testimony. . . ."

"Yes?"

She took his hand. "I had no idea . . ."

"I'm no hero. But it's nice to know you think so."

The horn blew again.

They kissed, and Tyson left quickly.

He got back into the MP car and sat beside Sergeant Larson, who didn't produce the handcuffs this time. Larson said, "BOQ. Correct?"

"Correct."

Tyson looked out the window as the car moved slowly to the BOQ, a short distance away. He remembered the route he used to take between his house and the BOQ. He had not been allowed to vary his route or make any stops or detours. Straight and narrow. He'd hated that, but now it looked like boundless freedom in comparison.

Filmy black clouds raced across the morning sky, blowing from east to west, and there was the smell of rain in the cool air. The few trees on the route looked more bare than they had the day before, and the limbs seemed blacker, giving them a forlorn appearance against the stark institutional buildings.

The car stopped in front of the BOQ, and Sergeant Larson said, "Nineteen-fifteen hours, sir."

"Right." Tyson got out, entered the far right door of the building, and went up three flights of stairs. He knocked on Corva's door. The door opened, and Corva showed him in.

They sat at the dining room table, and Tyson poured a cup of coffee from a mess hall thermos jug.

Corva said, "How is Marcy?"

"Fine. Sends you her regards."

Corva nodded as he rifled through a folder of yellow paper. "David?"

"Fine. All the Tysons are fine. How are the Corvas?"

"Fine. How's jail?"

"Jail sucks. I'm in charge of the latrine detail now—my first command since I was CO of Alpha Company."

Corva chewed absently on a Danish as he jotted notes on his pad. He said, "Today should be the last day."

Tyson nodded.

Corva continued, "Colonel Levin is prepared to testify on your behalf today."

"No."

"Why not?"

"Give the man a break, Vince. He's got enough problems being a middle-aged Jewish lieutenant colonel. He wants his full bird before he gets out."

Corva said impatiently, "How about Marcy, then?"

"No."

"Why not?"

"Because I'd like to keep it dignified, if you don't mind."

Corva thought about that a moment, then asked, "How about your minister, Reverend Symes? He is most anxious to speak for you."

"Symes is most anxious to speak, period. He'll begin at my baptism."

"Well, how about—?"

"No one. Not my ex-scout leader either. Let Kelly's statement stand by itself."

Corva leaned across the table. "Look, Ben, now that you've established that jail sucks beyond a reasonable doubt, let's try to make sure you don't go back this afternoon."

Tyson nodded.

Corva continued, "Testimony regarding your character is the last thing that board will hear before they go off to vote on a sentence."

"My character is irrelevant. The board has the facts." Tyson stood and went to the window. The sky was darkening, and a few drops of rain splattered against the glass.

Corva said, "You're not in the best humor this morning."

Tyson shook his head. "I woke up in jail this morning."

Corva stood and took a step toward Tyson. "Talk it out."

Without turning, Tyson said, "It's all hitting me now. Farley, looking so pathetic. Brandt, being destroyed by Kelly. Sadowski, Scorello, Beltran, Walker, Kalane . . . now they've got to live not only with what they've done and with everyone knowing about it, but also with the fact that they didn't take the stand like men . . . because some wimpy lawyers got to them."

Corva laid his hand tentatively on Tyson's shoulder.

Tyson went on, "And if I go to jail . . . what does a man say to his wife when he comes home after some years in jail? Do women wait? What is your experience?"

"Ben, that's enough."

Tyson said, "And David's life would be ruined—"

"Enough!" Corva grabbed Tyson's shoulder and with a surprising strength spun him around and shoved him toward the wall. "Enough!"

Tyson clenched his fist and glared down at the smaller man. Corva glared back. Finally Tyson said, "Okay. Had a bad night."

Corva went to the table and poured more coffee. He said, "Do you still want to take the stand?"

"Yes."

"Do you know what you want to say?"

Tyson nodded.

Still standing, Corva shuffled through some papers on the table. He said, "The last piece in this Oriental mosaic fell into place last night."

Tyson looked at his lawyer.

Corva picked up a telex message and glanced at it. He said, "At first I thought it was the government who was somehow keeping her under wraps, the way they kept Kelly under wraps. But I should have known. . . ."

"She's dead?"

"No, no. She's very much alive and well. It was the church who removed her from the world." Corva added, "I told you Interpol thought she was in Italy, and she is. In a place called Casa Pastor Angelicus. It is a sort of cloister for nuns built on a hill outside of Rome. She is effectively cut off from the outside world." Corva added with a half smile, "I don't think a subpoena would ever reach her."

Tyson stayed silent a few seconds before asking, "How . . . how is it that she is there?"

"Well, apparently when the first public stories of this appeared in May or June, someone, perhaps in the Vatican, got wind of it and had her sequestered. I would doubt that she knows anything about your difficulties."

Tyson nodded. "Well, I suppose it's just as well, isn't it? It's good that there are places left in this world where people can live in absolute peace. So," he said, "that is a closed chapter." He rubbed his brow. "Thank God somebody was spared from all of this."

"But perhaps someday, when this is over and she returns to her hospital work, you might visit her."

Tyson shook his head. "No. I think, as Kelly said, this is the end of the incident. Whoever walked away from that hospital should keep walking, in different directions, and never look back and never reach out to one another. Not ever again."

Corva replied, "Maybe you're right. No more reunions. Though," he said musingly, "I would have liked her to tell the court and everyone that you saved her life. That is a story that should be known."

"Is it? It doesn't fit, Vince. Vietnam means loss. Lost war, lost honor, lost innocence, lost souls. Don't confuse everyone with a story of two people who found something in each other."

"You're too cynical this morning."

"Well, then, let's say it is a private story and it's just as well that it won't be used for any public purpose. I would never have let you call her to the stand anyway."

"I know that. I just wanted to find her for you."

"Thank you."

"Time to go."

54

B en Tyson sat at the defense table. Pierce, Weinroth, and Longo were
already at their table. Tyson said, "Why do they always beat us here?"
"I once stole Pierce's water pitcher, and he's not going to let it happen
again."

At 10 A.M. sharp, the sergeant at arms called out, "All rise!"

Colonel Sproule entered the court and took his place behind the pulpit.
"The court will come to order."

Everyone sat. Tyson saw that the chapel was still filling with people and the
MPs didn't seem to be stopping anyone from cramming in. This was going to be
a short session.

He looked up into the dark choir and saw, standing at the railing, Chet
Brown. Brown waved a cheery greeting, but Tyson did not acknowledge it.

He looked into the front row and saw Marcy, who blew him a kiss. David was
there, as was his mother, as Corva had insisted. Also in the front pew now was
Karen Harper, minus her friend. She was sitting a few feet from Marcy, and
they occasionally exchanged a word or two.

The chapel smelled of damp clothing and chilly rain. The persistent drizzle
ran down the stained-glass windows, giving them a flat lifeless appearance,
making the depictions on them look like cartoons.

Tyson looked again at the prosecution table. Pierce, Weinroth, and Longo sat
talking in low whispers, and for the first time since Tyson had seen them at the
hearing, they looked quite human. In fact, he even credited them with human
attributes, such as love, money problems, and family cares. He noticed, too,
that Major Judith Weinroth was very much taken with Colonel Graham Pierce,
and he fantasized for them an affair.

Tyson looked at Colonel Sproule, shuffling papers behind the pulpit. The
man was a product of another era. He had sat there, day after day, literally and
figuratively looking down on the court. And clearly he had been shocked in an
old-fashioned sense of the word by what he'd heard.

Tyson looked now across the open space at the board table, which was empty.
Beyond the table, in the wing of the altar area, stood two armed MPs at parade
rest. Tyson spoke to Corva while still looking at the two MPs. "The armed and
the unarmed."

Corva nodded.

"That's another way to divide the world."

Again Corva nodded. "That's the way it's always been."

"I have a small sense of how the Viet peasants felt when they had to deal
with us. How do you deal with a man carrying an M-16 rifle if you're carrying a
basket of vegetables?"

"Very carefully."

"Right. The Aussie doctor didn't understand that."

"Apparently not," replied Corva as he looked through some papers on the
table. "Are you ready for your courtroom debut?"

"I ought to be."

"True."

Corva noted, "A jury often knows how they're going to vote on a verdict. There are only two choices. But sentencing is much more complex. What you say may make a difference."

"In other words, don't blow it."

Corva didn't respond.

Colonel Sproule caught Colonel Pierce's eye and indicated he was ready.

Colonel Pierce stood and said, "All the parties to the trial who were present when the court closed are now present except the members of the board." Pierce sat.

Colonel Sproule turned to the defense table. "Will the accused please rise?"

Tyson stood.

Sproule said, "Lieutenant Benjamin Tyson, you are advised that you may now present testimony in extenuation or mitigation of the offense of which you stand convicted. You may, if you wish, testify under oath as to these matters, or you may remain silent, in which case the court will not draw any inferences from your silence. In addition, you may, if you wish, make an unsworn statement in mitigation or extenuation of the offense of which you stand convicted. This unsworn statement is not evidence, and you cannot be cross-examined upon it, but the prosecution may offer evidence to rebut anything contained in the statement. The statement may be oral or in writing or both. You may make it yourself, or it may be made by your counsel or by both of you. Consult with your counsel if you need to, and advise this court what you wish to do."

Tyson replied, "I wish to make a sworn statement, your honor."

Sproule nodded as though in approval. He turned toward the sergeant at arms and said, "Sergeant, call the board to court."

Tyson felt his heart beating heavily for the first time since this began. He wanted a drink of water but didn't take the cup in front of him.

Corva leaned toward him. "I am not going to ask you questions or elicit anything from you. You are on your own, Lieutenant."

"That's fine. I've heard enough out of you to last me a lifetime."

Corva grunted.

The members of the court-martial board arrived in their usual single file and went to their chairs in order of rank, but this time, the court already having been called to order, they sat immediately.

Colonel Sproule wasted no time either. "Lieutenant Tyson, will you take the stand, please?"

Tyson walked unhesitantly toward the witness chair and reached it at the same time Pierce did. The two men stood less than three feet apart, and at this distance Tyson was able to see freckles on Pierce's remarkable scarlet skin.

Pierce said, "Raise your right hand."

Tyson raised his hand.

Pierce and Tyson looked directly at each other as Pierce recited, "Do you swear that the evidence you shall give shall be the truth, the whole truth, and nothing but the truth, so help you God?"

"I do."

"Please be seated."

Tyson sat.

Corva, still at the defense table but standing now, said, "Your honor, members of the board; Lieutenant Tyson will make a statement." Corva sat.

Tyson found himself looking at his surroundings from a different perspective. He could no longer see Sproule, whose fidgeting with his hearing aid was distracting. But he could see Pierce, sitting at the table ten feet away directly in front of him. Pierce was leaning forward over his crossed arms as though very eager to hear him. Tyson suspected this was meant to unnerve him, but realizing that, he found it somewhat ludicrous. Weinroth and Longo were sitting straight, which looked more appropriate to the military surroundings. The board was to his left, and he could see them by turning his head slightly in that direction.

Beyond the prosecution table but partly blocked by it was pew after pew of heads and shoulders, all eyes on him. Tyson said in a normal conversational tone of voice, "I realize that any statement I make here in extenuation and mitigation could only be construed as a self-serving one. But the military system of justice is unique in that it allows a convicted man to present certain facts that may diminish his sentence. But I'm not certain that it would be appropriate for me to go into personal details of my life, as you know them as well as anyone, due to the public attention that has surrounded not only this trial, but also my personal life. And I'm not certain it's necessary to attempt to convey to you any more of the horrors of war than you've already had conveyed to you. I understand that the Code specifically recognizes combat fatigue and all that this term implies as an extenuating factor in cases of murder such as these. But I know, and you know, that the crime for which I stand convicted was not the crime that occurred in that hospital, but the crime that occurred some days later in base camp, when I walked past battalion headquarters and failed to enter there and do my duty. That crime did not occur under conditions of battle fatigue. I cannot sit here in good conscience and tell you that if I had it to do over again, I would do my duty as I clearly understood it. On the contrary, if I had it to do over again, I would do the same thing. And though my life and freedom depend on it, I cannot tell you why I would again willfully commit the same crime. I know that I briefly considered reporting this crime of mass murder. But only briefly; and that was a result of my officer training and my other moral training such as it may have been. I did not wrestle long with my conscience before deciding that I would not do my duty. And after I had made the decision not to speak of this crime ever again, I felt that I had made the right decision. If I said otherwise to you, you would wonder, and properly so, why I did not rectify my original decision, which I know full well was both an immoral and illegal one. So I stand here convicted of a crime I did commit, and we should let the matter rest there."

Tyson surveyed the silent court, then continued, "As for my men, you may have the charitable thought that I was protecting them out of a sense of loyalty, comradeship, and that special paternalism that exists between officers and men. There would be some truth in that thought, but you know and I know that loyalty, comradeship, and paternalism should not extend that far. I do feel some natural regret for the lives that have been perhaps ruined or altered by the public testimony we have all heard here. But balanced against the lives that were ended at that hospital, there cannot and should not be too many tears shed for any of the men of the first platoon of Alpha Company. I do feel some sympathy for the families who have discovered things about their sons and husbands that were best left undiscovered. A day or so after I killed Larry Cane, I wrote his family a letter of condolence in which I said he died bravely. He was a brave man in many ways, but he did not die bravely, and I again offer my condolences to his family."

Tyson looked at the board and addressed them directly. "When my attorney, Mr. Corva, asked me if I would like to make a sworn statement in extenuation or mitigation on my own behalf, I told him I could think of no extenuating or mitigating circumstances that I could swear to." He paused and looked directly at the board, meeting each member's eyes. "Sitting here now, I still can't."

Colonel Sproule waited some time, expecting more. Finally realizing that Tyson had no intention of offering anything further, he addressed Colonel Pierce. "Does the prosecution wish to offer anything in rebuttal to the statement of the accused?"

Pierce stood and began to reply, but Corva had come across the floor and was standing in front of the pulpit. Corva said, "The accused has not finished, your honor."

Sproule's eyebrows rose. "It appeared he was, Mr. Corva."

"No, your honor." Corva turned to Tyson, who gave him a sharp look. Corva said to Tyson, "Would you characterize your state of mind after the incident as remorseful?"

Tyson sat back in the chair and crossed his legs. He stared at Corva awhile, then replied, "Yes."

"And do you feel remorse now?"

Tyson replied tersely, "I suppose."

"And would you also describe yourself as haunted by this incident?"

Tyson looked at his lawyer. Clearly Corva did not intend to let his statement stand as it was. He studied the man's face and saw he was very distraught.

"Are you *haunted* by what happened at that hospital?"

Tyson snapped, "Wouldn't you be?"

"Did you seek psychiatric help after you returned from Vietnam?"

Tyson could see the board out of the corner of his eye, and he noticed that some of them looked uncomfortable. He kept silent.

"You *did* seek psychiatric help, didn't you?" he went on without waiting for an answer. "By shooting Larry Cane did you believe you did everything humanly possible to stop the mutiny and massacre?"

"Hard to say."

Corva's voice rose. "Can't you give me more complete answers?"

There was a stirring in the spectator pews. Tyson looked past Corva at Pierce, who was no longer staring at him, but at Corva. Weinroth and Longo were glancing at each other.

"Don't you think," asked Corva, his voice becoming louder, "that combat fatigue mitigates what happened at that hospital? That if the UCMJ recognizes that, then maybe you should too?"

Tyson uncrossed his legs and leaned forward. His voice was taut. "I don't think I want to retry this case now."

"Were you or were you not suffering from combat fatigue? Answer the question."

Tyson stood. "I told the court what I had to say! There is no extenuation or mitigation."

Corva began to speak, but Sproule cleared his throat. "Mr. Corva, does your client wish to conclude his statement?"

"No."

"Yes," said Tyson, and stepped away from the chair. Corva blocked him. There was open talking in the court now. Sproule called for quiet and said to Corva, "This is most unusual."

Tyson looked into Corva's eyes. It suddenly occurred to him that Corva had been under tremendous strain, had hidden it well, and was now about to snap. Tyson took his seat and said in a calm voice, "I suppose battle fatigue could explain almost all of what happened."

Corva seemed to be getting himself under control and nodded quickly.

Sproule spoke. "Mr. Corva, do you want a recess?"

Corva rubbed his cheek. "No, your honor."

Tyson said, "Your honor, I've concluded my statement."

Corva stood silently, as though in a daze.

"Very well," said Sproule with a note of relief in his voice. Sproule looked at Pierce and asked for the second time, "Does the prosecution wish to offer anything in rebuttal to the statement of the accused?"

Pierce stood and made an exaggerated shrug. "It appears that defense counsel has already done that."

There were a few tentative laughs, which quickly died away.

Sproule looked at Colonel Moore. "Does the board have any questions for the witness?"

Colonel Moore, apparently without consulting the board, replied tonelessly, "We have no questions, your honor."

Sproule said to Tyson, "You are excused, Lieutenant."

"Yes, sir." Tyson rose and nudged Corva back toward the defense table. They both sat.

Colonel Sproule said, "We will take a five-minute break in place." Sproule made a show of concentrating on some paperwork as did the prosecution team and the board.

Tyson leaned toward Corva. "Are you all right?"

Corva sipped some water. "Better."

"Are you well enough for me to beat the shit out of you?"

Corva smiled wanly. "I just slipped a little."

"Don't get personally involved with your clients," advised Tyson.

Corva didn't reply. The minutes ticked by in silence. Sproule looked up from his papers and cleared his throat. He addressed Pierce. "Does the prosecution wish to present an argument for an appropriate sentence?"

Pierce let a few seconds pass, then replied, "The board has the facts and will reach a decision on an appropriate sentence."

Sproule turned to Corva. Sproule asked, "Does the defense wish to present an argument for an appropriate sentence?"

Corva, without standing, replied, "The defense, too, believes the board has the facts it needs to reach an appropriate sentence."

"So," said Sproule with uncharacteristic informality, "that's it." Sproule turned to the board and said, "It is my duty now to instruct the board on matters of punishment." He cleared his throat and began. "It is your sole responsibility to select an appropriate sentence, and you may consider all matters in extenuation and mitigation in arriving at that sentence. You may take into account the background and character of the accused, his reputation and service record, including awards, medals, conduct, efficiency, fidelity, courage, bravery, and other traits of good character.

"You must also consider that the desired effect of a sentence is not primarily punishment, deterrence, rehabilitation, or the protection of society. The end product of a conviction in a trial by military court-martial and the sentence arrived at is to reflect military goals, which include the maintenance of good order and discipline, the continued ability of the service to carry out its mission, and the preservation of the service concepts of duty and honor. In the case where the accused is a commissioned officer, he should, by custom and often by law, be held accountable to a higher degree for the preservation of these goals, concepts, and ideals than an enlisted man would be. However, he should not be held accountable to such a degree as would impose unrealistic or unattainable standards on the officer corps."

Sproule went on, "In considering your verdict, you should also take into consideration the prevailing conditions at the time of the offense. You should not take into consideration any outside influences, real or perceived, and you should not be subject in any way to command influence."

Sproule glanced around the room, then concluded, "Though there is not and should not be a statute of limitations for the crime of murder, you may consider in arriving at an appropriate sentence that the offense for which the accused stands convicted occurred over eighteen years ago. Also, due to the special circumstances of the accused having been a civilian for nearly eighteen years, you may take into account his civilian accomplishments, his community standing, his marital status, and his age in arriving at your sentence." Colonel Sproule looked at Colonel Moore. "Do you have any questions?"

Moore looked toward either side of the table, then said, "We have no questions."

Colonel Sproule instructed the board, "You may deliberate the sentence in the room set aside for that purpose. If you have not reached a sentence by fourteen-thirty hours, you may continue deliberating in the deliberation room until you do reach a sentence. Please keep the court informed of your progress. The court will be closed."

Tyson and Corva found themselves back in Rabbi Weitz's office. The rabbi, too, was present. He said to Tyson, "I came. I was there today for the first time. Whose side were you on?"

Corva said, "That's what I'd like to know. That was the absolute worst statement I ever heard from an accused."

Tyson saw that Corva was nearly himself again, though he seemed somewhat sulky.

Corva added, "It would serve you right if they took you at your word."

Rabbi Weitz joined in. "If that was supposed to be reverse psychology, my friend, I hope the board responds."

Tyson said irritably, "I said what I had to say."

Corva responded, "Your ego will be your downfall one of these days . . . maybe today."

"You said I could say what I wanted."

"You were supposed to say that the murderers were walking free. That before they imposed a prison sentence on you, they should consider that. I thought you understood what we have been driving at . . . oh, the hell with it."

Rabbi Weitz took his attaché case, headed for the door, and opened it. "While they are considering an appropriate sentence, maybe they will consider an appropriate place to hold courts-martial next time. God bless you both." He left.

Corva sat at the rabbi's desk, drinking ice water.

Tyson stood at the window and looked out into the rain. On the lawn, not ten feet away, stood two MPs in rain gear, M-16 rifles slung on their shoulders. "There's no place to run."

"What's that?"

"They have MPs with rifles out there."

"What did you expect?"

Tyson shrugged. He turned from the window. "Why did you do that?"

"Do what?"

"You know damned well what."

Corva stayed silent. At length he responded, "I did it because I couldn't sit there and watch you walk jauntily to a firing squad with your fucking stiff upper lip."

"Well, I did it my way, and you did it your way. And the result was a dog and pony show." He glanced at his watch and asked, "How long will this take, and how long will I get?"

Corva said, "They have a lot to consider. Sometimes this takes longer than the verdict. It could go on for days."

Tyson nodded. "Take a guess then. What's your experience with sentences, or shouldn't I ask?"

Corva smiled thinly, then said, "I could have fifty years' experience with sentences, and I couldn't call this one. It could be anywhere from no jail time to ten . . . fifteen years."

Tyson sat in a visitor's chair and looked at the clock. "Eleven-fifteen hours."

"What is that in real time?"

"Quarter after eleven."

"Well, be prepared for a wait."

"Is it your policy to stay with the accused while the sentence is deliberated?"

"I guess. We're authorized to go back to the lockup if somehow you'd feel more comfortable there."

"I think we'll stay here."

"Right."

They sat in silence for some time, then Corva began speaking. "You remember what we used to say in Nam—you can't tell the good guys from the bad guys. So kill them all and let Saint Peter sort them out. Well, the first time I heard that, I thought it was funny. Then when I saw it happen—the killing of civilians—it wasn't so funny. But by the time I was ready to go home, it started to make sense, and that scared the hell out of me. I think—I know—that when you're there, you lose touch with external reality and create your own inner reality. That was the missing piece in your little speech. The gap between knowing what your duty was, deciding not to do it, then feeling fine about deciding not to do it even though it went against what you believed in."

Tyson lit a cigarette. "I keep going back there in my mind. Trying to experience it again, trying to feel what I felt, think what I thought. But the more I try to do that, the more elusive the whole thing becomes. It's funny that my most vivid and, I think, accurate memories are of the first days and weeks in Nam. While I was still open to outside reality. But as the weeks went by, with each passing month I began to block, to distort, and especially to deny. We, all of us, got heavily into denial. You could have five men killed in the morning, and by lunch they didn't exist. You could kill a peasant through carelessness, and before you even reloaded, he was a hard-core VC armed to the teeth. So maybe what happened at the hospital was not what Brandt said or Farley said or what I told you or what Kelly told all of us. Maybe it was something else. Maybe if I'd gone into battalion headquarters and seen the colonel and told him what had happened, he'd have told me I was crazy. He'd wave an after-action report in my face, and show me my proposal for a Silver Star and tell me to get a grip on myself."

Corva said, "Oh, Christ, Ben, what a place that was. Are we sane now?"

"You bet."

"Right." Corva said, "By the way, I have a verbal message for you from a Major Harper. Want to hear it?"

"No."

"Okay."

Tyson drew on his cigarette. "What's she want?"

Corva said, "She wants you to know that she's being released from active duty at midnight tonight. She says she would like to buy you a drink tomorrow at a midtown bar of your choice."

Tyson thought about that awhile, then said, "There was a woman I could have gone for."

"You did. But, hey, that's another story. Make her take you to a hotel bar—then if it's going right, you just have to point up."

Tyson smiled. "You're disgusting. If I meet her, I want you along to chaperone."

"I'll be there. And so will you."

Tyson looked at him but said nothing. After a few minutes he said, "That Sindel woman isn't bad-looking either. Must be the uniform. Why am I so attracted to uniforms?"

"Don't know. Ask your shrink."

"My shrink once said that when a soldier goes to war, all is pre-forgiven."

"Did he? I wish I had him on the board."

"He's dead."

"Right."

They both glanced at their watches. Corva said, "Hungry?"

"No." Tyson lit another cigarette. "Why do you think I will be able to meet Karen Harper in a bar tomorrow?"

Corva replied, "I'm optimistic. So, apparently, is Harper. But I think some of them want to hand you a jail sentence—to show that the military doesn't give a damn *why* you failed to act like an officer. That's the traditional approach. They court-martialed that Captain Bucher who surrendered the *Pueblo.* They would have court-martialed Custer had he survived the massacre. The military gets off on showing toughness when compassion is called for and compassion when toughness is called for. What they say, in effect, is, 'We don't live by civilian concepts of right and wrong. We have our own code and our own requirements.' Where else can a man get five years in jail for dozing off at the wrong time and wrong place?"

Tyson nodded. "I thought about that. Sproule was telling them to go easy. But he's a judge. He's not really part of the corps. Those infantry officers are coming from someplace else. Aren't they?"

"We'll see."

"Tell me a war story, Corva. I'm bored. Tell me about the tunnel and the Bronze Star they gave you."

"Okay," Corva began with enthusiasm. "I crawled into this tunnel, and it narrowed and narrowed until I had less than a foot of free space around me."

"I know that."

"Right. So I flip on the miner's lamp, and there's this Oriental gentleman there who I assumed was a member of the People's Liberation Army, though I saw no shoulder or collar insignia on his black pajamas. So I reach back into my pocket—it was a tight space, remember—and pull out my little plastic card and quickly peruse the Rules of Engagement—"

Tyson laughed.

"Don't laugh at me. This is serious. So I'm up to rule six or seven now, and I think I find what I'm looking for—'Meeting a gook face-to-face in a dark tunnel.' And it says, 'Shoot first and issue a challenge afterward.' So—"

There was a knock on the door, and Tyson looked at the wall clock. Five after noon. *Lunch.* The door opened, and Sergeant Larson stepped into the office and, remembering last time, said immediately, "The board has reached a sentence. Will you come with me, sir?"

Tyson stood quickly, snatched his hat off the desk, and was out the door, followed by Corva and Larson. They strode quickly down the corridor, turned, and entered the chapel. Tyson walked directly to the defense desk and stood behind it. Corva caught up and took his place beside Tyson.

Tyson glanced out over the pews and saw they were half empty. Obviously no one expected this so soon. But Marcy, David, and his mother were being escorted up the aisle by an MP. Other people were hurrying in.

Pierce, Weinroth, and Longo sat at their table, but for the first time the table was clear of papers.

The board sat stoically in their seats, not speaking to one another as they'd sometimes done before Sproule arrived.

The sergeant at arms marched to the middle of the floor and called out, "All rise."

Colonel Sproule strode in and went to the pulpit. He squinted out over the pews, hesitated, then said, "The court will come to order."

Pierce stood. "All parties to the trial who were present when the court closed are now present."

Sproule turned to Colonel Moore. "I have a communication that you have reached a sentence. Is that correct?"

Moore replied from his seat, "That is correct."

Sproule turned to Tyson. "Lieutenant Benjamin Tyson, will you report to the president of the court?"

Tyson stood, and Corva stood with him.

There were still people coming into the chapel, but there was no noise beyond the sound of soft footsteps and from the open doors, the occasional splash of a car going through the wet street.

Tyson walked across the red-carpeted floor and stood again directly in front of Colonel Moore, who rose. Tyson saluted and stood at attention.

Colonel Moore looked him squarely in the eye, as he said, "Lieutenant Benjamin Tyson, it is my duty as president of this court to inform you that the court, in closed session, in full and open discussion, and upon secret written ballot, all of the members concurring, sentence you to dismissal from the Army of the United States and to forfeit all pay and allowances that may be due you or have accrued as a result of your past and present service as a commissioned officer in the Army of the United States."

There was no sound in the chapel, as if, Tyson thought, someone had turned off the audio portion. He waited for a sound, but there was none, and Colonel Moore seemed to have finished, but he couldn't have, and Tyson stood there until finally Colonel Moore sat down.

Someone in the pews was weeping, everyone was standing. Tyson found Corva beside him. Corva said, "Well, are you going to stand there, or do you want to go home?"

"Home. I want to go home."

Colonel Sproule looked at Colonel Pierce and asked the required question, "Has the prosecution any other case to try at this time?"

Pierce already had his briefcase in his hand and in a breach of military etiquette spoke as he was on his way to the side door, "No, your honor, I have nothing further."

Colonel Sproule announced, "The court will adjourn to meet on future call."

Tyson turned toward the side door, and Corva gently turned him toward the communion rail. "We're leaving through the front door this time. Lots of people out there want to say hello."

Two lines of MPs had formed up in the wide center aisle, and Tyson and

Corva walked between them, joined by Marcy, then David, and his mother, who kissed him. No one spoke as they headed out into the October rain. Marcy took his hand and squeezed it as they entered the vestibule.

Out on the rain-splashed steps, Tyson was greeted by the sight of umbrellas, hundreds of umbrellas, and as he walked down the steps with his family, the umbrellas tilted to cover them from the rain. Tyson kept his hand in Marcy's and put his arm around his son. "Let's go home," he said.

CATHEDRAL

For Lauren, age three,
an old hand at the alphabet,
and Alexander,
newly arrived in the world

Acknowledgments

I wish to thank the following people
for their editorial help, dedication, and, above all, patience:
Bernard and Darlene Geis, Joseph Elder, David Kleinman,
Mary Crowley, Eleanor Hurka, and Rose Ann Ferrick.
And very special thanks to Judith Shafran,
to whom this book would have been dedicated
had she not been an editor and therefore a natural enemy of authors,
albeit a noble and forthright one.
For their expertise and technical assistance I'd like to thank
Detective Jack Lanigan, NYPD, Retired; and Michael Moriarty,
Carm Tintle, and Jim Miller, Seanachies.
The following organizations have provided information for this book:
The New York Police Department Public Information Office;
The St. Patrick's Parade Committee; The 69th Infantry, NYARNG;
Amnesty International; the Irish Consulate;
the British Consulate; and the Irish Tourist Board.
There were other individuals and organizations
who gave of their time and knowledge,
providing colorful threads of the narrative tapestry presented here,
and to them—too numerous to mention—
I express my sincere appreciation.
And finally, I want to thank The Little People,
who refrained, as much as could be hoped, from mischief.

Nelson DeMille
New York
Spring 1980

Author's Note

Regarding places, people, and events: The author has learned that in any book dealing with the Irish, literary license and other liberties should be not only tolerated but expected.

St. Patrick's Cathedral in New York has been described with care and accuracy. However, as in any work of fiction, especially in one set in the future, dramatic liberties have been exercised in some instances.

The New York police officers represented in this novel are not based on real people. The fictional hostage negotiator, Captain Bert Schroeder, is not meant to represent the present New York Police Department Hostage Negotiator, Frank Bolz. The only similarity shared is the title of Hostage Negotiator. Captain Bolz is an exceptionally competent officer whom the author has had the pleasure of meeting on three occasions, and Captain Bolz's worldwide reputation as innovator of the New York Plan of hostage negotiating is well deserved. To the people of the City of New York, and especially to the people whose lives he's been instrumental in saving, he is a true hero in every sense of the word.

The Catholic clergy represented in this work are not based on actual persons. The Irish revolutionaries in this novel are based to some extent on a composite of real people, as are the politicians, intelligence people, and diplomats, though no individual character is meant to represent an actual man or woman.

The purpose of this work was not to write a roman à clef or to represent in any way, favorably or unfavorably, persons living or dead.

The story takes place not in the present or the past but in the future; the nature of the story, however, compels the author to use descriptive job titles and other factual designations that exist at this writing. Beyond these designations there is no identification meant or intended with the public figures who presently hold those descriptive job titles.

Historical characters and references are for the most part factual except where there is an obvious blend of fact and fiction woven into the story line.

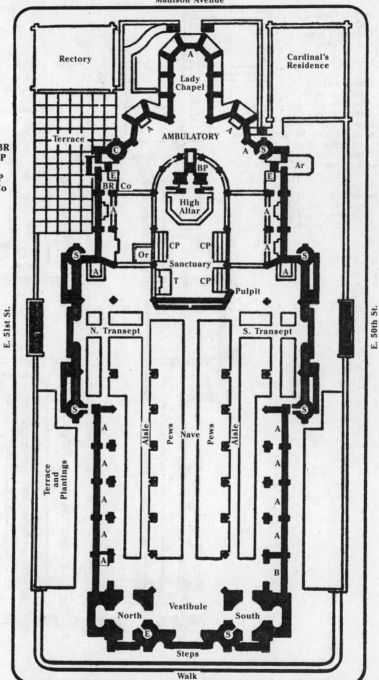

St. Patrick's
Cathedral
First Floor Plan

Keys

Altars—A
Archbishop's
Sacristy—Ar
Archbishop's
Throne—T
Bookstore—B
Bride's Room—BR
Bronze Plate—BP
Chimney—C
Clergy Pews—CP
Confessional—Co
Elevators—E
Organ
Keyboard—Or
Spiral
Staircases—S

← N

Madison Avenue

Rectory

Cardinal's
Residence

A

Lady
Chapel

Terrace

AMBULATORY

A

A

C

A   S

Ar

BP

E

E

BR   Co

A

High
Altar

A

A

CP   CP

A

S

Or

Sanctuary

A   S

A

T   CP

Pulpit

N. Transept

S. Transept

E. 51st St.

E. 50th St.

A

Aisle

Pews   Nave   Pews

Aisle

A

A

A

Terrace
and
Plantings

A

A

A

A

A

A

A

A   B

Vestibule

North

South

E

Steps

S

Walk

Fifth Avenue

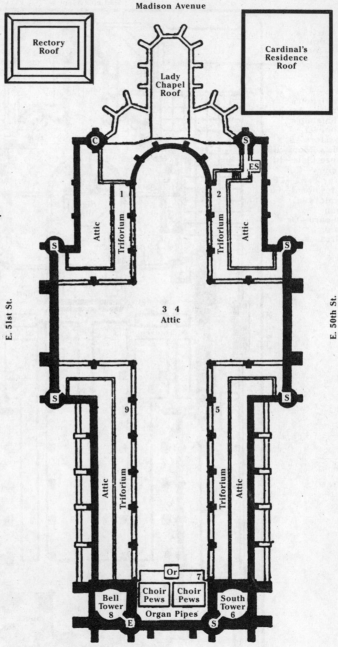

St. Patrick's Cathedral Triforium Plan and Attics

Key (clockwise):

Eamon Farrell—1
Frank Gallagher—2
Jean Kearney—3
Arthur Nulty—4
George Sullivan—5
Rory Devane—6
Jack Leary—7
Donald Mullins—8
Abby Boland—9

Chimney—C
Elevator—E
Elevator Shaft—ES
Organ Keyboard—Or
Spiral Staircases—S

← N

Madison Avenue

Rectory Roof

Cardinal's Residence Roof

Lady Chapel Roof

C

S

ES

1

2

Attic

Triforium

Triforium

Attic

E. 51st St.

E. 50th St.

S

S

3 4
Attic

S

S

9

5

Attic

Triforium

Triforium

Attic

Or   7

Choir Pews   Choir Pews

Bell Tower 8

South Tower 6

E

S

Organ Pipes

Fifth Avenue

BOOK I

Northern Ireland

Now that I've learned a great deal about Northern Ireland, there are things I can say about it: that it's an unhealthy and morbid place, where people learn to die from the time that they're children; where we've never been able to forget our history and our culture —which are only other forms of violence; where it's so easy to deride things and people; where people are capable of much love, affection, human warmth and generosity. But, my God! How much we know how to hate!

Every two or three hours, we resurrect the past, dust it off and throw it in someone's face.

Betty Williams,
Northern Irish peace
activist and winner of
the Nobel Peace Prize

1

"The tea has got cold." Sheila Malone set down her cup and waited for the two young men who sat opposite her, clad in khaki underwear, to do the same.

The younger man, Private Harding, cleared his throat. "We'd like to put on our uniforms."

Sheila Malone shook her head. "No need for that."

The other man, Sergeant Shelby, put down his cup. "Let's get done with it." His voice was steady, but his hand shook and the color had drained from under his eyes. He made no move to rise.

Sheila Malone said abruptly, "Why don't we take a walk?"

The sergeant stood. The other man, Harding, looked down at the table, staring at the scattered remains of the bridge game they'd all passed the morning with. He shook his head. "No."

Sergeant Shelby took the younger man's arm and tried to grip it, but there was no strength in his hand. "Come on, now. We could use some air."

Sheila Malone nodded to two men by the fire. They rose and came up behind the British soldiers. One of them, Liam Coogan, said roughly, "Let's go. We've not got all day."

Shelby looked at the men behind him. "Give the lad a second or two," he said, pulling at Harding's arm. "Stand up," he ordered. "That's the hardest part."

The young private rose slowly, then began to sink back into his chair, his body trembling.

Coogan grasped him under the arms and propelled him toward the door. The other man, George Sullivan, opened the door and pushed him out.

Everyone knew that speed was important now, that it had to be done quickly, before anyone's courage failed. The sod was wet and cold under the prisoners' feet, and a January wind shook water off the rowan trees. They passed the outdoor privy they had walked to every morning and every evening for two weeks and kept walking toward the ravine near the cottage.

Sheila Malone reached under her sweater and drew a small revolver from her waistband. During the weeks she had spent with these men she had grown to like them, and out of common decency someone else should have been sent to do it. Bloody insensitive bastards.

The two soldiers were at the edge of the ravine now, walking down into it.

Coogan poked her roughly. "Now, damn you! Now!"

She looked back toward the prisoners. "Stop!"

The two men halted with their backs to their executioners. Sheila Malone hesitated, then raised the pistol with both hands. She knew she would hit only their backs from that range, but she couldn't bring herself to move closer for a head shot. She took a deep breath and fired, shifted her aim, and fired again.

Shelby and Harding lurched forward and hit the ground before the echo of the two reports died away. They thrashed on the ground, moaning.

Coogan cursed. "Goddamn it!" He ran into the ravine, pointed his pistol at the back of Shelby's head, and fired. He looked at Harding, who was lying on his side. Frothy blood trickled from his mouth and his chest heaved. Coogan bent over, placed the pistol between Harding's wide-open eyes, and fired again. He put his revolver in his pocket and looked up at the edge of the ravine. "Bloody stupid woman. Give a woman a job to do and . . ."

Sheila Malone pointed her revolver down at him. Coogan stepped backward and tripped over Shelby's body. He lay between the two corpses with his hands still held high. "No! Please. I didn't mean anything by it. Don't shoot!"

Sheila lowered the pistol. "If you ever touch me again, or say anything to me again . . . I'll blow your fucking head off!"

Sullivan approached her cautiously. "It's all right now. Come on, Sheila. We've got to get away from here."

"He can find his own bloody way back. I'll not ride with him."

Sullivan turned and looked down at Coogan. "Head out through the wood, Liam. You'll pick up a bus on the highway. See you in Belfast."

Sheila Malone and George Sullivan walked quickly to the car waiting off the lane and climbed in behind the driver, Rory Devane, and the courier, Tommy Fitzgerald. "Let's go," said Sullivan.

"Where's Liam?" asked Devane nervously.

"Move out," said Sheila.

The car pulled into the lane and headed south toward Belfast.

Sheila drew from her pocket the two letters the soldiers had given her to mail to their families. If she were stopped at a roadblock and the Royal Ulster Constabulary found the letters . . . She opened the window and threw her pistol out, then let the letters sail into the wind.

Sheila Malone jumped out of her bed. She could hear motors in the street and the sounds of boots against the cobbles. Residents of the block were shouting from windows, and trash-can lids were being beaten to sound the alarm. As she began pulling her slacks on under her nightdress her bedroom door crashed open, and two soldiers rushed in without a word. A shaft of light from the hall made her cover her eyes. The red-bereted paratroopers pushed her against the wall and ripped the slacks from around her legs. One of them raised her nightdress over her head, and then ran his hands over her body, searching for a weapon. She spun and swung her fists at him. "Get your filthy hands . . ."

One of the soldiers punched her in the stomach, and she doubled over and lay on the floor, her nightdress gathered up around her breasts.

The second soldier bent down, grabbed her long hair, and dragged her to her feet. He spoke for the first time. "Sheila Malone, all I'm required to tell you is that you are being arrested under the Special Powers Act. If you make one fucking sound when we take you out to the trucks, we'll beat you to a pulp."

The two soldiers pushed her into the hall, down the stairs, and into the street, which was filled with shouting people. Everything passed in a blur as she was half-carried to the intersection where the trucks were parked. Voices called insults at the British soldiers and the Royal Ulster Constabulary who were assisting them. A boy's voice shouted, "Fuck the Queen." Women and children were crying, and dogs were barking. She saw a young priest trying to calm a group of people. An unconscious man, his head bloodied, was dragged past her. The soldiers picked her up and threw her into the back of a small truck filled with a dozen other prisoners. An RUC guard stood at the front of the truck, fondling a large truncheon. "Lie down, bitch, and shut your mouth."

She lay down by the tailgate and listened to her own breathing in the totally silent truck. After a few minutes the gates of the truck closed and it pulled away.

The guard shouted above the noise of the convoy. "The Pope is a fucking queer."

Sheila Malone lay against the tailgate, trying to calm herself. In the dark truck some men slept or were unconscious; a few were weeping. The guard kept up an anti-Catholic tirade until the truck stopped and the tailgate swung open, revealing a large, floodlit enclosure surrounded by barbed wire and machine-gun towers. Long Kesh, known to the Catholics of Northern Ireland as Dachau.

A soldier shouted into the truck, "Clear out! Quick! Move it!"

A few men scrambled over and around Sheila, and she heard the sounds of blows, shouts, and cries as the men left the truck. A voice cried out, "Take it easy, I'm an old man." A young boy clad in pajamas crawled over her and tumbled to the ground. The RUC guard was kicking everyone toward the tailgate now, like a trash man sweeping the floor of his truck clean at the dump. Someone pulled her out by her legs, and she fell on the soft, wet earth. She tried to stand but was knocked down.

"Crawl! Crawl, you bastards!"

She picked up her head and saw two lines of paratrooper boots. She crawled as quickly as she could between the gauntlet as blows fell on her back and buttocks. A few of the men made obscene remarks as she passed by on her hands and knees, but the blows were light and the obscenities were shouted by boyish, embarrassed voices, which somehow made it all the more obscene.

At the end of the gauntlet two soldiers picked her up and pushed her into a long Nissen hut. An officer with a swagger stick pointed to an open door, and the soldiers pushed her onto the floor of a small room and shut the door as they left. She looked up from where she lay in the center of the tiny cubicle.

A matron stood behind a camp table. "Strip. Come on, you little tramp. Stand up and take them off."

Within minutes she was stripped and searched and was wearing a gray prison dress and prison underwear. She could hear blows being struck outside the small cubicle and cries and shouts as the harvest of the sweep was processed—transformed from sleeping civilians into gray, terrified internees.

Sheila Malone had no doubt that a good number of them were guilty of some kind of anti-British or antigovernment activity. A few were actually IRA. A smaller number might even be arsonists or bombers . . . or murderers like herself. There was a fifty-fifty chance of getting out of internment within ninety days if you didn't crack and confess to something. But if they had something on you—something as serious as murder . . . Before she could gather her thoughts and begin to formulate what she was going to say, someone placed a hood over her head and she was pushed through a door that closed behind her.

A voice shouted directly in her ear, and she jumped. "I said, spell your name, bitch!"

She tried to spell it but found to her surprise that she could not. Someone laughed.

Another voice shouted, "Stupid cunt!"

A third voice screamed in her other ear. "So, you shot two of our boys, did you?"

There it was. They knew. She felt her legs begin to shake.

"Answer me, you little murdering cunt!"

"N-n-no."

"What? Don't lie to us, you cowardly, murdering bitch. Like to shoot men in the back, do you? Now it's your turn!"

She felt something poke her in the back of the head and heard the sound of a pistol cocking. The hammer fell home and made a loud, metallic thud. She jumped and someone laughed again. "Next time it won't be empty, bitch."

She felt sweat gather on her brow and soak the black hood.

"All right. Pull up your dress. That's right. All the way!"

She pulled her skirt up and stood motionless as someone pulled her pants down to her ankles.

After an hour of pain, insults, humiliation, and leering laughter, the three interrogators seemed to get bored. She was certain now that they were just fishing, and she could almost picture being released at dawn.

"Fix yourself up."

She let her aching arms fall and bent over to pull up her pants. Before she straightened up she heard the three men leave the room as two other people entered. The hood was pulled from her head, and the bright lights half-blinded her. The man who had taken the hood moved to the side and sat in a chair just out of range of her vision. She focused her eyes straight ahead.

A young British army officer, a major, sat in a chair behind a small camp desk in the center of the windowless room. "Sit down, Miss Malone."

She walked stiffly toward a stool in front of the desk and sat slowly. Her buttocks hurt so much that she would almost rather have remained standing. She choked down a sob and steadied her breathing.

"Yes, you can have a bed as soon as we finish this." The major smiled. "My name is Martin. Bartholomew Martin."

"Yes . . . I've heard of you."

"Really? Good things, I trust."

She leaned forward and looked into his eyes. "Listen, Major Martin, I was beaten and sexually abused."

He shuffled some papers. "We'll discuss all of that as soon as we finish with this." He picked out one sheet of paper. "Here it is. A search of your room has uncovered a pistol and a satchel of gelignite. Enough to blow up the whole block." He looked at her. "That's a dreadful thing to keep in your aunt's house. I'm afraid she may be in trouble now as well."

"There was no gun or explosives in my room, and you know it."

He drummed his fingers impatiently on the desk. "Whether they were there or not is hardly the point, Miss Malone. The point is that my report *says* a gun and explosives were found, and in Ulster there is not a great deal of difference between the charges and the realities. In fact, they are the same. Do you follow me?"

She didn't answer.

"All right," said the major. "That's not important. What is important," he continued as he stared into her eyes, "are the murders of Sergeant Thomas Shelby and Private Alan Harding."

She stared back at his eyes and displayed no emotion, but her stomach heaved. They had her, and she was fairly certain she knew how they had gotten her.

"I believe you know a Liam Coogan, Miss Malone. An associate of yours. He's turned Queen's evidence." An odd half smile passed over his face. "I'm afraid we've got you now."

"If you know so goddamned much, why did your men—"

"Oh, they're not my men. They're paratroop lads. Served with Harding and Shelby. Brought them here for the occasion. I'm in Intelligence, of course." Major Martin's voice changed, became more intimate. "You're damned lucky they didn't kill you."

Sheila Malone considered her situation. Even under normal British law she would probably be convicted on Coogan's testimony. Then why had she been arrested under the Special Powers Act? Why had they bothered to plant a gun and explosives in her room? Major Martin was after something else.

Martin stared at her, then cleared his throat. "Unfortunately, there is no capital punishment for murder in our enlightened kingdom. However, we're going to try something new. We're going to try to get an indictment for treason —I think we can safely say that the Provisional Irish Republican Army, of which you are a member, has committed treason toward the Crown."

He looked down at an open book in front of him. " 'Acts that constitute treason. Paragraph 811—Levies war against the Sovereign in her realm. . . .' I think you fill that bill nicely." He pulled the book closer and read, " 'Paragraph 812—The essence of the offense of treason lies in the violation of the allegiance owed to the Sovereign. . . .' And Paragraph 813 is my favorite. It says simply"—he looked at her without reading from the book—" 'The punishment for treason is death by hanging.' " He stressed the last words and looked for a reaction, but there was none. "It was Mr. Churchill, commenting on the Irish uprising of 1916, who said, 'The grass grows green on the battlefield, but never on the scaffold.' It's time we started hanging Irish traitors again. You first. And beside you on the scaffold will be your sister, Maureen."

She sat up. "My sister? Why . . . ?"

"Coogan says *she* was there as well. You, your sister, and her lover, Brian Flynn."

"That's a bloody lie."

"Why would a man turn Queen's evidence and then lie about who committed the murders?"

"Because *he* shot those soldiers—"

"There were two calibers of bullets. We can try two people for murder—any two. So why don't you let me work out who did what to whom?"

"You don't care who killed those soldiers. It's Flynn you want to hang."

"Someone must hang." But Major Martin had no intention of hanging any of them and making more Irish martyrs. He wanted to get Flynn into Long Kesh, where he could wring out every piece of information that he possessed about the Provisional IRA. Then he would cut Brian Flynn's throat with a piece of glass and call it suicide.

He said, "Let's assume that you escape the hangman's noose. Assume also that we pick up your sister, which is not unlikely. Consider if you will, Miss Malone, sharing a cell with your sister for the rest of your natural lives. How old are you? Not twenty yet? The months, the years pass slowly. *Slowly.* Young girls wasting their lives . . . and for what? A philosophy? The rest of the world will go on living and loving, free to come and go. And you . . . well, the real hell of it is that Maureen, at least, is innocent of murder. You are the reason she'd be there—because you wouldn't name her lover. And Flynn will have found another woman, of course. And Coogan, yes, Coogan will have gone to London or America to live and—"

"Shut up! For God's sake, shut up!" She buried her face in her hands and tried to think before he started again.

"Now there *is* a way out." He looked down at his papers, then looked up again. "There always is, isn't there? What you must do is dictate a confession naming Brian Flynn as an officer in the Provisional IRA—which he is—and naming him as the murderer of Sergeant Shelby and Private Harding. You will be charged as an accessory after the fact and be free within . . . let's say, seven years."

"And my sister?"

"We'll put out a warrant for her arrest only as an accessory. She should leave Ulster and never return. We will not look for her and will not press any country for extradition. But this arrangement is operative only if we find Brian Flynn." He leaned forward. "Where is Brian Flynn?"

"How the hell should I know?"

Martin leaned back in his chair. "Well, we must charge you with something within ninety days of internment. That's the law, you understand. If we don't find Flynn by the ninetieth day, we will charge you with double homicide— perhaps treason as well. So, if you can remember anything that will lead us to him, please don't hesitate to tell us." He paused. "Will you think about where Flynn might be?"

She didn't answer.

"Actually, if you really don't know, then you're useless to me . . . unless . . . You see, your sister will try to free you, and with her will be Flynn . . . so perhaps—"

"You won't use me for bait, you bastard."

"No? Well, we'll have to see about that, won't we?"

"May I have a bed?"

"Certainly. You may stand now."

She stood. "No more Gestapo tactics?"

"I'm sorry, I don't understand." He rose from his chair. "The matron will escort you to a cell. Good night."

She turned and opened the door. A hood came down over her head, but before it did she saw not the matron but two young Royal Ulster Constabulary men and three grinning paratroopers.

2

B rian Flynn looked up at Queen's Bridge, shrouded in March mist and darkness. The Lagan River fog rolled down the partially lit street and hung between the red-brick buildings of Bank Road. The curfew was in effect, and there was no traffic.

Maureen Malone looked at him. His handsome, dark features always seemed sinister at night. She pulled back the sleeve of her trench coat and looked at her watch. "It's after four. Where the hell are—"

"Quiet! Listen."

She heard the rhythmic footsteps coming out of Oxford Street. In the mist a squad of Royal Ulster Constabulary appeared and turned toward them, and they crouched behind a stack of oil drums.

They waited in silence, their breathing coming irregularly in long plumes of fog. The patrol passed, and a few seconds later they heard the whining of a truck changing gears and saw the headlights in the mist. A Belfast Gas Works truck pulled up to the curbstone near them, and they jumped in the open side door. The driver, Rory Devane, moved the truck slowly north toward the bridge. The man in the passenger seat, Tommy Fitzgerald, turned. "Road block on Cromac Street."

Maureen Malone sat on the floor. "Is everything set?"

Devane spoke as he steered slowly toward the bridge. "Yes. Sheila left Long Kesh in an RUC van a half hour ago. They took the A23 and were seen passing through Castlereagh not ten minutes ago. They'll be coming over the Queen's Bridge about now."

Flynn lit a cigarette. "Escort?"

"No," said Devane. "Just a driver and guard in the cab and two guards in the back, according to our sources."

"Other prisoners?"

"Maybe as many as ten. All going to Crumlin Road Jail, except for two women going up to Armagh." He paused. "Where do you want to hit them?"

Flynn looked out the rear window of the truck. A pair of headlights appeared on the bridge. "Collins's men are set up on Waring Street. That's the way they'll have to go to Crumlin Road." He wiped the fog from the window and stared. "Here's the RUC van." Devane cut off the engine and shut the lights.

The black, unmarked RUC van rolled off the bridge and headed into Ann Street. Devane waited, then restarted his truck and followed at a distance with his lights off. Flynn said to Devane, "Circle round to High Street."

No one spoke as the truck moved through the quiet streets. They approached Waring Street, and Tommy Fitzgerald reached under his seat and pulled out two weapons, an old American Thompson submachine gun and a modern Armalite automatic rifle. "The tommy gun is for you, Brian, and the light gun for my lady." He passed a short cardboard tube to Flynn. "And this . . . if, God forbid, we run into a Saracen." Flynn took the tube and stuck it under his trench coat.

They swung off Royal Avenue into Waring Street from the west at the same time the RUC van entered from the east at Victoria Street. The two vehicles approached each other slowly. A black sedan fell in behind the RUC van, and Fitzgerald pointed. "That'll be Collins and his boys."

Flynn saw that the RUC van was moving more slowly now, the driver realizing that he was being boxed in and looking for a way out.

"Now!" shouted Flynn. Devane swung the truck so that it blocked the road, and the RUC van screeched to a stop. The black sedan following the van came to a halt, and Collins with three of his men jumped out and ran toward the rear of the van with submachine guns.

Flynn and Maureen were out of the truck and moving toward the trapped van twenty-five yards up the road. The RUC guard and driver dropped below the windshield, and Flynn pointed his rifle. "Come out with your hands raised!" But the men didn't come out, and Flynn knew he couldn't shoot at the unarmored van filled with prisoners. He yelled to Collins, "I've got them covered! Go on!"

Collins stepped up to the van and struck the rear doors with his rifle butt. "Guards! You're surrounded! Open the doors and you won't be harmed!"

Maureen knelt in the road, her rifle across her knees. She felt her heart beating heavily in her chest. The idea of freeing her sister had become an obsession over the months and had, she realized, clouded her judgment. Suddenly all the things that were wrong with this operation crystallized in her mind —the van riding very low as though it were weighted, the lack of an escort, the predictable route. "Run! Collins—"

She saw Collins's surprised face under the glare of a streetlamp as the doors swung out from the RUC van.

Collins stood paralyzed in front of the open doors and stared at the British paratrooper berets over the top of a sandbag wall. The two barrels of the machine guns blazed in his face.

Flynn watched as his four men were cut down. One machine gun continued to pour bullets into the bodies while the other shifted its fire and riddled the sedan with incendiary rounds, hitting the gas tank and blowing it up. The street echoed with the explosion and the chattering sound of the machine guns, and the night was illuminated by the fire of the burning sedan.

Maureen grabbed Flynn's arm and pulled him toward their truck as pistol shots rang out from the doorway where the guard and driver had disappeared. She fired a full magazine into the doorway and the shooting stopped. The streets were alive with the sounds of whistles, shouting, and running men, and they could hear motor vehicles closing in.

Flynn turned and saw that the truck's windshield was shot out and the tires were flat. Fitzgerald and Devane were running up the street. Fitzgerald's body jerked, and he slid across the cobblestones. Devane kept running and disappeared into a bombed-out building.

Behind him Flynn could hear soldiers jumping from the RUC van and racing toward them. He pulled Maureen's arm, and they started to run as a light rain began to fall.

Donegall Street entered Waring Street from the north, and they turned into it, bullets kicking up chips of cobble behind them. Maureen slipped on the wet stone and fell, her rifle clattering on the pavement and skidding away in the darkness. Flynn lifted her, and they ran into a long alleyway, coming out into Hill Street.

A British Saracen armored car rolled into the street, its six huge rubber wheels skidding as it turned. The Saracen's spotlight came on and found them.

The armored car turned and came directly at them, its loudspeaker blaring into the rainy night. "HALT! HANDS ON YOUR HEADS!"

Behind him Flynn could hear the paratroopers coming into the long alley. He pulled the cardboard tube from his trench coat and knelt. He broke the seal and extended the telescoped tubes of the American-made M-72 antitank weapon, raised the plastic sights, and aimed at the approaching Saracen.

The Saracen's two machine guns blazed, pulverizing the brick walls around him, and he felt shards of brick bite into his chest. He put his finger on the percussion ignition switch and tried to steady his aim as he wondered if the thing would work. A disposable cardboard rocket launcher. Like a disposable diaper. Who but the Americans could make a throwaway bazooka? *Steady, Brian. Steady.*

The Saracen fired again, and he heard Maureen give a short yell behind him and felt her roll against his legs. "Bastards!" He squeezed the switch, and the 66mm HEAT rocket roared out of the tube and streaked down the dark, foggy street.

The turret of the Saracen erupted into orange flame, and the vehicle swerved wildly, smashing into a bombed-out travel agency. The surviving crew stumbled out holding their heads from the pain of the deafening rocket hit, and Flynn could see their clothes smoking. He turned and looked down at Maureen. She was moving, and he put his arm under her head. "Are you hit badly?"

She opened her eyes and began to sit up in his arms. "I don't know. Breast."

"Can you run?"

She nodded, and he helped her up. In the streets around them they could hear whistles, motors, shouts, tramping feet, and dogs. Flynn carefully wiped his fingerprints from the Thompson submachine gun and threw it into the alley.

They headed north toward the Catholic ghetto around New Lodge Road. As they entered the residential area they kept to the familiar maze of back alleys and yards between the row houses. They could hear a column of men double-timing on the street, rifle butts knocking on doors, windows opening, angry exchanges, babies wailing. The sounds of Belfast.

Maureen leaned against a brick garden wall. The running had made the blood flow faster through her wound, and she put her hand under her sweater. "Oh."

"Bad?"

"I don't know." She drew her hand away and looked at the blood, then said, "We were set up."

"Happens all the time," he said.

"Who?"

"Coogan, maybe. Could have been anyone, really." He was fairly certain he knew who it was. "I'm sorry about Sheila."

She shook her head. "I should have known they would use her as bait to get us. . . . You don't think *she* . . ." She put her face in her hands. "We lost some good people tonight."

He peered over the garden wall, then helped her over, and they ran through a block of adjoining yards. They entered a Protestant neighborhood, noticing the better built and maintained homes. Flynn knew this neighborhood from his youth, and he remembered the schoolboy pranks—breaking windows and running like hell—like now—through these alleys and yards. He remembered the smells of decent food, the clotheslines of white gleaming linen, the rose gardens, and the lawn furniture.

They headed west and approached the Catholic enclave of the Ardoyne. Ulster Defense League civilian patrols blocked the roads leading into the

Arodyne, and the Royal Ulster Constabulary and British soldiers were making house searches. Flynn crouched behind a row of trash bins and pulled Maureen down beside him. "We've gotten everyone out of their beds tonight."

Maureen Malone glanced at him and saw the half smile on his face. "You enjoy this."

"So do they. Breaks the monotony. They'll swap brave tales at the Orange lodges and in the barracks. Men love the hunt."

She flexed her arm. A stiffness and dull pain were spreading outward from her breast into her side and shoulder. "I don't think we have much chance of getting out of Belfast."

"All the hunters are here in the forest. The hunters' village is therefore deserted."

"Which means?"

"Into the heart of the Protestant neighborhood. The Shankill Road is not far."

They turned, headed south, and within five minutes they entered Shankill Road. They walked up the deserted road casually and stopped on a corner. It was not as foggy here, and the streetlights were working. Flynn couldn't see any blood on Maureen's black trench coat, but the wound had drained the color from her face. His own wound had stopped bleeding, and the dried blood stuck to his chest and sweater. "We'll take the next outbound bus that comes by, sleep in a barn, and head for Derry in the morning."

"All we need is an outbound bus, not to mention an appearance of respectability." She leaned back against the bus-stop sign. "When do we get our discharge, Brian?"

He looked at her in the dim light. "Don't forget the IRA motto," he said softly. "Once in, never out. Do you understand?"

She didn't answer.

A Red Bus appeared from the east. Flynn pulled Maureen close to him and supported her as they mounted the steps. "Clady," said Flynn, and he smiled at the driver as he paid the fare. "The lady's had rather too much to drink, I'm afraid."

The driver, a heavy-set man with a face that looked more Scottish than Irish, nodded uncaringly. "Do you have your curfew card?"

Flynn glanced down the length of the bus. Less than a dozen people, mostly workers in essential services, and they looked mostly Protestant—as far as he could tell—like the driver. Perhaps everyone looked like Prods tonight. No sign of police, though. "Yes. Here it is." He held his wallet up close to the driver's face.

The driver glanced at it and moved the door lever closed, then put the bus in gear.

Flynn helped Maureen toward the rear of the bus, and a few of the passengers gave them looks ranging from disapproval to curiosity. In London or Dublin they would be dismissed for what they claimed to be—drunks. In Belfast people's minds worked in different directions. He knew they would have to get off the bus soon. They sat in the back seat.

The bus rolled up Shankill Road, through the Protestant working-class neighborhood, then headed northwest into the mixed neighborhoods around Oldpark. Flynn turned to Maureen and spoke softly. "Feeling better?"

"Oh, quite. Let's do it again."

"Ah, Maureen . . ."

An old woman sitting alone in front of them turned around. "How's the lady? How are you, dear? Feelin' better, then?"

Maureen looked at her without answering. The citizens of Belfast were capable of anything from murder and treachery to Christian kindness.

The old woman showed a toothless smile and spoke quietly. "Between Squire's Hill and McIlwhan's Hill is a wee valley called the Flush. There's an abbey there—you know it—Whitehorn Abbey. The priest, Father Donnelly, will give you lodgings for the night."

Flynn fixed the woman with a cold stare. "What makes you think we need a place to stay? We're headed home."

The bus stopped, and the old woman stood without another word and trundled off to the front of the bus and stepped off.

The bus started again. Flynn was very uneasy now. "Next stop. Are you up to it?"

"I'm not up to one more second on this bus." She paused thoughtfully. "The old woman . . . ?"

Flynn shook his head.

"I think we can trust her."

"I don't trust anyone."

"What kind of country do we live in?"

He laughed derisively. "What a bloody stupid thing to say, Maureen. *We* are the ones who helped make it like it is."

She lowered her head. "You're right, of course . . . as usual."

"You must accept what you are. I accept it. I'm well adjusted."

She nodded. With that strange logic of his he had turned the world upside down. Brian was normal. She was not. "I'm going to Whitehorn Abbey."

He shrugged. "Better than a barn, I suppose. You'll be needing bandaging . . . but if the good rector there turns us in . . ."

She didn't answer and turned away from him.

He put his arm around her shoulders. "I *do* love you, you know."

She looked down and nodded.

The bus stopped again about a half-mile up the road, and Flynn and Maureen moved toward the door.

"This isn't Clady," said the driver.

"That's all right," answered Flynn. They stepped off the bus and into the road. Flynn took Maureen's arm. "That bastard will report us at the next stop." They crossed the road and headed north up a country lane lined with rowan trees. Flynn looked at his watch, then at the eastern sky. "Almost dawn. We have to be there before the farmers start running about—they're almost all Prods up here."

"I know that." Maureen breathed deeply as they walked in the light rain. The filthy air and ugliness of Belfast were far behind, and she felt better. Belfast—a blot of ash on the green loveliness of County Antrim, a blot of ash on the soul of Ireland. Sometimes she wished that the city would sink back into the bog it grew out of.

They passed hedgerows, well-tended fields, and pastures dotted with cattle and bales of fodder. An exhilarating sodden scent filled the air, and the first birds of morning began to sing.

"I'm not going back to Belfast."

He put his arm around her and touched her face with his hand. She was becoming feverish. "I understand. See how you feel in a week or two."

"I'm going to live in the south. A village."

"Good. And what will you do there? Tend pigs? Or do you have independent means, Maureen? Will you buy a country estate?"

"Do you remember the cottage overlooking the sea? You said we'd go there some day to live our lives in peace."

"Someday maybe we will."

"I'll go to Dublin, then. Find a job."

"Yes. Good jobs in Dublin. After a year they'll give you the tables by the window where the American tourists sit. Or the sewing machine by the window where you can get a bit of air and sun. That's the secret. By the window."

After a while she said, "Perhaps Killeen . . ."

"No. You can never go back to your own village. It's never the same, you know. Better to go to any other pig village."

"Let's go to America."

"No!" The loudness of his own voice surprised him. "No. I won't do what they all did." He thought of his family and friends, so many of them gone to America, Canada, or Australia. He had lost them as surely as he had lost his mother and father when he buried them. Everyone in Ireland, north and south, lost family, friends, neighbors, even husbands and wives and lovers, through emigration. Like some great plague sweeping the land, taking the firstborn, the brightest, and the most adventurous, leaving the old, the sick, the timid, the self-satisfied rich, the desperately poor. "This is my country. I won't leave here to become a laborer in America."

She nodded. Better to be a king of the dunghills of Belfast and Londonderry. "I may go alone."

"You probably should."

They walked quietly, their arms around each other's waists, both realizing that they had lost something more than a little blood this night.

3

The lane led into a small, treeless valley between two hills. In the distance they saw the abbey. The moonlight lit the white stone and gave it a spectral appearance in the ground mist.

They approached the abbey cautiously and stood under a newly budded sycamore tree. A small oblong cemetery, hedged with short green plants, spread out beside the abbey wall. Flynn pushed through the hedge and led Maureen into the cemetery.

The churchyard was unkempt, and vines grew up the gravestones. Whitehorn plants—which gave the abbey its name and which were omens of good luck or bad luck, depending on which superstition you believed—clogged the narrow path. A small side gate in a high stone wall led into the abbey's cloister. Flynn pushed it open and looked around the quiet court. "Sit on this bench. I'll find the brothers' dormitory."

She sat without answering and let her head fall to her chest. When she opened her eyes again, Flynn was standing over her with a priest.

"Maureen, this is Father Donnelly."

She focused on the elderly priest, a frail-looking man with a pale face. "Hello, Father."

He took her hand and with his other hand held her forearm in that way they had of claiming instant intimacy. He was the pastor; she was now one of his flock. Presto. Everyone's role had been carved in stone two millennia ago.

"Follow me," he said. "Hold my arm."

The three of them walked across the cloister and entered the arched door of a polygon-shaped building. Maureen recognized the traditional configuration of the chapter house, the meeting place of the monks. For a moment she thought she was going to face an assemblage, but she saw by the light of a table lamp that the room was empty.

Father Donnelly stopped abruptly and turned. "We have an infirmary, but I'm afraid I'll have to put you in the hole until the police and soldiers have come round looking for you."

Flynn didn't answer.

"You can trust me."

Flynn didn't trust anyone, but if he was betrayed, at least the War Council wouldn't think him too foolish for having trusted a priest. "Where's this hole, then? We don't have much time, I think."

The priest led them down a corridor, then opened the door at the end of the passage. Gray dawn came through stained glass, emitting a light that was more sensed than seen. A single votive candle burned in a red jar, and Flynn could see he was in the abbey's small church.

The priest lit a candle on a wall sconce and took it down. "Follow me up the altar. Be careful."

Flynn helped Maureen up to the raised altar sanctuary and watched the priest fumble with some keys and then disappear behind the reredos wall in back of the altar.

Flynn glanced around the church but neither saw nor heard anything in the shadows to signal danger. He noticed that the oppressive smell of incense and tallow was missing, and the church smelled like the outside air. The priest had told him that the abbey was deserted. Father Donnelly was apparently not the abbot but served in something like a caretaker capacity, though he didn't seem the type of priest that a bishop would exile to such a place, thought Flynn. Nor did he seem the type to hide members of the provisional IRA just to get a thrill out of it.

The priest reappeared holding his candle in the darkness. "Come this way." He led them to a half-open door made of scrolled wrought iron in the rear of the altar. "This is the place we use." He looked at the two fugitives to see why they weren't moving toward it. "The crypt," he added as if to explain.

"I know what it is. Everyone knows there's a crypt beneath an altar's sanctuary."

"Yes," said Father Donnelly. "First place they always look. Come along."

Flynn peered down the stone steps. A candle in an amber glass, apparently always kept burning, illuminated a wall and floor of white limestone. "Why is it I've not heard of this abbey as a place of safety before tonight?"

The priest spoke softly, evenly. "You had no need of it before tonight."

Typical priests' talk, thought Flynn. He turned to Maureen. She looked down the stairway, then at the priest. Her instincts, too, rebelled against entering the crypt. Yet her conditioned response was to do what the priest urged. She stepped toward the stairway and descended. Flynn glanced at the priest, then stepped through the doorway.

Father Donnelly led them along the limestone wall past the tombs of the former abbots of Whitehorn Abbey. He stopped and opened the bronze door of one of the tombs, marked *Fr. Seamus Cahill,* held up his candle, and entered the tomb. A wooden casket lay on a stone plinth in the middle of the chamber.

Father Donnelly passed the candle to Flynn and raised the lid of the casket. Inside was a body wrapped in heavy winding sheets, the linen covered with fuzz of green mold. "Sticks and straw," he said. He reached into the casket and released a concealed catch, and the coffin bottom swung downward with the bogus mummy still affixed to it. "Yes, yes. Melodramatic for our age, but when it was conceived, it was necessary and quite common. Go on. Climb in. There's a staircase. See it? Follow the passageway at the bottom until you enter a chamber. Use your candle to light the way. There are more candles in the chamber."

Flynn mounted the plinth and swung his legs over the side. His feet found the top step, and he stood in the casket. A dank, almost putrid smell rose out of the dark hole. He stared at Father Donnelly questioningly.

"It's the entranceway to hell, my boy. Don't fear. You'll find friends down there."

Flynn tried to smile at the joke, but an involuntary shudder ran up his spine. "I suppose we should be thanking you."

"I suppose you should. But just hurry on now. I want to be in the refectory having breakfast when they arrive."

Flynn took a few steps down as Father Donnelly helped Maureen up the plinth and over the side of the casket onto the first step. Flynn held her arm with one hand and held the candle high with the other. She avoided the wrapped figure as she descended.

Father Donnelly pulled the casket floor up, then shut the lid and left the tomb, closing the bronze door behind him.

Flynn held the candle out and followed the narrow, shoulder-width passageway for a distance of about fifty feet, grasping Maureen's hand behind him. He entered an open area and followed the wall to his right. He found candles in sconces spaced irregularly around the unhewn and unmortared stone walls and lit them, completing the circuit around the room. The air in the chamber was chilly, and he saw his own breath. He looked around slowly at the half-lit room. "Odd sort of place."

Maureen wrapped herself in a gray blanket she had found and sat on a footstool. "What did you expect, Brian—a game room?"

"Ah, I see you're feeling better."

"I'm feeling terrible."

He walked around the perimeter of the six-sided room. On one wall was a large Celtic cross, and under the cross was a small chest on a wooden stand. Flynn placed his hand on the dusty lid but didn't open it. He turned back to Maureen. "You trust him?"

"He's a priest."

"Priests are no different from other men."

"Of course they are."

"We'll see." He now felt the fatigue that he had fought off for so long, and he sank down to the damp floor. He sat against the wall next to the chest, facing the stairway. "If we awake in Long Kesh . . ."

"My fault. All right? Go to sleep."

Flynn drifted off into fitful periods of sleep, opening his eyes once to see Maureen, wrapped in the blanket, lying on the floor beside him. He awoke again when he heard the casket bottom swing down and strike the wall of the passageway. He jumped up and stood at the entrance to the passage. In a shaft of light from the crypt he could see the coffin floor hanging, its grotesque mockery of a dead man stuck to it like a lizard on a wall.

The torso of a man appeared: black shoes, black trousers, the Roman collar, then the face of Father Donnelly. He held a tea tray high above his head as he made his way. "They were here and they're gone."

Flynn moved down the passageway and took the tray that the priest passed to him. Father Donnelly closed the coffin, and they walked into the chamber, Flynn placing the tray on a small wooden table.

Father Donnelly looked around the chamber the way a host examines a guest room. He stared at Maureen's sleeping figure, then turned to Flynn. "So, you blew up a sixer, did you? Rather daring, I'd say."

Flynn didn't answer.

"Well, anyway, they traced you as far as the McGloughlin farm up the lane. Good, loyal Ulstermen, the McGloughlins. Solid Presbyterians. Family came over from Scotland with Cromwell's army. Another three hundred years and they'll think this is their country. How's the lady?"

Flynn knelt beside her. "Sleeping." He touched her forehead. "Feverish."

"There's some penicillin tablets and an army aid kit along with the tea and bacon." He took a small bottle from his pocket. "And some Dunphy's, if you've the need of it."

Flynn took the bottle. "Rarely have I needed it more." He uncorked it and took a long drink.

Father Donnelly found two footstools, pulled them to the table, and sat. "Let her sleep. I'll take tea with you."

Flynn sat and watched the priest go through the fussy motions of a man who took food and drink seriously. "Who was here?" asked Flynn.

"The Brits and the RUCs. As usual the RUCs wanted to tear the place apart, but a British army officer restrained them. A Major Martin. Know him, do you? Yes, he's quite infamous. Anyway, they all played their roles wonderfully."

"I'm glad everyone had a good time. I'm only sorry I had to waken everyone so early."

"You know, lad, it's as if the participants in this war secretly appreciate each other. The excitement is not entirely unwelcome."

Flynn looked at the priest. Here was one man, at least, who didn't lie about it. "Can we get out of here?" he asked as he sipped the hot tea.

"You'll have to wait until they clear out of the hedgerows. Binoculars, you understand. Two days at least. Leave at night, of course."

"Doesn't everyone travel at night?"

The priest laughed. "Ah, Mister . . ."

"Cocharan."

"Whatever. When will this all stop?"

"When the British leave and the northern six counties are reunited with the southern twenty-six."

The priest put down his teacup. "Not true, my boy. The real desire of the IRA, the most secret dark desire of the Catholics, no matter what we all say about living in peace after the reunification, is to deport all the Protestants back to England, Scotland, and Wales. Send the McGloughlins back to a country they haven't seen in three hundred years."

"That's bloody rubbish."

The priest shrugged. "I don't care personally, you understand. I only want you to examine your own heart."

Flynn leaned across the table. "Why are you in this? The Catholic clergy has never supported any Irish rebellion against the British. So why are you risking internment?"

Father Donnelly stared down into his cup, then looked up at Flynn. "I don't involve myself with any of the things that mean so much to you. I don't care what your policy is or even what Church policy is. My only role here is to provide sanctuary. A haven in a country gone mad."

"To anyone? A murderer like me? Protestants? British troops?"

"Anyone who asks." He stood. "In this abbey was once an order of fifty monks. Now, only me." He paused and looked down at Flynn. "This abbey has a limited future, Mr. Cocharan, but a very rich past."

"Like you and me, Father. But I hope not like our country."

The priest seemed not to hear him and went on. "This chamber was once the storage cellar of an ancient Celtic Bruidean house. You know the term?"

"Yes, I think so."

"The House of the Hostages, it was called. A six-sided structure where six roads met. Coincidentally—or maybe not so—chapter houses are traditionally polygons, and the chapter house we passed through is built on these foundations." He gestured above. "Here in the Bruidean a traveler or a fugitive could shelter from the cold, dark road, protected by tradition and the king's law. The early Celts were not complete barbarians, after all." He looked at Flynn. "So you see, you've come to the right place."

"And you've taken it upon yourself to combine a bit of paganism with Christian charity."

The priest smiled. "Irish Catholicism has always been a blend of paganism and Christianity. The early Christians after Patrick specifically built their churches on Druid holy spots such as this. I suspect early Christians burnt this Bruidean down, then constructed a crude church on its foundations. You can still see the charred foundation stones. Then the Vikings destroyed the original monastery, and the next one was destroyed by the English army when Cromwell passed through. This is the last abbey to be built here. The Protestant plantations took all the good land in Ireland, but the Catholics held on to most of the good church sites."

"What more could you want?"

The priest regarded Flynn for a long time, then spoke softly. "You'd better wake the lady before the tea gets cold."

Flynn rose and crossed the floor to where Maureen was lying, knelt beside her, and shook her. "Tea."

She opened her eyes.

He said, "Hold on to me." He stood her up and helped her to his stool. "How are you feeling?"

She looked around the candlelit room. "Better."

Flynn poured the tea, and Father Donnelly extracted a pill from a vial. "Take this."

She swallowed the pill and took some tea. "Did the British come?"

The priest felt her forehead. "Came and went. In a few days you'll be on your way."

She looked at him. He was so accepting of them, what they were and what they had done. She felt disreputable. Whenever her life was revealed to people not in the movement, she felt not proud but ashamed, and that was not the way it was supposed to be. "Can you help us?"

"I am, dear. Drink your tea."

"No, I mean can you help us . . . get out of this?"

The priest nodded. "I see. Yes, I can help you if you want. It's rather easy, you know."

Flynn seemed impatient. "Father, save souls on your own time. I need some sleep. Thank you for everything."

"You're quite welcome."

"Could you do one more favor for us? I'll give you a number to call. Tell the person who answers where we are. Tell them that Brian and Maureen need help. Let me know what they say."

"I'll use a phone in the village in case this one is tapped."

Flynn smiled appreciatively. "If I've seemed a bit abrupt—"

"Don't let it trouble you." He repeated the number Flynn gave him, turned, and disappeared into the narrow passageway.

Flynn took the bottle of Dunphy's from the table and poured some in Maureen's teacup. She shook her head impatiently. "Not with the penicillin, Brian."

He looked at her. "We're not getting along, are we?"

"I'm afraid not."

He nodded. "Well, let's have a look at the nick, then."

She stood slowly, pulled her wet sweater over her head, and dropped it on the stool. Flynn saw that she was in pain as she unhooked her bloodied bra, but he didn't offer to help. He took a candle from the table and examined the wound, a wide gash running along the outside of her right breast and passing under her armpit. An inch to the left and she would have been dead. "Just a graze, really."

"I know."

"The important thing is that you won't need a doctor." The wound was bleeding again from the movement of her undressing, and he could see that it had bled and coagulated several times already. "It's going to hurt a bit." He dressed the wound while she stood with her arm raised. "Lie down and wrap yourself in the blanket."

She lay down and stared at him in the flickering light. She was cold, wet, and feverish. Her whole side ached, and the food had made her nauseous, though she was very thirsty. "We live like animals, licking our wounds, cut off from humanity . . . from . . ."

"God? But don't settle for this second-class Popish nonsense, Maureen. Join the Church of England—then you'll have your God, your respectability, and you can sit over tea with the Ladies' Auxiliary and complain about the IRA's latest outrage."

She closed her eyes, and tears ran down her cheeks.

When he saw that she was sleeping, he took the cup of Dunphy's and drained it, then began walking around the cellar. He examined the walls again and saw the scorch marks. How many times had this place been put to the torch? What made this location holy to both the Druids and the Christians? What spirit lived here in the heart of the earth? He carried a candle to the wooden chest and studied it. After some time he reached out and lifted the lid.

Inside he saw fragments of limestone that bore ancient Celtic inscriptions and a few unidentifiable pieces of metal, bronze, rusted iron. He pushed some of the objects aside, revealing a huge oval ring crusted with verdigris. He slipped it on his ring finger. It was large, but it stayed on his finger well enough. He clenched his fist and studied the ring. It bore a crest, and through the tarnish he could make out Celtic writing around a crudely molded bearded face.

He rubbed his fingers over the ring and wiped away some of the encrustation. The crude face stared back at him like a child's rendering of a particularly fearsome man. He felt dizzy and sensed his legs buckling under him. He was aware of hitting the floor. Then he blacked out.

4

Brian Flynn woke to find a face staring down at him.

"It's noon," said Father Donnelly. "I've brought you some lunch."

Flynn focused on the ruddy face of the old man. He saw that the priest was staring at the ring on his finger. He got to his feet and looked around. Maureen was sitting at the table wearing a new pullover and eating from a steaming bowl. The priest had been there for some time, and that annoyed him. He walked over and sat opposite her. "Feeling better?"

"Much."

Father Donnelly pulled up a stool. "Would you mind if I joined you?"

"It's your food and your table," said Flynn.

The priest smiled. "One never gets used to dining alone."

Flynn took a spoon. "Why don't they send you a . . . monk or something?" He took a spoonful of stew.

"There's a lay brother who does the caretaking, but he's on leave." He leaned forward. "I see you've found the treasure of Whitehorn Abbey."

Flynn continued to eat as he spoke. "Sorry. Couldn't resist the temptation."

"That's all right."

Maureen looked up. "What are we talking about, please?"

Flynn slipped off the ring, passed it to her, and motioned toward the opened chest.

She examined the ring, then passed it to Father Donnelly. "It's an extraordinary ring."

Father Donnelly toyed with the ring. "Extraordinarily large, in any case."

Flynn poured a bottle of Guinness into a glass. "Where did it come from?"

The priest shook his head. "The last abbot said it was always here with the other things in that box. It may have been excavated here during one of the rebuildings. Perhaps under this floor."

Flynn stared at the ring in the priest's hand. "Pre-Christian?"

"Yes. Pagan. If you want a romantic story, it is said that it was a warrior king's ring. More specifically, Fenian. It's certainly a man's ring, and no average man at that."

Flynn nodded. "Why not MacCumail's ring? Or Dermot's?"

"Why not, indeed? Who would dare wear a ring larger than this?"

Flynn smiled. "You've a pagan streak in you, Father. Didn't Saint Patrick consign the departed Fenians to hell? What was their crime, then, that they must spend eternity in hell?"

"No crime. Just born at the wrong time." He smiled. "Like many of us."

"Right." Flynn liked a priest who could laugh at his dogma.

The priest leaned across the table. "When Oisin, son of Finn MacCumail, returned from the Land of Perpetual Youth, he found Ireland Christian. The brave warrior was confused, sad. Oisin rejected the ordered Christian society and longed with nostalgia for the untamed lustiness of old Erin. If he or his father, Finn MacCumail, came into Ulster today, they would be overjoyed at this Christian warfare. And they would certainly recognize the new pagans among us."

"Meaning me?"

Maureen poured tea into three mugs. "He's talking to you, Brian, isn't he?"

Father Donnelly rose. "I'll take my tea in the refectory."

Maureen Malone rose, too. "Don't leave."

"I really must." His demeanor had changed from paternal to businesslike. He looked at Flynn. "Your friends want you to stay here for two more days. They'll contact me and let me know the plan. Any reply?"

Flynn shook his head. "No."

Maureen looked at Flynn, then at Father Donnelly. "I have a reply. Tell them I want safe passage to Dublin, a hundred pounds, and a work visa for the south."

The priest nodded. He turned to go, hesitated, and came back. He placed the ring on the small table. "Mister . . ."

"Cocharan."

"Yes. Take this ring."

"Why?"

"Because you want it and I don't."

"It's a valuable relic."

"So are you."

"I won't ask you what you mean by that." He stood and looked hard at the priest, then took the ring from the table and placed it on his finger. Several new thoughts were forming in his mind, but he had no one to share them with. "Thank you." He looked at the ring. "Any curse attached to it that I should know about?"

The priest replied, "You should assume there is."

He looked at the two people standing before him. "I can't approve of the way you live your lives, but I find it painful to see a love dying. Any love, anywhere in this unloving country." He turned and made his way out of the cellar.

Flynn knew that Maureen had been talking to the priest while he'd been sleeping. He was having difficulty dealing with all that had happened in so short a time. Belfast, the old lady and the abbey, a priest who used pagan legends to make Christian statements, Maureen's aloofness. He was clearly not in control. He stood motionless for a time, then turned toward her. "I'd like you to reconsider about Dublin."

She looked down and shook her head.

"I'm asking you to stay . . . not only because I . . . What I mean is . . ."

"I know what you mean. Once in, never out. I'm not afraid of them."

"You should be. I can't protect you—"

"I'm not asking you to." She looked at him. "We're both better off."

"You're probably right. You understand these things better than I."

She knew that tone of voice. Remote. Sarcastic. The air in the cellar felt dense, oppressive. Church or not, the place made her uneasy. She thought about the coffin through which they had entered this hole, and that had been a little like dying. When she came out again she wanted to leave behind every memory of the place, every thought of the war. She looked at the ring on his hand. "Leave the damned thing here."

"I'm not only taking the ring, Maureen, I'm taking the name as well."

"What name?"

"I need a new code name . . . Finn MacCumail."

She almost laughed. "In any other country they'd treat you for megalomania. In Northern Ireland they'll find you quite normal, Brian."

"But I am normal."

"Not bloody likely."

He looked at her in the dim candlelight. He thought he had never seen anyone so lovely, and he realized that he hadn't thought of her in that way for a long time. Now she was flushed with the expectation of new beginnings, not to mention the flush of fever that reddened her cheeks and caused her eyes to burn bright. "You may well be right."

"About your being a lunatic?"

"Well, that too." He smiled at the small shared joke. "But I meant about you going off to Dublin."

"I'm sorry."

"Don't be. I'm only sorry I can't go with you."

"Perhaps, Brian, some day you'll get tired of this."

"Not bloody likely."

"No."

"Well, I'll miss you."

"I hope so," she said.

He stayed silent for a moment, then said, "I still don't know if we can trust him."

"He's a saint, for God's sake, Brian. Take him for what he appears to be."

"He appears different to me. Something odd about him. Anyway, we're not home free yet."

"I know."

"If anything happens and I don't have time to make a proper parting . . . well . . ."

"You've had time enough over the years to say what you felt. Time wasn't the problem. Tea?"

"Yes, please."

They sat silently, drinking their tea.

Flynn put down his cup. "Your sister . . ."

She shook her head. "Sheila is beyond our help."

"Maybe not."

"I don't want to see anyone else killed. . . ."

"There are other ways. . . ." He lapsed into silence, then said, "The keys to the jails of Ulster are in America."

A month later, when spring was firmly planted in the countryside and three weeks after Maureen Malone left for Dublin, Brian Flynn hired a car and went out to the abbey to thank Father Donnelly and to ask him about possible help in the future.

He found all the gates to the abbey locked, and no one answered any of the pull bells. A farmer riding by on a cart told him that the abbey was looked after by villagers employed by the diocese. And that no one had lived there for many years.

BOOK II

New York

English, Scotchmen, Jews, do well in Ireland—Irishmen, never; even the patriot has to leave Ireland to get a hearing.

George Moore,
Ave (Overture)

5

B rian Flynn, dressed in the black clothing and white collar of a Roman Catholic priest, stood in the dim morning light near the south transept entrance to St. Patrick's Cathedral. He carried a small parcel wrapped in white paper decorated with green shamrocks. A few older women and two men stood at the base of the steps near him, huddled against the cold.

One of the two large transept doors swung open, and the head of a sexton appeared and nodded. The small crowd mounted the steps and passed through the side vestibule, then entered the Cathedral. Brian Flynn followed.

Inside the Cathedral, Flynn knelt at the communion rail. The raised marble area, the altar sanctuary, was decked with fields of green carnations, and he studied the festive decorations. It had been four years since he had left Whitehorn Abbey; four years since he had seen her. Today he would see her again, for the last time.

He rose and turned toward the front of the Cathedral, slipping his right hand into his black overcoat pocket to feel the cold steel of the automatic pistol.

Father Timothy Murphy left his room in the rectory and made his way to the underground passage between the rectory and the Cathedral. At the end of a corridor he came to a large paneled door and opened it, then stepped into a dark room and turned on a wall switch. Soft lights glowed in the marble-vaulted sacristy.

He walked to the priests' chapel in the rear of the sacristy and knelt, directing his prayers to St. Patrick, whose feast day it was, and asking as he did every year for peace in Northern Ireland, his native land. He asked also for good weather for the parade and a peaceful and relatively sober day in his adopted city.

He rose, crossed the sacristy, mounted a short flight of marble stairs, and unlocked a pair of brass gates. He rolled the gates back on their tracks into the marble archway, then continued up the steps.

On the first landing he stopped and peered through a barred door into the crypt that contained the remains of the past archbishops of New York. A soft yellow light burned somewhere in the heart of the crypt.

The staircase split in two directions on the landing, and he took the flight to the left. He came around the altar and walked toward the high pulpit. He mounted the curving stone steps and stood beneath the bronze canopy high above the pews.

The Cathedral spread out before him, covering an entire city block. The lighter spots of the towering stained-glass windows—the flesh tones of faces and hands—picked up the early morning light, changing the focus of the scenes from the Scriptures depicted on them in a way that their artisans never intended. Disembodied heads and limbs stared out of the cobalt blues and fiery reds, looking more damned than saved.

Father Murphy turned away from the windows and peered down at the worshipers. A dozen people were widely scattered over the length and breadth of this massive-columned house, none of them with any companion but God. He lifted his eyes toward the great choir loft over the front portals. The large pipe organ rose up like a miniature cathedral, its thousands of brass pipes soaring like spires against the diffused light of the massive rose window above them.

From his pocket Father Murphy drew his typed sermon and laid it over the open pages of the lectionary, then adjusted the microphone upward. He checked his watch. Six-forty. Twenty minutes until Mass.

Satisfied with these small details, he looked up again and noticed a tall priest standing beside the altar of St. Brigid. He didn't recognize the man, but St. Patrick's would be filled with visiting priests on this day; in fact, the priest appeared to be sightseeing, taking in the wide expanses of the Cathedral. A country bumpkin, thought Murphy, just as he himself had been years before. Yet there was something self-assured about the man's bearing. He seemed to be not awed but critical, as though he were considering buying the place but was unhappy with some of the appointments.

Father Murphy came down from the pulpit. He studied the bouquets of green-dyed carnations, then snapped one off and stuck it in the lapel of his coat as he descended the steps of the altar sanctuary and walked down the center aisle. In the large vestibule under the bell tower he came within a dozen feet of the tall priest, that area of space within which greeting had to be made. He paused, then smiled, "Good morning, Father."

The tall priest stared. "Morning."

Father Murphy considered extending his hand, but the other priest had his right hand deep in his overcoat pocket and held a gift-wrapped box under his other arm. Murphy passed by the priest and crossed the cold stone vestibule to the front door. He drew the floor bolt, then pushed the door open and stepped out to the front steps of the Cathedral. His clear blue eyes drifted across Fifth Avenue and upward to the top of the International Building in Rockefeller Center. A glint of sunlight reflected from the bronze work of the building. It was going to be a sunny day for the Irish, a great day for the Irish.

He looked to his right. Approaching from the north was a vehicle with flashing yellow lights. Hissing noises emanated from it as it drew opposite the Cathedral. Murphy saw the stream of Kelly-green paint coming from the rear of the machine, drawing a line down the middle of Fifth Avenue and covering the white traffic line.

His eyes focused on the huge bronze statue of Atlas—facing him from across the street in front of the International Building—holding up the world in a classic pose, heroic but pagan. He had never liked that statue—it mocked his church. Rockefeller Center itself mocked his church, its gray masonry buildings a colossal monument to the ego of one man, soaring above the marble spires of the Cathedral.

He stared at the naked physique of the god opposite him and was reminded of the tall priest in the Cathedral.

Brian Flynn moved to an arched oak door in a wall of the vestibule below the bell tower, opened it, and stepped into a small elevator. He pushed the only button on the panel, and the elevator rose. Flynn stepped out into the choir practice room, walked through it into the choir loft, and stood at the parapet rail.

Flynn looked beyond the sea of wooden pews toward the raised altar, its bronze work bathed in soft illumination and its marble gleaming from unseen light sources. White statuary reflected the ambient lighting and seemed—as it was supposed to seem—ethereal and animated. The statue of St. Patrick opposite the pulpit appeared to be looking up at him. Behind the carnation-decked altar was the rounded apse that held the Lady Chapel, the tall, slender, stained-glass windows alight with the rising sun. The fifteen altars that stood on the periphery of the Cathedral were aglow with votive candles.

If the intention was to awe, to mystify, to diminish man in the face of God, then this Gothic structure accomplished its purpose very well. What masters of suspense and mystery these Catholics were, Flynn thought, what incredible manipulators of physical reality and, hence, inner reality. Bread and wine into flesh and blood, indeed. Yet inside this Cathedral the years of childhood programming had their effect, and his thinking was involved with too many forgotten emotions. Outside the Church was a world that didn't diminish him or play tricks with his mind and eyes. He gave the Cathedral a last look, then made his way to a small door off the choir loft and opened it.

A rush of cold air hit him, and he shivered as he stepped into the bell tower. When his eyes had adjusted to the darkness he moved forward and found a spiral staircase with handrails in the center of the tower and began to climb, steadying himself with one hand and holding the parcel with the other.

The tower was dark, but translucent glass let in a grayish light. Flynn could see his breath as he climbed. The stairs gave way to ladders, and the ladders became shakier at each succeeding landing. He wondered if anyone ever came up here; he couldn't imagine why they would. He stopped to catch his breath on a landing below what he believed to be the first bell room.

He saw some movement to his right and drew his pistol. He walked in a crouch toward the movement, but it was only the straps of the bells hanging down the wall in a sinister fashion, swaying in the drafts as they passed through a hole in the landing.

He looked around. The place was eerie. The diffused light added to the effect, and the sounds of the surrounding city were changed into odd noises that seemed to come from the tower itself. The draft was eerie also because he couldn't quite tell from which direction it came. It seemed to come from some hidden respiratory organ belonging to the Cathedral itself—in a way, the secret breath of St. Patrick's—or St. Patrick himself. Yet he felt somehow that this breath was not sanctified and that there was an evil about the place. He had felt that in Whitehorn Abbey, and afterward realized that what the faithful took to be the presence of the Holy Spirit was something quite different for the faithless.

He tried to light a cigarette, but the matches would not stay lit. The brief light illuminated the small, polygon-shaped chamber of the tower, and again his thoughts were drawn back to the subbasement of Whitehorn's chapter house. He rubbed his hand over the large ring that he still wore. He thought of Maureen and pictured her as he had last seen her in that basement: frightened, sick, saddened at their parting. He wondered what her first words to him would be after these four years.

He looked at his watch. In ten minutes the bells would ring the Angelus, and if he were near them he would be deafened. He mounted the ladder and ascended. He had an impulse to shout a blasphemy up into the dark tower to rouse those spirits in their aerie, to tell them that Finn MacCumail was approaching and to make way.

The ladder reached into the first bell room, which held three of the Cathedral's nineteen cast-bronze bells hanging from a crossbeam. Flynn checked his watch again. Eight minutes to seven. Setting a flashlight on a crossbeam, he worked swiftly to unwrap the package, exposing a black metal box. He found the electrical wire that led to the utility work light fixed on the beam and cut the wire, connecting each end to terminals in the metal box. He set an electrical timer on the box to 5:00 P.M., then pulled the chain of the utility light. The bell room was partially illuminated, revealing the accumulated dust and cobwebs of a century, and the timer began ticking loudly in the still room.

He touched one of the bronze bells and felt its coldness, thinking that today might be the last day New York would hear it.

6

Maureen Malone stood naked in front of the full-length door mirror, cold water clinging to her face and shoulders and glistening in the harsh bathroom light. Her hand moved to her right breast, and she felt the cold, jagged flesh along the side of it. She stared at the purple gash. God, the damage a tiny bullet could do. She had once considered plastic surgery, but the wound went down into her soul where no surgeon's hands could reach it.

She took a hotel bath towel, wrapped herself in it, and stepped into the bedroom. She walked slowly across the thick carpet, parted the heavy drapery, and looked out into the city from the forty-second floor of the Waldorf's north tower.

She tried to focus on the lights a few at a time. Strings of highway and bridge lamps cut across the waterways and flatlands around the island, and the island itself was jammed with incredibly huge buildings. She scanned the buildings closest to her and saw the Cathedral laid out in the shape of a cross, bathed in a cold blue light. The apse faced her, and the entrance was on a wide avenue. It's twin spires rose gracefully amid the rectangular hulks around it, and she could see traffic moving on many of the city's streets, an incredible thing at that hour, she thought.

The lights of the city blurred in her eyes, and her mind wandered back to the dinner in the Empire Room downstairs where she had been a speaker. What had she told those ladies and gentlemen of Amnesty International? That she was there for the living and dead of Ireland. *What was her mission?* they asked. To convince the British to release the men and women interned in Northern Ireland under the Special Powers Act. After that, and only after that, would her former comrades-in-arms talk peace.

The newspapers had said that her appearance on the steps of St. Patrick's Cathedral on the saint's feast day, with Sir Harold Baxter, the British Consul General in New York, would be a historical precedent. Never had a Cardinal allowed anyone remotely political to stand with him on the steps on this day. The political types mounted the steps, she was told, saluted the Prince of the Church and his entourage, then rejoined the parade and marched to the reviewing stands fourteen blocks farther north. But Maureen Malone, ex-IRA terrorist, had been invited. Hadn't Jesus forgiven Mary Magdalene? the Cardinal had asked her. Wasn't this what Christ's message was all about? She didn't know if she liked the comparison with that famous whore, but the Cardinal had seemed so sincere.

Sir Harold Baxter, she knew, was as uncomfortable with the arrangement as she was, but he could not have accepted without the approval of his Foreign Office, so that at least was a breakthrough. Peace initiatives, unlike war initiatives, always had such small, meek, tentative beginnings.

She felt a sudden chill by the window and shivered. Her eyes went back to the blue-lit Cathedral. She tried to envision how the day would end but couldn't, and this frightened her. Another chill, a different kind, ran down her spine. *Once in, never out.*

Somehow she knew Brian Flynn was close, and she knew he would not let her get away with this.

Terri O'Neal woke to the sound of early morning traffic coming through the second-story window. She sat up slowly in the bed. A streetlight outside the window partially illuminated the room. The man next to her—Dan, yes, Dan—turned his head and stared at her. She could see that his eyes were clear, unclouded by either drink or sleep. She suspected that he had been awake for some time, and this made her uneasy, but she didn't know why. "Maybe I should get going. Work today."

He sat up and held her arm. "No work today. You're going to the parade. Remember?"

His voice, a light brogue, was not husky with sleep. He *had* been awake—and how did he know she wasn't going to work today? She never told her pickups anything more than they had to know—in case it didn't go well. "Are *you* going to work today?"

"I am at work." He laughed as he took a cigarette from the night table.

She forced a smile, swung her legs out of bed, and stood. She felt his eyes taking in her figure as she walked to the big bay window and knelt in the window bench facing the street. She looked out. A lovely street. Sixty-something—off Fifth, a street of brownstone and granite town houses.

She looked westward. A big police van was parked on the corner of Fifth, and across the street from it was a television truck. On the far side of the Avenue were the reviewing stands that had been assembled in front of the park.

She looked directly below her. A long line of police scooters were angle-parked on the street. Dozens of helmeted police officers were milling about, blowing into their hands or drinking coffee. Their proximity made her feel better.

She turned and sat facing the bed. She noticed that he had put on his jeans, but he was still sitting on the bed. She became apprehensive again, and her voice came out low and tremulous. "Who—who are you?"

He got off the bed and walked to her. "I'm your lover of last evening, Mrs. O'Neal." He stood directly in front of her, and she had to crane her neck to look up into his face.

Terri O'Neal was frightened. This man did not act, look, or talk like a crazy—yet he was going to do something to her that she was not going to like. She was sure of that. She pulled free of his stare and turned her eyes slightly toward the side panel of the bay window. A loud scream would do it. She hoped to God it would do it.

Dan Morgan didn't follow her eyes, but he knew what was out there. "Not a peep, lass. Not a peep . . ."

Reluctantly she swung her head back toward him and found herself staring into a big, black silencer at the end of a bigger black pistol. Her mouth went dry.

". . . or I'll put a bullet through your pretty, dimpled kneecap."

It was several seconds before she could form a thought or a word, then she said softly, "What do you want?"

"Just your company for a while."

"Company?" Her brain wasn't taking in any of this.

"You're kidnapped, darlin'. Kidnapped."

7

Detective Lieutenant Patrick Burke sat huddled against the cold dawn on the top riser of the reviewing stands and looked down into the Avenue. The freshly painted green line glistened in the thin sunlight, and policemen stepped carefully over it as they crossed the street.

A bomb squad ambled through the risers picking up paper bags and bottles, none of them containing anything more lethal than the dregs of cheap wine. A bum lay covered with newspaper on the riser below him, undisturbed by the indulgent cops.

Burke looked east into Sixty-fourth Street. Police motor scooters lined the street, and a WPIX television van had taken up position on the north corner. A police mobile headquarters van was parked on the south corner, and two policemen were connecting the van's cables to an access opening at the base of a streetlamp.

Burke lit a cigarette. In twenty years of intelligence work this scene had not changed nearly so much as everything else in his life had. He thought that even the bum might be the same.

Burke glanced at his watch—five minutes to kill. He watched the uniformed patrolmen queue up to a PBA canteen truck for coffee. Someone at the back of the line was fortifying the cups of coffee with a dark liquid poured from a Coke bottle, like a priest, thought Burke, sprinkling holy water on the passing troops.

It would be a long, hard day for the uniformed cops. Over a million people, Irish and otherwise, would crowd the sidewalks of Fifth Avenue and the bars and restaurants of midtown Manhattan. Surprisingly, for all the sound and fury of the day there had never been a serious political incident in over two centuries of St. Patrick's days in New York. But Burke felt every year that it would happen, that it must happen eventually.

The presence of the Malone woman in New York disturbed him. He had interviewed her briefly in the Empire Room of the Waldorf the previous evening. She seemed likable enough, pretty, too, and undaunted by his suggestion that someone might decide to murder her. She had probably become accustomed to threats on her life, he thought.

The Irish were Burke's specialty, and the Irish, he believed, were potentially the most dangerous group of all. But if they struck, would they pick *this* day? This day *belonged* to the Irish. The parade was their trooping of the colors, their showing of the green, necessary in those days when they were regarded as America's first unwanted foreigners. He remembered a joke his grandfather used to tell, popular at the turn of the century: What is St. Patrick's Day? It's the day the Protestants and Jews look out the windows of their town houses on Fifth Avenue to watch their employees march by.

What had begun as America's first civil rights demonstration was now a reminder to the city—to the nation—that the Irish still existed as a force. This was the day that the Irish got to fuck up New York City, the day they turned Manhattan on its ear.

Burke stood, stretched his big frame, then bounded down the rows of benches and jumped onto the sidewalk. He walked behind the stands until he came to an opening in the low stone wall that bordered Central Park, where he descended a flight of stone steps. In front of him rose the huge, castlelike Arsenal—actually a park administration building—flying, along with the American flag, the green, white, and orange tricolor of the Republic of Ireland. He circled around it to his right and came to a closed set of towering wrought-iron gates. Without much enthusiasm he climbed to the top of the gates, then dropped down into the zoo.

The zoo was deserted and much darker than the Avenue. Ornate lamps cast a weak light over the paths and brick buildings. He proceeded slowly down the straight lane, staying in the shadows. As he walked he unholstered his service revolver and slipped it into his coat pocket, more as a precaution against muggers than professional assassins.

The shadows of bare sycamores lay over the lane, and the smell of damp straw and animals hung oppressively in the cold, misty air. To his left seals were barking in their pool, and birds, captive and free, chirped and squawked in a blend of familiar and exotic sounds.

Burke passed the brick arches that supported the Delacorte clock and peered into the shadows of the colonnade, but no one was there. He checked his watch against the clock. Ferguson was late or dead. He leaned against one of the clock arches and lit another cigarette. Around him he saw, to the east, south, and west, towering skyscrapers silhouetted against the dawn, crowded close to the black treelines like sheer cliffs around a rain forest basin.

He heard the sound of soft footsteps behind him and turned, peering around the arch into the path that led to the Children's Zoo deeper into the park.

Jack Ferguson passed through a concrete tunnel and stepped into a pool of light, then stopped. "Burke?"

"Over here." Burke watched Ferguson approach. The man walked with a slight limp, his oversized vintage trench coat flapping with every step he took.

Ferguson offered his hand and smiled, showing a set of yellowed teeth. "Good to see you, Patrick."

Burke took his hand. "How's your wife, Jack?"

"Poorly. Poorly, I'm afraid."

"Sorry to hear that. You're looking a bit pale yourself."

Ferguson touched his face. "Am I? I should get out more."

"Take a walk in the park—when the sun's up. Why are we meeting here, Jack?"

"Oh God, the town's full of Micks today, isn't it? I mean we could be seen anywhere by anybody."

"I suppose." Old revolutionaries, thought Burke, would wither and die without their paranoia and conspiracies. Burke pulled a small thermal flask from his coat. "Tea and Irish?"

"Bless you." Ferguson took it and drank, then handed it back as he looked around into the shadows. "Are you alone?"

"Me, you, and the monkeys." Burke took a drink and regarded Ferguson over the rim of the flask. Jack Ferguson was a genuine 1930s City College Marxist whose life had been spent in periods of either fomenting or waiting for the revolution of the working classes. The historical tides that had swept the rest of the world since the war had left Jack Ferguson untouched and unimpressed. In addition he was a pacifist, a gentle man, though these seemingly disparate ideals never appeared to cause him any inner conflict. Burke held out the flask. "Another rip?"

"No, not just yet."

Burke screwed the cap back on the Thermos as he studied Ferguson, who was nervously looking around him. Ferguson was a ranking officer in the Official Irish Republican Army, or whatever was left of it in New York, and he was as burnt out and moribund as the rest of that group of geriatrics. "What's coming down today, Jack?"

Ferguson took Burke's arm and looked up into his face. "The Fenians ride again, my boy."

"Really? Where'd they get the horses?"

"No joke, Patrick. A renegade group made up mostly from the Provos in Ulster. They call themselves the Fenians."

Burke nodded. He had heard of them. "They're here? In New York?"

"Afraid so."

"For what purpose?"

"I couldn't say, exactly. But they're up to mischief."

"Are your sources reliable?"

"Very."

"Are these people into violence?"

"In the vernacular of the day, yes, they're into violence. Into it up to their asses. They're murderers, arsonists, and bombers. The cream of the Provisional IRA. Between them they've leveled most of downtown Belfast, and they're responsible for hundreds of deaths. A bad lot."

"Sounds like it, doesn't it? What do they do on weekends?"

Ferguson lit a cigarette with unsteady hands. "Let's sit awhile."

Burke followed him toward a bench facing the ape house. As he walked he watched the man in front of him. If ever there was a man more anachronistic, more quixotic than Jack Ferguson, he had never met him. Yet Ferguson had somehow survived in that netherworld of leftist politics and had even survived a murder attempt—or an assassination attempt, as Ferguson would have corrected him. And he was unusually reliable in these matters. The Marxist-oriented Officials distrusted the breakaway Provisionals and vice versa. Each side still had people in the opposite camp, and they were the best sources of information about each other. The only common bond they shared was a deep hate for the English and a policy of hands-off-America. Burke sat next to Ferguson. "The IRA has not committed acts of violence in America since the Second World War," Burke recited the conventional wisdom, "and I don't think they're ready to now."

"That's true of the Officials, certainly, and even the Provisionals, but not of these Fenians."

Burke said nothing for a long time, then asked, "How many?"

Ferguson chain-lit a cigarette. "At least twenty, maybe more."

"Armed?"

"Not when they left Belfast, of course, but there are people here who would help them."

"Target?"

"Who knows? No end of targets today. Hundreds of politicians in the reviewing stands, in the parade. People on the steps of the Cathedral. Then, of course, there's the British Consulate, British Airways, the Irish Tourist Board, the Ulster Trade Delegation, the—"

"All right. I've got a list too." Burke watched a gorilla with red, burning eyes peering at them through the bars of the ape house. The animal seemed interested in them, turning its head whenever they spoke. "Who are the leaders of these Fenians?"

"A man who calls himself Finn MacCumail."

"What's his real name?"

"I may know this afternoon. MacCumail's lieutenant is John Hickey, code name Dermot."

"Hickey's dead."

"No, he's living right here in New Jersey. He must be close to eighty by now."

Burke had never met Hickey, but Hickey's career in the IRA was so long and so blood-splattered that he was mentioned in history books. "Anything else?"

"No, that's it for now."

"Where can we meet later?"

"Call me at home every hour starting at noon. If you don't reach me, meet me back here on the terrace of the restaurant at four-thirty . . . unless, of course, whatever is to happen has already happened. In that case I'll be out of town for a while."

Burke nodded. "What can I do for you?"

Ferguson acted both surprised and indifferent, the way he always did at this point. "Do? Oh, well . . . let's see. . . . How's the special fund these days?"

"I can get a few hundred."

"Fine. Things are a bit tight with us."

Burke didn't know if he was referring to himself and his wife or his organization. Probably both. "I'll try for more."

"As you wish. The money isn't so important. What is important is that you avoid bloodshed, and that the department knows we're helping you. And that no one else knows it."

"That's the way we've always done it."

Ferguson stood and put out his hand. "Good-bye, Patrick. *Erin go bragh.*"

Burke stood and took Ferguson's hand. "Do what you can, Jack, but be careful."

Burke watched Ferguson limp away down the path and disappear under the

clock. He felt very chilled and took a drink from his flask. *The Fenians ride
again.* He had an idea that this St. Patrick's Day would be the most memorable
of all.

8

Maureen Malone put down her teacup and let her eyes wander around
the hotel breakfast room.
"Would you like anything else?" Margaret Singer, Secretary of Amnesty International, smiled at her from across the table.
"No, thank you—" She almost added ma'am but caught herself. Three years
as a revolutionary didn't transform a lifetime of inbred deference.
Next to Margaret Singer sat Malcolm Hull, also of Amnesty. And across the
round table sat a man introduced only as Peter who had his back to the wall
and faced the main entrance to the dining room. He neither ate nor smiled but
drank black coffee. Maureen knew the type.
The fifth person at the table was recently arrived and quite unexpected: Sir
Harold Baxter, British Consul General. He had come, he said frankly, to break
the ice so there would be no awkwardness when they met on the steps of the
Cathedral. The British, reflected Maureen, were so civilized, polite, and practical. It made one sick, really.
Sir Harold poured a cup of coffee and smiled at her. "Will you be staying on
awhile?"
She forced herself to look into his clear gray eyes. He looked no more than
forty, but his hair was graying at the temples. He was undeniably good-looking.
"I think I'll go on to Belfast tonight."
His smile never faded. "Not a good idea, actually. London or even Dublin
would be better."
She smiled back at his words. Translation: After today they'll surely murder
you in Belfast. She didn't think he cared personally if the IRA murdered her,
but his government must have decided she was useful. Her voice was cool.
"When the Famine killed a million and a half Irish, it also scattered as many
throughout the English-speaking world, and among these Irish are always a few
IRA types. If I'm to die by their bullets, I'd rather it be in Belfast than anywhere else."
No one said anything for a few seconds, then Sir Harold spoke. "Certainly
you overestimate the strength of these people outside of Ulster. Even in the
south, the Dublin government has outlawed them—"
"The Dublin government, Sir Harold, are a bunch of British lackeys." There.
She had really broken the ice now. "The only hope for the Catholics of the six
counties—or Ulster, as you call it—has become the Irish Republican Army—
not London or Dublin or Washington. Northern Ireland needs an alternative to
the IRA, so Northern Ireland is where I must be."
Harold Baxter's eyes grew weary. He was sick to death of this problem but
felt it his duty to respond. "And you are the alternative?"
"I'm searching for an alternative to the killing of innocent civilians."
Harold Baxter put on his best icy stare. "But not British soldiers? Tell me,

why would Ulster Catholics wish to unite with a nation governed by British lackeys?"

Her response was quick, as his had been. They both knew their catechism. "I think a people would rather be governed by their own incompetent politicians than by foreign incompetents."

Baxter sat back and pressed his palms together. "Please don't forget the two-thirds of the Ulster population who are Protestant and who consider Dublin, not London, to be a foreign capital."

Maureen Malone's face grew red. "That bunch of Bible-toting bigots does not recognize any allegiance except money. They'd throw you over in a second if they thought they could handle the Catholics themselves. Every time they sing 'God Save the Queen' in their silly Orange Lodges, they wink at each other. They think the English are decadent and the Irish Catholics are lazy drunks. They are certain *they* are the chosen people. And they've guiled you into thinking they're your loyal subjects." She realized that she had raised her voice and took a deep breath, then fixed Baxter with a cold stare to match his own. "English blood and the Crown's money keep Belfast's industry humming —don't you feel like fools, Sir Harold?"

Harold Baxter placed his napkin on the table. "Her Majesty's government would no more abandon one million subjects—loyal or disloyal—in Ulster than they would abandon Cornwall or Surrey, madam." He stood. "If this makes us fools, so be it. Excuse me." He turned and headed toward the door.

Maureen stared after him, then turned toward her host and hostess. "I'm sorry. I shouldn't have picked an argument with him."

Margaret Singer smiled. "That's all right. But I'd advise you not to argue politics with the other side. If we tell the Russians what bullies they are and then try to get a Soviet Jew released from the camps, we don't have much luck, you know."

Hull nodded in assent. "You won't agree, but I can assure you that the British are among the fairest people in this troubled world. If you want to get them to end internment, you'll have to appeal to that sense of fairness. You broke with the IRA to travel this path."

Margaret Singer added, "We all must deal with our devils—and we do." She paused. "They hold the keys to the camps."

Maureen took the gentle rebuke without answering. The good people of the world were infinitely more difficult to deal with than the bad. "Thank you for breakfast. Excuse me." She stood.

A bellhop came toward the table. "Miss Malone?"

She nodded slowly.

"For you, miss." He held up a small bouquet of green carnations. "I'll put them in a nice vase in your room, ma'am. There's a card I can give you now, if you wish."

She stared at the small buff envelope, then took it. It was blank. She looked questioningly at Singer and Hull. They shook their heads. She broke the seal on the envelope.

Maureen's mind went back to London five years earlier. She and Sheila had been hiding in a safe house in an Irish neighborhood in the East End. Their mission had been secret, and only the Provisional IRA War Council knew of their whereabouts.

A florist had come to the door one morning and delivered a bouquet of English lavender and foxglove, and the Irishwoman who owned the house had gone up to their room and thrown the flowers on their bed. "Secret mission," she had said, and had spit on the floor. "What a bloody bunch of fools you all are."

She and Sheila had read the accompanying card: *Welcome to London. Her Majesty's government hope you enjoy your visit and trust you will avail yourself of the pleasures of our island and the hospitality of the English people.* Right out of a government travel brochure. Except that it wasn't signed by the Tourist Board but by Military Intelligence.

She had never been so humiliated and frightened in her life. She and Sheila had run out of the house with only the clothes on their backs, and spent days in the parks and the London Underground. They hadn't dared to go to any other contacts for fear they were being followed for that purpose. Eventually, after the worst fortnight she had ever passed in her life, they had made it to Dublin.

She pulled the card half out of its envelope to read the words. *Welcome to New York. We hope your stay will be pleasant and that you will take advantage of the pleasures of the island and the hospitality of the people.*

She didn't have to pull the rest of the card out to see the signature, but she did anyway, and read the name of Finn MacCumail.

Maureen closed the door of her room and bolted it. The flowers were already on the dresser. She pulled them from the vase and took them into the bathroom. She tore and ripped them and flushed them down the toilet. In the mirror she could see the reflection of the bedroom and the partly opened door to the adjoining sitting room. She spun around. The closet door was also ajar, and she hadn't left either of those doors open. She took several deep breaths to make sure her voice was steady. "Brian?"

She heard a movement in the sitting room. Her knees were beginning to feel shaky, and she pressed them together. "Damn you, Flynn!"

The connecting door to the sitting room swung open. "Ma'am?" The maid looked across the room at her.

Maureen took another long breath. "Is anyone else here?"

"No, ma'am."

"Has anyone been here?"

"Only the boy with the flowers, ma'am."

"Please leave."

"Yes, ma'am." The maid pushed her cart into the hall. Maureen followed her and bolted the door, then sat in the armchair and stared at the Paisley wallpaper.

She was surprised by her calmness. She almost wished he would roll out from under the bed and smile at her with that strange smile that was not a smile at all. She conjured up an image of him standing in front of her. He would say, "It's been a damned long time, Maureen." He always said that after they had been separated. Or "Where are my flowers, lass? Did you put them in a special place?"

"Yes, very special," she said aloud. "I flushed them down the goddamned john."

She sat there for several minutes carrying on her imaginary conversation with him. She realized how much she missed him and how she wanted to hear his voice again. She was both excited and frightened by the knowledge that he was close and that he would find her.

The phone next to her rang. She let it ring for a long time before she picked it up.

"Maureen? Is everything all right?" It was Margaret Singer. "Shall I come up and get you? We're expected at the Irish Pavilion—"

"I'll be right down." She hung up and rose slowly from the chair. The Irish Pavilion for a reception, then the steps of St. Patrick's, the parade, and the reviewing stands at the end of the day. Then the Irish Cultural Society Benefit Dinner for Ireland's Children. Then Kennedy Airport. What a lot of merrymaking in the name of helping soothe the ravages of war. Only in America. The Americans would turn the Apocalypse into a dinner dance.

She walked across the sitting room and into the bedroom. On the floor she saw a single green carnation, and she knelt to pick it up.

9

Patrick Burke looked out of the telephone booth into the dim interior of the Blarney Stone on Third Avenue. Cardboard shamrocks were pasted on the bar mirror, and a plastic leprechaun hat hung from the ceiling. Burke dialed a direct number in Police Plaza. "Langley?"

Inspector Philip Langley, head of the New York Police Department's Intelligence Division, sipped his coffee. "I got your report on Ferguson." Langley looked down from his thirteenth-story window toward the Brooklyn Bridge. The sea fog was burning off. "It's like this, Pat. We're getting some pieces to a puzzle here, and the picture that's taking shape doesn't look good. The FBI has received information from IRA informers that a renegade group from Ireland has been poking around the New York and Boston IRA—testing the waters to see if they can have a free hand in something that they're planning in this country."

Burke wiped his neck with a handkerchief. "In the words of the old cavalry scout, I see many hoofprints going in and none coming out."

Langley said, "Of course, nothing points directly to New York on Saint Patrick's Day—"

"There is a law that says that if you imagine the worst possible thing happening at the worst possible moment, it will usually happen, and Saint Patrick's Day is a nightmare under the best of circumstances. It's Mardi Gras, Bastille Day, Carnivale, all in one. So if I were the head of a renegade Irish group and I wanted to make a big splash in America, I would do it in New York City on March seventeenth."

"I hear you. How do you want to approach this?"

"I'll start by digging up my contacts. Barhop. Listen to the barroom patriots talk. Buy drinks. Buy people."

"Be careful."

Burke hung up, then walked over to the bar.

"What'll you be having?"

"Cutty." Burke placed a twenty-dollar bill on the bar. He recognized the bartender, a giant of a man named Mike. Burke took his drink and left the change on the bar. "Buy you one?"

"It's a little early yet." The bartender waited. He knew a man who wanted something.

Burke slipped into a light brogue. "I'm looking for friends."

"Go to church."

"I won't be finding them there. The brothers Flannagan. Eddie and Bob. Also John Hickey."

"You're a friend?"

"Meet them every March seventeenth."

"Then you should know that John Hickey is dead—may his soul rest in peace. The Flannagans are gone back to the old country. A year it's been. Drink up now and move along. You'll not be finding any friends here."

"Is this the bar where they throw a drunk through the window every Saint Patrick's Day?"

"It will be if you don't move along." He stared at Burke.

A medium-built man in an expensive topcoat suddenly emerged from a booth and stood beside Burke. The man spoke softly, in a British accent. "Could I have a word with you?"

Burke stared at the man, who inclined his head toward the door. Both men walked out of the bar. The man led Burke across the street, stopping on the far corner. "My name is Major Bartholomew Martin of British Military Intelligence." Martin produced his diplomatic passport and military I.D. card.

Burke hardly glanced at them. "Means nothing."

Martin motioned to a skyscraper in the center of the block. "Then perhaps we'd better go in there."

Burke knew the building without looking at it. He saw two big Tactical Policemen standing a few yards from the entrance with their hands behind their backs. Martin walked past the policemen and held open the door. Burke entered the big marble lobby and picked out four Special Services men standing at strategic locations. Martin moved swiftly to the rear of the lobby, behind a stone façade that camouflaged the building's elevators. The elevator doors opened, and both men moved inside. Burke reached out and pushed floor nine.

Martin smiled. "Thank you."

Burke looked at the man standing in a classical elevator pose, feet separated, hands behind his back, head tilted upward, engrossed in the progression of illuminated numbers. Despite his rank there was nothing military about Bartholomew Martin, thought Burke. If anything he looked like an actor who was trying to get into character for a difficult role. He hadn't mastered control of the mouth, however, which was hard and unyielding, despite the smile. A glimpse of the real man, perhaps.

The elevator stopped, and Burke followed the major into the corridor. Martin nodded to a man who stood to the left, dressed in a blue blazer with polished brass buttons.

On the wall of the corridor, opposite Burke, was the royal coat of arms and a highly polished bronze plaque that read: BRITISH INFORMATION SERVICES. There was no sign to indicate that this was where the spies usually hung out, but as far as Burke knew, nobody's consulate or embassy information office made that too clear.

Burke followed Martin through a door into a large room. A blond receptionist, dressed in a blue tweed suit that matched the Concorde poster above her desk, stood as they approached and said in a crisp British accent, "Good morning, Major."

Martin led Burke through a door just beyond the desk, through a microfilm reading room, and into a small sitting room furnished in a more traditional style than the rest of the place. The only detail that suggested a government office was a large travel poster that showed a black and white cow standing in a sunny meadow, captioned: "Find peace and tranquility in an English village."

Martin drew the door shut, locked it, and hung his topcoat on a clothes tree. "Have a seat, Lieutenant."

Burke left his coat on, walked to the sideboard and took the stopper out of a decanter, smelled it, then poured a drink. He looked around the well-furnished room. The last time he'd been in the consulate was a week before last St. Patrick's Day. A Colonel Hayes that time. Burke leaned back against the sideboard. "Well, what can you do for me?"

Major Martin smiled. "A great deal, I think."

"Good."

"I've already given Inspector Langley a report on a group of Irish terrorists called the Fenians, led by a Finn MacCumail. You've seen the report?"

"I've been apprised of the details."

"Fine. Then you know something may happen here today." Major Martin leaned forward. "I'm working closely with the FBI and CIA, but I'd like to work more closely with your people—pool our information. The FBI and CIA tell us things they don't tell you, but I'd keep you informed of their progress as well as ours. I've already helped your military intelligence branches set up files on the IRA, and I've briefed your State Department intelligence service on the problem."

"You've been busy."

"Yes. You see, I'm a sort of clearinghouse in this affair. British Intelligence knows more about the Irish revolutionaries than anyone, of course, and now you seem to need that information, and we have a chance to do you a good turn."

"What's the price?"

Major Martin played with a lighter on the coffee table. "Yes, price. Well, better information from you in future on the transatlantic IRA types in New York. Gunrunning. Fund raising. IRA people here on R and R. That sort of thing."

"Sounds fair."

"It *is* fair."

"So what do you want of me particularly?"

Major Martin looked at Burke. "Just wanted to tell you directly about all of this. To meet you." Martin stood. "Look here, if you want to get a bit of information to me directly, call here and ask for Mr. James. Someone will take the message and pass it on to me. And I'll leave messages for you here as well. Perhaps a little something you can give to Langley as your own. You'll make a few points that way. Makes everyone look good."

Burke moved toward the door, then turned. "They're probably going after the Malone woman. Maybe even after the consul general."

Major Martin shook his head. "I don't think so. Sir Harold has no involvement whatsoever in Irish affairs. And the Malone woman—I knew her sister, Sheila, in Belfast, incidentally. She's in jail. An IRA martyr. They should only know—but that's another story. Where was I?—Maureen Malone. She's quite the other thing to the IRA. A Provisional IRA tribunal has condemned her to death in absentia, you know. She's on borrowed time now. But they won't shoot her down in the street. They'll grab her someday in Ireland, north or south, have a trial with her present this time, kneecap her, then a day or so later shoot her in the head and leave her on a street in Belfast. And the Fenians, whoever they are, won't do anything that would preempt the Provos' death sentence. And don't forget, Malone and Sir Harold will be on the steps of Saint Patrick's most of the day, and the Irish respect the sanctuary of the church no matter what their religious or political beliefs. No, I wouldn't worry about those two.

Look for a more obvious target. British property. The Ulster Trade Delegation.
The Irish always perform in a predictable manner."

"Really? Maybe that's why my wife left me."

"Oh, you're Irish, of course . . . sorry. . . ."

Burke unbolted the door and walked out of the room.

Major Martin threw back his head and laughed softly, then went to the
sideboard and made himself a martini. He evaluated his conversation with
Burke and decided that Burke was more clever than he had been led to believe.
Not that it would do him any good this late in the game.

BOOK III

The Parade

Saint Patrick's Day in New York is the most fantastic affair, and in past years on Fifth Avenue, from Forty-fourth Street to Ninety-sixth Street, the white traffic lines were repainted green for the occasion. All the would-be Irish, has-been Irish and never-been Irish, seem to appear true-blue Irish overnight. Everyone is in on the act, but it is a very jolly occasion and I have never experienced anything like it anywhere else in the world.

Brendan Behan,
Brendan Behan's New York

10

In the middle of Fifth Avenue, at Forty-fourth Street, Pat and Mike, the two Irish wolfhounds that were the mascots of the Fighting 69th Infantry Regiment, strained at their leashes. Colonel Dennis Logan, Commander of the 69th, tapped his Irish blackthorn swagger stick impatiently against his leg. He glanced at the sky and sniffed the air, then turned to Major Matthew Cole. "What's the weather for this afternoon, Major?"

Major Cole, like all good adjutants, had the answer to everything. "Cold front moving through later, sir. Snow or freezing rain by nightfall."

Logan nodded and thrust his prominent jaw out in a gesture of defiance, as though he were going to say, "Damn the weather—full speed ahead."

The young major struck a similar pose, although his jaw was not so grand. "Parade'll be finished before then, I suspect, Colonel." He glanced at Logan to see if he was listening. The colonel's marvelously angular face had served him well at staff meetings, but the rocklike quality of that visage was softened by misty green eyes like a woman's. Too bad.

Logan looked at his watch, then at the big iron stanchion clock in front of the Morgan Guaranty Trust Building on Fifth Avenue. The clock was three minutes fast, but they would go when that clock struck noon. Logan would never forget the newspaper picture that showed his unit at parade rest and the clock at three minutes after. The caption had read: THE IRISH START LATE. Never again.

The regiment's staff, back from their inspection of the unit, was assembled in front of the color guard. The national and regimental colors snapped in a five-mile-an-hour wind that came down the Avenue from the north, and the multicolored battle streamers, some going back to the Civil War and the Indian wars, fluttered nicely. Logan turned to Major Cole. "What's your feel?"

The major searched his mind for a response, but the question threw him. "Feel . . . sir?"

"Feel, man. *Feel.*" He accentuated the words.

"Fine. Fine."

Logan looked at the battle ribbons on the major's chest. A splash of purple stood out like the wound it represented. "In 'Nam, did you ever get a feeling that everything was not fine?"

The major nodded thoughtfully.

Logan waited for a response that would reinforce his own feelings of unease, but Cole was too young to have fully developed that other sense to the extent that he could identify what he felt in the jungle and recognize it in the canyons of Manhattan Island. "Keep a sharp eye out today. This is not a parade—it's an operation. Don't let your head slide up your ass."

"Yes, sir."

Logan looked at his regiment. They stood at parade rest, their polished helmets with the regimental crest reflecting the overhead sunlight. Slung across their shoulders were M-16 rifles.

The crowd at Forty-fourth Street, swelled by office workers on their lunch hour, was jostling for a better view. People had climbed atop the WALK—DON'T WALK signs, the mailboxes, and the cement pots that held the newly budded trees along the Avenue.

In the intersection around Colonel Logan newsmen mixed with politicians and parade officials. The parade chairman, old Judge Driscoll, was patting everyone on the back as he had done for over forty years. The formation marshals, resplendent in black morning coats, straightened their tricolor sashes and top hats. The Governor was shaking every hand that looked as if it could pull a voting lever, and Mayor Kline was wearing the silliest green derby that Logan had ever seen.

Logan looked up Fifth Avenue. The broad thoroughfare was clear of traffic and people, an odd sight reminiscent of a B-grade science-fiction movie. The pavement stretched unobstructed to the horizon, and Colonel Logan was more impressed with this sight than anything else he had seen that day. He couldn't see the Cathedral, recessed between Fiftieth and Fifty-first Streets, but he could see the police barriers around it and the guests on the lower steps.

A stillness began to descend on the crossroads as the hands of the clock moved another notch toward the twelve. The army band accompanying the 69th ceased their tuning of instruments, and the bagpipes of the Emerald Society on the side street stopped practicing. The dignitaries, whom the 69th Regiment was charged with escorting to the reviewing stands, began to fall into their designated places as Judge Driscoll looked on approvingly.

Logan felt his heart beat faster as he waited out the final minutes. He was aware of, but did not see, the mass of humanity huddled around him, the hundreds of thousands of spectators along the parade route to his front, the police, the reviewing stands in the park, the cameras and the newspeople. It was to be a day of dedication and celebration, sentimentality and even sorrow. In New York this day had been crowned by the parade, which had gone on uninterrupted by war, depression, or civil strife since 1762. It was, in fact, a mainstay of Irish culture in the New World, and it was not about to change, even if every last man, woman, and child in old Ireland did away with themselves and the British to boot. Logan turned to Major Cole. "Are we ready, Major?"

"The Fighting Irish are always ready, Colonel."

Logan nodded. The Irish were always ready for anything, he thought, and prepared for nothing.

Father Murphy looked around him as a thousand guests crowded the steps of the Cathedral. He edged over and stood on the long green carpet that had been unrolled from the main portal between the brass handrail and down into the street. In front of him, between the handrails, stood the Cardinal and the Monsignor, shoulder to shoulder. Flanking them were the British consul, Baxter, next to the Cardinal, and the Malone woman next to the Monsignor. Murphy smiled. The arrangement wasn't strictly protocol, but they couldn't get at each other's throats so easily now.

Standing in loose formation around the Cardinal's group were priests, nuns, and church benefactors. Murphy noticed at least two men who were probably undercover police. He looked up over the heads of the people in front of him toward the crowd across the Avenue. Boys and girls had climbed to the top of the pedestal of the Atlas and were passing bottles back and forth. His eyes were drawn to a familiar face: Standing in front of the pedestal, with his hands resting on a police barricade, was Patrick Burke. The man towered above the crowd around him and seemed strangely unaffected by the animated throng pressing against him on the sidewalk. Murphy realized that Burke's presence reassured him, though he didn't know why he felt he needed that assurance.

The Cardinal turned his head toward Harold Baxter and spoke in a voice that had that neutral tone of diplomacy so like his own. "Will you be staying with us for the entire day, Mr. Baxter?"

Baxter was no longer used to being called mister, but he didn't think the Cardinal meant anything by it. He turned his head to meet the Cardinal's eyes. "If I may, Your Eminence."

"We would be delighted."

"Thank you." He continued to look at the Cardinal, who had now turned away. The man was old, but his eyes were bright. Baxter cleared his throat. "Excuse me, Your Eminence, but I was thinking that perhaps I should stand away from the center of things a bit."

The Cardinal waved to well-wishers in the crowd as he spoke. "Mr. Baxter, you *are* the center of things today. You and Miss Malone. This little display of ours has captured the imagination of political commentators. It is, as they say, newsworthy. Everyone loves these precedents, this breaking with the past." He turned and smiled at Baxter, a wide Irish smile. "If you move an inch, they will be pulling their hair in Belfast, Dublin, London, and Washington." He turned back to the crowds and continued moving his arm in a blending of cheery waving and holy blessing.

"Yes, of course. I wasn't taking into account the political aspect—only the security aspect. I wouldn't want to be the cause of anyone being injured or—"

"God is watching over us, Mr. Baxter, and Commissioner Dwyer assures me that the Police Department is doing the same."

"That's reassuring on both counts. You've spoken to him recently? The Police Commissioner, I mean."

The Cardinal turned and fixed Baxter with a smile that showed he understood the little joke but did not find it amusing.

Baxter stared back for a moment, then turned away. It was going to be a long day.

*   *   *

Patrick Burke regarded the steps. He noticed his friend Father Murphy near the Cardinal. It must be a strange life for a man, he reflected. The celibacy. The paternal and maternal concern of monsignors and mother superiors. Like being an eternal boy. His mother had wanted that for him. A priest in the family was the ultimate status for those old Irish, but he had become a cop instead, which was almost as good in the old neighborhoods, and no one was disappointed, least of all himself.

He saw that the Monsignor was smiling and talking with the ex-IRA woman. Burke focused on her. She looked pretty, even from this distance. Angelic, almost. Her blond hair moved nicely in the breeze, and she kept brushing wisps of hair from her face.

Burke thought that if he were Harold Baxter or Maureen Malone he would not be on those steps at all, and certainly not together. And if he were the Cardinal, he would have invited them for yesterday, when they could have shared the steps with indifferent pigeons, bag ladies, and winos. He didn't know whose idea it had been to wave this red flag in the face of the Irish rebels, but if it was supposed to bring peace, someone had badly miscalculated.

He looked up and down the Avenue. Workers and high school kids, all playing hooky to get in on the big bash, mingled with street vendors, who were making out very well. Some young girls had painted green shamrocks and harps on their faces and wore *Kiss Me, I'm Irish* buttons, and they were being taken up on it by young men, most of whom wore plastic leprechaun bowlers. The older crowd settled for green carnations and *Erin Go Bragh* buttons.

Maureen Malone had never seen so many people. All along the Avenue, American and Irish flags hung from staffs jutting out of the gray masonry buildings. A group in front of the British Empire Building was hoisting a huge green banner, and Maureen read the familiar words: ENGLAND GET OUT OF IRELAND. Margaret Singer had told her that this was the only political slogan she would see, the only one sanctioned by the Grand Marshal, who had also specified that the banners be neatly made with white lettering on green background. The police had permission to seize any other banner. She hoped Baxter saw it; she didn't see how he could miss it. She turned to Monsignor Downes. "All these people are certainly not Irish."

Monsignor Downes smiled. "We have a saying in New York. 'On Saint Patrick's Day, everyone is Irish!' "

She looked around again, as though she still didn't believe what she was seeing. Little Ireland, poor and underpopulated, with its humble patron saint, almost unknown in the rest of the Christian world, causing all this fuss. It gave her goose bumps, and she felt a choking in her throat. Ireland's best exports, it was said bitterly, were her sons and daughters. But there was nothing to be bitter about, she realized. They had kept the faith, although in an Americanized version.

Suddenly she heard a great noise coming from the crowd and turned her head toward the commotion. A group of men and women, about fifteen of them, had unfurled a green banner reading: VICTIMS OF BRITISH INTERNMENT AND TORTURE. She recognized a friend of her sister's.

A police mounted unit galloped south down the Avenue, Plexiglas helmet-visors down, long batons raised above their heads. From the north side of the Cathedral on Fifty-first Street, scooter police roared past the mobile headquarters truck and onto Fifth Avenue.

A man with a bullhorn shouted, "LONG KESH! ARMAGH PRISON!

CRUMLIN ROAD JAIL! CONCENTRATION CAMPS, BAXTER, YOU BASTARD! MAUREEN MALONE—TRAITOR!"

She turned and looked at Harold Baxter across the empty space left by the Cardinal and Monsignor who had been moved up the steps by the security police. He remained in a rigid position of attention, staring straight ahead. She knew there were news cameras trained on him to record his every movement, every betrayal of emotion, whether anger or fear. But they were wasting their time. The man was British.

She realized that cameras were on her as well, and she turned away from him and looked down into the street. The banner was down now, and half the demonstrators were in the hands of the police, but the other half had broken through the police barricades and were coming toward the steps, where a line of mounted police waited almost nonchalantly.

Maureen shook her head. The history of her people: forever attempting the insurmountable and, in the end, finding it indeed insurmountable.

Maureen watched, transfixed, as one of the last standing men cocked his arm and threw something toward the steps. Her heart skipped a beat as she saw it sailing through the air. It seemed to hang for a second before drifting downward slowly; the sunlight sparkled from it, making it difficult to identify. "Oh God." She began to drop to the ground but caught a glimpse of Baxter out of the corner of her eye. He hadn't moved a muscle and, whether it was a bomb or a carnation heading his way, he acted as if he could not care less. Reluctantly she straightened up. She heard a bottle crash on the granite steps directly behind her and waited for the sound of exploding petrol or nitro, but there was only a choked-off exclamation from the crowd, then a stillness around her. Green paint from the shattered bottle flecked the clothing of the people standing closest to where it hit. Her legs began to shake in relief, and her mouth became dry.

Sir Harold Baxter turned his head and looked at her. "Is this traditional?"

She could not control her voice sufficiently to speak, and she stared at him.

Baxter moved beside her. Their shoulders touched. Her reaction was to move away, but she didn't. He turned his head slightly. "Will you stand next to me for the rest of this thing?"

She moved her eyes toward him. Camera shutters clicked around them. She spoke softly. "I believe there's an assassin out there who intends to kill me today."

He didn't appear to react to this information. "Well, there are probably several out there who intend to kill me. . . . I promise I won't throw myself in front of you if you promise the same."

She let herself smile. "I think we can agree on that."

Burke stood firm as the crowd pushed and shoved around him. He looked at his watch. The episode had taken just two minutes. For a moment he had thought this was it, but within fifteen seconds he knew these were not the Fenians.

The security police on the steps had acted quickly but not really decisively in front of the partisan crowd. If that bottle had been a bomb, there would have been more than green paint to mop up. Burke took a long drink from his flask. He knew the whole day was a security problem of such magnitude that it had ceased to be a problem.

Burke considered the little he knew of the Fenians. They were veterans, said Ferguson, survivors, not suicidal fanatics. Whatever their mission they most probably intended to get away afterward, and that, thought Burke, would make their mission more difficult and make his job just a little easier. He hoped.

* * *

Colonel Dennis Logan was calming Pat and Mike, who had been aroused by shouts from the crowd.

Logan straightened up and looked at the stanchion clock. One minute past noon. "Oh, shit!" He turned to his adjutant, Major Cole. "Start this fucking parade."

"Yes, sir!" The adjutant turned to Barry Dugan, the police officer who for twenty-five years had blown the green whistle to begin the parade. "Officer Dugan! Do it!"

Dugan put the whistle to his lips, filled his lungs, and let out the longest, loudest whistle in all his quarter century of doing it.

Colonel Logan placed himself in front of the formation and raised his arm. Logan looked up the six blocks and saw the mass of newsmen and blue uniforms milling around a paddy wagon. They'd take their time if left to their own devices. He remembered his regiment's motto: Clear the way! He lowered his arm and turned his head over his right shoulder. "Foo-waard—MARCH!" The regiment stepped off.

The army band struck up the "Garryowen," and the two hundred and twenty-third St. Patrick's Day Parade began.

11

Patrick Burke walked across the Avenue to the curb in front of the Cathedral and stood by the barricades. The 69th Regiment came abreast of the Cathedral, and Colonel Logan called the regiment to a halt.

The barriers behind Burke were parted where the green carpet came into the street, and a group of men in morning dress left the parade line and approached the Cathedral.

Burke remembered that the Cardinal had mentioned, casually, to the newspapers the day before that his favorite song was "Danny Boy," and the army bandleader apparently had taken this as a command and ordered the band to play the sweet, lilting air. Some of the people on the steps and many in the crowd around the Cathedral broke into spontaneous song. It was difficult for an Irishman, thought Burke, not to respond to that music, especially if he had had a few already.

> "O Danny Boy, the pipes, the pipes are calling
> From glen to glen, and down the mountain side,
> The summer's gone, and all the roses falling,
> 'Tis you, 'tis you, must go and I must bide."

Burke watched the entourage of dignitaries as they mounted the steps: the marshals, Mayor Kline, Governor Doyle, senators, congressmen, all the secular power in the city and state, and many from the national level. They all passed through the space in those barriers, walked across the narrow carpet, and presented themselves to the Cardinal, then left quickly, as protocol demanded.

The faithful knelt and kissed the green-jeweled ring; others bowed or shook hands.

> "But come ye back when summer's in the meadow,
> Or when the valley's hushed and white with snow,
> For I'll be here in sunshine or in shadow,
> O Danny Boy, O Danny Boy, I love you so."

Maureen felt the excitement, the heightening of perceptions that led to fear, to apprehension. Everyone was smiling and bowing, kissing the Cardinal's ring, shaking her hand, the Monsignor's hand, Baxter's hand. Hands and wide smiles. The Americans had super teeth. Not a bad one in the lot.

She noticed a few steely-eyed men near her who wore the same expression of suppressed anxiety that she knew was on her face. Down by the space in the barriers she recognized Lieutenant Burke from the Waldorf. He was eyeing everyone who approached, as though they were all ax murderers instead of important citizens, and she felt a little comforted.

Around her the crowd was still singing, trying to remember the words and humming where they couldn't, as the flutes and horns of the army band played.

> "But when ye leave, and all the flowers are dying,
> And I am dead, as dead I may well be,
> Then will ye come and find the place where I am lying,
> And kneel and say an Ave there for me?"

Maureen shook her head. What a typically morbid Irish song. She tried to turn her thoughts to other things, but the intrusive words of the ballad reminded her of her own life—her own tragic love. Danny Boy was Brian, as Danny Boy was every Irish girl's lover. She could not escape its message and meaning for her as an Irishwoman; she found her eyes had gone misty, and there was a lump in her throat.

> "And I shall hear tho soft ye tread above me,
> And tho my grave will warmer, sweeter be,
> And you shall bend and tell me that you love me,
> And I shall sleep in peace until you come to me."

Burke watched the 69th move out. When the last unit was clear of the Cathedral, he breathed easier. The potential targets were no longer clustered around the Cathedral, they were scattered again—on the steps, moving around the regiment in small groups, some riding now in limousines up Park Avenue to the reviewing stands, some on their way home or to the airports.

At the end of the 69th Regiment Burke saw the regimental veterans in civilian clothes marching in a unit. Behind them was the Police Emerald Society Pipes and Drums, kilts swirling and their bagpipes wailing as their drums beat out a warlike cadence. At the head of the unit their longtime commander, Finbar Devine, raised his huge mace and ordered the pipers to play "Danny Boy" as they passed the Cathedral. Burke smiled. One hundred and ninety-six marching bands would play "Danny Boy" for the Cardinal today, such was the combined power of the press and the Cardinal's casual remark. Before the day was out His Eminence would wish he had never heard the song and pray to God that he would never hear it again as long as he lived.

Burke joined the last rank of the old veterans at the end of the 69th Regiment. The next likely point of trouble was the reviewing stands at Sixty-fourth Street, where the targets would again be bunched up like irresistibly plump fruit, and on St. Patrick's Day the fastest way to get uptown was to be in the parade.

Central Park was covered with people on hillocks and stone outcroppings, and several people were sitting in trees.

Colonel Logan knew that thousands of marchers had fallen in behind him now. He could feel the electricity that was passing through his regiment into the crowd around him and down the line of marchers, until the last units—the old IRA vets—had caught the tempo and the spirit. Cold and tired in the fading light, the old soldiers would hold their heads high as they passed the spectators, who by this time were jaded, weary, and drunk.

Logan watched the politicians as they left the march and headed toward the reviewing stands to take their seats. He gave the customary order of "eyes left" as they passed the stands and saluted, breathing more easily now that his escort mission had been accomplished.

Patrick Burke left the parade formation at Sixty-fourth Street, made his way through the crowd, and entered the rear door of the police mobile headquarters van. A television set was tuned to the WPIX news program that was covering the parade. Lights flashed on the consoles, and three radios, each tuned to a different command channel, crackled in the semidarkness. A few men occupied with paperwork or electronics sat on small stools.

Burke recognized Sergeant George Byrd from the Bureau of Special Services. "Big Byrd."

Byrd looked up from a radio and smiled. "Patrick Burke, the scourge of Irish revolutionaries, defender of the faith."

"Eat it, George." He lit a cigarette.

"I read the report you filed this morning. Who are the Finnigans? What do they want?"

Burke sat on a small jump seat. "Fenians."

"Fenians. Finnigans. Micks. Who are they?"

"The Fenians were a group of Irish warriors and poets. About 200 A.D. There was also an Irish anti-British guerrilla army in the nineteenth century who called themselves Fenians—"

Byrd laughed. "That's kind of old intelligence, Burke. Must have been held up in Police Plaza."

"Filed with your promotion papers, no doubt."

Byrd grunted and leaned back against the wall. "And who's Finn Mac—something?"

"Head of the original Fenians. Been dead seventeen hundred years now."

"A code name?"

"I hope so. Wouldn't want to meet the real one."

Byrd listened to the radios. The command posts up and down the Avenue were reporting: The post at the Presbyterian church at Fifty-fourth Street reported all quiet. The post on the twentieth floor of the General Motors Building reported all quiet. The mobile headquarters at the Cathedral reported all quiet. Byrd picked up the radiophone and hesitated, then spoke softly. "Mobile at Sixty-fourth. All quiet at the reviewing stands. Out." He replaced the phone and looked at Burke. "Too quiet?"

"Don't start that shit." Burke picked up a telephone and dialed. "Jack?"

Jack Ferguson glanced at the closed bedroom door where his wife slept fitfully, then spoke in a low voice. "Patrick"—he looked at a wall clock in the kitchen—"it's twelve-thirty. You're supposed to call me on the hour."

"I was in the parade. What do you have?"

Ferguson looked at some notes scribbled on a pad near the telephone. "It's hard to find anyone today."

"I know, Jack. That's why today is the day."

"Exactly. But I did learn that the man called MacCumail has recruited some of the more wild-eyed members of the Boston Provisional IRA."

"Interesting. Any line on weapons? Explosives?"

"No," answered Ferguson, "but you can buy anything you want in this country, from pistols to tanks."

"Anything else?"

"A partial description of the man called MacCumail—tall, lean, dark—"

"That could be my mother."

"He wears a distinctive ring. Always has it."

"Not very smart."

"No. He may believe it's a charm of some sort. The Irish are a superstitious lot. The ring is oversized, probably an antique or a family heirloom. Also, I did find out something interesting about this MacCumail. It's only hearsay . . . but apparently he was captured once and possibly compromised by British Intelligence."

"Hold on." Burke tried to arrange his thoughts. It occurred to him, not for the first time, that there was more than one game in town today. Where there was an Irish conspiracy, there was sure to be an English conspiracy. After eight hundred years of almost continuous strife, it was as though the two adversaries were inseparably bonded in a bizarre embrace destined to last eternally. If the Irish war was coming to America, then the English would be here to fight it. It was Major Bartholomew Martin's presence in New York, more than anything Ferguson said, that signaled an approaching battle. And Major Martin knew more than he was telling. Burke spoke into the mouthpiece. "Do you have anything else?"

"No . . . I'm going to have to do some legwork now. I'll leave messages with Langley at Police Plaza if anything turns up. I'll meet you at the zoo at four-thirty if nothing has happened by then."

"Time is short, Jack," Burke said.

"I'll do what I can to avoid violence. But you must try to go easy on the lads if you find them. They're brothers."

"Yeah . . . brothers. . . ." Burke hung up and turned to Byrd. "That was one of my informers. A funny little guy who's caught between his own basic decency and his wild politics."

Burke left the van and stood in the crowd at the corner of Sixty-fourth Street. He looked at the reviewing stands across Fifth Avenue, thick with people. If there was going to be trouble, it would probably happen at the reviewing stands. The other possible objectives that Major Martin suggested—the banks, the consulates, the airline offices, symbols of the London, Dublin, or Belfast governments—were small potatoes compared to the reviewing stands crowded with American, British, Irish, and other foreign VIPs.

The Cathedral, Burke understood, was also a big potato. But no Irish group would attack the Cathedral. Even Ferguson's Official IRA—mostly nonviolent Marxists and atheists—wouldn't consider it. The Provisionals were violent but mostly Catholic. Who but the Irish could have peaceful Reds and bomb-throwing Catholics?

Burke rubbed his tired eyes. Yes, if there was an action today, it had to be the reviewing stands.

Terri O'Neal was lying on the bed. The television set was tuned to the parade. Dan Morgan sat on the window seat and looked down Sixty-fourth Street. He noticed a tall man in civilian clothes step down from the police van, and he watched him as he lit a cigarette and stared into the street, scanning the buildings. Eventually the police, the FBI, maybe even the CIA and British Intelligence, would start to get onto them. That was expected. The Irish had a tradition called Inform and Betray. Without that weakness in the national character they would have been rid of the English centuries ago. But this time was going to be different. MacCumail was a man you didn't want to betray. The Fenians were a group more closely knit than an ancient clan, bound by one great sorrow and one great hate.

The telephone rang. Morgan walked into the living room, closed the door behind him, then picked up the receiver. "Yes?" He listened to the voice of Finn MacCumail, then hung up and pushed open the door. He stared at Terri O'Neal. It wasn't easy to kill a woman, yet MacCumail wasn't asking him to do something he himself wouldn't do. Maureen Malone and Terri O'Neal. They had nothing in common except their ancestry and the fact that both of them had only a fifty-fifty chance of seeing another dawn.

12

Patrick Burke walked down Third Avenue, stopping at Irish pubs along the way. The sidewalks were crowded with revelers engaged in the traditional barhopping. Paper shamrocks and harps were plastered against the windows of most shops and restaurants. There was an old saying that St. Patrick's Day was the day the Irish marched up Fifth Avenue and staggered down Third, and Burke noticed that ladies and gentlemen were beginning to wobble a bit. There was a great deal of handshaking, a tradition of sorts, as though everyone were congratulating each other on being Irish or on being sober enough to find his hand.

Burke approached P. J. Clarke's at Fifty-fifth Street, an old nineteenth-century brick relic, spared by the wrecker's ball but left encapsulated in the towering hulk around it—the Marine Midland Bank Building, which resembled a black Sony calculator with too many buttons.

Burke walked in through the frosted glass doors, made his way to the crowded bar, and ordered a beer. He looked around for familiar faces, an informant, an old friend, someone who owed him, but there was no one. Too many familiar faces missing this afternoon.

He made his way back into the street and breathed the cold north wind until his head cleared. He continued to walk, stopping at a half-remembered bar, an Irish-owned shop, or wherever a group of people huddled and spoke on the sidewalk. His thoughts raced rapidly and, unconsciously, he picked up his pace to keep abreast of the moving streams of people.

This day had begun strangely, and every incident, every conversation, added to his sense of unreality. He took a cigarette from his pocket, lit it, and headed south again.

Burke stared up at the gilt lettering on the window of J. P. Donleavy's, a small, inconspicuous pub on Forty-seventh Street. Donleavy's was another haunt of the quasi-IRA men and barroom patriots. Occasionally there would be a real IRA man there from the other side, and you could tell who he was because he rarely stood at the bar but usually sat alone in a booth. They were always pale, the result of Ireland's perpetual mist or as a result of some time in internment. New York and Boston were their sanctuaries, places of Irish culture, Irish pubs, Irish people without gelignite.

Burke walked in and pushed his way between two men who were talking to each other at the bar. He slipped into his light brogue for the occasion. "Buy you a drink, gentlemen. A round here, barkeeper!" He turned to the man on his left, a young laborer. The man looked annoyed. Burke smiled. "I'm to meet some friends in P.J.'s, but I can't remember if they said P. J. Clarke's, P. J. O'Hara's, P. J. Moriarty's, P. J. O'Rourke's or here. Bloody stupid of me—or of them." The beer came and Burke paid for it. "Would you know Kevin Michaels or Jim Malloy or Liam Connelly? Have you seen them today?"

The man to Burke's right spoke. "That's an interesting list of names. If you're looking for them, you can be sure they'll find *you.*"

Burke looked into the man's eyes. "That's what I'm counting on."

The man stared back but said nothing.

Burke smelled the sour beer on the man's breath, on his clothes. "I'm looking, too, for John Hickey."

Neither man spoke.

Burke took a long drink and put his glass down. "Thank you, gentlemen. I'm off to the Green Derby. Good day." He turned and walked down the length of the bar. An angled mirror reflected the two men huddled with the bartender, looking at him as he left.

He repeated his story, or one like it, in every bar that he thought might be promising. He switched from whiskey to stout to hot coffee and had a sandwich at a pub, which made him feel better. He crossed and recrossed Third Avenue, making his way southward. In every bar he left a forwarding address, and at every street corner he stopped and waited for the sound of shoes against the cold concrete to hesitate, to stop behind him. He was trolling, using himself as bait, but no one was rising to it today.

Burke picked up his pace. Time was running out. He looked at his watch; it was past four, and he had to be at the zoo at four-thirty. He stopped at a phone booth. "Langley? I need five hundred for Ferguson."

"Later. You didn't call for that."

Burke lit a cigarette. "What do you know about a Major Bartholomew Martin?"

There was a long silence on the phone, then Langley said, "Oh, you mean the British Intelligence guy. Don't worry about him."

"Why not?"

"Because I said so." Langley paused. "It's very complicated . . . CIA . . ."

"Tell me about it someday. Anything else I should know?"

"The FBI has finally decided to talk to us," Langley said. "They've uncovered an arms buy in New Jersey. A dozen M-16 rifles, a few sniper rifles, pistols, and plastic explosives. Also, a half dozen of those disposable rocket launchers. U.S. Army issue."

"Any other particulars?"

"Only that the buyers had Irish accents, and they didn't arrange for shipping to Ireland the way they usually do."

"Sounds ominous."

"I'll say—what are they *waiting* for?"

Burke shook his head. "I don't know. The parade has less than an hour to run. The weapons should be a clue to the type of operation."

"Martin thinks they're going to knock over a British bank down in the Wall Street area. The Police Commissioner has diverted detectives and patrolmen down there," said Langley.

"Why should they come all the way here to knock over a British bank? They want something . . . something they can only get *here.*"

"Maybe." Langley paused. "We're really not getting any closer, are we?"

"Too many targets. Too much beach to guard. The attackers always have the initiative."

"I'll remember that line when I stand in front of the Commissioner."

Burke looked at his watch. "I have to meet Ferguson. He's my last play." He hung up, stepped into Third Avenue, and hailed a cab.

Burke passed through the open gate beside the armory. The zoo looked less sinister in the light of day. Children with parents or governesses walked on the paths, holding candy or balloons, or some other object that was appropriate to their mission and the setting.

The Delacorte clock showed four thirty. Brass monkeys in the clock tower suddenly came to life, circled the bell with hammers raised, and struck it. As the mast gong sounded a recording played "MacNamara's Band."

Burke found Ferguson in the Terrace Restaurant at a small table, his face buried in *The New York Times.* Two containers of tea steamed on the table. Burke pulled up a chair opposite him and took a container.

Ferguson lowered the newspaper. "Well, the word on the street is that there is to be a robbery of a major British bank in the Wall Street area."

"Who told you that?"

Ferguson didn't answer.

Burke looked over the zoo, scanning the men on the benches, then turned back to Ferguson and fixed him with a sharp look.

Ferguson said nothing. "Major Martin," Burke said, "is what is known as an agent provocateur. What his game is, I don't know yet. But I think he knows more than he's telling any of us." Burke ground out his cigarette. "All right, forget what Martin told you. Tell me what *you* think. Time is—"

Ferguson turned up the collar of his trench coat against the rising wind. "I know all about time. It's very relative, you know. When they're kneecapping you in that new way with an electric drill instead of a bullet, then time moves very slowly. If you're trying to discover something by dusk, it goes quickly. If you were ten minutes early instead of late, you might have had the time to do something."

"About what?"

Ferguson leaned across the table. "I just came from the Cathedral. John Hickey, who hasn't been inside a church since he robbed Saint Patrick's in Dublin, was sleeping in the first pew. The old man wears a beard now, but I'd know him anywhere."

"Go on."

"The four o'clock Mass is ending soon, and there'll be thousands of people coming out of the Cathedral. Quitting time for most citizens is also at five."

"Right. It's called rush hour—"

"The counties and the IRA vets are marching now. Both groups are composed of people in civilian dress, and there are people who don't know each other in each unit. Anyone could be infiltrated among them."

"I'm listening, but hurry it up."

"I have to give you my thoughts so you can deduce—"

"Go on."

"All right. The police are tired. Some units are going off duty, the crowd is restless, drunk."

"I hear you."

"Events are moving inexorably toward their end. The gathering storm is about to break."

"No poetry, please."

"Finn MacCumail is Brian Flynn. Before Maureen Malone's desertion from the IRA, she and Brian Flynn were lovers."

Burke stood. "He's going after her."

"It's the kind of insane thing a man who calls himself Finn MacCumail, Chief of the Fenians, would do."

"At the Cathedral?"

"What better place? The Irish have a love of spectacle, grand gestures. Whether they win or not is unimportant. Ireland will always remember her martyrs and heroes for their style, not their success or lack of it. So, who will soon forget the resurrected Finn MacCumail and his Fenians when they kidnap or kill his faithless lover at Saint Patrick's Cathedral in New York on Saint Patrick's Day? No, it won't be soon forgotten."

Burke's mind raced. "I didn't believe they'd hit the Cathedral . . . but it fits the facts—"

"To hell with the facts. It fits their characters. It fits with history, with destiny, with—"

"Fuck history." Burke ran toward the terrace steps. "Fuck destiny, Jack." He tore down the path toward Fifth Avenue.

Ferguson called out after him. "Too late! Too late!"

Terri O'Neal watched the IRA veterans pass on the television screen. The scene shifted from Sixty-fourth Street to a view from the roof of Rockefeller Center. The County Tyrone unit passed in front of the Cathedral, and the camera zoomed in. She sat up and leaned closer to the television set. Her father's face suddenly filled the screen, and the announcer, who had recognized him, made a passing comment. She put her hand over her face as the enormity of what was going to happen—to her, to him, to everyone—at last dawned on her. "Oh, no. . . . Dad! Don't let them get away with this. . . ."

Dan Morgan looked at her. "Even if he could hear you, there's not a thing he can do now."

The telephone rang, and Morgan answered it. He listened. "Yes, as ready as I'll ever be." He hung up, then looked at his watch and began counting off sixty seconds as he walked into the bedroom.

Terri O'Neal looked up from the television and watched him. "Is this it?"

He glanced at the parade passing by on the screen, then at her. "Yes. And God help us if we've misjudged. . . ."

"God help you, anyway."

Morgan went into the bedroom, opened the side panel of the bay window, and waved a green shamrock flag.

13

B rendan O'Connor stood with the crowd on Fifth Avenue. He looked up
and saw the shamrock flag waving from the window on Sixty-fourth
Street. He took a deep breath and moved behind the reviewing stands
where pedestrian traffic was allowed to pass under the scrutiny of patrolmen.
He lit a cigarette and watched the smoke blow southward, over his shoulder.

O'Connor reached his right hand into the pocket of his overcoat, slid the
elastic off the handle of a grenade that had the pin removed, and held the
handle down with his thumb. As he moved through the closely pressed crowd
he pushed the grenade through a slit in his pocket and let it fall to the sidewalk.
He felt the detonator handle hit his ankle as it flew off. He repeated the
procedure with a grenade in his left pocket, pushing quickly through the tight
crowd as it fell.

Both seven-second fuses popped in sequence. The first grenade, a CS gas
canister, hissed quietly. The second grenade, a smoke signaling device, billowed huge green clouds that floated south into the stands. Brendan O'Connor
kept walking. Behind him he could hear the sounds of surprise as the CS gas
rose to face level, followed by the sounds of fear and panic as the smoke and
choking gas swept over the crowd on the sidewalk and up to the reviewing
stands. O'Connor released four more canisters through his pockets, then
walked through an opening in the stone wall and disappeared into the park.

Patrick Burke vaulted the low stone wall of Central Park and barreled into
the crowd on the sidewalk near the reviewing stands. Billowing green smoke
rolled over the stands toward him, and even before it reached him his eyes
began to tear. "Shit." He put a handkerchief to his face and ran into the
Avenue, but panic had seized the marchers, and Burke was caught in the middle of the confusion. The banner of the unit had fallen to the pavement, and
Burke glimpsed it under the feet of the running men—BELFAST IRISH RE-
PUBLICAN ARMY VETERANS. As he fought his way across the Avenue,
Burke could see that their ranks were laced with agitators and professional
shriekers, as he called them. *Well planned,* he thought. *Well executed.*

James Sweeney put his back to the streetlight pole at Sixty-fourth Street and
held his ground against the press of people around him. His hands reached
through the pockets of his long trench coat and grabbed a long-handled bolt
cutter hanging from his belt. He let the skirts of his coat fall over the cable
connections from the mobile headquarters van as he clipped the telephone
lines and then the electric power lines at the base of the pole.

Sweeney took three steps into the shoving crowd and let the bolt cutter slide
into the storm drain at the curb. He allowed himself to be carried along with
the flow of the moving mass of marchers and spectators up Sixty-fourth Street,
away from the Avenue and the choking gas.

* * *

Inside the mobile headquarters van the telephone operators heard an odd noise, and the four telephones went dead. All the lights in the van went out a second later. One of the operators looked up at George Byrd silhouetted against a small side window. "Phones out!"

Byrd pressed his face to the small window and looked down at the base of the streetlight. "Oh Christ! Sons of bitches." He turned back and grabbed at a radio as the van driver started the engine and switched to internal power. Byrd transmitted: "All stations! Mobile at Sixty-fourth. Power line cut. We're operating radios on generator. Telephone lines cut. Situation unclear—"

Burke burst through the door and grabbed the radiophone from Byrd's hand. "Mobile at Fifty-first—do you read?"

The second mobile van beside the Cathedral answered. "Roger. All quiet here. Mounted and scooter units headed your way—"

"No! Listen—"

As the nineteen bronze bells in the north spire of St. Patrick's Cathedral chimed five o'clock, the timer on the box resting on the crossbeam above the bells completed the electrical circuit. The box, a broad-band transmitter, began sending out static over the entire spectrum of the radio band. From its transmitting point, high above the street, the transmitter jammed all two-way radios in the midtown area.

A high, piercing sound filled Burke's earphone. "Mobile at Fifty-first—do you read? Action will take place at *Cathedral*. . . ." The sound grew louder and settled into a pattern of continuous high-pitched static. "Mobile at Fifty-first . . ." He let the radiophone fall from his hand and turned to Byrd. "Jammed."

"I hear it—shit!" Byrd grabbed at the radio and switched to alternate command channels, but they were all filled with static. "Bastards!"

Burke grabbed his arm. "Listen, get some men to the public telephones. Call Police Plaza and the rectory. Have them try to get a message to the police around the Cathedral. The mobile van there may still have telephone communication."

"I doubt it."

"Tell them—"

"I know, I know. I heard you." Byrd sent four men out of the van. He looked out the side window at the crowd streaming by and watched his men pushing through it. He turned around to speak to Burke, but he was gone.

On the steps of the Cathedral, Maureen watched the plainclothesman standing in front of her trying to get his hand radio to work. Several policemen were running around, passing on messages and receiving orders, and she could tell by their manner that there was some confusion among them. Police were moving in and out of the van on the corner to her right. She noticed the spectators on the sidewalks; they seemed to have received some message that those on the steps had not. There was a murmur running through the crowd, and heads craned north, up the Avenue, as though the message had come from that direction as in a child's game of Pass-It-On. She looked north but could see nothing unusual except the unsettled crowd. Then she noticed that the pace of the marchers had slowed. She turned to Harold Baxter and said quietly, "Something is wrong."

The bells struck the last of the five chimes, then began their traditional five o'clock hymns with "Autumn."

Baxter nodded. "Keep alert."

The County Cork unit passed slowly in front of the Cathedral, and behind them the County Mayo unit marked time as the parade became inexplicably stalled. Parade marshals and formation marshals spoke to policemen. Maureen noticed that the Cardinal looked annoyed but not visibly concerned about the rising swell of commotion around him.

Office workers and store clerks began streaming out of the lobbies of Rockefeller Center, the Olympic Tower, and the surrounding skyscrapers onto the already crowded sidewalks. They jostled to get away from the area, or to get a better view of the parade.

Suddenly there was a loud cry from the crowd. Maureen turned to her left. From the front doors of Saks Fifth Avenue burst a dozen men dressed in black suits and derbies. They wore white gloves and bright orange sashes across their chests, and most of them carried walking sticks. They pushed aside a police barricade and unfurled a long banner that read: GOD SAVE THE QUEEN. ULSTER WILL BE BRITISH FOREVER.

Maureen's pulse quickened, and her mind flashed back to Ulster, to the long summer marching season when the Orangemen paraded through the cities and villages, proclaiming their loyalty to God and Queen and their hate of their Catholic neighbors.

The crowd began to howl and hiss. An old IRA veteran fortified with spirits crashed through the police barrier and ran into the street, racing at the Orangemen, screaming as he ran, "Fucking bloody murdering bastards! I'll kill you!"

A half dozen of the Orangemen hoisted bullhorns and broke into song:

> "A rope, a rope, to hang the Pope!
> A pennyworth o' cheese to choke him!
> A pint o' lamp oil to wrench it down,
> And a big hot fire to roast him!"

Several of the enraged crowd broke from the sidewalks and ran into the street, spurred on by a few men who seemed to have materialized suddenly as their leaders. This vanguard was soon joined by streams of men, women, and teen-agers as the barriers began falling up and down the Avenue.

The few mounted police who had not headed to the reviewing stands formed a protective phalanx around the Orangemen, and a paddy wagon escorted by patrol cars began moving up Fiftieth Street to rescue the Orangemen from the crowd that had suddenly turned into a mob. The police swung clubs to keep the surging mob away from the still singing Orangemen. All the techniques of crowd control, learned in the Police Academy and learned on the streets, were employed in an effort to save the dozen Orangemen from being lynched, and the Orangemen themselves seemed finally to recognize their perilous position as hundreds of people ran out of control. They laid down their bullhorns and banner and joined the police in fighting their way to the safety of the approaching paddy wagon.

Patrick Burke ran south on Fifth Avenue, weaving in and out of the spectators and marchers who filled the street. He drew up in front of a parked patrol car, out of breath, and held up his badge. "Can you call mobile at the Cathedral?"

The patrolman shook his head and pointed to the static-filled radio.

"Take me to the Cathedral. Quick!" He grabbed the rear-door handle.

The uniformed sergeant sitting beside the driver called out. "No way! We can't move through this mob. If we hit someone, they'll tear us apart."

"Shit." Burke slammed the door and recrossed the Avenue. He vaulted the wall into Central Park and ran south along a path paralleling the Avenue. He came out of the park at Grand Army Plaza and began moving south through the increasingly disorderly mob. He knew it could take him half an hour to move the remaining nine blocks to the Cathedral, and he knew that the parallel avenues were probably not much better, even if he could get to them through a side street. He was not going to make it.

Suddenly a black horse appeared in front of him. A young policewoman, with blond hair tucked under her helmet, was sitting impassively atop the horse. He pushed alongside the woman and showed his badge. "Burke, Intelligence Division. I have to get to the Cathedral. Can you push this nag through this mob with me on the back?"

She regarded Burke, taking in his disheveled appearance. "This is not a nag, Lieutenant, but if you're in so much of a hurry, jump on." She reached down. Burke took her hand, put his foot in the stirrup, and swung heavily onto the rear of the horse.

The policewoman spurred the horse forward. "Giddyap! Come on, Commissioner!"

"I'm only a lieutenant."

The policewoman glanced over her shoulder as the horse began to move forward. "That's the horse's name—Commissioner."

"Oh. What's your . . . ?"

"Police Officer Foster . . . Betty."

"Nice. Good names. Let's move it."

The trained police horse and the rider were in their element, darting, weaving, cutting into every brief opening, and scattering knots of people in their path without seriously injuring anyone.

Burke held tightly to the woman's waist. He looked up and saw that they were approaching the intersection at Fifty-seventh Street. He shouted into her ear, "You dance good, Betty. Come here often?"

The policewoman turned her head and looked at him. "This run had damned well better be important, Lieutenant."

"It's the most important horse ride since Paul Revere's."

Major Bartholomew Martin stood at the window of a small room on the tenth floor of the British Empire Building in Rockefeller Center. He watched the riot that swirled around the Cathedral, then turned to the man standing beside him. "Well, Kruger, it appears that the Fenians have arrived."

The other man, an American, said, "Yes, for better or for worse." He paused, then asked, "Did you know this was going to happen?"

"Not exactly. Brian Flynn does not confide in me. I gave him some ideas, some options. His only prohibition was not to attack British property or personnel—like blowing up this building, for instance. But you never quite know with these people." Major Martin stared off into space for a few seconds, then spoke in a faraway voice. "You know, Kruger, when I finally caught up with the bastard in Belfast last winter, he was a beaten man—physically as well as mentally. All he wanted was for me to kill him quickly. And I wanted very much to accommodate him, I assure you, but then I thought better of it. I turned him around, as we say, then pointed him at America and set him loose. A dangerous business, I know, like grabbing that tiger by the tail. But it's paid off, I think."

Kruger stared at him for a long time, then said, "I hope we've calculated American public reaction correctly."

Martin smiled as he took some brandy from a flask. "If the American public was ambivalent about the Irish problem yesterday, they are not so ambivalent today." He looked at Kruger. "I'm sure this will help your service a bit."

Kruger replied, "And if it doesn't help, then you owe us a favor. In fact, I wanted to speak to you about something we have planned in Hong Kong."

"Ah, intrigue. Yes, yes, I want to hear all about it. But later. Enjoy the parade." He opened the window, and the sound of crashing windows, police sirens, and thousands of people filled the small room. *"Erin go bragh,* as they say."

14

Maureen Malone felt someone tap her on the shoulder. She turned to see a man holding a badge in front of her face. "Bureau of Special Services, Miss Malone. Some of the crowd is turning their attention up here. We have to get you into the Cathedral. Mr. Baxter, you too. Please follow us."

Baxter looked down at the crowd in the street and at the police line, arms locked, at the curb. "I think we're perfectly safe here for now."

The man answered, "Sir, you have to get out of here for the safety of the other people on the steps—please—"

"Yes, yes, I see. All right. Miss Malone, he's quite right."

Maureen and Baxter turned and mounted the steps. Maureen saw the red vestments of the Cardinal as he moved through the crowded steps in front of them, flanked by two men.

Other BSS men on the steps had moved around the Monsignor and the other priests and church people, eyeing the crowd closely. Two BSS men noticed that the Cardinal, Malone, and Baxter were being led away by unknown men and began to follow, pushing their way toward the portals. Two priests on the top step fell in behind them, and the two BSS men felt the press of something hard on their backs. "Freeze," said one of the priests softly, "or we'll blow your spines open."

The police in the mobile headquarters van beside the Cathedral had lost radio communication as static filled the frequencies, but they were still reporting by telephone. Without warning an ambulance coming down Fifty-first Street swerved and sideswiped the headquarters van. The van shot forward, and the lines connecting it to the streetlamp snapped. The ambulance drivers abandoned their vehicle and disappeared quickly into the crowded lobby of the Olympic Tower.

Maureen Malone, Harold Baxter, and the Cardinal walked abreast down the main aisle of the crowded Cathedral. Two men walked behind them, and two men set the pace in front. Maureen could see that the priest in the pulpit was Father Murphy, and another priest was kneeling at the communion rail. As she moved closer to the kneeling priest she was aware that there was something familiar about him.

The Cardinal turned and looked back up the aisle, then asked his escort, "Where is Monsignor Downes? Why aren't the others with us?"

One of the men answered, "They'll be along. Please keep moving, Your Eminence."

Father Murphy tried to continue the Mass, but he was distracted again by the shouts and sirens outside. He looked out over the two thousand worshipers in the pews and in the aisles, and his eye caught a movement of brilliant red in the main aisle. He stared at the disturbing sight of the Cardinal walking toward the altar, flanked by Malone and Baxter and escorted by security men. The thought that something was happening outside to mar this great day upset him. He forgot where he was in the Mass and said abruptly, "The Mass is ended. Go in peace." He added hurriedly, "No. Wait. Stay until we know what is happening. Stay in your seats, please."

Father Murphy turned and saw the priest who had been kneeling at the communion rail now standing on the top step of the pulpit. He recognized the tall priest with the deep green eyes and was, oddly, not surprised to see him again. He cleared his throat. "Yes?"

Brian Flynn slipped a pistol from under his black coat and kept it near his side. "Stand back."

Murphy took a deep breath. "Who the hell are you?"

"I'm the new archbishop." Flynn pushed Murphy into the rear of the pulpit and took the microphone. He watched the Cardinal approaching the altar, then began to address the worshipers who were still standing in the pews. "Ladies and gentlemen," he began in a carefully measured cadence, "may I have your attention. . . ."

Maureen Malone stopped abruptly in the open area a few feet from the altar rail. She stared up at the pulpit, transfixed by the tall, dark figure standing there in the dim light. The man behind her nudged her forward. She turned slowly. "Who are you?"

The man revealed a pistol stuck in his waistband. "Not the police, I assure you." The New York accent had disappeared, replaced by a light brogue. "Keep walking. You, too, Baxter, Your Eminence."

One of the men in front opened the gate in the marble altar railing and turned. "Come in, won't you?"

Patrick Burke, seated uneasily on the horse, looked over the heads of the crowd. Two blocks beyond he could see mass confusion, worse than that which swirled around him. The shop windows of Cartier and Gucci were broken, as were most of the other windows along the Avenue. Uniformed police stood in front of the displays of many of the shops, but there was no apparent looting, only that strange mixture of fighting and reveling that the Irish affectionately called a donnybrook. Burke could see the Cathedral now, and it was obvious that whatever had sparked this turmoil had begun there.

The crowd immediately around him was made up of marching units that were staying together, passing bottles, and singing. A brass band was playing "East Side, West Side," backed by an enthusiastic chorus. The policewoman spurred the horse on.

Midway down the block before the Cathedral the crowd became tighter, and the horse was straining to sidestep through. Bodies crushed against the riders' legs, then fell away as the horse made another lunge. "Keep pushing! Keep going!" called Burke.

The policewoman shouted, "God, they're packed so tight. . . ." She pulled back on the reins, and the horse reared up. The crowd scattered, and she drove into the opening, then repeated the maneuver.

Burke felt his stomach heave and caught his breath. "Nice! Nice! Good work!"

"How far do I have to get?"

"When Commissioner is kneeling at the communion rail, I'll tell you!"

Brian Flynn waited until the Cardinal and the others were safely inside the railing of the high altar, then said into the microphone, "Ladies and gentlemen, there is a small fire in the basement. Please stay calm. Leave quickly through the doors, including the front doors."

A cry went up from the congregation, and a few men interspersed throughout the Cathedral shouted, "Fire! Fire! Run!"

The pews emptied rapidly, and the aisles streamed with people pushing toward the exits. Racks of votive candles went down, spilling and cracking on the floor. The bookshop near the south spire emptied, and the first wave of people filled the vestibules and surged through the three sets of front doors, pouring out onto the steps.

The spectators on the steps suddenly found themselves pushed by a sea of people coming through the portals, and were swept down across the sidewalk, into the police barricades, through the line of policemen, and into the riot on Fifth Avenue.

Monsignor Downes tried to fight against the tide and get into the Cathedral, but found himself in the street squeezed between a heavy woman and a burly police officer.

The two bogus priests who had been pressing guns into the backs of the Bureau of Special Services men blended into the moving throng and disappeared. The two BSS men turned and tried to remount the steps but were carried down into the Avenue by the crowd.

Police scooters toppled, and patrol cars were covered with people trying to escape the crush of the crowd. Marching units broke ranks and became engulfed in the mob. Police tried to set up perimeters to keep the area of the disturbance contained, but without radio communication their actions were uncoordinated and ineffective.

Television news crews filmed the scene until they were overwhelmed by the surging mob.

Inspector Philip Langley peered down from the New York Police Department command helicopter into the darkening canyons below. He turned to Deputy Police Commissioner Rourke and shouted above the beat of the rotor blades. "I think the Saint Patrick's Day Parade is over."

The Deputy Commissioner eyed him for a long second, then looked down at the incredible scene. Rush hour traffic was stalled for miles, and a sea of people completely covered the streets and sidewalks as far south as Thirty-fourth Street and as far north as Seventy-second Street. Close to a million people were in the small midtown area at this hour, and not one of them was going to get home in time for dinner. "Lot of unhappy citizens down there, Philip."

Langley lit a cigarette. "I'll hand in my resignation tonight."

The Deputy Commissioner looked up at him. "I hope there's somebody around to accept it." He looked back at the streets. "Almost every ranking officer in the New York Police Department is down there somewhere, cut off from communication, cut off from their command." He turned to Langley. "This is the worst yet."

Langley shook his head. "I think the worst is yet to come."

In the intersection at Fiftieth Street, Burke could see the bright orange sashes of men being led into a paddy wagon. Burke remembered the Irish saying: "If you want an audience, start a fight." These Orangemen had wanted an audience, and he knew why; he knew, too, that they were not Orangemen at all but Boston Provos recruited to cause a diversion—dumb Micks with more courage than brains.

The policewoman turned to him as she urged the horse on. "Who are those people with orange sashes?"

"It's a long story. Go on. Almost there—"

Brian Flynn came down from the pulpit and faced Maureen Malone. "It's been a damned long time, Maureen."

She looked at him and replied in an even voice, "Not long enough."

He smiled. "Did you get my flowers?"

"I flushed them."

"You have one in your lapel."

Her face reddened. "So you've come to America after all, Brian."

"Yes. But as you can see, on my terms." He looked out over the Cathedral. The last of the worshipers were jamming the center vestibule, trying to squeeze through the great bronze doors. Two Fenians, Arthur Nulty dressed as a priest and Frank Gallagher dressed as a parade marshal, stood behind them and urged them on through the doors, onto the packed steps, but the crowd began to back up into the vestibule. All the other doors had been swung closed and bolted. Flynn looked at his watch. This was taking longer than he expected. He turned to Maureen. "Yes, on my terms. Do you see what I've *done?* Within half an hour all of America will see and hear this. We'll provide some good Irish theater for them. Better than the Abbey ever did."

Maureen saw in his eyes a familiar look of triumph, but mixed with that look was one of fear that she had never seen before. Like a little boy, she thought, who had stolen something from a shop and knows he might have to answer for his transgression very shortly. "You won't get away with this, you know."

He smiled, and the fear left his eyes. "Yes, I will."

Two of the Fenians who had posed as police walked around the altar and descended the stairs that led down to the sacristy. From the open archway on the left-hand wall of the sacristy, they heard footsteps approaching in the corridor that led from the rectory. Excited voices came from a similar opening on the opposite wall that led to the Cardinal's residence. All at once priests and uniformed policemen burst into the sacristy from both doors.

The two Fenians drew the sliding gates out of the wall until they met with a loud metallic ring, and the people in the sacristy looked up the stairs. A uniformed sergeant called out, "Hey! Open those gates!" He advanced toward the stairs.

The Fenians tied a chain through the scrolled brasswork and produced a padlock.

The sergeant drew his pistol. Another policeman came up behind him and did the same.

The Fenians seemed to pay no attention to the officers and snapped the heavy lock on the ends of the wrapped chain. One of them looked up, smiled, and gave a brief salute. "Sorry, lads, you'll have to go round." Both Fenians disappeared up the stairs. One of them, Pedar Fitzgerald, sat near the crypt door where he could see the gate. The other, Eamon Farrell, came around the altar and nodded to Flynn.

Flynn turned to Baxter for the first time. "Sir Harold Baxter?"

"That's correct."

He stared at Baxter. "Yes, I'd enjoy killing you."

Baxter replied without inflection, "Your kind would enjoy killing anyone."

Flynn turned away and looked at the Cardinal. "Your Eminence." He bowed his head, and it wasn't clear if he was mocking or sincere. "My name is Finn MacCumail, Chief of the new Fenian Army. This church is now mine. This is my Bruidean. You know the term? My place of sanctuary."

The Cardinal seemed not to hear him. He asked abruptly, "Is this Cathedral on fire?"

"That depends to a large extent on what happens in the next few minutes."

The Cardinal stared at him, and neither man flinched. The Cardinal finally spoke. "Get out of here. Get out while you can."

"I can't, and I don't want to." He looked up at the choir loft over the main doors where Jack Leary, dressed as a colonial soldier, stood with a rifle. Flynn's eyes dropped to the main doors nearly a block away. People still jammed the vestibule, and noise and light passed in through the open doors. He turned to Father Murphy, who stood next to him. "Father, you may leave. Hurry down the aisle before the doors close."

Murphy strode deliberately to a spot beside the Cardinal. "We are both leaving."

"No. No, on second thought, we may find a use for you later." Flynn turned to Maureen again and moved closer to her. He spoke softly. "You knew, didn't you? Even before you got the flowers?"

"I knew."

"Good. We still know each other, don't we? We've spoken over the years and across the miles, haven't we, Maureen?"

She nodded.

A young woman dressed as a nun appeared at the altar rail holding a large pistol. In the front pew a bearded old man, apparently sleeping on the bench, rose, stretched, and came up behind her. Everyone watched as the two people ascended the steps of the altar sanctuary.

The old man nodded to the hostages and spoke in a clear, vibrant voice. "Your Eminence, Father Murphy, Miss Malone, Sir Harold. I am John Hickey, fancifully code-named Dermot, in keeping with the pagan motif suggested by our leader, Finn MacCumail." He made an exaggerated bow to Flynn. "I am a poet, scholar, soldier, and patriot, much like the original Fenians. You may have heard of me." He looked around and saw the signs of recognition in the eyes of the four hostages. "No, not dead, as you can plainly see. But dead before the sun rises again, I'll wager. Dead in the ruins of this smoldering Cathedral. A magnificent funeral pyre it'll be, befitting a man of my rank. Oh, don't look so glum, Cardinal, there's a way out—if we all keep our senses about us." He turned to the young woman beside him. "May I present our Grania— or, as she prefers her real name, Megan Fitzgerald."

Megan Fitzgerald said nothing but looked into the face of each hostage. Her eyes came to rest on Maureen Malone, and she looked her up and down.

Maureen stared back at the young woman. She knew there would be a woman. There always was with Flynn. Flynn was that type of man who needed a woman watching in order to stiffen his courage, the way other men needed a drink. Maureen looked into the face of Megan Fitzgerald: high cheekboned, freckled, with a mouth that seemed set in a perpetual sneer, and eyes that should have been lovely but were something quite different. Too young, and not likely to get much older in the company of Brian Flynn. Maureen saw herself ten years before.

Megan Fitzgerald stepped up to her, the big pistol swinging nonchalantly from her left hand, and put her mouth close to Maureen's ear. "You understand that I'm looking for an excuse to kill you."

"I hope I find the courage to do something to give you one. Then we'll see how *your* courage stands up."

Megan Fitzgerald's body tensed visibly. After a few seconds she stepped back and looked around the altar, sweeping each person standing there with a cold stare and meeting Flynn's look of disapproval. She turned, walked down from the altar, and then strode down the main aisle toward the center doors.

Flynn watched her, then looked past her into the vestibule. The doors were still open. He hadn't counted on the crowd being so large. If they couldn't get the doors closed and bolted soon, the police would force their way in and there would be a fire fight. As he watched, Megan passed into the vestibule and raised her pistol. He saw the smoke flash from the upturned muzzle of her gun, then heard the report roll through the massive church and echo in and out of the vaults and side altars. A scream went up from the crowd in the vestibule, and their backs receded as they found a new strength and a more immediate reason to push through the crowd blocking the steps.

Flynn watched Megan bring the gun down into a horizontal position and aim it at the opening. Nulty and Gallagher maneuvered around, and each took up a position behind the doors, pushing them against the last of the fleeing worshipers.

Megan dropped to one knee and steadied her aim with both hands.

Patrick Burke shouted to the policewoman, "Up the steps! Up to the front door!"

Betty Foster spurred the horse up the steps where they curved around to Fifty-first Street, and moved diagonally through the crowd toward the center doors.

Burke saw the last of the worshipers flee through the doors, and the horse broke into the open space between them and the portals. The policewoman reined the horse around and kicked its flanks. "Come on, Commissioner! Up! Up!"

Burke drew his service revolver and shouted, "Draw your piece! Through the doors!"

Betty Foster held the reins with her left hand and drew her revolver.

A few yards from the portals the big bronze ceremonial doors—sixteen feet across, nearly two stories high, and weighing ten thousand pounds apiece—began closing. Burke knew they were pushed by unseen persons standing behind them. The dimly lit vestibule came into sight, and he saw a nun kneeling there. Behind her, the vast, deserted Cathedral stretched back a hundred yards, through a forest of stone columns, to the raised altar sanctuary where Burke could see people standing. A figure in bright red stood out against the white marble.

The doors were half closed now, and the horse's head was a yard from the opening. Burke knew they were going to make it. And then . . . what?

Suddenly the image of the kneeling nun filled his brain, and his eyes focused on her again. From her extended arm Burke saw a flash of light, then heard a loud, echoing sound followed by a sharp crack.

The horse's front legs buckled, and the animal pitched forward. Burke was aware of Betty Foster flying into the air, then felt himself falling forward. His face struck the granite step a foot from the doors. He crawled toward the small opening, but the bronze doors came together and shut in his face. He heard, above all the noise around him, the sound of the floor bolts sliding home.

Burke rolled onto his back and sat up. He turned to the policewoman, who was lying on the steps, blood running from her forehead. As he watched, she sat up slowly.

Burke stood and offered her his hand, but she got to her feet without his aid and looked down at her mount. A small wound on Commissioner's chest ran with blood; frothy blood trickled from the horse's open mouth and steamed in a puddle as it collected on the cold stone. The horse tried to stand but fell clumsily back onto its side. Betty Foster fired into his head. After putting her hand to the horse's nostrils to make certain he was dead, she holstered her revolver. She looked up at Burke, then back at her horse. Walking slowly down the steps, she disappeared into the staring crowd.

Burke looked out into the Avenue. Rotating beacons from the police cars cast swirling red and white light on the chaotic scene and across the façades of the surrounding buildings. Occasionally, above the general bedlam, Burke could hear a window smash, a whistle blow, a scream ring out.

He turned around and stared at the Cathedral. Taped to one of the bronze ceremonial doors, over the face of St. Elizabeth Seton, was a piece of cardboard with hand-lettering on it. He stepped closer to read it in the fading light.

THIS CATHEDRAL IS UNDER THE CONTROL
OF THE IRISH FENIAN ARMY

It was signed, FINN MACCUMAIL.

BOOK IV

The Cathedral: Siege

Friendship, joy and peace! If the outside world only realized the wonders of this Cathedral, there would never be a vacant pew.

Parishioner

15

Patrick Burke stood at the front doors of St. Patrick's Cathedral, his hands in his pockets and a cigarette in his mouth. Lightly falling sleet melted on the flanks of the dead horse and ran in rivulets onto the icy stone steps. The crowds in the surrounding streets were not completely under control, but the police had rerouted the remainder of the marching units west to Sixth Avenue. Burke could hear drums and bagpipes above the roar of the mob. The two hundred and twenty-third St. Patrick's Day Parade would go on until the last marcher arrived at Eighty-fourth Street, even if it meant marching through Central Park to get there.

Automobile horns were blaring incessantly, and police whistles and sirens cut through the windy March dusk. *What a fucking mess.* Burke wondered if anyone out there knew that the Cathedral was under the control of gunmen. He looked at his watch—not yet five thirty. The six o'clock news would begin early and not end until this ended.

Burke turned and examined the bronze ceremonial doors, then put his shoulder to one of them and pushed. The door moved slightly, then sprang back, closing. From behind the doors Burke heard a shrill alarm. "Smart sons of bitches." It wasn't going to be easy to get the Cathedral away from Finn Mac-Cumail. He heard a muffled voice call out from behind the door. "Get away! We're putting mines on the doors!"

Burke moved back and stared up at the massive doors, noticing them for the first time in twenty years. On a right-hand panel a bronze relief of St. Patrick stared down at him, a crooked staff in one hand, a serpent in the other. To the saint's right was a Celtic harp, to his left the mythical phoenix, appropriated

511

from the pagans, rising to renewed life from its own ashes. Burke turned slowly and started walking down the steps. "Okay, Finn or Flynn, or whatever you call yourself—you may have gotten in standing tall, but you won't be leaving that way."

Brian Flynn stood at the railing of the choir loft and looked out over the vast Cathedral spread out over an area larger than a football field. Seventy towering stained-glass windows glowed with the outside lights of the city like dripping jewels, and dozens of hanging chandeliers cast a soft luminescence over the dark wooden pews. Rows of gray granite pillars reached up to the vaulted ceiling like the upraised arms of the faithful supporting the house of God. Flynn turned to John Hickey. "It would take some doing to level this place."

"Leave it to me, Brian."

Flynn said, "The first priority of the police is that mob out there. We've bought some time to set up our defense." Flynn raised a pair of field glasses and looked at Maureen. Even at this distance he saw that her face was red, and her jaw was set in a hard line. He focused on Megan who had assembled three men and two women and was making an inspection of the perimeter walls. She had taken off the nun's wimple, revealing long red hair that fell to her shoulders. She walked quickly, now peeling off her nun's habit and throwing the black and white garments carelessly onto the floor until she was clad in only jeans and a T-shirt, which had a big red apple on it and the words *I Love New York*. She stopped by the north transept doors and looked up at the southeast triforium as she called out, "Gallagher!"

Frank Gallagher, dressed in the morning coat and striped pants of a parade marshal, leaned over the balcony parapet and pointed his sniper rifle at her, taking aim through the scope. He shouted back, "Check!"

Megan moved on.

Flynn unrolled a set of blueprints and rested them on the rail of the choir loft. He tapped the plans of the Cathedral with his open hand and said, as though the realization had just come to him, "We took it."

Hickey nodded and stroked his wispy beard. "Aye, but can we keep it? Can we hold it with a dozen people against twenty thousand policemen?"

Flynn turned to Jack Leary standing near the organ keyboard beside him. "Can we hold it, Jack?"

Leary nodded slowly. "Twenty thousand, or twenty, they can only come in a few at a time." He patted his modified M-14 rifle with attached scope. "Anyone who survives the mines on the doors will be dead before he gets three paces."

Flynn looked closely at Leary in the subdued light. Leary looked comical in his colonial marching uniform and with his green-painted rifle. But there was nothing funny about his eyes or his expressionless voice.

Flynn looked back over the Cathedral and glanced at the blueprints. This building was shaped like a cross. The long stem of the cross was the nave, holding the main pews and five aisles; the cross-arms were the transepts, containing more pews and an exit from the end of each arm. Two arcaded triforia, long, dark galleries supported by columns, overhung the nave, running as far as the transepts. Two shorter triforia began at the far side of the transepts and overlooked the altar. This was the basic layout of the structure to be defended.

Flynn looked at the top of the blueprints. They showed the five-story rectory nestled in the northeast quadrant of the cross outside the Cathedral. The rectory was connected to the Cathedral by basement areas under the terraces, which did not appear on the blueprints. In the southeast quadrant was the Cardinal's residence, also separated by terraces and gardens and connected underground. These uncharted connections, Flynn understood, were a weak point in the defense. "I wish we could have held the two outside buildings."

Hickey smiled. "Next time."

Flynn smiled in return. The old man had remained an enigma, swinging precipitantly between clownishness and decisiveness. Flynn looked back at the blueprints. The top of the cross was the rounded area called the apse. In the apse was the Lady Chapel, a quiet, serene area of long, narrow stained-glass windows. Flynn pointed to the blueprint. "The Lady Chapel has no outside connections, and I've decided not to post a man there—can't spare anyone."

Hickey leaned over the blueprints. "I'll examine it for hidden passages. Church architecture wouldn't be church architecture, Brian, without hollow walls and secret doors. Places for the Holy Ghost to run about—places where priests can pop up on you unawares and scare the hell out of you by whispering your name."

"Have you heard of Whitehorn Abbey outside of Belfast?"

"I spent a night there once. Did you get a scare there, lad?" Hickey laughed.

Flynn looked out over the Cathedral again, concentrating on the raised area of black and white marble called the altar sanctuary. In the middle of the sanctuary sat the altar, raised still higher on a broad marble plinth. The cold marble and bronze of the area was softened by fields of fresh green carnations, symbolizing, Flynn imagined, the green sod of Ireland, which would not have looked or smelled as nice on the altar.

On both sides of the sanctuary were rows of wooden pews reserved for clergy. In the pews to the right sat Maureen, Baxter, and Father Murphy, all looking very still from this distance. Flynn placed his field glasses to his eyes and focused on Maureen again. She didn't appear at all frightened, and he liked that. He noticed that her lips were moving as she stared straight ahead. Praying? No, not Maureen. Baxter's lips were moving also. And Father Murphy's. "They're plotting dark things against us, John."

"Good," said Hickey. "Maybe they'll keep us entertained."

Flynn swung the field glasses to the left. Facing the hostages across the checkered marble floor sat the Cardinal on his elevated throne of red velvet, absolutely motionless. "No sanctuary in the sanctuary," commented Flynn under his breath.

Leary heard him and called out, "A sanctuary of sorts. If they leave that area, I'll kill them."

Flynn leaned farther over the rail. Directly behind the altar were the sacristy stairs, not visible from the loft, where Pedar Fitzgerald, Megan's brother, sat on the landing holding a submachine gun. Fitzgerald was a good man, a man who knew that those chained gates had to be protected at any cost. He had his sister's courage without her savagery. "We still don't know if there's a way they can enter the crypt from an underground route and come up behind Pedar."

Hickey glanced again at the blueprints. "We'll get the crypt keys and the keys to this whole place later and have a proper look around the real estate. We need time, Brian. Time to tighten our defense. Damn these blueprints, they're not very detailed. And damn this church. It's like a marble sieve with more holes in it than the story of the Resurrection."

"I hope the police don't get hold of the architect."

"You should have kidnapped him last night along with Terri O'Neal," Hickey said.

"Too obvious. That would have put Intelligence onto something."

"Then you should have killed him and made it look like an accident."

Flynn shook his head. "One has to draw a line somewhere. Don't you think so?"

"You're a lousy revolutionary. It's a wonder you've come as far as you have."

"I've come farther than most. I'm here."

16

Major Bartholomew Martin put down his field glasses and let out a long breath. "Well, they've done it. No apparent casualties . . . except that fine horse." He closed the window against the cold wind and sleet. "Burke almost got himself killed, however."

Kruger shrugged. It never paid to examine these things too closely.

Major Martin put on his topcoat. "Sir Harold was a good sort. Played a good game of bridge. Anyway, you see, Flynn went back on his word. Now they'll want to kill poor Harry as soon as things don't go their way."

Kruger glanced out the window. "I think you planned on Baxter getting kidnapped."

Major Martin moved toward the door. "I planned *nothing,* Kruger. I only provided the opportunity and the wherewithal. Most of this is as much a surprise to me as it is to you and the police." Martin looked at his watch. "My consulate will be looking for me, and your people will be looking for you. Remember, Kruger, the first requirement of a successful liar is a good memory. Don't forget what you're not supposed to know, and please remember the things you *are* supposed to know." He pulled on his gloves as he left.

Megan Fitzgerald motioned to the three men and two women with her and moved quickly toward the front of the Cathedral. The five of them followed her, burdened with suitcases, slung rifles, and rocket tubes. They entered the vestibule of the north tower, rode up the small elevator, and stepped off into the choir practice room in the tower. Megan moved into the choir loft.

Jack Leary was standing at the end of the loft, some distance from Flynn and Hickey, establishing his fields of fire. Megan said curtly, "Leary, you understand your orders?"

The sniper turned and stared at her.

Megan stared back into his pale, watery eyes. Soft eyes, she thought, but she knew how they hardened as the rifle traveled up to his shoulder. Eyes that saw things not in fluid motion but in a series of still pictures, like a camera lens. She had watched him in practice many times. Perfect eye-hand coordination— "muscle memory" he had called it on the one occasion he had spoken to her. Muscle memory—a step below instinct, as though the brain wasn't even involved in the process—optic nerves and motor nerves, bypassing the brain, controlled by some primitive bundle of fibers found only in the lower forms of life. The others stayed away from Leary, but Megan was fascinated by him. "Answer me, Leary. Do you know your orders, man?"

He nodded almost imperceptibly as his eyes took in the young woman standing in front of him.

Megan walked along the rail and came up beside Flynn and Hickey. She placed the field phone on the railing and looked at the outside telephone on the organ. "Call the police."

Flynn didn't look up from the blueprints. "They'll call us."

Hickey said to her, "I'd advise you not to upset Mr. Leary. He seems incapable of witty bantering, and he'd probably shoot you if he couldn't think of anything to say."

Megan looked back at Leary, then said to Hickey, "We understand each other."

Hickey smiled. "Yes, I've noticed a silent communication between you—but what other type could there be with a man who has a vocabulary of fourteen words, eight of which have to do with rifles?"

Megan turned and walked back to the entrance of the choir practice room where the others were waiting, and she led them up a spiral iron staircase. At a level above the choir practice room she found a door and kicked it open, motioning to Abby Boland. "Come with me," she said.

The long triforium stretched out along the north side of the Cathedral, an unlit gallery of dusty stone and air-conditioning ducts. A flagpole of about twenty feet in length jutted out from the parapet over the nave, flying the white and yellow Papal flag.

Megan turned to Abby Boland, who was dressed in the short skirt and blue blouse of a twirler from Mother Cabrini High School, a place neither of them had heard of until a week before. "This is your post," said Megan. "Remember, the rocket is to use if you see a Saracen—or whatever they call them here— coming through your assigned door. The sniper rifle is for close-in defense, if they come through the tower door there—and for blowing your own brains out if you've a mind to. Any questions? No?" She looked the girl up and down. "You should have thought to bring some clothes with you. It'll be cold up here tonight." Megan returned to the tower.

Abby Boland unslung her rifles and put them down beside the rocket. She slipped off her tight-fitting shoes, unbuttoned her constricting blouse, and sighted through the scope of the sniper rifle, then lowered it and looked around. It occurred to her that rather than freeing her husband, Jonathan, she might very well end up in jail herself, on this side of the Atlantic, too long a distance to intertwine their fingers through the mesh wire of Long Kesh. She might also end up dead, of course, which might be better for both of them.

Megan Fitzgerald continued up the stairs of the bell tower and turned into a side passage. She found a pull chain and lit a small bulb revealing a section of the huge attic. Wooden catwalks ran over the plaster lathing of the vaulted ceiling below and stretched back into the darkness. The four people with her walked quickly over the catwalks, turning on lights in the cold, musty attic.

Megan could see the ten dormered hatches overhead that led to the slate roof above. On the floor, at intervals, were small winches that lowered the chandeliers to the floors below for maintenance. She turned and moved to the big arched window at the front peak of the attic. Stone tracery on the outside of the Cathedral partially blocked the view, and grime covered the small panes in front of her. She wiped a section with her hand and stared down into Fifth Avenue. The block in front of the Cathedral was nearly deserted, but the police had not yet cleared the crowds out of the intersections on either side. Falling sleet was visible against the streetlights, and ice covered the streets and sidewalks and collected on the shoulders of Atlas.

Megan looked up at the International Building in Rockefeller Center directly across from her. The two side wings of the building were lower than the attic, and she could see people moving through the ice, people sitting huddled on the big concrete tubs that held bare plants and trees. The uniformed police had no rifles, and she knew that the Cathedral was not yet surrounded by the SWAT teams euphemistically called the Emergency Services Division in New York. She saw no soldiers, either, and remembered that Americans rarely called on them.

She turned back to the attic. The four people had opened the suitcases and deposited piles of votive candles at intervals along the catwalks. Megan called out to Jean Kearney and Arthur Nulty. "Find the fire axes, chop wood from the catwalks, and build pyres around the candles. Cut the fire hoses up here and string the wire for the field telephone. Be quick about it. Mullins and Devane, grab an ax and come with me."

Megan Fitzgerald retraced her steps out of the attic, followed by the two men who had posed as BSS Security, Donald Mullins and Rory Devane. She continued her climb up to the bell tower. Mullins carried a roll of communication wire, which he played out behind him. Devane carried the weapons and axes.

Arthur Nulty offered Jean Kearney a cigarette. He looked over her Kelly-green Aer Lingus stewardess uniform. "You look very sexy, lass. Would it be a sacrilege to do it up here, do you think?"

"We'll not have time for that."

"Time is all we've got up here. God, but it's cold. We'll need some warming and there's no spirits allowed, so that leaves . . ."

"We'll see. Jesus, Arthur, if your wife—what happens to us if we get her out of Armagh?"

Arthur Nulty let go of her arm and looked away. "Well . . . now . . . let's take things one a time." He picked up an ax and swung it, shattering a wooden railing, then ripped the railing from its post and threw it atop a pile of votive candles. "Whole place is wood up here. Never thought I'd be burning a church. If Father Flannery could see me now." He took another swing with the ax. "Jesus, I hope it doesn't come to that. They'll give in before they see this Cathedral burned. In twenty-four hours your brothers will be in Dublin. Your old dad will be pleased, Jean. He thought he'd never see the boys again." He threw a post on the woodpile. "She called them pyres, Megan did. Doesn't she know that pyres refer only to places to burn corpses?"

17

P atrick Burke posted patrolmen at each of the Cathedral's portals with the warning that the doors were mined, then came back to the front of the Cathedral and approached a parked patrol car. "Any commo yet?"

The patrolman shook his head. "No, sir. What's going on in there?"

"There are armed gunmen inside, so keep pushing the crowd back. Tell the officer in charge to begin a cordon operation."

"Yes, sir." The patrol car moved away through the nearly deserted Avenue.

Burke remounted the steps and saw Police Officer Betty Foster kneeling in the ice beside her horse.

She looked up at him. "You still here?" She looked back at the horse. "I have to get the saddle." She unhooked the girth. "What the hell's going on in there?" She tugged at the saddle. "You almost got me killed."

He helped her pull at the saddle, but it wouldn't come loose. "Leave this here."

"I can't. It's police property."

"There's police property strewn up and down Fifth Avenue." He let go of the saddle and looked at the bell tower. "There'll be people in these towers soon, if they're not there already. Get this later when they recover the horse."

She straightened up. "Poor Commissioner. Both of them."

"What do you mean?"

"Police Commissioner Dwyer died of a heart attack—at the reviewing stands."

"Jesus Christ." Burke heard a noise from the bell tower overhead and pulled Betty Foster under the alcove of the front door. "Somebody's up there."

"Are you staying here?"

"Until things get straightened out."

She looked at him and said, "Are you brave, Lieutenant Burke?"

"No. Just stupid."

"That's what I thought." She laughed. "God, I thought I was going to pass out when I saw that nun—I guess it wasn't a nun—"

"Not likely."

"That woman, pointing a gun at us."

"You did fine."

"Did I? I guess I did." She paused and looked around. "I'm going to be on duty for a long time. I have to go back to Varick Street and get remounted."

"Remounted?" A bizarre sexual image flashed through his mind. "Oh. Right. Keep close to the wall. I don't know if those people up in the tower are looking for blue targets, but it's better to assume they are."

She hesitated. "See you later." She moved out of the alcove, keeping close to the wall. She called back, "I didn't just come back for the saddle. I wanted to see if you were all right."

Burke watched her round the corner of the tower. This morning neither he nor Betty Foster would have given each other a second glance. Now, however, they had things going for them—riots, gunpowder, horses—great stimulants, powerful aphrodisiacs. He looked at his watch. This lull would not last much longer.

Megan Fitzgerald climbed into the bell room and stood catching her breath as she looked around the cold room, peering into the weak light cast by the single bulb. She saw Flynn's radio jamming device on a crossbeam from which hung three huge bells, each with a turning wheel and a pull strap. Gusts of cold March wind blew in from the eight sets of copper louvers in the octagon-shaped tower room. The sound of police bullhorns and sirens was carried up into the eighteen-story-high room.

Megan grabbed a steel-cut fire ax from Rory Devane, turned suddenly, and swung it at one of the sets of louvers, ripping them open and letting in the lights of the city. Mullins set to work on the other seven louvers, cutting them out of their stone casements as Devane knelt on the floor and connected a field telephone.

Megan turned to Mullins, who had moved to the window overlooking Fifth

Avenue. "Remember, Mullins, report *anything* unusual. Keep a sharp eye for helicopters. No shooting without orders."

Mullins looked out at Rockefeller Center. People were pressed to the windows opposite him, and, on the roofs below, people were pointing up at the ripped louvers. A police spotlight in the street came on, and its white beam circled and came to rest on the opening where Mullins stood. He moved back and blinked his eyes. "I'd like to put that spot out."

Megan nodded. "Might as well set them straight now."

Mullins leaned out of the opening and squinted into his sniper scope. He saw figures moving around at the periphery of the spotlight. He took a long breath, steadied his aim, then squeezed the trigger. The sound of the rifle exploded in the bell room, and Mullins saw the red tracer round streak down into the intersection. The spotlight suddenly lost its beam, fading from white to red to black. A hollow popping sound drifted into the bell room, followed by sounds of shouting. Mullins stepped back behind the stonework and blew his nose into a handkerchief. "Cold up here."

Devane sat on the floor and cranked the field phone. "Attic, this is bell tower. Can you hear me?"

The voice of Jean Kearney came back clearly. "Hear you, bell tower. What was that noise?"

Devane answered. "Mullins put out a spot. No problem."

"Roger. Stand by for commo check with choir loft. Choir loft, can you hear bell tower and attic?"

John Hickey's voice came over the line. "Hear you both. Commo established. Who the hell authorized you to shoot at a spotlight?"

Megan grabbed the field phone from Devane. "I did."

Hickey's voice had an edge of sarcasm and annoyance. "Ah, Megan, that was a rhetorical question, lass. I knew the answer to that. Watch yourself today."

Megan dropped the field phone on the floor and looked down at Devane. "Go on down and string the wire from the choir loft to the south tower, then knock out the louvers and take your post there."

Devane picked up a roll of communication wire and the fire ax and climbed down out of the bell room.

Megan moved from opening to opening. The walls of the Cathedral were bathed in blue luminescence from the Cathedral's floodlights in the gardens. To the north the massive fifty-one-story Olympic Tower reflected the Cathedral from its glass sides. To the east the Waldorf-Astoria's windows were lit against the black sky, and to the south the Cathedral's twin tower rose up, partially blocking the view of Saks Fifth Avenue. Police stood on the Saks roof, milling around, flapping their arms against the cold. In all the surrounding streets the crowd was being forced back block by block, and the deserted area around the Cathedral grew in size.

Megan looked back at Mullins, who was blowing into his hands. His young face was red with cold, and tinges of blue showed on his lips. She moved to the ladder in the middle of the floor. "Keep alert."

He watched Megan disappear down the ladder and suddenly felt lonely. "Bitch." She was not much older than he, but her movements, her voice, were those of an older woman. She had lost her youth in everything but her face and body.

Mullins looked around his solitary observation post, then peered back into Fifth Avenue. He unfastened a rolled flag around his waist and tied the corners to the louvers, then let it unfurl over the side of the tower. A wind made it snap against the gray marble, and the Cathedral's floodlights illuminated it nicely.

From the street and the rooftops an exclamation rose from the reporters and civilians still in the area. A few people cheered, and a few applauded. There were a few jeers as well.

Mullins listened to the mixed reaction, then pulled his head back into the tower and wiped the cold sleet from his face. He wondered with a sense of awe how he came to be standing in the bell tower of St. Patrick's Cathedral with a rifle. Then he remembered his older sister, Peg, widowed with three children, pacing the prison yard of Armagh. He remembered the night her husband, Barry Collins, was killed trying to take a prison van that was supposed to contain Maureen Malone's sister, Sheila. He remembered his mother looking after Peg's three children for days at a time while Peg went off with hard-looking men in dark coats. Mullins remembered the night he went into the streets of Belfast to find Brian Flynn and his Fenians, and how his mother wept and cursed after him. But most of all he remembered the bombs and gunfire that had rocked and split the Belfast nights ever since he was a child. Thinking back, he didn't see how he could have traveled any road that didn't lead here, or someplace like it.

Patrick Burke looked up. A green flag, emblazoned with the gold Irish harp, hung from the ripped louvers, and Burke could make out a man with a rifle standing in the opening. Burke turned and watched the police in the intersection wheeling away the smashed spotlight. The crowd was becoming more cooperative, concluding that anyone who could put out a spotlight at two hundred yards could put them out just as easily. Burke moved into the alcove of the tower door and spoke to the policeman he had posted there. "We'll just stand here awhile. That guy up there is still manufacturing adrenaline."

"I know the feeling."

Burke looked out over the steps. The green carpet was white with sleet now, and green carnations, plastic leprechaun hats, and paper pompoms littered the steps, sidewalks, and street. In the intersection of Fiftieth Street a huge Lambeg drum left by the Orangemen lay on its side. Black bowlers and bright orange sashes moved slowly southward in the wind. From the buildings of Rockefeller Center news cameramen were cautiously getting it all on film. Burke pictured it as it would appear on television. Zoom-in shots of the debris, a bowler tumbling end over end across the icy street. The voice-over, deep, resonant—"Today the ancient war between the English and the Irish came to Fifth Avenue. . . ." The Irish always gave you good theater.

Brian Flynn leaned out over the parapet rail of the choir loft and pointed to a small sacristy off the ambulatory as he said to Hickey, "Since we can't see the outside door of the bishop's sacristy or the elevator door, the police could theoretically beat the alarms and mines. Then we'd have policemen massed in that small sacristy."

Leary, who seemed to be able to hear things at great distances, called out from the far end of the choir loft. "And if they stick their heads into the ambulatory, I'll blow—"

Hickey shouted back, "Thank you, Mr. Leary. We know you will." He said softly to Flynn, "God Almighty, where'd you get that monster? I'll be afraid to scratch my ass down there."

Flynn answered quietly, "Yes, he has good eyes and ears."

"An American, isn't he?"

"Irish-American. Marine sniper in Vietnam."

"Does he know why he's here? Does he even know where the hell he *is?*"

"He's in a perch overlooking a free-fire zone. That's all he knows and all he cares about. He's being paid handsomely for his services. He's the only one of us besides you and me who has no relatives in British jails. I don't want a man up here with emotional ties to us. He'll kill according to standing orders, he'll kill any one of us I tell him to kill, and if we're attacked and overcome, he'll kill any of us who survives, if he's still able. He's the Angel of Death, the Grim Reaper, and the court of last resort."

"Does everyone know all of this?"

"No."

Hickey smiled, a half-toothless grin. "I underestimated you, Brian."

"Yes. You've been doing that. Let's go on with this. The Archbishop's sacristy—a problem, but only one of many—"

"I wish you'd brought more people."

Flynn spoke impatiently. "I have a great deal of help on the outside, but how many people do you think I could find to come in here to die?"

A distant look came over the old man's face. "There were plenty of good men and women in Dublin on Easter Monday, 1916. More than the besieged buildings could hold." Hickey's eyes took in the quiet Cathedral below. "No lack of volunteers then. And faith! What faith we all had. In the early days of the First War, sometime before the Easter Rising, my brother was in the British Army. Lot of Irish lads were then. Still are. You've heard of the Angels of Mons? No? Well, my brother Bob was with the British Expeditionary Force in France, and they were about to be annihilated by an overwhelming German force. Then, at a place called Mons, a host of heavenly angels appeared and stood between them and the Germans. Understandably the Germans fell back in confusion. It was in all the papers at the time. And people *believed* it, Brian. They believed the British Army was so blessed by God that He sent His angels to intervene on their behalf against their enemy."

Flynn looked at him. "Sounds like a mass hallucination of desperate men. When we start seeing angels here, we'll know we've had it, and—" He broke off abruptly and looked at Hickey closely in the dim light. For a brief second he imagined he was back in Whitehorn Abbey, listening to the stories of the old priest.

"What is it, lad?"

"Nothing. I suppose one shouldn't doubt the intervention of the supernatural. I'll tell you about it tomorrow."

Hickey laughed. "If you can tell it tomorrow, I'll believe it."

Flynn forced a smile in return. "I may be telling it to you in another place."

"Then I'll surely believe it."

Megan Fitzgerald came up behind George Sullivan setting the last of the mines on the south transept door. "Finished?"

Sullivan turned abruptly. "Jesus, don't do that, Megan, when I'm working with explosives."

She looked at Sullivan, dressed splendidly in the kilts of a bagpiper of the New York Police Emerald Society. "Grab your gear and follow me. Bring your bagpipes." She led him to a small door at the corner of the transept, and they walked up a spiral stone staircase, coming out onto the long south triforium. A flagpole with a huge American flag hanging from it pointed across the nave toward the Papal flag on the opposite triforium. Megan looked to the left, at the choir loft below, and watched Flynn and Hickey poring over their blueprints like two generals on the eve of battle. She found it odd that such different men seemed to be getting on well. She hadn't liked the idea of bringing

John Hickey in at the last moment. But the others felt they needed the old hero to legitimize themselves, a bona fide link with 1916, as though Hickey's presence could make them something other than the outcasts they all were.

She saw no need to draw on the past. The world had taken form for her in 1973 when she had seen her first bomb casualties in downtown Belfast on the way home from school, and had taken meaning and purpose when her older brother Tommy had been wounded and captured trying to free Sheila Malone. The distant past didn't exist, any more than the near future did. Her own personal memories were all the history she was concerned with.

She watched Flynn pointing and gesturing. He seemed not much different from the old man beside him. Yet he had been different once. To Tommy Fitzgerald, Brian Flynn was everything a man should be, and she had grown up seeing Brian Flynn, the legend in the making, through her older brother's eyes. Then came Brian's arrest and his release, suspicious at best. Then the break with the IRA, the forming of the new Fenian Army, his recruiting of her and her younger brother Pedar, and, finally, her inevitable involvement with him. She had not been disappointed in him as a lover, but as a revolutionary he had flaws. He would hesitate before destroying the Cathedral, but she would see to it that this decision was out of his hands.

Sullivan called out from the far end of the triforium, "The view is marvelous. How's the food?"

Megan turned to him. "If you've no qualms about feasting on blood, it's good and ample."

Sullivan sighted through his rifle. "Don't be a beast, Megan." He raised the rifle and focused the scope on Abby Boland, noticing her open blouse. She saw him and waved. He waved back. "So near, yet so far."

"Give it a rest, George," said Megan impatiently. "You'll not be using it for much but peeing for yet a while." She looked at him closely. George Sullivan was not easily intimidated by her. He had that combination of smugness and devil-may-care personality that came with handling high explosives, a special gift of the gods, he had called it. Maybe. "Are you certain Hickey knows how to rig the bombs?"

Sullivan picked up his bagpipe and began blowing into it. He looked up. "Oh, yes. He's very good. World War Two techniques, but that's all right, and he's got the nerve for it."

"I'm interested in his skill, not his nerve. I'm to be his assistant."

"Good for you. Best to be close by if it goes wrong. Never feel a thing. It'll be us poor bastards up here who'll be slowly crushed by falling stone. Picture it, Megan. Like Samson and Delilah, the temple falling about our heads, tons of stone quivering, falling. . . . Someone should have brought a movie camera."

"Next time. All right, George, the north transept is your sector of fire if they break in. But if they use armor through that door, Boland will lean over the north triforium and launch a rocket directly down at it. Your responsibility for armor is the south transept door below you. She'll cover you and you'll cover her with rifle fire."

"What if one of us is dead?"

"Then the other two, Gallagher and Farrell, will divide up the sector of the dead party."

"What if we're all dead?"

"Then it doesn't matter, does it, George? Besides, there's always Leary. Leary is immortal, you know."

"I've heard." He put the blowpipe to his mouth.

"Can you play 'Come Back to Erin'?"

He nodded as he puffed.

"Then play it for us, George."

He took a long breath and said, "To use an expression, Megan, you've not paid the piper, and you'll not call the tune. I'll play 'The Minstrel Boy' and you'll damn well like it. Go on, now, and leave me alone."

Megan looked at him, turned abruptly, and entered the small door that led down to the spiral stairs.

Sullivan finished inflating the bagpipe, bounced a few notes off the wall behind him, made the necessary tuning, then turned, bellied up to the stone parapet, and began to play. The haunting melody carried into every corner of the Cathedral and echoed off the stone. Acoustically bad for an organ or choir, Sullivan thought, but for a bagpipe it was lovely, sounding like the old Celtic warpipes echoing through the rocky glens of Antrim. The pipes were designed to echo from stone, he thought, and now that he heard his pipes in here, he would recommend their use in place of organs in Ireland. He had never sounded better.

He saw Abby Boland leaning across the parapet, looking at him, and he played to her, then turned east and played to his wife in Armagh prison, then turned to the wall behind him and played softly for himself.

18

B rian Flynn listened to Sullivan for a few seconds. "The lad's not bad." Hickey found his briar pipe and began filling it. "Reminds me of those Scottish and Irish regiments in the First War. Used to go into battle with pipes skirling. Jerry's machine guns ripped them up. Never missed a note, though—good morale-builder." He looked down at the blueprints. "I'm beginning to think whoever designed this place designed Tut's tomb."

"Same mentality. Tricks with stone. Fellow named Renwick in this case. There's a likeness of him on one of those stained-glass windows. Over there. Looks shifty."

"Even God looks shifty in stained glass, Brian."

Flynn consulted the blueprints. "Look, there are six large supporting piers— they're towers, actually. They all have doors either on the inside or outside of the Cathedral, and they all have spiral staircases that go into the triforia. . . . All except this one, which passes through Farrell's triforium. It has no doors, either on the blueprints or in actuality."

"How did he get up there?"

"From the next tower which has an outside door." Flynn looked up at Eamon Farrell. "I told him to look for the way into this tower, but he hasn't found it."

"Aye, and probably never will. Maybe that's where they burn heretics. Or hide the gold."

"Well, you may joke about it, but it bothers me. Not even a church architect wastes time and money building a tower from basement to roof without putting it to some use. I'm certain there's a staircase in there, and entrances as well. We'll have to find out where."

"We may find out quite unexpectedly," said Hickey.

"That we may."

"Later," said Hickey, "perhaps I'll call on Renwick's ghost for help."

"I'd settle for the present architect, Stillway." Flynn tapped his finger on the blueprints. "I think there are more hollow spaces here than even Renwick knew. Passages made by masons and workmen—not unusual in a cathedral of this size and style."

"Anyway, you've done a superb job, Brian. It will take the police some time to formulate an attack."

"Unless *they* get hold of Stillway and his set of blueprints before our people on the outside find him." He turned and looked at the telephone mounted on the organ. "What's taking the police so long to call?"

Hickey picked up the telephone. "It's working." He came back to the rail. "They're still confused. You've disrupted their chain of command. They'll be more angry with you for that than for this."

"Aye. It's like a huge machine that has malfunctioned. But when they get it going again, they'll start to grind away at us. And there's no way to shut it down again once it starts."

Eamon Farrell, a middle-aged man and the oldest of the Fenians, except for Hickey, looked down from the six-story-high northeast triforium, watching Flynn and Hickey as they came out of the bell-tower lobby. Flynn wore the black suit of a priest, Hickey an old tweed jacket. They looked for all the world like a priest and an architect talking over renovations. Farrell shifted his gaze to the four hostages sitting in the sanctuary, waiting for some indication as to their fate. He felt sorry for them. But he also felt sorry for his only son, Eamon, Jr., in Long Kesh. The boy was in the second week of a hunger strike and wouldn't last much longer.

Farrell slipped his police tunic off and hung it over the parapet, then turned and walked back to the wooden knee-wall behind him. In the wall was a small door, and he opened it, knelt, and shone his flashlight at the plaster lathing of the ceiling of the bride's room below him. He walked carefully in a crouch onto a rafter, and played the light around the dark recess, moving farther out onto the wooden beam. There was a fairly large space around him, a sort of lower attic below the main attic, formed by the downward pitch of the triforium roof before it met the outside wall of stone buttresses.

He stepped to the beam on his right and raised his light to the corner where the two walls came together. In the corner was part of a rounded tower made of brick and mortar. He made his way toward it and knelt precariously on a beam over the plaster. He reached out and ran his hand over a very small black iron door, almost the color of the dusty brick.

Eamon Farrell unhooked the rusty latch and pulled the door open. A familiar smell came out of the dark opening, and he reached his hand in and touched the inside of the brick, then brought his hand away and looked at it. Soot.

Farrell directed the light through the door and saw that the round hollow space was at least six feet across. He angled the light down but could see nothing. Carefully he eased his head and shoulders through the door and looked up. He sensed rather than saw the lights of the towering city above him. A cold downdraft confirmed that the hollow tower was a chimney.

Something caught his eye, and he pointed the light at it. A rung set into the brick. He played the light up and down the chimney and saw a series of iron rungs that ran up the chimney to the top. He withdrew from the opening and closed the thick steel door, then latched it firmly shut. He remained crouched on the beam for a long time, then came out of the small attic and moved to the parapet, calling down to Flynn.

Flynn quickly moved under the triforium. "Did you find something, Eamon?"

Farrell hesitated, then made a decision. "I see the tower as it comes through behind the triforium. There's no doorway."

Flynn looked impatient. "Throw me the rope ladder, and I'll have a look."

"No. No, don't bother. I'll keep looking."

Flynn considered, then said, "That tower has a function—find out what it is."

Farrell nodded. "I will." But he had already found it, and found an escape route for himself, a way to get out of this mess alive if the coming negotiations failed.

Frank Gallagher looked out from the southeast triforium. Everyone seemed to be in place. Directly across from him was Farrell. Sullivan, he noticed, was making eyes at Boland across the nave. Jean Kearney and Arthur Nulty were in the attic building bonfires and discussing, no doubt, the possibility of getting in a quick one before they died. Megan's brother, Pedar, was on the crypt landing watching the sacristy gates. He was young, not eighteen, but steady as a rock. *For thou art Peter, and upon this Rock,* thought Gallagher, who was devoutly Catholic, *upon this Rock, I will build my church; and the gates of hell shall not prevail against it.* The Thompson submachine gun helped, too.

Devane and Mullins had the nicest views, Gallagher thought, but it was probably cold up there. Megan, Hickey, and Flynn floated around like nervous hosts and hostess before a party, checking on the seating and ambience.

Frank Gallagher removed the silk parade marshal's sash and dropped it on the floor. He sighted his rifle at the choir loft, and Leary came into focus. He quickly put the rifle down. You didn't point a rifle at Leary. You didn't do anything to, with, or for Leary. You just avoided Leary like you avoided dark alleys and contagion wards.

Gallagher looked down at the hostages. His orders were simple. *If they leave the sanctuary, unescorted, shoot them.* He stared at the Cardinal. Somehow Frank Gallagher had to square this thing he was doing, square it with the Cardinal or his own priest later—later, when it was over, and people saw what a fine thing they had done.

19

Maureen watched Flynn as he moved about the Cathedral. He moved with a sense of purpose and animation that she recognized, and she knew he was feeling very alive and very good about himself. She watched the Cardinal sitting directly across from her. She envied him for what she knew was his absolute confidence in his position, his unerring belief that he was a blameless victim, a potential martyr. But for herself, and perhaps for Baxter, there was some guilt, and some misgivings, about their roles. And those feelings could work to undermine their ability to resist the pressures that the coming hours or days would bring.

She glanced quickly around at the triforia and choir loft. *Well done, Brian, but you're short of troops.* She tried to remember the faces of the people she had seen close in, and was fairly certain that she didn't know any of them except Gallagher and Devane. Megan and Pedar Fitzgerald she knew of through their brother, Tommy. What had become of all the people she once called sisters and brothers? The camps or the grave. These were their relatives, recruited in that endless cycle of blood vengeance that characterized the Irish war. With that kind of perpetual vendetta she couldn't see how it would end until they were all dead.

She spoke to Baxter. "If we run quickly to the south transept doors, we could be in the vestibule, hidden from the snipers, before they reacted. I can disarm almost any mine in a few seconds. We'd be through the outer door and into the street before anyone reached the vestibule."

Baxter looked at her. "What in the world are you talking about?"

"I'm talking about getting out of here alive."

"Look up there. Five snipers. And how can we run off and leave the Cardinal and Father Murphy?"

"They can come with us."

"Are you mad? I won't hear of it."

"I'll do what I damned well please."

He saw her body tense and reached out and held her arm. "No, you don't. Listen here, we have a chance to be released if—"

"No chance at all. From what I picked up of their conversation, they are going to demand the release of prisoners in internment. Do you think your government will agree to *that?*"

"I'm . . . I'm sure something will be worked out . . ."

"Bloody stupid diplomat. I know these people better than you do, and I know your government's position on Irish terrorists. No negotiation. End of discussion."

". . . but we have to wait for the right moment. We need a plan."

She tried to pull her arm away, but he held it tightly. She said, "I wish I had a shilling for every prisoner who stood in front of a firing squad because he waited for the right moment to make a break. The right moment, according to your own soldier's manual, is as soon after capture as possible. Before the enemy settles down, before they get their bearings. We've already waited too long. Let go of me."

"No. Let me think of something—something less suicidal."

"Listen to me, Baxter—we're not physically bound in any way yet. We must act now. You and I are as good as dead. The Cardinal and the priest may be spared. We won't be."

Baxter took a long breath, then said, "Well . . . it may be that I'm as good as dead . . . but don't you know this fellow, Flynn? Weren't you in the IRA together . . . ?"

"We were lovers. That's another reason I won't stay here at his mercy for one more second."

"I see. Well, if you want to commit suicide, that's one thing. But don't tell me you're trying to escape. And don't expect me to get myself killed with you."

"You'll wish later you'd taken a quick bullet."

He spoke evenly. "If an opportunity presents itself, I *will* try to escape." He paused. "If not, then when the time comes I'll die with some dignity, I hope."

"I hope so, too. You can let go of my arm now. I'll wait. But if we're bound or

thrown into the crypt or something like that—then, as you're thrashing about
with two shattered kneecaps, you can think about how we could have run.
That's how they do it, you know. They kneecap you hours before they shoot you
in the heart."

Baxter drew a deep breath. "I suppose I lack a sufficiently vivid imagination
to be frightened enough to try anything. . . . But you're supplying me with the
necessary picture." He took his hand away from hers and sat watching her out
of the corner of his eyes, but she seemed content to sit there. "Steady."

"Oh, take your bloody British steady and shove it."

Baxter remembered her bravery on the steps and realized that part of that,
consciously or unconsciously, was for him, or more accurately, what he represented. He realized also that her survival was to some extent in his hands. As
for himself, he felt indignant over his present position but felt no loss of dignity.
The distinction was not a small one and would determine how each of them
would react to their captivity, and if they were to die, how they would die. He
said, "Whenever you're ready . . . I'm with you."

Pedar Fitzgerald looked up the right-hand stairs as his sister came down
toward him. He stood and cradled the Thompson submachine gun under his
arm. "How's it going, Megan?"

"Everything's set but the bombs." She looked down the stairs through the
gate into the empty sacristy. "Any movement?"

"No. Things are quiet." He forced a smile. "Maybe they don't know we're
here."

She smiled back. "Oh, they know. They know, Pedar." She drew her pistol
and descended the stairs, then examined the lock and chain on the gates. She
listened, trying to hear a sound from the four side corridors that led into the
sacristy. Something moved, someone coughed quietly. She turned and said to
her brother in a loud voice, "When you shoot, boys, shoot between the bars.
Don't damage the lock and chain. Those Thompsons can get away from you."

Pedar smiled. "We've handled them enough times."

She winked at him and climbed back up the stairs, sticking the pistol in the
waistband of her jeans. She moved close to him and touched his cheek lightly.
"We're putting all we've got on this, Pedar. Tommy is in for life. We could be
dead or in an American prison for life. Mum is near dead for worry. None of us
will see each other again if this goes badly."

Pedar Fitzgerald felt tears forming in his eyes but fought them back. He
found his voice and said, "We've all put everything on Brian, Megan. Do you
. . . do you trust him . . . ? Can he do it, then?"

Megan Fitzgerald looked into her brother's eyes. "If he can't and we see he
can't, then . . . you and I, Pedar . . . we'll take over. The family comes first."
She turned and climbed up to the sanctuary, came around the altar, and looked
at Maureen sitting in the pew. Their eyes met and neither looked away.

Flynn watched from the ambulatory, then called out, "Megan. Come take a
walk with us."

Megan Fitzgerald turned away from Maureen and joined Flynn and Hickey
as they began walking up the center aisle. "There are people in the sacristy
corridors," she said.

Flynn nodded as he walked. "They won't do anything until they've established who we are and what we want. We've a little time yet."

When they reached the front door, Flynn ran his hands over the cold bronze
ceremonial doors. "Magnificent. I'd like to take one with me." He examined
the mines, then turned back and motioned around the Cathedral. "We've set

up a perfect and very deadly cross fire from five long, concealed perches protected by stone parapets. As long as we hold the high spots we can dominate the Cathedral. But if we lose the high ground and the fight takes place on the floor, it will be very difficult."

Hickey relit his pipe. "As long as there's no fighting in the bookstore."

Megan looked at him. "I hope you keep your sense of humor when the bullets start ripping through the smoke around your face."

He blew smoke toward her. "Lass, I've been shot at more times than you've had your period."

Flynn interrupted. "If you were a police commander, John, what would you do?"

Hickey thought a moment, then said, "I'd do what the British Army did in downtown Dublin in 1916. I'd call in the artillery and level the fucking place. Then I'd offer surrender terms."

"But this is not Dublin, 1916," said Flynn. "I think the people out there have to act with great restraint."

"You may call it restraint. I'd call it cunning. They'll eventually have to attack when they see we won't be talked out. But they'll do it without the big guns. More tactics, less gunpowder—gas, helicopters, concussion grenades that don't damage property. There's a lot available to them today." He looked around. "But we may be able to hold on."

Megan said, "We *will* hold on."

Flynn added, "We have gas masks, incidentally."

"Do you, now? You're a very thorough man, Brian. The old IRA was always going off half-cocked to try to grab the British lion's balls. And the lion loved it —loved feasting on IRA." He looked up at the triforia, then down at the deserted main floor. "Too bad, though, you couldn't find more men—"

Flynn interrupted. "They're a good lot. Each of them is worth twenty of the old-type ruffians."

"Are they, then? Even the women?"

Megan stiffened and started to speak.

Flynn interjected, "Nothing wrong with women, you old bastard. I've learned that over the years. They're steady. Loyal."

Hickey glanced at the sanctuary where Maureen sat, then made an exaggerated pretense of looking away quickly. "I suppose many of them are." He sat at the edge of a pew and yawned. "Tiring business. Megan, lass, I hope you didn't think I included you when I spoke about women."

"Oh, go to hell." She turned and walked away.

Flynn let out a long breath of annoyance. "Why are you provoking her?"

Hickey watched her walk toward the altar. "Cold, cold. Must be like fucking a wooden icebox."

"Look, John—"

The telephone on the chancel organ beside the altar rang loudly, and everyone turned toward it.

20

Brian Flynn put his hand on the ringing phone and looked at Hickey. "I was beginning to believe no one cared—one hears such stories about New York indifference."

Hickey laughed. "I can't think of a worse nightmare for an Irish revolutionary than to be ignored. Answer it, and if it's someone wanting to sell aluminum siding for the rectory, I suggest we just go home."

Flynn drew a deep breath and picked up the receiver. "MacCumail here."

There was a short silence, then a man's voice said, "Who?"

"This is Finn MacCumail, Chief of the Fenians. Who is this?"

The voice hesitated for a moment, then the man said, "This is Police Sergeant Tezik. Tactical Patrol Unit. I'm calling from the rectory. What the hell is going on in there?"

"Not much of anything at the moment."

"Why are the doors locked?"

"Because there are mines attached to each one. It's for your own protection, actually."

"Why . . . ?"

"Listen, Sergeant Tezik, and listen very closely. We have four hostages in here—Father Timothy Murphy, Maureen Malone, Sir Harold Baxter, and the Cardinal himself. If the police try to force their way in, the mines will explode, and if they keep coming, the hostages will be shot and the Cathedral will be set afire. Do you understand?"

"Jesus Christ . . ."

"Get this message to your superiors quickly, and get a ranking man on the phone. Be quick about it, Sergeant Tezik."

"Yeah . . . all right. . . . Listen, everything's pretty screwed up here, so just take it easy. As soon as we get things sorted out, we'll have a police official on the phone with you. Okay?"

"Make it quick. And no nonsense or there will be a great number of dead people you'll have to answer for. No helicopters in the area. No armored vehicles on the streets. I have men in the towers with rockets and rifles. I've got a gun pointed at the Cardinal's head right now."

"Okay—take it easy. Don't—"

Flynn hung up and turned to Hickey and Megan, who had joined them. "A TPU sergeant—spiritual kin to the RUCs and the Gestapo. I didn't like the tone of his voice."

Hickey nodded. "It's their height. Gives them a sense of superiority." He smiled. "Easier targets, though."

Flynn looked at the doors. "We caused a bit *too* much confusion. I hope they reestablish some chain of command before the hotheaded types start acting. The next few minutes are going to be critical."

Megan turned to Hickey and spoke quickly. "Do you want Sullivan to help you place the bombs?"

"Megan, love, I want *you* to help me. Run along and get what we need." He waited until Megan left, then turned to Flynn. "We have to make a decision now about the hostages—a decision about who kills which one."

Flynn looked at the Cardinal sitting straight on his throne, looking every inch a Prince of the Church. He knew it wasn't vanity or affectation he was observing but a product of two thousand years of history, ceremony, and training. The Cardinal would be not only a difficult hostage but a difficult man to make a corpse of. He said to Hickey, "It would be a hard man who could put a bullet into him."

Hickey's eyes, which normally twinkled with an old man's mischief, turned narrow and malevolent. "Well, I'll do him, if"—Hickey inclined his head toward Maureen—"if you'll do her."

Flynn glanced at Maureen sitting in the clergy pews between Baxter and Father Murphy. He hesitated, then said, "Yes, all right. Go on and plant the bombs."

Hickey ignored him. "As for Baxter, anyone will kill him. You tell Megan to do the priest. The little bitch should draw her first blood the hard way—not with Maureen."

Flynn looked at Hickey closely. It was becoming apparent that Hickey was obsessed with taking as many people with him as possible. "Yes," he said, "that seems the way to handle it." He looked out over the vast expanse around him and said, more to himself than to Hickey, "God, how did we get in this place, and how can we get out?"

Hickey took Flynn's arm and pressed it tightly. "Funny, that's almost exactly what Padraic Pearse said when his men seized the General Post Office in Dublin, Easter Monday. I remember it very clearly. The answer then, as it is now, is that you got in with luck and blarney, but you'll not get out alive. . . ." He released Flynn's arm and slapped him on the back. "Cheer up, lad, we'll take a good number of them with us, like we did in 1916. Burn this place down while we're about it. Blow it up, too, if we get those bombs in place."

Flynn stared at Hickey. He might have to kill Hickey before Hickey got them all killed.

Megan Fitzgerald mounted the sanctuary, carrying two suitcases. She walked rapidly to the right side of the high altar, and placed them beside a bronze plate set into the marble floor, then lifted the plate. John Hickey came up beside her and picked up the suitcases. "Go on."

Megan descended a shaky metal ladder, found a light chain, and pulled it. Hickey climbed down and handed the suitcases to Megan, who placed them gently on the floor. They examined the unevenly excavated crawl space. Building rubble, pipes, and ducts nearly filled the space around them, and it was difficult to move or to see clearly. Megan called out, "Here's the outer wall of the crypt."

Hickey called back, "Yes, and here's the wall of the staircase that continues down into the sacristy. Come along." Hickey turned on a flashlight and probed the area to his front as he moved, dragging one of the suitcases behind him.

They followed a parallel course to the descending staircase wall, hunching lower as they progressed. The dirt floor turned to Manhattan bedrock, and Hickey called out, "I see it up ahead." He crawled to a protruding mound from which rose the footing of a massive column. "Here it is. Come closer." He played the light around the dark spaces. "See? Here's where they cut through the old foundation and footing to let the sacristy stairs pass through. If we dug down farther, we'd find the sacristy's subbasement. It's somewhat like the layout of a modern split-level home."

Megan was skeptical. "Damned confusing sort of place. The fire in the attic is much surer."

"Don't be getting cold feet, now, Megan. I'll not blow you up."

"I'm only concerned with placing them properly."

"Of course." Hickey ran his hand over the column. "Now the story is that when they blasted the new stairs through the foundation in 1904 they weakened these flanking columns. In architectural terms, they're under stress. The old boy whose father worked on the blasting told me that the Irish laborers believed only God Almighty kept the whole place from collapsing when they set the dynamite. But God Almighty doesn't live here anymore, so when we plant this plastic and it blows, nothing will hold up the roof."

"And if it does hold up, will you be a believer then?"

"No. I'll think we didn't place the explosives properly." Hickey opened the suitcase and pulled out twenty white bricks wrapped in cellophane. He tore the cellophane from the white, putty-like substance and molded a brick into the place where the bedrock met the hewn and mortared stone of the column footing. Megan joined him, and they sculpted the bricks around the footing. He handed her the flashlight. "Hold this steady."

Hickey implanted four detonators, connected by wires to a battery pack, into the plastic. He picked up an alarm clock and looked at his watch. "It's four minutes after six now. The clock doesn't know A.M. from P.M., so the most time I can give it is eleven hours and fifty-nine minutes." He began turning the clock's alarm dial slowly counter-clockwise, talking as he did. "So I'll set the alarm for five minutes after six—no, I mean three minutes after six." He laughed as he kept turning the dial. "I remember once, a lad in Galway who didn't understand that. At midnight he set the timer to go off at one minute after twelve, in what he thought would be the afternoon. British officer's club, I think it was. Yes, lunchtime, he thought. Anyway, at one minute past midnight . . . he was standing before his Maker, who must have wondered how he became so unmade." He laughed again as he joined the clock wire to the batteries.

"At least don't get us killed until we've set the one on the other side."

"Good point. Did I do that right? Well, I hope so." He pulled the clock switch, and the loud ticking filled the damp space. He looked at her. "And don't forget, my sharp little lass, only you and I know exactly where these are planted, which gives us some advantages and a bit of power with your friend, Mr. Flynn. Only you and I can decide if we want to give an extension of the deadline to meet our demands." He laughed as he pushed the clock into the explosives and molded the plastic around it. "But if the police have killed us before then, well, at three minutes after six—which incidentally happens to be the exact time of sunrise—they'll get a message from us, directly from hell." He took some earth from the floor and pressed it into the white plastic. "There. That looks innocent, doesn't it? Give me a hand here." He spoke as he continued to camouflage the plastic explosives. "You're young. You don't want it to end so soon, I know, but you must have some sort of death wish to get mixed up in this. Nobody dropped you in through the roof. You people planned this for over a year. Wish I'd had a year to think about it. I'd be home now where I belong."

He picked up the flashlight and turned it onto her face. Her bright green eyes glowed back at him. "I hope you had a good look at this morning's sunrise, lass, because the chances are you'll not see another one."

Patrick Burke moved carefully from under the portal of the bronze ceremonial doors and looked up at the north tower. The Cathedral's floodlights cast a blue-white brilliance over the recently cleaned stonework and onto the fluttering harp flag of green and gold, reminding Burke irreverently of a Disney World castle. Burke looked over the south tower. The louvers were torn open, and a man was looking down at him through a rifle scope. Burke turned his back on the sniper and saw a tall uniformed patrolman of the Tactical Patrol Unit hurrying toward him through the sleet.

The young patrolman hesitated, then said, "Are you a sergeant or better?"

"Can't you tell?"

"I . . ."

"Lieutenant, Intelligence."

The patrolman began speaking rapidly. "Christ, Lieutenant, my sergeant, Tezik, is in the rectory. He's got a platoon of TPU ready to move. He wants to hit the doors with trucks—I don't think we should do anything until we get orders—"

Burke moved quickly across the steps and followed the north wall of the Cathedral through the gardens and terraces until he came to the rear of the rectory. He entered a door that led to a large vestibule. Scattered throughout the halls and offices and sitting on the stairs were about thirty men of the Tactical Patrol Unit, an elite reaction force, looking fresh, young, big, and eager. Burke turned to the patrolman who had followed him. "Where's Tezik?"

"In the Rector's office." He leaned toward Burke and said quietly, "He's a little . . . high-strung. You know?"

Burke left the patrolman in the vestibule and moved quickly up the stairs between the sitting TPU men. On the next landing he opened a door marked RECTOR.

Monsignor Downes sat at his desk in the center of the large, old-fashioned office, still wearing his topcoat and smoking a cigarette. Burke stood in the doorway. "Monsignor, where's the police sergeant?"

Monsignor Downes looked up blankly. "Who are you?"

"Burke. Police. Where is—?"

Monsignor Downes spoke distractedly. "Oh, yes. I know you. Friend of Father Murphy . . . saw you last night at the Waldorf . . . Maureen Malone . . . you were—"

"Yes, sir. Where is Sergeant Tezik?"

A deep voice called out from behind a set of double doors to Burke's right. "I'm in here!"

Burke moved through the doors into a larger inner office with a fireplace and bookshelves. Sergeant Tezik sat at an oversized desk in the rear room. "Burke. ID. Get your men out of the rectory and on the street where they belong. Help with crowd control."

Sergeant Tezik stood slowly, revealing a frame six-and-a-half feet tall, weighing, Burke guessed, about two seventy-five. Tezik said, "Who died and left you in charge?"

Burke closed the door behind him. "Actually, Commissioner Dwyer *is* dead. Heart attack."

"I heard. That don't make *you* the PC."

"No, but I'll do for now." Burke moved farther into the room. "Don't try to take advantage of this mess, Tezik. Don't play macho man with other people's lives. You know the saying, Tezik: When a citizen is in trouble he calls a cop; when a cop is in trouble he calls Emergency Service."

"I'm using what they call personal initiative, Lieutenant. I figure that before those bastards get themselves dug in—"

"Who have you called? Where are your orders coming from?"

"They're coming from my brains."

"That's too bad."

Tezik continued, unperturbed, "I can't get an open line no place."

"Did you try Police Plaza?"

"I *told* you, I can't get through. This is a revolution, for Christ's sake. You know?" He hesitated, then added, "Only the interphone in the Cathedral complex is working. . . . I spoke to somebody . . ."

Burke moved to the desk. "Who did you speak to?"

"Some guy—Finn?—something. Name's on the Cathedral doors."

"What did he say?"

"Nothing." He thought a moment. "Said he had four hostages."

"Who?"

"The Cardinal—"

"Shit!"

"Yeah. And they got a priest, too—Murphy. And some broad whose name I don't remember—that peace woman, I think. Name was in the papers. And some English royalty guy, Baker."

"Jesus Christ. What else did he say, Tezik? Think."

Tezik seemed to be thinking. "Let me see. . . . He said he'd kill them—they always say that. Right? And burn the Cathedral—how do you burn a Cathedral—?"

"With matches."

"Not possible. Stone don't burn. Anyway, the doors are supposed to be rigged with explosives, but, shit, I have thirty-five TPU in the rectory, ready to go. I got a dozen more standing in the halls that lead to the sacristy. I got four-wheel-drive equipment from the Sanitation Department, with my men driving, ready to hit the doors, and—"

"Forget it."

"Like hell. Look, the longer you wait, the deeper the other guy digs in. That's a fact."

"Where did you learn that fact?"

"In the Marines. 'Nam."

"Sure. Listen, Tezik, this is midtown Manhattan, not Fuck Luck Province. A great cathedral full of art treasures has been seized, Tezik. And *hostages,* Tezik. The dinks never held hostages, did they? Police policy is containment, not cavalry charges. Right?"

"This is different. The command structure's broken down. One time, near Quang-tri, I was on patrol—"

"Who cares?"

Tezik stiffened. "Let me see your shield."

Burke held out his badge case, then put it away. "Look, Tezik, these people who've taken the Cathedral do not present a clear or immediate danger to anyone outside the Cathedral—"

"They shot out a spotlight. They hung a flag from the steeple. They could be Reds, Burke—revolutionaries. . . . Fenians . . . what the hell *are* Fenians?"

"Listen to me—leave this to Emergency Services and the Hostage Negotiator. Okay?"

"I'm going in now, Burke. Now, before they start shooting into the city—before they start shooting the hostages . . . or burning the Cathedral—"

"It's stone."

"Back off, Lieutenant. I'm the man on the spot, and I have to do what I have to do."

Burke unbuttoned his topcoat and hooked his thumbs into his belt. "No way."

Neither man spoke for several seconds, then Tezik said, "I'm walking to that door."

Burke said, "Try it."

The office was very still except for the ticking of a mantel clock.

They both sidestepped clear of the desk, then faced off, each man knowing that he had unwittingly backed the other against a wall, and neither knowing what to do about it.

21

Father Murphy addressed Maureen and Baxter sitting beside him on the pew. "I'm going to speak to His Eminence. Will you come with me?"

Maureen shook her head.

Baxter said, "I'll be along shortly."

Father Murphy crossed the marble floor, knelt at the throne and kissed the episcopal ring, then rose and began speaking to the Cardinal in a low voice. Maureen watched them, then said to Baxter, "I can't stay here another moment."

He studied her closely. Her eyes were darting around wildly, and he saw that her body was shaking again.

He put his hand on her arm. "You really must get a grip on yourself."

"Oh, go to hell! How could you understand? For me this is like sitting in a room full of nightmares come to life."

"Let me see if I can get you a drink. Perhaps they have tranquilizers—"

"No! Listen, I'm not afraid of . . ."

"Talk about it if it will help."

Maureen tried to steady her shaking legs. "It's lots of things. . . . It's *him*. Flynn. He can . . . he has a power . . . no, not a power . . . a way of making you do things, and afterward you wished you hadn't done them, and you feel awful. Do you understand?"

"I think—"

"And . . . these people . . . They're my people, you see, yet they're not. Not anymore. I don't know how to react to them. . . . It's like a family meeting, and I've been called in because I've done something terrible. They're not saying anything, just watching me. . . ." She shook her head. *Once in, never out.* She was beginning to understand what that really meant, and it had nothing to do with them but with oneself. She looked at Baxter. "Even if they don't kill us . . . There are worse things. . . ."

Baxter pressed her arm. "Yes . . . I think I understand—"

"I'm not explaining myself very well."

She knew of that total suppression of ego that made hostages zombies, willing participants in the drama. And afterward the mixed feelings, confusion, guilt. She remembered what one psychologist had said, *Once you're a hostage, you're a hostage for the rest of your life.* She shook her head. No. She wouldn't let that happen to her. No. "No!"

Baxter squeezed her hand. "Look here, we may have to die, but I promise you, I won't let them abuse you . . . us. There'll be no mock trial, no public recanting, no . . ." He found it difficult to say what he knew her fears were. "No sadistic games, no psychological torture . . ."

She studied his face closely. He had more insight into these things than she would have thought of a prim career diplomat.

He cleared his throat and said, "You're a very proud woman. . . . It's easier for me, actually. I hate them, and anything they do to me just diminishes *them* —not *me*. It would help if you established the proper relationship between yourself and them."

She shook her head. "Yes. I feel like a traitor, and I'm a patriot. I feel guilty, and I'm the victim. How can that be?"

"When we know the answers to that, we'll know how to deal with people like Brian Flynn."

She forced a smile. "I'm sorry I bothered you with all of this." Baxter started to interrupt, but she went on. "I thought you had a right to know, before I—"

Baxter grabbed at her arm, but she vaulted into the pew behind her, then jumped into the last row and grabbed at the two wooden columns of the carved screen, swinging her legs up to the balustrade before jumping down to the ambulatory six feet below.

Frank Gallagher leaned over the edge of the triforium. He pointed his rifle straight down at the top of her head, but the rifle was shaking so badly he didn't fire.

Eamon Farrell sighted across the sanctuary at her back but shifted his aim to her left and squeezed off a single round, which exploded into the stillness of the Cathedral.

George Sullivan and Abby Boland in the long triforium at the front of the Cathedral looked quickly at the source of the shot, then down at the aim of Farrell's rifle, but neither moved.

Leary had read the signs before Maureen even made her first move. As she came out of the pew he leaned farther over the parapet of the choir loft and followed her through his rifle scope. As she swung up to the balustrade he fired.

Maureen heard the sharp crack of Farrell's fire ring out behind her, then almost simultaneously heard the report roll down from the choir loft. Farrell's shot passed to her left. Leary's shot passed so close over her head she felt it touch her hair, and the wooden column near her left ear splintered in her face. Suddenly a pair of strong hands grabbed her shoulders and yanked her backward into the pew behind her. She looked up into the face of Harold Baxter. "Let go of me! Let go!"

Baxter was agitated and kept repeating, "Don't move! For God's sake, don't move!"

A sound of running footsteps came to the sanctuary, and Maureen saw Megan leaning into the pew, pointing a pistol at her face. Megan spoke softly. "Thank you." She cocked the pistol.

Baxter found himself sprawled over Maureen's body. "No! For God's sake, don't."

Megan screamed. "Move, you stupid bastard! Move!" She struck Baxter on the back of the head with her pistol, then pushed the muzzle into Maureen's throat.

The Cardinal was halfway across the sanctuary, shouting, "Stop that! Let them alone!" Father Murphy moved quickly behind Megan and grabbed her forearms. He picked her high into the air, spun around, and dropped her on the floor. Megan slid on the polished marble, then shot up quickly into a kneeling position, and pointed the gun at the priest.

Brian Flynn's voice came clearly from the communion rail. "No!"

Megan pivoted around and stared at him, her pistol still leveled in front of her.

Flynn jumped over the gate and mounted the steps. "Go into the choir loft and stay there!"

Megan knelt on the floor, the pistol shaking in her hand. Everyone stood around her, motionless.

John Hickey quickly mounted the sanctuary steps. "Come with me, Megan." He walked to her, bent over at the waist, and took her arms in his hands. "Come on, then. That's it." He pulled her to her feet, and pushed her gun-hand down to her side. He led her down the steps into the center aisle.

Flynn walked to the side of the pews and looked down. "Baxter, that was very gallant—very knightly. Stupid, too."

Harold Baxter picked himself up, then pulled Maureen up beside him.

Flynn looked at Maureen. "You won't get off that easy. And you almost got Sir Harry killed, too."

She didn't answer.

Baxter pressed a handkerchief to Maureen's cheek, where she had been hit by the wooden splinters.

Flynn's arm shot out and knocked Baxter's hand away. He went on calmly, "And don't think Mr. Leary is a bad shot. Had you gotten to the door he would have blown both your ankles away." Flynn turned. "And that goes as well for His Eminence and the good Father. And if by some miracle someone does get out of here, someone else dies for it." He looked at each of them. "Or should I just bind you all together? I'd rather not have to do that." He fixed each of the silent hostages with a cold stare. "Do not leave this sanctuary. Do we all understand the rules? Good. Everyone sit down." Flynn walked behind the altar and descended the steps to the crypt door landing. He spoke quietly to Pedar Fitzgerald. "Any movement down there?"

Fitzgerald answered softly. "Lot of commotion in the corridors, but it's quiet now. Is anyone hurt? Is my sister all right?"

"No one is hurt. Don't leave this post, no matter what you hear up there."

"I know. Look out for Megan, will you?"

"We're all watching out for Megan, Pedar."

A TPU man burst into the Monsignor's suite and ran to the inner office, out of breath. "Sergeant!"

Tezik and Burke both looked up.

The patrolman said excitedly, "The men in the corridors heard two shots fired—"

Tezik looked at Burke. "That's it. We're going in." Tezik moved quickly past Burke toward the door. Burke grabbed his shoulders and threw him back against the fireplace.

Tezik recovered his balance and shouted to the patrolman, "Arrest this man!"

The patrolman hesitated, then drew his service revolver.

The telephone rang.

Burke reached for it, but Tezik snatched the phone away and picked up the receiver. "Sergeant Tezik, NYPD."

Flynn sat at the chancel organ bench and said, "This is Finn MacCumail."

Tezik's voice was excited. "What happened in there? What's all that shooting?"

Flynn lit a cigarette. "Two shots hardly constitute 'all that shooting,' Sergeant. You ought to spend your next holiday in Belfast. Mothers fire two shots into the nursery just to wake the children."

"What—"

"No one is hurt," interrupted Flynn. "An automatic rifle discharged by accident." He said abruptly, "We're getting impatient, Sergeant."

"Just stay calm."

"The deadline for the demands I'm going to make is sunrise, and sunrise won't come any later because you're fucking around to find your chiefs." He hung up and drew on his cigarette. He thought about Maureen. He ought to tie her up for her own good, and for the good of them all, but perhaps he owed it to her to leave her options open and let her arrive at her own destiny without his interference. Sometime before sunrise they would be free of each other, or if not free, then together again, one way or the other.

22

Sergeant Tezik replaced the receiver and glanced at Burke. "An automatic rifle went off by accident—that's what he said. . . . I don't know." Tezik seemed to have calmed down somewhat. "What do you think?"

Burke let out a long breath, then moved to the window overlooking the Cathedral and pulled back the drapes. "Take a look out there."

Sergeant Tezik looked at the floodlit Cathedral.

"Have you ever seen the inside of that place, Tezik?"

He nodded. "Holy Name Society communions. Couple of . . . funerals."

"Yeah. Well, remember the triforia—the balconies? The choir loft? The acre or so of pews? It's a deathtrap in there, Sergeant, a fucking shooting gallery, and the TPU will be ducks." Burke let the drape fall and faced Tezik. "My intelligence sources say that those people have automatic weapons and sniper rifles. Maybe rockets. What do you have, Tezik? Six-shooters? Go back to your post. Tell your men to stand fast."

Tezik walked to a sideboard, poured a glass of brandy, drank it, then stared off at a point in space for a full minute. He looked at Burke and said, "Okay, I'm no hero." He forced a smile. "Thought it might be a piece of cake. Couple of medals. Mayor's commendation . . . media stuff. You know?"

"Yeah, I've been to a lot of funerals like that."

The other TPU man holstered his revolver and left as Tezik moved sullenly toward the door.

"And no funny stuff, Sergeant."

Tezik walked into the outer office, then called back. "They want to speak to a high-ranking police official. Hope you can find one."

Burke moved to the desk and dialed a special number to his office in Police Plaza. After a long delay the phone rang and a woman answered. "Jackson."

"Louise, Burke here."

Duty Sergeant Louise Jackson, a middle-aged black woman, sounded tired. "Lieutenant! Where are you?"

"In the rectory of Saint Patrick's Cathedral. Put Langley on."

"The Inspector's in a helicopter with Deputy PC Rourke. They're trying to establish a command structure, but we lost radio contact with them when they got close to the Cathedral. Jamming device there. Every telephone line in the city is overloaded except these special ones, and they're not so good either. Everything's pretty crazy here."

"It's a little messy here, too. Listen, you call the Hostage Negotiator's office upstairs. Have them get hold of Bert Schroeder, quick. We have a hostage situation here."

"Damn it. That's what we thought. The BSS guarding the VIPs on the steps just called in. They lost some people in the shuffle, but they were a little vague about who and how."

"I'll tell you who and how in a second. Okay, call the Emergency Service office—Captain Bellini, if he's available. Explain that the Cathedral is held by gunmen and tell them to assemble siege equipment, snipers, and whatever other personnel and equipment is necessary, in the Cardinal's residence. Got that?"

"This one's going to be a bitch."

"For sure. Okay, I have a situation report and a message from the gunmen, Louise. I'll give it to you, and you call the Commissioner's office. They'll call everyone on the Situation A list. Ready to copy?"

"Shoot."

"At approximately 5:20 P.M. Saint Patrick's Cathedral was seized by an unknown number of gunmen—" Burke finished his report. "I'm designating the rectory as the command post. Get Ma Bell on the horn and have them put extra phone lines into the rectory according to existing emergency procedures. Got that?"

"Yes. . . . Pat, are you authorized—?"

Burke felt the sweat collecting around his collar and loosened it. "Louise, don't ask those kinds of questions. We've got to wing this one. Okay?"

"Okay."

"Do your best to contact those people. Stay cool."

"I'm cool. But you ought to see the people here. Everybody thinks it's some kind of *insurrection* or something. Albany and Washington called the PC's office—couldn't get a straight answer from City Hall or Gracie Mansion—PC's office called here. Want to know if it's an insurrection—or a race riot. Can you tell if it's an insurrection? Just for the record."

"Tell Albany and Washington that nobody in New York cares enough to start an insurrection. As far as I can make out, the Fenians provoked a disturbance to cover their seizing of the Cathedral. It got out of hand—a lot of happy citizens cutting loose. Do you have any reports from our people in the field?"

"Not a one. You're the first."

"One more thing. Get John Hickey's file sent here as soon as possible. And see what we have on a Northern Irishman named Brian Flynn." He hung up.

Burke walked into the outer office. "Monsignor?"

Monsignor Downes put down his telephone. "I can't get through to *anyone*. I have to speak to the Vicar General. I have to call the Apostolic Delegate in Washington. What's happening? What is going on here?"

Burke looked into Downes's ashen face, moved to the coffee table, and picked up a bottle of wine and a glass.

"Have some of this. The phones will be clear later. Couple of million people are trying to call home at the same time, that's all. We're going to have to use this rectory as a command post."

Monsignor Downes ignored the wine. "Command post?"

"Please clear the rectory and evacuate all the office personnel and priests. Leave a switchboard operator on until I can get a police operator here." Burke looked at his watch and considered a moment, then said, "How do I get into the corridor that connects with the sacristy?"

Monsignor Downes gave him a set of involved and disjointed instructions.

The door swung open and a tall man in a black topcoat burst in. He held up his badge case. "Lieutenant Young. Bureau of Special Services." He looked at the Monsignor, then at Burke, and said, "Who are you?"

"Burke. ID."

The man went directly to the coffee table and poured a glass of wine. "Christ —excuse me, Father—damn it, we've accounted for every VIP on the steps except three."

Burke watched him drink. "Let me guess—ID guys are good at guessing. You lost the Cardinal, Baxter, and the Malone woman."

Lieutenant Young looked at him quickly. "Where are they? They're not in the Cathedral, are they?"

"I'm afraid they are."

"Oh, Christ—sorry—shit. That's it. That's my job. Forget it. Forget it."

"Three out of about a hundred VIPs isn't bad."

"Don't joke! This is bad. Very bad."

"They're unharmed as far as I know," added Burke. "They also have a parish priest—Murphy. Not a VIP, so don't worry about that."

"Damn it. I lost three VIPs." He rambled on as he poured himself another glass. "Damn it, they should have sent the Secret Service. When the Pope came, the President sent the Secret Service to help us." He looked at Burke and the Monsignor and went on. "Most of the BSS was up by the reviewing stands. Byrd had all the good men. I got stuck with a handful of incompetents."

"Right." Burke moved to the door. "Get some competent men to stay with Monsignor Downes here. He's a VIP. I'm going to try to speak with the gunmen. They're VIPs, too."

Young glanced at Burke and said fiercely, "Why didn't you tell us something like this was going to happen, Burke?"

"You didn't ask." Burke left the office, descended the stairs, and found an elevator that took him into the basement. He came upon a worried-looking Hispanic custodian. "Sacristy," said Burke without preamble.

The man led him to a passage and pointed. Burke saw six TPU men standing along the walls with guns drawn. He held up his badge case and motioned the men to draw back from the sacristy. He unholstered his revolver, put it in his topcoat pocket, then walked down the short staircase to the opening of the passage. Burke put his head slowly around the corner and looked into the marble vaulted sacristy.

A TPU man behind him whispered, "Guy's got a Thompson at the top of those stairs."

Burke moved carefully into the sacristy, down the length of a row of vestment tables that ran along the wall to the right. At the end of the tables was another arched opening, and through it he could see a dimly lit polygon-shaped room of stone and brick.

Burke moved slowly toward the gates, keeping out of sight of the staircase opening. He heard muffled voices echoing down the staircase. Burke knew he had to speak with Finn MacCumail, and he had to have it together when he did. He leaned back against the marble wall to the side of the stairs and listened to his heart beat. He filled his lungs several times but couldn't find his voice. His hands clutched around the revolver in his pocket, and he pulled his hand free and steadied it against the wall. He looked at his watch. One minute. In one minute he would call for Finn MacCumail.

Maureen sat in the pew, her face in her hands, and Father Murphy and the Cardinal sat flanking her, keeping up a steady flow of soothing words. Baxter returned from the credence table, where a canteen of water had been placed. "Here."

She shook her head, then rose abruptly. "Let me alone. All of you. What do you know? You don't know the half of it. But you *will.*"

The Cardinal motioned to the other two, and they followed him across the sanctuary and stood beside the throne. The Cardinal said quietly, "She has to make peace with herself. She's a troubled woman. If she wants us, she'll come to us." He looked up at the altar rising from the sanctuary. "God has brought us together in His house, and we are in His hands now—us, as well as them. His will be done, not ours. We must not provoke these people and give them cause to harm us or this church."

Baxter cleared his throat. "We have an obligation to escape if a clear opportunity presents itself."

The Cardinal gave him a look of slight annoyance. "We are operating from different sets of standards, I'm afraid. However, Mr. Baxter, I'm going to have to insist that in my church you do as I say."

Baxter replied evenly, "There's some question, I think, concerning whose church this is at the moment, Your Eminence." He turned to Father Murphy. "What are your thoughts?"

Father Murphy seemed to vacillate, then said, "There's no use arguing about it. His Eminence is correct."

Baxter looked exasperated. "See here, I don't like being pushed about. We *must* offer some resistance, even if it's only psychological, and we must at least *plan* to escape if we're going to keep our sanity and self-respect. This may go on for days—weeks—and if I leave here alive, I want to be able to live with myself."

The Cardinal spoke. "Mr. Baxter, these people have treated us reasonably well, and your course of action would provoke retaliation and—"

"Treated us *well?* I don't give a damn *how* they treat us. They have no right to keep us here."

The Cardinal nodded. "You're right, of course. But let me make my final point, which is that I understand that much of the brashness of young men is a result of the proximity of young women—"

"I don't have to listen to this."

The Cardinal smiled thinly. "I seem to be annoying you. I'm sorry. Well, anyway, don't think for a moment that I doubt these people will kill me and Father Murphy as surely as they would you and Miss Malone. That's not important. What is important is that we not provoke them into the mortal sin of murder. And also important to me is my obligation as guardian of this church. This is the greatest Catholic Cathedral in America, Mr. Baxter, Domus Ecclesiae, the Mother Church, the spiritual center of Catholicism in North America. Try to think of it as Westminster Abbey."

Baxter's face reddened. He drew a breath. "I have a duty to resist, and I will."

The Cardinal shook his head. "Well, we have no such duty to wage war." He moved closer to Baxter. "Can't you leave this in God's hands? Or, if you're not so inclined, in the hands of the authorities outside?"

Baxter looked the Cardinal in the eye. "I've made my position clear."

The Cardinal seemed lost in thought, then said, "Perhaps I *am* overly concerned about this church. It's in my trust, you see, and as with anyone else, material values figure into my calculations. But we *are* agreed that lives are not to be needlessly sacrificed?"

"Of course."

"Neither our lives"—he motioned around the Cathedral—"nor theirs."

"I'm not so certain about theirs," said Harold Baxter.

"All God's children, Mr. Baxter."

"I wonder."

"Come now."

There was a long silence, broken by Maureen Malone's voice as she crossed the sanctuary. "Let me assure you, Cardinal, that each one of these people was spawned in hell. I know. Some of them may seem like rational men and women to you—jolly good Irishmen, sweet talk, lilting brogues, and all that. Perhaps a song or poem later. But they're quite capable of murdering us all and burning your church."

The three men looked silently at her.

She pointed to the two clerics. "It may be that you don't understand real evil, only abstract evil, but you've got Satan in the sanctuary right now." She moved her outstretched hand and pointed to Brian Flynn, who was mounting the steps into the sanctuary.

Flynn looked at them and smiled. "Did someone mention my name?"

23

Burke moved closer to the stairway opening, drew a deep breath, and called out, "This is the police! I want to speak with Finn MacCumail!" He heard his words echo up the marble stairway.

A voice with a heavy Irish accent called back, "Stand at the gate—hands on the bars! No tricks. I've got a Thompson."

Burke moved into view of the stairway and saw a young man, a boy really, kneeling on the landing in front of the crypt door. Burke mounted the steps slowly and put his hands on the brass gate.

Pedar Fitzgerald pointed the submachine gun down the stairs. "Stand fast!" he called back up the stairs. "Get Finn! There's a fellow here wants a word with him!"

Burke studied the young man for a moment, then shifted his attention to the layout. The stairs split to the left and right at the crypt door landing. Above the crypt door was the rear of the altar, from which rose a huge cross of gold silhouetted against the towering ceiling of the Cathedral. It didn't look to him as if anyone could get through the gates and up those stairs without being cut to pieces by overhead fire.

He heard footsteps on the left-hand stairs, and a tall figure emerged and stood outlined against the eerie yellow light coming from the glass-paneled crypt doors. The figure passed beside the kneeling man and moved deliberately down the dimly lit marble stairs. Burke could not clearly see his features, but saw now that the man was wearing a white collarless shirt and black pants, the remains of a priest's suit. Burke said evenly, "Finn MacCumail?" To an Irishman familiar with Gaelic history, as he was, it sounded as preposterous as calling someone Robin Hood.

"That's right." The tall man kept coming. "Chief of the Fenians."

Burke almost smiled at this pomposity, but something in the man's eyes held him riveted.

Flynn stopped close to the gates and stared at Burke. "And to whom do I have the pleasure of speaking?"

"Chief Inspector Burke, NYPD, Commissioner's office." He met the stare of the man's deep, dark eyes, then looked down at his right hand and saw the large bronze ring.

Brian Flynn said, "I know who you are . . . *Lieutenant.* I have an Intelligence section too. That's a bit galling, isn't it? Well," he smiled, "if I can be Chief of the Fenians, you can be a Chief Inspector, I suppose."

Burke remembered with some chagrin the first rule of hostage negotiating—never get caught in a lie. He spoke in a slow, measured cadence. "I said that only to expedite matters."

"Admirable reason to lie."

The two men were only inches apart, but the gates had the effect of lessening the intrusion into their zones of protected territory. Still, Burke felt uncomfortable but kept his hands on the brass bars. "Are the hostages all right?"

"For the time being."

"Let me speak with them."

Flynn shook his head.

"There were shots fired. Who's dead?"

"No one."

"What is it you want?" Burke asked, though it didn't matter what the Fenians wanted, he thought, since they were not going to get it.

Flynn ignored the question. "Are you armed?"

"Of course. But I won't go against that Thompson."

"Some people would. Like Sergeant Tezik."

"He's been taken care of." Burke wondered how Flynn knew Tezik was crazy. He imagined that kindred spirits could recognize each other by the tone of their voices.

Flynn looked over Burke's shoulder at the sacristy corridors.

Burke said, "I've pulled them back."

Flynn nodded.

Burke said, "If you'll tell me what you want, I will see that your demands are passed directly to the top." He knew he was operating off his beat, but he knew also that he had to stabilize the situation until the Hostage Negotiator, Bert Schroeder, took over.

Flynn tapped his fingers on the bars, his bronze ring clanging against the brass in a nervous and, at the same time, unnerving way. "Why can't I speak directly to someone of higher rank?"

Burke thought he heard a mocking tone in his voice. "They are all out of communication. If you turn off the jamming device—"

Flynn laughed, then said abruptly, "Has anyone been killed?"

Burke felt his hands getting sticky on the bars. "Maybe in the riot . . . Police Commissioner Dwyer . . . died of a heart attack." He added. "You won't be implicated in that—if you surrender now. You've made your point."

"I haven't even begun to make my point. Were those people on the horse injured?"

"No. Your men saw the policewoman from the towers. The man was me."

Flynn laughed. "Was it, now?" He thought a moment. "Well, that makes a difference."

"Why?"

"Let's just say that it makes it less likely that you are working for a certain English gentleman of my acquaintance." Flynn considered, then said, "Are you wearing a transmitter? Are there listening devices in the corridors?"

"I'm not wearing a wire. I don't know about the corridors."

Flynn took a pencil-shaped microphone detector from his pocket and passed it over Burke's body. "I think I can trust you, even if you are an intelligence officer specializing in hunting Irish patriots like myself."

"I do my job."

"Yes. Too well." He looked at Burke with some interest. "The universal bloodhound. Dogged, nosy, sniffing about. Always wanting to know things. I've known the likes of you in London, Belfast, and Dublin." He stared at Burke, then reached into his pocket and pushed a piece of paper through the gate. "You're as good as anyone, I suppose. Here is a list of one hundred and thirty-seven men and women held by the British in internment camps in Northern Ireland and England. I want these people released by sunrise. That's 6:03 A.M. —New York time. I want them flown to Dublin and granted amnesty by the British and Irish governments plus asylum in the south if they want it. The transfer will be supervised by the International Red Cross and Amnesty International. When I receive word from these two organizations that this is accomplished, we will give you back your Cathedral and release the hostages. If this is not done by sunrise, I will throw Sir Harold Baxter from the bell tower, followed by, in random order, the Cardinal, Father Murphy, and Maureen Malone. Then I will burn the Cathedral. Do you believe me, Lieutenant Burke?"

"I believe you."

"Good. It's important that you know that each of my Fenians has at least one relative in internment. It's also important you know that nothing is sacred to us, not church or priests, not human life or humanity in general."

"I believe you will do what you say you will do."

"Good. And you'll deliver not only the message but also the essence and spirit of what I'm saying. Do you understand that?"

"I understand."

"Yes, I think you do. Now, for ourselves, our purpose is to be reunited with our kin, so we'll not trade their imprisonment for ours. We want immunity from prosecution. We will walk out of here, motor to Kennedy Airport by means of our own conveyances, and leave New York for various destinations. We have passports and money and want nothing from you or your government except a laissez-passer. Understood?"

"Yes."

Flynn leaned nearer the bars so that his face was very close to Burke's. "I know what's going through your mind, Lieutenant Burke—can we talk them out, or do we have to blow them out? I know that your government—and the NYPD—has a shining history of never having given in to demands made at gunpoint. That history will be rewritten before sunrise. You see, we hold all the cards, as you say—Jack, Queen, King, Ace, and Cathedral."

Burke said, "I was thinking of the British government—"

"That, for a change, is Washington's problem, not mine."

"So it is."

"From now on, communicate with me only through the telephone extension on the chancel organ. I don't want to see anyone moving down here."

Burke nodded.

"And you'd better get your command structure established before some of your cowboys try something."

Burke said, "I'll see that they don't."

Flynn nodded. "Stay close, Lieutenant, I'll be wanting you later." He turned and mounted the steps slowly, then disappeared around the corner of the right-hand staircase.

Burke stared up at the kneeling man with the Thompson, and the man jerked the barrel in a motion of dismissal. Burke took his hands off the brass gate and stepped down the stairs and out of the line of sight of the staircase. He wiped his sweaty palms across his topcoat and lit a cigarette as he walked to the corridor opening.

He was glad he wouldn't have to deal again with the man named Brian Flynn, or with the personality of Finn MacCumail, and he felt sorry for Bert Schroeder, who did.

Captain Bert Schroeder stood with his foot on the rim of the fountain in Grand Army Plaza, smoking a short, fat cigar. A light sleet fell on his broad shoulders and soaked into his expensive topcoat. Schroeder watched the crowd slowly trailing away through the lamplit streets around him. Some semblance of order had been restored, but he doubted if he would be able to pick up his daughter and make it to his family party.

The unit he had been marching with, County Tyrone, his mother's ancestral county, had dispersed and drifted off, and he stood alone now, waiting, fairly certain of the instinct that told him he would be called. He looked at his watch, then made his way to a patrol car parked on Fifth Avenue and looked in the window. "Any news yet?"

The patrolman looked up. "No, sir. Radio's still out."

Bert Schroeder felt a sense of anger at the undignified way the parade had ended but wasn't sure yet toward whom to direct it.

The patrolman added, "I think the crowd is thin enough for me to drive you someplace if you want."

Schroeder considered, then said, "No." He tapped a paging device on his belt. "This thing should still be able to receive a signal. But hang around in case I want you."

Schroeder's pager sounded, and he felt his heart pound in a conditioned response. He threw down his cigar and shut off the device.

The driver in the patrol car called out, "Somebody grabbed somebody, Captain. You're on."

Schroeder started to speak and found that his mouth was dry. "Yeah, I'm on."

"Give you a lift?"

"What! No . . . I have to . . . to call . . ." He tried to steady the pounding in his chest. He turned and looked up at the brightly lit Plaza Hotel on the far side of the square, then ran toward it. As he ran, a dozen possible scenarios flashed through his mind the way they always did when the call came—*hostages* —who? The Governor? The Mayor? Congressmen? Embassy people? But he pushed these speculations aside, because no matter what he imagined when the beeper sounded or the phone rang or the radio called his name, it always turned out to be something very different. All he knew for certain was that very shortly he would be bargaining hard for someone's life, or many lives, and he would do it under the critical eyes of every politician and police official in the city.

He bounded up the steps of the Plaza, ran through the crowded lobby, then down a staircase to the line of wall phones outside Trader Vic's. A large crowd was massed around the phones, and Schroeder pushed through and grabbed a receiver from a man's hand. "Police business! Move back!"

He dialed a special operator number and gave her a number in Police Plaza. He waited a long time for a ring, and while he waited he lit another cigar and paced around to the extent of the phone cord.

He felt like an actor waiting for the curtain, apprehensive over his rehearsed lines, panicky that the ad libs would be disastrous. His heart was beating out of control now, and his mouth went dry as his palms became wet. He hated this. He wanted to be somewhere else. He loved it. He felt alive.

The phone rang at the other end, and the duty sergeant answered. Schroeder said calmly, "What's up, Dennis?"

Schroeder listened in silence for a full minute, then said in a barely audible voice, "I'll be at the rectory in ten minutes."

He hung up and, after steadying himself against the wall, pushed away from the phones and mounted the steps to the lobby, his body sagging, his face blank. Then his body straightened, his eyes came alive, and his breathing returned to normal. He walked confidently out the front doors and stepped into the police car that had followed him.

The driver said, "Bad, Captain?"

"They're all bad. Saint Pat's rectory on Madison. Step on it."

24

Monsignor Downes's adjoining offices were filling rapidly with people. Burke stood by the window of the outer office sipping a cup of coffee. Mayor Kline and Governor Doyle came in looking very pale, followed by their aides. Burke recognized other faces as they appeared at the door, somewhat hesitantly, as though they were entering a funeral parlor. In fact, he thought, as people streamed in and exchanged subdued greetings the atmosphere became more wakelike, except that everyone still wore topcoats and green carnations—and there were no bereaved to pay condolences to, though he noticed that Monsignor Downes came close to filling that role.

Burke looked down into Madison Avenue. Streetlights illuminated the hundreds of police who, in the falling sleet, were clearing an area around the rectory. Police cars and limousines pulled up to the curb discharging police commanders and civilian officials. Lines were being brought in by the telephone company, and field phone wire was being strung by police to compensate for the lost radio communication. The machine was moving slowly, deliberately. Traffic was rolling; civilization, such as it was in New York, had survived another day.

"Hello, Pat."

Burke spun around. "Langley. Jesus, it's good to see someone who doesn't have much more rank than I do."

Langley smiled. "You making the coffee and emptying the ashtrays?"

"Have you been filled in?"

"Briefly. What a fucking mess." He looked around the Monsignor's office. "It looks like *Who's Who in the East* here. Has Commissioner Dwyer arrived yet?"

"That's not likely. He died of a heart attack."

"Christ. Nobody told me that. You mean that dipshit Rourke is in charge?"

"As soon as he gets here."

"He's right behind me. We put the chopper down in the courtyard of the Palace Hotel. Christ, you should have seen what it looked like from the air."

"Yeah. I think I would rather have seen it from the air." Burke lit a cigarette. "Are we in trouble?"

"We won't be invited to the Medal Day ceremonies this June."

"For sure." Burke tapped his ash on the windowsill. "But we're still in the game."

"You, maybe. You got a horse shot out from under you. I didn't have a horse shot out from under me. Any horses around?"

"I have some information from Jack Ferguson we can use when we're on the carpet." He took Langley's arm and drew him closer. "Finn MacCumail's real name is Brian Flynn. He's Maureen Malone's ex-lover."

"Ah," said Langley, "ex-lover. This is getting interesting."

Burke went on. "Flynn's lieutenant is John Hickey."

"Hickey's dead," said Langley. "Died a few years ago. . . . There was a funeral . . . in Jersey."

"Some men find it more convenient to hold their funeral before their demise."

"Maybe Ferguson was wrong."

"He saw John Hickey in Saint Pat's today. He doesn't make mistakes."

"We'll have the grave dug up." Langley felt chilled and moved away from the window. "I'll get a court order."

Burke shrugged. "You find a sober judge in Jersey tonight, and I'll dig it up myself. Anyway, Hickey's file is on the way, and Louise is checking out Brian Flynn."

Langley nodded. "Good work. The British can help us on Flynn."

"Right . . . Major Martin."

"Have you seen him?"

Burke inclined his head toward the double doors.

Langley said, "Who else is in there?"

"Schroeder and some police commanders, federal types, and people from the British and Irish consulates." As he spoke, Mayor Kline, Governor Doyle, and their aides went into the inner office.

Langley watched them, then said, "Has Schroeder begun his dialogue yet?"

"I don't think so. I passed on MacCumail's—Flynn's—demands to him. He smiled and told me to wait outside. Here I am."

Deputy Police Commissioner Rourke hurried across the room and into the inner office, motioning to Langley to follow.

Langley turned to Burke. "Listen for the sounds of heads rolling across the floor. You may be the next Chief of Intelligence—I have this vision of Patrick Burke captured for eternity in a bronze statue, on the steps of Saint Patrick's, astride a horse with flaring nostrils, charging up—"

"Fuck off."

Langley smiled and hurried off.

Burke looked at the people milling about the room. The Speaker of the

House of Representatives, past and present governors, senators, mayors, congressmen. It *was* a veritable *Who's Who in the East,* but they looked, he thought, rather common and frightened at the moment. He noticed that all the decanters on the coffee table were empty, then fixed his attention on Monsignor Downes, still sitting behind his desk. Burke approached him. "Monsignor—"

The Rector of St. Patrick's Cathedral looked up.

"Feeling better?"

"Why didn't the police know this was going to happen?"

Burke resisted several replies, then said, "We *should* have known. It was all there if we had only . . ."

Langley appeared at the double doors and motioned to Burke.

Burke looked at the Rector. "Come with me."

"Why?"

"It's your church, and you have a right to know what's going to happen to it. Your Cardinal and your priest are in there—"

"Priests make people uncomfortable sometimes. They get in the way . . . unintentionally."

"Good. That may be what this group needs."

Monsignor Downes rose reluctantly and followed Burke into the inner office.

In the big room about forty men and women stood or sat, their attention focused around the desk where Captain Bert Schroeder sat. Heads turned as Burke and Monsignor Downes came into the room.

Mayor Kline rose from his chair and offered it to Downes, who flushed and sat quickly. The Mayor smiled at his own beneficence and good manners, then held his hands up for silence. He began speaking in his adenoidal voice that made everyone wince. "Are we all here? Okay, let's begin." He cleared his throat. "All right, now, we have all agreed that the City of New York is, under law, primarily responsible for any action taken in this matter." He looked at his aide, Roberta Spiegel. She nodded, and he went on. "So, to avoid confusion, we will all speak to the perpetrators with one voice, through one man. . . ." He paused and raised his voice as though introducing a speaker. "The NYPD Hostage Negotiator . . . Captain Bert Schroeder."

The effect of the Mayor's delivery elicited some applause, which died away as it became apparent that it wasn't appropriate. Roberta Spiegel shot the Mayor a look of disapproval, and he turned red. Captain Schroeder rose and half acknowledged the applause.

Burke said softly to Langley, "I feel like a proctologist trapped in a room full of assholes."

Schroeder looked at the faces turned toward him and drew a deep breath. "Thank you, Your Honor." His eyes darted around the room. "I am about to open negotiations with the man who calls himself Finn MacCumail, Chief of the Fenian Army. As you may know, my unit, since it was started by Captain Frank Bolz, has concluded successfully every hostage situation that has gone down in this city, without the loss of a single hostage." He saw people nodding, and the terror of what he was about to undertake suddenly evaporated as he pictured himself concluding another successful case. He put an aggressive tone in his voice. "And since there's no reason to change tactics that have been so successful in criminal as well as political hostage situations, I will treat this as any other hostage situation. It will not be influenced by outside political considerations . . . but I do solicit your help and suggestions." He looked into the crowd and read expressions ranging from open hostility to agreement.

Burke said to Langley, "Not bad."

Langley replied, "He's full of shit. That man is the most political animal I know."

Schroeder went on. "In order to facilitate my job I'd like this room cleared of everyone except the following." He picked up a list written on Monsignor Downes's stationary and read from it, then looked up. "It's also been agreed that commanders of the field operations will headquarter themselves in the lower offices of the rectory. People connected with the negotiations who are not in this office with me will be in the Monsignor's outer office. I've spoken to the Vicar General by phone, and he's agreed that everyone else may use the Cardinal's residence."

Schroeder glanced at Monsignor Downes, then went on. "Telephones are being installed in the residence and . . . refreshments will be served in His Eminence's dining room. Voice speakers will be installed throughout both residences for paging and so that you may monitor my phone conversations with the perpetrators."

The room filled with noise as Schroeder sat down. The Mayor raised his hands for silence the way he had done so many times in the classroom. "All right. Let's leave the Captain to do his job. Everyone, Governor, ladies and gentlemen—please clear the room. That's right. Very good." The Mayor went to the door and opened it.

Schroeder mopped his brow and waited as the remaining people seated themselves. "All right. You know who I am. Everyone introduce themselves in turn." He pointed to the sole woman present.

Roberta Spiegel, a good-looking woman in her early forties, sat back in a rocking chair and crossed her legs, looking bored, sensual, and businesslike at the same time. "Spiegel. Mayor's aide."

A small man with flaming red hair, dressed in tweeds, said, "Tomas Donahue, Consul General, Irish Republic."

"Major Bartholomew Martin, representing Her Majesty's government in the . . . absence of Sir Harold Baxter."

"James Kruger, CIA."

A muscular man with a pockmarked face said, "Douglas Hogan, FBI."

A rotund young man with glasses said, "Bill Voight, Governor's office."

"Deputy Commissioner Rourke . . . Acting Police Commissioner."

A well-dressed man with a nasal voice said, "Arnold Sheridan, agent-in-charge, State Department Security Office, representing State."

"Captain Bellini, NYPD, Emergency Services Division."

"Inspector Philip Langley, NYPD, Intelligence Division."

"Burke, Intelligence."

Schroeder looked at Monsignor Downes, who, he realized, had not left. Schroeder considered for a moment as he sat at the man's desk with his gold-crossed stationery stacked neatly in a corner, then smiled. "And our host, you might say, Monsignor Downes, Rector of Saint Patrick's. Good of you to . . . come . . . and to let us use . . . Will you be staying?"

Monsignor Downes nodded hesitantly.

"Good," said Schroeder. "Good. Okay, let's start at the beginning. Burke, why the hell did you open negotiations? You know better than that."

Burke loosened his tie and sat back.

Schroeder thought the question may have sounded rhetorical, so he pressed on. "You didn't make any promises, did you? You didn't say anything that might compromise—"

"I told you what I said," interrupted Burke.

Schroeder stiffened. He glared at Burke and said, "Please repeat the exchange, and also tell us how he seemed—his state of mind. That sort of thing."

Burke repeated what he had said earlier, and added, "He seemed very self-assured. And it wasn't bravado. He seemed intelligent, too."

"He didn't seem unbalanced?" asked Schroeder.

"His whole manner seemed normal—except for what he was saying, of course."

"Drugs—alcohol?" asked Schroeder.

"Probably had less to drink today than anyone here."

Someone laughed.

Schroeder turned to Langley. "We can't get an angle on this guy unless we know his real name. Right?"

Langley glanced at Burke, then at the Acting Commissioner. "Actually, I know who he is."

The room became quiet.

Burke stole a look at Major Martin, who seemed impassive.

Langley continued. "His name is Brian Flynn. The British will certainly have a file on him—psy-profile, that sort of thing. Maybe the CIA has something, too. His lieutenant is a man named John Hickey, thought to have died some years ago. You may have heard of him. He's a naturalized American citizen. We and the FBI have an extensive file on Hickey."

The FBI man, Hogan, said, "I'll check."

Kruger said, "I'll check on Flynn."

Major Martin added, "Both names seem familiar. I'll wire London."

Schroeder looked a bit happier. "Good. Good work. That makes my job—our jobs—a lot easier. Right?" He turned to Burke. "One more thing—did you get the impression that the woman who fired at you was shooting to kill?"

Burke said, "I had the impression she was aiming for the horse. They probably have some discipline of firepower, if that's what you're getting at."

The policemen in the room nodded. Commissioner Rourke said, "Does anybody know anything about this group—the Fenians?" He looked at Kruger and Hogan.

Kruger glanced at Major Martin, then replied, "We have almost no funds to maintain a liaison section on Northern Irish affairs. It has been determined, you see, that the IRA poses no immediate threat to the United States, and preventive measures were not thought to be justified. Unfortunately, we are paying for that frugality now."

Douglas Hogan added, "The FBI thought it was the Provisional IRA until Major Martin suggested otherwise. My section, which specializes in Irish organizations in America, is understaffed and partly dependent on British Intelligence for information."

Burke nodded to himself. He was beginning to catch the drift. Kruger and Hogan were being petulant, taking an I-told-you-so line. They were also covering themselves, rehearsing for later testimony, and laying the groundwork for the future. Nicely done, too.

Commissioner Rourke looked at Major Martin. "Then you are . . . I mean . . . you are not . . ."

Major Martin smiled and stood. "Yes, I'm not actually *with* the consulate. I'm with British Military Intelligence. No use letting that get about, though." He looked around the room, then turned to Langley. "I told Inspector Langley that something was—what is the term?—coming down. But unfortunately—"

Langley said dryly, "Yes, the Major has been very helpful, as have the CIA and FBI. My own division did admirably too; and actually missed averting this act by only minutes. Lieutenant Burke should be commended for his resourcefulness and bravery."

There was a silence during which, Burke noticed, no one yelled "Hooray for Burke." It occurred to him that each of them was identifying his own objectives, his own exposure, looking for allies, scapegoats, enemies, and trying to figure how to use this crisis to his advantage. "I told Flynn we wouldn't keep him waiting."

Schroeder said, "I won't begin a dialogue until I clarify our position." He looked at Bill Voight, the Governor's aide. "Has the Governor indicated that he is willing to grant immunity from prosecution?"

Voight shook his head. "Not at this time."

Schroeder looked at Roberta Spiegel. "What is the Mayor's position regarding the use of police?"

Roberta Spiegel lit a cigarette. "No matter what kind of deal is concluded with London or Washington or anyone, the Mayor will enforce the law and order the arrest of anyone coming out of that Cathedral. If they don't come out, the Mayor reserves the right to send the police in to get them."

Schroeder nodded thoughtfully, then looked at Arnold Sheridan.

The State Department man said, "I can't speak for the administration or State at this time, and I don't know what the Attorney General's position will be regarding immunity from federal prosecution. But you can assume nobody in Washington is going along with any of those demands."

Schroeder looked at Tomas Donahue.

The Irish Consul General glanced at Major Martin, then said, "The Irish Republican Army is outlawed in the Irish Republic, and my government will not accept members of the IRA or offer them sanctuary in the unlikely event the British government decides to release these people."

Major Martin added, "Although I do not represent Her Majesty's government, I can assure you the government's position is as always regarding the IRA or whatever they're calling themselves today: Never negotiate, and if you do negotiate, never concede a single point, and if you do concede a point, never tell them you've conceded it."

Roberta Spiegel said, "Now that we know what uncompromising bastards we are, let's negotiate."

Commissioner Rourke said to Schroeder, "Yes, now all you have to do is talk them out, Bert. They've involved the Red Cross and Amnesty, so we can't easily lie to them. You've got to be very . . . very . . ." He couldn't come up with the word he wanted and turned to Captain Bellini, who had said nothing so far. "Captain, in the unlikely event Bert can't do it, is the Emergency Services Division ready to mount an . . . assault?"

Bellini shifted his massive frame in his small chair. The blue-black stubble on his face gave him a hard appearance, but the area under his eyes had gone very pale. "Yeah . . . yes, sir. When the time comes, we'll be ready."

Schroeder reached for the telephone. "Okay. I know where everyone's coming from. Right?"

Monsignor Downes spoke. "May I say something?"

Everyone looked at him. Schroeder took his hand off the receiver, smiled, and nodded.

Downes said softly, "No one has said anything about the hostages yet. Or about the Cathedral." There was a silence in the room and Monsignor Downes went on. "If, as I assume, your first responsibility is to the hostages, and if you make this clear to your superiors and to the people inside the Cathedral, then I don't see why a compromise can't be worked out." He looked around the room.

No one took it upon himself to explain the realities of international diplomacy to the Monsignor.

Schroeder said, "I haven't lost a hostage—or for that matter a building—yet, Monsignor. It's often possible to get what you want without giving anything in return."

"Oh . . . I didn't know that," said Monsignor Downes quietly.

"In fact," continued Schroeder assuringly, "the tack I am going to take is pretty much as you suggested. Stick around, you'll see how it's done." He picked up the telephone and waited for the police operator at the switchboard. He looked around the room and said, "Don't be disturbed if he seems to be winning a few rounds. You have to give them the impression they're scoring. By sunrise he'll tire—you ever go shark fishing? You let them run out the line until you're ready to reel them in." He said to the police operator, "Yes, get me the extension at the chancel organ." He put his elbows on the desk and waited. No one in the room moved.

25

Governor Doyle put down the telephone and looked around the crowded outer office. People were jockeying for the newly installed phones, and a cloud of blue smoke hung over the elegant furnishings, reminding him of a hotel suite on election night, and that reminded him of the next election. He spotted Mayor Kline talking to a group of city and police officials and came up behind the Mayor, taking his arm in a firm grip. "Murray, I have to speak to you."

The Mayor let himself be propelled by the bigger man into the hallway and up to a landing on the staircase that led to the priests' rooms. The Mayor escaped the Governor's grasp and said, "What is it, Bob? I have things to do."

"I just spoke to Albany. The main concern up there is civil disobedience."

"I didn't think enough people lived in Albany to have a riot."

"No, *here*. In *Manhattan*. That mob outside could explode again . . . with all the drinking. . . ."

The Mayor smiled. "What makes this Saint Patrick's night different from all other Saint Patrick's nights?"

"Look, Murray, this is not the time for your wisecracking. The seizure of this Cathedral may be just a prelude to a larger civil insurrection. I think you should call a curfew."

"*Curfew?* Are you crazy? Rush hour traffic is still trying to get out of Manhattan."

"Call it later, then." The Governor lowered his voice. "My analysts in Albany say that the only thing keeping this situation cooled down is the sleet. When the sleet stops, the bars will empty and there could be trouble—"

The Mayor looked incredulous. "I don't care *what* your analysts in Albany say. This is *Saint Patrick's Day* in New York, for God's sake. The biggest parade in the world, outside of the May Day Parade in Moscow, has just ended. The largest single party in New York—maybe in America—is just beginning. People plan this day all year. There are over a million people in midtown alone, jammed into bars, restaurants, and house parties. More liquor and food is consumed tonight than any other night of the year. If I called a curfew . . . the Restaurant Owners' Association would have me *assassinated.* They'd pour all the unconsumed beer into the Rockefeller Center skating rink and drown me in it. Shit, *you* try to enforce a curfew tonight."

"But—"

"And it's *religious.* What kind of an Irishman are you? That's all we need—a Jewish Mayor calling off Saint Patrick's Day. It'd be easier to call off *Christmas.* What kind of yo-yos are giving you advice in Albany? Fucking farmers?"

The Governor began pacing around the small landing. "Okay, Murray. Take it easy." He stopped pacing and thought a moment. "Okay, forget the curfew. But I *do* think you need the State Police and the National Guard to help keep order."

"No. No soldiers, no State Police. I have twenty thousand police—more than a full army division. Little by little we'll get them out on the street."

"The Sixty-ninth Regiment is mustered and in a position to lend a hand."

"Mustered?" Kline laughed. "Plastered is more like it. Christ, the enlisted men got off duty from the armory at two o'clock. They're so shitfaced by now they wouldn't know a rifle from their bootlaces."

"I happen to know that the officers and most of the noncoms are at a cocktail party in the armory right now; and—"

"What are you trying to pull?"

"Pull?"

"Pull."

The Governor coughed into his hand, then smiled goodnaturedly. "All right, it's like this—you know damned well that this is the biggest disturbance to hit New York since the blackout of '77, and I have to show that I'm doing *something.*"

"Fly to Albany. Let me run my city."

"Your city. It's my *state!* I'm responsible to *all* the people."

"Right. Where were you when we needed money?"

"Look . . . look, I don't need your permission to call out the National Guard or the State Police."

"Call your Attorney General and check on that." Mayor Kline turned and took a step toward the stairs.

"Hold on, Murray. Listen . . . suppose Albany foots the bill for this operation? I mean, God, this will cost the city *millions.* I'll take care of it, and I'll get Washington to kick in a little extra. I'll say it was an international thing, which it is—like the consulate protection money. Okay?"

The Mayor arrested his descent down the stairs and turned back toward the Governor. He smiled encouragingly.

The Governor went on. "I'll pay for it all if you let me send in my people—I need to show a state presence here—you understand. Okay? Whaddaya say, Murray?"

The Mayor said, "The money to be paid to the city within thirty days of billing."

"You got it."

"Including all overtime and regular time of all the city departments involved, including police, fire, sanitation, and other municipal departments for as long as the siege lasts, and all expenses incurred in the aftermath."

"All right. . . ."

"Including costs of repair to municipal property, and aid to private individuals and businesses who sustain a loss."

The Governor swallowed. "Sure."

"But only the Sixty-ninth Regiment. No other guard units and no State Police—my boys don't get along with them."

"Let me send the State Police into the boroughs to fill the vacuum left by the reassignment to Manhattan."

The Mayor considered, then nodded and smiled. He stuck out his hand, and they shook on it. Mayor Kline said loudly, so that the people in the hallway below could hear, "Governor, I'd like you to call out the Sixty-ninth Regiment and the State Police."

Colonel Dennis Logan sat at the head table in the 69th Regiment Armory hall on Lexington Avenue. Over a hundred officers, noncommissioned officers, and civilian guests sat or stood around the big hall. The degree of intoxication ranged from almost to very. Logan himself felt a bit unsteady. The mood this year was not boisterous, Logan noticed, and there was a subdued atmosphere in the hall, a result of reports of the disturbance in midtown.

A sergeant came toward Logan with a telephone and plugged the phone into a jack. "Colonel, the Governor is on the line."

Logan nodded and sat up straight. He took the receiver, glanced at Major Cole, then said, "Colonel Logan speaking, sir. Happy Saint Patrick's Day to you, Governor."

"I'm afraid not, Colonel. A group of Irish revolutionaries has seized Saint Patrick's Cathedral."

The Colonel felt a heaviness in his chest, and every part of his body went damp, except his throat. "Yes, sir."

"I'm calling the Sixty-ninth Regiment to duty."

Colonel Logan looked around the hall at the scene spread out before him. Most of the officers and NCOs were wobbling, a few were slumped over tables. The enlisted men were home by now or scattered throughout every bar in the metropolitan area.

"Colonel?"

"Yes, sir."

"Full gear, riot-control equipment, weapons with live ammunition."

"Yes, sir."

"Assemble outside the Cardinal's residence on Madison for further orders. Don't delay."

"Yes, sir."

"Is the Sixty-ninth ready, Colonel?"

Logan started to say something rational, then cleared his throat and said, "The Fighting Irish are always ready, Governor."

"This is Captain Bert Schroeder of the New York Police Department." Schroeder reached out and turned on the switches that activated the speakers in both residences.

A voice with an Irish accent came into the room and echoed from the outer office, which quickly became still. "What took you so long?"

Burke nodded. "That's him."

Schroeder spoke softly, pleasantly, a tone designed to be soothing. "Things were a bit confused, sir. Is this—?"

"Finn MacCumail, Chief of the Fenians. I told Sergeant Tezik and Lieutenant Burke I wanted to speak with a high ranking man. I'm only up to a captain now."

Schroeder gave his standard reply. "Everyone that you would want to speak to is present. They are listening to us from speakers. Can you hear the echo? We've all agreed that to avoid confusion I will do the speaking for everyone. They'll relay messages through me."

"Who are *you?*"

"I have some experience in this."

"Well, that's interesting. Are there representatives of the Irish, British, and American governments present?"

"Yes, sir. The Police Commissioner, the Mayor, and the Governor, too."

"I picked a good day for this, didn't I?"

Burke said to Schroeder, "I forgot to tell you, he has a sense of humor."

Schroeder said into the telephone, "Yes, sir. So let's get right down to business."

"Let's back up and establish the rules, Captain. Is everyone in contact with their capitals?"

"Yes, sir."

"Have Amnesty International and the Red Cross been contacted?"

"It's being done, sir."

"And you are the mouthpiece?"

"Yes, sir. It's less confusing. I think you'll find the arrangement acceptable." Schroeder sat at the edge of his chair. This was the most difficult part, persuading wild-eyed lunatics that it was better to speak to him than to the President of the United States or the Queen of England. "So, if we can proceed . . ."

"All right. We'll see."

Schroeder exhaled softly. "We have your demands in front of us, and the list of people you want released from Northern Ireland. We want you to know that our primary concern is the safety of the hostages—"

"Don't forget the Cathedral. It's ready to be burned down."

"Yes. But our *primary* concern is human life."

"Sorry about the horse."

"What? Oh, yes. We are too. But no one—no human—has been killed, so let's all work to keep it that way."

"Commissioner Dwyer is feeling better, then?"

Schroeder shot a look at Burke and covered the mouthpiece. "What the hell did you tell him about Dwyer?"

"Rule number one. The truth."

"Shit!" Schroeder uncovered the mouthpiece. "The Commissioner's death was from natural causes, sir. You have not killed anyone." He stressed again, "Our goal is to protect lives—"

"Then I can burn down the Cathedral after I get what I want?"

Schroeder looked around the room again. Everyone was bent forward in their chairs, cigars and cigarettes discharging smoke into the quiet atmosphere. "No, sir. That would be arson, a felony. Let's not compound the problem."

"No problem here. Just do what you're told."

"Are the hostages safe?"

"I told Burke they were. If I say something, that's what I mean."

"I was just reassuring everyone here. There are a lot of people here . . . Mr. MacCumail, to hear what you have to say to them. The Rector of the Cathedral is here. He's very concerned about the Cardinal and the others. They're all counting on you to come through. Listen, is it possible to speak with the hostages? I'd like to—"

"Perhaps later."

"All right. Fine. Okay. Listen, I'd like to speak to you about that spotlight. That was a potentially dangerous act—"

"Not if you have the County Antrim shooting champion in the bell tower. Keep the spotlights off."

"Yes, sir. In the future, if you want something, just ask me. Try not to take things into your own hands. It's easier, sometimes, to ask."

"I'll try to remember that. Where exactly are you calling from?"

"I'm in the Rector's office."

"Good. Best not to get too far from the center of things."

"We're right here."

"So are we. All right, I have other things to see to. Don't be calling me every minute on some pretext. The next call I receive from you will inform me that the three governments and the two agencies involved are ready to begin working out the details of the transfer of prisoners."

"That may be some time. I'd like to be able to call you and give you progress reports."

"Don't make a nuisance of yourself."

"I'm here to help."

"Good. You can start by sending the keys to me."

"The keys?" He looked at Monsignor Downes, who nodded.

Flynn said, "All the keys to the Cathedral—not the city. Send them now, with Lieutenant Burke."

Schroeder said, "I'm not sure I can locate any keys—"

"Don't be starting that bullshit, Captain. I want them within ten minutes or I raze the Altar of the Blessed Sacrament. Tell that to Downes and he'll produce all the keys he's got, and about a hundred he hasn't got."

Monsignor Downes came toward the desk, looking very agitated.

Schroeder said quickly into the phone, "All right. There was a misunderstanding. The Monsignor informs me he has a complete set of keys."

"I thought you'd find them. Also, send in corned beef and cabbage dinners for forty-five people. I want it catered by . . . hold on, let me check with my American friend here." There was a short silence, then Flynn said, "John Barleycorn's on East Forty-fifth Street. Soda bread, coffee and tea as well. And a sweet, if you don't mind. I'll pay the bill."

"We'll take care of that . . . and the bill, too."

"Captain, before this night is through there won't be enough money in the city treasury to buy you a glass of beer. I'll pay for the food."

"Yes, sir. One more thing. About the time limit . . . you've presented us with some complicated problems and we may need more time to—"

Flynn's voice became belligerent. "No extensions! The prisoners named had better be free in Dublin when the first light breaks through the windows of the Lady Chapel. Dawn or dead, Schaeffer."

"Schroeder. Look—"

"Whatever. Happy Saint Paddy's Day to you. *Erin go bragh.*"

There was a click, and the sound of the phone hummed in the room. Captain Schroeder put down his telephone, shut off the speakers, and relit his cigar. He tapped his fingers on the desk. It had not gone well. Yet he felt he'd dealt with harder men than Finn MacCumail. Never as well spoken, perhaps, but crazier, certainly.

He kept reminding himself of two facts. One was that he'd never had a failure. The other was that he'd never failed to get an extension of a deadline. And much of his success in the first fact was a result of his success in the second. He looked up at the silent assembly. "This one is going to be rough. I like them rough."

Captain Joe Bellini stood at the window with his tunic open, his thumbs hooked into his gun belt. His fingers ran over his cartridge loops. He had a mental picture of his Emergency Services Division assaulting the big gray lady out there. He didn't like them rough; he didn't like them easy. He didn't like them at all.

Brian Flynn sat at the chancel organ beside the sanctuary and looked at the book resting on the keycover. "Schaeffer." He laughed.

John Hickey picked up the book, titled *My Years as a Hostage Negotiator,* by Bert Schroeder. "Schaeffer. Very good, Brian. But he'll be on to you eventually."

Flynn nodded. "Probably." He pushed back the rolltop cover of the keyboard and pressed on a key, but no sound came from the pipes across the ambulatory. "We need the key to turn this on," he said absently. He looked up at Hickey. "We don't want to hurt him too badly professionally. We want him in there. And toward the end, if we have to, we'll play our trump card against him —Terri O'Neal." He laughed. "Did ever a poor bastard have so many cards stacked against him without knowing it?"

26

Flynn said, "Hello, Burke."

Burke stopped at the bottom of the sacristy stairs.

Flynn said, "I asked for you so you'd gain stature with your superiors."

"Thanks." Burke held up a large key-ring. "You want these?"

"Hand them through."

Burke climbed the steps and handed the keys through the bars.

Flynn produced the microphone sensor and passed it over Burke's body. "They say that technology is dehumanizing, but this piece of technology makes it unnecessary to search you, which always causes strained feelings. This way it's almost like trusting one another." He put the device away.

Burke said, "What difference would it make if I *was* wired? We're not going to discuss anything that I won't report."

"That remains to be seen." He turned and called out to Pedar Fitzgerald on the landing. "Take a break." Fitzgerald cradled his submachine gun and left. Flynn and Burke stared at each other, then Flynn spoke. "How did you get on to us, Lieutenant?"

"That's no concern of yours."

"Of course it is. Major Martin?"

Burke realized that he felt much freer to talk without a transmitter sending his voice back to the rectory. He nodded and saw a strange expression pass briefly over Flynn's face. "Friend of yours?"

"Professional acquaintance," answered Flynn. "Did the good Major tell you my real name?"

Burke didn't answer.

Flynn moved closer to the gate. "There is an old saying in intelligence work —'It's not important to know who fired the bullet, but who paid for it.' " He looked at Burke closely. "Who paid for the bullets?"

"You tell me."

"British Military Intelligence provided the logistics for the Fenian Army."

"The British government would not take such a risk because of your petty war—"

"I'm talking about people who pursue their own goals, which may or may not coincide with those of their government. These people talk of historical considerations to justify themselves—"

"So do you."

Flynn ignored the interruption. "These people are monumental egotists. Their lives are meaningful only as long as they can manipulate, deceive, intrigue, and eliminate their enemies, real or imagined, on the other side or on their own side. They find self-expression only in situations of crisis and turmoil, which they often manufacture themselves. That's your basic intelligence man, or secret policeman, or whatever they call themselves. That's Major Bartholomew Martin."

"I thought you were describing yourself."

Flynn smiled coldly. "I'm a revolutionary. Counterrevolutionaries are far more despicable."

"Maybe I should get into auto theft."

Flynn laughed. "Ah, Lieutenant, you're an honest city cop. I trust you." Burke didn't answer, and Flynn said, "I'll tell you something else—I think Martin had help in America. He had to. Be careful of the CIA and FBI." Again Burke didn't respond, and Flynn said, "Who gains the most from what's happened today?"

Burke looked up. "Not you. You'll be dead shortly, and if what you say is true, then what does that make *you?* A pawn. A lowly pawn who's been played off by British Intelligence and maybe by the CIA and FBI, for their own game."

Flynn smiled. "Aye, I know that. But the pawn has captured the archbishop, you see, and occupies his square as well. Pawns should never be underestimated; when they reach the end of the board, they turn and may become knights."

Burke understood Brian Flynn. He said, "Assuming Major Martin is what you say he is, why are you telling me? Am I supposed to expose him?"

"No. That would badly compromise me, you understand. Just keep an eye on him. He wants me dead now that I've served his purpose. He wants the hostages dead and the Cathedral destroyed—to show the world what savages the Irish are. Be wary of his advice to your superiors. Do you understand?"

"I understand that you've gotten yourself in a no-win situation. You've been sucked into a bad deal thinking you could turn it around, but now you're not so sure."

"My goal is uncompromised. It's up to the British government to release my people. It will be their fault if—"

"For God's sake, man, give it up," Burke said, his voice giving way to impatience and anger. "Take a few years for aggravated assault, false imprisonment, whatever the hell you can work out with the DA."

Flynn gripped the bars in front of him. "Stop talking like a fucking cop! I'm a soldier, Burke, not a bloody criminal who makes deals with DAs."

Burke let out a long breath and said softly, "I can't save you."

"I didn't ask you to—but the fact that you mentioned it tells me more about Patrick Burke, Irishman, than Patrick Burke, policeman, is willing to admit."

"Bullshit."

Flynn relaxed his grip on the bars. "Just take care of Major Martin and you'll save the hostages and the Cathedral. I'll save the Fenians. Now run along and bring the corned beef like a good fellow, won't you? We may chat again."

Burke put a businesslike tone in his voice. "They want to haul the horse away."

"Of course. An armistice to pick up the dead." He seemed to be trying to regain control of himself and smiled. "As long as they don't make corned beef out of it. One man with a rope and an open vehicle. No tricks."

"No tricks."

"No, there have been enough tricks for one day." Flynn turned and moved up the stairs, then stopped abruptly and said over his shoulder, "I'll show you what a decent fellow I am, Burke—everyone knows that Jack Ferguson is a police informer. Tell him to get out of town if he values his life." He turned again and ran up the stairs.

Burke watched him disappear around the corner on the landing. *I'm a soldier, not a bloody criminal.* It had been said without a trace of anguish in his voice, but the anguish was there.

Brian Flynn stood before the Cardinal seated on his throne. "Your Eminence, I'm going to ask you an important question."

The Cardinal inclined his head.

Flynn asked, "Are there any hidden ways—any secret passages into this Cathedral?"

The Cardinal answered immediately. "If there were, I wouldn't tell you."

Flynn stepped back and pointed to the towering ceiling at a point above the crypt where the red hats of the deceased archbishops of New York hung suspended by wire. "Would you like to have your hat hung there?"

The Cardinal looked at him coldly. "I am a Christian who believes in life everlasting, and I'm not intimidated by threats of death."

"Ah, Cardinal, you took it wrong. I meant I'd tell my people in the attic to take an ax to the plaster lathing until that beautiful ceiling is lying in the pews."

The Cardinal drew a short breath, then said softly, "To the best of my knowledge, there are no secret passages. But that doesn't mean there aren't any."

"No, it doesn't. Because I suspect that there are. Now, think of when you were first shown your new cathedral by the Vicar General. Surely there must be an escape route in the event of insurrection. A priest's hole such as we have in Ireland and England."

"I don't believe the architect considered such a thing. This is America."

"That has less meaning with each passing year. Think, Your Eminence. Lives will be saved if you can remember."

The Cardinal sat back and looked over the vast church. Yes, there were hollow walls with staircases that went somewhere, passages that were never used, but he could not honestly say that he remembered them or knew if they led from or to an area not controlled by these people. He looked out over the marble floor in front of him. The crypt lay below and, around the crypt, a low-ceilinged basement. But they knew that. He'd seen Hickey and Megan Fitzgerald descend through the bronze plate beside the altar.

Two thirds of the basement was little more than crawl space, a darkness where rats could scurry beneath the marble floor above. And above that darkness six million people passed every year to worship God, to meditate, or just to look. But the darkness below their feet stayed the same, until now—now it was seeping into the Cathedral and into the consciousness and souls of the people in the Cathedral. The dark places became important, not the sanctified places of light.

The Cardinal looked up at the figures standing tensely in the triforia and the choir loft, like sentinels on dark, craggy cliffs, guards on city walls. The eternal watchman, frightened, isolated, whispering, *"Watchman, what of the night?"*

The Cardinal turned to Flynn. "I can think of no way in and, by the same token, no way out for you."

"The way out for me will be through the front doors." He questioned the Cardinal closely about the suspected basement beneath the nave, passages between the basements outside the Cathedral, and the crawl space below.

The Cardinal kept shaking his head. "Nonsense. Typical nonsense about the church. This is a house of God, not a pyramid. There are no secrets here, only the mysteries of the faith."

Flynn smiled. "And no hoards of gold, Cardinal?"

"Yes, there is a hoard of gold. The body and blood of Christ that rests in the Tabernacle, the joy and goodwill and the peace and love that resides with us here—that is our hoard of gold. You're welcome to take some of that with you."

"And perhaps a few odd chalices and the gold on the altars."

"You're welcome to all of that."

Flynn shook his head. "No, I'll take nothing out of here but ourselves. Keep your gold and your love." He looked around the Cathedral and said, "I hope it survives." He looked at the Cardinal. "Well, perhaps a tour will refresh your memory. Come with me, please."

The Cardinal rose, and both men descended the steps of the sanctuary and walked toward the front of the Cathedral.

Father Murphy watched the Cardinal walk off with Flynn. Megan wasn't in sight, Baxter was sitting at the end of the pew, and John Hickey was at the chancel organ, speaking on the field phone. Murphy turned to Maureen. "You want desperately to do something, don't you?"

She looked at him. The catharsis of an escape from death made her feel strangely relaxed, almost serene, but the impulse for action still lay within her. She nodded slowly.

Father Murphy seemed to consider for a long time, then said, "Do you know any code—such as Morse code?"

"Yes. Morse code. Why?"

"You're in mortal danger, and I think you should make a confession, in the event something happens . . . suddenly. . . ."

Maureen looked at the priest but didn't answer.

"Trust me."

"All right."

Murphy waited until Hickey put down the field phone and called out, "Mr. Hickey, could I have a word with you?"

Hickey looked over the sanctuary rail. "Use the one in the bride's room—wipe the seat."

"Miss Malone would like to make a confession."

"Oh," Hickey laughed. "That would take a week."

"This is not a joking matter. She feels her life is in mortal danger, and—"

"That it is. All right. No one's stopping you."

Father Murphy rose, followed by Maureen.

Hickey watched them move toward the side in the rail. "Can't you do it there?"

Murphy answered. "Not in front of everyone. In the confessional."

Hickey looked annoyed. "Be quick about it."

They descended the side steps and walked across the ambulatory to the confessional booth beside the bride's room. Hickey raised his hand to the snipers in the perches and called out to the two retreating figures. "No funny business. You're in the cross hairs."

Father Murphy showed Maureen into a curtained booth, then entered the archway beside it. He went through the priest's entrance to the confessional and sat in the small, dark enclosure, then pulled the cord to open the black screen.

Maureen Malone knelt and stared through the curtain at the dim shadow of the priest's profile. "It's been so long, I don't know how to begin."

Father Murphy said in the low, intimate whisper cultivated for the confessional, "You can begin by locating the button on the door frame."

"Excuse me?"

"There's a button there. If you press it, it buzzes in the upstairs hall of the rectory. It's to call a priest when confessions are not normally held, in case you have a need for instant forgiveness." He laughed softly at what Maureen thought must be an occupational joke in the rectory.

She said excitedly, "Do you mean we can communicate—"

"We can't get any signal back, and in any case we wouldn't want one. And I don't know if anyone will hear us. Quickly, now, signal a message—something useful to the people outside."

Maureen drew the curtain farther to cover her hand, then ran her fingers over the oak frame and found the button. She pressed it several times to attract someone's attention, then began in halting Morse code.

THIS IS MALONE. WITH FR. MURPHY.

What should she say? She thought back to her training—*Who, what, where, when, how many?*

OBSERVED 13-15 GUNMEN IN CATHEDRAL. SNIPER IN EACH TRIFORIUM. ONE IN CHOIR LOFT. MAN AT SACRISTY STAIRS WITH THOMPSON SUB. ONE OR TWO MEN/WOMEN IN EACH TOWER. TWO OR MORE IN ATTIC. POSTS CONNECTED BY FIELD PHONES. HOSTAGES ON SANCTUARY.

She stopped and thought of the snatches of conversation she'd overhead, then continued in a faster, more confident signal.

VOTIVE CANDLES PILED IN ATTIC. BOMB? UNDER SANCTUARY.

She stopped again and tried desperately to think—*Who, what, where . . . ?* She went on.

MACCUMAIL IS BRIAN FLYNN. JOHN HICKEY, LIEUTENANT. MEGAN FITZGERALD THIRD IN COMMAND. OBSERVED MINES ON DOORS, SNIPER RIFLES, AUTOMATIC RIFLES, PISTOLS, M-72 ROCKETS, GAS MAS—

"Stop!" Murphy's voice came urgently through the screen.

She pulled her hand away from the buzzer.

Murphy said somewhat loudly, "Do you repent all your sins?"

"I do."

The priest replied, "Say the rosary once."

Hickey's voice cut into the confessional. *"Once?* By God, I'd have her on her knees until Easter if we had that long. Come on out."

Maureen came out of the confessional as Father Murphy came through the archway. Murphy nodded to Hickey. "Thank you. Later I'd like the Cardinal to hear my confession."

Hickey's wrinkled face broke into a mocking smile. "Now, what have you done, Father?"

He stepped very close to Hickey. "I'll hear the confessions of your people, too, before this night is over."

Hickey made a contemptuous sound. "No atheists in cathedrals, eh, Padre?" He stepped back from the priest and nodded. "Someone once said, 'By night an atheist half believes in God.' Maybe you're right. By dawn they'll all turn to you as they see the face of death, with his obscene gaping grin, pressed against the pretty windows. But I'll not make a confession to any mortal man, and neither will Flynn nor that she-devil he sleeps with."

Father Murphy's face reddened. He went on, "I think Harold Baxter will want to make his peace as well."

"That heathen? In a Catholic church? Don't bet the poor-box money on it." Hickey turned and looked up at the solitary figure sitting in the pew on the sanctuary. "This whole operation may have been worth the while just to see that Protestant bastard on his knees in front of a Catholic priest. All right, let's get back to the corral."

Maureen said to Hickey, "I hope I live long enough to see how *you* face death." She turned and walked with the priest in silence to the communion rail. She said, "That man . . . There's something . . . wicked . . ."

The priest nodded. As they came up to the communion rail she said, "Do you think we got through?"

"I don't know."

"Do you know Morse code?"

He reached out and opened the gate in the rail. "No, but you'll write out those dots and dashes for me before I make my confession." He waved her through the rail absently. As she passed him she reached out and squeezed his hand. He suddenly came alert. "Wait!"

She turned on the steps. "What is it?"

He looked at Hickey, who was standing near the confessional watching them. He reached into his vestment and handed her a set of rosary beads. "Get back here and kneel at the rail."

She took the beads and glanced at Hickey. "Stupid of me—"

"My fault. Just pray he doesn't suspect." The priest walked into the sanctuary.

Maureen knelt at the rail and let the string of beads hang loosely from her hands. She turned. Her eyes rose over the Cathedral, and she peered into the dimly appreciated places. Dark figures like ravens stared down at her from the murky balconies. Megan was moving near the front doors like a shadow, and an unearthly stillness hung over the cold, gray towering stonework. She focused on John Hickey. He was staring at the confessional and smiling.

27

Brian Flynn helped the Cardinal up into the bell room. The Cardinal looked at the torn copper louvers. Flynn said to Donald Mullins, "Have you formally met the Archbishop of New York?"

Mullins knelt and kissed the episcopal ring, then rose.

Flynn said, "Take a break, Donald. There's coffee in the bookstore."

Mullins went quickly down the ladder.

Flynn moved to the opening in the tower and looked out into the city. There was a long silence in the cold, drafty room. "That's incredible, you know . . . an armed revolutionary kneels in the dust and kisses your ring."

The Cardinal looked impatient. "Why are we up here? There can be no hidden passages up here."

Flynn said, "Have you had many dealings with Gordon Stillway?"

The Cardinal answered, "We planned the latest renovations together."

"And he never pointed out any curiosities to you? No secret—"

"I'm not in the habit of entertaining the same question more than once."

Flynn made an exaggerated bow. "Pardon me. I was only trying to refresh your memory, Your Eminence."

"What exactly do you want with me, Mr. Flynn?"

"I want you to speak with the negotiator, and I want you to talk to the world. I'm going to set up a conference in that press room so conveniently located in the subbasement below the sacristy. You will go on television and radio—"

"I'll do no such thing."

"Damn it, you've done enough talking on television and radio to damage our cause. You've used your pulpit long enough to speak out *against* the IRA. Now you'll undo that damage."

"I spoke out against murder and mayhem. If that equals speaking out against the IRA, then—"

Flynn's voice rose. "Have you seen a British internment camp? Do you know what they do to those poor bastards in there?"

"I've seen and heard reports, and I've condemned the British methods in Ulster along with the IRA methods."

"No one remembers that." He put his face close to the Cardinal's. "You'll announce to the world that as an Irish-American, and as a Catholic prelate, you are going to Northern Ireland to visit the camps."

"But if you clear them out, who is there left to visit, Mr. Flynn?"

"There are hundreds in those camps."

"And the ones to be released are the relatives of the men and women with you. Plus, I'm sure, a good number of important leaders. The rest can stay so you can still claim some moral justification for your bloody methods. I'm not as naïve as you believe, and I won't be used by you."

Flynn let out a deep breath. "Then I won't guarantee the safety of this church. I'll see that it's destroyed no matter what the outcome of the negotiations!"

The Cardinal moved near Flynn and said, "There is a price, Mr. Flynn, that each man must pay for each sin. This is not a perfect world, and the evildoers in it often escape punishment and die peacefully in their beds. But there is a higher court . . ."

"Don't try to frighten me with that. And don't be so certain that court would damn *me* and issue *you* wings. My concept of heaven and heavenly justice is a bit more pagan than yours. I picture Tirna-n'Og, where warriors are given the respect they no longer receive on earth. Your heaven has always sounded very effeminate to me."

The Cardinal didn't reply but shook his head.

Flynn turned away from him and looked into the blue city lights. After a time he said, "Cardinal, I'm a chosen man. I know I am. Chosen to lead the people of Northern Ireland out of British bondage."

He turned back to the Cardinal and thrust his right hand toward him. "Do you see this ring? This is the ring of Finn MacCumail. It was given me by a priest who wasn't a priest. A man who never was, in a place that never was what it seemed to be. A place sanctified by Druids a thousand years or more before the name Jesus Christ was ever heard in Erin. Oh, don't look so skeptical—you're supposed to believe in miracles, damn it."

The Cardinal looked at him sadly. "You've shut God's love out of your heart and taken into your soul dark things that should never be spoken of by a Christian." He held out his hand. "Give me the ring."

Flynn took an involuntary step back. "No."

"Give it to me, and we'll see if the Christian God, your true God, is effeminate."

Flynn shook his head and held up his hand balled into a fist.

The Cardinal dropped his outstretched arm and said, "I see my duty clearly now. I may not be able to save this church or save the lives of anyone in here. But before this night is over I'll try to save your soul, Brian Flynn, and the souls of the people with you."

Flynn looked down at the bronze ring, then at the Cardinal, and focused on the large cross hanging from his neck. "I wish sometimes that I'd gotten a sign from that God you believe in. But I never did. By morning one of us will know who's won this battle."

28

Monsignor Downes stood at the window of his inner office, chain-smoking unfiltered cigarettes and staring out at the floodlit Cathedral through a haze of blue smoke. In his mind's eye he saw not only smoke but fire licking at the gray stone, reaching from the stained-glass windows and twining around the twin spires. He blinked his eyes and turned toward the people in the room.

Present now besides himself was Captain Schroeder, who probably wouldn't leave until the end, and sitting in his chairs were Lieutenant Burke, Major Martin, and Inspector Langley. Captain Bellini was standing. On the couch were the FBI man, Hogan, and the CIA man, Kruger—or was it the other way around? No, that was it. All six men were rereading a decoded message brought in by a detective.

Patrick Burke looked at his copy of the message.

—DER SANCTUARY.
   MACCUMAIL IS BRIAN FLYNN. JOHN HICKEY, LIEUTENANT. MEGAN FITZGERALD THIRD IN COMMAND. OBSERVED MINES ON DOORS, SNIPER RIFLES, AUTOMATIC RIFLES, PISTOLS, M-72 ROCKETS, GAS MAS—

Burke looked up. "D-E-R Sanctuary. Murder? Ladder? Under?"

Langley shrugged. "I hope whoever that was can send again. I have two men in the upstairs hall waiting to copy." He looked at the message again. "I don't like the way it ended so abruptly."

Bellini said, "I didn't like that inventory of weapons."

Burke said, "Malone or Baxter sent it. Either of them would know Morse code and know that this is the stuff we're looking for. Right? And if, as the Monsignor says, the buzzer is in the confessional, then we might rule out Baxter if he's, as I assume, of the Protestant persuasion."

Major Martin said, "You can assume he is."

The Monsignor interjected hesitantly. "I've been thinking . . . perhaps Mr. Baxter *will* make a confession . . . so they can send again. Father Murphy will hear His Eminence's confession and vice versa—so we can expect, perhaps, three more messages. . . ."

"Then," said Martin, "we're out of sinners. They can't go twice, can they?"

Monsignor Downes regarded him coolly.

Bellini said, "Is that okay, Monsignor? I mean, to use the confessional to do that?"

Downes smiled for the first time. "It's okay."

Major Martin cleared his throat. "Look here, we haven't considered that this message might be a ruse, sent by Flynn to make us believe he's well armed. . . . A bit subtle and sophisticated for the Irish . . . but it's possible."

Langley replied, "If we had the complete message, we might have a better idea of its authenticity."

Schroeder said to Langley, "I need information on the personalities in there. Megan Fitzgerald. Third in command."

Langley shook his head. "I'll check the files, but I've never heard of her."

There was a period of silence in the room, while in the outer office men and women arrived and departed, telephones rang constantly, and people huddled in conversation. In the lower floors of the rectory police commanders coordinated crowd control and cordon operations. In the Cardinal's residence Governor Doyle and Mayor Kline met with government representatives and discussed larger issues around a buffet set up in the dining room. Phones were kept open to Washington, London, Dublin, and Albany.

One of the half-dozen newly installed telephones rang, and Schroeder picked it up, then handed it to the CIA man. Kruger spoke for a minute, then hung up. "Nothing on Brian Flynn or Megan Fitzgerald. Nothing on the Fenians. Old file on John Hickey. Not as good as yours." Two phones rang simultaneously, and Schroeder answered both, passing one to Hogan and one to Martin.

The FBI man spoke for a few seconds, then hung up and said, "Nothing on Flynn, Fitzgerald, or the Fenians. You have our file on Hickey. The FBI, incidentally, had an agent at his funeral checking out the mourners. That's the last entry. Guess we'll have to add a postscript."

Major Martin was still on the telephone, writing as he listened. He put the receiver down. "A bit of good news. Our dossier on Flynn will be Telexed to the consulate shortly. There's a capability paper on the Fenian Army as well. Your files on Hickey are more extensive than ours, and you can send a copy to London, if you will." He lit a cigarette and said in a satisfied tone, "Also on the way is the file on Megan Fitzgerald. Here's a few pertinent details: Born in Belfast, age twenty-one. Father deserted family—brother Thomas in Long Kesh for attacking a prison van. Brother Pedar is a member of the IRA. Mother hospitalized for a nervous breakdown." He added caustically, "Your typical Belfast family of five." Martin looked at Burke. "Her description—red hair, blue eyes, freckles, five feet seven inches, slender—quite good-looking according to the chap I just spoke to. Sound like the young lady who pegged a shot at you?"

Burke nodded.

Martin went on. "She's Flynn's present girl friend." He smiled. "I wonder how she's getting on with Miss Malone. I think I'm starting to feel sorry for old Flynn."

A uniformed officer stuck his head in the door. "Chow's here from John Barleycorn's."

Schroeder reached for the telephone. "All right. I'll tell Flynn that Burke is ready with his fucking corned beef." He dialed the operator. "Chancel organ." He waited. "Hello, this is Captain Schroeder. Finn MacCumail? . . ." He pushed the switches to activate all the speakers, and the next room became quiet.

"This is Dermot. MacCumail is praying with the Cardinal."

Schroeder hesitated. "Mr. . . . Dermot—"

"Just call me Hickey. John Hickey. Never liked these *noms de guerre!* Confuses everyone. Did you know I was in here? Have you got my file in front of you, Snider?"

"Schroeder." He looked down at the thick police file. Each man had to be played differently. Each man had his own requirements. Schroeder rarely admitted to having anyone's file in front of him as he negotiated, but it was equally important not to get caught lying to a direct question, and it was often convenient to play on a man's ego.

"Schroeder? You awake?"

Schroeder sat up. "Yes, sir. Yes, we knew you were in there. I have your file, Mr. Hickey."

Hickey cackled happily. "Did you read the part where I was caught trying to blow up Parliament in 1921?"

Schroeder found the dated entry. "Yes, sir. Quite"—he looked at Major Martin, who was staring tight-lipped—"quite daring. Daring escape too—"

"You bet your ass, sonny. Now look at 1941. I worked with the Germans then to blow up British shipping in New York harbor. Not proud of that, you understand; but a lot of us did that in the Second War. Shows how much we hated the Brits, doesn't it, to throw in with the bloody Nazis."

"Yes, it does. Listen—"

"The Dublin government and the British government both sentenced me to death in absentia on five different occasions. Well, as Brendan Behan once said, they can hang me five times in absentia, too." He laughed.

There was some laughter from the adjoining office. No one in the inner office laughed. Schroeder bit his cigar. "Mr. Hickey—"

"What do you have for February 12, 1979? Read it to me, Schaeffer."

Schroeder turned to the last page and read. "Died of natural causes, at

home, Newark, New Jersey. Buried . . . buried in Jersey City Cemetery. . . ."

Hickey laughed again, a high, piercing laugh. Neither man spoke for a few
seconds, then Schroeder said, "Mr. Hickey, first I want to ask you if the hostages are all right."

"That's a stupid question. If they weren't, would I tell *you?*"

"But they *are* all right?"

"There you go again. Same stupid question," Hickey said impatiently.
"They're fine. What did you call for?"

Schroeder said, "Lieutenant Burke is ready to bring the food you ordered.
Where—?"

"Through the sacristy."

"He'll be alone, unarmed—"

Hickey's voice was suddenly ill-tempered. "You don't have to reassure me.
For my part I'd like you to try something, because quicker than you can make it
up those stairs with a chaincutter or ram, the Cardinal's brains would be run-
ning over the altar, followed by a great fucking explosion that they'd hear in the
Vatican, and a fire so hot it'd melt the brass balls off Atlas. Do you understand,
Schroeder?"

"Yes, sir."

"And stop calling me sir, you candy-assed flatfoot. When I was a lad, if you
looked at a constable cross-eyed he'd knock you into next week. Now you're all
going round calling murderers sir. No wonder they picked New York for this.
Fucking cops would rather bat softballs with a bunch of slum brats than bat
heads. Also, while I'm on the subject, I don't like your voice, Schroeder. You
sound mealy-mouthed. How the hell did you get picked for this job? Your voice
is all wrong."

"Yes, sir . . . Mr. Hickey. . . . What would you like me to call
you . . . ?"

"Call me a son of a bitch, Schroeder, because that's what I am. Go on, you'll
feel better."

Schroeder cleared his throat. "Okay . . . you're a son of a bitch."

"Oh, yeah? Well, I'd rather be a son of a bitch than an asshole like you." He
laughed and hung up.

Schroeder put down the receiver, took a long breath, and turned off the
speakers. "Well . . . I think . . ." He looked down at Hickey's file. "Very
unstable. Maybe a little senile." He looked at Burke. "You don't have to go if
you . . ."

"Yeah. I have to go. I damn well have to go. Where's the fucking food?" He
stood.

Langley spoke. "I didn't like that part about the explosion."

Major Martin said, "I'd have been surprised if they hadn't set it up with
explosives. That's their specialty."

Burke moved toward the door. "The Irish specialty is bullshit." He looked at
Martin. "Not subtle or sophisticated bullshit, of course, Major. Just bullshit.
And if they had as much gelignite and plastic as they have bullshit, they could
have blown up the solar system." He opened the door and looked back over his
shoulder. "Forty-five meals. Shit, I wouldn't want to have to eat every meal
over the number of people they have in there."

Bellini called out at Burke's retreating figure. "I hope you're right, Burke. I
hope to Christ you're right." He turned back to the people in the room. *"He*
doesn't have to shoot his way in there."

Schroeder looked at Monsignor Downes, who appeared pale, then turned to

Bellini and said irritably, "Damn it, Joe, stop that. No one is going to have to shoot his way into that Cathedral."

Major Martin was examining some curios on the mantelpiece. He said, as though to himself but loud enough for everyone to hear him, "I wonder."

29

Flynn stood with Maureen on the landing in front of the crypt entrance. He found a key on the ring and opened the green, glass-paneled door. Inside, a set of stairs descended into the white-marbled burial chamber. He turned to Pedar Fitzgerald. "Somewhere in there may be a hidden passage. I'll be along shortly."

Fitzgerald cradled his submachine gun under his arm and moved down the stairs. Flynn shut the door and looked at the inscription in the bronze. *Requiescant In Pace*. "May they rest in peace," he said. Below the inscriptions were plaques bearing the names of the former archbishops of New York who were buried in the crypt. He turned to Maureen. "You remember how frightened we were to go down into Whitehorn Abbey's crypt?"

She nodded. "There have been too many graves in our lives, Brian, and too much running. God, look at you. You look ten years older than your age."

"Do I? Well . . . that's not just from the running. That's partly from not running fast enough." He paused, then added, "I was caught."

She turned her head toward him. "Oh . . . I didn't know."

"It was kept quiet. Major Martin. Remember the name?"

"Of course. He contacted me once, right after I'd gone to Dublin. He wanted to know where you were. He said it would go easier on Sheila . . . and he said they would cancel the warrant for my arrest . . . Pleasant sort of chap, actually, but you knew he'd pull your fingernails out if he had you in Belfast."

Flynn smiled. "And what did you tell this pleasant chap?"

"I would have told him to go to hell except I thought he might actually go and find you there. So I told him to fuck off."

Flynn smiled again, but his eyes were appraising her thoughtfully.

She read the expression in his face. "I want you to understand that I never turned informer. Traitor, if you like, but never informer."

He nodded. "I believe you. If I didn't, I'd have killed you long ago."

"Would you?"

He changed the subject. "You're going to get people hurt if you try to escape again."

She didn't respond.

Flynn took a key from his pocket and held it out. "This is the key to the padlock on that chain. I'll open it now, and you can go."

"Not without the others."

"But you'd try to escape without the others."

"That's different."

He smiled and kept the key in front of her. "Ah, you're still a street fighter, Maureen. You understand that there's a price to pay—in advance—for a bit of freedom. Most men and women in this world would leave here quickly through the offered gate, and they wouldn't even entertain the thought of escaping with bullets whistling about their ears. You see, your values and requirements are reversed from ordinary people's. We changed you forever in those years we had you."

She remembered the way he had of interpreting for her all of her motives and actions, and how he had once had her so confused about who and what she was that she'd fallen into his power, willingly and gladly. She looked at him. "Shut up."

Flynn hesitated, then pocketed the key and shifted to another topic. "I chatted with the Cardinal. He believes in the ring, you know. You didn't believe because you thought that as a halfhearted Christian you shouldn't. But His Eminence is about as good a Christian as they make, you'll agree, and for that reason he believes."

She looked at the crypt door. "I never said I didn't believe in such things. I told you in Whitehorn Abbey on the evening I left that I couldn't understand why any power—good or evil—would pick *you* as their mortal emissary."

He laughed. "That's a terrible thing to say. You're a master of the low blow, Maureen. You'd be a bitch except you've got a good heart." He moved closer to her. "How do you explain the fact of Father Donnelly's disappearance? I've searched for that man—if man he was—over these past years, and no one has even heard of him."

She stared through a glass pane into the white, luminescent crypt and shook her head.

Flynn watched her, then put a different tone in his voice and took her arm in a firm grip. "Before I forget, let me give you one good piece of advice—don't provoke Megan."

She turned toward him. "The fact that I'm still breathing provokes her. Let me give *you* a piece of advice. If you get out of here alive, get as far from her as you can. She draws destruction like a lightning rod, Brian."

Flynn made no response and let go of her arm.

She went on. "And Hickey . . . that man is . . ." She shook her head. "Never mind. I see you've fallen in with a bad lot. We hardly know each other anymore, Brian. How can we give each other advice?"

He reached out and touched her cheek. There was a long silence on the crypt landing. Then from the sacristy corridor came the sound of footsteps and the squeaking of wheels on the marble floor. Maureen said suddenly, "If Major Martin caught you, how is it that you're alive?"

Flynn walked down the stairs and stood at the gate.

She followed. "Did you make a deal with him?"

He didn't answer.

"And you call yourself a patriot?"

He looked at her sharply. "So does Major Martin. So do you."

"I would never—"

"Oh, you'd make a deal. Popes, prime ministers, and presidents make deals like that, and it's called diplomacy and strategy. That's what this life is all about, Maureen—illusion and semantics. Well, I'm making no deals today, no accommodations, no matter what names the negotiator gives me for it to make it more palatable. That should make you happy, since you don't like deals."

She didn't reply.

He went on. "If you agree that the deal I made with Major Martin wasn't so awful, I'll put Sheila's name on the list of people to be released."

She looked at him quickly. "You mean, it's not—"

"Changes things a bit, doesn't it? Looking ahead, were you, to a tearful reunion with little Sheila? Now you've nothing whatsoever to gain from this. Unless, of course, you see my point in trafficking with the enemy."

"Why is it so important to you that I tell you that?"

A voice called out, "This is Burke. Coming in."

Flynn said to Maureen, "We'll talk again later." He shouted into the sacristy, "Come on, then." He drew back his jacket and adjusted the pistol in his waistband, then said to her, "I respect your abilities as a fighter enough to treat you like a man. Don't try anything, don't make any sudden moves, don't stand behind me, and keep silent until you're spoken to."

She answered, "If that was a compliment, I'm not flattered. I've put that behind me."

"Aye, like a reformed whore puts the streets behind her, but the urge is still there, I'll wager."

She looked at him. "It is now."

He smiled.

Burke appeared from the sacristy corridor, pushing a serving cart. He rolled the cart over the marble floor and stopped at the bottom stair below the gate.

"Do you know Miss Malone?" Flynn asked.

Burke nodded to her. "We've met."

"That's right," said Flynn. "Last evening at the Waldorf. I have a report on it. Seems so long ago, doesn't it?" He smiled. "I've brought her here to assure you we haven't butchered the hostages." He said to her, "Tell him how well you've been treated, Maureen."

She said, "No one is dead yet."

Burke replied, "Please tell the others that we are doing all we can to see that you're safely released." He put a light note in his voice. "Tell Father Murphy he can hear my confession when this is over."

She nodded and gave him a look of understanding.

Flynn was silent a moment, then asked, "Is the priest a friend of yours?"

Burke replied, "They're all friends of mine."

"Really?" He came closer to the gate. "Are you wired, Burke? Do I have to go through the debugging routine?"

"I'm clean. The cart is clean. I don't want to be overheard either." Burke came up the seven steps and was acutely aware of the psychological disadvantage of standing on a step eight inches below Flynn. "And the food's not drugged."

Flynn nodded. "No, not with hostages. Makes all the difference in the world, doesn't it?"

Maureen suddenly grabbed the bars and spoke hurriedly. "His real name is Brian Flynn. He has only about twelve gunmen—"

Flynn pulled the pistol from his waistband and pressed it hard against her neck. "Don't be a hero, Maureen. It isn't required. Is it, Lieutenant?"

Burke kept his hands in full view. "Easy now. Nice and easy. Miss Malone, don't say anything else. That's right."

Flynn spoke to her through clenched teeth. "That's good advice, lass. You don't want to jeopardize others, such as Lieutenant Burke, who's already heard too much." He looked at Burke. "She's impulsive and hasn't learned the difference between bravery and recklessness. That's my fault, I'm afraid." He grabbed her arm with his free hand and pulled her away from the gate. "Leave."

Maureen looked at Burke and said, "I've made a confession to Father Murphy, and I'm not afraid to die. We'll *all* make our confessions soon. Don't give in to these bastards."

Burke looked at her and nodded. "I understand."

She smiled, turned, and mounted the steps to the altar.

Flynn held the pistol at his side and watched her go. He seemed to be thinking, then said, "All right, how much do I owe you?"

Burke slowly handed a bill to Flynn.

Flynn looked at it. "Five hundred sixty-one dollars and twelve cents. Not cheap to feed an army in New York, is it?" Flynn slipped the pistol into his waistband and counted out the money. "Here. Come closer."

Burke moved nearer the gate and took the bills and change.

Flynn said, "I deducted the sales tax on principle." He laughed. "Make certain you report that to the press, Lieutenant. They love that sort of nonsense."

Burke nodded. Brian Flynn, he decided, was not a complete lunatic. He had the uneasy feeling that Flynn was sharper than Schroeder, and a better performer.

Flynn looked down at the cart laden with covered metal dishes. "It wouldn't be Saint Paddy's Day without the corned beef, would it, Burke? Had yours?"

"No. Been busy."

"Well, come in and join us, then. Everyone would enjoy your company."

"I can't."

"Can't?" Flynn made a pretense of remembering something. "Ah, yes. Hostages will neither be given nor exchanged under any circumstances. Police will not take the place of hostages. But I'll not keep you prisoner."

"You seem to know a lot about this."

Flynn thrust his face between the bars, close to Burke's. "I know enough not to do anything stupid. I hope you know as much."

"I'm sure we've had more experience with hostage situations than you—see that *you* don't make any mistakes."

Flynn lit a cigarette and said abruptly, "So, I should formally introduce myself now that Miss Malone was thoughtful enough to tell you my name. I am as the lady said—as you might have known from other sources—Brian Flynn. Ring any bells?"

"A few. Back in the late seventies. Over there."

"Yes, over there. Over here now. Unlike John Hickey, I'm not officially dead, only unofficially missing. All right, let's talk about our favorite subject. Is Major Martin present at your war councils?"

"Yes."

"Get him out of there."

"He's representing the British consulate for now."

Flynn forced a laugh. "Sir Harry will be distressed to hear that. Let me tell you that Martin will double-cross his own Foreign Office, too. His only loyalty is to his sick obsession with the Irish. Get him the hell away from the decision-making process."

"Maybe I'd rather have him close where I can see him."

Flynn shook his head. "You never see a man like that no matter how close he is. Get him out of the rectory, away from your commanders."

Burke said softly, "So your people on the outside can kill him?"

A slow smile passed over Flynn's face. "Oh, Lieutenant, you are the sharp one. Yes, indeed."

"Please don't do anything without talking to me first."

Flynn nodded. "Yes, I'll have to be straight with you. We may still be able to work together."

"Maybe."

Flynn said, "Look here, there's a lot of double-dealing going on, Burke. Only the New York police, as far as I can tell, have no ulterior motives. I'll count on you, Lieutenant, to do your job. You must play the honest broker and avert a bloodbath. Dawn tomorrow or—I promise you—this Cathedral will burn. That's as inevitable as the sunrise itself."

"You mean you have no control over that?"

Flynn nodded. "Very quick-witted of you. I control my people up to a point. But at dawn each man and woman in here will act on standing orders unless our demands have been met. Without a word from me the prisoners will be shot or thrown from the bell tower, fires will be set, and other destructive devices will automatically engage."

Burke said, "You did a damned stupid thing to relinquish that kind of control. Stupid and dangerous."

Flynn pressed his face to the bars. "But you could do worse than dealing with me. If anything happened to me, you would have to deal with Hickey and the woman we call Grania, so don't you or Schroeder or anyone out there try to undermine me. Work with me and no one will die."

"Better the devil you know than the devils you don't know."

"Quite right, Lieutenant. Quite right. You may go."

Burke moved backward down a step, away from the gate. He and Flynn looked at each other. Flynn made no move to turn away this time, and Burke remembered the hostage unit's injunction against turning your back on hostage takers. "Treat them like royalty," Schroeder liked to say on television talk shows. "Never show them your back. Never use negative words. Never use words like death, kill, die, dead. Always address them respectfully." Schroeder would have had a stroke if he had heard this exchange.

Burke took another step backward. Schroeder had his methods, yet Burke was becoming convinced that this situation called for flexibility, originality, and even compromise. He hoped Schroeder and everyone else out there recognized that before it was too late.

He turned his back to Flynn, went down the steps past the serving cart, and moved toward the corridor opening, all the while aware of the deep, dark eyes that followed him.

30

Patrick Burke made the long underground walk from the sacristy past the silent policemen in the corridors. He noticed that the Tactical Patrol Unit had been replaced by the Emergency Services Division. They wore black uniforms and black flak jackets, they carried shotguns, sniper rifles, automatic weapons, and silenced pistols, and they looked very unlike the public image of a cop, he thought. Their eyes had that unfocused look, their bodies were exaggeratedly relaxed, and cigarettes dangled from tight lips.

Burke entered the rectory's basement and made his way upstairs to the Monsignor's office suite, through the crowded outer office, and into the next room, shutting the door firmly behind him. Burke met the stares of the twelve people whom he had labeled in his mind the Desperate Dozen. He remained standing in the center of the room.

Schroeder finally spoke. "What took you so long?"

Burke found a chair and sat. "You told me to get the measure of the man."

"No negotiating, Burke. That's my job. You don't know the procedure—"

"Anytime you want me to leave, I'm gone. I'm not looking to get on the cover of *Time.*"

Schroeder stood. "I'm a little tired of getting ribbed about that goddamned *Time* story—"

Deputy Commissioner Rourke cut in. "All right, men. It's going to be a long night." He turned to Schroeder. "You want Burke to leave after he briefs us?"

Schroeder shook his head. "Flynn has made him his errand boy, and we can't upset Mr. Flynn."

Langley broke in. "What did Flynn say, Pat?"

Burke lit a cigarette and listened to the silence for a longer time than was considered polite. "He said the Cathedral will more or less self-destruct at sunrise."

No one spoke until Bellini said, "If I have to take that place by force, you better leave enough time for the Bomb Squad to comb every inch of it. They've only got two mutts now—Sally and Brandy. . . ." He shook his head. "What a mess . . . damn it."

Schroeder said, "No matter what type of devices they have rigged, they can delay them. I'll get an extension."

Burke looked at him. "I don't think you understood what I said."

Langley interjected. "What else did he say, Pat?"

Burke sat back and gave them an edited briefing, glancing at Major Martin, who stood against the fireplace in a classic pose. Burke had the impression that Martin was filling in the missing sentences.

Burke focused on Arnold Sheridan, the quintessential Wasp from State, tight smile, correct manners, cultivated voice that said nothing. He was assigned to the security section but probably found it distasteful to be even a quasi-cop. Burke realized that, as the man on the scene, Sheridan might sway the administration either way. Hard line, soft line, or line straddling. Washington could push London into an accommodation, and then, like dominoes, Dublin, Albany, and the City of New York would tumble into line. But as he looked at Sheridan he had no idea of what was going on behind those polite, vacant eyes.

Burke looked back at Schroeder as he spoke. This was a man who was an accomplished listener as well as a talker. He heard every word, remembered every word, even interpreted nuances and made analyses and conclusions but ultimately, through some incredible process in his brain, never really *understood* a thing that was said. Burke flipped a cigarette ash into a coffee cup. "I don't think this guy is a textbook case. I don't think he's going to bend in his demands or give extensions, Schroeder."

Schroeder said, "They all give extensions, Burke. They want to play out the drama, and they always think a concession will come in the next minute, the next hour, the next day. It's human nature."

Burke shook his head. "Don't operate on the premise that you'll get more time."

Major Martin interrupted. "If I may say something—Lieutenant Burke's analysis is not correct. I've dealt with the Irish for ten years, and they are dreadful liars, fakes, and bluffers. Flynn will give you extensions if you keep him hopeful that—"

Burke stood. "Bullshit."

The Irish Consul General stood also and said hesitantly, "Look here, Major, I . . . I think it's unfair to characterize the Irish . . ."

Martin forced an amiable tone into his voice. "Oh, sorry, Tomas. I was speaking only of the IRA, of course." He looked around the room. "I didn't mean to offend Irish Americans either. Commissioner Rourke, Mr. Hogan, Lieutenant Burke"—he looked at Schroeder and smiled—"or your better half."

Commissioner Rourke nodded to show there were no hard feelings, and spoke. "Everyone is a little tense. Let's take it easy. Okay?" He looked at Burke. "Lieutenant, the Major has a lot of experience in these things. He's providing us with valuable information, not to mention insight. I know Irish affairs are your specialty, but this is not an Irish-American affair. This is different."

Burke looked around the room. "I'd like to make it an American affair for a few minutes. Specifically, I'd like to speak to the Commissioner, Captain Schroeder, Inspector Langley, Mr. Kruger, and Mr. Hogan—alone."

Commissioner Rourke looked around the room, unsure of what to say. Major Martin moved to the door. "I've got to get to the consulate." Tomas Donahue made an excuse and followed. Monsignor Downes nodded and left. Arnold Sheridan rose and looked at his watch. "I have to call State."

Bellini said, "You want me here, Burke?"

"It doesn't concern you, Joe."

Bellini said, "It better not." He left.

The Governor's aide suddenly looked alert. "Oh . . ." He stood. "I have to go. . . ." He left.

Roberta Spiegel sat back in her rocker and lit another cigarette. "You can either go talk in the men's room—though that's no guarantee I won't follow— or you can talk here."

Burke decided he didn't mind her presence. He took Langley to the far end of the room and said quietly, "Did we hear from Jack Ferguson yet?"

Langley said, "We got through to his wife. She's sick in bed. She hasn't heard from him either."

Burke shook his head. He usually felt his first responsibility was to an informant who was in danger, but now he had no time for Jack Ferguson. Ferguson understood that—and understood, he hoped, that he was in danger. Burke moved to the center of the room and addressed the remaining people. "I've dealt a few cards from the bottom of the deck myself over the years, but never have I seen a card game as stacked as this one. And since I'm the one who almost got his head blown off this afternoon, I think you'll understand why I'm a little pissed off." He looked at Kruger and Hogan. "You two have some explaining to do." Burke took a long pull on his cigarette and continued. "Consider this—we have here a well-planned, well-financed operation. Too much so, from what we know of the IRA, domestic and foreign. I see here the hand of not so much the revolutionary but the counterrevolutionary—the government man." He looked at Kruger and Hogan.

No one spoke.

"Brian Flynn has told me that Major Bartholomew Martin suggested an American operation to him and provided the necessary resources to carry it out. And if *that* is true, then I don't think Martin could have pulled it off without the help of some of your people—or at least without your well-known talent for looking the other way when it suits you."

Langley stood. "Careful."

Burke turned. "Come off it, Langley. You had your suspicions, too." He turned back to the people in front of him. "This whole thing has been a staged performance, but I think it got out of control because Brian Flynn wasn't playing his part as written. Maybe he was supposed to knock over an armory or blow a bank. But he got a better idea, and now we're all up to our asses in the consequences."

Kruger stood. "I've never heard such paranoid nonsense—"

Hogan reached out and put his hand on Kruger's arm, then sat forward. "Listen, Burke, what you say is not altogether untrue." He paused, then went on. "The FBI *did* stand to gain from this incident. Sure, when this is over they'll fire some people at the top, but then the analysis will show how powerless we were to stop it. And maybe we'll become the beneficiaries of a little power and money." He leaned farther forward and put an aggrieved tone in his voice: "But to even *hint* that *we*—"

Burke waved his arm to cut off the disclaimers. "I have no real evidence, and I don't want any. All I want you to know is that Patrick Burke knows. And I almost got my fucking head blown off finding out. And if Flynn starts making public statements, people will tend to believe him, and your two outfits will be in trouble—again."

Hogan shook his head. "He won't make any public charges about outside help, because he's not going to admit to the Irish people that he worked with British Intelligence—"

Kruger looked at him sharply. "Shut up, Hogan."

Douglas Hogan waved his hand in dismissal. "Oh, for Christ's sake, Kruger, there's no use trying to play it coy." He looked at the four policemen in the room. "We had some knowledge of this, but, as you say, it got out of control. I can promise you, though, that no matter what happens, we will cover you . . . so long as you do the same. What's happened is past. Now we have to work at making sure we come out of this not only blameless but looking good." Douglas Hogan spread his hands out in front of him and said coaxingly, "We have been handed a unique opportunity to make some important changes in intelligence procedures in this country. A chance to improve our image."

Commissioner Rourke stood. "You people are . . . crazy."

Langley turned to the Commissioner. "Sir, I think we have no choice but to keep to the problem at hand. We can't change the series of events that brought us here, but we can try to ensure that the outcome won't be disastrous . . . as long as we work together."

The Commissioner looked at the FBI man, the CIA man, then at his two intelligence officers. He understood very clearly that their logic was not his logic, their world not his world. He understood, also, that anyone who could do what Kruger and Hogan had apparently done were dangerous and desperate men. He looked at Roberta Spiegel. She nodded to him, and he sat down.

Burke glanced around the room and said, "It's important that you all understand that Bartholomew Martin is a danger to any negotiated settlement. He means to see that the Cathedral is destroyed and that blood is shed." He looked at Rourke and Schroeder. "He is not your good friend." He stared at Kruger and Hogan. "The most Martin hoped for was an arms steal or a bank heist, but *Flynn* presented him with a unique opportunity to influence public opinion in America the way the IRA murder of Lord Mountbatten did in the British Isles. However, if Flynn walks out of the Cathedral with no blood shed and the IRA prisoners are released, he'll be a hero to a large segment of the Irish population, and no one will ever believe he meant to harm anyone or destroy the Cathedral—and Major Martin cannot allow that to happen." Burke turned again to Kruger and Hogan. "I want him neutralized—no, that's not like one of your famous euphemisms for murder. Don't look so uncomfortable.

Neutralized—inoperative. Watched. I want a regular Foreign Office man representing the British government in New York, not Martin. I've given *you* a unique opportunity to save your own asses."

Kruger stared at Burke, unconcealed hostility in his eyes.

Hogan nodded. "I'll do what I can."

Roberta Spiegel said, "End of discussion." She looked at Schroeder. "Captain, you're on."

Schroeder nodded and turned on the speakers in the rectory offices and in the Cardinal's residence. He placed the call through the switchboard and looked around the room while he waited. *New ball game for them,* he thought. But his ball game hadn't changed substantially. His only concern was the personality of Brian Flynn. His whole world was reduced to the electronic impulses between himself and Flynn. Washington, London, and Dublin could make it easier for him by capitulating, but they couldn't make it any more difficult than it already was. A voice in the earphone made him sit up. "Hello, Mr. Flynn? This is Captain Schroeder."

31

B rian Flynn stood at the chancel organ and lit a cigarette as he cradled the receiver on his shoulder. "Schroeder, the corned beef was stringy. You didn't butcher the horse now, did you?"

The negotiator's voice came back with a contrived laugh in it. "No, sir. If there's anything else you want, please let us know."

"I'm about to do that. First of all, I'm glad you know my name. Now you know you're dealing with Ireland's greatest living patriot. Right?"

"Yes, sir. . . ."

"There'll be a monument erected to me someday in Dublin and in a free Belfast. No one will remember you."

"Yes, sir."

Flynn laughed suddenly. "I hear you writing, Schroeder. What are you writing? 'Megalomania'?"

"No, sir. Just keeping notes."

"Good. Now just listen and take notes on this. First . . ." Flynn leafed through Schroeder's autobiography as he spoke. ". . . make certain you leave the Cathedral's floodlights on. It looks so grand bathed in blue light. Also, that will make it difficult for your ESD men to climb up the sides. I've people in skyscrapers with field glasses. If they see anything moving outside, they'll signal the towers or call me directly. Which brings me to point two. Don't interfere with my outside telephone lines. Point three, if the lights in here so much as flicker, I'll shoot everyone. Point four, no psy-warfare, such as your usual prank of running that silly armored car you own around the Cathedral. My men in the towers have M-72 rockets. Anyway, we've seen more armored cars than you've seen taxis, Schroeder, and they don't frighten us. Point five, no helicopters. If my men in the towers see one, they'll fire on it. Point six, tell your ESD people that we've planned this for a long time, and an attack would cost them dearly. Don't waste them. You'll need them next time." Flynn wiped a line of sweat from his forehead. "Point seven, I say again, no extensions. Plan to wrap it up by dawn, Schroeder. Point eight, I want a nice twenty-one-inch color television set. I'll tell you when I want Burke to bring it. Point nine, I want to see continuous news coverage until dawn. Point ten, I want to hold a news conference in the press room below the sacristy. Prime time, 10:00 P.M., live. Got all that?"

After a long silence Schroeder's voice came through, sounding strained. "Yes, sir. We'll try to accommodate you on all those points."

"You *will* accommodate me. What have you heard from Dublin, London, and Washington?"

"They're tied into their representatives, who are here in the Cardinal's residence. They're making progress."

"It's good to see allies working so well together. I hope they're all keeping their tempers as we are doing, Captain. What have you heard from Amnesty and the Red Cross?"

"They are willing to cooperate in any way possible."

"Good for them. Good people. Always there to lend a hand. How about immunity from prosecution for my people in here?"

Schroeder cleared his throat. "The U.S. Attorney General and the State Attorney General are discussing it. So far, all I can promise you is—"

"A fair trial," interrupted Flynn. "Wonderful country. But I don't want *any* trial at all, Schroeder."

"I can't make that promise at this time."

"Let me make something clear—at the same time you tell me those prisoners are being released, you'd better have a guarantee of immunity for us or it's no deal. I'll shoot the hostages and blow this place apart." Flynn could hear Schroeder's breathing in the earpiece.

Schroeder said softly, "Everything you ask for is being considered very carefully, but these things take time. All I'm concerned with at the moment is the safety—"

"Schroeder, stop talking to me as though I were some sort of criminal lunatic. Save that for your next case, if you have one. I'm a soldier, and I want to be spoken to as a soldier. The prisoners in here are being treated correctly. And your tone is very patronizing."

"I'm sorry. I didn't mean to offend you. I'm only trying to assure you of our good intentions. My job is to negotiate a settlement we can all live with, and—"

Flynn suddenly stood and said, "How do you call it negotiation if you don't intend to *give* anything?"

Schroeder didn't reply.

"Have you *ever* made any real concessions in all of your career as a hostage negotiator, Schroeder? Never. You're not even *listening* to me, for Christ's sake. Well, you'd damn well *better* listen, because when this Cathedral is in ruins and the dead are lying everywhere, you'll wish to God you paid more attention, and that you'd acted in better faith."

"I *am* listening. I *am* acting—"

"You'll be known, Captain Bert Schroeder, as the man who failed to save Saint Patrick's Cathedral and who has innocent blood on his hands. You'll never hold your head up again, and you'll not accept many talk-show invitations, I think."

Schroeder's voice came back, agitated for the first time that anyone who was listening could remember. "I haven't lied to you, have I? We haven't tried to use force, have we? You asked for food, we gave you food. You asked—"

"I paid for the fucking food! Now listen to me closely. I know you're only a middleman for a lot of bastards, but . . ." Flynn looked at Schroeder's picture on the cover of his book. It was an action shot, taken during a bank robbery that had turned into a hostage situation. Schroeder, unlike his predecessor, who always wore a baseball cap and Windbreaker, was dressed nattily in a three-piece pinstripe. The face and massive body suggested was more the baseball-cap type, but Schroeder was reaching for his own style. Flynn studied the face on the cover. Good profile, firm jaw, erect carriage. But the eyes were unmistakably frightened. A bad picture. Flynn continued, "But I trust you, Schroeder—trust you to use your influence and your good offices. I want you to keep talking to me all night, Captain. I want you to carry my message to the people around you."

Schroeder's voice sounded surprised at the sudden expression of confidence. "Yes, sir. I'll do that. You can talk to me." Both men remained silent for a time, then Schroeder said, "Now I'd like to ask two favors of you."

Flynn smiled and flipped absently through the autobiography in front of him. "Go on."

"Well, for one thing, the jamming device is causing confusion in command and control, and we don't want an incident to occur because of a lack of communication. Also, it's causing interference with commercial radio and the sound portions of television broadcasts."

Flynn threw aside the book. "Can't have that. I'll think about it. What else?"

"I'd like to say a few words to each of the hostages."

"Maybe after the press conference."

"All right. That's fair. There is one other thing."

"There always is."

"Yes, well, since you and I are building a rapport—building confidence in each other—and I'm the only one talking to you, I wonder if you'd do the same for me. I mean, I spoke to Mr. Hickey before, and—"

Flynn laughed and looked around, but Hickey wasn't in sight. "John gave you a bit of a rough time, did he, Captain? He enjoys making unpleasant jokes. Well, just play along with him. He loves to talk—Irish, you know."

"Yes, but there could be a misunderstanding. You are the boss, and I want to keep my lines of communication open to *you,* and—"

Flynn dropped the receiver into its cradle and looked through a book of sheet music. He wanted to find something unchurchly that would take his mind away from the Cathedral. Of all the godforsaken places he'd ever found himself in, no place seemed more oddly forsaken than the Cathedral at this moment. Yet others, he knew, felt the presence of a divine spirit here, and he understood that the emptiness he felt was totally within himself. He found "The Rose of Tralee," turned the key into the organ, and played as he sang very softly.

> "The pale moon was rising above
> The green mountains,
> The sun was declining beneath
> The blue sea,
> As I strayed with my love to the
> Pure crystal fountain,
> That stands in the beautiful vale
> of Tralee. . . ."

Bert Schroeder looked for a long time at the dead speaker, folded his hands on the desk, and thought. Flynn talked about immunity, which showed he thought of a future, and by implication his desire to keep his crime from being compounded was strong. He had no intention of killing anyone, least of all himself. More importantly, Flynn was beginning to depend on him. That always happened. It was inevitable as he came to realize that Schroeder's voice was the only one that mattered. Schroeder looked up. "I think I'm getting an angle on this guy."

Burke said, "It sounds like he has an angle on *you.*"

Schroeder's eyes narrowed, and he nodded reluctantly. "Yes, he seems to know something of my methods. I'm afraid the media has given my bureau too much coverage." He added, "I never sought publicity."

"You mean your autobiography was unauthorized? Christ, you should have at least waited until you retired before you released it." Burke smiled. "And now you've missed the big chapter. Catch it on the second printing. Talk to your agent about it." Burke put a conciliatory tone in his voice. "Look, Bert, I don't have all the answers, but—"

Schroeder stood. "No, you don't. And I'm tired of your sideline quarterbacking!"

No one spoke. Burke stood and moved toward the door.

Schroeder said, "Don't go far. Flynn may want coffee later."

Burke turned and said, "Up to this point we've had double-crosses, incompetence, and some ordinary stupidity. And we've been damned lucky in spite of it. But if we don't get our act together by dawn, we're going to have a massacre, a desecration, and a lot of explaining to do."

Schroeder stared ahead and spoke placidly. "Just leave it to me."

32

Father Murphy walked across the sanctuary and stood before the Cardinal's throne. "Your Eminence, I would like to make my confession."

The Cardinal nodded. "Take my hands."

Murphy felt the scrap of paper sticking to his palm. "No . . . I would like to go into the confessional."

The Cardinal stood. "We'll go into the Archbishop's sacristy."

"No . . ." Murphy felt a line of sweat collect on his brow. "They won't let us. We can go into the confessional where I heard Miss Malone's confession."

The Cardinal stared at him curiously, then nodded. "As you wish." He came down from the throne and walked toward the rear of the sanctuary, then descended the side steps that led into the ambulatory. Father Murphy glanced back at Maureen and Baxter. They nodded encouragingly, and he followed the Cardinal.

Leary leaned over the choir loft parapet, placed the cross hairs in front of the Cardinal's face, and led him as he walked from right to left across his magnified picture. Everyone in the triforia began shouting warnings to the two priests, shouting at Leary who they knew was about to fire, shouting for Flynn or Hickey.

The Cardinal seemed oblivious to the warnings. He stopped at the archway that led to the priests' entrance to the confessional and waited for Father Murphy, who walked hesitantly across the ambulatory.

Leary centered his cross hairs on the gold cross that hung over the Cardinal's heart and took up the slack in the trigger.

Flynn suddenly appeared in front of the two priests with his arms raised and looked into the balconies. The shouting stopped. Leary straightened his body and stood with his rifle resting in the crook of his arm. Even from this distance Flynn could see that Leary had that distinctive posture of a hunter who had just been denied his quarry, motionless, listening, watching. Flynn saw Megan appear in the loft and move beside Leary, speaking to him as though she were soothing his disappointment. Flynn turned to the two priests. "What the hell do you think you're doing?"

The Cardinal answered evenly, "I'm going to hear a confession."

Flynn spoke between clenched teeth. "Are you *mad?* You can't come down from there without permission."

The Cardinal answered, "I don't need your permission to go anywhere in this church. Please stand aside."

Flynn fought down the anger inside him. "Let me tell you two something. Those people up there have standing orders to shoot. . . . All right, four of them may not be priest killers, but the fifth man would kill you. He would shoot his mother if that's what he's contracted to do. Just as you took your vows, he has taken his."

The Cardinal's face turned crimson; he began to speak, but Flynn cut him off. "That man has spent fourteen years as a sniper for a dozen different armies. By now he sees the world through cross hairs. His whole being is compressed into that solitary act. And he loves it—the sound of the gun, the recoil of the stock against his shoulder, the flash of the muzzle, the smell of burnt powder in his nostrils. It's like a sexual act to him—can you two understand *that?"*

Neither the Cardinal nor the priest answered. The Cardinal turned his head and looked up into the shadows of the choir loft, then turned back to Flynn. "It's hard to believe such a man exists. You should be careful he doesn't shoot *you."* He stepped around Flynn and entered the wooden archway, then turned into the door of the confessional.

Father Murphy glanced at Flynn, then pushed aside the curtain and entered the confessional.

John Hickey stood some distance off near the Lady Chapel and watched silently.

Murphy knelt in the dark enclosure and began, "Bless me, Father . . ." He peered through a space in the curtain and saw Flynn walking away. He spoke in whispered tones to the Cardinal, making a hasty confession, then broke off abruptly and said, "Your Eminence, I'm going to use the call buzzer to send a coded message."

The dark outline of the Cardinal's profile behind the black screen stayed motionless as though he hadn't heard, then slowly the head nodded.

Murphy drew the curtain gently over the doorjamb and pressed the button in a series of alerting signals. He looked closely at the paper in his hand and squinted in the darkness. He began:

THIS IS FR. MURPHY.

Suddenly a hand flew through the curtain and grabbed his wrist. Hickey's voice filled the confessional. "While you're in there, Padre, confess to using the confessional for treachery." He flung the curtain aside, and Murphy blinked in the sudden light. Hickey snatched the paper out of the priest's hand and pulled the curtain closed. "Go on, finish your damned confession. I'll finish the message."

Murphy slumped against the screen and spoke softly to the Cardinal. "I'm sorry. . . ."

Hickey stood outside the booth and looked around. Flynn was gone. No one was paying any attention to him except Malone and Baxter on the sanctuary, who looked both angry and disheartened. Hickey smiled at them, then read the coded message, put his finger on the buzzer, and began to send. He repeated the salutation—

THIS IS FR. MURPHY IN CONFESSIONAL WITH CARDINAL.

He continued, reproducing the halting wrist of a man who was sending for the first time. He modified the written message as he sent.

ESTIMATE OF FENIAN STRENGTH: NO MORE THAN EIGHT GUNMEN. ONE IN EACH OF EAST TRIFORIA. NONE IN WEST TRIFORIA. NONE IN CHOIR LOFT. ONE MAN AT SACRISTY STAIRS WITH THOMPSON—ONLY AUTO WEAPON SEEN. ONE MAN IN EACH TOWER. FIELD PHONES MALFUNCTIONING. HOSTAGES MOVED TO CRYPT. SAFE FROM FIRE.

He stopped and picked up the text of the message.

MACCUMAIL IS BRIAN FLYNN. JOHN HICKEY, LIEUTENANT. MEGAN THIRD IN COMMAND.

He improvised again.

NO MINES ON DOORS. GAS MASKS ARE OLD TYPE, INEFFECTIVE FILTERS.

He stopped and thought a moment. Then went on.

FENIANS LOYAL TO HICKEY. WILL NOT NEGOTIATE IN GOOD FAITH. SUICIDAL TALK. BAXTER TO BE HANGED BEFORE DAWN DEADLINE AS AN EXAMPLE. DO WHAT YOU MUST. WE ARE NOT AFRAID. GOD BLESS YOU— FATHER MURPHY.

Hickey took his finger off the buzzer and smiled. The people out there were a bit confused now . . . and frightened. Fright led to desperation. Desperation led to reckless acts. Hickey put himself in their place—discounting the possibility of negotiation, concerned over the hostages, underestimating the force holding the Cathedral. The police would submit a plan to take the Cathedral, and it would be accepted. And the politicians would have the message to justify that use of force. The police would burst through the doors, and they'd be met by explosions and an unexpected volume of killing fire.

Hickey pictured it in his mind as he looked around the Cathedral. Shattered marble, crumbling statues, dark red blood running over the altars and floors, the dead lying draped over the pews. The attic would be set aflame, and the ceiling would fall into the nave, blowing their precious stained glass into the streets. He saw dying bodies writhing among the rubble and the flames. And when they thought it was over, long after the last shot had been fired, as the dawn streaked in through dusty shafts revealing the rescuers and medics moving through the ruins, then the time bombs would detonate, and the two main columns would tremble and shudder and collapse in a deafening roar of granite and marble, plaster and bronze, wood and concrete. The Cathedral would die, brick by brick, stone by stone, column by column, wall by wall. . . . And in years to come when people looked on the most magnificent ruin in America they would remember John Hickey's last mission on earth.

Maureen Malone sat very still in the pew and watched as Hickey sent his message. She turned to Harold Baxter. "Bastard!"

Baxter looked away from Hickey. "Yes, well, that's his prerogative, isn't it? But, no harm done. Especially if the first message was received."

"I don't think you understand," she said. "The people outside still believe we control that signal. Hickey is not sending them a rude message or something of that sort. He's reading from our message and sending a misleading intelligence report over our signatures."

Baxter looked at Hickey, and the comprehension of what she was saying came to him.

"And God only knows what he's telling them. He's mad, you know. Flynn is a paragon of rationality compared to Hickey."

"Hickey is not mad," said Baxter. "He's something far more dangerous than mad."

She looked down at the floor. "Anyway, I'll not apologize for trying."

"I'm not asking you to. But I think the next plan should be mine."

"Really?" She spoke with a frigid tone in her voice. "I don't think we have the time to wait for either your plan or your much discussed right moment."

He answered without anger. "Just give me a few more minutes. I think I know a way out of here."

Burke walked into the Monsignor's inner office, followed by Inspector Langley. A uniformed officer handed them each a copy of the decoded message. Burke sat on Schroeder's desk and read the message. He looked around at the people present—Schroeder, Commissioner Rourke, Roberta Spiegel, and Bellini—the hard core of the Desperate Dozen, with Langley and himself added or subtracted as the situation changed.

Captain Bellini looked up from his copy and spoke to Commissioner Rourke. "If this is accurate, I can take the Cathedral with an acceptable risk to my people. If the hostages are in the crypt, they have a fair chance of surviving . . . though I can't guarantee that." He looked at the message again. "They don't seem to stand much chance with the Fenians anyway." He stood. "I'll need a few more hours to plan."

Burke thought of Maureen's statement at the sacristy gate. *Twelve gunmen.* Now Murphy said eight. He looked across the room at Bellini. "And if it's not accurate?"

Bellini said, "How far off can they be? They're heads-up people. Right? They can count. Look, I'm not real anxious to do this, but I feel a little better about it now."

Langley said, "We can't discount the possibility that one or both of these messages are from the Fenians." He looked at his copy and compared it to the earlier message, which he held in his hand. "I'm a little confused. Something is wrong here." He looked up. "Bellini, as an intelligence officer, I'd advise you not to believe either of these."

Bellini looked distraught. "Well, where the hell does that put me? Square fucking one, that's where."

Roberta Spiegel said, "Whether or not we believe either of these messages, everybody in the Cardinal's residence and in the next room is reading this last message, and they will come to their own conclusions." She looked at Rourke. "This justifies a preemptive attack, Commissioner. That's what's going through their minds out there." She turned to Bellini. "Captain, be prepared to mount an attack at very short notice."

Bellini nodded distractedly.

The door opened, and Monsignor Downes came into the office. "Did someone want to see me?"

The five men looked at each other questioningly, then Roberta Spiegel said, "Yes, I asked to see you."

Downes remained standing.

The Mayor's aide thought a moment, then said, "Monsignor, neither the Mayor nor myself nor anyone wants to do anything that will harm this church or endanger the lives of the hostages. However—"

The Monsignor's body stiffened.

"However, if the police and my office and the people in Washington decide that negotiation is no longer possible and that there is a clear and immediate danger to the hostages . . . will you and the diocese stand behind our decision to send in the Emergency Services Division?"

Monsignor Downes stood motionless without answering.

Spiegel said to Bellini, "Give the Monsignor a copy of that message."

Downes took the paper and read it, then looked at Roberta Spiegel. "I'll have to check with the Vicar General. I cannot take the responsibility for this on my own." He turned and left the room.

Roberta Spiegel said, "Every time we uncover another layer of this problem I see how much we've underestimated Flynn. We're sandbagged pretty badly all around, and as the time slips by it's obvious that the easiest course of action is surrender—ours, not Flynn's."

Langley said, "Even surrender is not so easy. We may give in, but that doesn't mean Washington, London, or Dublin will."

Commissioner Rourke said to Bellini, "Captain, the only thing we can do unilaterally, without anyone's permission except the Mayor's, is to attack."

Bellini answered, "That's always the easiest decision, sir—it's the execution that gets a little sticky."

Schroeder spoke up. "I get the feeling you've given up on the negotiations."

Everyone looked at him. Burke said, "Captain, you're still the best hope we've got. If there's any middle ground between our capitulation and an attack, I'm sure you'll find it. Brian Flynn said, however, that there was no middle ground, and I think he was telling us the truth. Dawn or dead."

Maureen watched Hickey as he spoke to the Cardinal and Father Murphy at the confessional. She said to Baxter, "He's questioning them about the buzzer and about the first message."

Baxter nodded, then stood. "Let's pace a bit and stretch our legs. We'll talk."

They began walking across the altar sanctuary toward the throne, a distance of forty feet, then turned and walked back. As they walked, Baxter inclined his head. "Look over there—at the brass plate."

Maureen glanced to the right of the altar. Beyond the sacristy staircase was the large brass plate through which Hickey and Megan Fitzgerald had descended with the suitcases.

Baxter looked over the length of the Cathedral. "I've been analyzing this building. When Hickey and Fitzgerald came up from that plate, they had earth on their hands and knees. So it must be mostly crawl space. There must be large areas that are unlit or badly lit. We have an area of almost a city block in which to disappear. If we can lift that plate quickly and drop into that space, they could never flush us out."

As they paced back toward the right side of the altar the plate came into view again. She said, "Even if we could raise the plate and drop below before we were shot, we wouldn't be free, and no one on the outside would know we were down there."

"We would know we weren't up *here.*"

She nodded. "Yes, that's the point, isn't it?" They walked in silence for a few minutes, then Maureen said, "How do you plan to do it?"

Baxter outlined his plan.

Father Murphy and the Cardinal entered the sanctuary, and both Maureen and Baxter noticed that the two priests looked very pale. Father Murphy looked from Maureen to Baxter. "Hickey knows, of course."

The Cardinal spoke. "I would have had no objection to trying to signal the rectory." He looked at Murphy sharply, then at Baxter and Maureen. "You must keep me informed—beforehand—of your plans."

Baxter nodded. "We're about to do that, Your Eminence. We're considering an escape plan. We want you both to come with us."

The Cardinal shook his head and said emphatically, "My place is here." He seemed lost in thought for a moment, then said, "But I'm ready to give you my blessing." He turned to Father Murphy. "You may go if you choose."

Murphy shook his head and addressed Maureen and Baxter. "I can't leave without His Eminence. But I'll help you if I can."

Maureen looked at the three men. "Good. Let's work out the details and the timing." She looked at her watch. "At nine o'clock, we go."

33

Captain Bellini said to Monsignor Downes as the Rector walked into the office, "Have you found the plans to the Cathedral yet?"

The Monsignor shook his head. "The staff is looking here and at the diocese building. But I don't believe we ever had a set on file."

Commissioner Rourke said to Langley, "What are you doing about finding the architect, Gordon Stillway?"

Langley lit a cigarette and took his time answering. He said finally, "Detectives went to his office on East Fifty-third. It was closed, of course—"

Rourke interrupted. "Are you getting a court order to go in?"

Langley noticed that the Deputy Commissioner was becoming more assertive. By midnight he'd probably try to give an order. Langley said, "Actually, someone already got in—without the benefit of a court order. No Cathedral blueprints. The detectives are trying to find a roster of employees. That's apparently missing also."

Monsignor Downes cleared his throat and said, "I don't approve of an assault . . . but it must be planned for, I suppose . . ." He looked at the bookcase and said, "Among those books you'll find about five that are pictorial studies of the Cathedral. Some have plans in them, very sketchy plans—for tourists to follow when they walk on the main floor. The interior pictures are very good, though, and may be helpful."

Bellini went to the bookcase and began scanning the shelves.

Burke stood. "There may be a set of blueprints in Stillway's apartment. No one's answering the phone, and the detective we have stationed there says no one's answering the door. I'm going over there now."

Schroeder stood also. "You can't leave here. Flynn said—"

Burke turned on him. "The hell with Flynn."

Roberta Spiegel said, "Go ahead, Lieutenant."

Langley ripped a page from his notebook. "Here's the address. Don't gain entry by illegal means."

Monsignor Downes said, "If you should find Gordon Stillway, remember he's a very old man. Don't excite him."

"I don't do anything illegal. I don't excite people." Burke turned and walked out into the adjoining office. A heavy cloud of blue smoke hung at face level over the crowded outer office. Burke pushed his way into the hall and went down the stairs. The rectory offices on the ground floor were filled with uniformed police commanders directing the field operations. Burke approached a captain sitting at a desk and showed his badge case. "I need a squad car and a maniac to drive it."

The captain looked up from a map of midtown. "Do you? Well, the area on the other side of the cordon is jammed solid with people and vehicles. Where is it you'd like to go in such a hurry, Lieutenant?"

"Gramercy Park. Pronto-like."

"Well, make your way to the IRT station on Lex."

"Bullshit." He grabbed a phone and went through the switchboard to the Monsignor's office. "Langley, is the helicopter still in the Palace courtyard? Good. Call and get it revved up."

Burke walked out of the rectory into Fifty-first Street and breathed in the cold, bracing air that made him feel better. The sleet was tapering off, but the wind was still strong. He walked into the deserted intersection of Fifty-first and Madison.

An eerie silence hung over the lamplit streets around the Cathedral, and in the distance he could see the barricades of squad cars, buses, and sanitation trucks that made up the cordon. Strands of communication wire ran over the sleet-covered streets and sidewalks. Sentries stood silhouetted against half-lit buildings, and National Guardsmen cruised by in jeeps, rifles pointed upward. Bullhorns barked in the wintry air, and policemen patrolled the sanitized area with shotguns. Burke heard their footsteps crunching in the unshoveled ice and heard his own quickening pace. As he walked, he thought of Belfast and, though he'd never been there, felt he knew the place. He turned up his collar and walked faster.

Across Madison Avenue a solitary figure on horseback rode slowly into the north wind. He stared at the rider, Betty Foster, as she passed beneath a streetlight. She didn't seem to notice him, and he walked on.

The wind dropped, and he heard in the distance, past the perimeter of the cordon, the sounds of music and singing. New York would not be denied its party. Burke passed the rear of the Lady Chapel, then approached the Cardinal's residence, and through the lace curtains on a ground-floor window he saw ESD men standing in a room. A lieutenant was briefing them, and Burke could see a chalkboard. *Win this one for the Gipper, lads.* Through another window on the corner Burke saw well-dressed men and women, the Governor and Mayor among them, crowded around what was probably a buffet. They didn't exactly look like they were enjoying themselves, but they didn't look as grim as the men around the chalkboard either.

In the intersection Burke turned and looked back at the Cathedral illuminated by its garden floodlights. A soft luminescence passed through the stained-glass windows and cast a colored shadow over the white street. It was a serene picture, postcard pretty: ice-covered branches of bare lindens and glistening expanses of undisturbed sleet. Perhaps more serene than it had ever been in this century—the surrounding area cleared of cars and people, and the buildings darkened. . . .

Something out of place caught his eye, and he looked up at the two towers where light shone through the ripped louvers. In the north tower—the bell tower—he saw a shadow moving, a solitary figure circling from louver to louver, cold, probably edgy, watchful. In the south tower there was also a figure, standing motionless. Two people, one in each tower—the only eyes that stared out of the besieged Cathedral. So much depended on them, thought Burke. He hoped they weren't the panicky type.

The police command helicopter followed Lexington Avenue south. Below, Burke could see that traffic was beginning to move again, or at least what passed for moving traffic in Manhattan. Rotating beacons at every intersection indicated the scope of the police action below. The towering buildings of midtown gave way to the lower buildings in the old section of Gramercy Park, and the helicopter dropped altitude.

Burke could see the lamps of the small private park encircled by elegant town houses. He pointed, and the pilot swung the craft toward the open area and turned on the landing lights. The helicopter settled into a small patch of grass, and Burke jumped out and walked quickly toward the high wrought-iron fence. He rattled the bars of a tall gate but found it was locked. On the sidewalk a crowd of people stared back at him curiously. Burke said, "Is anyone there a keyholder?"

No one answered.

Burke peered between the bars, his hands wrapped around the cold iron. He thought of the zoo gate that morning, the ape house, the sacristy gate, and all the prisons he'd ever seen. He thought of Long Kesh and Crumlin Road, Lubianka and Dachau. He thought that there were too many iron bars and too many people staring at each other through them. He shouted with a sudden and unexpected anger, "Come on, damn it! Who's got a key?"

An elderly, well-dressed woman came forward and produced an ornate key. Without a word she unlocked the gate, and Burke slipped out quickly and pushed roughly through the crowd.

He approached a stately old town house across the street and knocked sharply on the door. A patrolman opened the door, and Burke held up his badge, brushing by him into the small lobby. A single plainclothesman sat in the only chair, and Burke introduced himself perfunctorily.

The man answered through a wide yawn, "Detective Lewis." He stood as though with some effort.

Burke said, "Any word on Stillway?"

The detective shook his head.

"Get a court order yet?"

"Nope."

Burke began climbing the stairs. When he was a rookie, an old cop once said to him, "Everybody lives on the top floor. Everybody gets robbed on the top floor. Everybody goes nuts on the top floor. Everybody dies on the top floor."

Burke reached the top floor, the fourth. Two apartments had been made out of what was once probably the servants' quarters. He found Stillway's door and pressed the buzzer.

The detective climbed the stairs behind him. "No one home."

"No shit, Sherlock." Burke looked at the three lock-cylinders in a vertical row, ranging in age from very old to very new, showing the progression of panic with each passing decade. He turned to the detective. "Want to put your shoulder to that?"

"Nope."

"Me neither." Burke moved to a narrow staircase behind a small door. "Stay here." He went up the stairs and came out onto the roof, then went down the rear fire escape and stopped at Stillway's window.

The apartment was dark except for the yellow glow of a clock radio. There was no grate on the window, and Burke drew his gun and brought it through the old brittle glass above the sash lock. He reached in, unlatched the catch, and threw the sash up, then dropped into the room and moved away from the window in a crouch, his gun held out in front of him with both hands.

He steadied his breathing and listened. His eyes became accustomed to the dark, and he began to make out shadows and shapes. Nothing moved, nothing breathed, nothing smelled; there was nothing that wanted to kill him, and, he sensed, nothing that had been killed there. He rose, found a lamp, and turned it on.

The large studio apartment was in stark modern contrast to the world around it. Bone-white walls, track lighting, chromium furniture. The secret modern world of an old architect who specialized in Gothic restorations. *Shame, shame, Gordon Stillway.*

He walked toward the hall door, gun still drawn, looking into the dark corners as he moved. Everything was perfectly ordinary; nothing was out of place —no crimson on the white rug, no gore on the shiny chromium. Burke holstered his revolver and opened the door. He motioned to the detective. "Back window broken. Cause to suspect a crime in progress. Fill out a report."

The detective winked and moved toward the stairs.

Burke closed the door and looked around. He found a file cabinet beside a drafting table and opened the middle drawer alphabetized J to S. He was not too surprised to find that between St.-Mark's-in-the-Bouwerie and St. Paul the Apostle there was nothing but a slightly larger space than there should have been.

Burke saw a telephone on the counter of the kitchenette and dialed the rectory, got a fast busy-signal on the trunk line, dialed the operator, got a recording telling him to dial again, and slammed down the receiver. He found Gordon Stillway's bar in a shelf unit and chose a good bourbon.

The phone rang and Burke answered, "Hello."

Langley's voice came through the earpiece. "Figured you couldn't get an open line. What's the story? Body in the library?"

"No body. No Stillway. The Saint Patrick's file is missing, too."

Langley said, "Interesting . . ." He paused, then said, "We're having no luck in our other inquiries either."

Burke heard someone talking loudly in the background. "Is that Bellini?"

Langley said quietly, "Yeah. He's going into his act. Pay no attention."

Burke lit a cigarette. "I'm not having a good Saint Patrick's Day, Inspector."

"March eighteenth doesn't look real promising either." He drew a long breath. "There are blueprints in this city somewhere, and there are other architects, maybe engineers, who know this place. We could have them all by midmorning tomorrow—but we don't have that long. Flynn has thought this all out. Right down to snatching Stillway and the blueprints."

Burke said, "I wonder."

"Wonder *what?*"

"Hasn't it occurred to you that if Flynn had Stillway, then Stillway would be in the Cathedral where he'd do the most good?"

"Maybe he *is* in there."

Burke thought a moment. "I don't know. Flynn would tell us if he had the architect. He'd tell us he knows ways to blow the place by mining the hidden passages—if any. He's an intelligent man who knows how to get maximum mileage from everything he does. Think about it." Burke looked around the tidy room. A copy of the *New York Post* lay on the couch, and he pulled the telephone cord as he walked to it. A front-page picture showed a good fist-flying scene of the disturbance in front of the Cathedral at noon. The headline ran: DEMONSTRATION MARS PARADE. A subline said: BUT THE IRISH MARCH. The special evening editions would have better stuff than that.

Langley's voice came into the earpiece. "Burke, you still there?"

Burke looked up. "Yeah. Look, Stillway was here. Brought home the evening paper and . . ."

"And?"

Burke walked around the room holding the phone and receiver. He opened a closet near the front door and spoke into the phone. "Wet topcoat. Wet hat. No raincoat. No umbrella. No briefcase. He came home in the sleet, changed, and went out again carrying his briefcase, which contained, I guess, the Saint Patrick's file."

"What color are his eyes? Okay, I'll buy it. Where'd he go?"

"Probably went with somebody who had a good set of credentials and a plausible story. Somebody who talked his way into the apartment . . ."

Langley said, "A Fenian who got to him too late to get him into the Cathedral—"

"Maybe. But maybe somebody else doesn't want us to have the blueprints or Stillway. . . ."

"Strange business."

"Think about it, Inspector. Meanwhile, get a Crime Scene Unit over here, then get me an open line so I can call Ferguson."

"Okay. But hurry back. Schroeder's getting nervous."

Burke hung up and took his glass of bourbon on a tour around the apartment. Nothing else yielded any hard clues, but he was getting a sense of the old architect. Not the type of man to go out into the cold sleet, he thought, unless duty called. The phone rang. Burke picked it up and gave the operator Ferguson's number, then said, "Call back in ten minutes. I'll need to make another call."

After six rings the phone was answered, and Jack Ferguson came on the line, his voice sounding hesitant. "Hello?"

"Burke. Thought I'd get the coroner."

"You may well have. Where the hell have you been?"

"Busy. Well, it looks like you get the good-spy award this year."

"Keep it. Why haven't you called? I've been waiting for your call—"

"Didn't my office call you?"

"Yes. Very decent of them. Said I was a marked man. Who's on to me, then?"

"Well, Flynn for one. Probably the New York Irish Republican Army, Provisional Wing, for another. And I think you've outlived your usefulness to Major Martin—it *was* Martin you were playing around with, wasn't it?"

Ferguson stayed silent for a few seconds, then said, "He told me he could head off the Fenians with my help."

"Did he, now? Well, the only people he wanted to head off were the New York police."

Again, Ferguson didn't speak for a few seconds, then said, "Bastards. They're all such bloody bastards. Why is everyone so committed to this senseless violence?"

"Makes good press. What is your status, Jack?"

"Status? My status is I'm scared. I'm packed and ready to leave town. My wife's sister came and took her to her place. God, I wouldn't have waited around for anyone else, Burke. I should have left an hour ago."

"Well, why did you wait around? Got something for me?"

"Does the name Terri O'Neal mean anything to you?"

"Man or woman?"

"Woman."

Burke thought a moment. "No."

"She's been kidnapped."

"Lot of that going around today."

"I think she has something to do with what's happening."

"In what way?"

Ferguson said, "Hold on a moment. I hear someone in the hall. Hold on."

Burke said quickly, "Wait. Just tell me— Jack— Shit." Burke held the line. He heard Ferguson's footsteps retreating. He waited for the crash, the shot, the scream, but there was nothing.

Ferguson's voice came back on the line, his breathing loud in the earpiece. "Damned Rivero brothers. Got some señoritas pinned in the alcove, squeezing their tits. God, this used to be a nice Irish building. Boys would go in the basement and get blind drunk. Never looked at a pair of tits until they were thirty. Where was I?"

"Terri O'Neal."

"Right. I got this from a Boston Provo. He and some other lads were supposed to snatch this O'Neal woman last night if a man named Morgan couldn't pick her up in a disco. I assume Morgan picked her up—it's easy today, like going out for a pack of cigarettes. You know? Anyway, now these Boston lads think it was part of what happened today, and they're not happy about what the Fenians did."

"Neither are we."

"Of course," added Ferguson, "it could all be coincidence."

"Yeah." Burke thought. *Terri O'Neal*. It *was* a familiar name, but he couldn't place it. He was sure it wasn't in the files, because women in the files were still rare enough to remember every one of them. "Terri O'Neal."

"That's what the gentleman said. Now get me the hell out of here."

"Okay. Stay put. Don't open the door to strangers."

"How long will it take to get a car here?"

"I'm not sure. Hang on. You're covered."

"That's what Langley told Timmy O'Day last summer."

"Mistakes happen. Listen, we'll have a drink next week . . . lunch—"

"Fuck lunch—"

Burke hung up. He stared at the telephone for several minutes. He had a bad taste in his mouth, and he stubbed out his cigarette, then sipped on the bourbon. The telephone rang, and he picked it up. "Operator, get me Midtown North Precinct."

After a short wait the phone rang, and a deep voice said, "Sergeant Gonzalez, Midtown North."

"This is Lieutenant Burke, Intelligence." He gave his badge number. "Do you have clear radio commo with your cars?"

The harried desk sergeant answered, "Yeah, the jamming isn't affecting us here."

Burke heard the recorder go on and heard the beep at four-second intervals. "You check me out after you hang up. Okay?"

"Right."

"Can you get a car over to 560 West Fifty-fifth Street? Apartment 5D. Pick up and place in protective custody—name of Jack Ferguson."

"What for?"

"His life is in danger."

"So is every citizen's life in this city. Comes with the territory. West Fifty-fifth? I'm surprised he's not dead yet."

"He's an informant. Real important."

"I don't have many cars available. Things are a mess—"

"Yeah, I heard. Listen, he'll want to go to the Port Authority building, but keep him in the station house."

"Sounds fucked up."

"He's involved with this Cathedral thing. Just do it, okay? I'll take care of you. *Erin go bragh*, Gonzalez."

"Yeah, *hasta la vista.*"

Burke hung up and left the apartment. He went out into the street and walked back toward the park, where a crowd had gathered outside the fence. As he walked he thought about Ferguson. He knew he owed Ferguson a better shot at staying alive. He knew he should pick him up in the helicopter. But the priorities were shifting again. Gordon Stillway was important. Brian Flynn was important, and Major Martin was important. Jack Ferguson was not so important any longer. Unless . . . *Terri O'Neal.* What in the name of God was that all about? Why was that name so familiar?

34

J ohn Hickey sat alone at the chancel organ. He raised his field glasses to the southeast triforium. Frank Gallagher sat precariously on the parapet, reading a Bible; his back was to a supporting column, his sniper rifle was across his knees, and he looked very serene. Hickey marveled at a man who could hold two opposing philosophies in his head at the same time. He shouted to Gallagher, "Look lively."

Hickey focused the glasses on George Sullivan in the long southwest triforium, who was also sitting on the parapet. He was playing a small mouth organ too softly to be heard, except by Abby Boland across the nave. Hickey focused on her as she leaned out across the parapet, looking at Sullivan like a moonstruck girl hanging from a balcony in some cheap melodrama.

Hickey shifted the glasses to the choir loft. Megan was talking to Leary again, and Leary appeared to be actually listening this time. Hickey sensed that they were discovering a common inhumanity. He thought of two vampires on a castle wall in the moonlight, bloodless and lifeless, not able to consummate their meeting in a normal way but agreeing to hunt together.

He raised the glasses and focused on Flynn, who was sitting alone in the choir benches that rose up toward the towering brass organ pipes. Beyond the pipes the great rose window sat above his head like an alien moon, suffused with the night-lights of the Avenue. The effect was dramatic, striking, thought Hickey, and unintentionally so, like most of the memorable tableaux he had seen in his life. Flynn seemed uninterested in Megan or Leary, or in the blue-prints spread across his knees. He was staring out into space, and Hickey saw that he was toying with his ring.

Hickey put down the glasses. He had the impression that the troops were getting bored, even claustrophobic, if that were possible in this space. Cabin fever—Cathedral fever, whatever; it was taking its toll, and the night was yet young. Why was it, he thought, that the old, with so little time left, had the most patience? Well, he smiled, age was not so important in here. Everyone had almost the same lifespan left . . . give or take a few heartbeats.

Hickey looked at the hostages on the sanctuary. The four of them were speaking intently. No boredom there. Hickey cranked the field phone beside him. "Attic? Status report."

Jean Kearney's voice came back with a breathy stutter. "Cold as hell up here."

Hickey smiled. "You and Arthur should do what we used to do when I was a lad to keep warm in winter." He waited for a response, but there was none, so he said, "We used to chop wood." He laughed, then cranked the phone again. "South tower. See anything interesting?"

Rory Devane answered, "Snipers with flak jackets on every roof. The area as far south as Forty-eighth Street is cleared. Across the way there are hundreds of people at the windows." He added, "I feel as though I'm in a goldfish bowl."

Hickey lit his pipe, and it bobbed in his mouth as he spoke. "Hold your head up, lad—they're watching your face through their glasses." He thought, *And through their sniper scopes.* "Stare back at them. You're the reason they're all there."

"Yes, sir."

Hickey rang the bell tower. "Status report."

Donald Mullins answered, "Status unchanged . . . except that more soldiers are arriving."

Hickey drew on his pipe. "Did you get your corned beef, lad? Want more tea?"

"Yes, more tea, please. I'm cold. It's very cold here."

Hickey's voice was low. "It was cold on Easter Monday, 1916, on the roof of the General Post Office. It was cold when the British soldiers marched us to Kilmainham Jail. It was cold in Stonebreaker's Yard where they shot my father and Padraic Pearse and fifteen of our leaders. It's cold in the grave."

Hickey picked up the Cathedral telephone and spoke to the police switch-board operator in the rectory. "Get me Schroeder." He waited through a series of clicks, then said, "Did you find Gordon Stillway yet?"

Schroeder's voice sounded startled. "What?"

"We cleaned out his office after quitting time—couldn't do it before, you understand. That might have tipped someone as dense as even Langley or

Burke. But we had trouble getting to Stillway in the crowd. Then the riot broke."

Schroeder's voice faltered, then he said, "Why are you telling us this—?"

"We should have killed him, but we didn't. He's either in a hospital or drunk somewhere, or your good friend Martin has murdered him. Stillway is the key man for a successful assault, of course. The blueprints by themselves are not enough. Did you find a copy in the rectory? Well, don't tell me, then. Are you still there, Schroeder?"

"Yes."

"I thought you nodded off." Hickey saw Flynn moving toward the organ keyboard in the choir loft. "Listen, Schroeder, we're going to play some hymns on the bells later. I want a list of eight requests from the NYPD when I call again. All right?"

"All right."

"Nothing tricky now. Just good solid Christian hymns that sound nice on the bells. Some Irish folk songs, too. Give the city a lift. *Beannacht.*" He hung up. After uncovering the keyboard and turning on the chancel organ, he put his thin hands over the keys and began playing a few random notes. He nodded with exaggerated graciousness toward the hostages who were watching and began singing as he played. "In Dublin's fair city, where the girls are so pretty . . ." His voice came out in a well-controlled bass, rich and full, very unlike his speaking voice. "'Twas where I first met my sweet Molly Malone . . ."

Brian Flynn sat at the choir organ and turned the key to start it. He placed his hands over the long curved keyboard and played a chord. On the organ was a large convex mirror set at an angle that allowed Flynn to see most of the Cathedral below—used, he knew, by the organist to time the triumphal entry of a procession or to set the pace for an overly eager bride, or a reluctant one. He smiled as he joined with the smaller organ below and looked at Megan, who had just come from the south tower. "Give us the pleasure of your sweet voice, Megan. Come here and turn on this microphone."

Megan looked at him but made no move toward the microphone. Leary's eyes darted between Flynn and Megan.

Flynn said, "Ah, Megan, you've no idea how important song is to revolution." He turned on the microphone. Hickey was going through the song again, and Flynn joined in with a soft tenor.

> "As she wheeled her wheelbarrow
> Through streets wide and narrow
> Crying cockles, and mussels,
> Alive, alive-o . . ."

John Hickey smiled, and his eyes misted as the music carried him back across the spans of time and distance to the country he had not seen in over forty years.

> "She was a fishmonger,
> And sure 'twas no wonder,
> For her father and mother were
> Fishmongers, too,
> And they each wheel'd their barrow . . ."

Hickey saw his father's face again on the night before the soldiers took him out to be shot. He remembered being dragged out of their cell to what he thought was his own place of execution, but they had beaten him and dumped him on the road outside Kilmainham Jail. He remembered clearly the green sod laid carefully over his father's grave the next day, his mother's face at the graveside. . . .

> "And she died of a fever
> And no one could save her,
> And that was the end of sweet
> Molly Malone,
> But her ghost wheels her barrow . . ."

He had wanted to die then, and had tried to die a soldier's death every day since, but it wasn't in his stars. And when at last he thought death had come in that mean little tenement across the river, he found he was required to go on . . . to complete one last mission. But it would be over soon . . . and he would be home again.

35

Bert Schroeder looked at the memo given him by the Hostage Unit's psychologist, Dr. Korman, who had been monitoring each conversation from the adjoining office. Korman had written: *Flynn is a megalomaniac and probably a paranoid schizophrenic. Hickey is paranoid also and has an unfulfilled death wish.* Schroeder almost laughed. What the hell other kind of death wish could you have if you were still alive?

How, wondered Schroeder, could a New York psychologist diagnose a man like Flynn, from a culture so different from his own? Or Hickey, from a different era? How could he diagnose *anybody* based on telephone conversations? Yet he did it at least fifty times a year for Schroeder. Sometimes his diagnoses turned out to be fairly accurate; other times they did not. He always wondered if Korman was diagnosing *him* as well.

He looked up at Langley, who had taken off his jacket in the stuffy room. His exposed revolver lent, thought Schroeder, a nice menacing touch for the civilians. Schroeder said to him, "Do you have much faith in these things?"

Langley looked up from his copy of the report. "I'm reminded of my horoscope—the language is such that it fits anybody . . . nobody's playing with a full deck. You know?"

Schroeder nodded and turned a page of the report and stared at it without reading. He hadn't given Korman the psy-profiles on either man yet and might never give them to the psychologist. The more varying opinions he had, the more he would be able to cover himself if things went bad. He said to Langley, "Regarding Korman's theory of Hickey's unfulfilled death wish, how are we making out on that court order for exhumation?"

Langley said, "A judge in Jersey City was located. We'll be able to dig up Hickey . . . the grave, by midnight."

Schroeder nodded. *Midnight—grave digging.* He gave a small shudder and looked down at the psychologist's report again. It went on for three typewritten pages, and as he read Schroeder had the feeling that Dr. Korman wasn't all there either. As to the real state of mind of these two men, Schroeder believed only God knew that—not Korman or anyone in the room, and probably not the two men themselves.

Schroeder looked at the three other people remaining in the room—Langley, Spiegel, and Bellini. He was aware that they were waiting for him to say something. He cleared his throat. "Well . . . I've dealt with crazier people. . . . In fact, all the people I've dealt with have been crazy. The funny thing is that the proximity to death seems to snap them out of it, temporarily. They act very rational when they realize what they're up against—when they see the forces massed against them."

Langley said, "Only the two people in the towers have that visual stimulation, Bert. The rest are in a sort of cocoon. You know?"

Schroeder shot Langley an annoyed look.

Joe Bellini said suddenly, "Fuck this psycho-crap. *Where is Stillway?*" He looked at Langley.

Langley shrugged.

Bellini said, "If Flynn has him in there, we've got a real problem."

Langley blew a smoke ring. "We're looking into it."

Schroeder said, "Hickey is a liar. He knows where Stillway is."

Spiegel shook her head. "I don't think he does."

Langley added, "Hickey was very indiscreet to mention Major Martin over the phone like that. Flynn wouldn't have wanted Martin's name involved publicly. He doesn't want to make trouble between Washington and London at this stage."

Schroeder nodded absently. He was certain the governments wouldn't reach an accord anyway—or, if they did, it wouldn't include releasing prisoners in Northern Ireland. He had nothing to offer the Fenians but their lives and a fair trial, and they didn't seem much interested in either.

Captain Bellini paced in front of the fireplace. "I won't expose my men to a fight unless I know every column, pew, balcony, and altar in that place."

Langley looked down at the six large picture books on the coffee table. "Those should give you a fair idea of the layout. Some good interior shots. Passable floor plans. Have your men start studying them. Now."

Bellini looked at him. "Is that the best intelligence you can come up with?" He picked up the books in one of his big hands and walked toward the door. "Damn it, if there's a secret way into that place, I've got to know." He began pacing in tight circles. "They've had it all their way up to now . . . but I'll get them." He looked at the silent people in the room. "Just keep them talking, Schroeder. When they call on me to move, I'll be ready. I'll get those potato-eating Mick sons of bitches—I'll bring Flynn's balls to you in a teacup." He walked out and slammed the door behind him.

Roberta Spiegel looked at Schroeder. "Is he nuts?"

Schroeder shrugged. "He goes through this act every time a situation goes down. He's getting himself psyched. He gets crazier as the thing drags on."

Roberta Spiegel stood and reached into Langley's shirt pocket and took a cigarette.

Langley watched her as she lit the cigarette. There was something masculine and at the same time sensuously feminine about all her movements. A woman who had an obvious power over the Mayor—although exactly what type of power no one knew for sure. And, thought Langley, she was much sharper than

His Honor. When it came down to the final decision on which so many lives hung, *she* would be the one to make it. Roberta Spiegel, whose name was known to nobody outside of New York. Roberta Spiegel, who had no ambitions of elected office, no civil service career to worry about, no one to answer to.

Spiegel sat on the edge of Schroeder's desk and leaned toward him, then glanced back at Langley. She said, "Let me be frank while we three are alone—" She bit her lip thoughtfully, then continued. "The British are not going to give in, as you know. Bellini doesn't have much of a chance of saving those people or this Cathedral. Washington is playing games, and the Governor is—well, between us, an asshole. His Honor is—how shall I put it?—not up to the task. And the Church is going to become a problem if we give them enough time." She leaned very close to Schroeder. "So . . . it's up to you, Captain. More than any time in your distinguished career it's all up to *you*—and, if you don't mind my saying so, Captain, you don't seem to be handling this with your usual aplomb."

Schroeder's face reddened. He cleared his throat. "If you . . . if the Mayor would like me to step aside—"

She came down from the desk. "There comes a time when every man knows he's met his match. I think we've *all* met our match here at this Cathedral. We can't even seem to win a point. Why?"

Schroeder again cleared his throat. "Well . . . it always seems that way in the beginning. They're the aggressors, you understand, and they've had months to think everything out. In time the situation will begin to reverse—"

Spiegel slammed her hand on the desk. "They know that, damn it! That's why they've given us no time. *Blitzkrieg,* Schroeder, *blitzkrieg.* Lightning war. You know the word. They're not hanging around while we get our act together. Dawn or dead. That's the truest thing anyone's said all night."

Schroeder tried to control his voice. "Miss Spiegel . . . you see, I've had many years . . . let me explain. We are at a psychological disadvantage because of the hostages. . . . But put yourself in the *Cathedral.* Think of the disadvantages *they* must overcome. They don't want to die—no matter what they pretend to the contrary. That and that alone is the bottom line of their thinking. And the hostages are keeping them alive—therefore, they won't kill the hostages. Therefore, at dawn *nothing* will happen. *Nothing.* It never does. *Never.*"

Spiegel let out a long breath. She turned toward Langley and reached out not for another cigarette but for his pistol. She pulled it from his shoulder holster and turned to Schroeder. "See this? Men used to settle their arguments with this." She looked closely at the blue-black metal and continued. "We're supposed to be beyond that now, but I'll tell you something. There's more of this in the world than there are hostage negotiators. I'll tell you something else —I'd rather send Bellini in with his guns than wait around with my finger up my ass to see what happens at dawn." She dropped the pistol to her side and leaned over the desk. "If you can't get a firm extension of the dawn deadline, then we go in while we still have the cover of darkness—before that self-destruct response levels this block."

Schroeder sat motionless. "There is no self-destruct response."

Spiegel said, "God, I wish I had your nerves—it *is* nerves, isn't it?" She tossed the revolver back to Langley.

Langley holstered the gun. He looked at Spiegel. She got away with a great deal—the cigarettes, then the gun. She relieved him of his possessions with a very cavalier attitude. But maybe, he thought, it was just as well she didn't observe the cautious etiquette that men did in these situations.

Roberta Spiegel moved away and looked at the two police officers. "If you want to know what's really happening around you, don't listen to those politicians out there. Listen to Brian Flynn and John Hickey." She looked at a large wooden crucifix over Schroeder's head and then out through the window at the Cathedral. "If Flynn or Hickey say dawn or dead, they *mean* dawn or dead. Understand who you're dealing with."

Schroeder nodded, almost imperceptibly. For a split second he had seen the face of the enemy, but it disappeared again just as quickly.

There was a long silence in the room, then Spiegel continued softly, "They can sense our fear . . . smell it. They also sense that we're not going to give them what they want." She looked at Schroeder. "I wish the people out there could give you the kind of direction you should have. But they've confused your job with theirs. They expect miracles from you, and you're starting to believe you can deliver them. You can't. Only Joe Bellini can deliver them a miracle—a military miracle—none killed, no wounded, no damage. Bellini is looking better to the people out there. They're losing faith in the long hard road that you represent. They're fantasizing about a glorious successful military solution. So while you're stalling the Fenians, don't forget to stall the people in the other rooms, too."

36

Flynn and Hickey played the organs, and George Sullivan played the pipes. Eamon Farrell, Frank Gallagher, and Abby Boland sang "My Wild Irish Rose." In the attic Jean Kearney and Arthur Nulty lay huddled together on a catwalk above the choir loft. The pipes of the great organ reverberated through the board on which they lay. Pedar Fitzgerald sat with his back against the crypt door. He half closed his tired eyes and hummed.

Flynn felt the lessening of the tensions as people lost themselves in reveries. He could sense a dozen minds escaping the cold stone fortress. He glanced at Megan and Leary. Even they seemed subdued as they sat on the choir parapet, their backs to the Cathedral, drinking tea and sharing a cigarette. Flynn turned away from them and lost himself in the thunderous organ.

Father Murphy knelt motionless before the high altar. He glanced at his watch.

Harold Baxter paced across the sanctuary floor, trying to appear restless while his eyes darted around the Cathedral. He looked at his watch. No reason, he thought, to wait the remaining minutes. They might never get an opportunity as good as this. As he passed by Father Murphy, he said, "Thirty seconds."

Maureen lay curled up on a pew, her face buried in her arms. One eye peered out, and she saw Baxter nod to her.

Baxter turned and walked back toward the throne. He passed close to the Cardinal and said, "Now."

The Cardinal stood, came down from the throne, and walked to the communion rail. He opened the gate and strode swiftly down the center aisle.

Father Murphy heard Baxter say, "Go." Murphy made the sign of the cross, rose quickly, and moved toward the side of the altar.

Flynn watched the movements on the sanctuary in the organ mirror as he played. He continued to play the lilting melody as he called out to Leary. "Turn around."

Leary and Megan both jumped down from the parapet and spun around. Leary raised his rifle.

Hickey's organ stopped, and Flynn's organ died away on a long, lingering note. The singing stopped, and the Cathedral fell silent, all eyes on the Cardinal. Flynn spoke into the microphone as he looked in the mirror. "Stop where you are, Cardinal."

Father Murphy opened the circuit-breaker box recessed into the side of the altar, pulled the switch, and the sanctuary area went dark. Baxter took three long strides, passed the sacristy staircase, and hit the floor, sliding across the marble toward the brass floorplate. Maureen rolled off the pew and crawled swiftly toward the rear of the sanctuary. Baxter's fingers found the grip on the brass plate and lifted the heavy metal until its hinges locked in place. Maureen pivoted, and her legs found the opening in the floor.

The four people in the triforia were shouting wildly. A shot rang out from the choir loft, and the shouting stopped. Four shots exploded in quick succession from the triforia.

Maureen dropped through the hole and fell to the earth floor below.

Baxter felt something—a spent bullet, a piece of marble—slam into his chest, and he rocked backward on his haunches.

The Cardinal kept walking straight head, but no one looked at him any longer.

Father Murphy crawled to the sacristy staircase and collided with Pedar Fitzgerald running up the steps. Both men swung wildly at each other in the partial darkness.

Baxter caught his breath and lunged forward. His arms and shoulders hung into the opening, and his feet slid over the marble trying to find traction.

Maureen was shouting, "Jump! Jump!" She reached up and grabbed his dangling arm.

Five more shots rang out, splintering marble and ringing sharply from the brass plate. Baxter felt a sharp pain shoot across his back, and his body jerked convulsively. Five more shots whistled through the dark over his head. He was aware that Maureen was pulling on his right hand. He tried to drop headfirst into the hole, but someone was pulling on his legs. He heard a shout very close to his ear, and the firing stopped.

Maureen was hanging from his arm, yelling up to him, "Jump! For God's sake, jump!"

Baxter heard his own voice, low and breathless. "Can't. Got me. Run. Run." Someone was pulling on his ankles, pulling him back from the hole. He felt Maureen's grip on his arm loosen, then break away. A pair of strong hands rolled him over on his back, and he looked into the face of Pedar Fitzgerald, who was kneeling above him, holding the submachine gun to his throat. In the half-light Baxter saw that there was blood spreading over Fitzgerald's neck and across his white shirt.

Fitzgerald looked down at him and spoke between labored breaths. "You stupid son of a bitch! I'll kill you—you goddamned bastard." He pounded his fist into Baxter's face, then crawled over him to the hole and pointed the barrel of the gun down into the opening. He steadied himself and fired two long, deafening bursts into the darkness.

Baxter was dimly aware of a warm wetness seeping over the cold floor beneath him. His eyes tried to focus on the vaulted ceiling ten stories above his face, but all he saw were the blurry red spots of the Cardinals' hanging hats. He heard footsteps running toward the altar, coming up the stairs, then saw faces hovering over him—Hickey, then a few seconds later Flynn and Megan Fitzgerald.

Baxter turned his head and saw Father Murphy lying near the stairs, his hands pressed to his face and blood running between his fingers. He heard Megan's voice. "Pedar! Are you hit? Pedar?"

Baxter tried to raise his head to look for the Cardinal. Suddenly he saw Megan's shoe flying into his face, and a red flash passed in front of his eyes, followed by blackness.

Flynn knelt beside Pedar Fitzgerald and pulled the barrel of the gun out of the hole. He touched Fitzgerald's bloody neck wound. "Just grazed you, lad." He called to Megan. "Take him back to his post. Quickly."

Flynn lay prone at the edge of the opening and called down. "Maureen! Are you all right? Are you hit?"

Maureen knelt a few yards from the opening. Her body was trembling, and she took long breaths to steady herself. Her hands ran over her body, feeling for a wound.

Flynn called down again. "Are you hit?" His voice became anxious. "For God's sake, answer me."

She drew a deep breath and surprised herself by answering, "No."

Flynn's voice sounded more controlled. "Come back."

"Go to hell."

"Come back, Maureen, or we'll shoot Baxter. We'll shoot him and throw him down there where you can see him."

"They're all dead anyway."

"No, they're not."

"Let Baxter speak to me."

There was a pause, then Flynn said, "He's unconscious."

"Bloody murdering bastards. Let me speak to Father Murphy."

"He's . . . hurt. Wait. I'll get the Cardinal—"

"Go to hell." She knew she didn't want to hear any of their voices; she just wanted to run. She called back, "Give it up, Brian. Before more people are killed, give it up." Hesitantly she called, "Good-bye."

She drew away from the opening until her back came into contact with the base of a column. She stared at the ladder that descended from the opening. She heard someone speaking in half-whispered tones, and she had a feeling someone was ready to come down.

Flynn's voice called out again, "Maureen—you're not the kind who would run out on your friends. Their lives depend on you."

She felt a cold sweat break out over her body. She thought to herself, *Brian, you make everything so damned hard.* She stepped toward the opening but then hesitated. A new thought came into her mind. *What would Brian do?* He'd run. He always ran. And not out of cowardice but because he and all of them had long ago agreed that escape was the morally correct response to tight situations. Yet . . . he'd stayed with her when she was wounded. She vacillated between the column and the opening.

Flynn's voice cut into the dark basement. "You're a damned coward, Maureen. All right, then, Baxter's gone."

A shot rang out on the sacristy.

After the report died away he called out again. "Murphy is next."

Maureen instinctively moved back against the column. She put her face in her hands. "Bastards!"

Flynn yelled, "The priest is next!"

She picked up her head and wiped the tears from her eyes. She peered into the darkness. Her eyes adjusted to the half-light, and she forced herself to evaluate the situation calmly. To her right was the outer wall of the sacristy staircase. If she followed it she'd find the foundation wall, beyond which was freedom. That was the way she had to go.

She looked quickly back and saw a pair of legs dropping from the opening. More of the body was revealed as it descended the ladder—Hickey. Above Hickey's head another pair of legs appeared. Megan. Both of them held flashlights and pistols by their sides. Hickey turned his head and squinted into the blackness as he climbed down. Maureen crouched down beside the column.

Hickey's voice rolled through the black, damp air. He spoke as to a child. "Coming for you, darlin'. Coming to get you. Come to old John, now. Don't let the wicked Megan find you. Run to Mr. Hickey. Come on, then." He laughed and jumped down the last few steps, switched on the flashlight, and turned toward her.

Megan was right behind him, her fiery red features looking sinister in the overhead light.

Maureen drew a long breath and held it.

37

Schroeder stood tensed with the phone to his ear. He looked up at Langley, the only person left in the office. "Goddamn it—they're not answering." Langley stood at the window, staring intently at the Cathedral. On the other side of the double doors phones were ringing and people were shouting.

One of the doors burst open, and Bellini ran in looking more agitated than when he had last left. He shouted, "I have orders from fucking Kline to go in if you can't raise them!"

Schroeder looked up at him. "Get in here and close the door!" He yelled at the police operator, "Of course I want you to keep trying, you stupid ass!"

Bellini closed the door, walked to a chair, and fell into it. Sweat streamed down his pale face. "I . . . I'm not ready to go in. . . ."

Schroeder said to Bellini impatiently, "How fucking long does it take to kill four hostages, Bellini? If they're dead already, Kline can damned well wait until you have at least a half-assed idea of how to hit the place."

Suddenly Flynn's voice came over the speaker. "Schroeder?"

Schroeder answered quickly, "Yes—" He controlled his voice. "Yes, sir. Is everything all right?"

"Yes."

Schroeder cleared his throat and spoke into the phone. "What is happening in there?"

Flynn's voice sounded composed. "An ill-advised attempt to escape."

Schroeder sounded incredulous. *"Escape?"*

"That's what I said."

"No one is hurt?"

There was a long pause, then Flynn said, "Baxter and Murphy are wounded. Not badly."

Schroeder looked at Langley and Bellini. He steadied his voice. "We're sending in a doctor."

"If they needed one, I'd tell you."

"I'm sending in a doctor."

"All right, but tell him before you send him that I'll blow his brains out."

Schroeder's voice became angry, but it was a controlled anger, contrived almost, designed to show that shooting was the one thing he wouldn't tolerate. "Damn you, Flynn, you said there'd be no shooting. You said—"

"It couldn't be helped, really."

Schroeder made his tone ominous. "Flynn, if you kill anyone—so help me God, if you hurt anyone, then we're beyond the let's-make-a-deal stage."

"I understand the rules. Calm down, Schroeder."

"Let me speak to each of the hostages. Now."

"Hold on." There was silence, then the Cardinal's voice filled the room. "Captain, do you recognize my voice?"

Schroeder looked at the other two men, and they nodded. He said, "Yes, Your Eminence."

The Cardinal spoke in a tone that suggested he was being coached and closely watched. "I'm all right. Mr. Baxter has received what they tell me is a grazing wound across his back and a ricochet wound in his chest. He's resting and seems all right. Father Murphy was also hit by a ricocheting bullet—in the face—the jaw. He's stunned but otherwise appears all right. . . . It was a miracle no one was killed."

The three men in the room seemed to relax. There were murmurs from the adjoining office. Schroeder said, "Miss Malone?"

The Cardinal answered hesitantly, "She is alive. Not wounded. She is—"

Schroeder heard the phone being covered at the other end. He heard muffled voices, an angry exchange. He spoke into the receiver, "Hello? Hello?"

The Cardinal's voice came back, "That's all I can say."

Schroeder spoke quickly, "Your Eminence, please don't provoke these people. You must not endanger your own lives, because you're also endangering other lives—"

The Cardinal replied in a neutral tone, "I'll pass that on to the others." He added, "Miss Malone is—"

Flynn's voice suddenly came on the line. "Good advice from Captain Courageous. All right, you see no one is dead. Everyone calm down."

"Let me speak to Miss Malone."

"She stepped out for a moment. Later." Flynn said abruptly, "Is everything set for my press conference?"

Schroeder's voice turned calm. "We may need more time. The networks—"

"I have a message for America and the world, and I mean to deliver it."

"Yes, you will. Be patient."

"That's not one of the Irish virtues, Schroeder."

"Oh, I don't know if that's true." He felt it was time for a more personal approach. "I'm half Irish myself, and—"

"Really?"

"Yes, my mother's people were from County Tyrone. Listen, I understand your frustrations and your anger—I had a great-uncle in the IRA. Family hero. Jailed by the English."

"For what? Being a bore like his nephew?"

Schroeder ignored the remark. "I grew up with many of the same hates and prejudices that you—"

"You weren't there, Schroeder. You weren't *there*. You were *here*."

"This won't accomplish anything," said Schroeder firmly. "You might make more enemies than friends by—"

"The people in here don't need any more friends. Our friends are dead or in prison. Tell them to let our people go, Captain."

"We're trying very hard. The negotiations between London and Washington are progressing. I see a light at the end of the tunnel—"

"Are you sure that light isn't a speeding train coming at you?"

Someone in the next room laughed.

Schroeder sat down and bit the tip off a cigar. "Listen, why don't you show us some good faith and release one of the wounded hostages?"

"Which one?"

Schroeder sat up quickly. "Well . . . well . . ."

"Come on, then. Play God. Don't ask anyone there. You tell me which one."

"The one that's the most badly wounded."

Flynn laughed. "Very good. Here's a counterproposal. Would you like the Cardinal instead? Think now. A wounded priest, a wounded Englishman, or a healthy Cardinal?"

Schroeder felt an anger rising in him and was disturbed that Flynn could produce that response. "Who's the more seriously hurt?"

"Baxter."

Schroeder hesitated. He looked around the room. His words faltered.

Flynn said, "Quickly!"

"Baxter."

Flynn put a sad tone in his voice. "Sorry. The correct response was to ask for a Prince of the Church, of course. But you knew that, Bert. Had you said the Cardinal, I would have released him."

Schroeder stared down at the unlit cigar. His voice was shaky. "I doubt that."

"Don't doubt me on things like that. I'd rather lose a hostage and make a point."

Schroeder took out a handkerchief and wiped his neck. "We're not trying to make this a contest to see who's got more nerve, who's got more . . . more . . ."

"Balls."

"Yes. We're not trying to do that. That's the old police image. We're rolling over for you." He glanced at Bellini, who looked very annoyed. He continued, "No one here is going to risk the lives of innocent people—"

"*Innocent?* There are no innocent civilians in war any more. We're all soldiers—soldiers by choice, by conscription, by implication, and by birth." Flynn drew a breath, then said, "The good thing about a long guerrilla war is that everyone gets a chance for revenge at least once." He paused. "Let's drop this topic. I want that television now. Send Burke."

Schroeder finally lit his cigar. "I'm sorry, he's temporarily out of the building."

"I told you I wanted him around. You see, Schroeder, you're not so accommodating after all."

"It was unavoidable. He'll call you soon." He paused, then changed the tone of his voice. "Listen, along the same lines—I mean, we're building a rapport, as you said—can I ask you again to try to keep Mr. Hickey off the phone?"

Flynn didn't answer.

Schroeder went on, "I'm not trying to start any trouble there, but he's saying one thing and you're saying another. I mean, he's very negative and very . . . pessimistic. I just wanted to make you aware of that in case you didn't—"

The phone went dead.

Schroeder rocked back in his chair and drew on his cigar. He thought of how much easier it was dealing with Flynn and how difficult Hickey was. Then it hit him, and he dropped his cigar into an ashtray. *Good guy—bad guy.* The oldest con trick in the game. Now Flynn and Hickey were pulling that on *him.* "Sons of bitches."

Langley looked at Schroeder, then glanced at the note pad he'd been keeping. After each dialogue Langley felt a sense of frustration and futility. This negotiating business was not his game, and he didn't understand how Schroeder did it. Langley's instincts screamed at him to grab the phone and tell Flynn he was a dead motherfucker. Langley lit a cigarette and was surprised to see his hands shaking. "Bastards."

Roberta Spiegel took her place in the rocker and stared up at the ceiling. "Is anybody keeping score?"

Bellini stared out the window. "Can they fight as good as they bullshit?"

Schroeder answered, "The Irish are one of the few people who can."

Bellini turned back to the window, Spiegel rocked in her chair, Langley watched the smoke curl up from his cigarette, and Schroeder stared at the papers scattered on the desk. Phones rang in the other room; a bullhorn cut into the night air, and its echo drifted through the window. The mantel clock ticked loudly, and Schroeder focused on it. 9:17 P.M. At 4:30 he'd been marching in the parade, enjoying himself, enjoying life. Now he had a knot in his stomach, and life didn't look so good anymore. Why was someone always spoiling the parade?

38

Maureen slid behind the thick column and watched Hickey as he stood squinting in the half-light. Megan came up behind him, swinging her big pistol easily by her side, the way other women swung a handbag—the way she herself had swung a pistol once.

Maureen watched them whispering to each other. She knew what they were saying without hearing a word: Which way has she gone? Should they split up? Fire a shot? Call out? Turn on the flashlights? She waited close by, not fifteen feet away, because they'd never suspect she'd be this close, watching. To them she was a civilian, but they ought to have known her better. She was angry at their low regard of her.

Suddenly the flashlights came on, and their beams poked into the dark, distant places. Maureen pressed closer to the column.

Hickey called out, "Last chance, Maureen. Give up and you won't be hurt. But if we have to flush you out . . ." He let his voice trail off, the implied meaning more unnerving than if he had said it.

She watched them as they conferred again. She knew they expected her to go east toward the sacristy foundation. Flynn may even have heard the four of them discussing it. And that was the way she wanted to go but knew now she couldn't.

She prayed they wouldn't split up—wouldn't cut her off in both directions. She admitted, too, that she didn't want Megan to be away from Hickey . . . though perhaps if she *were* away from Hickey . . . Maureen slipped off her shoes, reached under her skirt, and slid off her panty hose. She twisted the nylon into a rope, wrapped the ends around her arms, and pulled it taut. She draped the nylon garrote over her shoulders and knelt, taking handfuls of earth and rubbing them across her damp face, her legs and hands. She looked down at her tweed jacket and skirt—dark but not dark enough. Silently she took them off, reversed them so the darker lining showed, and put them back on again. She buttoned the jacket over her white blouse and turned up the collar. All the while her eyes were fixed on Hickey and Megan.

Suddenly another pair of legs dropped into the hole, and a figure descended the ladder. Maureen recognized Frank Gallagher by the striped pants of his parade marshal's morning dress.

Hickey pointed toward the front of the Cathedral, and Gallagher drew a pistol and walked slowly west along the staircase wall toward the outer wall of the partially buried crypt. Hickey and Megan headed east toward the sacristy.

Maureen saw she had no way to go but south toward the crawl space beneath the ambulatory—the least likely place to find an exit, according to what Father Murphy knew of the layout. But as she watched Gallagher's flashlight moving slowly, she realized she could beat him to the end of the crypt, and from there she had more options. She moved laterally, to her left, parallel to Gallagher's course. Fifteen feet from the first column she came to another and stopped. She watched Gallagher's light almost directly opposite her. The shaft of light from the brass-plate opening was dimmer now, and the next column was somewhere in the darkness to her left.

She moved laterally again, running silently, barefoot, over the damp earth, hands feeling for pipes and ducts. The next column was irregularly spaced at about twenty-five feet, and she thought she'd missed it, then collided with it, feeling a sudden blow against her chest that knocked the wind out of her and made her give an involuntary gasp.

Gallagher's light swung out at her, and she stood frozen behind the column. The beam swung away, and she proceeded in a parallel course. She dashed toward the next column, counting her paces as she ran. At eight strides she stopped and felt in front of her, touching the stone column, and pressed against it.

She saw she was far ahead of Gallagher now, but his beam reached out and probed the place opposite her. The sanctuary floor above her ended a few feet beyond where she stood, and the steps that led to the communion rail sloped down to the crawl space below the main floor. She also saw, by the beam of light, the corner of the crypt where the wall turned away from her. She was no more than fifteen feet from it. She stooped down and passed her hands over the earth, finding a small piece of building rubble. She threw it back toward the last column she'd come from.

Gallagher's light swung away from her intended path toward the sound. She dashed forward, trying to judge the distance. Her hand hit the brick outer wall of the crypt, and she moved left toward the corner. Gallagher's light swung back. She ducked below the beam, then slid around the corner, bracing her back against the cold crypt. She sidestepped with her back against the wall, watching the beam of Gallagher's light as it passed off to her left. She felt for the nylon around her neck and swung it from her shoulders. She conjured up a picture of Frank Gallagher: pleasant looking, sort of vacuous expression. Big, too. She wrapped the nylon tightly around her hands and looped it.

The beam of light was growing in thickness and intensity, bobbing closer to the corner of the crypt. She could actually hear Gallagher's footsteps around the corner, could hear the tight-lipped nose-breathing she knew so well. *God,* she thought, *God, I never wanted to kill so badly.*

Discretion. When to run, when to fight. When in doubt, said Brian Flynn, run. Watch the wolves, he had said to her. They run from danger without self-recrimination. Even hunger wouldn't cloud their judgment. There'd be other kills. She steadied her hands and took a long breath, then swung the nylon around her shoulders and moved along the wall, to her right, away from Gallagher's approaching footsteps. *Next time.*

Something brushed across her face, and she stifled a yell as she swatted it away. Carefully she reached out and touched a hanging object. A pull chain. She reached up and found the light bulb, unscrewed it, and tossed it gently underhand into the crawl space in front of her. She pulled the chain, switching on the electricity. She thought, *I hope he sticks his fucking finger into it and burns.*

Gallagher came to the corner and knelt. He swung his light in a wide arc under the crawl space that began a few feet from the wall.

Maureen saw in the light in front of her the bottom of the steps that led down from the raised sanctuary above her. Farther back, in the crawl space, she saw the glowing red eyes of rats. She moved down the length of the crypt wall. It seemed to go on for a long way. Gallagher's light swung up from the crawl space and began probing the length of the wall.

She moved more quickly, stumbling over building rubble. After what she judged was about twenty-five feet her right hand felt the corner where the wall turned back toward the sacristy. The beam of light fell on her shoulder, and she froze. The light played off her jacket, then swung away. She slid around the corner just as the light came back to reexplore the suspicious thing it had picked out.

Maureen turned and kept her right shoulder to the wall as she moved toward the sacristy foundation. She found another light bulb and unscrewed it, then pulled the chain. Rats squealed around her, and something ran across her bare feet.

The crypt wall turned in to meet the outer wall of the sacristy staircase, and she judged that she was on the exact opposite side of the staircase from where she'd come down through the brass plate.

So far she had eluded them, gotten the better of them in a game that was the ultimate hide-and-seek. Every Belfast alley and factory park flashed through her mind. Every heart-thumping, dry-throated crawl through the rubble came back to her, and she felt alive, confident, almost exhilarated at the dangerous game.

The ground rose, and she had to stoop lower until finally she had to crawl on all fours. She felt to her front as she moved. A rat scurried across her hand, another across her legs. Sweat ran from her face and washed the dirt camouflage into her eyes and mouth. Her breathing was so loud she thought Gallagher must hear it clearly.

Behind her the beam of Gallagher's light probed in all directions. He could have no idea that he had actually been following her . . . unless he had heard her or had seen her footprints, or had found one of the empty light-sockets and guessed. . . . *Stick your goddamned finger in one of them and fry.* She hoped he was as frightened as she was.

She kept crawling until her hand came into contact with cold, moist stone. She ran her fingers over the jagged surface, then higher up, and she felt the rounded contour of a massive column. Her hand slid down again, and she felt something soft and damp and drew away quickly. Cautiously she reached out again and touched the yielding, putty-like substance. She pulled a piece of it and brought it to her nose. "Oh, my God," she spoke under her breath. "Oh, you bastards. You really would do it."

Her knee bumped into something, and her hands reached down and felt the suitcase that they had carried down into the hole—a suitcase big enough to hold at least twenty kilos of plastic. Somewhere, probably on the other side of the staircase, was the other charge.

She wedged into the space between the stairway wall and the column's footing and took the nylon from around her shoulders. She found a half brick and held it in her right hand.

Gallagher came closer, his flashlight focused on the ground in front of him. She could see in the light the marks she had made when she had to crawl through the earth.

Gallagher's light swung up and focused on the column footing, then probed the space where she was hiding. He crawled closer and poked the light between the column and the wall.

For a long second the light rested directly on her face, and they stared at each other from less than a yard away. Gallagher's face registered complete surprise, she noticed. A stupid man.

She brought her hand down with the half brick in it and drove it between his eyes. The light fell to the floor, and she sprang out of her niche and wrapped the nylon garrote around his neck.

Gallagher thrashed over the earth floor like a wounded animal. Maureen hooked her legs around his torso and rode his back, holding the garrote like a set of reins, drawing it tightly around his neck with all the strength she could summon.

Gallagher weakened and fell forward on his chest, pinning her legs beneath him. She pulled harder on the nylon, but there was too much give in it. She knew she was strangling him too slowly, causing him unnecessary suffering. She heard the gurgling coming from deep in his throat.

Gallagher's head twisted around at an unbelievable angle, and his face stared up at her. The fallen flashlight cast a yellow beam over his face, and she saw his bulging eyes and thick protruding tongue. His skin was split where she had hit him with the brick, and his nose was broken and bleeding. Their eyes met for a brief second.

Gallagher's body went limp and lay motionless. Maureen sat on his back trying to catch her breath. She still felt life in his body, the shallow breathing, the twitching muscles and flesh against her buttocks. She began tightening the garrote, then suddenly pulled it from his neck and buried her face in her hands.

She heard voices coming around the crypt, then saw two lights not forty feet away. She quickly shut off the flashlight and threw it aside. Maureen felt her heart beating wildly again as she groped for the fallen pistol.

The beam rose and searched the ceiling. A voice—Megan's—said, "Here's another missing bulb. Clever little bitch."

The other flashlight examined the ground. Hickey said, "Here are their tracks."

Maureen's hands touched Gallagher's body, and she felt him moving. She backed off.

Hickey called out, "Frank? Are you there?" His approaching light found Gallagher's body and rested on it.

Maureen crawled backward until she made contact with the base of the column. She turned and clawed at the plastic explosive, trying to pull it loose from the footing, feeling for the detonator that she knew was embedded somewhere.

The two beams of light came closer. Hickey shouted, "Maureen! You've done well, lass. But as you see, the hounds are onto the scent. We're going to begin probing fire if you don't give yourself up."

Maureen kept pulling at the plastic. She knew there would be no probing fire with plastic so close.

The sound of the two crawling people got closer. She looked back and saw two pools of light converging on Gallagher's body. Hickey and Megan were hovering over Gallagher now. Gallagher was trying to raise himself on all fours.

Megan said, "Here, I've found his light."

Hickey said, "Look for his gun."

Maureen gave one last pull at the plastic, then moved around the column until she ran into the foundation wall that separated her from the sacristy.

She put her right shoulder against the wall and crawled along it, feeling for an opening. Pipes and ducts penetrated the wall, but there was no space for her to pass through.

Hickey's voice called out again. "Maureen, my love, Frank is feeling a bit better. All is forgiven, darlin'. We owe you, lass. You've a good heart. Come on, now. Let's all go back upstairs and have a nice wash and a cup of tea."

Maureen watched as one, then two, then three flashlights started to reach out toward her.

Hickey said, "Maureen, we've found Frank's gun, so we know you're not armed. The game is over. You've done well. You've nothing to be ashamed of. Frank owes you his life, and there'll be no retributions, Maureen. Just call out to us and we'll come take you back. You've our word you won't be harmed."

Maureen huddled against the foundation wall. She knew Hickey was speaking the truth. Gallagher owed her. They wouldn't harm her while Gallagher was still alive; that was one of the rules. The old rules, Hickey's rules, her rules. She wondered about someone like Megan, though.

Her instincts told her that it was over—that she should give up while the offered amnesty was still in effect. She was tired, cold, aching. The flashlights came closer. She opened her mouth to speak.

39

Inspector Langley was reading Monsignor Downes's appointment book. "I think the good Rector entertained the Fenians on more than one occasion. . . . Unwittingly, of course."

Schroeder looked at Langley. It would never have occurred to him to snoop through another man's papers. That's why he had been such a bad detective. Langley, on the other hand, would pick the Mayor's pocket out of idle curiosity. Schroeder said acidly, "You mean you don't suspect Monsignor Downes?"

Langley smiled. "I didn't say that."

Bellini turned from the window and looked at Schroeder. "You didn't have to eat so much shit, did you? I mean that business about rolling over and all that other stuff."

Schroeder felt his fright turning to anger. "For Christ's sake, it's only a ploy. You've heard me use it a dozen times."

"Yeah, but this time you *meant* it."

"Go to hell."

Bellini seemed to be struggling with something. He leaned forward with his hands on Schroeder's desk and spoke softly. "I'm scared, too. Do you think I *want* to send my men in there? Christ Almighty, Bert, I'm going in, too. I have a wife and kids. But Jesus, man, every hour that you bullshit with them is another hour for them to get their defenses tightened. Every hour shortens the time until dawn, when I *have* to attack. And I won't hit them at dawn in a last desperate move to save the hostages and the Cathedral, because they *know* I have to move at dawn if they don't have what they want."

Schroeder kept his eyes fixed on Bellini's but didn't reply.

Bellini went on, his voice becoming more strident. "As long as you keep telling the big shots you can do it, they're going to jerk me around. Admit you're not going to pull it off and let me . . . let me know in my own mind . . . that I *have* to go in." He said almost in a whisper, "I don't like sweating it out like this, Bert. . . . My men don't like this. . . . I have to *know.*"

Schroeder spoke mechanically. "I'm taking it a step at a time. Standard procedures. Stabilize the situation, keep them talking, calm them down, get an extension of the deadline—"

Bellini slammed his hand on the desk, and everyone sat up quickly. "Even if you *could* get an extension of the deadline, how long would it be for? An hour? Two hours? Then I have to move in the daylight—while you stand here at the window smoking a cigar, watching us get massacred!"

Schroeder stood and his face twitched. He tried to stop himself from speaking, but the words came out. "If you have to go in, I'll be right next to you, Bellini."

A twisted smile passed over Bellini's face. He turned to Langley and Spiegel, then looked back at Schroeder. "You're on, Captain." He turned and walked out of the room.

Langley watched the door close, then said, "That was stupid, Bert."

Schroeder found his hands and legs were shaking, and he sat down, then rose abruptly. He spoke in a husky voice. "Watch the phone. I have to go out for a minute—men's room." He walked quickly to the door.

Spiegel said, "I took some cheap shots at him, too."

Langley looked away.

She said, "Tell me what a bitch I am."

He walked to the sideboard and poured a glass of sherry. He had no intention of telling the Mayor's aide she was a bitch.

She walked toward him, reached out, and took the glass from his hand. She drank, then handed it back.

Langley thought, *She did it again!* There was something uncomfortably intimate and at the same time unnervingly aggressive about the proprietary attitude she had taken with him.

Roberta Spiegel walked toward the door. "Don't do anything stupid like Schroeder did."

He looked up at her with some surprise.

She said suddenly, "You married? Divorced . . . separated . . . single?"

"Yes."

She laughed. "Watch the store. See you later." She left.

Langley looked at the lipstick mark on his glass and put it down. "Bitch." He walked to the window.

Bellini had placed a set of field glasses on the sill. Langley picked them up and saw clearly the man standing in the belfry. If Bellini attacked, this young man would be one of the first to die. He wondered if the man knew that. Of course he did.

The man saw him and raised a pair of field glasses. They stared at each other for a few seconds. The young man held up his hand, a sort of greeting. The faces of all the IRA men Langley had ever known suddenly coalesced in this face—the young romantics, the old-guard IRA like Hickey, the dying Officials like Ferguson, the cold-blooded young Provos like most of them, and now the Fenians—crazier than the Provos—the worst of the worst. . . . All of them had started life, he was sure, as polite young men and women, dressed in little suits and dresses for Sunday Mass. Somewhere something went wrong. But maybe they would get most of the worst crazies in one sweep tonight. Nip it in the bud here. He damn well didn't want to deal with them later.

Langley put down the glasses and turned from the window. He looked at his watch. Where the hell was Burke?

He had a sour feeling in his stomach. *Transference.* Somehow he felt he was in there with them.

Maureen watched the circle of light closing in on her and almost welcomed the light and Hickey's cajoling voice after the sensory deprivation she had experienced.

Hickey called out again. "I know you're frightened, Maureen. Just take a deep breath and call to us."

She almost did, but something held her back. A series of confused thoughts ran through her mind—Brian, Harold Baxter, Whitehorn Abbey, Frank Gallagher's ghostly face. She felt she was adrift in some foggy sea—with no anchor, misleading beacons, false harbors. She tried to shake off the lethargy and think clearly, tried to resolve her purpose, which was freedom. Freedom from Brian Flynn, freedom from all the people and things that had kept her feeling guilty and obligated all her life. *Once you're a hostage, you're a hostage the rest of your life.* She had been Brian's hostage long before he put a gun to her head. She had been a hostage to her own insecurities and circumstances all her life. But now for the first time she felt less like a hostage and less like a traitor. She felt like a refugee from an insane world, a fugitive from a state of mind that was a prison far worse than Long Kesh. *Once in, never out.* Bullshit. She began crawling again, along the foundation wall.

Hickey called out, "Maureen, we see you moving. Don't make us shoot."

She called back, "I know you don't have Gallagher's gun, because I have it. Careful I don't shoot *you.*" She heard them talking among themselves, then the flashlights went out. She smiled at how the simplest bluffs worked when people were frightened. She kept crawling.

The foundation curved, and she knew she was under the ambulatory now. Somewhere on the other side of the foundation were the fully excavated basements beneath the terraces outside that led back to the rectory.

Beneath the thin layer of soil the Manhattan bedrock rose and fell as she crawled. The ceiling was only about four feet high now, and she kept hitting her head on pipes and ducts. The ducts made a noise when she hit them and boomed like a drum in the cold, stagnant air.

Suddenly the flashlights came on again, some distance off. Megan's voice called, "We found the gun, Maureen. Come toward the light or we shoot. Last chance."

Maureen watched the beams of light searching for her. She didn't know if they had Gallagher's gun or not, but she knew she didn't have it. She crawled on her stomach, commando style, pressing her face to the ground.

The lights began tightening around her. Hickey said, "I'm counting to ten. Then the armistice is over." He counted.

Maureen stopped crawling and remained motionless, pressed against the wall. Blood and sweat ran over her face; her legs and arms were studded with pieces of embedded stone. She steadied her breathing and listened for a sound from the basement that was only feet away. She looked for a crack of light, felt for a draft that might be coming from the other side, then ran her hands over the stone foundation. Nothing. She began moving again.

Hickey's voice called out, "Maureen, you're a heartless girl, making an old man crawl in the damp like this. I'll catch my death—let's go back up and have some tea."

The light beams were actually passing over her intermittently, and she froze when they did. They didn't seem to be able to pick out her blackened features in the darkness. She noticed that the stone wall turned again, then ended. Brick wall ran from the stone at right angles, and she suspected the brick wall was not a stress-bearing foundation but a partition behind which the foundation had disappeared. She rose to a kneeling position, reached for the top of the wall, and discovered a small space near the concrete ceiling. She pressed her face to the space but saw no light, heard no noise, and felt no air. Yet she was certain she was close to finding a way out.

A voice called out. Gallagher's. "Maureen, please don't make us shoot you. I know you spared my life—come on, then, be a good woman and let's all go back."

Again she knew they wouldn't shoot, if not because of the explosives then for fear of a ricochet among all this stone. She was suddenly angry at their small lies. What kind of idiot did they think she was? Hickey might be an old soldier, but Maureen knew more about war than Megan or Gallagher would live to learn. She wanted to scream an obscenity at them for their patronizing attitude. She moved along the wall and felt it curve farther inward. She judged from the configuration of the horseshoe-shaped ambulatory that she was now below the bride's room or confessional. Suddenly her hand came into contact with dry wood. Her heart gave a small leap. She faced the wall and knelt in front of it. Her hands explored the wood, set flush into the brick. She felt a rusty latch and pulled on it. A pair of hinges squeaked sharply in the still air. The flashlight beams came toward her.

Hickey called to her. "You're leading us a merry chase, young lady. I hope you don't give your suitors as much trouble."

Maureen said under her breath, "Go to hell, you old bag of bones." She pulled slowly on the door. Cracks of light appeared around the edges, showing it to be about three feet square. She closed the door quickly, found a broken shard of brick, and threw it farther along the wall.

The light beams swung toward the noise. She pulled the door open a few inches and pushed her face to the small aperture. She blinked her eyes several times and focused on a fluorescent-lit hallway.

The hallway floor was about four feet below her—a beautiful floor, she thought, of white polished vinyl. The walls of the corridor were painted plasterboard; the ceiling a few feet above her head was white acoustical tile. A beautiful hallway, really. Tears ran down her face.

She swung the door fully open and rubbed her eyes, then pushed her hair away from her face. Something was wrong. . . . She put her hand out, and her fingers passed through a wire grill. A rat screen covered the opening.

40

Burke walked into the Monsignor's inner office and looked at Langley, the sole person present, staring out the window. Burke said, "Everybody quit?"

Langley turned.

Burke said, "Where's Schroeder?"

"Relieving himself . . . or throwing up, or something. Did you hear what happened—?"

"I was briefed. Damned fools in there are going to blow it. Everyone's all right?"

"Cardinal said so. Also, you missed two good showdowns—Schroeder versus Spiegel and Schroeder versus Bellini. Poor Bert. He's usually the fair-haired boy, too." Langley paused. "I think he's losing it."

Burke nodded. "Do you think it's him, or is it us . . . or is it that Flynn is that good?"

Langley shrugged. "All of the above."

Burke went to the sideboard and noticed there was very little left in the decanters. He said, "Why did God let the Irish invent whiskey, Langley?"

Langley knew the drill. "To keep them from ruling the world."

Burke laughed. "Right." His voice became contemplative. "I'll bet no Fenian has had a drink in forty-eight hours. Do you know a woman named Terri O'Neal?"

Langley concentrated on the name, then said, "No. I don't make it at all." He immediately regretted the common cop jargon and said, "I can't identify the name. Call the office."

"I called from downstairs. Negative. But they're rechecking. How about Dan Morgan?"

"No. Irish?"

"Probably Northern Irish. Louise is going to call back."

"Who are these people?"

"That's what I asked you." He poured the remainder of the brandy and thought a moment. "Terri O'Neal . . . I think I have a face and a voice, but I just can't remember. . . ."

Langley said, "Flynn's asked for a television in there. In fact, you're supposed to deliver it to him." Langley looked at Burke out of the corner of his eye. "You two get along real well."

Burke considered the statement for a few seconds. In spite of the circumstances of their meeting, he admitted that Flynn was the type of man he could have liked—if Flynn were a cop, or if he, Burke, were IRA.

Langley said, "Call Flynn now."

Burke went to the phone. "Flynn can wait." He made certain the speakers in the other rooms were not on, then turned on the voice box on the desk so that

Langley could monitor. He dialed the Midtown North Precinct. "Gonzalez? Lieutenant Burke here. Do you have my man?" There was a long silence during which Burke found he was holding his breath.

"He's a prick," said Gonzalez. "Keeps screaming about police-state tactics and all that crap. Says he's going to sue us for false arrest. I thought you said he needed protection."

"Is he still there?"

"Yeah. He wants a ride to the Port Authority Terminal. I can't hold him a minute longer. If I get hit with a false arrest rap, I'm dragging you in with me—"

"Put him on."

"My pleasure. Wait."

Burke turned to Langley while he waited. "Ferguson. He's onto something. Terri O'Neal—Dan Morgan. Now he wants to run."

Langley moved beside Burke. "Well, offer him some money to stick around."

"You haven't paid him for today yet. Anyway, there's not enough money around to keep him from running."

Burke spoke into the telephone. "Jack—"

Ferguson's voice came into the room, high-pitched and agitated. "What the hell are you *doing* to me, Pat? Is this the way you treat a friend? For God's sake, man—"

"Cut it. Listen, put me on to the people you spoke to about O'Neal and Morgan."

"Not a chance. My sources are confidential. I don't treat friends the way you do. The intelligence establishment in this country—"

"Save it for your May Day speech. Listen, Martin has double-crossed all of us. He was the force behind the Fenians. This whole thing is a ploy to make the Irish look bad—to turn American public opinion against the Irish struggle."

Ferguson didn't speak for a while, then said, "I figured that out."

Burke pressed on. "Look, I don't know how much information Martin fed you, or how much information about the police and the Fenians you had to give him in return, but I'm telling you now he's at the stage where he's covering his tracks. Understand?"

"I understand that I'm on three hit-lists—the Fenians', the Provos', and Martin's. That's why I'm leaving town."

"You have to stick. Who is Terri O'Neal? Why was she kidnapped by a man named Morgan? Whose show was it? Where is she being held?"

"That's *your* problem."

"We're working on it, Jack, but you're closer to it. And we don't have much time. If you told us your sources—"

"No."

Burke went on. "Also, while you're at it, see if you can get a line on Gordon Stillway, the resident architect of Saint Pat's. He's missing, too."

"Lot of that going around. I'm missing, too. Good-bye."

"No! Stick with it."

"Why? Why should I risk my life any further?"

"For the same reasons you risked it all along—peace."

Ferguson sighed but said nothing.

Langley whispered, "Offer him a thousand dollars—no, make it fifteen hundred. We'll hold a benefit dance."

Burke said into the phone, "We'd like to exonerate all the Irish who had nothing to do with this, including your Officials and even the Provos. We'll work with you after this mess is over and see that the government and the press don't crucify all of you." Burke paused, then said, "You and I as Irishmen"—he remembered Flynn's attempt to claim kinship—"you and I want to be able to hold our heads up after this." Burke glanced at Langley, who nodded appreciatively. Burke turned away.

Ferguson said, "Hold on." There was a long silence, then Ferguson spoke. "How can I reach you later?"

Burke let out a breath. "Try to call the rectory. The lines should be clear later. Give the password . . . leprechaun. . . . They'll put you through."

"Leper is more like it, Burke. Make it leper. All right. If I can't get through on the phone, I won't come to the rectory—the cordon is being watched by all sorts of people. If you don't hear from me, let's have a standing rendezvous. Let's say the zoo at one."

Burke said, "Closer to the Cathedral."

"All right. But no bars or public places." He thought. "Okay, that small park on Fifty-first—it's not far from you."

"It's closed after dark."

"Climb the gate!"

Burke smiled. "Someday I'm going to get a key for every park in this town."

Ferguson said, "Join the Parks Department. They'll issue one with your broom."

"Luck." Burke spoke to Gonzalez. "Let him go." He hung up and took a deep breath.

Langley said, "Do you think this O'Neal thing is important enough to risk his life?"

Burke drained off the glass of brandy and grimaced. "How do people drink this stuff?"

"Pat?"

Burke walked to the window and looked out.

Langley said, "I'm not making any moral judgments. I only want to know if it's *worth* getting Jack Ferguson killed."

Burke spoke as if to himself. "A kidnapping is a subtle sort of thing, more complicated than a hit, more sinister in many ways—like hostage taking." He considered. "Hostage taking—that's a form of kidnapping. Terri O'Neal is a *hostage.* . . ."

"Whose hostage?"

Burke turned and faced Langley. "I don't know."

"Who has to do what for whom to secure her release? No one has made any demands yet."

"Strange," agreed Burke.

"Really," said Langley.

Burke looked at Schroeder's empty chair. Schroeder's presence, in spite of everything, had been reassuring. He said half-jokingly, "Are you sure he's coming back?"

Langley shrugged. "His backup man is in another room with a phone, waiting like an understudy for the break of a lifetime. . . ." Langley said, "Call Flynn."

"Later." He sat in Schroeder's chair, leaned back, and looked at the lofty ceiling. A long crack ran from wall to wall, replastered but not yet painted. He had a mental image of the Cathedral in ruins, then pictured the Statue of Liberty lying on its side half submerged in the harbor. He thought of the Roman Coliseum, the ruined Acropolis, the flooded temples of the Nile. He said, "You know, the Cathedral itself is not that important. Neither are the lives of any of us. What's important is how we act, what people say and write about us afterward."

Langley looked at him appraisingly. Burke sometimes surprised him. "Yes, that's true, but you won't tell that to anybody today."

"Or tomorrow, if we're pulling bodies out of the rubble."

John Hickey's voice came to Maureen from not very far off. "So, what have we here? What light through yonder window breaks, Maureen?" He laughed, then said sharply, "Move back from there or we'll shoot you."

Maureen cocked her elbow and drove it into the rat screen. The wire bent, but the edges stayed fixed to the wall. She pressed her face to the grill. To her left the hallway ended about ten feet away. On the opposite wall toward the end of the passage were gray sliding doors—elevator doors—the elevator that opened near the bride's room above. She drove her elbow into the grill again, and one side of the frame ripped loose from the plasterboard. "Yes, yes . . . *please* . . ."

She could hear them behind her, scurrying over the rubble-strewn ground like the rats they were, faster, coming at the light source. Then John Hickey came out of the dark. "Hands on your head, darlin'."

She turned and stared at him, holding back the tears forming in her eyes.

Hickey said, "Look at you. Your pretty knees are all scratched. And what's that dirt all over your face, Maureen? *Camouflage?* You'll be needing a good wash."

He ran his flashlight over her. "And your smart tweeds are turned inside out. Clever girl. Clever. And what is *that* around your neck?" He grabbed the nylon garrote and twisted it. "My, what a naughty girl you are." He gave the garrote another twist and held it until she began to choke. "Once again, Maureen, you've shown me a small chink in our armor. What would we do without you?" He loosened the tension on the nylon and knocked her to the ground. His eyes narrowed into malignant slits. "I think I'll shoot you through the head and throw you into the corridor. That'll help the police make the decision they're wrestling with." He seemed to consider, then said, "But, on the other hand, I'd like you to be around for the finale." He smiled a black, gaping smile. "I want you to see Flynn die or for him to see you die."

In a clear flash of understanding she knew the essence of this old man's evil. "Kill me."

He shook his head. "No. I like you. I like what you're becoming. You should have killed Gallagher, though. You would have been firmly planted in the ranks of the damned if you had. You're only borderline now." He cackled.

Maureen lay on the damp earth. She felt a hand grab her long hair and pull her back across the floor into the darkness. Megan Fitzgerald knelt over her and put a pistol to her heart. "Your charmed life has come to an end, bitch."

Hickey called out, "None of that, Megan!"

Megan Fitzgerald shouted back. "You'll not stop me this time." She cocked the pistol.

Hickey shouted, "No! Brian will decide if she's to die—and if she's to die, he wants to be the one to kill her."

Maureen listened to this statement without any outward emotion. She felt numb, drained.

Megan screamed back. "Fuck you! Fuck Flynn! She'll die here and now."

Hickey spoke softly. "If you shoot, I'll kill you." Everyone heard the click of the safety disengaging from his automatic.

Gallagher cleared his throat and said, "Let her alone, Megan."

No one moved or spoke. Finally Megan uncocked her pistol. She turned on her light and shone it into Maureen's face. A twisted smile formed on Megan's lips. "You're old . . . and not very pretty." She poked Maureen's breast roughly with the muzzle of her pistol.

Maureen looked up through the light at Megan's contorted face. "You're very young, and you ought to be pretty, but there's an ugliness in you, Megan, that everyone can see in your eyes."

Megan spit at her, then disappeared into the dark.

Hickey knelt over Maureen and wiped her face with a handkerchief. "Well, now, if you want my opinion, I think you're very pretty."

She turned her face away. "Go to hell."

Hickey said, "You see, Uncle John saved your life again."

She didn't respond, and he went on. "Because I really want you to see what's going to happen later. Yes, it's going to be quite spectacular. How often can you see a cathedral collapsing around your head—?"

Gallagher made an odd gasping sound, and Hickey said to him, "Only joking, Frank."

She said to Gallagher, "He's not joking, you know—"

Hickey leaned close to her ear. "Shut up or I'll—"

"What?" She looked at him fiercely. "What can you do to me?" She turned toward Gallagher. "He means to see all of us dead. He means to see all your young friends follow him to the grave . . ."

Hickey laughed in a shrill, piercing tone.

The rats stopped their chirping.

Hickey said, "The little creatures sense the danger. They smell death. They know."

Gallagher said nothing, but his breathing filled the still, cold air.

Maureen sat up slowly. "Baxter? The others . . . ?"

Hickey said in an offhand manner, "Baxter is dead. Father Murphy was hit in the face, and he's dying. The Cardinal is all right, though." He said in an aggrieved whisper, "Do you see what you've *done?*"

She couldn't speak, and tears ran down her face.

Hickey turned from her and played his light over the open hatchway.

Gallagher said, "We better put an alarm here."

Hickey answered, "The only alarm you'll hear from down here is from about a kilo of plastic. I'll have Sullivan come back and mine it." He glanced at Maureen. "Well, shall we go home, then?"

They began the long crawl back.

Hickey spoke as they made their way. "If I was a younger man, Maureen, I'd be in love with you. You're so like the women I knew in the Movement in my youth. So many of the revolutionary women in other movements are ugly misfits, neurotics and psychotics. But we've always been able to attract clearheaded, pretty lasses like yourself. Why is that, do you suppose?" He said between labored breaths, "Well, don't answer me, then. Tired? Yes, me too. Slow down, Gallagher, you big ox. We've got some way to go yet before we can rest. We'll all rest together, Maureen. Soon this will be over . . . we'll be free of all our worries, all our bonds . . . before dawn . . . a nice rest . . . it won't be so bad . . . it won't, really. . . . We're going home."

41

Schroeder came through the double doors of the Rector's inner office. "Look who's back. Did you call Flynn?"

"Not without you here, Bert. Feeling better?"

Schroeder came around the desk. "Please get out of my chair, Lieutenant."

Burke vacated the chair.

Schroeder looked at Burke as he sat. "Can you carry a TV set?"

"Why didn't he ask for a television right away?"

Schroeder thought. Flynn *wasn't* a textbook case in many respects. Little things like not immediately asking for a television . . . little things that added up . . .

Langley said, "He's keeping the Fenians isolated. Their only reality is Brian Flynn. After the press conference he'll smash the TV or place it where only he and Hickey can use it for intelligence gathering."

Schroeder nodded. "I never know if this TV business is part of the problem or part of the solution. But if they ask, we have to give." He dialed the switchboard. "Chancel organ." He handed the receiver to Burke, turned on all the speaker switches, then sat back with his feet on the desk. "On the air, Lieutenant."

A voice came over the speakers: "Flynn here."

"Burke."

"Listen, Lieutenant, do me a great favor, won't you, and stay in the damned rectory—at least until dawn. If the Cathedral goes, you'll want to see it. Tape all the windows, though, and don't stand under any chandeliers."

Burke was aware that more than two hundred people in the Cathedral complex were listening, and that every word was being taped and transmitted to Washington and London. Flynn knew this, too, and was playing it for effect. "What can I do for you?"

"Aren't you supposed to ask first about the hostages?"

"You said they were all right."

"But that was a while ago."

"Well, how are they *now?*"

"No change. Except that Miss Malone took a jaunt through the crawl space. But she's back now. Looks a bit tired, from what I can see. Clever girl that she is she found a hatchway from the crawl space into the hallway that runs past the bride's-room elevator." He paused, then went on, "Don't touch the hatch, however, as it's being mined right now with enough plastic to give you a nasty bump."

Burke looked at Schroeder, who was already on the other phone talking to one of Bellini's lieutenants. "I understand."

"Good. And you can assume that every other entrance you find will also be mined. And you can assume the entire crawl space is seeded with mines. You can also suspect that I'm lying or bluffing, but, really, it's not smart to call my bluff. Tell that to your ESD people."

"I'll do that."

Flynn said, "Anyway, I want the television. Bring it round to the usual place. Fifteen minutes."

Burke looked at Schroeder and covered the mouthpiece.

Schroeder said, "There's one waiting downstairs in the clerk's office. But you have to get something from him in return. Ask to speak to a hostage."

Burke uncovered the mouthpiece. "I want to talk to Father Murphy first."

"Oh, your friend. You shouldn't admit to having a friend in here."

"He's not my friend, he's my confessor."

Flynn laughed loudly. "Sorry, that struck me funny, somehow. That was no lady, that was my wife. You know?"

Schroeder suppressed a smirk.

Burke looked annoyed. "Put him on!"

Flynn's voice lost its humor. "Don't make any demands on me, Burke."

"I won't bring a television unless I speak to the priest."

Schroeder was shaking his head excitedly. "Forget it," he whispered. "Don't push him."

Burke continued, "We have some talking to do, don't we, Flynn?"

Flynn didn't answer for a long time, then said, "I'll have Murphy at the gate. See you in no-man's-land. Fifteen . . . no, fourteen minutes now, and don't be late." He hung up.

Schroeder looked at Burke. "What the hell kind of dialogue are you two carrying on down there?"

Burke ignored him and called through to the chancel organ again. "Flynn?"

Brian Flynn's voice came back, a bit surprised. "What is it?"

Burke found his body shaking with anger. "New rule, Flynn. You don't hang up until I'm through. Got it?" He slammed down the receiver.

Schroeder stood. "What the hell is wrong with you? Haven't you learned *anything?*"

"Oh, go fuck yourself." He wiped his brow with a handkerchief.

Schroeder pressed on. "Don't like being at the receiving end, do you? Messes up your self-image. These bastards have called me every name under the sun tonight, but you don't see me—"

"Okay. You're right. Sorry."

Schroeder said again, "What do you talk to him about down there?"

Burke shook his head. He was tired, and he was starting to lose his temper. He knew that if he was making mistakes because of fatigue, then everyone else was, too.

The phone rang. Schroeder answered it and handed it to Burke. "Your secret headquarters atop Police Plaza."

Burke shut off all the speakers and carried the phone away from the desk. "Louise."

The duty sergeant said, "Nothing on Terri O'Neal. Daniel Morgan—age thirty-four. A naturalized American citizen. Born in Londonderry. Father Welsh Protestant, mother Irish Catholic. Fiancée arrested in Belfast for IRA activities. May still be in Armagh Prison. We'll check with British—"

"Don't check *anything* with their intelligence sections or with the CIA or FBI unless you get the go-ahead from me or Inspector Langley."

"Okay. One of those." She went on. "Morgan made our files because he was arrested once in a demonstration outside the UN, 1979. Fined and released. Address YMCA on West Twenty-third. Doubt if he's still there. Right?" She read the remainder of the arrest sheet, then said, "I've put it out to our people and to the detectives. I'll send you a copy of the sheet. Also, nothing yet on Stillway."

Burke hung up and turned to Langley. "Let's get that television."

Schroeder said, "What was that all about?"

Langley looked at Schroeder. "Trying to catch a break to make your job and Bellini's a little easier."

"Really? Well, that's the least you can do after screwing up the initial investigation."

Burke said, "If we hadn't blown it, you wouldn't have the opportunity to negotiate for the life of the Archbishop of New York or the safety of Saint Patrick's Cathedral."

"Thanks. I owe you."

Burke looked at him closely and had the impression that he wasn't being completely facetious.

Maureen came out of the lavatory of the bride's room and walked to the vanity. Her outer garments lay draped over a chair, and a first-aid kit sat in front of the vanity mirror. She sat and opened the kit.

Jean Kearney stood to the side with a pistol in her hand and watched. Kearney cleared her throat and said tentatively, "You know . . . they still speak of you in the movement."

Maureen dabbed indifferently at her legs with an iodine applicator. She didn't look up but said listlessly, "Do they?"

"Yes. People still tell stories of your exploits with Brian before you turned traitor."

Maureen glanced up at the young woman. It was an ingenuous statement, without hostility or malice, just a relating of a fact she had learned from the storytellers—like the story of Judas. The Gospel according to the Republican Army. Maureen looked at the young woman's bluish lips and fingers. "Cold up there?"

She nodded. "Awfully cold. This is a bit of a break for me, so take your time."

Maureen noticed the wood chips on Jean Kearney's clothing. "Doing some carpentry in the attic?"

Kearney turned her eyes away.

Maureen stood and took her skirt from the chair. "Don't do it, Jean. When the time comes, you and—Arthur, isn't it?—you and Arthur must not do whatever it is they've told you to do."

"Don't say such things. We're loyal—not like you."

Maureen turned and looked at herself in the mirror and looked at the image of Jean Kearney behind her. She wanted to say something to this young woman, but really there was nothing to say to someone who had willingly committed sacrilege and would probably commit murder before too long. Jean Kearney would eventually find her own way out, or she'd die young.

There was a knock on the door, and it opened a crack. Flynn put his head in, and his eyes rested on Maureen; then he looked away. "Sorry. Thought you'd be done."

Maureen pulled on her skirt, then picked up her blouse and slipped into it.

Flynn came into the room and looked around. He fixed his attention on the bandages and iodine. "History does have a way of repeating itself, doesn't it?"

Maureen buttoned her blouse. "Well, if we all keep making the same mistakes, it's bound to, isn't it, Brian?"

Flynn smiled. "One day we'll get it right."

"Not bloody likely."

Flynn motioned to Jean Kearney, and she left reluctantly, a disappointed look on her face.

Maureen sat at the vanity and ran a comb through her hair.

Flynn watched for a while, then said, "I'd like to speak to you."

"I'm listening."

"In the chapel."

"We're perfectly alone here."

"Well . . . yes. Too alone. People would talk. I can't compromise myself—neither can you. . . ."

She laughed and stood. "What would people talk *about?* Really, Brian . . . here in the bride's room of a cathedral. . . . What a lot of sex-obsessed Catholics you all still are." She moved toward him. "All right. I'm ready. Let's go."

He took her arms and turned her toward him.

She shook her head. "No, Brian. Much too late." His face had a look, she thought, of desperation . . . fright almost.

He said, "Why do women always say things like that? It's never too late; there are no seasons or cycles to these things."

"But there are. It's winter for us now. There'll be no spring—not in our lifetime."

He pulled her toward him and kissed her, and before she could react he turned and left the room.

She stood in the center of the bride's room, immobile for a few seconds, then her hand went to her mouth and pressed against her lips. She shook her head. "You fool. You damned fool."

Father Murphy sat in the clergy pews, a pressure bandage over the right side of his jaw. The Cardinal stood beside him. Harold Baxter lay on his side in the same pew. A winding bandage circled his bare torso, revealing a long line of dried blood across his back and a smaller spot of red on his chest. His face showed the result of Pedar Fitzgerald's blows. Megan's kick had swollen one eye nearly shut.

Maureen moved across the sanctuary and knelt beside the two men. They exchanged subdued greetings. Maureen said to Baxter, "Hickey told me you were dead and Father Murphy was dying."

Baxter shook his head. "The man's quite mad." He looked around. Flynn, Hickey, and Megan Fitzgerald were nowhere to be seen. That, for some reason, was more unnerving than having them in his sight. He felt his hold on his courage slipping and knew the others were feeling that way also. He said, "If we can't escape . . . physically escape . . . then we have to talk about a way to survive in here. We have to stand up to them, keep them from dividing us and isolating us. We have to *understand* the people who hold us captive."

Maureen thought a moment, then said, "Yes, but they're hard people to know. I never understood Brian Flynn, never understood what made him go on." She paused, then said, "After all these years . . . I thought I'd have heard one day that he was dead or had a breakdown like so many of them, or ran off to Spain like so many more of them, but he just keeps going on . . . like some immortal thing, tortured by life, unable to die, unable to lay down the sword that has become so burdensome. . . . God, I almost feel sorry for him." She had the uncomfortable feeling that her revelations about Brian Flynn were somehow disloyal.

The Cardinal knelt beside the three people. He said, "In the tower I learned that Brian Flynn is a man who holds some unusual beliefs. He's a romantic, a man who lives in the murky past. The idea of blood sacrifice—which may be the final outcome here—is consistent with Irish myth, legend, and history. There's this aura of defeat that surrounds the people here—unlike the aura of ultimate victory that is ingrained in the British and American psyche." The Cardinal seemed to consider, then went on. "He really believes he is a sort of incarnation of Finn MacCumail." He looked at Maureen. "He's still very fond of you."

Her face flushed, and she said, "That won't stop him from killing me."

The Cardinal answered, "He would only harm you if he thought you felt nothing for him any longer."

She thought back to the bride's room. "So what am I supposed to do? Play up to him?"

Father Murphy spoke. "We'll all have to do that, I think, if we're going to survive. Show him we care about him as a person . . . and I think at least some of us do. I care about his soul."

Baxter nodded slowly. "Actually, you know, it costs nothing to be polite . . . except a bit of self-respect." He smiled and said, "Then when everyone is calmed down, we'll have another go at it."

Maureen nodded quickly. "Yes, I'm willing."

The Cardinal spoke incredulously. "Haven't you two had enough?"

She answered, "No."

Baxter said, "If Flynn were our only problem, I'd take my chances with him. But when I look into the eyes of Megan Fitzgerald or John Hickey . . . Maureen and I spoke about this before, and I've decided that I don't want tomorrow's newspapers to speak of my execution and martyrdom, but I would want them to say, 'Died in an escape attempt.' "

The Cardinal said acidly, "It may read, 'A foolish escape attempt' . . . shortly before you were to be released."

Baxter looked at him. "I've stopped believing in a negotiated settlement. That reduces my options to one."

Maureen added, "I'm almost certain that Hickey means to kill us and destroy this church."

Baxter sat up with some difficulty. "There's one more way out of here . . . and we can all make it. . . . We *must* all make it, because we won't get another chance."

Father Murphy seemed to be struggling with something, then said, "I'm with you." He glanced at the Cardinal.

The Cardinal shook his head. "It was a miracle we weren't all killed last time. I'm going to have to insist that—"

Maureen reached into the pocket of her jacket and held out a small white particle. "Do any of you know what this is? No, of course you don't. It's plastic explosive. As we suspected, that's what Hickey and Megan carried down in those suitcases. This is molded around at least one of the columns below. I don't know how many other columns are set to be blown, or where they all are, but I do know that two suitcases of plastic, properly placed, are enough to bring down the roof." She fixed her eyes on the Cardinal, who had turned pale. She continued, "And I don't see a remote detonator and wire up here. So I have to assume it's set to go on a timer. What time?" She looked at the three men. "At least one of us has to get out of here and warn the people outside."

Brian Flynn strode up to the communion rail and spoke in an ill-tempered tone. "Are you plotting again? Your Eminence, please stay on your exalted throne. The wounded gentlemen don't need your comfort. They're comforted enough knowing they're still alive. Miss Malone, may I have a word with you in the Lady Chapel? Thank you."

Maureen stood and noticed the stiffness that had spread through her body. She walked slowly to the side steps, down into the ambulatory, then passed into the Lady Chapel.

Flynn came up behind her and indicated a pew toward the rear. She sat.

He stood in the aisle beside her and looked around the quiet chapel. It was unlike the rest of the Cathedral; the architecture was more delicate and refined. The marble walls were a softer shade, and the long, narrow windows were done mostly in rich cobalt blues. He looked up at one of the windows to the right of the entrance. A face stared back at him, looking very much like Karl Marx, and in fact the figure was carrying a red flag in one hand and a sledgehammer in the other, attacking the cross atop a church steeple. "Well," he said in a neutral tone, "you know you've arrived as a lesser demon when the Church sticks your face up in a window. Like a picture in the celestial post office. Wanted for heresy." He pointed up at the window. "Karl Marx. Strange."

She glanced at the representation. "You wish it was Brian Flynn, don't you?"

He laughed. "You read my black soul, Maureen." He turned and looked at the altar nestled in the rounded end of the chapel. "God, the money that goes into these places."

"Better spent on armaments, wouldn't you say?"

He looked at her. "Don't be sharp with me, Maureen."

"Sorry."

"Are you?"

She hesitated, then said, "Yes."

He smiled. His eyes traveled upward past the statue of the Virgin on the altar, to the apsidal window above it. "The light will break through that window first. I hope we're not still here to see it."

She turned to him suddenly. "You won't burn this church, and you won't kill unarmed hostages. So stop speaking as though you were the type of man who would."

He put his hand on her shoulder, and she slid over. He sat beside her and said, "Something is very wrong if I've given the impression I'm bluffing."

"Perhaps it's because I know you. You've fooled everyone else."

"But I'm not fooling or bluffing."

"You'd shoot me?"

"Yes . . . I'd shoot myself afterward, of course."

"Very romantic, Brian."

"Sounds terrible, doesn't it?"

"You should hear yourself."

"Yes . . . well, anyway, I've been meaning to speak with you again, but with all that's been going on . . . We have some time now." He said, "Well, first you must promise me that you won't try to escape again."

"All right."

He looked at her. "I mean it. They'll kill you next time."

"So what? Better than being shot in the back of the head—by you."

"Don't be morbid. I don't think it will come to that."

"But you're not sure."

"It depends on things out of my control now."

"Then you shouldn't have gambled with my life and everyone else's—should you? Why do you think the people out there will be rational and concerned about our lives if you're not?"

"They've no choice."

"No choice but to be rational and compassionate? You've developed quite a faith in mankind, I see. If people behaved like that, none of us would be here now."

"This sounds like the argument we never finished four years ago." He stared toward the windows for a while, then turned to her. "Would you like to come with me when we leave here?"

She faced him. "When you leave here it will be for the jail or the cemetery. No, thank you."

"Damn you. . . . I'm walking out of here as free and alive as I walked in. Answer the question."

"What's to become of poor Megan? You'll break her dear heart, Brian."

"Stop that." He held her arm tightly. "I miss you, Maureen."

She didn't respond.

He said, "I'm ready to retire." He looked at her closely. "Really I am. As soon as this business is done with. I've learned a good deal from this."

"Such as?"

"I've learned what's important to me. Look here, you quit when you were ready, and I'm doing the same. I'm sorry I wasn't ready when you were."

"Neither you nor I believe a word of that. 'Once in, never out.' That's what you and all of them have thrown up to me all these years, so I'm throwing it right back in your face. 'Once in—' "

"No!" He pulled her closer to him. "Right now I believe I'm going to get out. Why can't you believe it with me?"

She suddenly went limp and put her hand over his. She spoke in a despondent tone. "Even if it *were* possible—there are people who have plans for your retirement, Brian, and they don't include a cottage by the sea in Kerry." She slumped against his shoulder. "And what of me? I'm hunted by the Belfast IRA still. One can't do the kinds of things we've done with our lives and expect to live happily ever after, can we? When was the last time you heard a knock on the door without having a great thump in your chest? Do you think you can announce your retirement like a respected statesman and settle down to write your memoirs? You've left a trail of blood all over Ireland, Brian Flynn, and there are people—Irish and British—who want yours in return."

"There are places we could go—"

"Not on this planet. The world is very small, as a good number of our people on the run have found out. Think how it would be if we lived together. Neither of us could ever go out to buy a packet of tea without wondering if it would be the last time we'd see each other. Every letter in the mail could explode in your face. And what if there were . . . children? Think about that awhile."

He didn't reply.

She shook her head slowly. "I won't live like that. It's enough that I have to worry about myself. And it's a relief, to be honest with you, that I have no one else to worry about—not you, nor Sheila . . . so why should I want to go with you and worry about when they're going to kill you? . . . Why do you want to worry about when they're going to catch up with me?"

He stared at the floor between the pews, then looked up at the altar. "But . . . you would *like* to . . . I mean if it were possible . . . ?"

She closed her eyes. "I wanted that once. I suppose, really, I still do. But it's not in our stars, Brian."

He stood abruptly and moved into the aisle. "Well . . . as long as you'd like to . . . that's good to know, Maureen." He said, "I'm adding Sheila's name to the list."

"Don't expect anything in return."

"I don't. Come along, then."

"Would you mind if I stayed here in the chapel?"

"I wouldn't, no. But . . . you're not safe here. Megan . . ."

"God, Brian, you speak of her as though she were a mad dog waiting to kill a sheep who's strayed from the fold."

"She's a bit . . . vindictive. . . ."

"Vindictive? What have I ever done to her?"

"She . . . she blames you, in part, for her brother's capture. . . . It's not rational, I know, but she's—"

"Bloodthirsty. How in the name of God did you get mixed up with that savage? Is that what the youth of Northern Ireland's turning into?"

Flynn looked back toward the chapel opening. "Perhaps. War is all they've known—all Megan's known since she was a child. It's become commonplace, the way dances and picnics used to be. These young people don't even remember what downtown Belfast looked like before. So you can't blame them. You understand that."

She stood. "She goes a bit beyond war psychosis. You and I, Brian . . . *our* souls are not dead, are they?"

"We remember some of the life before the troubles."

Maureen thought of Jean Kearney. She pictured the faces of the others. "We started this, you know."

"No. The other side started it. The other side always starts it."

"What difference does it make? Long after this is over, our country will be left with the legacy of children turned into murderers and children who tremble in dark corners. We're perpetuating it, and it will take a generation to forget it."

He shook his head. "Longer, I'm afraid. The Irish don't forget things in a generation. They write it all down and read it again, and tell it round the peat fires. And in truth you, I, and Megan are products of what came long before the recent troubles. Cromwell's massacres happened only last week, the famine happened yesterday, the uprising and civil war this morning. Ask John Hickey. He'll tell you."

She took a long breath. "I wish you weren't so damned right about these things."

"I wish you weren't so right about us. Come along."

She followed him out of the quiet chapel.

42

Flynn descended the sacristy steps and saw Burke and Pedar Fitzgerald facing each other through the gate. A portable television sat on the landing beside Burke.

Flynn said to Fitzgerald, "Bring the priest here in five minutes."

Fitzgerald slung the Thompson over his shoulder and left.

Burke looked at Flynn closely. He appeared tired, perhaps even sad.

Flynn took out the microphone detector and passed it over the television. "We're both suspicious men by temperament and by profession. God, it's lonely though, isn't it?"

"Why the sudden melancholy?"

Flynn shook his head slowly. "I keep thinking this won't end well."

"I can almost guarantee you it won't."

Flynn smiled. "You're a welcome relief from that ass Schroeder. You don't bother me with sweet talk or with talk of giving up."

"Well, now, I hate to say this after that compliment, but you *should* give it up."

"I can't, even if I wanted to. This machine I've put together has no real head, no real brain. But it has many killing appendages . . . inside and outside the Cathedral, each spring-loaded to act or react under certain conditions. I'm no more than the creator of this thing—standing outside the organism. . . . I suppose I speak for it, but not *from* it. You understand?"

"Yes." Burke couldn't tell if this pessimism was contrived. Flynn was a good actor whose every line was designed to create an illusion, to produce a desired response.

Flynn nodded and leaned heavily against the bars.

Burke had the impression that Flynn was fighting some inner struggle that was taking a great deal out of him.

After a time Flynn said, "Well, anyway, here's what I wanted to speak to you about. Hickey and I have concluded that Martin's abducted the resident architect of Saint Patrick's. Why, you ask? So that you can't plan or mount a successful attack against us."

Burke considered the statement. There'd certainly be more optimism in the rectory and Cardinal's residence if Gordon Stillway was poring over the blueprints with Bellini right now. Burke tried to put it together in his mind. The Fenians had missed Stillway; that was obvious by now. Maureen Malone wouldn't have found an unsecured passage if Stillway was in there, because Stillway, no matter how brave a man he might be, would have been spilling it all out after fifteen minutes with this bunch.

And it wasn't too difficult to believe that Major Martin had anticipated Stillway's importance and snatched him before the Fenians could get to him. But to believe all that, you had to believe some very nasty and cold-blooded things about Major Martin.

Flynn broke the silence. "Are you seeing it now? Martin doesn't want the police to move too fast. He wants to drag this out—he wants the dawn deadline to approach. He's probably already suggested that you'll get an extension of the deadline, hasn't he?"

Burke said nothing.

Flynn leaned closer. "And without a firm plan of attack you're ready to believe him. But let me tell you, at 6:03 A.M. this Cathedral is no more. If you attack, your people will be ripped up very badly. The only way this can end without bloodshed is on *my* terms. *You* believe that we've beaten you. So swallow all that goddamned Normandy Beach-Iwo Jima pride and tell the stupid bastards out there that it's finished and let's all go home."

"They won't listen to that."

"Make them listen!"

Burke said, "To the people out there the Fenians are no more the peers of the police and government than the New York street gang that calls itself the Pagans. They *can't* deal with you, Flynn. They're bound by law to arrest you and throw you in the slammer with the muggers and rapists, because that's all terrorists are—muggers, murderers, and rapists on a somewhat larger scale—"

"Shut up!"

Neither man spoke, then Burke said in a gentler tone, "I'm telling you what their position is. I'm telling you what Schroeder won't tell you. It's true we've lost, but it's also true we won't—can't—surrender. You could surrender . . . honorably . . . negotiate the best terms possible, lay down your guns—"

"No. Not one person in here can accept anything less than we've asked for."

Burke nodded. "All right. I'll pass it on. . . . Maybe we can still work something out that will save you and your people and the hostages and the Cathedral. . . . But the people in internment . . ." He shook his head. "London would never . . ."

Flynn also shook his head. "All or nothing."

Both men lapsed into a silence, each aware that he had said more than he'd intended. Each was aware, too, that he had lost something that had been building between them.

Pedar Fitzgerald's voice came down the stairs. "Father Murphy."

Flynn turned and called back. "Send him down."

The priest walked unsteadily down the marble staircase, supporting his large frame on the brass rail. He smiled through the face bandages and spoke in a muffled voice. "Patrick, good to see you." He put his hand through the bars.

Burke took the priest's hand. "Are you all right?"

Murphy nodded. "Close call. But the Lord doesn't want me yet."

Burke released the priest's hand and withdrew his own.

Flynn put his hand to the bars. "Let me have it."

Burke opened his hand, and Flynn snatched a scrap of paper from him.

Flynn unfolded the paper and read the words written in pencil. *Hickey sent last message on confessional buzzer.* There followed a fairly accurate appraisal of the Cathedral's defenses. Flynn frowned at the first sentence: *Hickey sent last message* . . . What did that mean?

Flynn pocketed the paper and looked up. There was no anger in his voice. "I'm proud of these people, Burke. They've shown some spirit. Even the two holy men have kept us on our toes, I'll tell you."

Burke turned to Murphy. "Do any of you need a doctor?"

Murphy shook his head. "No. We're a bit lame, but there's nothing a doctor can do. We'll be all right."

Flynn said, "That's all, Father. Go back with the others."

Murphy hesitated and looked around. He glanced at the chain and padlock, then looked at Flynn, who stood as tall as he but was not as heavy.

Flynn sensed the danger and moved back. His right hand stayed at his side, but the position of his fingers suggested he was ready to go for his pistol. "I've been knocked about by priests before, and I owe you all a few knocks in return. Don't give me cause. Leave."

Murphy nodded, turned, and mounted the steps. He called back over his shoulder, "Pat, tell them out there we're not afraid."

Burke said, "They know that, Father."

Murphy stood at the crypt door for a few seconds, then turned and disappeared around the turn in the staircase.

Flynn put his hands in his pockets. He looked down at the floor, then lifted his head slowly until he met Burke's eyes. He spoke without a trace of ruthlessness. "Promise me something, Lieutenant—promise me one thing tonight. . . ."

Burke waited.

"Promise me this—that if they attack, you'll be with them."

"What—?"

Flynn went on. "Because, you see, if you know you're not involved on that level, then subconsciously you'll not see things you should see, you'll not say things you should say out there. And you'll not live so easily with yourself afterward. You know what I mean."

Burke felt his mouth becoming dry. He thought of Schroeder's foolishness. It was a bad night for rear-echelon people. The front line was moving closer. He looked up at Flynn and nodded almost imperceptibly.

Flynn acknowledged the agreement without speaking. He looked away from Burke and said, "Don't leave the rectory again."

Burke didn't reply.

"Stay close. Stay close especially as the dawn approaches."

"I will."

Flynn looked past Burke into the sacristy and focused on the priests' altar in the small chapel at the rear that was directly below the Lady Chapel altar. There were arched Gothic windows behind this altar also, but these subterranean windows with soft artificial lighting behind them, eastward-facing windows, were suffused with a perpetual false dawn. He kept staring at them and spoke softly, "I've spent a good deal of my life working in the hours of darkness, but I've never been so frightened of seeing the sunrise."

"I know how you feel."

"Good. . . . Are they frightened out there?"

"I think they are."

Flynn nodded slowly. "I'm glad. It's not good to be frightened alone."

"No."

Flynn said, "Someday—if there's a day after this one—I'll tell you a story about Whitehorn Abbey—and this ring." He tapped it against the bars.

Burke looked at the ring; he suspected it was some sort of talisman. There always seemed to be magic involved when he dealt with people who lived so close to death, especially the Irish.

Flynn looked down at the floor. "I may see you later."

Burke nodded and walked down the steps.

43

B rian Flynn stood beside the curtain entrance to the confessional and looked at the small white button on the jamb. *Hickey sent last message* . . . Flynn turned toward the sound of approaching footsteps.

Hickey stopped and looked at his watch. "Time to meet the press, Brian."

He looked at Hickey. "Tell me about this buzzer."

Hickey glanced at the confessional. "Oh, that. There's nothing to tell. I caught Murphy trying to send a signal on it while he was confessing—can you imagine such a thing from a *priest,* Brian? Anyway, I think this is a call buzzer to the rectory. So I sent a few choice words, the likes of which they've never heard in the good fathers' dormitory." He laughed.

Flynn forced a smile in return, but Hickey's explanation raised more questions than it answered. *Hickey sent last message* . . . Who sent the previous message or messages? He said, "You should have kept me informed."

"Ah, Brian, the burdens of command are so heavy that you can't be bothered with every small detail."

"Just the same—" He looked at Hickey's chalk-white face and saw the genial twinkle in his eyes turn to a steady burning stare of unmistakable meaning. He imagined he even heard a voice: *Don't go any further.* He turned away.

Hickey smiled and tapped his watch. "Time to go give them hell, lad."

Flynn made no move toward the elevator. He knew he had reached a turning point in his relationship with John Hickey. A tremor passed down his spine, and a sense of fear came over him unlike any normal fear he had ever felt. *What have I unleashed?*

Hickey turned into the archway beside the confessional, passing into the hallway of the bride's room. He stopped in front of the oak elevator door and turned off the alarm. Slowly he began to deactivate the mine.

Flynn came up behind him.

Hickey neutralized the mine. "There we are. . . . I'll set it again after you've gone down." He opened the oak door, revealing the sliding doors of the elevator.

Flynn moved closer.

Hickey said, "When you come back, knock on the oak door. Three long, two short. I'll know it's you, and I'll defuse the mine again." He looked up at Flynn. "Good luck."

Flynn stepped closer and stared at the gray elevator doors, then at the mine hanging from the half-opened oak door. *I'll know it's you, and I'll defuse the mine. . . .* He looked into Hickey's eyes and said, "I've got a better idea."

Inspector Langley and Roberta Spiegel waited in the brightly lit hallway of the subbasement. With them were Emergency Service police and three intelligence officers. Langley checked his watch. Past ten. He put his ear to the elevator doors. He heard nothing and straightened up.

Roberta Spiegel said, "This bastard has all three networks and every local station waiting for him. Mussolini complex—keep them waiting until they're delirious with anticipation."

Langley nodded, realizing that was exactly how he felt waiting for Brian Flynn to step out of the gray doors.

Suddenly the noise of the elevator motor broke into the stillness of the corridor. The elevator grew louder as it descended from the hallway of the bride's room into the subbasement. The doors began to slide open.

Langley, the three ID men, and the police unconsciously straightened their postures. Roberta Spiegel put her hand to her hair. She felt her heart in her chest.

The door opened, revealing not Brian Flynn but John Hickey. He stepped into the hall and smiled. "Finn MacCumail, Chief of the Fenians, sends his respects and regrets." Hickey looked around, then continued. "My chief is a suspicious man—which is why he's stayed alive so long. He had, I believe, a premonition about exposing himself to the dangers inherent in such a situation." He looked at Langley. "He is a thoughtful man who didn't want to place such temptation in front of you—or your British allies. So he sent me, his loyal lieutenant."

Langley found it hard to believe that Flynn was afraid of a trap—not with four hostages to guarantee his safety. Langley said, "You're John Hickey, of course."

Hickey bowed formally. "No objections, I trust."

Langley shrugged. "It's your show."

Hickey smiled. "So it is. And to whom do I have the pleasure of speaking?"

"Inspector Langley."

"Ah, yes. . . . And the lady?" He looked at Spiegel.

Spiegel said, "My name is Roberta Spiegel. I'm with the Mayor's office."

Hickey bowed again and took her hand. "Yes. I heard you on the radio once. You're much more beautiful than I pictured you from your voice." He made a gesture of apology. "Please don't take that the wrong way."

Spiegel withdrew her hand and stood silent. She had the unfamiliar experience of being at a loss for a reply.

Langley said, "Let's go."

Hickey ignored him and called down the corridor, "And these gentlemen?" He walked up to a tall ESD man and read his name tag. "Gilhooly." He took the man's hand and pumped it. "I love the melody of the Gaelic names with the softer sounds. I knew Gilhoolys in Tullamore."

The patrolman looked uncomfortable. Hickey walked up and down the hallway shaking each man's hand and calling him by name.

Langley exchanged looks with Spiegel. Langley whispered, "He makes Mussolini look like a tongue-tied schoolboy."

Hickey shook the hand of the last man, a big flakjacketed ESD man with a shotgun. "God be with you tonight, lad. I hope our next meeting is under happier circumstances."

Langley said impatiently, "Can we go now?"

Hickey said, "Lead on, Inspector." He fell into step with Langley and Spiegel. The three ID men followed. Hickey said, "You should have introduced those men to me. You ignored them—ignored their humanity. How can you get people to follow you if you treat them like jackstraws?"

Langley wasn't quite sure what a jackstraw was, and in any case chose not to answer.

Hickey went on. "In ancient days combatants would salute each other before battle. And a man about to be executed would shake his executioner's hand or even bless him to show mutual respect and compassion. It's time we put war and death on a personal basis again."

Langley stopped at a modern wooden door. "Right." He looked at Hickey. "This is the press room."

Hickey said, "Never been on television before. Do I need makeup?"

Langley motioned to the three ID men, then said to Hickey, "Before I take you in there, I have to ask you if you're armed."

"No. Are you?"

Langley nodded to one of the men who produced a metal detector and waved the wand over Hickey's body.

Hickey said, "You may find that British bullet I've been carrying in my hip since '21."

The metal detector didn't sound, and Langley reached out and pushed open the door. Hickey entered the room, and the sounds of conversation died abruptly. The press conference area below the sacristy was a long, light-paneled room with an acoustical tile ceiling. Several card tables were grouped around a long central conference table. Camera and light connections hung from trapdoors in the ceiling. Hickey looked slowly around the room and examined the faces of the people looking at him.

A reporter, David Roth, who had been elected the spokesman, rose and introduced himself. He indicated a chair at the head of the long table.

Hickey sat.

Roth said, "Are you Brian Flynn, the man who calls himself Finn Mac-Cumail?"

Hickey leaned back and made himself comfortable. "No, I'm John Hickey, the man who calls himself John Hickey. You've heard of me, of course, and before I'm through you'll know me well enough." He looked around the table. "Please introduce yourselves in turn."

Roth looked a bit surprised, then introduced himself again and pointed to a reporter. Each man and woman in the press room, including, at Hickey's request, the technicians, gave his name.

Hickey nodded pleasantly to each one. He said, "I'm sorry I kept you all waiting. I hope my delay didn't cause the representatives of the governments involved to leave."

Roth said, "They won't be present."

Hickey feigned an expression of hurt and disappointment. "Oh, I see. . . . Well, I suppose they don't want to be seen in public with a man like me." He smiled brightly. "Actually, I don't want to be associated with them either." He laughed, then produced his pipe and lit it. "Well, let's get on with it, then."

Roth motioned to a technician, and the lights went on. Another technician took a light reading near Hickey's face while a woman approached him with makeup. Hickey pushed her away gently, and she moved off quickly.

Roth said, "Is there any particular format you'd like us to follow?"

"Yes. I talk and you listen. If you listen without nodding off or picking your noses, I'll answer questions afterward."

A few reporters laughed.

The technicians finished the adjustments in their equipment, and one of them yelled, "Mr. Hickey, can you say something so we can get a voice reading?"

"Voice reading? All right, I'll sing you a verse from 'Men Behind the Wire,' and when I'm through, I want the cameras on. I'm a busy man tonight." He began to sing in a low, croaky voice.

> "Through the little streets of Belfast
> In the dark of early morn,
> British soldiers came marauding
> Wrecking little homes with scorn.
> Heedless of the crying children,
> Dragging fathers from their beds,
> Beating sons while helpless mothers
> Watch the blood flow from their heads—"

"Thank you, Mr. Hickey—"
Hickey sang the chorus—

> "Armored cars, and tanks and guns
> Came to take away our sons
> But every man will stand behind
> The men behind the wii-re!"

"Thank you, sir."
The camera light came on. Someone yelled, "On the air!"
Roth looked into the camera and spoke. "Good evening. This is David—"
Hickey's singing came from off camera:

> "Not for them a judge or jury,
> Or indeed a crime at all.

> Being Irish means they're guilty,
> So we're guilty one and a-lll—"

Roth looked to his right. "Thank you—"

> "Round the world the truth will echo,
> Cromwell's men are here again.
> England's name again is sullied
> In the eyes of honest me-nnn—"

Roth glanced sideways at Hickey, who seemed to have finished. Roth looked back at the camera. "Good evening, I'm David Roth, and we're broadcasting live . . . as you can see . . . from the press room of Saint Patrick's Cathedral. Not too far from where we now sit, an undisclosed number of IRA gunmen—"

"Fenians!" yelled Hickey.

"Yes . . . Fenians . . . have seized the Cathedral and hold four hostages: Cardinal—"

"They know all that!" shouted Hickey.

Roth looked upset. "Yes . . . and with us tonight is Mr. John Hickey, one of the . . . Fenians. . . ."

"Put the camera on me, Jerry," said Hickey. "Over here—that's right."

Hickey smiled into the camera and began, "Good evening and Happy Saint Patrick's Day. I am John Hickey, poet, scholar, soldier, and patriot." He settled back into his chair. "I was born in 1905 or thereabouts to Thomas and Mary Hickey in a small stone cottage outside of Clonakily in County Cork. In 1916, when I was a wee lad, I served my country as a messenger in the Irish Republican Army. Easter Monday, 1916, found me in the besieged General Post Office in Dublin with the poet Padraic Pearse, the labor leader James Connolly, and their men, including my sainted father, Thomas. Surrounding us were the Irish Fusiliers and the Irish Rifles, lackeys of the British Army."

Hickey relit his pipe, taking his time, then went on. "Padraic Pearse read a proclamation from the steps of the Post Office, and his words ring in my ears to this day." He cleared his throat and adopted a stentorian tone as he quoted: " 'Irishmen and Irishwomen—in the name of God and the dead generations from which she receives her old tradition of nationhood, Ireland, through us, summons her children to her flag and strikes for freedom.' "

Hickey went on, weaving a narrative blend of history and fancy, facts and personal prejudices, interjecting himself into some of the more famous events of the decades following the Easter Monday rebellion.

Most of the reporters leaned forward in interest; some looked impatient or puzzled.

Hickey was serenely unaware of them or of the cameras and lights. From time to time he would mention the Cathedral to keep everyone's interest piqued, then would swing into a long polemic against the British and American governments or the governments of the divided Ireland, always careful to exclude the people of these lands from his wrath.

He spoke of his sufferings, his wounds, his martyred father, his dead friends, a lost love, recalling each person by name. He beamed as he spoke of his revolutionary triumphs and frowned as he spoke darkly of the future of an Ireland divided. Finally he yawned and asked for a glass of water.

Roth took the opportunity to ask, "Can you tell us exactly how you seized the

Cathedral? What are your demands? Would you kill the hostages and destroy the Cathedral if—"

Hickey held up his hand. "I'm not up to that part yet, lad. Where was I? Oh, yes. Nineteen hundred and fifty-six. In that year the IRA, operating from the south, began a campaign against the British-occupied six counties of the North. I was leading a platoon of men and women near the Doon Forest, and we were ambushed by a whole regiment of British paratroopers backed by the murderous Royal Ulster Constabulary." Hickey went on.

Langley watched him from the corner, then looked around at the news people. They seemed unhappy, but he suspected that John Hickey was doing better with the public than with the media. Hickey had a hard-driving narrative style . . . a simplicity and almost crudeness—sweating, smoking, and scratching— not seen on television in a long time.

John Hickey—sitting now in fifty million American living rooms—was becoming a folk hero. Langley would not have been surprised if someone told him that outside on Madison Avenue vendors were hawking John Hickey T-shirts.

44

Brian Flynn stood near the altar and watched the television that had been placed on the altar.

Maureen, Father Murphy, and Baxter sat in the clergy pews, watching and listening silently. The Cardinal sat nearly immobile, staring down at the television from his throne, his fingertips pressed together.

Flynn stood in silence for a long while, then spoke to no one in particular. "Long-winded old man, isn't he?"

Maureen looked at him, then asked, "Why didn't you go yourself, Brian?"

Flynn stared at her but said nothing.

She leaned toward Father Murphy and said, "Actually, Hickey seems an effective speaker." She paused thoughtfully. "I wish there were a way to get this kind of public platform without doing what they've done."

Murphy added as he watched the screen, "He's at least venting the frustrations of so many Irishmen, isn't he?"

Baxter glanced at them sharply. "He's not venting anyone's frustrations— he's inflaming some long-cooled passions. And I think he's embellishing and distorting it a bit, don't you?" No one answered, and he went on. "For instance —if he'd been ambushed by a regiment of British paras, he wouldn't be here to talk about it—"

Maureen said, "That's not the point—"

Flynn overheard the exchange and looked at Baxter. "Harry, your chauvinism is showing. Hail Britannia! Britannia rules the Irish. Ireland—first outpost of Empire and destined to be the last."

Baxter said to Flynn, "The man's a bloody demagogue and charlatan."

Flynn laughed. "No, he's *Irish*. Among ourselves we sometimes tolerate a poetic rearrangement of facts mutually understood. But listen to the man, Harry—you might learn a thing or two."

Baxter looked at the people around him—Maureen, Murphy, Flynn, the Fenians . . . even the Cardinal. For the first time he understood how little he understood.

Megan Fitzgerald walked up to the sanctuary and stared at the television screen.

Hickey, in the tradition of the ancient seanachies, interrupted his narrative to break into song:

"Then, here's to the brave men of Ireland.
At home or in exile away;
And, here's to the hopes of our sire land,
That never will rust or decay.
To every brave down-trodden nation,
Here's liberty, glorious and bright. But,
Oh! Let our country's salvation,
Be toasted the warmest, to-niiight!"

Megan said, "Bloody old fool. He's making a laughingstock of us ranting like that." She turned to Flynn. "Why the hell did you send him?"

Flynn looked at her and said softly, "Let the old man have his day, Megan. He deserves this after nearly seventy years of war. He may be the world's oldest continuously fighting soldier." He smiled in a conciliatory manner. "He's got a lot to tell."

Megan's voice was impatient. "He's supposed to tell them that the British are the only obstacle to a negotiated settlement here. I've a brother rotting in Long Kesh, and I want him free in Dublin come morning."

Maureen looked up at her. "And I thought you were here only because of Brian."

Megan wheeled around. "Shut your damned mouth!"

Maureen stood, but Father Murphy pulled her quickly into the pew.

Flynn said nothing, and Megan turned and strode off.

Hickey's voice blared from the television. The Cardinal sat motionless staring at some point in space. Baxter looked away from everyone and tried to filter out Hickey's voice, concentrating on the escape plan. Father Murphy and Maureen watched the screen intently. Flynn watched also, but his thoughts, like Baxter's, were elsewhere.

John Hickey took out a flask and poured a dark liquid into his water glass, then looked up at the camera. "Excuse me. Heart medicine." He drained off the glass and let out a sigh. "That's better. Now, where was I? Right—1973—" He waved his arms. "Oh, enough of this. Listen to me, all of you! We don't want to hurt anyone in this Cathedral. We don't want to harm a Prince of the Roman Church—a holy man—a good man—or his priest, Father Murphy . . . a lovely man. . . ." He leaned forward and clasped his hands together. "We don't want to harm one single altar or statue in this beautiful house of God that New Yorkers—Americans—love so dearly. We're not barbarians or pagans, you know."

He held his hands out in an imploring gesture. "Now listen to me. . . ." His voice became choked, and tears formed in his eyes. "All we want is another chance for the young lives being wasted in British concentration camps. We're not asking for the impossible—we're not making any irresponsible demands. No, we're only asking—begging—begging in the name of God and humanity for the release of Ireland's sons and daughters from the darkness and degradation of these unspeakable dungeons."

He took a drink of water and stared into the camera. "And who is it who have hardened their hearts against us?" He thumped the table. "Who is it who'll not let our people go?" *Thump!* "Who is it that by their unyielding policy endangers the lives of the people in this great Cathedral?" He pounded the table with both fists. "The bloody fucking British—*that's* who!"

Burke leaned against the wall in the Monsignor's office and watched the screen. Schroeder sat at his desk, and Spiegel had returned to her rocker. Bellini paced in front of the screen, blocking everyone's view, but no one objected.

Burke moved to the twin doors, opened them, and looked into the outer office. The State Department security man, Arnold Sheridan, stood by the window in deep thought. Occasionally he would eye the British and Irish representatives. Burke had the impression that Sheridan was going to give them the unpleasant news from Washington that Hickey was scoring heavily and it was time to talk. An awkward, almost embarrassed silence lay over the office as Hickey's monologue rolled on. Burke was reminded of a living room he had sat in once where the adolescents and adults had somehow gotten themselves involved in watching an explicit documentary on teen-age sex. Burke turned back to the inner office and stared at the screen.

Hickey's voice was choked with emotion. "Many of you may question the propriety of our occupation of a house of God, and it was, I assure you, the hardest decision any of us has ever made in our lives. But we didn't so much *seize* the Cathedral as we took *refuge* in it—claimed the ancient privilege of *sanctuary*. And what better place to stand and ask for God's help?"

, He paused as though wrestling with a decision, then said softly, "This afternoon, many Americans for the first time saw the obscene face of religious bigotry as practiced by the Orangemen of Ulster. Right here in the streets of the most ecumenical city in the world, the ugliness of religious intolerance and persecution was made unmistakably clear. The songs you heard those bigots sing were the songs the little children are taught in homes, schools, and churches. . . ." He straightened his posture; on his face was a distasteful look that melted into an old man's sadness. He shook his head slowly.

Schroeder turned away from the screen and said to Burke, "What's the latest with those Orangemen?"

Burke kept staring at the screen as he spoke. "They still say they're Protestant loyalists from Ulster, and they'll probably keep saying that until at least dawn. But according to our interrogators they all sound like Boston Irish. Probably IRA Provos recruited for the occasion." Given all the externals of this affair, Burke thought, psychological timing, media coverage, tactical preparations, political maneuverings, and last-ditch intelligence gathering—it was clear that Flynn would not extend the deadline and risk the tide turning against him.

Spiegel said, "It was a tactical blunder to let Hickey on television."

Schroeder said defensively, "What else could I do?"

Bellini interjected, "Why don't I grab him—then we'll use him to negotiate for the hostages."

Schroeder said, "Good idea. Why don't you go cold-cock him right now before they break for a commercial?"

Burke looked at his watch. 10:25 P.M. The night was slipping away so fast that it would be dawn before anyone realized it was too late.

* * *

Hickey looked around the press room. He noticed that Langley had disappeared. Hickey leaned forward and spoke to the cameraman. "Zoom in, Jerry." He watched the monitor. "Closer. That's it. Hold it." He stared at the camera and spoke in low tones that had the suggestion of finality and doom. "Ladies and gentlemen of America—and all the unborn generations who will one day hear my words—we are outnumbered two thousand to one by police and soldiers, besieged and isolated by our enemies, betrayed by politicians and diplomats, compromised and undermined by secret agents, and censured by the world press. . . ." He placed his hand over his chest. "But we are not afraid, because we know that out there are friends who wish us success and Godspeed in our mission. And there are the men and women, old and young, in Long Kesh, Armagh, Crumlin Road—all the hellholes of England and Northern Ireland—who are on their knees tonight, praying for their freedom. Tomorrow, God willing, the gates of Long Kesh will be thrown open, and wives will embrace husbands, children will weep with parents, brothers and sisters will meet once more. . . ."

The tears were running freely again, and he took out a big bandanna and blew his nose, then continued, "If we accomplish nothing else this night, we'll have made the world aware of their existence. And if we die, and others die with us, and if this great Cathedral where I sit right now is a smoldering ruin by morning, then it will only be because men and women of goodwill could not prevail against the repressive forces of darkness and inhumanity." He took a long breath and cleared his throat. "Till we meet again in a happier place . . . God bless you all. God bless America and Ireland and, yes, God bless our enemies, and may He show them the light. *Erin go bragh.*"

David Roth cleared his throat and said, "Mr. Hickey, we'd like you to answer a few specific questions. . . ."

Hickey stood abruptly, blew his nose into the bandanna, and walked off camera.

Inspector Langley had returned; he opened the door, and Hickey moved quickly into the hall, followed by Langley and the three ID men. Langley came up beside Hickey and said, "I see you know when to quit."

Hickey put away his bandanna. "Oh, I couldn't go on any longer, lad."

"Yeah. Listen, you got your message across. You're way ahead. Now why don't you come out of there and give everyone a break?"

Hickey stopped in front of the elevator. His manner and voice suddenly became less teary. "Why the hell should we?"

Langley dismissed the three ID men. He took a notebook from his pocket and glanced at it. "Okay, Mr. Hickey, listen closely. I've just been authorized by representatives of the British and American governments to tell you that if you come out of the Cathedral now, the British will begin procedures to release— quietly and at intervals—most of the people on your list, subject to conditions of parole—"

"*Most?* What kind of *intervals?* What kind of *parole?*"

Langley looked up from the notebook. "I don't know anything more than I'm telling you. I just got this over the phone. I'm only a cop, okay? And we're the only ones allowed to speak to you people. Right? So this is a little difficult but just listen and—"

"Pimp."

Langley looked up quickly. "What?"

"Pimp. You're pimping for the diplomats who don't want to make a direct proposition to us whores."

Langley flushed. "Look . . . look you—"

"Get hold of yourself, man. Steady."

Langley took a breath and continued in a controlled voice. "The British can't release all of them at once—not when you've got a gun to their heads—to everyone's heads. But it *will* be done. And also the State and U.S. Attorney General have agreed to allow all of you in there to post a low bond and go free awaiting trial—you understand what that means?"

"No, I don't."

Langley looked annoyed. "It means you can skip out on the fucking bail and get the hell out of the country."

"Oh . . . sounds dishonest."

Langley ignored the remark and said, "No one has been killed yet—that's the main thing. That gives us a lot of leeway in dealing with you—"

"It makes that much difference, does it? We've committed a dozen felonies already, terrified half the city, made fools of you, caused a riot, cost you millions of dollars, ruined your parade, and the Commissioner of Police has dropped dead of a heart attack. But you're willing to let bygones be bygones—give us a wink and run us off like Officer Muldoon stumbling onto a crap game in an alley—as long as no one's been killed. Interesting. That says a great deal about this society."

Langley drew another breath and said, "I won't make this offer again—for obvious reasons, no one will ever mention it over the telephone. So that's it." He slapped the notebook shut. "It's a fair compromise. Take it or leave it."

Hickey pressed the elevator button, and the doors opened. He said to Langley, "We wouldn't look very good if we compromised, would we? You'd look good, though. Schroeder would be booked solid on TV for a year. But we'd not have access to the airwaves so easily. All anyone would see or remember is us coming out the front doors of Saint Patrick's with our hands up. We'd do that gladly if the camps were emptied *first.* Then there's no way anyone could hide or steal our victory with diplomatic or journalistic babble."

"You'd be *alive,* for Christ's sake."

"Did you get my grave dug up yet?"

"Don't pull that spooky shit on me."

Hickey laughed.

Langley spoke mechanically, determined to deliver the last lines he had been instructed to say. "Use your power of persuasion with the people in there and your influence as a great Irish Republican leader. Don't tarnish with senseless death and destruction what you've already accomplished." He added his own thoughts. "You snowed about half of America tonight. Quit while you're ahead."

"I had a horse at Aqueduct this afternoon that quit while he was ahead. . . . But I'll pass your kind offer on to Mr. Flynn and the Fenians, and we'll let you know. If we never mention it, then you can assume we are holding fast to all our demands."

Hickey stepped into the elevator. "See you later, God willing." He pushed the button, and as the doors slid closed he called out, "Hold my fan mail for me, Inspector."

45

B rian Flynn stood opposite the elevator's oak door, an M-16 rifle leveled at it. George Sullivan stood to the side of the door, listening. The elevator stopped, and Sullivan heard a soft rapping, three long and two short. He signaled in return, then defused the mine and opened the door.

John Hickey stepped out. Flynn lowered the rifle a half second too slowly, but no one seemed to notice.

Sullivan extended his hand. "Damned fine, John. You had me laughing and weeping at the same time."

Hickey smiled as he took Sullivan's hand. "Ah, my boy, it was a dream come true." He turned to Flynn. "You would have done even better, lad."

Flynn turned and walked into the ambulatory. Hickey followed. Flynn said as he walked, "Did anyone approach you?"

Hickey walked ahead to the chancel organ. "One fellow, that Inspector Langley. Gave us a chance to surrender. Promised us a low bail—that sort of thing."

"Did the British relay any information—any indication they would compromise?"

"The British? Compromise? They're not even *negotiating.*" He sat at the keyboard and turned on the organ.

"They didn't get word to you through anyone?"

"You'll not hear from them." He looked at Flynn. "You've got to play the bells now, Brian, while we still have everyone's attention. We'll begin with—let's see—'Danny Boy' and then do a few Irish-American favorites for our constituency. I'll lead, and you follow my tempo. Go on now."

Flynn hesitated, then moved toward the center aisle. Hickey began playing "Danny Boy" in a slow, measured meter that would set the tempo for the bells.

The four hostages watched Flynn and Hickey, then turned back to the television. The reporters in the Cathedral press room were discussing Hickey's speech. Baxter said, "I don't see that we're any closer to being let out of here."

Father Murphy replied, "I wonder . . . don't you think after this, the British . . . I mean . . ."

Baxter said sharply, "No, I don't." He looked at his watch. "Thirty minutes and we go."

Maureen looked at him, then at Father Murphy. She said, "What Mr. Baxter means is that he, too, thinks they were probably considering a compromise after Hickey's speech, but Mr. Baxter's decided that he doesn't want to be the cause of any compromise."

Baxter's face reddened.

Maureen continued. "It's all right, you know. I feel the same way. I'm not going to be used by them like a slab of meat to be bartered for what they want." She said in a quieter voice, "I've been used by them long enough."

Murphy looked at them. "Well . . . that's fine for you two, but I can't go unless my life is in actual danger. Neither can His Eminence." He inclined his head toward the Cardinal, who sat looking at them from his throne. Murphy added, "I think we all ought to wait. . . ."

Maureen looked back at the Cardinal and saw by his face that he was struggling with the same question. She turned to Father Murphy. "Even if Hickey's speech has moved the people out there toward a compromise, that doesn't move *Hickey* toward a compromise—does it?" She leaned forward. "He's a treacherous man. If you still believe he's evil and means to destroy us, destroy himself, the Fenians, and this church, then we *must* try to get out of here." She fixed her eyes on Murphy's. "Do you believe that?"

Murphy looked at the television screen. A segment of John Hickey's speech was being replayed. The volume was turned low, and Hickey's voice wasn't audible over the organ. Murphy watched the mouth moving, the tears rolling down his face. He looked into the narrow eyes. Without the spellbinding voice the eyes gave him away.

Father Murphy looked out over the sanctuary rail at Hickey playing the organ. Hickey's head was turned toward them as he watched himself on television. He was smiling at his image, then turned and smiled, a grotesque smile, at Father Murphy. The priest turned quickly back to Maureen and nodded.

Baxter looked up at the Cardinal's throne; the Cardinal bowed his head in return. Baxter glanced at his watch. "We go in twenty-seven minutes."

Flynn rode the elevator to the choir practice room, then stepped out into the loft. He walked up behind Leary, who was leaning over the parapet watching the hostages through his scope. Flynn said, "Anything?"

Leary continued to observe the four people on the sanctuary. At some point years ago he had realized that not only could he anticipate people's movements and read their expression, but he could also read their lips. He said, "A few words. Not too clear. Hard to see their lips." The hostages had reached a point in their relationships to each other where they communicated with fewer words, but their body language was becoming clearer to him.

Flynn said, "Well, are they or aren't they?"

"Yes."

"How? When?"

"Don't know. Soon."

Flynn nodded. "Warning shots first, then go for the legs. Understand?"

"Sure."

Flynn picked up the field phone on the parapet and called Mullins in the bell tower. "Donald, get away from the bells."

Mullins slung his rifle and pulled a pair of shooters' baffles over his ears. He snatched up the field phone and quickly descended the ladder to the lower level.

Flynn moved to a small keyboard beside the organ console and turned the switch to activate the nineteen keys that played the bells. He stood before the waist-high keyboard and turned the pages of bell music on the music desk, then put his hands over the big keys and joined with the chancel organ below.

The biggest bell, the one named Patrick, chimed a thunderous B-flat, and the sound crashed through the bell tower, almost knocking Mullins off his feet.

One by one the nineteen huge bells began tolling in their carillon, beginning at the first bell room where Mullins had been and running upward to a point near the top of the spire twenty-one stories above the street.

In the attic a coffee cup fell off a catwalk rail. Arthur Nulty and Jean Kearney covered their ears and moved to the Madison Avenue end of the Cathedral. In the choir loft and triforia the bells resonated through the stonework and reverberated in the floors. In the south tower Rory Devane listened to the steady chiming coming from the opposite tower. He watched as the activity on the rooftops slowed and the movement in the streets came to a halt. In the cold winter air the slow rhythmical sounds of "Danny Boy" pealed through the dark canyons of Manhattan.

The crowds around the police barricades began cheering, raising bottles and glasses, then singing. More people began moving outdoors into the avenues and side streets.

Television coverage shifted abruptly from the press room of the Cathedral to the roofs of Rockefeller Center.

In bars and homes all over New York, and all over the country, pictures of the Cathedral as seen from Rockefeller Center flashed across the screens, bathed in stark blue lighting. A camera zoomed in on the green and gold harp flag that Mullins had draped from the torn louvers.

The sound of the bells was magnified by television audio equipment and transmitted with the picture from one end of the continent to the other. Satellite relays picked up the signal and beamed it over the world.

Rory Devane slipped a flare into a Very pistol, pointed it up through the louvers, and fired. The projectile arched upward, burst into green light, then floated on a parachute, swinging like a pendulum in the breeze, casting an unearthly green radiance across the buildings and through the streets. Devane went to the eastward-facing louvers and fired again.

Remote cameras located in the streets, bars, and restaurants began sending pictures of men and women singing, cheering, crying. A kaleidoscope of images flashed across video screens—bars, street crowds, the green-lit sky, closeups of tight-lipped police, the bell tower, long shots of the Cathedral.

The flares suddenly changed from the illumination type to signal flares, star bursts, red, white, blue, then the green, orange, and white of the Irish tricolor. The crowd reacted appropriately. All the while the rich, lilting melody of "Danny Boy" filled the air from the bell tower and filled the airwaves from televisions and portable radios.

> "O Danny Boy, the pipes, the pipes are calling
> From glen to glen, and down the mountain side,
> The summer's gone, and all the roses falling,
> 'Tis you, 'tis you, must go and I must bide. . . ."

Finally, on each station, reporters after an uncommonly long period of silence began adding commentary to the scenes, which needed none.

In the sanctuary the hostages watched the television in fascinated silence. Hickey played the organ with intense concentration, leading Flynn on the bells. Both men glanced at each other from time to time across the hundred yards that separated them.

Hickey swung into "Danny Boy" for the third time, not wanting to break the spell that the bittersweet song had laid over the collective psyche of the Cathedral and the city. He laughed as tears rolled down his furrowed cheeks.

In the Cardinal's residence and in the rectory the only sound was the pealing of the bells rolling across the courtyard and resonating from a dozen television sets into rooms filled with people.

Burke stood in the Monsignor's inner office, where the original Desperate Dozen had reassembled along with some additional members whom Burke had labeled the Anguished Auxiliaries.

Schroeder stood to the side with Langley and Roberta Spiegel, who, Burke noticed, was becoming Langley's constant companion.

Langley stared at the screen and said, "If they'd had television on V-J day, this is what it would have looked like."

Burke smiled in spite of himself. "Good timing. Good theater . . . fireworks . . . really hokey, but Christ, it gets them every time."

Spiegel added, "And talk about your psychological disadvantages."

Major Martin stood in the rear of the room between Kruger and Hogan. He kept his head and eyes straight ahead and said in an undertone, "We've always underestimated the willingness of the Irish to make public spectacles of themselves. Why don't they suffer in silence like civilized people?"

The two agents looked at each other behind Martin's back but said nothing.

Martin glanced to either side. He knew he was in trouble. He spoke with a light tone in his voice. "Well, I suppose I've got to undo this—or perhaps in their typical Irish fashion they'll undo themselves if—Oh, sorry, Hogan. . . ."

Douglas Hogan moved away from Martin.

Monsignor Downes found his diary buried under Schroeder's paperwork and drew it toward him, opening it to March 17.

He wrote, *10:35 P.M. The bells tolled tonight, as they've tolled in the past to mark the celebration of the holy days, the ends of wars, and the deaths of presidents.* He paused, then added, *They tolled for perhaps the last time. And people, I think, sensed this, and they listened and they sang. In the morning, God willing, the carillon will ring out a glorious Te Deum—or if it is God's will, they will ring no more.* Monsignor Downes put aside his pen and closed the diary.

Donald Mullins swung his rifle butt and smashed a hole in the thick, opaque glass of the lower section of the tower. He knocked out a dozen observation holes, the noise of the breaking glass inaudible through his shooters' baffles and the chiming of the bells. Mullins slung his rifle and took a deep breath, then approached a broken window in the east side of the tower room and stared out into the cold night.

He saw that Devane was alternating star bursts with parachute flares, and the clearing night sky was lit with colors under a bright blue moon. The anxiety and despair he had felt all evening suddenly vanished in the clarity of the night, and he felt confident about meeting his death here.

46

Harold Baxter didn't consult his watch. He knew it was time. In fact, he thought, they should have gone sooner, before the bells and the fireworks, before Hickey's speech, before the Fenians had transformed themselves from terrorists to freedom fighters.

He took a long last look around the Cathedral, then glanced at the television screen. A view from the tallest building of Rockefeller Center showed the cross-shape of the blue-lit Cathedral. In the upper left corner sat the rectory; in the right corner, the Cardinal's residence. Within five minutes he would be sitting in either place, taking tea and telling his story. He hoped Maureen, the priest, and the Cardinal would be with him. But even if one or all of them were killed, it would be a victory because that would be the end of the Fenians.

Baxter rose from the pew and stretched nonchalantly. His legs were shaking and his heart was pounding.

Father Murphy rose and walked across the sanctuary. He exchanged quiet words with the Cardinal, then moved casually behind the altar and looked down the staircase.

Pedar Fitzgerald sat with his back to the crypt door, the Thompson pointed down the stairs toward the sacristy gate. He was singing to himself.

Father Murphy raised his voice over the organ. "Mr. Fitzgerald."

Fitzgerald looked up quickly. "What is it, Father?"

Murphy felt a dryness in his throat. He looked across the stairwell for Baxter but didn't see him. He said, "I'm . . . I'm hearing confessions now. Someone will relieve you if you want to—"

"I've nothing to confess. Please leave."

Baxter steadied his legs, took a deep breath and moved. He covered the distance to the right side of the altar in three long strides and bounded down the steps in two leaps, unheard over the noise of the organ. Maureen was directly behind him.

Father Murphy saw them suddenly appear on the opposite stairs and made the sign of the cross over Fitzgerald.

Fitzgerald sensed the danger and spun around. He stared at Baxter flying toward him and raised his submachine gun.

Father Murphy heard a shot ring out from the choir loft and dived down the stairs; he looked over his shoulder for the Cardinal but knew he wasn't coming.

Leary got off a single shot, but his targets were gone in less time than it took him to steady his aim from the recoil. Only the Cardinal was left, sitting immobile on his throne, a splash of scarlet against the white marble and green carnations. Leary saw Hickey climb across the organ and drop to the sanctuary beside the Cardinal's throne. The Cardinal stood, placing himself in Hickey's path. Hickey's arm shot out and knocked the Cardinal to the floor. Leary placed the cross hairs over the Cardinal's supine body.

Flynn continued the song on the bells, not wanting to alert the people outside that something was wrong. He watched the sanctuary in the mirror. He called out, "That will be all, Mr. Leary."

Leary lowered his rifle.

Baxter flew down the stairs, and his foot shot out, hitting Fitzgerald full in the face. Fitzgerald staggered back, and Father Murphy grabbed his arm from behind. Baxter seized the submachine gun and pulled violently. Fitzgerald wrenched the gun back.

The sound of the chancel organ had died away, but the bells played on, and for a second they were the only sound in the Cathedral until the air was split by a burst of fire from the submachine gun. The muzzle flashed in Baxter's face, and he was momentarily blinded. Pieces of plaster fell from the vaulted ceiling above, crashing over the sacristy stairs.

Father Murphy yanked back on Fitzgerald's arm but couldn't break Fitzgerald's grip on the gun. Maureen ducked around Baxter and jabbed her fingers into Fitzgerald's eyes. Fitzgerald screamed, and Baxter found himself holding the heavy submachine gun. He brought the butt up in a vertical stroke but missed Fitzgerald's groin and solar plexus, hitting him a glancing blow across the chest.

Baxter swore, raised the butt again, and drove it horizontally into the young man's throat. Father Murphy released Fitzgerald, and he fell to the floor. Baxter stood over the fallen man and raised the gun butt over Fitzgerald's face.

Maureen shouted, "No!" She grabbed Baxter's arm.

Fitzgerald looked up at them, tears and blood running from his unfocused eyes. Blood gushed from his open mouth.

Brian Flynn watched Hickey and Megan moving across the sanctuary. Leary stood beside him, fingering his rifle and murmuring to himself. Flynn turned his attention back to the bells.

The four people in the triforia had barely taken in what had happened in the last fifteen seconds. They stared down into the altar sanctuary and saw the Cardinal lying sprawled on the floor and Hickey and Megan approaching the two stairwells cautiously.

Maureen held the Thompson, steadied herself, and pulled back on the trigger. A deafening burst of automatic fire flamed out of the muzzle and slammed into the padlock and chain.

Murphy and Baxter crouched as bullets ricocheted back, cracking into the marble stairs and walls. Baxter heard footsteps on the sanctuary floor. "They're coming."

Maureen fired a long second burst at the gate, then swung the gun up at the right-hand staircase, placed Hickey in her sight, and fired.

Hickey's body seemed to twitch, then he dropped back out of view.

Maureen swung the gun around to the left and pointed it at Megan, who had stopped short on the first step, a pistol in her hand. Maureen hesitated, and Megan dived to the side and disappeared.

Baxter and Murphy ran down the stairs and tore at the shattered chain and padlock. Hot, jagged metal cut into their hands, but the chain began dropping away in pieces, and the padlock fell to the floor.

Maureen backed down the stairs, keeping the muzzle of the gun pointed up at the crypt door.

Police officers in the side corridors were shouting into the empty sacristy.

Baxter yelled to them. "Hold your fire! We're coming out! Hold it!" He tore the last section of chain away and kicked violently at the gates. "Open! Open!"

Father Murphy was pulling frantically on the left-hand gate, shouting, "No! They *roll—!*"

Baxter lunged at the right gate and tried to slide it along its track into the wall, but both gates held fast.

Flak-jacketed police began edging out into the sacristy.

Maureen knelt on the bottom stair, keeping the gun trained on the landing above. She shouted, "What's wrong?"

Baxter answered, "Stuck! Stuck!"

Murphy suddenly released the gate and straightened up. He grabbed at a black metal box with a large keyhole located where the gates joined and shook it. "They've locked it! The keys—they have the keys—"

Maureen looked back at them over her shoulder. She saw that the gate had its own lock, and she hadn't hit it even once. Baxter shouted a warning, and she spun around. She saw Hickey standing in front of the crypt door, his legs straddling Pedar Fitzgerald's body. Maureen raised the gun.

Hickey called down. "You can shoot me if you'd like, but that won't get you out of here."

Maureen screamed at him. "Don't move! Hands up!"

Hickey raised his hands slowly. "There's really no way out, you know."

She shouted, "Throw me the gate key!"

He made an exaggerated shrug. "I think Brian has it." He added, "Try shooting the lock out. Or would you rather use the last few rounds on me?"

She swore at him, spun around, and faced the gates. She shouted to Baxter and Murphy. "Move back!" She saw the police in the sacristy. "Get away!"

The police scattered back into the corridors. She pointed the muzzle at the boxlike lock that joined the gates and fired a short burst at point-blank range. The bullets ripped into the lock, scattering sparks and pieces of hot metal.

Baxter and Murphy yelled out in pain as they were hit. A piece of metal grazed Maureen's leg, and she cried out. She fired again, one round, and the rotating drum of .45-caliber bullets clicked empty. Murphy and Baxter seized the bars of the gates and pulled. The gates held fast.

Maureen swung back to find Hickey halfway down the steps, a pistol in his hand. Hickey said, "You don't see that kind of craftsmanship today. Hands up, please."

Megan Fitzgerald knelt at the landing beside her brother. She looked down at Maureen, and their eyes met for a brief second.

Hickey's voice was impatient. "Hands on your heads! Now!"

Father Murphy, Baxter, and Maureen stood motionless.

Hickey called out to the police. "Stay in the corridors, or I'll shoot them all!" He shouted to the three people, "Let's go!"

They remained motionless.

Hickey pointed the pistol and fired.

The bullet whistled past Murphy's head, and he fell to the floor.

Maureen reversed the Thompson, grabbing its hot barrel in her hands, and brought it down savagely on the marble steps. The gunstock splintered and the drum flew off. She threw the mangled gun to the side, then stood erect and raised her arms.

Baxter did the same. Murphy stood and put his hands on his head.

Hickey looked at Maureen appreciatively. "Come on, then. Calm down. That's right. Best-laid plans and all that." He moved aside to let them pass.

Maureen stepped up to the landing and looked down at Pedar Fitzgerald. His throat was already beginning to swell, and she knew he would die unless he reached a hospital soon. She found herself cursing Baxter for botching it and injuring Fitzgerald so seriously, cursing Father Murphy for not remembering the gate's lock, cursing herself for not killing Hickey and Megan. She looked down at Megan, who was wiping the blood from her brother's mouth, but it kept flowing up from his crushed throat. Maureen said, "Sit him up or he'll drown."

Megan turned slowly and looked up at her. Her lips drew back across her teeth, and she sprang up and dug her nails into Maureen's neck, shrieking, snarling.

Baxter and Murphy rushed up the remaining stairs and pulled the two women apart. Hickey watched quietly as the struggle and the shouting subsided, then said, "All right. Everyone feel better? Megan, sit the lad up. He'll be all right." He poked the pistol at the three hostages. "Let's go."

They continued up to the sanctuary. Hickey chatted amiably as he followed. "Don't feel too badly. Damned bad luck, that's all. Maureen, you're a terrible shot. You didn't come within a yard of me."

She turned suddenly. "I hit you! I hit you!"

He laughed, put his finger to his chest, and drew it away with a small drop of pale, watery blood. "So you did."

The hostages moved toward the pews. The Cardinal was slumped in his throne, his face in his hands, and Maureen thought he was weeping, then saw the blood running through his fingers. Father Murphy made a move toward the Cardinal, but Hickey shoved him away.

Baxter looked up into the triforia and choir loft and saw the five rifles trained on them. He was vaguely aware that the bells were still pealing, and the phone beside the chancel organ was ringing steadily.

Hickey called up to Gallagher. "Frank, get down here quickly and take Pedar's place." He pushed Baxter into a pew and said, as though complaining to a close friend, "Damned dicey operation I've gotten myself in, Harry. Lose one man and there's no one to replace him."

Baxter looked him in the eyes. "In school I learned that IRA stood for I Ran Away. It's a wonder anyone's stayed here."

Hickey laughed. "Oh, Harry, Harry. After this place explodes and they find your pieces, I hope the morticians put your stiff upper lip where your asshole was and vice versa." Hickey shoved Maureen into the pew. "And you—breaking up that gun—Like an old Celt yourself you were, Maureen, smashing your sword against a rock before dying in battle. Magnificent. But you're becoming a bit of a nuisance." He looked at Murphy. "And *you,* running out on your boss like that. Shame—"

Murphy said, "Go to hell."

Hickey feigned a look of shock. "Well, will you listen to this . . . ?"

Murphy's hands shook, and he turned his back on Hickey.

Baxter stared at the television on the table. The scene had shifted back to the press room below. Reporters were speaking excitedly to their newsrooms. The gunfire, he knew, had undone the effects of Hickey's speech and the tolling bells. Baxter smiled and looked up at Hickey. He started to say something but suddenly felt an intense pain in his head and slumped forward out of the pew.

Hickey flexed his blackjack, turned, and grabbed Father Murphy by the lapel. He raised the leather blackjack and stared into the priest's eyes.

Gallagher had come out of the triforium door and ran toward the sanctuary. "No!"

Hickey looked at him, then lowered the blackjack. "Cuff them." He moved to the television and ripped the plug from the outlet.

Maureen knelt over Baxter's crumpled body and examined the wound on his forehead. "Bloody bastards—" She looked at the choir loft where Flynn played the bells. Gallagher took her wrist and locked on a handcuff, then locked the other end to Baxter's wrist. Gallagher cuffed Murphy's wrist and led him to the Cardinal. Gallagher knelt, then passed the cuff through the arm in the throne and gently placed the cuff over the Cardinal's blood-streaked wrist. Gallagher whispered, "I'll protect you." He bowed his head and walked away.

Father Murphy slumped down on the top step of the raised platform. The Cardinal came down from the throne and sat beside him. Neither man spoke.

Megan came out of the stairwell carrying her brother in her arms. She stood in the center of the sanctuary looking around blankly. A blood trail led from the stairwell to where she stood, and the trail became a small pool at her feet. Hickey took Pedar from his sister's arms and carried the limp body down to the chancel organ. He propped Pedar Fitzgerald against the organ console and covered him with his old overcoat.

Gallagher unslung his rifle and went down to the crypt landing. He shouted to the police who were cautiously examining the gate. "Get back! Go on!" They disappeared to the sides of the sacristy.

Megan remained standing in the pool of blood, staring at it. The only sounds in the Cathedral were the pealing bells and the persistently ringing telephone.

Brian Flynn watched from the choir loft as he tolled the bell. Leary glanced at Flynn curiously. Flynn turned away and concentrated on the keyboard, completing the last bar of "Danny Boy," then began "The Dying Rebel." He spoke into the microphone. "Mr. Sullivan, the pipes, please. Ladies and gentlemen, a song." He began singing. Hesitantly, other voices joined him, and Sullivan's pipes began skirling.

> "The night was dark and the battle ended.
> The moon shone down O'Connell Street.
> I stood alone where brave men parted,
> Never more again to speak."

John Hickey picked up the ringing telephone.

Schroeder's voice came over the line, very nearly out of control. "What happened? What *happened?*"

Hickey growled, "Shut up, Schroeder! The hostages are not dead. Your men saw it all. The hostages are cuffed now, and there'll be no more escape attempts. End of conversation."

"Wait! Listen, are they injured? Can I send a doctor?"

"They're in reasonably good shape. If you're interested, though, one of my lads has been hurt. Sir Harold Baxter, knight of the realm, bashed his throat in with a rifle. Not at all sporting."

"God . . . listen, I'll send a doctor—"

"We'll let you know if we want one." He looked down at Fitzgerald. His throat was grotesquely bloated now. "I need ice. Send it through the gates. And a tracheal tube."

"Please . . . let me send—"

"No!" Hickey rubbed his eyes and slumped forward. He felt very tired and wished it would all end sooner than he had hoped.

"Mr. Hickey . . ."

"Oh, shut up, Schroeder. Just shut up."

"May I speak to the hostages? Mr. Flynn said I could speak to them after the press—"

"They've lost the right to speak with anyone, including each other."

"How badly are they hurt?"

Hickey looked at the four battered people on the sanctuary. "They're damned lucky to be alive."

Schroeder said, "Don't lose what you've gained. Mr. Hickey, let me tell you, there are a lot of people on your side now. Your speech was . . . magnificent, grand. What you said about your suffering, the suffering of the Irish—"

Hickey laughed wearily. "Yes, a traditional Irish view of history, which is at times in conflict with the facts but never inhibited by them." He smiled and yawned. "But everyone bought it, did they? TV is marvelous."

"Yes, sir, and the bells—did you see the television?"

"What happened to those song requests?"

"Oh, I've got some here—"

"Shove them."

After a short silence Schroeder said, "Well, anyway, it was really incredible, you know—I've never seen anything like that in this city. Don't lose that, don't—"

"It's already lost. Good-bye, Schroeder."

"Wait! Hold it! One last thing. Mr. Flynn said you'd turn off the radio jammer—"

"Don't blame your radio problems on us. Buy better equipment."

"I'm just afraid that without radio control the police might overreact to some perceived danger—"

"So what?"

"That almost happened. So, I was wondering when you were going to shut it off—"

"It will probably shut off when the Cathedral explodes." He laughed.

"Come on now, Mr. Hickey . . . you sound tired. Why don't you all try to get some sleep? I'll guarantee you an hour—two hours' truce—and send some food, and—"

"Or more likely it'll be consumed by the flames from the attic. Forty long years in the building— Poof—it'll be gone in less than two hours."

"Sir . . . I'm offering you a truce—" Schroeder took another breath, then spoke in a cryptic tone. "A police inspector gave you a . . . a status report, I believe. . . ."

"Who? Oh, the tall fellow with the expensive suit. Watch that man, he's taking graft."

"Are you considering what he said to you?"

"As the Ulster Protestants are fond of saying, 'Not an inch!' Or would they now say centimeter? Inch. Yes, inch—"

"It's a fair solution to—"

"Unacceptable, Schroeder! Don't bother me with it again."

Schroeder said abruptly, "May I speak with Mr. Flynn?"

Hickey looked up at the loft. There was a telephone extension on the organ, but Flynn had not used it. Hickey said, "He's come to a difficult passage in the bells. Can't you hear it? Have a little consideration."

"We haven't heard from him in a long time. We expected him at the press conference. Is he . . . all right?"

Hickey found his pipe and lit it. "He's as well as any young man can be who is contemplating his imminent death, the sorrow of a lost love, the tragedy of a lost country, and a lost cause."

"*Nothing* is lost—"

"Schroeder, you understand Irish fatalism, don't you? When they start playing melancholy songs and weeping in their beers, it means they're on the verge of something reckless. And listening to your whimpering voice will not improve Brian Flynn's mood."

"No, listen, you're close—it's not lost—"

"Lost! Listen to the bells, Schroeder, and between their peals you'll hear the wail of the banshee in the hills, warning us all of approaching death." He hung up.

Megan was staring down at him from the sanctuary.

Hickey glanced at Pedar Fitzgerald. "He's dying, Megan."

She nodded hesitantly, and he looked at her. She seemed frightened suddenly, almost childlike. He said, "I can give him over to the police and he may live, but . . ."

She understood clearly that there would be no victory, no amnesty for them, or for the people in Northern Ireland, and that soon she and everyone in the Cathedral would be dead. She looked at her brother's blue-white face. "I want him here with me."

Hickey nodded. "Yes, that's the right thing, Megan."

Father Murphy shifted around on the throne platform. "He should be taken to a hospital."

Neither Megan nor Hickey answered.

Father Murphy went on, "Let me administer the sacrament—"

Hickey cut him off. "You've got a damned ritual for everything, don't you?"

"To save his soul from damnation—"

"People like you give eternal damnation a bad name." Hickey laughed. "I'll wager you carry some of that holy oil with you all the time. Never know when a good Catholic might drop dead at your feet."

"I carry holy oil, yes."

Hickey sneered. "Good. Later we'll fry an egg with it."

Father Murphy turned away. Megan walked toward Maureen and Baxter. Maureen watched her approach, keeping her eyes fixed steadily on Megan's.

Megan stood over the two cuffed people, then knelt beside Baxter's sprawled body and ripped the belt from his pants. She stood with her feet spread and brought the belt down with a whistling sound across Baxter's face.

Father Murphy and the Cardinal shouted at her.

Megan raised the belt again and brought it down on Maureen's upraised arms. She aimed the next blow at Baxter, but Maureen threw herself over his defenseless body and the belt lashed her across the neck.

Megan struck at Maureen's back, then struck again at her legs, then her buttocks.

The Cardinal looked away. Murphy was shouting at the top of his lungs.

Hickey began playing the chancel organ, joining with the bells. Frank Gallagher sat on the blood-smeared landing where Fitzgerald had lain and listened to the sounds of blows falling; then the sharp sounds were lost as the organ played "The Dying Rebel."

George Sullivan looked away from the sanctuary and played his bagpipe. Abby Boland and Eamon Farrell had stopped singing, but Flynn's voice called to them over the microphone, and they sang. Hickey sang, too, into the organ microphone.

> "The first I saw was a dying rebel.
> Kneeling low I heard him cry,
> God bless my home in Tipperary,
> God bless the cause for which I die."

In the attic Jean Kearney and Arthur Nulty lay on their sides, huddled together on the vibrating floor boards. They kissed, then moved closer. Jean Kearney rolled on her back, and Nulty covered her body with his.

Rory Devane stared out of the north tower, then fired the last flare. The crowds below were still singing, and he sang, too, because it made him feel less alone.

Donald Mullins stood in the tower below the first bell room, oblivious to everything but the pounding in his head and the cold wind passing through the smashed windows. From his pocket he took a notebook filled with scrawled poems and stared at it. He remembered what Padraic Pearse had said, referring to himself, Joseph Plunkett, and Thomas MacDonagh at the beginning of the 1916 uprising: "If we do nothing else, we shall rid Ireland of three bad poets." Mullins laughed, then wiped his eyes. He threw the notebook over his shoulder, and it sailed out into the night.

In the choir loft Leary watched Megan through his sniper scope. It came to him in a startling way that he had never once, even as a child, struck anyone. He watched Megan's face, watched her body move, and he suddenly wanted her.

Brian Flynn stared into the organ's large concave mirror, watching the scene on the altar sanctuary. He listened for the sound of Maureen's cries and the sound of the steady slap of the belt against her body, but heard only the vibrant tones of the chimes, the high, reedy wail of the bagpipes, the singing, and the full, rich organ below.

> "The next I saw was a gray-haired father,
> Searching for his only son.
> I said Old Man there's no use in searching
> Your only son to Heaven has gone."

He lowered his eyes from the mirror and shut them, listening only to the faraway chimes. He remembered that sacrifices took place on altars, and the allusion was not lost on him, and possibly some of the others understood as well. Maureen understood. He remembered the double meaning of sacrifice: an implied sanctification, an offering to the Deity, thanksgiving, purification. . . . But the other meaning was darker, more terrible—pain, loss, death. But in either case the understanding was that sacrifice was rewarded. The time, place, and nature of the reward was never clear, however.

> "Your only son was shot in Dublin
> Fighting for his Country bold.
> He died for Ireland and Ireland only
> The Irish flag green, white and gold."

A sense of overpowering melancholy filled him—visions of Ireland, Maureen, Whitehorn Abbey, his childhood, flashed through his mind. He suddenly felt his own mortality, felt it as a palpable thing, a wrenching in his stomach, a constriction in his throat, a numbness that spread across his chest and arms.

A confused vision of death filled the blackness behind his eyelids, and he saw himself lying naked, white as the cathedral marble, in the arms of a woman with long honey-colored hair shrouding her face; and blood streamed from his mouth, over his cold dead whiteness—blood so red and so plentiful that the people who had gathered around remarked on it curiously. A young man took his hand and knelt to kiss his ring; but the ring was gone, and the man rose and walked away in disgust. And the woman who held him said, *Brian, we all forgive you.* But that gave him more pain than comfort, because he realized he had done nothing to earn forgiveness, done nothing to try to alter the course of events that had been set in motion so long before.

47

Brian Flynn looked at the clock in the rear of the choir loft. He let the last notes of "An Irish Lullaby" die away, then pressed the key for the bell named Patrick. The single bell tolled, a deep low tone, then tolled again and again, twelve times, marking the midnight hour. St. Patrick's Day was over.

The shortest day of the year, he reflected, was not the winter solstice but the day you died, and March 18 would be only six hours and three minutes long, if that.

A deep silence lay over the acre of stone, and the outside cold seeped into the church, slowly numbing the people inside. The four hostages slept fitfully on the cool marble of the altar sanctuary, cuffed together in pairs.

John Hickey rubbed his eyes, yawned, and looked at the television he had moved to the organ console. The volume was turned down, and a barely audible voice was remarking on the new day and speculating on what the sunrise would bring. Hickey wondered how many people were still watching. He pictured all-night vigils around television sets. Whatever happened would happen live, in color, and few would be willing to go to sleep and see it on the replays. Hickey looked down at Pedar Fitzgerald. There were ice packs around his throat and a tube coming from his mouth that emitted a hissing sound. Slightly annoying, Hickey thought.

Flynn began playing the bells again, an Irish-American song this time, "How Are Things in Glocca Morra?"

Hickey watched the television. The street crowds approved of the selection. People were swaying arm in arm, beery tears rolling down red faces. But eventually, he knew, the magic would pass, the concern over the hostages and the Cathedral would become the key news story again. A lot of emotional strings were being pulled this night, and he was fascinated by the game of manipulation. Hickey glanced up at the empty triforium where Gallagher had stood, then turned and called back toward the sacristy stairs, "Frank?"

Gallagher called from the stairwell, "All quiet!"

Hickey looked up at Sullivan and Abby Boland, and they signaled in return. Eamon Farrell called down from the triforium overhead. "All quiet." Hickey cranked the field phone.

Arthur Nulty rolled over and reached out for the receiver. "Roger."

"Status."

Nulty cleared his throat. "Haven't we had enough bells, for God's sake? I can't hear so well with that clanging in my ears."

"Do the best you can." He cranked the phone again. "Bell tower?"

Mullins was staring through a shattered window, and the phone rang several times before he was aware of it. He grabbed it quickly. "Bell tower."

Hickey said, "Sleeping?"

Mullins moved one earpiece of the shooters' baffles and said irritably, "Sleeping? How the hell could anyone sleep with *that?*" He paused, then said, "Has he gone mad?"

Hickey said, "How are they behaving outside?"

Mullins trailed the phone wire and walked around the tower. "They keep coming and going. Mostly coming. Soldiers bivouacked in the Channel Gardens. Damned reporters on the roofs have been drinking all night. Could use a rip myself."

"Aye, time enough for that. At this hour tomorrow you'll be—where?"

"Mexico City . . . I'm to fly to Mexico City. . . ." He tried to laugh. "Long way from Tipperary."

"Warm there. Keep alert." Hickey cranked again. "South tower."

Rory Devane answered. "Situation unchanged."

"Watch for the strobe lights."

"I know."

"Are the snipers still making you nervous, lad?"

Devane laughed. "No. They're keeping me company. I'll miss them, I think."

"Where are you headed tomorrow?"

"South of France. It's spring there, they tell me."

"So it is. Remember, a year from today at Kavanagh's in fair Dublin."

"I'll be there."

Hickey smiled at the dim memory of Kavanagh's Pub, whose front wall was part of the surrounding wall of Glasnevin Cemetery. There was a pass-through in the back wall where gravediggers could obtain refreshments, and as a result, it was said, many a deceased was put into the wrong hole. Hickey laughed. "Aye, Rory, you'll be there." He hung up and turned the crank again.

Leary picked up the phone in the choir loft. Hickey said, "Tell Brian to give the bells a rest, then." He watched Leary turn and speak to Flynn. Leary came back on the line. "He says he feels like playing."

Hickey swore under his breath. "Hold on." He looked at the television set again. The scenes of New York had been replaced by an equally dramatic view of the White House, yellow light coming from the Oval Office windows. A reporter was telling the world that the President was in conference with top advisers. The scene shifted to 10 Downing Street, where it was 5:00 A.M. A bleary-eyed female reporter was assuring America that the Prime Minister was still awake. A quick scene-change showed the Apostolic Palace in the Vatican. Hickey leaned forward and listened carefully as the reporter speculated about the closed-door gathering of Vatican officials. He mumbled to himself, "Saint Peter's next."

Hickey spoke into the phone. "Tell Mr. Flynn that since we can expect an attack at any time now, I suggest he stop providing them with the noise cover they need." He hung up and listened to the bells, which still rang. Brian Flynn, he thought, was not the same man who strode so cockily through this Cathedral little more than six hours before. Flynn was a man who had learned a great deal in those six hours, but had learned it too late and would learn nothing further of any consequence in the final six hours.

Captain Bert Schroeder was startled out of a half-sleep by the ringing telephone. He picked it up quickly.

Hickey's voice cut into the stillness of the office and boomed out over the speakers in the surrounding rooms, also startling some of the people there. *"Schroeder! Schroeder!"*

Schroeder sat up, his chest pounding. "Yes! What's wrong?"

Hickey's voice was urgent. "Someone's seized the Cathedral!" He paused and said softly, "Or was I having a nightmare?" He laughed.

Schroeder waited until he knew his voice would be steady. He looked around the office. Only Burke was there at the moment, sleeping soundly on the couch. Schroeder said, "What can I do for you?"

Hickey said, "Status report, Schroeder."

Schroeder cleared his throat. "Status—"

"How are things in Glocca Morra, London, Washington, Vatican City, Dublin? Anybody still working on this?"

"Of course. You can see it on TV."

"I'm not the public, Schroeder. *You* tell me what's happening."

"Well . . ." He looked at some recent memos. "Well . . . the Red Cross and Amnesty are positioned at all of the camps . . . waiting . . ."

"That was on TV."

"Was it? Well . . . Dublin . . . Dublin has not yet agreed to accept released internees—"

"Tell them for me that they're sniveling cowards. Tell them I said the IRA will take Dublin within the year and shoot them all."

Schroeder said emphatically, "Anyway, we all haven't agreed on terms yet, have we? So finding a place of sanctuary is of secondary importance—"

"I want to speak with all the governments directly. Set up a conference call."
Schroeder's voice was firm. "You know they won't speak to you directly."

"Those pompous bastards will be on their knees begging for an audience by six o'clock."

Schroeder put a note of optimism in his voice. "Your speech is still having favorable repercussions. The Vatican is—"

"Speaking of repercussions and concussions and all that, do you think—now this is a technical question that you should consider—do you think that the glass façade of the Olympic Tower will fall into the street when—"

Schroeder said abruptly, "Is Mr. Flynn there?"

"You have a bad habit of interrupting, Schroeder."

"Is Mr. *Flynn* there?"

"Of course he's here, you ass. Where else would he be?"

"May I speak to him, please?"

"He's playing the bells, for God's sake!"

"Can you tell him to pick up the extension beside the organ?"

"I told you, you don't interrupt a man when he's playing the *bells.* Haven't you learned anything tonight? I'll bet you were a vice cop once, busting into hotel rooms, interrupting people. You're the type."

Schroeder felt his face redden. He heard Hickey's voice echoing through the rectory and heard a few people laughing. Schroeder snapped a pencil between his fingers. "We want to speak with Mr. Flynn—privately, at the sacristy gate." He looked at Burke sleeping on the couch. "Lieutenant Burke wants to speak—"

"As you said before, it's less confusing to speak to one person. If I can't speak to the Queen, you can't speak to Finn MacCumail. What's wrong with *me?* By the way, what have you given up for Lent? Your brains or your balls? *I* gave up talking to fools on the telephone, but I'll make an exception in your case."

Schroeder suddenly felt something inside him come loose. He made a strong effort to control his voice and spoke in measured tones. "Mr. Hickey . . . Brian Flynn has a great deal of faith in me—the efforts I'm making, the honesty I've shown—"

The sound of Hickey's laughter filled the office. "He sounds like a good lad to you, does he? Well, he's got a surprise in store for *you,* Schroeder, and you won't like it."

Schroeder said, "We'd rather not have any surprises—"

"Stop using that imperial *we.* I'm talking about *you. You* have a surprise coming."

Schroeder sat up quickly, and his eyes became more alert. "What do you mean by that? What does that mean? Listen, everything should be aboveboard if we're going to bargain in good faith—"

"Is Bellini acting in good faith?"

Schroeder hesitated. This use of names by these people was unsettling. These references to him personally were not in the script.

Hickey continued, "Where is Bellini now? Huddled around a chalk board with his Gestapo? Finding sneaky little ways to kill us all? Well, fuck Bellini and fuck you."

Schroeder shook his head in silent frustration, then said, "How are the hostages?"

Hickey said, "Did you find Stillway yet?"

"Do you need a doctor in there?"

"Did you dig up my grave yet?"

"Can I send food, medicine—?"

"Where's Major Martin?"

Burke lay on the couch with his eyes closed and listened to the dialogue deteriorate into two monologues. As unproductive as the dialogue had been, it hadn't been as bizarre as what he was listening to now. He knew now, beyond any doubt, that it was finished.

Schroeder said, "What surprises does Flynn have planned for me?"

Hickey laughed again. "If I tell you, it won't be a surprise. I'll bet when you were a child you were an insufferable brat, Schroeder. Always trying to find out what people bought you for Christmas, sneaking around closets and all that."

Schroeder didn't respond and again heard the laughter from the next room.

Hickey said, "Don't initiate any calls to us unless it's to say we've won. I'll call you back every hour on the hour until 6:00 A.M. At 6:03 it's over."

Schroeder heard the phone go dead. He looked at Burke's still form on the couch, then shut off all the speakers and dialed again. "Hickey?"

"What?"

Schroeder took a deep breath and said through his clenched jaw, "You're a dead motherfucker." He put the phone down and steadied his hands against the desk. There was a taste of blood in his mouth, and he realized that he was biting into his lower lip.

Burke turned his head and looked at Schroeder. Their eyes met, and Schroeder turned away.

Burke said, "It's okay."

Schroeder didn't answer, and Burke could see his shoulders shaking.

48

Colonel Dennis Logan rode in the rear of a staff car up the deserted section of Fifth Avenue, toward the Cathedral. He turned to his adjutant, Major Cole. "Didn't think I'd be passing this way again today."

"Yes, sir. It's actually March eighteenth."

Colonel Logan overlooked the correction and listened to the bells play "I'll Take You Home Again, Kathleen," then said, "Do you believe in miracles?"

"No, sir."

"Well, see that green line?"

"Yes, sir, the long one in the middle of the Avenue that we followed." He yawned.

"Right. Well, some years ago, Mayor Beame was marching in the parade with the Sixty-ninth. Police Commissioner Codd and the Commissioner for Public Events, Neil Walsh, were with him. Before your time."

Major Cole wished that this parade had been before his time. "Yes, sir."

"Anyway, it rained that morning after the line machine went by, and the fresh green paint washed away—all the way from Forty-fourth to Eighty-sixth Street. But later that morning Walsh bought some paint and had his men handpaint the line right in front of the Cathedral."

"Yes, sir."

"Well, when we marched past with the city delegation, Walsh turns to Codd and says, 'Look! It's a miracle, Commissioner! The line's still here in front of the Cathedral!' "

Colonel Logan laughed at the happier memory and went on. "So Codd says, 'You're right, Walsh!' and he winks at him, then looks at Beame. 'Oh my gosh!' said the little Mayor. 'I always wanted to see a miracle. I never saw a miracle before!' " Logan laughed but refrained from slapping his or Cole's knee. The driver laughed, too.

Major Cole smiled. He said, "Sir, I think we've mustered most of the officers and at least half the men."

Logan lit a cigar. "Right. . . . Do they look sober to you?"

"It's hard to say, sir."

Logan nodded, then said, "We're not really needed here, are we?"

"That's difficult to determine, Colonel."

"I think the Governor is looking for high marks in leadership and courage, don't you?"

Major Cole replied, "The regiment is well trained in crowd and riot control, sir."

"So are twenty-five thousand New York police."

"Yes, sir."

"I hope to God he doesn't get us involved in an assault on the Cathedral."

The major replied, "Sir," which conveyed no meaning.

Colonel Logan looked through the window as the car passed between a set of police barriers and moved slowly past the singing crowds. "Incredible."

Cole nodded. "Yes, it is."

The staff car drew up to the rectory and stopped.

Captain Joe Bellini advised the newspeople that the press conference room might cave in if the Cathedral was blown up, and they moved with their equipment to less vulnerable places outside the Cathedral complex as Bellini moved in. He stood in the room beside a chalkboard. Around the tables and along the walls, were sixty Emergency Service Division men, armed with shotguns, M-16 rifles, and silenced pistols. In the rear of the room sat Colonel Logan, Major Cole, and a dozen staff personnel from the 69th Regiment. A cloud of gray tobacco smoke veiled the bright lights. Bellini pointed to a crude outline of the Cathedral on the chalkboard. "So, Fifth Squad will attack through the sacristy gates. You'll be issued steel-cut chainsaws and bolt cutters. Okay?"

Colonel Logan stood. "If I may make a suggestion . . . Before, you said your men had to control their fire. . . . This is your operation, and my part is secondary, but the basic rules of warfare . . . Well, anyway, when you encounter concealed enemy positions that have a superior field of fire—like those triforia and choir loft—and you know you can't engage them with effective fire . . . then you have to lay down *suppressing* fire." Logan saw some signs of recognition. "In other words you flip the switches on your M-16s from semiautomatic to full automatic—rock and roll, as the men say—and put out such an intense volume of fire that the enemy has got to put his head down. Then you can safely lead the hostages back down the sacristy stairs."

No one spoke, but a few men were nodding.

Logan's voice became more intense. He was suddenly giving a prebattle pep talk. "Keep blasting those triforia, blast that choir loft, slap magazine after magazine into those rifles, raking, raking, raking those sniper perches, blasting away so long, so loud, so fast, and so hard that it sounds like Armageddon and the Apocalypse all at once, and no one—*no one*—in those perches is going to pick his head up if the air around him is filled with bullets and pulverized stone." He looked around the silent room and listened to his heart beating.

There was a spontaneous burst of applause from the ESD men and the military people. Captain Bellini waited until the noise died away, then said, "Yes, well, Colonel, that's sound advice, but we're *all* under the strictest orders not to blow the place apart—as you know. It's full of art treasures. . . . It's . . . well . . . you know . . ."

Logan said, "Yes, I understand." He wiped his face. "I'm not advocating air strikes. I mean, I'm only suggesting you increase your use of small-arms fire, and—"

"Such an intense degree of even small-arms fire, Colonel, would do"—Bellini remembered the Governor's words—"irreparable . . . irreparable damage to the Cathedral . . . the ceiling . . . the stonework . . . statues . . ."

One of the squad leaders stood. "Look, Captain, since when are art treasures more important than people? My mother thinks *I'm* an art treasure—"

Several people laughed nervously.

Bellini felt the sweat collecting under his collar. He looked at Logan. "Colonel, your mission . . ." Bellini paused and watched Logan stiffen.

Logan said, "My mission is to provide a tight cordon around the Cathedral during the assault. I know what I have to do."

Bellini almost smirked. "No, that's been changed. The Governor wants you to take a more active part in the assault." He savored each word as he said it. "The police will supply you with their armored personnel carrier. It's army surplus, and you'll be familiar with it." Bellini noticed that Major Cole had gone pale.

Bellini stepped closer to Logan. "You'll take the vehicle up the front steps with fifteen men inside—"

Logan's voice was barely under control. "This is *insane.* You can't use an armored vehicle in such a confined space. They might have armor-piercing ordnance in there. Good Lord, we couldn't maneuver, couldn't conceal the vehicle . . . These Fenians are guerrilla veterans, Captain. They know how to deal with tanks—they've seen more British armored cars than you've seen—"

"Taxis," said Burke as he walked into the press room. "That's what Flynn said to Schroeder. Taxis. Mind if Inspector Langley and I join you?"

Bellini looked tired and annoyed. He said to Logan, "Take it up with the Governor." Glancing at the wall clock, he said, "Everyone take ten. Clear out!" He sat down and lit a cigarette. The men filed out of the conference room and huddled in groups throughout the corridors.

Burke and Langley sat across from Bellini. Bellini said softly, "That fucking war hero is spooking my men."

Burke thought, *They should be spooked. They're going to get creamed.* "He means well."

Bellini drew on his cigarette. "Why are those parade soldiers in on this?"

Langley looked around, then said quietly, "The Governor needs a boost."

Bellini sipped on a cup of cold coffee. "You know . . . I discussed a lot of options for this attack with the Mayor and Governor. Ever notice how people who don't know shit about warfare all of a sudden become generals?" Bellini chain-lit another cigarette and went on in a voice that was becoming overwrought. "So Kline takes my hand and squeezes it—Christ, I should've squeezed his and broken his fucking fingers. Anyway, he says, 'Joe, you know what's expected of you.' Christ Almighty, by this time I don't even know if I'm allowed to take my gun in there. But my adrenaline is really pumping by now, and I say to him, 'Your Honor, we have to attack *now,* while the bells are

ringing.' Right? And he says—check this—he says, 'Captain, we have an obligation'—a moral something or other—'to explore every possible avenue of negotiation'—blah, blah, blah—'political considerations'—blah, blah—'the Vatican'
—blah, blah. So I say . . . no, I didn't say it, but I should have . . . I should
have said, 'Kline, you schmuck, do you want to rescue the hostages and save the
fucking Cathedral, or do you want to make time with the White House and the
Vatican?' "

He paused and breathed hard. "But maybe then I would have sounded like
an asshole, too, because I don't really care about a pile of stone or four people
I don't even know. My responsibility is to a hundred of my men who I do know
and to their families and to myself and my wife and kids. Right?"

No one spoke for some time, then the telephone rang. Bellini grabbed it,
listened, then handed it to Burke. "Some guy called the Leper. You hang out
with classy people."

Burke took the receiver and heard Ferguson's voice. "Burke, Leper here."

Burke said, "How are you?"

"Cold, scared shitless, tired, hungry, and broke. But otherwise, well. Is this
line secure?"

"No."

"Okay, I have to speak to you face to face."

Burke thought a moment. "Do you want to come here?"

Ferguson hesitated. "No . . . I saw people hanging around the checkpoints
who shouldn't see me. I'm very close to our rendezvous point. See you there."

Burke put down the receiver and said to Langley, "Ferguson's on to something."

Bellini looked up quickly. "Anything that can help me?"

Burke wanted to say, "Frankly, nothing can help you," but said instead, "I
think so."

Bellini seemed to sense the lie and slumped lower in his chair. "Christ, we've
never gone up against trained guerrilas. . . ." He looked up suddenly. "Do I
sound scared? Do I look scared?"

Burke replied, "You look and sound like a man who fully appreciates the
problems."

Bellini laughed. "Yeah. I appreciate the hell out of the problems."

Langley seemed suddenly annoyed. "Look, you must have known a day like
this would come. You've trained for this—"

"Trained?" Bellini turned on him. "Big fucking deal trained. In the army I
was trained on how to take cover in a nuclear attack. The only instructor who
made any sense was the one who told us to hold our helmets, put our heads
between our legs, and kiss our asses good-bye." He laughed again. "Fuck
trained." Bellini stubbed out his cigarette and breathed deeply. "Oh, well.
Maybe Schroeder will pull it off." He smiled thinly. "He's got more incentive
now." He pointed to a black bulletproof vest and a dark pullover sweater at the
end of the table. "That's his."

Langley said, "Why don't you let him off the hook?"

Bellini shook his head, then looked at Burke. "How about you? What are
you doing later?"

Burke said, "I'll be with you."

Bellini's eyes widened.

Langley looked at Burke quickly. "Like hell."

Burke said nothing.

Bellini said, "Let the man do what he wants."

Langley changed the subject and said to Bellini, "I have more psy-profiles for you."

Bellini lit a cigarette. "Put a light coat of oil on them and shove them up your ass."

Langley stiffened.

Bellini went on, enjoying the fact that no one could pull rank on him any longer. "Where's the architect, Langley? Where are the blueprints?"

Langley said, "Working on it."

"Terrific. Everybody is working on something—you, Schroeder, the Mayor, the President. Everybody's working. You know, when this started nobody paid much attention to Joe Bellini. Now the Mayor calls about every fifteen minutes asking how I'm making out. Calls me Joe. Terrific little guy."

Men started drifting back into the room.

Bellini leaned over the table. "They've got me cornered. When they start calling you by your first name, they've got you by the balls, and they're not going to let go until I charge up those fucking steps—holding not much more than my cock in one hand and a cross in the other—and get myself killed." He stood. "Believe me, Burke, it's all a fucking show. Everybody's got to play his part. You, mc, the politicians, the Church, the bastards in the Cathedral. We *know* we're full of shit, but that's the way we learned how to play."

Burke stood and looked around at the ESD men, then looked closely at Bellini. "Remember, you're the good guys."

Bellini rubbed his temples and shook his head. "Then how come we're wearing black?"

49

Patrick Burke stepped out of the rectory into the cold, gusty air. He looked at his watch. Nearly 1:00 A.M., March 18. They would still call it the St. Patrick's Day massacre or something catchy like that. He turned up his collar and walked east on Fifty-first Street.

At Park Avenue a city bus was drawn up to form a barricade. Burke walked around the bus, passed through a thin crowd, and crossed the avenue. A small group had congregated on the steps and terraces of St. Bartholomew's Episcopal Church, passing bottles and singing the songs that were being played on St. Patrick's bells. People were entering the church, and Burke recalled that many churches and synagogues had announced all-night prayer vigils. A news van was setting up cameras and lights.

Burke listened to the bells. Flynn—if it was Flynn playing—had a good touch. Burke remembered Langley's speculation about the John Hickey T-shirts. He envisioned a record jacket: St. Patrick's Cathedral—green star clusters—*Brian Flynn Plays the Bells.*

Burke passed by the church and continued east on Fifty-first Street. Between two buildings lay a small park. A fence and gate ran between the flanking structures, and Burke peered through the bars. Café tables and upturned chairs stood on the terraces beneath bare sycamores. Nothing moved in the unlit park. Burke grasped the cold steel bars, pulled himself up to the top, and dropped into the park. As he hit the frozen stone walk below, he felt a sharp pain shoot through his numb legs and swore silently. He drew his pistol and remained crouched. A wind shook the trees, and ice-covered twigs snapped and fell to the ground with the sound of breaking crystal.

Burke straightened up slowly and moved through the scattered tables, pistol held at his side. As he moved, the ice crackled under his shoes, and he knew that if Ferguson were there he would have heard him by now.

An overturned table caught his attention, and he moved toward it. A chair lay on its back some distance away. The ice on the ground was broken and scattered, and Burke knelt to get a closer look at a large dark blotch that on closer inspection looked like a strawberry Italian ice but wasn't.

Burke rose and found that his legs had become unsteady. He walked up the shallow steps to the next level of the terrace and saw more overturned furniture. In the rear of the park was a stone wall several stories high where a waterfall usually flowed. At the base of the wall was a long, narrow trough. Burke walked to the trough and stared down at Jack Ferguson lying in the icy water, his face blue-white, very much, Burke thought, like the color of the façade of the Cathedral. The eyes were open, and his mouth yawned as if he were trying to catch his breath from the shock of the cold water.

Burke knelt on the low stone abutment of the trough, reached out, and grabbed Ferguson's old trench coat. He pulled the body closer and saw, as the folds of the trench coat drifted apart, the two bullet-shattered knees poking out of the worn trousers—bone, cartilage, and ligaments, very white against the deeper color of bluish flesh.

He slipped his pistol into his pocket and pulled the small man easily onto the coping stone of the abutment. A small bullet hole showed like black palm ash in the center of Ferguson's forehead. His pockets had been rifled, but Burke searched the body again, finding only a clean, neatly pressed handkerchief which reminded him that he would have to call Ferguson's wife.

Burke closed Ferguson's eyes and stood, wiped his hands on his overcoat and blew into them, and then walked away. He righted an ice-covered chair, drew it up to a metal table, and sat. Burke took a long, deep breath and steadied his hands enough to light a cigarette. He drew on the cigarette, then took out his flask and opened it, but set it on the table without drinking. He heard a noise at the fence and looked out across the park. He drew his pistol and rested it in his lap.

"Burke! It's Martin."

Burke didn't answer.

"Can I come up?"

Burke cocked his revolver. "Sure!"

Martin walked toward Burke, stopped, and looked past him at the low stone wall at the base of the waterfall. "Who's that?"

Burke didn't reply.

Martin walked up to the body and looked down into the frozen face. "I know this man . . . Jack Ferguson."

"Is it?"

"Yes. I've dealt with him—only yesterday, as a matter of fact. Official IRA. Marxist. Nice chap, though."

Burke said with no intonation in his voice, "The only good Red is a dead Red. Kill a Commie for Christ. Move here where I can see you."

"Eh?" Martin moved behind Burke's chair. "What did you say . . . ? See here, you didn't . . . did you?"

Burke repeated. "Here in front where I can see you."

Martin moved around the table.

Burke said, "Why are you here?"

Martin lit a cigarette. "Followed you from the rectory."

Burke was certain no one had followed him. "Why?"

"Wanted to see where you were going. You've been most unhelpful. I've been sacked from my consulate job, by the way. Is that your doing? People are starting to say the most incredible things about me. Anyway, I'm at loose ends now. Don't know what to do with myself. So I thought perhaps I could . . . well . . . lend you a hand . . . clear my name in the process. . . . Is that a gun? You can put that away."

Burke held the gun. "Who do you think killed him, Major?"

"Well, assuming it wasn't you . . ." He shrugged. "Probably his own people. Or the Provos or the Fenians. Did you see his knees? God, that's a nasty business."

"Why would the IRA want to kill him?"

Martin answered quickly and distinctly. "He talked too much."

Burke uncocked his revolver and held it in his pocket. "Where's Gordon Stillway?"

"Gordon . . . Oh, the architect." Martin drew on his cigarette. "I wish I were half as devious as you think I am."

Burke took a drink from his flask and said, "Look, the Cathedral is going to be stormed in the next few hours."

"Sorry it had to come to that."

"Anyway, I'm concerned now about saving as many lives as possible."

"I am, too. Our Consul General is in there."

"So far, Major, you've had it all your way. You got your Irish terrorism in America. We've had it pushed in our face. The point is made and well taken. So we don't need a burned-out Cathedral and a stack of corpses."

"I'm not quite sure I'm following you."

"It would help Bellini if he had the blueprints and the architect."

"Undoubtedly. I'm working on that also."

Burke looked at Martin closely. "Settle for what you've already got. Don't push it further."

"I'm sorry, I'm losing you again."

Burke stared at Martin, who put his foot on a chair and puffed on his cigarette. A gust of cold wind moved through the enclosed park and swirled around. Ice fell from the glistening trees, landing on Martin and Burke, but neither man seemed to notice. Martin seemed to reach a decision and looked at Burke. "It's not just Flynn, you see. My whole operation wasn't conceived just to kill Brian Flynn." Martin rubbed his chin with his gloved hand. "You see, I need more than Flynn's death, though I look forward to it. I also need a *lasting* symbol of Irish terrorism. I'm afraid I need the Cathedral to go down."

Burke waited a long time before he spoke. His voice was low, controlled. "It may become a symbol of Britain's unwillingness to negotiate."

"One gambles. But you see, London *did* offer a compromise, much to my surprise, and the Fenians, lunatics that they are, have not responded to it. And with the old man's speech and the bells and all that, it's the Fenians who are ahead, not me. Really, Burke, the only way I can influence public opinion, here and abroad, is if . . . well, if there's a tragedy. Sorry."

"It's going to backfire."

"When the dust clears, the blame will be squarely on the Irish. Her Majesty's government is very adept at expressing sorrow and pity for the loss of lives and property. Actually, the ruins of Saint Patrick's may have more value as a tourist attraction than the Cathedral did. . . . Not many good ruins in America. . . ."

Burke's fingers scratched at the cold, blue steel of the revolver in his pocket.

Martin went on, his eyes narrowing and long plumes of vapor exhaling from his nose and mouth. "And, of course, the funerals. Did you see Mountbatten's? Thousands of people weeping. We'll do something nice for Baxter, too. The Roman Church will do a splendid job for the Cardinal and the priest. Malone . . . well, who knows?"

Burke said, "You're not tightly wrapped, you know that?"

Martin lit another cigarette, and Burke saw the match quivering in the dark. Martin spoke in a more controlled voice. "You don't seem to understand. One has to spread the suffering, make it more universal before you get a sense of outrage." Martin looked at his glowing cigarette. "One needs a magnificent disaster—Dunkirk, Pearl Harbor, Coventry, Saint Patrick's . . ." He knocked the ash from his cigarette and stared down at the gray smudge on the ice-covered table. ". . . And from those ashes rises a new dedication." He looked up. "You may have noticed the phoenix on the bronze ceremonial door of Saint Patrick's. It inspired me to name this Operation Phoenix."

Burke said, "Flynn may accept the compromise. He hinted as much to me. He may also make a public statement about how British treachery almost got everyone killed."

"He wouldn't admit that the greatest IRA operation since Mountbatten's murder was planned by an Englishman."

"He doesn't want to die quite as badly as you want him to die. He'll take what he's already gotten and come out of there a hero." Burke took another drink to fire his imagination. "On the other hand . . . there's still the possibility that he may destroy the place at dawn. So the Mayor and Governor want to carry out a preemptive strike. Soon. But they need encouragement. They won't move unless Bellini says he can bring it off. But Bellini won't say that unless he gets the blueprints and the architect. . . ."

Martin smiled. "Very good. It's hereditary, I see—I mean the ability to manufacture heaps of malarkey at the drop of a hat."

"If we don't have the architect, we won't attack. At 6:03 Flynn will call a time out, wait until the city is full of people and the morning TV shows are rolling, then magnanimously spare the Cathedral and hostages. No funerals, no bangs, not even a broken stained-glass window."

"At 6:03 something more dreadful will happen."

"One gambles."

Martin shook his head. "I don't know. . . . Now you've got me worried, Lieutenant. It would be just like that bastard to double-cross me. . . ." He smiled. "Well, double-cross may not be the word. . . . These people are so erratic . . . you never know, do you? I mean, historically they always opt for the most reckless—"

Burke said, "You've got these Micks pretty well figured out, don't you, Major?"

"Well . . . no racial generalities intended, to be sure, but . . . I don't know . . ." He seemed to be weighing the possibilities. "The question is—do I gamble on an explosion at 6:03 or settle for a good battle before then . . . ?"

Burke came closer to Martin. "Let me put it this way. . . ." He breathed a long stream of cold fog in Martin's face. "If the Cathedral goes down"—he pulled his pistol, cocked it, and pressed it to Martin's temple—"then you're what we call a dead motherfucker."

Martin faced Burke. "If anything happened to me, you'd be killed."

"I know the rules." He tapped Martin on the forehead with the muzzle of the revolver, then holstered it.

Martin flipped his cigarette away and spoke in a businesslike tone. "In exchange for Stillway I want your word that you'll do everything you can to see that the assault is carried out before Flynn makes any overtures toward a compromise. You have his confidence, I know, so use that in any way you can—with him or with your superiors. And no matter what happens, you'll make certain that Flynn is not captured alive. Understood?"

Burke nodded.

Martin added, "You'll have Stillway and the blueprints in ample time, and to show you what a good sport I am, I'll give all this to you personally. As I said yesterday morning, you can look good with your superiors. God knows, Lieutenant, you need the boost."

Martin moved away from Burke and looked down at Ferguson's frozen body. He lit another cigarette and dropped the match carelessly on Ferguson's face. He looked at Burke. "You're thinking, of course, that like our late friend here, you know too much. But it's all right. I'm willing—obligated—to make an exception in your case. You're one of us—a professional, not an amateur busybody like Mr. Ferguson or a dangerous insurgent like Mr. Flynn. So act like a professional, Lieutenant, and you'll be treated like one."

Burke said, "Thank you for setting me straight. I'll do my best."

Martin laughed. "You can do your worst, if you like. I'm not counting only on you to see that things go my way. Lieutenant, there are more surprises inside and outside that Cathedral than even you suspect. And at first light, it will all unfold." He nodded his head. "Good evening." He turned and walked away at a leisurely pace.

Burke looked down at Ferguson. He bent over and picked the match from his face. "Sorry, Jack."

50

The clock in the rear of the choir loft struck 3:00 A.M. Brian Flynn tolled the hour, then stood and looked at Leary sitting on the parapet, his legs swinging out into space three stories above the main floor. Flynn said, "If you nod off, you'll fall."

Leary answered without turning. "That's right."

Flynn looked around for Megan but didn't see her. He moved around the organ, picked up a rifle, and walked toward Leary.

Leary suddenly spun around and swung his legs into the choir loft. He said, "That's an old trick."

Flynn felt his body tense.

Leary continued. "Learned it in the army. You perch in a position that will get you hurt or killed if you fall asleep. Keeps you awake . . . usually."

"Interesting." He moved past Leary and entered the bell tower, then took the elevator down to the vestibule. He walked up the center aisle, his footsteps echoing in the quiet Cathedral. Sullivan, Boland, and Farrell were leaning out over the triforia. Hickey was asleep at the chancel organ. Flynn passed through the open gate of the communion rail and mounted the steps. The four hostages slept in pairs on opposite sides of the sanctuary. He glanced over at Baxter beside Maureen and watched the steady rise and fall of her chest, then looked up at where the Cardinal and Father Murphy lay cuffed to the throne, sleeping. Flynn knelt beside Maureen and stared down at her bruised face. He sensed that eyes were watching him from the high places, that Megan was watching from the dark, and that Leary's scope was centered on his lips. Flynn leaned over, his back to Leary, and positioned himself to block Leary's view of Maureen. He stroked her cheek.

She opened her eyes and looked up at him. "What time is it?"

"Late."

She said, "You've let it become late."

He said quietly, "I'm sorry . . . I couldn't help you . . ."

She turned her face away. Neither one spoke, then Maureen said, "This standoff with the police is like one of those games of nerve with autos racing toward each other, each driver hypnotized by the other's approach—and at one minute to dawn . . . is anyone going to veer off?"

"Bloody nonsense. This is war. Bloody stupid women, you think men play games of ego—"

"War?" She grabbed his shirt and her voice rose. "Let me tell *you* about *war*. It's not fought in churches with handcuffed hostages. And as long as you're talking about war, I'm still enough of a soldier to know they may not wait for dawn—they may be burrowing in here *right now,* and within the time it takes to draw your next breath this place could be filled with gunfire and you could be filled with bullets." She released his shirt. "War, indeed. You know no more about war than you do about love."

Flynn stood and looked at Baxter. "Do you like this man?"

She nodded. "He's a good man."

Flynn stared off at some point in the distance. "A good man," he repeated. "Someone meeting me for the first time might say that—as long as my history wasn't known." He stared down at her. "You don't like me much right now, but it's all right. I hope you survive, I even hope Baxter survives, and I hope you get on well together."

She lay on her back looking up at him. "Again, neither you nor I believe a word of that."

Flynn stepped away from her. "I have to go. . . ." He looked over the sanctuary rail at Hickey and said suddenly, "Tell me about him. What's the old man been saying? What about the confessional buzzer?"

Maureen cleared her throat and spoke in a businesslike voice, relating what she had discovered about John Hickey. She added her conclusions. "Even if you win, he'll somehow make certain everyone dies." She added, "All four of us believe that, or we wouldn't have risked so much to escape."

Flynn's eyes drifted back to Hickey, then he looked around the sanctuary at the hostages, the bouquets of now-wilting green carnations, and the bloodstains on the marble below the high altar. He had the feeling he had seen this all before, experienced something similar in a dream or vision, and he remembered that he *had,* in Whitehorn Abbey. He shook off the impression and looked at Maureen.

Flynn knelt suddenly and unlocked the handcuff. "Come with me." He helped her up and supported her as he walked toward the sacristy stairs.

He was aware that Hickey was watching from the chancel organ, and that Leary and Megan were watching also, from the shadows of the choir loft. He knew that they were thinking he was going to let Maureen go. And this, he understood, as everyone who was watching understood, was a critical juncture, a test of his position as leader. Would those three in any way try to restrict his movements? A few hours before they wouldn't have dared.

He reached the sacristy stairs and paused, not hesitantly but defiantly, and looked up into the loft, then back at the chancel organ. No one made a sound or a movement, and he waited purposely, staring into the Cathedral, then descended the steps. He stopped on the landing beside Gallagher. "Take a break, Frank."

Gallagher looked at him and at Maureen, and Flynn could see in Gallagher's expression a look of understanding and approval. Gallagher's eyes met Maureen's; he started to speak but then turned and hurried up the stairs.

Flynn looked down the remaining steps at the chained gate, then faced Maureen.

She realized that Brian Flynn had reasserted himself, imposed his will on the others. And she knew also that he was going to go a step further. He was going to free her, but she didn't know if he was doing it for her or for himself, or to demonstrate that he could do anything he damned well pleased—to show that he was Finn MacCumail, Chief of the Fenians. She walked down the staircase and stopped at the gate. Flynn followed and gestured toward the sacristy. "Two worlds meet here, the worlds of the sacred and the profaned, the living and the dead. Have ever such divergent worlds been separated by so little?"

She stared into the quiet sacristy and saw a votive candle flickering on the altar of the priests' chapel, the vestment tables lining the walls, covered with neatly folded white and purple vestments of the Lenten season. *Easter,* she thought. *The spring. The Resurrection and the life.* She looked at Flynn.

He said, "Will you choose life? Will you go without the others?"

She nodded. "Yes, I'll go."

He hesitated, then drew the keys from his pocket. With a hand that was unsteady he unlocked the gate's lock and the chain's padlock, and began unwinding the chain. He rolled back the left gate and scanned the corridor openings but saw no sign of the police. "Hurry."

She took his arm. "I'll go, but not without you."

He looked at her, then said, "You'd leave the others to go with me?"

"Yes."

"Could you do that and live with yourself?"

"Yes."

He stared at the open gate. "I'd be imprisoned for a long time. Could you wait?"

"Yes."

"You love me?"

"Yes."

He reached out for her, but she moved quickly up the stairs and stopped halfway to the landing. "You'll not push me out. We leave together."

He stood looking up at her silhouetted against the light of the crypt doors. "I can't go."

"Not even for me? I'd go with you—for you. Won't you do the same?"

"I *can't* . . . for God's sake, Maureen . . . I *can't.* Please, if you love me, go. Go!"

"Together. One way or the other, *together.*"

He looked down and shook his head and, after what seemed like a long time, heard her footsteps retreating up the stairs.

He relocked the gate and followed, and when he walked up to the altar sanctuary, he found her lying beside Baxter again, the cuff locked on her wrist and her eyes closed.

Flynn came down from the sanctuary and walked to a pew in the center of the Cathedral and sat, staring at the high altar. It struck him that the things most men found trying—leadership, courage, the ability to seize their own destiny—came easily to him, a gift, he thought, of the gods. But love—so basic an emotion that even unexceptional men were blessed with loving women, children, friends—that had always eluded him. And the one time it had not eluded him it had been so difficult as to be painful, and to make the pain stop he made the love stop through the sheer force of his will. Yet it came back, again and again. *Amor vincit omnia,* as Father Michael used to preach. He shook his head. *No, I've conquered love.*

He felt very empty inside. But at the same time, to his horror and disgust, he felt very good about being in command of himself and his world again.

He sat in the pew for a long time.

Flynn looked down at Pedar Fitzgerald, lying in a curled position at the side of the organ console, a blanket drawn up to his blood-encrusted chin. Flynn moved beside John Hickey, who lay slumped over the organ keyboard, and stared down at Hickey's pale, almost waxen face. The field phone rang, and Hickey stirred. It rang again, and Flynn grabbed it.

Mullins's voice came over the line. "I'm back in the bell room. Is that it for the bells, then?"

"Yes. . . . How does it look outside?"

Mullins said, "Very quiet below. But out farther . . . there're still people in the streets."

Flynn heard a note of wonder in the young man's voice. "They celebrate late, don't they? We've given them a Saint Patrick's Day to remember."

Mullins said, "There wasn't even a *curfew.*"

Flynn smiled. America reminded him of the *Titanic,* a three-hundred-foot gash in her side, listing badly, but they were still serving drinks in the lounge. "It's not like Belfast, is it?"

"No."

"Can you sense any anxiety down there . . . movement . . . ?"

Mullins considered, then said, "No, they look relaxed yet. Cold and tired for sure, but at ease. No passing of orders, none of that stiffness you see before an attack."

"How are you holding up against the cold?"

"I'm past that."

"Well, you and Rory will be the first to see the dawn break."

Mullins had given up on the dawn hours ago. "Aye, the dawn from the bell tower of Saint Patrick's in New York. That needs a poem."

"You'll tell me it later." He hung up and picked up the extension phone. "Get me Captain Schroeder, please." He looked at Hickey's face as the operator routed the call. Awake, the face was expressive, alive, but asleep it looked like a death mask.

Schroeder's voice came through sounding slurred. "Yes . . ."

"Flynn here. Did I wake you?"

"No, sir. We've been waiting for Mr. Hickey's hourly call. He said . . . but I'm glad you called. I've been wanting to speak to you."

"Thought I was dead, did you?"

"Well, no. . . . You were on the bells, right?"

"How did I sound out there?"

Schroeder cleared his throat. "You show promise."

Flynn laughed. "Well, can it be you're developing a sense of humor, Captain?"

Schroeder laughed self-consciously.

"Or is it that you're so relieved to be talking to me instead of Hickey that you're giddy?"

Schroeder didn't answer.

Flynn said, "How are they faring in the capitals?"

Schroeder's tone was reserved. "They're wondering why you haven't responded to what Inspector Langley related to you."

"I'm afraid we aren't very clear on that."

"I can't elaborate over the phone."

"I see. . . . Well, why don't you come to the sacristy gate, then, and we'll talk."

There was a long pause. "I'm not at liberty to do that. . . . It's against regulations."

"So is burning down a cathedral, which is what will happen if we don't speak, Captain."

"You don't understand, Mr. Flynn. There are carefully worked out rules . . . as I think you know. . . . And the negotiator cannot expose himself to . . . to . . ."

"I won't kill you."

"Well . . . I know you won't . . . but . . . Listen, you and Lieutenant Burke have . . . Would you like to speak with him at the gate?"

"No, I would like to speak with *you* at the gate."

"I . . ."

"Aren't you even curious to see me?"

"Curiosity plays no part—"

"Doesn't it? It seems to me, Captain, that you of all people would recognize the value of eyeball-to-eyeball contact."

"There's no special value in—"

"How many wars would have been avoided if the chiefs could have just seen the other man's face, touched each other, got a whiff of the other fellow's sweaty fear?"

Schroeder said, "Hold on."

Flynn heard the phone click, then a minute later Schroeder's voice came through. "Okay."

"Five minutes." Flynn hung up and poked Hickey roughly. "Were you listening?"

Flynn took Hickey's arm in a tight grip. "Someday, you old bastard, you'll tell me about the confessional, and the things you've been saying to Schroeder and the things you've been saying to my people and to the hostages. And you'll tell me about the compromise that was offered us."

Hickey flinched and straightened up. "Let go! These old bones snap easily."

"I may snap the ones in your neck."

Hickey looked up at Flynn, no trace of pain in his face. "Careful. Be careful."

Flynn released his arm and pushed it away. "You don't frighten me."

Hickey didn't answer but stared at Flynn with undisguised malice in his eyes.

Flynn met his stare, then looked down at Pedar Fitzgerald. "Are you looking after him?"

Hickey didn't answer.

Flynn stared closely at Fitzgerald's face and saw it was white—waxy, like Hickey's. "He's dead." He turned to Hickey.

Hickey said without emotion, "Died about an hour ago."

"Megan . . ."

"When Megan calls, I tell her he's all right, and she believes that because she wants to. But eventually . . ."

Flynn looked up at Megan in the loft. "My God, she'll . . ." He turned back to Hickey. "We should have gotten a doctor. . . ."

Hickey replied, "If you weren't so wrapped up in your fucking bells, you could have done just that."

Flynn looked at him. *"You* could have—"

"Me? What the hell do I care if he lives or dies?"

Flynn stepped back from him, and his mind began to reel.

Hickey said, "What do you see, Brian? Is it very frightening?" He laughed and lit his pipe.

Flynn moved farther away from Hickey into the ambulatory and tried to get his thoughts under control. He reevaluated each person in the Cathedral until he was certain he knew each one's motives . . . potential for treachery . . . loyalties and weaknesses. His mind focused finally on Leary, and he asked the questions he should have asked months ago: Why was Leary here? Why would a professional killer trap himself in a perch with no way out? Leary had to be holding a card no one even knew existed. Flynn wiped the sweat from his brow and walked up to the sanctuary.

Hickey called out, "Are you going to tell Schroeder about his darling daughter? Tell him for me—use these exact words—tell him his daughter is a dead bitch!"

Flynn descended the stairs behind the altar. Gallagher stood on the crypt landing, an M-16 slung across his chest. Flynn said, "There's coffee in the bookshop." Gallagher climbed the stairs, and Flynn went down the remaining steps to the gate. Parts of the chain had been pieced together, and a new padlock was clamped to it. He examined the gate's mangled lock; another bullet or two and it would have sprung. But there were only fifty rounds in the drum of a Thompson. Not fifty-one, but fifty. . . . And an M-72 rocket could take a Saracen, and the Red Bus to Clady on the Shankill Road went past Whitehorn Abbey . . . and it was all supposed to be haphazard, random, with no meaning . . .

Flynn stared into the sacristy. He heard men speaking in the side corridors, and footsteps approached from the center opening in the left wall. Schroeder stepped into the sacristy, looked around, turned toward Flynn, and walked deliberately up the stairs. He stood on the steps below the gates, his eyes fixed on Flynn's. A long time passed before Flynn spoke. "Am I as you pictured me?"

Schroeder replied stiffly, "I've seen a photo of you."

"And I of you. But am I as you *pictured* me?"

Schroeder shook his head. Another long silence developed, then Flynn spoke abruptly. "I'm going to reach into my pocket." Flynn took the microphone sensor and passed it over Schroeder. "This is a very private conversation."

"I will report everything said here."

"I would bet my life you don't."

Schroeder seemed perplexed and wary.

Flynn said, "Are they any closer to meeting our demands?"

Schroeder didn't like face-to-face negotiating. He knew, because people had told him, that his face revealed too much. He cleared his throat. "You're asking the impossible. Accept the compromise."

Flynn noticed the extra firmness in Schroeder's voice, the lack of sir or mister, and the discomfort. "What *is* the compromise?"

Schroeder's eyebrows rose slightly. "Didn't Hickey—"

"Just tell it to me again."

Schroeder related the offer and added, "Take it before the British change their minds about parole. And for yourselves, low bail is as good as immunity. For God's sake, man, no one has ever been offered more in a hostage situation."

Flynn nodded. "Yes. . . . Yes, it's a good offer—tempting—"

"Take it! Take it before someone is killed—"

"It's a little late for that, I'm afraid."

"What?"

"Sir Harold murdered a lad named Pedar. Luckily no one knows he's dead except Hickey and myself . . . and I suppose Pedar knows he's dead. . . . Well, when my people discover he's dead, they'll want to kill Baxter. Pedar's sister, Megan, will want to do much worse. This complicates things somewhat."

Schroeder passed his hand over his face. "God . . . listen, I'm sure it was unintentional."

"Harry bashed his throat in with a rifle butt. Could have been an accident, I suppose. It doesn't make the lad any less dead."

Schroeder's mind was racing. He swore to himself, *Baxter, you stupid bastard.* "Look . . . it's a case of a POW trying to escape. . . . It's Baxter's duty to try. . . . You're a soldier . . ."

Flynn said nothing.

"Here's a chance for you to show professionalism . . . to show you're not a common crim—" He checked himself. "To show mercy, and—"

Flynn interrupted. "Schroeder, you are most certainly part Irish. I've rarely met a man more possessed of so much ready bullshit for every occasion."

"I'm serious—"

"Well, Baxter's fate depends mostly on what you do now."

"No. It depends on what *you* do. The next move is yours."

"And I'm about to make it." He lit a cigarette and asked, "How far are they along in their attack plans?"

Schroeder said, "That's not an option for us."

Flynn stared at him. "Caught you in a lie—your left eye is twitching. God, Schroeder, your nose is getting longer." He laughed. "I should have had you down here hours ago. Burke was too cool."

"Look—you asked me here for a private meeting, so you must have something to say—"

"I want you to help us get what we want."

Schroeder looked exasperated. "That's what I've been *doing.*"

"No, I mean *everything* we want. Your heart isn't in it. If the negotiations fail, you don't lose nearly as much as everyone in here does. Or as much as Bellini's ESD. They stand to lose fifty to a hundred men in an attack."

Schroeder thought of his imprudent offer to Bellini. "There will be no attack."

"Did you know Burke told me he'd go with Bellini? There's a man with a great deal to lose if you fail. Would *you* go with Bellini?"

"Burke couldn't have said that because Bellini's not going *anywhere.*" Schroeder had the uneasy impression he was being drawn into something, but he had no intention of making a mistake this late. "I'll try to get more for you only if you give me another two hours after dawn."

Flynn ignored him and went on. "I thought I'd better give you a very personal motive to push those people into capitulation."

Schroeder looked at Flynn cautiously.

"You see, there's one situation you never covered in your otherwise detailed book, Captain." Flynn came closer to the gate. "Your daughter would very much like you to try harder."

"What . . . ?"

"Terri Schroeder O'Neal. She wants you to try harder."

Schroeder stared for a few seconds, then said loudly, "What the hell are you talking about?"

"Lower your voice. You'll excite the police."

Schroeder spoke through clenched teeth. "What the *fuck* are you saying?"

"Please, you're in church." Flynn passed a scrap of paper through the bars.

Schroeder snatched it and read his daughter's handwriting: *Dad—I'm being held hostage by members of the Fenian Army. I'm all right. They won't harm me if everything goes okay at the Cathedral. Do your very best. I love you, Terri.*

Schroeder read the note again, then again. He felt his knees buckle, and he grabbed at the gate. He looked up at Flynn and tried to speak, but no sound came out.

Flynn spoke impassively. "Welcome to the Fenian Army, Captain Schroeder."

Schroeder swallowed several times and stared at the note.

"Sorry," said Flynn. "Really I am. You don't have to speak—just listen." Flynn lit another cigarette and spoke briskly. "What you have to do is make the strongest possible case for our demands. First, tell them I've paraded two score of well-armed men and women past you. Machine guns, rockets, grenades, *flamethrowers.* Tell them we are ready, willing, and able to take the entire six-hundred-man ESD down with us, to destroy the Cathedral and kill the hostages. In other words, scare the shit out of Joe Bellini and his heroes. Understand?" He paused, then said, "They'll never suspect that Captain Schroeder's report of seeing a great number of well-armed soldiers is false. Use your imagination—better yet, look up at the landing, Schroeder. Picture forty, fifty men and women parading past that crypt door—picture those machine guns and rockets and flamethrowers. . . . Go on, look up there."

Schroeder looked, and Flynn saw in his eyes exactly what he wanted to see.

After a minute Schroeder lowered his head. His face was pale, and his hands pulled at his shirt and tie.

Flynn said, "Please calm down. You can save your daughter's life only if you pull yourself together. That's it. Now . . . if this doesn't work, if they are still committed to an assault, then threaten to go public—radio, TV, newspapers. Tell Kline, Doyle, and all the rest of them you're going to announce that in all your years of hostage negotiating, that you, as the court of last resort for the lives of hostages, strongly and in no uncertain terms believe that neither an attack nor further negotiations can save this situation. You will declare, publicly, that therefore for the first time in your career you urge capitulation—for humanitarian as well as tactical reasons."

Flynn watched Schroeder's face but could see nothing revealed there except anguish. He went on, "You have a good deal of influence—moral and professional—with the media, the police force, and the politicians. Use every bit of that influence. You must create the kind of pressure and climate that will force the British and American governments to surrender."

Schroeder's voice was barely audible. "Time . . . I need time. . . . Why didn't you give me more time . . . ?"

"If I'd told you sooner, you wouldn't have made it through the night, or you may have told someone. The only time left is that which remains until the dawn —less if you can't stop the attack. But if you can get them to throw open the prison gates . . . Work on it."

Schroeder pushed his face to the bars. "Flynn . . . please . . . listen to me. . . ."

Flynn went on. "Yes, I know that if you succeed and we walk out of here free, they'll certainly count us, and they'll wonder where all the flamethrowers are. . . . Well, you'll be embarrassed, but all's fair in love and war, and *c'est la guerre,* and all that rot. Don't even think that far ahead and don't be selfish."

Schroeder's head shook, and his words were incoherent. All that Flynn could make out was "Jail." Flynn said, "Your daughter can visit you on weekends." He added, "I'll even visit you."

Schroeder stared at him, and a choked-off sound rose in his throat.

Flynn said, "Sorry, that was low." He paused. "Look, if it means anything to you, I feel bad that I had to resort to this. But it wasn't going well, and I knew you'd want to help us, help Terri, if you understood the trouble she was in." Flynn's voice became stern. "She really ought to be more selective about her bunkmates. Children can be such an embarrassment to parents, especially parents in public life—sex, drugs, wild politics . . ."

Schroeder was shaking his head. "No . . . you don't have her. You're bluffing. . . ."

Flynn continued. "But she's safe enough for the moment. Dan—that's her friend's name—is kind, considerate, probably a passable lover. It's the lot of some soldiers to draw easy duty—others to fight and die. Throw of the dice and all that. Then again, I wouldn't want to be in Dan's place if he gets the order to put a bullet in the back of Terri's head. No kneecapping or any of that. She's innocent, and she'll get a quick bullet without knowing it's about to come. So, are we clear about what you have to do?"

Schroeder said, "I won't do it."

"As you wish." He turned and began walking up the stairs. He called back. "In about a minute a light will flash from the bell tower, and my men on the outside will telephone Dan, and . . . and that, I'm afraid, will be the end of Terri Schroeder." He continued up the stairs.

"Wait! Listen, maybe we can work this out. Hold on! Stop walking away!"

Flynn turned slowly. "I'm afraid this is not negotiable, Captain." He paused and said, "It's awkward when you're involved personally, isn't it? Did you ever consider that every man and woman you've negotiated with or for was involved personally? Well, I'm not going to take you to task for your past successes. You were dealing with criminals, and they probably deserved the shoddy deals you got for them. You and I deserve a better deal. Our fates are intertwined, our goals are the same—aren't they? Yes or no, Captain? Quickly!"

Schroeder nodded.

Flynn moved down the stairs. "Good decision." He came close to the gate and put his hand out. Schroeder looked at it but shook his head. "Never."

Flynn withdrew his hand. "All right, then . . . all right. . . ."

Schroeder said, "Can I go now?"

"Yes. . . . Oh, one more thing. It's quite possible you'll fail even if you dwell on the flamethrowers and threaten public statements and all that . . . so we should plan for failure."

Schroeder's face showed that he understood what was coming.

Flynn's voice was firm and businesslike. "If Bellini is to attack, in spite of everything you can do to stop it, then I'll give you another way to save Terri's life."

"No."

"Yes, I'm afraid you'll have to get down here and tell me when, where, how, that sort of thing—"

"No! No, I would never—never get police officers killed—"

"They'll get killed anyway. And so will the hostages and the Fenians and Terri. So if you want to at least save her, you'll give me the operational plans."

"They won't tell me—"

"Make it your business to know. The easier solution is to scare Bellini out of his fucking mind and get *him* to refuse. You've a great many options. I wish I had as many."

Schroeder wiped his brow. His breathing was erratic, and his voice was shaky. "Flynn . . . please . . . I'll move heaven and earth to get them to surrender—I swear to God I will—but if they don't listen—" He drew up his body. "Then I won't betray them. Never. Even if it means Terri—"

Flynn reached out and grabbed Schroeder by the arm. "Use your head, man. If they're repulsed once, they aren't likely to try again. They're not marines or royal commandos. If I beat them back, then Washington, the Vatican, and other concerned countries will pressure London. I can almost guarantee there'll be *fewer* police killed if I stop them in their tracks . . . stop them before the battle gets too far along. . . . You *must* tell me if they've got the architect and the blueprints . . . tell me if they will use gas, if they're going to cut off the lights. . . . You know what I need. And I'll put the hostages in the crypt for protection. I'll send a signal, and Terri will be freed within five minutes. I won't ask any more of you."

Schroeder's head shook.

Flynn reached out his other hand and laid it on Schroeder's shoulder. He spoke almost gently. "Long after we're dead, after what's happened here is only a dim memory to an uncaring world, Theresa will be alive, perhaps remarried—children, grandchildren. Step outside of what you feel now, Captain, and look into the future. Think of her and think also of your wife—Mary lives for that girl, Bert. She—"

Schroeder suddenly pulled away. "Shut up! For God's sake, shut up. . . ." He slumped forward, and his head rested against the bars.

Flynn patted him on the shoulder. "You're a decent man, Captain. An honest man. And you're a good father. . . . I hope you're still a father at dawn. Well . . . will you be?"

Schroeder nodded.

"Good. Go on, then, go back, have a drink. Get yourself together. It'll be all right. No, don't go thinking about your gun. Killing me or killing yourself won't solve anyone's problem but your own. Think about Terri and Mary. They need you and love you. See you later, Captain, God willing."

51

Governor Doyle stood in a back room of the Cardinal's residence, a telephone in his hand. He listened to a succession of state officials: policemen, public relations people, legislators, the Attorney General, the commander of the state's National Guard. They spoke to him from Albany, from the state offices in Rockefeller Center, from their homes, and from their vacation hotels in warmer climates. All of these people, who normally couldn't decide on chicken or roast beef at a banquet, had decided that the time had come to storm the Cathedral. The Lieutenant Governor told him, frankly, if not tactfully, that his ratings in the polls were so low he had nothing to lose and could only gain by backing an assault on the Cathedral regardless of its success or failure. Doyle put the receiver into its cradle and regarded the people who were entering the room.

Kline, he noticed, had brought Spiegel, which meant a decision could be reached. Monsignor Downes took a seat beside Arnold Sheridan of the State Department. On the couch sat the Irish Consul General, Donahue, and the British Foreign Office representative, Eric Palmer. Police Commissioner Rourke stood by the door until Kline pointed to a chair.

Doyle looked at Bartholomew Martin, who had no official status any longer but whom he had asked to be present. Martin, no matter what people were saying about him, could be counted on to supply the right information.

The Governor cleared his throat and said, "Gentlemen, Miss—Ms.—Spiegel, I've asked you here because I feel that *we* are the ones most immediately affected by this situation." He looked around the room. "And before we leave here, we're going to cut this Gordian knot." He made a slicing movement with his hand. "Cut through every tactical and strategic problem, political consideration, and moral dilemma that has paralyzed our will and our ability to *act!*" He paused, then turned to Monsignor Downes. "Father, would you repeat for everyone the latest news from Rome?"

Monsignor Downes said, "Yes. His Holiness is going to make a personal appeal to the Fenians, as Christians, to spare the Cathedral and the lives of the hostages. He will also appeal to the governments involved to show restraint and will place at their disposal the facilities of the Vatican where they and the Fenians can continue their negotiations."

Major Martin broke the silence. "The heads of state of the three governments involved are making a point of *not* speaking directly to these terrorists—"

The Monsignor waved his hand in a gesture of dismissal. "His Holiness would not be speaking as head of the Vatican State but as a world spiritual leader."

The British representative, Palmer, said, "Such an appeal would place the American President and the Prime Ministers of Ireland and Britain in a difficult—"

Monsignor Downes was becoming agitated by the negative response. "His Holiness feels the Church must do what it can for these outcasts because that has been our mission for two thousand years—these are the people who need us." He handed a sheet of paper to the Governor. "This is the text of His Holiness's appeal."

Governor Doyle read the short message and passed it to Mayor Kline.

Monsignor Downes said, "We would like that delivered to the people inside the Cathedral at the same time it's read on radio and television. Within the next hour—before dawn."

After everyone in the room had seen the text of the Pope's appeal, Eric Palmer said, "Some years ago, we actually did meet secretly with the IRA, and they made it public. The repercussions rocked the government. I don't think we're going to speak with them again—certainly not at the Vatican."

Donahue spoke with a tone of sadness in his voice. "Monsignor, the Dublin government outlawed the IRA in the 1920s, and I don't think Dublin will back the Vatican on this. . . ."

Martin said, "As you know we've actually passed on a compromise to them, and they've not responded. The Pope can save himself and all of us a great deal of embarrassment if he withholds this plea."

Mayor Kline added, "The only way the Fenians can go to the Vatican is if I *let* them go. And I can't do that. I have to enforce the law."

Arnold Sheridan spoke for the first time, and the tone of his voice suggested a final policy position. "The government of the United States has reason to believe that federal firearm and passport laws have been violated, but otherwise it's purely a local affair. We're not going anywhere to discuss the release of Irish prisoners in the United Kingdom or immunity from prosecution for the people in the Cathedral."

Spiegel looked at Downes. "The only place negotiations can be held is right here—on the phone or at the sacristy gate. It is the policy of the police in this city to contain a hostage situation—not let it become mobile. And it is the law to arrest criminals at the first possible opportunity. In other words, the trenches are dug, and no one is leaving them under a truce flag."

The Monsignor pursed his lips and nodded. "I understand your positions, but the Church, which many of you consider so ironbound, is willing to try *anything.* I think you should know that personal appeals to all parties involved will be forthcoming from the Archbishop of Canterbury, the Primate of Ireland, and from hundreds of other religious leaders of every faith and denomination. And in almost every church and synagogue in this city and in other cities, all-night prayer vigils have been called. And at 5:00 A.M., if it's not over by then, every church bell in this city, and probably in the country, will begin ringing—ringing for sanity, for mercy, and for all of us."

Roberta Spiegel stood and lit a cigarette. "The mood of the people, notwithstanding bells and singing in the streets, is very hard line. If we take a soft approach and it explodes in our faces at 6:03, all of us will be out on our asses, and there'll be no all-night prayer vigils for us." She paused, then said, "So let's cut through the bullshit—or the Gordian knot—and decide how and when we're going to attack, and get our stories straight for afterward."

Cigarettes were being lit, and Major Martin was helping himself to the Cardinal's sherry.

The Governor nodded appreciatively. "I admire your honesty and perception, Ms. Spiegel, and—"

She looked at him. "This is why you asked us here, so let's get on with it, Governor."

Governor Doyle flushed but controlled his anger and said, "Good idea." He looked around. "Then we all agree that a compromise is not an option, that the Fenians won't surrender, and that they'll carry out their threats at dawn?"

There were some tentative nods.

The Governor looked at Arnold Sheridan and said, "I'm on my own?"

Sheridan nodded.

Doyle said, "But—off the record—the administration would like to see a hard-line approach?"

Sheridan said, "The message the government wants to convey is that this sort of thing will always be met by force—local force." Sheridan walked to the door. "Thank you, Governor, for the opportunity to contribute to the discussion. I'm sure you'll reach the right decision." He left.

Mayor Kline watched the door close and said, "We've been cut adrift." He turned to Donahue and Palmer. "You see, the federal system works marvelously—they collect taxes and pass laws, Mayor Kline fights terrorists."

Kline stood and began pacing. He stopped in front of Donahue and Palmer. "Do you understand that it is in my power, as the duly elected Mayor of this city, to order an assault on that Cathedral?"

Neither man responded.

Kline's voice rose. "It is my *duty*. And I don't have to answer to *anyone*."

Eric Palmer stood and moved toward the door. "We've offered all the compromises we can. . . . And if this is, as you indicate, a local matter, then there's no reason for Her Majesty's government to involve itself any further." He looked at Martin, who made no move to follow, then nodded to the others. "Good morning." He walked out.

Tomas Donahue stood. "I feel bad about all of this. . . . I've lived in this city for five years. . . . Saint Patrick's is my parish church. . . . I know the Cardinal and Father Murphy. . . ." He looked at Monsignor Downes. "But there's *nothing* I can do." He walked to the door and turned back. "If you need me, I'll be in the consulate. God bless. . . ." He left quickly.

Spiegel said, "Nice clean exits."

Governor Doyle hooked his thumbs on his vest pockets. "Well . . . there it is." He turned to Martin. "Major . . . won't you give us your thoughts. . . . As a man who is familiar with the IRA . . . what would be your course of action?"

Martin said without preamble, "It's time you discussed a rescue operation."

The Governor nodded slowly, aware that the phrase "rescue operation," as opposed to attack or assault, was a subtle turning point. The phraseology for the coming action was being introduced and refined. He turned abruptly to Monsignor Downes. "Are you willing to give your blessing to a rescue operation?"

The Monsignor looked up quickly. "Am I . . . ? Well . . ."

Governor Doyle moved close to Downes. "Monsignor, in times of crisis it's often people like ourselves, at the middle levels, who get stuck holding the bag. And *we* have to act. Not to act is more immoral than to act with force." He added. "Rescue, we have to *rescue*—"

Monsignor Downes said, "But . . . the Papal plea . . ."

Mayor Kline spoke from across the room. "I don't want to see the Pope or the other religious leaders make fools of themselves. If God himself pleaded with these Fenians, it would make no difference."

The Monsignor ran his hands across his cheeks. "But why *me* . . . ? What difference does it make what *I* say?"

Kline cleared his throat. "To be perfectly honest with you, Monsignor, I won't do a damned thing to rescue those people or save that Cathedral unless I have the blessing of a ranking member of the Catholic clergy. A Monsignor will do, preferably Irish like yourself. I'm no fool, and neither are you."

Monsignor Downes slumped into his chair. "Oh God . . ."

Rourke rose from his chair and walked to Downes. He knelt beside the Monsignor's chair and spoke with anguish in his voice. "My boys are mostly Catholic, Father. If they have to go in here . . . they'll want to see you first . . . to make their confessions . . . to know that someone from the Church is blessing their mission. Otherwise, they'll . . . I don't know. . . ."

Monsignor Downes put his face in his hands. After a full minute he looked up and nodded slowly. "God help me, but if you think it's the only way to save them . . ." He stood suddenly and almost ran from the room.

For a few seconds no one spoke, then Spiegel said, "Let's move before things start coming apart."

Mayor Kline was rubbing his chin thoughtfully. He looked up. "Schroeder will have to state that he's failed absolutely."

Governor Doyle said, "That should be no problem. He has." He added, "It would help also if we put out a news release—concurrent with the rescue—that the Fenians have made *new* demands in addition to the ones we were willing to discuss—" He stopped abruptly. "Damn it, there are *tapes* of every phone conversation. . . . Maybe Burke can—"

Kline interrupted. "Forget Burke. Schroeder is speaking in person to Flynn right now. That will give Schroeder the opportunity to state that Flynn has made a set of new demands."

The Governor nodded. "Yes, very good."

Kline said, "I'll have Bellini report in writing that he believes that there's a good chance of carrying out a rescue with a minimum loss of life and property."

Doyle said, "But Bellini's like a yo-yo. He keeps changing his mind—" He looked sharply at Rourke. "Will he write such a statement?"

Rourke's tone was anxious. "He'll carry out any orders to attack . . . but as for signing any statement . . . he's a difficult man. I know his position is that he needs more solid intelligence before he says he *approves*—"

Major Martin said, "Lieutenant Burke tells me he's very close to an intelligence breakthrough."

Everyone looked at Martin.

Martin continued. "He'll have at least the blueprints, perhaps the architect himself, within the next hour. I can almost guarantee it." Martin's tone suggested that he didn't want to be pressed further.

Kline said, "What we need from Inspector Langley are psy-profiles showing that half the terrorists in there are psychotic."

Governor Doyle said, "Will these police officers cooperate?"

Spiegel answered. "I'll take care of Langley. As for Schroeder, he's very savvy and politically attuned. No problem there. Regarding Bellini, we'll offer a promotion and transfer to wherever he wants." Spiegel walked toward the telephone. "I'll get the media right now and tell them that the negotiations are reaching a critical stage and it's absolutely essential they delay on those Church appeals."

Doyle said almost smugly, "At least I know *my* man, Logan, will do what he is told." He turned to Kline. "Don't forget, I want a piece of this, Murray. At least one squad has to be from the Sixty-ninth."

Mayor Kline looked out the window. "Are we doing the right thing? Or have we all gone crazy?"

Martin said, "You'd be crazy to wait for dawn." He added, "It's odd, isn't it, that the others didn't want to share this with us?"

Roberta Spiegel looked up as she dialed. "Some rats have perceived a sinking ship and jumped off. Other rats have perceived a bandwagon and jumped on. Before the sun rises, we'll know which rats saw things more clearly."

Bert Schroeder sat at his desk in the Monsignor's office. Langley, Bellini, and Colonel Logan stood, listening to Mayor Kline and Governor Doyle tell them what was expected of them. Schroeder's eyes darted from Kline to Doyle as his thoughts raced wildly.

Roberta Spiegel sat in her rocker staring into the disused fireplace, absently twirling a brandy snifter in her hands. The room had grown cold, and she had Langley's jacket draped over her shoulders.

Major Martin stood at the fireplace, occupied with the curios on the mantel.

Police Commissioner Rourke stood beside the Mayor, nodding agreement at everything Kline and Doyle said, trying to elicit similar nodding from his three officers.

The Governor stopped speaking and looked at Schroeder a moment. Something about the man suggested a dormant volcano. He tried to gauge his reaction. "Bert?"

Schroeder's eyes focused on the Governor.

Doyle said, "Bert, this is no reflection on you, but if dawn comes and there's no compromise, no extension of the deadline—and there won't be—and the hostages are *executed* and the Cathedral *demolished* . . . well, it will be *you*, Bert, who'll get most of the public abuse. Won't it?"

Schroeder said nothing.

Mayor Kline turned to Langley. "And it will be *you*, Inspector, who will get a great deal of the official censure."

"Be that as it may—"

Bellini said heatedly, "We can handle criminals, Your Honor, but these are guerrillas armed with military ordnance—intrusion alarms, submachine guns, rockets, and . . . and God knows what else. What if they have flamethrowers? Huh? And they're holed up in a national shrine. Christ, I still don't understand why the army can't—"

The Mayor put a restraining hand on Bellini with a look of disappointment. "Joe . . . Joe, this is not like you."

Bellini said, "It sure as hell is."

Governor Doyle looked at Logan, who appeared uncomfortable. "Colonel? What's *your* feel?"

Colonel Logan came to a modified position of attention. "Oh . . . well . . . I am convinced that we should act without delay to mount an att—a rescue operation."

The Governor beamed.

"However," continued Logan, "the tactical plan is not sound. What you're asking us to do is like . . . like shooting rats in a china cabinet without breaking the china . . . or the cabinet. . . ."

The Governor stared at Logan, his bushy eyebrows rising in an arc like squirrel tails. "Soldiers are often asked to do the impossible—and to do it well. National Guard duty is not all parades and happy hours."

"No, sir . . . yes, sir."

"Can the Fighting Irish hold up their end of the operation?"

"Of course!"

The Governor slapped Logan's shoulder soundly. "Good man."

The Mayor turned to Langley. "Inspector, you will have to come up with the dossiers we need on the Fenians."

Langley hesitated.

Roberta Spiegel fixed her eyes on him. "By no later than noon, Inspector."

Langley looked at her. "Sure. Why not? I'll do some creative writing with the help of a discreet police psychologist—Dr. Korman—and come up with psy-profiles of the Fenians that would scare the hell out of John Hickey himself."

Major Martin said, "May I suggest, Inspector, that you also show a link between the death of that informer—Ferguson, I think his name was—and the Fenians? That will tidy up that business as well."

Langley looked at Martin and understood. He nodded.

Kline looked at Bellini. "Well, Joe . . . are you on our team?"

Bellini looked troubled. "I am . . . but . . ."

"Joe, can you honestly say that you're absolutely convinced these terrorists will not shoot the Cardinal and the others at dawn and then blow up Saint Patrick's Cathedral?"

"No . . . but—"

"Are you convinced your men cannot conduct a successful rescue operation?"

"I never said anything like that, Your Honor. I just won't sign anything. . . . Since when are people required to sign something like that?"

The Mayor patted his shoulder gently. "Should I get someone *else* to lead your men against the terrorists in a rescue operation, Joe? Or should I just let Colonel Logan handle the whole operation?"

Bellini's mind was filled with conflicting thoughts, all of them unhappy.

Spiegel snapped, "Yes or no, Captain? It's getting late, and the fucking sun is due at 6:03."

Bellini looked at her and straightened his posture. "I'll lead the attack. If I get the blueprints, then I'll decide if I'm going to sign anything."

Mayor Kline let out a deep breath. "Well, that's about it." He looked at Langley. "You'll of course reconsider your resignation."

Langley said, "Actually, I was thinking about chief inspector."

Kline nodded quickly. "Certainly. There'll be promotions for everyone after this."

Langley lit a cigarette and noticed his hands were unsteady. Kline and Doyle, he was convinced, were doing the right thing in attacking the Cathedral. But with the sure instincts of the politician, they were doing it for the wrong reasons, in the wrong way, and going about it in a slimy manner. But so what? That was how half the right things got done.

Mayor Kline was smiling now. He turned to Schroeder. "Bert, all we need from you is some more time. Keep talking to them. You're doing a hell of a job, Bert, and we appreciate it. . . . Captain?" He smiled at Schroeder the way he always smiled at someone he had caught not paying attention. "Bert?"

Schroeder's eyes focused on Kline, but he said nothing.

Mayor Kline regarded him with growing apprehension. "Now . . . now, Bert, I need a signed statement from you saying that it is your professional opinion, based on years of hostage negotiating, that you recommend a cessation of negotiations. Right?"

Schroeder looked around the room and made an unintelligible noise.

The Mayor seemed anxious but went on. "You should indicate that when you saw Flynn he made *more* demands . . . crazy demands. Okay? Write that up as soon as possible." He turned to the others. "All of you—"

"I won't do that."

Everyone in the room looked at Schroeder. Kline said incredulously, "What —what did you say?"

Roberta Spiegel stood quickly, sending the rocker sliding into Governor Doyle.

Doyle moved the rocker aside and approached Schroeder. "Those are true statements! And you haven't accomplished shit so far!"

Schroeder stood and steadied himself against the desk. "I've listened to all of you, and you're all crazy."

Spiegel said to Langley, "Get the backup negotiator."

Schroeder shouted, "No! No one can speak with Flynn but me. . . . He won't speak to anyone else. . . . You'll see he won't speak. . . . I'll call him now. . . ." He reached for the telephone, but Langley pulled it away. Schroeder fell back in his chair.

Mayor Kline looked stunned. He tried to speak but couldn't get a word out.

Spiegel moved around the desk and looked down at Schroeder. Her voice was soft and dispassionate. "Captain, sometime between now and the time Bellini is ready to move, you will prepare a statement justifying our decision. If you don't, I'll see to it that you are brought up on departmental charges, dismissed from the force, and lose your pension. You'll end up as a bank guard in Dubuque—if you're lucky enough ever to get a gun permit. Now, let's discuss this intelligently."

Schroeder stood and took a deep breath. His voice had the control and tone of the professional negotiator again. "Yes, let's do that. I'm sorry, I became overwrought for a moment. Let's discuss what Brian Flynn really said to me, not what you'd have liked him to say." Schroeder looked at Bellini and Logan. "It seems those forty-five corned beef dinners were not a ruse—there were people to eat those dinners. I saw them. And flamethrowers . . . let me tell you about the flamethrowers. . . ." He lit a cigar with shaking hands, then continued.

Schroeder went on in cool, measured tones, but everyone could hear an undercurrent of anxiety in his voice. He concluded, "Flynn has assembled what amounts to the largest, best-equipped armed force of trained insurgents this country has seen since the Civil War. It's too late to do anything except call Washington and tell them we've surrendered what is in our power to surrender. . . ."

52

Langley found Burke lying on a bed in a priest's room. "They've decided to hit the Cathedral!"

Burke sat up quickly.

Langley's voice was agitated. "Soon. Before the Pope's appeal—before the church bells ring and Monsignor Downes comes to his senses—"

"Slow down."

"Schroeder spoke to Flynn at the gate—said he saw forty or fifty armed Fenians—"

"Fifty?"

"But he didn't. I *know* he didn't."

"Hold on. Back up."

Langley paced around the small room. "Washington perceived a sinking ship. Kline and Doyle perceived a bandwagon. See? Tomorrow they'll both be heroes, or they'll be in Mexico wearing dark glasses and phony noses—"

Burke found some loose aspirin in the night table and chewed three of them.

Langley sat down on a chair. "Listen, Spiegel wants to see you." He briefed Burke quickly, then added, "You're the negotiator until they decide about Schroeder."

Burke looked up. "Negotiator?" He laughed. "Poor Bert. This was going to be his perfect game. . . . He really wanted this one." He lit a cigarette stub. "So"—he exhaled a stream of acrid smoke—"we attack—"

"No! We *rescue!* You have to call it a rescue operation now. You have to choose your words very carefully, because it's getting very grim and none of them is saying what they mean anymore—they never did anyway—and they lie better than we do. Go on, they're waiting for you."

Burke made no move to leave. "And Martin told them I would produce Stillway!"

"Yes, complete with blueprints. That was news to me—how about you?"

"And he never mentioned Terri O'Neal?"

"No—should he?" Langley looked at his watch. "Does it matter anymore?"

Burke stared out the window into Madison Avenue. "Martin killed Jack Ferguson, you know."

Langley came up behind him. "No. The Fenians killed Jack Ferguson."

Burke turned. "Lots of phony deals going down tonight."

Langley shook his head. "Damned right. And Kline is passing out promotions like they were campaign buttons. Go get one. But you have to pay."

Langley began pacing again. "You have to sign a statement saying you think everything Kline and Doyle do is terrific. Okay? Make them give you a captain's pay. I'm going to be a chief inspector. And get out of ID. Ask for the Art Forgery Squad—Paris, London, Rome. Promise me you'll visit Schroeder in Dubuque—"

"Get hold of yourself."

Langley waved his arms. "Remember, Martin is in, Schroeder is out. Logan is in with Kline and Doyle but out with Bellini—are you following me? Watch out for Spiegel. She's in rare form—what a magnificent bitch. The Fenians are lunatics, we're sane. . . . Monsignor Downes blesses us all. . . . What else?" He looked around with wild darting eyes. "Is there a shower in this place? I feel slimy. You still here? Beat it!" Langley fell back on the bed. "Go away."

Burke had never seen Langley become unglued, and it was frightening. He started to say something, then thought better of it and left.

Burke walked beside Roberta Spiegel up the stairs. He listened to her brisk voice as they moved. Martin was climbing silently behind him.

Burke opened the stairshed door and walked onto the flat rooftop of the rectory. A wind blew from the north, and frozen pools of water reflected the lights of the tall buildings around them. Spiegel dismissed a team of ESD snipers, turned up her coat collar, and moved to the west side of the roof. She put her hands on the low wrought-iron fence that ran around the roof's perimeter and stared at the towering Cathedral rising across the narrow courtyard.

The streets below were deserted, but in the distance, beyond the barricades, horns blared, people sang and shouted, bagpipes and other instruments played intermittently. Burke realized it was after 4:00 A.M., and the bars had closed. The party was on the streets now, probably still a hundred thousand strong, maybe more, tenaciously clinging to the night that had turned magic for them.

Spiegel was speaking, and Burke tried to concentrate on her words; but he had no topcoat, and he was cold, and her words were blowing away in the strong wind. She concluded, "We've gotten our act together, Lieutenant, but before it comes apart, we're going to move. And we don't want any more surprises. Understand?"

Burke said, "Art Forgery Squad."

Spiegel looked at him, momentarily puzzled, then said, "Oh . . . all right. Either that or shower orderly at the academy gym." She turned her back to the wind and lit a cigarette.

Burke said, "Where's Schroeder?"

Spiegel replied, "He understands we don't want him out of our sight and talking to the press, so rather than suffer the indignity of a guard, he volunteered to stick with Bellini."

Burke felt a vague uneasiness pass through him. He said, "And I'm the negotiator?"

Spiegel said, "In fact, yes. But for the sake of appearances, Schroeder is still on the job. He's not without his political connections. He'll continue his duties, with some modifications, of course, and later . . . he'll go on camera."

Martin spoke for the first time. "Captain Schroeder should actually go back to the sacristy and speak with Flynn again. We have to keep up appearances at this critical moment. Neither Flynn nor the press should sense any problem."

Burke cupped his hands and lit a cigarette, looking at Martin as he did. Martin's strategy was becoming clear. He thought about Schroeder hanging around Bellini, about Schroeder meeting Flynn again at the gate. He thought, also, that Flynn did not have fifty well-armed people, and therefore Schroeder was mistaken, stupid, or gullible, which seemed to be the consensus. But he knew Schroeder was none of these things. *When you have excluded the impossible,* said Sherlock Holmes, *whatever remains, however improbable, must be the truth.* Schroeder was lying, and Burke was beginning to understand why. He pictured the face of a young woman, heard her voice again, and placed her at a promotion party five or six years before. Almost hesitantly he made the final connection he should have made hours ago. Burke said to Spiegel, "And Bellini's working on a new plan of attack?"

Spiegel looked at him in the diffused light and said, "Right now Bellini and Logan are formulating plan B—escalating the response, as they say—based on the outside possibility that there is a powerful force in that Cathedral. They won't go in any other way. But we're counting on *you* to give us the intelligence we need to formulate a plan C, an infiltration of the Cathedral and surprise attack, using the hidden passages that many of us seem to believe exist. That may enable us to actually save some lives and save Saint Patrick's."

She looked out at the looming structure. Even from the outside it looked labyrinthine with its towers, spires, buttresses, and intricate stonework. She turned to Burke. "So, do you feel, Lieutenant Burke, that you've put your neck on a chopping block?"

"There's no reason why my neck shouldn't be where yours is."

"True," she said. "True. And yours is actually a little more exposed, since I understand you're going in with Bellini."

"That's right. How about you?"

She smiled unpleasantly, then said, "You don't *have* to go. . . . But it wouldn't be a bad idea . . . if you don't produce Stillway."

Burke glanced at Martin, who nodded slightly, and said, "I'll have him within . . . half an hour."

No one spoke, then Martin said, "If I may make another suggestion . . .

let's not make too much of this architect business in front of Captain Schroeder. He's overwrought and may inadvertently let something slip the next time he speaks with Flynn."

There was a long silence on the rooftop, broken by the sounds of shoes shuffling against the frozen gravel and the wind rushing through the streets. Burke looked at Spiegel and guessed that she sensed Bert Schroeder had a real problem, was a real problem.

Spiegel put her hands in the pockets of her long coat and walked a few paces from Burke and Martin. For a few brief seconds she wondered why she was so committed to this, and it came to her that in those seven miserable years of teaching history what she had really wanted to do was make history; and she would.

Captain Joe Bellini rubbed his eyes and looked at the clock in the press conference room. 4:26 A.M. *The fucking sun is due at* 6:03. In his half-sleep he had pictured a wall of brilliant sunlight moving toward him, coming to rescue him as it had done so many times in Korea. *God,* he thought, *how I hate the sound of rifles in the night.*

He looked around the room. Men slept on cots or on the floor, using flak jackets for pillows. Others were awake, smoking, talking in low tones. Occasionally someone laughed at something that, Bellini guessed, was not funny. Fear had a special stink of its own, and he smelled it strongly now, a mixture of sweat, tobacco, gun oil, and the breath from labored lungs and sticky mouths.

The blackboard was covered with colored chalk marks superimposed on a white outline of St. Patrick's. On the long conference table lay copies of the revised attack plan. Bert Schroeder sat at the far end of the table, flipping casually through a copy.

The phone rang, and Bellini grabbed it. "ESD operations, Bellini."

The Mayor's distinctive nasal voice came over the line. "How are you holding up, Joe? Anxious to get rolling?"

"Can't wait."

"Good. . . . Listen, I've just seen your new attack plan. . . . It's a little excessive, isn't it?"

"It was mostly Colonel Logan's, sir," Bellini said.

"Oh . . . well, see that you tone it down."

Bellini picked up a full soft-drink can in his big hand and squeezed it, watching the top pop off and the brown liquid run over his fingers. "Approved or disapproved?"

The Mayor let a long time go by, and Bellini knew he was conferring, looking at his watch. Kline came back on the line. "The Governor and I approve . . . in principle."

"I thank you in principle."

Kline switched to another subject. "Is he still there?"

Bellini glanced at Schroeder. "Like dog turd on a jogger's sneakers."

Kline forced a weak laugh. "Okay, I'm in the state offices in Rockefeller Center with the Governor and our staffs—"

"Good view."

"Now, don't be sarcastic. Listen, I've just spoken to the President of the United States."

Bellini detected a note of self-importance in Kline's tone.

"The President says he's making definite progress with the British Prime Minister. He's also making noises like he might federalize the guard and send in marshals. . . ." Kline lowered his voice in a conspiratorial tone. "Between you and me, Joe, I think he's putting out a smokescreen . . . covering himself for later."

Bellini lit a cigarette. "Who isn't?"

Kline's voice was urgent. "He's under pressure. The church bells in Washington are already ringing, and there are thousands of people marching with candles in front of the White House. The British Embassy is being picketed—"

Bellini watched Schroeder stand and then walk toward the door. He said into the phone, "Hold on." Bellini called to Schroeder, "Where you headed, Chief?"

Schroeder looked back at him. "Sacristy." He walked out the door.

Bellini watched him go, then said into the phone, "Schroeder just went to make a final pitch to Flynn. Okay?"

Kline let out a long breath. "All right . . . can't hurt. By the time he gets back you'll be ready to move—unless he has something very solid, which he won't."

Bellini remembered that Schroeder had never had a failure. "You never know."

There was a long silence on the line, then the Mayor said, "Do you believe in miracles?"

"Never actually saw one." He thought, *Except the time you got reelected.* "Nope, never saw one."

"Me neither."

Bellini heard a click on the line, followed by a dial tone. He looked across the quiet room. "Get up! Off your asses! Battle stations. Move out!"

Bert Schroeder stood opposite Brian Flynn at the sacristy gate. Schroeder's voice was low and halting as he spoke, and he kept looking back nervously into the sacristy. "The plan is a fairly simple and classical attack. . . . Colonel Logan drew it up. . . . Logan himself will hit the front doors with an armored carrier, and the ESD will hit all the other doors simultaneously with rams. . . . They'll use scaling ladders and break through the windows. . . . It's all done under cover of gas and darkness . . . everyone has masks and night scopes. The electricity will be cut off at the moment the doors are hit. . . ."

Flynn felt the blood race through his veins as he listened. "Gas . . ."

Schroeder nodded. "The same stuff you used at the reviewing stands. It will be pumped in through the air ducts." He detailed the coordination of helicopters, snipers on the roofs, firemen, and bomb disposal men. He added, "The sacristy steps"—he looked down as though realizing he was standing in the very spot—"they'll be hit with steel-cut chain saws. Bellini and I will be with that squad. . . . We'll go for the hostages . . . if they're on the sanctuary . . ." He shook his head, trying to comprehend the fact that he was saying this.

"The hostages," said Flynn, "will be dead." He paused and said, "Where will Burke be?"

Schroeder shook his head, tried to go on, but heard his voice faltering. After some hesitation he slipped a sheaf of papers from his jacket and through the bars.

Flynn slid them under his shirt, his eyes darting between the corridor openings. "So there's nothing that the famous Captain Schroeder can do to stop this?"

Schroeder looked down. "There never was. . . . Why didn't you see that . . . ?"

Flynn's voice was hostile. "Because I listened to you all night, Schroeder, and I think I half believed your damned lies!"

Schroeder was determined to salvage something of himself from the defeat and humiliation he had felt at the last confrontation. "Don't put this on *me*. You knew I was lying. You *knew* it!"

Flynn glared at him, then nodded slightly. "Yes, I knew it." He thought a moment, then said, "And I know you're finally speaking the truth. It must be a great strain. Well, I can stop them at the doors . . . if, as you say, they haven't discovered any hidden passages and they don't have the architect—" He looked suddenly at Schroeder. "They *don't* have him, do they?"

Schroeder shook his head. He drew himself up and spoke rapidly. "Give it up. I'll get you a police escort to the airport. I know I can do that. That's all they really want—they want you out of here!"

Flynn seemed to consider for a brief moment, then shook his head.

Schroeder pressed on. "Flynn—listen, they're going to hit you hard. You're going to *die*. Can't you grasp that? You can't delude yourself any longer. But all you have to do is say you're willing to take less—"

"If I wanted less, I would have asked for less. No more hostage negotiating, please. God, how you go on. Talk about self-delusion."

Schroeder drew close to the gate. "All right. I've done all I could. Now you release—"

Flynn cut him off. "If the details you've given me are accurate, I'll send a signal to release your daughter."

Schroeder grabbed at the bars. "What *kind* of signal? When? The phones will be cut off. . . . The towers will be under sniper fire—What if you're . . . dead? Damn it, I've given you the plans—"

Flynn went on. "But if you've lied to me about any part of this, or if there should be a change in plans and you don't tell me—"

Schroeder was shaking his head spasmodically. "No. No. That's not acceptable. You're not living up to your end."

Flynn turned and walked up the stairs.

Schroeder drew his pistol and held it close against his chest. It wavered in his hand, the muzzle pointing toward Flynn's back, but his hand shook so badly he almost dropped the gun. Flynn turned the corner and disappeared.

After a full minute Schroeder holstered the pistol, faced around, and walked back to the side corridor. He passed grim-faced men standing against the walls with slung rifles. He found a lavatory, entered it, and vomited.

53

Burke stood alone in the small counting room close by the press room. He adjusted his flak jacket over his pullover and, after putting a green carnation in a cartridge loop, started for the door.

The door suddenly swung open, and Major Martin stood before him. "Hello, Burke. Is that what everyone in New York is wearing now?" He called back into the corridor, and two patrolmen appeared with a civilian between them. Martin smiled. "May I present Gordon Stillway, American Institute of Architects? Mr. Stillway, this is Patrick Burke, world-famous secret policeman."

A tall, erect, elderly man stepped into the room, looking confused but otherwise dignified. In his left hand he held a briefcase from which protruded four tubes of rolled paper.

Burke dismissed the two officers and turned to Martin. "It's late."

"Is it?" Martin looked at his watch. "You have fifteen full minutes to head off Bellini. Time, as you know, is relative. If you're eating Galway Bay oysters, fifteen minutes pass rather quickly, but if you're hanging by your left testicle, it drags a bit." He laughed at his own joke. "Bellini is hanging by his testicle. You'll cut him down—then hang him up there again after he's spoken to Mr. Stillway."

Martin moved farther into the small room and drew closer to Burke. "Mr. Stillway was kidnapped from his apartment by persons unknown and held in an empty loft not far from here. Acting on anonymous information, I went to the detectives in the Seventh Precinct and, *voilà*, Gordon Stillway. Mr. Stillway, won't you have a seat?"

Gordon Stillway remained standing and looked from one man to the other, then said, "This is a terrible tragedy . . . but I'm not quite certain what I'm supposed to—"

Martin said, "You, sir, will give the police the information they must have to infiltrate the Cathedral and catch the villains unawares."

Stillway looked at him. "What are you talking about? Do you mean they're going to attack? I won't have that."

Martin put his hand on Stillway's shoulder. "I'm afraid you've arrived a bit late, sir. That's not negotiable any longer. Either you help the police, or they go in there through the doors and windows and cause a great deal of death and destruction, after which the terrorists will burn it down and blow it up—or vice versa."

Stillway's eyes widened, and he let Martin maneuver him into a chair. Martin said to Burke, "You'd better hurry."

Burke came toward Martin. "Why did you cut it this close?"

Martin took a step back and replied, "I'm sorry. I had to wait for Captain Schroeder to deliver the attack plans to Flynn, which is what he's doing right now."

Burke nodded. Bellini's attack had to be canceled no matter what else happened. A new plan based on Stillway's information, if he had any, would jump off so close to 6:03 that it would probably end in disaster anyway. But Martin had delivered Stillway and therefore would be owed a great favor by Washington. He looked at Martin. "Major, I'd like to be the first to thank you for your help in this affair."

Martin smiled. "Now you're getting into the right spirit. You've been so glum all night, but you'll see—stick with me, Burke, and as I promised, you'll come out of this looking fine."

Burke addressed Stillway. "Are there any hidden passages into that Cathedral that will give the police a clear tactical advantage?"

Stillway sat motionless, contemplating the events that had begun with a sunny day and a parade, proceeded to his kidnapping and rescue, and ended with him in a subterranean room with two men who were obviously unbalanced. He said, "I have no idea what you mean by a clear tactical advantage." His voice became irritable. "I'm an architect."

Martin looked at his watch again. "Well, I've done my bit. . . ." He opened the door. "Hurry now. You promised Bellini you'd be at his side, and a promise is sacred and beautiful. And oh, yes, later—if you're still alive—you'll see at least one more mystery unfold in that Cathedral. A rather good one." He walked out and slammed the door.

Stillway regarded Burke warily. "Who was he? Who are *you?*"

"Who are *you?* Are you Gordon Stillway—or are you just another of the Major's little jokes?"

Stillway didn't answer.

Burke extracted a rolled blueprint from the briefcase, unfurled it, and stared at it. He threw the blueprint on the table and looked at his watch. "Come with me, Mr. Stillway, and we'll see if you were worth the wait."

Schroeder walked into the press conference room and hurried toward a phone. "This is Schroeder. Get me Kline."

The Mayor's voice was neutral. "Yes, Captain, any luck?"

Schroeder looked around the nearly empty room. Rifles and flak jackets had disappeared, and empty boxes of ammunition and concussion grenades lay in the corner. Someone had scrawled on the chalkboard:

> FINAL SCORE:
> CHRISTIANS AND JEWS——
> PAGANS AND ATHEISTS——

Kline's voice was impatient. "Well?"

Schroeder leaned against the table and fought down a wave of nausea. "No . . . no extension . . . no compromise. Listen . . ."

Kline sounded annoyed. "That's what everyone's been telling you all night."

Schroeder drew a long breath and pressed his hand to his stomach. Kline was speaking, but Schroeder wasn't listening. Slowly he began to take in more of his surroundings. Bellini stood across the table with his arms folded, Burke stood at the opposite end of the room, two ESD men with black ski masks stood very near him, and an old man, a civilian, sat at the conference table.

The Mayor went on. "Captain, right now you are still very much a hero, and within the hour you will be the police department's chief spokesman." Schroeder examined Bellini's blackened face and thought Bellini was glaring at him with unconcealed hatred, as though he *knew,* but he decided it must be the grotesque makeup.

Kline was still speaking. "And you will not speak to a newsperson until the last shot is fired. And what's this I hear about you volunteering to go in with Bellini?"

Schroeder said, "I . . . I have to. That's the least I can do. . . ."

"Have you lost your mind? What's wrong with you, anyway? You sound— have you been drinking?"

Schroeder found himself staring at the old man who, he now noticed, was studying a large unrolled length of paper. His eyes passed over the silent men in the room again and focused on Burke, who seemed . . . almost sad. Everyone looked as though someone had just died. Something was wrong here—

"Are you drunk?"

"No. . . ."

"Pull yourself together, Schroeder. You'll be on television soon."

"What . . . ?"

"Television! You remember, the red light, the big camera. . . . Now you get clear of that Cathedral—get over here as soon as possible."

Schroeder heard the phone go dead and looked at the receiver, then dropped it on the table. He extended his arm and pointed at Gordon Stillway. "Who is *that?*"

The room remained silent. Then Burke said, "You know who that is, Bert. We're going to redraw the attack plans."

Schroeder looked quickly at Bellini and blurted, "No! No! You—"

Bellini glanced at Burke and nodded. He turned to Schroeder. "I can't believe you did that." He came toward Schroeder, who was edging toward the door. "Where're you going, ace? You going to tip your pal, cocksucker?"

Schroeder's head was shaking spasmodically.

Bellini drew closer. "I can't hear you, you shit! Your golden voice sounds like a toilet flushing."

Burke called out. "Joe—no hard stuff—just take his gun." Burke moved closer to the two men. The two ESD officers held their rifles at their hips, not understanding exactly what was going on but ready to fire if Schroeder made a move for his gun. Gordon Stillway looked up from his blueprints.

Schroeder found his voice. "No . . . listen . . . I have to talk to Flynn . . . because . . . you see . . . I've got to try one more time—"

Bellini held out his hand. "Give me your gun—left hand—pinky in the trigger guard—nice and easy, and no one's going to get hurt."

Schroeder hesitated, then slowly reached into his jacket and carefully extracted the pistol with a hooked finger. "Bellini—listen—what's going on? Why—"

Bellini reached for the pistol with his left hand and swung with his right, hitting Schroeder a vicious blow to the jaw. Schroeder fell back against the door and slid down to the floor.

Burke said, "You didn't have to do that."

Bellini flexed his hand and turned to Burke. "You're right—I should've yanked his nuts out and shoved them up his nose." He looked back at Schroeder. "Tried to kill me, did you, scumbag?"

Burke saw that Bellini was contemplating further violence. "It had nothing to do with you, Bellini. Just cool out." He came up beside Bellini and put his hand on his shoulder. "Come on. You've got lots to do."

Bellini motioned to the ESD men. "Cuff this cocksucker and dump him in a closet somewhere." He turned to Burke. "You think I'm stupid, don't you? You think I don't know that you're all going to cover for that motherfucker, and as soon as the shit storm is over at dawn he's going to be the Mayor's golden boy again." He watched the ESD men carry Schroeder out and called after them, "Find some place with rats and cockroaches." He sat down and tried to steady his hands as he lit a cigarette.

Burke stood beside him. "Life is unfair, right? But someone handed us a break this time. Flynn thinks you're doing one thing, and you're going to do something else. So it didn't turn out so bad, right?"

Bellini nodded sulkily and looked at Stillway. "Yeah . . . maybe . . ." He rubbed his knuckles and flexed his fingers again. "That hurt . . . but it felt so good." He laughed suddenly. "Burke, come here. Want to know a secret? I've been looking for an excuse to do that for five years." He looked at the ceiling. "Thank you, God." He laughed again.

The room began filling with squad leaders hastily recalled from their jump-off points, and Bellini watched them file into the room. The absolutely worst feeling in the whole world, Bellini thought, was to get yourself psyched out of your mind for a fight and have it postponed. The squad leaders, he saw, were in a bad mood. Bellini looked at Burke. "You better call His fucking Honor and explain. You can cover Schroeder's ass if you want, but even if you don't, it won't matter to Kline, because they'll still promote him and make him a national hero."

Burke took off his flak jacket and pullover. "I have to see Flynn and come up with a good reason why Schroeder isn't staying in touch with him."

Bellini moved to the head of the conference table and took a long breath. He looked at each of the twelve squad leaders and said, "Men, I've got some good news and some bad news. Thing is, I don't know which is which."

No one laughed, and Bellini went on. "Before I tell you why the attack is postponed, I want to say something. . . . The people in the Cathedral are desperate men and women . . . guerrillas. . . . This is combat . . . war . . . and the goal is not to apprehend these people at the risk of your own lives—"

A squad leader called out, "You mean shoot first and ask questions later, right?"

Bellini remembered the military euphemism for it. "Make a clean sweep."

54

F ather Murphy stood on the crypt landing, a purple stole around his neck. Frank Gallagher knelt before him, making a hasty confession in a low, trembling voice. Flynn waited just inside the large crypt door, then called out to Gallagher, "That's fine, Frank."

Gallagher nodded to the priest, rose, and moved into the crypt. Flynn handed him a sheet of paper and said, "Here's the part of the attack plan which deals with the sacristy gate." He briefed Gallagher, then added, "You can take cover here in the crypt while you keep the gates under fire." As Flynn spoke, Gallagher focused on the brownish blood that had flowed so abundantly from Pedar Fitzgerald's mouth. Father Murphy was standing in the center of the bloodstain, apparently without realizing it, and Gallagher wanted to tell the priest to move—but Flynn was clasping his hand. "Good luck to you, Frank. Remember, Dublin, seventeenth of March next."

Gallagher made an unintelligible noise, but he nodded with a desperate determination.

Flynn came out of the crypt and took Murphy's arm. He led the priest up the stairs, across the sanctuary, and down the side steps into the ambulatory. Father Murphy disengaged himself from Flynn and turned toward the chancel organ. John Hickey sat talking on the field phone, Pedar Fitzgerald's covered body at his feet. The priest knelt and pulled the coat back from Pedar's head. He anointed his forehead, stood, and looked at Hickey, who had hung up the receiver.

Hickey said, "Sneaked that in, did you? Well, where now is Pedar Fitzgerald's soul?"

Father Murphy kept staring at Hickey.

Hickey said, "Now, like a good priest, you'll ask me to confess, and you assume I'll refuse. But what if I do confess? Would my entire past life, including every sin, sacrilege, and blasphemy that you can imagine, be forgiven? Would I gain the kingdom of heaven?"

Murphy said, "You know you must repent."

Hickey slapped the top of the organ. "I *knew* there was a catch!"

Flynn took Murphy's arm and pulled him away. They passed beside the confessional, and Flynn paused to look at the small white buzzer. "That was clever, Padre. I'll give you that." Flynn looked back across the ambulatory at Hickey. "I don't know what messages you, Maureen, or Hickey sent, but you can be sure none of you accomplished anything beyond adding to the confusion out there."

Father Murphy replied, "I still *feel* better about it."

Flynn laughed and began walking. Murphy followed, and Flynn spoke as they walked. "You feel better, do you? My, what a big ego you have, Father." Flynn stopped in the transept aisle between the two south triforia. He turned and looked up at the triforium they'd just passed beneath and called up to Eamon Farrell. "I know you're devout, Eamon, but Father Murphy can't fly, so you'll have to miss this confession."

Farrell looked as though this were the one confession he didn't want to miss.

Father Murphy called up, "Are you sorry for all your sins?"

Farrell nodded. "I am, Father."

Murphy said, "Make a good act of contrition—you'll be in a state of grace, Mr. Farrell. Don't do anything to alter that."

Flynn was annoyed. "If you try any of that again, you'll not hear another confession."

Murphy walked away, and Flynn outlined the coming attack to Farrell. He added, "If we stop them, your son will be free at dawn. Good luck."

Flynn walked to the wide transept doors. The priest was staring at the two khaki-colored mines attached to the doors and four more can-shaped mines placed at intervals on the floor. Trip wires ran from them in all directions. "You see," said Flynn conversationally, "when the doors are smashed in, these two mines explode instantly, followed at fifteen-second intervals by the other four, producing, so to speak, a curtain of shrapnel of a minute's duration. Every doorway in here will be clogged with writhing bodies. The screams . . . wait until you hear the screams. . . . You wouldn't believe that men can make such noises. My God, it makes the blood run cold, Father, and turns the bowels to ice water."

Murphy continued to stare at the mines.

Flynn motioned overhead. "Look at these commanding views. . . . How in the world do they expect to succeed?" He led the priest to the small door in the corner of the transept and motioned Murphy to go first. They walked wordlessly up the spiral stairs and came out in the long triforium five stories above the main floor.

Abby Boland stood by the door, an M-16 rifle cradled in her arms. She had found a pair of overalls in a maintenance closet, and she wore them over her cheerleader's uniform. Flynn put his arm around her and walked her away from the priest as he explained the coming attack and went through her assignments. Flynn looked across the nave at George Sullivan, who was watching them. He took his arm from her shoulder and said, "If we don't stop them . . . and if you determine in your own mind that killing more of them won't help anything, then get into the bell tower. . . . Don't try to cross the choir loft to get to George. . . . Stay away from Leary and Megan. Understand?"

Her eyes darted to the choir loft, and she nodded.

Flynn continued. "The attic will take a while to fall in, and the bombs won't damage the towers—they'll be the only things left standing. George will be all right in the south tower."

"George and I understood we'd not see each other again after this." She looked at Sullivan, who was still watching them.

"Good luck to you." Flynn moved toward the tower passage and left her with Father Murphy.

After a few minutes Murphy rejoined Flynn, and Flynn looked at his watch. "We don't have a great deal of time, so keep these things short."

"How do you know how much time you've got? Am I to understand that you know the details of this attack?" He looked at the sheaf of rolled papers in Flynn's hand.

Flynn tapped Murphy on the shoulder with the paper tube. "Each man has a price, as you know, and it often seems pitifully low, but did anyone ever consider that Judas Iscariot may have *needed* that silver?" He laughed and indicated the spiral stairs. They climbed three stories up into the tower, until they reached the level that passed beside the attic. Flynn opened a large wooden door, and they stepped onto a catwalk. Murphy peered into the dimly lit expanse, then walked to a pile of chopped wood and votive candles. He turned back and stared at Flynn, who met his stare, and Murphy knew there was nothing to be said.

Jean Kearney and Arthur Nulty moved out of the shadows and approached along a catwalk, their arms around each other. The expressions on their faces showed that they found the sight of Flynn and the priest to be ominous. They stopped some distance from the two men and looked at them, long plumes of breath coming from their mouths. Father Murphy was reminded of two lost souls who were not allowed to cross a threshold unless invited.

Flynn said, "The good Father wants to hear your sins."

Jean Kearney's face flushed. Nulty looked both embarrassed and frightened.

Flynn's eyebrows rose, and he let out a short laugh. He turned to the priest. "Self-control is difficult in times like these."

Murphy's face betrayed no anger or shock, but he let out a long, familiar sigh that Flynn thought must be part of the seminary training. Flynn motioned Murphy to stay where he was and strode across the catwalk. He handed Jean Kearney three sheets of paper and began briefing the two people. He concluded, "They'll come with the helicopters anytime after 5:15." He paused, then said, "Don't be afraid."

Jean Kearney answered, "The only thing we're afraid of is being separated." Nulty nodded.

Flynn put his arms around their shoulders and moved with them toward the priest. "Make Father Murphy a happy man and let him save your souls from the fires of hell at least." Flynn moved toward the door, then called back to Murphy. "Don't undermine the troops' morale, and no lengthy penances."

Flynn reentered the tower and waited in the darkness of a large, opaque-windowed room. He looked at his watch. According to Schroeder there were twenty minutes left until the earliest time the attack might begin.

He sat down on the cold, dusty floor, suddenly filled with a sense of awe at what he had done. One of the largest civil disturbances in American history was about to end in the most massive police action ever seen on this continent—and a landmark was going to be deleted from the guidebooks. The name of Brian Flynn would enter history. Yet, he felt, all that was trivial compared to the fact that these men and women were willingly following him into death.

Abruptly he pivoted around, drew his pistol, and knocked out a pane of thick glass, then looked out at the night. A cold wind blew feathery clouds across a brilliant blue, moonlit sky. Up the Avenue dozens of flags hung from protruding staffs, swaying stiff and frozen in the wind. The sidewalks were covered with ice and broken glass, sparkling in the light. *Spring,* he thought. "Dear God, I'll not see the spring."

Father Murphy cleared his throat, and Flynn spun around. Their eyes met, and Flynn rose quickly. "That was fast."

Flynn began the climb up the winding stairs that gave way to a series of ladders. Murphy followed cautiously. He'd never been this high in either tower, and despite the circumstances he was eager in a boyish sort of way to see the bells.

They climbed into the lowest bell room, where Donald Mullins crouched behind the stonework that separated two louvers. He wore a flak jacket, and his face and hands were blackened with soot from a burned cork whose odor still hung in the cold room.

Father Murphy looked at the ripped louvers with obvious displeasure and then stared up at the bells hanging from their cross-beams. Flynn said nothing but looked out into the Avenue. Everything appeared as before, but in some vague, undefined way it was not. He said to Mullins, "Can you tell?"

Mullins nodded. "When?"

"Soon." Flynn gave him two sheets of paper. "They've got to blind the eyes that watch them before the rest of the attack can proceed. It's all there in the order of battle."

Mullins ran a flashlight over the neatly typed pages, only vaguely interested in how Flynn came to have them. "My name here is Towerman North. Sounds like a bloody English lord or something." He laughed, then read, "If Towerman North cannot be put out with sniper fire, then high explosive and/or gas grenades will be fired into bell room with launchers. Helicopter machine gunners will be called in if Towerman North is still not neutralized. . . ." He looked up. "Neutralized . . . God, how they've butchered the language here. . . ."

Flynn saw that Mullins's smile was strained. Flynn said, "Try to keep us informed on the field phone. . . . Keep the receiver off the cradle so we can hear what's happening. . . ."

Mullins pictured himself thrashing around on the floor, small animal noises coming from his mouth into the open receiver.

Flynn went on, "If you survive the snipers, you'll survive the explosion and the fire."

"That barely compensates me for freezing half to death."

Flynn moved to the west opening and stared down at the green and gold harp flag, glazed with ice, and ran his hand over it. He looked out at Rockefeller Center. Hundreds of windows were still lit with bright fluorescent light, and figures passed back and forth. He took Mullins's field glasses and watched. A man was eating a sandwich. A young woman laughed on the telephone. Two uniformed policemen drank from cups. Someone with field glasses waved to him. He handed the glasses back. "I never hated them before . . ."

Mullins nodded. "It's so maddeningly commonplace . . . but I've gotten used to it." Mullins turned to Father Murphy. "So, it's that time, is it?"

"Apparently it is."

Mullins came close to Murphy. "Priests, doctors, and undertakers give me worse chills than ever a north wind did."

Father Murphy said nothing.

Mullins's eyes stared off at some indeterminate place and time. He spoke in a barely audible voice. "You're from the north, and you've heard the caoine— the funeral cry of the peasants. It's meant to imitate the wail of a chorus of banshees. The priests know this but never seem to object." He glanced at Murphy. "Irish priests are very tolerant of these things. Well, I've heard the actual banshees' wail, Father, whistling through the louvers all night . . . even when the wind was still."

"You've heard nothing of the sort."

Mullins laughed. "But I have. I *have*. And I've seen the coach-a-bower. Immense it was and black-polished, riding over these rooftops, a red coffin mounted atop it, and a headless Dullahan madly whipping a team of headless horses . . . and the coach drew past this window, Father, and the coachman threw in my face a basin of cold blood."

Murphy shook his head.

Mullins smiled. "Well . . . I fancy myself a poet, you see . . . and I've license to hear things. . . ."

Murphy looked at him with some interest. "A poet . . ."

"Aye." A faint smile played over his blue lips, but his voice was melancholy. "And some time ago I fell in love with Leanhaun Shee, the Gaelic muse who gives us inspiration. She lives on mortal life, as you may know, in return for her favor. That's why Gaelic poets die young, Father. Do you believe that?"

Murphy said, "They die young because they eat badly, drink too much, and don't dress well in winter. They die young because unlike most civilized poets they run off to fight in ill-conceived wars. Do you want to make your confession?"

Mullins knelt and took the priest's hands.

Flynn climbed down to the room below. A strong gust of wind came through the shattered windows and picked up clouds of ancient dust that had been undisturbed for a century.

Father Murphy came down the ladder. "This"—he motioned toward the broken windows—"this was the only thing that bothered him. . . . I suppose I shouldn't tell you that. . . ."

Flynn almost laughed. "Well, one man's prank may be another's most tormenting sin, and vice versa." He jumped onto the ladder and descended to the spiral stairs, Father Murphy following. They came out of the tower into the subdued lighting and warmer air of the choir loft.

As Father Murphy moved along the rail he felt that someone was watching him. He looked into the choir pews that rose upward from the keyboard, and let out a startled gasp.

A figure stood above them, motionless in the shadows, dressed in a hooded monk's robe. A hideous, inhuman face peered out from the recesses of the cowl, and it was several seconds before Father Murphy recognized it as the face of a leopard.

Leary's voice came out of the immobile face. "Scare you, priest?"

Murphy regained his composure.

Flynn said, "A bit of greasepaint would have done, Mr. Leary."

Leary laughed, an odd shrill laugh for a man with so deep a voice.

Megan rose from between the pews, dressed in a black cassock, her face covered with swirls of dull-colored camouflage paint, expertly applied, thought Flynn, by another hand.

She moved into the center aisle, and Flynn saw that it was an altar boy's robe and that it revealed her bare forearms. He saw also that her legs and feet were bare. He studied Megan's face and found that the paint did not make her features so impenetrable that he could not see the same signs he had seen in Jean Kearney. He said, "With death so near, Megan, I can hardly blame you."

She thrust her chin out in a defiant gesture.

"Well, if nothing else good comes of this, you've at least found your perfect mate."

Father Murphy listened without understanding at first, then drew in a sharp breath.

Megan said to Flynn, "Is my brother dead?"

Flynn nodded.

Her face remained strangely impassive. She motioned toward Leary as she fixed her deep green eyes on Flynn. "We won't let you surrender. There will be no compromises."

Flynn's voice was sharp. "I don't need either of you to explain my duty or my destiny."

Leary spoke. "When are they coming? How are they coming?"

Flynn told them. He said to Leary, "This may be your richest harvest."

"Long after you're all dead," said Leary, "I'll still be shooting."

Flynn stared up into the dark eyes that were as fixed as the mask around them. "Then what?"

Leary said nothing.

"I find it difficult, Mr. Leary, to believe you're prepared to die with us."

Megan answered, "He's as dedicated as you are. If we have to die, we'll die here together."

Flynn thought not. He had an impulse to warn Megan, but he didn't know what to warn her about, and it didn't seem to matter any longer. He said to her, "Good-bye, Megan. Good luck."

She moved back into the pews, beside Leary.

Murphy looked at the two robed figures. They stared back at him. He suspected they would snuff out his life from their dark perch with no more hesitation than a man swatting an insect. Yet . . . "I have to ask."

Flynn said, "Go ahead—make a fool of yourself again."

Murphy turned to him. "You're the fool who brought them here."

Megan and Leary seemed to sense what the discussion was about. Megan called out in a mocking voice, "Come up here, Father. Let us tell you our sins." Leary laughed, and Megan went on, "Keep you up nights, Father, and turn your face as scarlet as a cardinal's hat. You've never heard sins like ours." She laughed, and Flynn realized he had never heard the sound of her laugh.

Flynn took the priest's arm again and moved him into the south tower without resistance. They climbed the stairs and passed through a door into the long southwest triforium.

George Sullivan stood at the parapet staring down at the north transept door. Sullivan's kilts and tunic, thought Flynn, were incongruous with his black automatic rifle and ammunition pouches. Flynn called to him, "Confessions are being heard, George."

Sullivan shook his head without looking up and lit a cigarette. His mind seemed to be elsewhere. Flynn nudged him and indicated the empty triforium across the transept. "You'll have to cover Gallagher's sectors."

Sullivan looked up. "Why doesn't Megan go up there?"

Flynn didn't answer the question, and Sullivan didn't press him. Flynn looked out at Abby Boland. These personal bonds had always been the Fenian strength—but also the weakness.

Sullivan also glanced across the nave. He spoke almost self-consciously. "I saw she made a confession to the priest. . . . These damned women of ours are so guilty and ashamed. . . . I feel somehow betrayed . . ."

Flynn said lightly, "You should have told him your version."

Sullivan started to reply but thought better of it. Flynn extended his hand, and Sullivan took it firmly.

Flynn and Father Murphy walked together back into the south tower and climbed the ten stories into the louvered room where Rory Devane stood in the dark, his face blackened and a large flak jacket hanging from his thin shoulders.

Devane greeted them affably, but the sight of the priest wearing the purple stole was clearly not a welcome one.

Flynn said, "Sometime after 5:15 snipers will begin pouring bullets through all eight sides of this room."

"The room will be crowded, won't it?"

Flynn went on. "Yet you have to stay here and engage the helicopters. You have to put a rocket into the armored carrier."

Devane moved to a west-facing opening and looked down. Flynn briefed Devane, then said, "Father Murphy is interested in your soul."

Devane looked back at the priest. "I made my confession this morning— right here in Saint Pat's, as a matter of fact. Father Bertero, it was. I've done nothing in the meanwhile I need to confess."

Murphy said, "If you say an act of contrition, you can regain a state of grace." He turned and dropped into the ladder opening.

Flynn took Devane's hand. "Good luck to you. See you in Dublin."

"Aye, Brian, Kavanagh's Pub, or a place close by the back wall."

Flynn turned and dropped down the ladder, joining Murphy on the next level. The two men left the south tower and made their way across the choir loft. They entered the bell tower, and Flynn indicated the spiral staircase. "I have to speak with Mullins again."

Murphy was about to suggest that Flynn use the field phone, but something in Flynn's manner compelled him not to speak. They climbed until they reached a level where the stairs gave way to ladders somewhere below the first bell room where Mullins was.

Flynn looked at the large room they were in. The tower here was four-sided, with small milky-glass windows separated by thick stone. Mullins had knocked holes in some of the panes in the event he had to change his location, and Flynn pulled off a thick triangle of glass and looked at it, then looked at Murphy. "A great many people watching this on television are morbidly fascinated with the question of how this place will look afterward."

Murphy said, "I don't need any more revelations from you tonight. As a priest nothing shocks me any longer, and I still cling to my faith in humanity."

"That is truly a wonder. I'm in awe of that. . . ."

Murphy saw that he was sincere. "I observed how your people cared for each other, and for you. . . . I've heard some of their confessions. . . . There are hopeful signs amid all this."

Flynn nodded. "And Hickey? Megan? Leary? And me?"

"May God have mercy on all your souls."

Flynn didn't respond.

Murphy said evenly, "If you're going to kill me, do it quickly."

Flynn's face looked puzzled, then almost hurt. "No . . . why would you think that?"

Murphy automatically mumbled an apology but immediately felt it was unnecessary under the circumstances.

Flynn reached out and grabbed his arm. "Listen, I've kept my promise to you and let you run around doing your duty. Now I want a promise from you."

Father Murphy looked at him cautiously.

Flynn said, "Promise me that after this is finished, you'll see that all my people are buried together in Glasnevin with Ireland's patriots. You can have a Catholic ceremony, if that'll make you feel better. . . . I know it won't be easy. . . . It may take you years to convince those swine in Dublin. . . . They never know who their heroes are until fifty years after they're dead."

The priest looked at him without comprehension, then said, "I . . . won't be alive to . . ."

Flynn took the priest's big hand firmly as though to shake it, but slapped the end of a handcuff on his wrist and locked the other end around the ladder's rail.

Father Murphy stared at his tethered wrist, then looked at Flynn. "Let me loose."

Flynn smiled weakly. "You weren't even supposed to *be* here. Now just keep your wits about you when the bullets start to fly. This tower should survive the explosion."

Murphy's face went red, and he shouted again. "You've no right to do this! Let me go!"

Flynn ignored him. He pulled a pistol from his belt and jumped down into the ladder opening. "It may happen that Megan, Hickey . . . someone may come for you. . . ." He laid the pistol on the floor. "Kill them." He dropped down the ladder. "Good luck, Padre."

Murphy bent down and grabbed the pistol with his free hand. He pointed it at the top of Flynn's head. "Stop!"

Flynn smiled as he continued his climb down. *"Erin go bragh,* Timothy Murphy." He laughed, and the sound echoed through the stone tower.

Murphy shouted after him. "Stop! Listen . . . you must save the others too. . . . Maureen . . . For God's sake, man, she loves you. . . ." He stared down into the dark hole and watched Flynn disappear.

Father Murphy threw the pistol to the floor and tugged at the cuffs, then sank to his knees beside the ladder opening. Somewhere in the city a church bell tolled, then another joined in, and soon he could hear the sounds of a dozen different carillons playing the hymn "Be Not Afraid." He thought that every bell in the city must be ringing, perhaps every bell in the country, and he hoped the others could hear them, too, and know they were not alone. For the first time since it had all begun, Father Murphy felt tears forming in his eyes.

55

B rian Flynn came down from the tower and walked up the nave aisle, his footsteps echoing from the polished marble. He turned into the ambulatory and approached John Hickey, who stood on the raised platform of the chancel organ and watched him approach. Flynn walked deliberately up the steps and stood facing Hickey. After a short silence Hickey said, "It's 4:59. You let Murphy waste valuable time trying to save already damned souls. Does everyone know their orders at least?"

"Has Schroeder called?"

"No—that means either nothing is new or something is wrong." Hickey took out his pipe and filled it. "All night I've worried that my tobacco would run out before my life. It really bothered me. . . . A man shouldn't have to scrimp on his tobacco before he dies." He struck a match, and it sounded inordinately loud in the stillness. He drew deeply on his pipe and said, "Well, where's the priest?"

Flynn motioned vaguely toward the towers. "We've no grudge against him. . . . He shouldn't pay the price for being in the wrong place at the wrong time."

"Why not? That's why the rest of us are going to die." He flashed a look of feigned enlightenment. "Ah, I suppose playing God means you have to save a life for every ten score you take."

Flynn said, "Who *are* you?"

Hickey smiled with unrestrained glee. "Have I frightened you, lad? Don't be frightened, then. I'm just an old man who amuses himself by playing on people's fears and superstitions." Hickey stepped over the body of Pedar Fitzgerald and came closer to Flynn. He sucked noisily on his pipe, a pensive look on his face. "You know, lad, I've had more fun since I had myself buried than ever I did before I was interred. You get a lot of mileage out of resurrection—someone made a whole religion out of it once." He jerked a thumb toward the crucifix atop the altar and laughed again.

Flynn felt the old man's breath against his face. He put his right hand on the organ console. "Do you know anything about this ring?"

Hickey didn't look at it. "I know what you believe it is."

"And what is it *really?*"

"A ring, made of bronze."

Flynn slipped it from his finger and held it in his open palm. "Then I've held it too long. Take it."

Hickey shrugged and reached for it.

Flynn closed his hand and stared at Hickey.

Hickey's eyes narrowed into dark slits. "So, you want to know who I am and how I got here?" Hickey looked into the glowing bowl of his pipe with exaggerated interest. "I can tell you I'm a ghost, a thevshi, come from the grave to retrieve the ring and bring about your destruction and the destruction of the new Fenians—to perpetuate this strife into the next generation. There's the proper Celtic explanation you're looking for to make you feel better about your fears." He looked directly into Flynn's eyes. "But I can also tell you the truth, which is far more frightening. I'm *alive.* Your own dark soul imagined the thevshi, as it imagines the banshee, and the pooka, and the Far Darrig, and all the nightmarish creatures that walk the dark landscape of your mind and make you huddle around flickering peat fires. Aye, Brian, that's a fright, because you can't find sanctuary from those monsters you carry within you."

Flynn stared at him, examining the furrowed white face. Suddenly Hickey's eyes became benign, sparkling, and his mouth curled up in a good-natured smile. Hickey said, "You see?"

Flynn said. "Yes, I see. I see that you're a creature who draws strength from other men's weaknesses. It's my fault you're here, and it's my responsibility to see that you do no further harm."

"The harm is done. Had you stood up to me instead of wallowing in self-pity, you could have fulfilled your responsibility to your people, not to mention your own destiny."

Flynn stared at Hickey. "No matter what happens, I'll see you don't leave here alive." Flynn turned and walked to the sanctuary. He stood before the high throne. "Cardinal, the police will attack anytime after 5:15. Father Murphy is in a relatively safe place—we are not, and we will most probably die."

Flynn watched the Cardinal's face for a show of emotion, but there was none. He went on, "I want you to know that the people out there share in the responsibility for this. Like me they are vain, egotistical, and flawed. A rather sorry lot for products of so many thousands of years of Judeo-Christian love and charity, wouldn't you say?"

The Cardinal leaned forward in the throne. "That's a question for people who are looking for a path to take them through life. Your life is over, and you'll have all your answers very soon. Use the minutes left to you to speak to her." He nodded toward Maureen.

Flynn was momentarily taken aback. It was perhaps the last reply he expected from a priest. He stepped away from the throne, turned, and crossed the sanctuary.

Maureen and Baxter remained seated, cuffed together in the first pew. Without a word Flynn unlocked the handcuffs, then spoke in a distant voice. "I'd like to put you both in a less exposed place, but that isn't acceptable to some of the others. However, when the shooting starts, you won't be executed, because we may repel them and we'll need you again." He looked at his watch and continued in a dispassionate voice. "Sometime after 5:15 you'll see all the doors explode, followed by police rushing in. I know you are both capable of keeping a cool head. Dive between the pews behind you. As 6:03 approaches . . . if you're still alive . . . get out of this area no matter what's happening around you. That's all I can do for you."

Maureen stood and looked at him closely. "No one asked you to do anything for us. If you want to do something for everyone, get down those stairs right now and open the gates to them. Then go into the pulpit and tell your people it's finished. No one will stop you, Brian. I think they're waiting to hear from you."

"When they open the gates of Long Kesh, I'll open the gates here."

Her voice became angry. "The keys to the jails of Ulster are *not* in America, or in London or Dublin. They are in Ulster. Give me a year in Belfast and Londonderry, and I'll get more people out of jail than you've ever had released with your kidnappings, raids, assassinations—"

Flynn laughed. "A *year?* You wouldn't last a year. If the Catholics didn't get you, Maureen, the Prods would."

She drew a shallow breath and brought her voice under control. "Very well . . . it's not worth going into that again. But you've no right to con these people into dying. Your voice can break the spell of death that hangs over this place. Go on! Do it! Now!" She swung and slapped him on the face.

Baxter moved off to one side and looked away.

Flynn pulled Maureen to him and said, "All night everyone's been very good about giving me advice. It's odd, isn't it, how people don't pay much attention to you until you've set a time bomb ticking under them?" He released her arms. "You, for instance, walked out on me four years ago without much advice for my future. All the things you've said to me tonight could have been said then."

She glanced at Baxter and felt curiously uncomfortable that he was hearing all of this. She spoke in a low voice. "I said all I had to say then. You weren't listening."

"You weren't speaking so loudly, either."

Flynn turned to Baxter. "And you, Harry." He moved closer to Baxter. "Major Bartholomew Martin needed a dead Englishman in here, and you're it."

Baxter considered this and accepted it in a very short time. "Yes . . . he's a sick man . . . an obsessed man. I suppose I always suspected . . ."

Flynn looked at his watch. "Excuse me, I have to speak to my people." He turned and walked toward the pulpit.

Maureen came up behind him and put her hand on his shoulder, turning him toward her. "Damn it, aren't you at least going to say good-bye?"

Flynn's face reddened, and he seemed to lose his composure, then cleared his throat. "I'm sorry . . . I didn't think you . . . Well—good-bye, then. . . . We won't speak again, will we? Good luck . . ." He hesitated, then leaned toward her but suddenly straightened up again.

She started to say something, but Gallagher's deep voice called out from the sacristy stairs, "Brian! Burke's here to see you!"

Flynn looked at his watch with some surprise.

Hickey called out from the organ, "It's a trap!"

Flynn hesitated, then looked at Maureen. She nodded slightly. He held her eyes for a moment and said, "Still trusting." He smiled and walked quickly around the altar and descended the stairs.

Burke stood at the gate in his shirt-sleeves, his shoulder holster empty and his hands in his pants pockets.

Flynn approached without caution and stood close to the gate. "Well?" Burke didn't answer, and Flynn spoke curtly. "You're not going to ask me to give up or—"

"No."

Flynn called up to Gallagher, "Take a break." He turned to Burke. "Are you here to kill me?"

Burke took his hands out of his pockets and rested them on the bars. "There's an implied white flag here, isn't there? Do you think I'd kill you like that?"

"You should. You should always kill the other side's commander when you have a chance. If you were Bellini, I'd kill you."

"There're still rules."

"Yes, I just gave you one."

A few seconds passed in silence, then Flynn said, "What do you want?"

"I just wanted to say I have no personal animosity toward you."

Flynn smiled. "Well, I knew that. I could see that. And I've none toward you, Burke. That's the hell of it, isn't it? I've no personal hatred of your people, and most of them have none toward me."

"Then why are we here?"

"We're here because in 1154 Adrian the Fourth gave Henry the Second of England permission to bring his army to Ireland. We're here because the Red Bus to Clady passes Whitehorn Abbey. That's why I'm here. Why are you here?"

"I was on duty at five o'clock."

Flynn smiled, then said, "Well, that's damned little reason to die. I'm releasing you from your promise to join the attack. Perhaps in exchange you'll decide to kill Martin. Martin set up poor Harry to be here—did you figure that out?"

Burke's face was impassive.

Flynn glanced at his watch. 5:04. Something was wrong. "Hadn't you better go?"

"If you like. Also, if you'd like, I'll stay on the phone with you until 6:03."

Flynn looked at Burke closely. "I want to speak to Schroeder. Send him down here."

"That's not possible."

"I want to speak to him! Now!"

Burke answered, "No one is intimidated by your threats anymore. Least of all Bert Schroeder." He exhaled a deep sigh. "Captain Schroeder put the muzzle of his gun in his mouth . . ."

Flynn grabbed Burke's arm. "You're lying! I want to see his body."

Burke pulled away and walked down into the sacristy, then looked back

toward Flynn. "I don't know what pushed him off the edge, but I know that
somehow you're to blame." Burke stood at the corridor opening. Barely three
feet away stood a masked ESD man with a Browning automatic shotgun. Burke
edged toward the opening and looked back at Flynn. He seemed to vacillate,
then said, "Good-bye."

Flynn nodded. "I'm glad we met."

56

Bellini stood close to the conference table in the press room, his eyes
focused on four long, unrolled sheets of blueprints, their corners
weighted with coffee cups, ashtrays, and grenade canisters. Huddled
around him were his squad leaders. The first three blueprints showed the basement, the main floor, and the upper levels. The fourth was a cutaway drawing
of a side view of the Cathedral. Now that they were all in front of him, Bellini
was unimpressed.

Gordon Stillway was seated in front of the blueprints, rapidly explaining the
preliminary details. Bellini's brow was creased. He looked around to see if
anyone was showing signs of enlightenment. All he could read in the blackened, sweaty faces was impatience, fatigue, and annoyance at the postponement.

Burke opened the door and came into the room. Bellini glanced up and gave
him a look that didn't convey much gratitude or optimism. Burke saw Langley
standing by the rear wall and joined him. They stood side by side and watched
the scene at the table for a few seconds, then Burke spoke without looking
away from the conference table. "Feeling better?"

Langley's tone was cool. "I've never felt better in my life."

"Me too." He looked at the spot on the floor where Schroeder had fallen.
"How's Bert?"

Langley said, "A police doctor is treating him for physical exhaustion."

Burke nodded.

Langley let a few seconds go by. "Did Flynn buy it?"

Burke said, "His next move may be to threaten to kill a hostage if we don't
show him Schroeder's body . . . with the back of his head blown away."

Langley tapped the pocket that held Schroeder's service revolver. "Well . . .
it's important that Flynn believes the plans he has are the plans Bellini will
use. . . ." He inclined his head toward the squad leaders. "Lots of lives depend on that. . . ."

Burke changed the subject. "What are you doing about arresting Martin?"

Langley shook his head. "First of all, he's disappeared again. He's good at
that. Secondly, I checked with the State Department joker, Sheridan, and Martin has diplomatic immunity, but they'll consider expelling—"

"I don't want him expelled."

Langley glanced at him. "Well, it doesn't matter because I also spoke with
our FBI buddy, Hogan, and he says Martin has happily expelled himself—"

"He's gone?"

"Not yet, of course. Not before the show ends. He's booked on a Bermuda flight out of Kennedy—"

"What time?"

Langley gave him a sidelong glance. "Departs at 7:35. Breakfast at the Southampton Princess—forget it, Burke."

"Okay."

Langley watched the people at the conference table for a minute, then said, "Also, our CIA colleague, Kruger, says it's their show. Nobody wants you poking around. Okay?"

"Fine with me. Art Forgery Squad, you say?"

Langley nodded. "Yeah, I know a guy in it. It's the biggest fuck-off job anyone ever invented."

Burke made appropriate signs of attentiveness as Langley painted an idyllic picture of life in the Art Forgery Squad, but his mind was on something else.

Gordon Stillway concluded his preliminary description and said, "Now, tell me again what precisely it is you want to know?"

Bellini glanced at the wall clock: 5:09. He drew a deep breath. "I want to know how to get into Saint Patrick's Cathedral without using the front door."

Gordon Stillway spoke and answered questions, and the mood of the ESD squad leaders went from pessimism to wary optimism.

Bellini glanced at the bomb disposal people. Their lieutenant, Wendy Peterson, the only woman present in the room, leaned closer to the blueprint of the basement and pulled her long blond hair away from her face. Bellini watched the woman's cold blue eyes scanning the diagram. There were seventeen men, one woman, and two dogs, Brandy and Sally, in the Bomb Squad, and Bellini knew beyond a doubt that they were all certifiable lunatics, including the dogs.

Lieutenant Peterson turned to Stillway. Her voice was low, almost a whisper, which was a sort of trademark of this unit, thought Bellini. Peterson said, "If you wanted to plant bombs—let's assume you didn't have a great deal of explosives with you but you were looking for maximum effect—"

Stillway marked two *X*'s on the blueprints. "Here and here. The two big columns flanking the sacristy stairs." He paused reflectively and said, "About the time I was six years old they blasted the stairs through the foundation here and weakened the bedrock on which these columns sit. This is recorded information for anyone who cares to look it up, including the IRA."

Wendy Peterson nodded.

Stillway looked at her curiously. "Are you a bomb disposal person? What kind of job is that for a woman?"

She said, "I do a lot of needlepoint."

Stillway considered the statement for a second, then continued, "These columns are big, but with the type of explosives they have today, as you know, a demolition expert could bring them down, and half the Cathedral goes down with them . . . and God help you all if you're in there." He stared at Lieutenant Peterson.

Wendy Peterson said, "I'm not interested in the explosion."

Stillway again considered this obscure response and saw her meaning. He said, "But *I* am. There are not many like me around to rebuild the place. . . ." He let his voice trail off.

Someone asked the question that had been on many people's minds all night. *"Can* it be rebuilt?"

Stillway nodded. "Yes, but it would probably look like the First Supernatural Bank."

A few men laughed, but the laughter died away quickly.

Stillway turned his attention back to the basement plans and detailed a few other idiosyncrasies on the blueprints.

Bellini rubbed the stubble on his chin as he listened. He interrupted: "Mr. Stillway, if we were to bring an armored personnel carrier—weighing about ten tons . . . give or take a ton—up the front steps, through the main doors—"

Stillway sat up. *"What?* Those doors are invaluable—"

"Could the floor hold the weight?"

Stillway tried to calm himself and thought a moment, then said reluctantly, "If you have to do something so insane . . . destructive . . . Ten tons? Yes, according to the specs the floor will hold the weight . . . but there's always some question, isn't there?"

Bellini nodded. "Yeah. . . . One other thing . . . they said—these Fenians said—they were going to set fire to the Cathedral. We have reason to believe it may be the attic. . . . Is that possible . . . ?"

"Why not?"

"Well . . . it looks pretty solid to me—"

"Solid *wood."* He shook his head. "What bastards . . ." Stillway suddenly stood. "Gentlemen—Miss—" He moved through the circle of people. "Excuse me if I don't stay to listen to you work out the details—I'm not feeling so well—but I'll be in the next room if you need me." He turned and left.

The ESD squad leaders began talking among themselves. The Bomb Squad people moved to the far end of the room, and Bellini watched them huddled around Peterson. Their faces, he noted, were always expressionless, their eyes vacant. He looked at his watch. 5:15. He would need fifteen to twenty minutes to modify the attack plan. It was going to be close, but the plan that was forming in his mind was much cleaner, less likely to become a massacre. He stepped away from the squad leaders and walked up to Burke and Langley. He hesitated a second, then said, "Thanks for Stillway. Good work."

Langley answered, "Anytime, Joe—excuse me—*Inspector.* You call, we deliver—architects, lawyers, hit men, pizza—"

Burke interrupted. "Do you feel better about this?"

Bellini nodded. "I'll take fewer casualties, the Cathedral has a fifty-fifty chance, but the hostages are still dead." He paused, then said, "Do you think there's any way to call off Logan's armored cavalry charge up Fifth Avenue?"

Langley shook his head. "Governor Doyle really has his heart set on that. Think of the armored car as one of those sound trucks they use in an election campaign."

Bellini found a cigar stub in his pocket and lit it, then looked at his watch again. "Flynn expected to be hit soon after 5:15, and he's probably sweating it out right now. Picture that scene—good, *good.* I hope the motherfucker is having the worst time of his fucking life."

Langley said, "If he's not now, I expect he will be shortly."

"Yeah. Cocksucker." Bellini's mouth turned up in a vicious grin, and his eyes narrowed like little pig slits. "I hope he gets gut-shot and dies slow. I hope he pukes blood and acid and bile, until he—"

Langley held up his hand. "Please."

Bellini spun around and looked at Burke. "I can't believe Schroeder *told him—"*

Burke cut him off. "I never said that. I said I found the architect, and you should revise your attack. Captain Schroeder suffered a physical collapse. Right?"

Bellini laughed. "Of course he collapsed. I hit him in the face. What did you expect him to do—dance?" Bellini's expression became hard, and he made a contemptuous noise. "That cocksucker sold me out. He could have gotten a hundred men killed."

Burke said, "You forget about Schroeder, and I'll forget I heard you plant the idea in your squad leaders' heads about making a clean sweep in the Cathedral."

Bellini stayed quiet a minute, then said, "The attack is not going to be the way Schroeder told Flynn. . . . What's going to happen to his daughter?"

Langley took a file photo of Dan Morgan out of his pocket and laid it on a bridge table beside a snapshot of Terri O'Neal that he'd taken from Schroeder's wallet. "This man will murder her." He pointed to Terri O'Neal's smiling face.

The telephone rang, and Bellini looked at it. He said to the two men, "That's my buddy, Murray Kline. His Honor to you." He picked up the extension on the bridge table. "Gestapo Headquarters, Joe speaking."

There was a stammer on the other end, then the Mayor's voice came on, agitated. "Joe, what time are you moving out?"

Bellini felt a familiar heart-flutter at the sound of the military expression. Never again after today did he want to hear those words.

"Joe?"

"Yeah . . . well, the architect was worth the wait—"

"Good. Very good. What *time* are you jumping off?"

Jumping off. His heart gave another leap, and he felt like there was ice water in his stomach. "About 5:35—give or take."

"Can't you move it up?"

Bellini's voice had an insolent tone. "No!"

"I told you there are people trying to stop this rescue—"

"I don't get involved in politics."

Roberta Spiegel's voice came on the line. "Okay, forget the fucking politicians. The bombs, Bellini—"

"Call me Joe."

"You're leaving the Bomb Squad damned little time to find and defuse the goddamned *bombs,* Captain."

"Inspector!"

"Listen, you—"

"You listen, Spiegel—why don't you crawl around with the fucking dogs and help them sniff out the bombs? Brandy, Sally, and Robbie." He turned to Burke and Langley and smiled, a look of triumph on his face.

Langley winced.

Bellini continued before she could recover, knowing there was no reason to stop now. "They're short on dogs since your last fucking budget cuts, and they could use the help. You have your big nose into everything else."

There was a long silence on the line, then Spiegel laughed. "All right, you bastard, you can say what you want now, but later—"

"Yeah, later. I'd give my left arm for a guaranteed later. We move at 5:35. That's not negotiable—"

"Is Inspector Langley there?"

"Hold on." He covered the mouthpiece. "You want to talk to the Dragon Lady?"

Langley's face flushed, and he hesitated before taking the phone from Bellini, who moved back to the conference table. "Langley here."

Spiegel said, "Do you know where Schroeder is? His backup negotiator can't locate him."

Langley said, "He's collapsed."

"Collapsed?"

"Yeah, you know, like fell down, passed out."

"Oh . . . well, get him inflated again and get him here to the state offices in Rockefeller Center. He has to do his hero act later."

"I thought he was supposed to be the fall guy."

She said, "No, you're a little behind on this. . . . We've rethought that. He's the hero now no matter what happens. He's got lots of good press contacts."

"Who's the fall guy?"

She went on, "You see, there are no such things as victory or defeat anymore —there are only public relations problems—"

"Who's the fall guy?"

Spiegel said, "That's you. You won't be alone, though . . . and you'll come out of it all right. I'll see to that."

Langley didn't answer.

She said, "Listen, Philip, I think you should be here during the assault."

Langley's eyebrows went up at the use of his first name. He noted that her voice was pleasant, almost demure. "Rescue. You have to call it a rescue, Roberta." He winked at Burke.

Spiegel's voice was a little sharper. "Whatever. We—*I* want you up here."

"I think I'll stay down here."

"You get your ass up here in five minutes."

He glanced at Burke. "All right." He hung up and stared down at the phone. "This has been a screwy night."

"Full moon," said Burke. There was a lengthy silence, then Langley said, "Are you going in with Bellini?"

Burke lit a cigarette. "I think I should . . . to tidy up those loose ends . . . get hold of any notes the Fenians might have kept. There are secrets in that place . . . mysteries, as the Major said. And before Bellini starts blowing heads off . . . or the place goes up in smoke . . ."

Langley said, "Do what you have to do. . . ." He forced a smile. "Do you want to change places with me and go hold Spiegel's hand?"

"No thanks."

Langley glanced nervously at his watch. "Okay . . . listen, tell Bellini to keep Schroeder locked in that room. At dawn we'll come for Schroeder and parade him past the cameras like an Olympic hero. Schroeder's in, Langley's out."

Burke nodded, then said, "That mounted cop . . . Betty Foster . . . God, it seems so long ago. . . . Anyway, make sure she gets something out of this . . . and if I don't get a chance to thank her later . . . you can . . ."

"I'll take care of it." He shook his head. "Screwy night." He moved toward the door, then turned back. "Here's another one for you to work out when you get in there. We lifted the fingerprints off the glass that Hickey used." He nodded toward the chair Hickey had sat in. "The prints were smudged, but Albany and the FBI say it's ninety percent certain it was Hickey, and we've got a few visual identifications from people who saw him on TV—"

Burke nodded. "That clears that up—"

"Not quite. The Jersey City medical examiner did a dental check on the remains they exhumed and . . ." He looked at Burke. "Spooky . . . really spooky . . ."

Burke said quickly, "Come off it, Langley."

Langley laughed. "Just kidding. The coffin was filled with dirt, and there was a note in there in Hickey's handwriting. I'll tell you what it said later." He smiled and opened the door. "Betty Foster, right? See you later, Patrick." He closed the door behind him.

Burke looked across the room. More than a dozen ESD leaders, completely clad in black, grouped in a semicircle around the table. Above them a wall clock ticked off the minutes. As he watched they all straightened up, almost in unison, like a football team out of a huddle, and began filing out the door. Bellini stayed behind, occupied with some detail. Burke stared at his black, hulking figure in the brightly lit room and was reminded of a dark rain cloud in a sunny sky.

Burke walked over to the conference table and pulled on a black turtleneck sweater, then slipped back into his flak jacket. He adjusted the green carnation he'd gotten from an ESD man who had passed out a basketful of them. Burke looked down at the blueprints and read the notations of squad assignments hastily scrawled across them. He said to Bellini, "Where's the safest place I can be during the attack?"

Bellini thought a moment, then said, "Los Angeles."

57

Brian Flynn stood in the high pulpit, a full story above the main floor. He looked out at the Cathedral spread before him, then spoke into the microphone. "Lights."

The lights began to go out in sections: the sanctuary, ambulatory, and Lady Chapel lights first, the switches pulled by Hickey; then the lights in the four triforia controlled by Sullivan, followed by the choir-loft lights, and finally the huge hanging chandeliers over the nave, extinguished from the electrical panels in the loft. The vestibules, side altars, and bookstore darkened last as Hickey moved through the Cathedral pulling the remaining switches.

A few small lights still burned, Flynn noticed. Lights whose switches were probably located outside the Cathedral. Hickey and the others smashed the ones that were accessible, the sound of breaking glass filling the quiet spaces.

Flynn nodded. The beginning of the attack would be signaled when the last lights suddenly went out, a result of the police pulling the main switch in the rectory basement. The police would expect a dark Cathedral where their infrared scopes would give them an overwhelming advantage. But Flynn had no intention of letting them have such an advantage, so every votive candle, hundreds and hundreds of them, had been lit, and they shimmered in the surrounding blackness, an offering of sorts, he reflected, an ancient comfort against the terrors of the dark and a source of light the police could not extinguish. Also, at intervals throughout the Cathedral, large phosphorus flares were placed to provide additional illumination and to cause the police infrared scopes to white out. Captain Joe Bellini, Flynn thought, had a surprise in store for him.

Flynn placed his hands on the cool Carrara marble of the pulpit balustrade and blinked to adjust his eyes to the dim light as he examined the vast interior. Flickering shadows played off the walls and columns, but the ceiling was obscure. It was easy to imagine there was no roof, that the towering columns had been relieved of their burden and that overhead was only the night sky—an illusion that would be reality on the following evening.

The long black galleries of the triforia above, dark and impenetrable in the best of light, were nearly invisible now, and the only sense he had of anything being up there was the sound of rifles scraping against stone.

The choir loft was a vast expanse of blackness, totally shrouded from the murky light below as if a curtain had been drawn across the rail; but Flynn could feel the two dark presences up there more strongly than when he had seen them, as though they basked in blackness and flourished in the dark.

Flynn drew a long breath through his nostrils. The burning phosphorus exuded an overpowering, pungent smell that seemed to alter the very nature of the Cathedral. Gone was that strange musky odor, that mixture of stale incense, tallow, and something else that was indefinable, which he had labeled the Roman Catholic smell, the smell that never changed from church to church and that evoked mixed memories of childhood. *Gone, finally gone,* he thought. *Driven out.* And he was inordinately pleased with this, as though he'd won a theological argument with a bishop.

He lowered his eyes and looked over the flares and the dozens of racks of votive candles. The light seemed less comforting now, the candles burning in their red or blue glass like brimstone around the altars, and the brilliant white phosphorus like the leaping flames of hell. And the saints on their altars, he noticed, were moving, gyrating in obscene little dances, the beatific expressions on their white faces suddenly revealing a lewdness that he had always suspected was there.

But the most remarkable metamorphosis was in the windows, which seemed to hang in black space, making them appear twice their actual size, rising to dizzying heights so that if you looked up at them you actually experienced some vertigo. And above the soaring choir loft, atop the thousands of unseen brass pipes of the organ, sat the round rose window, which had become a dark blue swirling vortex that would suck you out of this netherworld of shadows and spirits—which was only, after all, the anteroom of hell—suck you, finally and irretrievably, into hell itself.

Flynn adjusted the microphone and spoke. He doubted his voice would break the spell of death, as she had said, and in any case he had the opposite purpose. "Ladies and gentlemen . . . brothers and sisters . . ." He looked at his watch. 5:14. "The time, as you know, has come. Stay alert . . . it won't be much longer now." He drew a short breath, which carried out through the speakers. "It's been my great honor to have been your leader. . . . I want to assure you we'll meet again, if not in Dublin, then in a place of light, the land beyond the Western Sea, whatever name it goes by . . . because whatever God controls our ultimate destiny cannot deny our earthly bond to one another, our dedication to our people. . . ." He felt his voice wavering. "Don't be afraid." He turned off the microphone.

All eyes went from him to the doors. Rockets and rifles were at the ready, and gas masks hung loosely over chests where hearts beat wildly.

John Hickey stood below the pulpit and threw a rocket tube, rifle, and gas mask to Flynn. Hickey called out in a voice with no trace of fear, "Brian, I'm afraid this is good-bye, lad. It's been a pleasure, and I'm sure we'll meet again in a place of incredible light, not to mention heat." He laughed and moved off into the half-shadows of the sanctuary.

Flynn slung the rifle across his chest, then broke the seal on the rocket and extended the tube, aiming it at the center vestibule.

His eyes became misty, from the phosphorus, he thought, and they went out of focus, the clear plastic aiming sight of the rocket acting as a prism in the dim candlelight. Colors leaped all around the deathly still spaces before him like fireworks seen at a great distance, or like those phantom battles fought in his worst silent nightmares. And there was no sound here either but the steady ticking of his watch near his ear, the rushing of blood in his head, and the faraway pounding of his chest.

He tried to conjure up faces, people he had known from the past, parents, relatives, friends, and enemies, but no images seemed to last more than a second. Instead, an unexpected scene flashed into his consciousness and stayed there: Whitehorn Abbey's subbasement, Father Donnelly talking expansively, Maureen pouring tea, himself examining the ring. They were all speaking, but he could not hear the voices, and the movements were slow, as if they had all the time in the world. He recognized the imagery, understood that this scene represented the last time he was even moderately happy and at peace.

John Hickey stood before the Cardinal's throne and bowed. "Your Eminence, I have an overwhelming desire," he said matter-of-factly, "to slit your shriveled white throat from ear to ear, then step back and watch your blood run onto your scarlet robe and over that obscene thing hanging around your neck."

The Cardinal suddenly reached out and touched Hickey's cheek.

Hickey drew back quickly and made a noise that sounded like a startled yelp. He recovered and jumped back onto the step, pulled the Cardinal down from his throne, and pushed him roughly toward the sacristy stairs.

They descended the steps, and Hickey paused at the landing where Gallagher knelt just inside the doors of the crypt. "Here's company for you, Frank." Hickey prodded the Cardinal down the remaining stairs, pushing him against the gates so that he faced into the sacristy. He extended the Cardinal's right arm and handcuffed his wrist to the bars.

Hickey said, "Here's a new logo for your church, Your Eminence. Been a good while since they've come up with a new one." He spoke as he cuffed the other extended arm to a bar. "We've had Christ on the cross, Saint Peter crucified upside down, Andrew crucified on an X cross, and now we've got you hanging on the sacristy gates of Saint Patrick's. Lord, that's a natural. Sell a million icons."

The Cardinal turned his head toward Hickey. "The Church has survived ten thousand like you," he said impassively, "and will survive you, and grow stronger precisely because there are people like you among us."

"Is that a fact?" Hickey balled his hand into a fist but was aware that Gallagher had come up behind him. He turned and led Gallagher by the arm back to the open crypt doors. "Stay here. Don't speak to him and don't listen to him."

Gallagher stared down the steps. The Cardinal's outstretched arms and red robes covered half the grillwork. Gallagher felt a constriction in his stomach; he looked back at Hickey but was not able to hold his stare. Gallagher turned away and nodded.

Hickey took the staircase that brought him up to the right of the altar and approached Maureen and Baxter. They rose as he drew near.

Hickey indicated two gas masks that lay on the length of the pew that separated the two people. "Put those on at the first sign of gas. If there's one thing I can't stand, it's the sight of a woman vomiting—reminds me of my first trip to Dublin—drunken whores ducking into alleys and getting sick. Never forgot that."

Maureen and Baxter stayed silent. Hickey went on, "It may interest you to know that the plan of this attack was sold to us at a low price, and the plan doesn't provide much for your rescue or the saving of this Cathedral."

Baxter said, "As long as it provides for your death, it's a fine plan."

Hickey turned to Baxter. "You're a vindictive bastard. I'll bet you'd like to bash in another young Irishman's throat, now you've got the hang of it and the taste for it."

"You're the most evil, twisted man I've ever met." Baxter's voice was barely under control.

Hickey winked at him. "Now you're talking." He turned his attention to Maureen. "Don't let Megan or Leary shoot you, lass. Take cover between these pews and lie still in the dark. Very still. Here's your watch back, my love. Look at it as the bullets are whistling over your head. Keep checking it as you stare up at the ceiling. Sometime between 6:03 and 6:04 you'll hear a noise, and the floor will bounce ever so slightly beneath your lovely rump, and the columns will start to tremble. Out of the darkness, way up there, you will see great sections of ceiling falling toward you, end over end, as in slow motion, right onto your pretty face. And remember, lass, your last thoughts while you're being crushed to death should be of Brian—or Harry . . . any man will do, I suppose." He laughed as he turned away and walked toward the bronze plate on the floor. He bent over and lifted the plate.

Maureen called after him: "My last thought will be that God should have mercy on all our souls . . . and that your soul, John Hickey, should finally rest in peace."

Hickey threw her a kiss, then dropped down the ladder, drawing the bronze plate closed over him.

Maureen sat back on the pew. Baxter stood a moment, then moved toward her. She looked up at him and put out her hand. Baxter took it and sat close beside her so that their bodies touched. He looked around at the flickering shadows. "I tried to picture how this would end . . . but *this* . . ."

"Nothing is ever as you expect it to be. . . . I never expected you to be . . . ."

Baxter held her more tightly. "I'm frightened."

"Me too." She thought a moment, then smiled. "But we made it, you know. We never gave them an inch."

He smiled in return. "No, we never did, did we?"

Flynn peered into the darkness to his right and stared at the empty throne, then looked out through the carved wooden screen to where the chancel organ keyboard stood on its platform beside the sanctuary. A candle was lit on the organ console, and for a moment he thought John Hickey was sitting at the keys. He blinked, and an involuntary noise rose in his throat. Pedar Fitzgerald sat at the organ, his hands poised over the keys, his body upright but tilted slightly back. His face was raised toward the ceiling as if he were about to burst into song. Flynn could make out the tracheal tube still protruding from his mouth, the white dead skin, and the open eyes that looked alive as the flame of the candle danced in them. "Hickey," he said softly to himself, "Hickey, you unspeakable, filthy, obscene . . . ." He glanced up into the choir loft but could not see Megan, and he concentrated again on the front doors.

5:20 came, then 5:25—

Flynn looked around the column to his rear and saw Maureen and Baxter huddled together. He watched them briefly, then turned back to the vestibule.

5:30.

A tension hung in the still, cold air of the Cathedral, a tension so palpable it could be heard in the steady beating chests, felt on the sweaty brows, tasted in the mouth as bile, seen in the dancing lights, and smelled in the stench of burning phosphorous.

5:35 came, and the thought began to take hold in the minds of the people in the Cathedral that it was already too late to mount an attack that would serve any purpose.

In the long southwest triforium George Sullivan put down his rifle and picked up his bagpipes. He tucked the bag under his arm, adjusted the three drone pipes over his shoulder, and put his fingers on the eight-holed chanter, and then put his mouth to the blowpipe. Against all orders and against all reason he began to play. The slow, haunting melody of "Amazing Grace" floated from the chanter and hummed from the drone pipes into the candlelit silence.

There was a very slight, almost imperceptible lessening of tension, a relaxing of vigilance, coupled with the most primitive of beliefs that if you anticipated something terrible, imagined it in the most minute detail, it would not happen.

Book V

Assault

==

For the great Gaels of Ireland
Are the men that God made mad,
For all their wars are merry,
And all their songs are sad.

G.K. Chesterton

Bellini stood at the open door of the small elevator in the basement below the Archbishop's sacristy. An ESD man stood on the elevator roof and shone a handheld spotlight up the long shaft. The shaft began as brick, but at a level above the main floor it was wood-walled and seemed to continue up, as Stillway had pointed out, to a level that would bring it through the triforium's attic.

Bellini called softly, "How's it look?"

The ESD man replied, "We'll see." He took a tension clamp from a utility pouch, screwed it tightly to the elevator cable at hip level, and then stepped onto it and tested its holding strength. He screwed on another and stepped up to it. Step by step, very quickly now, he began working his way up the shaft to the triforium level eight stories above.

Bellini looked back into the curving corridor behind him. The First ESD Assault Squad stood silently, laden with equipment and armed with silenced pistols and rifles that were fitted with infrared scopes.

On the floor just outside the elevator a communications man sat in front of a small field-phone switchboard that was connected by wire to the remaining ESD Assault Squads and to the state office in Rockefeller Center. Bellini said to the man, "When the shit hits the fan, intersquad communication takes priority over His Honor and the Commissioner. . . . In fact, I don't want to hear from them unless it's to tell us to pull out."

The commo man nodded.

Burke came down the corridor. His face was smeared with greasepaint, and he was screwing a big silencer onto the barrel of an automatic pistol.

Bellini watched him. "This don't look like Los Angeles, does it, Burke?"

Burke stuck the automatic in his belt. "Let's go, Bellini."

Bellini shrugged. He climbed the stepladder and stood on the roof of the elevator, and Burke came up beside him in the narrow shaft. Bellini shone his light up the wall until it rested on the oak door that opened on the Archbishop's sacristy twenty feet above. He said to Burke in a quiet voice, "If there's a Fenian standing there with a submachine gun and he hears us climbing, there'll be a waterfall of blood and bodies dropping back on this elevator."

Burke shifted Bellini's light farther up and picked out the dim outline of the climbing man, now about one hundred feet up the shaft. "Or there may be an ambush waiting up there at the top."

Bellini nodded. "Looked good on paper." He shut off his light. "You got about one minute to stop being an asshole and get out of here."

"Okay."

Bellini glanced up at the dark shaft. "I wonder . . . I wonder if that door or any door in this place is mined?" Bellini was speaking nervously now. "Remember in the army . . . all the phony minefield signs? All the other bullshit psywarfare . . . ?" He shook his head. "After the first shot everything is okay . . . it's all the shit before. . . . Flynn's got me psyched out. . . . He understands . . . I'm sure he's crazier than me. . . ."

Burke said, "Maybe Schroeder told him how crazy you really are . . . maybe Flynn's scared of *you.*"

Bellini nodded. "Yeah . . ." He laughed, then his face hardened. "You know something? I *feel* like killing someone. . . . I have an *urge* . . . like when I need a cigarette . . . you know?"

Burke looked at his watch. "At least this one can't go into overtime. At 6:03 it's finished."

Bellini also checked his watch. "Yeah . . . no overtime. Just a two-minute warning, then a big bang, and the stadium falls down and the game is over." He laughed again, and Burke glanced at him.

The ESD climber reached the top of the shaft. He tied a nylon rope ladder to the pulley crossbeam and let the ladder fall. Bellini caught it before it hit the metal roof of the elevator. The communications man threw up a field-phone receiver, and Bellini clipped it to the shoulder of his flak jacket. "Well, Burke . . . here goes. Once you get *on* the ladder, you're not getting *off* the ladder so easy." He began climbing. Burke followed, and one by one the ten ESD men climbed behind them.

Bellini paused at the oak door of the Archbishop's sacristy and put his ear to it. He heard footsteps and froze. Suddenly the crack of light at the bottom of the door disappeared. He waited several more seconds, his rifle pointed at the door and his heart pounding in his chest. The footsteps moved away. His phone clicked, and he answered it quietly. "Yeah."

The operator said, "Our people outside report all the lights are going out in there—but there's . . . like candlelight . . . maybe flares lighting up the windows."

Bellini swore. The flares, he knew, would be white phosphorus. *Bastards.* Right from the beginning . . . right from the fucking beginning . . . He continued up the swaying ladder.

At the top of the shaft the climber sat on the crossbeam, pointing his light farther up, and Bellini saw a small opening where the shaft wall ended a few feet from the sloping ceiling of the triforium attic. Bellini mumbled, "Caught a fucking break at least." He stood precariously on the crossbeam, eight stories above the basement, and stretched toward the opening, grabbing at the top of the wooden wall. He pulled himself up, squeezing his head and broad shoulders into the space, a silenced pistol in his hand. He blinked in the darkness of the half attic, fully expecting to be shot between the eyes. He waited, then turned on his light, cocking his pistol at the same time. Nothing moved but his pounding chest against the top edge of the wall. He slid down headfirst five feet to a beam that ran over the plaster lathing, breaking his fall with his outstretched arms and righting himself silently.

Burke's head and shoulders appeared in the opening, and Bellini pulled him through. One by one the First Assault Squad dropped into the small side attic behind the triforium.

Bellini crawled over the beams, sidled up to the wooden knee-wall and moved along it until he felt a small door Stillway had described. On the other-side of the door was the southeast triforium, and in the triforium, he was certain, were one or more gunmen. He put a small audio amplifier to the door and listened. He heard no footsteps, no sound of life in the triforium, but somewhere in the Cathedral a bagpipe was playing "Amazing Grace." He mumbled to himself, "Assholes."

He backed carefully away from the wall and led his squad to the low, narrow space where the sloping roof met the stone of the outside wall. He unclipped the field phone from his jacket and spoke quietly to his switchboard below. "Report to all stations—First Squad in place. No contact."

The Second Assault Squad of ESD men climbed the rungs of the wide chimney, fire axes slung to their backs. They passed the steel door in the brick and continued up to the chimney pot.

The squad leader attached a khaki nylon rappelling line to the top rung and held the gathered rope in his hands. The cold night air blew into the chimney, making a deep, hollow, whistling sound. The squad leader stuck a periscope out of the chimney pot and scanned the towers, but the Fenians were not visible from this angle, and he pointed the scope at the cross-shaped roof. Two dormers faced him, and he saw that the hatches on them were open. "Shit." He reached back, and the squad commo man cranked the field phone slung to his chest and handed him the receiver. The squad leader reported, "Captain, Second Squad in position. The damned hatches are open now, and it's going to be tough crossing this roof if there're people leaning out those dormers shooting at us."

Bellini answered in a barely audible voice. "Just hold there until the towers are knocked out. Then move."

The Third Assault Squad climbed the chimney behind the Second Squad but stopped their ascent below the steel door. The squad leader maneuvered to a position beside the door, directing a flashlight on the latch. Slowly he reached out with a mechanical pincher and tentatively touched the latch, then drew it away. He called Bellini on the field phone. "Captain. Third in position. Can't tell if there are alarms or mines on the door."

Bellini answered, "Okay. When Second Squad clears the chimney, you open the door and find out."

"Right." He handed the phone back to the commo man hanging beside him, who said, "How come we never rehearsed anything like this?"

The squad leader said, "I don't think the situation ever came up before."

* * *

At 5:35 the ESD sniper-squad leader in Rockefeller Center picked up the ringing field phone on the desk in a tenth-floor office. Joe Bellini's voice came over the line, subdued but with no hesitation. He gave the code word. "Bull Run. Sixty seconds."

The sniper-squad leader acknowledged, hung up, drew a long breath, and pushed the office intercom buzzer in an alerting signal.

Fourteen snipers moved quickly to the seven windows that faced the louvered sections of the towers across Fifth Avenue and crouched below the sills. The intercom sounded again, and the snipers rose and threw open the sashes, then steadied their rifles on the cold stone ledges. The squad leader watched the second hand of his watch, then gave the final short signal.

Fourteen silenced rifles coughed, and the metallic sound of sliding operating rods clattered in the offices, followed by whistling sounds, then the coughs of another volley, breaking up into random firing as the snipers fired at will. Spent brass cartridge casings dropped silently on the plush carpets.

Brian Flynn looked down at the television sitting on the floor of the pulpit. The screen showed a close-up shot of the bell tower, the blue-lit shadow of Mullins staring out through the torn louvers. Mullins raised a mug to his lips. The scene shifted to another telescopic close-up of Devane in the south tower, a bored look on his face. The audio was tuned down, but Flynn could hear the droning voice of a reporter. The reporter gave the time. Everything seemed very ordinary until the camera panned back, and Flynn caught a glimpse of light from the rose window, which should have been dark. He realized he was seeing a video replay from early in the evening. Flynn reached for the field phone.

A dozen Fenian spotters in the surrounding buildings watched the Cathedral through field glasses.

One spotter saw movement at the mouth of the chimney. A second spotter saw the line of windows in Rockefeller Center open.

Strobe lights began signaling to the Cathedral towers.

Rory Devane knelt behind a stone mullion, blowing into his cold hands, his rifle cradled in the bend of his arms. His eye caught the flashing strobes, and then he saw a line of muzzle flashes in the building across the Avenue. He grabbed for the field phone, and it rang simultaneously, but before he could pick it up, shards of disintegrating stone flew into his face. The dark tower room was filled with sharp pinging sounds and echoed with the metallic clatter of tearing copper louvers.

A bullet slammed into Devane's flak jacket, sending him reeling back. He felt another round pass through his throat, but didn't feel the one that ricocheted into his forehead and fractured his skull.

Donald Mullins stood in the east end of the bell room staring out across the East River trying to see the predawn light coming over Long Island. He had half convinced himself that there would be no attack, and when the field phone rang he knew it was Flynn telling him the Fenians had won.

A strobe light flashed from a window in the Waldorf-Astoria, and his heart missed a beat. He heard one of the bells behind him ring sharply, and he spun around. Muzzle flashes, in rapid succession like popping flashbulbs, ran the width of the building across the Avenue, and more strobe lights flashed in the distance; but these warnings, which he had been watching for all night, made no impression on his mind. A series of bullets slammed into his flak jacket, knocked the breath out of him, and picked him up off his feet.

Mullins regained his footing and lunged for the field phone, which was still ringing. A bullet shattered his elbow, and another passed through his hand. His rifle fell to the floor, and everything went black. Still another round entered behind his ear and disintegrated a long swath of his skull.

Mullins staggered in blind pain and grabbed at the bell straps hanging through the open stairwell. He felt himself falling, sliding down the swinging straps.

Father Murphy huddled against the cold iron ladder in the bell tower, half unconscious from fatigue. A faint peal of the bell overhead made him look up, and he saw Mullins falling toward him. Instinctively he grabbed at the man before he passed through the opening in the landing.

Mullins veered from the gaping hole and landed on the floor, shrieking in pain. He lurched around the room, his hands to his face and his sense of balance gone along with his inner ear, blood running between his fingers. He ran headlong toward the east wall of the tower and crashed through the splintered glass, tumbling three stories to the roof of the northwest triforium.

Father Murphy tried to comprehend the surrealistic scene that had just passed before his cloudy eyes. He blinked several times and stared at the shattered window.

Abby Boland thought she heard a sound on the roof of the triforium's attic behind her and froze, listening.

Leary thought he heard the pealing of a bell from the tower and strained to listen for another.

Flynn was calling into the field phone, "South tower, north tower, answer."

In the chimney the commo men with the two squads answered their phones simultaneously and heard Bellini's voice. "Both towers clear. Move!"

The Second Squad leader threw the gathered rope up and out of the chimney and scrambled over the top into the cold air. They had gambled that by leaving on the blue floodlights that bathed the lower walls of the Cathedral, they wouldn't alert the Fenian spotters in the surrounding buildings or in the attic. But the squad leader felt very visible as he rappelled down the side of the chimney. He landed on the dark roof of the northeast triforium, followed by his ten-man Assault Squad. They moved quickly over the lower roof to a slender pinnacle that rose between two great windows of the ambulatory. The squad found the iron rungs in the stone that Stillway said would be there and climbed up to a higher roof, partially visible in the diffused lighting. Dropping onto the roof, they lay in the wide rain gutter where the wall met the sloping expanse of gray slate shingles, then began crawling in the gutter toward the closest dormer. The squad leader kept his eyes on the dormer as he moved toward it. He saw something poke out of the open hatchway, something long and slender like a rifle barrel.

The Third Assault Squad leader at the steel door watched the last dark form disappear from the chimney pot overhead and hooked his pinchers on the door latch, muttered a prayer, and lifted the latch, then slowly pushed in on the door, wondering if he was going to be blown up the chimney like soot.

Jean Kearney and Arthur Nulty stood in dormered hatchways, which were on opposite sides of the pitched roof, scanning the night sky for helicopters. Nulty, on the north slope of the roof, thought he heard a sound below. He looked straight down at the triforium roof but saw nothing in the dark. He heard a sound to his immediate right and turned. A long line of black shapes, like beetles, he thought, was crawling through the rain gutter toward him. He couldn't imagine how they got there without helicopters or without the spotters in the surrounding buildings seeing them climb the walls. Instinctively he raised his rifle and drew a bead on the first man, who was no more than twenty feet away.

One of the men shouted, and they all rose to one knee. Nulty saw rifles coming into firing position, and he squeezed off a single round. One of the black-clad men slapped his hand over his flak jacket, lost his balance and fell out of the rain gutter; he dropped three stories to the triforium roof below, making a loud thud in the quiet night.

Jean Kearney turned at the sound of Nulty's shot. "Arthur! What—?"

The dormer where Nulty stood erupted in flying splinters of wood, and Nulty fell back into the attic. He rose very quickly to his feet, took two steps toward Jean Kearney, his arms waving, then toppled over the catwalk and crashed to the plaster lathing below.

Kearney stared down at his body, then looked up at the dormer hatch and saw a man hunched in the opening. She raised her rifle and fired, but the man jumped out of view.

Kearney ran along the catwalk and dived across the wooden boards, reaching a glowing oil lamp. She flung it up in an arc, and it crashed into a pile of chopped wood. She rolled a few feet farther and reached for the field phone, which was ringing.

Men were dropping into the attic from the open hatches, scrambling over the catwalks and firing blindly with silenced rifles into the half-lighted spaces. Bullets hit the rafters and floor around her with a thud.

Kearney fired back, and the noise of her rifle attracted a dozen muzzle flashes. She felt a sharp pain in her thigh and cried out, dropping her rifle. Blood gushed through her fingers as she held a hand under her skirt against the wound. With her other hand she felt on the floor for the ringing phone.

The woodpile was beginning to blaze now, and the light silhouetted the dark shapes moving toward her. They were throwing canisters of fire-extinguishing gas into the blazing wood, but the fire was growing larger.

She picked up her rifle again and shot into the blinding light of the fire. A man cried out, and then answering shots whistled past her head. She dragged herself toward the bell tower passage, leaving a trail of blood on the dusty floor. She reached another oil lamp and flung it into the pile of wood that lay between her and the tower, blocking her escape route.

She lay in a prone position, firing wildly into the flame-lit attic around her. Another man moaned in pain. Bullets ripped up the wood around her, and the windows in the peak behind her began shattering. The fires were reaching toward the roof now, curling around the rafters. The smell of burning wax candles mixed with the aroma of old, seasoned oak, and the heat from the fires began to warm her chilled body.

* * *

In the northeast triforium Eamon Farrell heard a distinct noise on the roof in the attic behind him. His already raw nerves had had enough. He held his breath as he looked down into the Cathedral at Flynn in the pulpit cranking the field phone. Sullivan and Abby Boland across from him were leaning anxiously out over the balustrades. Something was about to happen, and Eamon Farrell saw no reason to wait around to see what it was.

Farrell turned slowly from the balustrade, lay down his rifle, and opened the door in the knee wall behind him. He entered the dark attic and turned his flashlight on the steel door in the chimney. God, he was certain, had given him an escape route, and he had been right to keep it from Flynn and right to use it.

Carefully he approached the door, put the flashlight in his pocket, then lowered himself through the opening until his feet found an iron rung. He closed the door and stepped down to the next rung in the total darkness. His shoulder brushed something, and he gave a startled yelp, then reached out and touched a very taut rope.

He looked upward and saw a piece of the starlit sky at the mouth of the chimney, which was partly obscured by a moving shape. His stomach heaved as he became aware that he was not alone.

He heard someone breathe, smelled the presence of other bodies in the sooty space around him, pictured in his mind dangling shapes swinging on ropes in the darkness like bats, inches from him. He cleared his throat. "Wha— who . . . ?"

A voice said, "It ain't Santa Claus, pal."

Farrell felt cold steel pressed against his cheekbone, and he shouted, "I surrender!" But his shout panicked the ESD man, and darkness erupted in a silent flash of blinding light. Farrell fell feet-first and then somersaulted into the black shaft, blood splattering over his flailing arms.

The Third Squad leader said, "I wonder where *he* was going?" The squad moved silently through the chimney door and assembled in the dark attic over the bride's room.

Flynn turned off the television. He spoke into the pulpit microphone. "It's begun. Keep alert. Steady now. Watch the doors and windows. Rockets ready."

Bellini squatted at the door in the knee wall and listened to Flynn's voice through the public address system. "Yeah, motherfuckers, you watch the doors and windows." The First Squad knelt to the sides with rifles raised. Bellini put his hand to the latch, raised it, and pushed. The ESD men behind him converged on the door, and Bellini threw it open, rolling onto the floor into the dark triforium. The men poured through after him, diving and rolling over the cold floor, weapons pointing up and down the long gallery.

The triforium was empty, but on the floor lay a black morning coat, top hat, and a tricolored sash with the words Parade Marshal.

Half the squad crawled along the parapet, spacing themselves at intervals. The other half ran in a crouch to where the triforium turned at a right angle overlooking the south transept.

Bellini made his way to the corner of the right angle and raised an infrared periscope. The entire Cathedral was lit with candles and phosphorus flares and, even as he watched, the burning phosphorus caused the image to white out and disappear. He swore and lowered the periscope. Someone handed him a daylight periscope, and he focused on the long triforium across the transept. In the flickering light from below he could see a tall man in a bagpiper's tunic leaning over the balustrade and aiming a rifle at the transept doors across the nave. He shifted the periscope and looked down toward the dark choir loft but saw nothing, then scanned right to the long triforium across the nave and caught a glimpse of what looked like a woman in overalls. He focused on her and saw that her young face looked frightened. He smiled and traversed farther right to the short triforium across the sanctuary where the chimney was. It appeared empty, and he began to wonder just how many people Flynn had used to take the Cathedral and fuck up everyone's day.

Burke came up behind him, and Bellini whispered in his ear, "This is not going so bad." Bellini's field phone clicked, and he put it to his ear. The Third Squad reported to all points. "In position. One Fenian in chimney—KIA."

A voice cut in, and Bellini heard the excited shouts of the Second Squad leader. "Attic ablaze! Fighting fire! Three ESD casualties—one Fenian dead—one still shooting. Fire helicopters in position, but they won't come in until attic is secure. May have to abandon attic!"

Bellini looked up to the vaulted ceiling. He cupped his hand around the mouthpiece and spoke quickly. "You stay there and fight that fucking fire, you kill the fucking Fenian, and you bring those fire choppers in. You piss on that fire, you spit on that fire, but you do not leave that fire. Acknowledge."

The squad leader seemed calmer. "Roger, Roger, okay. . . ."

Bellini put down the field phone and looked at Burke. "The attic is burning."

Burke peered up into the darkness. Somewhere above the dimly outlined ceiling, about four stories up, there was light and heat, but here it was dark and cold. Somewhere below there were explosives that could level the entire east end of the Cathedral. He looked at his watch and said, "The bombs will put the fire out."

Bellini looked at him. "Your sense of humor sucks, you know?"

Flynn stood in the pulpit, a feeling of impotence growing in him. It was ending too quietly, no bangs, not even whimpers, at least none that he could hear. He was becoming certain that the police had finally found Gordon Stillway, compliments of Bartholomew Martin, and they weren't going to come in through the doors and windows—Schroeder had lied or had been used by them. They were burrowing in right now, like rot in the timbers of a house, and the whole thing would fall with hardly a shot fired. He looked at his watch. 5:37. He hoped Hickey was still alive down there, waiting for the Bomb Squad in the darkness. He thought a moment, and the overwhelming conviction came over him that Hickey at least would complete his mission.

Flynn spoke in the microphone. "They've taken out the towers. George, Eamon, Frank, Abby, Leary, Megan—keep alert. They may have found another way in. Gallagher, watch the crypt behind you. Everyone, remember the movable blocks on the floor; watch the bronze plate on the sanctuary: scan the bride's room, the Archbishop's sacristy, the bookstore and the altars; keep an ear to the walls of the triforium attics—" Something made him look up to his right at the northeast triforium. "Farrell!"

No one answered.

Flynn peered into the darkness above. "Farrell!" He slammed his fist on the marble balustrade. "Damn it!" He cranked the field phone and tried again to raise the attic.

Bellini listened to the echoes of Flynn's voice die away from the speakers. The squad leader beside him said, "We have to move—now!"

Bellini's voice was cool. "No. Timing. It's like trying to get laid—it's all timing." The phone clicked, and Bellini listened to the Third Squad leader in the attic of the opposite triforium. "Captain, do you see anyone else in this triforium?"

Bellini answered, "I guess the guy called Farrell was the only one. Move into the triforium." He spoke to the operator. "Get me the Fourth Squad."

The Fourth Squad leader answered, and his voice resonated from the duct he was crawling through. "We jumped off late, Captain—got lost in the duct work. I think we're through the foundation—"

"*Think!* What the hell is wrong with you?"

"Sorry—"

Bellini rubbed his throbbing temples and brought his voice under control. "Okay . . . okay, we make up the time you lost by moving your time of last possible withdrawal from 5:55 to 6:00. That's fair, right?"

There was a pause before the squad leader replied, "Right."

"Good. Now you just see if you can find the block-square crawl space. Okay? Then I'll send the Bomb Squad in." He hung up and looked at Burke. "Glad you came?"

"Absolutely."

Flynn cranked the field phone. "Attic! Attic!"

Jean Kearney's voice finally came on the line, and Flynn spoke hurriedly. "They've taken out the towers, and they'll be coming through the roof hatches next—I can hear helicopters overhead. There's no use waiting for it, Jean—light all the fires and get into the bell tower."

Jean Kearney answered, "All right." She stood propped against a catwalk rail, supported by two ESD men, one of whom had the big silencer of a pistol pressed to her head. She shouted into the phone, "Brian—!" One of the men pulled the phone out of her hand.

She steadied herself on the rail, feeling lightheaded and nauseous from the loss of blood. She bent over and vomited on the floor, then picked her head up and tried to stand erect, shaking off the two men beside her. Hoses hung from hovering helicopters and snaked their way through the roof hatches, discharging billows of white foam over the flickering flames. She felt defeated but relieved that it was over. She tried to think about Arthur Nulty, but her thigh was causing her such pain that all she could think about was that the pain should go away and the nausea should stop. She looked at the squad leader. "Give me a pressure bandage, damn it."

The squad leader ignored her and watched the firemen coming through the hatches, taking over the hoses from his Assault Squad. He shouted to his men. "Move out! Into the bell tower!"

He turned back to Jean Kearney, noticing the tattered green Aer Lingus uniform; he looked at her freckled features in the subdued light and pointed at a smoldering pile of wood. "Are you *crazy?*"

She looked him in the eye. "We're loyal."

The squad leader listened to the sound of his men double-timing over the catwalks toward the tower passage. As he reached for the aid kit on his belt his eyes darted around at the firemen who were occupied with the large chemical hoses.

Jean Kearney's hand flew out and expertly snatched his pistol, put it to her heart, and fired. She back-pedaled, her arms swinging in wide circular motions until she toppled over to the dusty catwalk.

The squad leader looked at her, stunned, and then bent over and retrieved his pistol. "Crazy . . . crazy."

A thick mass of foam moved across the catwalk and slid over Jean Kearney's body; the white billowing bubbles tinged with red.

Flynn used the field phone to call the choir loft. He spoke quickly to Megan. "I think they've taken the attic. They'll be coming through the side doors into the choir loft. Keep the doors covered so Leary can shoot."

Megan's voice was angry, nearly hysterical. "How the hell did they take the attic? What the bloody hell is going on, Brian? What the *fuck* is going wrong here?"

He drew a long breath. "Megan, when you've been on fifty missions, you'll know not to ask those questions. You just fight, and you die or you don't die, but you never ask— Listen, tell Leary to scan Farrell's post—I think they're also up there—"

"Who the hell ever said you were a military genius?"

"The British—it made them feel more important."

She hesitated, then said, "Why did you let Hickey do that to my brother?"

Flynn glanced at Pedar Fitzgerald's body propped up on the organ bench. "Hickey—like Mr. Leary—is a friend of yours, not mine. Ask Hickey when next you meet. Also, tell Leary to scan Gallagher's triforium—"

Megan cut in. "Brian . . . listen . . . listen . . ."

He recognized the tone of her voice, that childlike lilt she used when she became repentant about something. He didn't want to hear what she had to say and hung up.

Bellini scanned with the periscope as he reported to all points on the field phone. "Yeah . . . they're starting to look over their shoulders now. Man at the chancel organ . . . but he looks . . . dead . . . Still don't see Hickey. . . . Might be in the crawl space. Two hostages . . . Malone and Baxter . . . Murphy still missing . . . shit . . . Cardinal still missing—"

The Fifth Squad leader in the octagon room to the side of the sacristy gates cut in. "Captain, I'm looking at the gates with a periscope . . . bad angle . . . but someone—looks like the Cardinal—is cuffed to them. Advise."

Bellini swore softly. "Make sure it's him, and stand by for orders." He turned to Burke. "These Mick bastards still have some tricky shit up their shillelaghs— Cardinal's cuffed to the gates." He focused the periscope on Flynn in the pulpit directly below. "Smart guy. . . . Well, this potato-eating bastard is mine . . . but it's a tough shot. . . . Canopy overhead and a marble wall around him. He knows it's going down the tube, but he can't do shit about it. Cocksucker."

Burke said, "If the attic is secure and you get the bombs . . . you ought to try negotiating. Flynn will talk with twenty rifles pointing down at him. He's a lot of things, but stupid isn't one of them."

"Nobody told me nothing about asking him to surrender." Bellini put his face close to Burke's. "Don't get carried away with yourself and start giving orders, or I swear to God I'll grease you. I'm doing okay, Burke—I'm doing fine—I'm golden tonight—fuck you and fuck Flynn—let him squirm—then let him die."

The Fifth Assault Squad dropped one at a time from the duct opening and lay on the damp floor of the crawl space, forming a defensive perimeter. The squad leader cranked his field phone and reported, "Okay, Captain, we're in the crawl space. No movement here—"

Bellini answered, "You sure you're not in the fucking attic now? Okay, I'm sending the dogs and their handlers through the ducts with Peterson's Bomb

Squad. When you rendezvous, move out. Be advised that Hickey may be down there—maybe others. Keep your head out of your ass."

Bellini signaled to Wendy Peterson. "Perimeter secure. Move through the ducts. Follow the commo wire and don't get lost."

She answered in a laconic voice that echoed in the ducts, "We're already moving, Captain."

Bellini looked at his watch. "Okay . . . it's 5:45 now. At 6:00—at 5:55 my people are getting the hell out of there, whether or not you think you got all the bombs. I suggest you do the same."

Peterson answered, "We'll play it by ear."

"Yeah, you do that." He hung up and looked at Burke. "I think it's time—before our luck turns."

Burke said nothing.

Bellini rubbed his chin, hesitated, then reached for the phone and called the garage under Rockefeller Center. "Okay, Colonel, the word is Bull—fucking—Run. Ready?"

Logan answered, "Been ready a while. You're cutting it close."

Bellini's voice was caustic. "It's past close—it's probably too damned late, but that doesn't mean you can't earn a medal."

Colonel Logan threw the field phone down from the commander's hatch of the armored carrier and called to the driver, "Go!"

The twenty thousand pounds of armor began rumbling up the ramp of the underground garage. The big overhead door rose, and the carrier slid into Forty-ninth Street, turned right, and approached Fifth Avenue at twenty-five miles per hour, then veered north up the Avenue gathering speed.

Logan stood in the hatch with an M-16 rifle, the wind billowing his fatigue jacket. He stared at the Cathedral coming up on his right front, then glanced up at the towers and roof. Smoke billowed over the Cathedral, and helicopters hovered, beating the smoke downward, thick hoses dropping into the attic hatches. "Good Lord . . ."

Logan looked into the silent predawn streets, empty except for the police posted in recessed doorways. One of them gave him a thumbs up, another saluted. Logan stood taller in the hatch; his mind raced faster than the carrier's engines, and his blood pounded through his veins.

The armored carrier raced up to the Cathedral. The driver locked the right-hand treads, and the carrier pivoted around, ripping up large slabs of the blacktop. The driver released the treads as the carrier pointed toward the front doors, and he gunned the engines. The vehicle fishtailed and raced across the wide sidewalk, bounced, and hit the granite steps, tearing away the stone as the treads climbed upward. The brass handrails disappeared beneath the treads, and the ten tons of armor headed straight for the ten tons of bronze ceremonial doors.

Logan made the sign of the cross, ducked into the hatch, and pulled the lid shut. The truck tires attached to the front of the carrier hit the doors, and the bolts snapped, sending the massive doors flying inward. The alarms sounded with a piercing ring. The carrier was nearly into the vestibule when the delayed mines on the doors began to explode, scattering shrapnel across the sides of the vehicle. The carrier kept moving through the vestibule and skidded across the marble floor to a stop beneath the choir loft overhang.

Harold Baxter grabbed Maureen and pulled her down beneath the clergy pews.

Brian Flynn raised a rocket launcher and took aim from the pulpit.

The rear door of the carrier dropped, and fifteen men of the 69th Regiment, led by Major Cole, scrambled over the door and began fanning out under the choir loft.

Frank Gallagher was speaking to the Cardinal when the sound of the exploding doors rolled through the Cathedral. For a moment he thought the bombs beneath him had gone off, then he recognized the sound for what it was. His chest heaved, and his body shook so badly that his rifle fell from his hands. He lost control of his nerves as he heard the reports of rifle fire in the Cathedral behind him. He let out a high-pitched wail and ran down the sacristy steps, falling to his knees beside the Cardinal. He grabbed at the hem of the red robe, tears streaming from his eyes and snatches of prayer forming on his lips. "God . . . O God . . . Father . . . Eminence . . . dear God . . ."

The Cardinal looked down at him. "It's all right, now. There . . . there . . ."

Colonel Logan rose quickly through the carrier hatch and rested his automatic rifle on the machine gun mount in front of him. He peered into the darkness as he scanned to his front, then saw a movement in the pulpit and zeroed in.

The First Squad, including Bellini and Burke, had risen up in unison from behind the balustrade, rifles raised to their shoulders.

Abby Boland saw the shadows appear along the ledge, black forms, eerie and spectral in the subdued light. She saw the tiny pinpoint flashes and heard the silencers cough like a roomful of old people clearing their throats. She screamed, "George!" Sullivan was intent on the transept doors opposite him but looked up when she screamed.

The Third Squad had burst out of the attic and occupied Farrell's triforium. They lined up along the parapet and searched the darkness for targets.

Brian Flynn steadied the M-72 rocket as a burst of red tracers streaked out of the commander's hatch of the carrier and cracked into the granite column behind him. He squeezed the detonator. The rocket roared out of the tube, sailed over the pews with a fiery red trail, and exploded on the sloping front of the armored carrier.

The carrier belched smoke and flame through ruptured seams, and the driver was killed instantly. Logan shot up from the hatch, flames licking at his clothing, and nearly hit the overhang of the loft. His smoking body fell back toward the blazing carrier, spread-eagled like a sky diver, and disappeared in clouds of black smoke and orange flame.

The First and Third ESD squads in the triforia were firing into the candlelit Cathedral, the operating mechanisms of their rifles slapping back and forth as the silencers wheezed, and spent brass piled up on the stone floors.

Abby Boland stood rigid for a split second as the scream died in her throat. She got off a single shot, then felt something rip the rifle from her hands, and the butt rammed her face. She fell to the floor, picked up a rocket, and stood again.

Sullivan fired a long automatic burst into Farrell's triforium and heard a scream. He shifted his fire to the triforium where Gallagher had been, but a single bullet hit him squarely in the chest. He tumbled to the floor, landing on his bagpipes, which emitted a sad wail that pierced the noises in the Cathedral.

Abby Boland saw him go down as she fired the rocket across the Cathedral.

Bellini watched the trail of red fire illuminating the darkness. It came toward him with a noise that sounded like a rushing freight train. "Duck!"

The rocket went high and exploded on the stonework above the triforium. The triforium shook, and the window above blew out of its stone mullions, sending thousands of pieces of colored glass raining down in sheets past the triforium to the sanctuary and pulpit below.

Bellini's squad rose quickly and poured automatic fire onto the source of the rocket.

Abby Boland held a pistol extended in both hands and fired at the orange flashes as the stonework around her began to shatter. The loud pop of a grenade launcher rolled across the Cathedral, and the top of the balustrade in front of her exploded. Her arms flew up and splattered blood and pistol fragments across her face. She fell forward, half blinded, and her mangled hands clutched at the protruding staff of the Papal flag. In her disorientation she found herself hanging out over the floor below. A burst of fire tore into her arms, and she released her grip. Her body tumbled head over heels and crashed into the pews below with a sharp splintering sound.

Pedar Fitzgerald's dead body took a half-dozen hits and lurched to and fro, then fell against the keyboard and produced a thundering dissonant chord that continued uninterrupted amid the shouting and gunfire.

Flynn crouched in the pulpit, fired long bursts at Farrell's triforium, then shifted his fire toward the vestibules where the men of the 69th Regiment had retreated from the burning carrier. Suddenly the carrier's gasoline exploded. Flames shot up to the choir loft, and huge clouds of black smoke rose and curled around the loft. The National Guardsmen retreated back farther through the mangled doors onto the steps.

Bellini leaned out of the triforium and sighted his rifle almost straight down and fired three shots in quick succession through the bronze pulpit canopy.

Flynn's body lurched, and he fell to his knees, then rolled over the pulpit floor. Bellini could see his body dangling across the spiral stairs. He took aim at the twitching form. Burke hit Bellini's shoulder and deflected his shot. "No! Leave him."

Bellini glared at Burke for a second, then turned his attention to the choir loft. He saw a barely perceptible flash of light, the kind of muzzle fire that came from a combination silencer/flash suppressor and that could only be seen from head on. The light flashed again, but this time in a different place several yards away. Bellini sensed that whoever was in there was very good, and he had a very good perch, a vast sloping area completely darkened and obscured by rising smoke. Even as he watched he heard a scream from the end of the triforium, and one of his men fell back. He heard another moan coming from the opposite triforium. In a short time everyone was on the floor as bullets skimmed across the ledge of the balustrade a few feet above their heads. Burke sat with his back against the wall and lit a cigarette as the wood above him splintered. "That guy is good."

Bellini crouched across from him and nodded. "And he's got the best seat in the house. This is going to be a bitch." He looked at his watch. The whole thing, from the time Logan had hit the doors to this moment, had taken just under two minutes. But Logan was dead now, the National Guardsmen were nowhere to be seen, and he had lost some good people. The hostages might be dead, the people in the crawl space weren't reporting, and someone in the choir loft was having a good day.

Bellini picked up the field phone and called Fifth Squad in the corridor off the sacristy. "All the bastards are dead except one or two in the choir loft. You have to go for the Cardinal and the two hostages under the pews."

The squad leader answered, "How the hell do we rush that gate with the Cardinal hanging there?"

"Very carefully. Move out!" He hung up and said to Burke, "The sniper in the choir loft isn't going to be easy."

The ESD men from the Fifth Assault Squad moved out of the octagon rooms on both sides of the sacristy gate and slid quickly along the walls, converging on the Cardinal.

The squad leader kept his back to the wall and peered carefully around the opening. His eyes met the Cardinal's, and both men gave a start; then the squad leader saw a man kneeling at the Cardinal's feet. Gallagher let out a surprised yell, and the squad leader did the same as he fired twice from the hip.

Gallagher rocked back on his haunches and then fell forward. His smashed face struck the bars, and he rolled sideways, sliding down the Cardinal's legs.

The Cardinal stared down at Gallagher lying in a heap at his feet, blood rushing from his head over the steps. He looked at the squad leader, who was staring at Gallagher. The squad leader turned and looked up at the top landing, saw no one, and gave a signal. ESD men with bolt cutters swarmed around the gates and severed the chain that tied them together. One of the men snapped the Cardinal's handcuffs while another one opened the gate lock with a key. So far no one had spoken a word.

The assault squad slid open the gates, and ten men ran up the stairs toward the crypt door.

The Cardinal knelt beside Gallagher's body, and a medic rushed out of a side corridor and took the Cardinal's arm. "Are you okay?" The Cardinal nodded. The medic stared down at Gallagher's face. "This guy don't look so good, though. Come on, Your Eminence." He tugged at the Cardinal's arm as two uniformed policemen lifted the Cardinal, steering him toward the corridor that led back to his residence.

One of the ESD men stood to the side of the crypt door and lobbed a gas canister down into the crypt. The canister popped, and two men wearing gas masks rushed in through the smoke. After a few seconds one of them yelled back, "No one here."

The squad leader took the field phone and reported, "Captain, sacristy gate and crypt secured. No ESD casualties, one Fenian KIA, Cardinal rescued." He added impulsively, "Piece of cake."

Bellini replied, "Tell me that after you get up those stairs. There's a mother-fucker in the choir loft that can circumcise you with two shots and never touch your nuts."

The squad leader heard the phone click off. "Okay. Hostages under the pews —let's move." The squad split into two fire teams and began crawling up the opposite staircases toward the sanctuary.

Maureen and Baxter stayed motionless beneath the clergy pews. Maureen listened to the sounds of striking bullets echoing through the Cathedral. She pressed her face close to Baxter's and said, "Leary—maybe Megan—is still in the loft. I can't tell who else is still firing."

Baxter held her arm tightly. "It doesn't matter as long as Leary is still there." He took her wrist and looked at her watch. "It's 5:36. At 6:00 we run for it."

She smiled weakly. "Harry, John Hickey is a man who literally would not give you the right time of day. For all we know it's 6:03 right now. Then again, my watch may be correct, but the bombs may be set for right now. Hickey does not play fair—not with us nor with Brian Flynn."

"Why am I so bloody naïve?"

She pressed his arm. "That's all right. People like Hickey, Flynn . . . me . . . we're treacherous. . . . It's as natural as breathing. . . ."

Baxter peered under the pews, then said, "Let's run for it."

"Where? This whole end of the Cathedral will collapse. The doors are mined. Leary's in the loft, and Gallagher is at the gate."

He thought a moment. "Gallagher owes you. . . ."

"I wouldn't put myself at the mercy of any of them. We couldn't reach those stairs anyway. I won't be shot down by scum like Leary or Megan. I'm staying here."

"Then you'll be blown up by John Hickey."

She buried her face in her hands, then looked up. "Over the back of the sanctuary, keeping the altar between us and the choir loft. Into the Lady Chapel—the windows are about fifteen feet from the floor. Climb the chapel altar—one of us boosts the other up. We won't get that far, of course, but—"

"But we'll be heading in the right direction."

She nodded and began moving under the pews.

The Fifth Assault Squad crouched on the two flights of steps behind the high altar. The squad leader peered around the south side of the altar and looked to his left at the bronze floor-plate. He turned to the right, put his face to the floor, and tried to locate the hostages under the clergy pews, but in the bad light and at the angle he was looking he saw no one. He raised his rifle and called softly, "Baxter? Malone?"

They were both about to spring out toward the rear of the sanctuary but dropped to a prone position. Baxter called back, "Yes!"

The squad leader said, "Steps are clear. Cardinal's safe. Where is Father Murphy?"

Maureen peered across the sanctuary floor to the stairwell thirty feet away. "Somewhere in the towers, I think." She paused, then said, "Gallagher? The man who—"

The squad leader cut her off. "The bomb under us hasn't been found yet. You have to get out of there."

"What time is it?" Baxter asked.

The squad leader looked at his digital watch. "It's 5:46 and twenty seconds."

Maureen stared at the face of her watch. Ten minutes slow. "Bastard." She reset it and called back. "Someone's got to get the snipers in the loft before we can move."

The squad leader poked his head around the altar, looked up at the choir loft illuminated by candles and flares, and tried to peer into the blackness beyond. "He's too far away for us to get him or for him to get you."

Baxter shouted with anger in his voice, "If that were so, we wouldn't be here. That man is very good."

The squad leader said, "We're sitting on a *bomb*, and so far as I'm concerned it could go off *anytime.*"

Maureen called out to the squad leader, "Listen, two people planted the bombs, and they were down in the crawl space less than twenty minutes. They carried two suitcases."

The squad leader called back, "Okay—I'll pass that on. But you have to understand, lady, that the Bomb Squad could blow it—you know? So you have to make a break."

Maureen called back, "We'll wait."

"Well, *we* won't." The squad leader looked up at the triforium directly over-head where Bellini was, but saw no one at the openings. He called on the field phone. "Captain, Malone and Baxter are under the pews below you—alive." He passed on the information about the bombs and added, "They won't try to cross the sanctuary." Bellini's voice came over the line. "I don't blame them. Okay, in thirty seconds everyone fires into the loft. Tell them to run for it then."

"Right." He hung up and relayed the message to Maureen and Baxter.

Maureen called back, "We'll see—be careful—"

The squad leader turned and shouted to his men on the opposite stairs. "Heavy fire into the loft!" The men moved up the steps and knelt on the floor, firing down the length of the Cathedral. The squad leader moved the remain-der of his squad around the altar and opened fire as the two triforia began shooting. The sound of bullets crashing into stone and brass in the loft rolled back through the Cathedral. The squad leader shouted to Malone and Baxter. "Run!"

Suddenly two rifles started firing rapidly from the choir loft with extreme accuracy. The ESD men on both sides of the altar began writhing on the cold sanctuary floor. Both teams pulled back to the staircases, dragging their wounded and leaving a trail of blood on the white marble.

The squad leader swore loudly and peered around the altar. "Okay, okay, stay there!" He glanced quickly up at the choir loft and saw a muzzle flash. The marble in front of him disintegrated and hit him full in the face. He screamed, and someone grabbed his ankles, dragging him back down the stairs.

Medics rushed up from the sacristy and began carrying away the wounded. The commo man cranked his field phone and reported to Bellini in a shaky voice. "Hostages pinned down. This altar is the wrong end of a shooting gallery. We can't help them."

The Fourth Assault Squad moved slowly through the dark crawl space, the squad leader scanning his front with an infrared scope. The two dogs and their handlers moved with him. Behind the advancing line of men moved Wendy Peterson and four men of the Bomb Squad.

Every few yards the dogs strained at their leashes, and the Bomb Squad would uncover another small particle of plastic explosive without timers or detonators. The entire earth floor seemed to be seeded with plastic, and every column had a scrap of plastic stuck to it. A dog handler whispered to the impatient squad leader, "I can't stop them from following these red herrings."

Wendy Peterson came up beside the squad leader and said, "My men will follow up on these dogs. Your squad and I have to move on—faster—to the other side."

He stopped crawling, lay down an infrared scope, and turned his head to-ward her. "I'm moving like there were ten armed men in front of me, and that's the only way I know how to move when I'm crawling in a black fucking hole . . . Lieutenant."

The Bomb Squad men hurried up from the rear. One of them called, "Lieu-tenant?"

"Over here."

He came up beside her. "Okay, the mine on the corridor hatchway is dis-armed, and we can get out of here real quick if we have to. The mine had a det-cord running from it, and we followed it to the explosives around the main column on this side." He paused and caught his breath. "We defused that big mother—about twenty kilos of plastic—colored and shaped to look like stone

—simple clock mechanism—set to go at 6:03—no bullshit about that." He held out a canvas bag and pressed it into Peterson's hands. "The guts."

She hunched over and lit a red-filtered flashlight, emptying the contents of the bag on the floor. Alarm clock, battery pack, wires, and four detached electric detonators. She turned on the clock, and it ticked loudly in the still air. She shut it off again. "No tricks?"

"No. We cut away all the plastic—no booby traps, no anti-intrusion devices. Very old techniques but very reliable, and top-grade plastic—smells and feels like that new C-5."

She picked off a clinging piece of plastic, kneading it between her thumb and forefinger, then smelled it.

The squad leader watched her in the filtered light and was reminded of his mother making cookie dough, but it was all wrong. "Really good stuff, huh?"

She switched off the light and said to the squad leader, "If the mechanism on the other one is the same, I'd need less than five minutes to defuse that bomb."

He said, "Good—now all you need is the other bomb. And *I* need about eight minutes to get the hell out of here and into the rectory basement. So at 5:55, no matter what's coming down, I say adios."

"Fair enough. Let's move."

He made no move but said, "I have to report the good news." He picked up the field phone. "Captain, the north side of the crawl space is clear of bombs."

Bellini answered, "Okay, very good." He related Maureen's information. "Move cautiously to the other side of the crypt. Hickey—"

"Yeah, but we can't engage him. We can move back to the hatchway, though, so you can have somebody drop concussion grenades through that bronze plate in the sanctuary. Then we'll move in and—"

Bellini cut him off. "Fifth Squad is still on the sacristy stairs. Took some casualties. . . . They're going to have trouble crossing the sanctuary floor—sniper up in the loft—"

"Well, blow him the fuck away and let's get it moving."

"Yeah . . . I'll let you know when we do that."

The squad leader hesitated, then said, "Well . . . we'll stay put. . . ."

Bellini let a few seconds pass, then said, "This sniper is going to take awhile. . . . I'm not *positive* Hickey or anyone is down there. . . . You've got to get to the other column."

The squad leader hung up and turned to the dog handlers. "Okay, drag those stupid mutts along, and don't stop until we get to the other side." He called to his men. "Let's go."

The three teams—ESD Assault Squad, Bomb Squad, and the dog handlers, twenty people in all—began moving. They passed the rear wall of the crypt and turned left, following the line of columns that would lead them to the main column flanking the sacristy stairs and what they hoped would be the last bomb.

They dropped from their hands and knees to a low-crawl position, rifles held out in front of them, the squad leader scanning with the infrared scope.

Peterson looked at her wristwatch as they moved. 5:47. If the mechanism on this side wasn't tricky, if there were no mines, if there were no other bombs, and if no one fired at them, then she had a very good chance of keeping St. Patrick's Cathedral from blowing up.

As she moved, though, she thought about triggers—all the ways a bomb could be detonated besides an electric clock. She thought about a concussion grenade that would set off an audio trigger, a flashlight that would set off a photo trigger, movement that would set off an inertial trigger, trip wires, false clocks, double or triple mechanisms, spring-loaded percussion mechanisms, remote mechanisms—so many nasty ways to make a bomb go off that you didn't want to go off. Yet, nothing so elaborate was needed to safeguard a time bomb until its time had come if it had a watchdog guarding it.

John Hickey knelt beside the main column, wedged between the footing and the sacristy stairwell, contemplating the mass of explosives packed around the footing and bedrock. His impulse was to dig out the clock and advance it to eternity. But to probe into the plastic in the dark might disconnect a detonator or battery connection. He looked at his watch. 5:47. Sixteen minutes to go. He could keep them away that long—long enough for the dawn to give the cameras good light. He grinned.

Hickey pushed himself farther back into the small space and peered up through the darkness toward the spot where the bronze plate sat in the ceiling. No one had tried to come through there yet, and as he listened to the shooting overhead, he suspected that Leary and Megan were still alive and would see to it that no one did. A bullet struck the bronze plate, and a deep resonant sound echoed through the dark. Four more bullets struck the plate in quick succession, and Hickey smiled. "Ah, Leary, you're showing off now, lad."

Just then his ears picked up the sound of whimpering. He cupped his ear and listened. Dogs. Then men breathing. He flipped the selector switch on his rifle to full automatic and leaned forward as the sound of crawling came nearer. The dogs had the scent of the massed explosives and probably of him. Hickey pursed his lips and made a sound. "Pssst!"

There was a sudden and complete silence.

Hickey did it again. "Pssst!" He picked up a piece of rubble and threw it.

The squad leader scanned the area to his front, but there was not even the faintest glimmer of light for the infrared scope to pick up and magnify.

Hickey said, "It's me. Don't shoot."

No one answered for several seconds, then the squad leader called out in a voice that was fighting to maintain control. "Put your hands up and move closer."

Hickey placed his rifle a few inches from the ground and held it horizontally. "Don't shoot, lads—please don't shoot. If you shoot . . . you'll blow us all to hell." He laughed, then said, "I, however, can shoot." He squeezed the trigger and emptied a twenty-round magazine across the ground in front of him. He slapped another magazine into the well as the reports died away, and he heard screaming and moaning. He emptied another full magazine in three long bursts of grazing fire. He heard a dog howling, or, he thought, perhaps a man. He mimicked the howling as he reloaded and fired again.

The ESD snipers in both triforia were shooting down the length of the Cathedral into the choir loft, but the targets there—at least two of them—were moving quickly through the darkness as they fired. ESD men began to fall, dead and wounded, onto the triforium floors. An ESD man rose up beside Bellini and leaned out over the balustrade, putting a long stream of automatic fire into the loft. The red tracer rounds arched into the loft and disappeared as they embedded themselves into the woodwork. The organ keyboard was hit, and electrical sparks crackled in the darkness. The man fired again, and another stream of tracers struck the towering brass pipes, producing a sound like pealing bells. The tracer rounds ricocheted back, spinning and dancing like fiery pinwheels in the black space.

Bellini shouted to the ESD man and pulled at his flak jacket. "Too long! Down!"

All of a sudden the man released his rifle and slapped his hands to his face, then leaned farther out and rolled over the balustrade, crashing to the clergy pews below.

An ESD man with a M-79 grenade launcher fired. The small grenade burst against a wooden locker with a flash, and robes began to burn. Bellini picked up his bullhorn and shouted, "No grenades." The fire blazed for a few seconds, then began to burn itself out. Bellini crouched and held the bullhorn up. "Okay —First and Third squads—all together—two full magazines—automatic—on my command." He grabbed the rifle beside him and shouted into the bullhorn as he rose, "Fire!"

The remaining men in both triforia rose in unison and fired, producing a deafening roar as streams of red tracers poured into the black loft. They emptied their magazines, reloaded, fired again, then ducked.

There was a silence from the choir loft, and Bellini rose carefully with the bullhorn, keeping himself behind a column. He called out to the loft. "Turn the lights on and put your hands up, or we'll shoot again." He looked down at Burke sitting crosslegged beside him. "That's negotiating!" He raised the bullhorn again.

Leary knelt at the front of the loft in the north corner and watched through his scope as the bullhorn came up behind the column, diagonally across the Cathedral. He lay flat on top of the rail and leaned out precariously like a pool player trying to make a hard shot, putting the cross hairs of his scope over a small visible piece of Bellini's forehead. He fired and rolled back to the choir loft floor.

The bullhorn emitted an oddly amplified moan as Bellini's forehead erupted in a splatter of bone and blood. He dropped straight down, landing on Burke's crossed legs. Burke stared at the heavy body sprawled across him. Bellini's blackened temple gushed a small fountain of red . . . like a red rosebud, Burke thought abstractedly. . . . He pushed the body away and steadied himself against the parapet, drawing on his cigarette.

There was very little noise in the Cathedral now, he noted, and no sound at all from the survivors of the First Squad around him. Medics had arrived and were treating the wounded where they lay; they carried them back into the attic for the descent down the elevator shaft. Burke looked at his watch. 5:48.

Father Murphy listened to the sounds of footsteps approaching from below. His first thought was that the police had arrived; then he remembered Flynn's words, and he realized it might be Leary or Megan coming for him. He picked up the pistol and held it in his shaking hand. "Who is it? Who's there?"

An ESD team leader from the Second Assault Squad two levels below motioned his fire team away from the open well. He raised his rifle and muffled his voice with his hand. "It's me. . . . Come on down . . . attic burning."

Father Murphy put his hand to his face and whispered, "The attic . . . oh . . . God . . ." He called down. "Nulty! Is that you?"

"Yes."

Murphy hesitated. "Is . . . is Leary with you? Where's Megan?"

The team leader looked around at his men, who appeared tense and impatient. He called up the ladder well, "They're here. Come down!"

The priest tried to collect his thoughts, but his mind was so dulled with fatigue he just stared down into the black hole.

The team leader shouted, "Come down, or we're coming up for you!"

Father Murphy drew back from the opening as far as his cuffed wrist permitted. "I've got a gun!"

The team leader motioned to one of his men to fire a gas canister into the opening. The projectile sailed upward through the intervening level and burst on the ladder near Father Murphy's head. A piece of the canister struck him in the face, and his lungs filled with gas. He lurched back, then stumbled forward, falling through the opening. He hung suspended from his handcuffs, swinging against the ladder, his stomach and chest heaving as choked noises rose from his throat.

An ESD man with a submachine gun saw the figure dropping out of the darkness and fired from the hip. The body jerked, then lay still against the ladder. The ESD team moved carefully up to the higher level.

City lights filtered through the broken glass and cast a weak, shadowy illumination into the tower room. A cold wind blew away the smell of gas. An ESD man drew closer to the ladder, then shouted, "Hey! It's a priest."

The team leader dimly recalled some telephone traffic regarding the missing hostage, the priest. He cleared his throat. "Some of them were dressed as priests . . . right?"

The man with the submachine gun added, "He said he had a gun. . . . I heard it fall. . . . Something fell on the floor here. . . ." He looked around and found the pistol. "See . . . and he called them by name. . . ."

The man with the grenade launcher said, "But he's *cuffed!*"

The team leader put his hands to his temples. "This is fucked up. . . . We might have fucked up. . . ." He put his hand on the ladder rail and steadied himself. Blood ran down the rail and collected in a small pool around his fingers. "Oh . . . oh, no . . . no, no, *no—*"

The other half of the Second Squad from the attic made its way carefully down through the dark bell tower, then rushed into the long triforium where Abby Boland had been. They hit the floor and low-crawled down the length of the dark gallery, passing over the blood-wet floor near the flagstaff and turning the corner overlooking the north transept. Two men searched the triforium attic as the team leader reported on the field phone, "Captain, northwest triforium secured. Anything you see moving up here is us."

A voice came over the wire. "This is Burke. Bellini is dead. Listen . . . send some men down to the choir loft level. . . . The rest of you stay there and bring fire down on that loft. There're about two snipers there—at least one of them is very accurate."

The team leader acknowledged and hung up. He looked back at his four remaining men. "Captain got greased. Okay, you two stay here and fire down into the loft. You two come with me." He reentered the tower and ran down the spiral stairs toward the loft level.

One of the remaining two men in the triforium leaned out over the balustrade, steadying his rifle on the protruding flagstaff, which he noticed was splintered and covered with blood. He looked down and saw in the light of a flare a young woman's body lying in a collapsed pew.

"Jesus . . ." He looked into the dark loft and fired a short burst at random. "Flush those suckers out. . . ."

A single shot whistled up out of the loft, passed through the wooden staff and punched into his flak jacket. He rose up off his feet, and his rifle flew into the air. The man lay stretched out on the floor for a few seconds, then rolled over on his hands and knees and tried to catch his breath. "Good God . . . Jesus H. Christ . . ."

The other man, who hadn't moved from his kneeling position, said, "Lucky shot, Tony. Bet he couldn't do it again."

The injured man put his hand under his flak jacket and felt a lump the size of an egg where his breast bones met. "Wow . . . fuck-ing wow. . . ." He looked at the other man. "Your turn."

The man pulled off his black stocking cap and pushed it above the balustrade on the tip of his rifle. A faint coughing sound rolled out of the choir loft, followed by a whistle and crack, then another, but the hat didn't move. The ESD man lowered the hat. "He stinks." He moved to a position several yards down the triforium and peered over the edge of the balustrade. The huge yellow and white Papal flag was no longer hanging from the staff but was stretched across the pews below, covering the body of the dead woman. The ESD man stared back at the staff and saw the two severed flag-ropes swaying. He ducked quickly and looked at the other man. "You're not going to believe this . . ."

Someone in the choir loft laughed.

An ESD man beside Burke picked up Bellini's bullhorn and began to raise it above the balustrade, then thought better of it. He pointed it upward from his kneeling position and called out, "Hey! You in the loft! Show's over. Nobody left but you. Come to the choir rail with your hands up. You won't be harmed." He shut off the bullhorn and said, "You'll be blasted into hamburger, mother-fucker."

There was a long silence, then a man's voice called out from the loft. "You'll never take us." There were two sharp pistol shots, followed by silence.

The ESD man turned to Burke. "They blew their brains out."

Burke said, "Sure."

The man considered for a moment. "How do we know?" he finally asked.

Burke nodded toward Bellini's body.

The ESD man hesitated, then wiped Bellini's face and forehead with a hand-kerchief, and Burke helped him heft Bellini's body over the parapet.

Immediately there was a sound like a bee buzzing, followed by a loud slap, and Bellini's body was pulled out of their hands and crashed to the triforium floor behind them. An odd shrillish voice screamed from the loft, "Live ones! I want *live* ones!"

For the first time since the attack began Burke felt sweat forming on his brow.

The ESD man looked pale. "My God. . . ."

The Second Squad leader led his remaining two men down the dark bell tower until they found the choir practice room. They searched it carefully in the dark and located the door that led out to the loft. The squad leader listened quietly at the door, then stood to the side and put his hand on the knob and turned it, but there was no alarm. The three men hugged the walls for a second before the squad leader pushed the door open, and they rushed the opening in a low crouch.

A shotgun exploded five times in the dark in quick succession, and the three men were knocked back into the room, their faces, arms, and legs ripped with buckshot.

Megan Fitzgerald stepped quickly into the room and shone a light on the three contorted bodies. One of the men looked up at the black-robed figure through the light and stared at her grotesquely made-up face, distorted with a repulsive snarl. Megan raised a pistol, deliberately shot each of the writhing figures in the head, then closed the door, reset the silent light alarm, and walked back into the loft. She called to Leary, who was moving and firing from positions all over the loft. "Don't let Malone or Baxter get away. Keep them pinned there until the bombs explode!"

Leary shouted as he fired, "Yeah, yeah. Just watch the fucking side doors."

A long stream of red tracers streaked out of the long northwest triforium and began ripping into the choir pews. Leary got off an answering shot before the last tracer left the muzzle of the ESD man's rifle, and the firing abruptly stopped.

Leary moved far back to the towering organ pipes and looked out at the black horizon line formed by the loft rail across the candle- and flare-lit Cathedral. It was strictly a matter of probability, he knew. There were thirteen hundred square feet of completely unlit loft and less than twenty police in a position to bring fire into the loft. And because of their overhead angle they couldn't bring grazing fire across the sloping expanse, but only direct fire at a specific point of impact, and that reduced the killing zone of their striking rounds. In addition, he and Megan had flak jackets under their robes, his rifle was silenced and the flash was suppressed, and they were both moving constantly. The ESD night scopes would be whited out as long as the phosphorus below kept burning, but he was firing into a lit area, and he could see their shapes when they came to the edge of the triforia. Probability. Odds. Skill. Vantage point. All in his favor. Always were. Luck did not exist. God did not exist. He called to Megan, "Time?"

She looked at her watch and saw the luminous minute hand tick another minute. "Fourteen minutes until 6:03."

He nodded to himself. There were times when he felt immortal and times when immortality only meant staying alive for just long enough to get the next shot off. Fourteen minutes. No problem.

Burke heard the field phone click and picked up the receiver from the floor. "Burke."

Mayor Kline's voice came through the earpiece. "Lieutenant, I didn't want to cut in on your command network—I've been monitoring all transmissions, of course, and not being there to see the situation, I felt it was better to let Captain Bellini handle it—but now that he's—"

"We appreciate that, sir." Burke noticed Kline's voice had that cool preciseness that was just a hair away from whining panic. "Actually, I have to get through to the crawl space, Mr. Mayor, so—"

"Yes—just a second—I was wondering if you could fill us in—"

"I just did."

"What? Oh, yes. Just one second. We need a situation report from you as the ranking man in there—you're in charge, by the way."

"Thanks. Let me call you right back—"

"Fine."

He heard a click and spoke to the police operator. "Don't put that asshole through again." He dropped the receiver on the floor.

The Sixth Assault Squad of ESD rappelled from police helicopters into the open attic hatches. They ran across the foam-covered catwalks to the south tower and split up, one team going up toward Devane's position, the other down toward the triforium and choir loft levels.

The team climbing into the tower fired grenades ahead of them, moving up level by level until they reached the copper-louvered room where Devane had been posted. They looked for the body of the Fenian sniper in the dark, smoke-filled room but found only bloodstains on the floor and a gas mask lying in the corner.

The squad leader touched a bloodstain on the ascending ladder and looked up. "We'll go with gas from here."

The men pulled on gas masks and fired CS canisters to the next level. They moved up the ladder, floor by floor, the gas rising with them, into the narrowing spire. Above them they heard the echoing sounds of a man coughing, then the deep, full bellow of vomiting. They followed the blood trail on the rusty ladder, cautiously moving through the dark levels until they reached a narrow, tapering, octagonal room about fifteen stories above the street. The room had clover-shaped openings, without glass, cut into the eight sides of the stonework. The blood trail ended on the ladder, and the floor near one of the openings was smeared with vomit. The squad leader pulled off his gas mask and stuck his head and shoulders out of the opening and looked up.

A series of iron rungs ran up the last hundred feet of the tapering spire toward the copper cross on top. The squad leader saw a man climbing halfway up. The man lost his footing, then recovered and pulled himself up to the next rung. The squad leader dropped back into the small, cold room. He unslung his rifle and chambered a round. "These fucks blew away a lot of our people—understand?"

One of his men said, "It's not too cool to blow him away with all those people watching from Rockefeller Center."

The squad leader looked out the opening at the buildings across the Avenue. Despite orders and all the police could do, hundreds of people were at the windows and on the rooftops watching the climber make his way up the granite spire. A few people were shouting, making encouraging motions with their hands and bodies. The squad leader heard cheering and applauding and thought he heard gasps when the man slipped. He said, "Assholes. The wrong people are *always* getting the applause." He released the safety switch, moved toward the opening, and looked up. He shouted, "Hey, King Kong! Get your ass back here!"

The climber glanced down but continued up the spire.

The squad leader pulled his head back into the room. "Give me the rappelling line." He took the nylon rope and began hooking himself up. "Well, as the homicide detectives say, 'Did he fall or was he pushed?' That is the question."

The other half of the Sixth Assault Squad descended through the south tower and, following a rough sketch supplied by Gordon Stillway, located the door to the long southwest triforium. One of the men kicked the door in, and the other four rushed down the length of the long gallery in a crouch. An ESD man spotted a man dressed in kilts lying crumpled at the corner of the balustrade, a bagpipe sticking out from under his body.

Suddenly a periscope rose from the triforium across the transept, and a bullhorn blared. "Get down! The loft! Watch the loft!"

The men turned in unison and stared down at the choir loft projecting out at a right angle about thirty feet below them. A muzzle flashed twice, and two of the five men went down. The other three dove for the floor. "What the hell . . . ?" The team leader looked wildly around the long dark gallery as though it were full of gunmen. "Where did that come from . . . the loft?" He looked at the two dead men, each shot between the eyes. "I never saw it. . . . I never heard anything. . . ."

One of the men said, "Neither did they."

* * *

The fifteen men of the 69th Regiment had moved back into the Cathedral after the carrier had stopped burning, and they lay on the floor under the choir loft, sighting their rifles down the five wide aisles toward the raised sanctuary. Major Cole rose to one knee and looked over the pews with a pair of binoculars, then scanned the four triforia. Nothing seemed to be moving in the Cathedral, and the loudest sound was the striking of bullets from the Fenian sniper overhead. Cole looked at the smoking armored carrier beside him. The smell of burnt gasoline and flesh made his stomach heave.

A sergeant came up beside him. "Major, we have to *do* something."

The major felt his stomach heave again. "We are not supposed to interfere with the police in any way. There could be a misunderstanding . . . an accident . . ."

A runner came up the steps, moved through the battered doors, and crossed the vestibule, finding Major Cole contemplating his watch. The runner crouched beside him. "From the Governor, sir."

Cole took the handwritten report without enthusiasm and read from the last paragraph. "Father Murphy still missing. Locate and rescue him and rescue the other two hostages beneath the sanctuary pews. . . ." Cole looked up at the sergeant.

The sergeant regarded Cole's pale face. "If I found a way into that loft and zapped the sniper, you could dash up the aisle and grab the two hostages—" He smiled. "But you got to move quick because you'll be racing the cops for them."

Major Cole said stiffly, "All right. Take ten men into the loft." He turned to the runner. "Acknowledge message. Have the police command call their men in the triforia and tell them to hold fire on the loft for . . . five minutes." The runner saluted and moved off. Cole said to the sergeant, "Don't get anyone hurt."

The sergeant turned and led ten Guardsmen back into the south vestibule and opened the door to the spiral staircase. The soldiers double-timed up into the tower until they saw a large wooden door in the wall. The sergeant approached it cautiously and listened, but heard nothing. He put his hand on the knob and turned it slowly, then drew open the door a crack. There was complete blackness in front of him. At first he thought he wasn't in the loft, but then he saw in the distance candlelight playing off the wall of the long northern triforium above, and he recognized the empty flagstaff. He drew open the door, crouched with his rifle held out, and began walking in one of the cross aisles. The ten soldiers began following at intervals.

The sergeant slid his shoulder along the pew enclosure on his left as he moved, blinking into the darkness, listening for a sound somewhere in the cavernous loft. His shoulder slipped into an opening, and he turned, facing the wide aisle that ran up the center of the sloping loft. The entire expanse was pitch black, but he had a sense of its size from the massive rose window looming in the blackness, larger than a two-story house, glowing with the lights of Rockefeller Center across the Avenue. The sergeant took a step up the rising aisle, and he heard a sound like rustling silk in the pews above him.

A woman stood a few feet in front of him on the next higher step. The sergeant stared up at two points of burning green light that reflected the candlelight rising from the Cathedral behind him. The piercing eyes held him for a fraction of a second before he raised his rifle.

Megan screamed wildly and discharged a shotgun blast into his face. She jumped up on a pew and began firing down into the aisle below. The soldiers scrambled back along the aisle, buckshot pelting their helmets, flak jackets, and limbs as they retreated into the tower.

Leary shouted, "Keep them away, Megan! Keep me covered. I'm shooting like I never shot before. Give me time." He fired and moved, fired again and moved again.

Megan picked up her automatic rifle and fired quick bursts at the tower doors. Leary saw a periscope poking over the parapet in the southeast triforium and blew it away with a single shot. "I'm hot! God, I'm hot today!"

Burke heard the shotgun blasts from the loft, followed by the short, quick bursts of the M-16 and then the whistling of the sniper's rifle as rounds chipped away at the balustrade over his head.

The ESD man beside him said, "Sounds like the weekend commandos didn't capture the choir loft."

Burke picked up the field phone and spoke to the other three triforia. "At my command we throw everything we've got into the loft." He called the sacristy stairs. "Tell Malone and Baxter we're putting down suppressing fire again, and if they want to give it a try, this is the time to do it—there won't be another time."

Burke waited the remainder of the five minutes he had given the 69th, to be sure they were not going to try again to get into the loft, then put the field phone to his mouth. "Fire!"

Twenty-five ESD men rose in the four triforia and began firing with automatic rifles and grenade launchers. The rifles raked the loft with long traversing streams, while the launchers alternated their loads, firing beehive canisters of long needles, buckshot, high explosives, gas grenades, illumination rounds, and fire-extinguishing gas.

The choir loft reverberated with the din of exploding grenades, and thick black smoke mingled with the yellowish gas. The smoke and gas rose over the splintering pews, then moved along the ceiling of the Cathedral like an eerie cloud, iridescent in the light of the burning flares below.

Megan and Leary, wearing gas masks, knelt in the bottom aisle below the thick, protruding parapet that ran the width of the loft. Leary fired into the triforia, moved laterally, fired, and moved again. Megan sent streams of automatic fire into the sanctuary as she raced back and forth along the parapet.

Burke heard the sounds of the grenade launchers tapering off as the canisters were used up, and he heard an occasional exclamation when someone was hit. He stood and looked over the balustrade, through the smoke, and saw small flames flickering in the loft. From the field phone in his hand came excited voices as the other triforia called for medics. And still the firing from the loft went on. Burke grabbed an M-16 from one of the ESD men. "Goddamned sons of bitches—" He fired a full magazine without pause, reloaded and fired again until the gun overheated and jammed. He threw the rifle down savagely and shouted into the field phone, "Shoot the remaining fire-extinguishing canisters and get down."

The last of the canisters arched into the loft, and Burke saw the fires begin to subside. Impulsively he grabbed the bullhorn and shouted toward the loft, "I'm coming for you, cocksuckers. I'm—" He felt someone knock his legs out from under him, and he toppled to the floor as a bullet passed through the space where he had stood.

An ESD man sat cross-legged looking down at him. "You got to be cool, Lieutenant. There's nothing personal between them and us. You understand?"

Another man lit a cigarette and added, "They're giving it their best shot, and we're giving it our best shot. Today they got the force with them—see? And we don't. Makes you wonder, though. . . . I mean in a cathedral and all that . . ."

Burke took the man's cigarette and got control of himself. "Okay. . . . okay. . . . Any ideas?"

A man dabbing at a grazing wound across his jaw answered, "Yeah, offer them a job—my job."

Another man added, "Somebody's got to get *into* the loft through the towers. That's the truth."

Burke saw the dial of the other man's watch. He picked up the phone and called the sacristy stairs. "Did the hostages make it?"

The commo man answered, "Whoever's behind that M-16 up there wasn't shooting at you guys—it was raining bullets on the floor between the pews and the stairs—Christ, somebody up there has it in for these two."

"I'm sure it's not personal." Burke threw the phone down. "Still, I'm getting a little pissed off."

"What the hell is driving those two Micks on?" an ESD man asked. "Politics? I mean, I'm a registered Democrat, but I don't get *that* excited about it. You know?"

Burke stubbed out a cigarette and thought about Bellini. He looked down at the coagulated gore on his trousers that had been part of Bellini, those great stupid brains that had held a lot more knowledge than he had realized. Bellini would know what to do, and if he didn't, he would know how to inspire confidence in these semi-psychotics around him. Burke felt very much out of his element, unwilling to give an order that would get one more man killed; and he appreciated—really and fully appreciated—the reason for Bellini's erratic behavior all night. Unconsciously he rubbed at the stains on his trousers until someone said, "It doesn't come off."

Burke nodded. He realized now that he had to go to the loft, himself, and finish it one way or the other.

Maureen listened to the intense volume of fire dying away. The arm of the policeman who had fallen from the triforium above dangled between the pews, dripping blood into a large puddle of red. Through the gunfire she had thought she heard a sound coming from the pulpit.

Baxter said, "I think that was our last chance, Maureen."

She heard it again, a low, choked-off moan. She said, "We may have one more chance." She slid away from Baxter, avoiding his grasp, and rolled beneath the pews, coming out where they ended near the spiral pulpit staircase a few feet across a patch of open floor. She dove across the opening and flattened herself on the marble-walled steps, hugging the big column around which the steps circled. As she reached the top she noticed the red bloodstains on the top stairs. She looked into the pulpit and saw that he had dragged himself up to a sitting position, his back to the marble wall. His eyes were shut, and she stared at him for several seconds, watching the irregular rising and falling of his chest. Then she slid into the pulpit. "Brian."

He opened his eyes and focused on her.

She leaned over him and said quietly, "Do you see what you've done? They're all dead, Brian. All your trusting young friends are dead—only Leary, Megan, and Hickey are left—the bastards."

He took her hand and pressed it weakly. "Well . . . you're all right, then . . . and Baxter?"

She nodded, then ripped open his shirt and saw the bullet wound that had entered from the top of his shoulder. She moved her hands over his body and found the exit wound on his opposite hip, big and jagged, filled with bone splinters and marrow. "Oh, God . . ." She breathed deeply several times, trying to bring her voice under control. "Was it *worth* it?"

His eyes seemed clear and alert. "Stop scolding, Maureen."

She touched his cheek. "Father Murphy . . . Why did you . . . ?"

He closed his eyes and shook his head. "We never escape what we were as children. . . . Priests awe me. . . ." He drew a shallow breath. "Priests . . . cathedrals . . . you attack what you fear . . . primitive . . . self-protecting."

She glanced at her watch, then took him by his shoulders and shook him gently. "Can you call off Leary and Megan? Can you make them stop?" She looked up at the pulpit microphone. "Let me help you stand."

He didn't respond.

She shook him again. "Brian—it's over—it's finished—stop this killing—"

He shook his head. "I can't stop them. . . . You know that. . . ."

"The bombs, then. Brian, how many bombs? Where are they? What time—?"

"I don't know . . . and if I did . . . I don't know . . . 6:03 . . . sooner . . . later . . . two bombs . . . eight . . . a hundred. . . . Ask Hickey. . . ."

She shook him more roughly. "You're a damned fool." She said more softly, "You're dying."

"Let me go in peace, can't you?" He suddenly leaned forward and took her hands in a surprisingly tight grip, and a spasm shook his body. He felt blood rising from his lungs and felt it streaming through his parted lips. "Oh . . . God . . . God, this is slow. . . ."

She looked at a pistol lying on the floor and picked it up.

He watched her as she held the pistol in both hands. He shook his head. "No. . . . You've got enough regrets . . . don't carry that with you. . . . Not for me. . . ."

She cocked the pistol. "Not for you—for *me.*"

He held out his hand and pushed her arm away. "I *want* it to be slow. . . ."

She uncocked the pistol and flung it down the steps. "All right . . . as you wish." She looked around the floor of the pulpit, and from among a pile of ammunition boxes she took an aid kit and unwrapped two pressure bandages.

Flynn said, "Go away. . . . Don't prolong this. . . . You're not helping. . . ."

"You want it to be slow." She dressed both wounds, then extracted a Syrette of morphine from the kit.

He pushed her hand away weakly. "For God's sake, Maureen, let me die my way. . . . I want to stay clearheaded . . . to think. . . ."

She tapped the spring-loaded Syrette against his arm, and the morphine shot into his muscle. "Clearheaded," she repeated, "clearheaded, indeed."

He slumped back against the pulpit wall. "Cold . . . cold . . . this is bad. . . ."

"Yes . . . let the morphine work. Close your eyes."

"Maureen . . . how many people have I done this to . . . ? My God . . . what *have* I done all these years . . . ?"

Tears formed in her eyes. "Oh, Brian . . . always so late . . . always so late. . . ."

* * *

Rory Devane felt blood collecting in his torn throat and tried to spit, but the blood gushed from his open wound again, carrying flecks of vomit with it. He blinked the running tears from his eyes as he moved upward. His hands had lost all sensation, and he had to look at them to see if they were grabbing the cold iron rungs.

The higher he climbed, the more his head throbbed where the ricochet had hit him, and the throbbing spread into his skull, causing a pain he wouldn't have believed possible. Several times he wanted to let go, but the image of the cross on the top drew him upward.

He reached the end of the stone spire and looked up at the protruding ornamental copper finial from which rose the cross. Iron spikes, like steps, had been driven into the bulging finial. He climbed them slowly, then threw his arms around the base of the cross and put his head down on the cold metal and wept. After a while he picked up his head and completed his climb. He draped his numb arms over the cross and stood, twenty-eight stories above the city.

Slowly Devane looked to his front. Across the Avenue, Rockefeller Center soared above him, half the windows lit and open, people waving at him. He turned to his left and saw the Empire State Building towering over the Avenue. He shifted his body around and looked behind him. Between two tall buildings he saw the flatland of Long Island stretching back to the horizon. A soft golden glow illuminated the place where the earth met the dark, starlit sky. "Dawn."

Burke knelt on the blood-covered floor of the triforium. The wounded had been lowered down the elevator shaft, and the dead, including Bellini, were laid out in the attic. Four ESD men of the First Assault Squad remained, huddled against the parapet. The sniper in the choir loft was skimming bullets across the top of the balustrades, but from what Burke could hear, few of the ESD men in the three other triforia were picking their heads up to return the fire. Burke took the field phone and called the opposite triforium. "Situation."

The voice answered, "Squad leader got it. Wounded evacuated down the chimney, and replacements moving up but—listen, what's the word from Rockefeller Center? It's late."

Burke had a vivid image of Commissioner Rourke throwing up in a men's room, Murray Kline telling everyone to be calm, and Martin, looking very cool, giving advice that was designed to finish off the Cathedral and everyone in it. Burke glanced at his watch. It would be slow going down that chimney. He spoke into the phone. "Clear out."

"I hear you."

Burke signaled the switchboard. "Did you get through to the towers or attic yet?"

The operator answered, "Attic under control. Upper parts of both towers are secure, except for some clown climbing the south tower. But down at the loft level everything's a fucking mess. Some weird bitch dressed like a witch or something is blasting away at the tower doors. Some ESD guys got wasted in the choir room. Army guys got creamed coming into the loft from the other tower. Very unclear. You want to speak to them? Tell them to try again?"

"No. Tell them to stand by. Put me through to the crawl space."

The operator's voice was hesitant. "We can't raise them. They were reporting fine until a few minutes ago—then I lost them." The man paused, then added, "Check the time."

"I know the fucking time. Everybody knows the fucking time. Keep trying the crawl space. Connect me with Fifth Squad."

An ESD man on the sacristy stairs answered, and Burke said, "Situation."

The man reported, "Sacristy behind me is filled with fresh Assault Squads, but only two guys at a time can shoot from behind the altar. We definitely cannot reach that bronze plate. We cannot reach the hostages, and they can't reach us. Christ, those two bastards up there can *shoot.*" He drew a deep breath. "What the hell is happening?"

"What's happening," Burke answered, "is that this end of the Cathedral will probably collapse in ten minutes, so send everyone back to the rectory basement except two or three men to keep contact with the hostages."

"Right."

Langley's voice came on the line. "Burke—get the hell out of there. Now."

Burke answered, "Have the ESD and Bomb Squad send more people into the crawl space—Hickey must've nailed the others. There's at least one bomb left, and he's probably guarding it like a dog with a meaty bone. Get on it."

Langley said, "The bomb could blow *any* time. We can't send any more—"

Mayor Kline cut in, and his voice had the tone of a man speaking for the tape recorders. "Lieutenant, *on your advice,* I'll put one more Assault Squad and bomb team in there, but you understand that their chances—"

Burke ripped the wire out of the phone and turned to the man beside him. "Get everyone down the elevator shaft, and don't stop until you reach the basement of the Cardinal's residence."

The man slung his rifle. "You coming?"

Burke turned and moved around the bend in the triforium that overlooked the south transept. He stood and looked over the balustrade. The line of sight of the choir loft was blocked by the angle of the crossed-shaped building, and the ESD men had shot a line across the transept to the long triforium. Burke slipped into a rope harness and began pulling himself, hand over hand, across the hundred-foot-wide transept arm.

An ESD man on the far side reached out and pulled him over the balustrade. The two men walked quickly to the corner where Sullivan lay sprawled across his bagpipes, his kilts and bare legs splattered with blood. Both men crouched before they turned the corner, and Burke moved down the length of the triforium, passing six kneeling ESD snipers and two dead ones. He took a periscope and looked over the balustrade.

The choir loft was about three stories below, and from here he could see how huge and obscure it was, while the police perches were more defined by the candlelight playing off the window-like openings. Still, he thought, it was incredible that anyone in the loft had survived the volleys of fire, and he wondered why those two were so blessed.

He lowered the scope and moved farther to his right, then stood higher and focused the periscope on the floor below. The shattered front of the armored vehicle stuck out from under the loft, and he saw part of a body sprawled over it—Logan. Two blackened arms stuck straight out of what had been the driver's compartment. Major Cole and a few men knelt to the side of the carrier, looking grim but, he thought, also relieved that the day's National Guard exercises were nearly over.

A shot whistled out of the loft, and the periscope slapped Burke in the eye and flew out of his hands. Burke toppled and fell to the floor.

The ESD man beside him said, "You held it up too long, Lieutenant. And that was our last scope."

Burke rubbed his eye and brought his hand away covered with watery blood. He rose to one knee and looked at the man, who appeared blurry. "Any word from the towers?"

Before the man answered, a short staccato burst of fire rolled out of the loft, followed by another, and the man said, "That's the word from the towers—the witch wants nobody near her doors." He looked at his watch and said, "What a fucking mess. . . . We almost had it. Right?"

Burke looked at the ESD man across from him, who was a sergeant. "Any ideas?"

"The thing hinges on knocking out the loft so that Malone and Baxter can make it to the stairs and so the ESD people there can drop concussion grenades through the plate and turn that guy Hickey's brains to mashed potatoes. Then the bomb guys can get the bombs. Right?"

Burke nodded. This seemed to be the inescapable solution to the problem. The choir loft dominated the entire Cathedral, as it was meant to do for a different purpose. And Flynn had placed two very weird people up there. "What are our options for knocking out the loft?"

The ESD sergeant rubbed his jaw. "Well, we could bring new spotlights into the triforia, have helicopters machine-gun through the rose window, break through the plaster lathing in the attic over the loft. . . . Lots of options . . . but all that ordnance isn't handy . . . and it takes time. . . ."

Burke nodded again. "Yeah . . ."

"But the best way," said the sergeant, "is for somebody to sneak into that loft from one of the towers. Once you're past the door, you've got space to maneuver, just like them, and you're as invisible as they are."

Burke nodded. The alternate answer was to get to the explosives through the crawl space and worry about the sniper and the hostages later. Then 6:03 wouldn't matter anymore. Burke picked up the field phone and spoke to the switchboard. "What's the situation in the crawl space?"

The operator answered, "The new ESD squad is in—found some survivors dragging wounded back. Dogs and handlers dead. Bomb Squad people all out of it except Peterson, who's wounded but still functioning. There's a crazy guy down there with an automatic weapon. The survivors say there's no way to get to any remaining bombs except through the bronze plate." The operator hesitated, then said, "Listen . . . Peterson said this guy could probably set off the bombs anytime he wants . . . so I'm signing off because I'm a little close to where the bombs are supposed to be. Commo is going to be broken until I get this switchboard set up someplace else. Sorry, Lieutenant." He added, "They're searching both towers and the attic for the radio jammer, and if they find it, you'll have radio commo. Okay? Sorry."

The phone went dead. Burke turned on a radio lying near his feet, and a rush of static filled the air. He shut it off.

The ESD commo man beside him said, "That's it. Nobody is talking to nobody now. We can't coordinate an attack on that loft if we wanted to—or coordinate a withdrawal. . . ."

Burke nodded. "Looks like getting in was the easy part." He looked around the dark gallery. "Well, it's a big place. Looks pretty solid to me. The architect seemed to think this end would stand if the main columns over there went. . . ."

One of the men asked, "Anybody guaranteeing that? Is anybody sure there aren't bombs under these columns?" He tapped one of the columns.

Burke responded, "Logically, they wouldn't have bothered with fires in the attic if the whole place was rigged to explode. Right?" He looked at the men huddled around him, but no one seemed relieved by his deductions.

The sergeant said, "I don't think logic has anything to do with how these cocksuckers operate."

Burke looked at his watch. 5:54. He said, "I'm staying . . . you're staying." He entered the south tower and began to climb down to the loft level.

Maureen looked at her watch, then said to Flynn, "I'm going back."

"Yes . . . no . . . don't leave. . . ." His voice was much weaker now.

She wiped his brow with her hand. "I'm sorry . . . I can't stay here."

He nodded.

"Do you have much pain, Brian?"

He shook his head, but as he did his body stiffened.

She took another Syrette of morphine and removed the cap. With the blood he had lost, she knew this would probably kill him, but there would be no pain. She bent over and put her arm around his neck, kissing him on the lips as she brought the Syrette to his chest, near his heart.

Flynn's lips moved against hers, and she turned her head to hear. "No . . . no . . . take it away. . . ."

She drew the Syrette back and looked at him. He had not opened his eyes once in the last several minutes, and she did not understand how he knew . . . unless it was that he just knew her too well. She held his hand tightly and felt the large ring pressing into her palm. She said, "Brian . . . can I take this . . . ? If I leave here . . . I want to return it . . . to bring it home. . . ."

He pulled his hand away and clenched his fingers. "No."

"Keep it, then—the police will have it."

"No. . . . Someone must come for it."

She shook her head and then kissed him again. Without a word she slid back toward the winding stairs.

He called to her, "Maureen . . . listen . . . Leary . . . I told him . . . not to shoot at you. . . . He follows orders. . . . You can tell when Megan is covering the tower door . . . then you can run. . . ."

She lay still on the stairs, then said, "Baxter . . . ?"

"Baxter is as good as dead. . . . You can go . . . go . . ."

She shook her head. "Brian . . . you shouldn't have told me that. . . ."

He opened his eyes and looked at her, then nodded. "No, I shouldn't have . . . stupid. . . . Always doing the wrong thing. . . ." He tried to sit up, and his face went white with pain. "Please . . . run . . . live . . . " His chest began to rise and fall slowly.

Maureen watched him, then slid slowly down the stairs and rolled quickly over the few feet of exposed floor and crawled between the pews, coming up beside Baxter.

Baxter said, "I wanted to follow you . . . but I thought perhaps . . ."

She took his hand and pressed it.

"He's dead?"

"No."

They lay side by side in silence. At 5:55 Baxter asked, "Do you think he could —or would—call off Leary and Megan?"

She said, "I didn't ask."

Baxter nodded. "I see. . . . Well, are you ready to run for it?"

"I'm not certain that's what I want to do."

"Then why did you come back here?"

She didn't answer.

He drew a short breath and said, "I'm going. . . ."

She held his arm tightly and peered under the pew at the long expanse of blood-streaked white marble that seemed to radiate an incandescence of its own in the candlelight. She heard the staccato bursts of Megan's fire hitting the tower doors but no longer heard the sound of Leary's bullets striking in the Cathedral. "Leary is waiting for us."

"Then let's not keep him waiting." He began moving toward the end of the pew.

She kept a grip on his arm. "No!"

A policeman's voice called out from the sacristy stairwell behind the altar. "Listen, you're keeping two men here—I don't like to put it this way, but we'd rather be gone—you know?—so are you coming or not?" He thought he spoke just loud enough for them to hear, but the acoustics carried the sound through the Cathedral.

Two shots whistled out of the loft and cracked into the marble midway between the pews and the altar. Maureen slid beside Baxter and turned her face to him. "Stay with me."

He put his arm around her shoulders and called out to the stairwell. "Go on —there's no point in waiting for us."

There was no answer, and Maureen and Baxter edged closer to each other, waiting out the final minutes.

Wendy Peterson knelt behind the back wall of the crypt as a medic wound a bandage around her right forearm. She flexed her fingers and noticed that they were becoming stiff. *"Damn."*

The medic said, "You better go back." Another medic was tying a pressure bandage around her right heel.

She looked around the red-lit area. Most of the original group had been left behind, dead from head wounds as a result of the ground-skimming fire. The rest were being evacuated, suffering from wounds in the limbs or buttocks or from broken clavicles where the flak jackets had stopped the head-on bullets. In the red light, pale faces seemed rosy, red blood looked black, and, somehow, the wounds seemed especially ugly. She turned away and concentrated on moving her fingers. "Damn it."

The new ESD squad leader assembled his men at the corner of the crypt and looked at his watch. "Eight minutes." He knelt down beside Peterson. "Listen, I don't know what the hell I'm supposed to be doing down here except collecting bodies because, let me tell you, there's no way to get that joker out of there, Lieutenant."

She moved away from the medics and limped to the edge of the vault. "You sure?"

He nodded. "I can't fire—right? He's got a gas mask, and concussion grenades are out. But even if we got him, there's not much time to defuse even one bomb, and we don't know how many there are. The damned dogs are dead, and there aren't any more dogs—"

"Okay . . . okay. . . . Damn it . . . we're so close."

"No," said the squad leader, "we are not close at all." Some of the men around him coughed nervously and pointedly. The squad leader addressed Peterson. "They said this was your decision . . . and Burke's decision." He picked up the field phone beside him, but it was still dead. "Your decision."

A voice called out from the dark, an old man's voice with a mocking tone. "Fuck you! Fuck all of you!"

A nervous young policeman shouted back, "Fuck you!"

The squad leader stuck his head around the crypt corner and shouted, "If you come out with your hands—"

"Oh, baloney!" Hickey laughed, then fired a burst of bullets at the red glow coming around the corner of the crypt. The gunfire caused a deafening roar in the closed space and echoed far into the quarter-acre of crawl space. Hickey shouted, "Is there a bomb squad lad there? Answer me!"

Peterson edged toward the corner. "Right here, Pop."

"Pop? Who are you calling Pop? Well, never mind—listen, these bombs have more sensitive triggers to make them blow than . . . than Linda Lovelace." He laughed, then said, "Terrible metaphor. Anyway, lass, to give you an example you'll appreciate professionally—I mean demolitions, not blowing—where was I? Oh, yes, I've lots of triggers—photosensitive, audio—all kinds of triggers. Do you believe that, little girl?"

"I think you're full of shit."

Hickey laughed. "Well, then send everyone away, darlin', and toss a concussion grenade at me. If that doesn't blow the bombs, then a demo man can come back and defuse them. *You* won't be able to with your brains scrambled, and I won't be able to stop him with *my* brains scrambled. Go on, lassie. Let's see what you're made of."

Wendy Peterson turned to the squad leader. "Give me a concussion grenade and clear out."

"Like hell. Anyway, you know we don't carry those things in spaces like this."

She unsheathed the long stiletto that she used to cut plastic and moved around the corner of the crypt.

The squad leader reached out and pulled her back. "Where the hell are you going? Listen, I thought of that—it's over sixty feet to where that guy is. *Nobody* can cover that distance without making some noise, and he'll nail you the second he hears you."

"Then cover me with noise."

"Forget it."

Hickey called out, "What's next, folks? One man belly-crawling? I can hear breathing at thirty-forty feet. I can smell a copper at sixty feet. Listen, gentlemen—and lady—the time has come for you to leave. You're annoying me, and I have things to think about in the next few minutes. I feel like singing—" He began singing a bawdy version of the British army song:

> "Fuck you aaa-lll, fuck you aaa-lll,
> The long and the short and the taa-lll.
> Fuck all the coppers, and fuck all their guns,
> Fuck all the priests and their bastard sons.
> S-o-oo, I'm saying good-bye to you all,
> The ones that appeal and appall.
> I stall and tarry,
> While you want to save Harry,
> But nevertheless fuck you aaa-lll."

Wendy Peterson put the stiletto back in its sheath and let out a long breath. "Let's go."

The procession began making its way back toward the open hatch to the corridor, moving with an affected casualness that disguised the fact that they were retreating at top speed. No one looked back except Wendy Peterson, who glanced over her shoulder once or twice. Suddenly she began running in a crouch, past the moving line of men, toward the open hatch.

John Hickey squeezed out of the tight space and sat down against the column footing, the mass of plastic explosive conforming to his back. "Oh . . . well . . ." He filled his pipe, lit it, and looked at his watch. 5:56. "My, it's late. . . ." He hummed a few bars of "An Irish Lullaby," then sang softly to himself, ". . . too-ra-loo-ra-loo-ra, hush now don't you cry. . . ."

The Sixth Squad leader climbed the iron rungs of the south spire alone, a nylon line attached to his belt. He moved quietly through the cold dark night to a point five feet below Rory Devane, who still clung to the arms of the cross. The ESD man drew his pistol. "Hey! Jesus! Don't move, or I'll blow your ass off."

Devane opened his eyes and looked down behind him.

The squad leader raised his pistol. "You armed?"

Devane shook his head.

The squad leader got a clear look at Devane's bloodied face in the city lights. "You're really fucked up—you know that?"

Devane nodded.

"Come on down. Nice and easy."

Devane shook his head. "I can't."

"Can't? You got up there, you bastard. Now get down. I'm not hanging here all fucking day waiting for you."

"I can't move."

The squad leader thought that about half the world was watching him on television, and he put a concerned expression on his face, then smiled at Devane good-naturedly. "You asshole. For two cents I'd jam this gun between your legs and blow your balls into orbit." He glanced at the towering buildings of Rockefeller Center and flashed a resolute look for the telescopic cameras and field glasses. He took a step upward. "Listen, sonny boy, I'm coming up with a line, and if you pull any shit, I swear to God, motherfucker, you're going to be treading air."

Devane stared down at the black-clad figure approaching. "You people talk funny."

The squad leader laughed and climbed up over the curve of the finial and wrapped his arms around the base of the cross. "You're okay, kid. You're an asshole, but you're okay. Don't move." He circled around to the side and pulled himself up until his head was level with Devane's shoulder, then reached out and looped a line around Devane's torso. "You the guy who fired the flares?"

Devane nodded.

"Real performer, aren't you, Junior? What else do you do? You juggle?" He tied the end of the long line to the top of the cross and spoke in a more solemn voice. "You're going to have to climb a little. I'll help you."

Devane's mind was nearly numb, but something didn't seem right. There was something incongruous about hanging twenty-eight stories above the most technologically advanced city in the world and being asked to climb, wounded, down a rope to safety. "Get a helicopter."

The squad leader glanced at him quickly.

Devane stared down into the man's eyes and said, "You're going to kill me."

"What the hell are you talking about? I'm risking my goddamned life to save you—shithead." He flashed a smile toward Rockefeller Center. "Come on. Down."

"No."

The squad leader heard a sound and looked up. A Fire Rescue helicopter appeared overhead and began dropping toward the spire. The helicopter dropped closer, beating the cold air downward. The squad leader saw a man in a harness edging out of the side door, a carrying chair in his hands. The squad leader hooked his arms over Devane's on the cross and pulled himself up so that they were face to face, and he studied the young man's frozen blue features. The blood had actually crystallized in his red hair and glistened in the light. The squad leader examined his throat wound and the large discolored mass on his forehead. "Caught some shit, did you? You should be dead—you know?"

"I'm going to live."

"They're stuffing some of my friends in body bags down there—"

"I never fired a shot."

"Yeah. . . . Come on, I'll help you into the sling."

"How can you commit murder—*here?*"

The squad leader drew a long breath and exhaled a plume of fog.

The Fire Rescue man was dangling about twenty feet above them now, and he released the carrying chair, which dropped on a line to within a few feet of the two men. The squad leader put his hands on Devane's shoulders. "Okay, Red, trust me." He reached up and guided the chair under Devane, strapped him in, then untied the looped rope. "Don't look down." He waved off the helicopter.

The helicopter rose, and Devane flew away from the spire, swinging in a wide arc through the brightening sky. The squad leader watched as the line was reeled in and Devane disappeared into the helicopter. The squad leader turned and looked back at Rockefeller Center. People were leaning from the windows, civilians and police, and he heard cheering. Bits of paper began sailing from the windows and floated in the updrafts. He wiped his runny eyes and waved toward the buildings as he began the climb down from the cross. "Hello, assholes —spell my name right. Hi, Mom—fuck you, Kline—I'm a hero."

Burke ran down the spiral stairs of the south tower until he reached a group of Guardsmen and police on the darkened choir loft level. Burke said, "What's the situation?"

No one answered immediately, then an ESD man said, "We sort of ran into each other in the dark." He motioned toward a neat stack of about six bodies against the wall.

"Christ. . . ." Burke looked across the tower room and saw a splintered door hanging loosely from its hinges.

An ESD man said, "Stay out of the line of fire of that door."

"Yeah, I guessed that right away."

A short burst of rifle fire hit the door, and everyone ducked as the bullets ricocheted around the large room, shattering thick panes of glass. A National Guardsman fired a full magazine back through the door.

The steady coughing of the sniper's silencer echoed into the room, but Burke could not imagine what was left to fire at. He circled around the room and slid along the wall toward the door.

Wendy Peterson ran to the top step of the sacristy stairs behind the altar. Her breathing came hard, and the wound on her heel was bleeding. She called back to the crypt landing where the two remaining ESD men stood. "Concussion grenade."

One of the men shrugged and threw up a large black canister.

She edged out and glanced to her right. About thirty feet separated the hostages under the pews from the stairs. To her left, toward the rear of the sanctuary, five feet of floor separated her from the bullet-scarred bronze plate.

How heavy, she wondered, was that plate? Which way did it hinge? Where was the handle? She turned back to the crypt landing. "The hostages?"

One of the men answered, "We can't help them. They have to make a break when they think they're ready. We're here in case they make it and are wounded . . . but they're not going to make it. Neither are we if we hang around much longer." He cleared his throat. "Hey, it's 5:57—can those bombs go before 6:03?"

She motioned toward the bronze plate. "What are my chances?"

The man looked down at the blood-streaked stairs and unconsciously touched his ear, which had been nicked by a shot from the loft—a shot fired from over a hundred yards away through the dim lighting. "Your chances of getting to the plate are good—fifty-fifty. Your chances of opening it, dropping that grenade, waiting for it to go, then dropping in yourself, are a little worse than zero."

"Then we let the place go down?"

He said, "No one can say we didn't try." He ran his foot across the sticky blood on the landing. "Cut out."

She shook her head. "I'll hang around—you never know what might happen."

"I *know* what's going to happen, Lieutenant, and this is not the place to be when it happens."

Two shots struck the bronze plate and ricocheted back toward the Lady Chapel. Another shot struck the plaster ceiling ten stories above. Peterson and the two ESD men looked up at the black expanse and dodged pieces of falling plaster. A second later one of the Cardinal's hats that had been suspended over the crypt dropped to the landing beside one of the ESD men. The man picked it up and examined the tassled red hat.

Leary's voice bellowed from the loft. "Got a cardinal—on the wing—in the dark. God, I can't miss! I can't *miss!*"

The ESD man threw the hat aside. "He's right, you know."

Peterson said, "I'll talk to the hostages. You might as well go."

One of the men bounded down the stairs toward the sacristy gates. The other climbed up toward Peterson. "Lieutenant"—he looked down at the bloody, soiled bandages wrapped around her bare foot—"it takes about sixty seconds to make it to the rectory basement. . . ."

"Okay."

The man hesitated, then turned and headed for the sacristy gates.

Peterson sat down on the top step and called out to Baxter and Malone, "How are you doing?"

Maureen called back, "Go away."

Peterson lit a cigarette. "It's okay . . . we have time yet. . . . Anytime you're ready . . . think it out." She spoke to them softly as the seconds ticked away.

Leary grazed a round over each of the four triforium balustrades, changed positions, fired at the statue of St. Patrick, moved laterally, picked out a flickering votive candle, fired, and watched it explode. He moved diagonally over the pews, then stopped and put two bullets through the cobalt blue window rising above the east end of the ambulatory. The approaching dawn showed a lighter blue through the broken glass.

Leary settled back into a bullet-pocked pew near the organ pipes and concentrated on the sanctuary—the stairwell, the bronze plate, and the clergy pews. He flexed his arm, which had been hit by shrapnel, and rubbed his cheek where buckshot had raked the side of his face. At least two ribs had been broken by bullets where they had hit his flak jacket.

Megan was firing at each of the tower doors, alternating the sequence and duration of each burst of automatic fire. She stood in the aisle a few feet below Leary and watched the two doors to her right and left farther down the loft. Her arms and legs were crusted with blood from shrapnel and buckshot, and her right shoulder was numb from a direct bullet hit. She suddenly felt shaky and nauseous and leaned against a pew. She straightened up and called back to Leary, "They're not even trying."

Leary said, "I'm bored."

She laughed weakly, then replied, "I'm going to blast those pews and flush those two out. You nail them."

Leary said, "In about six minutes half the Cathedral will fall in on them . . . or I'll get them if they make a break. Don't spoil the game. Be patient."

She knelt in the aisle and raised her rifle. "What if the police get the bombs?"

Leary looked at the sanctuary as he spoke. "I doubt they got Hickey. . . . Anyway, I'm doing what I was told—covering that plate and keeping those two from running."

She shouted as she took aim at the clergy pews. "I want to *see* her die— before I die. I'm going to flush them. You nail them. Ready?"

Leary stared down at Megan, her silhouette visible against the candlelight and flares below. He spoke in a low, contemplative voice. "Everyone's dead, Megan, except Hickey and, I guess, Malone and Baxter. They'll all die in the explosion. That leaves only you and me."

She spun around and peered up into the blackness toward the place from which his voice had come.

He said, "You understand, I'm a professional. It's like I said, I only do what I'm told—never more, never less—and Flynn told me to make especially sure of you and Hickey."

She shook her head. "Jack . . . you can't. . . . Not after we . . ." She laughed. "Yes, of course. . . . I don't want to be taken. . . . Brian knew that. . . . He did it for me. Go on, then. Quickly!"

He raised a pistol, aimed at the dark outline, and put two bullets in rapid succession through her head. Megan's body toppled back, and she rolled down the aisle, coming to rest beside the Guard sergeant she had killed.

Burke stood in his stocking feet with his back to the wall just inside the tower door, a short, fat grenade launcher nestled in the bend of his elbow. He closed his eyes against the glare of the lights coming through the broken windows and steadied his breathing. The men in the tower room were completely still, watching him. Burke listened to the distant sound of a man and woman talking, followed by two pistol shots. He spun rapidly into the doorway and raced up the side aisle along the wall, then flattened himself in the sloping aisle about halfway up the loft. From farther back near the organ pipes came the sound of breathing. The breathing stopped abruptly, and a man's voice said, "I *know* you're there."

Burke remained motionless.

The man said, "I see in the dark, I smell what you can't smell, I hear *everything*. You're dead."

Burke knew that the man was trying to draw him into a panic shot, and he was not doing a bad job of it. The man was good. Even in a close-in-situation like this he was very cool.

Burke rolled onto his back, lifted his head, and looked out over the rail into the Cathedral. The cable that held the chandelier nearest the choir loft swayed slightly as it was being drawn up by the winch in the attic. The chandelier rose level with the loft, and Burke saw the Guardsman sitting on it, his rifle pointed into the loft. He looked, Burke thought, like live bait. *Live ones,* he wanted live ones. Burke's muscles tensed.

Leary fired, and the body on the chandelier jerked.

Burke jumped to his feet, pointed the grenade launcher at the direction of the sound, and fired its single beehive round. The dozens of needle darts buzzed across the quiet loft, spreading as they traveled. There was a sharp cry, followed immediately by the flash of a rifle that Burke saw out of the corner of his eyes as he turned and dove for the floor. A powerful blow on the back of his flak jacket propelled him headfirst into the wall, and he staggered, then collapsed into the aisle. Another shot ripped through the pews and passed inches over his head.

Burke lay still, aware of a pain in the center of his spine that began to spread to his arms and legs. Several more shots struck around him. The firing shifted to the doors, and Burke tried to crawl to another position but found that he couldn't move. He tried to reach the pistol in his belt, but his arm responded in short, spastic motions.

The firing shifted back toward him, and a round grazed his hand. His forehead was bleeding where he had crashed into the wall, and throbbing pains ran from his eyes to the back of his skull. He felt himself losing consciousness, but he could hear distinctly the sound of the man reloading his rifle. Then the voice said, "Are you dead, or do you just wish you were?"

Leary raised his rifle, but the persistent stabbing pain in his right leg made him lower it. He sat down in the center aisle, rolled back his trouser leg, and ran his fingers over his shin, feeling the tiny entry hole where the dart had hit him. He brought his hand around to his calf and touched the exit wound, slightly larger, with a splinter of bone protruding from the flesh. "Ah . . . shit . . . shit . . ."

He rose to his knee and emptied his rifle toward the doors and the side aisle, then ripped off his rubber mask and pulled the gas mask from around his neck. He tore off the long robe, using it to wipe his sniper rifle from end to end as he crawled down the center aisle. Leary placed the rifle in Megan's warm hands, reached into the front pew, and retrieved another rifle. He rose and steadied himself on the edge of the pew and slid onto the bench. Leary called out, "Martin! You out there?"

There was a silence, then a voice called back from the choir practice room. "Right here, Jack. Are you alone?"

"Yeah."

"Tell the police you're surrendering."

"Right. Come out here—alone."

Martin walked briskly into the choir loft, turned on a flashlight, and made his way through the dark into the center aisle. He stepped over Megan's body. "Hello, Jack." He approached Leary and edged into the pew. "Here, let's have that. That's a good lad." He took Leary's rifle and pistol, then called out, "He's disarmed."

ESD men began to move cautiously from both towers into the choir loft. Martin called to them. "It's all right—this man is an agent of mine." Martin turned to Leary and gave him a look of annoyance. "A bit early, aren't you, Jack?"

Leary spoke through clenched teeth. "I'm hit."

"Really? You look fine."

Leary swore. "Fitzgerald was starting to become a problem, and I had to do her when I had the chance. Then someone got into the loft, and I took a needle dart in the shin. Okay?"

"That's dreadful . . . but I don't see anyone in here. . . . You really should have waited."

"Fuck you."

Martin shone his light on Leary's shin. Like so many killers, he thought, Leary couldn't stand much pain. "Yes, that looks like it might hurt." He reached out and touched Leary's wound.

Leary let out a cry of pain. "Hey! God . . . that feels like there's still a needle in there."

"Might well be." Martin looked down at the sanctuary. "Malone and Baxter . . . ?"

A policeman shouted from the side of the loft. "Stand up!"

Leary placed his hands on the pew in front of him and stood. He said to Martin, "They're both under the sanctuary pews there—"

The lights in the loft went on, illuminating the sloping expanse of ripped pews, bullet-pocked walls, burnt lockers, and scarred aisles. The towering organ pipes shone brightly where they had been hit, but above the pipes the rose window was intact. Leary looked around and made a whistling sound. "Like walking in the rain without getting wet." He smiled.

Martin waved his hand impatiently. "I don't understand about Baxter and Malone. They're dead, aren't they?"

The police stepped over the bodies in the aisle and moved up carefully into the pews, rifles and pistols raised.

Leary automatically put his hands on his head as he spoke to Martin. "Flynn told me not to kill her—and I couldn't shoot into the pews at Baxter without taking the chance of hitting her—"

"*Flynn?* You're working for *me*, Jack."

Leary pushed past Martin and hobbled into the aisle. "You give orders, he gives orders. . . . I do only what I'm told—and what I'm paid for—"

"But Flynn's money came from *me*, Jack."

Leary stared at Martin. "Flynn never bullshitted me. He told me this loft would be hell, and I knew it. You said it would be—how'd that go?—relatively without risk?"

Martin's voice was peevish. "Well, as far as I'm concerned you didn't fulfill your contract. I'll have to reconsider the nature of the final payment."

"Look, you little fuck—" Two ESD men covered the remaining distance up the aisle and grabbed Leary's upraised arms, pulling them roughly behind his back, then cuffing him. They pushed him to the floor, and he yelled out in pain, then turned his head back toward Martin as the police searched him. "If they got Hickey from below, they got the bombs anyway. If they didn't get him, you'll still get your explosion."

Martin noticed Burke moving toward him, supported by two ESD men. Martin cleared his throat. "All right, Jack—that's enough."

But Leary was obviously offended. "I lived up to my end. I mean, Christ, Martin, it's after six—and look around you—enough is enough—"

"Shut up."

Two ESD men pulled Leary to his feet. Leary said, "This leg . . . it feels funny . . . burns . . ."

Martin said nothing.

Leary stared at him. "What did you . . . ? Oh . . . no . . ."

Martin winked at him, turned, and walked away.

An ESD man raised a bullhorn and called out into the Cathedral. "Police in the choir loft! All clear! Mr. Baxter—Miss Malone—run! Run this way!"

Baxter picked up his head and looked at Maureen. "Was that Leary?"

She forced a smile. "You're learning." She listened to the bullhorn call their names again. "I don't know . . ." She pressed her face against Baxter's, and they held each other tightly.

Wendy Peterson looked around the altar and stared up into the choir loft. It was completely lit, and she saw the police moving through the pews. Without looking at her watch she knew there were probably not more than three minutes left—less, if the bomb were set earlier, and she didn't remember one that was set for later than the threatened time.

She ran to the bronze plate, pulling the pin on the concussion grenade as she moved and calling back to the pews. "Run! Run!" She bent over and pulled up the heavy bronze plate with one hand.

Maureen stood, looking first at Wendy Peterson and then toward the illuminated expanse at the upper end of the Cathedral as Baxter came up beside her.

A bullhorn was blaring. "Run! Run this way!"

They began to run, but Maureen suddenly veered and dashed up the pulpit stairs, grabbing Flynn's arm and dragging him back down the steps. Baxter ran up behind her and pulled at her arm. She turned to him. "He's alive. Please . . ." He hesitated, then put Flynn over his shoulders, and they ran toward the communion rail.

Wendy Peterson watched silently until they reached a point in the center aisle where she thought they would be safe if the grenade detonated the bomb. She released the safety handle and flung the grenade into the hole with a motion that suggested *What the hell.* . . . She dropped the plate back and stood off several feet, holding her hands over her ears.

The grenade exploded, ripping the bronze plate from its hinges and sending it high into the air. A shock wave rolled through the Cathedral, and the sanctuary trembled beneath her feet. Everything seemed to hang in suspension as she waited for a secondary explosion, but there was nothing except the ringing in her ears. She dropped through the smoke down the ladder.

Burke moved slowly toward Martin as the echoes of the shock wave passed through the loft.

Martin said, "Well, Lieutenant Burke, this is a surprise. I thought you'd be . . . well, somewhere else. You look terrible. You're walking strangely. Where are your *shoes?*" Martin checked his watch. "Two minutes . . . less, I think. Good view from here. Do you have cameras recording this? You won't see this again." He peered over Burke's shoulder at the sanctuary. "Look at all that metalwork, that marble. Magnificent. It's going to look exactly like Coventry in about three minutes." He patted the lapel of his topcoat as he turned back to Burke. "See? I've kept my carnation. Where's yours?" He looked anxiously into the sanctuary again. "What *is* that crazy woman up to? Turn around, Burke. Don't miss this."

Martin brushed past Burke and drew closer to the rail. He watched Baxter and Maureen approaching, accompanied by Major Cole and four Guardsmen. Brian Flynn's limp body was being carried on a stretcher by two of the Guardsmen. Martin said to Burke, "Governor Doyle will be pleased with his boys—Mayor Kline will be *furious* with you, Burke." Martin called down. "Harry, old man? Up here!" He waved. "Nicely done, you two."

Martin turned and looked back as Leary, almost unconscious, was being carried into the choir practice room. He said to Burke, "Ballistics will show that the rifle I took from him never fired a shot that killed anyone. He did kill that young woman sniper, though, the very moment he had—what do you call it?—the drop on her. Well, at least that's the way he's made it appear. He'll go free if he is tried." Martin looked back over his shoulder. "Good-bye, Jack. I'll see you later in the hospital." He called to an ESD squad leader. "Easy with that man—he works for me." Martin turned back to Burke as Leary disappeared into the choir room. "Your people are in an ugly mood. Well . . . the mysteries are unfolding now . . . Burke? Are you listening to me? Burke—" Martin looked at his watch, then at the sanctuary, and continued in a new vein. "The problem with you people is no fire discipline. Shoot first and ask questions later—great tradition. That's why Father Murphy is hanging dead from a ladder in the bell tower here—oh, you didn't know that, Burke?"

Martin walked to the edge of the loft and rested his hands on the parapet, looking straight down. Baxter and Malone were standing with their backs to him now. Flynn was lying near them on the floor, a National Guard medic crouched over him. Baxter, Martin noticed, had his arm around Maureen Malone's shoulder, and she was slumped against him. Martin said to Burke, "Come closer—look at this, Burke. They've made friends." He called down, "Harry, you old devil. Miss Malone. Get down, you two—there'll be a bit of falling debris." He turned to Burke behind him. "I feel rather bad about being the one who pushed for Baxter being on the steps. . . . If I had had *any* idea it would be so risky . . ."

Burke moved beside Martin and leaned on the rail. The feeling began to return to his legs and arms, and the numbness was replaced by a tingling sensation. He looked out into the Cathedral, focusing on the sanctuary. A dead ESD man lay in the clergy pews, and black smoke drifted out of the hole. Green carnations were strewn across the black-and-white marble floor, and hundreds of fragments of stained glass glittered where they'd fallen from above. Even from this distance he could see the blood splattered across the raised altar, the bullet marks everywhere. The police in the choir pews behind him fell silent and began to edge closer to the rail. The towers and attic had emptied, most of the police leaving the Cathedral through the only unmined exit—the damaged ceremonial doors. Some congregated in the two long west triforia, away from the expected area of destruction. They stared at the sanctuary, a block away, with a mesmerized fascination. Burke looked at his watch: 6:02, give or take thirty seconds.

Wendy Peterson shone her light into Hickey's face and poked his throat with her stiletto, but he was dead—yet there was no blood running from his nose, mouth, or ears, no protruding tongue or ruptured capillaries to indicate he had been killed by concussion. In fact, she thought, his face was serene, almost smiling, and he had probably died peacefully in his sleep and with no help from her or anyone else.

She set the light down pointing at the base of the column and switched on the lamp of her miner's helmet. "Photosensitive, my ass," she said aloud. "Bullshitting old bastard." She began speaking to herself, as she always did when she was alone with a bomb.

"Okay, Wendy, you silly bitch, one step at a time. . . ." She drew a deep breath, and the oily smell of the plastic rose in her flaring nostrils. "All the time in the world . . ." She passed her hands gently over the dusty surface of the plastic, feeling for a place where the mechanism might be embedded. "Looks

like stone. . . . Clever . . . all smoothed over . . . okay . . ." She slipped
her wristwatch off and stuck it into the plastic. "Ninety seconds, Wendy, give or
take. . . . Too late to clear out . . . stupid . . ." She was cutting with the
stiletto, making a random incision into the plastic. "You get only two or three
cuts now. . . ." She thrust her right hand into the opening but felt nothing.
The wound on her arm had badly stiffened her fingers. "Sixty seconds . . .
time flies when you're . . ." She put her ear to the plastic and listened, but
heard nothing except the blood pounding in her head. ". . . when you're having a good time. . . . Okay . . . cut here. . . . *Okay,* God? Careful . . .
nothing here. . . . Where'd you put it, old man? Where's that ticking heart?
Cut here, Wendy. . . . When you wish upon a star, makes no difference . . .
There . . . *there,* that's it." She pushed back the plastic, enlarging the incision
and revealing the face of a loudly ticking alarm clock. "Okay, clock time, 6:02.
My time, 6:02—alarm time, 6:03. . . . You play fair, old man. . . . All
right. . . ." She wanted to yank the clock out, rip away the wires, or squash the
crystal and advance the alarm dial, but that, more often than not, set the
damned thing off. "Easy, baby . . . you've come so far now. . . ." She thrust
her hand into the plastic and worked her long, stiff fingers carefully through the
thick, damp substance, feeling for anti-intrusion detonators as she dug toward
the rear of the clock. "Go gently into this crap, Peterson. . . . Hand behind
the clock . . . there . . . simple mechanism. . . . Where's the off switch?
Come on . . . damn it . . . 6:03—shit—*shit*—no alarm yet . . . few more
seconds . . . steady, Wendy. Dear God, steady, *steady* . . ." The alarm rang
loudly, and Wendy Peterson listened to it carefully, knowing it was the last
sound she would ever hear.

A deep silence came over the Cathedral. Martin rested his folded arms on
the rail as he stared into the sanctuary. He tapped his fingers on the watch
crystal. "What time do you have, Burke? Isn't it late? What seems to be the
problem?"

In the rectory and in the Cardinal's residence people had moved back from
the taped windows. On all the rooftops around the Cathedral police and newspeople stood motionless. In front of televisions in homes and in the bars that
had never closed, people watched the countdown numbers superimposed on
the silent screen showing an aerial view of the Cathedral brightening slowly in
the dawn light. In churches and synagogues that had maintained all-night vigils,
people looked at their watches. 6:04.

Wendy Peterson rose slowly from the hole and walked to the middle of the
sanctuary, blinking in the brighter lighting. She held something in both hands
and stared at it, then looked slowly up at the triforia and loft. Her face was very
pale, and her voice was slightly hesitant, but her words rolled through the silent
Cathedral. "The detonating device . . ." She held up a clock connected by
four wires to a large battery pack, from which ran four more wires. She raised it
higher, as though it were a chalice, and in her other hand she held four long
cylindrical detonators that she had clipped from the wires. White plastic still
clung to the mechanism, and in the stillness of the Cathedral the ticking clock
sounded very loud. She ran her tongue over her dry lips and said, "All clear."
    No one applauded, no one cheered, but in the silence there was an audible
collective sigh, then the sound of someone weeping.
    The quiet was suddenly broken by the shrill noise of a long scream as a man

fell headfirst from the choir loft. The body hit the floor in front of the armored carrier with a loud crack.

Maureen and Baxter turned and looked down at the awkwardly sprawled body, a splatter of blood radiating over the floor around the head. Baxter spoke in a whisper. "Martin."

Burke walked haltingly across the floor beneath the choir loft. The tingling in his back had become a dull pain. A stretcher was carried past him, and he caught a glimpse of Brian Flynn's face but couldn't tell if he was dead or alive. Burke kept walking until he came to Martin's body. Martin's neck was broken, his eyes were wide open, and his protruding tongue was half bitten off. Burke lit a cigarette and dropped the match on Martin's face.

He turned and looked absently at the huge, charred carrier and the blackened bodies on it, then watched the people around him moving, speaking quickly, going about their duties; but it all seemed remote, as though he were watching through an unfocused telescope. He looked around for Baxter and Malone but saw they were gone. He realized he had nothing to do at the moment and felt good about it.

Burke moved aimlessly up the center aisle and saw Wendy Peterson standing alone in the aisle and looking, like himself, somewhat at loose ends. Weak sunlight came through the broken window above the east end of the ambulatory, and she seemed, he thought, to be deliberately standing in the dust-moted shaft. As he walked past her he said, "Very nice."

She looked up at him. "Burke . . ."

He turned and saw she held the detonating mechanism. She spoke, but not really, he thought, to him. "The clock is working . . . see? And the batteries can't all have failed. . . . The connections were tight. . . . There're four separate detonators . . . but they never . . ." She looked almost appalled, he thought, as though all the physical laws of the universe that she had believed in had been revoked.

He said, "But you—you were—"

She shook her head. *"No.* That's what I'm telling you." She looked into his eyes. "I was about two seconds late. . . . It *rang* . . . I *heard* it ring, Burke. . . . I *did.* Then there was a strange sort of a feeling . . . like a presence. I figured, you know, I'm dead and it's not so bad. They talk about—in this business they talk about having an Angel on your shoulder while you work— you know? God Almighty, I had a regiment of them."

Book VI

Morning, March 18

*And the Green Carnation withered, as
in forest fires that pass.*

G. K. Chesterton

Patrick Burke blinked as he walked out through the ceremonial doors, down the center of the crushed steps between the flattened handrails, and into the thin winter sunlight.

The night's accumulation of ice was running from rooftops and sidewalks and melting over the steps of St. Patrick's into the littered streets. Burke saw on the bottom step the hand-lettered sign that the Fenians had stuck to the front doors, half torn, the words blurring over the soggy cardboard. The splatter of green paint from the thrown bottle bled out across the granite, and a long, barely visible trail of blood from the dead horse led into the Avenue. You wouldn't know what it all was, thought Burke, if you hadn't been there.

A soft south wind shook the ice from the bare trees along Fifth Avenue, and church bells tolled in the distance. Ambulances, police vehicles, and limousines splashed through the sunlit pools of water, and platoons of Tactical Police and National Guardsmen marched in the streets, while mounted police, half-asleep on their horses, moved in apparently random directions. Many of the police, Burke noticed, had black ribbons on their badges, most of the city officials wore black armbands, and many of the flags along the Avenue were at half-mast, as though this had all been thought out for some time, anticipated, foreseen.

Burke heard a sound on the north terrace and saw the procession of clergy and lay people who were completing their circle of the Cathedral walls, led by the Cardinal wearing a white stole. They drew abreast of the main doors and

751

faced them, the Cardinal intoning, "Purify me with hyssop, Lord, and I shall be clean of sin. Wash me, and I shall be whiter than snow."

Burke stood a few yards off, listening as the assembly continued the rite of reconciliation for the profaned church, oblivious to the people swarming around them. He watched the Cardinal sprinkle holy water against the walls as the others prayed, and he wondered how so obscure a ritual could be carried out so soon and with such Roman precision. Then he realized that the Cardinal and the others must have been thinking about it all night, just as the city officials had rehearsed their parts in their minds during the long black hours. He, Burke, had never let his thoughts get much beyond 6:03, which was one reason why he would never be either the Mayor or the Archbishop of New York.

The procession moved through the portal two by two and past the smashed ceremonial doors into the Cathedral. Burke took off his flak jacket and dropped it at his feet, then walked slowly to the corner of the steps near Fiftieth Street and sat down in a patch of pale sunlight. He folded his arms over his knees and rested his head, falling into a half-sleep.

The Cardinal moved at the head of the line of priests who made up the Cathedral staff. A cross-bearer held a tall gold cross above the sea of moving heads, and the Litany of the Saints was chanted as the line went forward through the gate of the communion rail.

The group assembled in the center of the sanctuary where Monsignor Downes awaited them. The altar was entirely bare of religious objects in preparation for the conclusion of the cleansing rite, and police photographers and crime lab personnel were hurrying through their work. The assembly fell silent, and people began looking around at the blood-splattered sanctuary and altar. Then heads began to turn out toward the ravaged Cathedral, and several people wept openly.

The Cardinal's voice cut off the display of emotion. "There will be time enough for that later." He spoke to two of the priests. "Go into the side vestibules where the casualties have been taken and assist the police and army chaplains." He added, "Have Father Murphy's body taken to the rectory."

The two priests moved off. The Cardinal looked at the sacristans and motioned around the sanctuary. "As soon as the police have finished here, make it presentable for the Mass that will be offered at the conclusion of the purification." He added, "Leave the carnations."

He turned to Monsignor Downes and spoke to him for the first time. "Thank you for your prayers, and for your efforts during this ordeal."

Monsignor Downes lowered his head and said softly, "I . . . they asked me to sanction your rescue . . . this attack . . ."

"I know all of that." He smiled. "More than once during the night I thanked God it wasn't I who had to deal with those . . . questions." The Cardinal turned and faced the long, wide expanse of empty pews. "God arises, His enemies are scattered, and those who hate Him flee before Him."

Captain Bert Schroeder walked unsteadily up the steps of St. Patrick's, a bandage covering the left side of his chalk-white jaw. A police medic and several Tactical Police officers escorted him.

Mayor Kline raced up to Schroeder, hand extended. "Bert! Over here! Bring him here, men."

A number of reporters had been let through the cordon, and they converged on Schroeder. Cameras clicked and newsreel microphones were thrust in his face. Mayor Kline pumped Schroeder's hand and embraced him, taking the opportunity to say through clenched teeth, "Smile, damn it, and look like a hero."

Schroeder looked distraught and disoriented. His eyes moved over the throng around him to the Cathedral, and he stared at it, then looked around at the people talking excitedly and realized that he was being interviewed.

A reporter called out, "Captain, is it true you recommended an assault on the Cathedral?"

Schroeder didn't answer, and Kline spoke up. "Yes, a rescue operation. The recommendation was approved by an emergency committee consisting of myself, the Governor, Monsignor Downes, Inspector Langley of Intelligence, and the late Captain Bellini. Intelligence indicated the terrorists were going to massacre the hostages and then destroy the Cathedral. Many of them were mentally unbalanced, as our police files show." He looked at each of the reporters. "There were no options."

Another reporter asked, "Who exactly was Major Martin? How did he die?" Kline's smile dropped. "That's under investigation."

There was a barrage of questions that Kline ignored. He put his arm around Schroeder and said, "Captain Schroeder played a vital role in keeping the terrorists psychologically unprepared while Captain Bellini formulated a rescue operation with the help of Gordon Stillway, resident architect of Saint Patrick's." He nodded toward Stillway, who stood by himself examining the front doors and making notes in a small book.

Kline added in a somber tone, "The tragedy here could have been much greater—" A loud Te Deum began ringing out from the bell tower, and Kline motioned toward the Cathedral. "The Cathedral stands! The Cardinal, Sir Harold Baxter, and Maureen Malone are alive. For this we should thank God." He bowed his head and after an appropriate interval looked up and spoke emphatically. "This rescue *will* be favorably compared to similar humanitarian operations against terrorists throughout the world."

A reporter addressed Schroeder directly. "Captain, did you find this man, Flynn—and the other one, Hickey—very tough people to negotiate with?"

Schroeder looked up. "Tough . . . ?"

Mayor Kline hooked his arm through Schroeder's and shook him. "Bert?"

Schroeder's eyes darted around. "Oh . . . yes, yes I did—no, no, not . . . not any tougher than— Excuse me, I'm not feeling well. . . . I'm sorry . . . excuse me." He pulled loose from the Mayor's grip and hurried across the length of the steps, avoiding reporters. The newspeople watched him go, then turned back to Kline and began asking him about the large number of casualties on both sides, but Kline evaded the questions. Instead, he smiled and pointed over the heads of the people around him.

"There's the Governor crossing the street." He waved. "Governor Doyle! Up here!"

Dan Morgan stood near the window, his eyes focused on the television screen that showed the Cathedral steps, the milling reporters, police and city officials. Terri O'Neal sat on the bed, fully dressed, her legs tucked under her body. Neither person spoke nor moved.

The camera focused on Mayor Kline and Captain Schroeder, and a reporter was speaking from off camera commenting on Schroeder's bandaged jaw.

Morgan finally spoke. "It appears he didn't do what he was asked."

Terri O'Neal said, "Good."

Morgan let out a deep sigh and walked to the side of the bed. "My friends are all dead, and there's nothing good about that."

She kept looking at the television as she spoke in a hoarse whisper. "Are you going to kill . . . ?"

Morgan drew his pistol from his belt. "No. You're free." He placed his hand on her shoulder as he pointed the silencer at the center of her head.

She put her face in her hands and began weeping.

He squeezed back on the trigger. "I'll get your coat. . . ."

She suddenly took her face out of her hands and turned. She realized she was looking into the barrel of the pistol. "Oh . . . no . . ."

Morgan's hand was shaking. He looked at her and their eyes met. The end of the silencer brushed her cheek, and he jerked the pistol away and shoved it in his belt. "There's been enough death today," he said. He turned and walked out of the bedroom. Terri O'Neal heard the front door open, then slam shut.

She found the cigarettes Morgan left behind, lit one, and stared at the television. "Poor Daddy."

Burke shifted restlessly, brought out of his short sleep by the noise around him and the pounding pain in his back. He rubbed his eyes and noticed that the injured eye was blurry again, and every inch of his body felt blurry; numb, he supposed, was a better word, numb except the parts that hurt. And his mind seemed numb *and* blurry, free-floating in the sunny light around him. He stood unsteadily, looked over the crowded steps, and blinked. Bert Schroeder and Murray Kline were holding court—and it was, he realized, just as he would have pictured it if he had allowed himself to think of the dawn. Schroeder surrounded by the press, Schroeder looking very self-possessed, handling questions like a pro—but as he watched he saw that the Hostage Negotiator was not doing well. He saw Schroeder suddenly break loose and make his way across the steps, through the knots of people like a broken-field runner, and Burke called out as he passed, "Schroeder!"

Schroeder seemed not to hear and continued toward the arched portal of the south vestibule. Burke came up behind him and grabbed his arm. "Hold on." Schroeder tried to pull away, but Burke slammed him against the stone buttress. "Listen!" He lowered his voice. "I know—about Terri—"

Schroeder looked at him, his eyes widening. Burke went on. "Martin is dead, and the Fenians are all dead or dying. I had to tell Bellini . . . but he's dead, too. Langley knows, but Langley doesn't give away secrets—he just makes you buy them back someday. Okay? So just shut your mouth and be very cool." He released Schroeder's arm.

Tears formed in Schroeder's eyes. "Burke . . . God Almighty . . . do you *understand* what I did . . . ?"

"Yeah . . . yeah, I understand, and I'd really like to see you in the fucking slammer for twenty, but that won't help anything. . . . It won't help the department, and it won't help me or Langley. And it damn sure won't help your wife or daughter." He moved closer to Schroeder. "And don't blow your brains out, either. . . . It's a sin—you know? Hang around long enough in this job and someone will blow them out for you."

Schroeder caught his breath and spoke. "No . . . I'm going to retire—re-sign—confess . . . make a public—"

"You're going to keep your goddamned mouth shut. No one—not me or Kline or Rourke or the DA or anyone—wants to hear your fucking confession, Schroeder. You've caused enough problems—just cool out."

Schroeder hung his head, then nodded. "Burke . . . Pat . . . thanks. . . ."

"Fuck you." He looked at the door beside him. "You know what's in this vestibule?"

Schroeder shook his head.

"Bodies. Lots of bodies. The field morgue. You go in there and you talk to those bodies—and say something to Bellini—and you go into the Cathedral and you make a confession, or you pray or you do anything you have to do to help you get through the next twenty-four hours." He reached out and opened the door, took Schroeder's arm, and pushed him into the vestibule, then shut the door. He stared down at the pavement for a long time, then turned at the sound of his name and saw Langley hurrying up the steps toward him.

Langley started to extend his hand, then glanced around quickly and withdrew it. He said coolly, "You're in a little trouble, Lieutenant."

Burke lit a cigarette. "Why?"

"Why?" He lowered his voice and leaned forward. "You pushed a British consulate official—a *diplomat*—out of the choir loft of Saint Patrick's Cathedral to his *death.* That's *why."*

"He fell."

"Of course he fell—you pushed him. What could he do but fall? He couldn't *fly."* Langley ran his hand over his mouth, and Burke thought he was hiding a smile. Langley regained his composure and said caustically, "That was very stupid—don't you agree?"

Burke shrugged.

Roberta Spiegel walked unnoticed through the crowd on the steps and came under the portal, stopping beside Langley. She looked at the two men, then said to Burke, "Christ Almighty, right in front of about forty policemen and National Guardsmen. Are you crazy?"

Langley said, "I just asked him if he was stupid, but that's a good question, too." He turned to Burke. "Well, are you stupid or crazy?"

Burke sat down with his back to the stone wall and watched the smoke rise from his cigarette. He yawned twice.

Spiegel's voice was ominous. "They're going to arrest you for *murder.* I'm surprised they haven't grabbed you yet."

Burke raised his eyes toward Spiegel. "They haven't grabbed me because you told them not to. Because you want to see if Pat Burke is going to go peacefully or if he's going to kick and scream."

Spiegel didn't answer.

Burke glared at her, then at Langley. "Okay, let me see if I know how to play this game. A file on Bartholomew Martin—right? He suffered from vertigo and fear of heights. Or how about this?—twenty police witnesses in the loft sign sworn affidavits saying Martin took a swat at a fly and toppled— No, no, I've got it—"

Spiegel cut him off. "The man was a *consulate official—"*

"Bullshit."

Spiegel shook her head. "No one can fix this one, Lieutenant."

Burke leaned back and yawned again. "You're Ms. Fixit in this town, lady, so you fix it. And fix me up with a commendation and captain's pay while you're about it. By tomorrow."

Spiegel's face reddened. "Are you *threatening* me?" Their eyes met, and neither turned away. She said, "And who's going to believe *your* version of anything that was discussed tonight?"

Burke stubbed out his cigarette. "Schroeder, who is a hero, will corroborate *anything* I say."

Spiegel laughed. "That's absurd."

Langley cleared his throat and said to Spiegel. "Actually, that's true. It's a long story. . . . I think Lieutenant Burke deserves . . . well, whatever he says he deserves."

Spiegel looked at Langley closely, then turned back to Burke. "You've got something on Schroeder—right? Okay, I don't have to know what it is. I'm not looking to hang you, Burke. I'll do what I can—"

Burke interrupted. "Art Forgery Squad. It would be a really good idea if I was in Paris by this time tomorrow."

Spiegel laughed. "Art Forgery? What the hell do you know about art?"

"I know what I like."

"That true," said Langley. "He does." He stuck his hand out toward Burke. "You did an outstanding job tonight, Lieutenant. The Division is very proud of you."

Burke took his hand and used it to pull himself up. "Thank you, Chief Inspector. I shall be clean of sin. Wash me, and I shall be whiter than snow."

Langley said, "Well . . . we'll just get you a commendation or something. . . ."

Spiegel lit a cigarette. "How the hell did I ever get involved with cops and politicians? God, I'd rather be on the stroll in Times Square."

Burke said, "I thought you looked familiar."

She ignored him and surveyed the steps and the Avenue. "Where's Schroeder, anyway? I see lots of news cameras, but smiling Bert isn't in front of any of them. Or is he at a television studio already?"

Burke said, "He's in the Cathedral. Praying."

Spiegel seemed taken aback, then nodded. "That's *damned* good press. Yes, yes. Everyone's out here sucking up on the coverage, and he's in there praying. They'll eat it up. Wow . . . I could run that bastard for councilman in Bensonhurst . . ."

Stretcher-bearers began bringing the bodies out of the Cathedral, a long, silent procession, through the doors of the south vestibule, down the steps. The litters carrying the police and Guardsmen passed through a hastily assembled honor guard; the stretchers of the Fenians passed behind the guard. Everyone on the steps fell silent, police and army chaplains walked beside the stretchers, and a uniformed police inspector in gold braid directed the bearers to designated ambulances. The litters holding the Fenians were placed on the sidewalk.

Burke moved among the stretchers and found the tag marked Bellini. He drew the cover back and looked into the face, wiped of greasepaint—a very white face with that hard jaw and black stubble. He dropped the cover back and quickly walked a few steps off, his hands on his hips, staring down at his feet.

The bells had ended the Te Deum and began to play a slow dirge. Governor Doyle stood with his retinue, his hat in his hand. Major Cole stood beside him holding a salute. The Governor leaned toward Cole and spoke as he lowered his head in respect. "How many did the Sixty-ninth lose, Major?"

Cole looked at him out of the corner of his eye, certain that he had detected an expectant tone in the Governor's voice. "Five killed, sir, including Colonel Logan, of course. Three wounded."

"Out of how many?"

Cole lowered his salute and stared at the Governor. "Out of a total of eighteen men who directly participated in the attack."

"The *rescue* . . . yes . . ." The Governor nodded thoughtfully. "Terrible. Fifty percent casualties."

"Well, not quite fif—"

"But you rescued two hostages."

"Actually, they saved themselves—"

"The Sixty-ninth Regiment will be needing a new commander, Cole."

"Yes . . . that's true."

The last of the police and Guardsmen were placed in ambulances, and the line of vehicles began moving away, escorted by motorcycle police. A black police van pulled up to the curb, and a group of stretcher-bearers on the sidewalk picked up the litters holding the dead Fenians and headed toward the van.

An Intelligence officer standing beside the van saluted Langley as he approached and handed him a small stack of folded papers. The man said, "Almost every one of them had an identifying personal note on him, Inspector. And here's a preliminary report on each one." The man added, "We also found pages of the ESD attack plan in there. How the hell—?"

Langley took the loose pages and shoved them in his pocket. "That doesn't go in your report."

"Yes, sir."

Langley came up beside Burke sitting under the portal again, with Spiegel standing in front of him.

Burke said, "Where are Malone and Baxter?"

Spiegel answered, "Malone and Baxter are still in the Cathedral for their own protection—there may still be snipers out there. Baxter's in the Archbishop's sacristy until we release him to his people. Malone's in the bride's room. The FBI will take charge of her."

Burke said, "Where's Flynn's body?"

No one answered, then Spiegel knelt on the step beside Burke. "He's not dead yet. He's in the bookstore."

Burke said, "Is that the Bellevue annex?"

Spiegel hesitated, then spoke. "The doctor said he was within minutes of death . . . so we didn't . . . have him moved."

Burke said, "You're murdering him—so don't give me this shit about not being able to move him."

Spiegel looked him in the eye. "Everybody on both sides of the Atlantic wants him dead, Burke. Just like everyone wanted Martin dead. Don't start moralizing to me. . . ."

Burke said, "Get him to Bellevue."

Langley looked at him sharply. "You know we can't do that now . . . and he knows too much, Pat. . . . Schroeder . . . other things. . . . And he's dangerous. Let's make things easy on ourselves for once. Okay?"

Burke said, "Let's have a look."

Spiegel hesitated, then stood. "Come on."

They entered the Cathedral and passed through the south vestibule littered with the remains of the field morgue that smelled faintly of something disagreeable—a mixture of odors, which each finally identified as death.

The Mass was beginning, and the organ overhead was playing an entrance song. Burke looked at the shafts of sunlight coming through the broken windows. He had thought that the light would somehow diminish the mystery, but it hadn't, and in fact the effect was more haunting even than the candlelight.

They turned right toward the bookstore. Two ESD men blocked the entrance but moved quickly aside. Spiegel entered the small store, followed by Burke and Langley. She leaned over the counter and looked down at the floor.

Brian Flynn lay in the narrow space, his eyes closed and his chest rising and falling very slowly. She said, "He's not letting go so easily." She watched him for a few seconds, then added, "He's a good-looking man . . . must have had a great deal of charisma, too. Very few are born into this sorry world like that. . . . In another time and place, perhaps, he would have been . . . something else. . . . Incredible waste . . ."

Burke came around the counter and knelt beside Flynn. He pushed back his eyelids, then listened to his chest and felt for his pulse. Burke looked up. "Fluid in the chest . . . heart is going . . . but it may take a while."

No one spoke. Then Spiegel said, "I can't do this . . . I'll get the stretcher-bearers. . . ."

Flynn's lips began to move, and Burke put his ear close to Flynn's face. Burke said, "Yes, all right." He turned to Spiegel. "Forget the stretcher . . . he wants to speak to her."

Maureen Malone sat quietly in the bride's room while four policewomen tried to make conversation with her.

Roberta Spiegel opened the door and regarded her for a second, then said abruptly, "Come with me."

She seemed not to have heard and sat motionless.

Spiegel said, "He wants to see you."

Maureen looked up and met the eyes of the other woman. She rose and followed Spiegel. They hurried down the side aisle and crossed in front of the vestibules. As they entered the bookstore Langley looked at Maureen appraisingly, and Burke nodded to her. Both men walked out of the room. Spiegel said, "There." She pointed. "Take your time." She turned and left.

Maureen moved around the counter and knelt beside Brian Flynn. She took his hands in hers but said nothing. She looked through the glass counter and realized there was no one else there, and she understood. She pressed Flynn's hands, an overwhelming feeling of pity and sorrow coming over her such as she had never felt for him before. "Oh, Brian . . . so alone . . . always alone . . ."

Flynn opened his eyes.

She leaned forward so that their faces were close and said, "I'm here."

His eyes showed recognition.

"Do you want a priest?"

He shook his head.

She felt a small pressure on her hands and returned it. "You're dying, Brian. You know that, don't you? And they've left you here to die. Why won't you see a priest?"

He tried to speak, but no sound came out. Yet she thought she knew what he wanted to say and to ask her. She told him of the deaths of the Fenians, including Hickey and Megan, and with no hesitancy she told him of the death of Father Murphy, of the survival of the Cardinal, Harold Baxter, Rory Devane, and of the Cathedral itself, and about the bomb that didn't explode. His face registered emotion as she spoke. She added, "Martin is dead, also. Lieutenant Burke, they say, pushed him from the choir loft, and they also say that Leary was Martin's man. . . . Can you hear me?"

Flynn nodded.

She went on. "I know you don't mind dying . . . but I mind . . . mind terribly. . . . I love you, still. . . . Won't you, for me, let a priest see you? Brian?"

He opened his mouth, and she bent closer. He said, ". . . the priest . . ."

"Yes . . . I'll call for one."

He shook his head and clutched at her hands. She bent forward again. Flynn's voice was almost inaudible. "The priest . . . Father Donnelly . . . here . . ."

"What . . . ?"

"Came here. . . ." He held up his right hand. "Took back the ring. . . ."

She stared at his hand and saw that the ring was gone. She looked at his face and noticed for the first time that it had a peaceful quality to it, with no trace of the things that had so marked him over the years.

He opened his eyes wide and looked intently at her. "You see . . . ?" He reached for her hands again and held them tightly.

She nodded. "Yes . . . no . . . no, I don't see, but I never did, and you always seemed so sure, Brian—" She felt the pressure on her hand relax, and she looked at him and saw that he was dead. She closed his eyes and kissed him, then took a long breath and stood.

Burke, Langley, and Spiegel stood at the curb on the corner of Fifth Avenue and Fiftieth Street. The Sanitation Department had mobilized its huge squadrons, and the men in gray mingled with the men in blue. Great heaps of trash, mostly Kelly-green in color, grew at the curbsides. The police cordon that had enclosed two dozen square blocks pulled in tighter, and the early rush hour began building up in the surrounding streets.

None of the three spoke for some time. Spiegel turned and faced the sun coming over the tall buildings to the east. She studied the façade of the Cathedral, then said, "In class I used to teach that every holiday will one day have two connotations. I think of Yom Kippur, Tet. And after the Easter Monday Rising in 1916, that day was never the same again in Ireland. It became a different sort of holiday, with different connotations—different associations—like Saint Valentine's Day in Chicago. I have the feeling that Saint Patrick's Day in New York may never be the same again."

Burke looked at Langley. "I don't even *like* art—what the hell do I care if someone forges it?"

Langley smiled, then said, "You never asked me about the note in Hickey's coffin." Langley handed him the note, and Burke read: *If you're reading this note, you've found me out. I wanted to spend my last days alone and in peace, to lay down the sword and give up the fight. Then again, if something good comes along—In any case, don't put me here. Bury me beneath the sod of Clonakily beside my mother and father.*

There was a silence, and they looked around for something to occupy their attention. Langley saw a PBA canteen truck that had parked beside the wrecked mobile headquarters. He cleared his throat and said to Roberta Spiegel, "Can I get you a cup of coffee?"

"Sure." She smiled and put her arm through his. "Give me a cigarette."

Burke watched them walk off, then stood by himself. He thought he might make the end of the Mass, but then decided to report to the new mobile headquarters across the street. He began walking but turned at the sound of an odd noise behind him.

A horse was snorting, thick plumes of fog coming from its nostrils. Betty Foster said, "Hi! Thought you'd be okay."

Burke moved away from the spirited horse. "Did you?"

"Sure." She reined the horse beside him. "Mayor make you nervous?"

Burke said, "That idiot. . . . Oh, the horse. Where do you *get* these names?"

She laughed. "Give you a lift?"

"No . . . I have to hang around. . . ."

She leaned down from the saddle. "Why? It's over. *Over,* Lieutenant. You *don't* have to hang around."

He looked at her. Her eyes were bloodshot and puffy, but there was a determined sort of recklessness in them, brought on, he supposed, by the insanity of the long night, and he saw that she wasn't going to be put off so easily. "Yeah, give me a lift."

She took her foot from the stirrup, reached down, and helped him up behind her. "Where to?"

He put his arms around her waist. "Where do you usually go?"

She laughed again and reined the horse in a circle. "Come on, Lieutenant—give me an order."

"Paris," said Burke. "Let's go to Paris."

"You got it." She kicked the horse's flanks. "Gi-yap, Mayor!"

Maureen Malone rubbed her eyes in the sunlight as she came through the doors of the north vestibule flanked by FBI men, including Douglas Hogan. Hogan indicated a waiting Cadillac limousine on the corner.

Harold Baxter came out of the south vestibule surrounded by consulate security men. A silver-gray Bentley drew up to the curb.

Maureen moved down the steps toward the Cadillac and saw Baxter through the crowd. Reporters began converging first on Baxter and then around her, and her escort elbowed through the throng. She pulled away from Hogan and stood on her toes, looking for Baxter, but the Bentley drove off with a motorcycle escort.

She slid into the back of the limousine and sat quietly as men piled in around her and the doors slammed shut. Hogan said, "We're taking you to a private hospital."

She didn't answer, and the car drew away from the curb. She looked down at her hands, still covered with Flynn's blood where he had held them.

The limousine edged into the middle of the crowded Avenue, and Maureen looked out the window at the Cathedral, certain she would never see it again.

A man suddenly ran up beside the slow-moving vehicle and held an identification to the window, and Hogan lowered the glass a few inches. The man spoke with a British accent. "Miss Malone . . ." He held a single wilted green carnation through the window. "Compliments of Sir Harold, miss." She took the carnation, and the man saluted as the car moved off.

The limousine turned east on Fiftieth Street and passed beside the Cathedral, then headed north on Madison Avenue and passed the Cardinal's residence, Lady Chapel, and rectory, picking up speed as it moved over the wet pavement. Ahead she saw the gray Bentley, then lost it in the heavy traffic. She said, "Lower the window."

Someone lowered the window closest to her, and she heard the bells of distant churches, recognizing the distinctive bells of St. Patrick's playing "Danny Boy," and she sat back and listened to them. She thought briefly of the journey home, of Sheila and Brian, and she recalled a time in her life, not so long ago, when everyone she knew was alive—parents, girl friends and boyfriends, relatives and neighbors—but now her life was filled with the dead, the missing, and the wounded, and she thought that most likely she would join those ranks. She tried to imagine a future for herself and her country but couldn't. Yet she wasn't afraid and looked forward to working, in her own way, to accomplish the Fenian goal of emptying the jails of Ulster.

The bells died in the distance, and she looked down at the carnation in her lap. She picked it up and twirled the stem in her fingers, then put it in the lapel of her tweed jacket.

BY THE RIVERS OF BABYLON

This book is dedicated to Bernard Geis, who took a chance;
my wife, Ellen, who took a bigger chance;
and my parents, who had no choice.

Acknowledgments

I wish to thank Captain Thomas Block
for his invaluable technical assistance
and Bernard Geis and his staff at Bernard Geis Associates,
particularly Judith Shafran and Jessie Crawford,
for their superb editorial guidance.

Our struggle has barely begun. The worst is yet to come. And it is right for Europe and America to be warned now that there will be no peace. . . . The prospect of triggering a third world war doesn't bother us. The world has been using us and has forgotten us. It is time they realized we exist. Whatever the price, we will continue the struggle. Without our consent, the other Arabs can do nothing. And we will never agree to a peaceful settlement. We are the joker in the pack.

Dr. George Habash, Leader,
The Popular Front
for the Liberation of
Palestine (PFLP)

We Jews just refuse to disappear. No matter how strong, brutal, and ruthless the forces against us may be—here we are. Millions of bodies broken, buried alive, burned to death, but never has anyone been able to succeed in breaking the spirit of the Jewish people.

Golda Meir
Brussels, February 19, 1976
The Brussels II Conference
on the Plight of Soviet Jewry

FRANCE: ST. NAZAIRE

N uri Salameh, apprentice electrician, patted the oversized pockets of his white coveralls again. He stood, slightly bowed, in the middle of the huge Aérospatiale plant, unsure of his next step. Around him, other immigrant French-speaking Algerians seemed to move with an unreal balletlike slowness as they marked time in anticipation of the bell that would signal the end of their work shift.

The late afternoon sun streamed in dusty, moted shafts through the six-story-high windows and suffused the badly heated plant with a warm golden glow that contrasted with Salameh's breath fog.

Outside the plant, the airport lights were coming on. A flight of metallic blue Mirages floated over the airfield in a V-formation. Buses began lining up to take the Aérospatiale workers to their homes in St. Nazaire.

Inside the plant, additional rows of fluorescent lights flickered on, momentarily startling the Algerian. Salameh looked around quickly. At least one other countryman avoided his darting eyes. Salameh knew that his fate was no longer in his own hands nor, he suspected, in the hands of Allah.

With the Arab's ancient character flaw, he soared on the wings of hope and rose from the depths of despair to the most dangerous peaks of overconfidence. He began walking briskly across the concrete floor.

In front of him, the huge Concorde sat on metal scaffolding. Forming jigs, to guide the assemblers, arched over, under and around the fuselage and wings.

Much of the aircraft's skin was missing and workers were crawling over the long body, like ants crawling over the half-eaten carcass of a giant dragonfly.

Salameh climbed the stairs to the top platform of the scaffolding and crawled onto the forming jig that ran along the base of the twelve-meter-high tail. On one of the unpainted aluminum tail plates was stenciled the production number, 4X-LPN.

Salameh looked at his watch. Ten minutes until the end of the shift. He had to do it now, before the night riveters closed the tail section. He grabbed a clipboard hanging from the jig and scanned it quickly. He looked back down over his shoulder. Below, an Algerian looked up as he swept metal filings from the floor, then turned away.

Salameh felt the sweat form on his face, then turn cold in the concrete and steel chill of the factory. He wiped his forehead with his sleeve, then lowered himself between two stringers into the rear of the partially skinned aluminum fuselage. The tail section was a maze of laser-welded struts and curved braces. His feet rested on the supporting cross members directly over the number eleven trim tank. He crouched down and crab-walked from strut to strut toward the half-finished pressure bulkhead.

Salameh peered over the bulkhead and looked down the length of the cavernous fuselage. Six men walked over the temporary plywood floors, laying bats of insulation between the passenger cabin and the baggage compartment in the belly of the craft. They alternately lifted the plywood, laid the bats, then placed the plywood back between the struts and beams. Salameh noticed that, along with the insulation, the men were laying sections of honeycombed porcelain and nylon armor. Overhead, fluorescent work lights were strung along the top of the cabin. There was a light strung into the tail also, but Salameh did not turn it on. He crouched for a few minutes in the darkness of the tail section behind the half-finished bulkhead.

At length, Nuri Salameh cleared his throat and called into the cabin, "Inspector Lavalle."

A tall Frenchman turned from the emergency door which he had been examining and walked toward the chest-high wall. He smiled in recognition at the Algerian. "Salameh. Why are you hiding like a rat in the darkness?"

The Algerian forced an answering smile. He waved the clipboard at the structures inspector. "It is ready to be closed up, no?"

Henri Lavalle leaned over the bulkhead. He shined his high-intensity light into the tapering tail section and made a cursory inspection. He took the clipboard from the Arab with his other hand, and flipped the pages quickly. You could not trust these Algerians to read the schedules of inspection correctly. Inspector Lavalle checked each page again. Each inspector had made his mark. The electrical, hydraulic, and fuel-tank inspection marks were in order. He rechecked his own structures inspection marks. "Yes. All the inspections have been accomplished," he answered.

"And my electrical?" asked Salameh.

"Yes. Yes. You did fine. It is complete. It can be closed up." He handed the clipboard back to the Algerian, bade him good night, and turned away.

"Thank you, Inspector." Salameh hooked the clipboard onto his belt, turned, and made his way carefully, in a crouch, over the beam work. He looked surreptitiously over his shoulder as he moved. Inspector Lavalle was gone. Salameh could hear the insulators packing their tools, climbing out of the fuselage and down the scaffolding. Someone shut most of the work lights off in the cabin and the tail section grew darker.

Nuri Salameh turned on his flashlight and pointed it up into the hollow tail. He climbed slowly up the strutwork until he could almost touch the point where the two sides of the tail met. From one of his bulging side pockets, he removed a black electrical box, no larger than a packet of cigarettes. The box had a metal parts number plate on it that identified it as S.F.N.E.A. #CD-3265-21, which it was not.

From his top pocket he took a tube of epoxy and squeezed the glue onto an aluminum plate, then pressed the box firmly against the side of the plane and held it for a few seconds. He then pulled a telescoping antenna from the black box and rotated it until it was clear of the metal sides of the tail.

He shifted his position quietly and braced his back against a strut and his feet against a crossbar. It was not warm in the confining tail, but sweat formed on his face.

With an electrical knife, he stripped a section of insulation from a green wire with black hatch marks that led to the tail navigation light. He pulled a length of matching wire from his pocket. On the end of the wire was attached a small, bare metal cylinder the size of a Gauloise cigarette. The other end was bare copper wire. He spliced the copper end onto the navigation light wire and taped the splice carefully.

Salameh began slowly climbing down the framework. As he descended, he ran the green wire along a bundle of multicolored wires until he reached the bottom of the fin where it joined with the fuselage. He let the wire drop through the cross struts beneath his feet.

Salameh stretched face down on the cold aluminum cross struts and reached down until he could touch the number eleven fuel trim tank below. Through the few missing plates on the bottom of the fuselage, he could see the tops of men's heads as they passed beneath the great plane. Sweat streamed from his face and he imagined that it must be dripping onto the men, but no one looked up.

From another pocket Salameh took a mass of white puttylike substance weighing about half a kilo. He molded the substance carefully over the tip of the number eleven trim tank. He found the dangling green wire and ran his fingers down to the end of it until he felt the small metal cylinder that was attached. He pushed the cylinder into the soft putty and pressed the putty firmly around the cylinder. The shift bell rang loudly, startling him.

Salameh rose quickly and wiped the clammy sweat from his face and neck. His whole body shook as he clawed his way through the confining struts toward the open section of the tail. He heaved himself out of the dark tail onto the jig, then jumped onto the platform of the scaffolding. The whole operation, lasting an eternity, had taken less than four minutes.

Salameh was still shaking as the two riveters from the second shift stepped onto the platform. They regarded him curiously as he tried to regain his composure.

One of the riveters was a Frenchman, the other an Algerian. The Algerian spoke to him in French. "This is ready?" He held out his hand.

Salameh was momentarily confused until he saw that both men's eyes were fixed on the clipboard that still hung from his belt. He quickly unhooked it and handed it over. "Yes. Yes. Ready. Electrical. Structures. Hydraulic. All inspected. It can be closed up."

The two men nodded as they checked the schedules of inspection. They then set about preparing the aluminum plates, rivets, and rivet guns. Salameh stood watching for a moment until his knees stopped trembling, then climbed unsteadily down the ladder and punched his time card.

* * *

Nuri Salameh boarded one of the waiting buses and sat silently among the workers, watching them drink wine from bottles, as the bus made its way back to St. Nazaire.

Salameh got off the bus in the center of town and walked through the winding, cobbled streets to his roach-infested flat above a *boucherie*. He greeted his wife and four children in Arabic, then announced that dinner should be delayed until he returned from an important errand.

He took his bicycle from the dark, narrow stair landing and walked it into the alley, then pedaled onto the street. He rode down to the waterfront where the Loire met the Bay of Biscay. His cold breath streamed from his mouth as he panted from his exertions. The tires needed air and he cursed as the bicycle bounced against the uneven cobbles.

The traffic thinned out in the darkening streets as he pedaled past the active waterfront area to the deserted area that held the great concrete U-boat pens built by the Germans during World War II. The bombproof pens rose up from the black water, grey, ugly, and blast-scarred. Tall loading booms towered over the docks on the waterfront and caught the last of the sunlight from the bay.

Nuri Salameh wheeled his bicycle to the rusted stairs that descended to the pens and pushed it into a clump of wild bay laurel shrubs. He carefully descended the creaking stairs.

At the water's edge, he made his way over the top of the moss- and barnacle-covered retaining wall and approached one of the covered pens. The smells of diesel oil and sea water filled his nostrils as he stood and read the faded, flaking sign painted on the mossy concrete. There was the usual *Achtung!*, then some other words in German, then the number 8. Salameh approached slowly, and entered the submarine pen through a rusty iron door.

Inside, he could hear the sound of water gently lapping against the walls. The only illumination came through the open entrance from the lights across the river. Salameh felt his way along the length of the catwalk toward the open end of the tunnellike pen. He was shivering in the damp, stagnant air. Several times he suppressed a cough.

Suddenly, a light from a flashlight struck him in the eyes, and he covered his face. "Rish?" he whispered. "Rish?"

Ahmed Rish shut off the light and spoke softly in Arabic. "It is done, Salameh?" It was more a statement than a question.

Nuri Salameh could sense the presence of other men on the narrow catwalk. "Yes."

"Yes," answered Ahmed Rish. "Yes." There was a malignant satisfaction in his voice.

Salameh thought back to those dark Algerian eyes that had followed him all day. The Algerian riveter with the Frenchman—and the others—had looked at him with thinly veiled complicity.

"The inspections were completed? The tail is to be closed tonight?" Rish's voice had the tone of a man who knew the answers.

"Yes."

"You placed the radio on the highest point inside the tail—close to the outer skin?"

"Right on the outer skin, Ahmed."

"Good. The antenna?"

"It is extended."

"The splice? The radio will receive a constant trickle charge from the aircraft's batteries?"

Salameh had rehearsed this in his mind many times. "The splice was from the tail navigation light. The splice wire is not conspicuous even on close inspection. I even matched the wire color. Green. No one will ever see the radio, but if that should happen, I placed an Aérospatiale parts number plate on it. Only an electrical engineer would not be fooled by it. Any other maintenance people would either not see it, or if they did, they would think it belonged."

Rish seemed to nod in the darkness. "Excellent. Excellent." He did not speak for a moment, but Nuri Salameh could hear Rish's breathing and smell the man's damp breath. Rish spoke again. "The electrical detonator was properly fixed to the other end?"

"Of course."

"The *plastique?*" He used the universal French word for the explosive.

Salameh recited what he had been taught. "I molded it over the tip of the fuel tank. The tank at that point is slightly rounded. The *plastique* was approximately ten centimeters thick from the tip of the tank to the detonator, which was placed in the exact rear center of the charge. The result was a natural shape-charge which will blow inward and penetrate the tank." Salameh licked his cold lips. He had no sympathy for these people or their cause and he knew he had committed a great sin. From the start, he had no wish to get involved with this thing. But every Arab was a guerilla, according to Rish. From Casablanca, in Morocco, across five thousand kilometers of burning desert to Bagdad, they were all guerrillas, all brothers. Over one hundred million of them. Nuri Salameh didn't believe a word of it, but having his parents and sisters still in Algiers helped to persuade him to carry out this deed. "I was proud to do my part," said Salameh, to fill the silence, but he knew it would do no good. He suddenly realized that his fate had been sealed the moment he had been approached by these men.

Rish seemed not to have heard. He had other things on his mind. "The *plastique.* Would you say it blended in well with the shape of the tank? Perhaps we should have had you spray it with aluminum paint," he said absently.

Salameh was eager to pass on good news, to placate, to dispel the demons of doubt. "No one goes back there. It is sealed off from the pressurized cabin by the pressure bulkhead. All hydraulics and electrical are serviced from small access panels on the outside. Only a failure of some component would make it necessary to remove the riveted plates. That side of the fuel tank should never be seen by human eyes again." He could definitely hear the impatient breathing of at least three other men in the shadow behind Rish. It had become completely dark at the end of the tunnel. Occasionally, a ship's klaxon would sound on the river or bay, the muted dissonance rolling across the water and into the cold submarine pen.

Rish murmured something.

Salameh waited for the worst. Why meet in a dark place when a comfortable bistro or apartment would have done as well? In his heart he knew the answer, but he sought desperately to reverse his preordained destiny. "I have applied for the transfer to Toulouse, as you wished. It will be approved. I would be honored to do the same thing on the other one there," he said hopefully.

Rish made a noise that sounded like a laugh and it sent a chill down Salameh's spine. The charade would not last long now. "No, my friend," said the voice in the darkness. "That is already attended to. Your joker is in the deck and the other will be safely in the deck shortly."

Salameh recognized the metaphor. That was what these people called themselves and their operations—the jokers in the deck. The game was played among civilized nations until the joker turned up—in an airport massacre, a

hijacking, a letter bomb. Then, the game of the diplomats and ministers became confused and frantic. No one knew the rules when that joker landed on
the green baize table. People screamed at each other. Guns and knives were
produced from under the table. The polite game turned ominous.

Salameh swallowed a dry lump. "But surely—" He heard a noise. Rish had
clapped his hands.

Quickly and expertly, Salameh was pinioned to the slimy wall of the sub pen
by many hands. He felt the cold steel slice across his throat, but he could not
scream because of the hand across his mouth. He felt a second and third knife
probing for his heart, but in their nervousness, the assassins only succeeded in
puncturing his lungs. Salameh felt the warm blood flow over his cold, clammy
skin and heard the gurglings from his lungs and throat. He felt another knife
come down on the back of his neck and try to sever his vertebrae, but it slid off
the bone. Salameh struggled mechanically, without conviction. In his pain, he
knew that his killers were trying to do the thing quickly but in their agitation
were making a bad job of it. He thought of his wife and children waiting for
their dinner. Then a blade found his heart, and he heaved free of his tormentors in a final spasmodic death throe.

Rish spoke softly as the shadows knelt down over Salameh. They took his
wallet and watch, turned his pockets inside out, and removed his good work
boots. They slid him over the side of the catwalk and held him suspended by his
ankles above the black, stagnant water that lapped rhythmically against the
sides of the pen. The water rats, which had chirped incessantly during the short
struggle, became still, waiting. They stared with beady red eyes that seemed to
burn with an inner fire of their own. Salameh's face, running with rivulets of
blood, touched the cold, black water, and the murderers released him. He
disappeared with a barely discernible splash. The sound of the water rats diving
from the catwalks into the rank, polluted waters filled the long gallery.

The masked workers made a final sweep with their pneumatic spray guns.
The guns shut down with a hiss. The Concorde gleamed enamel white in the
cavernous paint room. There was a stillness in the room where there had been
sound and movement a short time before. Infrared heat lamps began to glow
eerily. The paint fog hung in the unearthly atmosphere around the aircraft
which glowed red with reflected light. Air evacuators pulled the fog from the
great room.

The evacuators turned themselves off and the infrared lamps dimmed and
blackened. Suddenly, the dark room filled with the blue-white light of hundreds
of fluorescents.

Later, white coveralled men filed in quietly as one might enter a holy place.
They stood and stared up at the long, graceful bird for a few seconds. It seemed
as though the craft were standing long-legged and proud, looking down its beak
at them with the classical birdlike haughtiness and indifference of the sacred
Ibis of the Nile.

The men carried stencils and spray guns. They rolled in 200-liter drums of a
light blue paint. Scaffolding was rolled up and long stencils for the striping
were unfurled.

They worked with an economy of words. The foreman, from time to time,
checked the designer's sketches.

An artist placed his stencils over the tail section where the production number still showed a faint outline under the new white enamel. The production
number would now become the permanent international registration number.
He stenciled on the 4X, the international designation for the nation that owned

and would fly the aircraft. He then stenciled LPN, the individual registration of the craft.

Above him, on a higher scaffold, two artists peeled off the black vinyl stencil attached to the tail. What remained against the field of white was a light blue six-pointed Star of David, under which were the words, EL AL.

Book I

ISRAEL
THE PLAIN OF SHARON

*They have healed also the hurt of . . . my people . . . saying,
Peace, peace; when there is no peace.*

Jeremiah 6:14–16

*. . . they have seduced my people saying,
Peace; and there was no peace. . . .*

Ezekiel 13:10–11

1

In the Samarian hills, overlooking the Plain of Sharon, four men stood quietly in the predawn darkness. Below them, spread out on the plain, they could see the straight lights of Lod International Airport almost nine kilometers in the distance. Beyond Lod were the hazy lights of Tel Aviv and Herzlya, and beyond that, the Mediterranean Sea reflected the light of the setting moon.

They stood on a spot that, until the Six Day War, had been Jordanian territory. In 1967, it had been a strategic spot, situated as it was almost half a kilometer above the Plain of Sharon on a bulge in the 1948 truce line that poked into Israel. There had been no Jordanian position closer to Lod Airport in 1967. From this spot, Jordanian artillery and mortars had fired a few rounds at the airport before Israeli warplanes had silenced them. The Arab Legion had abandoned the position, as they had abandoned everything on the West Bank of the Jordan. Now this forward position had no apparent military significance. It was deep inside Israeli territory. Gone were the bunkers that had faced each other across no man's land and gone were the miles of barbed wire that had separated them. More importantly, gone too were the Israeli border patrols.

But in 1967 the Arab Legion had left behind some of its ordnance and some of its personnel. The ordnance was three 120mm mortars with rounds, and the personnel were these four Palestinians, once members of the Palestinian Auxiliary Corps attached to the Arab Legion. They were young men then, left behind and told to wait for orders. It was an old stratagem, leaving stay-behinds and equipment. Every modern army in retreat had done it in the hopes that those agents-in-place would serve some useful function if and when the retreating army took the offensive again.

The four Palestinians were natives of the nearby Israeli-occupied village of Budris, and they had gone about their normal, peaceful lives for the last dozen years. In truth, they had forgotten about the mortars and the rounds until a message had reminded them of their pledge taken so long ago. The message had come out of the darkness like the recurrence of a long-forgotten nightmare. They feigned surprise that such a message should come on the very eve of the Peace Conference, but actually they knew that it would come precisely for that reason. The men who controlled their lives from so great a distance did not want this peace. And there was no way to avoid the order to action. They were trapped in the shadowy army as surely as if they were in uniform standing in a parade line.

The men knelt among the stand of Jerusalem pines and dug into the soft, dusty soil with their hands. They came upon a large plastic bag. Inside the bag were a dozen 120mm mortar rounds packed in cardboard canisters. They pushed some sand and pine needles over the bag again and sat back against the trees. The birds began to sing as the sky lightened.

One of the Palestinians, Sabah Khabbani, got up and walked to the crest of the hill and looked down across the plain. With a little luck—and an easterly wind sent by Allah—they should be able to reach the airport. They should be able to send those six high-explosive and six phosphorus rounds crashing into the main terminal and the aircraft parking ramp.

As if in answer to this thought, Khabbani's *kheffiyah* suddenly billowed around his face as a hot blast of wind struck his back. The Jerusalem pines swayed and released their resinous scent. The *Hamseen* had arrived.

The curtains billowed around the louvered shutters of the third-floor apartment in Herzlya. One of them slammed shut with a loud crack. Air Force Brigadier Teddy Laskov sat up in his bed as his hand reached into his night table. He saw the swinging shutters in the dim light from the window and settled back, his hand still on his .45 automatic. The hot wind filled the small room.

The sheets next to him moved and a head looked out from under them. "Is anything wrong?"

Laskov cleared his throat. "The *Sharav* is blowing." He used the Hebrew word. "Spring is here. Peace is coming. What could be wrong?" He took his hand away from the pistol and fumbled for his cigarettes in the drawer. He lit one.

The sheets next to Laskov stirred again. Miriam Bernstein, the Deputy Minister of Transportation, watched the glowing tip of Laskov's cigarette as it moved in short, agitated patterns. "Are you all right?"

"I'm fine." He steadied his hand. He looked down at her. He could make out the curves of her body under the sheets, but her face was half-buried in the pillow. He turned on the night light and threw back the sheets.

"Teddy." She sounded mildly annoyed.

Laskov smiled. "I wanted to see you."

"You've seen enough." She grabbed for the sheets, but he kicked them away. "It's cold," she said petulantly and curled into a tight ball.

"It's warm. Can't you feel it?"

She made an exasperated sound and stretched her arms and legs sensuously. Laskov looked at her tanned naked body. His hand ran up her leg, over her thick pubic hair, and came to rest over one of her breasts. "What are you smiling at?"

She rubbed her eyes. "I thought it was a dream. But it wasn't."

"The Conference?" His tone revealed an impatience with this subject.

"Yes." She placed her hand over his, breathed in the sweet-smelling air, and closed her eyes. "The miracle has happened. We've started a new decade, and now the Israelis and the Arabs are going to sit down together and make peace."

"*Talk* peace."

"Don't be skeptical. It's a bad start."

"Better to start skeptical. Then you won't be disappointed with the outcome."

"Give it a chance."

He looked down at her. "Of course."

She smiled at him. "I have to get up. She yawned and stretched again. "I have a breakfast date."

He removed his hand. "With whom?" he asked, against his better judgment.

"An Arab. Jealous?"

"No. Just security conscious."

She laughed. "Abdel Majid Jabari. My father figure. Know him?"

Laskov nodded. Jabari was one of the two Israeli-Arab Knesset members who were delegates to the peace mission. "Where?"

"Michel's in Lod. I'll be late. May I get dressed, General?" She smiled.

Only her mouth smiled, Laskov noticed. Her dark eyes remained expressionless. That full, rich mouth had become quite accomplished at showing the full range of human emotion, while the eyes only stared. The eyes were remarkable because they conveyed absolutely nothing. They were only for seeing things. They were not a window into her soul. The things she must have seen with those eyes, Laskov thought, she wished no one to know.

He reached out and stroked her long, thick black hair. She was exceptionally pretty, there was no doubt about that, but those eyes . . . He saw her lips turn up at his stroking. "Don't you ever *smile?*"

She knew what he meant. She put her face in the pillow and mumbled. "Maybe when I get back from New York. Maybe then."

Laskov stopped stroking her hair. Did she mean if the peace mission was a success? Or did she mean if she got good news of her husband, Yosef, an Air Force officer, missing over Syria for three years? He had been in Laskov's command. Laskov had seen him go down on the radar. He was fairly certain Yosef was dead. Laskov had a feel for these things after so many years as a combat pilot. He decided to confront her. He wanted to know where he stood before she went to New York. It might be months before he saw her again. "Miriam . . ."

There was a loud knock on the front door. Laskov swung his feet over the side of the bed and stood. He was a solid bearlike man with a face more Slavic than Semitic. Thick, heavy eyebrows met on the bridge of his nose.

"Teddy. Take your gun."

Laskov laughed. "Palestinian terrorists hardly ever knock."

"Well, at least put your pants on. It might be someone for me, you know. Official."

Laskov pulled on a pair of cotton khaki trousers. He took a step toward the door, then decided that bravado was foolish. He took the American Army Colt .45 automatic out of the night table and shoved it into his waistband. "I wish you wouldn't tell your staff where you spend the night."

The knock came again, louder this time. He walked barefoot across the oriental rug of the living room and stood to the side of the door. "Who is it?" As he looked back across the living room, he noticed that he hadn't closed the bedroom door. Miriam lay naked on the bed in a direct line with the front door.

Abdel Majid Jabari stood in the darkened alcove of Michel's in Lod. The café, owned by a Christian Arab, sat on the corner near the Church of St. George. Jabari looked at his watch. The café should have opened already, but there was no sign of life inside. He huddled into the shadow.

Jabari was a dark, hawk-nosed man of the pure, classical Saudi-peninsula type. He wore an ill-fitting dark business suit and the traditional black and white checked headdress, the *kheffiyah,* secured with a crown of black cords.

Throughout the last thirty years, Jabari rarely went out alone during the hours of darkness. Ever since the time he had decided to make a personal and private peace with the Jews in the newly formed state of Israel. Since that day, his name had been on every Palestinian death list. His election to the Israeli Knesset two years before had put his name at the top of those lists. They'd come close once. Part of his left hand was missing, the result of a letter bomb.

A motorized Israeli security patrol went by and eyed him suspiciously but did not stop. He looked at his watch again. He had arrived early for his appointment with Miriam Bernstein. He couldn't think of another person, man or woman, who could bring him to such a deserted rendezvous. He loved her, but he believed his love was strictly platonic. This was an unusual Western notion, but he felt comfortable with it. She filled a need in him that had existed since his wife, children, and all his blood relatives had fled to the West Bank in 1948. When the West Bank had come into Israeli hands in 1967, he could think of nothing for days but the coming reunion. He had followed in the wake of the Israeli army. When he got to the refugee camp where he knew his family was, he found his sister dead and everyone else fled into Jordan. His sons were reported to be with the Palestinian guerilla army. Only a female cousin remained, wounded, lying in an Israeli mobile hospital. Jabari had marveled at the hate that must have filled these people, his countrymen, as his cousin lay dying, refusing medical aid from the Israelis.

Jabari had never known such despair before or since. That day in June 1967 was far worse than the original parting in 1948. But he had rallied and traveled a long road since then. Now he was going to discuss the coming peace over breakfast with a fellow delegate to the UN Conference in New York.

Shadows moved in the street around him and he knew that he should have been more careful. He'd come too far to have it end here. But in his excitement and anticipation of seeing Miriam Bernstein and going to New York, he had become lax in his security. He had been too embarrassed to tell her to meet him after sunrise. He couldn't fault her for not understanding. She simply didn't know the kind of terror he had lived with for thirty years.

The *Hamseen* blew across the square picking up litter, rustling it across the pavement. This wind didn't blow in gusts but in one long, continuous stream, as though someone had left the door open on a blast furnace. It whistled through the town, each obstruction acting as a reed in a woodwind instrument, making sounds of different pitch, intensity, and timbre. As always it made one feel uneasy.

Three men came out of the shadow of a building across the road and walked toward him. In the predawn light, Jabari could see the outlines of long rifles tucked casually under their arms. If they were the security patrol, he would ask them to stay with him awhile. If they weren't . . . He fingered the small nickel-plated Beretta in his pocket. He knew he could get the one in front, anyway.

Sabah Khabbani helped the other three Palestinians roll a heavy stone across the ground. Lizards scurried from the place where the stone had stood. Revealed under the stone was a hole a little more than 120mm wide. Khabbani pulled a ball of oiled rags out of the opening, reached his arm into the hole, and felt around. A centipede walked across his wrist. He pulled his arm out. "It's in good condition. No rust." He wiped the packing grease from his fingers onto his baggy pants. He stared at the small, innocuous-looking hole.

It was an old guerilla trick, originated with the Viet Cong and passed on to other armies of the night. A mortar tube is placed in a large hole. The tube is held by several men and mortar rounds are dropped into the tube. One by one the rounds begin to hit downrange. Eventually, one round strikes its target: an airfield, a fort, a truck park. The firing stops. Now the mortar is registered for elevation, deflection, and range. Rocks and earth are quickly packed around the mortar with care to insure that the aim is not changed. The muzzle of the tube is hidden with a stone. The gunners flee before the overwhelming firepower of the conventional army is brought to bear on their position. The next time they wish to fire—a day, a week, or a decade later—they must only uncover the preaimed muzzle. There is no need to carry the cumbersome paraphernalia of the big mortar. The heavy baseplate, bridge, and standard, weighing altogether over 100 kilograms, are not needed. The delicate boresight is not needed, nor are the plotting boards, compass, aiming stakes, maps, or firing tables. The mortar tube is already registered on its target, lying buried, waiting only for rounds to be dropped into its muzzle.

Khabbani's gunners would fire four rounds each, then cover the muzzles with the stones. By the time the high angle rounds began hitting, one by one, the gunners would be far away.

Khabbani took a rag soaked in alcohol solvent, reached into the long tube, and swabbed the sides. He worried about these buried tubes. Were they really well aimed in 1967? Had the ground shifted since then? Were the rounds safe? Had trees grown up into the trajectory of the rounds?

His rag showed dead insects, dirt, a little moisture, and just a trace of rust. He would find out shortly if it was safe to fire.

"Richardson." The voice was muffled, but Laskov was sure of it. He unbolted the door.

Miriam Bernstein got out of bed naked and leaned against the doorjamb in the pose of a Parisian lady of the night against a lamppost. She smiled and tried on a sexy come-hither look. Laskov was not amused. He opened the door slowly. Tom Richardson, the U.S. air attaché, stepped in at the moment Laskov heard the bedroom door close behind him. He looked at Richardson's face. Had he seen her? He couldn't decide. No one registered much emotion at that hour. "Is this business or social?"

Richardson spread his arms out. "I'm in full uniform and the sun isn't even up."

Laskov regarded the younger officer. He was a tall, sandy-haired man who was chosen for the attaché job more for his ability to charm than for his ability to fly. A diplomat in uniform. "That doesn't answer my question."

"Why do you have that hardware stuck in your pants? Even in D.C. we don't answer the door like that."

"You should. Well, have a seat. Coffee?"

"Right."

Laskov moved toward the small kitchenette. "Turkish, Italian, American, or Israeli?"

"American."

"I've only got Israeli and it's instant."

Richardson sat in a club chair. "Are we going to have one of those days?"

"Don't we always?"

"Get in the spirit of things, Laskov. There's going to be peace."

"Maybe." He put a kettle on the single gas jet. He could hear the shower running on the other side of the wall.

Richardson looked at the closed bedroom door. "Am I disturbing something? Were you making a separate peace with a local Arab boy's sister?" He laughed, then said seriously, "Can we speak freely?"

Laskov came out of the kitchen. "Yes. Let's get this business out of the way. I have a full day ahead of me."

"Me too." Richardson lit a cigarette. "We have to know what kind of air cover you have planned for the Concordes."

Laskov walked over to the window and threw open the shutters. Below his apartment ran the Haifa-Tel Aviv Highway. Lights shone from private villas near the Mediterranean. Herzlya was known as the air attaché ghetto. It was also Israel's Hollywood and Israel's Riviera. Herzlya was the place where El Al and Air Force personnel lived if they could afford it. Laskov detested the place because of its privileged atmosphere, but an accident of social grouping had put most of the important people he had to deal with in Herzlya.

The smell of the western sea breezes, which usually carried into the apartment, was replaced by the dry east wind carrying scents of orange and almond blossoms from the Samarian hills. Across the highway, the first shaft of sunlight revealed two men standing in the alcove of a shop. They moved further into the shadow. Laskov turned from the window and walked to a high-backed swivel chair. He sat down.

"Unless you came with a chauffeur and a footman, I think someone is watching this apartment."

Richardson shrugged. "That's their job, whoever they are. We have ours." He leaned forward. "I'll need a full report on today's operation."

Laskov sat back in his chair. His dogfighter chair. At get-togethers his friends would regale each other with the old fights. The Spitfires. The Corsairs. The Messerschmitts. Laskov looked at the ceiling. He was flying his mission over Warsaw again. Captain Teddy Laskov of the Red Air Force. Things were simpler then. Or so they seemed.

Shot down for the third time, in the last days of the war, Laskov had returned to his village of Zaslavl, outside Minsk, on convalescent leave. He found the remainder of his family, barely half of whom had survived the Nazis, murdered in what the Commissars called a civil disturbance. Laskov called it a pogrom. Russia would never change, he decided. A Jew was as much a Jew in unholy Russia as in Holy Russia.

Captain Laskov, highly decorated officer of the Red Air Force, had returned to his squadron in Germany. Ten minutes after arriving, he had climbed into a fighter, bombed and strafed an encampment of his own army outside of Berlin, and flown on to an airfield occupied by the American Second Armored Division on the west bank of the Elbe.

From the American internment camp, he had made his way, finally, to Jerusalem, but not before seeing what had become of West European Jewry.

In Jerusalem, he had joined the underground Haganah Air Force, which consisted of a few scrapped British warplanes and a few American civilian light aircraft hidden in palm groves. A far cry from the Red Air Force, but when Laskov saw his first Spitfire with the Star of David on it, his eyes misted.

Since that day in 1946, he had fought in the War of Independence of 1948, the Suez War of 1956, the Six Day War of 1967, and the 1973 Yom Kippur War. But the war dates meant nothing to him. He had seen more action between those wars than during them. He'd flown 5,136 sorties, been hit five times and shot down twice. He carried scars from shattered plexiglas, burning aviation fuel, flak, and missile shrapnel. He walked slightly bent as a result of having had to eject out of a burning Phantom in 1973. He was getting old and he was tired. He rarely flew combat missions anymore, and he hoped, and almost believed, that after the Conference there would be none that would have to be flown again. Ever.

The kettle whistled and Laskov stared at it. Richardson got up and shut it off. "Well?"

Laskov shrugged. "We have to be careful who we give that kind of information to."

Richardson walked quickly up to Laskov. He was white and almost trembling. "What? What the hell do you mean? Look, I've got reports to make. I've got to coordinate our carrier fleet in the Med. Since when have you kept anything from us? If you're insinuating that there's a leak . . ."

Laskov wasn't prepared for Richardson's outburst. They had always bantered prior to getting to the point. It was part of the game. The reaction to what Laskov thought was a joke was inappropriate. He decided that Richardson was tense, as everyone else would probably be today. "Take it easy, Colonel." He stared hard at the young man.

The mention of his rank seemed to snap him out of it. Richardson smiled and sat down. "Sorry, General."

"All right." Laskov got up and picked up the telephone with a scrambler attached to it. He dialed The Citadel, Israeli Air Force Headquarters. "Patch me into the E-2D," he said.

Richardson waited. The E-2D Hawkeye was the newest of Grumman's flying radar craft. The sophisticated electronic systems on board could detect, track, and classify potential belligerents or friendlies on land, sea, and air at distances and with an accuracy never before possible. Its collected information was fed into a computer bank and transmitted via data link back to Strike Force Control, Civilian Air Traffic Control, and Search and Rescue units. It also had electronic deception capabilities. Israel had three of them and one was airborne at all times. Richardson watched as Laskov listened.

Laskov replaced the phone.

"They see anything?" Richardson asked.

"Foxbats. Four of them. Probably Egyptian. Just maneuvers, I suspect. Also a Mandrake recon in the stratosphere. Probably Russian."

Richardson nodded.

They discussed the technical data as Laskov made two cups of passable coffee. The water stopped running in the bathroom.

Richardson blew steam off the cup. "You using your 14's for escort?"

"Of course." The Grumman F-14 Tomcat was the best fighter craft in the world. But so was the Mig-25 Foxbat. It depended on who was flying each craft. It was that close. Laskov had a squadron of twelve Tomcats that had cost Israel eighteen million dollars apiece. They were sitting, at that moment, on the military end of Lod Airport.

"You going up, too?"

"Of course."

"Why don't you leave that to the younger men?"

"Why don't you go fuck yourself?"

Richardson laughed. "You have a good command of American idiom."

"Thank you."

"How far are you going with them?"

"Until we run out to the edge of our range." He walked to the window and looked into the dawn. "With no bombs or air-to-ground stuff, and on a day like this, we should be able to do a thousand klicks out and then back again. That should take them out of the range of the Land of Islam, in case anyone has any crazy ideas today."

"Not out of range of Libya, Tunisia, Morocco, and Algeria. Look, you can land at our base in Sicily if you want to stay with them that far. Or, we can get a bunch of KAGD's to refuel you in flight, if you want."

Laskov looked away from Richardson and smiled. The Americans were all right except when they were getting panicky about trying to keep the peace at any cost. "They're not going all the way over the Med. The Concordes are going to file a last-minute flight-plan change that will take them up the boot of Italy. We've gotten them special clearance to fly supersonic over Italy and France. We'll break with them east of Sicily. I'll give you the coordinates and your carrier 14's can pick them up if you want. But I don't think that will be necessary. Don't forget, they can go Mach 2.2 at 19,000 meters. Nothing but the Bat can match that, and they'll be out of range of any of their bases—Arab or Russian—by the time we leave them."

Richardson stretched. "You expecting any trouble? Our intelligence tells us it looks O.K."

"We always expect trouble here. But frankly, no. We're just being cautious. There will be a lot of important people on those Concordes. And everything is at stake. *Everything.* All it takes is one crazy to fuck things up."

Richardson nodded. "How's ground security?"

"That's the Security Chief's problem. I'm just a pilot, not a guerilla fighter. If those two goofy-looking birds get airborne, I'll escort them to hell and back without a scratch on them. I don't know from the ground."

Richardson laughed. "Right. Me, neither. By the way, what are you packing besides your .45?"

"The usual ironmongery of death and destruction. Two Sidewinders and two Sparrows, plus six Phoenix."

Richardson considered. The Sidewinder missiles were good at five to eight kilometers; the Sparrows, at sixteen to fifty-six kilometers; and the Phoenix, at fifty-six to a hundred and sixty. The Hughes-manufactured Phoenix was critical to get the Foxbat before it came into dogfight range with its greater maneuverability. "Take a tip, Laskov. There's nothing up there at 19,000 and Mach 2.2 but Foxbats. Leave your 20mm cannon rounds home. There are 950 of them and they weigh. The Sidewinder will get anything that gets in close. We did it on a computer once. It's O.K."

Laskov ran his hand through his hair. "Maybe. Maybe I'll keep them in case I feel like knocking down a Mandrake."

Richardson smiled. "You'd hit an unarmed reconnaissance plane in international air space?" He spoke softly, as though there were someone close by who shouldn't hear. "What's your tactical frequency and call sign today?"

"We'll be on VHF channel 31. That's 134.725 megahertz. My alternate frequency is a last-minute security decision. I'll get it to you later. Today my name will be Angel Gabriel plus my tail number—32. The other eleven Cats will also be Gabriel plus their tail numbers. I'll send you the particulars later."

"And the Concordes?"

"The company call sign for aircraft number 4X-LPN is El Al 01. For 4X-LPO, it's El Al 02. That's what we'll call them on the Air Traffic Control and El Al frequencies. On my tactical frequency, they have code names, of course."

"What are they?"

Laskov smiled. "Some idiot clerk at The Citadel probably spends all day on these things. Anyway, the pilot of 01 is a very religious young man, so 01 is the Kosher Clipper. The pilot of 02 is a former American, so in honor of that great American airline slogan, 02 is the Wings of Emmanuel."

"That's awful." Miriam Bernstein walked into the living room, dressed in a smartly tailored lemon-yellow dress and carrying an overnight bag.

Richardson stood up. He recognized the beautiful, much talked about Deputy Minister of Transportation, but was enough of a diplomat not to mention it.

She walked toward Richardson. "It's all right, Colonel, I'm not a working girl. I have a high clearance. The General has not been indiscreet." Her English was slow and precise, the result of seldom used formal classroom English.

Richardson nodded.

Laskov could tell that Richardson was somewhat unsettled by Miriam. It amused him. He wondered if he should make an introduction, but Miriam was already at the door. She turned and addressed Laskov. "I saw the men in the street. I've called a taxi. Jabari is waiting. I must rush. See you at the final briefing." She looked past Laskov. "Good day, Colonel."

Richardson decided not to let them think he was totally in the dark. *"Shalom.* Good luck in New York."

Miriam Bernstein smiled and left.

Richardson looked at his coffee cup. "I'm not going to drink any more of this swill. I'll take you to breakfast and drop you at The Citadel on my way to my embassy."

Laskov nodded. He walked into the bedroom. He slipped on a khaki cotton shirt that might have been civilian except for two small olive branches that designated his rank. He pulled the automatic from his waistband. He buttoned his shirt with one hand and held the .45 with the other as he walked to the window. Below, the two men, whoever they were, looked quickly down at their shoes. Miriam got into a waiting taxi and sped off. Laskov threw the .45 on the bed.

He felt uneasy. It was the wind. Something to do with an imbalance of negative ions in the air, they said. The ill wind went by many names—the *Foehn* of Central Europe, the *Mistral* of Southern France, the *Santa Ana* of California. Here it was called *Hamseen* or *Sharav.* There were people, like himself, who were weather-sensitive and suffered physically and psychologically from the effect. It wouldn't matter at 19,000 meters, but it mattered here. It was a mixed blessing, this first hot wind of spring. He looked into the sky. At least it was turning out to be a perfect day for flying.

2

Abdel Majid Jabari sat staring at a cup of black Turkish coffee laced with arak. "I don't mind telling you I was badly frightened. I came very close to shooting a security man."

Miriam Bernstein nodded. Everyone was jumpy. It was a time of celebration, but also a time of apprehension. "My fault. I should have realized."

Jabari put up his hand. "Never mind. We see Palestinian terrorists everywhere, but in fact, there are not many left these days."

"How many does it take? You especially should be careful. They really *do* want you." She looked at him. "It must be difficult. A stranger in a strange land."

Jabari was still high-strung from his dawn encounter. "I'm no stranger here. I was born here," he said pointedly. "You weren't," he added, then regretted the remark. He smiled in a conciliatory manner and spoke in Arabic. " 'If you mingle your affairs with theirs, then they are your brothers.' "

Miriam thought of another Arabic saying. " 'I came to the place of my birth and cried, "The friends of my youth, where are they?" And Echo answered. "Where are they?" ' " She paused. "That applies to both of us, I suppose. This is no more your land now, Abdel, then it was mine when I landed on these shores. Displaced persons displacing other wretched persons. It's all so damned . . . cruel."

Jabari could see that she was on the verge of slipping into one of her darker moods. "Politics and geography aside, Miriam, there are many cultural similarities between the Arabs and the Jews. I think they have all finally realized that." He poured a glass of arak and raised it. "In Hebrew, you—we—say *shalom alekhem,* peace unto you. And in Arabic, we say *salaam aleckum,* which is as close as we've gotten to it up to now."

Miriam Bernstein poured herself a glass of arak. *"Alekhem shalom,* and unto you, peace." She drank and there was a burning in her stomach.

As they sat at breakfast they spoke about what might happen in New York. She felt good talking to Jabari. She was apprehensive about sitting face to face with Arabs across a conference table at the UN—the long-heralded confrontation—and Jabari was a good transition for her. She knew he had been far from the mainstream of Arab thought for thirty years, and his loyalties were with Israel; but if there were such a thing as a racial psyche, then perhaps Abdel Jabari reflected it.

Jabari watched her closely as she spoke in that husky voice that sometimes sounded weary and often sounded sensuous. Over the years, a bit at a time, he had come to know her story as she had come to know his. They had both known what it was to be the flotsam and jetsam of a world in upheaval. Now they both sat at the top of their society and they were both in a position to change the currents of history for better or worse.

Miriam Bernstein was a fairly typical product of the European holocaust. She had been found by the advancing Red Army in a concentration camp, whose purpose was as obscure as its name, although the words *Medizinische*

Experimente stuck out in her mind. She remembered that she had once had parents and other family—a baby sister—and that she was Jewish. Beyond that, she knew little. She spoke a little German, probably learned from the camp guards, and a little Polish, probably learned from the other children in the camp. She also knew a few words of Hungarian, which had led her to believe that this was her nationality. But mostly she had been a silent child, and she neither knew nor cared if she was a German, Polish, or Hungarian Jew. All she knew for certain, or cared about, was that she was a Jew.

The Red Army had taken her and the other children to what must have been a labor camp, because the older children worked at repairing roads. Many of them died that winter. In the spring, they all worked in the fields. She had wound up in a hospital, then was released into the custody of an elderly Jewish couple.

One day, some people came from the Jewish Agency. She and the old couple, along with many others, traveled across war-ravaged Europe for weeks in crowded railroad cars that gave her nightmares. They boarded a boat and went to sea. At Haifa, the boat was turned away by the British. The boat attempted to unload the people further up the coast at night. A fierce battle broke out on the beach between the Jews, who were trying to secure the beachhead, and the Arabs, who didn't want the boat to unload. Eventually, British soldiers broke up the fight and the boat sailed away. She never knew where it went because she had been one of the people who had been landed on the beach before the fight. The old couple, whose name she could not remember, disappeared— dead on the beach or still on the boat.

Another Jewish couple picked her up from the beach and told the British soldiers that her name was Miriam Bernstein and that she was their child. She had strayed from their house and gotten caught in the fighting. Yes, she was born in Palestine. She remembered that the young couple were very poor liars, but the British soldiers just looked at her and walked away.

The Bernsteins had taken her to a new kibbutz outside Tel Aviv. When the British left Palestine, the Arabs raided the settlement. Her new father went to defend the kibbutz and never returned. As the years passed, she discovered that her older stepbrother, Yosef, was also an adopted refugee. She found nothing unusual about that because she imagined that most children in the world—or in her world—came from the camps and rubble of Europe. Yosef Bernstein had seen what she had seen, and more. Like her, he knew neither his real parents nor his real name, his nationality nor his age. They became young lovers and eventually married. During the Yom Kippur War, their only son, Eliahu, was killed in action.

Miriam Bernstein had taken an early interest in private peace groups and had cultivated the good will of the local Arab communities. Her kibbutz, like most, was hawkish, and she felt increasingly isolated from her friends and neighbors. Only Yosef had understood, but it was not easy for him, a fighter pilot, to have a dovish wife.

After the 1973 War her party appointed her to a vacant seat in the Knesset in recognition of her popularity with the Israeli Arabs and with the women's peace movement.

She quickly came to the attention of Prime Minister Meir and the two became personal friends. When Mrs. Meir resigned in 1974, it was understood that Miriam Bernstein was her voice in the Knesset. With Mrs. Meir's backing, she rose quickly to a deputy minister's post. Long after the grand old woman no longer sat in the wings of the Knesset, Miriam Bernstein held on to her seat and her post through one government crisis after another. On the surface, it appeared—and she believed—that she survived every Cabinet shuffle because she was exceedingly good at whatever she did. Her enemies said that she survived at least in part because of her striking good looks. In fact, she survived in the high-mortality world of parliamentary politics because she was an instinctive survivor. She was not consciously aware of this side of her character, and if she were ever confronted with a synopsis of her political machinations or a list of the people she had politically eliminated, she would not have recognized that it was Miriam Bernstein who had done those things.

Whenever she thought back on Mrs. Meir's help and support, it was always the small things that stood out, such as the times the Prime Minister took her back to her apartment after an all-night Cabinet session and made her coffee. Then there was the time the Cabinet requested that she adopt a Hebrew name in keeping with government policy for office holders. Mrs. Meir—formerly Mrs. Meyerson—understood her reluctance to sever the only thread she had with the past and supported her resistance to the change.

There were people who thought that Miriam Bernstein was being groomed to fill Mrs. Meir's old job someday, but Miriam Bernstein denied any such ambitions. Still, it had been said that Mrs. Meir was appointed Prime Minister *because* she didn't want the job. The Israelis liked to put people in power who didn't want power. It was safer.

Now she held a job that she coveted more than Prime Minister: Peace Delegate. It was a job that hadn't existed a few months before, but she always knew it would exist someday.

There was much to do in New York, and there was personal business to attend to there, also. Yosef had been missing for three years now. She wondered if she could find out something about his fate from the Arabs when she got to New York.

Jabari noticed a small disturbance outside and instinctively put his hand in his pocket.

Miriam Bernstein seemed not to notice. She was caught up in what she was saying. "The people have elected a government ready to exchange concessions for solid guarantees, Abdel. We have shown the world that we will not go under. Sadat was one of the first modern Arab leaders to understand that. When he came to Jerusalem he was following in the footsteps of countless others who have come to Jerusalem since the beginning of recorded time to find peace, and yet he shattered a precedent of thirty years' standing." She leaned forward. "We have fought well and have won the respect of many nations. The enemy is no longer at the gate. The long siege is ended. The people are in a mood to talk."

Jabari nodded. "I hope so." He looked over her shoulder at the crowd gathered in the street as she continued to talk. He felt her hand over his. "And you, Abdel? If they founded a new Palestine, would you go?"

Jabari stared straight ahead for a long moment. "I am an elected member of the Knesset. I don't think I would be welcome in any new Palestine." He held up his mangled hand. "But even so, I might take that chance. Who knows—I might be reunited with my family there."

Miriam Bernstein was sorry she had asked the question. "Well, we will all have decisions to make in the future. What's important now is that we are going to New York to discuss a lasting peace."

Jabari nodded. "Yes. And we must strike now while the mood is in the air. I have this fear that something will happen to break the spell. An incident. A misunderstanding." He leaned forward. "All the stars—social, historical, economic, military, and political—are aligned for peace in the Holy Land as they have not been in millennia. And it's spring. So it can't hurt to talk. Right?" He stood. "But I wish we were in New York already and the Conference were under way." He looked into the street. "I think our planes are coming in. Let's have a look."

People from the café were hurrying into the street. Approaching Lod Airport from the north were two Concordes. As the first aircraft began its descent, the crowd could see the blue Star of David against the white tail. There was some scattered applause from the mixed Arab and Jewish crowd.

Miriam Bernstein shielded her eyes as the Concorde dropped lower and approached from out of the sun. Beyond the airfield, the Samarian hills rose up off the plain. She noticed that new almond blossoms had come out during the night and the hills were smudged with pink and white clouds. The rocky foothills were softly green and carpeted with brilliant red anemones, cream-colored lupins, and yellow daisies. The yearly miracle of rebirth had returned, and along with the wildflowers brought into bloom by the *Hamseen*, peace was breaking out in the Holy Land.

Or so it seemed.

Tom Richardson and Teddy Laskov left the café in Herzlya and got into Richardson's yellow Corvette. They hit the heavy Friday traffic of Tel Aviv and the car slowed to a crawl. At a traffic light a block from The Citadel, Laskov opened the door. "I'll walk from here, Tom. Thanks."

Richardson looked over. "O.K. I'll try to see you before you scramble."

Laskov put one foot out of the door, then felt Richardson's hand on his shoulder. He looked back at Richardson.

Richardson regarded him for a long second. "Listen, don't get trigger-happy up there. We don't want any incidents."

Laskov stared back with cold, dark eyes. His brows came together. He spoke loudly, above the noise of Tel Aviv's traffic. "Neither do we, Tom. But the best we've got are going to be on board those birds. If anything that looks military gets on my radar screen, and if it's in missile range, so help me, I'll knock it out of the goddamn sky. I'm not putting up with any fly-bys, reconnaissance, or harassment horseshit from *anyone*. Not today." Laskov slid his big bulk out of the low-slung car and moved as if he were heading for a barroom brawl.

The light was green, and Richardson edged ahead. He wiped the sweat from his upper lip. At King Saul Boulevard, he made a right turn. Laskov, big and burly, was still in his mind's eye. He could actually see the great burden on the man's broad shoulders. There wasn't a top military commander in the world who didn't wonder if he was going to be the fool to start World War III. The old warrior, Laskov, liked to bellow, but Richardson knew that if and when a quick, tactical decision had to be made, Laskov would make the right one.

Richardson turned onto Hayarkon Street and stopped in front of the American Embassy. He finger-combed his damp hair in the rear view mirror. The day had gotten off to a bad start.

Through the car's sun roof, he could see two white Concordes overhead. The bright sunlight gave them an ethereal glow. One was in a holding pattern, heading out to sea. The other was heading in the opposite direction as it began its final descent to Lod. For a split second, the aircraft seemed to cross paths and their delta wings formed the Star of David.

Sabah Khabbani chewed slowly on a piece of pita bread as he stood looking through his field glasses at Lod Airport. He shifted the glasses. Below, on the Plain of Sharon, the plowed earth was a rich chocolate. Between the cultivated fields, the Rose of Sharon and the lilies of the valley flowered as they had done since long before Solomon. A distinctive grey area marked Ramla Military Prison where so many of his brothers were wasting away their lives. To the south, the rocky Judean hills, brown a few days before, had turned red and white, yellow and blue, as wildflowers blossomed. Around him, the Jerusalem pines, part of the reforestation program, swayed as the *Hamseen* came over the crest. The old Palestine of his boyhood had been beautiful in a wild way. He had to admit the Jews had improved on it. Still . . .

Khabbani removed his strapless old watch from his pocket and looked at it. In less than one hour, the VIP lounge should be full. Any time between then and takeoff was all right, according to his instructions. Khabbani considered. The terminal was actually a little beyond the maximum effective range of his mortars, but if the *Hamseen* held, he could reach it. If he did not reach the terminal, the rounds would fall short and land in the parking ramp where the Concordes would be. It didn't matter. It was only necessary to cause an incident and have the flight canceled. Khabbani wasn't sure he liked this thing he was doing. He shrugged.

One of his men gave a low call. Khabbani looked to where the man was pointing. Two Concordes, traveling in trail, were heading for Lod from the north. Khabbani studied them in his field glasses. Such beautiful aircraft. He had read that they each held 113,000 kilograms of fuel. A quarter-million kilograms together. That would make an explosion that they would feel in Jerusalem.

3

The city of Lod, the ancient Lydda, baked in the early spring heat wave. The first *Hamseen* of the year was unusually early. The scorching, dry, Sirocco-like desert wind from the east blew across the city with increasing strength. The *Hamseen* would last a few days, then the weather would become balmy. According to Arab tradition, there were fifty such dog days a year—the Arabic word *Hamseen* meaning fifty. The only *Hamseen* that was welcome was the first, for with it, the wildflowers of the Judean and Samarian hills and fields opened and the air was thick with sweet scents.

At Lod International Airport, the tarmac shimmered. On the ramps, where the air liners were parked, an unusually large contingent of Israeli soldiers stood with their weapons slung. In the passenger terminal, security men in nondescript clothing and wearing sunglasses stood with newspapers held in front of them.

Throughout the day, *sherut* taxis and private cars, carrying well-dressed men and women, pulled up to the doors of the main terminal. The occupants were quickly ushered inside the terminal and into the VIP lounge or the El Al Security office on the top floor.

At the far end of the field stood a cluster of military huts. Commandos in camouflage fatigues stood in various degrees of alertness. Behind the huts, a squadron of twelve American-made F-14 Tomcats stood on the concrete hardstands. Mechanics and armorers worked on the fighters and spoke to pilots and flight officers.

The road coming down from Jerusalem wound through Lod and the ancient Moslem quarter of Ramla on the way to Lod International Airport. Since morning, the inhabitants of Lod and Ramla had noticed the unusually heavy civilian and military traffic. In the past, such activity had been a prelude to yet another crisis. This time it was different.

In Lod, the Greek Orthodox Church of St. George was filled with Christian Arabs and other native Christians of indeterminate Crusader and Byzantine ancestry. No special service was being conducted, but people had come, drawn out of a sense of wanting to be in a special place with others—of wanting to participate in some small way in events that were to touch their lives.

In the city's synagogues, men sat in small groups hours before the sundown service and spoke in quiet voices. In the market square, near St. George's, Jewish women shopped for the Sabbath meal among the pitched stalls. There seemed to be a touch of lightheartedness in the bargaining and purchasing, more so than on a usual Friday afternoon, and people tarried in the market place much longer than was necessary to complete their business.

In Ramla, the square in front of the Great Mosque, Jami-el-Kebir, was crowded long before the Muezzin called the faithful to prayer.

The Arab market was as crowded, but noisier than the one in Lod. The Arabs, lingerers by nature, seemed more so as the market and streets filled with every manner of conveyance, from Land Rovers and Buicks to Arabian stallions and camels.

In Ramla Military Prison, Palestinian terrorists were able to hope that at least some of them might soon be free men.

The mood of Lod and Ramla was like that of the rest of Israel and the rest of the Middle East. Here in this part of the world, virtually every powerful, historical force had met at one time or another and had used the terrain as a battleground. Trying to live in peace in this area, said one proverb, was like trying to sleep in the middle of a crossroad. Thousands of armies, millions of men, had marched over this small spot on the map known as the Holy Land. But more than just armies had met in those seemingly desolate hills and deserts. Ideologies and faiths had met, clashed, and left a legacy of blood. Nearly every culture in the East and West was represented by ruins, standing like gravestones over the countryside, or buried like corpses beneath it. It was difficult to dig in modern Israel without uncovering the ruins—and, mingled with the ruins, the bones.

Ramla and Lod typified the agonizing history of the ancient land; the divisiveness and the unity of modern Israel. They reflected the mood of the complex, multireligious state. Hope without celebration. Despair without weeping.

El Al's Security Chief, Jacob Hausner, dropped the ornate French telephone receiver back into its cradle. He turned to his young assistant, Matti Yadin. "When are these bastards going to stop bothering me?"

"Which bastards, Chief?" asked Yadin.

Hausner brushed a speck from the top of his satinwood Louis XV desk. He had decorated his office out of his own funds, and he liked to keep it neat. He walked over to the big picture window that overlooked the aircraft parking ramp and opened the heavy velvet drapes. Fabric-fading sunlight poured in. "All of them." He waved his arm to indicate the world at large. "That was The Citadel. They're a little concerned."

"I don't blame them."

Hausner regarded Yadin coolly for a second.

Yadin smiled, then looked at his boss with an expression of sympathy. It was a tough job at the best of times. For the past few weeks it had been hell for everyone in Security. He studied Hausner's profile as the man stared out the window, lost in thought.

Jacob Hausner was a child of the Fifth *Aliya,* the fifth wave of immigration to Palestine. This *Aliya* had been made up mostly of German Jews who had left their old homeland to return to their more ancient one after Hitler came to power in 1933. They were a lucky or, perhaps, farsighted group. They had all escaped the holocaust in Europe while it was still possible to do so. They were also an affluent, well-educated group, and they had brought with them much-needed capital and skills. Many of them had settled around the older German colony in the seaport of Haifa, and they prospered. Hausner's early years were typical of the rich German Jews in Haifa during the prewar period.

When World War II broke out, Hausner, just seventeen, had joined MI-6, British Secret Intelligence Service. Being trained by the British in that occupation, he approached it in much the same fashion as his teachers—with the attitude of a dilettante. But also like so many British spies with this attitude, he was exceedingly good at his job. If he considered it only as a necessary wartime hobby, so much the better. He was a rich young man who looked and acted like anything but a spy, which was the idea.

Outside of Haifa, he easily passed as a German. The job called for a lot of party going and social climbing among the German colonies in Cairo and Istanbul, and Hausner was good at it. His mind grasped the most intricate details of that strange and shady business of leading two lives, and he loved it almost as much as he loved Chopin, Mozart, and *Sachertorten.*

Hausner had joined a private British flying club in a fit of boredom before the war and had become one of the few licensed civilian pilots in Palestine. Between intelligence assignments, he pestered the British to let him log hours in Spitfires and Hurricanes so that he could keep his skills sharp.

After the war, he went to Europe and bought scrapped warplanes for the illegal Haganah Air Force. He had bought the first British Spitfire that General Laskov had flown in, but neither man was aware of the fact.

After the 1948 war, it was natural that Hausner, with a background of intelligence work and flying skill, should become one of El Al's first security men.

Compared to most Jews who came of age during that period, his life had been one of relative ease. He now lived in Herzlya in a small villa on the Mediterranean. He kept a series of mistresses and more casual acquaintances there but still faithfully visited his family in Haifa on the religious days.

In appearance, he reminded most people of a European aristocrat. He had a thin, aquiline nose, high cheekbones, and thick white hair.

Hausner looked at Yadin. "I hope they let me go on this flight."

Yadin shook his head and smiled. "Who would they crucify if the planes blew up, Chief?"

"We don't use the words *blow up* in the same sentence as the word *plane,* Matti." He smiled. He could afford to smile. Everything was going well. He had a perfect record and he saw no reason why Concordes 01 and 02 should spoil that record.

Matti Yadin got up and stretched. "Do we hear any rumblings from our intelligence services?"

Hausner kept staring out the window. "No. Our Palestinian friends are very quiet—whatever is left of them."

"Too quiet?"

Hausner shrugged. He was a man who refused to make guesses based on no information. No news simply meant no news. He had faith in his country's intelligence services. They had rarely failed him. If an insect hit any part of the web of Israeli Intelligence, the web quivered and the spider, at the center, felt it. Anything outside the web was too far removed to worry about.

Hausner drew the drapes and turned away from the window. He straightened his tie and jacket in a wall mirror, then walked across the office and opened the door into the adjoining conference room.

Yadin followed him and moved off toward the far wall, where he found a seat.

The conference room, which was crowded and noisy, became quiet. Everyone turned toward Hausner.

Around the large circular table sat some of the most powerful people in Israel. There was Chaim Mazar, head of Shin Beth, Israel's Internal Security Service; Brigadier General Itzhak Talman, the Air Force Chief of Operations; General Benjamin Dobkin, representing the Army's Chiefs of Staff; Miriam Bernstein, Deputy Minister of Transportation; and Isaac Burg, head of Mivtzan Elohim, "The Wrath of God," the anti-terrorist group.

There were also five members of the Knesset present besides Bernstein. Along the walls, junior aides sat in chairs and a secretary was preparing to take notes at a small desk. Hausner came toward the table.

The group was an *ad hoc* committee put together to ensure the safety of the Concorde flight. One of their jobs was to question Hausner, and they meant to do it.

Hausner noticed that he was the only one present who was wearing a suit, as usual. He looked at Miriam Bernstein directly. Those eyes again. Nothing. Why, then, did he feel that she was always judging him? And then there was her sexuality. Hausner did not wish to admit to himself that she did not so much *use* it as that it was simply there. A fact. A sensual woman. He looked away from her. Strictly speaking, the Minister of Transportation was his boss. Perhaps, he thought, that produced the tension. He remained standing and cleared his throat. "I agreed to be at this meeting so that we wouldn't have any more doubts about my ability to get an airplane off the ground." He held up his hand to stifle a half-dozen incipient protests. "Okay. Forget it."

The sparsely decorated room was illuminated by a large picture window with the same view as from Hausner's office. He walked to the window. At the far end of the parking ramps, away from the other planes, the two long, sleek Concordes, each with a Star of David on its tail, stood gleaming in the bright sunlight. Around the aircraft stood Hausner's security guards, armed with Uzi submachine guns and sniper rifles. The army had sent over a ten-man squad of infantry, too, which did nothing to improve Hausner's mood.

Everyone was conscious of the quiet. Hausner pointed dramatically. "There they are. Pride of the fleet. They cost a mere eighty million dollars each, with the spare tire and radio. We charge all passengers first-class fare, plus a twenty-percent surcharge, and yet we haven't made a *shekel* from them, as you know." He looked at Bernstein, who was one of his severest critics in the Knesset. "And you know one of the reasons El Al hasn't made a profit? Because *I* demand the tightest security that is humanly possible. And good security has a high price." Hausner moved a few feet down the length of the bright window. Squinting eyes followed him. "Some of you," he began slowly, "were worried about profit a few short months ago, and you were willing to let security become lax because of it. Now, the same people," he looked at Miriam Bernstein, "are concerned that I have not done enough." Hausner walked back toward an empty seat and sat down. "O.K. Let's get this over with." He looked around the table. He spoke in a fast staccato voice. "We've had those birds on the line for thirteen months. Since the time that we got them, they have never left the sight of my security people. We've had the bulkheads and baggage holds armored while they were being built at the factories in St. Nazaire and Toulouse. All maintenance is done only by El Al mechanics here at Lod. Today, I personally checked the fuel going into the craft. It was pure Jet A kerosene, I assure you. When we first got the Concordes, I demanded and got an auxiliary power unit installed in the front wheel well. The rest of the world's Concordes have to be started by an external ground power unit. By installing the APU, I can dispense with two trucks going up to my birds at foreign airports—the preconditioned air truck and the ground power unit truck. We can start our own engines anywhere, any time, after which the birds are self-supportive. We took the extra weight penalty of the nine-hundred kilogram APU, as we've always taken the extra weight penalty in the name of security. You can't make money that way, of course, but I won't have it any other way. And neither will you."

Hausner looked around, waiting for a comment, but there was none. He continued. "We also go through the extra expense and bother of performing most services only here at Lod. For instance, no water bowser gets near my birds except here at Lod. If you fly El Al, you're pissing Jordan water in Tokyo. The toilet service is only done here, also. Furthermore, after every flight, the cleaning service, supervised by my personnel, goes over each plane very thoroughly, in case anyone decided to leave a package for us. We probe the seats, examine the toilets, and even open the barf bags. Another point—the galley service is done at Lod and nowhere else. As for the food on these Concordes, I checked it myself as it was being stowed in the galleys. You have my assurance that everything is kosher. In fact, the company rabbi ate the meal and all he got was indigestion." Hausner leaned back and lit a cigarette. He spoke more slowly. "Actually, in one very important respect, this flight is more secure than any other. On this flight we don't have to worry about the passengers."

Hausner nodded toward Matti Yadin. "My assistant has volunteered to head the security team on Concorde 01. I have volunteered to do the same on 02. However, the Prime Minister has not yet informed me if I am to go with the mission." He looked slowly around the table. "Are there any other questions regarding El Al security? No? Good."

There was a long silence. Hausner decided that since it was his conference room, he was supposed to be chairman. He turned to Chaim Mazar of Shin Beth. "Would you like to make a report?"

Mazar got up slowly. He was a tall, thin man with the eyes of someone who had been in Internal Intelligence for a long time. His manner was abrupt— some thought rude. He began without preamble. "The big worry, of course, is some maniac with a small, shoulder-fired, heat-seeking missile standing on a roof somewhere between here and the coast. I can assure you that there is no one standing on any roof between here and the coast. Nor will there be anyone standing around anywhere in the flight path at takeoff. I have asked the Defense Minister to call short air-raid drills in the flight path. There will be helicopters over the whole area. There has been no sign of guerilla activity of any sort inside of Israel. I am confident there will be no problems. Thank you." He sat down.

Hausner smiled. Short and to the point. Good man. He turned to Isaac Burg, the head of Mivtzan Elohim.

Burg remained seated but leaned slightly forward. He was a short, gentlemanly looking, white-haired man with a twinkle in his blue eyes. He affected fussy habits and mannerisms that were very disarming. In reality, he had no such habits. He was much younger than he looked, and he was capable of killing in cold blood while he searched his pockets for a nasal spray. No one would have believed that he was the man who had nearly completed the job of wiping out the multitude of Palestinian guerilla organizations around the world. His men had been brutal in hunting down the last of the disorganized groups, but the result had been an almost complete end to terrorist attacks at home and abroad. Burg smiled. "We ran into a Palestinian guerilla just the other day in Paris. He was an important member of Black September. One of the last. We questioned him with much vigor. He assures us that there are no plans that he is aware of to disrupt the peace mission. The guerillas are so dispersed and untrusting these days that we can't be sure they speak even to each other. But one of my men, who is a ranking member of one of the Palestinian intelligence services, informs me that there is nothing planned."

Burg fumbled for his pipe and finally located it. He stared at the pipe for a long second, then looked up. "Anyway, as far as we know, the Arab governments now want this Conference to succeed as much as we do. They've let us know through various sources that they are keeping a close watch on known and suspected guerillas in their nations. In case they are a little lax, we are doing the same thing." He stuffed an aromatic blend into his pipe bowl. "John McClure of the CIA, who is attached to us, informs me that his agency has not picked up any rumblings from Arab groups around the world. Mr. McClure, incidentally, is beginning his home leave tomorrow and will be flying with the peace mission as a courtesy." Isaac Burg smiled pleasantly as he lit his pipe. The sweet smoke billowed over the table. He looked at General Dobkin. "How about the Arab hinterlands?"

Benjamin Dobkin rose and looked around the room. He was a solidly built man with a thick neck and close-clinging, curly black hair. Like most Israeli generals, he wore plain combat fatigues with the sleeves rolled up. His massive arms and hands were what most people noticed first. He was an amateur archeologist, and the strenuous digs into the ancient tells had added a lot of bulk to his already massive frame. When he had commanded an infantry brigade, every man in the brigade became a willing or unwilling archeologist. Not a drainage trench, a latrine, a foxhole, or anti-tank ditch was dug without the soil being sifted at the first possible opportunity. Benjamin Dobkin was also a religious man, and he took no pains to hide his deep faith. Officer Evaluation Reports on Dobkin always included words like "solid," "steady," and "self-possessed."

He clasped his massive hands behind him and began. "The problem is—has always been—that guerillas can get away with the most outrageous antics in the hinterlands of underdeveloped countries. Israeli Army Operations cleaned out many of these Fatahlands. The Arab governments themselves partially finished the job." He looked around. "But unlike some of my friends here, the Army cannot and will not exclude the possibility of some sort of aggression by Palestinians or other Arabs originating out of these rural Arab areas where there are still pockets of guerillas. The Army has only limited access, but we do send many Army Intelligence people there, where, with luck, they pass as Arabs. We spy out the land." He hesitated. "As we've always done. As we did three thousand years ago. 'And Moses sent them up to spy out the land of Canaan, and said unto them, "Get you up this way southward, and go up into the mountain: and see the land, what it is, and the people that dwelleth therein, whether they be strong or weak, few or many." ' "

Ya'akov Sapir, a left-wing Knesset member who was anything but religious, interjected. "And these army spies of Moses, if I remember correctly, reported that this land was a land flowing with milk and honey. I don't think anyone has trusted an army reconnaissance report since then."

There were a few tentative laughs around the table and from the chairs along the wall.

General Dobkin regarded Ya'akov Sapir for a long moment. "And as a member of the Knesset Postal Committee, I think you might be interested to know that the Corinthians' replies to Paul's letters are still sitting in the Jerusalem Post Office."

This brought more laughter.

Hausner looked annoyed. "Can we dispense with these learned Biblical barbs, please? General? Would you continue, please?"

Dobkin nodded. "Yes. All in all, it looks good. My counterparts in the Arab countries have sent word that they are moving to neutralize the remaining guerilla pockets where they can be located."

Chaim Mazar leaned forward. "What kind of operation *could* they mount against this peace mission if they weren't neutralized, General?"

"Sea and air. We are still concerned about sea and air. The Navy Department has assured me, however, that the flight path of the Concordes over the Mediterranean is being thoroughly patrolled not only by their craft and the American Sixth Fleet but also by the navies of Greece, Turkey, and Italy, who are staging a NATO exercise along the flight path. In addition, a sea-to-air missile, of the type that would be needed to bring down an aircraft flying at the height and speed of the Concordes is much too sophisticated to be either owned or operated by terrorists. And even if they did own one and managed to launch it at sea, the Air Force escort would have ample time to identify it, track it, and shoot it down. Isn't that correct, General?" He looked at Itzhak Talman, Air Force Chief of Operations. Everyone turned toward Talman.

Itzhak Talman rose. He walked toward the picture window and looked into the distance. He was a tall, handsome man with a clipped British military mustache and the look of a dashing ex-RAF pilot. He spoke a mixture of bad Hebrew and worse Yiddish with an upper-class British accent. Like the British officers whom he emulated, he had a cool, detached, and imperturbable manner. But like a lot of those old officers of the Empire, Talman was play-acting. Actually, he had a highly nervous, emotional nature, but he kept it very well hidden.

Talman turned back and faced the table. He spoke in a dispassionate voice. "My very best fighter officer, Teddy Laskov, is personally leading a squadron of hand-picked pilots, who are in turn flying the best fighter craft in the world. They are, at this moment, supervising the arming and maintenance of those twelve craft at the far end of this airfield. Teddy Laskov assures me that he can spot, track, intercept, and shoot down anything in the sky, including Foxbats, SAM's, and Satan himself, if he gets on the radar." He looked around the room over the heads of the men and women assembled there. "Air Force Intelligence informs me that not only have the guerillas never had the capability to make an aerial attack, but they have none now. But *if* anyone were to mount an attack against those Concordes, they would have to put up, into the air, what would amount to the most powerful air fleet in the Mediterranean." Talman stroked his mustache. "Teddy Laskov is the best we've got. As soon as those birds break over the coast, they are my responsibility, and I accept that responsibility with no hesitation." He walked back to his seat.

Teddy Laskov, who had been in the corridor listening, opened the door quietly. Several heads turned toward the object of Talman's praise. Laskov smiled self-consciously and waved his hand to indicate that no one was to pay him any attention. He stood against the wall.

Miriam Bernstein had been trying to catch Hausner's eye. Hausner studiously ignored her. He looked around the table and toward the seats along the wall, but no one appeared to have anything further to add. "All right, then—"

Miriam Bernstein rose. "Mr. Hausner."

"Yes?"

"I'd like to add something here."

"Oh."

"Thank you." She offered Hausner a smile which he seemed not to notice. She looked down and shuffled through some papers in front of her, then looked up. "I've been listening very carefully to what has been said here, and while I'm impressed with the precautions that have been taken, I am frankly worried about the spirit they were taken in and especially the language used to describe these precautions. Gentlemen, we are going to this *veida,* this Conference, to make a *Brit Shalom,* a Covenant of Peace."

Miriam Bernstein paused and looked around the table, meeting the eyes of each man in turn. "Talking of shooting things from the sky, of questioning suspected Arabs in friendly countries with much vigor, of sending Army spies into Arab lands—these are justifiable under some circumstances, but at this moment in our history, I would take the risk of keeping a very low, nonaggressive profile. We don't want to go into the United Nations like a bunch of cowboys with our six-shooters blazing. We want to go there looking as if we came to talk peace."

She drew her lips together as she thought of the words she would use to speak reason without appearing to speak surrender. She had been associated with the peace wing of her party for many years and felt obligated to give this warning as they stood on the threshold of seeing peace become a reality. She had not lived in a place that was at peace for one day in her entire life. She extended her hands, palms up, in a conciliatory gesture. "I'm not trying to create a problem where none exists. I'm just saying that all military and intelligence operations should come to an almost complete halt during the weeks ahead. This is an act of faith on our part. Somebody has to holster his gun first. Even if you should see Satan himself on your radar screen, General Talman, don't shoot him out of the sky with one of your missiles. Just explain to him that you are going on a peace mission and that you will not be goaded into an aggressive act. He will see that you mean to have your peace, and that—and Providence—will send him away." She looked around the room and her eyes fixed on Teddy Laskov for a split second.

He looked back and found something in those eyes that few people had ever seen, but he wasn't quite sure what to call it.

She looked up over the heads of the people around her. Outside, past the airfield, were the rocky hills where Khabbani and his men were arguing about when to fire. The heat of the *Hamseen* permeated the small room.

Miriam Bernstein looked around the room again. "There are those among us who do not want to give up at the peace table what they bought in blood. I understand this. I do. And I know all the rebuttals to the peace-at-any-cost philosophy. We all do. I even believe many of them. I'm just asking you all to think about what I've said over the next few days. Thank you." She sat down and busied herself with the papers in front of her.

No one made a reply. The room was very still.

General Talman rose and walked over to Teddy Laskov. He took him by the arm and they both walked out into the corridor.

Eventually, people began speaking in quiet voices to those sitting near them. Then the meeting broke into small groups as final plans were coordinated.

Jacob Hausner tuned out the low voices around him and regarded Miriam Bernstein for a long time. There was a subtle undercurrent between them. He felt it. Unresolved, it would surface at the most unexpected moment. He remembered suddenly and vividly the time she had refused an invitation to spend the weekend at his villa. He bristled now at the thought of it. Then he sat back and looked at the ceiling. To hell with her. He had other things besides Miriam Bernstein to occupy his thoughts.

There had been a lot of practice over the years for this moment. The Palestinians had always considered El Al a military objective, and the attacks had begun almost the same day El Al had in 1948. But it was the more spectacular terrorist operations of the 1960s and 1970s that had grabbed the headlines.

The last incident had been the attempted hijacking of an El Al 747 out of Heathrow Airport. Ahmed Rish had been the mastermind of that plot. Hausner's face grimaced at the name. Rish. One of the last—and probably the best—of a bad lot. They'd had him in Ramla Military Prison once, too, after he had been arrested at Lod Airport on an unknown mission. In 1968, before Israel adopted a policy of refusing to negotiate with terrorists, they had exchanged him, along with fifteen other terrorists, for the Israeli passengers on the El Al flight that had been hijacked in the attempt to capture General Sharon. Hausner had thought it was a mistake then, and later events had proved him correct.

He wished that Ahmed Rish had turned up dead in one of the Mivtzan Elohim raids over the years. Rish's specialty was airplanes, and the thought of Rish on the loose, an unrepentant and deeply committed terrorist, disturbed him. Hausner had been one of his principal interrogators at Ramla. Rish was one of the few terrorists who had made him lose his temper. Hausner remembered striking him. In his report, he concluded that Rish was a very dangerous man who ought to be locked up forever. But he had been released.

Rish had turned up in a lot of places since then, each one of them too close to an El Al plane. There were rumors that Rish had been one of the terrorists who had escaped the Entebbe raid. Probably true, thought Hausner.

When Isaac Burg had mentioned a guerilla caught in France, Hausner's memory had been jogged. Rish had been spotted in France over a year ago, after the Heathrow operation. Why France? Hausner recalled that something about that had bothered him at the time. What was it? France. Rish. Rish's *modus operandi*. That was it. There was something about Rish's *modus operandi* that had struck him at the time. Rish wasn't a gun-toting, half-crazed hijacker. He didn't take many personal risks. Rish operated in a very remote, circumspect manner.

Why France? Why not the big Arab communities in Germany? The only Arab group of any size in France was the Algerians. Rish was an Iraqi, though he was fighting for the Palestinian cause. To the rest of the world, Arabs were all the same. But to each other they were not. Also, to the French police, who were used to Algerians, an Iraqi would stick out.

Yes, Rish was an insect who had touched the net of Israeli Intelligence not so long ago, and it had quivered. They had spotted him not in Paris but in the countryside. Strange. Once in Brittany and once in the South by the Spanish border. Why? Suddenly, the thought struck Hausner that there was a weak link in this whole security chain somewhere, and he didn't know what or where it was. A chill ran down his spine.

There was a psychological profile of Rish on file, plus a standard identikit. He'd get them out. And he'd place a call to the French SDECE. Hausner looked around. Everyone was still conversing in small groups. He rose. "If no one needs me any longer, I'll get back to my job."

No one answered.

"Madame Deputy Minister?"

"Don't let us keep you," said Miriam Bernstein.

"I won't." He looked around the room. "Please feel free to use my conference room as long as you wish. Excuse me." He turned and walked to the door, then looked back. *"Shalom,"* he said sincerely.

4

Captain David Becker, pilot of El Al Concorde 02, sat in the Operations Room next to his First Officer, Moses Hess. Across the long table from Hess sat the flight engineer, Peter Kahn, an American Jew, like Becker.

On the walls were maps, charts, and bulletins. One wall was a large window that faced out onto the airplane parking ramp. The two Concordes sat beyond the partially shaded ramp in the harsh sunlight.

On the other side of a glass partition in the Operations Room was the Dispatcher's Office with its teletypes and weather maps.

On the far end of the long table, in the Operations Room, sat the flight crew of El Al Concorde 01. There was Asher Avidar, the pilot, a hot-headed Sabra whom Becker considered much too young and impulsive to fly anything but the military fighters that he had formerly flown. Next to Avidar was Zevi Hirsch, the First Officer, who Becker thought would have been the pilot except for his age, and Leo Sharett, the flight engineer, who also counterbalanced Avidar's brashness.

Avidar was speaking to his crew, and Becker strained to hear and understand the rapid Hebrew. This was a very carefully planned flight, and Becker wanted none of Avidar's lone-eagle antics. He had to follow Avidar on the long trip, and fuel was a critical factor at Mach 2.2.

Becker checked the most recent weather maps for the flight while he listened to Avidar briefing his crew.

Becker was an exceptionally tall man, and for that reason he had been denied fighter training in the American Air Force when he entered service at the start of the Korean War. In ROTC, they had failed to point this height limit out to him, and he found himself ferrying troops on C-54 transports. Eventually, he partially satisfied his lust for combat by joining the Strategic Air Command. He waited patiently through the 1950s for his chance to vaporize the city in Russia that was assigned to him, though he knew he would not see the destruction. The city was Minsk, or, more precisely, the airport to the northwest of the city. His bomb would have also incinerated Teddy Laskov's hometown of Zaslavl, which was a coincidence that neither man had become aware of during their chance conversations.

Eventually, with age, his aggressive tendencies waned, and with the coming of the Intercontinental Ballistic Missiles, he found himself in cargo planes

again. Then came Vietnam and he was put back into a B-52. He vaporized lots
of people there, but he had long since lost the appetite for it. During the 1967
War, he volunteered for the re-supply flights to Israel. His enlistment ran out
on his last flight to Lod, at the same time that his twenty-year marriage did, so
he stayed and married the Israeli Air Force girl who always gave him a hard
time about the shipment manifests.

The Israeli Air Force did not have nor need anything like the huge long-
range bombers he knew so well, and there were only a few C-130 military
transports in the Hel Avir, the Air Corps. But he really didn't want to go back
into the military, anyway. He just wanted to fly. Eventually, he landed a job
flying El Al DC-4 cargo planes.

In the U.S. Air Force, he had logged thousands of hours of heavy jet flying.
He had also been checked out on the American FB-111 supersonic bomber and
thus was one of the few men in Israel who knew how to fly big planes at
supersonic speeds. When El Al bought the Concordes, Becker went to Toulouse for training. Now he was going to fly the single most important flight in
his career, and he meant to make certain that it went well.

Becker glanced into the Dispatch Room as the door from the corridor swung
open. He could see Generals Talman and Laskov enter. They spoke with the
personnel for a few minutes, then came through the connecting door.

Everyone in the Operations Room, all reserve officers in the Hel Avir, stood.
Talman and Laskov smiled and motioned for everyone to be seated. Talman
spoke. "Good afternoon. Well, we have just come from a security meeting and I
want to tell you all that everything looks fine. But for added security, we are
going to advance your takeoff time to three-thirty. In addition, you are not
flying over the Med to Madrid, but instead you will go up the Italian boot and
head for Orly to refuel. We have permission to fly supersonic over Italy and
France. Everything, including new flight plans, maps, and weather charts, is
taken care of. No one will deplane at Orly. Same procedure as the Madrid
plan." He looked at each man. "Gentlemen," he paused, looking for the right
words as he stroked his clipped mustache, then said only, "have a good flight.
Shalom." He turned and walked back to the Dispatch Room.

Teddy Laskov sat on the table. "All right. We have a minute for a last bit of
coordinating. I'll monitor you on Air Traffic Control and on the company frequency the whole time I'm with you. But if we want to speak to each other, we
must do so on my tactical frequency, channel 31. That is your 134.725. If, for
some reason, I believe that the frequency is no longer secure—or if you do—
say the words, 'My number three fuel tank indicator has become inop,' and we
will all meet on the alternate tactical which will be channel 27, your 129.475.
Clear? All right. I'll stay with you until you get to 19,000 meters and Mach 2.2.
Maybe I'll hang around if my fuel is good. You'll be all right after that. Are
there any questions?"

Avidar stood up. "Let me lay it on the line, General. Who's got tactical
control of this flight? I mean, I'm the flight leader of these two Concordes and
you're in charge of your people and you outrank me in the Hel Avir—but this is
a civilian flight. Let's say we're attacked. Let's say I want to take evasive action,
but you want us to hold a steady course so you know where we are. Who's the
boss?"

Laskov regarded Avidar for a long time. Whatever else people thought of the
young pilot, at least he didn't waste time beating around the bush. Also, he had
no qualms about verbalizing the unthinkable. Laskov nodded. "All right. Fair
question, Asher. Let me repeat what you've already been told. We foresee no
trouble. But if . . . if we are attacked, you will follow the rules for heavy

bomber missions. Since Israel has no heavy bombers, let me acquaint you with those rules. They are simple. The first rule is you hold course until you get instructions from the fighter escort leader—me—to take individual evasive action or for everyone to change course, speed, or altitude. For rule number two, see rule number one. Does that answer your question?"

"No." He sat down and looked away.

Laskov tried a conciliatory tone. "Look, Asher, flying escort is always a pain in the ass for everyone. We don't have these long-range escort situations in Israel, so it's new to you—but in a war I was in a thousand years ago, it was proved time and again that the sheep have to stay with the flock and listen to the sheep dogs, or else the wolves get them. No matter how many sheep in the flock seem to be getting picked off by the wolves, I assure you, it is worse trying to go it alone. Now, the analogy is not exact, but you get the message." He tried a fatherly look, but Avidar was having no part of it. Laskov shrugged and turned toward Becker. "David? Anything on your mind?"

"No, General. I think that wraps it up, except for the call signs on the tactical frequencies."

Laskov stood up. "Right. I am the Angel Gabriel plus my tail number, which is 32. My squadron is Gabriel with their tail numbers. You, David, are the Wings of Emmanuel. Asher, you are the Kosher Clipper. Well, anyway, it will be Emmanuel and Clipper on the air." Laskov looked at his watch. It was just two P.M. "One more thing. In addition to the regular peace mission delegates who appear on your passenger manifest, you might get a few extra VIP's. There will be an American on board, too. John McClure. Some sort of embassy man going home on leave. Tell your Chief Stewards to expect an addendum to the manifest."

Becker flipped through his clipboard and found the manifest. "There's another compatriot of mine coming, too, General. Tom Richardson, the air attaché. You must know him. He has some business in New York."

Laskov paused. That must have been a last minute development. Laskov knew it meant something, but he didn't know what. Maybe just a friendly gesture. He nodded. "He's sort of a professional acquaintance—a friend when he's not trying to tell us our business. If he doesn't like the kosher food, kick his ass out over Rome. Avidar, if he's on your flight, don't try to argue politics or religion with him. He has neither."

Becker smiled. "He asked to be on my ship. I'll take good care of him."

"Do that," said Laskov, absently. He walked toward the connecting door to the Dispatch Room where he could see Talman talking to the Chief Dispatcher. He turned around and faced the men who had all stood up again. "David. You said he *picked* your ship?"

"Yes, sir." Becker handed Laskov the manifest.

Laskov looked at it. Next to Richardson's name, which was penned in at the bottom, were the numbers "02." He knew the combined manifest showed neither plane nor seat selection at this point. Plane selection was a state security matter and would be decided at the last moment. Seat selection was to be left to the individual delegates so that they could group into committees and get some work accomplished on the flight. Laskov wondered why Richardson requested a specific plane since he didn't know if any friends or acquaintances would be on that plane. Why not wait until he saw how the delegation broke up? Both planes would only be a little over half full. Maybe he wanted to fly with Becker. He looked up. "Did he know you were flying 02?"

"I think so. I guess he figured he could sit in the jump seat and chat on the way over. He doesn't speak Hebrew that well."

"I guess so. All right, men. Have a good flight. See you at about 5,000 meters. *Shalom.*"

The VIP lounge, down the corridor from both the Operations Room and Hausner's office, was crowded with about a hundred people. The drapes had been drawn to help the air conditioners, but the lounge was still warm. The darkness, however, gave an illusion of coolness. Every minute or so, someone would part the drapes a bit and look at the two Concordes, standing by themselves and ringed by soldiers.

Yaakov Leiber, the Chief Steward on Becker's aircraft, walked into the VIP lounge. Little Yaakov Leiber, as almost everyone called him, was very nervous. He wished someone else were briefing the passengers on this flight. He was used to giving his little speech in the VIP lounge, but this group was different. He recognized many of the faces and names.

In addition to the twenty Peace Delegates, there was an unusually large support group of aides, research assistants, secretaries, interpreters, and security people. The lounge was quite smoky, Leiber noticed, and the bar was, as usual, empty.

Yaakov Leiber cleared his throat. "Ladies and gentlemen. Ladies and gentlemen." He raised his hands.

The room became quiet in stages. Heads turned. They noticed the small man in the oversized white uniform, who wore bifocals so thick that his eyes looked like oysters.

Leiber put his back to the bar. "Good afternoon. I am Yaakov Leiber, Chief Steward on El Al Concorde 02."

"I'm glad he's not our pilot," observed a man in the back. A few people laughed.

Leiber smiled. "Actually, I used to be a pilot, but once I forgot to bring a telephone book to sit on and I crashed into a hangar."

There was laughter and even some applause.

Leiber stepped closer to the crowd. "I just want to acquaint you with some things." He spoke about seat selection and the new boarding time for several minutes. "Are there any questions?"

The mission's Orthodox Rabbi, Chaim Levin, stood up. "You understand, young man, that today is Friday—and you are confirming for me that we are going all the way to New York and will still land before the Sabbath begins. Is that correct?"

Leiber held back a smile. It was a peculiarity of El Al flights that there was hardly ever a rabbi on board, even during the week. Some rabbis wouldn't fly on the national carrier because the El Al crews had all broken the Sabbath at one time or another. They flew on foreign carriers because it didn't matter to them if those crews broke the Jewish Sabbath or their own Sabbath. The two rabbis on the peace mission, one Orthodox and one Conservative, had decided to make an exception and fly El Al for the appearance of national unity. "Yes, sir," said Leiber. "Sundown in New York is at 6:08. But we'll be going a little faster than the sun, so we'll land at about two P.M. New York time."

Rabbi Levin looked at Leiber for a long time.

"In other words, Rabbi, we'll land one and a half hours before the time we started," said Leiber. "You see—"

"All right, I understand. I've flown before, you know." He regarded Leiber, the Sabbath-breaker, with a stare he usually reserved for pork-eating Jews. "If we land one second after sundown, you'll hear from me."

There were some laughs, and Leiber smiled, too. "Yes, sir." He looked around. "The meal is pot roast and potato kugel. There will be several movies available if anyone is interested. My wife, Marcia, who is much prettier than I am, will be one of your stewardesses on 01." Like many couples who flew often, it was the Leibers' policy never to fly together. They had children. He hoped no one would infer anything from this arrangement. "Are there any questions? Then, thank you for flying El Al—although I don't see how you could have done otherwise." He held up both hands. *"Shalom."*

Captain David Becker completed his line check of Concorde 02. He stood in the shadow cast by the drooping nose cone. A squad of infantry stood around the aircraft and glanced at him from time to time. An El Al security man, Nathan Brin, approached. "How's it going, Captain?"

"Good."

"We're satisfied. You?"

Becker looked at the plane and nodded.

"See you upstairs." He walked off.

"Right." Becker stared up at the craft. This white bird of peace looked like anything but a dove. It was a sea bird of some sort, Becker decided. A stork. A gull, maybe. It sat up high on long legs because of the high-pitch angles you had to use with a delta wing. If it weren't for the long legs, it would drag its ass on the ground when it took off or landed. God made sea birds with long legs for that reason. The technicians at British Aircraft Corporation and Aérospatiale had come to the same design conclusion. So had the Russians when they built their supersonic airliner, the TU-144. Brilliant. It was good to see that God was right, thought Becker.

Then there was the nose cone. The beak. It stayed down during takeoffs and landings, like a bird's, for better visibility. It was raised during flight for aerodynamic streamlining. The British, French, Russians, and God—not necessarily in that order—had independently found the same solutions for the problems of flight. Aircraft had started off as rigid structures and their performance was, therefore, confined to rigid parameters. Birds were flexible. Man started making aircraft flexible with movable ailerons and rudders. Then came the retractable landing gear. Then the swing-wing jets. Now there were noses that dropped.

Becker looked down the length of the plane. It was not really a big aircraft. The fuselage was fifty-two meters long and the delta span was only twenty-seven meters. Gross weight with passengers and fuel was 181,000 kilograms, about half as heavy as a 747.

One of the last refuges of the old English system of weights and measures was to be found in the cockpit of an airplane. All the world's pilots had been trained in both the English language and the English system of measurement. It was a world standard, and it was not easy or necessarily desirable to do away with it altogether. Most instruments were dual marked and pilots shifted easily from one system to the other in their conversations. Next to the Mach air speed indicator in the Concorde was the quaint knot indicator. To Becker, it was a fixed point in a rapidly changing world. He pictured an old square-rigger bravely trying to make five knots against a headwind.

Becker began a final walk-around. He stood under the portside delta and looked up. No, it wasn't built to move a couple of hundred tourist-class passengers around. It was built to move seventy VIP types faster than sound to their peace missions, oil deals, and foreign lovers. An elitist aircraft. Maximum speed was Mach 2.2—about 2,300 kilometers per hour, depending on air temperature. The speed of a high-velocity rifle bullet. And at that speed, flying was an aeronautical limbo where many of the standard rules of flight were suddenly changed.

There were a lot of peculiar demands at supersonic speeds. There was the big drag factor at the speed of sound. The delta wings helped there, but deltas had poor handling characteristics. They yawed and rolled and the plane became difficult to fly. Delta wings had to approach at high angles of attack, and if you got on the back of a thrust curve, air speed management was very difficult.

If you lost an engine in a regular commercial jet, nobody got too upset. Lose one at supersonic, and you could easily lose control of the aircraft. Then the plane would flip-flop and disintegrate.

The skin temperature could get up to 127 degrees Celsius at Mach 2. If you got above that, the plane wouldn't immediately become unglued, but you would weaken the structure and you might pay for it on another flight.

At Mach 2.2, you have to think fast. If you wanted to level at 19,000 meters, for instance, you had to start doing it at 17,000. If you corrected too fast, you'd have the passengers hanging from the baggage racks.

Then there was the thing that had bothered Becker from the first day he had taken the Concorde up to 19,000 meters. It was the problem of sudden cabin decompression of the type that can happen if you are hit by a missile, or if there is a small explosion on board, or if someone shatters a window with a bullet. In a conventional commercial aircraft, flying at relatively low altitudes, about 9,000 meters, cabin decompression was not a critical problem. The crew and passengers put on overhead oxygen masks and breathed until the aircraft descended into thicker air. But at 19,000 meters, you needed a pressure suit to make breathing possible, even with an oxygen mask. Lacking pressure suits, you had only a few seconds of usable consciousness to get down to where you could breathe with a mask. There was no way to do that at 19,000 meters. You put the mask on, but you blacked out anyway. The on-board computer sensed the problem and brought the plane down nicely, but by the time you got down to where you could breathe with the mask, you woke up with brain damage.

Becker had a recurring nightmare: a brain-damaged crew coming out of their blackout—sucking on the oxygen masks, if they still had the wits to grasp that simple necessity—trying to figure out what all those funny lights and dials in front of them were, while their eyes rolled and saliva drooled from their mouths. And all the while, the computerized Concorde held steady, waiting for a human hand to guide it. Neanderthals in Apollo. And in the back, seventy idiot passengers, in different states of mental debility, making faces and grunting. In his nightmare, the Concorde always landed and there were people on the observation deck waving. Won't they be surprised when their friends and lovers come down the stairway? Becker closed his eyes. He knew it wasn't possible to bring it home from those altitudes after more than thirty seconds' loss of oxygen. It was only an irrational nightmare. Yet he kept feeding a simple command to the conditioned-response part of his brain: *If nothing in the cockpit looks familiar anymore, touch nothing.* The fuel would eventually run out.

Becker wiped the sweat from his face and looked out across the field. Fifty meters away, Avidar was looking up at Concorde 01. He wondered if Avidar had nightmares like that. No, not Avidar.

5

Miriam Bernstein sat in the VIP lounge, drinking coffee with Abdel Jabari. Jabari saw the other Arab delegate, Ibrahim Ali Arif, come in, and he excused himself to speak with him.

Bernstein saw Jacob Hausner sitting alone at the bar. She stood up, hesitated, then walked toward him, but he didn't turn. "Hello."

He glanced over his shoulder. "Oh. Hello."

"Look, I'm sorry if I made some people uncomfortable before."

He stirred his drink. "No problem."

"Good." She stood silent for a moment. "So. Are you coming with us?"

"Yes. I just heard from the PM. I'll be on 02."

She didn't know why that should be good news, but she felt a sudden surge of something like well-being before she could sublimate it. "I'll be on 02 also."

There was silence.

She forced a smile and spoke again. "Do you want to change planes—or do you want me to?"

Why did he feel so strongly that the remark was made to provoke him? Hausner had a gut feeling that she was repressing some strong emotion and that it had to do with him. He looked at her. There was absolutely nothing in that face to reinforce his feeling, but it persisted. "I don't think that's necessary."

She looked into the mirror. Her eyes drifted between her own expression and Hausner's as if to make sure no one's mask had slipped. Her expression was all right, but she could see the tension in her body. She realized that she was almost standing on tiptoes. He always had that effect on her. She relaxed and smiled neutrally. "Nice of you to come. Can they spare you here?"

Hausner drained off his drink. "They had their choice of keeping me here for a crucifixion or letting me go and hoping I'd go down with the ship if something happened."

She nodded. "So you chose to go down with the ship."

"They chose. I think they'd like to see me go down and the ship stay up. But you can't have it both ways. Buy you a drink?"

"I don't drink, but—"

"Nobody in this goddamn country drinks. When I was in the RAF, nobody flew unless they were blind." He pushed his glass toward the bartender. "Well, see you on board."

She looked at him. "Right." She turned and walked off.

Matti Yadin came up to the bar when he saw Miriam Bernstein move away. "That bitch giving you a hard time again, boss?"

Hausner thought a moment. "I'm not sure."

Teddy Laskov walked into the VIP lounge, looking for Tom Richardson. He had some things to ask him. He was also supposed to give Richardson the alternate tactical frequency that he and Talman had just selected. He considered calling it into the American air attaché office, then thought better of it.

For a reason that he couldn't fully explain, even to himself, he decided to keep the information from Richardson. If the Americans really needed it when he got airborne, they could get it from Talman at The Citadel.

Laskov saw Hausner and Miriam speaking at the bar. He saw her turn and walk off. If he didn't know that they detested each other, he'd have to say that she looked hurt by something Hausner had said. He was surprised at the jealousy he suddenly felt. Laskov watched her. She didn't see him. They had already said their good-byes. He turned and walked with his bearlike gait down the back stairs where a jeep waited to take him to his squadron.

General Benjamin Dobkin stood near the coffee bar, speaking with Isaac Burg.

Dobkin looked at Burg. "So you're coming to New York with us?"

Burg nodded. "I think I should check on my agents in New York. Also, I have a lady friend there and she is going to feel the Wrath of God in about seven hours." He laughed and his eyes twinkled.

Dobkin stared into his cup, then looked down at Burg. "It's their last chance, isn't it? I mean, if ever they were going to strike, it would have to be now. If they don't, they are completely washed up in the eyes of their supporters. This is the biggest and most important target they have ever had. It is now or never for them, isn't it?"

Burg gave a slight nod. "Yes." He looked at Dobkin. "You know, when I got out of that meeting before, I was very confident. But human beings are very resourceful and cunning creatures. If they have the will, they will find the way. That much I know, after dealing with the Arabs for all these years. They are not the buffoons the press makes them out to be, as you and I know very well." He nodded again. "Yes, I'm worried."

Concorde 01 and Concorde 02 stood in the sunlight with their doors thrown open. Already on board each craft were six men from Hausner's security squad. Matti Yadin sat with the six men in 01 and briefed them. They each carried a Smith & Wesson .22 caliber automatic pistol. The .22 caliber round wasn't supposed to go completely through a human body and puncture the cabin. In theory, it looked safe, but shooting guns in small pressurized cabins was never a good idea.

The security men also had on board, as standard equipment, an old American M-14 rifle which had been fitted to accept a starlight scope for night shooting and a 10X Crossman sniper scope for day shooting. There was also on board an Israeli-made Uzi submachine gun. This was a very small weapon, forty-six centimeters long, and weighing only four kilograms but capable of firing a magazine of twenty-five 9mm rounds with much effect. The M-14 and the Uzi were to be used only outside the aircraft.

There was another piece of ordnance on board that none of the people in the airplanes knew about. In the tail of each Concorde was a half-kilo of plastic explosive stuck to the fuel trim tank, put there over a year before by two now-deceased Algerians, in faraway St. Nazaire and Toulouse. When the aircraft accelerated, fuel would be pumped into the empty tank in order to change the aircraft's center of gravity, making supersonic flight possible. If and when the explosive was detonated, the aircraft would be blown out of the sky.

Teddy Laskov sat in the cockpit of his F-14 and played with a pocket calculator, figuring his flying range based on such variables as fuel consumption, gross weight, expected maneuvers, and air temperature. Laskov, the old dogfighter, wanted very much to keep his 20mm cannon rounds, but he had to concede that they were not only too heavy but redundant as well. Missiles. That's what it was all about today. Maybe Richardson had been right about that. He called out of the open cockpit to the armorers. "Take out the twenty millimeters."

When the cannon rounds had been removed from each craft, he looked to his left and right and spoke into his headset. "Start your engines."

Twenty-four Pratt and Whitney engines, with over 9,000 kilograms of thrust each, exploded into a ground-shaking, ear-piercing wail.

A minute later, Laskov held up his thumb and shouted into his microphone. *"Zanek!"* Scramble.

The twelve fighters rolled toward the runway.

Tom Richardson realized too late that he hadn't gotten Laskov's alternate frequency. It wasn't the kind of information he could solicit from The Citadel over the phone and, for some reason, his own office hadn't gotten it yet. Also, the change in takeoff time, although he'd expected it, had caused him some inconvenience. He wondered if Laskov had taken his suggestion about not carrying the cannon rounds. It wasn't that critical, one way or the other, he decided.

The Peace Delegation was filing out of the lounge, down the back stairs, and into the waiting buses. Richardson ducked into a phone booth near the bar and dialed a number in Jericho, in the occupied West Bank. He didn't trust telephones, but he had little choice and less time.

Jacob Hausner stuck his head into his outer office. "Did the French SDECE call back yet?"

His secretary looked up. "No, sir."

"Damn it." He looked past her toward the window. The buses were almost filled. "I have to go. I'll probably fly back with one of the Concordes tomorrow. If anything important comes in while I'm in the air, call The Citadel and they'll put it out to the Concorde over the scrambler. I'll be on 02."

"Have a good trip. *Shalom.*"

"That's what this whole goddamned thing is all about. *Shalom.*" He walked quickly down the corridor.

Matti Yadin looked out the window of the bus that was going to Concorde 01. He saw Hausner hurrying by below him. "Boss!"

Hausner turned and looked up.

Yadin leaned out. "If you don't want to ride with—you know—I'll switch with you."

Hausner shook his head. "No. That's all right. It's a short flight. Besides, it's bad luck to change flight plans." Hausner hesitated. He was still worried about something, but he didn't know exactly what. He'd developed a bad feeling about this flight, all of a sudden, and he could see in Yadin's eyes the same uneasiness. "Remember Ahmed Rish?"

"How could I forget him?" said Yadin.

"How, indeed? Just think about him and radio me if anything clicks. See you in New York."

Yadin forced a smile. *"Shalom."*

Hausner reached up and grasped Yadin's hand, something he had never done before.

* * *

Chaim Mazar stood in the control tower of Lod Airport with a pair of field glasses to his eyes and looked out at the buses approaching the Concordes. A glint of light from the roof of an apartment house in Lod caught his eye and he swung the glasses toward it. He grabbed for his field radio as he kept his glasses trained on the building. He spoke rapidly into the mouthpiece. "Chopper Control, this is Tower. I saw a flash of light in quadrant thirty-six. Pink stucco apartment house. The roof. Get somebody up there."

Mazar watched as a Huey helicopter descended on the roof of the house within seconds. Four of his men jumped out with Uzi sub-machine guns before the helicopter landed. A few seconds later, a voice sounding out of breath came over his squawk box. "Tower, this is Huey seven-six."

"Roger, seven-six. Go ahead."

"No problem, Tower. Young lady with a sun reflector." There was a pause. The voice sounded amused. "Sunbathing in the nude, over."

Mazar wiped the beads of sweat from his forehead and sipped from a glass of water. "Roger. There's supposed to be an air-raid drill in progress. Get her something to wear and place her under arrest. Keep her in the chopper until you can turn her over to the police."

There was a long pause. "Roger, Tower."

"Tower, out. Mazar slumped back into his chair next to the air traffic controllers. He turned to one of them. "That was a little rough, but it's been a long day."

Sabah Khabbani lay at the crest of the hill and looked hard through his field glasses. The day was bright and clear, but nine kilometers was a long distance. It appeared as though the Concordes were loading. This was as good a time as any. He raised his hand. He waited until a helicopter passed over.

Behind him, in the pines, the three men knelt a few meters from each other. They each held a mortar round poised above the small hole in the ground. Next to each man were three additional rounds. They would each alternate two high explosive rounds with two white phosphorus rounds. The twelve rounds should blanket the entire area between the terminal and the Concordes. If one piece of incendiary matter punctured a fuel tank—and there was no reason why that shouldn't happen—no one would survive.

They watched Khabbani closely. His arm dropped. With shaking hands, each of the men let his round slip out of his fingers. They could hear the rounds slide down the long tubes. They covered their ears and opened their mouths to equalize the pressure of the impending blast.

Brigadier General Itzhak Talman stood in the Operations Room of The Citadel and looked at the radar and visual displays from the E-2D Hawkeye. He could see Laskov's twelve F-14's as they maintained a holding pattern off the coast. Indicated on other display consoles were scheduled airline traffic, a few private planes, and ships at sea. A computer flashed several messages on various cathode ray tubes and printed readout tapes. Talman turned up the volume on one of the radios and heard Laskov speaking to his squadron. So far, so good. He poured a cup of coffee and took a seat. All he could do now was wait.

Captain Ephraim Dinitz waited until he heard the dull thud of the rounds striking the firing pins at the bottom of the tubes. That should satisfy the military court if there should be a question later concerning intent. He and his men ran out from the trees and rocks. Dinitz shouted in Arabic. "I arrest you under military law! Place your hands on your heads!"

The three Palestinian gunners stared alternately between the silent mortars and the closing Israeli soldiers. Slowly they rose to their feet and placed their hands over their heads.

Khabbani looked back over his shoulder and watched the whole scene unfold thirty yards behind him. His heart sank and a lump came to his throat. He saw himself in Ramla Prison staring vacantly through the barbed wire for the rest of his life. He would never touch his wife or children again except through that barbed wire. He got up and leaped from the crest of the hill. A soldier shouted. Khabbani ran stumbling over the rocks, the wildflowers going by in a blur beneath his feet. Another shout. The staccato report of an automatic weapon. He saw the bullets hit around him and it was several seconds before he realized he was no longer running but lying on the ground, bleeding quickly to death.

Chaim Mazar picked up his field radio. From the tower he could see the hills where it had all happened. He nodded. "All right, Dinitz. Interrogate them immediately and call me back." He sat back in his chair. He realized that those miserable Palestinian peasants knew less than he did about who was behind that pathetic attempt. Those mortars had been spotted ten years before and left there to see who would come around and use them. The detonators had been removed from the rounds, of course. He'd had the spot watched more closely than usual for the last week. In addition, someone had tipped off one of his agents earlier in the day.

It was such a clumsy and foolhardy attempt that Mazar couldn't believe it was meant to succeed. All he could think of was the English expression, red herring, or the Hebrew words, sacrificial lamb. That's what those unfortunate Palestinians were. Everyone was supposed to relax their guard now that the great terrorist attempt had been foiled. But Mazar didn't see it that way. If this *was* a red herring, then that could only mean that there must still be an undiscovered plot to sabotage this peace mission. But for the life of him, he couldn't imagine what it could be. He shrugged.

The Air Traffic Controller looked up from his radio. "Concordes are ready to roll, sir."

Mazar nodded. "Then give them clearance and get them the hell out of here."

The flight crew of El Al Concorde 01 completed their checklist. The Concorde rolled out to the edge of the 4,000-meter runway. The radio crackled. "Cleared for takeoff, El Al 01 and 02. Two-minute intervals. Have a good flight."

"Roger." Avidar pushed the throttles forward and the big bird screamed down the runway.

David Becker sat in the left-hand seat and watched through the windshield as 01 lifted gently from the earth. He turned to Moses Hess. "Count off two minutes for me, will you, Moses?"

Hess nodded and looked at his watch.

Behind them, on the port side of the flight deck, Peter Kahn sat in front of the flight engineer's long control console. The lights and gauge needles were all steady. He turned to Becker and said in English, "All systems still go."

Becker smiled at the English idiom. "Right."

"One minute."

In the cabin, the passengers and flight attendants spoke in low voices. The manifest showed ten delegates and twenty-five support personnel. There were also two stewards and two stewardesses, plus the Chief Steward, Leiber. They sat in a group, immediately behind the flight deck. Scattered among the passengers were six security men with Jacob Hausner in charge. Tom Richardson had found a seat next to John McClure and was carrying on a one-sided conversation with the taciturn man. General Dobkin was reviewing the notes he would present to the Pentagon brass. Isaac Burg sat by himself, reading a newspaper and sucking on his unlit pipe. Rabbi Levin had picked a religious argument with one of the delegates. The total manifest, with crew and flight attendants, numbered fifty-five. The extra baggage allowance had placed the Concorde very near its maximum takeoff weight, especially considering the existing air temperature.

Miriam Bernstein sat behind Abdel Jabari, who was sitting with Ibrahim Arif, the other Arab delegate on board 02. A nervous young Security man, Moshe Kaplan, stared at the two black and white checked *kheffiyahs* from across the aisle.

The cabin was small and the seats were two-and-two across, with barely enough room for a man 180 centimeters tall to stand. But the French had designed the interior with their typical flair for such things, and the appearance was one of luxury. The lack of space didn't matter much because the Concorde was seldom airborne for more than three and a half hours at a time.

A final touch to the decor was provided by a large wall-mounted Machmeter which let the passengers see the aircraft's speed. The red neon lights read MACH 0.00.

In the cockpit, Hess looked up from his watch. "Let's go."

Becker released the brakes and pushed the throttles forward. The aircraft began to move. It gathered speed as it rolled down the long, shimmering runway.

"Sixty knots," Hess announced.

"Everything's good," called Kahn, as he ran his eyes across his panel.

Becker called for the afterburners.

The flight engineer moved his poised fingers to ignite the two outboard afterburners, then the inboard pair. "Afterburners—all four," he called. Simultaneously, there was the sound and sensation of a two-phased thud that made the procedural words unnecessary.

"One hundred knots," said Hess.

The runway was already half-gone and the undulating waves of heat that rose from the blacktop made the remaining length look even shorter than it was. Pools of mirage water formed and evaporated with increasing speed. Becker blinked his eyes. *Concentrate on the instruments. Forget the visual.* But he kept staring out of the windshield. The heat waves mesmerized him. They also distorted and foreshortened the end of the runway. It looked as though they had run out of blacktop. He felt beads of sweat form on his forehead and hoped Hess wouldn't notice. He pulled his eyes away from the sunlit windshield and stared down at the console. The air-speed needles were moving rapidly now. His left hand squeezed more tightly on the wheel as he nudged the column slightly rearward. Involuntarily, the muscles in his buttocks tightened and he rose imperceptibly from his seat. *Up, up, damn you!*

"V-one," said Hess. His monotone masked the significance of his words as the air speed rose through 165 knots. They were now committed to fly, even if a blinking light or flickering gauge indicated otherwise. "V-R," he said.

Becker began tugging more earnestly on the control column. The nose tire of the aircraft lifted off the hot blacktop. The Concorde's wings canted themselves skyward, biting into the air flow at a greater angle. They were eating up runway at the rate of 75 meters a second, and for a brief moment Becker felt his nerve slip away. All the old demons of doubt that had haunted him since flight school began chattering in his brain. *Why should it fly? There's something wrong, Becker, and no one has the balls to speak up. Why is the gauge over there flickering? Who built this plane, anyway? Why do you think you can fly it? Becker! Abort! Abort! You're going to die, Becker! Abort!* He felt his neck muscles tighten and his hands and knees were shaking.

"V-two," said Hess with what Becker thought was just a hint of anxiety in his voice.

Becker felt the wheel loosen in his hand as the main wheels rose from the runway. He looked down at the console. Two hundred twenty knots on the airspeed gauge. The rates of climb were moving rapidly and the altimeter was winding even faster. Becker held the airplane by the palm and fingers of one hand. He smiled and cleared his throat. "Gear up." The sound of his own voice, steady and even, seemed to chase the perverse imps from the cockpit. But he heard their familiar parting promise. *We'll kill you next time, Becker.* He waited out a sequence of lights, then said, almost too loudly, "Climb power." He lowered his voice. "After-takeoff check." He banked the aircraft slightly to follow in the flight path of his sister ship. "And when you get a chance, Peter, ring the cabin for some coffee." He settled back and his muscles loosened. There would be a landing and takeoff at Orly and then again in New York. He would be back at Lod within twenty-four hours. Then he would resign, effective immediately. He knew it had been coming for a long time. He felt it every time his sphincter tightened on takeoff and landing, every time his loins went loose when he hit an insignificant air pocket, every time he had to wipe the sweat from his palms when he flew through a line of thunderstorms. But it was all right. It had happened to better pilots than himself. The trick was to look it in the eye and say, "I quit."

"Quit what?" asked Hess.

Becker swung his head and stared at him. "What?"

"Quit what? What do you quit?" Hess was going over his checklist as he spoke.

"Quit . . . drinking coffee. Coffee. I forgot. I don't want any."

Hess looked up from his checklist and stared at him. His eyes met Becker's and they both knew. "Right." He called out to Kahn. "Only two coffees, Peter."

Becker wiped his palms and face openly. It was all right now. Hess had a right to know. He lit a cigarette and inhaled deeply.

6

Concorde 02 began its steep, graceful climb. The long landing gear assemblies had already risen into the belly of the craft. Hess pulled another hydraulic lever, retracting the flaps and activating the droop-nose to its streamlined position. The flight deck became very still, with only the murmur of electronic noises in the background. Becker banked the craft 30 degrees and put it on a due west heading over Tel Aviv. The dual altimeter indicated 6,000 feet and 1,800 meters and air speed was 300 knots. He lit another cigarette. So far, so good.

Becker rolled the Concorde out of its turn and sat back in his seat. His eyes took in all the instruments. The Concorde was an electronically controlled aircraft, somewhat like a space capsule. When the wheel or rudder pedals were moved, for instance, an electrical signal was sent to the hydraulic control activators. It was this, rather than cables or rods, that moved the exterior control surfaces. The computer would feed artificial stability and resistance back into the controls for the pilot to sense. Without this pressure to fly against, there would be nothing for the pilot to feel as he moved his controls. Pilots weren't used to that, and so the men at Aérospatiale and British Airway Corporation told the computer to put artificial resistance into the control movement. It was all psychological, reflected Becker, and all very strange and becoming stranger with each new technological breakthrough. Long before he felt the fear, he had felt this alienation in the cockpit. Yes, it was time to let the next generation take the controls.

They were over the beach outside of Tel Aviv. Becker took a pair of field glasses out of his flight kit and scanned the ground. Normally, the beach would be covered with thousands of bikinis, but the air-raid drill had sent everyone indoors. Becker saw his home in Herzlya, as he always did. He saw the empty chaise longue in his yard and wondered if his wife knew that he was part of the reason that everyone had to interrupt their first spring sunbathing. Ahead of him stretched the dark blue Mediterranean and a cloudless azure sky. Becker eased back on the wheel a bit more and gave it more throttle. The aircraft picked up speed and altitude.

Ahead, he could see 01. The Concorde might be an ungainly looking bird on the ground, but in flight it was the technocrats' contribution to pure aesthetics. It was a beautiful aircraft to fly, also, but Becker always had the uneasy feeling that the computers would fail him someday. Not really fail so much as betray. Those marvelous computers that could do a thousand things simultaneously; things that three human crewmen could not do, no matter how hard they worked. Those computers would lure him up to 60,000 feet—19,000 meters— and Mach 2.2 one day, and then quit. A message would flash on the cathode tube: *Fly It Yourself, Stupid.* Becker forced a smile. Two more takeoffs and three more landings.

He hit the transmit button on his console and spoke into his headset microphone. "Air Traffic Control, this is El Al Concorde 02. Over."

"Go ahead, 02."

"Roger. Company aircraft in sight. I'm at 380 knots, indicated. Accelerating to point-eight-zero, Mach."

"Roger. Level off at 5,000 meters."

"Roger." He pushed the selector switch to the company frequency. "El Al 01, 02 here. I have you dead ahead. I'm about eight kilometers back. I'll close to about five and get a little below you. Don't stop short."

Avidar acknowledged. They spoke for a while and coordinated speeds.

Becker got to 5,000 meters and closed in on Avidar. He spoke to Air Traffic Control. "El Al 01 and 02 in formation. Holding at 5,000 and now at point-eight-six, Mach. Waiting for unrestricted clearance to 19,000."

"Roger. Stand by. There's an Air Iran 747 at flight level six-zero-zero. Maintain 5,000 meters.

Avidar called Becker on the company frequency. "El Al 02, this is 01. See if you can raise our sheep dog. I don't see him."

Becker switched to 134.725. "Gabriel 32, this is Emmanuel."

Teddy Laskov had been monitoring the El Al and ATC frequencies and switched to channel 31 to meet Becker. "Emmanuel, this is Gabriel 32. I hear you fine. I can see you and Clipper at my eleven o'clock low position. Leave one radio on this frequency."

"Roger, Gabriel. When we get unrestricted clearance from ATC, we're climbing to 19,000 and accelerating to Mach 2.0 on a heading of 280 degrees."

"Roger. I'll be with you. So far, so good."

"So far. I'm going back to company frequency. The copilot will monitor you."

"Roger—break—Hawkeye, this is Gabriel 32. How are your blips?"

The E-2D Hawkeye was almost five kilometers directly above the Concordes and F-14's. It had been simultaneously monitoring all three frequencies. The Air Control officer on board picked up his radiophone. "I have you all spotted and plotted, Gabriel. Do you see a craft approaching from a bearing of 183 degrees? About 180 kilometers distance from you? Not a scheduled airliner."

Laskov spoke into the intercom to his flight officer behind him. "See anything, Dan?"

Daniel Lavon looked down at the combined television and cathode ray tube. "Possible. Something's at the southwest edge of our radar. A little over 160 kilometers and approaching our intended flight path at right angles."

The E-2D Hawkeye, with a crew of five and a cabin full of the latest electronic equipment, was in a better position to detect and classify aircraft than the F-14's. The flight technician on the Hawkeye spoke to Laskov. "We're trying to contact this craft, but we can't raise him."

Laskov acknowledged.

The E-2D command information controller got on the phone. "Gabriel, the unidentified craft is moving at approximately 960 kilometers per. He is on a course and speed that will bring him across your intended flight path, but at 1,800 meters below you and Emmanuel and Clipper at your present altitude."

"Roger, Hawkeye. Contact the son-of-a-bitch and tell him to change course and speed, or both."

"Roger, Gabriel. We're trying."

Laskov considered. In about a minute, the unidentified craft would be within the 160 kilometer range of his Phoenix. If this craft had a pair of Russian Acrid missiles, it couldn't engage the Concordes until it was within 130 kilometers. This 30-kilometer difference in range between the Russian Acrid and the American Phoenix was all the difference in the world. It was the reason why the F-14 was king of the sky. It had a longer reach. It was like two knights, one with an eight-foot lance and one with a ten-foot lance. In a few more minutes, though, Laskov would no longer have the advantage. "Hawkeye, I'm going to engage this target before he gets within 130 kilometers, unless you can identify him or he identifies himself."

General Talman rose from his chair in the Operations Room of The Citadel. He grabbed a radiophone and cut in quickly. "Gabriel, this is Operation Control. Look—you're the man on the spot. You have to make the decision, but for God's sake, consider all the angles." He paused. "I'm behind you, whatever happens. Out." Talman didn't want to tie up the radio net with a political discourse. It had all been argued long before this. He stood and watched the converging radar blips on his screen as he stroked his mustache.

What Laskov had wanted from Talman was an unequivocal order to fire at will. But he knew better.

"Gabriel, this is Hawkeye. Listen. He is not—repeat, not—military because we do not pick up any sophisticated radar emissions from him."

"Then what the hell goes 960 kilometers per hour?"

"Probably a civilian jet, Gabriel. Wait one. I have something coming in on the radio."

Laskov shouted into his microphone. "I don't give a good goddamn if it *is* a civilian jet. A civilian jet can be fitted to fire an air-to-air missile, too. Get me an I.D. on this guy, or he goes!"

There was no reply.

Danny Lavon spoke into the intercom. "General, this is a lot of bullshit. I'll take the responsibility. You can say I panicked and pushed a button. I've got him locked in now on—"

Laskov broke squelch on the intercom and cut him off with an electronic whine. When he released the squelch button, Lavon had stopped speaking. "Listen, son. You just follow orders. No more of that."

The Air Control officer came back on the air. "Gabriel, this is Hawkeye. Listen, we just spoke to Air Traffic Control in Cyprus. Our unidentified is a civilian Lear jet, Model 23, with a French registration. He filed a flight plan from Cairo to Cyprus to Istanbul to Athens. Six on board. Businessmen. French passports. We have their frequency and call sign. Trying to raise them now."

Laskov wasn't satisfied. "Trying to? Bullshit. They are within 130 kilometers and you have their frequency and you have the best radios made. What's the problem, Hawkeye?"

"It might be theirs, Gabriel."

"Roger." Laskov let out a long breath. He looked out of his plexiglas windshield. The two Concordes floated below him like paper airplanes. "Clipper and Emmanuel, this is Gabriel. Are you monitoring all of this?"

Becker and Avidar responded affirmatively.

"All right. Tell ATC you want to change to a due north heading and you want permission to climb unrestricted to 19,000, *now.*"

Becker and Avidar acknowledged. Avidar called Air Traffic Control and he received word that there was a TWA 747 and a Lufthansa 707 above them and that they would have to wait five minutes for their unrestricted climbs.

Laskov didn't think he wanted to wait even five seconds. He spoke to Lavon on the intercom. He didn't speak to the rest of the squadron on the radio because he didn't want Talman or anyone else to hear. "Arm the Phoenix, Daniel. Prepare to engage the target." He thought of Miriam Bernstein. *Even if you should see Satan himself on your radar screen . . . don't shoot him out of the sky with one of your missiles.* And Richardson. *Listen, don't get trigger-happy up there. We don't want any incidents.* Then, he thought of what lousy jobs he had had all his adult life. "Hawkeye, this guy has about sixty seconds to live unless he speaks to us."

It was the Hawkeye pilot who responded this time. "Roger, Gabriel. We can't raise him. I'm sorry. I can't do anything else. I understand your position. Do what you think is best."

"Thanks."

Talman broke into the net. "I'm with you, Gabriel." Talman was beginning to think there was something wrong. If the Lear's radios were bad, he would probably have headed back and landed at Alexandria. If they weren't bad, why wasn't he answering? He'd heard the Hawkeye call on Lear's frequency. Hawkeye had spoken to the Lear in French, then English, the international language of flight, and finally, even Arabic. Talman spoke into the radio. "It stinks, Gabriel."

"Right." Laskov spoke into the intercom. "Where is he?"

Lavon glanced at his radar. "About sixty-five kilometers—and climbing."

It was already too late for the Phoenix. "Arm the Sparrow and . . . engage the target."

"Right, General." Lavon moved an electrical switch and then slid back a small plate on the armament console. Under the panel was a red button. He put his finger on it.

"Gabriel, this is Emmanuel." Becker's voice sounded strained.

Laskov held up his hand to stop Lavon and acknowledged Becker.

"The Lear is calling us on company frequency."

"Roger." Laskov quickly turned up the radio on the El Al frequency. Lavon called the rest of the squadron and instructed them to monitor also.

"El Al Concorde 01 and 02. This is Lear number five-four. Can you hear me?"

Laskov felt a cold chill run down his spine. The accent was unmistakably Arabic.

Becker and Avidar acknowledged.

The Lear spoke again. The voice was slow and precise. "Listen very carefully. We have important information for you."

Becker and Avidar again acknowledged. There was an apprehensive tone in their voices.

Laskov realized that the Lear was stalling for time. He spoke to Lavon. "When I raise my hand, fire."

Talman stood motionless in the center of the Operations Room. He stared in disbelief at the radio speakers. He whispered to himself, "What the hell . . . ?"

The Lear came back on the air. The voice spoke very quickly now. "In the tail of each Concorde is a radio-controlled bomb. *Radio-controlled,*" he stressed. "Have no doubts about that. It was placed in 01 at St. Nazaire and in 02 at Toulouse. It is attached to the number eleven fuel tank. I know you have an escort of twelve F-14's. If I see the smoke trail of their missiles coming at me, or if I see the flash of their cannon, I will push the buttons on my radio detonator and blow you both up. Do you understand that? Are the F-14's monitoring? Do *you* understand that?"

Laskov refused to acknowledge. He sat and stared.

Avidar, his voice shaking with rage, shouted into the radio. "Bastard!"

Becker spoke evenly into his radio. "Roger." He pushed the PA button and spoke calmly. "Would Mr. Hausner, General Dobkin, and Mr. Burg come up to the flight deck, please?"

Laskov hung his head on his chest. He simply couldn't believe it. All that planning and all that security . . . He removed a pair of field glasses from an old leather case by his feet. He placed them in his lap and stared down at them. The glasses were the only thing besides his uniform that he had taken out of Russia. He raised them and looked out into the blue sky. He could see the green and white Lear 23 approaching now, trailing a long, thin line of exhaust from its two turbojet engines. He was close. In fact he was too close for the minimum 16-kilometer range of the Sparrow and too far for the maximum 8-kilometer range of the Sidewinder. The Lear turned 90 degrees and flew along-side Concorde 02. Laskov could see that a plexiglas observation bubble had been cut into the rear of the cabin roof. There appeared to be someone looking out of the bubble, and Laskov knew the man probably had field glasses trained on *him.* He lowered his glasses.

The Lear, either by luck or by design, stayed inside the 8-kilometer dead space between the Sparrow and the Sidewinder. That dead area had bothered a lot of Western military people, but it wasn't considered critical under most circumstances. In a conventional fight, Laskov would have just pulled up or held back until he could use the appropriate missile. But he was afraid to make any sudden maneuvers because he knew the Lear's observer was watching his squadron out of the rear bubble. He held his flight on a steady course. He spoke softly to Lavon. "Arm the Sidewinder, in case he gets in closer." But he knew it was no good. The Lear was holding too close to the Concordes even to consider missiles now.

The Lear made a small correction in course and positioned itself about 150 meters under Concorde 02 and just forward of 02's nose cone. From where Laskov was positioned, above the Concordes, he could barely see the Lear.

Talman sat slumped in his chair. The personnel in the Operations Room were completely still. Talman saw the blips of the Lear and 02 merge, and he knew Laskov was powerless to do anything with his missiles. The whole damned thing had happened so fast. He looked at the digital chronometer on the wall. From the time Laskov had seen the Lear on his radar to now had been less than ten minutes. Somehow, he had always known it would happen. All it took was one or two madmen. With modern technology, anything was possible. A single insignificant nobody could alter the destiny of nations. An atomic bomb planted in a city. A biological agent in a water supply. A bomb on a Concorde. How could you guard against something as preposterous as that?

Hausner, Dobkin, and Burg stood on the flight deck as Becker explained what had happened. Tom Richardson and John McClure had come into the cockpit, uninvited. They had seen the Lear approach and they knew something was wrong.

McClure slouched against the flight engineer's console, chewing on a wooden match. He was an extremely tall, thin man, who reminded some people of the unbearded Lincoln. A Midwestern twang completed the image. "Should've taken Pan Am home," was all he said when Becker had announced that they were being hijacked.

Burg turned to Becker. "Do you want me to get the Foreign Minister up here?"

Becker shook his head. "I don't need any politicians to give me advice. We will make the decisions right here. Just stand by." From time to time, Becker could see the nose of the Lear poke out from under his long nose cone. It reminded him of what an infantryman had told him once in Vietnam, of how the VC liked to get very close during a firefight so the Americans couldn't use their heavy weapons without killing their own men. He knew Laskov was in a bind. They were *all* in a bind.

Hausner seemed far away, almost disinterested. Then an odd smile came to his face. He remembered now what it was he couldn't remember before. Rish had been seen in those small villages of France. The names of the villages had meant nothing to him then. Israel had had no Concordes at the time. Now he realized that those obscure French villages were near St. Nazaire and Toulouse. He remembered his words at the security meeting. *We've had those birds on the line for thirteen months. Since the time that we got them, they have never left the sight of my security people.* That was the weak link. *Since the time we got them.* . . . St. Nazaire. Toulouse. What an idiot he had been.

Becker looked over his shoulder and addressed Hausner. "Could it be possible? A bomb, I mean?"

Hausner nodded. "Sorry."

Becker began to say something, then turned away.

The radio crackled, again, and Matti Yadin's voice came over the speaker. He knew Hausner would be in the cockpit, too. "You were right, boss."

Hausner didn't respond.

Becker called Laskov on the tactical frequency. "What do we do, Gabriel?"

"Stand by." Laskov could see the nose of the Lear poke out from the nose of Concorde 02. He looked at the cannon button on his control wheel. In his mind's eye, he fired and sent sixty 20mm cannon rounds a second streaking over the Concorde's windshield and into the cockpit of the Lear. But he didn't have any 20mm cannon rounds, and even if he did, he wondered if he would risk it. There was a chance before, but not now. He thought of Richardson and Bernstein and felt betrayed. Betrayed by well-intentioned people, but betrayed nonetheless. He pushed the cannon button. The combat camera rolled and made a movie for the men at The Citadel. Laskov pounded on the console in front of him.

The voice from the Lear came back on the Concordes' radios. "I assume your escort is monitoring El Al frequencies. Listen closely, fighter pilots. I have an observer looking back at you. If I see the flash of your cannon, I will push the button and blow up the Concordes. I do not mind dying. Now, listen to me —you must break off and return to base. You can do nothing here. If you do not turn away in sixty seconds, I will blow up the lead Concorde to make you understand that I am very serious.

Avidar called Laskov on the tactical frequency. "All right, sheep dog. What now?"

Laskov considered opening his throttles, ducking under the Concorde and ramming the Lear. They might not expect to see a quarter-million kilograms of airplane screaming down on them. They might panic. But even if he hit them, the mid-air explosion would certainly damage Concorde 02.

Avidar's voice came back on the radio. "What do we *do*, Gabriel?"

The Lear came over the El Al frequency. "Concordes. I think you are talking to your escort. It will do no good. They have fifteen seconds to turn back."

Laskov wondered if the Lear would blow up the Concordes as soon as his F-14's moved off. Or did the Lear—whoever the hell he was—want hostages? He switched to the El Al frequency and spoke to the Lear for the first time. "Lear, this is the fighter escort. We are not—repeat, not—leaving. We are all returning to Lod. You must follow and land with us. If you do not comply, I am going to—" suddenly, the term "engage you" was not appropriate. "I will kill you," he said softly.

The voice from Lear laughed back at him. "Your time is up. Go away or these deaths will be on *your* head."

Hausner knew who was speaking to them. He put his hand on Becker's shoulder. "I know that man. Tell Laskov his name is Ahmed Rish. He will do whatever he says he will do. Tell Laskov to go away."

Richardson nodded. "They can't mean to harm us or they would already have detonated the bombs. This is a hijacking, pure and simple. Ask them what they want." He paused. "And tell Teddy Laskov that I'm sorry about the 20mm."

Becker turned to Dobkin and Burg. They nodded. He passed Hausner's and

Richardson's messages to Laskov, then called the Lear. "Who are you people and what do you propose?"

Rish's voice came back loud and clear. "It doesn't matter who we are. Our purpose is to escort you somewhere and to hold you as hostages until it suits our purposes to let you go. No one will be harmed if you do exactly as we say. However, if your escort doesn't leave in one second, I am blowing up the lead aircraft."

Danny Lavon spoke on the intercom. "If he has a bomb on board, there is nothing we can do here anymore, General. Maybe we can pull off and engage him from 160 kilometers out."

Laskov called Talman. "Control, I'm coming home."

Talman spoke quietly into the radio. "My fault, Gabriel."

Laskov knew it wasn't anyone's fault, but there would be a lot of people saying that in the coming days.

The Lear came over the radio again. It was the same voice, Laskov noticed—Rish—but this time it had lost some of its composure. Rish was screaming to him to turn back. Laskov ignored the voice for a few seconds and took stock of the situation. He wondered how the Lear could have filed a flight plan that would bring him so close in time and space to the Concordes. Especially since the Concordes' takeoff time had been moved up half an hour. He also had the distinct impression that the Lear was able to hear him on his tactical frequency. He spoke the words, "My number three fuel tank indicator has become inop," and the F-14's, plus the E-2D, Talman and the Concordes switched to the alternate tactical frequency. Laskov called Clipper and Emmanuel on the new frequency. He spoke quickly. "Listen. That son-of-a-bitch was monitoring the primary tactical frequency. I don't know how he got it and he may have this one, too, but I'm going to talk to you, anyway. We're not abandoning you. The E-2D will keep you spotted. We'll hang back a few hundred kilometers. Call me on this frequency and let me know what's happening. If the time comes when you decide to risk it, we'll charge in and let loose with Phoenix at 160 kilometers distance. There's a good chance they won't spot the vapor trail if they're not looking for it. Do you understand?"

Everyone acknowledged in turn.

Ahmed Rish screamed into his radio over the El Al frequency. "I know you are talking! Enough of this nonsense. Enough! Five seconds." He put his finger on a radio detonator button labeled 01. "One, two, three—"

Laskov spoke on the El Al frequency. "Good luck." He gave the order and the flight of F-14's banked steeply to the right. They completed a 180-degree turn and were out of sight in seconds.

Becker couldn't see them go, but suddenly he felt very alone.

7

Avidar didn't like the way the situation was being handled. He had been slowly increasing his speed and he estimated that he was at least ten kilometers ahead of the Lear and Concorde 02. How much range could a radio detonator have? Certainly not more than ten or twelve kilometers. He looked at his altimeter. He was slightly over the 5,000 meters assigned to them by Air Traffic Control.

Air Traffic Control had seen the Lear blip merge into the El Al 02 blip and had seen the flight of F-14's pull away, but hadn't monitored any of the conversation on the El Al frequency. Still, the controller knew something was wrong. He called the Concordes. "If everything is all right with you, you can proceed unrestricted to 19,000 meters. Sorry about the delay."

Rish, who was apparently also monitoring ATC, told them to acknowledge.

Avidar and Becker acknowledged. Avidar looked at his speed indicator. He was flying at an air speed of 1,000 kilometers per hour. If he gave it full throttle and kicked in his afterburners, he could be at Mach 1 and at least three more kilometers away in less than fifteen seconds.

Rish's voice came back on the radio. "Very good. Very sensible. Now, you will leave your navigation lights on and follow me. I am going to proceed on a magnetic heading of 160 degrees, at 300 knots indicated air speed. El Al 02 will follow directly behind me. El Al 01 will fall in behind 02. We are going to descend to 150 meters. Do you understand?"

Becker and Avidar acknowledged.

The Lear began its bank to the left and Becker prepared to follow.

Asher Avidar hit the afterburner switches. He then began pushing forward on the throttles as fast as the engines could take the fuel. He aimed for the center of a cumulus cloud to his front. The four huge Rolls Royce Olympus engines generated 70,000 kilograms of thrust and the Concorde streaked off.

Zevi Hirsch screamed at Avidar. "What the hell—"

Leo Sharett turned from the flight panel. "Asher, *don't*—"

Matti Yadin, who was still on the flight deck, grabbed Avidar's arm, but Avidar pushed him away. Yadin pulled his Smith & Wesson .22 and put it to Avidar's head. Avidar quickly brushed it away as though it were an annoying insect.

In Concorde 02, Moses Hess grabbed Becker's arm and pointed out the windshield. Becker watched as Avidar's aircraft disappeared inside the cloud.

In the passenger cabin of 02, everyone knew by now that something was wrong. Yaakov Leiber leaned over an empty seat and watched the plane carrying his wife disappear off the starboard side. Then he saw it reappear again out of the cloud.

One of the six Arabs in the Lear shouted to Ahmed Rish. Rish watched as the Concorde streaked off. He grabbed the radio detonator from the seat. There were two red buttons. Without looking, he put his finger on the one marked 02 and began to press, then realized his mistake. He slid his finger onto the button marked 01.

Concorde 01 sailed upward. The number eleven fuel tank automatically began to fill with kerosene as the computer determined that the center of gravity should be more aft for the speed and angle at which the aircraft was moving. In the passenger cabin, the large digital Machmeter read MACH 0.97 and the seat belt lights came on. The passengers looked concerned when the G forces pushed them into their seats as the aircraft banked. The Machmeter read MACH 0.98, then MACH 0.99.

Ahmed Rish pressed the button. A radio signal, keyed only to the receiver on El Al 01, flashed across the sky.

The radio detonator barely received the signal at eleven kilometers. The receiver transformed the weak signal into an impulse that closed the switch and allowed the current from the tail navigation lights to flow down the wire into the detonator embedded in the plastic explosive.

The Machmeter read MACH 1.00 and the Concorde broke through the sound barrier. The tail tank, with 4,000 liters of fuel in it, exploded and blew out the pressure bulkhead. A tongue of flame shot into the passenger cabin as the Machmeter flashed MACH 1.10. The oxygen masks dropped from their overhead compartments as the cabin lost pressure.

Asher Avidar knew he had lost his gamble even before he heard the explosion. The controls suddenly went loose in his hands and the lights on the flight console began blinking on one by one. The door between the cabin and the cockpit blew open and the crew could hear screams behind them. Hirsch turned around and looked down the length of the aircraft. He saw daylight. All he could say was, "Oh, God!" Behind him, Matti Yadin lay on the floor, bleeding from where the door had hit him in the face. Avidar turned to Zevi Hirsch. He screamed above the sounds of rushing air. "It's better this way! You can't give in to these bastards!" Hirsch stared at him.

Becker watched as his sister ship fought to maintain control. With a cool detachment, he realized from the billowing orange flames that the bomb *was* on the number eleven trim tank—a place that was inaccessible from the cabin. He assumed that the bomb itself was a small device—the bigger danger was the exploding fuel. He spoke softly to Peter Kahn. "Override the computer and pump number eleven dry." He turned to Hess. "Get on the PA and tell the passengers to move toward the front of the cabin." He wondered if the pressure bulkhead would contain the blast. He hoped he wouldn't have to find out.

Becker stared out of the windshield, mesmerized by the sight. Hausner, Dobkin, Burg, Richardson, and McClure crowded behind the flight seats riveted to the same scene.

El Al 01 began its incredibly beautiful dance of death. The delta wing aircraft yawed and rolled like a graceful glider. Becker knew what Avidar was going through as he pulled and pushed at levers, throttles, switches, and buttons. But it was a losing battle.

Concorde 02 closed in on its dying sister. Becker called for field glasses and watched. A small propeller dropped out of the belly of the fiery bird and Becker knew that at least the computer was still functioning. Like the damaged brain of a big animal, it realized that it was in danger, but unlike the brain of a human, it didn't comprehend that the wound was mortal, and it continued to struggle to stay alive. The computer had sensed the electrical and hydraulic failures, so the propeller—really a windmill—was released to turn an electric generator and hydraulic pump. The French had called this feature *très pratique,* but the British called it desperate. Becker knew that, in this case, the new power source would only make the problem worse. Broken electrical wires would come alive and hydraulic fluid would squirt from open pipes. Damaged nerve endings and severed arteries. But the mechanical heart still beat and the mechanical brain still functioned. Becker was sickened by the picture in his field glasses. He put the glasses down and rubbed his eyes and temples.

In the dying Concorde, Avidar and Hirsch were reacting out of pure instinct —responding to each new crisis—because there was nothing else to do in the pilots' seats of a doomed aircraft. Leo Sharett sat calmly in front of his flight engineer's console, performing his job of systems management long after there were any systems left to manage. His instrument lights began to blink off one by one. The Concorde began to tumble tail over nose, like a silver leaf in a gentle wind. Then, mercifully, it disintegrated in a flash.

Becker could hear the anguished cries coming from the cabin behind him. Above all the voices, he could hear little Yaakov Leiber screaming for his wife.

Becker could see some debris floating toward them, and he made a violent maneuver to avoid it. The five men standing on the flight deck fell to the floor. In the cabin, passengers were thrown from their seats. Peter Kahn belatedly put the seat belt sign on and spoke into the PA microphone. "Everyone stay seated. Everything is going to be all right." He quickly explained the situation.

Everyone got up from the floor of the flight deck. Hausner looked at Dobkin and Burg. They turned away from him.

The Lear jet came back on the radio. It was Rish's voice again. It sounded high-pitched and near hysteria. "They forced me to do that!" he screamed. "Now, you listen to me! You will follow me and do exactly as I say, or you will share their fate!"

Hausner grabbed the microphone from the console. "Rish, you bastard! This is Jacob Hausner. You goddamned murderer. When we get down, I'm going to kill you, you son-of-a-bitch!" He began a long string of peculiarly Middle Eastern invectives in Arabic.

Rish's voice came back over the speaker after Hausner finished. Rish was clearly fighting for self-control. He spoke slowly. "Mr. Hausner, when we get down, the first thing I am going to do is kill *you.*"

Hausner began another tirade in Arabic, but Becker grabbed the microphone from him. He switched to the alternate tactical frequency to call Laskov, but all he could hear was a high-pitched, whining sound.

Rish's voice came over the company frequency, barely audible above the radio interference. "You are no longer able to communicate with your escort or with me. Just follow." The high-pitched whine became louder.

Becker turned down the volume on all the radios. "He jammed us. Probably has a broad band transmitter on board." He looked around the flight deck. "I think he holds all the cards." He looked at Burg, who was the senior man present.

Burg nodded. He looked very pale. Everyone did. The image of El Al Concorde 01 hurtling nose over tail had made them literally sick. Burg nodded again. "Let me go and speak to the Foreign Minister and the passengers. They should all know what is happening." His voice was choked. "Excuse me." He walked out of the cockpit.

Tom Richardson cleared his throat. "Maybe we should just let the pilots fly now."

Dobkin nodded. "Yes. We must speak to each of the passengers and tell them what we expect of them when we land. We must start organizing a psychological defense against the pressures of being held hostage. That is very important."

"Yes," said Hausner. "Good thinking. I imagine it's going to be a long captivity. At least for you."

Richardson spoke up. "Don't worry about that, Mr. Hausner. That son-of-a-bitch was just trying to scare you."

McClure spoke for the first time since he'd announced his preference for Pan Am. "Don't be an ass, Richardson. That man just murdered fifty people. If he said he was going to kill Hausner, he'll kill him."

"Thanks," said Hausner.

"Got to tell it like it is," said McClure. He produced another wooden match from his inexhaustible supply and put it between his lips.

The Concorde followed the Lear southward. Hausner stayed on the flight deck while the others went back into the passenger cabin. He couldn't face anyone just then. He felt totally responsible, although in fact it was Talman's word of caution and Laskov's minute of indecision that had put the situation beyond saving. It was Laskov's mellowing with age, his sharp military instincts blunted by the promise of peace. It was the anxious voices from the Hawkeye assuring Laskov that the Lear was only a group of businessmen. It was bad French security at the assembly plants. And it was everything else that had happened over the past several thousand years, all coming together under those cloudless skies, thousands of feet above the Mediterranean. But Hausner dismissed these thoughts. He was wishing that he had switched planes with Matti Yadin.

8

General Talman sat in his chair in the middle of the Operations Room at The Citadel. He avoided the eyes of his staff and the technicians around him. They had all seen Concorde 01 disintegrate on the radar screen.

Talman could still see the Lear and Concorde 02. They were approaching the Sinai coast. As long as the E-2D picture remained clear, he could track them. But, eventually, he knew the Lear would force the Concorde to fly at treetop level, and they might be lost in the ground clutter over the land.

Teddy Laskov's flight officer, Danny Lavon, watching on his radar, came to the same conclusion. "They're losing altitude fast, General. We're not going to be able to see them over the Sinai."

Laskov didn't answer.

Talman picked up a scrambler phone and called out every squadron he had. He ordered them to violate Egyptian air space and fly a course that might enable them to spot the Concorde on their radar. One of Talman's aides placed a call to Cairo. The Egyptians would cooperate, but it would be a while before the call could be routed through.

David Becker followed the Lear as it dropped to within a hundred meters of the water. The Sinai coast came up very quickly and they shot over it. Becker lowered the nose cone for better visibility. The desert streaked by below in a blur and the big Concorde bumped wildly in the updrafts. Becker didn't know what Rish had in mind, but he had no doubt that the man was insane. The Lear was relatively easy to maneuver through this low-level turbulence, but it was all Becker could do to keep the huge Concorde straight and level. His indicated air speed was only 250 knots, and he knew that if he went much slower he would stall. Yet the Lear seemed oblivious to his problems. It alternately gained and lost speed as he followed it. The small craft made slight corrections in heading and altitude that were difficult for Becker to follow. He concluded that the Lear's pilot wasn't much of a flyer. Becker had already extended the initial flaps for an extra margin, and he was constantly adjusting the power. Kahn pumped fuel into the number ten midsection tank in an attempt to help keep the aircraft in the proper balance.

Becker's mouth was dry and his heart thumped as he grasped the controls. On his right was the Suez Canal, below him the Mitla Pass. To his front, the ground was rising quickly. His sea level altimeter read 330 meters or 1,100 feet, but he could see that he was still no more than the same 100 meters above the ground that he had been when he crossed the coast. In the distance, he could make out the hazy brown peaks of the southern Sinai range that he knew were 800 meters high. He wondered if the pilot of the Lear understood that they should begin climbing now if they didn't want to meet those mountains.

Hess looked at Becker. "Dave, this guy is going to kill us."

Becker turned up the radio volume, but all he could hear was the jamming device. "Son-of-a-bitch!" He screamed into his headset. "Rish! Lear! We can't hold this altitude! You are the dumbest son-of-a-bitch who ever sat in a cockpit!" The jamming continued and he turned down the volume. "Bastard!"

Peter Kahn called out from the flight engineer's station. "Captain, we're burning 585 kilograms of fuel a minute."

"How much flight time do we have left?"

"Less than two and a half hours."

Becker looked at his watch. It was a little after four. If Rish was planning another Entebbe, they would never make it. "Well, if I knew where the bastard was leading us, I'd know if we should be scared shitless or not." Becker cursed his bad luck. Two more takeoffs and three more landings. Now, it looked like only one more landing and no more takeoffs.

The Lear banked sharply to the left and Becker followed, but his turn was not as steep as the Lear's and he wound up to the right of it when he came out of the turn. He quickly corrected and got behind it again. He asked Kahn to pass him the field glasses. He looked at the Lear, which was now about a thousand meters to the front of him. He could see the plexiglas observation bubble clearly. Someone was staring back at him with field glasses. "Sons-of-bitches." He put down the glasses. He waited for the imps in his head to start laughing at him. But they were not there. He breathed deeply. He felt strangely calm, more assured than he had felt in a very long time. Was this the way it was when you knew it was all over?

Hausner, who had been sitting quietly in the jump seat, looked up. "What are the chances of our people tracking us on radar?"

Hess looked over his shoulder. "At this altitude, over land, just about zero. The E-2D has a computer thing of some kind that can sort out images from the ground clutter, but we've been over Egypt for some time and I don't think he would follow."

"How about the Egyptians?"

Hess shook his head. "They have those Barlock ground radar units from the Russians that can see low-flying craft, but we're behind Henry Kissinger's line now. The Egyptian radar is pointed east toward the Israeli lines. We've probably been spotted visually from the ground, but by the time the Egyptians figure out what the hell is going on we'll be over the Red Sea if we hold this course. They can't help us, anyway, even if they wanted to. Right?"

"I was thinking of Laskov's offer to send a missile out," said Hausner. "Would we go for that if he still has us on his radar?"

Becker spoke as he held the plane steady. "*If* he has us on his radar, and *if* we're still airborne after dusk, I might consider it. This time of day, it's not too hard to see a missile's vapor trail. Electronic detonator signals go faster than missiles." Becker worked the rudder pedals as the Concorde's trail yawed left and right. "But we're damn close to the Lear. On a radar screen we look very, very close. It would have to be one hell of a shot to hit him instead of us."

Hausner stood up. "I'm going to take a look at that pressure bulkhead."

"Go ahead," said Becker. "But I've already thought of that. There's no way to get back there from here—as you know. But you're welcome to climb out on the tail if you'd like." Becker regretted the remark immediately, but his nerves were becoming more frayed with each minute of flight.

Hausner walked out of the cockpit. He began the long walk down the aisle. No one spoke to him. Little Yaakov Leiber stared at him through tear-filled eyes. The men who had been at the security meeting turned away from him.

Miriam Bernstein touched his arm as he went by, but he ignored it. He tapped two of his men on the shoulder as he walked by, and they got up and followed him.

Hausner entered the rear galley and walked through it into the small baggage compartment where the crew and flight attendants kept their luggage. There were also passengers' jackets and coats on hangers along the wall. He flung aside the clothing and stared at the pressure bulkhead.

Talman listened as each of his ten squadrons over the Sinai reported in to the Operations Room. No visual sighting. No radar sightings. Laskov reported last. "I'm coming into Eilat to refuel. I want fuelers waiting for us on the strip. When I get up again, I'm not coming back down until I find them. I want you to get American tankers on station to refuel us in mid-air next time. I'm going to fly over every inch of this area until I find them. The pilots and flight officers will take turns sleeping and flying."

Talman shook his head. "Wait one, Gabriel." He looked at his illuminated situation map. With every minute that passed, the extent of the air space in which the Concorde could conceivably be increased geometrically. He looked at the concentric circles on his map that encompassed the last spot where they were sighted, over the coast. They had been flying for a half an hour since they were last seen, at a speed of about 500 kilometers per hour. They could have headed off in any direction after that. The radius of the last concentric circle was 250 kilometers, if he assumed that last speed. He punched the information into a computer and read the digital display. The air space to be searched was already 196,350 square kilometers, without taking into account altitudes from 150 meters up to 8 kilometers. Every minute of flight time would increase the number of square kilometers and cubic kilometers. He pushed his radio button. "Gabriel, they could be heading for Lod, for all we know. Come home. We'll know where they are soon enough. We've violated enough foreign air space for one day. So far, the Egyptians have been very patient. But now they want us out. They promised to send aircraft up to look. Don't push, Gabriel. That's what the hijackers want and that's what we're trying to avoid. Come back to the barn, old man." He paused. "That's an order."

Laskov gave a crisp acknowledgment.

Talman sighed and called in the rest of his squadrons. What he didn't say over the unsecured air waves was that American satellites were already trying to spot the Concorde. Also, American Lockheed SR-71 reconnaissance craft, successors to the U-2, were already in the troposphere, flying at Mach 3, photographing the entire Sinai Peninsula. The satellite and SR-71 information would take days to be interpreted. It was a long shot, but it was better than doing nothing. Talman suspected, also, that Russian satellites and Mandrakes were doing the same thing. He wondered if the Russians would give Tel Aviv a call if they had any luck. His last ace in the hole was electronic eavesdropping. The powerful electronic ears of both the American National Security Agency and Israeli Intelligence might eventually vector in on the sound of the broad bank jamming device. In almost every country of the world, men and women, paid agents, sat in the upper levels of their houses and took shifts listening and recording every radio transmission that was broadcast in their vicinity. Eventually, one of these people might pick up the sound of the airborne broad band transmitter that they were instructed to listen for. But Talman knew that the Lear, so close to the Concorde, would be transmitting a very weak signal. The chances of picking it up were small, though not impossible.

Talman was satisfied that he had done everything that could be done, for the moment. He picked up the telephone and called the Prime Minister. He gave a situation report, then turned in his resignation. He hung up before he received a reply. He got up from his chair, walked over to his Deputy Chief of Operations, General Hur, and spoke to him for a moment. Then he took his hat and walked out of the Operations Room. Everyone watched quietly as the door shut behind him.

The Concorde climbed in slow stages over the mountains of the Sinai. Becker could see that the Lear wanted to keep within 150 meters of the ground, but the sudden rises and falls in the land made for a sickening roller coaster ride. Several of the passengers were already ill.

Mount Sinai rose up in front of them and the Lear skipped over the top with barely fifty meters to spare. Becker pushed forward on the throttles and cleared the peak. His ground altimeter bounced wildly between fifty and a hundred meters as the huge delta wings were buffeted by updrafts. He'd had enough. He pushed the throttles forward again and began to climb over the Lear. The Lear suddenly accelerated and rose up directly in front of him. Becker chopped back on the throttles and the Concorde shuddered as it approached a stall. He quickly moved the throttles forward once more until he got well above stall speed, then held it steady.

"That was too close," commented Hess. His voice was a little shaky. "I guess he means for us to follow, no matter how hard we have to work at it. He must know what a terrific pilot you are, Dave."

Becker wiped the cold sweat from his forehead. The Lear descended to its previous altitude and reduced its speed again, and again Becker fell in behind him. He felt like an obedient child following a truant officer to some undisclosed place of punishment, and the feeling was humiliating. He knew that Rish was prepared to cause a mid-air collision if things didn't go exactly his way. Becker's hands shook from rage more than from fear.

Hausner's men were stripping away the plastic laminate from the steel bulkhead with their commando knives. Hausner watched as the steel wall was revealed, piece by piece. There was no possible way to get through it. "Any good ideas?"

One of his men, Nathan Brin, steadied himself on the bouncing floor and looked up. "How about a desperate idea?"

"Let's hear it."

The young man rose and spoke quickly. "We can take the powder from our rounds and a container from the galley and make a shapecharge, put an electric wire to it, and blow a hole in the bulkhead. With a few coat hangers and a flashlight we can snag the wire that leads to the bomb and pull it off."

Hausner turned to the other man, Moshe Kaplan. "Kaplan, is this the kind of man I'm hiring these days?"

Brin turned red. "What's wrong with that idea?" he demanded.

"It's dangerous. And what makes you think there is a wire instead of a battery?"

Brin thought. "There must be an aircraft power source to the radio receiver and to the detonator. *Something* detonated the bomb on 01 and it wasn't a battery planted over a year ago."

Hausner nodded. "All right, if it is a wire, then it must be connected to something with a constant and stable voltage. Something like the tail navigation light." He thought a moment, then rushed out of the baggage room and back up the aisle toward the flight deck.

Becker turned around as he heard Hausner enter the cockpit. "Any luck?"

"Listen, the power source for this radio and detonator might be the tail navigation light. Turn it off."

Becker considered. He remembered that Rish had made a point of telling them to leave their navigation lights on. All aircraft always flew with them on, anyway. Why emphasize it? "There are other power sources back there. All the hydraulics in the tail are also electrically activated and monitored, including my tail bumper wheel and the rudder. I can certainly shut off the tail navigation light and I can even cut off the power to my tail bumper wheel, but I can't shut off the rudder. I need it to fly."

Kahn spoke up from the flight engineer console. "I thought of all that, too. There's a good chance that the power source *is* the tail navigation light. But any radio-controlled bomb would have a battery back-up, and the battery would get a steady trickle charge from one of those sources in the tail. Even if it's been in place for years, the radio battery is fully charged every time we start our engines. But I may be wrong. I can shut off the tail navigation light and bumper wheel assembly, and we can fly away from here. Maybe we'll be blown up. Maybe we won't. Anybody want to try it?"

Nobody did.

Hausner sat in the jump seat and lit a cigarette. The momentary elation was gone. "Maybe we could lift a section of the cabin floor and then we could also lift the armor mesh and insulation and stamp through the aluminum roof of the baggage compartment. In the baggage compartment it might be easier to get through the bulkhead into the tail."

Becker shook his head again. He didn't like people making holes in his plane and burrowing around in it. "You know the baggage compartment is pressurized. The bulkhead down there is just as thick as the one in the cabin. Even if you could get through—I don't want any holes. No going through floors. I can't risk it. Too many wires."

Hausner stood up and forced a smile. "Then I don't suppose you'd like the idea of using cartridge powder to blow a hole in the pressure bulkhead?"

Becker laughed in spite of the situation. "Sorry." He knew that Hausner was a man who would rather die than face life after what had happened here, unless he could personally save the situation. He also knew that Hausner was a man under sentence of death, anyway. He couldn't trust his judgment any longer. "Mr. Hausner, thank you for what you're trying to do. But as Captain of this aircraft I have to veto any ideas that would endanger this craft or the people on it. As long as we're airborne, I'm in command. Not you, not Burg, not the Foreign Minister. Me." He glanced over his shoulder. "Look, Jacob, I know what you're going through, but just take it easy. We have about two hours of flying time left. Let's see what happens."

Hausner nodded. "All right." He left the flight deck.

9

The Concorde passed over the tip of the Sinai Peninsula and headed toward the Red Sea, following the Lear as it banked sharply left and headed toward Saudi Arabia. Becker was curious about where they were going, but their destination seemed less and less important.

With its nose dropped and its tail and flaps down, the Concorde looked more than ever like a big, forlorn seabird that wanted to land on the water below, but, for some reason, could not. Becker looked at the whitecaps on the Red Sea until he was mesmerized by them.

"Coast coming up, Dave."

The Saudi Arabian shoreline slid by quickly. The ground was flat as far as he could see. He breathed a sigh of relief. "It won't be so bad now."

Hess glanced over at him. "That's one way of looking at it. Want me to take the wheel for a while?"

Becker looked at him. He wondered if Hess could fly a formation with the Concorde under these conditions. He decided to be blunt. "Can you fly it?"

"I can fly the crate it came in."

Becker smiled and let go of the controls. He fished in his pocket for a cigarette. He almost felt good. If ever a pilot had reason to lose his nerve, the flight over the Sinai was it. No matter what happened now, he was comforted by the thought that this, his last flight, had been his best.

The Lear picked up speed quickly and was doing about 800 kilometers per hour. Hess fought to keep the Concorde at 150 meters above the ground.

Ahead, Becker could see a few Bedouins on camels, staring at them. The sinking sun cast the huge delta shadow in front of the aircraft, over the Bedouins. The camels spooked and bolted clumsily as it passed. He drew on his cigarette. Now, over the flatlands, the flight looked safe enough, but Becker knew that, with the increased speed and the 150-meter altitude, any small dip in the nose would send them screaming into the ground before there was a chance to correct.

Peter Kahn looked up from his instruments. "One hour and fifty minutes fuel remaining, skipper."

Dobkin came onto the flight deck. He put this hand on Becker's shoulder. "How is it going?"

"All right. Any thoughts?"

Dobkin nodded. "We had a little meeting back there."

"And?"

"Well . . . we have concluded that they are very clever fellows. First of all, they didn't go into a long political harangue, like these chaps usually do, so we don't even know who they are, except that they're probably Palestinians. If Hausner hadn't recognized Rish's voice, we wouldn't even know that. This all makes it very hard for our intelligence people to begin work on this."

"Not good," said Becker.

"Not good at all," agreed Dobkin. "They further changed their *modus operandi* by jamming our radios. That can only mean that we're going to a secret destination. This time, there won't be a thousand newsmen at an international airport when we land. There will be no Entebbe rescue, either, because no one will know where we are. We're going to be held incommunicado."

Becker had come to similar conclusions. He had suspected he'd be putting the Concorde down in the desert, and now he was sure of it. He hoped, at least, it would be a hard-packed airstrip like Dawson's Field.

Dobkin seemed to be reading his thoughts. "Can you put it down anywhere?"

"Anywhere but a swine yard. No problem. Don't worry about it."

"I'll try not to."

Hausner took a seat next to Miriam Bernstein. They spoke quietly for a while. They both shared a sense of guilt that they were trying to relieve by speaking to each other. A steward, Daniel Jacoby, had taken charge of the flight attendants and was giving instructions to serve a meal and drinks, whether anyone wanted them or not. Hausner ordered a double Scotch. He stirred his drink. "I can't believe I could have overlooked that."

Miriam Bernstein took a sip from his drink. "They would have found another way to do it."

"Whatever way they found, I would have been responsible."

"I keep thinking about Teddy . . . General Laskov. He fell into the same trap we all did. I know he would have reacted differently if I hadn't . . ."

"I can't believe those sons-of-bitches really pulled this off."

"Jacob . . . I heard someone saying that this Rish knows you. He threatened—"

"I should have shot the son-of-a-bitch when I had him."

"Did he say, on the radio, that he was going—"

"Don't listen to rumors. There will be a lot of those in the days ahead."

She put her hand on his arm. "Remember when you asked me . . . if I would come out to your place . . ."

Hausner laughed. "Don't start saying things you'll be sorry for when we're back in Tel Aviv. I might hold you to it."

She smiled. "I never really understood you. I've always admired you . . . but you frighten people."

"I don't want any deathbed confessions. We are not quite ready for that yet."

"All right."

They spoke about other things. Dinner came, but neither of them could eat.

Abdel Majid Jabari spoke to Ibrahim Ali Arif, the other Arab delegate on board. He spoke in a rapid, soft, susurrant Arabic. "This is a tragedy beyond measure."

Arif ate rapidly as he spoke. "I feel very awkward at this moment. I feel like Daniel in the lions' den."

Jabari watched as the portly man stuffed food into his mouth. "Don't always think of your own discomfort, my friend. This tragedy transcends that." He lit a cigarette. "I feel worse for the Jews who staked their reputations and careers on Arab goodwill."

"I still feel personally uncomfortable. And I don't believe in blood guilt. Uncomfortable, yes—guilty, no. Guilt is a Jewish emotion." He looked at Jabari's untouched tray. "Do you mind?" He placed it over his own tray.

Jabari sipped his arak. "Anyway, the lions' den is out *there*," he pointed in the direction of the Lear. "These are our countrymen in here. You must be able to look them in the eye—without discomfort. Have no doubts that we will share their fate."

Arif laughed between bites. "We should be so lucky, my friend. Even if *they* are eventually released, you know very well that *we* are marked for special attention. This is the lions' den and that is the lions' den. We are men who have no country, no people, no haven. We are doomed men. I think I could eat another meal. Steward!"

The Lear turned northward and the Concorde followed. They left Saudi Arabia and flew into Iraq. The sun was low on the horizon and there were long purple shadows over the land. Becker began to become more worried. "Flight time?"

"Half an hour," answered Kahn.

One of the things that had always fascinated Becker about the Middle East was the absence of any real dusk. One minute it was light, and the next it was dark. Landing on something other than an airfield in the daylight was bad; landing at night could be a disaster. "What's going to run out first, Peter?"

Kahn knew what he meant. He already had a chart book open. "Sun sets officially at 6:16 around here. End-of-evening nautical twilight is five minutes later. It is now 6:01. We have twenty minutes of usable light and twenty-nine minutes of fuel. Approximately."

Becker could see the moon above the darkening horizon in front of him. A few stars showed in the dark edge of night. To the north, out his left windshield, Polaris was rising. Below, the shadows became longer and changed from purple to black. The desert was incredibly beautiful, thought Becker.

Hess called out to him. "Look."

Becker looked out the front windshield. In the distance, the ground sloped downward and he could make out a strip of lush green land. A river wound its way through clusters of date palms. Beyond the river, which was almost below him now, he could see another large meandering river. The Tigris and Euphrates. Beyond the Tigris, the mountains of Iran rose up over a thousand meters. His altimeter showed that the land had dropped from 180 meters above sea level to nearly sea level. They were indicating nearly 300 meters above the ground now and the Lear made no move to descend to its previous 150 meters.

"This has to be the end of the line," said Hess.

Becker looked down at the land between the rivers. Mesopotamia. The Fertile Crescent. Cradle of civilization. After the expanse of stark brown desert, it was a relief to see it. He wondered if they might fly north to Baghdad. Subconsciously, he was looking for the vapor trail of Laskov's missile. He put out his cigarette and turned to Hess. "I'll take it from here."

The Lear began a wide left-hand circle and Becker followed. The Lear started to lose altitude and Becker knew they weren't going on to Baghdad.

Hess hit the seat-belt and smoking-light signals. He took the PA microphone. "We are making a landing approach. Please remain seated. No smoking."

"Tell them, thank you for flying El Al," said Becker.

"Not funny," said Kahn.

"Fuel?" said Becker.

"Technically empty," said Kahn.

"Never mind the technical." After all the computers and electronics there was still that other thing that fliers called by many names.

Kahn hesitated. "Maybe 2,000 kilograms."

Becker nodded. That was less than five minutes' flight time under good conditions. He could make a perfect landing in five minutes if they began soon.

In a bad landing or an aborted landing that necessitated a turn-around, he wouldn't make it. He waited to hear the awful sound of silence as the engines flamed out one by one.

The Lear pulled out of the turn at a 90-degree angle to his circle and began heading due north on a straight descending flight path.

In the distance, Becker could see a straight road running north and south. "I think that's our landing field. He rolled out of his turn and fell in behind the Lear.

Hess extended the landing gear and put down the initial approach flaps. "I've seen better."

The sun was almost gone and the road was barely visible. On both sides of the road, Becker could make out low scrub bushes and uneven terrain. They began their final approach.

Dobkin and Hausner burst into the cabin. Dobkin shouted something to him.

Becker was angry. "Go back to your seats! I'm trying to land this damned thing."

They made no move to leave. "We've taken a vote," said Hausner.

"This is not the Knesset. Be quiet!"

Below, four pair of headlights came on, strung out on either side of the road and partially illuminating it. Someone was waving a high-powered light at what Becker assumed to be the intended threshold of the approach. The Lear flew over the threshold and Becker could see its flaps go down. Becker shook his head to clear the fatigue. He scanned his instruments. They were blurry. He looked up, out the windshield. The lights below bothered his eyes. He knew he could become quickly disoriented in this kind of situation. Pilots had been known to try to land upside down on the Milky Way when they were fatigued, and transferred their eyes from their instruments to visual contact. They could mistake the stars for landing beacons and rivers for runways. He rubbed his eyes.

Hausner stepped behind Becker. "The vote was unanimous. Otherwise we wouldn't consider it."

Becker eased off on the throttle and called to Hess for full flaps. He held the wheel in one hand and the throttles in the other. He tried to line the nose up between the headlights. He kept his eyes on the Lear's navigation lights. "What vote? What the hell are you talking about? I'm making a final approach on the most fucked-up runway I've ever landed at. What do you want?"

Hausner spoke quickly. "The bomb is no good on the ground. Becker! The most it will do is mangle the tail."

"Go on." Becker could see the Lear touch down and bounce. The Concorde passed over the threshold and Becker pulled off more power. The big aircraft began to settle to earth.

"We've voted to fight on the ground," said Hausner. "My men have some weapons. Can you put us down somewhere else?" Hausner was almost shouting.

Becker could feel the cushion of air forming below the big delta wings. He shouted back. "Why didn't you ask me two minutes ago? Trucks and men flashed by on both sides under the delta wings. The road was bad and the aircraft bounced dangerously. About two kilometers ahead, at the point where his rollout should end, was another group of vehicles with their headlights on.

To his left front was a high, gently rising hill that he knew must overlook the Euphrates. Hausner screamed something at him. Becker made a quick decision before he had time to think about it rationally. He pushed the throttles forward and the huge aircraft rose again. He pushed heavily against the control wheel and rudder pedals. The Concorde yawed to the left toward the Lear.

The Lear had taxied off the left side of the road and rested among the groups of vehicles that Becker had seen at the end of his intended rollout. Ahmed Rish watched from where he was standing on the wing of his Lear. At first, he thought that the Concorde had bounced badly and was skidding off the road. Then he noticed the position of the rudder and flaps. He dove into the Lear, shut off the jamming device, and screamed into the radio. "STOP! STOP!" He reached for the radio detonator, as the Concorde came hurtling directly at him, only a few meters from the ground.

The Concorde was doing 180 knots and its landing gear barely cleared the earth. The delta wing provided more of a cushion of air than a conventional straight wing could. Becker aimed at the rising terrain to his left. The low-volume squeal on the radio stopped, and he could hear Rish's voice screaming at him. In fact, he saw the Lear less than fifty meters in front of him, directly in his path. For a wild moment, Becker considered ramming the Lear, but he realized that killing Rish wouldn't save them and hitting the Lear might kill them all at that speed. He had to clear Rish's aircraft.

There was no possibility of using the throttle or afterburners now. If he did, the Concorde would rise, and when the tail went, they would all die. Or if the afterburners used the last of the fuel and the engines flamed out, they would die. He had to keep the aircraft down, but not so low that they would hit the Lear or any other ground obstruction. Becker held his breath as the Concorde shot over the Lear. The landing gear missed the Lear and the Concorde sailed on. Now the ruins of a wall rose up in front of him. He took a chance and pulled back gradually on the wheel. The nose lifted slightly. As he streaked over the wall, he felt the rear bumper wheel hit it. The Concorde shuddered. Becker pulled back on the wheel again, and the nose came up to meet the rising hill. He would have liked to vault over the river, but he knew he had about two seconds before Rish pushed the button.

The Lear bounced wildly against its tie-downs as the Concorde shot over. Swirling debris pummeled the small aircraft and the men and vehicles around it. A huge dust cloud rose up and blinded everyone on the ground. Rish fumbled for the radio detonator, found it, and felt for the buttons.

Becker snapped back the throttles. Rish was still screaming on the radio. The main landing gear touched the side of the hill as the Concorde's nose flared upward. Becker reversed the thrust of the engines. The rear bumper wheel hit and bounced. The nose fell and the nose landing gear hit the ground. The aircraft bounced violently, throwing the men standing behind Becker to the floor. The computerized wheel-braking system alternately applied and released pressure on the wheel brakes. Most of the tires blew out. Then the tail exploded.

Becker shut down all four engines. Hess pulled the fire-extinguishing lever. Kahn shut down all the systems. The Concorde rolled wildly up the incline, sucking debris into its engines with a sickening sound. The engines spooled down, and the only sound left was that of the remaining tires bumping over the rocky slope.

Becker felt the rudder pedals go slack even before he heard the explosion. He knew there were still fuel fumes in the number eleven tank, and he tried to imagine how bad the damage might be. He wondered if the bulkhead had held. A secondary explosion of a full fuel tank would completely destroy the aircraft.

Without the tail and rudder, the aircraft was completely uncontrollable, even on the ground.

Suddenly, the front landing gear collapsed and everyone on the flight deck pitched forward violently. The nose plowed a deep furrow into the ground as the aircraft continued its rollout. Debris turned up by the nose cone began striking the windshield, causing spider-web cracks. Becker instinctively hit a hydraulic switch and the outer protective visor began rising into place over the windshield. He crouched down in his seat and looked up and out of the downward-sloped cockpit. A ruined structure loomed up a hundred yards ahead. Becker braced for the crash. Something flew up and punctured the windshield before the outer visor was fully raised in place. The glass slivers flew into the cockpit and slashed Becker's hand and face. He shouted, "Hold on!" The Concorde slowed, then came to a quiet halt some meters from the structure.

Becker looked up. "Everyone all right?" He looked to his right. Moses Hess lay slumped over the control column, blood pouring from his head. There was a huge hole in the windshield directly in front of him.

Becker shouted behind him. "If you're going to make a fight of it, get the hell out of the airplane!"

Peter Kahn got up and shouted into the cabin. "Evacuate! Flight attendants! Emergency evacuation!"

Yaakov Leiber had unfastened his seat belt even before the aircraft came to a halt. He ran to the forward port door, rotated the handle, and threw the door open. The opening door activated the pressure bottles and inflated the emergency chute tucked under the doorsill. Hausner's six men were the first ones out. The other two stewards were leading the passengers down the aisle toward the chute. The stewardesses opened the two emergency doors next to the seats over the wings. They led the passengers out onto the wings and down to the leading edge of the big deltas. People began jumping off the wings and sliding down the chutes.

Hausner picked himself up from the flight deck and half-ran, half-crawled to the starboard door on the flight deck. He opened it and jumped down before the chute inflated. He was barely on the ground before he started shouting orders to his men. "Down the slope! Move! The bastards will be coming up from the road! Over there! Get out a hundred meters!"

Dobkin followed Hausner out the door. He made a quick appraisal of their situation. They were on high ground, which was good. The area around the aircraft was flat and the ground fell away on all sides. To the east it sloped gently down to the road. To the west it fell off sharply down to the river. He could not see the north and south extremities in the dark. As for weapons, they only had perhaps a half-dozen .22 pistols, one Uzi submachine gun, and one rifle. He knew the Arabs had a lot more than that. He looked up at the tail assembly. It was badly mangled, but that didn't matter any longer. The rear pressure bulkhead must have been blown in because there was baggage strewn in the wake of the Concorde. Toilet kits, shoes, and pieces of clothing lay in the deep furrow like seeds waiting to be covered for the spring planting. The last of the sun died away, and the sky was filled with cold white stars. Dobkin suddenly felt a chill and realized that the *Hamseen* was blowing here. It would be a long, cold night. He wondered if any of them would see the sun rise.

*   *   *

Isaac Burg stood on the tilted delta wing as the other passengers jumped off. He turned and climbed up the fuselage and made his way toward the mangled tail. He braced himself against a twisted longeron and stared down toward the road about half a kilometer away. He could see truck lights bouncing across the uneven slope and the shadows of men as they ran in front of the slow-moving vehicles. He drew his pistol, an American Army Colt .45, and waited.

Jabari and Arif slid down the chute and ran clear of the aircraft, Jabari helping the big Arif as he stumbled. They fell and crawled behind a small rise in the ground. After several seconds, Jabari looked over the top of the hillock. "I don't think it will explode."

Arif panted heavily. He wiped his face. "I can't believe I voted to fight."

Jabari leaned back against the earth. "You said yourself you were doomed anyway. As doomed as Jacob Hausner. Did you hear what was being said before? Hausner slapped Rish when he was in Ramla."

"Bad luck for Hausner. But at least he will die for a reason. I never slapped anyone except my wife, but Rish will cut my throat with as much glee as he cuts Hausner's."

Jabari lit a cigarette. "You are a very self-centered man, Ibrahim."

"When it comes to *my* throat, yes."

Jabari stood up. "Come. Let's see where and in what manner they propose to fight. Perhaps we can help."

Arif remained seated. "I'll sit here. You go ahead." He removed his checkered headdress. "Do I look Jewish now?"

Jabari laughed in spite of himself. "How is your Hebrew?"

"Better than half the members of the Knesset."

"Well, Ibrahim, if the time comes, it's worth a try."

"Avraham . . . Aronson."

Tom Richardson stood at the river side of the slope and looked down at the Euphrates. John McClure walked up behind him and put his foot on a low mound. Richardson could see a revolver in the hand resting across his knee. Richardson rubbed his cold hands together. "This was a bad move."

McClure spit out his match and found another one. "Maybe."

"Look, I don't feel obligated to hang around. There doesn't seem to be anyone on the river bank. Let's go. We could be in Baghdad by this time tomorrow."

McClure looked at him. "How do you know where we are?"

Richardson remained motionless.

"I asked you a question, Colonel."

Richardson forced himself to look into McClure's eyes and hold contact. He said nothing.

McClure let the silence drag out for a few seconds, then raised his revolver. He spun the chambers and noticed Richardson flinch. He spoke softly. "I think I'll stick around."

Richardson eyed the big pistol. "Well, I'm going," he said in a calm voice.

McClure could see several flashlights moving along the river bank. Three football fields away. That was the only way he would ever estimate distance. Three hundred yards. About 270 of those ridiculous meters. "They've already gotten around us." He pointed.

Richardson didn't bother to look. "Could be civilians."

"Could be." McClure raised the revolver, a big Ruger .357 Magnum, with both hands and fired two shots at the lights. The shots were answered by a burst of automatic weapon fire. Both men ducked as green tracer rounds streaked up at them. McClure reloaded. "Settle back and relax. We might be here a long time."

Nathan Brin rested the M-14 on a rock. He turned on the battery-powered starlight scope and looked across the landscape. The scope gave everything an eerie green color. He twirled the knobs until the image was clear. He saw that they were among the ruins of a city. It all looked very lunar to Brin. All except the twenty or so Arabs walking nonchalantly up the slope from the direction of the road. A few hundred meters behind them, the trucks had stopped at the beginning of the slope. The Arabs were about 200 meters away now. He placed the cross hairs over the heart of the man in front. The man was Ahmed Rish, but Brin didn't recognize him. He squeezed the trigger slightly, then remembered his training and swung the rifle to the last man in the file. He squeezed back harder on the trigger. The silencer-flash suppressor spit, and the only sound was the operating rod working back and forth. The man dropped silently. The file, oblivious of the dead man lying behind them, continued up the slope.

Brin swung the rifle to the man who was now the last in line. He pulled the trigger again. Again, the only sound was the metallic slamming of the bolt and operating rod. The man fell. Brin smiled. He was enjoying himself, despite all his upbringing to the contrary. He swung the rifle and fired again. The third man fell but apparently let out a sound. Suddenly, the Arabs scattered among the rocks. Brin straightened up and moved behind the rock. He lit a cigarette. He'd done it. For better or worse, they were committed to the fight. He rather enjoyed the prospect. He heard a noise behind him and swung the rifle around. Hausner was staring at him. Brin smiled. "All right?"

Hausner nodded. "All right."

Becker stared out into the dark night. "Where the hell are we?"

Peter Kahn had noted the coordinates on the Inertial Navigation System readout before the impact. He was reading an air chart by the lights of the emergency power system. "Good question."

Becker unstrapped his seat belt and pulled himself out of his seat. He took Hess's head in his hands. His skull had been crushed by a large brick that lay now in his lap. There was no sign of life. He let the head fall gently and wiped his bloody hands on his white shirt. He turned to Kahn. "He's dead, Peter."

Kahn nodded.

Becker wiped his sweating face. "Well, get back to work. Where the hell are we?"

Kahn looked down at the chart again and made a mark along a protractor. He looked up. "Babylon. We are by the rivers of Babylon."

Becker placed his hand on Kahn's shoulder and leaned over the map. He nodded. " 'Yea,' " he said, " 'yea, we wept when we remembered Zion.' "

Book II

BABYLON
THE WATCHTOWERS

By the rivers of Babylon, there we sat down,
yea, we wept, when we remembered Zion.
We hanged our harps upon the willows in the midst thereof.
For there they that carried us away captive required of us a song;
and they that wasted us required of us mirth, saying,
Sing us one of the songs of Zion.
How shall we sing the Lord's song in a strange land?

If I forget thee, O Jerusalem,
let my right hand forget her cunning.
If I do not remember thee,
let my tongue cleave to the roof of my mouth;
if I prefer not Jerusalem above my chief joy.

Psalms 137:1–6

And Babylon, the glory of kingdoms,
the beauty of the Chaldees' excellency,
shall be as when God overthrew Sodom and Gomorrah.
It shall never be inhabited,
neither shall it be dwelt in from generation to generation:
neither shall the Arabian pitch tent there;
neither shall the shepherds make their fold there.
But wild beasts of the desert shall lie there;
and their houses shall be full of doleful creatures;
and owls shall dwell there,
and satyrs shall dance there.
And the wild beasts of the islands shall cry in their desolate houses,
and dragons in their pleasant palaces:
and her time is near to come,
and her days shall not be prolonged.

Isaiah 13:19–25

10

There was a stillness on the hilltop, broken only by the ticking sounds made by the cooling of the four Rolls-Royce Olympus engines. The great white aircraft, with its front landing gear collapsed and its nose in the dirt, resembled some sort of proud creature brought to its knees. For a moment time seemed to falter, then a nightbird chirped tentatively, and all the other nocturnal creatures resumed their sounds.

Jacob Hausner knew that everything—their lives, their futures, and perhaps the future of their nation—depended on what happened in the next few minutes. A determined assault by the Palestinians right then would carry the hill, and that would be the end of all their brave talk of defense. He looked around. In the weak light he could see people moving aimlessly around the Concorde. Some, he suspected, were still in shock from the crash. Now that the time had come, no one knew what to do. The actors were willing, but they lacked a script. Hausner decided to write one on the spot, but he wished he had Dobkin and Burg nearby to coauthor it with him.

Hausner took the M-14 from Brin and looked down the slope through the telescopic lens. The three Arabs lay among the rocks where they had fallen. Hausner could see at least two AK-47 automatic rifles on the ground. If he could get those, it would put more substance behind their bluff.

He turned to Brin. "I'm going down there to retrieve those weapons. Keep me covered." He handed him the M-14 and drew his Smith & Wesson .22.

One of Hausner's other security men, Moshe Kaplan, saw him start down the hill and caught up with him. "Deserting already?"

Hausner whispered. "If you're coming along, keep low and keep quiet." He noticed that Kaplan's .22 had a silencer on it.

They made their way in short rushes from rock to rock. One man would cover and the other would move. Hausner noticed that what he took to be rocks were actually huge pieces of dried clay and earth that had apparently broken off and fallen from the face of the hill. His movements caused other hardened slabs to break loose and slide downward. It would be difficult for an enemy to attack upward if they had to duck bullets as they moved through shifting clay and sand.

From the crest of the hill, Brin watched through the starlight scope. A half-kilometer farther down the hill, he could see the Palestinians regrouping near the trucks. As he watched, he could tell by their motions that they were working themselves into a frenzy. Brin knew their style. If they were surprised, as this group had been, they would generally flee. Then would come the embarrassment and the recriminations. Then the working up of rage and courage that he was observing now. When they were sufficiently aroused, they would act, and they could be very resolute when they did. In fact, as he watched, a group of about twenty started up the hill again. Someone took something from a truck. Three rolled up litters. They were coming back for the bodies.

Hausner could not see much in the dark. He tried to maintain a straight line from where he had started. The bodies should be near a geological formation that looked like a ship's sail. He scanned the outlines of the land, but he knew it must look different from down here. He used the approved method of night vision—looking sideways out of the corners of the eyes as the head moved in short motions. He was becoming disoriented in the strange terrain.

As he moved down the slope, he wondered what they were doing back at the airplane. He hoped Brin had let everyone with guns know he was downhill. He thought about what kind of firepower they could muster. There were his five men still on the hill. They each had their own Smith & Wesson .22. In addition, Brin had the M-14 and someone else, probably Joshua Rubin, had the 9mm Uzi submachine gun. He suspected that there were a lot of other handguns on board as well. But handguns were not accurate beyond twenty meters or so. The Uzi and the M-14 were their only hope, but once the ammunition ran out, that would be it. The key lay in recovering those AK-47's. If there was enough ammunition, they could hold out for a day or so on the hill. But Hausner doubted now if he could find the bodies among these jagged, eroded earth formations.

Hausner heard a sound and stopped in his tracks. Kaplan froze against a rock. They heard it again. A low wailing voice, calling in Arabic. "I am over here," said the voice. "Over here."

Hausner responded in whispered Arabic that he hoped wouldn't betray his accent. "I'm coming," he said. "Coming."

"I am *here,*" said the voice. "I am hurt."

"I'm coming," repeated Hausner.

He crawled through a shallow gully, then looked up across an open space dominated by the formation that looked like the sail of a ship. Three bodies lay in the light of the newly risen moon. One of them had an AK-47 cradled in his arms. Hausner cursed under his breath.

Kaplan came up beside him and whispered in his ear. "Let me take him. I've got a silencer."

Hausner shook his head. "Too far." If Kaplan didn't kill him with the first round, the bullet might make a sound as it struck, and then there would be AK-47 rounds splattering all over the place. "I'll take him."

Hausner removed his tie and suit jacket. He pulled his blue shirt out from his pants and opened a few buttons at the top. He ripped the white silk lining out of the jacket and tied it on his head in what he hoped would pass for a *kheffiyah*. He began to crawl out to the wounded Arab.

Kaplan cocked his pistol and crouched in a moon shadow.

Brin watched the Palestinians come up the hill. They were less than a hundred meters from the last place he had seen Hausner and Kaplan. The Palestinians were not offering good targets this time. They were practicing cover and concealment techniques like trained infantrymen. Brin swung the rifle and scanned for Hausner. He saw a man crawling over a bare spot between the piles of earth. A man with a dark *kheffiyah*.

Hausner whispered. "I'm here. I'm here."
The wounded Arab squinted into the darkness.
Hausner moved faster toward him.

Brin watched through the scope as the Arab in the slightly irregular *kheffiyah* traveled across the ground like a lizard. He noticed now the wounded Arab whom the crawling man was approaching. The wounded man must be the one he had hit before, the one who had made the sound that alerted the others. He swung the rifle and put his cross hairs on the crawling man. He began squeezing on the trigger. He hesitated. There was something dishonorable about shooting a man who was risking his life to help a wounded comrade. Yet he could see no alternative. He compromised. He would shoot the crawling man, but he wouldn't hit the wounded one again. Why that convoluted decision should satisfy the god or gods of war that put men in these situations, he didn't know. He only knew that it was important that you try to play the game fairly. He scanned the slope again quickly. He couldn't see Hausner or Kaplan. He did see the advancing Arabs who were less than fifty meters from the wounded man and his crawling comrade. But they still didn't present good targets in the terrain they were moving in. Brin aimed at the crawling man in the open.

Hausner whispered. "It's all right." He could hear the sounds of men rushing up the slope.
The wounded Arab picked himself up on one elbow. He forced a smile as Hausner came near. He looked at Hausner from a distance of less than a meter. He let out a surprised sound and raised his rifle. Hausner leaped at him.
Brin eased off on the trigger.
The Arab yelled again. Hausner's hand found a half brick in the dust. He gripped it and swung at the Arab, catching him full in the face.
Kaplan dashed across the open space. He located the two dead Arabs and collected their automatic rifles and several banana clips of ammunition for each. Hausner took the wounded man's rifle and ammunition.
Brin waited until the lead Arab was into the clear area, then fired. The silencer coughed gently. The man pitched backwards.
Hausner and Kaplan looked toward where they heard the noise of the falling man. They could see the Arabs now, coming over and around the piles of earth and clay not twenty meters away.
Brin fired again, and the Arabs scattered as another of them fell.
Hausner hefted the wounded Arab onto his back and passed the rifle and ammunition to Kaplan. They began running up the hill under their heavy burdens. They wove around ridges of earth and then through erosion gullies, bent

down below the hard crust of the slope. Automatic fire suddenly burst out behind them. Earth, clay, and brick splinters flew up around them.

Kaplan could never forget that distinctive, hollow popping sound that an AK-47 makes, like a string of Chinese firecrackers. His blood ran cold as he heard the whistling go by his ears. Several times he thought he was hit, but it was only flying earth or ricochets, hot but spent. "Put him down!" he yelled at Hausner. They weren't going to make it with the Arab.

"No," panted Hausner. "Need him. Go on ahead."

"My ass!" Kaplan turned and leveled one of the AK-47's. He fired off a complete banana clip of thirty rounds. From the crest of the hill, he could hear the pathetic sounds of Smith & Wesson .22's. Then came the more authoritative sound of the Uzi submachine gun. He turned and caught up to Hausner. They were less than fifty meters from the crest now. Several men ran down the hill. Someone took the Arab from Hausner. Kaplan stumbled and lay, sweating and exhausted, on the ground. Someone helped him up. They ran a zigzag course as the earth kicked up around them. Near the crest of the hill, Kaplan could see Brin slowly aiming and firing with that terrible silent gun. Kaplan felt something hit him. Not a clay chip or a ricochet this time, but something searing and hot. He lost consciousness.

Hausner lay on the ground fighting for air. He put his arms out to each side and felt that he was on level ground. He'd made it. He could hear Dobkin calmly giving orders concerning the placement of the three AK-47's. He heard the gunfire coming up the slope and then the answering fire from their own positions. As soon as the three AK-47's cut in, the Arab fire stopped abruptly. Then all the firing stopped, and as the reports died away there was an eerie silence on the hill.

Dobkin leaned over Hausner. "That was damned foolish, Jacob. But they won't try that again for a while."

"Kaplan?"

Dobkin crouched down beside him. "Hit. But not bad. In the butt."

Hausner sat up. "He called that shot. Last thing he said to me was 'my ass.' Where is he?"

Dobkin pushed him down with one big hand. "Get your breath first. Don't want you having a heart attack."

The big man blotted out Hausner's whole view of the sky. "All right." He felt foolish lying on the ground. "Did we hit any? Take any weapons?"

"We hit a few. But they didn't make the same mistake again. They took their wounded and all the weapons. They've left a few dead, though."

"My prisoner?"

"Alive."

"Talking?"

"He will."

Hausner nodded. "I'd like to get up and check on my men."

Dobkin stared at him. "All right. Easy now."

"Right." Hausner got up slowly. He looked around. "Anyone else hurt?"

"Moses Hess is dead."

Hausner remembered the shattered windshield. "Anyone else?"

"A few people got banged up in the landing. Becker and Hess did an unbelievable job."

"Yes." Hausner took a few steps toward Brin, who was still looking through the starlight scope. Brin's position was the key defensive terrain feature on the east slope. It was a sort of promontory of earth that jutted out from the side of the hill. There was a low ridge of earth around it that would have to be heightened and thickened. It looked like a balcony and was a perfect sniper's perch. Hausner put his foot up on the earth bank and looked out over the dark countryside, then back to Dobkin. "Where are we?"

"Babylon."

"Be serious."

"Babylon."

Hausner was quiet for a moment. "You mean as in 'Babylon is fallen, is fallen'? Or 'By the rivers of Babylon'?"

"That's the place."

Hausner's senses reeled. A few short hours ago he had been in a comfortable, modern aircraft flying to New York City. Now he was crawling in the dust of Babylon. It was surreal. Dobkin might as well have said Mars. "Babylon," he said aloud. It was one of those evocative names in the lexicon of world geography. A name that was more than just a name. A place that was more than just a place. Like Hiroshima or Normandy. Camelot or Shangri-La. Auschwitz or Masada. Jerusalem or Armaggedon. "Why?"

Dobkin shrugged. "Who knows? Some sort of joke on Rish's part, I suppose. The Babylonian Captivity and all that."

"Odd sense of humor."

"Well, not a joke maybe, but some sort of historical—"

"I understand." Hausner turned to Brin. "You hear that, Nathan? You're a Babylonian captive. What do you think of that?"

Brin lit a cigarette cupped in his hand. "Captive, hell! At sunrise I am personally going down to those sons-of-bitches and give them an ultimatum to surrender."

Hausner laughed and slapped him on the back. He turned to Dobkin. "You see? My men are ready to take on these bastards, General."

Dobkin had little patience with paramilitary outfits like police and security men. He just grunted.

"What's our position?" asked Hausner. "Tactically, I mean."

"It's a little early to tell. I made a quick recon of this hill while you were doing your John Wayne."

"And?"

"Well, this is an elevation of about seventy meters. I suspect that it's not a natural hill at all, but a tell, a mound covering a structure. You can see it's fairly flat on the top like a table mesa—like Masada." The analogy was inevitable. "I think this used to be the citadel on the northern city wall. It's covered with drifting dust, but if it were excavated, you'd see walls and towers. That small hillock over there was probably the top of a tower. And this promontory where Brin is standing was a tower coming out of the side of the wall."

Hausner looked at him. "You know this place." It was more a statement than a question. "How?"

"From maps and models. I never thought I'd ever get to see it. It's a Jewish archeologist's dream." He smiled.

Hausner stared at him through the dark. "I'm really happy for you, General. I must remember to congratulate El Al for taking advantage of an unexpected situation and arranging this excursion. Maybe we'll put it on our regular schedule. Crash and all."

"Take it easy, Jacob."

Hausner let the silence drag out, then let out a long breath. "All right. Can we defend this place?"

Dobkin ran his hand through his hair. "I . . . I think so." He paused. "It's an oblong-shaped mound, about the size and configuration of a standard race track. It runs north and south along the bank of the Euphrates. The river is at full flood this time of year and the waters come up to the western slope of this mound. The Arabs have put some men down by the flood bank. The American, McClure, took a few pot shots at them before. He has some sort of big cowboy six-shooter. Colonel Richardson is with him."

"They are the only ones there?"

"I have lots of sentries posted along the crest, but McClure is the only one with a gun. It's an open, exposed slope and very steep. It was, I think, the river wall of the citadel about 2,500 years ago. What we call in military engineering a glacis. I don't think we can expect a serious attack from there now that we've shown we're watching it and can shoot back."

Hausner lit a cigarette. "How about this side of the hill?"

"That's the problem. From north to south it's about half a kilometer. The slope is gradual down to the road and plain. There are erosion gullies and earth formations in some areas, as you well know. Those are the most likely areas of approach. In other places it's very exposed with clear fields of fire for us. I don't think we could expect an attack from those areas. I've placed the three AK-47's to cover those most likely avenues of approach. Three of your men are handling them. Another of your men, Joshua Rubin, has the Uzi, and Brin here has the 14. Your men have passed their .22's to passengers whom I've designated, and they're supplementing this defensive perimeter. I'm going to place combination observation posts and listening posts further down the slope." He took a deep breath. "Still, it's a thin line. If it weren't for the AK's, I'd have to recommend asking for terms."

Hausner took a long pull from Brin's cigarette and handed it back. He looked to Dobkin. "Do you think they'll attack again tonight?"

"Any military commander worthy of the name would. The longer they wait, the more organized the defense becomes. A half-hour ago the odds against us were overwhelming. Now, we might just make it through the night."

"They wouldn't attack at daylight, would they?"

"I wouldn't."

"Is Becker sending out an SOS?"

"He's operating the radios on batteries. Let's get back to the Concorde. The Foreign Minister wants you at a meeting."

"Even here," said Hausner wryly.

Brin was scanning through the starlight scope. Every few minutes he would shut it off to save the batteries and rest his eyes. Hausner patted him on the shoulder. "I'll have someone relieve you later."

"He's going to have to be very big to take my rifle away."

Hausner smiled. "Have it your way." He followed after Dobkin.

11

T he Concorde sat near the middle of the flattened mound. At the north and south extremities of the oblong-shaped mound were the ruins of the river walls that now formed ramps leading up to the mound. It was the southern ramp that the Concorde had taken to the top. Hausner and Dobkin intersected the plowed furrow made by the Concorde's nose cone and walked in it toward the aircraft. Hausner had trouble keeping up with the big man. "Who's in charge?"

Dobkin didn't respond.

"Let's get down to it now, General. Chain of command. You understand that. There can only be one head man."

Dobkin slowed down. "The Foreign Minister is the ranking man, of course."

"Who's next?"

"I suppose Isaac Burg."

"Who's next?"

Dobkin let out a sound of exasperation. "Well, a politician would be next."

"Who?"

"Bernstein. She's in the Cabinet."

"I know that. But that hardly qualifies her here."

Dobkin shrugged. "Don't get me involved. I'm just a soldier."

"Who's next?"

"You or me, I guess."

"I have six men, all armed. They're loyal to me. They are the only effective fighting force on this hill."

Dobkin stopped. "One of them has a bullet in his ass. And it remains to be seen how effective the rest are. Those two actions tonight were only probes. The next time it will be an all-out attack."

Hausner turned and began walking again.

Dobkin came up beside him and clapped him on the back. "All right. I understand. But you've already atoned, Jacob, and you almost got killed in the process. Calm down a little, now. There are going to be a lot of tough hours ahead of us."

"More like days, I think."

"No way. We couldn't hold out much past sundown tomorrow. If that long."

"We may not be rescued by then."

Dobkin nodded. "You're right. This is the worst time of year to be here. The spring floods make the area damn near inaccessible. The tourist season won't start for a month. If Becker can't raise someone on the radio, it could very well be days before anyone realizes we're here. And more time before they act."

"Do you think the Iraqis would attempt a rescue?"

"Who knows? The Arabs are capable of the most chivalrous acts imaginable and the most treacherous—all within the same day."

Hausner nodded. "I think they want this peace mission to succeed. If Baghdad finds out we're here, we can expect help."

Dobkin waved his hand in a gesture of dismissal. "Who can say? The peace may already be lost. But I'm not a politician. Militarily, it would be difficult for them to aid us in this terrain. That's all I know for certain."

Hausner stopped. They were near the Concorde. He could see people standing and speaking in small groups. He lowered his voice. "Why?"

Dobkin spoke softly also. "Well, according to our latest intelligence, the Iraqis have very little helicopter mobility. They have less paratroop capability and virtually no amphibious craft, which would be needed to move troops this time of year. They're well equipped for desert warfare, but there's a lot of marsh and mud flats and swollen streams between the Tigris and Euphrates during the flood season. A lot of armies have come to grief in Mesopotamia in the spring."

"How about regular light infantry? Doesn't anyone use them anymore?"

Dobkin nodded. "Yes. Light infantry could reach us. But it would take a lot of time. There's a small town a little south of here—Hillah—but I don't know if they have a garrison or if they could reach us. And even if they could, would they stand up to the Palestinians?"

"Let's keep all this to ourselves."

"It's military secret Number One. And I'll tell you military secret Number Two. There are whole units of the Iraqi Army made up of displaced Palestinians. I'd hate to be the Iraqi military commander who had to test their loyalty by asking them to fight their compatriots. But we don't want to lower everyone's morale, so that's not for public information, either."

Dobkin and Hausner moved toward the Concorde and stopped near the nose cone. Some meters beyond the nose cone was the structure that they had almost hit. It looked like a ruined shepherds' shelter, but it wasn't stone as Hausner had thought when they were careening toward it. It was baked brick. The baked brick of Mesopotamia. It was partly roofed with date palms. Hausner noted that it was not much different from the shepherds' huts of Israel, or probably anywhere else in the Middle East. It was an ageless monument to the world's loneliest profession. A link with the world of Abraham. He could see through a partly collapsed wall. Men and women were standing inside talking. This was the Foreign Minister's meeting.

Hausner turned toward a sound in the dark. He could make out the majority of the passengers standing under the starboard delta wing. Rabbi Haim Levin was beginning Sabbath services a little late. Hausner recognized the short silhouette of Yaakov Leiber supported by the other two stewards.

Hausner saw something move under the fuselage. Suddenly Peter Kahn dropped down from the wheel well of the collapsed nose gear. He had a flashlight in his hand that he quickly shut off.

Dobkin walked up to him. "How's it look?"

"Bad."

"What's bad?" asked Hausner.

Kahn looked at him and smiled. "That was a hell of a thing you did, Mr. Hausner."

"What's bad?"

"The auxiliary power unit. It got damaged when the landing gear collapsed."

"So what? Are we taking off?"

Kahn forced a smile. "No. But there's still a few hundred liters of fuel left in the bottom of two of the wing tanks. If we can start the APU, we can run the generators and we'll have electricity to broadcast. The batteries won't last forever."

Hausner nodded. Forever might be only a matter of hours for them, in which case the batteries were good enough. "Where's the captain?"

"On the flight deck."

Hausner looked up the sloping nose cone. A greenish glow came through the windshield. He could make out Becker's outline. I'm going to talk to him."

Dobkin shook his head. "The Foreign Minister wants to speak to you." He indicated the shepherds' hut.

Hausner didn't feel up to it. "Not just yet."

"I'm afraid I have to insist."

There was a long silence. Hausner looked up at the flight deck, then back at the shepherds' hut. Kahn became uncomfortable and walked away. Hausner spoke. "In my carry-on luggage, I have an identikit and a psychological profile on Ahmed Rish. I want to get it."

Dobkin hesitated. "Well, I suppose . . ." Dobkin suddenly looked surprised as it hit him. "Why the hell do you have that with you?"

"A hunch."

"I'm impressed, Jacob. I really am. All right. They'll want to see that."

Hausner jumped up to the leading edge of the delta which was a few meters from the ground. He walked up the sloping wing to the emergency door.

The sloping cabin was dark, but an eerie green light came through the door leading to the flight deck. The seat belt and smoking lights were still on and the Machmeter still functioning. It read MACH 0.00 And always would. The cabin was empty. It smelled of burnt kerosene. Hand luggage, blankets, and pillows were scattered everywhere. Hausner could hear Rabbi Levin's clear voice coming through the split pressure bulkhead where the tail used to be.

He walked into the pitched flight deck. Becker was adjusting knobs on the green-glowing radios. There was the sound of electronic humming and the crackle of static. Moses Hess lay slumped over the instruments where he had died. Becker was speaking in a low voice and Hausner realized he was not speaking into the radio, but to Hess. He cleared his throat. "David."

Becker turned his head but said nothing. He went back to the radio.

Hausner stepped up to the seats. He felt uncomfortable with Hess's body lying there. "You did one hell of a job."

Becker began going through the frequencies again, monitoring but not attempting to transmit.

Hausner moved closer, between the seats, and his leg brushed Hess. He stepped back. If he had his way, the body would be buried in ten minutes. But he knew the rabbi wouldn't allow it on the Sabbath. Unless he or someone else could successfully plead health reasons, Hess's body wouldn't be buried until sundown. "I'll get him out of here, David."

"It doesn't matter." A loud radio whine filled the cabin. Becker cursed and shut it off, then shut down the emergency power. The dim lights went out, and moonlight filled the flight deck. "The bastard is still jamming us. He can't do a very good job of it from where he is, but he's trying."

"What kind of chance do we have to contact someone?"

"Who knows?" Becker leaned back and lit a cigarette. He stared through the windshield, then turned back to Hausner. "The high frequency radio seems to be completely dead. That's not unusual. It's very sensitive. If we can get it to work, we could theoretically call any place in the world, depending on atmospheric conditions. The VHF radio is working fine and I'm broadcasting on 121.5—the International Emergency Frequency. I'm also broadcasting and monitoring our last El Al frequency. But I don't hear anyone, and I'm not getting any responses."

"Why not?"

"Well, the VHF radio works on line of sight only. I haven't looked, but I imagine there are hills around us that are higher than we are."

"There are."

"And the batteries are not as powerful as a generator. And don't forget that Rish is broadcasting static on every frequency with his broad band transmitter, and he can keep his engines and generator running." Becker blew out a long stream of smoke. "That's why not."

"All right." Hausner stared out the windshield. He could see people moving in the shepherds' hut below him. "But we could probably contact an airplane overhead without much difficulty. Right?"

"Right. All we need is an airplane overhead."

Hausner noticed the blood-smeared brick that had killed Hess now sitting atop the flight console. In the green glow of the instruments he could make out the ancient cuneiforms pressed into it. He couldn't read cuneiforms, but he was certain that the brick said what most of the bricks of Babylon said: NEBU-CHADNEZZAR, KING OF BABYLON, SON OF NABOPOLASSAR, KING OF BABYLON, AM I. The brick was very much out of place and time in the flight deck of the supersonic craft. He turned away from it. "I'll mount an aircraft watch from the top of the fuselage. We'll work out a system to signal you when one is spotted."

"Sounds good." He looked for a long time at his dead copilot, then back at Hausner. "Kahn's working on the APU."

"I saw him. He says it looks bad. How long will the batteries last?"

"It's really hard to say. I can monitor for quite a while, but every time I try a transmission I'm really pulling a lot of juice. I don't know how much more power is being pulled off on the emergency circuit. The batteries are nickel cadmium. They're good, but they don't give much warning that they're on the way out. They perform pretty well right up until the time they die."

Hausner nodded. He knew that. He worried about it. The starlight scope had nickel cadmium batteries also. "Do you think you want to hold off and save the batteries to turn over the APU if Kahn can fix it?"

Becker rubbed his hand through his hair. "I don't know. Shit. Everything we do from now on is going to have to be some sort of trade-off, isn't it? I don't know just yet. I'll think about it."

"Right." Hausner grabbed onto the flight engineer's chair and pulled himself forward toward the door. He caught hold of the jamb and turned. "See you later."

Becker turned in his chair. "Are we going to make it?"

"Of course." Hausner walked up into the steeply tilted cabin and located his flight bag.

Hausner went out into the wing and jumped off the leading edge. He could see that the Sabbath service had just finished. Most of the men and women headed quickly back toward the perimeter. Some were walking toward the shepherds' hut, among them, Rabbi Levin. Hausner fell into step with him. "Can we bury Moses Hess?"

"No."

"We have to begin building some sort of defensive works. Would you object to some work on the Sabbath?"

"Yes."

They stopped by the wall of the shepherds' hut. A few people from the Sabbath service walked past them and into the hut. Hausner looked at the rabbi. "Are we going to work together or are we going to be in conflict, Rabbi?"

The rabbi slipped his prayer book and *tallit* into his jacket. "Young man, it's the nature of religions to be in conflict with rational secular goals. Of course Moses Hess should be buried tonight, and of course you should start working on defenses. So we'll compromise. You order everyone to work over my objections, and I'll take charge of Moses Hess's body and forbid his burial. These are the kinds of compromises Israel has made since 1948."

"And they're damned stupid. It's all a lot of hypocrisy. Well, have it your way for now." Hausner stepped toward the opening of the hut.

Rabbi Levin took Hausner's arm and drew him back. "Survival is often a mixture of stupidity, hypocrisy, and compromise."

"I have no time for this."

"Wait. You're an Anglophile, Hausner. Did you ever wonder why the English stopped for tea at four P.M. in the middle of a battle? Or why they dressed for dinner in the tropics?"

"It's their style."

"And it's good for morale. Good for morale," he repeated and tapped Hausner on the chest. "We don't want people running amok just because we happen to be sitting on a hilltop in Babylon surrounded by hostile Arabs. So we do everyday things in everyday ways. We hold Sabbath services. We don't bury our dead on the Sabbath. We don't work on the Sabbath. And we won't be reduced to eating lizards or something of that sort because lizards are not kosher, Jacob Hausner." He tapped Hausner again on the chest, harder this time. "Nor will we break any other religious laws." He brushed some dust off Hausner's shirt. "Ask General Dobkin why soldiers in combat have to shave every day. Morale, Jacob Hausner. Form. Style. Civilization. That's how to keep this group functioning. Keep the men shaving and the women's hair and lipstick straight. It will follows from there. I used to be an Army chaplain. I know."

Hausner smiled in spite of himself. "That's an interesting theory. But I asked you if we were going to get along."

Rabbi Levin lowered his voice. "I'll rant and rave about The Law, and you rant and rave about military expediency. People will take sides. Internal strife is not always bad. It works to make people forget what a hopeless position they're in when they're arguing about trifles. So you and I will argue over trifles. Privately, we'll compromise. Like now. I'm attending this meeting on the Sabbath. I'm a reasonable fellow. See?" He walked into the hut.

Hausner stood staring at the spot where the rabbi had been. He couldn't follow all the logic. It was a mixture of Machiavellian, Byzantine, and convoluted thinking with a dash of plain Jewish for good measure. He half suspected that the rabbi didn't understand all he was saying himself. The man was definitely eccentric. But what he said had a good gut feeling.

Hausner walked toward the entrance to the hut.

About fifteen people were standing, talking in low voices. Everyone became quiet and heads turned toward Hausner. He paused at the doorway. A blue-white moonbeam shone through the date palms and lit up the spot where he stood. Ariel Weizman, the Foreign Minister, came across the small room and took his hand. "You did a splendid job, Mr. Hausner."

Hausner allowed his hand to be shaken. "Do you mean in allowing the bombs to be placed aboard my aircraft, Mr. Minister?"

The Foreign Minister looked at him closely in the moonlight. "Jacob," he said softly, "enough of that." The Foreign Minister turned around. "Let us begin. We're here to define our objectives and estimate our chances of carrying out those objectives."

Hausner set his flight bag down and looked around the room as the Foreign Minister went on in his parliamentary speech patterns.

Kaplan was lying on his stomach, against a wall. A blue El Al blanket covered him from the waist down. His bloody pants lay on the floor next to him. Two stewardesses, Beth Abrams and Rachel Baum, were looking after him, and Kaplan seemed to be enjoying it. Hausner was grateful that El Al stewards and stewardesses received quite a bit of medical training.

The ten official delegates to the peace mission were there, including the two Arabs, Abdel Jabari and Ibrahim Arif. Miriam Bernstein stood near the cleft in the wall. She looked good by moonlight, reflected Hausner. He found himself staring at her.

The Arab prisoner sat in the corner, his wrists bound to his ankles. His face was caked with dried blood where Hausner had hit him. His fatigue shirt was stiff with blood from his shoulder wound. Someone had opened the shirt and put a dressing on his shoulder. He appeared to be half asleep, or drugged.

Hausner listened as everyone took a turn speaking. A regular Knesset meeting. Arguments and points of order and calls for votes. They couldn't even decide what they were there for, why they had decided to fight, or what to do next. And all the while his five men, with a few other volunteers were manning an impossibly long defensive perimeter. It was a microcosm of Israel: democracy in action, or inaction. Churchill was right, he reflected. Democracy is the worst form of government—except for all the others.

Hausner could see that Dobkin was also becoming impatient, but his training had taught him to defer to the politicians. Hausner interrupted someone. "Has anyone questioned the prisoner?"

There was a silence. Why was this man speaking out of turn? What did the prisoner have to do with anything? A Knesset member, Chaim Tamir, looked down at the prisoner, who was apparently sleeping soundly now. "We tried. He's reluctant to talk. Also, he is hurt badly."

Hausner nodded. He walked casually over to the sleeping Arab and kicked him in the leg. There were a few surprised exclamations, including one from the Arab. Hausner turned around. "You see, ladies and gentlemen, the most important speaker in this room is this young man. What he says about the military capacity of the other side will determine our fate. I risked my life to bring him to you, and you are speaking only to each other."

Hausner could see that Burg and Dobkin looked relieved and anxious. No one spoke. Hausner continued. "And if this young man has very bad news for us, it should not become general knowledge. So, I suggest everyone except the Foreign Minister, the general, and Mr. Burg leave."

The room exploded into shouts of indignation and outrage.

The Foreign Minister called for quiet. He turned to General Dobkin with a questioning look.

Dobkin nodded. "It really should have been the first priority. We must question him no matter what condition he is in. And we must do it without delay."

The Foreign Minister looked surprised. "Then why didn't you say so, General?"

"Well, the prisoner was hurt and the stewardess had given him pain killers, and then you called this meeting—"

Hausner turned to Burg. "Will you do it?"

Burg nodded. "It's my specialty." He lit his pipe.

The Arab prisoner knew that he was the subject of conversation, and he looked unhappy about it.

The Foreign Minister nodded. "We will continue this meeting elsewhere and leave you alone with the prisoner, Mr. Burg."

Burg nodded.

The assembly began filing out after the Foreign Minister. They looked angry and almost rebellious.

Miriam Bernstein stopped in front of Jacob Hausner and looked up at him. He turned his back to her, but she surprised him and herself by grabbing his arm and half turning him back around. "Who the hell do you think you are?"

"You know very well who and what I am."

She tried to bring her anger under control. "The ends, Mr. Hausner, do not justify the means."

"Tonight they do."

She spoke slowly and precisely. "Look, if we get out of here alive, I want us to have our humanity and self-respect intact. In a very short time, you have disbanded a democratic assembly and gotten permission to torture a wounded man."

"I'm only surprised it took me so long." He lit a cigarette. "Look, Miriam, round one goes to us bully boys. And probably every round from now on. So you people just get it through your heads that you're superfluous except as soldiers. I'm going to save this fucked-up situation even if I have to turn this goddamned hill into a concentration camp."

She slapped him hard across the face. His cigarette flew through the air.

The people remaining in the hut pretended not to see or hear the slap in the dark. The room was still.

Hausner cleared his throat. "Mr. Burg has work to do and you're holding him up, Mrs. Bernstein. Please leave."

She left.

Hausner turned to Dobkin. "We'll inspect the perimeter and see how we stand." He stepped across the room. "Isaac, as soon as you get something concrete, send a runner out to us." He indicated his flight bag on the floor. "Here is an identikit and psychological profile on Rish. Take care of it."

Burg stared at the flight bag, then looked up. "How, in the name of God—?"

"Just a very lucky guess. Nothing more." He knelt beside Kaplan. He was almost asleep now, probably drugged. He was not likely to be awakened by the sounds of an interrogation. "Will you be all right, Moshe? Do you want to be moved?"

Kaplan shook his head. "I've seen it before," he said weakly. "Get out to the perimeter. Come up with a good defense."

"What other kind of defense is there for us, Moshe?"

"No other kind."

As Hausner and Dobkin walked, a scream from the hut pierced the still night air. If Brin's first shot committed them to the fight, thought Hausner, then torturing the Arab committed them to a policy of no surrender. They could not ask for better treatment than they gave. There was no turning back now.

They walked along the river side of the hill. Every fifty meters or so men and women stood or sat in pairs or singly, looking down at the Euphrates.

They were mostly the junior aides, Hausner noticed. The secretaries and interpreters. The young men and women of any major diplomatic mission. They had looked forward to New York. Some of them might make it.

Hausner mentioned to Dobkin that they'd have to see to it that the ten delegates pulled guard duty along with everyone else. "That will cut down on their time for meetings," Hausner said. Dobkin smiled.

They found McClure and Richardson sitting on a sand rise in the ground. Hausner approached them. "Bad luck for you two."

McClure looked up slowly. "Could've been worse. Could've spent my home leave with my wife and in-laws."

Richardson stood. "What's the situation?"

"Grim," replied Hausner. He briefed them, then asked, "Do you two want to leave under a white flag? You're in an American Air Force uniform, Colonel. And you, Mr. McClure, I'm sure have proper identification as an American State Department employee. I'm fairly certain they wouldn't harm either of you. The Palestinians are trying not to antagonize your government these days."

McClure shook his head. "Funny coincidence. I had a great-uncle who was killed at the Alamo. Used to wonder how it felt being under siege. You know? Rejecting offers of surrender. Seeing the Mexos pouring over the walls. That must've been one hell of a fight."

Dobkin understood enough of the English to be confused. "Is that supposed to be an answer?"

Hausner laughed. "You are a strange man, Mr. McClure. But you're welcome to stay. You, by the way, have the only gun on this side of the hill."

"Kind of figured I did."

"Right," said Hausner. "So if someone on this side yells, get over there and pop off some rounds until I can send a few automatic weapons men over from the east slope."

"Will do."

Hausner felt confident with McClure. "Actually, I don't think they will try this side."

"Probably not." McClure looked at the sky, then at Hausner. "You better get some organization in this defense before the moon sets."

"I know," said Hausner. "Thanks, Mr. McClure." He turned to Richardson. "You too, Colonel."

"Call me Tom," said Richardson. He switched to Hebrew which surprised Hausner and Dobkin. "Listen, I'm with you, but I think you should try to negotiate."

Dobkin stepped closer to Richardson and answered him in Hebrew. "Negotiate for what? We were on a mission of peace and half of us are dead now. What are we supposed to negotiate?"

Richardson didn't answer.

Hausner spoke. "We'll take it under advisement, Colonel. Thank you."

McClure seemed unconcerned that everyone was speaking a language he couldn't understand. Hausner felt the tension between the two Americans. There was something wrong here.

12

Hausner and Dobkin continued to walk the perimeter. It was almost a perfect oval, or as Dobkin had described it, the size and shape of a race track, which led Hausner to agree with Dobkin that it was probably not a natural formation. The top of the mound or hill was fairly level, further evidence of a man-made structure underneath. The flat top was broken only by blown dunes and water-eroded gullies or wadis. There were places where a round knoll stuck up from the flat surface. Dobkin explained that these were most likely watchtowers that had risen above the walls of the citadel. Dobkin placed men and women on each one of them.

They counted thirty men and women who had somehow gotten themselves into position. Most of them had just placed themselves instinctively. Dobkin had placed only a few right after the crash.

Hausner stood by as Dobkin considered the problems of cover, concealment, and fields of fire. Dobkin shifted and adjusted the line to take better advantage of the terrain. He issued orders to start piling bricks and dirt for breastworks and to dig foxholes wherever it was possible to dig in the dusty soil. Hausner wondered if it weren't really a useless exercise, since there was virtually no firepower among the defenders.

Burg had given Dobkin his Colt .45 automatic and Dobkin in turn had given it to one of the stewards, Abel Geller, whom he placed in a strategic position. Hausner handed his Smith & Wesson .22 to a young stenographer named Ruth Mandel. "Do you know how to use this?"

She looked at it in her small hand. "I spent my time in the Army."

Hausner counted three handguns of small caliber plus his men's six Smith & Wesson .22's. His own made ten. Then there was Joshua Rubin with the Uzi, Brin with the M-14, and his other three security men, Jaffe, Marcus, and Alpern, with the three AK-47's. The AK's were placed to cover the entire east slope of the hill with intersecting fire. There was an average of one person every thirty meters. It wasn't good, but it wasn't hopeless, either.

Dobkin found a steward, Daniel Jacoby, and asked him to figure out a way of making coffee to take out to the perimeter.

Hausner and Dobkin stopped at Brin's position. A young girl in a bright blue jumpsuit was asleep sitting up with her back to a mound of earth near Brin. Hausner spoke. "Who's she?"

Brin looked up from the scope. "Naomi Haber, a stenographer. She volunteered to be my runner. I'll need someone to pass the word if I see anything."

Hausner nodded. "Have you seen anything?"

"No."

"After the moon sets you will."

"I know."

Hausner and Dobkin stood a distance from Brin and the sleeping girl. They both stared silently down into Babylon.

Hausner lit a cigarette. "Well?"

Dobkin shook his head. "I don't know. It depends on how determined the assault is. A regular infantry unit of platoon size could take this hill if they were good. On the other hand, a five-hundred-man battalion couldn't take it if they were bad. To assault a defensive position, no matter how lightly defended, takes a special kind of nerve.

"Do you think that bunch has it?"

"Who knows? How charismatic a leader is Rish? Will men die for him? For their cause? We don't even know how many there are. Let's wait for Burg's report."

"Right." Hausner looked eastward down the slope. He could make out ribbons of water shining in the moonlight and large stretches of glistening marsh. Yet the area was basically dead. Sand and clay. It was hard to believe that Mesopotamia had supported millions of people in ancient times. He could see a low wall almost a kilometer away and beyond that the road they had started to land on. "Do you really know this place, Ben?"

"I can probably draw a map of it from memory. In fact, in the morning, when I get my landmarks oriented, I will draw us a nice military map."

"How did these Palestinians get here, I wonder."

"How do guerrillas get anywhere?"

"They had a few trucks."

"I noticed."

"Heavy weapons? Mortars?"

"I hope to God not," said Dobkin.

"They wanted to keep us hostage—captive—in Babylon. That's almost funny."

"It wouldn't have been if we'd landed on that road," said Dobkin. "I wonder if we made the right move?"

"We might never know," said Hausner. He lit a cigarette and put his cold hands in his pockets. "Maybe Asher Avidar made the right move."

"Maybe."

Hausner looked to the north. About three-quarters of a kilometer away was a tall hill that rose dramatically from the flat plain. Hausner recognized it as a tell. "What's that?"

Dobkin followed his stare. "That's the hill of Babil. Some archeologists identify it as the location of the Tower of Babel."

Hausner stared. "Do you believe it?"

"Who knows?"

He looked around. "Can we see the Hanging Gardens from here?"

Dobkin laughed. "I don't give tours on the Sabbath." He put his big hand on Hausner's shoulder. "I'm curious to see what I can identify from here when the sun comes up. The main ruin is to the south. There."

"Does anyone live around here?"

"The Arabs don't like it. They think it's haunted. Do you know the verses from Isaiah?"

"You mean . . . 'neither shall the Arabian pitch tent there; neither shall the shepherds make their fold there. . . . But wild beasts . . . shall lie there. . . . And dragons in their pleasant palaces. . . .' That one?"

"That's the one."

"Yet, there's a shepherds' hut here."

Dobkin nodded. "And there is a small village located among the ruins, in spite of the Biblical injunction against this place."

Hausner put out his cigarette and saved the stub. "Can that village be any help to us?"

"I don't think so. I used to debrief Army Intelligence men back from Iraq. A lot of Iraqi villages are primitive beyond belief. Some of these people don't even know they are Iraqi citizens. They live like the first Mesopotamian peasants who began civilization here five thousand years ago."

"Then we're not near any type of modern transportation or communication?"

"Hillah to the south. But I wouldn't count on their knowing we're here." He paused and seemed to remember something. "There *is* a small museum and a guest house in the south part of the ruins by the Ishtar Gate."

Hausner turned his head quickly toward Dobkin. "Go on."

"The Iraqi Department of Antiquities built both structures about twenty years ago. I know the curator of the museum. Dr. Al-Thanni. I saw him in Athens only six months ago. We write via a mutual friend in Cyprus."

"Are you serious?" Hausner began pacing. "Could you get there?"

"Jacob, we are what is called in military siege terminology, invested. That means surrounded. Just as we have sentinels and firing positions up here, you can be sure they have the same around this entire mound."

"But if you could slip through—"

"The chances are that Dr. Al-Thanni won't be there until the end of April when the tourist season begins."

"There must be a telephone."

"There probably is. And running water. And I'll give you one guess where Rish's command post must be."

Hausner stopped pacing. "Still, if you could get there—to the guest house or the museum—it's a link with civilization. Al-Thanni may be there. You may be able to get a jeep. Or the telephone might be unguarded. What do you say, Ben?"

Dobkin looked south across the uneven landscape. He could make out the silhouettes of some excavated ruins. It was at least two kilometers to the Ishtar Gate excavation. There would be only a thin line of sentinels surrounding the hill. Still, he'd want to see it by daylight at least once. "I'm game. But if I'm caught they will make me tell them all I know about our setup here. Everyone talks, Jacob. You know that."

"Of course I know that."

"I'd have to have a pistol to . . . to make sure I didn't fall into their hands. Can we spare that?"

"I don't think so, Ben."

"Neither do I."

"A knife," offered Hausner.

Dobkin laughed. "You know, I never understood where our ancestors got the balls to fall on their own swords. That takes a bit of nerve. And it must be very, very painful." He looked off into the distance. "I don't know if I could do that."

"Well," said Hausner, "let's ask around and see if anyone has some kind of medicine that's fatal in an overdose."

"I appreciate the pains you're taking to facilitate my suicide."

"There are over fifty people—"

"I know. Yes, I'll go. But only after I've seen it in the daylight. I'll leave at nightfall tomorrow."

"We may not be alive that long."

"It's worth the wait. I'll have a better chance of success. If I go tonight, I'll only be throwing my life away. I don't want to do that. I want to succeed."

"Of course."

Isaac Burg approached, puffing on his pipe. He walked heavily like someone who has just completed a disagreeable task.

Hausner and Dobkin walked to meet him. Hausner spoke first. "Did he talk?"

"Everyone talks."

Hausner nodded. "Is he . . . ?"

"Oh, no. He's alive. Actually, I didn't have to lean on him very hard. He wanted to talk."

"Why?"

"They're all like that. Dobkin will tell you. You've seen it yourself at Ramla. It's a mixture of bragging, shock, nervousness, and fright." He studied his pipe for a second. "Also, I promised him I'd send him back to his friends."

Dobkin shook his head. "We can't do that. Military regulations. Anyone who sees the inside of a defensive area can't be repatriated until hostilities are ended. It's the same here as anywhere else."

"Well," said Burg, "in my world—spies and secret agents, I mean—we do things differently. I promised. And you can make an exception for medical reasons. Besides, he hasn't seen much. There's no use letting a man die just because we don't have medical facilities."

"I'll think about it," said Dobkin.

Hausner listened to them argue. It wasn't a heated argument but purely a disagreement over the interpretation of the rules. Burg was, at best, an enigma, thought Hausner. One minute he was prepared to torture a man to death and the next he was trying to save his life. And if he did let the Arab go, and they came back and took the hill and captured Burg alive, the Arabs would make certain that Burg died very slowly. If he were Burg, reflected Hausner, he would kill the man and bury him deep. And Dobkin—he was the perfect soldier. Loyal, intelligent, even inventive. But he *did* like his book of regulations. Hausner became impatient with their argument. "Never mind this. What did he *say?*"

Burg knocked his pipe on his shoe. "Say? He said lots of things. He said his name was Muhammad Assad and that he was an Ashbal. You know the word. A Tiger Cub—a Palestinian orphan of the wars with Israel. In fact, that outfit down there is all Ashbals. They were all raised by Palestinian guerilla organizations. Now they are all grown up. And they don't like us."

Dobkin nodded. "War leaves many legacies. This is the worst." He thought about the Ashbals. How many hollow-eyed, tattered waifs had he seen sobbing over the bodies of their parents amid the rubble of Arab villages? War. Now they were all grown up, these young victims. They were nightmares that came back in the day. "They don't like us at all," agreed Dobkin.

"Quite right," said Burg. "They are a dangerous lot. They've been indoctrinated with hate since the day they could comprehend. They reject all normal standards of behavior. Hatred of Israel is their tribal religion." He patted his pocket for his tobacco pouch and found it. "Also, they've been taught military skills since they could walk. They are a damned well-trained group."

"How many?" asked Dobkin.

"A hundred and fifty."

There was a silence.

"You're certain?" asked Hausner.

Burg nodded.

"How can you be certain?"

Burg smiled. "That's one of the things all soldiers lie about, isn't it, Ben? How many. At first, he said five hundred. I didn't buy that. That's what all the screaming was about. Finally, we agreed on a hundred and fifty."

Dobkin nodded. "Heavy weapons?"

Burg shook his head. "They weren't expecting resistance. Almost all of them are armed with AK-47 rifles, however."

"They must have a base close by," said Dobkin.

"Not so close. In the Shamiyah Desert. That's on the other side of the Euphrates. A good hundred kilometers from here. The Iraqi government suffers the existence of the camp for a variety of very familiar reasons. Anyway, they came here in late January by truck, before the floods. They have been waiting for orders ever since. Then a few hours ago, Rish flew in and called them on the radio. The rest is history—in the making."

"Rish is the boss, I take it?" asked Hausner.

"None other. And his lieutenant is a fellow named Salem Hamadi, another old friend. Hamadi is both a Palestinian and an Ashbal. In fact, he was in charge of the Ashbal program. Rish, as you know, is neither an Ashbal nor a Palestinian. He is Iraqi. His village is not far from here. Anyway, some time ago, they joined forces and began culling both male and female orphans from various camps. About twenty of these Tiger Cubs are tigresses. Muhammad says they trained for years in the Shamiyah Desert for special assignments that never seemed to come off."

"Did they know what they were here for?" asked Dobkin.

"They were told only when Rish's Lear began to make its final approach. There was some confusion as to whether there would be one Concorde or two." He paused as he remembered 01. "They were told they would keep us hostage here for a variety of political reasons, some of which were not too clear to Mr. Muhammad Assad. He admits they were pretty shaken up by our antics. I suspect that they were not psychologically prepared to fight and lose men. They were prepared to push around two planeloads of Israeli civilians. Then all of a sudden, they had people getting killed."

"But they're crack troops," said Hausner. "That's what you said."

Burg shook his head. "I didn't say they were crack troops. I said they were well trained. There is a difference. None of them has ever seen combat." He seemed to be thinking. "You know, this is not the first time that orphans have been trained from childhood as soldiers. There are a lot of cases of that in history. And you know what? They were never really better or worse than regular draftees. In fact, many times they were much worse. These orphan soldiers, like institutional children everywhere, were a little duller than their peers raised in a home environment. That is the case with the Ashbals, I'm sure. They do not make especially good soldiers. They lack imagination and they have virtually no personal goals in life. They lack any experiences outside of military life, and their emotional development is arrested. They have only a vague conception of what they are fighting for, since they have no home outside the barracks. I'm sure they would fight to the death to defend their comrades and their camps, but outside of that, there's no notion of family or country. Everything is vague when they go beyond their squads, their platoons, and their companies. There are a dozen other reasons why they don't make ideal soldiers. I could see it in our young friend, Muhammad." He looked at Dobkin. "Ben?"

Dobkin nodded. "I agree. But there are still over a hundred of them, and they outgun us. They are not going to pack their tents like your proverbial Arabs and steal away in the night."

"No," said Hausner. "They are not. Because they have two good leaders."

Dobkin nodded again. "That is the key. The leadership." He seemed to be remembering the old fights and nodded to himself several times. He looked at Hausner and Burg. "Here is what I know about the Arabs as soldiers. First, they are romantics whose mental picture of warfare is of men on white Arabian stallions charging across the desert. In truth, the Arabs of today are not known for their successes on the offensive. The days when they carried the banner of Islam across half the civilized world are long gone." He lit a cigarette. "But don't get me wrong. They are not such bad fighters as they are made out to be. They are generally brave and steadfast, especially in a static defensive situation. Like many soldiers from low social and economic backgrounds, they will endure the most extreme hardships and deprivations. But they have flaws as soldiers. They are reluctant to press an attack. They are unable to shift tactics with changing situations. Their officers and sergeants, while not the best, are critical for control and discipline. The average Arab soldier will show little initiative and less discipline when his leader is killed. Also, the Arabs have not completely come to grips with modern military equipment. The Ashbals in particular, from what little I know of them, seem to fit into this description. And further, they are so blinded by hate propaganda that they are not very cool or professional as soldiers."

Burg nodded. "I agree. And I think they *might* run off if they lose enough leadership or if the losses in the ranks become unacceptable—which I admit isn't very likely in this case. On the other hand, *we* can't run anywhere. We are fighting for our lives. All losses are acceptable to us. There is no alternative."

Hausner spoke. "There is an alternative. They'll ask for a conference."

"But not before they try one more attack," said Dobkin. He looked into the sky. "We'll have a chance to see if we can inflict unacceptable losses on them in a short while. The moon is setting."

13

B rin saw them first, even before the two-man OP/LP—Outpost/Listening Post—halfway down the slope saw them.

They came like shadows, wearing tiger fatigues and carrying their automatic rifles. The starlight scope amplified the smallest amount of natural light so that Brin could see things that even night creatures could not see—things that the men could not even see on themselves. He could see their shadows, cast by starlight. He could see the white skin under their eyes, symptomatic of fear. He could see the most intimate movements made in what was believed to be a shroud of darkness—the lips murmuring prayers, the quick urinations brought on by fear, the pulling of hair locks. A girl squeezed a young man's hand. Brin felt as though he were peeking through a keyhole.

He put down the rifle and whispered to Naomi Haber. "They're coming."

She nodded, touched his arm, and ran off to give the alarm.

The long meandering defensive line on the eastern slope of the hill became alert as the warning moved more rapidly than the swift runner.

On the western slope there was silence. The luminescent Euphrates would silhouette anything moving up that slope. Men and women pressed their faces to the ground at the crest of the slope to try to pick out a moving form. But there was only the silver-gray Euphrates flowing silently southward.

Dobkin, Burg, and Hausner stood on a small knoll—one of the covered watchtowers—near the middle of the eastern crest, about fifty meters in back of it.

The knoll had been designated as the CP/OP, the Command Post/Observation Post. From that vantage point, they hoped to direct the fight along the five-hundred-meter eastern slope.

A long aluminum brace from the Concorde's tail section, bent and twisted, was stuck in the hard clay earth atop the knoll. From the top of this unlikely standard flew a more unlikely banner, a child's T-shirt, salvaged from one of the suitcases, an intended gift for someone in New York. The T-shirt showed a cityscape of the Tel Aviv waterfront painted in day-glo colors. The purpose of the CP/OP was to establish command control in the dark—a place where runners could go to impart information and collect orders. It was also to be the last rallying point, the citadel within the citadel from which the last stand was to be made in the event the line was broken or penetrated. It was an old tactic, one that belonged to an age before radios, telegraphs, and field phones. The three commanders took their places on the high knoll, under their flag, and waited.

The two men from the OP/LP, halfway down the slope, fell breathless at the foot of the knoll and reported what was already known from Nathan Brin and Naomi Haber. "They're coming."

Brin watched as the Ashbals continued their silent movement up the hill. They didn't come in file as they had done the last time, but they moved on line along the whole width of the five-hundred-meter slope, approximately a hundred of them, men and women, well-spaced at five meters apart. They kept their line straight like well-trained infantry of another era. There was no wavering and no bunching up. They didn't linger or congregate around areas of natural cover and concealment as their instincts cried out for them to do. They held their AK-47's with fixed bayonets thrust out in front of them. It was an awesome sight to anyone who could see it. But to Brin, it was all show. Parade-ground training. He was interested to see how they would react when the bullets began flying down at them. Then, he suspected, they would quickly revert to their modern training. They would find what little cover and concealment was available and burrow into it. They would move from rock to gully to pothole. But for now, in the dark, they were putting on a show of the classic infantry attack—more for themselves than for the Israelis who could not see them.

The knowledge that he was the only one who could see them brought Brin to the verge of panic several times. Sweat formed on the rubber eye guard of his scope and ran down his cheek. They were still very far. About five hundred meters. Then four hundred meters.

General Dobkin and Isaac Burg disagreed on tactics. Dobkin wanted to engage them with heavy fire as far out as possible with the idea of keeping them out of assault range of the thin defensive line. With luck, that would precipitate a panicky flight down the hill. The prisoner had said that they had no hand grenades, but Dobkin couldn't be sure of that. He didn't want them in grenade range in any case.

Burg wanted to engage them as near as possible—within handgun range—in order to cause heavy casualties with as little expenditure of ammunition as possible.

Hausner wasn't consulted, but he thought that Dobkin's arguments were more realistic, considering their situation. In the end, however, he knew that Dobkin, soldier to the core, would defer to a civilian government official. It was a subjective type of decision that had to be made, and rank would always carry that type of argument.

Hausner excused himself, jumped from the hillock, and walked the fifty meters to where Brin was kneeling.

Brin was visibly shaking as he watched the wave of Ashbals approach. Hausner couldn't blame him. He spoke softly. "Range?"

Brin didn't look up. "Three hundred and fifty meters."

"Deployment?"

"Still on line. Most are in the open. Bayonets fixed."

Naomi Haber was sitting on the ground breathing heavily from her exertions. Hausner turned to her. "Go to an AK-47 position and tell him to begin the firing." She got up quickly and ran down the line. He turned back to Brin. "Range?"

"Three hundred."

"Commence firing," he said softly.

Brin squeezed the trigger, swung the rifle, squeezed again, swung, and

squeezed again. The silenced muzzle coughed faintly again and again. Then the
first AK-47 cut in, a signal to begin firing at will. Up and down the line, along
the crest of the hill, came gunshots. The hollow popping of the three AK-47's
drowned out the small handguns. Above all the other sounds could be heard
the sharp staccato of the little 9mm Uzi submachine gun.

The Arabs immediately replied with heavy fire from their own AK-47's. The
noise quickly rose to a deafening pitch. Hausner could see the incoming rounds
digging away at the improvised Israeli breastworks. He couldn't tell if anyone
had been hit yet.

Brin's assignment was to try to identify unit commanders and eliminate
them. He swung the rifle and spotted the antenna of a field radio, carried as a
backpack by a radio operator. At the end of a corkscrew wire coming out of the
radio was a radiophone. A young man was crouched down, holding the radiophone to his face. Brin aimed at the young man's mouth and fired. The phone
and the man's face erupted into a scatter of disjointed pieces. He swung the
rifle back and shot the radio operator through the heart.

The Ashbal's return fire ceased as their long line broke up quickly into small
groups centered around natural areas of cover. Their progress was slowed, but
they still moved forward. Brin scanned the area behind the Ashbals, looking for
the senior leaders. He thought once that he saw Rish, but then the head disappeared, replaced a second later by that of a young woman. Without hesitation,
Brin fired. He could see the head jerk sideways. The beret flew off and the long
hair swirled as the girl spun to the earth.

Dobkin could see the fiery bursts as the Arabs moved up the hill. He shook
his head. They may have been well trained, but he gave them a low grade on
tactics. The approved method of night attack, developed in large part by the
Israeli Army, was quite different from what the Ashbals were doing. It was
known now that night attacks should begin silently, not with the sound and fury
of artillery barrages and screaming men, as in the past wars. The Ashbals had
done that at the beginning, but they had moved too slowly and returned fire too
soon. The Israelis had, in past engagements, shown that a quick silent run was
the most effective method of night attack. The enemy was generally only half-
alert, and when they saw what was coming at them in the dark, they only half-
believed their eyes. By the time they reacted, the attackers were within hand
grenade range, then a second later, they were in the trenches. Even a fully
loaded infantryman could cover half a kilometer on the run in less than two
minutes.

Dobkin watched as the flashes moved in the darkness. These Ashbals fired
on the run and fell behind cover afterward, the exact opposite of what was good
sense. The defenders on the hill fired at the flash of the muzzles while the
attackers were running. As far as Dobkin could see, the Ashbal's fire was so far
without effect on his concealed positions, except for one casualty reported to
him. Looking downslope, Dobkin could see what appeared to be muzzle flashes
cut short by what he hoped were hits.

It had taken a lot of battles over a lot of years for him to be able to stand on a
high place and tell how a fight was progressing by flashes and noises, by sounds
of men and the smell of the night air. And most of all, some kind of warrior
instinct told him when everything was all right and when it was lost.

In total, despite all the noise, Dobkin knew that casualties would be very
light on both sides until the battle was joined up close. That's the way it had
always been in the past. This time, however, he felt it was not going to be a
victory. He turned to Burg. "They're very sloppy troops. But very determined.

We will probably be out of ammunition very shortly. Maybe we should give the order to pull back to this knoll."

Burg shook his head. Long before he had entered intelligence work, he had been a battalion commander in the War of Independence. He had a sense for these things also. "Let's wait. I have a feeling they will break off the engagement."

Dobkin didn't answer.

"At sunrise we will court-martial Hausner," said Burg matter-of-factly.

"We can't be sure he gave the order to fire," said Dobkin.

"You know he did." Burg stood with one hand grasping the twisted aluminum standard. He seemed mesmerized by the flash of weapons and the incessant whistling of bullets. He realized that what was missing was the sound of the heavy weapons that gave a fight a distinctive military flavor. This fight sounded like an American gangster movie—all pistols and submachine guns. "Well, General? Do you think Hausner gave the order to commence firing against our orders?" asked Burg.

Dobkin didn't feel like arguing. "I suppose he did. It doesn't really make a lot of difference, does it?"

"It makes a great deal of difference to me," snapped Burg. "A great deal of difference."

All along the defensive line, the volume of gunfire remained constant, for to begin conserving ammunition was a signal to the attackers that the end was near if only they would persevere. But the number of rounds left to the Israelis dwindled rapidly and, in fact, a few handguns were already without ammunition. The AK-47's kept up a three-piece symphony of short bursts, while Joshua Rubin with the Uzi fired continuously, stopping only to let the barrel cool. Brin, firing a relatively small amount of ammunition, was the most deadly with ten hits.

The Ashbals were within a hundred meters of the line now, but their casualties went up geometrically with every ten meters they gained.

Someone was running toward the command post from the direction of the west slope. Burg and Dobkin waited for the bad news that the Ashbals had launched a secondary attack up the slope on the river side. The entire line there was held by McClure with his pistol and a dozen men and women with bricks and pieces of aluminum braces fashioned into spears. The runner jumped onto the knoll and caught his breath. "All quiet on the western slope." He grinned.

Dobkin grinned in return and slapped him on the back. "That's the only good news I've had since a lady said yes to me last night in Tel Aviv."

Hausner, kneeling beside Brin, estimated that the end would come within the next few minutes. There simply wasn't enough ammunition to keep up that rate of fire.

As though the defenders read his thoughts, they began increasing the rates of fire in a last desperate gamble to panic the attackers. Hausner watched the oncoming Arabs, who were partially visible now through the darkness. The Ashbals wavered as the increased volume of fire tore into their ranks. They slowed but held firm. The momentum of their attack was stopped, however, but while they were afraid to go forward, they weren't falling back, either. Their commanders yelled and kicked at them and tried to regain the initiative. Some groups moved forward again, reluctantly.

Brin took advantage of the commanders' increased visibility and took two of them out in less than thirty seconds. The others began taking cover when they realized what was happening. Brin then began to search desperately for Rish. He had studied the photo from Hausner's identikit so intently for the past hour that all he could see in his mind's eye was Rish's face on every Arab. But he knew that when he actually saw that face, he would be certain of it.

The Israelis heard the Arabic shouts and could see some of what was happening. They deduced that there was a problem in the Ashbals' ranks. The veterans among the Israelis knew what to do. As Hausner watched, amazed, without any orders from anyone, about twenty men and women began running and screaming down the hill.

Dobkin knew what was happening. With cool detachment, he weighed the possibilities of success. The idea behind a primitive screaming counterattack was to strike fear into the hearts of the attackers. If it were done with enough élan and conviction, and if it were spontaneous like this one, it could make the enemy's blood run cold. They would turn, first the most cowardly among them, then even the most stouthearted would be caught up in the panicky flight as the attackers became the attacked. Lacking prepared defenses, they would run until they dropped.

But would that happen here? What would happen if the Ashbals had another force on the river side? If they attacked on that side, Dobkin could no longer send any reinforcements there. They were all halfway down the eastern slope in an unauthorized counterattack. That's what happened when people didn't obey orders. Dobkin ran toward the crest of the eastern slope.

Hausner took the M-14 from Brin and watched through the starlight scope. For a moment, everything hung in the balance. If the Ashbals did not break ranks, there would be a massacre. The attacking Israelis were outnumbered five to one and lightly armed. They were within fifty meters of the Ashbals and were firing into their ranks with increasing accuracy. Joshua Rubin had gone completely crazy. He ran and fired his Uzi in a long burst that Hausner thought would melt the barrel. Hausner could hear his primeval war cry above the din of the shooting.

Hausner began firing the M-14 at targets around Rubin to try to protect him. He saw what he thought was the first man to break ranks and run. Then two young girls followed. Then others followed. He could hear the Arabic word for retreat shouted by the fleeing Ashbals. A few leaders, officers, and sergeants tried to turn them around. Hausner put the cross hairs on one who was having some success and fired. The man fell. It was already apparent to the leaders that someone with a very good scope was causing them an inordinate number of casualties. Now that they were more conspicuous by trying to organize a stand, they were virtually committing suicide. Hausner aimed again. He had trained with every weapon that his men were issued, but this wasn't his job, and Brin was becoming impatient. Hausner fired, hit another leader, and passed the weapon back to Brin.

Finally, amid the shouts for medics and stretcher bearers for the leaders who were hit, the other Arab officers became disheartened and joined in the flow of retreat.

The retreat became more orderly as the Ashbals put distance between themselves and the Israelis, who by now had lost the madness born of desperation that had made them counterattack.

The Ashbals gathered up fallen equipment, picked up their dead and wounded, and organized a rear guard to allow them more time to get away. As they made their way down the slope, earthslides toppled them over and caused dead and wounded to be dropped.

The Israelis followed close on the heels of the rear guard but finally stopped when a runner sent by Dobkin ordered them back. They gathered what fallen equipment they could find in the darkness and climbed back to the crest of the hill, dirty, sweating, and exhausted. Rubin and a female stenographer, Ruth Mandel, were hit, but not seriously.

There was still no word from the river slope, but Dobkin sent two men with AK-47's there to be certain. A silence fell over the hill and the smell of cordite hung in the still air.

Hausner took the M-14 from Brin and, with the scope, took a last look at the retreating Arabs. They were out of range of the M-14 now, but he could see them clearly. Standing alone on a mound of earth with the body of a long-haired woman slung over his shoulder was a solitary man. He remained motionless as the last of the Ashbals filed past him. The man looked up at the hill that had cost so many of his brothers their lives. He made some sort of movement with his arm—a salute or a motion of damnation. Hausner could not be sure which. He couldn't identify the face at that distance, but he knew for a certainty that it was Ahmed Rish.

14

The Prime Minister of Israel walked, unannounced, into the Operations Room of The Citadel in Tel Aviv. The Air Force personnel allowed themselves one quick glance, then returned to their work.

The noise of telephones, teletypes, and electronic machinery was loud—louder than the Prime Minister remembered it on Yom Kippur, 1973.

The Prime Minister instinctively scanned the big room for General Talman. Then he remembered and walked over to Talman's replacement, General Mordecai Hur. His entourage dispersed throughout the room to gather information and pass on orders.

The Prime Minister stood close to General Hur. "Any survivors from 01?" Hur was a copy of his former boss, British-trained, reserved, correct, well-spoken, and well-dressed. The Prime Minister was none of these things, but he had gotten on well with Talman and he hoped for the same relationship with Hur.

General Hur shook his head almost imperceptibly. "No, sir. But we've recovered about half the bodies." He paused. "There won't be any survivors, you know."

"I know." He looked around at the electronic displays. "Where's 02, Motty?"

Hur was slightly taken aback by the diminutive of his name. "I don't know, sir. And every minute that we don't know increases the area where they could be if they have refueled and are still airborne. We're at the limits of our resources now."

The Prime Minister nodded. "How about that American satellite photo in the Sudan?"

Hur took a sheet of paper from a long counter. "Here's a report from our agent on the ground there. The object on the photo turned out to be sheets of aluminum lying on the sand. General size and configuration of a Concorde."

"Ruse or accident?"

"There's a difference of opinion on that. I say a clever ruse. Some people think it was just coincidence. But we've got three or four more photos like that to follow up. We'll have to try to verify with infrared heat pictures and spectrograph analysis if we can't get a reliable agent on the spot. Also, we have radar, radio, and visual reports which seem more like red herrings than anything else."

"This was a well-planned operation. But it needed an inside man, didn't it?"

"That's not my area, sir. Ask Shin Beth."

The Prime Minister had had Mazar on the carpet for over an hour, but Internal Security was just as surprised at the whole thing as everyone else. Mazar, however, unlike a dozen other people, had not offered his resignation. The Prime Minister had to admire a man who said in effect, "Screw you, my resignation is not going to help matters." But he knew that Mazar would have to go eventually.

An aide carried a telephone to him. "The Secretary General of the United Nations, sir."

The Prime Minister took the receiver. "Yes, Mr. Secretary?" He listened as the Secretary General gave the situation report that he had asked for earlier. The Secretary General spoke in guarded terms. The Arab peace delegations were still in New York. No one had been recalled. The mood was apprehensive. Would Israel overreact in some way and put the Arabs in a difficult position? The Prime Minister would not make any statements one way or the other. They spoke politely for several minutes. The Prime Minister looked at the chronometer displays on the wall. It was midnight in New York. The Secretary General sounded tired. "Thank you, Mr. Secretary. Can you have me switched to the Office of the Israeli Mission? Thank you."

He spoke to his Permanent Ambassador to the UN, and then to the advance personnel of the peace mission who had been working for months to prepare for the Conference. Many had friends and relatives with the lost peace delegation. There was a mixture of outrage, despair, and optimism among them. The Prime Minister could hear his own voice echoing on the amplifiers in their offices. He addressed them all. "You have prepared fertile ground for peace to grow." He was a farmer and he liked these metaphors. "We will plant that seed yet. Keep the ground ready. But *if* it becomes necessary to plow the earth with salt—" he paused. The line was unsecured, and at the very least, the FBI and the CIA were listening and he wanted them—and everyone else—to know, "—then we will plow it with salt and it will lie dead for a decade." He hung up.

He turned back to General Hur. "It will take a few minutes before the American State Department hears the tape of that call and rings us up. Let's have some coffee."

They walk over to the coffee bar and poured mugs for themselves. A nearby counter top was becoming piled with foreign and domestic newspapers showing the same front page picture of a Concorde with El Al markings—the Prime Minister recognized it as an old public relations photo sent out on the occasion of the inaugural flight of 01. They all carried headlines announcing the same news in different ways and different languages. The Prime Minister looked cursorily through a few of the newspapers. "Sometimes I feel we are very much alone on this big planet. Other times, I feel that people care about us."

General Hur looked down into the blackness of his cup. He sensed, rather than actually saw, the red eyes, the puffy skin, the slightly tousled hair. He had never believed in the Peace Conference while it was being talked about. But now he saw how much other people had believed in it, and he felt some guilt over the fact that he had hoped something—something minor, of course—would cause it to be canceled. He looked up at the Prime Minister. "My experience as a military man has been that people only care about peace at the eleventh hour. By then it's often impossible to reverse the course of events."

"And what time do you figure it is now, General?"

"I couldn't say, sir. That's the thing about the eleventh hour. You never know when it's a quarter to—you only know when it's five after, and counting."

An aide carried another telephone to the Prime Minister. "Washington. State Department."

The Prime Minister glanced at General Hur, then picked up the receiver. "Yes, Mr. Secretary. How is that farm of yours in Virginia? Yes, I know, the Tidewater region has become quite salty since your ancestors settled there. Times change. The tide is relentless. We have similar problems here. The sea has so much room to roam, yet it seems to want the land." They spoke in a roundabout manner for a few minutes, then the Prime Minister placed the receiver back into the cradle and turned to Hur. "Our reputation for overreacting to terrorism has not hurt us, General. Everyone wants to make certain that we are still in a mood to talk."

General Hur forgot his professionalism and his place and asked, "And are we?"

The Prime Minister looked around the Operations Room. He stayed silent for a long time, then said, "I don't know, General. We can't change what happened to 01. But I think the mood of the people will depend very much on what has happened to 02. Why haven't we heard from their captors, General?"

"I can't imagine."

The Prime Minister nodded. "Maybe they are not . . ."

"Not what, sir?"

"Never mind. Have you seen the report we received from Aerospatiale?"

"Yes. A classic example of closing the pasture gate after the cattle have gone. There's no help for us there."

The Prime Minister nodded again. "The Palestinian mortar men don't seem to know anything."

"I'd be surprised if they did."

"Are we forgetting anything, Motty?"

Hur shook his head. "No. I don't think so. We're doing all we can here. We've linked up with other air force operation centers from Tehran to Madrid, and they're helping. It all depends on an intelligence break now."

"Either that, or Mr. Ahmed Rish will get around to calling us and let us know what is happening."

"I'd rather we found out what is happening ourselves."

The Prime Minister took a last look around the room. "Keep at it, Motty. I'll speak to you later."

"Yes, sir. Where can I reach you if something comes up?"

The Prime Minister considered. Tel Aviv had far superior communication and transportation facilities. It was also less exposed and safer in other ways. A War Ministry study had reaffirmed that Tel Aviv should be the center of all operations during any crisis. Yet, Jerusalem was the capital—not only the political capital, but the heart and soul of Israel. It was a concept, a state of mind, a spiritual and eternal entity. Even if it were just rubble—or salted earth, as the

Romans had left it—it would be Jerusalem nonetheless. "Jerusalem. I am going to Jerusalem."

Hur nodded and allowed himself a smile.

The Prime Minister left.

Teddy Laskov stood alone on the tarmac at the military end of Lod Airport. A false dawn lit up the eastern sky and outlined the hills of Samaria rising up from the Plain of Sharon. He stared into the sky for a long time until the light faded and the darkest hour began.

He turned away and looked out across the black runways to where the twelve F-14's stood silhouetted against the lights of the International Terminal in the distance. They stood silent, like sentinels guarding the frontiers of civilization and humanity. People called them warplanes, but they could just as easily have been called peace planes, reflected Laskov. He would miss them. Miss the smell of their leather and their hydraulics. Miss the coffee bar in the ready rooms, the static of the radios. Especially, he would miss the men and women who made the Hel Avir more than just a collection of overpriced metal. From his first aircraft in Russia to his last in Israel—or from chock to chock, as pilots put it—it had been forty years. That was too long, anyway, he thought.

He turned and began walking toward a waiting jeep. He allowed himself one backward glance as he mounted the jeep.

The driver turned on the lights, put the vehicle in gear, and lurched across the runway toward the airport access road.

Laskov removed his hat and tunic and laid them in his lap. The night wind whipped around the windshield and tousled his greying hair. He settled back. He thought of Miriam. Her fate had actually been in his hands for a few minutes. In fact, he had held the fate of his nation in his hands while he held the control column of his warplane. Now he held nothing but his hat and coat. He was ambivalent about leaving the pressure cooker of command. It felt good to leave it, but he felt an emptiness as well. And it felt lonely very quickly, he noticed. Without Miriam, it would feel more so.

The driver ventured a sideward glance.

Laskov turned his head and forced a smile.

The young man cleared his throat. "Home, General?"

"Yes. Home."

15

The beginning of morning nautical twilight—BMNT—was at 6:03 A.M. The sky lightened into perfect cloudless blue. There was a slight chill in the air and the damp morning smell of the river lay over the hill. A mist rose off the water as the air became warmer. Somewhere, birds began to sing in the pale light. At 6:09 the sun rose above the distant peaks of the Zagros Mountains in Iran and burnt off the ground mist.

Hausner wondered what those ancient valley dwellers of the Tigris and Euphrates must have thought of those mysterious snow-peaked mountains as the sun came out of them every day. And then one day, the Persians had come out of them, semibarbarous and full of blood lust, and they had defeated the old civilizations of the Tigris and Euphrates. But eventually, the conquerors were absorbed into the culture of the ancient valley dwellers.

Every century or so, a new group of lean and ferocious mountain men would burst out of the surrounding highlands of what was now Iran and Turkey. The ancient cities and towns and farms would absorb the destruction and pillaging, the rape and the massacres, and then carry on under new rulers after the dust had settled and the killing had stopped. Then came the Arabians from the deserts of the south and swept away the old gods.

But the worst were the Mongols. They had come and wrought such utter destruction on the cities and ancient irrigation works that Mesopotamia never recovered. What was once a land of twenty or thirty million people—the most concentrated population in the world outside of Egypt and China—became a desert with a few million disease-ridden and terror-stricken inhabitants. Land that had been under continuous cultivation for four thousand years turned to dust. Malarial swamps and sand dunes shifted alternately over the land as the twin rivers ran wild over the alluvial plain. Some centuries later with the coming of the Turks, the land and the people declined even further. When the British pushed the Turks out in 1917, they couldn't believe that this was the Fertile Crescent. The legendary site of the Garden of Eden at Qurna was a pestilent swamp. The Tommies would joke, "If this is the Garden of Eden, I'd hate to see hell."

No wonder the modern Iraqis were the way they were, thought Hausner—a mixture of bitterness at their historical fate and pride in their ancient heritage. That was one of the keys to the complex personality of Ahmed Rish. If someone in Tel Aviv or Jerusalem would understand that, then maybe someone would say, "Babylonian Captivity."

Hausner shook his head. No. It was easy to come to that conclusion when you were standing in Babylon. It would not be as obvious to Military Intelligence people who were looking at reports of radio traffic and radar sightings, aerial photographs and agents' memos.

But still, the Israeli Intelligence services were known for imagination and unconventional thinking. If they looked hard at Rish's psychological profile—a romantic with illusions of historic grandeur and all the rest—then maybe they would come to the right conclusions. Hausner hoped so.

Hausner began inspecting the thin defensive line. There were two more AK-47's now and perhaps enough ammunition to hold off an attack such as had been mounted the previous night.

Everyone was working on the defensive positions except for a small party that had volunteered to comb the eastern slope again for abandoned equipment. They brought with them aluminum struts and sheets to be used as shovels to bury the two dead Arabs that were left behind.

The Israelis had suffered seven wounded; one, Chaim Tamir, a delegate to the peace mission, was hurt badly. They were all resting comfortably with Kaplan in the shepherds' hut, which Hausner designated as the infirmary, under the supervision of the two stewardesses.

An earth and clay ramp was being constructed up to the leading edge of the starboard-side delta to make access to the Concorde easier. The work was done by sweating, bare-chested men using crude tools made from scraps of the Concorde. Earth was carried in suitcases and blankets and packed onto the ramp by hand and foot.

Hausner stepped onto the partially completed ramp and jumped the remainder of the way onto the wing. He entered the cabin through the emergency door.

Sitting in the back of the aircraft, facing him, were Burg and Dobkin. His court-martial board.

Hausner moved down the aisle. The sun illuminated the small portholes, and a shaft of dusty sunlight streamed in from the gaping hole in the rear bulkhead. "Good morning." He remained standing in the aisle. The smell of burnt kerosene still permeated the cabin.

The two men nodded.

Dobkin cleared his throat. "Jacob, this grieves us very much. But if there is to be any discipline here, we must be brutal with anyone who disobeys orders."

"I quite agree."

Dobkin leaned forward. "Then you concur that we have the authority to try you?"

"I didn't say that."

"It's not important that you do," said Dobkin. "We *are* the law here. Whether you agree or not."

"I agree that *we* are the law. *We* can try people and mete out punishment."

Dobkin frowned. "Jacob, you are drawing a very fine line. Now this is serious. If we try you, it will be in open court, with observers and all of that, but I can tell you already that the verdict will be cut and dry. Guilty. And the only sentence possible under these circumstances is. . . ." He looked toward Burg for support. Burg had instigated this proceeding, but Burg was a pragmatist and a survivor to the core. He sat back and said nothing. He lit his pipe with a lot of flourish and made noncommittal noises. He wanted to see which way it would go. Dobkin was a military man. He was used to demanding total loyalty and getting it. Burg, in his world, accepted disloyalty and compromises that would make the generals reach for their court-martial manuals.

Hausner looked at his watch pointedly. "Listen, the only thing you have wrong here is the fact that I can't be charged with disobeying an order because *I* am in charge. Now, if anyone else disobeys an order—including either of you —we will convene this group and try him. Is there anything else?"

Dobkin leaned forward. "Are you mutinying?"

"I wouldn't call it that."

"I would. The highest ranking man among us is the Foreign Minister. As an elected member of the Knesset, he—"

"Forget it, General. I have the loyalty of the majority of the armed men out there. The Foreign Minister may be in charge *de jure,* but *de facto* we have taken over and you know it. That's why you didn't even bother to invite him to this little meeting. The only point of contention here is which of us three is the head man. I say it is me. But if you want the orders to come through the Foreign Minister or through either of you, that's fine with me. As long as you all understand who's giving those orders. All right?"

There was a long silence, then Burg spoke for the first time. "You see, it was a classical maneuver, based on the von Neumann-Morgenstern game plan theory, I believe. Jacob usurped the power from the Foreign Minister with our tacit approval. After we had taken that step, there was no going back for us. And now Jacob is finessing *us.* Very Machiavellian." Burg's tone was neutral.

Hausner said nothing.

There was another long silence. Dobkin spoke softly. "Why are you doing this, Jacob?"

Hausner shrugged, "I guess because I'm the only one who understands how to handle this situation. I trust *me.* I'm a little nervous about *you.*"

Dobkin shook his head. "No. It's because you got us here. Now you want to get us out. You want to be the hero so you can face life if—when—we get home. And you don't care who gets stepped on as long as you can square this thing with yourself."

Hausner's face turned red. "Whatever you say, General." He turned, walked toward the door, then looked over his shoulder. "Staff meeting at noon sharp. Here in the aircraft." He left.

On the ground, Hausner found Becker and Kahn. They were sitting over a schematic of the APU. He crouched down beside them in the shade of the delta wing. "Why didn't we have any luck with the radio last night?"

Kahn spoke. "We were having trouble concentrating with all the damned noise out here."

Hausner smiled. "Sorry. We'll try to keep it quiet tonight."

"I hope to God we're out of here by nightfall," said Kahn.

Hausner looked at him. "I think that might depend to a large extent on you two."

Becker stood. "On me. I'm the captain. If we make radio contact, I'll take the credit. If we don't, I'll take the blame." Becker's tone was cool.

Hausner stood also. "Of course. Everyone is looking for planes. As soon as someone spots one they have orders to run at top speed back here and tell you. The ramp up to the aircraft will be finished in a few hours. You can be inside and broadcasting within about two minutes of an aircraft being spotted. Is that satisfactory?"

"Sounds good," said Becker.

Hausner looked up at the delta wing. He seemed to come to a decision. "I'm draining off the remaining fuel."

Becker stared. "I need the fuel to run the auxiliary power unit so that we can generate power to run the radios."

"The APU is not working, nor will it ever work. The first priority is to keep the Arabs out of here. Even if you do get the APU working, it will be damned little use to us with Ahmed Rish sitting in the cockpit. I need the fuel to make things that will explode, Captain."

"I can't let you take the fuel."

Hausner stared at him. Technicians got away with a lot more than ordinary mortals. "You're wasting time on this APU. The damned thing isn't worth it. Go back to the flight deck and operate the radios until the batteries are gone. We have no time to worry about generating our own electricity for later. There may not be a later unless we shoot the works with what we've got like we did last night." He looked evenly at Becker, then at Kahn. He lowered his voice. "Besides, I don't want all that fuel in the wing tanks. One tracer round could set it off and cook you two in the cockpit."

Becker knew that Hausner had a point. But then again, so did he. For every problem that lay ahead, there were several conceivable solutions. "Look," he said, "let us try to fix the APU while radio reception is bad. You take the fuel you need. I think there might be more left than we thought. You can only hold so much in the containers available. The rest will stay in the tanks. Agreed?"

Hausner smiled. "When we were up there, you demanded and got complete obedience from me and everyone else with no arguments and no compromise. You were the captain. Now I am the commander on the ground. Why shouldn't I demand the same?"

Becker shook his head. "It's different up there. That's technical. Here it's all subjective. There's room for discussion."

"Bullshit." Hausner looked up at the Concorde. Its white paint glowed a pale yellow in the rising sun. "I'll make a final decision later. Meanwhile, I'm going to start making Molotov cocktails with the fuel. See you later." He turned and walked away.

Under the damaged tail section of the aircraft, the Foreign Minister sat on the ground with two junior aides, Shimon Peled and Esther Aronson. Also seated with him were two delegates, Ya'akov Sapir, a left-wing member of the Knesset, whom Hausner didn't care for, and Miriam Bernstein, whom Hausner did care for.

Hausner could see that they had taken a break from whatever they had been doing and were engaged in a lively parliamentary debate. He walked over to them.

The Foreign Minister looked up. At first he seemed surprised to see Hausner. Then he nodded to himself. He guessed correctly that Dobkin and Burg had come off second best in their attempt to discipline Hausner. He made a quick evaluation of the situation and stood up to meet Hausner. "I didn't have time to thank you properly for your role in last night's action."

Hausner nodded. "Thank you, Mr. Minister." He looked down at the four people sitting in the dust, trying to ignore him. "I'm sorry I didn't have time this morning to assign you any duties."

"Quite all right. We would be happy to have some direction in the expenditure of our energies and—"

"What I had in mind, Mr. Minister, was this—you should gather all the loose luggage that fell in the wake of the aircraft. Some of it is down the hill, so be careful when you go outside the perimeter. Empty the luggage and sort the contents. Carry all empty bags and clothes to the men and women on the perimeter. They will fill the luggage with sand and clay to make breastworks. Then they will fashion dummies out of the clothes, stuffing them with sand and rags. I want a nice job of it. The dummies will be placed in position at dusk. Save some clothing for bandages and catalogue anything else you find that may be of use, such as liquor, medicines, food, and that sort of thing." He paused, then spoke in a low voice. "Also, I want you to look among the drugs for one that will kill quickly and painlessly if taken in an overdose. But keep that quiet." He said loudly, "Is everything clear?"

The Foreign Minister nodded. "Of course. We'll begin as soon as we adjourn."

Hausner shook his head almost imperceptibly.

"Well, perhaps we should adjourn now," said the Foreign Minister. He turned around and faced the group that was still sitting. "All for adjournment say aye."

A few voices mumbled in return. They all stood slowly and sullenly and walked off, except for Miriam Bernstein.

Hausner turned and began walking in the opposite direction.

Bernstein caught up with him. "You humiliated a fine man back there."

He didn't answer.

"Did you hear me, damn you?"

He stopped but did not turn to face her. "Anyone who insists on playing games with me is exposing himself to humiliations, if not worse. And I don't have the time or patience for one of your lectures, Miriam."

She walked around him and looked him in the face. She spoke softly. "What's come over you, Jacob? I can't believe you're acting like this."

He stepped closer to her and stared down into her eyes. There were tears starting to form there, but he couldn't tell if they were tears of rage or sorrow. It struck him that he could never read her expressions. Sometimes she seemed like a robot programmed to deliver peace and conciliation sermons. Yet he suspected there was flesh and blood there. Passion. Real passion. He had discovered that much while they sat together on the Concorde. But then he had been at a low point and she had become human. She was one of those women who responded warmly to need and weakness. Strength and self-assurance in a man put her off. He supposed it had something to do with the black uniforms of her childhood. God, he would never understand the Jews of the camps. He could understand the arrogant, cocky Sabras, although he wasn't one of them, either. His own peers were a small group and getting smaller every year. He never felt really at home in the new Israel. He never felt at ease with Jews of the camps like Miriam Bernstein. He looked down, against his will, to her wrist where the numbers were tattooed. Many people had them removed by a plastic surgeon. Hers were distorted and lighter than was usual. The result of growth. The numbers of a child.

"Aren't you going to answer me?"

"What? Oh. Yes. What's come over me? Well, I'll tell you, Miriam. A few minutes ago, General Dobkin and Mr. Burg were at the point of putting me in front of a firing squad." He raised his hand to stifle her exclamation of disbelief, then went on. "Don't get me wrong. I'm not angry with them. I agree with the thought processes that brought them to that point. I just didn't agree with their choice of victim. You see, they perceive things a lot more clearly than the rest of you do. They know what has to be done here. I can guarantee you, Miriam, that if this situation lasts another forty-eight hours, you will all be clamoring for the execution of food-hoarders, malingerers, traitors, and people who fall asleep on guard duty. But we don't have the luxury of waiting for a consensus. What seems brutal to you today will seem lenient to you tomorrow."

She wiped away a tear and shook her head. "You have very little faith in humanity. Most of us are not like that. I'd rather die than vote for someone else's execution."

"You *will* die if you maintain that attitude. And for a person who saw what you saw, I don't know how you can have so much faith in the basic goodness of human beings."

"I said *most* human beings were decent. There are always a few fascists."

"What you really mean is that there is a little fascist in all of us. And that's the part of you that will become dominant when things get tough. The part of me that I've called on to survive. Called on knowingly and willingly. The beast. The heart of darkness." He looked at her. She was pale. "You know, for someone who spends so much time with an Air Force general, I would have thought that some of the hawk would have rubbed off."

She looked quickly up at him. Color came into her pale cheeks. "You—" She turned and walked quickly away from him.

16

Hausner sat with Brin and Naomi Haber at their firing position. He looked down the eastern slope, smoking a cigarette and speaking to the young couple. "Are you teaching her to use the scope and rifle?" he asked Brin.

Brin shrugged. "She doesn't want to learn."

Hausner turned to her. "Why not?"

She brushed some dust off her blue jumpsuit. "I can't shoot anyone. I'm a good and fast runner, and that's what I volunteered to do."

Hausner started to answer her, but Dobkin suddenly appeared. Hausner glanced at him quickly and looked for a gun, but did not see one. Brin tensed up, also.

Dobkin seemed to have forgotten the incident in the Concorde. He nodded and sat down on the ground. No one spoke for a long while.

Hausner turned and pointed across the top of the flat mound toward the southwest. "What's that?"

Dobkin looked. The morning shadows lay over the brown land. Swirls of mist rose out of the scattered marsh. "The Greek amphitheater. Built by Alexander the Great. When he captured Babylon in 323 B.C.E., the city was already ancient and on the skids. He attempted to revive it, but its day was over. Alexander died here. Did you know that?"

"No." Hausner chain-lit a cigarette.

"They'll be coming to parley soon," said Dobkin.

"Who? The Greeks?"

Dobkin allowed himself a smile. "The Greeks I could parley with. It's the Arabs I'm worried about."

Hausner smiled back. There was a little less tension between them. "*Maybe* they'll come." He turned to Brin and Naomi Haber. "Why don't you two take a break in the shade?"

The girl stood. Brin hesitated, then stood also. He took the M-14 and walked off, followed by the girl.

When they were out of earshot, Dobkin spoke. "No maybes about it. They won't try a daylight assault, and they don't want to wait for nightfall to resolve this thing."

"You're right," said Hausner.

"What are we going to tell them?"

Hausner looked at him. "Are you with me?"

Dobkin hesitated. "I . . . the Foreign Minister and Burg are *our* superiors."

"We'll see about that."

Dobkin changed the subject. "I'm going on a one-way mission tonight."

"I know that."

"There isn't much chance for me to get through. I'm going only so that the people here can keep their hopes and morale up."

"That's why I'm sending you. I don't think you'll make it either. There are not many people who would go after figuring that out. You're all right, General." He looked at him. "So, are you with me?"

Dobkin shrugged. "What difference does it make? You hold all the cards. The political leaders are cowed. Your men hold five of the six automatic weapons."

"I just want to know for myself." He pointed to the south. "What's that, by the way?"

"I'm not going to make you feel good by going along with you. Let's just say I'm neutral." He looked to the south. "That should be the Kasr mound. On the other side are the excavations of the palace of Nebuchadnezzar and the ruins of the Hanging Gardens. Close to that is the Ishtar Gate and the museum and guest house." He paused. "I'm looking forward to seeing it tonight."

"Glad to hear it," said Hausner. There was a long silence.

Suddenly, Hausner came to attention. He pointed southwest toward the Euphrates. "Is that smoke? It looks like a village among the ruins."

Dobkin nodded without looking. "It is. The village of Kweirish."

"I wonder if they would be of any help."

"I don't think so. They're peasants. They have no connection with the outside world. Besides, I'm sure the Ashbals are running the place."

Hausner could see the squalid mud huts, huddled like some medieval Italian village in a corner of a ruined Roman city in order to survive.

The whole of the surrounding countryside was a spectacular study of contrasts. Patches of desert and marshland to the east and beyond that the Tigris and then the towering mountains. On the west bank of the Euphrates, endless mud flats stretching to the horizons, wet now, but soon to be cracked by the hot sun like a jigsaw puzzle. A few bulrushes and date palms struggled on both banks of the Euphrates.

In the foreground, around the mound they were on, Hausner could make out bricks and rubble, smaller mounds and marsh. There were the low ridges of straight city walls, punctuated every now and then by higher mounds that had been the watchtowers. Wind, water, sand, and thousands of years of brick quarrying by peasants had combined to obliterate what was once the wonder of the world's cities. Hausner knew that scenes of desolation such as this were common in Mesopotamia. The largest and most opulent cities of the ancient world lay for thousands of years undisturbed beneath the dust. A sense of emptiness assailed him as he looked out across the Euphrates. Flat, bare plains of wet mud were crisscrossed here and there by the fabled irrigation canals, now disused. The very wildlife that should have flourished here seemed to have abandoned the place. This was a strange and somehow malevolent corner of the world. A place where huge temples had been raised long ago to gods that no one remembered and palaces built for kings and kingdoms that had vanished without a trace.

The silence of the place screamed in his ears as if he were hearing the ghostly crashing of Babylonian chariots, the fleeing enemy, and the shouts of her victorious armies. Opulent Babylon. In the Old and New Testaments, a symbol of human pride, carnality, and sin. To modern Jews and Christians, its utter desolation was a symbol of Biblical prophecy fulfilled. Hausner knew that there must be some meaning in all the nothingness that stretched before him. Yet, perhaps the meaning was nothingness. Sand. Dust. Death.

Why had Rish brought them here? The Babylonian Captivity? Hausner imagined that was it. Or maybe it was something less melodramatic. Perhaps it was just convenient for his purposes—close to the Palestinians' camp. But their camp was a hundred kilometers across the desert. . . . Well, the Babylonian Captivity it was, then. In the libraries of the world there were tomes on Babylon, and when they were revised and rewritten, there would be a footnote with an asterisk and it would read, *a curious incident involving a supersonic Concorde aircraft and.* . . . Hausner put out his cigarette and saved the stub. "Here they come," he said softly.

From the direction of the road, a group of five men were walking up the slope of the mound. The man in front held up a white flag.

Haber and Brin, who had not gone far, came hurrying back. Brin had changed to the ten-power day scope and watched them approach. "I don't think Rish is with them." Brin handed the rifle to Hausner who knelt and sighted through the scope. Hausner put the rifle down and shook his head. "He doesn't trust us. He thinks that we would not honor a white flag. That makes me damned angry. General?"

Dobkin nodded. "It does show a lack of faith on his part." He thought for a moment. "He really doesn't understand us—and *that* scares me."

Hausner stood and turned to Brin and Haber. "Pass the word to hold fire. I want everyone to remain out of sight. No one is to leave the perimeter, Nathan. If anyone tries, stop him." He brushed off his clothes. "General, will you accompany me?"

"Of course." He stood, also, and straightened his uniform. "You know, it's ironic. They want to talk *now*. That's what we wanted to do in New York—and on the Concorde. Now I'm not so sure *I* want to talk."

"I agree," said Hausner. "But I'm sure the peace delegation wants to talk. I don't trust that bunch, Ben. They are professional peacemakers. They are spring-loaded to see the good side of any proposal. Cursed are the peacemakers for they make the next war harder than the last."

Dobkin laughed. "Amen. The generals should negotiate the peaces and the peacemakers should run the armies." He became serious. "Actually, we are not being fair to the delegation. They are not all alike—some—most are very hard bargainers. They are realists as much as we are."

Hausner stepped down onto the slope. "I doubt it. Come on. Let's go before a dozen professional negotiators descend on us." He began making his way downhill. Dobkin followed.

They lost sight of the Arabs for a while as their group descended into a deep draw. A hundred meters down the slope, they spotted the white flag, then they saw the Arabs again. They were armed and advancing fast. Hausner felt a moment of doubt, but he waved a white handkerchief and shouted in Arabic. The Arabs spotted him and responded. Both groups approached each other slowly. The Arabs stopped on a level shelf in the side of the slope.

Hausner walked quickly up to them and stood very close to the leader, in the Arab manner. "Where's Rish? I will speak only with Rish."

The man stared at him for a very long moment. His dark eyes seemed to burn with hate and contempt. Obviously he didn't like this mission. He spoke softly and slowly. "I am Salem Hamadi, lieutenant of Ahmed Rish. He sends his respects and requests your immediate surrender."

Hausner looked at the man. Unlike Rish, Hamadi had never been captured and there existed neither an identikit nor a psychological profile on him. There was not even a comprehensive listing of his activities. All Hausner knew was that the man had started life as a Palestinian orphan and then became head of the Ashbal program for the various Palestinian liberation organizations. Values? Morality? Honor? It was hard to say. You couldn't even count on the strong religious upbringing that most Arabs were exposed to. The man who stood less than a meter from Hausner was short but well proportioned. He wore a neatly clipped goatee and apparently practiced somewhat more rigorous personal hygiene than Hausner had observed among the terrorists at Ramla. Hausner moved even closer. "Where is he? I demand to speak to him."

Hamadi nodded slowly. "You are Jacob Hausner."

"I am."

"Will you accompany me?"

"I might."

Hamadi hesitated. "You have my personal assurances."

"Really?"

Hamadi literally bit his lip to control his growing impatience. "My word." He paused. "Believe me, we want to talk this over as much as you do." He smiled suddenly. "This is not a trap to kill Jacob Hausner. We could do that right here and now. Besides, you are not that important."

"Rish seemed to think I was. He said he would kill me when we landed."

Salem Hamadi looked off into space. "He rescinds that vow."

Hausner turned and waved to Brin, who was watching through the scope. Brin acknowledged. Hausner could see heads staring discreetly over the newly fabricated breastworks of baggage and earth. He noticed that some of the baggage was too brightly colored. He would have to see that a layer of dust was put on everything. He turned back to Hamadi. Hamadi had seen the glint of light from the scope and was committing its location to memory. Hausner bumped him on purpose as he moved past him. "Well, let's go. I have other things to do."

The group started down the slope. They came off the incline and began walking parallel to a meter-high ridge that Dobkin explained was the city's inner wall. Hausner saw the spot where the Concorde's rear bumper wheel had hit it, what seemed like a century before. They turned south and headed toward the main ruins.

The ruins of the city were barely excavated. It took a lot of imagination to picture a teeming metropolis of living souls—young girls with jangling bracelets, soldiers eating and drinking, colorful bazaars, awesome processions, and the famous astrologers of Babylon drawing up horoscopes on wet clay for a few coppers. But Hausner, as an inhabitant of the Middle East, was used to excavations. He could see it all, and more. He could almost feel the presence of the spirits as they jostled him on the busy street. A ringing in his ears seemed to turn into semidistinct voices speaking an ancient Semitic language. Then there was a word or a snatch of a phrase in ancient Hebrew. He suddenly felt that right where he was walking, a Jew had walked and had spoken with his wife. They had their children with them. They were going somewhere. Toward the Ishtar Gate. Out of the city. They were leaving Babylon, and captivity, for good.

Hamadi said something, and Hausner became aware that they had come a long distance. He looked around. The excavations were more thorough here. Hamadi was speaking to Dobkin, who was asking incessant questions about the ruins. Hamadi seemed unsure of his answers and finally told Dobkin to be quiet.

Hausner knew something of the history of Babylon even if he did not know the city itself. He knew Babylon as a name, a symbol, a conception, a state of mind. He hardly credited the fact that it existed as brick and mortar. Dobkin was interested in the brick and mortar. Hausner, if he was interested at all, was interested in something more enduring. And what could be more enduring than total obliteration and destruction? That's what made Babylon a living symbol. Its place in history was secured by the fact that it had fallen as predicted.

So Babylon had died as cities do die, and the dust blew over her endlessly through the centuries, covering it all. The site could hardly be located by modern archeologists, and even local legend, which had kept alive the location of the sites of other buried cities, ceased to mention Babylon, so utter and complete was the desolation.

And now the digging out had begun, as it had in Israel and other parts of the Middle East. Each mound that was excavated was a reminder not only of the transitory nature of man's works, but also of the human peculiarity for self-destruction. For Hausner, the associations with Babylon, with Jews being here again, was both ludicrous and sad. The fact that they had arrived by supersonic transport was beside the point. The point was that they were there—there against their will. The human dimension had not undergone any major changes in thousands of years. Only the externals had changed.

When the small group reached the heights where the Greek amphitheater stood, they turned west toward the Euphrates River and followed a goat path. An emaciated donkey nibbled on the ubiquitous salt-white clumps of thorn. A slight breeze rustled through the yellow-green fronds of a solitary date palm. The heat was growing more oppressive. Hausner was reminded that there was less than twenty-four hours' supply of liquids on the hill. The available food might last twice as long. Sections of the aircraft's aluminum skin had been shaped into basins to collect rainwater, but rain seemed as unlikely here as snow.

They walked silently, Dobkin taking both a military and an archeological interest in the route. They stopped on a small ridge. Hausner could see the hill where the Concorde rested, about a kilometer and a half to the north. The top of the Concorde was barely visible from here. The hill—or the buried citadel—looked formidable from this perspective, and he could see why the Ashbals wished to negotiate.

To the west was the Euphrates, about five hundred meters further down the goat trail. Hausner could see the squalid village of Kweirish, on the bank of the Euphrates, more clearly now. It was a village of *sarifa*—rough mud huts, unwhitewashed and unadorned. As they came closer, he could see women wrapped to the eyes in long black *abbahs* and men in long shirtlike *gellebiahs,* their heads draped in *kheffiyahs.* Someone was scraping a thin music from a stringed instrument. Goats, the color of the earth, grazed the scrub and were herded by Biblical-looking figures in long robes and flowing headdresses, doing the same work under the same conditions as their ancestors had done thousands of years before. The whole scene, Hausner realized, had hardly changed in four or five thousand years. The people were Moslems instead of idol worshippers, they no longer kept swine herds, and Babylon was no more. But otherwise, life on the Euphrates went on and, in fact, changed considerably less than the course of the wandering, restless river.

The group turned off the goat trail and began climbing a huge mound. They reached a flight of steep brick steps and ascended further. On the way, they came to a flat area hollowed out of the side of the mound. Here, mounted on a stone plinth, stood the Lion of Babylon. Nothing was known of it, neither its age nor its significance, but it looked awesome, striding perpetually over a fallen victim. Hamadi spoke. "We search you and blindfold you here."

Hausner shook his head. "No."

Hamadi turned to Dobkin. "It is standard military procedure throughout the world when bringing an enemy into your lines. You know this. It is no humiliation."

Dobkin had to agree.

Hausner agreed reluctantly.

They undressed and were searched thoroughly. They dressed again and were blindfolded and taken slowly up the remaining steps. The ground leveled out, but it was covered with what seemed to be clay bricks. They descended a flight of steps and the air suddenly felt cooler. The blindfolds were removed. Hausner strained to see in the darkened room. He heard voices whispering.

"I am Ahmed Rish," said a soft voice from the shadow in passable Hebrew. "It is an event to see Jacob Hausner—again. And an honor to meet the famous General Dobkin."

Hausner and Dobkin remained silent. They both sensed that there were other men in the shadows along the walls. The ruined chamber had no roof, but the sun was too low to penetrate into it. They looked around slowly, as their eyes adjusted to the darkness.

Rish spoke again. "We are in the excavated ruins of the South Palace. The throne room where Belshazzar, grandson of Nebuchadnezzar, saw the fatal handwriting on the wall. You will be familiar with the story from the Book of Daniel, of course."

Silence.

Rish spoke again from the darkness. "I am standing where the royal throne stood, in a recess of the wall. If you squint into the darkness you may visualize the scene of feasting—the gold and silver vessels taken by Nebuchadnezzar when he sacked Jerusalem, the flickering candle, the apparition of the hand that emerged from the shadows and wrote the words of Babylon's doom upon the wall." He paused for effect. "That is one of the Jews' favorite stories. That is why I brought you here. A special treat."

Hausner and Dobkin did not respond.

Rish went on. "Close by, there has been uncovered a huge furnace. It is no doubt the fiery furnace into which Nebuchadnezzar threw Shadrach, Meshach, and Abed-nego. A miracle was wrought by God and they survived. However, the Jews have not always been saved by such miracles." He paused and the sound of men breathing filled the dark chamber. Rish spoke softly, almost below the threshold of hearing. "Babylon is a place of infinite sadness for the Jews, but it is also a place of miracles. Which will it be this time, Mr. Hausner?"

Hausner lit a cigarette. "You have been very eloquent, Ahmed Rish. I shall be very brief. What do you want?"

"That was foolhardy, landing that huge aircraft on that mound. You could have all been killed."

"What do you want?"

"Excuse me. I neglected to ask you if you would like some refreshments. Water? Food?"

Dobkin answered. "We have plenty of both, Rish."

Rish laughed. "I think not."

Hausner almost shouted. He didn't have any patience with this Arab habit of circumlocution. "Get to the point. What do you *want?*"

Rish's voice sounded a little harder. "I want you all to be my hostages while I negotiate with your government. I want to avoid further bloodshed."

Hausner's eyes were adjusting to the light. He could make out Rish standing in a recess of the wall. He was wearing a simple white *gellebiah* and sandals. He looked about the same as Hausner remembered him from Ramla. He was exceptionally tall and fair for an Arab. Hausner remembered that he was thought to have some Circassian or Persian blood. "You took a bit of a beating last night. You lost about thirty killed and wounded, I suspect."

"I am not here to trade after-action reports, Mr. Hausner. And I am not going to go into a long political harangue about why we did what we did, what our objectives are, or any of that with you. I will take those matters up with your government. I am only going to give you one guarantee and one ultimatum. The guarantee is that no Israelis will be killed if you surrender. The ultimatum is that you surrender before sundown. Is that acceptable?"

Hausner spoke. "What if my country rejects whatever demands you make? How then can you guarantee that we will be safe as hostages?"

"If they call our bluff, I will release you anyway. Only you and I know that, of course. But you have my word on it."

Hausner and Dobkin conferred quietly. Hausner spoke. "I think we know your game, Mr. Rish. Your primary objective was to create an incident to try to wreck the Peace Conference. You may have succeeded there. Maybe not. But your second objective was to grab two planeloads of top-ranking Israelis and interrogate them for political and military intelligence. That intelligence would be worth a fortune on the open market, wouldn't it? And your last objective was to hold us hostage for some unspecified demands. And even if you are willing to let us go if those demands are not met, it would not be before we are vigorously debriefed. Am I right? Do I have your guarantee that none of us will be interrogated or subject to duress of any sort?"

Rish did not answer.

Hausner went on. "How about the Israeli Arabs? I don't think you included them in your guarantee."

Again Rish did not answer, but Hausner could see, even in the bad light, a remarkable change come over his expression. Rish considered the Jews his traditional enemy. But as nonbelievers, by a curious quirk in Arab and Moslem thinking, they were not liable to the ultimate penalty for most offenses. However, a Moslem, especially if he were also Arab, could expect no mercy for transgressions against his people or his religion. Jabari and Arif were dead men as far as Rish was concerned, and Hausner knew it. Rish spoke. "You are making me angry, Mr. Hausner. The lions' den is not the place to be when you wish to provoke the lion. Do it from a distance, Mr. Hausner."

Hausner nodded and looked at Rish closely. He wanted very much to ask Rish about the girl he had seen him carrying away from the battle. But *was* that Rish, and if it was, who was the girl? Was she dead? To ask, however, would confirm what Rish must already suspect about the existence of a night scope. And to ask might send him into an uncontrollable rage. Rish seemed calm enough now, but you couldn't tell with unstable personalities. And that's what the psychiatrists at Ramla had labeled him. Unstable and psychopathic. But like a lot of psychopathic killers, he had a certain charm. The charm could lull you, and then you would make a mistake and that's when he would tear your throat out. "How do I know that you are not so filled with hate that you will not kill us all? What guarantee do I have that you are not . . . insane?"

Dobkin spoke quickly in a low voice. "For God's sake, Hausner." He grabbed his arm.

There was a very long stillness, during which time Hausner knew that Rish was trying to overcome his urge to murder them. But Hausner knew, as Rish knew, that to murder them was to end all chances of a surrender.

Rish got his emotions under control with considerable difficulty, then spoke with an even voice. "I can only repeat my guarantee and my ultimatum. You have until dusk. Not one moment longer. After dusk, as we both know, radio reception is better. So don't ask for an extension at dusk." Rish moved a little out of the alcove. "Also, as we both know, it is only a matter of time before the

Iraqi authorities discover our little problem here. But don't count on them to act for at least twenty-four hours after they learn we are here. They will hesitate before they move. I can assure you of that. I have friends in the government. They will delay any move and notify me of all decisions. And when the Iraqi Army does move, it moves with painful slowness, Mr. Hausner. Still, I must consider them in my calculations. And so, again I say—at dusk, if we do not hear from you, we attack."

Hausner and Dobkin remained silent. Rish held out his hands in a gesture of solicitation. "Think of the consequences of a defeat. My men are all Ashbals. You know this from your captive?"

There was no answer.

Rish went on. "Well, I cannot be responsible for what might happen in the heat of battle. If my men take the hill tonight, they may be carried away with the madness of killing. They lost many friends last night. They would want revenge. Then there are your women to consider . . . you understand?"

Hausner used one of the most offensive Arabic profanities he could think of.

There was silence except for the sound of men murmuring along the walls.

Then Rish stepped a little further out of the shadows. He smiled. "Your command of the more colorful parts of my native tongue is interesting. Where did you learn that?"

"From you—in Ramla."

"Really?" He moved out of the alcove and stood in the middle of the throne room about two meters from Hausner and Dobkin. "Once I was your prisoner. Now you are about to be mine. When I was in Ramla, you could have had me murdered by my fellow Arabs in exchange for a pardon or an extra privilege. It is done. I know it. But as much as you wanted to have it done, you did not. You had a sense of fair play. Yet I swore to kill you for the insult of slapping me. But really, in a way, I owe you my life. I will be fair with you if you surrender to me now." He looked closely at Hausner, then stepped to within a meter of him. "You know that I still burn with that blow, don't you?" He swung at Hausner and hit him across the face with an open palm.

Hausner was taken aback for a second, then lunged at Rish. Dobkin grabbed him and held him firmly.

Rish nodded his head. "Now that is over. The insult is canceled. *Al ain bel ain al sen bel sen.* An eye for an eye, a tooth for a tooth. Nothing more. Nothing less."

Hausner regained his composure and pulled away from Dobkin. "Yes, I agree, Rish. But there's still the small insult of blowing up a planeload of fifty people."

Rish looked away and spoke. "I won't discuss that. You have an opportunity to save the other fifty." He looked at Dobkin. "From a military point of view you must know it is hopeless."

Dobkin moved closer to Rish. He could hear the sounds of rustling garments in the shadows. Rish made an imperceptible movement with his hand and the shadows retreated back into the walls. Dobkin came within a few centimeters of Rish. "Last night it was indeed hopeless from a military standpoint. Yet we beat you. Tonight the odds will be better."

Rish shook his head. "Tonight we take the hill, General."

Hausner grabbed Dobkin's shoulder. "I've had enough. I want to get back."

Rish nodded. "You will be democratic enough to let everyone vote, I hope, Mr. Hausner."

"Yes. We do everything by vote up there, Rish. I'll let you know before sundown. In the meantime, I'm sending our prisoner down to you. He needs medical attention. Are you equipped?"

Rish laughed. "That is a clumsy way of finding out about our medical situation. But we will take the man. Thank you." He looked slowly from one to another. "Again, I must warn you that if my men take the hill in the dark I cannot control them."

Dobkin spoke. "You're either a bad commander or a bad liar."

Rish turned and walked back into the shadow of the alcove. His retreating voice echoed through the throne room. "I am a realist, gentlemen. Which you are not. Save those people, General. Save their lives, Mr. Hausner."

"I'll do that," said Hausner. He turned to leave.

"Oh. One more thing," said Rish. "This might help you reach a decision. I have some information that some of your people might find interesting." He paused.

Hausner felt a cold chill of apprehension run up his spine. He did not turn around and he did not respond. Dobkin stood with his back to Rish also.

"Some of your people have members of their families—loved ones—who are in Arab countries. I know the fates of those people. Would *you* like to know them? If you surrender, I will give your people true accounts of each one of them. It would end so much suffering and uncertainty for them. The knowledge of their whereabouts, if they are alive, might help their families to secure their return to Israel."

Silence.

"Abdel Jabari's family, for instance. Or Rachel Baum's brother, missing in action since 1973."

Hausner began walking away. Dobkin followed.

"Wasn't one of your wife's cousins missing in the Sinai since 1967, General?"

Dobkin continued walking without a falter in his step.

"Miriam Bernstein's husband, Yosef. He was in a Syrian POW camp until six months ago. Then one night they took him out and shot him."

Hausner slowed his pace.

"Or was that Rachel Baum's brother? I think Yosef Bernstein is still in a Syrian POW camp. Well, no matter, I have it all written down somewhere. I'll check on it later."

Hausner's body shook with rage and he found it difficult to keep walking. Behind him, Rish's low, taunting laugh echoed through the throne room.

They were led up and out of the chamber into the full sunlight. The escort was slow in putting the blindfolds back on. Dobkin had a glimpse of the towers and battlements of the Ishtar Gate about a hundred meters to the east. Nearby, there was the verandahed guest house and the small museum. The restored gate area gleamed with its blue-glazed bricks in the sunlight. Gold lions of Babylon and mythical beasts shone on the glazing in bas-relief. The walls of the Hanging Gardens stood close by, dusty and cracked with not a trace of vegetation, not even moss.

In the brief time that his eyes were uncovered, Hausner noticed that the mound they were on was approximately the same height as the one the Concorde stood on about two kilometers away, across a small depression in the land. He could see the Concorde from where he stood and his people moving about on the top of the mound.

The blindfolds were put on and they were led away.

After the Arabs left them, Dobkin let out a long breath. "You almost pushed him too far. You're crazy." He glanced back over his shoulder as the Arabs moved farther away. "You know, somehow I expected someone more purely evil."

"He's more evil than you can ever imagine."

"I wonder. He's insane. I'm sure of that. But during his moments of sanity, I think that he really wants to be liked and admired."

"He does. And we'll play on that if we get another chance." Hausner was breathing hard from the climb. He looked up and waved at Brin, who waved back. He turned to Dobkin, who was making the climb without any effort. "You're right, of course. To the people up there, Rish is the Devil incarnate, which is fine for our purposes—and theirs, too. But somehow our devils are never quite what we expect when we meet them face to face."

Brin called out. "Are they going to surrender?"

Hausner looked up and smiled. He yelled back. "I gave them your ultimatum." He noticed again how the positions looked from this perspective. He noted the crumbling crust of earth, the treacherous potholes, and the washed-out gullies. In the dark it must be a nightmare. If he were an attacker he would become demoralized very quickly.

The two men reached the crest. Everyone who wasn't standing sentry duty crowded around them. Dobkin briefly related some of what had happened. There were many questions and the discussion began to become heated. Hausner cut off further comment and promised to take a vote before sundown. He asked everyone to go back to work on the defenses, which indicated to a lot of people what they all knew anyway—there would be no surrender.

The men and women of the peace mission continued the work of building defenses for the expected onslaught. They improvised and invented on the spot. There were virtually no tools available except the flight engineer's tool kit, but from this small beginning, larger instruments were fashioned.

The seats and floor sections were removed from the cabin in some areas and the armor mesh was lifted out. The mesh was strung between aluminum braces, like laundry on a line, to absorb gunfire and shrapnel from hand grenades.

A Knesset member recalled the Greek physicist Archimedes' defense of Syracuse. The legend had it that Archimedes constructed giant magnifying lenses to burn the Roman fleet. In the same spirit, but with a different purpose, aluminum sections were taken off the twisted tail and set between aluminum braces around the perimeter. The aluminum served to reflect the blazing sunlight back into the eyes of the Ashbals if they should decide to attack during the daylight hours. It also made it extremely difficult for snipers to focus on a target. It had still another purpose of being used to send heliographic messages to possible sympathizers on land or in the air. A few men and women took turns manipulating different sections of the aluminum sheets to send out a constant international SOS signal.

More cast aluminum braces and crosspieces were broken from the tail section and stuck into the side of the slope, pointing outward. This line of pickets formed what the military called an abatis. Its function was to make it difficult to scale the breastworks without running into one of these impaling stakes in the dark.

Firing positions became more sophisticated as the day progressed. Holes became deeper and breastworks became longer and stouter. Luggage and armor mesh used on the perimeter were camouflaged with the monochromatic dust that was Babylon. At Dobkin's urging men and women also covered their clothes and faces with a paste made from the dust mixed with their sweat and, in some cases, urine.

Fields of fire were cleared downslope by pushing the giant clumps of earth and clay down to the base of the mound. Small walls of earth and clay were built in the erosion gullies so that an attacker using the gullies as an avenue of approach would have to expose himself at ground level to get over the top of them.

The sparse thorn scrub that grew on the slope and offered some pathetic concealment was cut away. The thorn, used as a local fuel, was brought into the perimeter for that purpose.

Clay and earth plaques were hacked out of the hard crust of the hilltop. Some weighed up to a hundred kilos. They were balanced atop one another to be pushed over the edge of the slope onto attackers below.

Man-traps were dug into the slope and impaling stakes made from the aircraft's aluminum braces were set in the bottom of the holes. The holes were covered with fabric torn from the seats, and the fabric was covered with dust.

Early-warning devices made from wire, string, and cans filled with pebbles were improvised and set out at intervals of one, two, and three hundred meters.

The cannibalization of the aircraft was accomplished with a great deal of difficulty because of the lack of tools. The work went faster when a crude torch was fashioned from the aircraft's oxygen bottles and the aviation fuel. The aluminum was burnt, ripped, pulled, and twisted from the aircraft. Most of the material came from the blasted tail section. The Israelis crawled over and through the great aircraft much as the workers in St. Nazaire had done. They stood on the same cross struts that Nuri Salameh had when he planted his bomb. They saw the twisted, scorched results of that explosion and used the torn material to their advantage.

Small weapons for close-in self-defense, knives and spears, were fashioned from the hydraulic piping. Glass jars from the baggage and the galley were emptied into other containers and filled with aviation fuel. To some jars were added soap from the lavatories and other soap products from the baggage. The result was a crude napalm that would stick and burn.

The men and women of the peace mission took to the work with a mixture of enthusiasm and desperate urgency. Short and informal idea sessions were held. At times, the classical sieges of ancient times were discussed and ideas and innovations gleaned from those past battles. Archimedes and da Vinci were recalled. The sieges of Troy, Rome, Syracuse, Carthage, Jerusalem, and Babylon were dragged out of the memories of school days. What were the elements of the successful defenses? What were the elements that led to the defeats? It was impossible not to think of Masada. There was a similarity that went beyond the tabletop configuration of the terrain.

The question that began to form in the minds of the defenders was: Could a group of intelligent and civilized individuals, given limited resources, stand off a group of less civilized but better armed attackers? Hausner watched as the long line of defensive works took shape. Sitting as they did on a high piece of ground, with the flanks and the western slope almost too steep to climb, the defenses looked very impressive, he thought. An observer looking down from the air—as Ahmed Rish was evidently now doing in his Lear jet—would have concluded that it was too formidable a citadel to storm if there had been any real firepower behind those hastily formed barricades. But there wasn't.

The real question, Hausner knew, was not how long they could hold out. A day might be long enough, yet a week might not be long enough. It all depended on when they would be found. Would they be found in time? What the hell was going on back in Israel?

17

Lod was hot. Almost too hot to bear. Teddy Laskov sat over a glass of beer at a sidewalk table in front of Michel's. Shops were shuttered and the Sabbath traffic was thin, but Michel's, Christian-owned, was crowded. The *Hamseen* showed no signs of letting up. Laskov looked down at the sweating glass. A puddle collected around it, and a stream wound its way across the marble table top and dripped on his leg. He watched it. The blue civilian pants confirmed that he was Teddy Laskov, private citizen. After almost forty years in one uniform or another, it felt very strange. There was a great difference, reflected Laskov, in wearing mufti off duty and wearing civilian clothes as a civilian. The clothes were the same, but they hung differently somehow.

Michel's brought back memories of Miriam, but he was not there for that reason. It was simply a convenient place to conduct business on the Sabbath. His inactivity and indecision had lasted exactly one hour as he paced the floor of his apartment. Then he had decided to act.

General Talman came down the street with what Laskov thought was his usual jaunty gait. He always looked like an RAF officer in a World War II movie. Even out of uniform, as he was now, he looked as if he were wearing a fifty-mission crush cap and silver wings. But as he approached, Laskov could see that his former boss was in no better spirits than he was. Talman's mustache twitched slightly as he nodded and sat down. "Damn hot."

"I noticed."

"All right, then. Let's get down to it. Is Mazar coming?"

"He should be here."

"Let's begin without him," said Talman.

"Good." Laskov pulled some loose notes from his pockets. "I took all the hunches, all the gut reactions, all the possible and probable radar sightings and all the Israeli and American security agency radio reports that I could collect before I packed it in." He looked down at his papers. "I think they headed east. Due east from the tip of Sinai."

Talman tapped his fingers on the table. "I've spoken to Hur. Off the record, of course. He tells me that the Palestinians have dragged a number of red herrings across their path. But the final consensus of all the Intelligence people is that they went west. Libya. That would make sense politically. A few men in Operations, however, are convinced that they continued south into the Sudan. That might make sense politically, also. They could have put down in the Sahara, refueled, and gone on to Uganda if they wanted. There's little radar in that part of the world and a lot of open space with few people who might spot them visually. It all makes sense politically, logistically, and practically. Libya or the Sudan." He paused and looked Laskov in the eye. "But I don't think so. I think they went east, also."

Laskov smiled. "Good. Now I'll show you why." He went through his notes. Talman ordered gin and tonic and listened.

* * *

Chaim Mazar walked past them and continued down the street. He turned and came back. He looked around as if for a table, spotted Laskov and Talman, smiled in apparent surprise, and went over to them. "Do you mind if I join you?" He folded his tall, lanky frame into a small wire chair.

Laskov shook his head. "I'm glad you're the head of Shin Beth and not an operative. You're the worst actor I've ever seen."

"I try." He looked around. "I just came from a press conference. If you think the hot wind is blowing out here, you should have been in there."

Talman leaned forward. "It's good of you to do this."

Mazar shrugged. "Look, I should probably have resigned or been fired myself."

"Why?" asked Laskov. "You're the hero of the hour after spiking that mortar attack. The government needs a hero now, and you're all we've got."

Mazar shrugged. "For the moment. I'll get the ax when the dust settles. I told you that mortar attack was a setup. The same people who produced and directed that farce also brought you the hijacking. It was like this—if for some reason Rish's Lear couldn't get into position, then they were going to try to let the mortar thing succeed. But the Lear *was* set up, and someone—the Palestinians themselves, of course—tipped us about the mortars. Actually, I already knew about them."

"So how are you responsible?" asked Laskov. "As head of Internal Security you did all you were supposed to do. It was . . . Hausner . . . and us. . . ."

"Only partially. You see, in order for the Lear to intercept the Concordes, it was necessary to have the exact time of departure. That information had to go to Rish at Cairo Airport, and that information could only have come from someone in Israel. Someone at the airport. A spy working in our country. That is my area of responsibility. And I can't identify that spy. I don't even have a clue." He lit a cigarette. "Whoever it was had to call a contact from Lod and give him the new flight plan and departure time, not to mention the fact that you both think Rish had the primary tactical frequency. I checked with Cairo. They were cooperative. Rish and his group—under pseudonyms and posing as businessmen—filed a flight plan to Cyprus. But they changed it suddenly. Alexandria Air Traffic Control gave them a hard time about their request for an earlier departure, but I suspect a little *baksheesh* did the trick, as it will do the trick in all the Land of Islam. Anyway, the rest is history."

Talman nodded. "That's interesting, but as you say, history. What matters now is where Concorde 02 is."

"That's what matters to the state of Israel and her external intelligence people and her armed forces. What matters to me as head of Shin Beth is who the spy is. And what makes the job of finding him more difficult is that I have to pull in most of my agents and Arab informers."

"Why?" asked Talmen.

"Because Isaac Burg, head of Mivtzan Elohim, knows one hell of a lot about Shin Beth. That's why. And if they've got him, they are squeezing his nuts, and they could very well have not only his whole organization but mine as well."

Laskov shook his head. "Absurd. He'd kill himself before he'd let them put him through the wringer."

Mazar nodded. "He carried a gun. I only hope he has the time to use it."

Talman ordered another gin. "How about Dobkin? He was actually in the Aman, wasn't he?"

"Yes. Dobkin was closely connected to Military Intelligence. In addition, he knew Cabinet secrets. The Foreign Minister knew . . . everything. And I don't think he will blow his brains out for anyone." Mazar looked down at the table, then stared at Laskov. "Miriam Bernstein was privy to all Cabinet information. I don't think she would stand up well under torture. Do you?" He waited for an answer.

Talman turned to Laskov but could see nothing in his expression. The silence dragged out.

Finally, Mazar let out a long breath. "I'm speaking as an intelligence man of thirty years when I say I hope they're all dead." He paused. "Hausner is, I'm sure."

No one spoke for several minutes. They sipped their drinks and watched the heat waves in the road. Laskov cleared his throat. "What do you have for us on Rish?"

Mazar opened his attaché case and took out a file. "This is insane. Neither of you have any intelligence experience, clearance, or need-to-know. Or common sense." He handed Talman the file. "I don't have any common sense, either."

"We know that," said Talman as he flipped through the file. "The strength of this country is its smallness. The flow of information has always been accomplished in a family-type atmosphere. There is nothing to keep privates from speaking directly to generals and heads of one service from helping the heads of others. But as we get older as a nation, I'm afraid we are going to get bureaucratized and compartmentalized like the rest of the world. You are only helping to delay that dangerous trend, Chaim."

Mazar grunted. "You're full of shit. We'll all wind up in jail if this goes wrong."

Laskov looked impatient. "Did you get any aerial photographs?"

"Yes," said Mazar. "There are thousands of them from the American satellites and the SR-71 recon craft. Here are some suspect ones. The Americans are being very cooperative with the Aman. But I had a lot of trouble explaining what Shin Beth needed them for. Anyway, you can read these as well as any photo analyst, I suppose."

"After forty years, I hope so," said Laskov. He took a stack of photos from Mazar and glanced at the top one. A grease-pencil notation in the margin gave longitude and latitude. The photo was of the Sinai tip. "Lots of cloud cover this time of year."

"It's spring," said Mazar, unnecessarily. "Anyway, they're mostly of Egypt, the Sudan, and Libya. I take it you still suspect points east?"

"We do," said Laskov. "Rish is Iraqi, isn't he?"

Mazar smiled. "I wish it were that easy. Rish's group is almost all Palestinian. They are the wanderers of Islam, like the Jews were the wanderers of the world. Ironic. They could be anywhere from Morocco to Iraq."

Laskov was only half listening. He was looking at a series of high-angle photos taken of the Tigris and Euphrates. They were taken at a height of twenty-five kilometers by the SR-71 recon craft at seven A.M. that morning. There was another series of the Shamiyah Desert in Iraq. The sun was low and cast clongated and distorted shadows over the land. He glanced at Mazar. "Were there any photos of Iraq taken at noon?"

Mazar looked in his notebook. "Only satellite photos. At 12:17. No more recon craft photos scheduled by the Americans until late afternoon tomorrow."

"Get me the satellite photos, then," said Laskov.

"I'll try." Mazar stood. "I've committed a court-martial offense but I don't feel so bad about it." He closed his empty attaché case. "Let me know if you receive a divine message. Meanwhile, I must look for our traitor."

Talman looked up from Rish's psychological profile and background dossier. "Have you questioned the three Palestinian mortar men?"

"Yes," said Mazar. "They really don't know anything, of course. At least they thought that they didn't. But we were able to interpret little things that seemed irrelevant to them. You know the procedure."

"Learn anything?" asked Talman.

"I'm convinced it was Rish who set them up, poor bastards. There are a few other clues, but I have to run them down before I can draw any conclusions. I'll keep you both informed."

Laskov stood and took Mazar's hand. "Thank you. You're a fool to do this."

"Yes." He wiped the sweat from his forehead with a handkerchief. "You owe me. And I'll be around to collect someday."

"How about right now?" Laskov scrawled something on a wet cocktail napkin. "Here's your payment." He handed Mazar the wet paper.

Mazar looked at it and his eyes widened. "Are you sure?"

"No. That's your job. To be sure."

Mazar put the napkin in his shirt pocket and walked quickly into the square toward St. George's, where he hailed a cab.

18

The Lear jet came in low, but not too low.

"Let's shoot it down," suggested Brin.

Hausner shook his head. "We've agreed to a truce until sundown, and we can well use the break. So don't mess it up, Brin."

"Bullshit. They wouldn't attack in the daylight, anyway. They didn't give us any break."

Dobkin looked up from a range card he was drawing. "That's not completely true. They could be sniping all day and causing other unpleasantness. I don't like having to accept a truce any more than you do, son, but let's be realistic." He went back to the card. He drew in rises and depressions in the slope in front of him. A gunner using that position at night or in other times of limited visibility should be able to place effective fire downrange by using the information written and drawn on the range card in relation to aiming stakes placed directly in front of the firing position. He handed it to Brin. "Here."

"I don't need it, General. I have the starlight scope."

"The batteries are almost gone. Also the lens could get broken."

"God forbid," said Hausner. "That's our early warning and best weapon, all in one."

"That's why I'm handling it," said Brin. He took the range card reluctantly.

Naomi Haber sat against the packed earth parapet with a towel wrapped around her head in the style of a *kheffiyah*. "You're very modest."

Brin ignored her.

Dobkin looked at her. The towel hid her long black hair and covered her forehead. She looked familiar now. "Your last name is Haber, isn't it?"

She looked at him warily. "Yes."

"Well, no wonder you teamed up with Davy Crockett here."

"Who?"

"Never mind." He turned to Hausner. "This girl used to be on the Army match-shooting team."

Brin looked honestly surprised. "Why didn't you mention that?"

She stood up and turned to Dobkin. "General . . . I . . . I mean, I just volunteered to be his assistant . . . his runner. Well, maybe I came to this position because I knew there was a rifle and scope here. But . . . shooting at targets and shooting at human beings are worlds apart, aren't they? I don't think—"

Dobkin looked sympathetic and began to speak. "Jacob—"

Hausner stood and grabbed her roughly by the arm. "Look, young lady, not one of my men is anywhere near the marksman that Brin is, and no one else on this hill came forward when I asked if anyone had this kind of training. You kept information from me, and by God, you'll answer for it! But for now, consider yourself a sniper. When you see one of those young buck Ashbals coming up the hill tonight, think of what he's going to do to you if he makes it to the top."

The girl turned away and stared down the hill.

Brin looked embarrassed. "I'll take care of it, boss."

"Do that," said Hausner. He walked away in the direction of the Concorde. Dobkin followed.

The work had not let up all morning, but now at midday, when the sun was at its hottest, most of the people were stopping for a break as they did in Israel and throughout the Middle East. They sat under the Concorde, the big delta wings protecting them from the blinding sunlight.

The garbage disposal unit on board gave up the previous day's partially eaten meal, and it was being reheated on aluminum sheets over fires of thorn. Liquids of all types were stored separately in a hole dug under the aircraft. There were bottles of sweet wine from the luggage and cans of juices and drink mixers from the galley. The extra baggage allowance had enabled everyone to bring a lot of packaged Israeli foods as gifts or for personal consumption. Still, the tremendous work load had resulted in big appetites.

Yaakov Leiber was put in charge of the stores by Hausner, and he seemed to be functioning well. Hausner put his hand on the little man's shoulder. "What's the situation, Steward?"

Leiber forced a smile. "We can eat and drink like kings . . . for one day."

"What can we do for, let's say, two more days?"

"We can go hungry and thirsty . . . but survive."

"Three days?"

"*Very* thirsty."

Hausner nodded. If the physical labor continued and the heat kept up, dehydration would begin setting in within three days. Maybe a lot sooner. Then no one would be able to think rationally. All thoughts would be of water. That would be the end, even if the defenses held. How many sieges had ended like that? Water. Food was not the problem. Humans could go for weeks on almost nothing. Besides, there was an abundance of lizards and scorpions. He'd heard jackals the night before. They could be snared with bait . . . the buried Arabs. . . . To hell with Rabbi Levin.

Leiber was speaking to him. "I've measured the water tanks carefully. There's enough for half a liter a day per person."

"Not enough."

"No, sir." He looked at the ground and kicked a clump of clay. "We could dig."

Hausner called to Dobkin, who was near the shepherd's hut. "Is this a tell or isn't it?"

"I'm certain it is," he called back. "A crumbled citadel. Covered with dust and debris." He came closer. "Why?"

"I want to dig for water," said Hausner.

Dobkin shook his head. "You'd find some interesting things down there, but not water. Not until you reached the level of the Euphrates." He walked up to Hausner and Leiber. "Why don't we send a water party down the slope?"

Hausner shook his head. "They have sentries, as you know."

"Tonight. It can be done if they don't attack up the river slope. I'll lead the party."

"You're going to make a telephone call from the guest house tonight."

Dobkin laughed. "I don't have a local coin."

Hausner smiled back.

Dobkin looked down at the ground and then at the Euphrates below them. "They would put the mud and slime into wooden forms and lay them in the sun," he said, apropos of nothing. His voice became distant. "The brickyards would stretch to the horizons in every direction. The sun would bake the bricks and they would use slime from the Euphrates for mortar. They would press designs into the brick. Lions and mythical beasts. And the kings would press their cuneiform inscriptions into each brick. NEBUCHADNEZZAR, KING OF BABYLON, SON OF NABOPOLASSAR, KING OF BABYLON, AM I. Over and over again. And sometimes they would fire-glaze the brick with reds and blues, yellows and greens. They built one of the most beautiful and colorful cities that man has ever seen. It sat like an iridescent pearl in the green silk of the Euphrates valley." Dobkin kicked at the brown dirt, then walked a few paces. He stared west across the endless mud flats into the sinking sun, as it burned reddish-yellow, still high on the horizon. "And they captured Israel and led Israel away to live by the rivers of Babylon. Right here, Jacob. A Jew stood right here and laid brick with slime to strengthen this citadel against Cyrus of Persia. Over twenty-five hundred years ago. But Cyrus took Babylon, and one of his first acts was to let the Jews go. Why? Who knows? But they went. Back to Israel. And they found Jerusalem in ruins. But they returned to it. That's what's important." He looked up and seemed to come out of his reverie. "But what's more important to us is that not all of them returned."

"What do you mean?"

"There may still be Jews of the Captivity living by the rivers of Babylon."

"Are you serious?" asked Hausner.

Leiber seemed a little confused by Dobkin. He stood a few meters off and listened politely.

"I'm serious," replied Dobkin. "Unless they've been moved to Baghdad by the Iraqi government, which is a distinct possibility. I'm talking about the Iraqi Jews who we've been trying to get the hell out of here. About five hundred of them all together. That was to be one of the points in the peace proposal."

"Do you think they're still here?"

"They've been here for twenty-five hundred years. Let's hope they still are. Their main village was on the opposite bank of the Euphrates. A place called Ummah. About two kilometers downstream. Almost across from Kweirish, the Arab village that we saw."

"Would they help?"

"Ah. That's the question. What is a Jew? Who is a Jew? Why did the ancestors of these Jews choose to stay in sinful Babylon? Who knows? They *have* remained Jews after all these years, cut off from the mainstream of Judaism.

We know that much. Though God knows what kind of Hebrew they speak . . .
if any." He opened his tunic. "But they'll know this." He pulled out a silver Star
of David.

Leiber spoke. "I wonder if they know we're here."

Hausner put his hand on Leiber's shoulder. "You can be sure, Steward, that
everyone knows we're here except the people who count—the Israeli and the
Iraqi governments." He patted Leiber's shoulder. "But they'll find us soon.
Now, I want you to comb every centimeter of this place and find more supplies."

Leiber nodded and moved off.

Dobkin spoke. "From what I saw this morning, I don't think I can make it to
the Ishtar Gate alone at night. The terrain is bad and unfamiliar, there are
deep unmarked excavations all over, and there will be sentries along the way,
I'm sure."

"Then, what do you propose?"

"The land on the other side of the Euphrates is flat and presumably without
Palestinians. I'll go down there tonight—with a water party if you want. They'll
collect some of the Euphrates—I'll swim it."

"The sentries," said Hausner.

Dobkin shrugged. "Once the shooting starts on the east side of the hill, the
sentries on the river bank won't hear much or even care about much. By two or
three in the morning, they will be cold and tired and thanking their stars they're
not part of the assault. I could make it."

Hausner looked doubtful. "And if you make it across the river and then
down to this village of Jews, then what? What do you expect to find there?"

Dobkin didn't know what to expect. Even if they had a communal farm
vehicle of some sort, the roads were impassable. There was certainly no telephone. A donkey would take days to get to Baghdad. Hillah was a possibility,
but then he'd have to recross the river. A boat maybe. A motorized boat could
get upriver to Baghdad in five or six hours. An unmotorized boat could be
downriver to Hillah in less than an hour. Then what? Hello, I'm General Dobkin of the Israeli Army and . . .

"What are you smiling at?" asked Hausner.

"A private joke. Listen, I didn't just remember about this village. I thought of
it the moment I knew we were in Babylon. But do we want to drag these people
into this? Don't they have enough problems?"

"No more than we do," said Hausner. "And I'll advise you not to hold back
that type of information in the future, General. As I see it you have two choices
—the guest house at the Ishtar Gate or the Jewish village of Ummah."

Dobkin nodded. There was a good possibility that Ummah was no longer
inhabited. There was also a chance that it was occupied by Palestinians. The
third possibility was that the Jews there wouldn't help. But *was* that possible?
Was it possible for him to walk up to a primitive Jew who lived in a squalid mud
hovel on the banks of the Euphrates, claim kinship, and demand help? Dobkin
thought it was. And would Rish take retribution against those miserable
wretches if he found out? Of course he would. But what were the alternatives?
There were none. "I'll try Ummah tonight."

"All right. I would have preferred that you take a shot at the guest house, but
it's your decision." He turned and walked toward the shepherds' hut with Dobkin. He turned to the big man as they walked. "I still can't spare a gun."

"All right."

They walked on for a few more paces in silence. Hausner cleared his throat.
"I asked the Foreign Minister to—"

"Yes," interrupted Dobkin. "I've got it. Digitalis. The Foreign Minister's aide, Peled, has a bad heart. He has a month's supply with him. I took two weeks of it."

"I hope that's enough."

"Me too."

Burg came out of the shepherds' hut with the two stewardesses, Rachel Baum and Beth Abrams. Their light-blue uniforms were soaked with sweat and what looked like blood and iodine. They gave Hausner an undisguised look of something that resembled a mixture of fear and disgust and kept walking.

Burg shrugged. "They look at me like that, too. They were doing so well with their patient, Muhammad, until I sent him into remission. No one understands us, Jacob."

"Has he said anything new?" asked Hausner.

Burg chewed on his empty pipe. "A few things." He watched as the Lear headed west over the Euphrates. "I wonder if he's going to base camp to get mortars and grenades?"

Hausner watched as the Lear disappeared into the sun. "That would make it a little tougher tonight."

Dobkin lit a cigarette. "I'm glad I won't be around."

"You're going, then?" asked Burg.

"Right. I'll be eating matzoh and roasted lamb and dancing the *horah* tonight while you're ducking bullets."

"I think you've had too much sun, General."

Dobkin told Burg about the Jewish village.

Burg listened and nodded. "Pardon the joke, but it doesn't sound kosher, Ben. Stick with the original plan."

"I have a better feeling about this."

Burg shrugged. Either way, it was suicide. "By the way, Muhammad says that Rish's lieutenant, Salem Hamadi, is a homosexual. That would be consistent with institutional upbringing."

"Who cares?" said Hausner.

"Salem Hamadi will when we broadcast it at top volume over the plane's PA tonight."

Hausner smiled. "That's low."

"All's fair. Did you get the PA boxes strung out to the perimeter yet?"

"It's done," said Dobkin.

Hausner moved into the shade of the delta wing. The earth and clay ramp was completed and he leaned back against the side of it. He felt the first stirring of a hot wind. Becker had reported that the Concorde's barometer had been dropping rapidly all day. "Does anyone know the name of the east wind here?"

"The *Sherji*," said Dobkin. "Do you feel it?"

"I think so."

"That's not good. I understand it's worse than the *Hamseen* in Israel."

"Why is that?"

"It's hotter, for one thing," said Dobkin. "And there is only sand and dust here. It picks up the dust. It can choke you. Kill you. Especially on a hill like this. That's how Babylon and all of Mesopotamia disappeared. Someone once said that a civilization would always survive if everyday people did everyday things every day. Well, that was true in Mesopotamia throughout every invasion —except the Mongol invasion. As soon as the women stopped sweeping the streets and the farmers stopped cultivating the land, the dust built up as the *Sherji* came out of the Persian mountains and carried the desert with it."

Hausner looked across the landscape toward the distant mountains. Dust devils began to form around the drifting sand dunes. They swirled across the hillocks and disappeared into the wadis, then appeared again, heading west toward them.

Dobkin followed Hausner's gaze. "From a military point of view, I honestly don't know to whose advantage a dust storm would be."

"We have enough problems," said Hausner. "I could do without another one." He looked at Burg. "We'll get rid of the prisoner if you're through with him."

"I assume you mean let him go."

"Yes."

Dobkin objected.

Hausner offered him a cigarette. "Let me tell you a story or two." He settled back against the cool earth ramp. "During the siege of Milan, in the twelfth century, the inhabitants filled grain bags with sand and used them to reinforce the battlements. The besiegers under the German Emperor, Barbarossa, thought the bags were filled with grain and became disheartened. Actually, the city was starving, but Barbarossa didn't know that. Some years later, Barbarossa besieged the Italian city of Alessandria. A peasant took his cow out of the city for pasture and was captured by Barbarossa's forces. When they slaughtered the cow for food, they saw that its stomach was filled with good grain. The peasant explained that hay and fodder were in short supply in the city, but there was so much grain that it was fed to the livestock. Barbarossa again became discouraged and lifted the siege. Actually, the Alessandrians were starving and the peasant and the cow were a ruse."

"You're trying to make a point," said Burg.

"Yes. First we have a party. A little singing and dancing. Some feigned eating and drinking. Store every weapon we've got in the shepherd's hut. Put a single round in all the spare magazines so that they look fully loaded. Look casual about food and ammunition. Set up a mock machine gun far enough away so that it will pass. Come up with more *ruses de guerre*. Make it look as if we have the Third Armored Division up here on rest and recreation. Then let Mr. Muhammad Assad loose."

Dobkin looked thoughtful. "It's kind of obvious."

"To Rish and his officers. But the Ashbals will think about it." He looked at Burg.

"Why not?" said Burg. "I'm through with him."

The three men went into the hut. Kaplan was still on his stomach, but looking well. Four other lightly wounded men, including Joshua Rubin, were playing cards. The wounded stenographer, Ruth Mandel, was wrapped in blankets and looked feverish. The Palestinian looked fearfully at Burg. Hausner could see that his nose was broken. He didn't like the idea of keeping the man with the wounded, but the hut was the only enclosed area except for the Concorde, which was like an oven in the sun. The wounded, between them, could keep watch on him. And all in all, casualties were very light, so Mr. Muhammad Assad could report that piece of intelligence as well.

The stewardesses were back and one of them, Beth Abrams, uncovered Kaplan's wound. It was starting to fester and it smelled very bad. The whole mud-brick hut smelled of ripe bandages and sweating bodies. Beth Abrams put some sort of yellow pulp on the open gangrenous wound. "What's that?" demanded Hausner.

Beth Abrams looked up at him for a long second, then spoke. "It's a local plant that is astringent. Like a witch-hazel bush."

"How do you know?"

"I read it in an Army medical manual when I was in." She dabbed it gently on the open wound as she spoke. "The fruit are lemon-yellow, about the size of tennis balls, and smooth. They lie on the ground tethered to long stalks. I forget the name, but these fit the description. They grow on the slope. I'm using the pulp on everyone. There's no alcohol left." She covered up the wound and moved away.

"All right." Hausner turned to Kaplan. "How's your ass?"

Kaplan managed a laugh. "These two stewardesses keep putting that yellow slime on it. When they say fly El Al and be treated like King Solomon, they're not kidding."

Hausner smiled. Kaplan reminded him of Matti Yadin. He'd have to see that Kaplan got a good promotion. "The smaller one, Beth Abrams, is a bit of a bitch, but she keeps looking at your ass in a non-medical way. Keep that in mind when you get back to Lod."

"I'll keep that in mind tonight."

Hausner noticed that Chaim Tamir, badly wounded the previous night in the counterattack, was sleeping fitfully.

Hausner crossed the small room to where the lightly wounded men were playing cards. He spoke to Joshua Rubin. "You never told me you were psychotic."

Rubin, a small red-haired man of about twenty, folded his cards and looked up. "You never asked. Who's got my Uzi?"

"It's retired. There were only three rounds left in the magazine when they brought you in."

"Give it back, then. I want it here. In case we get overrun. I want to take the first bastard who comes through that door."

"All right. I'll get it for you." Hausner looked around at the men, who went back to their cards. They were ordinary men, civilians, who had gone off the deep end for a few minutes the night before. Now they looked normal—were normal, arguing over a game of cards. What did Miriam Bernstein think of that? Did she understand that nice people were killers and killers were nice people? Did she understand that a man like Isaac Burg could smile and fumble around disarmingly with his pipe, then break a wounded prisoner's nose and still be a nice guy? The bottom line was survival. If it had to be done in order to survive, it was done.

19

The sun seemed hotter than usual as it reflected off the skin of the Concorde. Hausner and Burg stood with their eyes shielded from the glare, watching the tail section being disassembled. Hausner wondered again why he had never thought of checking the inaccessible parts. The Concorde had been X-rayed once for metal stress, but no one had thought to look for shadows that didn't belong there. Why hadn't *he* thought of it? If you accepted a job such as his and people got killed because of an oversight on your part, how much was your fault? How much was the fault of your subordinates? How much did you have to do to atone for the resulting tragedy? Did you have to atone at all? Weren't there some things that no one could reasonably be expected to foresee?

The one man he couldn't blame was Ahmed Rish. Rish was just doing *his* job as he saw it had to be done. It was Hausner's job to stop Rish from doing that job. Hausner knew that what bothered him most, although he tried to keep it in its proper perspective, was that Ahmed Rish had outfoxed *him.* That was very personal. Like a slap in the face. Was he leading these people to their certain death because of his excessive pride?

Excessive pride was always considered a sin in Jewish thinking. Babylon was a symbol of excessive pride, and Babylon was cursed. Babylon was brought to her knees. Was he acting out of wounded ego? No. He was following precedents set by Israel over the years. No negotiation with terrorists. Hard line. Unbending. It happened to fit his mood and personality, but it was not personal. Yet the thought nagged at him. He turned to Burg. "Is there anything else that is urgent?"

Burg turned away from the tail section and pointed to a depression in the earth about two hundred meters away. Abdel Majid Jabari and Ibrahim Ali Arif were digging a latrine trench. They used the same tools as everyone else: lengths of aluminum braces to break up the hard crust and aluminum sheets to scoop out the broken clay and dust. Their hands were wrapped in clothing to protect them from the jagged aluminum. "I questioned them," said Burg. "They are both Knesset members and it was not my place to doubt their loyalty, but the situation called for it. They were a little hurt and very angry. Maybe you can smooth it out."

Hausner watched the two Arabs for a while. "Yes. We'll all have to answer for our actions if we get back, won't we, Isaac? Here, Jabari and Arif are just two Trojan horses inside the walls of Troy, if you'll pardon the metaphor. Back in Jerusalem, they could have you in front of a Knesset committee in a second, couldn't they?"

Burg shot Hausner a dark look. "I did what I thought had to be done. Do you back me up?"

"Of course." He watched the two men as they straightened up and wiped the sweat from their faces. Their *kheffiyahs* kept the sun off their heads better than any of the headgear most of the other people were wearing. "They are in an awkward position. But I don't think turning traitor would help them with Rish. They don't want Rish on this hill any more than we do. Less. He will do more than kill them. You know what they do to traitors."

Burg nodded. "It's unpleasant." He reamed out his pipe. "Incidentally, your friend, Mrs. Bernstein, gave me a hell of a hard time about casting aspersions on the loyalty of Jabari and Arif. And also about my methods of questioning our prisoner. She said that we have all turned into perfect barbarians. She's right, of course. But we don't think that's so bad—do we, Jacob? But she does. Why is it that bleeding hearts refuse to see this world as it is?"

"They see it fine, Burg. They just can't pass up an opportunity to play the moral superiority game with bastards like us who have to slug it out in the shit so they can go do seminars on world peace and disarmament."

"Well, I don't think as unkindly as you do of that type. Anyway, she's causing trouble and I think you should do something."

"Like what?" He stared at Burg.

Burg stared back. "That's up to you."

Hausner wiped his palms on his pants. "I'll see."

As Hausner walked away, he noticed that the ground sunk into a shallow depression near the south ridge. Dobkin thought that this was the courtyard of the citadel and the south ridge was actually the city wall that ran from the citadel along the river to the Kasr mound in the south. The north ridge was similarly a covered wall. If the ridges weren't so narrow-backed, they would have made likely avenues of approach for the Ashbals. Hausner admitted that neither ridge looked like a natural formation, but how Dobkin could see walls, citadels, watchtowers, and even courtyards was beyond him. It all just looked like dirt. It was much more completely obliterated than anything he'd seen in Israel. Dobkin said to picture a thick shroud over a corpse. If you had a previous knowledge of human anatomy, then it was not difficult to pick out legs, arms, face, stomach, and chest by the rises and falls of the shroud. So it was with cities. Courtyards and watchtowers. Walls and citadels.

The two Arabs looked up at Hausner as he approached. Jabari spoke. "I didn't have an opportunity to congratulate you on your defense of Babylon last night."

"That's rather a dramatic way to put it," said Hausner.

Arif tried to catch his breath. He was bare-chested, and his stomach quivered as he panted. "I wish to congratulate you, also."

Hausner nodded. He stayed silent for a long while, then spoke. "Is there any reason for me to doubt you?"

Jabari came close. A few centimeters from him. "No."

"That's all you'll hear on it, then. I suspect Mr. Burg would like to apologize, but his training makes that impossible." He looked around. "I have a very important job for you two tonight."

"Even more important than digging the latrine?" asked Arif.

"I hope so," said Hausner. He sat with his feet dangling in the unfinished trench. They sat with him as he explained.

Dobkin and Burg called for another work break. They passed the word around to put on a show for the prisoner. Everyone complied, although the dancing and singing took more energy than anyone had to spare. The five AK-47's and about ten pistols were stacked carelessly in the shepherds' hut, as if they were extra weapons, and ammunition was left lying on the dirt floor. A security man, Marcus, came into the shepherds' hut with the Uzi submachine gun slung on his shoulder and gave it to Rubin, who put it ostentatiously under his blanket. He spoke with Rubin for a while and left. Another security man, Alpern, came in to visit with Kaplan and Rubin. He, too, had a Uzi, a little dustier than the other. It was the same one—the only one—passed through the cleft in the mud wall by Rubin.

The M-14 with the daylight scope was paraded into the hut by Brin. Muhammad Assad looked at it. He stared at the scope. Brin saw him staring at it. The only secret weapon they had was the starlight scope, and Hausner ordered that it not be shown. Brin spoke to Assad in Hebrew, which the man couldn't understand. "No, my friend, this is not the scope that put the bullet into you. We have another. But you'll just have to wonder about it."

Assad was given a very big lunch of airline food and packaged delicacies from the luggage. He seemed mystified by some of it, but tried everything. One of the stewardesses poured water from a galley pitcher into plastic glasses for the wounded. They sipped at it. Joshua Rubin drank half of his and threw the rest out the cleft in the wall. If Assad had noticed that they weren't as careless with water before, he did not show it.

Assad was taken out of the hut by two security men. Jaffe and Alpern. Before he was blindfolded, he saw the dozens of glass jars that held the aviation fuel stacked in a hole dug next to the hut. A steward, Daniel Jacoby, was filling more jars from an aluminum pitcher filled with fuel. One of the aides, Esther Aronson, was fashioning wicks made from strips of cloth. This was no ruse, and Muhammad Assad was duly impressed.

Alpern yelled to Esther Aronson to throw him a strip of cloth for a blindfold. She was slow about it—as she was told to be—and Alpern yelled angrily to hurry it up.

In the interim, Jaffe spun Assad around and pointed him toward the perimeter. Assad glimpsed what he took to be a heavy machine gun on a tripod, but was only a broken strut from the front landing gear, blackened with soot and sitting on a truncated camera tripod recovered from the luggage. Spent shell casings tied together with string gleamed in the sunlight like links of belt ammunition. If Assad wondered how the Israelis came to be carrying a heavy machine gun on board, he didn't ask. He saw all he was supposed to see in those few seconds, then the blindfold was quickly tied around his head. He was led to the edge of the perimeter where he was guided between two big aluminum reflectors and over the trench and earth wall. Halfway down the slope, the blindfold was removed and he was given a white handkerchief fixed to a length of aluminum hydraulic tubing. Jaffe, with the same tone in his voice that the Lord must have used with Lot's wife, told Assad not to look back. Despite his wound, Assad made good speed down the slope.

Hausner called an end to the festivities and found Burg and Dobkin standing on the high mound—the buried watchtower—that was the previous night's Command Post/Observation Post. They were looking over the progress of the work. The Tel Aviv waterfront moved slightly as the hot wind picked up the T-shirt flag. "What's the next priority?" he asked.

Burg suggested, "We should speak with Becker again. He's on the flight deck."

They walked back to the Concorde. A flattened platform of earth had been raised up under the collapsed nose wheel assembly, and Kahn was lying on it, supine, with his arms thrust up into the wheel well. He was covered with grease and sweat. Hausner wondered if his energies couldn't be better spent digging man-traps, but said nothing.

Dobkin called to him. "Any luck?"

Kahn slid out and stood up. "No. Not yet. But I think I'm getting closer."

Dobkin nodded. "Good."

"I only hope we have enough batteries and enough fuel left to turn it over and run it if I fix it." He looked pointedly at Hausner.

"Why?" asked Hausner. "So we can run the air conditioners?" He stepped onto the ramp. "If you two can't make contact with the radio using the batteries, I don't think the generator will make any difference."

Kahn didn't answer.

Hausner began walking up the ramp. He looked back toward the nose. "Technicians are tinkerers by nature. If something is broken you want to fix it. Your ego is involved with that goddamned APU, Kahn, but what good it's going to do us fixed is beyond me."

Kahn was red-faced but remained quiet.

Hausner took a few steps and shouted over his shoulder. "The radio is a

quick ticket out of this place, but you two don't seem to have the touch with it."
He jumped onto the delta wing.

Dobkin and Burg stayed behind and spoke quietly with Kahn.

The cabin was like an oven and Hausner, in spite of having gone without
water for some time, began to sweat. There were sounds coming into the cabin
from the work being done on the dismantling of the tail. As he passed the
galley, Hausner could see that it was stripped bare. The Machmeter was lit,
indicating that Becker was using the emergency power. It still read MACH
0.00, which somehow annoyed Hausner. What bright electrical engineer in
France had wired the passengers' Machmeter into the emergency power? Why
would the passengers want to know how fast they were going during an emergency situation? It occurred to him that the passengers on 01 must have
watched the speed bleed off after the explosion. He wondered how it read in
the cabin of 01 when the craft was somersaulting across the sky.

Hausner was assailed by the smell from the flight deck before he reached it.
He looked inside. Hess was still sitting slumped over the controls, but rigor had
set in and Hess's body had shifted and looked very unnatural. A hot wind blew
in through the hole in the windshield. Becker was listening at the radio with
earphones.

Hausner stopped in. "I want him out of here," he said loudly.

Becker removed his earphones. "He's my responsibility. I'll keep him here
until they're ready to bury him."

Hausner didn't know what was going on in Becker's mind and didn't want
even to begin to try and fathom it. What difference did it make where the body
was kept? Maybe it was better that the rest of the people didn't see it. If only
that damned rabbi wasn't . . .

Levin was an enigma. Religious people were all enigmas to Hausner. They
wouldn't fly El Al; they wouldn't eat lizards even if they were starving, they
wouldn't bury bodies on the Sabbath. In short, they wouldn't come to grips with
the twentieth century. They let people like Hausner break The Law so that the
water flowed into their homes on the Sabbath and the radar was manned and
surgery was performed. Levin was just another version of Miriam Bernstein,
Hausner decided. They were sure they were on the way to Heaven, and
Hausner was in training for Hell. It occurred to him that either he was making
very astute observations or he was becoming a paranoiac. But was there a
despot anywhere who wasn't?

"I *said,* do you want to fool around with the radio yourself?" said Becker.

"What? No. I don't. Did you hear anything? Did you try transmitting?"

"As I said before, it's very difficult to transmit in the daytime."

"Right. Maybe we'll have more luck tonight."

"No, we won't."

"Why not?"

"Well, I did get one transmission."

Hausner came closer. "Who?"

"Fellow by the name of Ahmed Rish. Before, when he was flying overhead.
He said that he hoped Jacob Hausner considered all the lives at stake and all
that. He also complimented me on my flying. Nice guy." Becker allowed himself a laugh. "He also said that he'd be back at dusk to circle overhead and jam
me if we weren't surrendering."

"Son-of-a-bitch."

"He's certainly full of surprises. All bad." Becker turned off the radio.
"Could you shoot him down?"

Hausner wiped the sweat from his neck. "How high could he fly and still jam you?"

"As high as he wants. He has the power, and it's line of sight through the clear sky."

"Then we can't shoot him down unless you have a SAM on board that you're keeping under wraps."

Becker stood and pulled at his wet clothes. "Incidentally, I want final authority concerning what is taken off this aircraft, Hausner. A little while ago two of your men tried to take the goddamned wiring that connects this radio to the batteries."

Hausner nodded. "All right." He saw that Becker was sallow and his lips were cracked. "Get some water."

Becker moved toward the door. "I think I'm going to dig the grave." He left the flight deck.

Hausner stared at the radio. After a few minutes he also left.

He didn't want to run into her, but it was inevitable. She was standing on the delta wing with some other men and women from the peace delegation. He had noticed how all the peer groups had stuck together. She didn't mingle with the junior aides or the flight crew.

They were all going up to the tail to help with the work. She stood with her hands wrapped in cloth to protect them from the jagged metal. She was covered with sweat and dust. She walked slowly across the unbearably hot wing as the others went on up the fuselage. She stood with her legs spread to keep her balance on the pitched wing. "Everyone seems to think you're a hero."

"I am."

"So you are. No one really likes heroes. They fear—detest heroes. Did you know that?"

"Of course."

"Have you made amends for the sin of overlooking a bomb planted in that tail section," she pointed to it, "over a year ago in France? Can you rejoin the human race now?"

"You almost make it sound inviting."

"Then do it."

He didn't answer.

"What else did Rish say?"

"He just wanted to talk about old times at Ramla."

"We have a right to know."

"Let's not start this again."

"What terms did he offer?"

"Would you consider surrendering under any circumstances?"

She hesitated. "Only to save lives."

"Our precious lives are not worth the national humiliation."

She shook her head. "What is it that I thought I found likeable in you? You are a loathsome person, really."

"Don't you want to tame the beast, Miriam? Aren't you a doer of good deeds?" He remembered her warmth on the plane when she thought he needed someone.

She seemed confused. "Are you playing with me?"

He took out a cigarette stub and stared at it for a long time. She suddenly seemed so defenseless. He looked up. "Listen, Burg is complaining about you. He says you're bad for morale. So shape up and keep your opinions to yourself until you have the floor in the Knesset. I'm serious, Miriam. If he decides to charge you with causing dissension, I can't help you."

She looked at him, but it took some time before the words registered. Her mind was on what he had said before. She suddenly flushed red. "What? What the hell kind of charge is 'causing dissension'? I won't be bullied like that. This is a democracy, damn it."

"This is Babylon. This is where the law of retaliation—the law of an eye for an eye, a tooth for a tooth—was codified by Hammurabi long before Moses gave it to us. Our origins are brutal and cruel, and there was a reason for that— it was a brutal world. Then we became the world's professional pacifists, and look what happened to us. Now we're raising young men and women who are fighters again after all these centuries. We may not like their manners, but they don't care. They don't much like our European background and all it connotes. If my parents had stayed in Europe, they would have gone into the boxcars like yours. They were the type. Asher Avidar was a damned fool—but you know what? I like that type of damned fool. People like you scare the hell out of me."

She began to shake and her voice came in short breaths. "If . . . if your parents had stayed in Europe—you would have grown up a Nazi. They would have recognized one of their own."

Hausner hit her with his open palm. She fell onto the wing and rolled a few meters down the incline before she came to a stop. She lay there with the metal burning her bare legs. She refused to stand up, although she was able to do so.

Hausner finally reached down and yanked her to her feet.

The people on the tail section were staring openly.

Hausner held her up by her arms and pressed her face near his. "We're never going to get it together if we keep knocking each other around, Miriam." He stared into her eyes and saw the tears well up and roll down her cheeks. "I'm sorry," he said.

She pulled away from him with surprising strength. "Go to hell!" She raised her fist, but he caught her by the wrist and held her.

"That's the spirit, Miriam. Now, doesn't that feel better than turning the other cheek? You'll be a fighter yet."

She pulled loose, walked quickly across the shimmering delta wing, and disappeared through the emergency door of the fuselage.

20

Hausner walked slowly down the earth ramp. Burg was waiting for him. Hausner sighed. "Well, what's next?"

"I feel like your adjutant."

"Yes. And my intelligence officer. Dobkin is my executive officer. Leiber is my supply sergeant. Everyone has a function, or will have within the next few hours."

"Even Miriam Bernstein?" ventured Burg.

Hausner looked at him. "Yes. She has a function, also. She keeps us honest. She reminds us that we are civilized."

"I'd rather not be reminded of that now. Anyway, she's only an amateur guilt-producer. The professional wants a word with you. That's what's next."

"The rabbi?"

"The rabbi. Then I think you should speak with McClure and Richardson. As your intelligence officer, I think there is something there that is not entirely kosher."

"Like what?"

"I'm not sure. Anyway, as your adjutant, I think they could use some morale boosting, being the only foreigners with us. If I were them, I would have taken a walk long ago."

"McClure is steady as a rock. Richardson is a little shaky, I think. I'll speak to them. Anything else?"

"Not that I can think of, unless you want to take that vote about accepting Rish's terms. It's getting late."

Hausner smiled. "We'll take it in the morning."

Burg nodded. "Yes. We'll sleep on it."

"Where's Dobkin?"

"The last time I saw him, he was giving a class in breastworks, trenches, foxholes, and parapets."

"Is that a graduate course?"

"I think so. And the final exam is tonight."

Hausner nodded. "Tell him that before nightfall I also want him to give a class in weapons training. I want as many people as possible cross-trained. If a gunner falls, I want anyone to be able to pick up the weapon."

"All right. If you need me I'll be at the shepherds' hut. I promised those two stews I'd pull a few hours of orderly duty."

"If we do nothing else right up here, we'll do our best for them. See that they have everything they need."

"Of course."

Hausner found Rabbi Levin speaking with Becker. Becker was digging a grave on a little knoll that overlooked the Euphrates.

Hausner stood some meters off until the rabbi saw him.

The rabbi said something to Becker, then walked over to where Hausner stood. "Jacob Hausner, the Lion of Babylon. Did you see your namesake on your journey to the Ishtar Gate?"

"What can I do for you, Rabbi?"

"You can begin by telling me precisely the terms that Rish offered."

"What difference does it make? We're not accepting them."

"You're not and I'm not and most people here are not. But there are some people who wish to. The Law teaches us that each man should make his own decision as to his fate in situations like this."

"I don't remember that in the Bible or the Talmud. I think you make these laws up to fit your needs."

Rabbi Levin laughed. "You're a hard man to fool, Jacob Hausner. But I'll tell you what The Law does say. It says suicide is a sin."

"So?"

"So? You should keep better informed. There are about six young interpreters and secretaries—two girls and four boys, I think—who are members of the hardcore Masada Defense League."

"And?"

"And they are running around proselytizing a Masada solution if we can't hold out. I won't have that, and I suspect you won't either." He looked at Hausner sharply.

Hausner wiped the sweat from his neck. The wind was creating swirls of dust across the top of the mound. On the far side of the Euphrates, the flat mud plain stretched forever. There had been trees there once and fields of high grain, but still it must have been possible to see Babylon as you approached with a caravan from the Western Desert along the ancient Damascus road. That's how the Jews of the Captivity came. Across the burning deserts of Syria. Then they would have seen the cultivated alluvial flood plains in the distance, not at all the way Hausner had seen it from the flight deck of Concorde 02, but it must have looked inviting, even though they knew it was the place of their bondage. And the Babylonians would have stood in the fields and on the walls of the city and watched their great army approach with Israel in chains and with carts loaded with the silver and gold from the sack of Jerusalem.

"Well?"

Hausner looked at him and spoke slowly and softly. "The Captivity . . . the camps . . . the pogroms. . . . You need warm human bodies to commit atrocities against. . . . I mean, when resistance becomes impossible . . . *physically* impossible . . . then you just . . . you just end it, damn it. You don't deliver yourself up for humiliation, rape, and slaughter. You end it yourself before they—"

"God decides who dies and who doesn't! Not man. Not Jacob Hausner. I won't have this! We have no moral right to end our own lives. And I'll tell you something else about Masada. It was brave beyond comprehension, but not everyone there wanted to commit suicide, either. There were some who were slain by their own kin before the mass suicide. That's murder. And I think that is what is going to happen here if those hotheads get control. What the hell kind of young men and women are we raising, anyway? I've never seen such recklessness."

Hausner thought of Avidar again. Then of Bernstein. There must be a compromise between the two philosophies. "In the end, when the situation is beyond saving, those who wish to be taken captive will find a way to surrender. Those who wish to fight to the end will do so. Those who wish to take their own lives will arrange it. Is there anything else, Rabbi?"

Rabbi Levin looked at him with a mixture of pain and disgust. "The wisdom of Jacob Solomon Hausner. Here's another little piece of unconventional wisdom for you. If those two women had called Solomon's bluff and agreed to let the baby be split in two, then that would have put King Solomon in the position of murderer and not a revered judge. That's what you will become—a murderer. Your compromise is not acceptable to me." The rabbi waved his arm and his voice became louder. "I insist that you let those who wish to surrender do so now, and that you forbid suicide and talk of suicide!"

Hausner noticed that the rabbi was holding something. He stared at the object as it made its way through the air in the rabbi's hand. Levin was still shouting, but Hausner had tuned him out. He suddenly put his hand on Rabbi Levin's shoulder and spoke softly. "I don't know." He lowered his head. "I just don't know, Rabbi. I'm getting tired of this. I don't think I want to be in charge here after all. I don't feel up to it. I . . . ."

Rabbi Levin took Hausner's hand gently. "I'm sorry. Look, let's let it rest for now. You look very tired. Listen, you have my word that I won't bother you for a decision until later—when you're feeling better."

Hausner recovered very quickly. He took his hand away from the rabbi's.

"Good. Then that's the last I expect to hear about it—until later." He looked down at the object in the rabbi's other hand. "What the hell is that?"

The rabbi knew he'd been taken by a sharp operator. He was angry, but impressed. "What?" He looked down at his hand. "Oh. This. It's an abomination. I hate to touch it. A false idol." He held it up to the sunlight. "Becker found it in the grave he's digging."

Hausner moved closer. It was some sort of winged demon fashioned out of what appeared to be terra cotta, although Hausner thought for a wild moment that it was something mummified. It had the body of an emaciated man with an oversized phallus and the most hideous face Hausner could ever remember seeing represented in any type of art. "I think this should make old Dobkin's day complete. He's been annoying everyone about sifting through the rubble on their breaks. Let me have it."

The rabbi turned it in his hand so it faced him. "It's really too obscenely ugly to be exposed in the sunlight of God's world. It belongs to another time. It should have stayed in darkness." He gripped the clay figure tightly until his knuckles went white.

Hausner stood transfixed. A gust of scorching wind picked up the fine dust around him and obscured everything in front of him for a second. He yelled through the wind and dust. "Don't be a damned fool. We don't do that in the twentieth century. Give it to me!"

Rabbi Levin smiled and loosened his grip on the demon. The wind dropped and the brown cloud settled to the earth. He held the figure out toward Hausner. "Here. It's meaningless. God would laugh at my superstition if I smashed it. Give it to General Dobkin. My compliments."

Hausner took it. "Thank you." They stared at each other for a few seconds, then Hausner turned and walked off.

Hausner strode quickly along the crest of the steep slope overlooking the Euphrates. He looked down. It was about a hundred meters to the river, and he wondered how Dobkin thought he was going to descend it without being seen, even at night.

At the base of the slope, once the foot of the citadel, a few dusty little bushes that looked like castor oil plants grew along the bank. There were also clumps of bulrushes, and Hausner knew that Ashbals were posted there.

The Euphrates looked cool and inviting. Hausner licked his parched lips as he made his way south along the perimeter. Men and women stopped digging at their positions to look at him as he walked by. He moved faster.

Hausner stopped at McClure and Richardson's location. He noticed that they had erected quite an elaborate position. There was a chest-deep firing position with a crenelated wall of earth around it like a miniature castle. There was a small sun shield fashioned from seat covers and straightened seat springs. It blew in the growing wind and looked as though it might not hold up. "It looks like the Alamo."

McClure bit a matchstick in half and spit out one end. "It *is* the Alamo."

Both men were covered from head to foot with grime and sweat. Richardson's blue Air Force tunic lay in a hollowed shelf of the hole, neatly folded and partly wrapped in a pair of women's panties. Hausner wasn't angry to see that Richardson was thinking ahead. He gave him credit for it. Hausner assumed a more formal attitude. "We have been offered terms, as you have probably heard. We cannot accept those terms. *You* can, however. And you can accept them with no shame and no fear. Rish will hold you only as long as it is necessary to keep this location secret from the world. No matter what happens, you go free. I'm fairly certain he will live up to that. They don't want any trouble with your government. I ask you to please leave here. It would be better for everyone."

McClure sat down on the edge of the hole and swung his long legs in front of him. "I feel kind of important here. I mean, being the only gun on the west side of the hill. I was the first one here last night, and I think I might have stopped those fellers from trying this slope. Besides, I put a lot of improvements into this real estate. I think I'll stay here."

Hausner shook his head. "I don't want you two here. You're a complication."

McClure looked down at his shoes for a while. "Well, if you want to know the truth, I don't want to be here myself. But I don't want to take my chances with that Rish feller, either. If you start beating the shit out of him tonight, he'll forget we're neutrals damn quick and start squeezing our nuts for information about the weak points in this setup. Think about *that.*"

Hausner thought about it. He looked at Richardson. "Colonel?" He could see that Richardson looked unhappy. Clearly, something was going on between these two.

Richardson cleared his throat. "I'm staying. But, goddamn it, I think you might try to parley again before sundown."

"I'll take your advice under consideration, Colonel. And if either of you change your mind . . . then I'll have to think about it in light of what Mr. McClure has said."

"You do that," said McClure. "And send over some of them kerosene bombs you're making. I can chuck one right down into those bushes and bulrushes tonight and light up the whole river bank."

Hausner nodded. "I'd like that. Incidentally, General Dobkin is leaving the perimeter tonight after sundown and before moonrise. He will be exiting here from your position. Try to observe the patterns and habits of the sentries down there. Give him whatever help you can."

McClure didn't ask any questions. He just nodded.

Dobkin was standing near a large, round black ball that came up to his chest.

Hausner, walking back from McClure and Richardson's position, saw him examining it under the tip of the port-side delta. He walked up to him. "Where the hell did that come from?"

Dobkin looked up. "It was thrown out of the tail section when it blew. It was lying there on the southern ridge, hidden by the terrain. Leiber found it when he was looking for stores. I had it brought here."

"That's nice. What the hell is it?"

Dobkin patted it. "Kahn says it's the compressed-nitrogen bottle."

Hausner nodded. The bottle was a backup to the hydraulic system. The compressed gas performed hydraulic functions in an emergency, until it ran out. "Can we use it?"

"I think so. It's a muscle. Energy waiting to do something."

"Is it full?"

"Kahn says it is. There's a lot of raw energy here if we can tap it. It has a valve, see?"

Hausner tapped on it with his knuckles. "Put the word out that I want some inspired thinking on this. Another little problem to keep our group of super-achievers busy. Idle minds are the playthings of the Devil. . . . Which reminds me . . ." Hausner held up the winged demon, "What's this?"

Dobkin took it carefully and held it cradled in his hands. He looked at its face for a long time before he spoke. "It's Pazuzu."

"I beg your pardon?" He smiled, but Dobkin did not smile back.

Dobkin scratched some dirt away from the enlarged penis with his thumbnail. "The wind demon. It brings sickness and death."

Hausner watched Dobkin examining it for a minute. "Is it . . . valuable?"

Dobkin looked up. "Not as such. It's terra cotta. And it's not an unusual example, but it's in good condition. Who found it?"

"Becker. He's digging a grave for Hess."

"Appropriate." He cleaned off the face with a bit of saliva. "I really didn't expect to find much here. This was the top of the citadel. The battlements and watchtowers. There must be meters of dust piled on top of them. Strange to find anything in so shallow a hole." He looked up at Hausner. "Thank you."

"Thank the rabbi. He overcame an irrational urge to smash it."

Dobkin nodded. "I wonder if it was irrational."

The remainder of the afternoon was spent in fatiguing labor. Trenches grew longer and deeper and snaked toward each other. In some places they joined, and, in fact, the object was to join them all—if they were to be there long enough—to make up an integral system, stretching from the Euphrates at the north ridge to the Euphrates at the south ridge. The defenses along the western slope consisted only of individual foxholes.

Before dusk, Hausner ordered a rest period for personal grooming. The men were ordered to shave. Hausner expected an argument, but got none. The shaving water was reused to make mud for face camouflage.

The nitrogen bottle posed a diversionary problem for the mechanically minded. It rose out of the brown earth like a monolith, black and mute. Hausner offered a half-liter of water to anyone who could find a use for it.

The *Sherji* grew stronger and hotter, and dust began to cover everyone and everything. People with respiratory problems had difficulty breathing.

The sun set at 6:16. The truce was over, and their fate was again in their own hands. Hausner watched as the blazing red circle sank into the western mud flats. Overhead, where the night met the day, the first stars showed in the darkness. In the east, the sky was already black as velvet. By the ancient Hebrew conception of measuring time, the day was nearly finished. The Sabbath was ended. The rabbi's influence would be slightly reduced.

Hausner walked toward the lightly guarded western slope. He found a small depression in the earth, away from anyone else, and lay down in the dust. He stared up at the changing sky. The air rapidly cooled as it does on the desert, and the *Sherji* dropped to a soft breeze. Hausner stared without blinking at the marvelous black sky studded with stars brighter and closer than he had seen them since childhood. Then, the days were all sun-splashed and the nights were all starlight and magic. It had been a long time since he had lain outdoors on his back under the stars.

He stretched sensuously in the warm, yielding dust. The dark half of the sky fell westward and pushed the light half down further into the west. It was all so incredibly beautiful. It was no wonder, he thought, that the desert peoples of the world had always been more fanatical than other groups about their gods. You could almost touch them and see them in the stunning interplay of terrestrial and celestial phenomena.

Out on the mud flats, a pack of jackals howled. Their howling got closer very quickly, and Hausner guessed that they were running toward the Euphrates. They were pursuing some unfortunate small prey that had ventured out to drink under cover of darkness. They howled again, long and malevolently, then came the awful shrieks and sounds of struggle, then quiet. Hausner shuddered.

The strange dusk of the desert lasted only a few minutes after the sun set, followed by what pilots and military people euphemistically called EENT, end of evening nautical twilight—darkness.

The moon would not rise for hours. Would Rish attack, like the jackals, during this period of darkness, or would he wait until much later when the moon set? Brin had not seen the Ashbals moving from the Ishtar Gate area toward their attack during this period of darkness, he would move his men into the attack positions. There was only the thin line of sentries at the base of the hill. But that didn't mean anything. If Rish were going to attack positions after dark. Any commander would. That gave the Israelis about half an hour before an attack could be launched. Enough time to bury Moses Hess.

Hausner considered not going to the funeral. It was meaningless. He could draw more spiritual strength from staring at the heavens than from looking into a hole in the ground and listening to Rabbi Levin talk about them.

Hausner tried to pick out the constellations, but it had been a long time. Ursa Major was easy and so were Orion and Taurus, but the rest were meaningless groupings. He had more luck with the individual stars. Castor and Pollux. Polaris and Vega.

It was the Babylonians who were the primary astrologers of the ancient world. Like the inhabitants of modern Iraq, they slept on the flat roofs of their houses at night. How could they fail to develop a vast amount of lore concerning the heavenly bodies? Their learning was jealously guarded and at first did not spread to the other civilizations. But after the downfall of Babylonia, they traveled the ancient world as professional astrologers. Long after Babylon was forgotten by the ancients, the name Chaldean, synonymous with Babylonian, became another name for astrologer, magician, and sorcerer. The fate of Babylon as a state was to be remembered for her haughtiness and corruption. The fate of her people was to wander the world, selling their ancient mysteries for bread, and in the end to be remembered only as magicians. But the world gained a profound knowledge of the stars in the process. It was strange, reflected Hausner, that of all the learned people of the ancient world, only the Jews never took an interest in astrology or astronomy. He could probably develop an entire theory as to why that was so, but he felt too lazy and too tired to bother.

She knelt down next to him and stared at him in his shallow hole. "That's morbid. Come out of there."

"It's a womb." He couldn't see her at all. How in the world did she find him, and how did she know it was he? She must have been close by when it was light.

"It's far from that. It's dry and dead. Get up. The funeral is beginning."

"Go on ahead."

"I'm afraid. It's totally black. Walk me there."

"I never go to funerals on a first date. We have about fifteen minutes. Let me make love to you."

"I can't."

"Laskov?"

"Yes. And my husband. I can't bear another complication."

"I am a lot of things, Miriam, but a complication is not one of them." He could hear her breathing. She was very close, probably less than a meter. He could reach out . . .

"It's wrong. Teddy, I could justify. You, I could not justify to—to anyone. Least of all to myself."

He laughed, and she laughed and sobbed at the same time. She caught her breath. "Jacob, why me? What do you see in me?" She paused. "What do I see in *you?* I loathe everything about you. I really do. Why do these things happen to people? If I loathe you, why am I here?"

Hausner reached out and found her wrist. "Why *did* you follow me?" She tried to pull away, but he would not let go. "If you follow a dangerous animal," he said, "you should know what you are going to do when you track him to his lair. Especially when you turn to leave and you find him standing at the entrance. If he could talk, he would ask you what you had in mind when you followed him. And you should have a good answer."

She didn't speak, but Hausner could hear her breathing getting heavier. Some kind of animal reaction subtly passed through her body, and Hausner felt it in those few square centimeters of her skin that were pressed to his. The pitch of her breathing changed, and he could swear that he could smell something that told him she was ready. In the dark, without any visual message, he knew that she had gone from alert and guarded to passive and submissive. He was surprised at his own heightened perceptions—and very confident of their accuracy. He pulled gently on her wrist and she rolled, unresisting, into his dusty resting place.

She lay on top of him and he helped her undress, then they lay on their sides facing each other and he undressed. Her skin was smooth and cool, as he expected it would be. He pressed his lips onto her mouth and felt her respond. She lay back on their crumpled clothes and raised her legs. Hausner lay between them and felt her firm thighs come around and grip his back with surprising strength. He went into her easily and lay still for a second. He wanted to see her face and was sorry he couldn't. He told her so. She replied that she was smiling. And when he asked her if her eyes were smiling, too, she said that she believed they were.

He moved slowly and she responded immediately. He could feel her nipples harden on his chest, and her breath blew in a rhythmic hot stream on his cheek and neck.

He put his hands under her buttocks and lifted her. She let out a little sound of pain as he thrust too far. He picked up his head and stared at her face, trying to see it. It was an incredibly black night, but the stars were growing stronger and he could finally see her eyes—black as the sky itself—pinpoints of reflected starlight. He thought he could read the expression in them, but he knew that it must be only a trick of the remote starlight.

She began to move spasmodically beneath him. Her buttocks rolled sensuously into the warm dust. Hausner heard his own voice speaking softly to her, saying things he would never have said except in total darkness. And she answered him in kind, protected also by that invisibility, like a child who covers his face while disclosing his deepest secrets. Her voice became rich and throaty and her breath came in short convulsive gasps. A soft ripple passed through her body, followed by a long spasm. Hausner's body tensed for a second, then shuddered violently.

They lay still, holding on to each other. The wind passed over them, cooling the sweat on their bodies.

Hausner rolled onto his side. He ran his hand over her breasts, feeling them rise and fall. His thoughts were not clear yet, but they included the knowledge that he had compromised his position. In Tel Aviv, this would have been fine. Here, it was not. But it could only have happened here. Strategic and tactical considerations aside, he was fairly certain that he loved her, or would love her very soon. He wanted to ask her about Laskov and about her husband, but these were things that had to do with the future. Therefore, they were irrelevant now. He tried to think of something to say that he thought she would like to hear, but couldn't think of anything. So he asked, "What would you like me to say? I don't know what to say."

"Say nothing," she said and held his hand to her breast.

The stars were stronger and there were more of them now. The Euphrates magnified the thin, cold starlight, and Hausner could see the group of about twenty dark shapes standing around the grave and silhouetted against the wide river. He moved closer but stayed behind the group. Miriam stood beside him for a second, then moved among the people to the graveside.

Moses Hess was lowered gently into his grave. The rabbi said the *El Male Rachimim,* the Prayer for the Dead, in a loud, clear voice that rolled down the slope, across the river, and onto the mud flats.

Becker also stood back from the ring of people around the grave, and Hausner could see that he was visibly upset.

How strange, thought Hausner. The bones of thousands of Jews were buried at Babylon. How strange to be burying another today. The rabbi's voice reached him from the edges of his mind. *". . . yea, we wept, when we remembered Zion. We hanged our harps upon the willows in the midst . . ."* Hausner realized that those famous willows no longer existed. He had not seen one.

Miriam Bernstein spoke quietly with the rabbi. He nodded. She turned and spoke softly, almost inaudibly, to the people gathered in the darkness. "Many of you know what has come to be called the Ravensbrück Prayer," she began, "written by an anonymous author on a scrap of wrapping paper and found at the camp after it was liberated. It is proper that we hear it now, at this service, so that we remember, whether we be in Babylon, Jerusalem, or New York, that we are on a mission of peace." She turned and looked down into the open grave and began.

> *Peace be to men who are of bad will,*
> *and may an end be put to all vengeance*
> *and to all talk about punishment and chastisement.*
> *The cruelties mock all norms and principles,*
> *they are beyond all limits of human understanding*
> *and there are many martyrs.*
> *Therefore, God*
> *does not weigh their sufferings on the scales of your justice,*
> *so that you would demand a cruel account,*
> *but rather let it be valid in a different way.*
> *Rather, write in favor of all executioners, traitors, and spies,*
> *and all bad men, and credit to them*
> *all the courage and strength of soul of the others. . . .*

Miriam's voice wavered as she continued reciting the prayer. Then, as she came to the end, her voice strengthened.

> *. . . All the good should count and not the evil.*
> *And for the memories of our enemies,*
> *we should no longer remain their victims,*
> *no longer their nightmare and their shuddering ghosts,*
> *but rather their help, so that they may cease their fury.*
> *That is the only thing that is asked of them,*

and that we, after it is all over,
may be able to live as humans among humans,
and that there may be peace again on this poor earth
for the men of good will
and that this peace may come also to the others.

Hausner only half-listened as the last sounds of Miriam's voice died in the darkness. It was a senseless prayer—a dangerous prayer for people who were going to have to live with revenge and hate in their hearts if they were to survive. Miriam, Miriam. When will you learn?

The funeral service was ended. Hausner realized that everyone was gone and he was alone. He looked out across the Euphrates, out across the black mud plains, out to where the black velvet sky met the black horizon, out toward Jerusalem. He fancied he saw the lights of the Old City, but it was only a star setting on the horizon. It disappeared, and in that moment, he knew he would never go home again.

Book III

BABYLON
THE ISHTAR GATE

*Go ye forth of Babylon,
    flee ye from the Chaldeans,
with a voice of singing declare ye, tell this,
    utter it even to the end of the earth;
say ye, The Lord hath redeemed his servant Jacob.
    And they thirsted not when he led them through the deserts: he caused
the waters to flow out of the rock for them:
    he clave the rock also, and the waters gushed out.*

Isaiah 48:20–21

21

They came soon after the funeral service was ended. They did not come on line as they had the night before, but in small squad groups and fireteam groups—in threes and sixes and nines. They moved quickly and silently from one area of cover and concealment to the next. They picked out the best avenues of approach, having found them the hard way the previous night. They were surprised to find the low walls built across the gullies, but they crawled up and over them like snakes and continued in the erosion gullies upward, toward the crest. Noise control and light discipline were excellent, equipment was taped down, faces were blackened, and the death penalty was in force for any breach of orders.

Ahmed Rish crawled with his lieutenant, Salem Hamadi, some distance behind their advancing army. Both of them knew that this might be their last effort. If they failed, it would mean humiliation and eventual death at the hands of their own men or at the hands of a tribunal made up of other Palestinians. Worse yet, they might be hunted for the rest of their lives by Mivtzan Elohim. They might spend the remainder of their lives at Ramla. The irony was that the head of Mivtzan Elohim, Isaac Burg, was within their grasp, as was fame, fortune, and glory. For Rish and Hamadi this was the most important night in both their lives. Rish covered his eyes as a swirl of sand blew in his face. He put his mouth to Hamadi's ear. "The ancient gods are with us. Pazuzu has sent us this wind."

Hamadi wasn't sure *whom* the wind was sent for. He spit some sand out of his mouth and grunted.

* * *

Nathan Brin rubbed his eye and looked again, then shut off the scope. He put his arm around Naomi Haber, who was nestled next to him. "My eyes are strained. I've been seeing things since sundown." He pushed the rifle sideways across the earth wall. "Here. Take a look."

Naomi ran her hand through his hair and wiped the sweat and camouflage dirt from his forehead. The inevitable had happened, after hours of forced company and a high state of nervous tension, combined with the fact that neither of them knew if they would be alive very much longer. She doubted if she would look twice at him in a café in Tel Aviv. But this was Babylon, and perhaps some of the wantonness of the place hung in the air like a vapor.

Their lovemaking, accomplished between sunset and the end of the funeral service, had been as hurried as Hausner's and Bernstein's, but much more frantic. It was interrupted whenever either of them had had a premonition or a panicky moment and they had stopped to scan the slope. They had laughed over the clumsy affair. But that was before, when there was little chance of the Ashbals being in the area. Now they were dressed, and the threat of attack was very serious.

Naomi Haber put the scope to her eyes and scanned. This was much different from match shooting. Much different. She could hit moving and still targets with uncanny accuracy, but she never was much good at picking out targets from a cluttered background. She was not yet familiar with the night view of the terrain. The eerie green glow further confused her.

"See anything?" asked Brin.

"I don't think so. That damned wind."

"I know," said Brin. The *Sherji* was picking up dust and sending wispy shadows across the land that could only be seen in the powerful scope.

She cursed silently and handed the rifle back to Brin. "I'm not good at this."

Brin took the rifle and pointed it straight into the air. He scanned for a full three minutes before he spotted the Lear overhead. He estimated its altitude at better than two kilometers. Well out of range of his rifle. Hausner had told him to look for the Lear and to try to knock it down. He considered sending one round at it, but decided against wasting the ammunition. They were jammed, and that's all there was to it. He switched off the scope and sat back. "Let's give us and the batteries five minutes rest." He lit a cigarette in his cupped hands.

The Ashbals took their time, resting between areas of concealment, then moving quickly to the next. They knew that the Israelis would have put out early warning devices and outposts, and they were on the lookout for both. In addition, they were under orders not to return any probing fire. But had they practiced the tactic of the quick, silent run just then, they might have been over the Israeli breastworks and into the Israeli trenches within minutes. But they continued to move in short, silent rushes.

Far ahead of the main body of Ashbals was a two-man sniper-killer team. One man, Amnah Murad, was armed with a Russian Dragunov sniper rifle. Mounted on the rifle was an infrared scope. Murad cradled the rifle carefully in his arms as he moved. The other man, Moniem Safar, carried a compass and an AK-47. Murad and Safar had trained as a team since they were five years old. They were closer than blood brothers. They were bound by the brotherhood of the hunt and the kill, and each could anticipate every move and every emotion of the other. They could literally communicate without speaking. A touch, a raised eyebrow, an imperceptible twitch of the mouth, a breath. The Lear had flown them in that afternoon from the desert base camp.

The two young men followed a compass heading that they were told would bring them to the promontory where the suspected Israeli night scope was located.

The two men looked up the slope and picked out the outline of the black ridge against the star-studded sky. They estimated the distance at half a kilometer. Murad knelt down, turned the scope on, and sighted through it as he adjusted the knobs. The hillside appeared red-glowing, and it reminded him of blood or of hell and made him uneasy for a moment. He scanned and spotted the promontory. He looked for the telltale light of a night scope, but saw nothing. He lay on his belly and rested the rifle on a small rise in the ground. He relaxed as he continued to stare.

Outpost/Listening Post, OP/LP No. 2, was located in the central section of the slope, almost a half-kilometer down from the promontory. It was manned by Yigael Tekoah, the Knesset member, and Deborah Gideon, his secretary. Tekoah thought he heard something to his front, then to his left, then, with a frightened start, to his rear. He touched the girl's shoulder and whispered into her ear. "I think they've gotten around us."

She nodded in the dark. They had both been too frightened to move when they first heard the noises, and now they were behind the enemy lines with no way to get back to their own. They were lost.

Tekoah knew that in a real military unit he would have had sound-amplifying devices, night-seeing devices, weapons and radios or line phones to speak with the main body. But here, OP/LP was tantamount to suicide. They were sacrificial lambs. Still, it had not been difficult to find six volunteers for the three posts.

Tekoah felt he had failed. He had not done his duty of alerting the others. There was still no fire coming from the Israeli positions, and he knew that the Arabs were making a successful surprise attack. They might very well infiltrate the Israeli positions before a shot was fired. "I am going to shout and warn them."

Deborah stayed frozen like a small rabbit.

"I'm sorry. I must."

She seemed to come out of it. She touched his cheek. "Of course."

Tekoah could hear footsteps very close now. He stood in their shallow foxhole, cupped his hands to his mouth, and faced the top of the slope. He took a deep breath.

An Ashbal tripped a wire that had hanging from it cans of pebbles and metal filings. The pebbles and metal rattled noisily in the still air. There was complete silence on the slope. Tekoah froze in mid-breath.

Brin grabbed the M-14, turned on the scope, and sighted. Nothing moved downslope, not even the cloud and dust shadows. All along the defensive perimeter the Israelis held their breath, and all across the slope the Arabs did the same. Brin wondered if it was the wind rattling the cans or an animal or a small earthslide. There had been a lot of that all day. He relaxed but continued to scan.

The two-man sniper-killer team came alert. Murad stared intently at the promontory now. He saw the light of the Israeli scope as it went on. He noticed that it was green. An American starlight. He knew it would be. The starlight picture was better than his, but that didn't mean that the man who had it was a better shot than a man with an infrared. Murad felt confident. He sighted on the green light and waited to see the head behind it.

Brin leaned out further over the small earth balcony. He whispered to Naomi Haber. "You might as well pass the word that I don't see anything yet."

She nodded and ran silently, barefoot, back toward the Command Post/ Observation Post.

Murad saw Brin's reddish-white skin where Naomi Haber had wiped the sweat and camouflage from his forehead. Murad fired three times in quick succession. The silencer coughed very gently like a weak old man clearing his throat.

Brin felt nothing but a tap on his forehead, then nothing at all. He pitched backward and lay in the dust, the rifle thrown out and down the slope in his death throe.

After a few minutes, the Ashbals began advancing again. Another man hit another wire, and cans again rattled in the night.

Hausner stood with Dobkin and Burg at the CP/OP.

Naomi Haber had had trouble finding the CP/OP in the dark, but she finally spotted the phosphorescent banner. She ran up to the three men and reported.

Hausner listened again for the rattling, but heard nothing. He turned to Haber and the two other young runners at the Command Post. "Go down the line and tell them to fire a mad-minute when they hear my whistle. But make the minute only ten seconds," he added.

The runners took off in different directions.

After a short interval, Hausner whistled. Those closest to him heard the whistle and began firing at full rates of fire, which was a signal for everyone down the line to begin.

The Ashbals froze, then stretched themselves out on the ground. A few were hit, but they did not call out in pain for fear of being strangled by their officers. The officers and non-coms whispered frantically to hold fire. "It is only probing fire. Probing fire. Do not shoot," they said through clenched teeth. But as the seconds dragged out, each second seeming like a year, and with the five Israeli AK-47's pounding automatic fire down the slope, even the most disciplined among them began to feel for their safety catches and triggers. Just as one young man was about to return the fire, the Israeli fire ceased as suddenly as it had begun. The "mad-minute," ten seconds long for want of ammunition, was over.

The smell of burnt cordite blew away with the east wind, and the last of the gunshots reverberated off the surrounding hills and died in the ears of the defenders. There was not one among them who believed that the Ashbals were disciplined enough to hold their fire under that barrage, or to choke down a cry of pain if they were hit, or to stifle a panicky scream as the earth churned up around their faces.

Hausner turned to Burg and Dobkin. "I think we're getting jumpy."

Burg spoke. "I hope the OP/LP's are not hurt."

Dobkin answered. "If everyone followed his range cards and the OP/LP's stayed where they were supposed to, then they should be all right." He looked toward the eastern slope. "And speaking of outposts, if they haven't heard anything, then I don't think there is anything out there. Animals, wind, and earthslides. That's the bane of trip-wire devices. Once a sparrow landed on a trip flare wire in Suez in '67 and—but who gives a damn about Suez in '67?"

"Nobody," Hausner assured him.

Micah Goren and Hannah Shiloah, typists, manned Outpost/Listening Post No. 1 on the north end of the slope. They also knew, too late, that they had been surrounded. They sat huddled in their small foxhole until the mad-minute ended. They contemplated their next move. Out of the darkness, three young Ashbals jumped with flashing knives and cut the throats of the two unarmed Israelis.

Reuben Taber and Leah Ilsar, interpreters, sat at OP/LP No. 3 toward the south end of the slope. They also knew what had happened. They moved out of their hole and began making their way back to the top of the slope.

Murad spotted them with the infrared scope not forty meters from where he was lying. The Arab raised his silenced rifle and shot each of them neatly through the head.

The Ashbals began crawling now, feeling ahead for trip wires. Their progress was slow but nonetheless unrelenting. The closest squad was within three hundred meters of the crest.

Tekoah realized what the mad-minute was and knew that the Israelis had not seen anything. He turned to Deborah Gideon. "Good luck." He swung and hit her on the jaw. She fell silently to the bottom of their foxhole. He quickly pushed clay and dirt over her from the rim of the hole, then jumped out of it and began to run up the slope. He cupped his hands to his mouth again and shouted. "TEKOAH HERE! OUTPOST NUMBER TWO! THEY ARE ALL OVER THE SLOPE!"

Whether it was an Arab or Israeli-fired AK-47 that cut him down, he never knew, nor would it have mattered to him if he had.

The Ashbals charged. The first of the man-traps collapsed under the weight of one of them, a young girl. She fell onto the stakes and became impaled but did not die. Her screams were much louder than the guns at first but soon faded.

The Israelis were somewhat demoralized to hear the Ashbals so near. What had happened to the outposts? To the early warning devices? Why didn't the mad-minute work? Where was Brin and that marvelous scope?

A three-man fire team of Ashbals made it to the crest but ran into the abatis. One was impaled in the neck, another in the chest. Abel Geller, a steward, shot the third man at close range with Dobkin's Colt .45.

The man-traps were taking their toll, but there were not as many of the arduously dug holes as there should have been. Once they were collapsed, the screams of the victims kept everyone else away. The dead absorbed the stakes in their bodies and rendered the traps useless.

The Israelis had five AK-47's now and there were fewer Ashbals than in the first attack, but the Arabs had achieved surprise and that was always a critical factor. And there was no Joshua Rubin with his Uzi. Neither was there Nathan Brin with his M-14 and starlight scope, though no one knew that yet.

A squad of Ashbals made its way toward the promontory over ground that was not covered by any weapon. They keyed on the green glow of the starlight scope lying in the dust at the base of the promontory.

All along the line, as the Ashbals got closer they positioned themselves between the Israeli gun positions, which they could spot from the muzzle flashes. The Israeli guns had to swing farther right and farther left to cover these dead spots with effective fire.

The Ashbals had another advantage: This night they were veterans. The previous night they were untried young men and women who were taken by surprise by the Israeli resistance. Incoming gunfire held no irrational terror for them now, only the healthy fear that comes with experience. They had lost many brothers and sisters, and they wanted revenge. Hamadi had promised them that, with victory, they could use the Israelis—men or women—as they pleased. Ahmed Rish had promised all of them personal wealth after the ransom. Another difference between this night and the previous night was a long inspirational talk by Hamadi. Everyone knew, or thought he did, what he was fighting for now.

Hausner's man, Jaffe, leaped over the breastworks and went between the impaling stakes of the abatis to recover the AK-47's of the men who had become impaled. He threw the rifles into the perimeter but was hit as he tried to get back and rolled down the slope. Another of Hausner's men, Marcus, recovered the AK-47's and ammunition of the Ashbal whom Abel Geller shot with the .45.

The three extra rifles were given to two men and a woman trained by Dobkin. Still, the Ashbals had the initiative and they were in that peculiar situation that happens sometimes in battle, where there would be more casualties in retreating than in advancing. They were too near the crest.

The Israelis had cleared the slope well in front of their positions and they had leveled the land and flattened the clay mounds, but the Ashbals were so close that they were able, with their superior firepower and almost unlimited ammunition, to pour overwhelming fire into the breastworks on the crest. The defenders spent more and more time keeping their heads down and less and less time returning the fire. Each time they raised their heads, they saw that the muzzle flashes had gotten closer than the last time.

Bullets ripped into the breastworks, eating away at them and causing small earthslides as they fell away, leaving exposed holes in the defensive walls. Bullets also ripped into the aluminum reflectors, knocking most of them off their posts. The armor mesh from the Concorde was effective, but after several thousand hits, the nylon began to fray and the posts holding the sections were cut in two and toppled over. The aluminum impaling stakes were severed or uprooted by rifle fire, leaving openings in the abatis. To those Israelis who had never seen battle, there was amazement at how much damage small arms fire could do.

Hausner, Burg, and Dobkin stood at their posts and received reports from the runners. Dobkin knew that the Ashbals had the initiative and that the next few minutes might bring them over the top. He put his hand on Hausner's shoulder. "I'm staying."

Hausner roughly pushed his arm away. "You're going, General. Now. That's an order."

Dobkin's voice rose, which was a rarity. "Now you listen—you need a military commander here. There's no need for me to go for help any longer."

"That's right," said Hausner. "It's all over. But you were willing to go when it looked safer up here. So now I want you to go in order to save yourself. And I want someone out there so that the survivors here can have hope during their captivity. Now, go!"

Dobkin hesitated.

"Go!" shouted Hausner.

Burg spoke. "Go, Ben. The best commander in the world couldn't save this situation. It's in the hands of the troops—and God. So go."

Dobkin turned and jumped off the small knoll. Without a word of parting to anyone, he made his way toward McClure's position on the west slope.

On the east slope, two Ashbals managed to make it to the breastworks where there were no AK-47's or pistols. The two Israelis there, Daniel Jacoby, a steward, and Rachel Baum, a stewardess, hurled makeshift aluminum spears and shouted a warning. The Ashbals ducked the spears and opened fire. Jacoby and Baum were both hit. The two Ashbals slid between the impaling stakes of the abatis and jumped the breastworks and trenches. They were inside the perimeter.

Alpern, another security man, ran down the line with his AK-47 blazing. The two Ashbals fell into the Israeli trench. Alpern jumped into the trench and finished them with one of the homemade spears. Two men, carrying a make-shift litter made out of alumimun spears and carpeting, collected Daniel Jacoby and Rachel Baum and carried them back to the shepherds' hut. Alpern called to two unarmed women and handed them the Ashbals' weapons. They had been lucky this time, but Alpern, a veteran of the 1973 war, knew that it was coming close to the end unless their last desperate defensive plan worked.

22

On the flight deck of Concorde 02, Captain David Becker sat back in his chair and lit his last cigarette. He thought about his children in the States and about his new Israeli wife. The radio gave off a high, piercing squeal, but he did not seem to notice it. Occasionally, a bullet struck the fuselage and made a popping sound as it broke the thin skin. A few ricochets bounced around the cabin. Two bullets had come through the windows of the flight deck and caused spider-web shatters in them. Becker crushed out his cigarette and threw it on the floor. He reached to turn off the emergency power, but remembered that they wanted it left on for some last minute ruses they had planned. He shrugged. All the resourcefulness in the world meant nothing against hordes. The hordes. That had been an American infantryman's joke during the Korean War. A Chinese squad was made up of three hordes and a mob, or something like that. Funny. The hordes were taking over the civilized world. Little by little. Like the end of Rome. He got up to leave.

The radio went silent, then hummed pleasantly. A voice in bad Hebrew came out of the speaker. "You must give up," said the voice quickly. "Tell H he must give it up." Becker stared at the radio. The Arab spoke quickly and cryptically in the event the transmission was being monitored somewhere. In a second the jamming was back on. "Fuck you," said Becker. He left the flight deck and went out to join the flight.

The Ashbal squad under the promontory was within a hundred meters of the green-glowing starlight scope. The two-man sniper-killer team near them had set up a position, and Murad was firing silently and accurately at heads looking over the breastworks on the ridge.

Burg turned to Hausner. "They're close enough, I think."

Hausner nodded. Dobkin had told them to hold off on what was termed their final protective measures and their psy-warfare until it was absolutely necessary. Hausner knew it could not get any more necessary than it was now. He gave the order to his runner to set in motion the last defensive measures. He turned to Burg. "I'm going to see how Brin is doing. You are the commander. Stay here."

Burg acknowledged. As Hausner moved off, a young girl, one of the runners, came up behind him. "They're coming up the river slope," she reported.

Burg lit his pipe. Directing battles from hilltops was not his strong suit. It had been over thirty years since he was a soldier. Dobkin had left, and Hausner had gone out to the perimeter to commit suicide—he had no doubt about that. No one had heard anything from the Foreign Minister for some time. He was dead, wounded, or fighting for his life like everyone else. And he, Burg, was left holding the bag. He would have to negotiate the surrender if there was a chance to negotiate. He, who was always careful to remain detached and on the fence. But this time he was on the spot, and he was alone on that spot. No more runners were reporting the course of the battle. They were all fighting on the perimeter, he supposed. There was no staff to consult, no meetings to be held. He had a glimpse of how Hausner must have felt, and he was sorry for him. The runner stood beside him. He looked at her closely. It was Esther Aronson, one of the Foreign Minister's aides. She was shaking and her voice was breaking as she gave a fragmentary appraisal. "What are we going to *do?*" she asked.

Burg pulled on his pipe. He heard at least ten AK-47's on the east slope now. He had no doubt that they needed everyone of them, but he couldn't let the Arabs come up the west slope unopposed. The Foreign Minister was in charge of that side of the perimeter, and Burg supposed that he knew he was unqualified for the task. The line was held by only about eight people. Then there were Richardson and McClure. He pointed out to the east slope. "Go out there and beg, borrow, or steal two AK-47's and at least two loaded pistols. Take them back to the west slope. Tell Mr. Weizman to begin all the last defensive measures as soon as you get back. All right?"

She nodded quickly in the dark.

Burg looked at her. That was a lot of responsibility for one person, he decided. Alone, it was up to her to appropriate weapons and ammunition, then take them several hundred meters in the dark and place them where they would do the most good, and at the same time pass on orders to the Foreign Minister, who was probably beside himself with doubt by now. And all this had to be done before the Arabs could make the climb up the slope. He patted her shoulder. "It'll be all right. Just take it one step at a time."

"I'm all right."

"Good. Did you happen to see General Dobkin over there?"

"No."

"All right. Just go ahead, then. Good luck."

She ran off toward the sound of gunfire.

Dobkin stood in the foxhole with McClure and Richardson. "I knew they'd try this slope eventually."

McClure leaned forward and held out his pistol with both hands. He aimed cross-slope to the right and fired twice, then fired twice more to his front, then fired his final two rounds cross-slope to his left. He drew fire before he got the last round off. He leaned back. "Hard as hell to hold a five-hundred-meter front with a six-shooter." He fished around in his pockets for loose rounds.

"They'll send something over here from the other side," Dobkin assured him.

"I sure hope so," answered McClure. He began to reload.

Richardson looked down over the steep slope when the gunfire stopped. At short intervals a tin of pebbles would rattle, or the sound of an Arab cursing as he slipped would carry up the slope. "When the hell are they going to begin the final protective defenses? Where the hell did that runner go? Where are our AK-47's?"

Dobkin lifted himself out of the hole. "Ask General Hausner. I don't work here anymore." He crouched down in a runner's stance. "Adios, Tex," he said to McClure. "See you in Haifa or Houston." He sprang out of his crouch and took a long step that brought him over the crest. He seemed to hang in the air for a long moment. He looked down and realized how steep the drop was. It was a wall, he remembered, a glacis. A sloping wall built up from the river bank. His fall intercepted the slope and jolted him with a shock. His next step was ten meters farther down the almost perpendicular slope, the next, twenty meters. He ran, dropped actually, almost vertically to the ground below. He covered half the slope in less than three seconds. To his front, two surprised-looking Arabs suddenly appeared climbing out of the dark. They reacted instinctively and held their AK-47's, with bayonets fixed out in front of them.

Hausner found Naomi Haber cradling Nathan Brin's mutilated head in her lap. He knew now what at least part of the problem had been with the defenses. "Where's the rifle?" he snapped.

She looked up. "He's dead."

"I can see that, damn it! Where's the goddamned rifle?"

She shook her head.

Hausner crouched on the promontory. He half-felt and half-saw where Brin had rested his rifle on the ledge. There was a furrow in the soil where a bullet had ripped through. There was something warm and wet there as well. He wiped his hand. It was no stray shot, he decided. The Arabs had at least one sniper rifle now. They'd have another when they recovered Brin's gun. Were they still keeping this sniper's perch under observation? He'd find out very soon. He leaped over the earth wall and slid down the slope below. He saw the green glow very easily and dived at it.

Murad saw him in his scope. He called out to the nine-man infantry squad that was moving toward the rifle, but they could not see Hausner.

Hausner picked up the rifle, rolled to another position, and raised it. He saw the squad less than thirty meters off and fired five rounds in quick succession. He hit one or two men, and the rest scattered. They were no match for the starlight scope in the dark and knew it.

Murad drew a bead on Hausner. He had had his heart set on owning that scope. Now this madman might get it damaged when Murad shot him. He fired.

Hausner was already moving. He heard the round kick up dirt near his feet. He flattened himself on the sloping hill and scanned the terrain to his front. The Arab knew where he was, but Hausner didn't know where the Arab was. If he couldn't spot him in the next few seconds, he would be dead.

Murad had Hausner directly in his cross hairs. He squeezed the trigger. It was an impossible shot to miss.

The Ashbal infantry squad directly behind Murad began firing blindly at the scope, their streams of green tracer rounds making crisscross patterns in the blackness. Burning tracers lodged in the earth and glowed like dying fireflies while ricochets shot off at all angles.

Murad squeezed the trigger as the picture in his infrared scope began disappearing. The major disadvantage of the scope in battle was that it whited-out when it was aimed at burning phosphorus. The tracers of his backup squad arched across his red picture and left white streaks that thickened and bled into each other. That was why he had wanted the starlight scope. He cursed loudly and fired blindly. "Stop, you fools! Stop!" He fired blindly again and again. His teammate, Safar, shouted over the sound of the AK-47's, and the squad ceased fire.

Hausner knew what had happened. Another man would have said that God was with him again. But Hausner felt that he was being toyed with. The bomb. The crash. The recovering of the AK-47's. Now this. He wasn't charmed, he decided. He was cursed. Why wouldn't it end?

Murad's picture returned, and he scanned the spot where Hausner had been but saw nothing.

Hausner had found a very shallow depression in the slope, under the steep rise of the promontory—the watchtower—and had fallen into it. Like infantrymen everywhere, he knew how to shrink. Every muscle contracted, the air left his lungs, and he seemed to deflate into his pitiful hole. His chest, thighs, and even his loins collapsed in some metaphysical way known only to men under fire, and the bottom of the depression seemed to drop a few more precious centimeters.

Murad suddenly became frightened. He felt naked, exposed. He, too, found a cavity in the earth and burrowed into it.

The sounds of battle along the ridge filled the air, but in that spot, there seemed to be silence. Hausner and Murad waited for each other. The two night scopes. Two flash suppressors. Two silencers and two fine rifles. Silent, invisible, and deadly.

The main body of the Ashbals was within a hundred meters of the perimeter, but a few squads of trained sappers, infiltrators, had penetrated to positions directly beneath the breastworks and abatis. They lay there, silent and frozen, armed only with knives and pistols, every inch of their exposed skin blackened, waiting for the main group to make the final assault. Had they had hand grenades, bangalor torpedoes, or satchel charges, as sappers are supposed to have, they could have wreaked havoc on the Israeli lines. But no one had expected that they would have to storm a hill to take these hostages. They felt ill used in this attack. They were professionals, the elite of any infantry unit. It was a suicide mission to crawl up to the enemy lines in front of the main advance. And here they were, but they could do nothing until the main body got within final assault range. Then they would jump into the Israeli trenches and kill with knife and pistol. But if only they had those explosives to send in first . . .

Dobkin leaped and flew past the two astonished Arabs. They swiveled and lay with their backs on the slope, and their heels dug into the shifting clay and sand. They pointed their AK-47's downward and fired. The reports from the automatic weapons shook their bodies and they slid down the glacis, breaking off the crust of age and exposing the original brickwork.

Dobkin literally flew forward. He heard the pop and zip of the bullets as they went by him. His feet came down again and he sprang off again. His heels crashed through the castor oil bushes and his feet hit the flood bank. He leaped again like a high diver and sailed into the air.

An arch of green tracers followed him. He seemed to somersault around and through the long, deadly green fingers. He hung in mid-air for what seemed like an eternity. Above him was the starry black sky of Mesopotamia. Then the ridge line sped past in a blur, then below was the luminescent Euphrates, then, as his body spun again, the mud flats flashed past his eyes, and then again the sky. Out of the corner of his eye, those green phosphorus streaks, like death rays in a science fiction movie, came closer and closer, following him, and those hollow staccato sounds grew louder as more and more guns joined in. He wondered why he wasn't falling, why he seemed to be suspended above the river. Then a sharp green light hit him with searing pain and everything resumed normal speed as if he had just awakened from a dream. He heard a splash and the muddy Euphrates closed over him.

Hausner decided he was not going to make it back to the Israeli lines. It was too open, and the Arab sniper had his position fixed now. Yet from where Hausner lay, he could not deliver effective fire anywhere except to his front. The scope was not being utilized to its fullest advantage, and in any case, he was almost out of ammunition.

A round knocked off the heel of his shoe, and his leg jerked spasmodically. He cursed as he stuck his head up. He took aim, but the Arab was invisible in his hole. The infantry squad had switched to non-tracer rounds and began firing in his general direction. He spotted the sniper's teammate traversing the terrain toward the infantry squad—bringing them a definite fix on his position. Hausner fired, and the man, Safar, went down holding his side.

Murad fired, and Hausner felt a sting on his ear. He swung toward the sniper and fired at his form as it disappeared into the hole. He felt a warm wetness on his ear as he settled back in his shallow concavity. He thought, briefly, irrationally, of Miriam.

Hausner had had enough. He wasn't accomplishing anything, and he could sense that the Ashbals on both sides of him were approaching the crest. He called out behind him, above the sound of the shooting. "Haber!"

There was no answer.

He called again. "Haber!"

She looked up. Brin's bloody and brain-splattered head still lay in her lap. She remembered that Hausner was there a few minutes before, but didn't know what had become of him. She heard him shout again, but didn't answer.

Hausner ripped off his shirt and wrapped it around the starlight scope. He reversed the rifle and gripped its red-hot silencer/flash suppressor. He stood and swung the rifle around his head and released it into the air. It sailed upward and over the top of the ruined watchtower above his head. It fell into the soft dust some distance from Naomi Haber. She heard it fall and knew instinctively what it was and what she was supposed to do. She lowered her head and placed a kiss on Nathan Brin's shattered forehead.

The order for the final protective defenses had gone up and down the perimeter, and the carefully rehearsed operations began to be set in motion. All the ruses and all the makeshift weaponry that looked so clever and inspired in the daylight were about to be put to the test, and there were many doubts now in the dark.

An Arab voice shouted loudly a hundred meters to the north of the promontory. "Here! There is a hole in the lines here! Here! Follow me!"

Two Ashbal squads, eighteen men, converged on the voice. They charged upward, following the commanding voice. No one fired at them. They came within fifty meters of the apparently deserted breastworks. Another few seconds and they would be inside and the fight would be virtually over.

The voice called again. "Here! Quickly! Over the top!"

If the Ashbals noticed in the din of the firing that the voice had a slightly metallic quality, or that the Palestinian accent was not quite right, they did not act on that knowledge. One of their commanders must be using a bullhorn. They kept coming on toward the voice which was so close to the Israeli defenses.

Ibrahim Arif lay in back of the breastworks in a small dugout and shouted into the PA microphone again. "NOW, UP AND OVER!"

The PA speaker box, thirty meters in front of the breastworks, beckoned the Ashbals forward. "NOW, UP AND OVER! SHOUT! SHOUT! DEATH TO ISRAEL!"

The Ashbals stood straight, ran forward, and shouted: "DEATH TO ISRAEL!"

Kaplan, who had checked himself out of the infirmary, Marcus, and Rebecca Livni, a young stenographer who had just acquired an AK-47, opened fire. They each poured two thirty-round magazines into the Ashbal ranks.

The Ashbals stood in the glare of the muzzle flashes, paralyzed and bewildered. The 7.62mm rounds ripped into them. They collapsed on top of one another like a pile of jackstraws. It was their single biggest loss so far, and it left a sizable gap in their frontal attack.

Esther Aronson had been pleading with everyone she ran into in the dark to listen to her. Burg said to beg, borrow, or steal. And begging wasn't working. Everyone was too involved with his own survival to worry about the strategic problems of an attack from the rear. Everyone who listened to her sympathized, but that was all she got. She searched desperately for Hausner. Hausner could give a simple order, and she would have what she wanted. But no one knew where he was. Missing, presumed dead.

She saw and heard the ruse of the PA box and knew that the last desperate tricks and defenses were beginning. On the west slope there was hardly anything of that sort. She needed arms. She ran over to where Marcus and Rebecca Livni were cautiously making their way through the breastworks and abatis to recover the rifles of the slain squads. Kaplan was covering them. Esther Aronson ran past Kaplan, vaulted over the trench and over the top of the breastworks, and slid through the stakes of the abatis past a surprised Marcus and Livni. "Sorry," she yelled. "I need guns for the west slope. They're attacking." She stepped quickly among the carnage, among the dead and still living, and quickly and expertly stripped off bandoliers and web gear that were loaded down with ammunition pouches. She grabbed at the AK-47's in the dark, more often than not finding their hot barrels instead of their stocks. Her hands and body burned as she slung them one after the other over her shoulders.

Marcus and Livni had run to Aronson and were helping her. Marcus kept shouting to watch out for live men, but Esther Aronson didn't seem to care or hear. Marcus shot a man who appeared to reach for his rifle as it was being pulled away.

Aronson yelled, "Thank you," and disappeared over the breastworks under that incredible load.

Marcus and Livni quickly gathered up the remaining rifles under cover of Kaplan's AK-47. The PA box was screaming, "BACK! BACK! STAY AWAY, COMRADES! THE JEWS ARE WELL ARMED OVER HERE." The Ashbals kept their distance.

*   *   *

Naomi Haber put a fresh magazine into the M-14 and sighted. The entire slope was covered with crawling, crouching figures. She scanned the area directly below her perch. She spotted Hausner lying very still in his hole. Had he been hit? She couldn't tell. He must have stood up to throw the rifle that distance. The Arab sniper would certainly have gotten him.

A bullet brushed the knuckles of her right hand and she let out a scream and almost lost the rifle. She crouched below the earth wall until the shock wore off. She licked at the wound like an animal, and this seemed to have a calming effect on her. She knew that the man who had almost killed her was the same man who had killed her lover. And she knew that for that reason, more than any other, he must die. She got up slowly and peeked over the earth wall.

Murad realized by now that Safar was dead. Safar, his childhood friend. His only real friend. His lover. And that Jew had killed him. Had he hit the Jew when he threw the rifle up? And the rifle and scope were gone. Who had it? He scanned between Hausner's hole and the sniper's promontory. The danger was on the promontory now, but his emotions wouldn't let him take his eyes off the last place he had seen the cursed Jew.

Haber sighted slowly as she took a breath. She could see the sniper's full body lying prone below her about eighty meters away. A shot toward the head area would, with luck, destroy the scope as well as the head, but a shot at the back was more certain. She put the cross hairs over the small of his back and fired twice.

Along the perimeter, the Israelis were setting up the dummies that had taken so long to construct. As they were set up, they drew fire, were knocked down and set up again.

A dozen unarmed men and women held up aerosol spray cans and ignited their vapor mists in short spurts, simulating muzzle flashes. The Arabs fired at these flashes, which they could see all along the ridge. Their estimation of the number of weapons captured by the Israelis went up considerably.

Meanwhile, the real AK-47's, newly captured with sufficient ammunition, were beginning to operate.

Two unarmed women, who had spent the last half hour tape-recording the sounds of battle on the peace mission's two dozen cassette tape recorders, now began placing those recorders at various points and pushing the playback buttons. The volume of fire from the Israeli lines seemed to increase.

Things were beginning to function again. Runners were coming to the CP/OP and reporting to Burg and asking for orders. Burg gave orders as though he had been doing it all his life. The final protective defenses were apparently working and morale was going up. But Burg knew that it was still a very close thing.

Esther Aronson staggered in the dark toward the west slope. She called out, but no one seemed to hear.

The Ashbals, temporarily confused by Dobkin's one-man charge, had stopped moving for a while, but eventually they began crawling up toward the top of the wall again. They could make out the top against the starry sky, less than fifty meters off. Their commander, Sayid Talib, couldn't believe their good luck. Except for the single pistol shooting intermittently at them, there was no one on the crest. But that wouldn't last forever. He exhorted his men to move faster. He had believed this to be a suicide mission for himself and his forty men, but Ahmed Rish had calmed him, with a story about an English general who took his army up a cliff more impregnable than this one and captured Canada for the English. And it was true. No one could have expected an attack here.

Talib's blood flushed his face as he climbed. He could not wait to get among the Israelis. He touched his half-mutilated face. When he had lived in Paris he had received a letter from the French Ministry of Immigration. He had opened it and discovered that it was in fact from Mivtzan Elohim. That carelessness had cost him the right side of his face, and life had never been the same since. Women let out a little cry when they saw his once handsome features. Even men looked away.

Talib prayed that he would find Isaac Burg alive. Of all the torture fantasies he had played out in his mind, he had decided that flaying would be ideal for the head of Mivtzan Elohim. He would strip his skin off over a period of twenty-four hours—maybe longer. He would feed it to the dogs while Burg watched. He looked up. They were less than twenty-five meters from the top.

McClure put his last six rounds in the chamber of his pistol. He turned to Richardson, who was standing very still. "How do you say, 'Take me to the American consulate,' in Arabic?"

"You should have asked Hausner that yesterday."

"You don't speak any Arabic, then?"

"No. Why should I?"

"Don't know. Just figured you did." He leaned out of the foxhole and looked downslope. He could see men, like lizards, crawling up out of the darkness. He aimed at one and fired.

Miriam Bernstein and Ariel Weizman found Esther Aronson crawling along the ground. They took the eight AK-47's and ammunition without any formalities and ran along the half-kilometer-long perimeter in opposite directions. At each position, they dropped off a rifle and ammunition. Bernstein skipped McClure's foxhole. At the south end of the perimeter she found herself alone with the last AK-47. An Ashbal girl lifted herself up onto the flat ground and stood five meters away with her AK-47 slung. She saw Bernstein and unslung her weapon, slowly and deliberately.

Bernstein did not have any idea of how to use the AK-47 and didn't know if she wanted to use it in any case. Was the safety off? Was it loaded? Did it have to be cocked? The previous owner, of course, had it cocked with the safety off for the attack, but she did not think of this. All she knew for certain was that the gun had a trigger. She found it and hesitated.

The Ashbal girl fired a full burst at her at point-blank range.

Miriam Bernstein saw the muzzle flashes and they blinded her. She thought of a blindingly sunny day in a café in Jerusalem. A young infantryman was telling a story of how an Arab had popped out of a house on the Golan Heights and fired a submachine gun at him from a distance of a few meters. The young infantryman had been standing in front of a tree, and the tree, directly behind him, was hit again and again and bark and wood splinters flew off and hit the young man all over his head, neck, and back. Then the Arab disappeared. The infantryman had said, "An angel was standing in front of me that day."

Bernstein heard another burst of fire and the automatic rifle jumped in her hands. The young girl appeared to leap backwards over the edge.

Miriam Bernstein sank to her knees and covered her face.

* * *

In the Concorde, Yaakov Leiber sat and watched an American war movie. He'd seen the movie that afternoon and had made notes. The projector was set on "fast forward." When a portion with authentic war sounds came on, he returned it to normal speed and turned up the volume. The movie sound speakers, set up on the perimeter, reproduced the deep throaty sounds of a heavy machine gun. Rumors of this heavy machine gun had run rife in the Ashbal camp ever since Muhammad Assad had been released by the Israelis. Before his execution for treason, Assad had apparently told his guards many stories of Israeli strengths.

The Ashbals were wavering now. Flashes of gunfire twinkled up and down the Israeli line. More and more sounds of increasingly rapid gunfire rolled down the slope. Above the sounds of the small arms came the rumble of the heavy machine gun. It seemed as though the Israelis had more weapons than they had people. The Ashbal fighters smelled defeat in the air. They began throwing anxious glances at their commanders.

Naomi Haber watched as the Arab sniper's body bounced. Her whole body shook as she realized that she had actually put two bullets into the man's back. She called out, trying to keep her voice even. "Mr. Hausner! He is finished. I will cover you!" She looked down on Hausner's still body below her. "Mr. Hausner! He is finished! I will—" She saw his arm move slightly in a wave. She turned the rifle downslope and began firing at the targets. Forward-moving target at eighty meters. Fire! Hit! Stationary target at ninety meters. Fire! Hit! Right-to-left at fifty meters. Fire! Miss. Adjust for range. Fire same target. Hit! Next target.

Hausner clawed at the steep sides of the overhanging watchtower, but there was no way up. He moved to his right where the slope was gentle and began running uphill. Ahead of him, to the left, he could hear the metallic operating rod of the M-14 slide back again and again. To his front, the Israeli breastworks rose up. There was not supposed to be anyone there—the M-14 was supposed to cover the entire area—but he could see an incredible number of muzzle flashes along the defensive perimeter. Where the hell had they found all those rifles? Or were they all aerosol cans? Flashes appeared in front of him, and he knew they were not aerosol cans. Bullets went buzzing past his ears from behind as well. He yelled out above the gunfire. "For God's sake, stop firing! Hausner! Hausner!" The sand gave way under him and he crawled and stumbled directly into the Israeli guns, shouting at the top of his lungs between gulps of air. Then he found himself at the bottom of a trench. A young man and woman with AK-47's looked down at him curiously. Hausner stood up. "You're the worst goddamned shots I have ever seen."

"Lucky for you," said the girl.

The unarmed fighters began pushing the stacked plaques of clay over the side. The heavy plaques tumbled down the slope, breaking off the hard crust as they went and picking up more mass and energy. The earth slides tore into the Ashbal ranks and snapped legs and crushed ribs as they hit.

Suddenly, torchlike flames illuminated the Israeli lines as dozens of Molotov cocktail wicks were lit. The incendiary devices arched high into the air and began landing among the Ashbals. To make sure that they burst on impact, the Israelis used half bricks, tied with thongs onto each device, to act as clappers. The jars and bottles broke on impact and the kerosene or the more deadly crude napalm ignited, splattering flames over the side of the slope.

For greater distance, brassieres were used as slings to hurl the bombs down the slope. The side of the slope lit up, and the Israeli gunfire became more accurate as the Ashbals stood revealed against the flames.

The Ashbals became confused and milled about. Some ran for dark areas where the burning kerosene would not illuminate them. Occasionally, a man would be splattered with burning fuel, and his screams would carry above the other ghastly sounds of battle.

The last few man-traps that had not caught anyone were soon occupied. A half-dozen young men and women screamed and squealed their lives away when the impaling stakes drove deeper into their rumps, their necks, their bellies, and their genitals as they squirmed to get off of them.

The sappers, who were playing dead directly beneath the Israeli breastworks, knew that they were in fact dead men. Their own army's fire had already killed some of them, and the chances of their men assaulting the Israeli lines were diminishing. They were caught almost in the jaws of the enemy. But their training had provided for almost every contingency. Slowly, a few at a time, they rolled downhill, stopping every few meters and playing dead again. They knew that the defenders' attention was riveted elsewhere. Meter by meter, they closed in on the main body of their comrades. It was slow and torturous, and almost every one of them was hit at least once, but half of the twenty-man elite team eventually made it back to their comrades. They were by no means out of danger there, however.

The fight on the west slope was over within sixty seconds of the time the first Israeli AK-47 opened up. Molotov cocktails incinerated the entire line of castor oil bushes, silhouetting the climbing Ashbals. Clay plaques and AK-47 fire swept the flat, steep slope clean. The glacis was as unassailable as when Darius first saw it over twenty-five hundred years before, or when Alexander remarked on the defenses some years later. Almost every man was killed outright or burned to death in the castor oil bushes below. The few who fell into the Euphrates, like most Arabs, could not swim and drowned in the deep, muddy waters.

Sayid Talib, his dreams of flaying Isaac Burg now forgotten, ran screaming through the burning bushes. The searing pain of two bullets almost made him lose consciousness. He stumbled and crawled and finally saw the Euphrates below him. He threw himself in. Swimming was one thing he had learned in Europe, and he let the river carry him southward. A few of his men splashed and shrieked around him and finally drowned. He believed he was the only survivor.

Hausner walked up to Burg who was standing on the CP/OP. "You are either the best commander since Alexander the Great or you had the good sense to stand here and do nothing."

Burg was surprised to see Hausner alive but didn't remark on it. "A little of both, I think." He could see that Hausner was bare-chested and missing both his shoes. Blood was smeared across his face. "Where the hell were you?"

"Downslope." He stood on top of the rise and looked out toward the perimeter. "Brin was killed by a sniper."

"I see." Burg lit the pipe that had been hanging dead in his mouth for some time. "We took a lot of casualties. The outposts are done for, I'm afraid."

"I suppose they are," said Hausner. Two girls approached the CP/OP from the direction of the west slope. They each had several rifles slung on their shoulders. One of them was Esther Aronson. She spoke. "It's all over for them over there. No casualties for us. One missing, though."

"You did a marvelous job," said Burg.

"I think these rifles could be put to better use on the east slope," she continued.

"Yes," said Burg. "Who's missing?"

"Miriam Bernstein. They're looking for her."

Hausner didn't seem to react.

The two young women hurried off into the darkness.

Hausner put out his hand. "Give me a pull on that damned thing."

Burg handed him the pipe. "Was this a miracle?"

"It doesn't qualify," said Hausner. His hands were shaking.

"Why not?"

"Because I didn't hear the voice of the Lord."

"You have to hear it? Only *you* are supposed to hear it?"

"That's right."

Burg laughed.

Hausner handed back the pipe. "Dobkin?"

Burg shrugged. "There's the miracle—if he's alive."

"Right. Listen—I'm going over to the west slope."

"No need. It's all over there."

"Don't tell me how to run this battle, Burg." He jumped down off the rise and walked very quickly west.

Burg stared after him.

Ibrahim Arif spoke into a PA microphone. He pitched his voice to carry above the deep bass sounds of battle and at the same time made it sound mocking. "Go home, little children. You have been soundly spanked. Now, go home and hide your faces! Salem Hamadi! Can you hear me? Go home and go to bed with your young boyfriend! Who is it this week? Ali? Abdel? Salman? Or is it Abdullah? Muhammad Assad said you were making love to Abdullah this week!"

Arif went on, taunting in that high wailing manner peculiar to the Arabs. As he spoke his heart thumped heavily in his chest, and his mouth, already dry from lack of water, felt like the sands of the desert. Between him and Rish's cruel, mutilating knife was a handful of Jews whose weapons were again running out of ammunition. And even if, by some miracle of Allah, he did get out of this alive, he would be hunted for the rest of his life with a renewed vengeance by the people he had once called brothers and sisters. But that was tomorrow's worry. Tonight's worry was staying away from Rish's knife and carrying out the orders of Jacob Hausner. "Or is it a camel or an ass for you tonight, Salem? Or perhaps it is your lord and master, Ahmed Rish?"

The young Ashbals, in their confusion and misery, shouted back. Two got up and charged the crest and were shot down. Some held the triggers of their weapons like a man in a helpless rage clenches his fists, and the barrels of the AK-47's overheated and the weapons exploded.

Ahmed Rish squatted in a gully with his radio operator. Salem Hamadi sat a few meters off. He appeared, in the dark, to be weeping or praying, or perhaps just muttering to himself. Rish called to him. "Get up! We must make one last effort. Their ammunition must be low. The moon is not yet risen. One last effort. Come! We must personally lead it."

Hamadi stood and advanced alongside Rish. Most of the remaining Ashbals followed mechanically.

Molotov cocktails rained down on the stalled attackers and bullets ripped their ranks. Earthslides knocked their feet out from under them or covered their prone bodies.

Finally, the call to retreat came loud and clear from behind them. "Back! Back! It is finished! Fall back!"

Abdel Jabari sat near the shepherds' hut and spoke authoritatively into the PA microphone. "Back! Back! It is finished! Fall back!" The PA speaker, its wire miraculously unscathed, blared from the hole of Outpost No. 2 "Back! Back!" Deborah Gideon awoke to its sound. She brushed the clay off her face and looked up out of the hole at the sky. An incredibly beautiful cluster of dazzling blue-white stars sat right above her. Footsteps hurried past her, heading downslope. She closed her eyes as a silhouette blotted out the stars above her.

"Back!" shouted Jabari. Though by now the young Ashbals knew it was yet another ruse, they pretended they did not and fell back as ordered by that strong voice. Another voice, as strong and as compelling, the voice of Ahmed Rish (or was it another ruse?), ordered them forward. The voice called out in the darkness and, in fact, it even crackled over the few functional field radios. "Forward! Attack! Follow me!" But the other voice, further down the slope, said, "Back! Go back!" And it was certainly easier to direct one's footsteps downslope than up—and less deadly. In fact, the Israeli fire seemed to abate as though they were waiting to see how it would go. The meaning, as the Ashbals saw it, was clear. The Israelis seemed to be saying, "You are no longer trapped on the slope. The back door is open. Go."

Near the center of the eastern defensive line and twenty meters behind it, Peter Kahn and David Becker stood by the big nitrogen bottle. Attached to its nozzle was a telescoping strut from the front nose wheel assembly. Balanced on top of the strut was a seat from the Concorde. On the seat was a tire from the nose assembly. Kahn gave the signal and Becker put a match to the kerosene-soaked seat and tire. They burst into flames and Kahn released the pressure valve. The nitrogen shot into the hollow strut and pushed its telescoping section into the air. The seat and wheel hurled upward and arched over the breast-works like a fiery image from the Book of Ezekiel. It hit the slope and bounced high, spewing burning particles and throwing off its flaming wheel. The seat and the tire bounced again down the slope through the ranks of the Ashbals.

Kahn and Becker retracted the strut and fastened another seat and the second and last tire to it. They lofted the burning, bouncing missile into the air, then put a third seat on the strut, pointed the whole assembly farther southward, and fired again.

The Ashbals turned back, only a few at first, then all of them, including their remaining officers and sergeants. They moved quickly, but did not run or break into a disorderly route. They picked up the wounded when and where they could, but left the dead and near-dead for the buzzards and jackals. The unaided wounded crawled and rolled down the slope.

The Israelis had ceased firing even before Burg's runners got the order out to the line. The unspoken understanding called for an unhampered and unharassed line of retreat for the Ashbals. The Ashbals were recovering a lot of loose equipment because of the lack of Israeli fire, but it seemed a small price in exchange for their ending the attack. And it was the Ashbal rank and file, not the officers, who had tacitly accepted the Israeli deal. Burg felt this was an important point.

* * *

There was a stillness on the hill and down the slope, a stillness that penetrated into the dark, out to the mud flats, and into the surrounding hills. The steady east wind blew off the smells of cordite and kerosene and impartially covered the living and the dead with a film of fine dust. As the din cleared from everyone's ears, they noticed that the stillness was only a temporary postbattle deafness. Now the east wind could be heard as well as felt, and it carried with it the sounds of crying and moaning men and women from the littered slope. The jackals began howling in the night—howling like a Roman crowd that had just witnessed an excellent fight in the gladiator pits—like a crowd mesmerized into a temporary silence, then suddenly bursting forth with approval at the slaughter.

Burg looked at his watch. The whole thing had taken just thirty-nine minutes.

23

Dobkin lay bleeding on the west bank of the Euphrates. He heard the silence and wondered what it meant. It had two interpretations, of course. He tried to replay the sounds of the past fifteen minutes in his mind—to interpret them like the old campaigner that he was. But the pain in his thigh bothered his concentration. Still, he felt certain that he would hear the Arabic victory shouting if that was the way it had gone. He listened intently through the pain. Nothing. Silence. He let the pain and fatigue take him into unconsciousness.

Hausner found her near the south end of the west slope. She was staring over the edge of the drop, down into the river. She held a rifle by one hand at her side. Hausner stood a few meters to the side of her and stared at her face, illuminated by the reflection from the river. "You killed someone."

She turned her head quickly. "I . . . but you're all right. You're all right." She let the rifle fall and turned toward him.

He seemed to hesitate. Making love was one thing. Showing affection on the morning after implied a deeper commitment. He didn't know if he was ready for that. "You . . . you're an MIA."

She hesitated also. "I'm here. Not missing." She laughed softly, a nervous laugh.

"Me, too," said Hausner with what sounded like a touch of disbelief. "We made it."

"I killed a young girl."

"Everyone who fires a gun in battle for the first time thinks he has killed someone."

"No. I really did. She fell down the slope."

"She may have been nicked a bit and run off."

"No. I hit her in the chest . . . I think."

"Nonsense." But he knew it was not. He wanted to say, "Good for you, Miriam. Welcome to the club," but he couldn't bring himself to say it. "You fired the gun and you thought you killed someone. Did you hear her yell?"

"I . . . I don't know. It happened . . ."

"Come with me. I have to get back."

She picked up the rifle and followed. She wanted to say something neutral like, "Thank you." Instead it came out, "I love you." She said it again, louder. "I love you."

He stopped but would not turn. He knew that he was not going to make it. He knew that with more certainty then he'd ever known anything. But maybe she was fated not to make it, either. If she were to die and he hadn't told her that he loved her, too, then that would be a tragedy. But if she lived, then his "I love you" could only cause her further grief. He began walking again and he could hear her soft footsteps in the dust, falling farther and farther behind.

Rabbi Levin ministered spiritually and physically to the wounded. He helped carry bodies from the line to the hut, then assisted in dressing wounds. He looked like a casualty himself, smeared with blood and hollow-eyed, and he smelled like a charnel house.

After the wounded were all assembled in and around the hut, the rabbi began making an accounting of them in a small book. He added the wounded of the second night to the wounded of the first night and made notes on their progress or lack of it. Tamir, unchanged. Hausner's three men—Rubin, up and around; Jaffe, unchanged; and Kaplan, bleeding again. Brin was dead, they'd told him, leaving only Marcus and Alpern still fit for full duty out of Hausner's original six men. Ruth Mandel was still feverish. Neither Daniel Jacoby nor Rachel Baum, wounded together, was doing well. Abel Geller, the steward, lay bleeding to death all over the floor of the hut, his white uniform an incredible red. A pool of mixed blood had collected on a low point in the ancient brick floor, and it made a splashing sound whenever Rabbi Levin walked through it. There were six other wounded whom he didn't know by sight, and he gave them numbers until he had time to identify them.

The rabbi needed air. He walked outside, but there was only more carnage there. Shimon Peled, the Foreign Minister's aide, lay dead against a wall of the hut. He had died not of his moderate wound but of a heart attack. He'd been ruled unfit for combat duty, but had insisted on being given a rifle. Levin shook his head. There would be a lot of stupidity and stubbornness that would pass for bravery in the hours and days ahead. He found some towels and covered Peled's face with one of them. Strange custom, this covering of the face of the dead. There were two girls lying against the wall, dead also. He arranged their bodies in a more restful position, closed their eyes—another strange custom when you thought about it—and covered their faces with towels also. He'd get their names later.

The biggest loss was the six men and women on the outposts. Rabbi Levin entered their names in his book. Deborah Gideon, Yigael Tekoah, Micah Goren, Hannah Shiloah, Reuben Taber, and Leah Ilsar. He'd say a prayer as soon as he had a minute or two.

And where was Hausner? He'd been reported as missing, as dead, and as alive. Even Jacob Hausner couldn't be all three at once. Levin wondered if they would be better or worse off without him. And General Dobkin? Did Ben Dobkin make it? He'd have to say a special prayer for Ben Dobkin.

As the rabbi walked back into the hut, Beth Abrams collapsed from the heat and the stench, and Levin carried her outside. She revived before he even set her down and insisted on going back to her nursing. The rabbi sighed and let her go. Yes, it *was* going to be a long and terrible night. The rabbi had an unorthodox thought: If everyone looked out for himself first, then everyone would have at least one person looking out for him. That didn't sound as if it should come from a rabbi, but he liked it. He took a deep breath and went back into the hut.

There was no celebration among the Israelis this night. Although they had accomplished the incredible feat of arms, not only was the price high, but they knew that the worst was yet to come. Now would set in the hunger and the thirst. The wounded were consuming vast quantities of water. Their moans and cries carried across the still hilltop, wearing away at the morale of the others.

A party went downslope and began looking for abandoned equipment. Three other teams went off to search for the outposts. When they brought back the hacked-up bodies of Micah Goren and Hannah Shiloah, there was a great deal of weeping among the defenders. The bodies of Reuben Taber and Leah Ilsar, each with a neat hole in the head, were added to the dead in back of the shepherds' hut.

Occasionally, a shot would be heard on the slope. The men and women on the hill pretended not to notice the shots, but they could not help noticing that there wasn't as much moaning from the Arab wounded left behind.

The Israelis badly needed a morale booster, and they found it in Yigael Tekoah. He was already a hero—presumably a dead one—for disregarding his own life to shout the warning. Now he was a live hero, found with multiple, but not mortal, wounds. He was brought back into the perimeter. Between periods of unconsciousness, he told them what he had done to try to save Deborah Gideon and asked about her. He was assured that she was fine and a runner was quickly sent out to pass on to the search parties what Tekoah had told them about her.

At Outpost No. 2, they could see where she had lain in the dust, but she was no longer there. They called for her and searched the area, but it was apparent that she had been taken prisoner.

Jacob Hausner stood with Burg on the promontory and watched the full moon rise in the east. If the full moon really made lunatics restless, then Ahmed Rish would be howling tonight. The entire slope turned blue-white, and the full extent of the carnage could be seen clearly now. "That's it until moonset," said Hausner.

Burg nodded. The next period of darkness between moonset and the beginning of morning nautical twilight would be about an hour and a half long. He wondered if Rish would attempt an attack then. Twilight might catch them on the slope, and then that would be the end of Ahmed Rish and company. "Maybe they've had it," he said aloud.

The awful post-action sounds hung in the night air: the moaning, the cries of pain, the weeping, the labored breathing from the necessary exertions, the heavy, shuffling footsteps of people fatigued beyond their limits, the sounds of retching, and the occasional sharp report of a *coup de grâce* being administered on the slope.

These sounds were far more unsettling than the sounds of the battle that had created them, reflected Hausner. He stared at the body of Nathan Brin, not yet removed from the place where he had fallen. He wanted to say something aloud or touch the man, but Naomi Haber, on duty with the starlight scope, was already tottering on the edge of hysteria. His low reserve of compassion was better expended on the living, he thought. He said a silent good-bye to the young man who had been such a fountainhead of optimism and strength, then walked over to the girl and put his arm around her. He marveled at how young people became so attached to each other in so short a period of time, but then remembered his own situation. "A lady who means very much to me was also forced to kill tonight. She is a professional pacifist, but she is coping with it."

Haber put down the rifle. "I'm all right. I can cope with that. Let me do my job." She wiped her eyes and went back to her protective scanning.

Hausner walked away and began his lonely circuit of the line.

As the night wore on and the shock wore off, most of the defenders on the hill returned to a more normal state of mind. Everything began functioning again. The dwindling supplies of water and ammunition were distributed, the wounded were cared for, and repairs were made on the defenses wherever possible.

After Hausner completed his inspection of the defenses, he found Burg and they both moved to the cockpit of the Concorde. As they entered, Becker was working the radio. Its squeal shot through the still cockpit. He switched it off and spoke to the two men behind him. "The Lear is still on station. Probably won't have to go and refuel until daylight."

"Well, we'll try again at daylight, then." Hausner took a long drink from a bottle of sweet Israeli wine that was Becker's ration. He made a face. He couldn't see the label, but he knew it wasn't a Trockenbeerenauslese. He sat in the jump seat, took Rish's psychological profile from the floor, and flipped through it absently. "One of our brilliant Army psychiatrists says here that Ahmed Rish would respond to treatment. He didn't say what kind of treatment, but I presume he meant decapitation." He looked up. "If you were Ahmed Rish, Isaac, what would you do next?"

Burg swiveled around in the flight engineer's seat and crossed his legs as he drew on his pipe. "If I were a paranoiac I think I would be so filled with desire for revenge that I'd lead those poor bastards back up the hill."

"But would they *follow?*" asked Becker.

"That's what we were trying to resolve before," said Hausner. "I think Rish will convince them that we are through. He can do that. He has a prisoner now, and no matter what she says about us, Rish will translate it to fit his own needs."

There was a long silence in the cockpit. Each man conjured up his own image of Deborah Gideon at the mercy of Ahmed Rish—naked, brutalized, broken, alone . . . dying. Hausner hoped that she would save herself a lot of pain and tell them everything she knew. It wasn't much and it wasn't worth the torture to keep it secret. But he feared they might torture her anyway, just for the pleasure of it. He found it hard to work up anger for Rish, just pity for the girl. Anger at Rish would have been the purest type of hypocrisy, as Muhammad Assad would attest to.

Becker rolled a cigarette from some of Burg's pipe tobacco and weather-map paper. He cleared his throat and broke the silence. "How are the odds now?"

Hausner knew that Becker was discreet. "The same, really." He seemed to be thinking out loud. "We have almost thirty guns but no more ammunition per gun than before—about a hundred rounds apiece, I think. Our defenses are in a shambles, and we don't have the water or energy to rebuild them. We've shot all our ruses and they won't be fooled by the same ones twice. Brin is dead, and the scope may be at the end of its life, too. Anyway, there are only ten rounds left for the M-14. I have two men trying to adapt the scope to an AK-47." He took another long pull from the wine bottle and swallowed it before it ran over his tongue. "By the way, how is the kerosene holding out?"

Becker smiled. "It's hard to believe that the instruments were that inaccurate. I don't know where the stuff is coming from."

Hausner nodded. "Don't let the rabbi know, or we'll get a sermon on the miracle of the holy oil. Anyway, we are completely out of containers and almost every Molotov cocktail is gone." He finished the wine and let the bottle drop to the deck. "But you asked about the odds. The odds are still dependent on the Ashbals. We still are not the odds-makers here. We can only wait for their next move." He looked down at the portfolio in his lap. He stared at a picture of Rish. "Ahmed," he said softly, "if you had an ounce of sanity, you would get the hell out of Babylon before it becomes your grave. But of course you won't."

24

Teddy Laskov looked down at Rish's picture. "Speak to me, Ahmed."
Itzhak Talman sipped on a glass of port and flipped through his own portfolio of Rish. "Why haven't we heard from him yet? What does he want?"

Michel's was noisy and crowded, and almost every conversation had to do with the peace mission. It seemed unpatriotic to speak of anything else. Everyone in the café recognized the two ex-Hel Avir generals, but no one stared at them or made them uncomfortable.

Laskov sipped a vodka. "I don't believe he has them under his control. If they were captives, then we would have heard from Rish."

"If they are not captive, then they are dead, Teddy."

Laskov leaned across the table, spilling the vodka from his glass. "Alive! I know it. I feel it."

"Captive where, then?"

"Babylon." The word surprised him as much as it did Talman. Perhaps it was because they had been using the Hebrew word, *shrym*—"taken captive"—instead of an expression like "held hostage" or "held prisoner." The association of words was inevitable. Perhaps the vodka helped. Or perhaps it was more than just an association of words mixed with alcohol. "Babylon," Laskov repeated and felt it was so. "Babylon," he said again, standing up and overturning his chair. "Babylon!" he shouted, and heads turned toward him. Talman took his arm, but Laskov pulled away. He stuffed his papers into his case and ran into the street, leaving Talman to throw a handful of pound notes on the table.

Outside, Talman jumped into a cab alongside Laskov, just as it began moving.

"Jerusalem!" Laskov shouted to the driver. "National emergency!"

Talman pulled the door closed as the driver, who was not unfamiliar with breaking the speed laws when someone yelled "national emergency," accelerated across St. George Square and turned onto the Jerusalem road.

"Babylon," said Laskov, more quietly this time.

The driver glanced over his shoulder, then watched his passengers' faces in his mirror.

"Babylon," said Talman with not as much conviction. "Yes. Maybe. Babylon."

* * *

"Babylon," said Jacob Hausner. He stared at Rish's psychological profile. "Babylon in all its desolation is a sight not so awful as that of the human mind in ruins." He had read that somewhere. Hausner had found Kahn's half-bottle ration of wine and picked it up from the floor. "Nice. Appropriate." He took a long drink from the bottle but could not stomach it any longer and spit it out. "If I ever get back to Haifa, I'm going to devote my energies and wide-ranging talents to the development of a good local wine."

Becker was unimpressed with both Hausner's erudition and his plans for the future. "What really galls me," he said, "is that we have to wait here for this lunatic. We are not the odds-makers."

"Perhaps we should be," said Hausner. "Perhaps it's time *we* went on the offensive."

Burg caught a danger signal. He sat up. "Meaning?"

Hausner stretched out in the jump seat. "They're probably back at their bivouac around the Ishtar Gate by now. If they are going to attack again at moonset, they will first come back here and assemble at a staging area, a jump-off point, some distance from the base of the slope. That's military procedure. The most distinguishable landmark for that purpose would be the city wall. We can place an ambush there. About ten or fifteen men should do it."

Burg shook his head. "For God's sake, Hausner, don't start thinking you're a general. It's all we can do to hold them off from up here. We can't send anyone out of this perimeter. If the ambush party didn't find them, then we'd be ten or fifteen men and guns short when the attack began."

"Then the ambush party could attack from the rear," said Hausner. "Or attack their bivouac, kill their wounded and the orderlies, smash their communications equipment, burn their stores, and maybe even rescue Deborah Gideon."

Burg stared over his glowing pipe for a few seconds. "Who are you, Hausner . . . Attila the Hun or head of El Al Security? Kill their wounded—burn their stores—have you gone mad? Stay out of the moonlight."

Becker spoke. "He's been mad at least as long as I've been with El Al," he said, not altogether jokingly.

"We have to *do* something," said Hausner. "The least we could do is send a party down the west slope for water."

Burg shook his head again. "If there is even one Ashbal left there, that water party will never make it. That slope—wall, really—is suicide. We can find plenty of volunteers to go, I'm sure, but I really have to object to sending anyone outside of this perimeter again. And that includes, I'm afraid, observation posts. That was a massacre." Burg felt more confident in his ability to lead men now. Also, Hausner had abandoned him, in a way, and he felt that his position was stronger because of it. The people had seen him on the hill as the commander, and he rather enjoyed the sensation. He was not satisfied with being non-committal any longer. He could butt heads with Hausner, and Hausner would have to listen to his point of view. "A tight defense. No excursions. The water will have to last. No OP's. We pull in like a turtle in a shell and hang on until someone realizes that we are here."

Hausner rose from the jump seat. He stared at Burg for a long time. "You know, I thought that converting our pacifists to dedicated killers was a miracle. The bigger miracle, I see, was transforming Isaac Burg from a shadowy, wispy, translucent little intelligence man into a man of substance. Flesh and blood. Opinions, even. Field Marshal von Burg. So you liked it, did you? It's nice to be king of the hill, master of your own fate, and to hold so many other fates in your hands. If you had made a mistake tonight you wouldn't be any more dead than if I'd made the mistake. But if you win—ah—that's the thing, Isaac. If you win, they'll parade you through the Jaffa Gate like a Roman emperor."

Burg stood up. "That's a lot of shit. I just think you could use some input here. My God, Hausner, don't you want help?"

Becker turned back to his log book and busied himself with it.

"The only help I can accept," said Hausner, "is from competent military people. That would be Dobkin. Not you." He lowered his voice. "I like you, Isaac, but don't get in my way."

"I'm in your way whether you like it or not. And I mean to have a say in the decision-making process around here." His pipe twitched in his mouth.

Hausner could see that he meant it. He suddenly laughed. "You bastard!" He moved toward the cockpit door. "All right, then, as long as you want it badly enough to stand up for it, it's yours. Welcome to the top of the pyramid. If I jump off, you're alone again." He laughed as he walked through the cabin, out the emergency door, and onto the wing. He shouted back into the aircraft. "You poor bastard!"

Benjamin Dobkin looked up into the faces of six or seven Arabs who were all bent over staring down at him. One of them bent further and shook Dobkin's shoulder. They were speaking to him in broken Arabic. Why should Arabs speak in broken Arabic?

He remembered crawling along the river bank, passing out, and crawling again. He had no idea of how much time had gone by since he left the perimeter. The moon was high and it was cold. He moved his hand slowly so as not to alarm them. He reached into his pocket and felt for the digitalis. It was gone.

One of the Arabs dangled the plastic bag containing the pills in front of his face. He grabbed for it, but the man pulled it away. The man said, in bad Arabic, "Medicine? Need?"

"Yes," said Dobkin. "Medicine. Need."

This caused some mumbling. Another man bent over and held something up to his face. "Pazuzu. Evil."

Dobkin stared at the blurry demon a few inches from his eyes. In the moonlight, the feral grin seemed wet and obscene. He supposed that having that with him was not going to get him on the right side of these Moslems. He said the Arabic word for archeologist, but they seemed not to be listening. The man dropped the demon on the ground and turned away.

They began talking among themselves now. It was with a slow realization that Dobkin recognized that they were using Hebrew words mixed with their strange Arabic.

He thrust his hand into his shirt and felt for the star. It was still there. He pulled it out and held it up by its chain. It gleamed in the cold, blue moonlight. "Shema Yisroel Adonoi Elohenu Adonoi Echod."

The effect was as if he had dropped out of the sky in a space suit—which in a way he had. The men stopped talking to one another and looked down at him wide-eyed.

He spoke in slow Hebrew, sticking to the classical words that he knew they would recognize from the Scriptures. "I am Benjamin Dobkin, *Aluf*"—he used the ancient Hebrew word for general—"*Aluf* of the Israelites. I came with the—" They would not understand that Hebrew construction, so he used the Arabic word for aircraft. "I need help. The Jews on the hill—in Babylon—need your help. Will you help?"

The oldest among them knelt beside him. He was what Dobkin would have expected of a Babylonian Jew—swarthy, white-bearded, dark-eyed, and dressed in a flowing robe that was not quite a *gellebiah*. "Of course we will help an *Aluf* of the Israelites. We are kin," he added.

"Yes," said Dobkin. "You have not forgotten Jerusalem."

Hausner walked the perimeter again and again. He was alone. He was tired, thirsty, hungry, and in pain from a dozen cuts and bruises. His ear was mangled from the bullet and felt as if it were on fire. The wine was whirling around his head, and he felt nauseous.

He stared up at the stars, then down at the moonlit landscape. There was something compelling about those expanses of blue-white terrain. He was sick to death of the hilltop, the big broken Concorde sitting with its torn tail, mocking his tragic error. He was sick of the people, the smells, the closeness of everyone and everything. He was suffering from what so many men in fortresses suffer from—claustrophobia mixed with contempt, born of familiarity, for everyone around him. Yet he had been there only a little more than twenty-four hours. But in his mind he had been there forever. The hilltop was big enough, physically. The people made it small. Their eyes followed him wherever he went.

He came around to the west side and looked out at the endless mud flats. He threw his hands into the air. "God, I want to go home! I am tired and I want to go home!" He thought of the famous question, "Why me, God?" and the sardonic answer, "Why not?" He laughed and shouted, "Yes, why not? Jacob Hausner is as good as anyone else to bully around! Thanks, God! I'll remember this!"

He laughed again, then broke into soft sobs and sank to the warm earth. Through his tears he could see the domes, spires, and towers of Jerusalem suffused with the warm golden glow of sunset. He was standing on the heights above the town, and lambs were being shepherded home by young boys outside the walls of the Old City. It was Passover and Easter Sunday as well, and the city was filled with people. Then, suddenly, he was home in Haifa on the terrace of his father's villa, overlooking the blue bay. It was autumn now—Succoth, the thanksgiving festival. His father's house was decked with harvest decorations and the tables were laden with food. He was a young man about to leave home for the war—to work with British Intelligence. Life was good. It always was. The war was great fun. Lots of girls. There was one who looked like Miriam, he remembered. Miriam. Miriam was a child then. While she and her family were being herded around naked by the Nazis, he was sitting in his father's house in Haifa reading German philosophers. Or he was playing war between leaves. That wasn't his fault, of course, but it was a fact. For every victim there is a wife, a husband, a son, a daughter, a friend, or a lover who lives.

But why feel guilty? Everyone has his turn at suffering sooner or later. For him it had come much later, but when it came it was complete—disgrace, humiliation, guilt, physical suffering, futile and futureless love, and . . . death. Death. When and how? Why not now? He looked down at the wide Euphrates and stood up. Why not just step off this ridge? But he wanted to go *home*. He wanted to take Miriam home to his father's house and sit her down to Passover dinner and fill her with food—all the food she had missed as a child—and he wanted to explain to her that life was not really that pleasant for him during the war, either. His mother's family had been killed. Did she know that? That's what he wanted—to sit Miriam down to dinner, to invent some retroactive suffering so that she would accept him as a fellow victim, and then to declare that the suffering was finished.

He wiped his eyes and face. He wondered how much of his sudden sentimentality was the alcohol, how much was Miriam Bernstein, and how much was battle fatigue. In any case, he didn't believe he would ever again be in Haifa for Passover, and if by some miracle he were, it would not be with Miriam Bernstein.

The wind rose noticeably and picked up great quantities of sand and dust. The *Sherji* was coming in force. Hausner could hear the wind whistling through the dead aircraft. He could hear it moan as though it were taunting the suffering men and women in the shepherds' hut. If God had a voice, it was the wind, thought Hausner, and it said anything you wanted to hear.

He turned eastward and saw it coming toward him. He could see it coming out of the hills, carrying more dust for Babylon. Under the blue-white moon, huge dust devils chased headlong down the mountains and over the foothills. Behind the twisters, clouds and sheets of dust blotted out the hills and mountains. He spun around. The Euphrates was unsettled, and he could hear its waters lapping against the banks. The dark pools on the mud flats stirred restlessly. Jackals became quiet and flocks of night birds flew east by the thousands, across the flatlands. The water lilies of the river were swamped, and the frogs became quiet as they abandoned them and found their mud holes on the banks. A herd of wild boar made grotesque sounds as they gathered on the far shore. Hausner shivered.

He looked up at the sky and wondered if the wind would throw up enough earth to blot out the full moon.

25

Teddy Laskov stood at the end of a long table in a long, plain room. The wind rattled the window panes and shutters. Full-length portraits of Theodor Herzl and Chaim Weizmann hung on the wall. On another wall was a color photograph of Israel taken by the American astronaut, Wally Schirra, from an Apollo spacecraft. The conference table and the floor around it were cluttered with attaché cases. The Prime Minister sat staring at the two interlopers. The room was as quiet as anyone ever remembered it to be during a combined session of the Cabinet, the Chiefs of Staff, and the National Security Committee.

The Prime Minister spoke. "Babylon?"

"Yes, sir."

"Not the pyramids along the Nile, now, General? Babylon?"

"Yes, sir."

"Just a hunch? A feeling? A divine inspiration?"

"Sort of." Laskov licked his lips. In Israel it was still possible to go right to the top if you screamed and yelled at the aides and lackeys long enough. In any event, the Prime Minister's provisional office in Jerusalem was small enough for the man himself to have heard Laskov screaming at the portal. Laskov glanced at Talman standing next to him. The man was trying to look very dignified—very British—although it was obvious that he was uneasy and not quite certain of his right to be there. Laskov spoke again to break the silence.

"Some of the electronic data that we have—radar sightings, radio transmissions, and that sort of thing—points, I think, to Iraq."

"Really? And where did you get that information, General?"

Laskov shrugged. There was a lot of mouth-to-ear whispering in the long room. Laskov waited and looked over the heads of the assembly. The small red-tiled building had seen a lot of history. It had originally housed the Knights of the Order of the Temple. During World War II, the British used the building to intern German civilians who were suspected of Nazi espionage or sympathies. Jacob Hausner had sent his share of Germans there, but Laskov was not aware of this. After the war the building was a British military headquarters during the Mandate period. Coincidentally, Laskov had been questioned in the very next room as a suspected member of the underground Israeli Air Force. Now he was here again, and the dryness in his mouth reminded him of the kind of life he had led. Some people would call it exciting and romantic. He called it worrisome and dangerous. Why didn't he accept his forced retirement and fade away? Let the government worry about the whereabouts of the peace mission. He might have done that if Miriam weren't among the missing.

"All right, General," said the Prime Minister. "We'll come back to the question of your sources of information later." The Prime Minister put a handkerchief into the open collar of his sport shirt and wiped his neck. He was a tall, thin man with nervous habits, one of which—tearing pieces of paper—he was engaged in at the moment. "Well, what do you propose we do with your information—or should I say, inspiration?"

Laskov spoke loudly and clearly. "I propose that we send a low-level reconnaissance craft to Babylon now—tonight. Take pictures and make visual sightings, if possible. If they're there, we'll try to show them our colors, fly low, give them hope. Behind the recon craft should be an airborne strike force—the F-14's for preparatory fires and behind them C-130's with commandos, if there's a place where they can land, or C-130's with airborne troops if they can't land. Maybe troop helicopters instead. That's for the army to worry about. If the recon craft can confirm their presence, then the strike force goes in."

The Prime Minister tapped a pencil on the table. "Would you object violently if I called the King of Jordan and told him I was sending an air armada over his sovereign kingdom?" There was a lot of laughter, and the Prime Minister paused with the timing of an accomplished performer. He leaned forward. "Surely you wouldn't be too hard on me if I called the President of Iraq and told him, by the by, that I was invading his country—shooting up Babylon, for old time's sake?"

Laskov waited for the laughter to subside. The Prime Minister had an acerbic sense of humor, but after he had his fun with Knesset members or generals, he became more attentive and was actually more open-minded than the average politician. "Mr. Prime Minister, surely a contingency plan of this sort exists. Where did we expect to find the peace mission? On Herzlya beach? And what did we intend to do when we found them?"

The Prime Minister settled back in his chair. His expression darkened. "Actually, rescue plans do exist. But Iraq is on that list of countries not friendly enough to get full cooperation from . . . and potentially unfriendly enough to declare war on us, I might add."

"I'm sorry, Mr. Prime Minister, but like all generals, I don't understand politics."

"Like all generals, you understand politics damn well, and you don't want to be bothered with them. Don't play the innocent with me, Laskov. You know the situation with Iraq. Now, the first thing I must do is place a call to Baghdad."

Laskov nodded his head enough to acknowledge the deserved rebuke, but he wasn't willing to concede the whole point. "Mr. Prime Minister," he said, his voice filled with emotion, "since when have we left the safety of Israeli citizens to foreign governments?"

"When they are in foreign lands, General Laskov."

"Uganda."

"A different time, a different place."

"The same old cutthroats." He took a deep breath. "Look, sir, the West German commandos did it in Somalia. We did it in Uganda—and we can do it again in Babylon."

The Prime Minister made a sound of exasperation. "I really must call first, if you don't mind." He leaned forward. "Anyway, if they are in Babylon, we have no idea of their condition. Dead? Alive? Captive? Really, General, I'm meeting you more than halfway on this. We've been in session for thirty hours and we're damned tired—and you come busting into this meeting yelling Babylon, and we give you the damned floor. Any other government would have had you thrown out on your ass—or worse." He took a sip from a cup of coffee.

The sound of the wind filled the quiet room, and the shutters began clattering again. The Prime Minister raised his voice over the noise. "But what you say makes sense. And I believe in God and I believe that He has whispered in your ear, Teddy Laskov—although why you and not me is a great mystery. Anyway, we will call the President of Iraq at once and then *he* will send a recon craft and his air force people will call us after they've interpreted the data from the craft. All right?"

"No, sir. Too much wasted time."

The Prime Minister rose. "Damn you, Laskov—get out of here before I call you back to active duty and put you on permanent latrine detail." He turned to Talman. "Do you have anything to say before you both leave, General?"

Talman swallowed and his mustache quivered. He took a deep breath and his voice escaped with the exhale. "Well, sir, I think that we should really do the reconnaissance ourselves, you know—I mean, we are rather good at it and the Iraqis may not be as accomplished, you see, and we have no direct data link with them and these things do get fouled up and at least we can ask the American SR-71 to take a high-level photo in the meantime—they won't go down low, but maybe they can get a clear shot and—"

The Prime Minister held up his hand. "Hold on." He turned to the members of the Joint Chiefs who were becoming fidgety. He beckoned to them, and they crowded around the Prime Minister's chair and spoke in whispers. The Prime Minister looked up. "Thank you, gentlemen. We'll handle it from here. Thank you. Yes, you may leave. Please."

Laskov walked slowly behind Talman toward the door. It felt strange—worse than strange—reflected Laskov, to be asked to leave a room when state secrets were about to be discussed. That was one of the consequences of leaving the halls of power. Your need-to-know was limited to monthly memos in the mail telling you what was being taken off the classified list. In exchange for the loss of power you got tranquility and peace of mind. And boredom. Laskov reached the door and turned. He didn't know what the Joint Chiefs were whispering about, but he was somewhat eased to see that they, rather than the Cabinet, had the Prime Minister's ear. He felt obligated to deliver a parting shot. "They are in Babylon and they are alive. I can feel it. We have no right to play it safe. Whatever you decide to do must be based on *their* welfare and the long-range welfare of this nation. Don't make a decision based on your own immediate career goals."

Somebody—Laskov didn't see who—called out, "That's easy to say when your own career is finished, General."

Laskov turned and left.

The Prime Minister waited until Laskov and Talman were out of hearing range. "I don't know where Laskov got his information on this, and as you just reminded me, we don't know where Chaim Mazar got his information, either. But if Mazar is correct about our American air attaché—Richardson—then the Americans owe us one, I think." He looked at the color photograph on the wall —a gift from the Americans. "Yes, we can ask them to make a special SR-71 flight over the Euphrates for us. Then we can see if Laskov is correct." He took a sip of coffee. "Apparently there is an angel or some other celestial entity flying around whispering in the ears of certain people. Has anyone here received a piece of intelligence in this manner? No? Well, we are not among the chosen, then. Ten-minute break, ladies and gentlemen."

26

The *Sherji* swept across Babylon, carrying tons of dust and sand with it. Trenches and foxholes that had been laboriously dug into the clay were filled to the brim in minutes. Man-traps were covered and early warning devices blown away. The pit containing the remaining stores of Molotov cocktails was covered with sand, and the aluminum reflectors and crude sunshields flew away with the wind. Many of the palm fronds on the roof of the shepherds' hut blew off and sand began raining in on the wounded. Weapons had to be wrapped in plastic or clothing to protect their moving parts. Men and women pulled clothing around their faces like desert Bedouins and walked bent into the dustladen wind.

Only the Concorde stood upright on the hill, enduring yet another indignity with the same haughty indifference it had shown since the beginning of its ordeal. The wind screamed through its torn skin and left deposits of dirt throughout its interior.

Hausner and Burg looked in on the wounded and spoke to the rabbi and Beth Abrams. Most of the wounded were stable, explained Rabbi Levin, but infection and other complications would kill most of them if they did not receive medical care soon.

Hausner and Burg left the hut and began walking the perimeter again. Burg shouted into Hausner's ear. "I know the Arabs. They'll take this wind as an omen to attack."

Hausner shouted back. "I should think they'd take it as an omen to get the hell out of here." He looked up at the sky. The moon was near its zenith and would begin to set soon. The dust clouds nearly obscured the moonlight. Occasionally, the dust would rise high enough to actually blot out the moon itself, and for a few seconds there would be almost complete darkness across the hilltop. It occurred to Hausner, as he looked down the east slope, that the Ashbals could be ten meters away and no one would see or hear them.

Burg pulled a T-shirt closer around his face. "Even if by some miracle someone knows where we are, a rescue is impossible under these circumstances."

Hausner was more interested in the subject of being overrun. "Unless we put out some sort of listening posts we are going to be taken by surprise."

"It's suicide to send anyone down there."

It felt odd sharing authority, thought Hausner. Not odd, actually—annoying. "All the same, Field Marshal, I'm sending at least one man—or woman—downslope. In fact, I may go myself."

Burg wondered if that wouldn't be a good idea. He remained silent.

As they turned west across the flat hill, the wind pushed them so that they had to strain in order not to be forced into a run. At the first position they came to, overlooking the river, they found what appeared to be two women sleeping in the remains of a foxhole. A blue El Al blanket lay over them and sand drifted over the blanket and their partially exposed limbs.

Hausner was reminded of Dobkin's lecture on the similarity between buried cities and people under shrouds. He stared down at the two restless forms. There was little chance of an Ashbal attack up this slope. In fact, there might not be any Ashbals left on the west slope. And if there were, could they negotiate the slope in the wind? But that was irrelevant. As soon as he had seen the two sleeping figures, Hausner's heart had made a small flutter. On all his inspections, he, like a million officers and sergeants-of-the-guard before him, had hoped that he would never see a guard asleep. Sleep, natural and innocent in civilian life, was a capital offense for a man or guard in probably every army in the world.

Hausner crouched down beside the two figures and cleared his throat. He hoped they would jump up so he could pass it off lightly, but neither seemed to be aware of his presence. He felt Burg's eyes on him. The two were unmistakably sleeping. He reached out and pulled back the blanket. Esther Aronson. He pulled it back further. Miriam.

One of the two sleeping women had the duty. The other was legitimately sleeping. One would live to share the fate of them all, the other might be shot within the next hour. "Miriam." Neither figure moved.

Burg moved around into Hausner's view and crouched down also. He gently picked up the AK-47 lying near the two women. Hausner knew this was prescribed military procedure, and he also knew that the situation was going downhill fast.

He looked closely at Burg but could not read anything in his face. The man had assumed his inscrutable expression. Was Burg willing to let it go? Hausner wondered if he himself would let it go if he were alone, as he usually was. Of course he would. Hausner put his hand on Miriam's shoulder and shook her. "Miriam." He noticed that his voice was tremulous and his hand was shaking. "Miriam!" He was suddenly angry—angry at having to be put in this position—angry at having another dilemma thrown at him by fate. "Miriam, God damn you!"

She sat up quickly. "Oh!"

Burg moved in and grabbed her arm. "What are your hours for guard?" he demanded suddenly.

She was still half-asleep. "What? Oh! Guard. Midnight to two—four to dawn. Why?" She looked around bewildered and saw Hausner, then saw Esther Aronson sleeping next to her. She understood.

Burg looked at his watch quickly. It was a quarter after twelve. "Did Esther Aronson wake you for duty?" he asked loudly. "Well?"

She stared hard at Hausner, who looked away.

"Did she wake you for duty?" repeated Burg as he shook her.

"Yes."

"Then I place you under arrest for sleeping on duty. I must warn you that this is a capital offense, Mrs. Bernstein."

Miriam rose to her feet and stood in the wind. Her hair and clothes billowed and sand pelted her face. "I see." She straightened up and looked at Burg. "Of course, I understand. I've endangered the lives of everyone else and I must pay for it."

"That's correct," said Burg. He turned to Hausner. "Isn't it?"

Hausner fought back an impulse to knock Burg over the side of the glacis. He looked down at the sleeping Esther Aronson, then at Miriam. His unpopularity, past and present, was due largely to what people called his Teutonic discipline. That had never bothered him in the least. In the civilization that he lived in, there were always people who stepped in to soften his tyranny. Now he had met a man who was either calling his bluff or, in fact, really wanted to shoot Miriam Bernstein as an example to the others. It was incredible, but anything was possible here. Hadn't they made threatening noises about shooting *him?*

"Isn't that correct?" Burg repeated. "Isn't that correct—that Miriam Bernstein must pay for jeopardizing the lives of close to fifty men and women?"

Hausner stared at Miriam, clothed in darkness and dust, a scarf held up to her face like a lost child. "Yes," he said. "We must try her—in the morning."

"Now," said Burg. "There may be no morning for us. Discipline in the field must be sure and swift. That's how it's done. Now."

Hausner moved close to Burg. "In the morning."

General Dobkin lay on the straw pallet in a mud hut. The wind came in through the closed shutters and deposited fine sand over his body. The oil lamp flickered but stayed lit. The man lying next to him stirred, then groaned. Dobkin could tell he was awake. He spoke to the man in passable Arabic. "Who are you?"

"Who are *you?*" asked the man.

Dobkin had been told that the man had been taken out of the river also. He was shoeless and shirtless, but wore what looked like tiger fatigue pants. Dobkin had been asked by the old man, whose name was Shear-jashub, if this injured man was also a Jew. Dobkin had lied and said he did not know. He was fairly certain now that the man he was speaking to was an Ashbal, but he could not be positive. Shear-jashub, who was a rabbi in the older sense of the word—an unordained teacher, a master—had asked Dobkin if there was any reason why the injured man should not be cared for or should not be placed in the hut of the Aluf. Dobkin had told the rabbi that there was no reason why these things should not be done.

Now, he regarded the man for a long time before he spoke. "I am a fisherman whose *dhow* overturned in the wind and I was injured. These Jews found me and helped me."

The man lay on his side and faced Dobkin. The oil lamp flickered across his face and Dobkin almost gasped when he saw it. He kept his eyes fixed on the grotesque man's eyes. The mutilation, he noticed, was old and scarred, not a part of his recent injuries. He saw that the Ashbal—he was sure of it now—was sizing him up: his haircut, his hands, his bare arms, which lay outside the blanket. Dobkin's boots were off and lying in a shadow, and the man seemed not to see them, but Dobkin could tell that he'd seen enough to know he was not a Euphrates fisherman.

The man rolled casually on his back. "Well, fisherman, this is quite a thing—being obliged to these Jews for our aid and comfort."

"Misfortune makes strange bedfellows," agreed Dobkin. He glanced at the man. Yes. He had seen him on the glacis. He remembered the face as a blurred nightmare—but it was real. He *had* seen it. "How shall I call you?"

"Sayid Talib. And you?"

Dobkin hesitated. He had a perverse desire to say, Benjamin Dobkin, Israeli Army, General of Infantry. "Just call me fisherman." His Arabic was not good, but he had to keep it passable so that Talib could find reason to continue the farce. Each of them was only waiting for the chance to rip the other's throat out, and a wrong word would do it. He wondered if Talib had gotten a good look at his face on the glacis.

How badly wounded was the man, Dobkin wondered. How badly wounded was *he* himself? He flexed his muscles under the blanket and took a deep breath. He seemed to have regained some of his strength.

The clay oil lamp, a dish with a wick floating in some fat, flickered on the floor between them. Dobkin looked around him slowly. There was nothing but his blanket. He felt casually over his body. His knife was gone. He should have gotten a knife from someone. He felt something hard inside his top pocket. Pazuzu. They had given him back his obscene little statue.

Dobkin and Talib lay on their sides staring at each other, listening to the wind blow and watching the lamp flicker.

"How is the fishing, fisherman?"

"It was good until tonight. What did you say your trade was?"

"I am a buyer of dates."

Occasionally, the mask would slip and each could see in the other's eyes the hate and the fear and the threat.

"How did you come to be in the river?"

"The same as you."

The conversation died and neither man moved for a very long time. Dobkin could feel his mouth becoming drier and his muscles fluttering.

Then the wind blew open a shutter and the lamp went out, and each man let out a long animal scream as he lunged for the other's throat in the dark.

Deborah Gideon lay naked on the tiled floor in the manager's office of the guest house. Long welts from a whip and small burn marks from a cigarette covered her back. There was blood on her thighs, legs, and buttocks as well, from wounds caused, apparently, by some animal.

Ahmed Rish washed his hands and face in a bowl of water. "Have her shot," he said to Hamadi.

Hamadi called out to the duty man at the front desk. "Kassim."

Rish dried his hands. What the girl had told him about Israeli numbers, defenses, and dispositions was not much more than he had already found out the hard way. But now he could fabricate his own intelligence report and his men would believe him. "We can be on that hill within an hour, Salem, if the *Sherji* stays with us. It will literally propel the men up that slope and hide their movements and sounds as well."

Hamadi nodded. The wind must have been sent by Allah, for if it hadn't come, he knew that he and Rish would have been murdered by their own men. Strangely, only Rish seemed unaware of this. "I will assemble our people."

"Good." He looked down at Deborah Gideon, then at the duty man who was staring at her. "Yes, yes, Kassim, you may use her. Then shoot her and burn the body and throw the ashes in the river. I want no evidence." He turned to Hamadi. "A military operation is one thing. Torture and murder are another. We still have to negotiate for the hostages with Israel tomorrow."

Hamadi nodded. Rish drew fine and meaningless lines as only an insane man could. If he weren't a hero to the whole Palestinian people, Hamadi would himself have murdered him long ago. The image of Rish, on his hands and knees biting that girl, turned his stomach. He, Hamadi, had tortured before, but this thing that Rish had done was something quite different. The whips and cigarettes had undoubtedly hurt the girl more than the bites, but it was the sheer animal terror of the madman snapping and howling and ripping into her flesh that had made her scream out everything he wanted to know. Hamadi could hardly blame her. He only hoped that the men outside did not understand what was happening. Hamadi turned and walked out of the room and through the small lobby onto the veranda.

The last of his men and women, about fifty of them, sat crosslegged, huddled under their open pavilions, holding up the supporting poles. Hamadi blew his whistle and the Ashbals struck the tents and came scrambling toward the veranda. They stood in the wind with long trailing veils wrapped around their mouths and their *kheffiyahs* pulled low over their eyes. Hamadi held up his hand and shouted above the wind. "Allah has sent us this *Sherji,"* he began.

Hausner stood on the delta wing and watched the people swathed in all sorts of strange garments, walking like phantoms in the wind and dust, making their way under the failing moonlight.

He turned and went into the cabin. The noise of the wind through the rent skin and the sand grating against the craft made it difficult to hear or speak inside. Holes that had been punched in the roof to let the heat out during the day now let the sand sift in, and there were little hills of it in the aisles. He made his way to the rear of the cabin through the door that led to the aft galley. Across the aisle from the galley was the small baggage compartment that abutted the split pressure bulkhead. The compartment was a shambles and still smelled faintly from the kerosene, melted plastic, and burnt garments.

Miriam Bernstein had made a pallet of some half-burnt clothing and sat on the floor with her back against the hull and her legs pulled up to her chin. She was reading a book by the illumination of a small penlight that someone had given her. There was also a small emergency light on overhead. Hausner could see through the split bulkhead out to the twisted aluminum skin and braces in the tail. Swaying electrical wires and hydraulic tubing lent a phantasmagoric touch in the cold, blue moonlight. There was a grotesque sort of beauty in any ruin, thought Hausner—even this technological ruin which stood as a monument to insult him and remind everyone of how they got there. He looked down at Miriam.

She glanced up over her book. "Is it time?"

He cleared his throat and spoke above the wind. "She said she did not wake you. She said she fell asleep on her watch and never woke you."

Miriam closed the book gently and rested it on her knee. "She's lying to cover for me. She woke me and I fell asleep."

"Don't be noble, Miriam." He looked at the book on her knee. Camus's *The Stranger.*

"Why not?" She shut off the penlight. "It would be a change of pace for this group."

"Don't criticize what we've done here or how we've done it."

"Condemned people may criticize anything they wish. Well—is it time?"

"Not yet."

They both let the silence drag out. Finally, she spoke. Her voice was belligerent and taunting. "I'm sorry. I shouldn't criticize. I'm one of you now. I mean, I killed that girl."

"Yes. You probably did."

"I had no choice, of course. You have a choice in this case."

"No, I don't. Self-defense is many things to many people. To some of us, it's shooting someone who threatens us. To others it's shooting someone only after they shoot at you first. This case is also a case of self-defense, Miriam. Society defending itself against slackers and malingerers. It's just a matter of projecting the facts. It's a matter of what your perception of immediacy and exigency is."

She understood, had understood all along, really. "So, who goes on trial?"

"Both of you. Unless whoever was at fault confesses."

"I've already confessed."

"You know what I mean."

"We'll both lie."

"I'm sure you will. There's an army procedure for that, too. It's happened before. You'll both be found guilty on the testimony of Burg and myself."

"Is this all show or do you actually intend to shoot one or both of us?"

Hausner lit a cigarette. He wondered if he could even get anyone to sit on a court-martial board, let alone form a firing squad. What, then, was the purpose of this exercise? To show the rank and file that the game had to be played by the rules right to the end? To instill fear in all the fatigued men and women who wanted to sleep on guard duty or who might be slow in obeying orders in other situations? Or was this Burg's way of bringing him down a peg or two?

"Well? Do you intend to shoot us or not? If not, let me out of here. I have things to do. If you're going to have a trial, have it now and don't keep us waiting until morning."

Hausner threw his cigarette on the floor and looked down at her. Moonlight from the porthole illuminated her face. She was staring up at him, and her face did not look as angry or hard as her voice sounded. It looked open and trusting, ready to accept whatever he said. He suddenly realized that any meeting could be their last.

"Would you pull the trigger yourself, Jacob?" The voice was inquisitive, as though she were asking his views on capital punishment in general.

Hausner stepped toward her. He seemed undecided about what to do or say. He suddenly knelt in front of her and put his hands on her bare knees. "I . . . I would kill myself before I would harm you. I would kill anyone who tried to harm you. I love you." The words didn't surprise him as much as they seemed to surprise her.

She turned her face away and stared out through the hole in the bulkhead. He grasped her knees and shook them. "I love you."

She turned her head back and nodded. She put her hands over his. Her voice was low and husky. "I'm sorry I put you in a compromising position, Jacob."

"Well . . . you know, one's lifelong beliefs don't amount to a hell of a lot when it comes to these decisions—decisions of the heart, as they say." He forced a smile.

She smiled back. "That's not true. You've been pretty consistent. A consistent bastard, I might point out." She almost laughed. "I *am* sorry I put you in this position. Would you have had an easier time shooting Esther Aronson?"

"That's enough of that. I'll get you both out of this."

She squeezed his hands. "Poor Jacob. You should have stayed in your father's villa. Idle and rich."

"Would you come to my father's house for Passover?" He suddenly felt that if he asked her that question, he might make it there himself.

She smiled, then took his hands and pressed them to her face.

He felt a heaving in his chest that he hadn't felt in many, many years. He waited a moment before he trusted himself to speak. "I . . . I'm sorry I . . . walked away from you before."

Her voice was deep and soft. "I understand."

"Do you?"

"The future. We have no future." She put her cheek against his chest.

He pulled her closer. "No. We don't." He wanted to live. He wanted a future. But even if he lived, he knew he would lose her. Laskov or her husband. Or someone else. This was not a match that was destined to last. Then he would wish that he had died in Babylon.

She was weeping now, and she sounded to Hausner like the wind, overwhelming and perpetually sad.

He felt her tears against his face and thought at first they were his own, and then they were. It was all so sad, he thought; like waking after a bittersweet dream of your childhood and finding that you had a lump in your throat and your eyes were misty. It made the whole day sad and there was nothing you could do about it because it was a dream. It was that kind of sadness that he felt with her.

They both clung to each other and she cried uncontrollably. He couldn't think of anything to say to make her stop because, he thought, she had every right to cry if she wanted. That's right, he thought, scream, cry, do anything you want, Miriam, only don't suffer silently. That's for fools. That's the Miriam that everyone knows in Tel Aviv and Jerusalem. Let the world know your pain. If everyone howled at every injustice, every act of barbarism, every act of unkindness, then we would be taking the first step toward a real humanity. Why should people walk, unprotesting, to their deaths? Scream. Cry. Howl.

As if she could read his thoughts, she threw back her head and let out a long wail.

That's right, Miriam. Scream. They've extinguished your blood, slaughtered your family, stolen your childhood, taken your husband, killed your son, murdered your friends, and left you here alone with a man like Jacob Hausner. You have a right to cry.

Her sobs became louder, louder than the wind, and Hausner knew that Becker could hear her and that they could probably hear her outside, and he didn't care if they did. "If I could do something to make it a little better, I would, Miriam."

She nodded to show that she understood, then suddenly she grabbed his head in her hands and kissed him the way she had kissed her husband on the day he went to war. "Yosef," she sobbed his name. "Jacob." She mumbled something else that Hausner could not make out.

He put his lips to her face and neck and tasted her tears. Yosef. Teddy. Jacob. What difference did it make? As long as they brought her comfort and did not hurt her any further. Hausner wished that her husband would turn up alive. Should he tell her that Rish knew? No, never. He would never tell her that. But while she waited for Yosef Bernstein, he hoped that Teddy Laskov, or anyone, could give her what she needed. He wished it could be he, but he knew it could not be. He would not see Jerusalem again, and even if he did, he would be no comfort to her outside of Babylon. He licked her tears the way an animal licks another's wounds.

Dobkin had never tasted blood, or another man's sweat, for that matter, and he was surprised at how salty they both were. The Arab had him by the testicles and he had his teeth in the Arab's windpipe. They both meant to kill the other, but without weapons, they had been uncertain at first of how to go about it.

They had begun by battering each other about and striking at the obvious places—the head—the chest. Talib had smashed the oil lamp on Dobkin's head, and blood and fat ran over the big man's back and neck. But these spots had been protected by nature's armor. Then the old instincts, buried so deep in the psyche, returned. Each man felt a tingling down his spine, and his neck hair raised and his testicles drew up as each became aware of what he had become. They found the weak spots that nature had inexplicably left exposed.

Dobkin concentrated on forcing his jaws closed and tried to ignore the searing pain. He had missed the Arab's jugular, but he knew that the cartilage of the windpipe would collapse if he persevered.

Talib was trying to get a better hold of Dobkin's testicles, but the big man's knees kept battering at him as they rolled across the mud floor. Talib reached around and poked at Dobkin's eyes, but Dobkin squeezed them tight and buried his face deeper into Talib's neck. Each man was fighting the battle of his life in almost absolute silence. Neither man ever once considered asking for mercy.

In another hut, across the crooked lane, the two appointed attendants made herbal tea over a crackling fire of thistle and told stories to keep each other amused. They heard nothing unusual, just the whistling of the wind and the slapping of the shutters.

Dobkin could take the pain no longer. His thigh wound was open and hemorrhaging, and he felt that he was going to lose consciousness. He found the terra cotta figure in his pocket and brought it down hard on Talib's ear. The wing of the wind demon shattered as it struck. The Arab's scream was lost in a sudden loud rush of wind that threw open the shutters.

Talib, stunned, loosened his grip long enough for Dobkin to pull away. Dobkin raised his huge hand and smashed the jagged edge of the Pazuzu down on Talib's good eye. The man let out a long scream and covered his face. Dobkin took the sharply pointed fragment of the demon's wing and plunged it into Talib's jugular. A stream of blood spurted up into Dobkin's face.

Talib thrashed across the room holding his throat with his hand and making gurgling sounds. The two men collided several times in the small, dark room, each time letting out primal noises as they touched. In his death throes Talib splattered blood across the floor and walls.

Finally, Dobkin fell back into a corner and remained still. He listened until he was certain the Arab was dead, then he lay back, fighting to remain conscious. He spit and spit to get the taste of blood out of his mouth, but he knew he never would.

27

Laskov and Talman were as surprised as anyone to have been invited back to the Prime Minister's meeting.

Laskov listened to the photo-analyst, Ezra Adam, as the young man gave his report. The analyst spoke apparently without passion, but Laskov could tell that the man was saying, "I have found the missing Concorde. Believe me. Go and get them." Laskov had heard too many photo-analysts over the years to mistake the tone. The man went through each of the dozen high-altitude SR-71 infrared photographs that the Americans had taken only hours before at the Israelis' request.

The various ministers and generals, most of whom could not discern anything from the light and dark blotches, followed Adam with their own set of photographs as he spoke.

Adam laid down another photograph and looked up at the Prime Minister. "So you can see, sir, it's somewhat difficult to read night photos with the—what do you call it?—the *Sherji* kicking up dust, and the high altitudes and all. We really should have our own low-level shots, but of course I understand there are political—"

"Get on with it, young man," snapped an air force general. "Let the PM worry about that."

"Yes, sir. Well, here—photo number ten, then. Similar to the others. I've seen this pattern before. Small scattered and random residues of heat. Suggestive of a battle, perhaps."

"Or a shepherd's encampment," said an army general.

"Or a village," added a Cabinet minister who didn't know anything about infrared photography an hour before but was catching on fast.

"Yes," agreed Adam. "It could be any of those. But one gets a feel for these things after a while. First of all, there is no known village on this spot. Please look at your transparent overlays of the archeologist map of Babylon. The village of Kweirish is a kilometer to the south of these heat sources, near the Ishtar Gate. Also, villages look different. And the cooking fires and lamps of a village or an encampment leave a different heat residue. You can see this in Kweirish. Based on a spectrographic analysis of these photos, I have reason to believe that there was phosphorus burned here on this slope. And here, in quadrant one-three—look at the size of that heat source. It's dim, you see, but it must be large. See? An aircraft whose engines haven't been running in perhaps twenty-four hours or more. Then a series of streaks here like trucks moving—or a light aircraft taking off. See these spots on each photo? That may be a small aircraft flying over the mound."

Laskov knew that to the laymen in the room it was all very suspect. But to his surprise, the Prime Minister suddenly stopped Adam in mid-sentence. "I believe you, Sergeant Adam. God knows why, but I do." Then more surprisingly, he turned to Laskov instead of to his military aides. "Well, Laskov, tell me a story based on these ridiculous smears."

Laskov looked around the room. "It would appear—that is, we can only surmise—"

"No. No," interrupted the Prime Minister. "No suppositions. I want one of your divine flashes. What does this—" he waved a particularly cryptic photograph in the air, "—what does *this* mean, General?"

Laskov wiped his face with a handkerchief. "Well, it means, sir, that the Concorde was forced down in Babylon—by the Lear—we know how that was done. There was no hijacker on board, of course, so the pilot of the Concorde —Becker—after a vote, I'm sure—put the craft down outside of the area controlled by the terrorists, who were waiting on the ground."

Laskov closed his eyes. He seemed to be thinking. After a few seconds, he opened his eyes again, but they were far away now. He continued. "At that point, the passengers had the choice of fleeing or fighting. No, they didn't have the choice. The Concorde appears to be against the Euphrates. So they were cut off—unable to flee except into the river. The terrorists would have immediately surrounded them to seal off all escape routes. So they decided to stay and fight. They are on a buried citadel. Not a bad defensive position. Look at the maps. And they had one Uzi and one M-14 with a starlight scope and perhaps a half-dozen handguns. The terrorists would come up that slope, perhaps not expecting anything, and would be fired on. The Arabs would become confused. Perhaps they would leave a weapon or two in their retreat. They would try again, of course. . . ."

Laskov paused. "The Concorde radio is jammed. They can't signal. We know from our sources that there is a transmitter causing radio interference somewhere near Hillah. That's not unusual in itself—we have dozens of such reports. But now, that one takes on a special meaning." He paused again and looked around the room. "So they hang on and wait—wait for someone to come to their aid." He looked at the Prime Minister.

The Prime Minister looked back at him. "That's quite a story, General. See if you can get me into that celestial radio net that you're tuned in to." He paused and tapped a pencil on the table. "So there are only a few terrorists then? Few enough for the people on the Concorde to defend themselves against successfully?"

The photo analyst spoke up. "Sir, if this was a battle that we see on these photographs, then it was one hell of a fight. The whole slope area for a length of a half-kilometer shows heat residues."

"Well, then," said the Prime Minister, "it was not our people. They could hardly have fought a full-scale battle with a large Arab force. Perhaps what we're looking at here," he tapped his pictures, "is a local insurrection of some sort."

"The large aircraft, sir," Adam reminded him. "And the aircraft overhead."

"Large aircraft, my ass," shot back the Prime Minister. "Blurry, streaky nonsense." He pushed his stack of photos away. He tapped his pencil awhile, shredded some paper, then sat back and sighed. "All right. Large aircraft. Big battle. Why not?" He turned to his communications man sitting in an alcove and called to him. "Do we have Baghdad yet?"

"Baghdad is on station, sir. Their President will be on station in one minute."

There was a silence in the room as the seconds dragged out.

The communications man called out. "The President of Iraq. Line four."

The Prime Minister looked around the room and picked up the receiver. He hit the number four button and spoke in passable Arabic. "Good morning, Mr. President. Yes, sir, it concerns the Concorde, of course. Babylon, Mr. President. Yes, *Babel.*"

Miriam Bernstein and Esther Aronson were kept, technically still under arrest, in the cabin of the Concorde. Hausner had stalled Burg's plans for an immediate court-martial, but the man was insistent—insistent, Hausner knew, on using the incident to bring him down. Hausner suspected that Burg no longer had faith in his, Hausner's, ability to lead. Burg believed that he was acting in the best interests of the group, and, thought Hausner, if that included shooting one or two women, while at the same time taking from him the last two things that were keeping him going—Miriam and his position as leader—then that was perfectly justifiable. Burg knew about him and Miriam, but that seemed not to change his attitude in the least, and Hausner could only respect him for that. Hausner was unhappy that he couldn't develop a healthy hatred for Isaac Burg. It was Hausner's misfortune that he liked the man. If he hadn't, Burg would never have gotten as far as he had.

To add to the internal problems, the Foreign Minister was making his own belated power play, and he had a lot of followers, not only because of his position as legal head of the group, but because he had a compellingly attractive solution to their problems. It was Ariel Weizman's theory that there were no longer any Arabs on the banks of the Euphrates. Therefore, the Israelis could escape down the west wall and flee across the Euphrates. The Concorde's life jackets would be given to the wounded and the nonswimmers.

Hausner and Burg had agreed to a short conference to discuss the Foreign Minister's proposal. The meeting convened in the littered cabin of the Concorde. The Foreign Minister presided.

Hausner spoke. "I admit that the idea has a certain appeal, but I very much doubt that Ahmed Rish would neglect the most fundamental military tactic of cutting off the enemy's line of withdrawal." He tried to explain this to the most civilian-minded of the group, but there was increasing resistance to anything he said.

Hausner's original power base was his six fanatically loyal men: Brin, Kaplan, Rubin, Jaffe, Marcus, and Alpern. Brin was dead, and Kaplan, Rubin, and Jaffe were wounded. And his men were no longer the only armed people on the hill. Now, even when he gave good advice, it generated negative responses.

Burg came to Hausner's defense and pointed out that if they did manage to cross the river, they would not get far if Rish discovered their absence. "You would be run down on the open mud flats and massacred like rabbits caught in the open by a pack of jackals—or worse, you would be forced to surrender."

Yet more than half the people wanted to flee Babylon. Hausner knew that he had to do everything in his power to keep the group together. It would be a pity —a tragedy—to see all their sacrifices and bravery wiped out in a precipitate flight.

The Foreign Minister insisted on discussing the question of Miriam Bernstein and Esther Aronson with Burg, but Burg refused. The women would remain under arrest until he, Burg, got around to selecting a court-martial board. Rabbi Levin called him an ass and walked off in disgust. The short conference was adjourned with no provision made for convening again.

Neither Hausner nor Burg nor a lot of others regretted the quick subversion of the democratic process. They knew, for example, that a vote taken just then would probably authorize the Foreign Minister to lead them out of Babylon and that this exodus would end in disaster. Ariel Weizman was not Moses and the waters were not going to open for him and swallow the army of Ahmed Rish. If Hausner and Burg agreed on anything, they agreed that the successful conduct of a war was too important to be left to politicians.

Ahmed Rish and Salem Hamadi led the remains of their army through the Ishtar Gate and up the Sacred Way until they reached the temple of the goddess Ninmakh, where they turned west toward the Greek theatre. They walked in the bed of an old canal and passed through the inner city wall. A kilometer farther west, they intersected the outer city wall and followed it north, toward the Northern Citadel.

Rish came up beside Hamadi and spoke into his ear. "We will walk right into their midst before they even know we are there."

"Yes." Hamadi listened to the wind coming down out of the hills. They were walking on the lee side of the wall, but nowhere were the ruined defenses more than two meters high and the sand and dust were choking the hard-breathing men as they tried to keep up with Rish's pace. "We must slow down, Ahmed."

"No. The wind may die at any moment."

Hamadi was no desert Arab, and the blowing sand was as alien to him as it was to the Israelis on the hill. He looked around at his men moving like specters through the swirling darkness. Many wore bandages and some were lame. It was obvious that they were no longer completely disciplined or reliable troops. If the fight did not go their way, Hamadi knew they might mutiny and kill their commanders. If the fight did go their way, they would massacre the Israelis and take no hostages. Without hostages, he and Rish would have no power to negotiate. Either way, Hamadi knew that it was over for him and Rish. But Rish seemed not to understand this and Hamadi would not tell him.

Rish increased his pace and the Ashbals did the same. They were almost running now, and Hamadi had the sense that they were all rushing headlong toward their fate, toward a collision with history, toward their personal destinies, and toward a clash that would affect the relationship between the Jews and the Arabs for the next decade or more. Hamadi had been listening closely to Radio Baghdad during the past twenty-four hours, and he knew that if they had accomplished nothing else, they had at least seriously jeopardized the Peace Conference. But the possibility of changing world history paled when compared to personal passions and motivations. He thought of Hausner during the body search—Hausner standing naked under the burning sun beside the Lion of Babylon. He remembered how his skin felt as he ran his hands over him. He was filled with an overwhelming desire to rape—to sodomize Jacob Hausner. To humiliate him and finally to torture and mutilate him.

Hausner walked away from the Foreign Minister's conference alone, hunched into the *Sherji*. The sand blew in his face and the wind billowed his tattered clothes. The incessant noise of the wind was driving him slightly mad and he wanted to shout against it.

He found Kaplan huddled in the spot that Brin had occupied for so long. The starlight scope had been adapted to an AK-47, but it was no more an aid in seeing into that wild night than the obscured moon was. Kaplan was shivering with fever from his wound, but he had insisted that he was the best qualified night-scope man on the hill.

Naomi Haber was looking over the parapet wall, trying to spot movement in the dust. She wore one of the newly fashioned windscreens on her face. The device was made of plexiglas from the Concorde's portholes and had foam rubber, taken from the seats, around the edges to keep out the sand the way a diver's mask keeps out the water. The device was secured to her head with a band of elastic.

Hausner drew Kaplan to the side. "They don't have to wait for moonset with this dust storm, you know."

"I know." And Kaplan also knew Hausner. He knew his tones of voice and his mannerisms, and he knew something was coming, and he knew it was not going to be pleasant.

"There are no more OP/LP's or early warning devices. We are blind."

"I know," He saw it taking shape now.

"My assistant commander—Burg—has absolutely forbidden anyone to leave the perimeter."

"I know that, too." Hausner had come to him out of the blackness and dust and touched him like the Angel of Death. And now he was going to die.

"But the best defense is a good offense, as they say. We can't wait here like a herd of frightened deer hoping that our numbers will be sufficient to make the wolves think twice before they attack. And if they do attack, then all we can do is stand shoulder to shoulder like the deer and kick. We must carry the fight to them. Take the offensive. Like last night."

"Yes."

"If we don't they will come out of that dust and be on this hill before we can do a thing. Take a look out there."

Kaplan looked obediently out into the swirling dust. The defenses were covered with drifting sand, and visibility was not more than five meters beyond the perimeter. They could be out there now for all he knew—six meters out, and he wouldn't know. A sudden apprehension, almost panic, came over him and he tightened his grip on his rifle. He had an overwhelming impulse to run out into the night, to penetrate the blackness with his body and see what was on that slope.

"What's out there, Moshe? What's out there?"

"I don't know."

"Wouldn't you like to know?"

Kaplan didn't answer.

Hausner waited, then went on with his evaluation of the situation. "The most effective military stratagem at this point would be to send an ambush patrol downslope. I would place such an ambush by the outer wall. The Ashbals would have to follow that wall from the Ishtar Gate to get here. Not only would an ambush decimate their attacking force, but it would alert us well in advance." He sighed. "But Burg refuses to risk any more people or to split our forces. It's a subjective decision, and I have to go along with it." He paused. "On the other hand . . . on the other hand, if one person with an automatic weapon and a few hundred rounds of ammunition were to be lying out there as the Ashbals walked along that wall, he could take out about a dozen of them before they even fired back." He paused again. "You know?" Hausner lit a cigarette in his cupped hands and passed it to Kaplan, a gesture more intimate than Kaplan could ever remember seeing or hearing of from Jacob Hausner.

Kaplan took a long pull on the cigarette and did not pass it back. "I . . . I suppose that's right—if they are not already halfway up the slope."

"Yes," agreed Hausner. "There's that. And there are undoubtedly sentries still posted at the base of the slope. But a single man should have no difficulty slipping by them in this darkness."

Kaplan had no doubt that Hausner would go himself if necessary. If Hausner had decided not to do it himself, it was only because he felt he had a more important mission to complete on the hill. But Kaplan, after risking his life once for Hausner, had developed an overwhelming desire to live to a ripe old age. Hausner was trying to undermine that desire. "A man who went down there would have damned little chance of getting back."

"Damned little."

"Especially if he had a wound that limited his mobility."

Hausner nodded. "You know, Moshe, there were only a few real soldiers on this hill. Your six men, Dobkin . . . a few other veterans . . . Burg. The number is dwindling. Professional soldiers know that someday they will be called on to do something that the conscripts would not be asked to do. You understand?"

"Of course." Kaplan wondered why Hausner had not gone to Marcus or Alpern. They were not wounded. He supposed it was the classical "this is an honor" type of thing. There were other reasons, he was sure, but Kaplan could not fathom the motives of Jacob Hausner.

"Well . . . thanks for listening to my ramblings, Moshe."

"Don't mention it." He hesitated. When he saw that Hausner made no move to leave, he said, "Actually, a person could get some good ideas of his own by just listening to other people's ideas."

"That's right."

Kaplan hesitated again, then turned and took a step. He felt Hausner's hand on his shoulder and heard Hausner's voice saying something appropriate, but the exact words did not register. The hell of it was that he couldn't even say any good-byes to the people who had come to mean so much to him over the past twenty-four hours. He felt very much alone walking out into the night.

28

The Prime Minister sat upright as he held the telephone to his ear. His eyes darted around the room toward the other men and women who were monitoring on earphones. The call to Baghdad was not going well. The Iraqi President had run the gamut of emotions from surprise at the call, to incredulity at the information, and finally to a lack of commitment on the Israeli Prime Minister's suggestions. The Prime Minister spoke evenly and firmly. "Mr. President, I *cannot* divulge to you the source of my information, but it is a *usually* reliable source." He looked across the room as if to confirm the reliable source.

Teddy Laskov and Itzhak Talman stood near the door. The Prime Minister's gaze seemed to be reevaluating them.

The Iraqi President sighed, which the Prime Minister knew in Arabic meant, "It's a great pity, but we're not getting any closer to a deal," or words to that effect. The Iraqi spoke. "In any case, a low-level reconnaissance is out of the question. The *Sherji* is blowing. However, I am sure your American friends have made an illegal overflight with one of their high-altitude craft. That should be sufficient."

"I wouldn't know anything about that."

The Iraqi President ignored the denial and began recounting his objections to adopting any hasty measures.

The Prime Minister listened to the wind rattle the shutters as he half-listened to the Iraqi. He knew that between the floods, the sandstorm, and the darkness, any land transportation, as well as air flights, were out of the question. The more he prodded the Iraqi, the more he knew that the inadequacies of Iraq's transportation and communication network would be revealed, not to mention the inadequacy of their armed forces in navigating through their own country. To have to admit to those problems only made the President more irascible. But Hillah was so close and it was a fair-sized town, thought the Prime Minister. He said, "Isn't there a garrison in Hillah?" His intelligence had told him there was.

There was a long pause. The Iraqi President seemed to be speaking to his aides. He finally spoke into the telephone. "That is classified information, I'm afraid."

The Prime Minister's fingers tightened on the telephone and his knuckles went white. "Mr. President . . . what do *you* suggest?" He glanced at his watch.

"Wait for the storm to end or at least wait until daylight."

"There may not be time."

"Mr. Prime Minister—it is the old question of risking lives to save lives. You tell me there are fifty Israelis under siege at Babylon, and you want me to risk an operation that could cost as many lives in accidents alone . . . not to mention money. . . . Anyway, we have *no* idea of what—if anything—is going on in Babylon."

"But you know that there *is* something going on there. Don't you?"

The Iraqi hesitated. "Yes. Something. We have just confirmed from our government office in Hillah that something is going on around the ruins of Babylon."

There was an immediate rustle of excitement in the room when the Iraqi made this admission.

The Prime Minister leaned forward over the telephone. He saw no reason to play his cards carefully any longer. He spoke abruptly. "Then for God's sake, send the Hillah garrison."

There was another long pause. When the voice came back it sounded almost apologetic, embarrassed. "The Hillah garrison is the 421st Battalion—your military intelligence will know them. They are a unit composed almost entirely of Palestinians. They fought against you in 1967 and 1973. The officers are Iraqi, but the men are refugees and sons of refugees. It would be unfair to put them in a position where their loyalties would be divided. You understand."

The Prime Minister understood. He looked around him. The people who were monitoring looked angry. A hard-line attitude was forming in the room. "Mr. President, could you speak to Hillah now—I'll hold. Ask your government people there—or your loyal officers—to find out exactly what is happening in Babylon."

"There is unfortunately much difficulty with the land lines at the moment. The storm and the floods. We will raise them by radio and see what they can discover."

"I see." The Prime Minister had no reason to believe that the Iraqi was lying about the land lines. He had one more card to play with the Iraqi. "Mr. President, my military people inform me that it is entirely possible to reach Babylon by river. An expedition from another garrison town on the Euphrates could be at Babylon within hours."

The Iraqi President's voice came back, hard now and impatient. "Do you think the Euphrates is like your little River Jordan? This is a great, mighty river. This time of the year it wanders like a lost sheep across the plain—it joins with lakes and swamps and with many, many small streams which are now swelled in size and are mistaken for the river. There are many false rivers to get lost on tonight."

The Prime Minister already knew this. In fact Babylon itself was no longer on the modern Euphrates but on the ancient, narrower course of the river. Still, a modern army or river unit should be able to navigate it. The ancient Mesopotamians had mastered it. "Mr. President, we are all aware of the great tribulations your country goes through each spring, and we know that any other time of the year we could count on a quick and sure response to our request. We know that one of the reasons these . . ." he didn't want to say terrorists, ". . . these guerillas picked your country was because of the inaccessibility of Babylon for these few weeks. However, Mr. President, I know that you will provide every assistance that is in your power to provide."

There was no answer.

The Prime Minister was aware that the Iraqi had already had to swallow a lot of pride in admitting to potential disloyalties and the inability to move armed forces around the country, to say nothing of the fact that a Concorde could have been hijacked into the middle of the country without his knowledge.

Added to that was the fact that a small private army of Palestinians was operating in his sovereign state. The Prime Minister sensed that the Iraqi President was, understandably, not in a good mood. The only thing left to do was to add insult to injury and try to provoke him into some sort of action. "Are you aware, Mr. President, that there is a Palestinian base camp in the Shamiyah Desert? That is probably where these Palestinians in Babylon come from."

Again, there was no answer.

The Prime Minister looked around the table. A psy-warfare colonel, who had spent some time over the years studying the Iraqi President, scribbled a note and slid it down the table. The Prime Minister read it. *As long as you've goaded him this far, finish it. Too late to be diplomatic.* The Prime Minister nodded and spoke into the telephone. "Are your armed forces *capable* of mounting an expedition at this late hour, Mr. President?"

There was still no response. Finally the President's voice came back. He sounded very cold. "Yes. I will give the orders to mount a river expedition. But they will not disembark until dawn. That is the best I can do."

"That will be fine," said the Prime Minister, knowing that it was anything but fine and yet not wanting to jeopardize what little he had gained.

"What do you expect us to find there?"

"I have no idea."

"Well, neither do we. For your sake, I hope there is something there. It will be somewhat embarrassing for you if there isn't."

"I know." The Prime Minister paused. It was time for the big question. "Would you allow us to assist you? We can make this a joint operation."

There was not even a small pause this time. "That is absolutely out of the question."

There was no use arguing that point. "All right. Good luck to you."

The Iraqi let the silence drag, then he spoke softly. "Babylon. The Captivity. Strange."

"Yes. Strange." You couldn't make a political or diplomatic move in the Middle East without tripping over five thousand years of history and bad blood. That was something the Americans, for instance, never understood. Events that took place three millennia ago were brought up at international conferences as though they had taken place the week before last. Given all that, was there hope for any of them? "But not so strange."

"Perhaps not." The Iraqi paused. "You must not think we are unsympathetic. Terrorists do not do us any service, either. No responsible Arab government endorses what they have done." He paused again, and the Israelis could hear a noise over the electronic speaker like a deep melancholy sigh. It was so Arabic, and at the same time so Jewish, that many people in the room were overcome with feelings of empathy, even kinship. The Iraqi President cleared his throat. "I must go."

"I'll call you before dawn, Mr. President."

"Yes."

The phone went dead. The Prime Minister looked up. "Well, do we go in now or not?" He looked at the wall clock. There was a little over six hours until first light in Babylon. "Or do we wait for the Iraqis?" He lit a cigarette and the striking match sounded loud in the quiet room. "You understand this is the first dialogue an Israeli Prime Minister and an Iraqi President have ever had. Do we want to jeopardize what might come out of this? Do we want to jeopardize the whole climate of peace that launched those Concordes?" He looked around the room and tried to read the faces at the long table. Many of those faces had been at the Entebbe conferences, but this was much more complicated than the

Entebbe situation, and *that* had taken days before a military solution was agreed upon.

One by one the generals and the politicians got up. Each was allowed two minutes to present his views. The room seemed fairly evenly divided and the division was not along military and civilian lines. Fully half of the military cautioned restraint and fully half of the civilians were in favor of a military solution. If a vote were taken, the result would have been very close.

Amos Zevi, Deputy Minister of Foreign Affairs, now Acting Foreign Minister, stood. He pointed out that if Foreign Minister Ariel Weizman and Deputy Minister of Transportation Miriam Bernstein were present, they would vote for restraint.

General Gur stood and quipped, "That might be true if they were *present,* Mr. Minister. But if they could send in a proxy vote from Babylon, I'm sure they would vote for an air attack without delay." This brought the only laughter in an otherwise somber debate.

There were those who still believed that Ahmed Rish was in control of the Israelis and that he would make his demands known very soon. This splinter group wanted to be prepared to negotiate when the terms of the ransom were announced.

One of the ministers, Jonah Galili, stood. He reminded the conference that at the time of Entebbe two of the chief rabbis in Israel had interpreted the *Halacha,* the collection of legal precedents in Jewish religious tradition, as allowing for the exchange of terrorists for hostages.

The Minister of Justice, Nathan Dan, himself a rabbi and a lawyer, jumped to his feet. "I take exception to that interpretation."

The Prime Minister slammed his hand on the table, causing his little pile of shredded paper to jump. "That's enough. This is neither a Yeshiva nor a café in Tel Aviv. I'm not interested in ancient *Halachas* or ancient Hebrew or semantics. I'm interested in here and now. Laskov! Your turn. Two minutes."

Teddy Laskov stood at the end of the long table. He spoke in general terms, citing the classical military arguments for action, but he saw he was not making an impression. It was clear that the lack of resolution was based on the fear of mounting an airborne assault on Babylon and finding no one there but the wild beasts of the desert. In a parliamentary government, one fiasco like that could send the whole government and half the Knesset home to write their memoirs. If the government acted and they found the Concorde with the peace mission missing—or God forbid, all dead—then at least they could justify their attempt to the world on humanitarian grounds. But if he, Laskov was wrong—if the photo-analysts were wrong—if there was nothing there . . .

Laskov decided to gamble. "I see what the problem is. All right, then. If I can prove conclusively that our people are at Babylon, can anyone then have any objection to going in there and getting them?"

The Prime Minister stood. "That is the crux of it, General. If you can prove to me conclusively that our people are there, I will vote for going in."

Here was an out for everyone. If later events showed that they should have authorized a raid, they could explain their inaction to the Israeli people on the very solid grounds of faulty and incomplete intelligence. They could state categorically that they never *knew* that the peace mission was at Babylon. It was more than just an excuse. It was the truth.

"And where do you propose to get this conclusive evidence, General?" asked the Prime Minister. "We really can't accept another divine message, I'm afraid, unless we are all permitted to tune in."

Laskov ignored the scattered laughter. "Do I have full authority to act in your name?"

"That's rather a lot to ask."

"Until dawn."

"Well, you can't do much damage in that short a time, I suppose. All right. In the meantime the airborne operation will be standing by on full alert. If you come back here before 5:30 A.M. and show me incontestable proof that at least the Concorde is at Babylon, then I'll push the red button and we'll all cross our fingers and hope for the best. However, if we hear from the Iraqis before then and they state that they have obtained intelligence that there is no one at Babylon, then whatever proof you bring me will be *ipso facto* no longer incontestable. In any case, after dawn, I will have to rely on the Iraqis to keep their word that they will send a force to Babylon. I don't want our forces bumping into theirs, so 5:30 is the cutoff time for mounting an operation. Fair enough?"

"I'd like to lead the fighter wing that goes in."

The Prime Minister sat down and shook his head. "What incredible balls. You're not even in the armed forces any longer. Why did I just give you the full authority of my office? I must be insane."

"Please."

There was a stillness in the room. The Prime Minister seemed to be lost in thought for a long time, then he rose again and looked at Laskov. "If you convince me to go, then I'd like it very much if you would lead the fighter wing. I can't think of anyone else I'd rather send," he said ambiguously.

Laskov saluted, turned, and strode briskly into the hall. Talman followed quickly.

Talman spoke in a low voice as they walked past people in the crowded hall. "What the hell kind of information could you possibly obtain in so short a time?"

Laskov shrugged. "I don't know."

They stepped outside and passed through the columned façade, through an iron gate, and into the street. They both walked in silence. Jerusalem was quiet except for the hot, dry wind. The night, in spite of the heat, was spectacular in the way that only Jerusalem can be in the spring. The air was sweet with the smell of blossoms and the sky was crystal clear. The waxing moon was nearly full overhead. Its light was yellow and warm. Flowers, vines, and trees grew in all the empty spaces as in a country village. The street itself was paved with ancient stone and the houses could have been anywhere from twenty to two thousand years old. It didn't seem to matter in Jerusalem. Everything was ageless and ancient at the same time.

Talman spoke. "What the hell did you say it for, then? There was an outside chance they would have voted to go. Now you've given them an out."

"They would never have voted to go."

Talman looked at Laskov in the weak light. "Are you having doubts?"

Laskov stopped abruptly. "I have absolutely no doubts. They are in Babylon, Itzhak. I know it." He hesitated, then said, "I can *hear* them."

"That's nonsense. You Russians are incurable mystics."

Laskov nodded. "That's true."

Talman reasserted his old authority. "I insist on knowing what you had in mind when you said you'd bring conclusive proof."

Laskov began walking again. "Let's suppose that you wanted to get a message to a high-level recon craft. How would you do it without a radio?"

Talman thought a moment. "You mean a photographic message? Well, I'd make a big sign on the ground—you know. Or if that were impossible, or if the craft were very high and it was dark or overcast—or if there was a sandstorm, then I'd—I'd create a heat source, I suppose. But we saw those heat sources. They are not conclusive."

"They *would* be if one of them were in the shape of the Star of David."

"But there was no such shape."

"But there was."

"There wasn't."

Laskov seemed to be speaking to himself as he walked. "With all that brain power, I'm surprised no one thought of it. But that's an arcane field—high-level infrared reconnaissance, I mean. Maybe they have a star waiting to be ignited if they *see* an aircraft. They don't understand that if they lit it, it could be photographed from an aircraft for some time after it burned out. Dobkin and Burg should have thought of that. But I'm being too critical. It may very well be that there is no kerosene left, or for one reason or another they could not do it, or the kerosene was critical to make bombs. And why would they think anyone would make a recon over Babylon? I mean, why—"

Talman interrupted him. "Teddy, the point is that they did not ignite a Star of David or a message that said, 'Here we are folks!' or anything of the sort. Maybe they had no time before . . ." His voice trailed off. "Anyway, there is no such sign or mark."

"If there *were* . . . ?"

"I'd be convinced. And so would most people."

"Well, then we'll have to look at the pictures that Air Force Intelligence didn't think were worth sending over to the Prime Minister. I'm sure we'll see the residual heat from a burning kerosene Star of David. It's just a matter of knowing what you're looking for—then you'll see it."

Talman stopped suddenly. His voice was low, almost a whisper. "Are you insane?"

"Not at all."

"Do you mean you would actually try to alter one of those photos?"

"Do you believe they are—or were—in Babylon?"

Talman believed it, but he didn't know why. "Yes."

"Do the ends justify the means?"

"No."

"If your wife were there—or your daughters—would you think differently?"

Talman knew about Laskov and Miriam Bernstein. "No."

Laskov nodded. Talman was not lying. He'd spent too many years among the British. Emotions played little or no part in his decision-making process. That was a good trait most of the time. But Laskov thought he should be a little more Jewish sometimes. "Will you promise to forget what I just said and go get some sleep?"

"No. In fact I feel it's my duty to place you under arrest."

Laskov put his big hands on Talman's arms. "They're dying in Babylon, Itzhak. I know it. The Russians *are* mystics and the Russian Jews are the worst of the lot. I can *see* them, I tell you. Last night I saw them in a dream. I saw Miriam Bernstein playing a zither—a harp—and crying by a stream. It was only before, in the café, that I understood what that meant. Do you think I'd lie to you about that? No. Of course you don't. Itzhak, let me help them. Let me do what I must do. Forget what I told you. When you were my commander, you looked the other way for me once or twice—yes, yes, I know you did—don't be flustered. Go home. Go home and sleep until noon, and when you wake up it will all be over. It will be a national celebration—or, yes, a tragedy—maybe even war. But what choice is there? Let me do this. I don't care what happens to me afterwards. But let me walk away now." He grasped Talman's arms tightly at his sides.

Talman was uncomfortable with Laskov's sudden intimacy, both physical and emotional. He made a small movement to indicate that he'd rather not be held, but Laskov would not release his grip. This was a crossroads for Talman, and he thought he could make the decision better if Laskov were standing off a bit. The Israelis stood too close, not as close as the Arabs, but close enough. Too close for Talman's comfort. "Well . . ." But Laskov's nearness made him . . . what? He could feel the man's warmth, his breath . . . he could feel something pass through Laskov's fingers and into his body. "I really . . ." This was terribly awkward. The man's face was less than half a meter from his. And he could . . . feel what Laskov was feeling. "I . . . think I'll go home. . . . No. . . . I'll come with you. Yes, damn it! It's insane, you know . . . insane, really . . . but I'll help you. Yes!"

Laskov smiled slowly. Yes, he knew Talman as well as he thought he did. Even Talman could be moved. The dream was a nice touch. "Good." He released Talman and stepped back. "Listen. I know an Air Force photo lab tech in Tel Aviv. We can pick him up on the way to the Citadel. He can make a storage dump look like a nude of Elizabeth Taylor if we want. He'll do anything I say, with no questions asked."

Talman nodded and they began walking again, almost running, back to the taxi rank outside the Prime Minister's office. They jumped into a cab. "Tel Aviv," said Laskov, out of breath. "National emergency!"

29

Benjamin Dobkin took the hand of Shear-jashub. They stook on the mud quay that jutted into the Euphrates. The entire village of a few dozen persons stood at the foot of the quay and watched them quietly. The moon revealed the dust clouds on the opposite shore. On this shore, the wind blew, but most of the dust fell into the river. The river itself was choppy, and small waves lapped against the quay. It would not be an easy crossing, nor would it be an easy journey on the land. Dobkin looked back at the old man. "Carry him out onto the mud flats for the jackals, and in the morning go about your business."

The old man nodded politely. He didn't need any instructions on how to survive. His village had survived for over two thousand years through episodes that were second to the European Holocaust only in scale. "May God go with you on your journey, Benjamin."

Dobkin was wearing the bloodstained tiger fatigues and the *kheffiyah* of the dead Ashbal. The man himself would soon be in the bellies of the jackals, but Dobkin couldn't get out of his mind the troubled feeling that Rish would eventually come to this village to avenge Talib and would swiftly complete the job that two millennia of attrition had not completed. "Would your people want to come—to come home to Israel—if that could be arranged?"

Shear-jashub looked at Dobkin. "Jerusalem?"

"Yes. Jerusalem. Anywhere in Israel. Herzlya beach, if you want." He could dimly understand what was going on in the old man's mind. Israel to him was just a Biblical name, along with Judah and Zion. It was hardly a real place and had not much more meaning than Babylon had had to Dobkin two days before. "It's a good place," said Dobkin. "The land is good." How the hell could he possibly bridge two millennia? Not only was the Hebrew different, but the concepts and values were worlds apart. "You may be in danger here."

"We are always in danger here."

What right did he have to hold out the promise of return to Jerusalem anyway? How could he deliver if they accepted? But he continued. "You have been in Babylon too long. It is time to go home." He'd have to be insistent. They were like children, and they did not know how good it could be for them in Israel. And he did not like to see Jews living in subjugation. When he traveled and saw Jews in some countries keeping a low profile, it angered him and he wanted to scream to them, "Come home, you idiots! Come home and hold your heads up. There is a place for you now. We bought it for you with our blood." He tightened his grip on the old rabbi's hand. "Come home."

Shear-jashub placed his free hand on Dobkin's shoulder. *"Aluf,"* he began. "Have you come to lead us out of the Captivity? Or are you to be the unwitting instrument for our final destruction? Wait. Let me finish. In the Book it says, 'Then rose up the chief of the fathers of Judah and Benjamin, and the priests, and the Levites, with all them whose spirit God had raised, to go up to build the house of the Lord which is Jerusalem.' But God did not raise the spirit of my forefathers and they stayed. But let me tell you this, Benjamin. When this house of God of the returned exiles, the Second Temple, was also destroyed and the populace was dispersed and wandered the world, it was the Jews who had remained in Babylon who kept the flame of learning lit. Babylon, not Jerusalem, was the first city of Jewish learning and culture in those years. Israel will always need her exiles, Benjamin, in order to insure that there will always be someone left to carry on the Law and to return to Jerusalem if it is ever again destroyed." He smiled and his shiny brown face wrinkled in the moonlight. "I hope the spirit of God moves you someday to build the Third Temple. And if you do, remember this—if Jerusalem falls again, then there are always the Jews of the Diaspora, and even us of the Captivity, to return and build the Fourth." He squeezed Dobkin's hand and shoulder, then gently pushed him away. "Go, Benjamin. Go and complete your work. And when it is done, then perhaps we will speak again of Jerusalem."

Dobkin turned quickly and walked to the end of the quay. He looked back over his shoulder and gave a half wave to the robed figures standing motionless in the moonlight. A sense of unreality came over him, not for the first time. The sights, sounds, and especially the smells of this place made it difficult for him to think rationally—to think like a twentieth century military man.

Dobkin stared down into the Euphrates. An odd-looking craft called a *gufa* sat in the river. It was no more than a large round basket, coated with the famous bitumen of Babylon. It looked as if it had just been freshly coated with the slime. It may have been a few days or a few thousand years old. Dobkin lowered his big frame into it, and it sank almost to the gunwales. A young man named Chislon jumped in after him, apparently without worrying about the few centimeters of freeboard remaining. The *gufa* bobbed dangerously low in the water, but finally settled with about ten centimeters of freeboard on Chislon's side and about five on Dobkin's. Chislon took a long pole from the quay, cast away the mooring rope, and pushed off.

* * *

Dobkin guessed correctly that the *gufa* was never used when the Euphrates was at high flood as it was now. Within minutes his guess was confirmed when he noticed that the pole was no longer touching bottom no matter how far over Chislon leaned. Chislon looked up and smiled at him several times.

The *gufa* picked up speed. Dobkin knew that they had to make a landfall on the opposite bank within two kilometers or they would overshoot the southern end of Babylon and he would have to backtrack on foot. He didn't feel strong enough for that. He smiled at the young man who was trying to look very calm, but Dobkin could see that he was scared.

Another possibility that had nagged at Dobkin's mind was to go on to Hillah. They might help in Hillah. He could go directly to the Hillah garrison and explain the situation. They would call Baghdad. But the Hillah garrison or the local government people must know that something was going on in Babylon. Why, then, weren't they investigating? He thought about it. The Jews had never completely trusted any outside group to show them charity or give them aid. They expected treachery and were not often disappointed. No, he should not go to Hillah. He should go to the guest house or the museum and get his hands on a telephone and call Israel. That was where he could expect help. That was where there were people who cared if he and the rest lived or died—cared very much, in fact.

The *Sherji* blew over the water and what it lacked in sand, it made up for in velocity. The *gufa* bobbed and swayed and waves splashed over the gunwales on all sides. The round craft began to spin around like a top, and Dobkin was becoming nauseous. His groin ached and his thigh was on fire. He put his head over the side and vomited up his meal of hot lemon tea and an unidentifiable fish that was called *masgouf*.

He felt better and leaned over the side and washed his face in the river. Chislon looked a little unwell also, he noticed.

Dobkin could see a few lights on the far bank and pointed to them.

"Kweirish," said Chislon.

Dobkin was certain now that the young man was clearly worried about the weather. Westerners always had an inordinate faith in native guides, but the truth of the matter was that natives rarely or never did the things that Western adventurers expected they did as part of their routine. Undoubtedly, Chislon had never before had any reason to cross the Euphrates at full flood in the middle of the night when the *Sherji* was blowing.

Dobkin looked at both banks as they spun past him. On the east bank, great masses of dust veiled the land and blotted out the moon. He knew that this meant the last act would be unfolding on the hill long before the moon set.

The river bent below Kweirish and the *gufa* gathered more speed as it came out of its turn. The small craft was caught in the high-velocity water between narrowing banks. Chislon continued to feel for the bottom with the pole and almost caused the craft to be swamped as he leaned farther over the side.

Dobkin tried to estimate when their course would intersect the far shore. Ahead, the river made a turn westward, and if the *gufa* didn't sink first, they might make landfall there. That should put them in the vicinity of the southernmost wall of the city. He would have to backtrack at least two kilometers to the Ishtar Gate and guest house. He wondered what he was going to do if he got there.

* * *

"Disasters and victories are very closely related," observed Hausner.

Burg stuffed a few cigarette stubs into his pipe and lit it as only a nicotine addict can light tobacco in a driving wind.

Both men huddled in what was left of the trenches on the east slope. Sand drifted into the cut in the earth, bringing it slowly and inexorably back up to grade level.

"Where is Kaplan?" asked Burg, for the second time.

How Burg knew that Kaplan was gone was anyone's guess, thought Hausner. Maybe Naomi Haber. Burg had his followers. "You know, not too far from here, at a place called Kut, a whole British army was besieged by the Turks during the First World War." He lit a full cigarette. "The British Expeditionary Force came from India and landed on the Persian Gulf at the mouths of the Tigris and Euphrates. They were going to wrest ancient Mesopotamia from the Turk. The Arab populace—the desert Arabs and the marsh Arabs—were like vultures. After every clash between the two armies, they would strip the dead and finish off the wounded. They harassed both armies and killed stragglers for their clothes and equipment. There's a lesson there and the lesson is, don't go out on the mud flats. If we do and the Ashbals don't get us, marauding Arabs will."

Burg pulled a scarf closer around his face and stuck his pipe into a fold and drew on it. He looked at Hausner. "I absolutely agree with you there. We'll tell the Foreign Minister that story later. Meanwhile, where is Kaplan?"

"This story has another part and another lesson to be learned, Isaac."

Burg exhaled his smoke on a sigh of resignation. "All right."

"Well, after a large battle with the Turks, the British had to hole up at this town called Kut. They had outrun their supplies. The Turks laid siege to the town, and the siege lasted for months. The relieving British force actually got within a kilometer of Kut, but the Turks drove them back again and again. The British in Kut finally had to surrender when their supplies ran out. One of the most severe criticisms of the British commander—this was stated in the War Office report—concerned his lack of forays and sallies from Kut into the encircling Turkish ranks. The report called for an end to static defenses and recommended mobile and fluid defenses. No more walls. Fire and maneuver. Military science has accepted that now. Why don't you?"

Burg forced a laugh. "I hardly see the parallel in your parable. Where is Kaplan? Downslope?"

"There *is* a parallel, and it is that good tactics are good tactics whether it is at Kut, Khartoum, or Babylon. And speaking of Khartoum, Burg, don't forget that the British relief force was only one day late in arriving *there*. But that didn't make General Gordon and his men and the civilians any less dead. If outside help does not reach us in the next few hours, we will suffer the same fate, Burg. While we sit here and no one is trying to hack us to pieces we lull ourselves into a false sense of security. But when that slope comes alive with screaming, bloodthirsty Ashbals, we will all be saying, 'Why didn't we try this?' or, 'Why didn't we try that?' Well, I'm telling you now, Burg, that any desperate method to buy more time is worth the risk."

"Where did he go? The Ishtar Gate?"

"No. Only down to the outer city wall. That will be the route they take."

"How can you be sure?"

"All field problems have only a finite number of solutions."

"I'm going to get you a job at the War College when we get back."

Hausner lay back against the side of the trench and closed his eyes as he smoked.

"When are we trying Bernstein and Aronson? Before or after *your* court-martial?"

Hausner had had enough of humility and deference. It didn't suit him. He didn't like sharing anything, least of all his authority. He sat up quickly and tapped Burg on the chest, "Don't push me, Isaac, or it will be you in the dock, not me. If it goes to a vote, they will pick the genuine bastard to lead them out of the wilderness, not the ersatz bastard like you or the statesman like Weizman. They can trust a real bastard to drive them on. They know they can't trust you or Weizman to make unpopular decisions or to enforce them. So back off. I'll be out of your way—and out of your life—soon enough."

Burg stared down into the glowing bowl of his pipe. "I don't trust you, Jacob. Anyone who thinks victories and disasters are very closely related is the kind of man who calls for another card when he already has twenty points on the black-jack table. That's not the way we play it in intelligence. We accept minimum gains in exchange for minimum losses. We never go for the big gain if there's a chance of a big loss. That's the way all armies, intelligence services, and foreign ministries play the game today. You're the last of the big gamblers. But you shouldn't do it with other people's lives. Even the life of one man—Moshe Kaplan—a brave man—shouldn't be gambled away—thrown away—on the outside chance that the loss of his life may do us some good."

"You know damn well that one life is considered a small risk. By the rules of your own damn game theory, that was an acceptable loss for a possibly large gain."

"It's very subjective, I suppose. I don't consider the loss of one life a small loss."

"You're a damned hypocrite, Burg. You've done worse than this in your lifetime. And don't pretend that you weren't glad I asked Dobkin to go. That mission is almost certain death, you know, and you didn't seem so goddamned upset about that."

"That was different. Dobkin is a professional. A man like that knows that a time like this comes at least once in his life."

"That doesn't make it any easier for him or any easier for me. Do you think I enjoyed sending either of them down there?"

"I didn't say that. Lower your voice. I'm only playing Devil's Advocate here."

"I don't need any more devils or their advocates, Burg. I do what I think I have to do. And I hope to God that the people in Jerusalem and Tel Aviv forget about their game plan theories, because if they're not willing to take that big gamble on us, if and when they find out where we are, then we are all dead."

Burg looked off downslope and spoke in an offhand manner. "Well, better dead than that we should be the cause of another war or that our rescue should jeopardize the Peace Conference."

Hausner saw it all in a flash of insight. Burg was willing to sacrifice them all for what he thought was a higher good. He would rather they die bravely—and quietly—than see them used as an instrument to put Israel in a difficult position. It was a matter of degree, if you thought about it. He, Hausner, was willing to sacrifice Kaplan, himself, or anyone else for higher goals. But where did the sacrifice stop? If Israel were being overrun, would she refuse to use her atomic weapons "for the sake of humanity and the higher good"? Did anyone, nation or citizen, have the right to say, "Higher good, my ass. I deserve to live and I'll kill anyone who tries to put an end to my life"?

But people did make sacrifices for higher goals; Kaplan was doing that now. Kaplan, lying so very alone in the dark—he could count his remaining time on earth in minutes. And Burg was willing to let them all—including himself—die rather than force Israel to make a decision.

Hausner thought about it. He was willing to sacrifice his life. But that was because fate had put him in a position where to continue to live might be worse than dying. And he had put Kaplan in that position. Kaplan could never have lived a normal life after refusing Hausner's kind of invitation to lay down his life. But it wasn't the lives or the deaths that bothered him, he realized. It was the principle of aggressive intervention that was at stake. The Jews of Israel couldn't let themselves slip into that passive role that had been the cause of the death of European Jewry.

It went against Hausner's personality to accept Burg's argument. If he, Hausner, were asked directly by the Prime Minister, he would say, "Damn right I want you to blast your way in here and get us. What the hell is taking you so long?" Certainly Burg believed that, too. Burg was only playing Devil's Advocate again. Burg was speaking like the Foreign Minister—and Miriam—would speak. Burg, the spy, had many personalities and spoke many tongues. But if Burg really believed what he said, then Burg was wrong. Burg would have to be watched. Burg might have to go.

Hausner sat alone in the trench. The dust and sand sifted into the slit and began covering his legs. The place where Burg had sat opposite him was already obliterated. Soon everything that they had constructed would also be obliterated. The Concorde, too, would be covered someday and only its vague outline would remain. Their bones would lay buried in the dust and all that would remain of them and their deeds would be another written record of suffering and martyrdom to go into the Jerusalem library. He grabbed a handful of dust from his leg and flung it into the wind. Babylon. He hated the place. He hated every square centimeter of its dead dust and clay. Babylon. Corrupter of men. Killer of souls. A million acts of moral depravity had been committed here. Massacres. Slavery. Illicit couplings. Blood sacrifices. How could his love for her have flowered in such a place?

He'd sent for her, but there was no guarantee that she would come. His heart beat heavily in his chest. His mouth, already dry, became sticky, and his hands trembled. Miriam, come quickly. The wait became insufferable. He looked at his watch. Five minutes since Burg had left. Three minutes since he had sent a runner to the Concorde. He wanted to get up and leave, but he couldn't bring himself to move from the place where she would come looking for him.

He heard two voices and saw two silhouettes. One figure pointed, turned and walked off. The other came toward him. He licked his lips and tried to steady his voice. "Here."

She slipped into the trench and knelt beside him in the dust. "What is it, Jacob?"

"I . . . just wanted to speak to you."

"Am I free?"

"No. No, I can't do that. Burg—"

"You can do anything you want here. You are King of Babylon."

"Stop it."

She leaned toward him. "A little bit of you is in complete agreement with Burg. A little bit of you is saying, 'Lock the bitch up and keep her locked up. I'm Jacob Hausner and I make the tough decisions and I stick to them.' "

"Don't Miriam . . ."

"Don't misunderstand me. I'm not concerned about me—or Esther, for that matter. I'm concerned about you. Part of you will die if you let this farce continue. Every minute you allow it to go on you become less of a human being. Take a stand for kindness and compassion for once. Don't be afraid to let everyone know the Jacob Hausner I know."

Hausner shook his head slowly. "I can't. I *am* afraid. Afraid things will fall apart here if I show mercy. Afraid—"

"Afraid *you* will fall apart if you show mercy."

He thought of Moshe Kaplan. How could he have done such a thing to that man? He thought of other Moshe Kaplans over the years. He thought back on Miriam reciting the Ravensbrück Prayer.

As if she read his mind, she said, "I don't want to be your victim, your nightmare, your shuddering ghost. I want to be your help."

He drew his legs up and rested his head on his knees. It was a posture he hadn't assumed since he was a child. He felt himself losing control. "Go away."

"It's not that easy, Jacob."

He picked his head up. "No. It's not." He stared at her through the darkness. He looked so lost, she thought. So alone. "What did you want with me?"

He shook his head. His voice cracked. "I don't know."

"Did you want to tell me you love me?"

"I'm shaking like a schoolboy on his first date and my voice is an octave higher."

She reached out and ran her hand across his temple and through his hair.

He took her hand and brought it to his lips.

Hausner wanted to kiss her, caress her, but instead he only took her in his arms and held her tightly. Then he moved her away gently and knelt on one knee. He reached into his shirt pocket and removed something. He held it out toward her in his open palm. It was a silver Star of David. It was fashioned from two separate triangles riveted together. Some of the rivets had apparently broken off and the triangle had shifted. He tried to sound nonchalant. "I bought it in New York on my last trip. Tiffany's. Drop it off for me and have it fixed. All right?"

He handed her the Star of David. She smiled. "Your first gift to me, Jacob— and you have to pretend it isn't even a gift. Thank you."

Suddenly her expression became very serious. She knelt in the bottom of the trench and stared down at the silver star in her open hand. "Oh, Jacob," she whispered, "please don't throw your life away." She made a fist over the star and clutched it to her breast. The points of the star dug into her hand until it bled. She lowered her head and fought back the tears until her body shook. "Oh, damn it. Damn it!" She pounded her fists against the ground. She shouted into the wind. "No, damn it. I won't let you die here!"

He said nothing but there were tears in his eyes, too.

With unsteady hands she removed a silver chain from her neck. On the chain were the Hebrew letters חי —life. She clasped the chain around his neck and pulled his head toward her. "Life," she said, through her sobs. "Life, Jacob."

Moshe Kaplan lay in a small ravine and scanned with the starlight scope. The moonlight was weak and the dust was thick, but he had no trouble seeing the file of Ashbals in tiger fatigues against the low wall less than twenty meters away. He was reminded of a nineteenth-century print called *The Gathering of the Werewolves*. It showed grotesque semi-humans gathering against the wall of a churchyard cemetery in the moonlight. It was a frightening picture, but far less frightening than the greenish picture in his scope.

As he watched, the picture suddenly dimmed and he knew the batteries had finally given out. He took one last look before the picture became darker and pulled back on the trigger.

On the hill, everyone knew that the time had come.

30

D obkin pushed Chislon forcibly back into the *gufa,* then shoved the craft away from the shore. There was considerably more freeboard now, and Chislon was far better off taking his chances with the Euphrates than sharing Dobkin's fate. Also, Chislon was the only connection between Dobkin and the village of Ummah, and Dobkin did not want that connection known by Rish should they be caught. He watched the *gufa* float downriver toward Hillah until he lost sight of it. He turned inland.

Dobkin was totally disoriented and could not be sure exactly where he was in relation to the Ishtar Gate. He walked through the blinding dust storm, keeping count of his paces. There were unmarked excavations everywhere and he almost fell into a few of them. At least their presence confirmed that he was indeed in Babylon. He navigated across that peculiar blanched, nitrous soil which had been produced from the walls of ancient buildings and which stunted and destroyed vegetation, making the site of Babylon an awful and naked waste.

When he had traveled three hundred meters, he climbed onto a high piece of ground and peered out at the surrounding terrain. He assumed that the guest house would have lights and looked for them through the darkness, but saw nothing.

He heard a noise behind him and spun around. Something moved in the dark. He saw it move again and saw its slanted yellow eyes glowing through the darkness.

The jackal stood on a crumbled wall, its hindquarters to the wind and its face pointing at Dobkin. Its eyes were half-closed and it stood stoically, accepting its miserable lot. Dobkin suddenly felt an empathy with this predator. "I don't know what you're looking for here, old hunter, but I hope you find it—as long as it isn't me."

The jackal moved gracefully along the wall toward Dobkin, sized him up, and stopped. He raised his muzzle and howled. There was no answer from his pack, and the jackal leaped from the wall and disappeared into the night.

Dobkin also came down from the high place and took temporary shelter in a partly excavated house. There were owls in the dark corners and they hooted at his presence. Dobkin settled onto the floor and fought down the numbing pain and fatigue. He let his eyes close, and his mind drifted.

Babylon. What an incredibly dead place. And the dead city was trying to kill him and add his bones to its bleached earth. "And Babylon shall become heaps, a dwelling place for dragons, an astonishment, and an hissing, without an inhabitant." Jeremiah's prophecy had been as accurate as Isaiah's.

In the fourth century, recalled Dobkin, a Persian king had turned the city into a royal game reserve. Its incredible walls, sometimes listed in place of the

Hanging Gardens as the Second Wonder of the World, still stood in those days, though most of the 360 watchtowers along its ramparts had fallen. This bizarre fate, the transformation of the largest city in the world into a place for wild animals—a zoo, really—recalled even more dramatically to Dobkin the prophesies of Isaiah and Jeremiah. A dwelling place for wild beasts.

By the beginning of the fifth century the Euphrates had changed course and Babylon had become a vast marsh, and the final prophesies of Isaiah and Jeremiah were fulfilled when, as Jeremiah wrote eight hundred years before the fact, "The sea is come up upon Babylon: she is covered with the multitude of the waves thereof."

Dobkin felt himself slipping off and lurched to his feet. He took some water from the goatskin and cleared his eyes. It was a strange world that he had been catapulted into, and he suspected that there was some meaning in all of it, but he could not begin to fathom what it was.

He climbed out of the half-buried house and onto a trail that ran over the sunken ruins. He turned north and picked his way along the flood bank of the Euphrates. He walked on for nearly a kilometer, his body hunched over against the wind and his face wrapped in his *kheffiyah*.

The wind dropped briefly, and he thought he heard a noise and lifted his head. An Arab stared at him from the alcove of a doorway. Dobkin realized that he was in Kweirish. He stared back at the Arab, then approached him. "The guest house," he said in what he hoped was Palestinian-accented Arabic.

The man believed that he was speaking to an Ashbal who had lost his way in the darkness. He had little love for these Palestinians, but they seemed to be the local authority at the moment. He had never seen an Ashbal without a rifle and he wondered about that. He stepped out of the alcove and walked past Dobkin, looking closely at him as he brushed by.

As Dobkin followed, he reached into his belt and took out the knife that the Jews of Ummah had given him. They walked up a crooked street for a few minutes, then the man disappeared into an alley between two buildings.

Dobkin followed carefully. He looked down the alley, but the Arab had disappeared. Dobkin put his back to the wall on his right and sidestepped in, the knife at his side ready to move.

The Arab suddenly stepped out of a niche in the wall opposite him and held out his arm. "This is the way."

Dobkin was certain this was the goat path down which Hamadi had taken him and Hausner and which led to the Ishtar Gate. He nodded and made an appropriate expression of gratitude, adding a mild benediction. He realized he would have to pass very close to the man to get by. He tightened his grip on his knife and walked, his right shoulder slightly out front, until he was abreast of the Arab.

The Arab gripped his own dagger. He meant to murder the Ashbal for his clothes and boots and whatever else he happened to have in his pockets. The Ashbals would never trace the man back to Kweirish.

Dobkin passed within a meter of the man and fixed his eyes on him.

The Arab realized how big the Ashbal was and saw also that he was alert. In fact, he wondered if the man had plans to murder *him*. His eyes glanced downward and he saw the big man's knife. Should he strike first or should he stand back and pray to Allah that the big man had no murderous designs on him? Certainly the man would not murder him for his poor *gellebiah* and his old sandals? "Allah go with you," he said and bowed his head, leaving himself at the big man's mercy.

Dobkin hesitated. All the reasons for murdering the man and not murdering him flashed through his mind. "And with you," Dobkin answered. He slid by and disappeared up the goat path between the houses.

Again, as before, a feeling of déjà vu came over him as he walked up into the city. He knew it was only a combination of fatigue and stress coupled with all those old maps and conjectural restorations he had seen of the place, but nevertheless it was haunting. He supposed that like most Jews—if the stories of the Captivity were substantially correct—he had had ancestors living in this place. But his ancestors had not tarried when Cyrus said "Go." They went, only to be dispersed again by the Romans some centuries later. From then until 1948 there had been no place to call home. Somehow the family known as Dobkin, after two millennia of wandering, had come to live in Russia, and from Russia they completed their journey and returned to Palestine. And from Palestine—Israel—Benjamin Dobkin had come back to Babylon. It remained to be seen if he would return to Jerusalem.

Dobkin found the ancient bed of the Euphrates, and from there it was easy to follow the old river wall into the palace area. Within a quarter of an hour, he found himself staring up at the glazed lions on the towers of the Ishtar Gate. He passed through the gate and followed the Sacred Processional Way until he saw the lights of the guest house. There appeared to be no sentry. Across from the guest house was a bivouac of struck tents. Some distance off he could make out the small museum. The Ashbals appeared to be gone. Gone to attack the hill again. As he stood and caught his breath, he heard a long burst of AK-47 fire coming from the direction of the hill, then silence. He wondered who had fired the burst. An outpost, he imagined. Another martyr to add to the very long list.

He thought for a moment of trying to find Dr. Al-Thanni in the museum, but decided against that. Time was crucial now. Besides could he trust Al-Thanni? And if he could, did he want to involve him in this? He realized that he had no specific plans beyond making a very important telephone call, and in fact he did not want to think too long about making any plans. The whole incredible operation could only work because of boldness, daring, and luck. So far he had been very lucky. He had found the village of Ummah and had acquired a set of tiger fatigues. He had found the guest house, and the Ashbals seemed to be gone from the tents. Now all he had to do was go inside and kill the duty man and anyone else left behind. But the wounded would probably be in there, and that meant orderlies, too. Perhaps a lot of them.

He walked up to the front veranda and opened the door into the small lobby. He blinked his eyes to adjust them to the light. A young Arab in tiger fatigues sat behind the clerk's counter reading a newspaper. It was all so commonplace, thought Dobkin. The young man looked up, and Dobkin could see his features straining as he tried to place him.

"Yes?" The man, Kassim, had just decided to rape the Jewess again—if she wasn't dead yet. Now this interruption. "Yes?" There was something wrong— those ill-fitting fatigues. They were wet and the dust was plastered on them with dark blotches that looked like blood. No rifle—a goatskin—the *kheffiyah* didn't sit quite right. Kassim stood up.

Dobkin walked to the counter quickly, but not too quickly, reached over and grabbed the young man by the hair with his left hand as his right hand thrust his knife into the man's larynx. He twisted the knife, then let the man slide down gently to the floor. He wiped his hand on the newspaper, then blotted the counter with it and dropped the paper behind it. He could still hear a bubbling sound from the other side of the counter. He turned and walked to the door marked in Arabic "Manager's Office," and opened it.

The small office was lit by a single floor lamp, and in the pool of light on the floor lay a naked women—or a girl—on her stomach, covered with blood and apparently dead or close to it. Dobkin knew by the skin and haircut that it was no local peasant girl who had been abducted for the obvious reason. He walked quickly over to the body and turned it over. She looked familiar even though her face was battered. His worst fear—that she was one of his—was realized as he slowly recognized Yigael Tekoah's secretary, but he could not remember her name. He knelt down and put his ear to her heart. She was alive. He looked at her bloody body. It appeared as if they had let some kind of wild animal attack her.

He picked her up and laid her on a small ottoman against the wall. A long woolen *gellebiah* hung on a coat hook on the door and he took it down and slipped it over her. He found a pitcher of water standing next to a basin of bloody water on a sideboard. He poured the water from the pitcher over the girl's face. She stirred slightly. Dobkin put the pitcher down. He could not spare one more second for the suffering girl. He walked to the desk and picked up the telephone. The single, commonplace act felt strange, the way it had during the Sinai Campaign when he had once found a working telephone in a destroyed village. He had called the next village—still in Egyptian hands—and announced his imminent arrival. That had been a lark. This was not. He waited impatiently for a dial tone. Overhead, he could hear the sound of footsteps and groaning. Orderlies and wounded. On the other side of the wall he heard men speaking. Outside, the wind shook the louvers and rattled the window panes. Dobkin wondered if the line was dead. He looked down at the telephone. There was no dial face. It was completely operator-controlled, but how did one raise the operator? He tapped on the cradle for what seemed like a very long time.

Suddenly, a man's voice came on, annoyed and churlish. "Yes? Hillah exchange! Yes?"

Dobkin took a breath. "Hillah, get me the international operator in Baghdad, please."

"Baghdad?"

"Baghdad." Dobkin knew that he would have to route this call with all the care and patience of a man building a house of cards. One slip and the connection could be broken.

"Who is calling Baghdad?"

Dobkin never fully appreciated his own country until he traveled to controlled societies. He hesitated, then spoke. "This is Dr. Al-Thanni." No. The Hillah operator would certainly know that voice. A bad mistake. "That is, I am Dr. Omar Sabbah, a *house guest* of Dr. Al-Thanni of the museum, Baghdad please."

There was a pause. "Wait."

Dobkin wondered if Al-Thanni was in his quarters in the guest house, or if he was staying at the museum. Or was he home in Baghdad? He held the receiver to his ear and waited. A clock on the wall ticked away the minutes. He found himself staring into the bowl of bloody water and turned away. His eyes burned and his whole body felt as though it wanted to fall. He carried the telephone across the room and knelt beside Deborah Gideon. He wet her lips from his goatskin and let some water slide between them. He felt her pulse and her pale skin and forced back her eyelid. She was in shock, but she was young and healthy looking enough to come out of it. He touched some of her wounds and looked at them closely. He did not feel so bad about killing the duty man now.

He ministered to her as best he could while he waited, the receiver cradled between his shoulder and ear. The clock ticked off a quarter of an hour. The voices on the other side of the wall got louder. A card game. Overhead there was a thump on the floor. A patient fell out of bed—or died and was thrown onto a stretcher.

Someone walked into the lobby and shouted. "Kassim! Kassim! Where are you?"

That was probably the dead man's name, thought Dobkin. Would anyone think to lean over the counter and look on the floor?

Footsteps approached the door. The doorknob turned. Dobkin kept the receiver to his ear and reached up and shut off the lamp. The door opened, and a shaft of light from the lobby passed a meter away from him and illuminated the place on the floor where the girl had lain. The edge of the shaft fell on her bare foot hanging over the sofa. "Kassim! Where are you, you son of an ass?"

The Hillah operator spoke. "Babylon? Babylon? Baghdad is on. Babylon, are you there? Are you there?"

Dobkin stood motionless, not even drawing a breath.

The Hillah operator spoke to the Baghdad operator. "Babylon is gone."

The door closed and the room went dark.

Dobkin spoke softly. "Babylon is here."

"What? Speak up. Speak up."

"Babylon is here."

"Can you hear Babylon, Baghdad?"

"I hear Babylon, Hillah," said the female operator to the male Hillah operator.

They are very up to date in Baghdad, thought Dobkin.

"Go ahead, Babylon," said the Baghdad international operator.

Dobkin thought again about asking for an Iraqi government office, or explaining to the operator who he was and what he wanted, but he would then have to have the international operator get him a regular operator. And what government office was open at this hour? And what reaction would the operator have to his story? Several scenarios played themselves out in his mind and each one ended with a dead telephone.

"Go *ahead,* Babylon."

"Get me . . ." There was no way that a call from the Land of Islam was going to reach Israel. Istanbul would call Israel, but he didn't speak Turkish so he would have to speak to an Arabic-speaking international operator in Istanbul. And if Baghdad or another exchange were still listening they would become very suspicious when he asked for Tel Aviv.

"Babylon. Are you *there?*"

"Yes. Athens. Get me Athens."

"Why are you calling Athens? Who are you?"

Bitch. "I am Dr. Omar Sabbah, young lady, and I wish to call an associate in Athens. Put me through without delay."

There was silence for some time, then the voice said, "That will take some time, Doctor. I will ring you back when I complete the call."

"No." Why not?

"Why not?"

"The . . . bell doesn't work properly here. I can never tell when I have incoming calls."

Silence.

"Did you hear me, Baghdad?"

"Yes. Yes. Wait. I will route your call. Stay on the line, then."

"Thank you." He heard Baghdad speak to Damascus and Damascus speak to Beirut. Beirut, the big exchange in the Middle East, reached Istanbul quickly. There was a time—and in fact there were still days—when Beirut would have rung Tel Aviv only two hundred kilometers down the coast. But today might not be one of those days, and he didn't want to risk it. The easy flowing Arabic became halting Turkish and equally bad Arabic as the Beirut and Istanbul international operators spoke to each other. The clock ticked on. Dobkin could not believe that he had gotten this far. He waited for the connection to be broken or the door to open. Sweat ran down his face and his mouth turned dry. He listened to his heart beat in the dark.

The card game in the next room was ending. There was another shout for the duty man. Some crying from the wounded. Dobkin thought he could hear automatic weapons fire to the north. The girl on the sofa cried out in her sleep, and Dobkin held his breath.

Istanbul spoke to Athens. Athens spoke better Turkish than Istanbul spoke Greek. Istanbul spoke to Beirut. Beirut bypassed Damascus and spoke directly to Baghdad. Hillah was no longer on station and Baghdad spoke directly to Babylon. "Athens is connected."

"Thank you." The last Athens operator spoke Turkish, but they automatically switched him over to an Arabic-speaking operator. "Number, please?"

Was anyone in Islam still on the line? He wanted to ask for an English-speaking operator but didn't want to cause any confusion. He stalled to give the way stations time to get off the line. Operators were nosy and would listen until they had another call or until they were bored. "Is this Athens?" he asked in Arabic.

"Yes, sir. Number, please."

"Can you look up a number for me?"

"Certainly, sir. Who is the party?"

Dobkin paused. He thought of an archeological acquaintance. "Dr. Adamandios Stathatos. He lives in the Kipseli district." He spelled it out slowly.

"Hold on, please."

Dobkin was certain that by now the Arabic operators had hung up, but there was still a chance that there was a security man on the line somewhere along the way. International phone calls were not that common in this part of the world and certainly not at that hour. Even in Israel, international calls were spot-monitored by Shin Beth.

The operator came back. "Dr. Stathatos in Kipseli. I'm ringing."

"Stop the call."

"Sir?"

"Stop the call. I just remembered another call." He could have spoken to Dr. Stathatos and perhaps accomplished his mission, but he wanted more than anything in the world to talk directly to Tel Aviv, and he was so close. "Cancel that call."

The Athens operator stopped the call. She was obviously annoyed. "Yes, sir."

"Get me . . . Tel Aviv."

"Tel Aviv?" There was a pause. This had happened before. It was no concern of hers. Greece and Israel were on good terms. Politics were silly. But that poor man had better be careful though, calling Tel Aviv from Iraq. "Hold on, please." There was another transfer of operators and more clicking, buzzing, humming, and ringing down the line.

A new voice came on and said, "Tel Aviv is on the line, sir."

A girl's voice in Hebrew, brisk and efficient, came through very weak. "Number, please?"

Dobkin's heart pounded in his chest. He wanted to crawl into the receiver and come out in Tel Aviv. He wanted to shout into the mouthpiece and tell this girl all there was to tell.

"Number, please."

He controlled his voice. "Wait." There were several numbers. His own, for one, but his wife would be with one of her innumerable relatives. There were lots of numbers. Friends, officers, politicians. But if he spoke to an intermediate party, there would be unnecessary confusion when that person spoke to the government.

"Sir, you—"

"The Prime Minister's office in Tel Aviv." He could not give the secure number on an international line, and he would have to speak to the regular office operator. He wondered if the government was in Tel Aviv or Jerusalem. At the very least he would be able to speak to a responsible duty officer in Tel Aviv. Dobkin heard noises in the lobby again. It was only a matter of time before they found the lost Kassim. He could hear the phone ringing on the line.

"Prime Minister's office," said a female operator.

"Yes. Is the security meeting there or in Jerusalem?"

There was a pause. That information was in the newspapers, so there was no reason not to answer. Still . . . "Who is this, please?"

"General . . ." He didn't know what her reaction would be to his name. "General Cohen."

She paused. "I'll have the Tel Aviv operator ring you through to the Jerusalem operator . . . General."

"Thank you." He heard a busy signal. Everyone in Israel must be calling the Prime Minister's office tonight with advice and complaints. That happened during every crisis. Everyone in Israel thought they were Prime Minister material.

"All the lines to Jerusalem are busy, sir."

"I'm calling long distance. Government business. Copy this number." He gave her the secure number for Jerusalem.

The phone rang almost immediately.

"Yes," said a tired-sounding male voice without identifying himself or his office. "Who's calling?"

Dobkin could hear the regular operators in the background. It was a busy night there. He drew some comfort from the fact. "Listen to me carefully and don't hang up."

"No, sir." The man had taken a lot of calls that evening and few of them had been pleasant, but he never considered hanging up on anyone who called on the VIP line.

"I am General Benjamin Dobkin." He gave his code name and number.

"Yes, sir." The man hit a button, and one of Chaim Mazar's Shin Beth men picked up in another room.

"I am calling from Babylon. Iraq. The place where they forced the Concorde down."

"Yes, sir."

"Have you authenticated my code?"

"Yes, sir."

"But you still don't believe it's General Dobkin?"

"No, sir."

"I don't blame you, son. Now listen, I must speak to someone who knows my voice and can authenticate it."

"Yes, sir."

Dobkin spoke slowly and clearly, but not too loudly. "Write down the names of these generals. If one of them is there, put him on so that he can identify my voice."

"Yes, sir."

Dobkin rattled off the names of a dozen army and air force generals. "If you put one of them on, he can verify my identity." He wondered if his connection would be broken somewhere along the line. Would the operator listen in just to confirm if he was still on and hear the Hebrew? What would an operator do in that case? "All right, young man?"

"Yes, sir."

The Internal Security man spoke to one of the Prime Minister's aides in the conference room over an intercom while he monitored.

The aide quickly scribbled a note and handed it to the Prime Minister.

Teddy Laskov opened his attaché case and pulled out six high-level photos, each showing a blowup of a blurred Star of David, put there by an expert airbrush. He felt strangely numb and indifferent about what he was about to do. One way or the other, the ruse would be discovered sooner or later, of course. His career was already over, but after this his name would be discredited and he might very well wind up in jail. But as long as his deception was discovered *after* the operation he didn't care. But *would* they discover it? Or would people believe that the photo was just a fortuitous illusion . . . or a miracle? In a way it was, the way it came to him that they were in Babylon, the way he was still so certain of it—so certain that he would risk jail and disgrace to make everyone else believe it. He picked up the stack of photographs on the table and straightened them. Talman, standing across the room, caught his eye. He looked sad, thought Laskov. Sad, frightened, guilty, and confused. But Talman stared at Laskov and managed a smile and a nod.

The Prime Minister pushed the note aside, unread. "Well, General? What do you have there? Color pictures and map coordinates of the Concorde delivered to Teddy Laskov by Gabriel from God? Come on. Let's see it."

Laskov seemed not to hear.

The Prime Minister's aide tapped his finger insistently on the note, and the Prime Minister finally looked down at it. He picked up and read it.

Benjamin Dobkin could hear them calling for Kassim again. The girl cried out again. An Arab on the other side of the wall heard her and made an obscene remark and laughed. The sound of rapid-fire weapons rose above the wind, and Dobkin knew there was not much time. He heard a click on the line. "Jerusalem? Jerusalem? Are you still there?"

31

Kaplan's ambush was deadly, but more than that, it gave the Israelis on the hill a warning.

The Ashbals nearly broke and ran under the withering fire, but the few remaining leaders, including Rish and Hamadi, kept their heads and returned the fire.

Kaplan might have been able to withdraw, but a madness overcame him as he slapped magazine after magazine into the hot AK-47. The sound and the smell and the vibration combined with the orange-red muzzle flash to mesmerize him. At the rate of about two hundred rounds a minute, he sent nearly a thousand rounds downrange, tearing into the Ashbal ranks. Hausner had not been stingy with the ammunition, and Kaplan meant to use it all.

Rish, Hamadi, and a few others had the presence of mind to notice that there was only one man firing at them. They maneuvered around and came up behind Kaplan. They rushed forward under the cover of the noise from Kaplan's gun and the whistling of the wind and fell on him from behind.

The Israelis on the hill heard his screams above the wind as clearly as if he had been in the next trench. He was taking a long time to die, and his screams had the dual effect—as is usually the case—of strengthening the resolve of the defiant ones and shaking the will of the faint-hearted.

Hausner took the PA microphone and screamed into it. His voice carried into the wind and down to the city wall. "Rish! Hamadi! You are animals! You are subhumans! I'll rip your balls off, Rish! When I get you, I'll rip your balls off!" Hausner's screams became shrill and took on a frenzied quality, almost indistinguishable from the agonized shrieks of Moshe Kaplan or the wild baying of the jackals which had begun again around the base of the mound.

Men and women on the hill looked away from one another as Hausner howled, bellowed, and roared with primeval sounds mixed with the most vulgar and obscene threats and invectives that anyone could imagine. The man had clearly lost control.

Someone—it sounded like Burg—took the microphone from Hausner and shouted words of encouragement and comfort to Kaplan. It did little good. The man continued to die slowly and horribly.

The Israelis began probing fire down the slope. The few remaining Molotov cocktails were thrown out into the night to try to illuminate the slope, but the wind and the sand smothered them before they could burn for very long.

The last of the Ashbals, fewer than forty, came up the slope in pairs, spread far apart. The wind pushed at their backs, driving them onward. The sand and dust masked their movements, while the noise of the wind covered their sounds. Even their muzzle flashes couldn't be seen clearly in the blinding dust.

The Israelis bailed sand from their shredded defenses and began returning the fire. AK-47's began jamming almost immediately, but specially trained teams ran up and down the line field stripping the malfunctioning rifles and swabbing them with lubricants from the Concorde. Still, the sand took its toll of guns on both sides, but more so among the defenders who lacked the cleaning and protective paraphernalia of the Ashbals.

The odds appeared to be even for this round, but Hausner, Burg, and for that matter just about everyone else knew that the *Sherji* was going to be the Israelis' downfall. Also, the defenses were weakened, the ruses were used up, and the ammunition was running out. Hunger and the intermediate stages of dehydration completed the job of reducing Israeli fighting effectiveness. There also seemed to be a crisis in leadership, and it was infectious down to the last man and woman.

In addition, many believed, along with Ariel Weizman, that the back door was open, that the west slope and the Euphrates were unguarded. But, in fact, Hamadi had sent a party from the east slope to the river bank within minutes of losing radio communication with Sayid Talib. Those Ashbals at the base of the west wall had been anxiously waiting for an attempted retreat down the steep slope and were still waiting.

The Ashbals used ammunition as though it were sand, spraying it into the Israeli lines. They fired long bursts as they angled horizontally over the side of the slope, advancing a few meters upward each time they made a sideward run.

Hausner stood on his command mound with Burg. He had calmed down considerably, and Burg thought he looked all right. But to Burg's annoyance and discomfort, he had asked Miriam Bernstein to act as his special messenger and aide. Technically, she and Esther Aronson were still under arrest, but no one objected when Hausner removed any restrictions on their movements. Miriam did not mention Kaplan or the scene with the PA microphone.

Hausner spoke above the noise. "When the ammunition is almost gone, some of our people will make a run for the west slope."

Burg nodded. "And I'm certain there are Ashbals there waiting for that very thing. We have to reiterate our orders to stand fast and fight hand to hand."

"They're not soldiers," Hausner reminded him. "They will do whatever their instincts tell them to do, in the end." He lowered his voice so that it was barely audible. "Some of them have formed a suicide pact. . . . After what happened to Kaplan, suicide looks inviting . . . I can't blame them. . . ."

There was a long silence on the small mound. The makeshift banner stood out straight in the steady wind, but brown dust had muted the colors of Tel Aviv's waterfront, and the aluminum staff tilted farther and farther downward.

Miriam began to say something, then stopped.

"What is it?" asked Hausner.

She began again. "Well . . . while we still have the ammunition and while the Ashbals are still some distance down the east slope, perhaps we should . . . withdraw quickly, cross the hilltop, and drop down the west slope—in force and organized—not a disorderly retreat. We should be able to break through whatever small force they have placed at the river bank. We can take to the river and float away in the darkness."

Hausner and Burg looked at each other, then at her for a few seconds. Hausner spoke. "Aren't you forgetting the wounded?"

"They will be just as lost in an orderly retreat as in a disorderly flight. We have a responsibility to the majority."

Burg spoke. "You've come a long way. But which way?"

"Why does it sound so awful coming from me?" she asked rhetorically. "Yet it does, doesn't it?" She paused. "Anyway, I would stay behind with other volunteers to look after the wounded, of course. I am practically under sentence of death anyway. Aren't I?"

Hausner shook his head. "Even when you make hard decisions, you somehow make them sound soft. The hard fact is that if we retreat—orderly or disorderly—or if we are being overrun and are fighting hand to hand—the first thing we do is shoot the wounded." He put his hand up to quiet her. "Don't be a fool, Miriam. You heard what they did to Kaplan. God knows what they did to Deborah Gideon."

"But . . . they want hostages."

"Maybe," interjected Burg. "But maybe not anymore. Maybe all they want now is revenge. Anyway, if Rish and Hamadi—if either of them is still alive—could stop them from massacring everyone, then the best we can hope for is to be subjected to a slow, more refined torture until we give up whatever state secrets we possess. No, we are not leaving wounded or nurses behind, and we are not going to try to move in the dark. The best trained and most disciplined armies are wary of night maneuvers. If *we* try it I'm convinced it will be a disaster."

"Then what *are* our options?" asked Bernstein. "You refuse to order a retreat or a surrender, and you are not encouraging mass suicide. What is going to become of us then?"

Hausner turned away from her. "I don't know," he said. "The best ending I can envision, outside of rescue, is that each and every man and woman dies in battle. That won't happen, of course. There will be surrenders and captures. There will be suicides, and there will be murders. Maybe some of us will be overlooked in the dark and escape. It will be very much like every other siege when the besiegers break through."

No one spoke. The sound of battle settled into an orderly pattern. Both sides were tired and both sides sensed that this was the last fight. Everyone moved mechanically as though it were a formalized dance—a ritual whose end would come at a fixed time regardless of what they did to hasten it.

The Ashbals kept a respectable three hundred- to four hundred-meter distance and maneuvered mostly laterally, trying to keep the Israelis off balance and at the same time seeking out their weakest sectors.

There was still over three hours left until dawn, but actual daylight would come somewhat later unless the wind dropped and the dust settled.

This was to be a battle of attrition and logistics, and the Ashbals still had a small advantage in manpower and guns and an overwhelming superiority in ammunition, food, medical supplies, and water. They had only to remain deployed and draw fire until they were certain that the Israelis were at the end of their ammunition. They gambled on the principle that even with strict fire discipline the Israelis' ammunition could not hold out until dawn.

Burg tried to formulate several plans in his mind. Flee now? Counterattack? Wait until the end and fight hand to hand? Kill the wounded? Kill Hausner? Would they be rescued at the eleventh hour? Not likely. "What happened to Dobkin?"

Hausner turned and looked southwest, out to where the village of Ummah was supposed to be. He stared as though he were trying to make contact with Dobkin. He turned again, due south, toward the Ishtar Gate. "I have a feeling he is all right."

Miriam was holding onto his arm, openly showing Burg how matters stood. "I wonder if he's made contact with anyone?"

"Well," said Burg. "I can tell you this—even if by some miracle he is speaking to some kind of authority right now, I don't believe help would arrive in time." He looked at Hausner as if for confirmation, but what he was really inviting now was one of Hausner's contradictions.

Hausner turned his back to the wind and looked west. He pointed toward the invisible horizon. "I can't help but think that Teddy Laskov will be as good as his word—that he is out there now with his squadron of fighters, looking for us, getting closer . . ."

Burg looked at Hausner, pointing into the sky. "That's a rather optimistic statement for you, Jacob," he said carefully. "I hope you're right."

Hausner folded his arms across his chest. "You know, Burg, I can't seem to accept the idea that all those very clever fellows in Tel Aviv and Jerusalem could still be sitting around with their fingers up their asses. I expected more from them. Is that patriotism? I suppose. Well, perhaps I'm expecting too much. After all, I was one of those clever fellows, too, and look how I fouled things up, Isaac. They're entitled to a few days off, too."

Burg couldn't help but laugh. "Not today." Whenever he started doubting Hausner's reasoning, the man showed a flash of insight.

A runner approached, and Burg walked to meet her.

Miriam had been standing off a few meters listening silently to Hausner and Burg. She came up beside Hausner now and took his arm again and squeezed it tightly. She thought of Teddy Laskov. She had been thinking of him less and less lately. After they crashed, she pictured him doing just what Hausner had said—swooping down in that big steel charger and rescuing her . . . everyone. But in reality she knew that he was probably in disgrace, and she knew that she was partly responsible for that. At first she refused to make the connection between her influence on him and his actions in the air, but the connection was there for anyone who knew them both, and she had finally faced up to it at about the same time she had faced up to a lot of other realities.

Hausner made realities real for her as no other man ever would or could. Other men in her life went along with her conception of the world in order to flatter her or be polite. That was the type of man she attracted. Thin men with glasses who sat next to her at seminars and committee meetings. Men who spoke in party jargon and repeated clichés and bromides as if they had made them up that morning.

Laskov had been different from most of the men she had known, and so had her husband. They were somewhat alike, and in her mind she characterized them both as noble savages. Jacob Hausner was another variation of the type but more extreme. She might have gone through this whole experience in Babylon without having changed her perceptions of the world very drastically. Hausner had *forced* her eyes open. She didn't like what she saw, but now she could objectively weigh the pros and cons of a proposal to shoot the wounded without going into fits of moral outrage. Was that good or bad? It was neither. It just *was*.

"Do you know Teddy Laskov well?" she asked Hausner.

"Not well. Our paths cross now and then."

She nodded. After a few seconds she said, hesitantly. "Do you like him?"

"Who?" He let the silence drag out. "Oh. Laskov. I suppose. He's easier to deal with than you political types."

She smiled in the dark. After a while she said, "He reminds me of you."

"Who? Laskov? Is that so?"

She squeezed his arm tighter. Friends her age who remembered the camps were bitter and disillusioned with mankind. Many had psychological problems. She was determined not to be scarred, and she had overcompensated. She was well adjusted and optimistic to the point where a psychiatrist friend had jokingly called it a neurosis. Yet she was scarred, of course. People said they saw it in her eyes, and she saw it herself in the mirror. "I'm certain he thinks this is all his fault."

"Well, then, we do have something in common."

"You're both egocentric, and you think that all the good and all the bad that happens around you is a result of your actions."

"Isn't it?"

"Teddy Laskov and I were lovers," she said suddenly.

Burg overheard her as he walked back toward the mound. He was still annoyed at her presence. Now this. It was really too much. He turned his back on them and walked away.

"And you will be again," said Hausner.

"I don't think so."

"The question is irrelevant right now, Miriam." He sounded impatient.

"You're not—?"

"Not at all. Listen. You go on to the Concorde and see how Becker is doing with his radios. If there's nothing to report—and there won't be—stay there."

"Why?"

"Just stay there, damn it! I don't have to explain my orders to anyone else, and I don't have to explain them to you."

She took a step, then turned. "I won't see you again, will I?"

"You will. I promise."

She looked up at him. "I won't see you again."

He didn't know what to say.

She reached up and took his head and pulled it down to her and kissed him.

He took her hands and disengaged himself. "Don't leave the aircraft," he said softly. "No matter what happens, promise?"

"Will I see you again?"

"Yes."

They stood looking at each other for some time. She reached up slowly, touched his face, then turned quickly and ran off into the dark.

Hausner watched her until he could not see her any longer.

He coughed some dust up out of his throat and wiped his running eyes. If there was any divine meaning or message in this senseless ordeal, if there was any secular lesson to be learned here, he couldn't think of what it could be. It was the same old human circus of bravery and cowardice, selfishness and self-lessness, cleverness and stupidity, mercy and heartlessness. Only the clowns were different. How many times did the show have to be performed for who-ever was up there watching? And why didn't it all end quickly? Why did God give them the cleverness and strength to prolong their own suffering when the end was preordained? Hausner had that uneasy feeling again—that it was a great cosmic joke directed at him. He turned toward Burg and shouted. "This is God's way of punishing me for not giving up smoking as I promised my father I would." He laughed into the wind.

Burg put his hand in his pocket and fingered the small .22 pistol there.

32

"**A**re you *there*, Jerusalem?"

"Still here . . . General. Stand by," said the duty operator.

The Prime Minister tapped his pencil on the table for several seconds and looked down at the note again, then looked up. "I assume many of you could recognize General Dobkin's voice if you heard it." He tried to control the edge of excitement in his voice.

There was a loud outburst of questions and exclamations, and people rose to their feet. The Prime Minister slapped the table for silence. "Be quiet and listen carefully." He signaled to the communications man in the alcove, and a loud rushing sound came over several speakers in the room. The Prime Minister pressed a button on the console in front of him and spoke into a microphone mounted on the console. "Who is this?"

Dobkin recognized the slightly mocking voice at once. His senses reeled for a second, then he steadied himself and swallowed. "This is General Benjamin Dobkin, Mr. Prime Minister." He paused. "Do you recognize my voice?"

"No." But it was obvious to the Prime Minister that there were people in the room who thought they did.

Dobkin tried to bring his voice under control, to sound as natural as possible. "Is there anyone there who can recognize my voice, sir?"

"You better hope there is." The Prime Minister looked around the table. A few heads nodded tentatively. A general who had been a colonel under Dobkin added, "Or a very good impersonation."

"Go ahead, General," said the Prime Minister, still not fully convinced, but very excited. "Where are you calling from?"

Teddy Laskov held the forged photographs tightly in his hands. Slowly, he began moving them back toward his attaché case.

"Babylon," said the voice over the speaker.

The room exploded with exclamations and most heads turned toward Laskov and Talman. The Prime Minister hit the table for silence, but he could not quiet the room. He spoke loudly into the microphone. "Where are you calling from, General? The telephone, I mean? Are you at *liberty?*"

"Yes, I'm at liberty. I'm calling from the guest house here, sir. Near the museum." Dobkin tried to control his voice, but it wavered slightly.

The Prime Minister tried, also, to sound composed, but his voice was becoming tremulous. "Yes. All right. Can you give us a situation report, General? What the hell is going on?"

Dobkin knew that the entire Cabinet, and most of the important men in the military were listening. He collected his thoughts and gave a clear, concise recapitulation of everything that had happened since they were lost over the Mediterranean.

A half-dozen aides ran in and out of the conference room with army ordnance maps of the area, facts and figures about flight times to Babylon, ground elevations, weather, time of first light and sunrise, and a hundred other items of input that had been assembled ever since Laskov had made his statement about

Babylon. It would all have to be considered before any final operational decisions could be made.

As Dobkin spoke, he could hear men and women passing through the lobby outside his door. The walking wounded going somewhere. A door opened and shut off the lobby. A radio went on in the room where the card game had ended. A woman's husky voice came out of the radio singing one of those interminable Arab songs. A few of the Ashbals joined in. The noise masked his voice, but it also kept him from hearing if anyone was near the door.

"What do you suggest, General?"

Dobkin recognized the voice of General Gur. "Suggest? I suggest, General Gur, that you come and get us the hell out of here."

"How are those mud flats on the west bank?" asked Air Force General Katzir.

"Still wet," said Dobkin truthfully. "But it looks drier farther from the river."

"The road you landed on," said Katzir, "do you think it would support a C-130?"

"I can't say, General. I think we ripped it up when we put down."

"We may have to use helicopters," said an unidentified voice.

"No," said Dobkin. "No time for that. They're being attacked right *now.*"

Another voice said something about sending a squadron of fighter craft in first. Dobkin could hear several voices being picked up by the microphone now. He heard Teddy Laskov's name mentioned. He'd thought that the man would be in retirement by now, but apparently he was at the meeting. Dobkin answered a few more questions as he listened to the debate heat up. Suddenly, he interrupted in a loud voice, "Mr. Prime Minister. I'm afraid I have to go. There are three gentlemen here with AK-47's, and when they comprehend what is happening, they will surely want me to get off the telephone."

In Jerusalem they heard what sounded like a scuffle, then a sharp crack like a gunshot, or perhaps something breaking. Then the telephone went dead.

Miriam Bernstein sat in the copilot's seat next to David Becker. "You don't think *anyone* heard your SOS, then?"

"No." He turned the radio down but left it on so that he could monitor. "The Lear is still up there, but I suspect he's in trouble."

"Why?"

"Why?" The fact that Hausner had sent a messenger to get a report from him and not come himself was an indication of how little faith everyone had in his end of this operation. Miriam Bernstein was, however, the Deputy Minister of Transportation and, therefore, both Hausner's and Becker's boss. But that didn't seem to matter anymore. "Why? Because he can't land in this dust, that's why. He will have to land and refuel somewhere where the dust is not so thick. Then *maybe* I can get a call through." He glanced sideways at her. "Do you want to go and make your report? That's all I have."

"Later." She stared out the shattered windshield. "Are you afraid to die?" she asked suddenly.

He turned his head and looked at her in the glow of the instrument panels. He hardly expected such a question from this very reserved woman. "No. I don't think so. I . . . I'm afraid to fly again . . . but not to die. Funny . . ." He had no idea why he let himself be drawn into such intimacy. "And you?"

"Almost everyone I've been close to is dead." She changed the subject. "What do you think of Jacob Hausner?"

He looked up from the book that he had begun to write in. He suspected that

Hausner and Bernstein had become very close. But that didn't change his public or private opinion of Jacob Hausner. "A Nazi."

"He likes you."

Becker didn't understand where the conversation was going or why. Apparently she was overwrought and just wanted to talk. People did funny things when they were staring death in the face. He had just admitted that he was afraid to fly, and he wouldn't have admitted that to his psychiatrist. "Don't get me wrong, Mrs. Bernstein. I'm glad we had him along for the ride. Things would probably have been all over for us by now without him." He kept looking at her. She didn't *look* overwrought. She appeared to be . . . happy, excited. He looked down and began writing again.

"I'm in love with him."

Becker broke the point on his pencil. "Oh." The gunfire seemed to grow louder, and Becker looked up. The night looked more frightening, more hideous and ominous through the glass of the flight deck than it did when he was outside in it. Every frightening thing he had seen he had seen through a piece of plexiglas, and he was increasingly associating horror with plexiglas, danger with plexiglas. Death with plexiglas. When he looked through a car windshield or even a house window, his stomach would churn, and he had never been consciously aware of the reason until now. That was an interesting discovery, but it was a little late. "Oh. That's . . . I'm . . ."

"What are you writing . . . David . . . may I call . . . ?"

"Yes. Of course." He closed the book. "The log. The ship's log."

She leaned toward him. "A log? You mean you've been keeping a record of all that's happened?"

"Well, only in a very dry, officialese way."

"May I see it?" She held out her hand and he passed it to her. She sat back, opened it, and flipped through the pages. She read a random entry. *16:02 hrs: Switch to alt. tac. freq. Gen. Laskov broadcast last message: E-2D will keep us on radar. Laskov leaves decision to use Phoenix to us. Squadron turns back.* She flipped a few more pages. *18:31 hrs: Flt. off. Hess dead from skull fracture caused by brick through windshield during rollout. Pilot should have had supersonic visor raised sooner in prep. for crash land. Might have averted death.* She stared at that entry for a few seconds, then closed the book and looked up. She forced a smile. "We are called the People of the Book, and we are also a bookish people. The written word has kept us together since the Diaspora. It's odd that no one else thought to keep a chronicle of what we did here."

"Well . . ." Becker found a cigarette stub and lit it. "It's hardly a chronicle, Mrs. Bernstein—"

"Miriam."

He hesitated. "Miriam, it's just my job to—"

"But that's the point, David. It's always someone's job. A scribe. A keeper of the books. A scholar. A ship's captain. Throughout history someone has always had the job of keeping the written records, and sometimes those records have been powerful and illuminating documents. Ezra was a scribe, and he has left us the only account of the repatriation of the exiles from Babylon. In modern circumstances, it can be an airline captain who performs this function." She smiled at him.

"I suppose."

She leaned toward him. "I can't convince you of your own importance, but can I convince you to hide this book in some way?"

"I suppose that's a good idea."

She started to pass the book back to him, but hesitated. "Would you mind if I sat awhile and wrote my own account of what has happened here? I'll try not to take up much space."

Becker forced a laugh. "Take as much space as you like. I made what I believe was the final entry just now."

"Thank you. Do you have carbon paper? I'd like to make a second copy of what I write. We can bury the book and leave the copy of my writing on the craft."

Becker found a piece of carbon paper in his flight kit. "The book itself has to remain on board. We can bury your copy."

"All right." She took the carbon paper. "Thank you."

"No one is going to see either of them, you know."

She looked up at him. "The Ravensbrück Prayer was written on a scrap of paper, David."

"That prayer has a lot of meaning for you."

"It did." She looked out the windshield for some time. "It was unsigned, you know, but the camp was mostly for women, and so perhaps that can give us a clue to the author." She passed a hand over her face. "They told me that . . . that my mother died at Ravensbrück. And so I like to think that perhaps she wrote it." She lowered her voice, and it was barely audible above the noise outside. "The words once had greater meaning for me, but what still does have meaning is that the human being who wrote it had faith. Faith that it would be found, but more importantly, faith that there would be free people left in the world after that terrible time who would find something of value in those words. And so it survived on a scrap of paper, although the author probably did not survive. It has been reproduced a million times, and it will survive the next holocaust." She smiled again at Becker. "Genesis was originally written with lampblack on papyrus, David. If that first scribe had listened to someone like you, we would never have known how the world began."

He forced a smile. "I'm convinced."

"Good." She took a pen from him and bent over the logbook. She wrote in quick, flowing Hebrew characters.

Suddenly she looked up, and there were tears in her eyes. "That prayer *had* meaning for me, but it has very little now because it was a prayer of forgiveness —a call to turn the other cheek. The person who wrote it was tested in the extreme for those qualities and was not found wanting. I have been tested here —not very hard, mind you, not the way the testing was done at Ravensbrück— and I am no longer forgiving. The fact is, I'm happy the way it has turned out. I look forward to shooting the first enemy soldier who puts his head in here. If I make widows and orphans and childless parents and grieving friends before I die, I'll be sorry for those unfortunate people, but it's nothing personal. Do you understand that? Does it sound so terrible?"

He shook his head. "An eye for an eye."

"Yes. And a tooth for a tooth." She turned a page in the logbook and continued writing.

Hausner sensed, without looking at his watch, that it was close to dawn. The battle was nearly finished, and only a few Israeli rounds were being fired downslope.

The Ashbals were advancing cautiously yet casually, laughing and shouting to each other through the blowing sand. They were not unaware that this apparent exhaustion of Israeli ammunition might be yet another ruse, but if it were, then the Israelis were playing it very close. In fact, an advance party of sappers had actually breached the perimeter at the south end near the promontory and had found the trenches deserted.

They moved slowly through the windblown darkness. They could sense the kill now and they were savoring it. They came through the fallen abatis and over the crest. They paused curiously at the trenches, then moved over them. They experienced that strange, subdued exultation that comes with violating the long-forbidden lair of the enemy.

Occasionally, a round or two of Israeli fire sent them scattering and slowed down their movements, but for the most part, except for the steady wind, which no one consciously heard any longer, there was an eerie silence on the hilltop.

In military terms, resistance was light and scattered. The Ashbals were having everything their own way, but patience and caution were still called for. After coming so far, none of the survivors wanted to meet his end within minutes of the final victory. They all wanted to share in the fruits of that victory.

The Ashbals refrained from answering the scattered Israeli fire for fear of drawing return fire on themselves. They signaled quietly to one another in the dark and tried to join up and form a single search line to sweep across the flat terrain. They did not want anyone slipping through their advance. The Ashbals in the center of the evolving line could begin to distinguish the outline of the Concorde whenever there was a break in the dust clouds.

The Israelis moved back slowly and quietly, firing only enough to keep the Ashbals at a distance and slow down their advance. There was no final plan, no last orders from the command post, but the retreat was orderly. About half the Israelis had decided to try to escape down the western slope and half had decided to stay and meet their fate where they stood.

The wounded were moved out of the shepherds' hut and into the Concorde where it was felt they might have a better chance to survive a massacre if they were temporarily out of the way during the worst of it. There were, however, persistent rumors that the wounded were to be killed before the Ashbals could get to them. There seemed to be some confusion on that point.

The Israelis on the west slope fired down toward the Euphrates to try to determine if there were any Ashbals there.

Ahmed Rish spoke on his field radio and ordered his small force there to return the fire. He didn't want the Israelis to run inadvertently into a massacre down there. He wanted them for himself on the hill.

The Ashbals on the river bank fired up the glacis, and everyone's heart sank as they discovered what they really had known all along—there was no escape route. There was a great deal of confusion, and some of the people who had counted on escaping that way began to weep.

Hamadi took a call over the radio from the officer in charge of their rear area, Al-Bakr. "Hamadi here. What? Who is he? Well, find out! Did he complete the call? The Baghdad operator confirms that? What was he saying? Yes, I know you don't speak Hebrew, damn it! I'm sure he speaks Arabic. After you take his first eye out, he will speak it for you. Yes. Keep me informed." He handed the phone back to the operator. He looked at Rish. "Ahmed."

Rish turned to him as they advanced slowly through the dust. "I understood enough of it. It is of no importance."

"But if he got through—"

"No importance!"

Hamadi turned away. More and more he felt that their fate was sealed. They were being hemmed in on all sides by forces over which they had no control. If he were to turn around and walk away into the night, he would live to see the sun come out of Persia. But he could not do that any more than he could kill Rish.

John McClure watched the green tracer rounds arc up from the base of the glacis and pass in front of his foxhole. "Well, we're not going to get down that way." He put his last two cartridges into his Ruger. "Well, Colonel, did you learn how to say 'take me to the American ambassador' yet?"

Richardson carefully put on his blue tunic and buttoned it. "We're going to have to be very careful in the next few minutes, McClure. Our lives may hang on a misunderstood word or gesture."

McClure placed the first loaded chamber to the right of the hammer. "Why'd you do it, Tom?"

Richardson straightened his tie and uselessly brushed some dust from his shoulders.

"I said, why'd you do it?"

Richardson looked at him across the small foxhole. "Do what?"

McClure cocked the pistol, and the cylinder turned left so that the cartridge was under the raised hammer.

Richardson found his cap and poured sand out of it. He looked down the big open muzzle. "Money. I have a weakness for expensive things."

"How much money, Tom?"

"A cool million. American."

McClure gave a low whistle. "Not bad."

"No. Safely deposited in a Swiss bank, I should add. I was supposed to get another mil afterwards, but I don't think so now."

"Maybe they'll still come across, Tom. Those people have lots of it."

"That's right, John. Those people have more petrodollars—our dollars— than they know what to do with. The West is hemorrhaging money and getting transfusions of oil."

"Interesting figure of speech, Tom. But we're not talking about that or about Israel, either. We're talking about you, Tom—a Colonel in the United States Air Force—selling out to a foreign power. That's still against the law—even in America."

Richardson straightened the cap on his head. "Well, I haven't been home in some time so I can't verify that, John. It used to be all right to publish classified Pentagon papers. Are you sure it's still against the law to sell out to a foreign power?"

"Don't temporize, Tom."

"Right. Well, I'll take my punishment when I get home. I wish you'd put that thing down. I'm not running off."

"People talk better when they're looking down a muzzle, Tom." McClure spit out a matchstick. "I thought you liked these people."

"It's not very fashionable to be an open anti-Semite these days."

"I see."

Richardson's face underwent a remarkable change. His mouth hardened and his eyes became narrow slits. "So, I went and had a celebration drink down at the Officers' Club with Israeli flyers who I was training at Travis in 1967. And I commiserated with them in 1973 after the near disaster. The next thing I know, someone puts in a good word for me and I'm posted here. I almost vomited when I got the assignment."

McClure did not respond.

After several long seconds, Richardson looked up at McClure. "Anyway, no one was supposed to get hurt," he said softly.

"But we're not talking about them, Tom. I may not like them either, but I'd hold out under torture before I'd betray them. Know why, Tom? 'Cause that's what Uncle says I got to do. That's what I get paid for . . . Tom."

Richardson ignored the entire exchange. His face softened again. "That reminds me, John," he said brightly. "Can I purchase you? A hundred thou?"

"Sorry."

"Half?"

"Nope." McClure found his last match.

"Plus the whole second mil if I get it?"

McClure seemed not to be paying attention. He chewed on the matchstick and spoke as he chewed. "You said no one was supposed to get hurt. But a lot of people got real hurt, Tom. Real hurt."

"I know. And I *am* sorry about all of this, John. None of this was supposed to happen. Who could have foreseen this? That's my real regret. All these casualties." He stared out into the dust.

"If no one was supposed to get hurt, Tom, why'd you *pick* 02?"

Richardson licked his dry lips. "Well . . . all right . . . *if* there was to be any trouble, then 01 was to be the . . . demonstration. We knew any trouble would come from Avidar. Not Becker."

McClure let out a short laugh. *"Knew?* How can you know these things? Suppose that against all we know about human nature and that kind of thing, Becker had gassed it and Avidar had played your game? That would have left you trying to tread sky at a couple thousand meters, my boy."

"Calculated gamble, John. You see, I gamble with my own life, too. I'm no coward." He continued to stare out into the dust. "I hear voices. Should we go out and surrender or should we sit tight and wait for them to get here?"

"You're awfully goddamned anxious to surrender to these young gerbils or whatever the fuck they call themselves, Tom. Do you think they're going to give you a hero's welcome, Richardson? They're going to murder you, you stupid son-of-a-bitch. And then they're going to murder me to make sure no one knows about you."

Richardson shook his head and smiled. "No, they won't kill me. Rish has a boss, and that boss and I worked out a guarantee for my safety. We foresaw problems with Rish. If I'm killed, then a letter in my safe at the Embassy will be opened, and it names names—Arab terrorist agents in Israel, including my contacts and others. I think ahead, John." He paused. "I won't let them harm you, either."

"Thanks, Tom. You're better than the American ambassador. Well, I wonder if Rish is in control of these guys . . . or in control of himself. I think maybe they're all so worked up they'll shishkebob you. . . . But maybe they won't." He seemed to be thinking. "You know, Tom, American justice *is* very lenient these days. That's why you don't care if I get you home. In most countries they'd hang you up by your left nut in a dungeon and forget about you. In the good old U.S. of A., a general court-martial or a Federal trial will get you ten to twenty—if we can get a conviction at all—and you'll walk in six . . . or less. Walk right to Switzerland. And the U.S. won't turn you over to Israel afterwards because that would raise one hell of a squawk."

"I don't make the rules." Richardson looked wary.

"No, but I do, sometimes. When I'm authorized to." He paused. "Did you say if you died, that would blow the cover on a whole lot of terrorists?"

"Wait! There's no need for any wet stuff, John. There's lots of things to consider here."

"Yes, there are, and if we had more time, then maybe we could work something out. But time is something we don't have."

"Hold it!" Richardson instinctively put his hands out in front of him. "I can guarantee your safety. These people—"

McClure thrust out his big .357 Magnum between Richardson's hands and fired a few inches from his heart. The impact sent Richardson's head snapping back and his officer's hat flew off and was taken up into the wind and sailed westward.

David Becker moved quickly down the ramp. In his hand was a metal can that contained a carbon copy of Miriam Bernstein's short chronicle, wrapped in oil rags and plastic. He picked a spot at the base of the earth ramp and dug a quick hole with a length of aluminum brace. He thought it was a useless exercise, but she seemed so intent on it. She appeared to be brave enough about death and didn't show any signs of hysteria, but she also seemed a little irrational about this chronicle, so he thought it best to go along with her. He placed the can in the hole and covered it quickly. The logbook itself, containing the original of her chronicle, was tucked under a loose floor section in the cabin. There *was* a chance that Israel would repatriate the Concorde someday, and so perhaps a worker would find the log. But as for the buried chronicle he wondered if it would ever be uncovered. Perhaps it would. After all, he had uncovered Pazuzu.

He straightened up and wiped his hands. He could hear two Arabs shouting to each other above the wind. They weren't more than two hundred meters away. An Israeli took a shot at the voices, and one of them let out a sound of pain. No, thought Becker, they will not be in a good mood when they get here. Yet he never once regretted the decision to fight, and he had never heard anyone else say they regretted it, either.

He moved over to the front wheel well and spoke to Peter Kahn, who was still working on the auxiliary power unit. "Come on, Peter. It's a little late for that. Come onto the flight deck."

Kahn took his head out from the well. "What the hell for? Look, when they get here, I want them to see Peter Kahn breaking his ass on this son-of-a-bitching power unit. Maybe they'll feel sorry for me and give me a ticket to Lod."

Becker smiled. "All right. . . . I . . . I'll see you around."

Kahn looked at him. "Right. See you around, Captain."

Becker turned toward the ramp and slowly mounted, oblivious to the rounds whistling through the air around him.

He walked across the wing and passed into the cabin. He had to pick his way through the wounded to reach the flight deck.

Inside the flight deck he took his seat next to Miriam. "It's done."

"Thank you."

There was a long silence. Becker finally spoke. "I always knew I'd die in this thing."

Miriam reached out and touched his arm. "I think you're the bravest man I've ever met."

Becker looked down at the control panel. He felt that he should be doing something, but he had orders from Hausner to stay in the cockpit no matter what happened. He turned the radio up and began scanning the frequencies. He would do that until someone put a bullet in his back. He felt sorry for Miriam—for all the women. He was certain the Ashbals had a special fate reserved for them. "Do you want to stay here? I mean . . ."

"I'm under orders, too." She smiled.

He looked out the windshield. "There are people gathering in the shepherds' hut. I think they are going to—"

"Yes, I see them. I'll stay with you, if you don't mind."

He hesitated, then reached out and took her hand and squeezed it.

The group of Israelis who were intent on suicide gathered in the blood-soaked, fetid shepherds' hut after the wounded had been removed.

Arabs, as a people, did not often take their own lives, but no one in the hut was surprised when Abdel Majid Jabari and Ibrahim Arif entered. It was understood that these two, above everyone else, were far better off dead.

The hut was completely dark, and that made things easier for everyone. There was little talking, only some dangling, whispered half-sentences as someone new entered.

After a few minutes, it became apparent that no one else was coming, but no one present knew what to do next, and a stillness fell over the hut.

In all, there were eleven men and women gathered in three small groups in separate corners. In one group was Joshua Rubin, who was the prime mover behind the suicide pact. Lying on the floor near him was Yigael Tekoah. Tekoah was bitter over the fact that he had not died when the Arab bullets cut him down as he shouted the warning from his outpost. Now he had to face death again. With Rubin and Tekoah were four young Knesset aides, two men and two women, all members of the Masada Defense League.

In another corner was the steward, Yaakov Leiber, and the two stewardesses, Beth Abrams and Rachel Baum. Beth Abrams had spent the last two days caring for the wounded and watching them suffer. She had changed from a happy girl to a despondent one in a very short time. Rachel Baum was lying on the floor between Leiber and Abrams. She, like Tekoah, had refused to be moved to the Concorde with the rest of the wounded. She was in terrible pain from her wounds and didn't see much sense in waiting on the Concorde for more pain. She had nursed Kaplan and had heard him die, and she was frightened enough to take this way out.

Yaakov Leiber had considered his three children before he made his decision, but Rubin had convinced him that no one would survive what the Ashbals had planned for them. Still, he was having second thoughts about it. He could see that the two stewardesses needed him there. He spoke softly to them in the dark. Beth Abrams was crying but Rachel Baum was quiet. He knelt next to her and took her hand. Beth Abrams also knelt and took both their hands.

In the third corner, Abdel Jabari and Ibrahim Arif sat back on their haunches. They had lived alone among these people for over thirty years, and now they were to die alone among them.

Jabari lit his last cigarette and whispered to Arif. "You know, Ibrahim, I always knew that I would not die a natural death."

Arif was pale and shaking. He, too, lit a cigarette in the black room and drew heavily on it. He tried to make a joke. "I may die of a heart attack yet." He drew again on the cigarette. "How are we going to work this?"

"I think there are two or three pistols. They will pass them around."

Arif's hands were shaking so badly he could barely hold the cigarette. He didn't see how he was going to hold a pistol. "I don't think I can do it, Abdel." He stood.

Jabari grabbed his arm and pulled him violently back into the corner. "Don't be an idiot," he hissed. "Did you hear what they did to Moshe Kaplan? Can you conceive of all the things they will do to *you?* Save yourself from that, old friend."

Arif began to cry, and Jabari comforted him. Jabari's only regret was that he had not said good-bye to Miriam. In fact, he had hardly seen her at all in the past two days. He had not wanted to burden her with his company, but now he wished that he had spent more time with her. He suspected that she was in love with Jacob Hausner, and he had been concerned over her choice. Jabari believed that there was an actual place called Heaven, as the Koran so vividly described, and he believed he was going there, but he could not believe that Miriam Bernstein would not be there, too. "Come, Arif. Calm yourself. It's a better world on the other side. Cool gardens, fountains, flowing wine, and virgins. Is that a reason to weep?"

Yigael Tekoah, who did not like Arabs and did not like the idea of having them on the peace mission, called softly across the room. "Abdel. Ibrahim. Courage."

Jabari called back. "We are all right, Yigael. Thank you." Jabari was still troubled that he could not see Miriam before he died. He was tempted to leave the hut and look for her, but he did not want to leave Arif alone. The Ashbals were too close. He wanted to make certain that he cheated Rish of his fun. But this waiting was not good for anyone. Finally, he broke the silence and asked what was the procedure. No one answered.

The sounds of firing got closer, and the Israelis who were still returning fire took up positions not far from the hut. A burst of rounds slammed into the mud wall outside. This acted as a catalyst for action, and Rubin walked into the middle of the hut. He cleared his throat and spoke. "We must act soon." He waited. "If it will be easier, I will do it for you. I have the two pistols."

Jabari stood quickly and walked to the center of the room. "If you please. Quickly."

Rubin did not answer, but raised one pistol and held it up between the two points of light that he knew were Jabari's eyes. He kept the pistol from touching Jabari and fired a single bullet into his forehead.

When the loud report died away the sound of praying could be heard along with soft sobbing.

Rubin was covered with wetness and instinctively wiped it from his face and arms. He began to shake and couldn't trust himself to speak. He didn't know what to do next. His resolve to finish the job for everyone left him, and he turned the pistol and shot himself through the heart. He fell backwards into the corner and landed among the four young aides. One of the girls screamed and fainted. The three others laid him gently on the floor. The two young men recovered the pistols. They whispered hurriedly between themselves, then rose and walked over to the corner where Leiber, Abrams, and Baum were huddled together. They lit cigarette lighters and aimed the pistols, then extinguished the lighters and began squeezing on the triggers. Beth Abrams let out a sob and Leiber threw his body between the two girls and the men. One of the men fired but didn't appear to hit anything. The other young man lit his lighter again to fix his aim.

Rabbi Levin burst into the hut and saw all he wanted to see before the cigarette lighter went out. He grabbed the two young men by the collars and threw them to the floor. He screamed and swore as he delivered kicks and punches in the dark. "Did you think you could outwit me? I found you! I knew what you were up to! Out! Out! Get out!" He ran around the small hut in a frenzy, kicking and punching blindly in the dark. He tripped several times over the bodies of Uri Rubin and Abdel Jabari. He repeatedly kicked both bodies until he realized they were dead. "Out! Out! Get out of here! How dare you! How dare you do this! Take the wounded into the plane! Out!"

As soon as he had entered, his presence broke the strange spell that had hung over the room, and everyone who could move quickly ran out.

Rabbi Levin was left standing alone in the center of the hut, his body shaking and tears streaming down his face. He had done what he had to do, but he was in no way certain that he was right and they were wrong. He wondered how he was going to get the two bodies buried in the short time remaining. He wondered who they were.

The Foreign Minister, Ariel Weizman, assembled a small, lightly armed group on the west side of the perimeter near McClure's foxhole. Weizman saw Richardson lying at the bottom of the hole, a layer of dust already covering his blue uniform, but he did not have time to speculate on the meaning of that or on McClure's absence.

Ariel Weizman was determined to lead his small group down the steep glacis. His plan was to drop quickly down the slope and vault into the river the way Dobkin had done. Without wounded, it might be possible. He wished that Miriam Bernstein would reconsider and join him, but she was very much under Hausner's influence and would not budge from the Concorde. He lined up his group of men and women, all of whom were wearing the orange life jackets from the Concorde, at the edge of the steep drop. He crouched in a runner's stance and instructed them to do the same. "When I count to three, we go. Steady. Wait for my count, now."

Few orders were coming from the command post. The runners who were still operating brought only bad news to Hausner and Burg and carried away no commands, only suggestions and encouragement.

Hausner and Burg had agreed that there came a time when the best orders were no orders, and so they let the civilian instincts for individual action and survival take over.

Hausner turned to Burg. "Would you want to take complete charge now, Isaac? I'm ready to step down."

Burg smiled wryly and shook his head. "No, thank you."

"Do you believe there was anything that I could have done that I did not do?"

Burg thought a moment. "No. Frankly, you did an excellent job. You might have been a touch more diplomatic . . . maybe not." He listened to the approaching gunfire. "Our people were marvelous, too."

"Yes. They were."

The last two of Hausner's men who were in action, Marcus and Alpern, came up to the command post. Marcus gave a half salute. "What should we do now, boss?"

Hausner didn't know what to tell him. He felt obligated to say something, but couldn't think of an order to give or an expression of gratitude to pass on. "Just take as many of the bastards with you as possible." He paused. "And thank you. You were the backbone and the heart of this defense. You did a hell of a job here. No one who survives will forget that."

The two men nodded and moved off into the darkness.

Burg put his hand on Hausner's shoulder. "I think you'd better get to the Concorde before you get cut off. You promised, and she's waiting for you. I'll stay here and try to do what I can."

Hausner shook his head. "No. I don't want to see what they're going to do to her any more than she wants to see what they're going to do to me. She knows that and she's not expecting me."

"I see. Are you going to—you know."

"No. I'm not the type. I have a few things I want to say to Ahmed Rish before I go."

Burg nodded. A crooked smile passed across his face. "We did do one hell of a job, didn't we?"

"Yes, we sure as hell. . . . Listen!"

"What?"

"Did you hear—?"

"Yes. Yes!"

Hausner stared upward. He thought he saw a flash of light. He could hear the distant shrill whining of jet engines. He yelled to Burg. "They found us, Isaac. They found us, damn it!"

Burg began gesticulating wildly. "Here! We're here!" Hausner forced a smile. "They're too late to help us but not too late to blow away Rish and his gang." He turned to Burg. "My faith in Israeli military intelligence is restored."

Burg was so excited he could hardly comprehend what Hausner was telling him. Then he understood. The air force had arrived—Israeli or Iraqi—but they were too late. Burg calmed down and his body seemed to sag. He nodded. "I hope Dobkin made it," was all he could think to say.

Hausner and Burg stared upward and saw the fiery trail of a missile cut across the sky.

33

The first thing Laskov did was the last thing he had promised Becker he would do. He fixed the Lear on his radar and engaged it with the long-range Phoenix missile at 160 kilometers.

The Lear pilot yawned as he looked sleepily out the windshield. The automatic pilot had kept the craft in a continuous left bank for longer than he cared to remember, and he thought he was developing vertigo. Below, the ground was obscured by the dust, but up here everything was very clear and moonlit. The dawn was creeping out of Persia, and it looked as if it would be a good day to fly. In a while he might have to fly to their camp in the Shamiyah Desert, refuel quickly, and come back—unless those fools on the ground could get it over with. He yawned again.

He glanced out of his left window and noticed a flame streaking across the sky. A second later he realized with astonishment that the light was coming toward him. He tapped the sleeping copilot on the shoulder, and they both watched the thing change course and follow them as they moved in their circle. The pilot let out a long shrill scream when he realized what it was. The Phoenix flamed up at them and seemed to hang outside their cockpit. The Israeli armorers had painted a likeness of the beautiful phoenix on its terrible namesake. The great bird seemed to smile in the first rays of sunlight, and an eye on the warhead appeared to wink at the two pilots in that split second before it consumed itself and its prey in an awful orange ball of flame. Unlike its namesake, however, there was no chance that it would rise up from its own ashes and begin a new life.

Laskov had guided his squadron in with radar. Their computers had enabled the automatic pilots to hug the terrain during the entire night flight, and they had flown under Jordanian and Iraqi radar. They had very little time to familiarize themselves with the terrain, but each pilot knew what he lacked from the briefing could be made up in skill and desire. The Mach 2 flight across Jordan and western Iraq, a thousand kilometers' distance, had taken less than forty-five minutes. Except for Laskov's craft, which carried two Phoenix missiles, the fighters carried only air-to-surface ordnance.

As soon as the Lear disappeared from his radar, Laskov spoke into his mouthpiece. "Concorde 02, this is Gabriel 32. Can you hear me?"

Miriam Bernstein heard the explosion overhead as she sat alone in the flight deck and couldn't imagine what it was, but didn't really care, either.

"Concorde 02, this is Gabriel. Do you hear me, Concorde?"

She thought she heard a faraway voice. It sounded vaguely familiar.

"Concorde 02, Concorde 02, do you *hear* me?"

She looked down at the radio as though she had never seen one before.

"Concorde 02, this is Gabriel 32. Can you hear me? Come in, please."

She fumbled with the volume dials and the microphone but really didn't understand the procedure. She yelled at the console. "Teddy! Teddy! I hear you!" She dropped the microphone in frustration and rushed from the flight deck. She yelled into the darkened cabin filled with nurses and wounded. "They're here! The air force! The air force!" The cabin erupted with noise, and she stood there for a second, transfixed. From behind her she could hear Teddy Laskov's voice as if from a dream. "Concorde 02, this is Gabriel 32. Can you hear me? Can you hear me?" She rushed out onto the wing and shouted. "David! Captain Becker!"

Becker had gone under the craft again to try to talk Kahn into coming up on the flight deck, or failing that, to say a proper good-bye. He had heard the sound of the rocket and the explosion and had known immediately what it was. He was already halfway up the earth ramp when Miriam called him. He pushed past her, tore into the cabin, and fought his way through the crowded aisle into the flight deck.

"Concorde 02, this is Gabriel 32. Concorde 02. Concorde 02. Acknowledge, please."

Becker grabbed the microphone with a trembling hand and squeezed the button as his other hand worked the dials. He squeezed so hard on the talk button that he was afraid the plastic instrument would cave in. "Loud and clear, Gabriel! Loud and clear! Position critical! Critical! Arabs inside perimeter! Can you read me, Gabriel?"

Laskov almost came out of his seat. "Loud and clear! Loud and clear! Understand situation critical, 02. Hold on. Hold on. Charlie-one-three-zero on the way with commandos. Can you hold?"

Becker's voice was quavering. "Yes. No. I don't know. Can you give support?"

"I'm a little far out yet, and I have to pull off speed to come in on you. I'll be on station in . . . four minutes. Can you mark your position with illumination?"

"Yes! I'll turn on my landing lights."

"Roger. How about JP-4?"

"Yes. Yes. We have Molotov cocktails. Will mark boundaries of our positions with fire. Also, look for tracers, Gabriel. Heavy incoming theirs—light outgoing ours."

"Roger that."

Several lightly wounded men and women were jammed into the flight deck behind Becker. Hausner's man, Jaffe, wounded but ambulatory, pushed his way out of the flight deck, through the cabin and out onto the wing. He stood on the wing and yelled out into the storm. "The air force is coming! The air force is coming! Mark our positions with kerosene! Where's Hausner? Where's Burg? Hold on! They're coming!"

Esther Aronson ran past Jaffe and jumped down off the wing. She stumbled, fell, and rose to her feet again. She raced west across the hilltop to try to stop the Foreign Minister and his group from fleeing down the west slope.

There was a lot of shouting on the hilltop and within a few minutes the Ashbals, as well as the Israelis, knew what was happening.

Rish and Hamadi spurred their remaining troops on. They converged on the Concorde as the Israelis fell back toward it. The last few Molotov cocktails were ignited and thrown. The Israelis began using the last reserves of their ammunition that they had hoarded for the final face-to-face confrontations, and their rate of fire picked up.

The Ashbals, who had suffered so many dead and wounded already, had been moving ahead reluctantly. Each new Ashbal casualty brought general cursing and wailing. They had been caught in an understandable conflict between wanting to go in and finish the job, and lying back and hoping it would resolve itself without their having to become casualties and miss out on the inevitable rape and massacre. Now the arrival of the Israeli Air Force had suddenly altered the situation. They had to capture at least some Israelis alive, and they had to do it fast if they were to have hostages to use as bargaining points.

They fired at the Concorde when the landing lights went on, but Rish did not want a fuel explosion to kill the Israelis, and he ordered the firing on the Concorde to be directed only at the flight deck. In the first illumination of the early dawn light, the outline of the long craft could be discerned whenever the wind dropped.

After the explosion overhead, a few pieces of the Lear had fallen to the ground, and the Ashbals knew they had not much more time. Ironically, the safest place to be when the jets came was as close to the Israelis as possible. Preferably right in the Concorde with them as hostages. It was going to be a close race. A matter of minutes either way would decide it.

The Foreign Minister led his group back to the Concorde. They carried the body of Colonel Thomas Richardson, United States Air Force. They had looked for McClure but could not find him. The Foreign Minister spoke with Rabbi Levin, who reported what had happened in the hut. They both decided that the only proper course of action was to place the remaining men and women from the hut under restraint and the seven unwounded ones, including Leiber, were ordered into the rear baggage compartment.

Uri Rubin's body was carried out of the hut by the two men of the Masada Defense League and placed in a trench that had been dug for that purpose.

Ibrahim Arif carried the body of Abdel Jabari cradled in his arms like a child. He staggered under the weight and wove around with tears blinding his eyes. He refused to let anyone bury the body.

Miriam Bernstein crouched on the wing and saw the body of her friend in

Arif's arms. Tears welled up in her eyes. She stood watching as the men argued over the fate of the corpse. "Arif," she shouted.

The big man looked up. "Arif, I loved him as you loved him. But he is dead and he must be put in the ground. Both our religions make that imperative. Please understand. Time is running out. Please do as they say."

Arif looked up and tried to speak but could not get his voice under control. Finally, he took a deep breath and called out. "He loved you—" He turned quickly and ran as best he could under the weight. He reached the slit trench and looked at Uri Rubin lying at the bottom of it. He looked into Jabari's open eyes. Well, good-bye, old friend. He gently lowered his friend atop the body of Uri Rubin and pushed some dirt over them both. Just then, two Israelis with rifles ran up and squeezed into the narrow trench. They felt, then saw the bodies under their feet but did not want to give up the only cover for some distance around because of it. They began firing out into the dust. One of them turned to Arif. "If you don't have a weapon, you'd better fall back. They're closing in."

Arif nodded and turned his steps back toward the Concorde. Life, he reflected, was made up of equal parts of idiocy, fear, irony, and pain. He envied Abdel his cool gardens, flowing wine, and virgins.

Laskov's copilot, Danny Lavon, spotted the kerosene fires first. The small points of light formed a more or less oblong shape around the points of the Concorde's landing lights. Streams of green tracer rounds streaked in from east to west toward the Concorde. A very few tracer rounds moved the opposite way. From time to time, a particularly large billow of dust would obscure the light sources below. From his altitude, Lavon could see the sun above the peaks of the Zagros Mountains, but the direct rays had not yet touched Babylon. The refracted rays would have brought on first light by now, but the sand and dust looked too thick to be penetrated. He called Laskov on the intercom. "Fires at one o'clock, skipper. At the small bend in the river. We're almost overhead."

"Roger. I see it." Laskov ordered the squadron to make a close dry run at the target.

The twelve F-14's came down in tandem. They swooped out of the sky like the big birds of prey that they were. They came screaming in at low level out of the western desert and banked sharply right. Laskov came in first. He let his computer make the first run to make sure he didn't lead his squadron into an obscured piece of terrain. He cleared the hilltop by less than twenty meters and the Concorde by even less than that. The thunder of the twelve F-14's as they came in, one after the other, was deafening and frightening. The already unsettled dust rose up in huge clouds, and the earth beneath the Concorde shook.

Each fighter came down in the same fashion, its computer and sensing devices following the terrain of the ground, keeping the awesome jets close to the earth. Instinctively, everyone on the hill threw themselves down or ducked as the big fighters blotted out all visual and auditory senses.

After the pass, Laskov ordered half of his squadron south to stand by and be prepared to protect the C-130's and the intended landing strips with fire if necessary. He doubted if there were any Ashbals there, but that was the procedure.

Hausner knelt on one knee and helped Burg up. "They almost took the pipe out of your mouth, Isaac. All right, this is where we part company, my friend. You go back and take charge of the aircraft and the people on it. I'm going to take charge of the delaying action."

"If I thought I had the time to argue with you, I would. Good-bye, Jacob. Good luck." He slapped Hausner on the back and ran off.

Hausner could hear the Ashbals approaching his command post knoll from the east. There were also noises coming from the south as the Ashbal line swung around in an arc. Hausner took a .22 pistol, knelt, and waited.

Out of the dust came Marcus and Alpern. Hausner called out to them, and they ran over to him. "Give me one AK-47 and all of your ammunition. I'll be able to delay them from the cover of this knoll. You get back to the Concorde on the double and help organize a defense there. Use the armor mesh and make the earth ramp and the hut your strongpoints. We should have dug secondary defenses around the craft, but there's no use thinking about that now. All right, you'll take your orders from Burg. No arguing. Do it."

They passed him one rifle and two half-filled magazines. Hausner pulled the bent standard from the ground with the T-shirt that showed the Tel Aviv waterfront and passed it to Alpern. "A souvenir, Sam. Always wear it when you're telling your grandchildren this story. They'll think you're a real moron."

Alpern smiled and took the banner. Both men moved off with only a half wave as a good-bye.

Hausner got himself into position behind the knoll. He fired a few tentative rounds and drew a few rounds of return fire.

Hausner was as happy to see Laskov and his F-14's as he had been to see anything else in his life. But the reality of the situation was that it was too late. Jaffe had reported to him about the C-130's and the commandos on the way, but even if they landed right then, it would be too late. They would have to land on the mud flats, unload, inflate rafts, and cross the Euphrates. If, instead, they landed on the road and their rollout ended where the Concorde had gone off the road, then they would still be almost a kilometer away. And as yet he didn't hear the heavy droning of the four-engine propeller craft.

Paratroopers might have saved them, but that was suicidal in this darkness and dust; the terrain was terrible, and half of them would land in the river. No, it was a good show of force, but it didn't change much. In fact, it made it worse. Before, the Ashbals were intent on massacre, and that at least would have ended the whole affair. Now they would have to take hostages in order to save themselves. After they got hostages, the whole affair would just be beginning. Hausner hoped that Laskov would foresee this and know when they were finished and would not hesitate to napalm the entire hill. If nothing else worthwhile came out of this, at least they would get Rish—and Hamadi, who Hausner thought might be a far more cunning adversary in the future.

In his mind, Hausner made up a long good-bye to Miriam. He was torn between going back to the Concorde to deliver it or staying there, where at least his emotions, if nothing else, were safe.

From his position under the front nose wheel, Peter Kahn had listened to everything that was happening as he worked on the APU. He heard the shouting and the hurried footsteps running toward the aircraft. He saw some people without weapons climbing the earth ramp up to the Concorde's wing. In the distance he could see others kneeling and firing at muzzle flashes. Firing holes had been knocked into the walls of the mud hut. A few men and women took up shooting positions around the earth ramp, and one girl took cover behind his little earth platform. The end was coming one way or the other, but still he continued to labor on the APU.

Suddenly, he rolled off his earth mound under the wheel well, stepped over the prone girl with the rifle, and wiped his hands and face. He walked quickly to the ramp and climbed it, along with a few other fatigued and tattered-looking people. On the wing, Miriam Bernstein took his arm. "Have you seen Jacob Hausner?"

"No, Mrs. Bernstein. I've been under the front wheel. Actually, I'm looking for him myself." He could see that some of the armor mesh that had been on the perimeter was being taken into the aircraft. It was being pressed against the inside of the hull and windows. He liked to see resourcefulness and good thinking right up until the last minute. It was a damned good try if nothing else. "Look, Mrs. Bernstein, you'd better get inside the craft. We're drawing fire here." He disengaged himself from her and walked over to Burg, who was standing at the farthest point of the starboard wing tip. A half-dozen men and women were lying prone on the wing near him and firing out into the darkness.

It had become apparent to Burg and others that the Ashbals did not want to fire at the wings and take a chance on blowing up the aircraft and their potential hostages. The wings had become a relatively safe perch from which to deliver fire.

Kahn tapped Burg on the shoulder. "Excuse me."

Burg spun around. "Oh. Hello, Kahn. Nice try with the APU, son."

"Right, sir. That's what I want to talk to you . . . or Mr. Hausner . . . about."

"Talk to me, son. Hausner's still out there." He pointed.

"Yes, sir. Well, I think I've fixed it."

"Fixed . . . ?" Burg suddenly burst out with an involuntary laugh. "What? Who gives a damn, son? Get inside the aircraft and keep your head down."

Kahn stood fast. "I don't think you understand, sir. They're not going to reach us in time. We can—"

A loud explosion shook them off their feet. An F-14 streaked by overhead. Another F-14 came in with its 20mm cannon blazing. A third came in off the Euphrates and released air-to-surface rockets over the top of the Concorde. The rockets left a fiery trail overhead and crashed out by the old trenches. Another F-14 released a laser-guided SMART bomb which crashed into the west slope and blew apart the millennia-old crust of earth, sending ancient brick flying into the air and tons of earth careening down the steep glacis, over the bank, and into the river, taking a few Ashbals with it.

The F-14's went through their repertory. The earth shook and quaked, and shock waves filled the air as tons of ordnance detonated on the old citadel that, for over a thousand years, had guarded the northern approaches to Babylon, and for over two thousand years had guarded nothing at all.

The earth split and heaved and threw up sand and clay hundreds of meters into the air. Orange billows burned up the dust and man-made shock waves collided with the ancient *Sherji*. Rockets' red trails slashed across the sky like the shooting stars that had so fascinated the ancient Babylonian astrologers. The F-14's put on a show the likes of which Babylon had never seen. But it was just that. A show. Laskov did not dare deliver any of the ordnance close enough to be effective. Still, it kept heads down and slowed the pace of the ground action. The idea was to buy time. Time for the commandos to arrive. Time.

Burg lay where he had fallen. "What?" he shouted over the explosions. "What?"

"I think we can start the APU and turn over the engines," shouted Kahn.

"So what? What the hell difference does that make? We don't want to run the air conditioning, Kahn."

"We can get the hell out of here! That's so what!"

"Are you crazy?"

A rocket fell short and plowed into the earth near the tail and blew up, sending clods of earth and shrapnel into the Concorde.

Kahn picked up his head. "No, I'm not. We can move this big bird."

"Move it where?"

"Who gives a damn where? Just move it the hell out of *here*. Any place."

Burg looked behind him. He hoped to see Hausner coming up the earth ramp with that by now famous mixture of nonchalance and menace. But only Miriam Bernstein was there, looking out into the fiery night. He wanted to shout to her, but she would not have heard. He turned back to Kahn. "Tell the captain to try to start his engines."

Kahn jumped up before Burg could add any restrictions to his order and dashed for the emergency door. He barreled into the aircraft and fought his way to the flight deck. "David!"

Becker was speaking to Laskov on the radio and waved to Kahn to be quiet. "David!"

Becker had taken an American Air Force course in calling and adjusting air strikes, and it was proving very profitable at the moment. He could not see much from the flight deck, but he was trying to make himself useful. And, he had to admit, he was having a pretty good time. "All right, Gabriel. If you have any SMART bombs left, now's the time to bring them in. Make one run along the river bank at the base of the slope in case we missed anyone down there. We may still try to make a run for it that way, and I want the bank cleared. Put another to my right front, about two hundred meters out. I'm going to start blinking my taxi lights now."

"Roger the river, 02, but negative outside your window. Too close."

Kahn was shaking Becker by the shoulder. He was shouting in English, their native tongue. "Didn't you hear me, goddamn it? The fucking APU is fixed." He liked the American idiom and couldn't reproduce it in Hebrew. "Get this big-assed mother-fucking bird fired up and let's haul ass out of this shithole!"

Becker was speechless for only a split second. "Fixed?"

"Fixed. Fixed." Maybe, thought Kahn.

Becker's fingers went to the APU ignition switch. He didn't believe there was enough battery charge left to turn the APU over, but it didn't hurt to try. He hit the switch and looked at the instruments. He tried to listen above the wind and explosions that poured into the cockpit through the shattered plexiglas. The APU was definitely turning over, but it wouldn't ignite. Becker turned off the aircraft lights. Did the batteries have enough remaining power to keep motorizing the APU until the fuel ignited? Without a word between them, Becker and Kahn watched the APU temperature gauge. Their eyes searched for any hint of motion from the needle that would indicate the beginnings of a successful start. The white needle continued to sit rigidly on the bottom mark of the temperature gauge. Becker tried the familiar "Just this once, God. Just this once." But nothing happened.

34

The two huge C-130 cargo craft came in low over the western desert. They had left Israel well before the F-14's, but at a top speed of only 585 kilometers per hour, the flight had taken nearly two hours.

The King of Jordan had quickly given permission to use Jordan's northern air corridor to the Iraq border. It was not until the Baghdad government was presented with the *fait accompli* of the F-14's already in Iraq and the C-130's approaching their border that they reluctantly agreed to let the unarmed cargo craft in. The alternative was to refuse the C-130's entry and to order the F-14's out, which would have necessitated an embarrassing explanation of how they had reached so deep into Iraq in the first place.

After a lot of ominous pronouncements had traveled over the circuitous telephone lines, Baghdad had agreed with Jerusalem that it was a joint operation, and the Israeli Prime Minister and the Iraqi President had prepared a joint news release to that effect. To give credibility to that news release, Baghdad sent a small river unit of the Iraqi Army from Hashimiyah up the Euphrates and ordered the Hillah garrison to stand by, although both governments knew that the unreliable troops were in fact not standing by but standing down. It was felt that many of the troops were in the pay of Ahmed Rish, and their Iraqi officers kept a very close watch over them. Both governments knew that the river unit from Hashimiyah would not make it to Babylon in time to participate in the operation, but the gesture of support was important.

Other Iraqi Army officers from Hillah, plus civil servants and personnel from the small Hillah airstrip, went by motor vehicle north toward Babylon. At a spot somewhat south of where the Concorde had touched down, they secured the Hillah-Baghdad road and set out flares to mark it in the dust-swept dawn. Another contingent crossed the Euphrates by motor launch to mark off a landing strip with flares on the mud flats. Neither action was absolutely necessary to land the C-130's, but it cut down considerably on the risks involved in the procedure.

The Iraqis had made their contribution and the Baghdad government settled back to watch the outcome. An Israeli military disaster wouldn't be viewed as a tragedy in some Iraqi circles, while a successful operation would obviously be the result of the Iraqi participation. Baghdad could not lose. They might come in for a lot of censure from Palestinian groups and perhaps some Arab governments, but the times were such that many Arab governments would officially applaud the move on humanitarian grounds, and Baghdad would reap some goodwill from the West—goodwill that could be turned into something more concrete at a later date. On balance, it seemed the thing to do—especially since Israel had already done so much that was irreversible.

Captain Ishmael Bloch and Lieutenant Ephraim Herzel, piloting the first of the two C-130's, saw the flares along the Hillah road and banked left as they pulled off more power. Three of the F-14's assigned to cover the landings shot past their windshield and dove in along the intended landing approach.

The big cargo craft dropped in very quickly as it was designed to do in a combat situation.

In the cabin, fifty Israeli commandos tightened their straps and braced themselves for the jolt that came with an assault landing. The tie-downs on the two jeeps, one mounted with a 106mm recoilless rifle and the other with a dual .50 caliber machine gun, were checked and tightened.

The doctors and nurses again checked the fastenings on their mobile operating unit and their surgical supplies.

Captain Bloch cut the power again and watched the speed bleed away on his indicator. He turned to Lieutenant Herzel. "When we flipped a coin for the road or the mud flat and I won and picked the road, why didn't you say something?" The giant aircraft seemed to float a few meters above the windswept road. Bloch tried to keep the nearly powerless craft lined up between the flares, but the strong crosswind pushed the plane to the left of the road, and when Bloch tried to slip it back, it yawed badly.

Herzel kept his eyes on the instruments. "I thought you picked the road because you *knew* it was more challenging."

Bloch thought for a moment that he would have to pull up and come around again, but the wind dropped for a few seconds and he lined the craft up over the road and came down hard.

The underinflated tires hit the crumbling blacktop and sent tremendous sections of it flying off at all angles. The wind pushed the high-profile aircraft left, and as Bloch compensated, the craft fishtailed, causing the C-130 literally to eat up the road as it taxied north, leaving a sand trail in the place of what had been a paved road. "My wife is a challenge. My girlfriend is a challenge. Why would I want another challenge?" He reversed the engines and stood on the brakes. The noise of the screaming engines and wheels was deafening, and the men and women inside the cabin covered their ears.

Herzel looked back out of the side window as the aircraft made a small turn to follow the road. He shouted. "Leave some blacktop so we can take off, Izzy."

"Take off, my ass. We're taxiing into Baghdad after this is over."

Outside, by the illumination of their landing lights and the flares, they could see a few Iraqi vehicles sitting off the side of the road at long intervals. A few of the men in them waved as the C-130 lumbered by, and Bloch and Herzel waved back. "Are the natives friendly?" asked Herzel.

"As long as we have fifty commandos back there, they will be very friendly."

The big craft began rolling to a stop at almost the same spot where the Concorde had first touched down. Bloch could see by his landing lights where the Concorde had begun chewing up the road. The C-130 was built for that type of thing. The Concorde was built for wide expanses of smooth runway. He admired the damned fool of a pilot who brought it in. Bloch looked up. He could see the high mounds of Babylon in the distance, silhouetted against the brightening sky. "Babylon."

Herzel looked out the windshield. "Babylon . . . Babylon."

The rear gate was down before the aircraft came to a complete halt, and the commandos began jumping out and deploying on both sides of the road. A group of Iraqi officers and government workers eyed them curiously from a cluster of khaki-painted vehicles on a small hillock. The commandos were jittery, and so were the Iraqis. Both sides spent some time waving and making other friendly gestures.

The two jeeps rolled down the ramp and squeezed by either side of the C-130, keeping to the roadbed as they passed under the huge wings. One squad

of commandos formed a perimeter to secure the aircraft. The medical personnel on board began preparing for the casualties.

Three rifle squads, each commanded by a lieutenant, with the overall command under Major Seth Arnon, fanned out on either side of the road, jogging
to keep abreast of the jeeps. They headed toward their first objectives—the
Ishtar Gate area and the guest house and museum.

Captain Bloch watched them from his high vantage point in the cockpit of
the C-130. "It's no fun being an infantryman."

Lieutenant Herzel looked up from his landing checklist. "They slept all the
way here, and they'll sleep all the way back. Feel sorry for your copilot for a
change."

Captain Bloch looked from the cockpit of the C-130 off to where the Northern Citadel was erupting in orange, yellow, red, and white flames. The sounds
of the thunder rolled down from Babylon onto the roadway. "It's those poor
bastards up there I feel sorry for. You know, Eph, when they took off Friday
afternoon, I said to myself, lucky sons-of-bitches, going to New York all expenses paid for as long as it takes to bring home a scrap of paper that says
peace."

Herzel glanced up and looked out the windshield at the light flashes on the
far mound. "I guess it's no fun being on a peace mission, either."

Captain Baruch Geis and Lieutenant Yosef Stern could not spot the Iraqis'
flares on the wide expanse of mud flats, nor could the three F-14's that were
assigned to them. Geis considered waiting for the sun to poke over the distant
mountain, but as he monitored David Becker's voice speaking to General Laskov and as he watched the flaming consequences of their conversations, he
knew that there was not much time left. In fact they were probably too late
already, but he was determined to complete his portion of the mission.

Captain Geis wanted to get as close to the fighting as possible without coming into range of small arms fire from the citadel mound. He gave up looking
for the flares and picked an area barely a kilometer south of the fighting—a
spot that was marked Ummah on his map. Strange, thought Geis, Arabic was
so like Hebrew. Ummah. Community. He radioed to the lead pilot of the three
F-14's that were with him. "I want to land so that my rollout will end somewhere near the spot marked Ummah. Can you give me light?"

The fighter pilot, Lieutenant Herman Shafran, radioed back.

"Roger. Flare on the way, over."

The F-14 came in on a west-east axis and released a 750,000 candlepower
parachute flare. The sky and earth were transformed with a brilliant, eerie
glow.

Geis pointed the nose of the aircraft directly into the hard-blowing *Sherji* and
began pulling off power. Ahead he saw the outlines of Ummah under the
artificial light. He placed the aircraft to the left of the village and put down his
flaps. The wind added tremendous lift to the aircraft and it seemed to hover
over the mud flats.

Lieutenant Stern looked over his right shoulder out his side window. There
appeared to be cooking fires lit among the houses of Ummah. The *Sherji* carried the flare west, and it swung like a pendulum under its sailing parachute,
casting distorting shadows across the earth. The flare sailed past the cockpit of
the aircraft, and Geis and Stern looked away as it cast a blinding light in the
flight deck. The F-14 released another flare over the river, and it too began to
float westward toward them.

In the cabin, the fifty commandos listened to the wind blow and the engines whine. In place of the jeeps were a dozen motorized rubber rafts. Everyone in the cabin had a sense of the aircraft hanging, hovering, making no headway at all. Muscles tensed, and as the flare lit up the windows of the cabin, sweat could be seen glistening on brows and upper lips.

The doctors and nurses spoke to each other in whispers. Each C-130 was prepared to handle twenty-five casualties. But what if there were nearly that many casualties among the peace mission alone? There were bound to be some casualties among the commandos. What if there were wounded prisoners?

Captain Geis was finally able to push the airplane firmly down and hold it down. Thousands of cubic meters of mud flew up and covered the aircraft as it charged through the quagmire and headed toward the village. The parachute flare overhead began to burn out and the land became darker.

A few of the mud houses of Ummah loomed up out of the weak light. Beyond Ummah, Geis could see the Euphrates. He reversed his engines and stood on his brakes. The big craft came to a halt and rocked backwards less than a hundred meters from the nearest hut.

The back gate opened, and three squads of commandos charged out of the aircraft, formed a line, and advanced on the village. A fourth squad fanned out a hundred meters and surrounded the C-130. They immediately began digging foxholes in the mud.

Major Samuel Bartok fired his Uzi into the air, but no one fired back. To the north, across the river, Bartok could hear the sounds of the fight, and he could see flashes of light. He glanced down at his map. If they met no resistance in this village and if they were able to navigate upriver to the hill where the fight was taking place, it would still take them about twenty minutes to get into position to bring effective fire on the Arabs. But even then he couldn't guarantee that he could keep them from advancing on the Concorde if they were to fight a rearguard action against his commandos. How many Palestinians were there? According to the pilot of the Concorde, there were not more than three dozen left out of over a hundred and fifty. That sounded like an incredible feat of arms for a peace mission. Major Bartok smiled grimly. No, that wasn't possible. He'd have to be prepared for any number.

The commandos' line became concave as it bent around the village. To the north, the first Israeli squad reached the Euphrates. The first man actually to stand on the bank of the river, Private Irving Feld, urinated in it.

A few minutes later, the third squad also radioed that they had reached the Euphrates south of the village.

The second squad, with Major Bartok in the lead, advanced up the middle toward the first huts.

An old man appeared in the small crooked street and walked slowly toward them. He looked over the heads of the commandos at the high-tailed aircraft on the barren mud flats, its blue Star of David catching the first rays of the sun. He raised his right hand. *"Shalom alekhem."*

"Salaam," answered Major Bartok in Arabic.

"Shalom," said the old man, with emphasis.

Major Bartok was only slightly surprised. He had been told that there might be a Jewish community somewhere near Babylon. If he had had the time, he would have spoken to the old man, but he had not one minute to waste. He waved. *"Alekhem shalom."* By the number of mud huts, he estimated that there couldn't be more than fifty people living in the village. He shouted over his shoulder to the radio operator as he led the squad through the village. "Tell Jerusalem we have found a Jewish village." He looked at his map. "Ummah.

Ask them if we can take them home. Even if we don't reach the Concorde in time, we can at least accomplish this."

Captain Geis in the C-130 took the message from the radio operator and radioed Jerusalem.

The Prime Minister listened as Captain Geis relayed the message. He nodded slowly to himself. Jews of Babylon. But they were Iraqi citizens. Kidnapping Iraqi citizens was hardly a friendly gesture. And if he authorized it over the radio, Baghdad would hear and the rest of the operation might be jeopardized. Still, the Law of Return provided that any Jew who wished to come to Israel could do so. Sometimes they needed a little help getting there. There were precedents for this. He looked around at the full room. Some of the men and women nodded. Some shook their heads. Many faces revealed the agonizing dilemma they all felt. But it was his decision. There was no time for debate. He spoke into the microphone. "Do you have room?"

Captain Geis smiled. "How could we not have room for them?"

"Well . . . well, if they want to go . . . to come home, then let them come. Out." He settled back into his chair. History in the making. Disaster in the making, perhaps. He had gone so far already that it was easy to ignore the consequences of any further perilous decisions. Once you took that initial plunge, everything else was easier. He asked for another cup of coffee.

35

Laskov watched as the sun spread its first rays over the mountains and the flatlands below. He caught a glimpse of Babylon as he flew by and wondered what it was like down there. He had the same sense of wanting to land as he had had when he flew over the pyramids of Egypt. But his fate was to observe the world from the aerie of his leather seat, with the smell of hydraulic oil in his nostrils. He had spent too much of his life above this teeming earth, and he was looking forward to mixing more with its inhabitants on the ground after this.

He took transmissions from the aircraft protecting the two C-130's. "Roger. Change missions with me now and unload some of your ordnance on the hill. Be careful." He came in low for a last strafing run. The sky was bright, but on the ground the dust storm was still keeping visibility down to a few hundred meters or less.

He pressed a button on his flight column, and the 20mm cannon ripped a path from east to west starting from the outer city wall up to the east slope. He released the button quickly as the rounds passed through the deserted Israeli trenches. There was still not enough visibility to bring effective fire on the advancing Arabs without a risk of hitting his own people.

The Concorde suddenly loomed up in front of him and he pulled back on the stick and cleared it. He saw, in that split second, a woman on the delta wing, and he imagined that it was Miriam. She seemed to be calling for someone.

Laskov wanted very much to ask Becker about Miriam. He ached with the unasked question. But there were hundreds of other people in Israel who wanted to know about their loved ones, also. He'd have to wait and find out along with everyone else.

He banked sharply as he passed over the Euphrates and headed south with his six F-14's to exchange assignments with the other half of his squadron. They would have a chance to lighten up on their load now. He looked at his fuel gauges. The low-level, top-speed flight had burned too much. The combat maneuvers were burning too much. They were cutting it close for the trip home. He hit the intercom button. "Isn't there a gas station down this street?"

"Right," said Danny Lavon. "Turn left here, go a thousand klicks to the light and stop at Lod. All major credit cards accepted."

Laskov smiled. He had alerted Lavon to keep an eye on the gauges without saying, "Keep an eye on the gauges." Why did pilots talk in circumlocution and bad jokes? Even the Red Air Force had practiced that idiocy. The Americans were masters at it. Invented it, probably. It must be universal now.

As he passed over the C-130 on the mud flats he saw the commandos launching their rubber rafts off the quay of a small mud village. He looked at his watch. It had been seven minutes since the C-130 came to a stop. Not bad time. He radioed Captain Geis. "Gabriel 32 overhead now. Nice landing. I still don't see those flares. I'll keep an eye open for foul play."

"Roger, 32. Nice performance in Babylon. How are they doing on the ground?"

"Touch and go. Out."

One of the F-14's peeled off and circled the C-130. Two others took up a pattern around the rafts.

Laskov was on the east bank of the river now. He passed over the C-130 on the Hillah road. Great gusts of wind buffeted the big cargo craft, and Laskov could see that the pilot had left the engines running in order to control it on the ground.

Laskov picked out the guest house and museum and the towers of the Ishtar Gate. His impulse was to put his last SMART bomb into the guest house, but Jerusalem had vetoed that. They had the idea that Dobkin might still be alive in there. Laskov doubted that very much. There was also some speculation based on one of Becker's transmissions, and Dobkin's report, that there might also be a female prisoner alive there. He doubted that, too. But they would find out soon enough. He could see the line of commandos and the jeeps approaching the area. Laskov knew there would be a fight there, and if the commandos were held up for more than ten minutes and couldn't bypass the area, then he had permission to take out the guest house and the museum, if necessary. If there were Israeli prisoners in there, he knew they would understand. He knew he would if the situation were reversed. He wouldn't like it but he would understand. So would Dobkin. Dobkin was a soldier.

David Becker hit the auxiliary power unit switch again. It began to turn over —more slowly this time. The batteries were weakening rapidly—but still no ignition and temperature rise. He looked over at Kahn in the copilot's seat. "Sorry, Peter."

A bullet passed into the flight deck and they both ducked. Becker could smell kerosene and he knew that some of the fuel tanks or the feeder lines had been hit.

"Try again," said Kahn. "Try again, David. We've nothing to lose."

Becker shouted over the noise. "Everything to lose. Can't you smell the kerosene?"

"I don't smell anything but hot lead. Hit it!"

"I need the last of the batteries to transmit!"

"For God's sake, try again!"

Becker wasn't used to Kahn being anything but polite and laconic, and he was surprised. He looked down at the APU switch, then up out of the shattered windshield. Three or four Ashbals were moving across the hilltop less than a hundred meters away. Someone, it looked like Marcus, took a single shot at them with his AK-47, and they fell to the ground, scratching for cover and concealment in the flat terrain. The first light was trying to penetrate the sandstorm, and visibility was somewhat better now. Becker could actually see shadowy figures moving in the distance through the grey and dusty dawn. He wondered who they were.

An F-14 came in so low that the Concorde shook, and tremendous clouds of sand pelted the craft and wrapped it in a shroud of dust. Without any conscious thought, Becker hit the APU switch. He looked slowly at Kahn. "Am I hearing things?"

Kahn heard nothing but felt it in the seat of his pants. He shouted above the noise of an exploding rocket. "We have ignition! I fixed the fucking thing with a wrench and a screw driver! I fixed it! Fuck Hausner!"

It flashed through Becker's mind that Kahn didn't care what happened next. He had fixed it, and that was the end of it. It was Becker's show now. He let the APU run for a minute, all the while waiting for it to ignite the thick kerosene fumes and blow them all into next week. But the wind was apparently carrying the fumes away. He relaxed a bit. The emergency power had gone off as the generator charged the batteries, and the primary system took over again. The cabin lights became brighter, and gauges and instrument lights came alive in the flight deck.

Becker wiped his face, then ran his hands over the front of his shirt. He hurried through the starting sequence for the outboard starboard engine. It ignited as easily as if it had just come out of the El Al maintenance shop. He glanced over at Kahn, and Kahn gave him a thumbs-up. Becker looked down at the fuel gauges. The indicators weren't even bouncing. They just lay in the red, hard against the zero mark. The single engine was burning tremendous quantities of the nonexistent fuel. Becker couldn't understand it. It had to have something to do with a malfunctioning sensor. Somewhere in this craft, he was certain, one of the thirteen fuel tanks was sloshing with kerosene. He hit the switch for the outboard port engine; it began turning over quickly, hesitating to ignite for only a few seconds. Then, after one puff of white smoke from its exhaust, it began spooling up normally. He hit the inboard starboard switch and the engine balked. He played with it and coaxed it.

Kahn got up and stood in front of the flight engineer's panels where he could be more help. He scanned the gauges and noted the multiple systems malfunctions. Concorde 02 would never fly again, but with any luck it would make its last taxi. "Come on, you old buzzard!"

The inboard starboard engine ignited, but sounded bad. Becker hit the inboard port engine switch. Nothing happened. He hit it again. Absolutely nothing. Like turning an ignition key in a car without a battery.

Kahn called out. "There's no power going to that engine. The wires must be severed. Forget it."

"Right." Becker locked the brakes and ran up the three functioning engines. The sand that they were ingesting might kill all three of them in a matter of seconds, or they might run out of fuel any moment, but Becker didn't want to release the brakes prematurely—not until he coaxed every last gram of thrust out of them. He shouted to Kahn, "Get everyone inside the aircraft!"

Kahn threw open the door of the flight deck. In the cabin, the wounded lay in the places where the seats had been removed, or sat up if they were able and held sections of the nylon armor mesh against the hull. The people who were caring for them crouched as they moved around the cabin. A few men and women with rifles pointed them through shattered portholes and waited for the expected final Ashbal assault.

Kahn ran out of the emergency door and onto the wing. The huge delta was throbbing with the pulse of the two starboard engines. At least a dozen men and women were kneeling or lying on the huge aluminum surface and firing out into the dust. A few people on the ground were using the desperate infantryman's trick of dry firing their empty rifles and simulating a recoil in order to keep the approaching Ashbals ducking. A few cassette tape recorders were still turning out the sounds of firing, but that and the dry firing were the only ruses still being used. Kahn saw Burg where he had left him on the wing tip and rushed toward him, shouting as he ran. "We're going to move it! Get everyone on the aircraft!"

Burg waved in acknowledgement. He had been trying to keep a tally of everyone. The Foreign Minister's group was accounted for, and the survivors of the group that had tried to commit suicide were safely under guard in the baggage compartment. All the wounded were on board, and he was fairly certain that everyone else was either on the wing, under the craft, or firing from the shepherds' hut. Everyone except Hausner and John McClure, neither of whom had been seen for some time. Burg shouted from the wing but he needn't have bothered. Everyone, including the Ashbals, knew what was happening by now.

The last of the armed men and women on the ground came up the earth ramp. Some climbed over the fuselage and took up positions on the port wing. Others lay prone on the edges of the starboard wing, and two men positioned themselves on top of the fuselage. Alpern came running up the earth ramp carrying the lifeless body of Marcus. The five other men and women of the delaying force followed close behind. Burg looked quickly at his list of names again. It seemed correct. The commandos would exhume the buried dead. They would also find Kaplan's body, he was sure, and perhaps Deborah Gideon and Ben Dobkin as well. Everyone except Hausner and McClure seemed to be accounted for, yet he couldn't be certain. He made a few quick notes in the small book, removed his shoe, stuffed the book into it, and threw the shoe away from the aircraft. If the Concorde burned, at least the commandos would find his notes when they combed the hill, and they would have an idea of how to begin accounting for the dead.

Burg ran over to Alpern who was pulling Marcus's body through the emergency door. "Hausner?"

Alpern shrugged as he drew Marcus inside the craft. "You know he's not coming."

Burg nodded. He caught Miriam Bernstein's eye. She had heard Alpern.

She ran toward the edge of the wing and started to jump. Burg caught her arm and pulled her back. She kicked and flailed her arms out at him, but he held her firm. She shouted at him to let her go, but he dragged her, with the help of another woman, toward the emergency door.

The Ashbals knew that the Israeli commandos were closing in on their rear. They were at the limits of their bravery, and for many the limits had already been exceeded. They were so fatigued that they were numb and barely aware of their surroundings, and every step forward became torturous. Their mouths, nostrils, and ears were clogged with dust, and their eyes were blinded by the sand. They began to think not of the Israelis in front of them but of the Israelis behind them. Each man and woman began plotting an escape route for himself in the event they could not capture hostages before the commandos overtook them.

But still they went on, driven not only by the knowledge that they had to lay hands on the Israelis in order to live, but also by the shouts and threats of Ahmed Rish and Salem Hamadi. And the Ashbals were still a dangerous force, even in their present state. They were like tigers and tigresses—for if nothing else, they were no longer cubs—who, though wounded, must still be respected and given a wide berth.

Rish caught two young girls, sisters, who were moving in the wrong direction. They pleaded that they were confused by the gunfire that was coming from behind them and disoriented by fatigue, dust, and darkness. Rish seized the opportunity to stiffen discipline. He forced the two girls to kneel and shot each in the back of the head with his pistol.

For a moment, Hamadi wondered if that was to be the proverbial straw that would break the camel's back. But the executions had the effect that Rish had anticipated. The small group, not more than two dozen now, moved more quickly toward the thundering Concorde. He marveled at how much tyranny men and women would put up with before they would rebel. There was a lesson there for him if ever again he should be in a position to lead men.

Hausner had been surprised at first to hear the Concorde's engines exploding into life. Then he remembered Kahn's untiring determination, and smiled. He doubted if Becker could produce enough thrust to move the injured aircraft with its long pointed nose buried in the dirt and its main tires flattened. Still, it was a splendid attempt. Even if the commandos moved fast, it could not be nearly fast enough. It might make a big difference if the Concorde could meet them on the east slope. That should surprise everyone, including, Hausner suspected, David Becker. Kahn always knew he would fix it, and he always knew he would taxi out of there.

Hausner knelt, fired, and moved back again and again. Some of the fire from the Concorde had come close to him, but that could not be helped. Now he noticed that the Israeli fire was very erratic, and as he listened it tapered off to almost nothing. Suddenly, the engines whined and he knew Becker was about to release his brakes. He glanced back over his shoulder and saw the red glow of the engines. He turned back, and out of the dust a line of Ashbals came running and stumbling toward him. He could hear Ahmed Rish's voice above the F-14's, above the AK-47's, and above the big engines. "Faster! Faster! This is your last effort! It is now or it is not at all! Come, my tiger cubs, follow me for the kill!"

Hausner understood why men and women followed Rish. The pitch and tone of the voice was familiar, and if the language had been German instead of Arabic he would have had no trouble placing it. Some men were born with command presence, and when their minds were disturbed, the result was deadly.

Hausner fell back to where he knew the burial trench was. He found it and lowered himself into it. He felt the bodies under his feet and wondered who had come to an end in this way. He crouched down and waited for Ahmed Rish in the dark.

* * *

Lieutenant Joshua Giddel's commando squad stayed behind at the small museum as the other two squads, with one jeep, bypassed the guest house and moved up the Processional Way.

Giddel's ten men lined up, five on each side of the jeep with the 106mm recoilless rifle mounted on it. They began moving across the flat dust field that separated the museum from the guest house.

With Lieutenant Giddel in the jeep were a driver, a two-man gun crew, and Dr. Al-Thanni, the museum curator. Lieutenant Giddel had discovered him in his office in the small museum. Dr. Al-Thanni had been checking his spring inventory lists as though nothing were amiss outside his window. It reminded Giddel of the story of Archimedes, who was working on a mathematics problem when the besieging Romans entered his city. The Greek inventor had refused to let external events break his train of thought, and an infuriated Roman soldier had killed him. And so, thought Giddel, Archimedes became an instant hero and martyr to intellectuals, and soldiers got another black mark. Giddel had overcome the urge that he knew the Roman soldier had succumbed to and settled for sweeping the inventory lists onto the floor.

Now the curator was in Giddel's jeep, bouncing over the few hundred meters that separated Giddel from his next objective. He spoke to Al-Thanni above the sound of the engine. "How many Ashbals would you estimate are in the guest house?"

Dr. Al-Thanni had a suite in the house, but had taken to sleeping on a cot in the museum. He still took his meals in the guest house and used the sanitary facilities. "They don't confide in me, young man." He straightened his glasses.

Giddel looked at him meaningfully.

"However, I would estimate that there are at least fifty with varying degrees of wounds and about ten or more orderlies with one doctor and a few sentries and duty officers."

"Is there a basement in the building?"

"No."

"All concrete?"

"Yes."

"Any guests in there? Guest house staff?"

"No. The season has not begun."

"Any other civilians or other noncombatants in there?"

"Sometimes a few village girls. You know."

"Is there a radio? Do they speak with the Ashbals in the field?"

"Yes. A radio in the lobby. At the clerk's counter where the duty man sits."

"Do the wounded have their weapons?"

"Yes."

"Any heavy weapons? Machine guns? Rocket launchers? Mortars? Hand grenades?"

"I did not see anything of that sort."

"Where would they keep a prisoner?"

"They had a prisoner—a girl—in the manager's office."

"An Israeli?" Giddel knew of the prisoner from General Dobkin's report to Jerusalem.

"I believe so."

"How about the general?" Giddel had already told him all he knew of General Dobkin, but he could see that Al-Thanni had been very skeptical of this information and probably believed that the Israelis were playing on his friendship with General Dobkin to use him. "But you did not see the general?"

"I told you, no."

"You heard nothing about the general?"

"I would tell you."

"Where else might they keep a prisoner?"

"I don't know. Not the rooms. They are filled with wounded. Not the kitchen. The dining hall is used for meals. There is a recreation room, but this is also used. I think the manager's office is the most likely. I have not been in the guest house since the time you say you received a call from him, so perhaps he is there."

Giddel glanced up at the guest house. He could make out its outline and saw some lights in the windows. "Where is the manager's office located?"

"To the left of the lobby as you walk in. Immediately to the left of the front doors. The windows face the front."

"Who is the senior man there?"

"A man named Al-Bakr."

"Is he reasonable?"

Dr. Al-Thanni allowed himself a small laugh.

"I mean, do you think he would negotiate rather than have his wounded caught in a firefight?"

"Ask him."

Lieutenant Giddel looked out at the squat building. Incredibly, no one seemed to notice his movement. The jeep maintained a steady 5 KPH, and the commandos jogged along with it. The guest house was more clearly visible now, and Giddel put his starlight field glasses to his eyes. He could see struck tents lying in front of the building. There were a few eucalyptus trees around the house, and they partly blocked the views from the verandas. Some vehicles were parked off to the left of the house. He could see lights in a few of the windows and smoke coming out of the chimneys. Breakfast. A few men sat on the verandas on each floor. No one seemed to see them yet. He turned to Al-Thanni. "But do you think he would listen to *reason?* Do you have any influence with him?"

"Me?" He shook his head. "I am—or was—their prisoner. Make no mistake about that. I am not a part of these people."

Giddel turned his attention back to the guest house.

Dr. Al-Thanni cautiously put his hand on the lieutenant's shoulder. "Young man, if I thought that my friend, General Dobkin, was in there and was alive, I would do anything in my power to get him out of there, but nothing I say can make a difference with these people. I have seen what they did to the other captive. Take my word for it—if General Dobkin was their prisoner, he is dead or he should be shot as a mercy. Don't waste time or men on this thing."

Lieutenant Giddel focused his field glasses. He could see several men looking intently over the railing of the side verandas. They were in white robes, and he could make out bandages on some of them. They were looking toward the Northern Citadel where the sound and light show had attracted their attention. They didn't seem to notice him, but then he saw a few men staring intently in his direction from the top front veranda. He spoke to Dr. Al-Thanni as he watched. "Thank you, Doctor. Please jump off the jeep. Unless you want to come in with us."

"No, thank you. Good luck." He jumped off the side and rolled away from the moving jeep.

Lieutenant Giddel saw several men run into the building. "Increase speed." The jeep moved faster, the commandos went from a jog to a run. "Load a concrete-piercing shell and prepare to fire the gun." The 106mm gun crew loaded and adjusted their aim.

Suddenly, two long streams of green tracer rounds shot out of the guest house and passed overhead.

Lieutenant Giddel gave up any hope of negotiating now.

Another gun joined in, then another. Green tracers arched over the jeep, then dropped lower as the Ashbals began to get the range.

The jeep driver handed Lieutenant Giddel the radiophone. "It's air cover."

Lieutenant Giddel took the phone. "East bank two-six, here."

"Roger. This is Gabriel 32. Can I make that house disappear for you guys?"

"Negative, Gabriel. Possible friendlies inside. We'll do it the hard way."

"Roger. If you change your mind, give us a yell."

"Roger. Thanks." Giddel turned to his gun crew. "Keep away from the left front ground floor. Commence firing."

The gun crew fired a .50 caliber spotter round from the aiming rifle attached to the 106mm barrel. The .50 caliber tracer hit the building on the second story above the front doors, and the crew immediately fired the main round after it. The 106mm round streaked across the open plain and hit the building a meter from the spotter round. There was a deafening explosion, and the concrete shattered. Flames, smoke, and debris erupted from nearby windows. All the lights in the building went out. Lieutenant Giddel told the driver to increase his speed again. The commandos began firing their M-79 grenade launchers, Uzi submachine guns, and M-16 automatic rifles from the hip as they advanced on the run. The 106mm crew reloaded and fired again. The round smashed through the front doors and exploded in the lobby. Two commandos stopped running and set up their M-60 light machine gun. They began raking the building with long bursts of 7.62mm rounds.

The jeep and the commandos were within two hundred meters of the building. The Ashbal firing had stopped immediately after the first 106mm round hit. A third 106mm round entered a shuttered window to the right of the front doors and exploded inside. The right half of the building began to sag. Flames and smoke poured out of the windows, and the front verandas collapsed on top of each other. Men and women in white robes began jumping out of the windows and fleeing toward the vehicles. The M-60 machine gun shifted its fires and began pumping incendiary rounds into the vehicles. One after the other exploded and the men and women running toward them fled out into the darkness.

Lieutenant Giddel had little stomach for firing on a place where wounded were kept, but it was also a place, according to Dr. Al-Thanni and General Dobkin, where prisoners were kept, and it was a headquarters as well. In addition, they had been fired at from there. The Ashbals had broken the cardinal rule about mixing medical and military facilities, and now they were paying for it.

At fifty meters the 106mm recoilless rifle fired again through the front door, and again the round exploded in the lobby, this time with a CS tear gas canister.

The façade was a mass of bullet scars, and the wooden louvers were splintered and burning. Smoke billowed from every window, and the smell of cordite was heavy. Screams could be heard from inside the building.

The jeep rolled over the struck tents, up the front steps, over the rubble of the verandas, and into the lobby. The driver turned his headlights on. Each of the commandos picked a window and dove through.

Inside the ruined guest house, dead and dying lay among heaps of rubble and plaster. Part of the floor above the lobby had fallen through, and burning beds and patients lay in a heap in the corner. The Israelis donned gas masks and threw canisters of CS into the doors that came off the lobby. Two commandos fired their grenade launchers with CS rounds up the stairwell and through the hole in the ceiling. Two other commandos ran out the back door onto the terrace in time to see about a dozen men and women in robes and in uniform disappear into the grey dawn. They let them go.

In the lobby, the sounds of screaming and moaning could be heard from overhead. Men and women, in shock, wearing burned and bloodstained night clothes, came marching down the stairs with their hands on their heads, coughing, blinded, and vomiting from the gas.

Lieutenant Giddel burst into the manager's office. It was undamaged except for the expected cracks in the plaster. Calcimine dust lay over everything and some of it still sifted down from the ceiling. Giddel spotted the girl first, and as he ran toward her he stumbled over a body on the floor. It was a man lying face down with his hands and legs tied. He recognized General Dobkin from his bulk and height. He turned him over carefully. There was blood smeared over his face and one eye had been gouged out. It was hanging by the optic nerve, resting on his cheek. Lieutenant Giddel had to steady himself and turned away for a second. He took a deep breath and looked back. Apparently his torturer had been in the middle of his work when the first 106mm round hit. He still couldn't tell if the man was alive or not until he saw blood-tinted bubbles forming around his broken nose and puffed lips.

The squad medic ran in and went straight to the girl. "She's alive. In shock." He turned and knelt down beside Dobkin. He examined him quickly. "The General's fading." He looked at his bloody, tattered clothes. "God knows what his injuries are. Let's get them both in the jeep and back to the C-130."

"Right." Giddel called out the window to the jeep driver. "Instruct C-130 to prepare to receive two casualties. Shock and hemorrhaging. Have them radio Jerusalem. We've got our first two Babylonian captives . . . alive. . . ." He turned to the medic. "But I hope to hell the others are in better shape than this." He looked at the miserable men and women being marched outside. He called to the driver. "And report that we have some Babylonians, too."

36

The two surviving Ashbals at the base of the glacis saw the Israeli force coming upriver in their rubber rafts. There were at least thirty Israelis, but the clear target was irresistable to trained infantrymen. The two Ashbals took cover behind an earth mound and fired on the exposed craft with automatic weapons. Water splashed up all around the rafts. Three rubber rafts were immediately hit and several men wounded. The Israelis quickly returned the fire, but they were in the worst tactical position possible. Major Bartok ordered the craft to beach on the east bank.

The Israeli commandos came ashore and began moving in single file along the flood bank. They were still a half-kilometer from the place where the steep glacis started, and Major Bartok doubted if he could dislodge the Ashbals, who were still firing at them, in less than ten minutes. To save time he would have to cut inland and bypass the Ashbals, then head up the narrow-backed southern approach to the old citadel, traveling atop what was once the river wall. If everything went well, he could be in sight of the Concorde in fifteen minutes. As Bartok ran along with his long file of men, he took the radiophone from his operator. He called Major Arnon. "East Bank 6, this is West Bank 6. How are you making out there, Yoni?"

Major Arnon sounded out of breath, and Bartok could tell he was also running. Arnon spoke in short, choppy sentences. "Passed the outer wall of city —Found one friendly KIA—Mutilated—Thirteen enemy KIA—Apparent ambush—Heading direction of east slope—Half a klick to top—Wait." He paused and stopped running. "I can hear something that sounds like jet engines. Is it possible that they started the Concorde?"

"Wait one." Bartok switched frequencies and monitored Becker and Laskov, speaking on the El Al frequency. He switched back. "Roger. They say the Concorde is started. I don't know what the hell they plan, but keep your head up."

"Roger. Out."

Laskov had been called back on station over the Concorde by one of his pilots. He spoke angrily into his mouthpiece. "What do you think you're doing, 02?"

Becker had put his uniform cap on, and it felt good. He spoke into his microphone. "We're getting the hell out of here!"

"Don't do it! You'll kill everyone!"

"I just asked my marvelous computer about that, and it said, 'Do whatever the hell you want, stupid. Just leave me out of it.' So I'm taking its advice. Sorry, Gabriel."

"You'll kill everyone, damn you!" Laskov almost lost control of himself. He lowered his voice. "David . . . listen—" Becker broke squelch and cut him off. Laskov released his talk button.

Becker's voice came on. "We're all dead anyway. Can't you understand that? You're too late to help us. Too late."

"No. I absolutely—" The squelch cut him off again, and again he released his talk button.

Becker spoke softly. "Sorry, General. You did a marvelous job. Really. Wish us poor sons-of-bitches luck. Out."

"Luck. Out."

David Becker released the brakes and waited. Nothing. He watched the instruments for signs of an engine explosion, but outside of that there was nothing he could do. It was out of his hands. The aircraft seemed to strain forward and it began vibrating ominously. He shot a look at Kahn over his shoulder.

Kahn looked up from the flight engineer's console. "Don't shut it down, David. Just wait."

Becker nodded. One way or the other the aircraft was going to fall apart. Even if they were able to taxi it to the east slope by the sheer thrust of the three remaining engines, the slide down would probably cause it to break up on the way or it would crash when it hit the base of the slope. Even the stationary vibrations now wracking the abused aircraft could cause structural failure before they went even one centimeter. The worst—or maybe the best—that could happen was that the leaking fuel would ignite and blow them all up. In a way he hoped that the fuel would either ignite or run out, and he could not understand why it didn't do either.

With a strange calm, he looked out the windshield. He could actually see men and women firing at the Concorde. Bullets passed into the flight deck and a sharp electrical crackling sound told him that the instrument console was hit.

The Concorde did not move.

Kahn tried to read a message in the flight engineer's instruments, but there was too much damage, and he couldn't tell if it was to the instruments or to the systems.

The two outboard engines were producing near maximum thrust, but the starboard inboard was operating at barely half its capacity. Kahn tried everything he could think of to get more power out of it. If only they could overcome that initial inertia. *Objects at rest tend to stay at rest.* Once the aircraft began to move, it should be all right. *Objects in motion tend to stay in motion.* Come on, you son-of-a-bitch. Kahn suddenly called to Becker. "Pull off power on the outboard port."

Becker understood. If the aircraft wouldn't go forward, then maybe they could swivel it to the left. He pulled back on the port engine throttle. The two starboard engines whined. Slowly, almost imperceptibly at first, the right wing began moving forward.

The Concorde began turning left, its nose moving through the dust in a sweeping motion. The right wing skimmed the top of the shepherds' hut, taking off the roof as it came around. The right main carriage assembly hit the earth ramp. The aircraft nearly came to a halt, but the forward motion continued, and the carriage cleaved through the corner of the ramp.

With the initial inertia overcome, Becker now opened up the left port engine. The aircraft moved forward slightly but continued to slide left as it moved. Instinctively, Becker began operating the rudder pedals and nose wheel to steer the aircraft, but then remembered with some chagrin that he had neither tail nor nose wheel.

Kahn saw him and called out. "Nice trick if you can do it, David."

Becker forced a smile. "I'll have to give it its head and see where it takes us. Listen, if I don't get a chance later let me congratulate you now." He glanced back over his shoulder. "No matter what—" Kahn's body was all the way forward in his chair, his face against the instrument panel in front of him. His white shirt was soaked with blood. "Oh, God!"

Jacob Hausner ran along close behind the slow, lumbering Concorde, firing short bursts all around him as he moved, hidden in the dust blown up by the engines. He had not been able to get to Rish from the latrine trench. Rish was no fool. Rish traveled in the middle of a diamond-shaped formation of seven or eight men, and even if Hausner had let him go by, he would not have been able to come up behind him. He could have taken out Hamadi if he had wanted to, but he didn't want to throw away his life on a second-stringer. He had been forced to retreat to the next place of cover and concealment, the shepherds' hut, but that almost cost him his life when they nearly surrounded it. Now he was running again, covering the Concorde and looking for a place to slip into until he could get close enough to Ahmed Rish to fill his guts with hot, searing lead.

As the Concorde gathered momentum and bounced over the terrain, a dozen men and women fired wildly from the trailing edge of the wings. Alpern clung to the mangled braces of the tail and fired down at the Ashbals through the tremendous billows of dust the aircraft left in its wake.

Several of the people on the wing shouted to Hausner to hurry before the plane picked up speed, but Hausner seemed not to hear. They tied shirts together and hung them over the trailing edge for him to grab, but he did not seem interested.

In the rear baggage compartment, the men and women who had tried to commit suicide were still bunched together, more for convenience than as a punishment. Miriam Bernstein had been placed, nearly hysterical, among them. Beth Abrams was trying to calm her and was holding on to her arm as the tail bounced and shook.

Ibrahim Arif was pressed against the gaping opening of the split pressure bulkhead. As he watched the ground sliding by below the highpitched tail, he saw a man running through the billows of dust behind the aircraft. He yelled to the young interpreter, Ezekiel Rabbath, who was assigned to watch them. Rabbath forced his way to the bulkhead, put his head through, and stuck his AK-47 out and pointed it so that it wouldn't hit any of the aluminum braces. As he was about to fire, he recognized the tattered, shoeless, dust-covered figure. "It's Jacob Hausner!"

Miriam Bernstein pushed her way through the closely packed bodies and squeezed by Arif and Rabbath. With incredible speed, she began crawling through the open bulkhead before anyone could react. Arif caught one ankle and Rabbath the other. She almost kicked free, but Yaakov Leiber got hold of her leg, and between the three of them they began pulling her in. Beth Abrams fell on them from behind and screamed, "Let her go! Let her go if she wants to go!"

There was a great deal of confusion as Beth Abrams was pulled away.

Miriam got hold of two cross braces out in the tail section that had supported the number eleven trim tank and held on to them. She shouted and kicked wildly as they held her legs. They could not pull her in, but neither could she get out.

Miriam shouted herself hoarse, and tears ran down her face. "Jacob! Jacob!"

The Concorde began to gather speed, and it pulled away from Hausner. Hausner fell as he turned to fire at an approaching figure. He lay in the dust and looked back at the blue and white Concorde disappearing through the wind-blown sand. He gave a parting wave to the aircraft. Miriam Bernstein believed that he saw her, and she waved back. "Jacob! Jacob!" She sobbed his name over and over again.

Every time Becker tried to control the aircraft by pulling off power on one engine or another, the aircraft slowed threateningly, and he had to open the throttles again. The result was that the Concorde half-spun and half-sideslipped to the left. Becker wondered if the main carriage wheel would snap off, moving like that. Every few seconds, he would glance over his shoulder at Kahn and look for some sign of life, but he saw none.

Occasionally he could see an Arab appear briefly out of the dust, then disappear again from his view as the aircraft spun slowly while it moved generally westward away from the slope that he wanted to reach.

Becker knew that a few more people had been hit in the cabin. He had the feeling that by the time the aircraft came to rest, it might be full of corpses. He had a mental picture of blood running from holes in the aluminum skin. Then, for some reason, he had a picture of everyone staggering down an earth ramp from the main boarding door. Everyone was covered with blood and their eyes were black and hollow. They were . . . brain-damaged. He felt the sweat run down his collar, and his hands shook. He had to get the damned thing over the edge someplace. Dying at the bottom of the mound was better than this.

He saw the edge of the west slope through his left windshield. What would happen, he wondered, if he went down that steep slope into the river? Would the aircraft break up in the fall? Would it sink quickly in the river and drown everyone? There was only one sure way of finding out. He took a chance and chopped the power off the port engine. The starboard wing swung around quickly; then he gave the port engine full power and at the same time chopped the power off the damaged inboard starboard. Both wings had equal thrust now, and the maneuver had pointed the Concorde directly toward the edge of the slope. The craft's momentum carried it forward. Both running engines sounded as though they had all the sand they could digest and they began making sickening, rattling noises.

The Concorde approached the edge of the glacis a few meters from where McClure and Richardson had dug their position. Becker prayed that a wheel strut wouldn't get stuck in a foxhole as the Concorde moved over the old positions. To his right he saw the small mound that was Moses Hess's resting place. The place that he had chosen for him, overlooking the Euphrates. Becker shouted back into the cabin. "Everybody inside! Crash positions! Pillows! On the floor! Heads down!"

The men and women on the wings had already begun moving inside the craft. In the cabin everyone faced rearward and sat or lay on the floor. Pillows and blankets were stuffed against the hull and bulkheads. Everyone tried to hold the wounded as best they could.

The long, damaged nose of the Concorde poked over the edge of the glacis. Becker imagined the aircraft must have looked like some creature from a fantasy—or nightmare—kneeling at the edge of a precipice, its wings—or cape —spread out, ready to spring up and jump into the sky.

Becker opened up the malfunctioning engine for an extra measure of thrust. The Concorde seemed to hang as though it were unable to make the decision— and perhaps reflected the ambivalence of its pilot. Becker looked out over the nose and watched the wide Euphrates below. The grey dawn light brought out highlights on the river's restless, wind-driven ripples.

Becker looked down at his console. His instruments showed the outboard starboard engine spooling down, and, in fact, he heard it dying. Whether it was out of fuel or filled with sand was irrelevant—it was dying. Then the outboard port flamed out suddenly and the inboard starboard, never operating at more than half power, began to cough black smoke. The Concorde hung halfway out into space.

Spurred on by the half-crazed shouts of Ahmed Rish, the remaining Ashbals doggedly continued their pursuit of the aircraft as it thrashed across the ground like a great wounded bird. There was only some light fire from the aircraft, coming from one or two portholes. There was, however, a man braced in the mangled tail section. He had not gone inside with everyone else and he was delivering accurate fire from his perch. Rish ordered all guns turned on him, and tracer rounds streaked through the half-light, up toward the high-raised tail. The man seemed to have taken many hits, but he continued to fire.

The Ashbals called on their last reserves of energy, and in a burst of speed, led by Salem Hamadi, they closed in on the tottering aircraft. Ahmed Rish ran behind them, alternately firing his rifle into the dust at their feet and using the butt to strike their backs and buttocks. Led by a near madman and pursued by a certified one, fewer than twenty wretched young men and women ran, stumbled, and crawled forward.

To anyone who was familiar with the myth, it must have looked like the scene of Charon, the ferryman of Hell, beating the damned souls with an oar as he took them across the River Styx. And it had all started so well, too. A proud fighting unit of over one hundred fifty men and women, reduced now to fewer than two dozen terrified, humiliated, and miserable human beings who looked and sounded more like jackals than tiger cubs.

Rish shot a man who fell and could not get up fast enough. Behind him, as he pursued the Concorde, he heard the firing of the approaching Israeli commandos as they pursued *him*.

Laskov watched from overhead. He wanted to try to take out the Ashbals who were intermittently visible now, but they were clinging too close to the Concorde and he was unable to get an accurate fix on the approaching commandos. The stall speed of the F-14 was too high to make it very effective for close-in support. It was because of their speed and range that the F-14's had been chosen for this mission. To try to put a bomb or rocket accurately on the racetrack-sized hilltop, in the dawn light, with high buffeting winds and obscuring dust, traveling at a minimum speed of 195 kilometers per hour, was out of the question with so many friendlies in the area. He considered asking the commandos to pull back, but in the final analysis, it was they who had to effect the rescue. Again, he settled for buzzing the area at low levels and setting up strafing patterns that would not come near the Concorde on the west side of the hill or the commandos approaching from the south and east. He led his six Tomcats in on a last strafing run that exhausted the remainder of their 200mm cannon rounds.

Hausner lay in a shallow depression, covered with dust, and listened to the small cannon rounds exploding around him. The Ashbals had not seen him fall in the dust and had run past him.

As he took cover he heard the whining down of the Concorde's engines as they died one by one. He looked up cautiously. The Concorde hung precariously at the edge of the slope. In the weak light of dawn he could see the fire dying in its huge engines. The Ashbals were closing in on the aircraft. From the east he could hear the random firing of the commandos as they worked their way up the slope. He got up on one knee and checked the mechanism on his AK-47. As he reloaded, he looked around him and realized that he was kneeling in the same hole where he and Miriam had made love. He ran his hand through the warm dust that had been their bed.

He looked up again at the Concorde as he finished reloading. His plan had been to kill Rish although he knew he himself would die whether he succeeded or not. But now it appeared that he would survive and that everyone else would die, because even if Rish did not reach them and massacre them or take them hostage, then this foolhardy attempt to slide into the river would surely kill them. All Hausner had to do now was to wait until the commandos reached him and he could go home. But he couldn't do that and he knew it. He rose to his feet and made off in the direction of the Concorde.

Becker couldn't decide if he wanted to go over the side or not. The longer he looked at the river, the farther away it seemed. But what were his options?

Burg had come into the flight deck and was strapping Kahn into the flight engineer's seat. Kahn was breathing, but a sucking chest wound was making that increasingly more difficult. Burg looked around, found a map, and stuffed it into the foaming hole. The sucking sounds quieted.

Becker watched for a second, then yelled to Burg. "Get a dozen people in the forward galley!"

Burg nodded and ran out the cockpit door and barked an order.

A dozen unwounded and ambulatory wounded got up quickly and crowded into the small forward galley. The Concorde tipped further and slid forward. Burg ran into the flight deck and strapped himself into the copilot's chair.

Salem Hamadi, well in the lead of the straggling Ashbals, ran at an angle alongside the leading edge of the upturned starboard wing until he reached the point where it came within two meters of the edge of the glacis. A second before he would have run off the side, Hamadi slung his rifle over his shoulder and leaped into the air.

Hamadi landed flat on the wing with his arms and legs spread out. At that moment, the ground that the underside of the flight deck was resting on gave way. The Concorde pitched further down and slid a few meters forward. Hamadi scrambled upward and tried to find some purchase on the sleek supersonic wing. His foot found a tear that had been made by a burst of bullets, and he vaulted toward the open emergency door and grabbed the door frame. No one seemed to be looking out the windows or the door. He pulled himself toward the opening.

More ground gave way under the aircraft, and the Concorde seemed to spring over the crumbling edge. It careened down the steep gracis toward the Euphrates. It looked very graceful to the fighter pilots in the air.

Salem Hamadi saw through the open door that everyone was in the crash position with their heads between their legs and pillows and blankets in front of their faces. He dropped into the dark cabin and let go of the door frame. The steeply pitched aircraft propelled him toward the flight deck door and he smashed into it. He put his back to the steel door and waited for the crash. Hamadi could not imagine what kind of fate awaited him—drowning, shooting, capture, maiming—but he knew he did not want to be around Ahmed Rish when the end came.

Becker saw the line of burnt castor oil bushes come up very fast. He saw two badly wounded Ashbals running off in opposite directions along the river bank. He felt the main wheel assembly collapse, and the Concorde slid faster on its belly. The nose cleaved through the high bank and the belly slid over it, lifting the aircraft slightly like a sled going over a bump. The Concorde belly-dived into the Euphrates, and Becker heard the thump of the impact at the same time he felt it hit. He saw the river come up to his windshield and pour through, sending shards of glass and sheets of water over him and Burg. Then everything went black.

Great billows of steam rose as the hot Olympus engines vaporized thousands of liters of the Euphrates. There was a rushing sound inside the aircraft as the belly filled with water and it settled into the river, then a stillness as it reached a level at which it could float. The passengers began to look up.

Salem Hamadi slid quickly through the door into the half-lit flight deck. He saw first a crewman strapped into the flight engineer's seat. He was bleeding and his blood colored the water sloshing on the deck. There was also a crewman sitting in the pilot's seat, slumped over the control column. Next to him in the copilot's seat was a man in civilian clothes who also seemed to be unconscious. There was sparkling plexiglas lying over everything. As he watched, the instrument lights began to fade, then the overhead lights went out. Hamadi pulled out his long knife. He knew instinctively that the man in civilian clothes was important and went for him first.

37

J acob Hausner stopped short of the line of Ashbals. He watched them as they began firing down into the river at the Concorde as it began floating slowly downstream. He raised his rifle and tried to pick out Rish among them, but they all looked the same with their layer of whitish dust.

Overhead, Laskov's F-14 circled lazily over the mud flats, then suddenly came streaking in toward the crest of the hill, directly at the Ashbals. Laskov had instructed Major Arnon's force to stop their advance and take cover until further notice. Major Bartok's force had changed direction and was heading at top speed back down the ridge line toward their rafts in an attempt to intercept the Concorde.

The sky was brightening noticeably and the wind was dropping. The Ashbals, who had traveled clothed in the dust and the darkness for so long, suddenly realized that they were naked. The F-14 released his last four rockets and pulled up sharply. The line of Ashbals on the crest disappeared in an inferno of orange flame and shrapnel.

The concussion knocked Hausner down, and when he looked up, he saw Ahmed Rish standing by himself well back of the crest where the dismembered bodies of his last soldiers lay smoldering. A smell of burning hair and flesh hung around the crest until the wind blew it away.

Hausner rose and looked around him. He and Rish were the only men left standing on the hill as far as he could see. Rish appeared to be contemplating the safest line of retreat. He had his back to Hausner as Hausner walked casually over to him. "Hello, Ahmed."

Rish did not turn. "Hello, Jacob Hausner."

"We won, Rish."

Rish shook his head. "Not completely. Hamadi is on that aircraft. Also, it may sink yet. And I'm sure the Peace Conference is finished. And please don't forget all your dead and wounded. Shall we call it a draw?"

Hausner tightened his grip on the AK-47. "Drop the rifle and your pistol. Turn slowly around, you son-of-a-bitch. Hands on your head."

Rish did as he was told. He smiled at Hausner. "You look terrible. Would you like a drink?" He inclined his head toward a canteen on his web belt.

"Shut your goddamn mouth." Hausner's hands were shaking, and the muzzle of the rifle moved with short, quick movements. He couldn't seem to make up his mind what to do next.

Rish smiled at Hausner. "This was all your fault, you know. None of this would have been possible without your incompetence. You don't know how many nights over the past year I've awakened in a sweat dreaming that Jacob Hausner would think of making a complete nose-to-tail search of his Concordes. Jacob Hausner. Legendary genius of El Al Security. Jacob Hausner. You don't know how we worried about the overrated Jacob Hausner." He laughed. "No one told us that Jacob Hausner was just a creation of Israeli public relations. The real Jacob Hausner has no more brains than a camel." He spit on the ground. "You may live and I may die, but I wouldn't change places with you." He laughed.

Hausner wiped the dust from his mouth and eyes. He knew Rish was trying to goad him into pulling the trigger. "Are you through?"

"Yes. I have said what I wanted to say to you. Now kill me quickly."

"I'm afraid that's not what I had in mind." He thought he could see Rish turn pale under his layer of dust. "Did you capture General Dobkin? How about the girl that was on the outpost? Do you have them? Come on, Rish. Answer me truthfully, and I'll put a bullet into your head, clean and quick. Otherwise . . ."

Rish shrugged. "Yes, we captured both of them. They were both alive the last I saw them. However, I received a radio transmission from the guest house where they were kept saying that your soldiers were blowing it up and machine-gunning the wounded." He shrugged again. "So, who can say if they are still alive?"

"Hospitals and headquarters don't mix, Rish, so don't give me that shit." He coughed and spit up some dust.

"Some water?"

"Shut up." Rish would be the intelligence prize of the decade. Rationally, he should take him alive. Rish would answer a lot of questions that had been bothering Israeli Intelligence for some time. Hausner wanted to know a few things himself. "Who passed on the flight information to you?"

"Colonel Richardson."

Hausner nodded. He asked suddenly, "Miriam Bernstein's husband? The others? What of them?"

Rish smiled.

"Answer me, you son-of-a-bitch."

"I think I'll take that information with me to the grave."

Hausner's finger tensed on the trigger. If he took Rish alive, he would spend the rest of his life staring through the barbed wire at Ramla. Life imprisonment was harsher justice than a bullet in the head and oblivion. But on a more primitive level Hausner wanted an eye for an eye. He was filled with all the primal passions and hate of mankind and wanted to see Rish's blood run. Rish was an unspeakable evil, and even barbed wire was no guarantee that his malevolence would be contained. While he lived and breathed, he was as dangerous and threatening as a contagion. "We killed your lover, didn't we? And it was a double blow to you because she was your sister, wasn't she?" The psychological profile had been vague on that point, but he knew now that it was so.

Rish did not answer, but his lips drew back in a feral grin that sent a shiver up Hausner's spine. Standing there in the dawn wind with his hands spread out, his face and clothes the color of the dead earth, and the rising sun showing a malignant gleam in his eyes, Hausner saw Pazuzu, the East Wind, harbinger of plague and death. Hausner's whole body began to shake with exhaustion and emotion. He lowered the barrel of the rifle and fired.

Rish's kneecap shattered and he fell in the dust. He howled with pain. "A quick bullet! You promised!"

Hausner was inexplicably relieved to see blood coming from Rish, to see the shattered bone splinters and marrow, and to hear the howling. Irrationally, he had thought there would be no blood and no pain.

"You promised!"

"When have we ever kept promises to each other?" He fired again and blew off the other kneecap.

Rish howled like an animal. He pounded his fists into the dust and bit his tongue and lips so hard they gushed blood. "For the love of Allah! For the love of God, Hausner!"

"Were your ancestors Babylonian, Rish? Were mine a part of the Captivity? Is that why we're here in the dust all these centuries later? Was that your purpose?" He fired twice and splintered Rish's right wrist and right elbow.

Rish collapsed with his face in the dust and sobbed "Mercy! Mercy. Please."

"Mercy? We Semites have never shown mercy to each other. Did you show mercy to Moshe Kaplan? Did he show mercy to you, for that matter? Our people have slaughtered each other without mercy since the Flood receded and probably before. The land between the Tigris and the Mediterranean is the biggest graveyard on this earth, and we made it that way. If the dead rise up on Judgment Day, there won't be room to stand." He fired a full burst and the rounds caught Rish on his left forearm and partially severed it.

Rish fainted, and Hausner walked up to him, reloaded a fresh magazine, and fired a bullet into the base of his head.

Hausner gave the lifeless body a violent kick. It rolled over the crest, slid down the steep glacis, and dropped into the Euphrates.

As he watched the body sinking, he noticed that there were still two Ashbals at the base of the glacis. They were firing at the floating Concorde, and by the look of their tracers they were scoring hits. Hausner aimed his rifle down at them and moved the selector switch back to automatic fire. Out of the corner of his eye, he saw the F-14 diving straight down at him out of the brightening sky. He thought that if he dropped his rifle and waved his arms, the pilot might not fire at him. He hesitated, then fired down at the two Ashbals with a long, unrelenting burst.

Teddy Laskov held back for a split second, then hit the switch for his last rocket.

Hausner's rifle clicked empty. There was no more movement at the base of the glacis, and there were no more tracer rounds following the Concorde. He heard the rocket coming at him over his shoulder, then saw the F-14 as it pulled up over the Euphrates. He knew that all his actions, not only over the past days, but over the past years, had been self-destructive. God—the Perverse One, not the Benevolent One—had only waited until Hausner imagined that he had something to live for before he pulled the rug from under him. Hausner knew it would happen that way and was neither bitter nor sorry. If he felt any sorrow at all, it was for Miriam.

The last thing Hausner saw was Laskov's tail number. Gabriel 32. A blinding light enveloped him, then he was suffused with a golden warmth, and an image of Miriam, looking very serene and eating dinner in a sunlit room, passed through his consciousness.

Laskov looked back and saw the top of the western crest erupt in orange flame.

Salem Hamadi moved forward quickly. The high-backed bucket seats did not show much target, and he wondered for a moment about the best way to proceed. He came up behind Burg and grabbed his thin white hair, pulled his head back, and exposed his throat. He looked down at the man and recognized the chief of the hated Mivtzan Elohim. His hands shook. It was like having Satan himself at the mercy of his long knife. His blade came across and cut into the side of Burg's neck. He was about to draw the knife across the jugular and windpipe when he saw a movement to his left. He looked at Becker, who had regained consciousness and was staring at him. All he could see in Becker's eyes was contempt and disgust. Not one bit of fear. Hamadi's hands began to shake and his eyes and lips twitched. He looked down at Burg. It occurred to him that killing this man was not going to make any real difference in the outcome of events. Not killing him might make a difference at least in regard to his own life. It would be the first time he had not killed an enemy when he had the chance. He wondered if he could do that. He took the knife away from Burg's neck.

Becker pointed to the shattered windshield.

Hamadi nodded. He spoke in slow Hebrew. "Tell them in Israel that Salem Hamadi spared a life. Tell Isaac Burg that he is in my debt for one favor." Perhaps he could collect on that someday. You never knew. Most agents on both sides carried these favors around with them as life insurance. "Salem Hamadi. One favor." He slid between Becker and Burg, over the instrument panels and squeezed through the shattered windshield and onto the nose cone. He rolled off and disappeared into the water.

Becker was fully awake now. He knew it wasn't a dream because he could see the gash on Burg's neck. It was too strange to dwell on. A strange incident in a strange land. Hamadi. Salem Hamadi. He'd report that, if he ever saw Jerusalem again.

Becker shouted over his shoulder into the cabin. He looked at Kahn and called to him. "Peter!" There was no answer. He could not see the foaming at the chest, which meant that either the hole was sealed or he was dead.

The Concorde was floating mostly as a result of the tremendous surface area of its wings, but Becker knew that the wings wouldn't keep them afloat much longer. Even as he looked back out of his side window, small waves broke over the big deltas. The water in the compartments below deck was pulling the craft down, and the heavy engines were causing the broken tail to sit low in the water. Becker felt the nose beginning to rise as the tail sat deeper in the water.

The door from the cabin was thrown open. Yaakov Leiber rushed in. "Captain, the rear baggage—" He saw Kahn and Burg slumped in their seats.

Becker noticed that Leiber seemed to be in full control of his faculties now that he was needed in his professional capacity again. "Go on, Steward. Make your report."

"Yes, sir. The rear baggage compartment and galley are swamped, and I've evacuated the—the potential suicides, and I can see water through the floor in the compartments below. Also, we can't account for Alpern. I think he was on the tail when we went over."

Becker nodded. "All right. Please get Beth Abrams and someone else in here to take care of Mr. Kahn and Mr. Burg. Then instruct everyone to put on the life jackets that are still available, if they haven't done so already. And get a more complete damage report for me."

"Right, sir." Leiber ran into the cabin. The passengers had come through the fall with barely an injury, but they were all anxiously eyeing the six-potential exits and beginning to cluster around them. Leiber found Beth Abrams sitting against the galley bulkhead with Miriam Bernstein. He whispered in her ear, then moved off and spoke to Esther Aronson and the Foreign Minister.

Beth Abrams, Esther Aronson, and Ariel Weizman moved quickly up to the flight deck. The two women immediately unstrapped Kahn and Burg. They began carrying the men, one at a time, back into the cabin.

The Foreign Minister leaned over Becker's shoulder and spoke quietly. "Are we sinking?"

Becker waited until the two women were out of the door with Burg. "Yes. We are. If we sink suddenly, we will all be drowned. You may want to order an evacuation now."

"But the wounded—"

"Put life jackets on them, sir. They can't stay here."

"Can't we get to land?"

Becker looked out the side windows. To his left he saw the mounds of Babylon slide by. He looked back at the citadel mound where he had thought he was going to meet his end. He could see a few commandos on the top of the glacis and a few on the bank waving to him. Some of the commandos had lowered rubber rafts in the river and were pursuing the Concorde. Ahead on the west bank, he could see an earth quay in the distance and a small village. There appeared to be commandos there as well. Help was all around them, but it might as well be in Jerusalem. The Euphrates had him caught in midstream, and he didn't see how he was going to beach the aircraft. No one could say that he should have thought of that when he took it over the side. He had thought of it, but it seemed like a totally inconsequential question ten minutes before. He looked out the right window. The aircraft might beach itself if it could float on for some distance. But it couldn't. "We've come so far," he said.

"And we're so close," said Ariel Weizman. "And we did *not* come this far to drown like rats in this cursed river of our sorrow." He looked out at the muddy water encircling them.

"Did Hausner ever get aboard?" asked Becker.

"No. He stayed."

Becker nodded. "How's Miriam—Mrs. Bernstein?"

Weizman shot a glance at Becker. "She'll be fine, Captain," he said formally.

Becker turned as the two women carried Peter Kahn out into the cabin. He looked at the bloody water on the floor running back into the cabin as the aircraft tilted upwards. He turned back in his chair. "Salem Hamadi was in here."

"What's that?"

"Nothing, sir. Just thinking out loud." He watched the two banks slide by. The aircraft was moving more slowly now as they took on more water. Someone—the commandos, the fighter pilots, or he himself—would have to think of something very quickly.

Becker settled back in his chair. He had finally become accustomed to sitting in a downward-pitched flight deck, and now it was pitched upward. Strange how these minor irritations loomed so large during a crisis. He tried the radio just to satisfy the requirement that it be tried, but it was as dead as everything else that was electrical. He spoke to the Foreign Minister, who had sat down in the copilot's chair. "I'm the Captain and I could order the evacuation if you'd prefer not to, sir."

Ariel Weizman kept his head and eyes straight ahead. "Will we have *any* warning if it is going to sink?"

Becker turned and faced the Foreign Minister. "It's sinking *now,* sir. It's only a question of the *rate* at which it is sinking. If it continues to sink slowly, we can ride it a while longer. If it suddenly slips into the river, then that's it."

The Foreign Minister looked at the earth quay in the distance, then back out the side window at the rubber rafts gaining on them. "We'll wait," he said hesitantly.

"Fine." Becker settled back and stared out the window at the new day. They had done some remarkable things with Concorde 02, but now the innovations and cleverness had come to an end. Great seabird that she seemed, she couldn't float worth a damn.

* * *

Miriam Bernstein stared out the porthole at the Euphrates. She looked up and watched the desolate east bank slide by. Her vision was blurred by her tears and the shattered glass distorted her view of the terrain, but she knew she was still looking at Babylon. A mud village appeared and people moved on the bank. A great assembly of them lined the shore and stared. The prismatic effect of the shattered glass gave the black *gellebiahs* and dun-colored huts a rainbow hue. Like Babylon of the colored brick. She thought she could feel, sense, almost see the Jews of the Captivity as they labored on the banks of the river, their harps hanging on the ghostly willows. She sighed and pressed her forehead to the glass and tears ran down her face. She knew he was dead. He had a preordained rendezvous with Ahmed Rish—or someone like him. She only hoped that he had found some peace at the end.

Danny Lavon spoke into his intercom. "Fuel, General."

Laskov looked at his fuel gauges. The aerial combat maneuvers had burned more than he had figured on. "Roger. Send everyone home. We're going to have to hang around a little longer."

"Roger." Lavon radioed the squadron.

The squadron went into a V-formation and flew by Laskov. They came in low over the river and dipped their wings in unison, then turned west and headed home.

Laskov looked out of his cockpit as they disappeared, then turned away. The sun sat on the highest peak in Iran, and its rays came down into Mesopotamia and turned the grey land golden. The wind had dropped, and he could see only an occasional line of dust clouds racing across the flat alluvial plains. He looked down at the two C-130's, the smoking guest house, the ruins of Babylon and the village of Arabs sitting in the middle of them. He stared down at the village of Jews on the opposite shore, and the huge, white, delta-winged Concorde floating toward it. "Incredible," he said into the intercom.

"Incredible," agreed Danny Lavon.

Laskov wondered if she were on the Concorde. He could see that the wings looked blurry now, which meant that they were awash. He didn't give the aircraft another two minutes. He tried the El Al frequency again. "Concorde 02, this is Gabriel 32. Bail out, damn it! Bail out! Can you hear me?" There was no answer. Laskov could see five rubber rafts closing in on the Concorde from the rear. He wondered if Becker knew they were there. They weren't much, but at least some of the wounded could get on them. The rest would have to swim or float if they had life jackets. Why the hell didn't they get out? Laskov spoke to the two ground commandos and the two C-130 captains. Everyone had ideas, but no one really knew quite what to do. There were contingency plans for just about every situation, but no one, not even the think-tank boys in Tel Aviv, had foreseen this. Major Bartok in the rafts seemed to have the closest shot at rescuing them. The squad of commandos in Ummah had recruited the villagers and many of them took to the water in *gufas* and tried to pole upriver to meet the approaching Concorde.

The Foreign Minister nodded. "We'll lose some, but what can we do? Let's evacuate."

"Wait one minute." Becker watched Laskov bank sharply to stay with them over the river. Bank sharply. Bank right. He looked down at his dead instruments. He moved his hands over to the emergency power switch. He turned it on. Dead. He already knew that. But he needed power. Power. The engines were dead and so the generator was dead. The batteries were under water. The nitrogen bottle was back in Babylon, and the primary hydraulic pumps were submerged or damaged. Still, there was a source of power left, and he didn't know why he hadn't thought of it sooner. He quickly reached down under his seat and pulled a manual handle that he never imagined he would use and never wanted to have to use in the air. A nonelectric hydraulic pump activated itself, and the trap door beneath the Concorde opened and the small generator propeller dropped out.

Instantly, Becker saw a few gauges come alive as the propeller turned under water and activated a generator. The propeller also worked an emergency hydraulic pump, and he saw that he had pressure again in some of the systems. The Concorde was being powered by a water wheel. Desperate—but *trés pratique*. If Kahn were sitting at the flight engineer's console, he would say that everything was looking good.

Becker knew that he had only a few seconds before the water caused this emergency system to fail also. Already the electrical and electronic components were flickering on the instrument panel. The hydraulic pressure, however, was holding. Becker turned his wheel, and the big starboard aileron went down as the portside aileron went up. The right wing dragged in the water and the left wing began to come around.

The Foreign Minister shook his shoulder. "David! I said—"

"Wait!" The Concorde began moving—banking—to the right. It partly changed direction and partly sideslipped toward the west bank. Ahead, Becker could see the earth quay of Ummah sticking into the river. Becker wanted to hit that quay and nestle the aircraft between its protective arm and the river bank. If he hit the bank downstream of the quay, the aircraft might not beach itself but only slide and spin along the shore and come apart.

The Concorde was going down as fast as it was turning now. The change of direction had jolted it out of its lethargic sinking and speeded up the rate at which it was taking water. Becker gripped the wheel so hard his knuckles turned white. As he alternately watched the gauges and the ailerons, he could see that the hydraulic as well as the electrical power was failing. The gauges flickered and the ailerons began to straighten out. Now they were both horizontal again, trailing loosely in the water. Becker swore in English.

Still, the Concorde had begun its turn, and as with an aircraft in its proper element, thought Becker, inertia should carry the motion through.

But a flowing river was not exactly like the thin air, as Becker was rapidly learning. The Concorde again assumed the position of least resistance, with its nose and tail lined up in the direction of the current. But at least they were now closer to the shore, and the water moved faster here, giving the Concorde an almost imperceptible quantum of added buoyancy. Becker thought they might just hit the quay.

Suddenly, Becker heard cheers and yelling coming from the cabin, and he looked over his shoulder. Yaakov Leiber appeared at the door and ran into the flight deck. "The commandos are alongside in their rubber rafts!"

The Foreign Minister looked back out the side window. "Perhaps I should try to evacuate the wounded."

"Nobody moves," said Becker. "And I mean that literally. No moving around back there. We're about five degrees from sliding ass backwards into the Euphrates."

Leiber walked more gingerly into the cabin and passed on Becker's orders.

Becker saw a rubber raft come alongside the flight deck on his side. The officer in it, Major Bartok, shouted something about evacuating. Becker shook his head and made a motion with his hand to indicate that both the situation and the aircraft were very shaky.

Major Bartok nodded in understanding. He gave a thumbs-up and shouted something about Becker being not a bad pilot.

Becker turned his face away from the side window and looked downriver. The quay was about 150 meters away now—about twice the length of the Concorde. The *gufas* were sliding past him on both sides, and he could see the strange-looking Jews in their primitive boats. He looked back to his front. It did not appear to Becker that the Concorde could intersect the quay. Yet he knew that somehow it would. He suddenly felt that their trials were over and that there would be no more tests and no more tribulations. An easy calm came over him for the first time in a very long time, and he relaxed as he stared through the broken windshield, a breeze blowing on his face. As he watched, the Concorde seemed to slide right. Or was it a visual distortion caused by the light on the rippling water? Were they headed for the quay ever since he'd gotten the Concorde to turn? He'd have to ask General Laskov later.

His right wing suddenly skimmed the shore and rode over the top of it, cleaving through mud huts as it went. The drag caused the Concorde to turn more sharply to the right, and as the shore got higher, the right wing rode higher and pushed the opposite wing deeper into the water.

The quay came up fast. The commandos and the villagers moved back and to the sides but stayed on it. The downward-pointed nose of the Concorde hit it first, just below the water line, like a Roman warship with an iron ramming prow. The quay trembled and split as the nose buried itself in the ancient mud brick and slime. Becker found himself staring at someone's boots outside his windshield less than a meter away. The Concorde sank perceptibly, and Becker could feel its main undercarriage, or what was left of it after the slide, settling onto the bottom. People were all over the aircraft now—commandos, villagers, and survivors. He heard them on the roof of the fuselage, and he heard them wading over the left wing and coming in through the aircraft's doors. He was vaguely aware of people shouting, weeping, and embracing. The next thing he was aware of was standing on the quay, saluting the Concorde. Someone led him away.

38

Miriam Bernstein and Ariel Weizman found Major Bartok in the confusion of the quay. The Foreign Minister identified himself and asked quickly, "The Peace Conference?"

The Major smiled and nodded. "They are still waiting for Israel in New York."

At the C-130, a crewman asked David Becker if they weren't short of water during their ordeal.

Becker replied. "Yes, of course. Can't you see everyone is very thirsty?"

"I see that," said the crewman. "But I wondered why all the men are clean-shaven."

"Shaven?" Becker ran his hand over his face. "Oh. He made us shave."

Rabbi Levin had cornered Major Bartok at the edge of the quay and was demanding that he be taken by raft to Major Arnon, who was now on the hill, so that he could supervise the locating and exhuming of the bodies. Major Bartok assured the rabbi that there was no need for him to go back, but Rabbi Levin proceeded to tell Major Bartok why he was wrong.

The village of Ummah had never seen anything quite like the procession marching through its one crooked street and was not likely to see anything like it again. The villagers helped carry stretchers and passed food and wine to those who wanted it. There was a mixture of crying and shouting and impromptu songs and dances. Flutes appeared, and their haunting notes lay over the quay and village as the people of the Concorde moved slowly toward the huge, towering C-130. An old man gave Miriam Bernstein a stringed instrument. A harp.

Everything was happening too fast for the survivors, and very little of it was registering consciously. Everyone had questions to ask, and the more questions the commandos asked, the more questions the people of the Concorde asked.

Major Bartok picked up his radiophone and called Captain Geis, whom he could see sitting up in the big flight deck of the C-130. "Tell Jerusalem . . . Tell Jerusalem they have freed themselves from their Captivity. We will carry them home. Casualties and after-action report to follow."

"Roger," said Geis, and relayed the radio message.

The Prime Minister sat back and wiped his eyes as the radio message came over the loudspeaker. He thought of how they had been unsure of themselves and how they had doubted. But in the end they had said *Zanek*—"Go"—and that was what was important. He wondered who had lived and who had died. Was the Foreign Minister alive? The delegates? Bernstein? Tekoah? Tamir? Sapir? Jabari? Arif? How about Burg? And how about Dobkin? Would he live? And Hausner. The great enigma and troublemaker. How long had the Deputy Minister of Transportation—Miriam Bernstein—kept the Minister of Transportation from firing him? He had a lot of questions to answer if he were alive. The Prime Minister opened his eyes and looked around the room. "Heroes, martyrs, fools, and cowards. We're going to need at least a month to sort out who is who."

Captain Ishmael Bloch taxied his C-130 up the Hillah road. On board were all Major Arnon's commandos, fifteen exhumed or unburied bodies from the hill, including Alpern's, plus a mutilated corpse from the base of the hill. The commandos had found Burg's shoe with his daybook stuffed inside, and this enabled them to move quickly to complete their unpleasant assignment.

There was also a body so badly torn by the shrapnel that it was almost left behind as an Arab, but a sharp-eyed soldier had noticed the Hebrew letters חי hanging from a heavy chain around the neck. Also on board were thirty-five wounded Ashbals along with half a dozen Arab dead who were identified as possible wanted terrorists. Ahmed Rish and Salem Hamadi were not believed to be among them.

On the operating tables were General Dobkin and Deborah Gideon. The two surgeons were waiting for the aircraft to lift off before they could go back to work.

Rabbi Levin, who had gotten his way about being returned to the hill, came over to the operating tables and looked up at the surgeons. The man operating on Deborah Gideon looked up and nodded quickly. The woman who was operating on General Dobkin pulled down her surgical mask. "I have never seen such brutality." She paused. "But he'll live. You're not needed here, Rabbi." She smiled and pulled her mask back in place.

Rabbi Levin turned and walked to the rear of the aircraft to find Lieutenant Giddel so that he could continue their argument on the necessity of serving only kosher foods during field operations.

The C-130 was taking a long time to lift, and Captain Bloch was becoming impatient. "I told you we'd roll to Baghdad."

"I hope this isn't a toll road, Izzy."

The big aircraft finally lifted off, and Bloch banked it sharply to the left over the Euphrates. He looked down at the Concorde, almost directly below him. "You know, Eph, I'd like to meet the crazy bastard who flew that thing in here and sailed it out."

"Becker. I've flown with him on reserve training. He's pretty good."

Bloch smiled. "Hey, this was one hell of an operation, wasn't it?"

Major Bartok watched the old man on the donkey as he made his way at his own speed across the mud flats. The C-130 was nearly loaded and its engines were turning, but that didn't seem to impress the old man in the least. Bartok stood patiently on the huge tailgate and waited.

Shear-jashub seemed to have no fear of the monstrous machine, and neither did his donkey. The old man rode the beast up onto the ramp and stopped when he came abreast of the Major. He did not dismount but asked abruptly, "What has become of *Aluf* Dobkin?"

"He is in that aircraft, Rabbi." He pointed overhead. "He is well."

The old man nodded. "You will give him a message for me?"

"Of course."

"It is also the answer to your question." Shear-jashub straightened himself on the donkey. "We of Ummah thank you for your kind offer, but we cannot go to Israel with you."

The major shook his head in frustration. "Why not? There is no future for you here."

"We are not concerned with the future here," said Shear-jashub, stressing the last word.

"Come home to Jerusalem, Rabbi. We have room. March everyone into this airplane right now. There is nothing to be frightened of. Go. Gather your people. Bring your goods and your animals, if you wish. Ummah will fit nicely in the belly of this big bird. Go and gather them up, Shear-jashub. The Captivity is over. Come away from Babylon."

The old man peered into the cavernous craft. Strange lights and noises came out of it. He could see those other Jews in there—the Israelites—walking, sitting, weeping, laughing. He had not understood all that had happened, but he understood enough to know that they came from a powerful nation and that Ummah could join that nation and the sons and daughters of Ummah could grow up in this nation. "We have many friends and kin in Hillah and Baghdad. What will they think when they come to Ummah and find that we are gone? We cannot go like that."

Bartok made a gesture of impatience. "I can't believe you would want to *stay* here. This is a terrible place."

"It is *our* place. Let me tell you that which I told the *Aluf*. There must always be a remnant left behind. In every nation there must always be we of the Diaspora. Nevermore can they lay hands on us all by taking Jerusalem. Do you understand that?"

Major Bartok looked out over the mud flats, then back at the old man. "Yes, I understand that. But this land is different. There is something evil about this place. You who are in this land came here as slaves, and you are still thought of as slaves." He saw that he was getting nowhere and he sighed. The last of the wounded were taken aboard, and he knew he could not wait. His first obligation was to them. He forced a smile. "Rabbi, remember this—if this Brit Shalom that everyone is speaking of goes well, then all the Jews of this land will be able to come to Israel if they wish. Tell them in Hillah and in Baghdad that we are waiting for them. And we are waiting for Ummah . . . and for Shear-jashub."

"I will remember."

Major Bartok nodded. "I wish I had the words to convince you. Perhaps if the *Aluf* were here . . . Well, good-bye Shear-jashub. We must go . . . to Jerusalem."

The old man smiled at the name of the city. "It is a strong and powerful city now."

"Yes."

"Good-bye." He reined the donkey around and rode down the ramp.

Major Bartok watched him for a few seconds, then turned and signaled the crew chief. The gate began to rise and the major walked along it into the big cabin. He turned to the crew chief. "Tell the pilots, please, that we are ready to go home."

In the cabin, he could hear a group reading from Jeremiah: . . . *a great company shall return thither. They shall come with weeping. . . .*

EPILOGUE

For thus saith the Lord; Sing with gladness for Jacob,
*   and shout among the chief of the nations:*
publish ye, praise ye,
*   and say, O Lord, save thy people,*
*   the remnant of Israel.*
Behold, I will bring them from the north country,
*   and gather them from the coasts of the earth,*
*   and with them the blind and the lame,*
*   the woman with child and her that travaileth with child together:*
*   a great company shall return thither.*
They shall come with weeping,
*   and with supplications will I lead them:*
I will cause them to walk by the rivers of waters
*   in a straight way, wherein they shall not stumble. . . .*

Hear the word of the Lord, O ye nations,
*   and declare it in the isles afar off, and say,*
He that scattered Israel will gather him,
*   and keep him, as a shephered doth his flock.*
For the Lord hath redeemed Jacob,
*   and ransomed him from the hand of him that was stronger than he.*

                                        Jeremiah 31:17–11

The two C-130's flew west, in formation, over the Iraqi desert.

Isaac Burg sat on a canvas chair and spoke quietly with Major Bartok, who was filling out his after-action report. Burg's arms and bare torso were splotched with iodine, and he had a white pressure bandage on his neck, which he kept touching questioningly.

Bartok kept shaking his head in disbelief at Burg's answers to his questions. Bartok, the soldier, was trying very hard to understand how the peace mission had decimated a full rifle company of trained soldiers. Out of professional inquisitiveness and personal curiosity, he was trying to discover the element or elements that had made that military miracle possible. "Perhaps we could use a few battalions of peace delegates in the army," he said.

Burg smiled. "It was just that they believed so much in peace, I think, that when someone tried to spoil that peace, they were so angry that they reacted like a lioness defending her cubs. It is a paradox, I know, but it is the best I can offer you."

"Sounds good," said Major Bartok. "But I'll just write that it was a combination of good leadership, good defensible terrain, and innovative defenders."

"Sounds good," said Burg.

Burg accepted another cup of coffee from a flight steward and settled back. It was a short flight, but it was the longest flight of his life.

The major began reading back what he euphemistically called his Line Ones,

Line Twos, and Line Threes. Killed in Action. Wounded in Action. Missing in Action.

Burg looked around the big cabin. There were so many absent. So many who deserved to be there instead of in green body bags on the other aircraft.

"Your security people took a hell of a beating," said Bartok.

Burg nodded. An incredible five out of the six security men were dead. Brin, Kaplan, Rubin, Alpern, and Marcus. Only Jaffe remained, and he was wounded. Hausner's palace guard. His instrument to effect his *coup d'état*. They were loyal to him and he was loyal to them. What more could men ask of one another? They were professionals, and professionals always suffered disproportionate casualties, but that was the way it should be.

And the El Al crew. They were professionals as well, and they had suffered disproportionately, too. It was their aircraft, and whether it was in Lod or in Babylon, they had felt a responsibility for the passengers. Daniel Jacoby and Rachel Baum were both wounded very badly, but Burg could see that they were still on the operating tables, and that was better than being under the green tarpaulin that was lying on the tailgate. Peter Kahn was serious, also, but stable. He was off the table now. The surgeon had shown Burg the bloody map that Burg had stuffed in Kahn's wound. "It saved his life," said the surgeon. "He owes you one when he gets out of the hospital." He crumpled it up and threw it into his surgical waste pail.

There were the dead among the secretaries, interpreters, and aides. There were the four slaughtered men and women of the outpost, and there were those who would die before the plane touched down in Jerusalem. But Burg did not know them all, and he was glad that he did not because there was no more room in his heart for sorrow just then.

And then there were the missing. That was the cruelest statistic of all. Did you mourn for their death or hope they were lying somewhere, suffering but alive? Did you pray that they were interned in some Arab hellhole? Miriam Bernstein could answer that better than anyone. Now she had two to wonder about.

Naomi Haber was missing. Burg thought he had accounted for everyone, but apparently he had not. No one had any idea what had become of her. Someone had suggested that she might have slipped off downslope and actually gotten close enough to put a bullet into Moshe Kaplan. Everyone had heard that bullet fired and it made no sense that Kaplan's tormentors had suddenly shown mercy and shot him. But where was she? The commandos had not found her.

And then there was John McClure. The shadowy man had disappeared. Burg understood McClure's world because it was his own. Anything was possible in their world, but disappearing from one's rescuers was a little odd even by their standards. Did he kill Richardson? Burg suspected that he had, and he knew why. The doctors on the other C-130 had reported that the bullet that killed Richardson was not recovered. It had been fired at close range and had gone through him.

But where was McClure now? Probably at the American Embassy in Baghdad by now, or perhaps at the home of a CIA contact in Hillah. He'd turn up someday posing as an archivist in the United States Information Service Library in Beirut. They always turned up like that.

Major Bartok wanted to know if Burg knew Jacob Hausner well. "Was he the actual leader?"

"Very much so." Hausner. Where was Jacob Hausner? Dead, probably. Would they ever know?

The man was so complex that his death—or disappearance—left one with complex feelings. His staying wasn't simply a matter of his wanting personal revenge against Ahmed Rish, although that was certainly part of it. It was more involved than that. He had wanted to die, but he had also wanted to live. You couldn't lose on a deal like that. And Hausner *was* a winner up to and including the end. Returning to Jerusalem would have exposed him to questions that any excessively proud man would not care to answer. So he had stayed.

Miriam Bernstein sat on the deck with her back against a bulkhead. Her legs were drawn up and her cheek rested on her knees. The quiet drone of the engines lulled her numb body. The Foreign Minister sat next to her on a canvas bench pulled down from the wall. The euphoria had passed. Around her some people were drifting off to sleep. A few were still manic and talked incessantly to people who were barely conscious. Even the soldiers seemed not to want to listen or to speak and had moved off and segregated themselves toward the tail. The whole cabin smelled of bodies, anesthetic, and medicine.

She looked at David Becker sitting on the deck a short distance from her with his back against the hull. He was awake, but he seemed far away. There were many heros, thought Miriam, but if there was any single hero, it was surely David Becker. He had accepted the professional praise of Captain Geis and Lieutenant Stern with self-effacement and almost boyish charm. He was a good-looking aviator. The perfect hero material. They would treat him royally in Jerusalem. The American background would help. She found herself staring at him. He seemed alone.

Becker's mind came back to the present as he found he was staring at Miriam Bernstein. He tried a smile, but he knew it came out wrong. He cleared his throat and spoke softly. "We lost our logbook."

She smiled. "And my chronicle was probably blown up by a bomb."

"We are not very good scribes."

"It was the thought."

"Yes." He smiled and closed his eyes.

Miriam saw that he was sleeping and felt like doing the same. She closed her eyes.

The Foreign Minister leaned over and tapped her on the shoulder. "We will have to prepare a single statement for when we land. Above all, we must separate what happened here from the Peace Conference. We must rebuild and recapture the spirit that existed before this . . ." he waved his hand, ". . . before this happened."

Miriam Bernstein looked up at him. "I won't be going to New York with you."

The Foreign Minister looked startled. "Why not?"

"I don't believe in it."

"Nonsense."

She shrugged. What would Jacob Hausner have advised? He had always been cynical of the peace mission, but maybe he'd advise her to go and make them know that she was going to be one hell of a tough negotiator. If the Arabs had counted on her as the weakest link in the Israeli mission, then they had better think again.

"You'll feel differently in a day or two, Miriam."

"Perhaps I will." She didn't feel like arguing. She heard the voice of Esther Aronson coming from somewhere in the mid-section of the cavernous compartment. She was reading from Jeremiah: . . . *for, lo, I will save thee from afar, and thy seed from the land of their captivity; and Jacob shall return. . . .*

Seed? His seed? His seed out of Babylon? Maybe. Unconsciously, her hand moved to her abdomen.

The Foreign Minister reached over and tapped her again. "I said, that was a truly selfless and altruistic act . . . for him, I mean . . . staying behind and keeping the Ashbals at bay."

Miriam forced a smile. "Altruistic? Jacob Hausner didn't know the meaning of the word. No, it was purely selfish, I can assure you. He didn't want to face an inquiry—not only concerning the bombs, but also concerning his leadership —his usurpation of leadership and all those killed while he was in command. He'd rather die, I think, than stand in a dock." She tried to smile again, but tears rolled down her cheeks.

Ariel Weizman was uncomfortable. He patted her arm. "Well now, maybe he's not dead."

She thought of her husband. That's what they kept telling her about him. And there were still Jews in Europe pinning pathetic notes on public bulletin boards, looking for their husbands and wives and sons and daughters after all these years. She looked at Ariel Weizman and her face became harder than he ever remembered seeing it. She spoke through clenched teeth. "He's dead, damn it. Dead. And damn him for throwing away his life." She buried her face in her arms and wept.

They were both dead, and there was no place where she could go to visit their graves any more than she could visit the graves of her parents, her sister, or her stepfather. There was nothing palpable about her past, nothing she could reach out and touch. It was as if these people had never existed. And so many of the places associated with them were outside her world. Europe. Babylon. She was engulfed by a sense of loss, a sense of overpowering sadness. Jacob said scream and shout and carry on and let the world know how you suffer, but she couldn't and wouldn't do that. And even if she did, it would not stop the pain. If only he hadn't told her that he loved her. Then it would have been so much easier for her to pass it off as passion or insecurity or something other than what it was.

Someone tapped her on the shoulder and she looked up. A young crewman was staring down at her, smiling. He handed her a scrap of folded paper. "Radio message."

She stared at it for a few seconds, then opened it and read the scribbled pencil lines to herself. *I love you. Teddy.*

"Any answer?"

She wiped her eyes with both hands. She hesitated, then shook her head. "No. Thank you."

The surprised crewman turned and walked off.

Miriam looked down at the note again, then slipped it into her pocket. Her fingers touched the silver star Jacob had given her. She drew her hand out of her pocket. She'd have to see about Jacob's seed before she knew about Teddy Laskov.

Teddy Laskov made a final pass over Babylon. Nothing seemed to move on the ground except the wind and the sand and a solitary man riding a donkey westward across the mud flats, looking up into the sky. The big blue and white Concorde lay submerged at the quay of Ummah. It should have looked more out of place than it did, reflected Laskov. The village and the aircraft were the culmination of twenty-five hundred years of separate development, yet there was a common thread there.

Laskov banked sharply and streaked west, away from the Cradle of Civilization, away from the land of Captivity, out over the Shamiyah Desert, west toward Jerusalem. The swing-wings on his jet, which had been spread out for combat, now folded back like a cape as he soared upward.

In a few minutes he came abreast of the two C-130's.

Miriam had not responded to his public announcement of his love, and he felt a bit of a fool—still he knew that he should show the colors to the people on board. It was good for morale. He shot between the two aircraft and tilted his wings. He banked around, pulled off speed, and extended the wings so that he could fly more slowly. He passed by again and waved from his cockpit bubble.

From every porthole on the C-130's people waved back as he circled the big craft.

Miriam Bernstein rose hesitantly and stood along with the others who were looking out of the portholes. She gave a belated half wave to the fighter as it passed by again, then turned away from the porthole, sunk to the floor, and fell asleep before she was completely stretched out. David Becker laid a blanket over her.

Laskov had had enough of the acrobatics and did not bank around again, but climbed west out of sight of the transports. He put the aircraft on a heading toward Jerusalem and passed through the sound barrier. He would be on the ground to meet them—showered and back in civilian clothes—when they arrived with the dust of Babylon still clinging to them. Situations changed with incredible speed in the modern world. There seemed to be no fixed point, like Polaris, that you could navigate by. He wondered if Miriam had changed much in Babylon. No. Not Miriam. She was steady, almost indifferent. There would be that initial strangeness and coolness that sometimes comes when two lovers meet after a separation, but it would pass.

Laskov soared up into the stratosphere for no reason other than that he wanted to see the curve of the earth below and the perpetual stars in their black heavens above. One's perspective changed up here. Babylon. Jerusalem. God. Miriam Bernstein. Teddy Laskov. They all began to sort themselves out in this cold, airless void. He would figure it all out before he saw the domes and spires of Jerusalem.

It was ten P.M. in New York. The Arab and Israeli delegations had assembled in the Conference Building of the United Nations. Status reports out of Baghdad and Jerusalem had been circulated every fifteen minutes. The most recent teletype reports had finally brought encouraging news to the assembled delegates.

Someone broke out a bottle of arak and it was passed around. There wasn't much talking in the meeting room, but as the tension eased, a feeling of confidence, even friendship, was developing between the two groups gathered there. An Arab delegate made a toast. Soon everyone was proposing toasts, and the arak and sweet wine flowed.

Saul Ezer, a permanent delegate of the Israeli Mission to the UN, reflected that this was probably the most congenial group of advance personnel he had ever seen at a conference. The arriving delegates from Israel and the Arab countries would land on very fertile ground. He got up quietly and went to a telephone in an adjoining office. He dialed a midtown hotel and rebooked the Israeli peace delegation.

* * *

Shear-jashub lost sight of the aircraft and turned his donkey east, across the mud flats, back toward Ummah. It had been a strange interlude in the timeless, changeless life of the Euphrates.

A remnant had again returned from Babylon, and a remnant had again chosen to stay behind. Shear-jashub imagined there would be great feasting in Jerusalem, but for Ummah there would be uncertainty. If Ummah did not survive, however, the communities in Baghdad and Hillah would. And if they did not, Jerusalem, or some other place, would. One day, God would cease His testing of His children, and then all the scattered remnants could return to the Promised Land, safe in the knowledge that they of the Diaspora were not needed outside of Zion to insure that their blood would survive.

In the distance, the sun came over the mounds of Babylon. Shear-jashub lifted his head and sang out in a clear voice that carried across the desolate plains and rolled across the Euphrates and into the ruins of Babylon: "And I will gather the remnant of my flock out of all countries whither I have driven them, and will bring them again to their folds; and they shall be fruitful and increase. And I will set up shepherds over them which shall feed them: and they shall fear no more, nor be dismayed, neither shall they be lacking, saith the Lord."